D1552915

A GREAT CIRCLE

BOOKS BY

REYNOLDS PRICE

REYNOLDS PRICE

A GREAT CIRCLE

The Mayfield Trilogy

THE SURFACE OF EARTH

THE SOURCE OF LIGHT

THE PROMISE OF REST

SCRIBNER CLASSICS

NEW YORK   LONDON   TORONTO   SYDNEY   SINGAPORE

SCRIBNER
1230 Avenue of the Americas
New York, NY 10020

SCRIBNER and design are trademarks of Macmillan Library Reference USA, Inc., used under license by Simon & Schuster, the publisher of this work.

For information regarding special discounts for bulk purchases, please contact Simon & Schuster Special Sales at 1-800-456-6798 or *business@simonandschuster.com*

Set in Electra

Manufactured in the United States of America

1   3   5   7   9   10   8   6   4   2

Library of Congress Cataloging-in-Publication Data
Price, Reynolds, 1933–
A great circle : the Mayfield trilogy / Reynolds Price.
p.   cm.
Includes a preface by the author.
Contents: The surface of earth—The source of light—The promise of rest.
1. Mayfield family (Fictitious characters)—Fiction. 2. Historical fiction, American.
3. Domestic fiction, American. 4. North Carolina—Fiction. I. Title.

PS3566.R54 G7 2001
813'.54—dc21   2001032026

ISBN 0-7432-1186-3

CONTENTS

PREFACE

Before my first novel was published in the spring of 1962, I began to make notes for what seemed a long story, perhaps a second novel. Those notes were glimpses of what would become—thirty-three years later—*A Great Circle*, a three-part fictional account of the Mayfield and Kendal families, their surrounding world (which includes black kin), and the more than 170 years of American history through which they live—the oldest character is born in 1815, though an older woman is recalled in another character's memory; and the final scene occurs in 1993.

When those first hints began to arrive, I set them down in my notebook with no sense that they'd result in something as substantial as what came—a trilogy of novels that would occupy me intermittently for more than three decades, that would consume the better part of what I thought I'd seen in my life and what I could do till that point, and that appears now for the first time in a single volume. Any workman might be glad to have lasted to see such an object.

It's even tempting to take the occasion as a chance to expand on the growth of the novels, but I'm cautioned by the famous late-life prefaces which Henry James fabricated for his novels. Instructive as those confidences may once have seemed—and in my college years, the 1950s, they were commended to us as holy writ—they now read like further works of fiction, outlays of self-regard that claim an impossible awareness of old motive and spent fuel. And though they make often impressive old-master comments on a younger master's work, they tell us very little that's reliable about the growth of books which had left James's hands decades earlier.

While I enjoy, as much as anyone, the creation of fictional memory or the elaboration of firm recall, what I hope for in this preface is at least some encouragement for anyone valiant enough (in these days of the threatened book) to take up such a large handful of words. The track of a vital story is as inexplicable as the path of a dream. At bottom, stories are what narrative writers can make, though they can no more prescribe that process to others than a mother can prescribe the making of a child. The reader may be interested, however, to know that I am certain of two concerns which were central in the years of work—they're down in my notes.*

First, the conscious aim was to make an arresting, decidedly fictional metaphor of the deeply shadowed yet benign relation I shared with my father from the time of my birth till he died when I was twenty-one. But I was wrong to think I could launch a long story in the midst of an intricate kinship between two invented characters, a relation haunted by the father's prior life. Because a gold wedding band plays an important role in the trilogy, joking friends have sometimes called it "Price's *Ring*." And my attempt to begin the story with a father and son who were well along in their mutual dependency soon had me frozen in the kind of Wagnerian-Ring moment when characters are compelled to halt, gaze backward, and explain long swatches of the past to another character and of course the audience.

In the winter of 1972, I slogged up that looping course for several weeks before I stopped and forced myself to the daunting realization that my story didn't start in the mid-1940s after all—when the father was in his thirties and the son in his mid-teens—but decades earlier. I saw then that I must scrap my first start and roll the story as far back as 1903, to the elopement of the father's oddly matched parents. And even then I'd be making an arbitrary plunge into the inextricably tangled nexus which eventually leads to the primal coupling that launched the species *Homo sapiens*, presumably somewhere in Africa. Practically speaking, however, my reader would need a straightforward account of at least one prior generation of craving and love and failure, in two families, before he or she could begin to respond to my intended present.

Yet in 1963, nine years before I discovered that feasible beginning, I'd sensed my destination and written in my notebook—

> The idea of this rather brief, shapely story . . . has been suspect to me for
> sometime now: made so a little by the finishing of "The Names and Faces
> of Heroes" [a story about my father and me] . . . which rather knocked the

---

*An especially avid reader can find all the notes I made while writing the three novels in a larger collection of my notes—*Learning a Trade: A Craftsman's Notebooks, 1955–1997* (Duke University Press).

props out of the *need* for such a story—, by a letter from Wally late last summer urging me to do a really sizable "Family novel," and by my own growing desire to do something a little—I don't know—maybe grander, in scale, scope. Then too I've seen the marvellous film of O'Neill's *Long Day's Journey Into Night* twice in the past five days, and that has made me think hard again about the idea of a novel which would examine intensely, unflinchingly and forgivingly the interlocked members of a family.

That early intention remained a guide through the decades of work, as it's guided Western narrative from the visible start.

My own suspicion of why humankind invented storytelling and continues to pursue it so relentlessly, waking and sleeping, is grounded in a sense of our ancient and unavoidable obsession with family. We narrate in the constant hope of escaping self-entrapment, a constraint that's closed around us in the dense net woven from our genetic legacies and the crying hungers, fears, and strengths which are given or denied us in our first years at home. And we narrate to *others*. If not, we're soon addressing ourselves to buildings and bus stops and are hauled away or left to spend the remainder of our lives huddled on subway gratings and under bridges.

Think only of the earliest stories in our culture. Though they're more than three millennia old, they're readily available in the oldest Hebrew scriptures and are still the most frequently consulted words in the world. Except for occasional lunges into rapt prophesy, those texts drive themselves onward as a narrative family journey. The marital tragedy of Adam and Eve becomes the fraternal tragedy of their sons Cain and Abel which becomes the nomadic fate of the father-son patriarchs which becomes the brotherly rivalries of Moses and Aaron which become the palace blood-intrigues of David and his sons and descendants which cross a short bridge into the Christian stories of the Jewish family of Jesus which raises an eldest son who rejects his kin, goes to the city to find his true Father, is gruesomely killed for his pains and (childless himself) breeds the gains and losses of at least two more millennia of family tales which show no sign of stopping.

Even Proust's *In Search of Lost Time*, the supreme Jewish novel of the twentieth century—though written by a man whose sexual nature precluded fatherhood—is propelled by family through its thousands of pages as remorselessly as the book of Genesis. And most attempts at devising an alternate engine for fictional narrative, by writers from whatever origins, have resulted in a stupefying vapidity or the airless fiction of prank and puzzle by which a few writers of our recent *fin de siècle* attempted to galvanize their own numb faculties.

Toward the end of *The Surface of Earth*, when the bruised Rob Mayfield visits his case-hardened uncle Kennerly Kendal, Kennerly remarks on a failure that's implicit in Rob's expectations of escape and reward—

> "Let me tell you this story that you don't understand. You'd have known it all your life if you'd ever woke up. We are very plain people. We're the history of the world; nothing one bit unusual in any of our lives. You are just one of us; you have not been singled out for special mistreatment."

Though the novel never says so, it's plain that Kennerly has read a great deal, pondered the meaning of the written record of human life, and watched the world itself intently.

The second concern of which I was certain in writing these novels is that, before I was more than a few pages into my new start, I saw how it might also deduce a compelling and perhaps useful story from what I'd witnessed of the central and ongoing catastrophe of American life—the enslavement, emancipation, and renewed subjection of men and women of African origin who were brought to America in violence. What I most hoped for in this respect was a demonstration of the fact that, despite the cage in which they labored, those same black men and women and their heirs became our chief messengers of spiritual and worldly freedom, both sources of actual joy.

In short, I soon realized that I was writing as a veteran of the last generation of white Americans who'd known former slaves and who'd lived steadily in the terrible and often miraculous symbiosis of two races. I was born only sixty-eight years after the Civil War ended (and am writing this preface at the age of sixty-eight); so the ground of my youth was thick with still-standing human reminders and with all the enigmas which the war had failed to solve, not to mention the new ones launched by emancipation.

But my sense of how that evil was maintained, and continues to be, by so many otherwise decent men and women is very different from the feelings of my kin and other imposing predecessors—writers with the keen faculties of Faulkner, Welty, and O'Connor who were sometimes silent on both the brutality implicit in the lives of their white subjects and on the inexplicably benign relations which often grew between black and white people caught in the monstrous cage of the system. The intensity with which my sense of the dilemma is conveyed in the novels arises from my conviction that, without a renewed effort at comprehension and remedy, the failure of racial justice in America—in the Northeast, the Plains, the Middle West, the West as well as the old Confederacy—is the failure most likely to doom our national enterprise still (plainly the failing is far from exclusive to us as a nation).

When I'd completed the third volume in 1994, I thought of taking Kennerly Kendal's bitter phrase as the title of the whole endeavor—*The History of the World*. A dread of the grandiose stopped me, but these years later I'll admit that I wonder what emotional fact this story omits. Certainly its choice to employ large families connected by blood as a lens to focus the story's gaze implies a central fact of the American South and of most of the rest of the country (the South alone, far from being the quaint backwater so often imagined, is a country larger than western Europe, one that plunged the nation into a war which killed some 640,000 men, and a country that's been uniquely emblematic—in its combination of magnanimity and maddog self-righteousness—of the entire republic). That central fact is the characteristic loneliness at the heart of American society and has been its motor force through the past four centuries.

Americans hardly invented loneliness—Russian fiction, not to mention French or Spanish or German or Japanese, groans with the weight of solitary souls—but American solitude has proved its own creature. What fueled the families best known to me—and all the enduring characters of American fiction—was a loneliness of such fierce proportions that it drove men, women, and children to fill what they felt as gaping holes in their own lives with other human beings when they might have learned from sustained witness of the world that human beings are never satisfactory stops against the howling winds of bafflement and melancholy. The epigraphs to the first and second novels speak to that constant, and constantly doomed, human effort.

This further variety of universal blindness—a necessity, to be sure, for propagating the race—gives A *Great Circle* its steady tone of comedy, a comedy that threads through sadness and disaster as it does in virtually all human lives. Yet it's a comedy that's proved oddly elusive for some readers, especially those unaccustomed to the sly irony native to the old South and far from dead yet—a culture of Native American, English, Scottish, Welsh, Irish, French, Spanish, and African peoples with mainly slim or desperately scarce resources who made their way through the dangerous world of men and nature by their mother wit alone.

Any reader, though, who listens closely to the voices of the numerous characters—in their conversations, their thoughts and solitary acts, and in their letters—is likely to hear why this trilogy is at least as nearly a *Comedy* as a tragic *Ring*. The failure of so many of the characters to imagine other than human consolations for their solitude is only one such comic strand in the story, a strand braided with far darker strands. All honest comedies of course comprise dark tragedy and long outlast it—tragedy being mainly a luxury in which only the fortunate can afford to dwell.

Since I'm no longer the man who wrote this slowly grown story, I'm reluctant to alter it in any respect. To do so now would be to employ whatever skills I presently have, whatever ideas and aims I hold all these years later to overwrite a younger man's work and to risk betraying its voice and spirit, even if I managed to curb his shortcomings. I've likewise made no attempt to homogenize diction and punctuation among the parts; the story stands as it was first published in separate volumes. In the interest of sustained chronology, however, I've taken this chance to make a scant nineteen one-word changes in the previous texts of the three novels. I've corrected obvious typographical errors and a few errors of usage. But at a time when large fictional undertakings may be less welcome to readers than they've sometimes been, I've made no cuts. I could find no entirely dispensable scene. In any case, since childhood the novels to which I've returned most gladly are those that ask to detain us for weeks, even months—the novels of Lady Murasaki, Samuel Richardson, Stendhal, Dickens, Tolstoy, Dostoevsky, Proust, and Thomas Mann.

Their first claim on us is the vitality of a particular saga and the language in which it conveys apparent life as it spins into hundreds of forms called men, women, children, animals, trees. That protean spectacle, with the right guidance, is never less than compelling. But many of us also feel that a sizable part of the pleasure of reading the hundreds of pages in a mammoth narrative is a parallel to the pleasure of mountain climbing or the granule-by-granule excavation of an ancient city to find its intact treasury or its sealed royal tomb—the sheer elation of a long effort that ends in conquest.

The candid writer of a book with any such ambitions may well acknowledge the slow pleasure of learning how, for even the sanest readers, words on a page can become actual other lives. Long years of hearing the reactions of strangers, and of monitoring my own, indicate that people read fiction primarily in the hopes of alternate life. If the dozens of lives in *The Surface of Earth* hadn't found their initial way toward numerous hospitable and responsive strangers, it hardly seems likely that two other volumes—the same lives and more—would have volunteered themselves.

Now that these thousand pages have been gathered, I can hope that new readers will find in *A Great Circle* the same kind of persuasion that brought me, in early childhood, to accept a seductive writer's lead till an alternate world began to grow round me and beckon my captive imagination through an earnest piece of real clock-time—an experience like a low-grade fever that nonetheless gives us needed rest or a seasonal love affair that leaves us cured of a few more illusions.

My generous publisher has made it possible to include two additions I've long hoped to provide—a chart of the three entwined families and a list of primary characters with brief notes on their lives. The family tree and the list were prepared by a hawk-eyed friend and scholar, Frances Kunstling. I've trimmed her list and concurred in her instinct that, for narrative pleasure, one small omission should be made from the family tree and the notes. Any reader who persists to the end can easily supply the omission and will, I hope, agree that the withholding is justified.

Finally, it may be useful to know that the *Encyclopedia Britannica* defines a great circle as, among other things, "the shortest course between two points on the surface of a sphere." It's the course desired by most human beings in our ideal relations but the one we find hardest to take.

R.P.

2001

THE MAYFIELD-KENDAL FAMILY

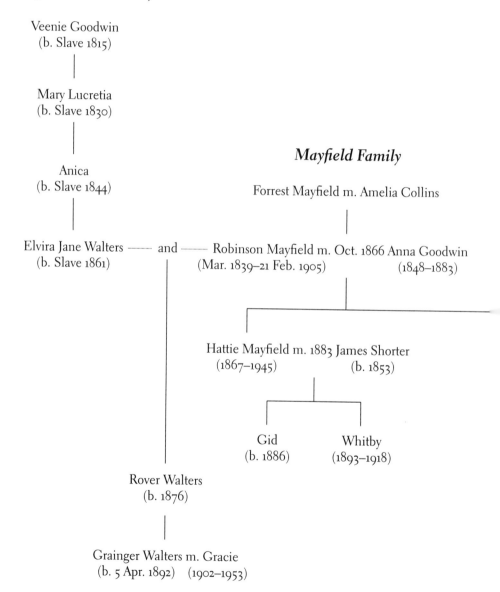

Grainger Walters Family

Veenie Goodwin
(b. Slave 1815)

Mary Lucretia
(b. Slave 1830)

Anica
(b. Slave 1844)

Mayfield Family

Forrest Mayfield m. Amelia Collins

Elvira Jane Walters ——— and ——— Robinson Mayfield m. Oct. 1866 Anna Goodwin
(b. Slave 1861)   (Mar. 1839–21 Feb. 1905)   (1848–1883)

Hattie Mayfield m. 1883 James Shorter
(1867–1945)   (b. 1853)

Gid   Whitby
(b. 1886)   (1893–1918)

Rover Walters
(b. 1876)

Grainger Walters m. Gracie
(b. 5 Apr. 1892)   (1902–1953)

Kendal Family

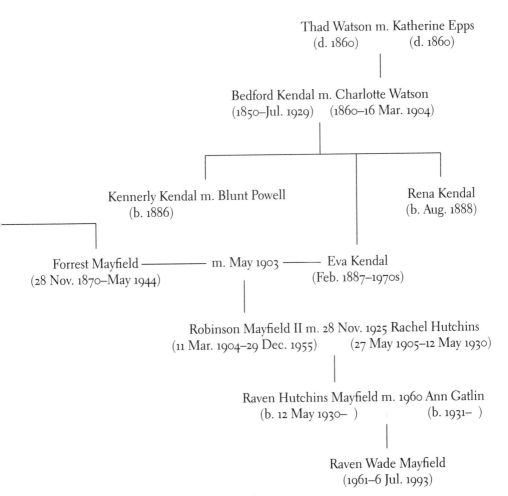

Thad Watson m. Katherine Epps
(d. 1860)   (d. 1860)

Bedford Kendal m. Charlotte Watson
(1850–Jul. 1929)   (1860–16 Mar. 1904)

Kennerly Kendal m. Blunt Powell
(b. 1886)

Rena Kendal
(b. Aug. 1888)

Forrest Mayfield ———— m. May 1903 ———— Eva Kendal
(28 Nov. 1870–May 1944)   (Feb. 1887–1970s)

Robinson Mayfield II m. 28 Nov. 1925 Rachel Hutchins
(11 Mar. 1904–29 Dec. 1955)   (27 May 1905–12 May 1930)

Raven Hutchins Mayfield m. 1960 Ann Gatlin
(b. 12 May 1930–)   (b. 1931–)

Raven Wade Mayfield
(1961–6 Jul. 1993)

For a list and description of primary characters, see page 1189.

A GREAT CIRCLE

THE
SURFACE
OF
EARTH

FOR

CHRISTOPHER BEEBE

AND

WILLIAM SINGER

But You, the Good which needs no good,
rest always, being Yourself Your rest.
What man can teach another man that?
What angel an angel?
What angel a man?

AUGUSTINE, *Confessions*, XIII, 38

BOOK ONE   ABSOLUTE PLEASURES

BOOK TWO   THE HEART IN DREAMS

BOOK THREE   PARTIAL AMENDS

O N E

ABSOLUTE PLEASURES

MAY 1903

"Who told Thad she was dead?" Rena asked.

"Thad killed her," Eva said. "He already knew."

Their father—from his rocker, almost dark in the evening—said, "Hush your voices down. Your mother's on the way. And never call him *Thad.* He was her dear father, your own grandfather; and of course he never killed her."

Kennerly said, "He gave her the baby. The baby killed her. So I think he did justice, killing himself."

"Shame," their father said. He drew at his cigar. "I hope none of you lives to face such a choice." Another draw. "But one of you will. Then remember tonight—the cruelty you've talked against the helpless dead."

He had started directing his answer to Kennerly—Kennerly was leaving home in a week: a job, his life—but he ended it on Eva. His middle child, his choice of the three, the thing in the world (beside his own mother, dead twenty years) that he'd loved and still loved, for sixteen years.

Dark as it was, Eva met his eyes and waited him out. Then she said, "What's shameful, sir, in wanting the truth? We're all nearly grown. We've heard scraps of it all our lives—lies, jokes. We are asking to know. It's our own story."

Her father nodded. "It would kill your mother to hear it."

They all were silent. The street beyond was empty. Hector the dog surrendered to Kennerly's scratching hands. Their mother's voice came from the kitchen, still talking—"Mag, you can take this bread on with you and bake fresh for breakfast if you get here in time. You'll get here, won't you?"—Some grumble from Mag, amounting to Yes.—"And you too, Sylvie? We got to iron curtains." A younger docile voice said "Yes'm."

Rena and Kennerly also looked to Eva. She was running this.

Eva said "Safe."

Their father said, quickly and as near to whispering as he ever came, "Thad Watson married Katherine Epps and, much as he loved her, he wanted a son. Three, four years passed—no son, no daughter. Katherine told him it was God's will, to calm down and wait. *Wait* was the one thing Thad couldn't do; and within another year, Katherine had a baby and died in the act. It had been a hard labor; and Dr. Burton had sent Thad out to wait in the yard, anywhere out of sight. He waited on the porch, really sat and waited for once in his life."

Eva said, "How do you know that?"

"My mother was there, helping what she could."

"Which wasn't much," Kennerly said.

"Not much. What could you have done with God set against you?"

Kennerly said, "I could have asked Him why."

"You'd have stood there and talked, and she'd have died anyhow. My mother gave the ether, little bits at a time on a clean cotton rag. So she died at ease—no pain, not a sound, no signal to Thad twenty feet away. When the doctor had listened to Katherine's still chest—Mother said he listened for the length of a song—and seen Mother safely washing the baby, he washed his own hands and put on his coat and stepped to the porch and said, 'Thad, I lost her. But I saved you a girl.' Thad waited on a minute. Then he stood up and looked Dr. Burton in the face as calm as this evening and told him 'Thank you' and headed indoors. The doctor assumed he was going to Katherine—there were plenty more women in there with her to meet him—so he stood on the porch to clear his own head. It had lasted all night; it was past dawn, May. The next thing he heard was a single shot. Thad had walked to the bedroom, straight through the women—never looked to your mother, herself nearly killed in Katherine's labor—and taken his pistol off the mantelpiece and walked to the bed where Katherine lay—they had still not washed her—and blown his brains out and fallen on her body." He drew at his cold cigar. "Now you know."

"It was Mother," Eva said. "The baby that killed his wife was Mother?"

"You knew that," he said. "But never say *killed*. She was innocent as if she had come from the moon, and her own father stopped her life in its tracks before she could move. Part of it anyhow."

Rena said, "Why would he do that, Father?—not wait for his child?"

A long wait. No answer, though voices still rose and fell in the kitchen.

"He knew his life had stopped," Eva said.

Kennerly made his sound of disgust.

"—Thought it had," their father said. "Then why not take the ruined baby with him?"

Nobody offered an answer to that.

But Eva said, "Did you ever see them, Father?"

"I remember him—I was ten when he died—and I must have seen her any number of times. But I don't have a shred of memory of her. A perfect blank. Your mother even—I still have to look at pictures of her to see her as a girl, and she all but lived with us."

Rena said "Why was that?"

"She was a quiet child."

They all waited silently and listened to her come slowly forward through the house; stop in her bedroom (the left front room) and brush at her hair; then stand in the door and say, "Eva, take a chair"—Eva sat on the steps—"You're too dressed-up anyhow. Commencement's *tomorrow.*"

"Yes ma'm," Eva said.

Their mother went on to her usual place—the far corner swing where Kennerly waited, gently rocked as though by a breeze.

Eva stayed still.

Her mother stared at her—the side of her face; she was lovely, brown curls in swags to her shoulders. "Eva, go change. You'll smother in that."

Eva looked to the street. "I'm breathing," she said.

"Rena, make her go change."

Rena budged, vibrated by the words themselves; but she also watched the street and stayed in place.

"*Eva*, look here."

Eva turned and looked and before her mother could speak, even study her face in the dusk, Eva said "Be good to me—" She looked to her father.

Their mother said, "What is that supposed to mean?"

Hector barked once.

Rena said—and pointed—"Mr. Mayfield."

He was almost on them, having come up the stone walk that quietly; and everyone but Mrs. Kendal stood to welcome him, though she spoke first—"Did she fail, Mr. Mayfield?"

"No'm, she passed," he said. "She barely passed." He was at the steps and paused there, three feet from Eva. So no one but Eva could see the smile that rose in his face as he turned to her father. "Ninety-six in English. One hundred in Latin. Be proud, Mr. Kendal."

"Thank you, sir," he said. "She'll graduate then?"

"Far as I'm concerned, she's graduated now; could have two years ago. Knows more than I do," Forrest Mayfield said.

"Too kind," Mrs. Kendal said. "Sit down and rest. Have you eaten your supper? You'll be starved and blind from reading children's papers."

"No I'm not," he said. "Good young eyes like mine—I can see in the dark."

"You're thirty," Mrs. Kendal said, "and thin as a slat. You'll lose your looks. *Then* where will you be?" She got to her feet. "Mag's still in the kitchen. Come on and eat."

"Thank you, no," he said. "I'm thirty-two and I've got to move on. Just wanted to tell you the fresh good news."

"Are you leaving for the summer?" Mr. Kendal said.

"Yes sir," he said, "when I get myself together."

"To your sister's again?"

"Not at first," he said. "I'll wander a little."

Mrs. Kendal said "To where?"

He smiled again, though entirely dark by now; spread his arms wide and sang it as music—"To my heart's true home."

Mrs. Kendal said "I thought so," and all of them laughed.

He joined them but then he looked to Mr. Kendal. "But you've got all I ever wanted, here." He gestured round with one arm again, a single place in which to gather, people made in the place, made by the place and grown firmly to it.

"*I* love them," Mr. Kendal said. "Thank you, Forrest."

Through all that, Forrest had shuddered with fear but showed only calm, the only lie he told them till then. And when he left, he had not lied again.

2

He had hardly vanished when Eva rose from the steps and walked to the door.

As she passed, her father said "Proud of you. *Proud.*"

Her mother said, "I hope you are going to change."

Eva nodded. "Yes ma'm." Then she turned the doorknob and looked back quickly at them all. She settled on her father and said to him "Thank you." Then she opened the door and said "Rena, come help me."

Her mother said "Spoiled."

But Rena stood and followed her.

They were silent in the hall and on the dark stairs, Indian-file; but when Eva had entered their own shared room (the back left room), Rena gently shut the door behind them and said "You've decided" to Eva's back.

"I decided long ago."

"You're leaving," Rena said.

Eva turned, nodding. "Tonight. This minute."

Rena said "Wait—" not meaning to stop her but to hold her an instant longer, for study.

Eva said "No" and took a step forward.

"Go," Rena said. "I just meant *why?*"

Eva touched her sister at the damp elbow-bend. "In a year or so you'll know."

"I'm eighteen months your junior," Rena said. "Eighteen more months won't answer me why you are killing us like this."

"You're glad," Eva said. "Mama'll surely be glad. Kennerly's leaving—"

"Father will die."

"No he won't," Eva said.

"He loves you more than the rest of us together."

Eva thought through that. "Even so," she said, "my life is separate. I'm going to *that*. He's been through worse than this. He'll live. I'll write him."

Rena said again "He'll die."

Eva touched her again, on the back of the neck, and smiled at her fully but stepped on past her to the door and opened it.

"Your grip?" Rena whispered and pointed to a brown leather case on the wardrobe.

Eva shook her head No.

"I've promised," Rena whispered. "Silence till tomorrow. They'll kill me then."

Eva smiled. "No they won't. They'll be glad of news. Now wait in here for as long as you can—till Mother calls us. Try to give me time."

Rena went to the wide bed they'd shared for years and sat on the edge, both hands on her knees. "Will I ever see you again, do you think?"

Eva listened to the sounds from the porch—still safe—then came back across to the bed and touched Rena. On the part in her hair. Then kissed the spot she'd touched. "That's up to Father," she said. "Help him." Then she was gone, no sound on the stair.

3

From the foot of the stairs there were two ways out—the front door, the porch, Mother, Father, Brother; and the kitchen where Mag and Sylvie still tinkered. No choice. She aimed herself there and went, still silent, ignoring the pieces of her life on all sides, snags in a river. But she stopped in the kitchen at the corner washstand and lifted one dipper of water from the bucket and drank it dry, from thirst and the fresh need to say one more goodbye in her home. When she lowered the dipper, both women were watching—Mag from the sink where she picked over white beans to soak all night, Sylvie from the midst of the room where she stood like the black greased axle of the whole dark house: Eva's age, one more piece of the permanent furniture of old safe life that Eva now abandoned. She took a step toward Sylvie—the door was beyond her—and said in a low voice, not whispering, "Take anything of mine you want."

"Who going to give it to me?"

"Tell Mama it's yours; tell her Eva said it's yours."

"She'll laugh," Sylvie said.

Eva pointed backward and overhead. "Go up now and take any stitch you want. Rena's waiting there."

Mag turned full around. Her face took the lamplight, darker than her daughter's. "You go," she said. "If you going, go."

Still facing Sylvie, Eva shut her eyes once and forced out the tears that Mag had pressed from her. Then she looked again and cracked her lips to say, "I'll send for you, Sylvie"; but waves of expulsion still pumped from Mag. Silent, Eva scissored one step to the left and was out the door.

Sylvie said "She gone."

"Thank Jesus," Mag said.

Sylvie said "I loved her."

"Me too," Mag said. "But she gone now. She out of my mind. Scratch her out of yours. What she don't know—people worth loving grow on trees in the ditch."

"Yes'm," Sylvie said and watched the shut door where dark air still churned in Eva's empty place.

4

Forrest Mayfield was drowning in gratitude, kneeling above his wife, taking the last of what she freely offered—the sight of her body in morning light laid safely beside him on linen marked only by proofs of their love. Till half an hour ago, at dawn, he had never seen more of her than head and arms—what showed to the world at the limits of her clothes. So he'd loved her because of her face and her kindness, the mysterious rein she accepted from the first on his oldest need—free flight outward from his own strapped and drying heart, that he be permitted after decades of hoarding to choose one willing girl and love her entirely, the remainder of his life. Almost no matter that she love in

return, only that she wait and endure his love, his endless thanks; acknowledge them with smiles. Now she was here—by her own will, unforced, still
offering (though the room had filled with light) her entire brilliant body, perfect beyond any dream or guess and visibly threaded with the narrow blue
channels that pulsed on, warm from their first full juncture.

The memory of that—crown of this past night—was the deepest flood he
swam in now, the union and its rising preparations: that she met him as
promised at the edge of the field behind her home (had got there before him
and the Negro he'd paid to drive the hired buggy six miles to the train—standing, arms at her side, her hands clenched, dark; and when he had said
"Your grip? Your clothes?" she had said, "I told you if I came, I'd just be yours.
Nothing with me belongs to another soul. This one dress was thrown off by
my Aunt Lola"). Then she'd sat beside him silent through the ride to the
train, only nodding Yes or No to his muffled questions, and walked silent to
the train and mounted one step and then turned to their driver, who carried
Forrest's trunk, and said "You know Sylvie" and opened her clenched hand
and gave him a five-dollar goldpiece and said, "This is Sylvie's from Eva; to
remember Eva." Then once on the train, they had spoken of nothing but the
school-year behind them as though they were vanishing now for the summer
to separate worlds and would meet in the fall again, master and pupil. And
then two hours later, here in Virginia, had accepted their marriage at the
trembling hands of an old Clerk of Court and his housekeeper-witness who
said to Eva as the clerk took the money, "God above help you." Then had
walked with him two hundred yards in the dark to this old hotel and, once
concealed by a black pine door from whatever slim dangers the world still
held, had welcomed him. Not at once, in a rush, but gravely in her own time,
the reins in her ringed hand still firmly clutched. When the porter had lit
their lamp and gone and the door was bolted, he had stood in place and
looked through the three yards of dimness toward her, by the bed—the
light was behind her, she shone at the edges—he had said "I thank you." She
had smiled—"For what?"—"For standing here." She had said, "I am where
I want to be" and slowly drew the wide green ribbon from her hair and began
on the numerous buttons of her dress, looking down at them, till—finished
and her undergarments folded—she stood bare and faced him. In her place,
he in his. *Simplex munditiis* was all he could think—Horace, "To Pyrrha,"
Plain in thy neatness in Milton's translation which Forrest had thought
nearly perfect till now when his own version came: *Simple in courtesy.* Inaccurate for Horace but true for this girl. Then she had said, "I'm sorry to ask
it, but can we just rest for a while now?" He had said, "Tired or not, you may
call me *Forrest.*" She had nodded, smiling, and entered the fresh bed; and

when he had blown out the lamp and stripped, he joined her and lay on the
cool edge, separate, till she reached out and took his hand before sleep. By
then it was nearly three o'clock. She held him three hours—not turning
once, only flinching now and then as she sank one layer deeper toward rest—
and he never shut an eye but waited in the dark, appalled by his joyous luck,
his hopes; inventing for the thousandth time their life. Then first-day woke
her, nacreous light like a fog seeping in; and she turned her head and studied him a long minute, gravely as though he had things still to teach or maybe
because she was still half-dreaming; but when she spoke she said "I am
rested."

   And when he had drawn their long-joined hands from the covers and
thanked them with slow dry kisses and had slowly uncovered his body, then
hers—all but stopped by the simple plainness of the answer this new sight
promised to all his needs—and had knelt above her in the space she offered
between smooth knees and bent to the work he had craved since birth, then
she'd welcomed him. Had shut her clean eyes and with two hands as powerful
as ice in stone had implored him into the still-sealed door of her final solitude,
final secret—only looking outward again at the instant of violation when she
smiled and drew herself further around him and he said, "You must know: it's
as strange to me as you."

   All was shared space now, shared news, shared messages freely exchanged
of gratitude, trust.

Pitiful fool. He had not seen because he had not looked, had never known
he should learn to look—at her true final stronghold, the delicate skull that
seemed in their struggle to press forward toward him (another fragile gift) but
in which her mind in every cell was howling its terror, loss, loneliness.

   Her three hours' sleep had been no rest but a punishment and, worse, a
revelation—vision of the ruin she had willed on her home. In the dream that
lasted every minute of those hours, she witnessed this—her father, this same
night, in their sleeping house, flat on his back beside her sleeping mother in
their high black bed, his face tilted slightly forward in the total dark, eyes wide
open and straining to pierce the floors and walls between his room and Eva's.
When the eyes had succeeded and for whole minutes ransacked the empty
side of the bed (beyond sleeping Rena), he shut them and slowly rolled his
huge body leftward till he lay full-length on her sleeping mother—who
remained asleep as he fastened his open mouth over hers and drew up each
shallow breath she exhaled till she lay empty, dead. Then he rose and
walked in the dark—no help; he was competent in darkness—to the next bedroom and performed the same smothering theft on Kennerly, who could have

refused but—awake, his own wide eyes on his father—accepted the death. Then up the stairs to Rena, who fought him uselessly until her whole head and body vanished under his, not only drained of breath and life but absorbed into him, food for his need. Then he rolled over off Rena's vacant place and lay on his back in the midst of the bed and stared up again—in darkness still, through plaster and lathing—and said "Eva. Now."

Forrest had separated from her and covered them both with sheet and quilt. She was on her back. He was on his left side, lying at her right, facing her profile. Now he must see if speech were still possible, feasible, between them— *words* after what they had finally swapped. He looked on, working for suitable words—it must be a question—till he felt convicted of mooning and said,"What will we do when we stand up from here?"

Eva faced the ceiling but her voice was kind. "You are making the plans."

He lay flat and thought; then beneath the cover, he touched her flank. "We will buy you three dollars' worth of clothes, send my sister a wire to say we're coming."

"Don't tell me," Eva said.

His eyes asked her meaning.

"Make all the plans and lead me through them, but don't tell me first."

He thought that through and decided to smile. "*Made,*" he said, "made years ago" and took her hand again and drew it out to kiss before rising.

But, his fingers round her wrist, she pulled her arm inward toward her body.

Thinking she drew back from reluctance or pain, Forrest turned her loose and nodded, smiling, and half-turned to rise.

But her hand strained out and took his shoulder and with more strength, even than before, drew him down and over her body—now cold to his touch—and quickly in. Then with her hands on the back of his head, she fastened his mouth over hers and endured in silence the gift she required.

5

May 12, 1903

My dear Sister,

I am sending this letter care of Kate Spencer in the hope she can get it safe to your hands. If so, you will know when you finish this sentence that I am well and happy as I dreamed. I only hope you have not suffered for me or that, if you have, the cloud is past and that when you read the following description you will think whatever you have suffered worth the pain and can live in the trust of someday having what I have now.

I will not write down all the story of the night I last saw you. This letter may yet fall into cruel hands and several more of those who helped us on might suffer for their kindness. Suffice to say that within three hours of kissing you good-bye, Mr. Mayfield and I were husband and wife, joined forever in that waiting bower of trust and joy made for us by our long delayed union. For the same reason I have just expressed, I cannot here answer in any detail the main question you put to me weeks ago; but a short answer is—Yes, two become one and are better for it.

I can tell you more of that if and when we meet. Surely there is not any real "if" between us—not with you, I know; but please tell me quickly that Father and Mother and Kennerly have healed and wish us well in the life we needed, and hope to see us as we do them. Tell me that, Rena—that my hopes are met by loving hopes at home. I have prayed each hour that they be so met. I have not yet thought of another answer or another prayer and will not until you have set me right or joyously confirmed my only dream that is still unfulfilled.

So write by return of post, no fail—if only the one word Yes or No. The address below is care of Forrest's sister; and when I have seen the word "safe" from your hand, I will tell you the rest of how I live through these first happy days.

You and everyone there are in my thoughts and will always be. Please tell them that, whatever the result.

Your loving sister,
Eva Mayfield

Care Mrs. James Shorter
Bracey, Virginia

May 12, 1903

Dear Thorne,

I am alive, as you will see by this, and only wish that I had some surety the news would come as a pleasure to you. It has been the only blot on my recent days—the thought that you and your dear mother and two or three more of my colleagues at the Academy might have put me down in your books as a liar, a cheat, a traitor to friendship and solemn duty.

The fact that my hand writes such words here will be sign enough that the words themselves are only bare counters for the doubts I've had, the moments of anguish, all of which come to me in the hard form of pictures—your mother's head shaking side to side at me, No; or your own eyes calm above slow lips opening to say "Forrest, leave us." Am I piercing the veil of distance, see-

ing truth? Or only, as so often, vainly flailing myself? You can answer me that, dear friend of the past, much hoped-for still.

But in the event there is no answer yet—that you and yours have waited in friendship through slander and rumor for mine and Eva's facts—here they are, set down with God as my witness. You may tell them to any man who claims to know different; he knows a lie.

I have loved her for the best part of two years now, since she entered my classes two falls ago. Your question will be Why? And my truthful answer, an answer I have searched and tested for months, is "I do not know." You have seen her, known her far longer than me—all her life; I have chiefly envied your memories of her in simpler childhood—so I need not offer descriptions of her loveliness. I have known, as you have, grander beauties who entered rooms with their armaments blazing or drew at me like great magnets in the earth—and left me less moved than a toddling child. Eva filled—from the moment I saw her, it seems—every valley in me and bore in herself the press of every height. No one has done that before for me, ever—even my mother, despite her early death from the strain to be all in all for my sister and me after Father's leaving—and it came to seem as the months raced on and no error was made, no flaw revealed, that no one would ever do it again, that if I should scorn this offered chance, there would never come another; and I should be sentenced (self-sentenced as always) to the gradual parching of solitude, concealment, self-contemplation, which I'd felt already at the rims of my heart. And of which I told you.

So in April I seized at the chance, and won. Did you notice at all? How can you not have? The day we took the two classes to The Springs, after the meal when everyone else had gone off to change in the woods before bathing, she and I found ourselves—with no prior intent, I gravely believe—alone together in the ruined springhouse. We were separated by all the trapped air, by the clogged springs at our feet, by the cold half-dark; but we drew at one another like moons at the full. Thorne, I did not touch her—a solemn oath. I said "Eva Kendal." She said "Yes sir." I said, "May we live together all our lives, beginning now?" and she said "Yes sir." I could not touch her—we heard the sound of someone approaching—I did not even move a step closer toward her. We had sealed our lives at four yards' distance—and none the less indissolubly for that, is my strongest prayer. Then you stepped in, having worried at our absence and come to see. But what did you see? Till that hour, I had opened my heart to you fully—no secret held back, no hunger not stated—yet, though you stood a moment in the bright doorway, staring, you never spoke a word to me of question or caution in those few ensuing weeks. Thorne, tell me that also—is there

some imperfection in our bond (mine and Eva's) that to you it appeared transparent as day, as the water of those springs we loomed above (had we bent, as
perhaps we should have, to clean them)?

And in those weeks, of April and May, we barely came closer than we stood
that moment with you as apex to the triad we formed. Nor said much more than
"Remember?" — "Yes." Till the week of our leaving when, with no word to Eva,
I made what minimum of plans were required for transport and marriage, for
ending my work and withdrawing those roots of devotion and thanks I had sunk
in the ground of your home, Thorne. Withdrawn never—transplanted, I hope.
And then two days in advance of the absolute end of my duties—all my exam-
inations given, hers all taken—I asked her to see me at the end of the day. She
came and stood before my desk—I sat, I remember now—and said "Are you
tired?" She said "Of what?" and her face gathered in on itself in fear. I said "Of
work." "Oh," she said, "Yes. I thought you meant our plan." Till then I had not
known she saw it as a plan, that we'd worked in silence to a single end. So in
two minutes more I told her the plan and asked did it suit her, and she said
"Yes sir." I said, "Could you live if your family disowns you?" She said, "Mr.
Mayfield, I am sixteen years old"—meaning, I think, that she knew her own
mind. So I told her again the place and time and signal, and she nodded
unsmilingly and turned to go. She had got within two, three steps of the
door—it was open; people passed in the hall every second—but I said to her,
"Eva, why are you doing this?" She waited and met my face straight on and
said, "Mr. Mayfield, I don't know that. I only know we promised, and I'm keeping to the promise if you want me to." The room was darkening, a cloudy day;
but she also faced the windows and had never, in all my looking, seemed so
needed, as urgent as the silent air I drew. Nor had her lean face, her wideset
eyes that can hold on me whole long minutes, never shutting, seemed so perfectly preserved from error, from the chance of speaking either lie or delusion
or destructive innocence. So I said, "I do. I want you to keep it." And she nodded and left; and I didn't see her till two nights later when she kept it, firmly.

And now we are here at my sister Hattie's, discovering each hour the degree
of accuracy in our wager—miraculous luck. I am borne up, Thorne; there are
arms beneath me where before—thirty years—there was vacancy, a shaft into
dark single death.

Forgive me then. And beg your mother to believe the truth—that I never
defiled the trust of her house, that my one room there was honored to the end.
Believe—please, both of you—that all I have done was done from long and
desperate need but also from careful study of the sustenance offered to that
need: study of the danger of my crushing that food in the act of acceptance,
of consuming it utterly. That I have hurt the present feelings and the memo-

ries of people who had trusted me fully, I bear as my heaviest burden. That I meant them permanent wounds, even harm, I passionately deny. Who, in the world, is harmed by the troth of two single souls unbound to others? Who would deny them their impulse to join? Who could not see that, far from diminished, the lives of our friends and families, perhaps of the world, stand to be enforced at their very foundations by the simple news that Eva and I are sworn to love?

And speak to me soon. When I know if you've so much as read on to here, if you care to know present and future as well as past, then I'll write again with word of both. Till then, for the past at least, loving thanks. But I will not believe Time suffers herself to be broken in three. She is whole and extends her whole self always—then, now, then. Thorne, you are found in all my time—your name, the sight of your generous face, your low kind voice.

In strong hope,
Forrest Mayfield

May 15, 1903

Dear Eva,

I got your letter and nobody but me has seen it or knows about it but Kate who'll be quiet, and nobody will. You ask me to say whether we have all healed and wish you well and want to see you. You always saw more than I ever could in Mother and Father, so I'll let you get those answers yourself by direct application. I've done enough, Eva—almost all I contracted for—and I'm relishing the peace now.

But I will tell you what happened the rest of the evening you left. You may not need any other answers. I waited in our room and read fifteen chapters of First Corinthians before they sent Kennerly upstairs to get us. He said "Where is Eva?" and I said, "Gone, with Mr. Mayfield, for good"; and he said "Thank Jesus." Then he sat in the rocker while I finished chapter sixteen; and then he said, "What do we do now, Rena?" (and him the one with the job and the life— he has already gone to it). I said, "I have promised to lie till morning, so you must too" and he agreed.

And we honestly tried. When Mother came up half an hour later, we were both sitting reading; and when she asked for you, he said you had gone up to Kate Spencer's house to borrow something. She took that, long enough to climb back down and tell it to Father; but in thirty more minutes—and no sign of you; we were back on the porch—he stood up and went in and got his hat and Mother said, "Where in the world are you aimed?" and he said "To the Spencers." So we sat through that—Mother talking every second—and then when we heard Father coming back alone, just his feet on the walk, I thought in my heart, "I'm about to kill him." But I waited and he came up and stopped at my feet—I was on the steps—and, far as I could see in the dark, sought my eyes and said, "Rena, I don't intend to harm you." I said "Yes sir." And he said "Is she gone?" I said "Yes sir." Mother said "With Forrest?" and I said "Yes." Everybody was quiet. Nobody moved for quite some time. Then Mother got up and kissed Kennerly and me and went in to bed, not a word to a soul. Then Father went in and, though I never saw him light a lamp, undressed and went to bed, I guess. The other thing he could have done was sit all night in the dark and study (we heard him and Mother saying two or three things, the noise not the words; but their voices were calm and they quickly stopped). Then we went in ourselves and closed the doors—they had left it to us, first time in our lives— and slept through till morning.

Breakfast went as usual till toward the end when Sylvie was passing the last plate of biscuits, and Father told her to get Mag and come in. So the two of them came; and when they were standing by the sideboard, he said, "There is one new rule; everybody please obey—we are going to give her a rest in our minds. Won't mention her name, speak of her for a while." Everybody nodded and Mother shed a tear. And that same night we went to the commencement. Your name was called.

Since then most everything has gone as planned. Brother left for his job and writes that he hates it but we knew that. Father works hard. Mother has not felt well, but it's already hot here. I am loving the weather, and bed is cooler with just me in it. I will write again if anything happens.

> *Your sister,*
> *Rena Kendal*

> *May 16, 1903*

Dear Forrest,

I accept with thanks your word to Mother and me that you did not abuse our home.

To the rest of what you offer and ask, I can only say that—as ever—you are begging for both the cake and its consumption. You have indeed gone toward something—its present name is Eva. You have also gone from a number of things, whose names are trust and—more necessary to life—the world's belief that love is a rational flame, consuming only what offers itself precisely as fuel, not the innocent or unwilling combustibles which I accuse you of igniting: Eva's mother and father, her sister, me.

Yet not I but the Time of which you speak will be your judge, and you err in referring to Time as she. Any child you taught two months of Latin will know

Time *is neuter. And neuter Time in its future aspect will uncover—in your face, your heart, and in those of your chosen—the true origin, intent, the end of your act; and any sane sighted man will be easily able to read off the news: sentence or praise. He need only be present, and that I will not be.*

Believe me,
Thorne Bradley

May 17, 1903

Dear Mother and Father,

I am married to Forrest Mayfield, and at present we are living with his sister in Bracey, Virginia. She is a recent widow with two children and is the one who raised Forrest when his own mother died, so we will be staying on here through the summer at least till Forrest can get a post at a school.

Out of all that I might want to tell you or you might ask, let me say five things—

What we did was as much my wish as his. I was never forced or even led but walked with him, side by side to now.

My wish did not come out of any weakness in my gratitude to you but out of my needing what I knew you'd forbid.

I am not now, and have never been, expecting a child.

I am happy.

I am hoping, as strongly as for all but our happiness here, that you can find it in your heart to wish us well; to say you have forgotten the few days of shock, and that you can entertain at least the memory of my face and word of my name.

If you have a kind answer to that last thing, may I hear it soon?

Your daughter,
Eva Kendal Mayfield

Care Mrs. James Shorter
Bracey, Virginia

October 5, 1903

Eva,

Flora writing this for me. Me and her out here taking in the fair and thinking we would send you this postal with the news. We won it throwing balls. No news but to say everything here the same. Don't answer me back. You know my mama.

Goodbye again from
Sylvie

November 23, 1903

Dear Mrs. Mayfield,

I am Undine Phillips, Mrs. Walker Phillips; and I write this on behalf of your brother Kennerly, who has roomed here with me since late in the spring. I write in pain and oddly to a stranger, but I've thought and prayed and believe it my duty to say this much.

Your letters to your brother have arrived here since July, but he has not received them. I have laid them each time on the front-hall table where I lay all the mail, and he has not touched them. In July when your first had waited three days and he had walked past, I remarked the fact to your brother who said it was not for him. I said that it bore his name and address; but he said nonetheless he could not take letters from Bracey, Virginia. As others have come, I have laid them out; and they too have been refused.

So I've taken the liberty of keeping them safe in the table drawer, with the thought he would change. I admire him so highly; he is such a fine gentleman, so helpful to me. But this afternoon when he saw your latest, he came straight to me on the backporch and said would I kindly return it to you with no message. I said I could not consider throwing myself into such a private matter unless he explained; he had never explained. He said you were his sister and offended his parents by early marriage. I knew of his devotion to your parents.

Since I offended my own mother briefly by marrying for love—and had a grand life till he died last year, not an hour's regret—I accepted the sad task. Hence these lines.

I enclose all the letters that have reached my house—three, unopened—and I take the further liberty of going beyond my commission and adding a message, one which I trust your brother will come to himself in time: that you and Mr. Mayfield know long years of unbroken love and care. You have after all only followed Christ's command—cleave then and prosper.

Truly yours,
Undine Phillips

DECEMBER 1903

Hatt Shorter stood at the foot of the bed on which Eva had lain for the past three hours, shoes on, fully dressed, face up, eyes closed (at the sound of the noon train, she'd put on her thin coat and walked to the post office; waited half an hour, then walked back in silence and come straight here). Hatt said "No word?"

Eva shook her head No, not looking up.

So Hatt moved round and sat at the end by Eva's feet and touched her far ankle. "May I speak now?—you noticed I've held off."

Eva said "Yes" and sat up enough to prop herself and look Hatt in the face—a long face, smooth for its age and the work it had volunteered to bear in thirty-six years or had not refused.

Hatt smiled as best she could, her hand in reflex flying up to cover the gaps in her teeth. "I've stood by and watched for seven months now; and was glad to do so, glad if that was a help. *I* know what you've been through; and can make a good guess at what's still waiting for you—tearing up every root the way you done, leaving your mother and coming off here in the night with a stranger to live with strangers (two of them, loud boys), and your own people punishing you with silence, and Forrest in his silliness giving you this child." Hatt waited a moment, long enough to stare at her own flat belly and draw a little wind into her own empty spaces. "It was *happiness*, Eva—not silliness. Believe him in that much. And whether he took it from you or whoever— some sow in the road—it was past time he got it. Believe *me* in that. From the day our mother died when he was twelve till the day him and you stood yonder in my door, I never knew Forrest to look less than hungry—for what *I* couldn't give him, God knew, I trust, with my own life sucking hard at me, every pap on my body (and I've felt covered, Eva; pardon me for truth)—but that day in May and many days since, he has looked like some boy fed in

Heaven; and whether you are actually his nourishment or not, he thinks you are. He has told me so, many times in private; and I won't lie to you—it comes hard to me to know that the one boy I really failed to love enough has found love and brought it up under my nose for me to smell in my own destitution. But the whole thing has been far harder on you. I've granted you that and I've tried to guess at little ways to help you, and you've thanked us all and carried on kindly; but Eva, you're a soul in misery—am I wrong?"

"No," Eva said.

"It's your mother, isn't it?—no word since leaving her?"

"I never loved my mother," Eva said.

Hatt waited again and, this time, studied Eva. "That has got to be a lie, always is."

Eva nodded. "Till now. I hated her till now."

"What's different now?"

"That's what I don't know. Nobody will tell me."

Hatt said, "What's the one thing you want to do?"

"To hear them say 'Come.' "

"To you and him both or just to you?"

Eva waited. "Either one."

Hatt said, "That is what I was waiting to hear. Listen, Eva—*I* know—they are not going to ask you. And in your condition you can't go alone. Make Forrest take you."

"My people wouldn't have us."

"Are they human beings?"

"Yes."

"Then send them a wire and say you and Forrest are coming for Christmas on such and such train and to meet you please since your health is poor."

"What if they refuse?"

"Then go to a hotel and sit two days—they'll know you're there—and if they still refuse, come back to me. You'll have your answer."

Eva said, "If it's that—the answer you mentioned—I'm not sure I could live on with that."

"Sure you could," Hatt said. "People don't just die. Has it ever dawned on you what a strange thing it is that so few people ever die broken-hearted? They'll moan eighty years but they won't end their pain."

"No," Eva said. "I never thought that."

Hatt said, "You work it out sometime. It's too hard for me." She smiled, leaned over; laid an ear to Eva's belly and rose, smiling wider. "Wait till *he's* here though. Don't worry him now—a strong boy's heart if I ever heard one."

Eva said, "You were serious?—about me going home?"

"Yes," Hatt said, "but the both of you got to go, not one."

"Then will you tell Forrest?"

"No."

"He obeys you, Hatt."

"But it's you he loves. You got to make him do it."

Eva pushed back against her pillow silently until she lay flat-out again. She shut her eyes and said, "Let me just think now. This all matters."

Hatt touched the extended ankle once more, cold through its stocking. She reached behind her and took the blundering apprentice afghan Eva had knitted for Forrest's birthday and spread it across her. Then she stood and went to the door and looked back.

Eva's eyes were still shut, but her brow and the ridges of her cheeks worked intensely.

From the porch came the shuffling of the boys home from school.

Hatt said, "You think. You're the one here with sense. Only one in this place, in all these hills." Her own face was fierce, seen by no one.

2

She had stayed on upstairs for the rest of the day. Hatt had shamed the boys and sent them out into drizzling cold to hunt a Christmas tree; and then they played—a distant muffled din. And when Forrest had returned at five and passed a few inaudible sentences with Hatt and climbed up to Eva, she had said little more than the simplest answers to his simple questions—her head? the baby's movements? would she feel up to joining a tree-decorating in the front room after supper? Her answers had been No.

So Forrest had brought her a supper-tray (by now she was in her gown, in bed) and watched her eat it, then had gone down and eaten with Hatt and the boys and helped them awhile with the Christmas tree, then had climbed back up to sit at his table near the foot of the bed and mark a set of papers on Cicero.

He sat as always, sideways to Eva. ("Facing you," he'd said, "I'd just see you; and with my back turned, I'd exhaust myself looking round to check." "Check for what?" she'd said—this was months before—and he'd said "That you're there" and had quoted her something new he'd found: St. Augustine, "Volo ut sis," *I want you to be*. She'd said "I be" and he'd settled for that, never asking "For whom?") And in her present misery, her wish was to turn her face to the wall and sink to oblivion, instant and long. But the light of his lamp was warmer than the dying stove; and falling on his profile, it offered her a clear chance to comprehend. She felt that, actually said to herself, "Why is he in this room? Why do I stay?" For months she had known the answer to the first, his answer at least—that she filled his life—and watching him now, she knew he believed himself and would always. Change or deceit had less chance in his face than in Jesus'.

What was unknown still was her own full reply—could she bear his presence? Could she go on doing this undoubted service, unending charity, for a smiling stranger? He was strange to Eva. Not mysterious or threatening, never likely to surprise, but simply and terribly strange through *not pertaining* to her. In all these months of stifling nearness—all the happy unions of bodies; she knew they were happy, could think of them calmly: their beautiful competence in one shared action—her heart had never accepted his offer; the offer he had made in the springhouse last April, to which she had spoken a ready Yes: *May we live together, beginning now?* Some days her answer was a flat No that slammed in on her like a runaway cart or that rose like sudden sour cud in her throat and demanded spitting. Always in direct reply to his presence, the looks of unassuaged gratitude he would still fasten on her. And always till now she had swallowed the answer, maintained silence, but looking away at whatever was handy (which was desperately little in this house like a robbed ship with skeleton crew; Hatt had stripped it the day of her husband's death of all that might remind her of him, till the healing of time—every picture or book that had borne his breath: even her sons in the scrubbings she gave them, the square clothes she sewed, were having their father's shapes leeched from their own in the general erasure).

Forrest looked up now from his work and faced her.

The No rose. She held it by smiling, lips shut.

"Answer quick," he said, "—the one thing you want most, that anyone could give you."

Eva no longer answered anything quickly; there were choices of answers, all true and contradictory. The one that came first now was "Stand up from here, dress, vanish in the night." But a question followed in her silent head—"Vanish to where?" No answer yet.

"Cheating," he said and smiled. "Tell me. Now."

She said "To die."

He stared on a moment, then adjusted the lamp for a little more light, then began to stand.

"No. Stay," she said.

He stayed but he said, "I am not meant to stay. I am meant to help you."

She nodded but held out a hand, palm toward him. "Help me there," she said.

Then they waited, studying their helpless faces, for actual minutes.

He said "Please answer."

She said, "I am not as old as I thought. Get me word from my home please."

He nodded but said what he'd never said before in the face of any question—"How? Tell me and I will."

She said, "Wire them tomorrow and say that we're coming when school lets out and will stay all Christmas."

Forrest said "No."

"You said you would."

He nodded. "I lied. No I was wrong. I will not do anything to make you unhappy."

"You have brought me here." She thought she meant this room, and she gestured slowly round it; but then she knew she meant this house, town, his presence.

"You told me you were old enough to know your mind, and you claimed you wanted to be with me. I have to be here."

"Why?" Eva said.

"Because, but for you and that baby growing, Hatt is what I have. Has been for years. She's destitute now as I was once."

"She's got those boys."

"Those boys don't make money."

Eva said, "Forrest, you are lying to us both. You are here in this house, like a whale's dark belly, because you're afraid."

"Of what?" he said. He could smile a little.

"Of asking to go elsewhere to work and meeting refusal because of me."

"That may be," he said. "May partly be."

"You have got to *test* me, Forrest," she said.

"I've never stopped," he said. "You pass each one."

"You are speaking of love again. I'm not."

"Then what?" he said.

"The world. Strangers. I think I am strong, but how can I know?"

"You are," he said.

"Oh for you," she said. "I am speaking of me."

"You are," he said. "And you know that the question is—am I?"

"We can try together," Eva said. "Against my father." Till then she had not blamed her father or seen him as the foe.

"We'd lose," Forrest said. "*You'd* win, I know, but the two of us would lose. Then where would I be?"

"Back at the start, alone but for Hatt."

"Correct," he said, the last question answered. He was bare to her now as a stove-in turtle. He looked down from her so as not to ask mercy.

But she gave it—or tried. "Tell me now please. I need to know."

He nodded and began to deliver it slowly but still to the floor in a low voice flatter than his normal tone, determined to spare her unfair demands. "My father and Hatt's was some sort of scoundrel. Drink, women—what? I never really knew. I was too young to ask when Mother died; and if Hatt knows, it's one more kindness she's done me—to keep it hid. It must have had something to do, though, with appetite. My own memories of him are very dim—I was five when he vanished the final time—but they all represent some form of famine. Anyhow when he'd left—"

"Wait please," Eva said. "Explain the famine."

He looked up quickly to test her seriousness, then down again. "This is my main memory. However he acted in his spare time, he seemed to work hard on the days of the week. And he'd spend Sundays with us. I remember several Sundays—every one, it seems, but surely just a few; maybe no more than one. But that one Sunday then, summer and hot, I was laid out on my little narrow bed in the cubicle I had at the top of the house; and it was barely light. He came in silent in a cotton nightshirt with plumcolored stripes and lay down on me; I was stretched on my back. Laid his whole weight on me—a tall broad man. Expected me to bear it. Well, I did and it woke me—I had not heard his footsteps—and when I looked up for the first sight that day of what the world offered, there were my father's eyes staring down at me, four inches from mine. Could he see from that close? I could and I looked; and that's my memory—the neediest eyes I've seen, asking me. I waited still—"

"Asking what?" Eva said, the dream of her wedding night long buried in her, far beyond memory.

He looked up and faced her fully. "Tell *me*. I'm the one must know."

She thought awhile, taking Forrest's offered face as text; then she shook her head. "Tell on please," she said.

"About him?"

"Yes."

"There's nothing else. Nothing strange as that."

"That was enough."

"Plenty," Forrest said. "Then in what few other memories I have, I turn round from staring out at the road or look up from playing and catch those same eyes fastened on me, never on Hatt."

"Why?" Eva said.

"I've wondered. I guess she was too old by then. He knew she was hopeless, could never save him. She was nine when he left. So she knows more than me but I've never asked. Sometimes she tells little pieces though. She remembers him leaving. I don't at all—why? I lived right there. But Hatt says—or *said*; she told me just once long years ago—that he left in the night with everything he owned which was two books, two shirts, his pants. And when Mother woke there was just a note laid on the washstand beside her. She'd always slept lightly—a leaf could wake her—but she missed his leaving."

Eva said "The note?"

"Hatt saw it right before Mother burned it—*Gone. Tell the children I kissed them. Also you. With thanks, Robinson Mayfield.*"

"Any news after that?" Eva said.

"Not a piece—that got through to us anyhow. Mother may have known every step he trod, but she kept it to herself through her seven years alone. And took it with her."

"Leaving you what?" Eva said.

"Very little. Hatt thinks I loved our mother. I did, I guess—I was lost when she died—but I knew then and since that I'd chosen Father; and he'd have loved me if he'd had a chance. Hatt may not remember or may say she can't; but when Mother died and she came to wake me and say we were alone, the first thing I said was 'Now he'll come back.' And in fact our only living relative wrote a letter in the effort to hunt him but he'd vanished successfully. He wanted to. That has been the hard thing in my life—thinking of that: that after coming to me and begging for God knows what as food and getting no gift, then he wanted to go. Go away from us, three people with names which he meant to forget. Compared to that, Mother's death was easy and Hatt's quick marriage—she married at sixteen, three weeks after Mother died; the first man that asked her: James Shorter, a fool. Everything else was easy. And now even that is fading for me. I trust you know why."

She nodded. "Thank you."

"*You*," he said. He was aware that, through all that last, he had gone on facing her. It occurred to him now to look away again before proceeding, though he also thought clearly, "I am no claim on her, not this face and eyes. Have never been on anyone." But as he gazed downward, he saw Eva move.

Not her whole body. Not even her arms. Her perfect hands rose from the cover above her flanks and waited steady in the air, open for him.

Forrest was held by the doctor's ban; but she waited still, open still. No one had ever asked him before for a thing that mattered, except his drowning father. Now this girl.

She was smiling, to be where she was and with him. For now at least.

He went. And slowly, carefully found that the ban was as useless to her as himself. Useless and needless. Every entrance was free; every channel conductive to the center of joy that had waited in darkness but blossomed enormous and rank in their sight now. So, bare in the cold, oiled with their sweat, they strove all night round their swelling child who rocked with their laughter. Or they slept at intervals to wake to themselves. Once he, once her. Their lovely self, young and savable. Equal in gifts. Christmas of the heart.

MARCH 1904

Blood poured from Eva.

It was all he could see as he entered the room—called by a Negro sent by Hatt to the school, and his own heart near rupture from the two-mile run in freezing rain.

Her legs up and spread, gown bunched round her waist, and steady blood pouring from the wide slack wound.

"*Mine*," Forrest thought. "Made by me." Then he thought "Again," with no sane cause; and seized in both hands the frame of the doorway to hold himself up, to hold back from fleeing the room filled with people like spokes round the hub of Eva dying. Hatt at the washstand bathing a silent child. Dr. Moser with his dirty mustache, in his shirtsleeves, blood to his elbows—silent above Eva, his hands at the wound. Pauline, the Negro midwife, at the bed-head, a bottle of ether and a rag in her hands.

Eva strained up and saw him. She had shrunk, since he left her four hours ago, to a dry death's head—skin like a chalky lacquer on her skull. Not dry but draining, rushing to empty. Her lips said "Come." Her hands were hid in her hair and did not move.

He went through the others toward her. Pauline drew back. No one else looked up from the urgent work. No one spoke. He could not.

Eva spoke. Her voice was appallingly intact as though every other part could leave but her voice remain. Her hands stayed in her hair; but her face and eyes found him and she said, "It was nobody's fault, remember. Mine if anybody's. Never yours, Forrest."

He again said "Thank you."

Dr. Moser snorted through his nose and looked up as if Forrest—con-victed, last appeal exhausted—had been blessed by a doting lying mother.

Forrest said "Are you hurting?"

"Yes. Dying."

They looked to the doctor. He did not deny her.

Eva said *"You* stay."

"I'll stay," he said. She had never told him of her grandmother's death, her grandfather's suicide; and so he believed she spoke of the present, that he not leave the room. He realized the sizable distance between them. He was still on his feet, had not yet so much as knelt at her side. He took off his overcoat and dropped it behind him; then moved to kneel, wondering where to find and hold her hand.

Dr. Moser said, "No. Get out of here. Quick."

Forrest looked.

The blood on the doctor's hand was dark, browning, dry.

Eva's eyes had sunk and shut. Every tooth was plain through the skin of her lips, tight as if blown by a monstrous wind. The room was filling with a high steady sound—some durable thread being spun through her nose, which mounted round him, excluding air.

Forrest left, for his life.

2

For thirty minutes he sat in the kitchen in a black straight chair with a cardboard seat, his arms extended on the table before him among the remains of interrupted breakfast, his own eyes shut. In all that time, aside from shallow breaths, he moved once. The fingers of his left hand had come down beside a cold half biscuit; and he'd raised that and chewed till the small dry bite swelled and galled on his tongue, the mouth of his gullet—alive from his spit and an agent of punishment. He spat it in the same hand and flung it to the floor and scrubbed the hand dry on his rough serge trousers, still wet from the run. Otherwise he existed only in his head—in a square space, a room two inches wide behind his eyes—where over and over he spoke a silent phrase: *I kill what I touch.* Every other thought was a variant of that—that if he had failed this second time, he could not try again but must do the world the grace of withdrawal, though again he did not think of death: withdrawal from human intimacy. And that in itself, a return to solitude, seemed now the least of his causes to grieve—the world lived alone, his world at least. In thirty years of steady searching, he had never observed a calm contingency—two human beings in a single space as easy as dogs, as mutually helpful—but only the mute or howling lonely: his father wandering perhaps to this day, his mother dissolving in soaked earth a mile from where he sat (a mile from Eva's body), his sister Hatt, the Kendals from whom he had stolen the last bond that held them in harness.

He was interrupted once by black Pauline coming for the black iron kettle that had groaned on the stove behind his wait. He had seen her movements; but he did not know her—she never faced him squarely, volunteered nothing but the surface of her act: *This kettle is boiling; I am taking it somewhere where water is used.* So he asked her nothing and waited on for the doctor or Hatt or a voice through walls and floors to call him. Call what?—*Come?* or *Go? Go farther, forever?*

It was Hatt who came, and to end the wait. When he saw her face, he knew it held news—held news back from flooding, like a wall.

She shut the door behind her, pressed against it a moment; then went to the stove and moved the second kettle, still steaming, to the back. Then she came to the table and stood above him. "What's his name?" she said.

He shook his head, baffled.

"The boy, your boy."

At first he thought he could not remember, then recalled that they had never decided. Eva had said, "I'll make you a bargain—a boy, you name it; a girl, I do." But he had said, "No both of us, when we see what we get." He searched Hatt's face—still a holding wall, blank—so he said, "We were going to name it together."

"It's a him," Hatt said. "Then he'll have to wait for Eva to speak again."

Thirty-three years—he could still not fathom Hatt's tone or purpose. For all he could read in her face or voice, she might be referring to an Eva resurrected on Judgment Day to name a nameless boy. "When will that be?" he said.

She took the chair opposite. "Once she has slept."

"She's asleep?"

"Yes," she said.

"You are telling me Eva is alive?" he said.

Hatt nodded, pointed behind her upward. "When I came down, she was. Her and the boy both." She stood but as though against enormous weight, the exhaustion of one more day half-done. "I got to go back." She went to the stand beside the stove, raised a dipper of water, took a long drink and attempted to swallow but was forced to bend to the low slop-pail and spit it there with a noise she'd have given a week of her life to strangle down. A little low howl. Then she rose and was facing the mantel clock, loudly ticking noon. "Are you hungry?" she said.

Forrest said "No."

"Thank Jesus," Hatt said.

3

By four o'clock the rain had stopped; but the yard and the bare trees were locked in ice, and full dark was shutting down like a lid. Forrest had stayed out the whole four hours in his one school suit, no overcoat—splitting pine quarters into sodden kindling with a dulling axe and stacking it beside him till now there was more than enough to last till spring, into early May: warmth, leafshade. He could not believe these trees overhead would leaf again; that they would not refuse and stand in their skeletons, black through summer. He had spoken, again, once in the time—to meet Hatt's boys as they slogged up from school and send them on to the Palmers' for supper and maybe the night. Whitby, the younger, had said "Is she live?" and Forrest had said, "She was at noon. I am waiting to know"; and they had obeyed and wandered on. Then he'd begun again chopping with his back to the upstairs window as before—Eva's room—and listened for nothing but a knuckle rattling on the loose pane to tell him.

It came at four and though he was in the midst of a swing, the cry of the wood, it took Hatt only two slight taps to call him. He picked up the split halves and stacked them and turned.

Hatt beckoned with her whole hand. Her face was obscured; she stood far back and the window was misted.

Forrest drew out his watch and checked the time. Then he wiped the blood of his hands on his trousers.

4

Hatt met Forrest at the top of the stairs. "She is asking for you." She pointed behind her—the open door; the hum of desperate waiting poured through it.

"The doctor's gone?"

"Downstairs in the kitchen. Pauline's making coffee. He wants to see you too, when Eva's done."

"Is she all right?" Forrest also pointed.

"Oh no," Hatt said. She lowered to a whisper. "She is walking the line. Which is why I called you—doctor agreed. She may have wishes. Messages. Go."

He had held the dark pine stair-rail through that. Now he used it as a sling to force him up and on through the door. He stopped by Eva's head, an empty chair there on which he sat.

Her hands were still hid, beneath the cover now; and her face was in danger at least as grave as when he'd last left her. But though she was past spending energy to smile, her eyes at once knew him—crouched a little farther in, then fixed on his face. "Don't contradict me. I am not strong enough to help you now, but I want to know in case I die; so name the boy."

He thought five seconds. "Robinson," he said.

She nodded. "Why?"

"My father," he said.

"All right," she said. She did not say the name. "Now listen again. When I go to sleep or die or whatever, you write a letter to my mother please. My *mother*, no one else. And tell her what's happened—whatever that is by the time you post it—and tell her if this child had been a girl, I'd have named it for her. You'd have let me, wouldn't you?"

"You know I would. We could do it now, name him Robinson Watson Mayfield. Wasn't that her name?"

Eva shook her head. "She wouldn't want that. Don't cross me please."

Forrest smiled—"I won't"—and bent to kiss the spot on the cover which seemed to be her hand. Right hand.

"Have you seen him?" she said.

"Not really," he said. "I've been waiting for you."

"You feed him," she said. Her face was no fiercer than usual.

Forrest looked behind him to the wicker cradle pushed near to the stove. "They've fed him; rest easy. Pauline and Hatt."

"They're feeding him off of *me*," she said.

"Dr. Moser's here, drinking coffee downstairs. What they've done was his orders."

"You too," Eva said. "All of you feeding this man off me till I'm brought to here, facing death, young as I am. I am not ready. Hold him off."

He had thought she spoke of their sleeping son, and he said "All right." But she did not know or did not remember that she had a son. It was Forrest's father who roamed her weakness, now and as she slept and for days to come. Whenever he turned in his flight to face her or came to this bed to press her and beg, he wore the face of her own lost father and spoke in his voice—"Eva. Now."

5

March 11, 1904

Dear Mrs. Kendal,

Eva is near death. Forgive me for saying it so harshly first; but I do it, as I'll alter my hand on the cover, in the sole hope of telling you before you con-

sign this paper to flames, unread. And in further hope of reviving the care of her parents and kin for one who has only intended them kindness.

This morning she bore your first grandson, in strong good health; but suffered the issue of so much blood as to leave her weakened most dangerously for the trials of fever which lurk for her now. Her perfect mind is already assaulted; but as I spoke with her an hour ago, she made two wishes entirely plain—that I name our son now in case of her death (so she know his name—it is Robinson, my father's) and that I write you at once and tell you this news and add her words: if this first child had been a girl, Eva herself would have named it for you. And with my full consent.

Mrs. Kendal, I have never told you and Mr. Kendal I was sorry; and I do not believe that Eva has. Will you understand that at first—in May and in all the months till now—I did not think I was; and neither did Eva if I read her aright. But now I am. And if Eva were strong enough to write, I am almost sure she would sign this with me. Isn't that indeed the message she sends you as reported above?

Beyond saying that, I will end for now, having made no drafts on your time or mercy—only fulfilled my promise to one in danger and voiced my own delayed regret to your family, that I now know myself to have injured. And pledged my intent to engage in repair of all my damage if life now will only give me the chance.

> *Faithfully yours,*
> *Forrest Mayfield*

Care Mrs. James Shorter
Bracey, Virginia

> *March 24, 1904*

Dear Forrest,

I do not know that Eva is alive; but if so, I trust you to use this wisely. It is heavy news and could press her gravely if she herself has not already gone.

Your letter to my wife, with Eva's message, arrived on the 14th. Our Sylvie always goes for the mail after I have left home; so I did not see it, and my wife did not tell me that night or the next day. She did not tell another soul. But on the 16th at ten in the morning, having already finished a dress for Rena and laid it on the bed in Rena's room and written a letter of calm news to Kennerly (no mention of Eva), she went to the kitchen and with Mag standing not six feet away, preparing dinner, she mixed a strong solution of lye in a water glass and drank it down.

She was gone well before Sylvie fetched me back, and not until that evening when Rena put on the new dress to meet callers did we have your news. She had folded it into the pocket of the dress with no word of comment or message from herself.

It was all her doing, Forrest. You are not to suffer for it, whatever her aim, nor is Eva nor your child. Her own life was ruined by the carelessness of others before she had drawn a hundred breaths; and never in all the available years did she rise from that. I miss her dreadfully and mourn her choice of eternal separation from the one who had pledged her eternal troth, but that is my grief which I will not share.

Now tell me what these days have held for you, and the look of the future. I assume you have found a post in Bracey, and I trust that your life is rooting there near its natural home.

This letter like yours makes no requests. Only the first—that you use it wisely. I pray you know how.

Truly,
Bedford Kendal

April 3, 1904

Dear Mr. Mayfield,

Rena has showed me the letter you wrote her, which came here yesterday. She did not feel she knew what to tell you or how and had no wish to disturb Father now, so I answer for her. I think I know how.

No Rena cannot visit Eva now or soon. You must not count on Rena or any of us for any kind of help in the visible future. We regret Eva's weakness and well understand that she may wish to reforge the links she ruptured, but we have our hands full here with the pieces of her latest harm on us and cannot spare time or strength to come there and cheer one who cheered herself at our hard expense.

You know of Mother's death; Rena says Father wrote you. It has been more than two weeks now. We move along.

But so you don't low-rate the damage done, I can tell you that Father went out this morning just before daybreak when I was asleep and shot my old dog Hector with his pistol, one time through the left eye, and came back to bed. When I had left home in May, I turned Hector over to Mother's good care; and she quickly grew fond, despite his bad habits. He settled his feelings on her in return, so had barked a good deal since she disappeared. I tried every way I knew of to calm him—let him sleep in my room the first few nights, even put paregoric in his evening scraps; but he started up awhile before light this morning, and Father found the way.

Will that show you what I mean?—why none of us will come.

Truly,
Kennerly Kendal

MAY 1904

May 1, 1904

My dear Father,

I have just been told the news of Mother—this afternoon, a Sunday, our third warm day. I was also told that you understand my own long weakness, the only cause this time for my ignorance and silence, and so will have pardoned me of that much at least.

The weakness itself is far from gone—I lost much blood—but the health of my boy and the sight of sun and the green light of leaves were making slow but daily amends when this last stroke landed.

What am I to do? Is anyone with you but Rena and the help? What I want to do is come home as soon as possible for a visit. In spite of this blow, Forrest seems to think I am making headway; and it looks like to me that by the time he has finished his school term here, the baby and I will be safe to travel; and the three of us can come down there and help you.

Say Yes to that please. I have lived in pain a good part of twelve months because of my choice that has harmed so many when I meant it to help. And now Mother's dying with no further word to me. How is someone to live with that on her heart, as well as a new son, a needful husband? I think you are my only hope again, Father; the one to excuse me. And I think, though I know you have gone without me for a whole silent year, that if you can extend me forgiveness and welcome—just simple permission—then I and my family can go on healing in the shadow of your own certain recovery, and aid in the work. The thought that we might find our true place beside you, and spend our lives, is now my dream.

Soon, I pray.

Love from
Eva

May 7, 1904

Dear Eva,

Father has gotten your letter and thought it all over and asked me to write you.

He thanks you certainly for what is kind. But as to your plans, he foresees troubles which he does not desire. An example would be that, whether or not he resents Mr. Mayfield, there are many here that do—worse than ever, right or wrong, since Mother's being forced to desperation. So he not only thinks that there's no hope at all of a life for you three in this place again but also that in his own strained condition he does not want to be tested for patience and charity.

Those are truly his words. I will add on my own that, so far as help goes, there is plenty of that. Though they wouldn't stop Mother in her last decision, Mag and Sylvie are here and Kennerly who came home of course for the funeral has only left for long enough to close down his job and move back here and be Father's man on the farms and in timber. I will go on another year and finish my schooling, and then I will no doubt be staying forever. I have no other plans; and no one has them for me, thank God.

So study the above and think what it means; and if you have further intentions, write back.

> *Your sister,*
> *Rena Kendal*

I do not guess I would know your face. Or you mine, either. It has been a year.

2

Forrest had taken Kennerly to walk on the hill behind Hatt's while Eva finished packing. In an hour, at noon, they would sit down to dinner; then drive to Bracey in the Palmers' buggy for the two-thirty train that would put Eva, Rob, and Kennerly at home by dark. Kennerly the escort and nurse, here for that.

At the top of the green rise, Forrest stopped and turned and faced the long valley. He shaded his eyes with a hand against the sun and said, "Leaves are due to be full-grown today." It was May fifteenth, a peaceful Sunday.

The nearest tree was a quarter-mile down, at the edge of Hatt's yard. Kennerly studied that, face bare to the light. "Never make it," he said. "Dying anyhow."

Forrest said "How's that?"

Kennerly pointed to the tree, ran his long white finger up and down in the air as though stroking its bark from crown to root. Then he turned to Forrest, who was uphill from him; and said, "Better take that down tomorrow; kill all your others. May be too late."

Forrest said "How's that?"

"Blight," Kennerly said.

Forrest said, "Tell Hatt when we get back then."

"This is not yours?" Kennerly said and pointed back, gestured round in an arc.

"No my sister's," Forrest said.

"Will you get it one day?"

"Oh no. Her boys. It was her husband's place."

"Where's the Mayfield place?"

Forrest looked again and pointed across to the opposite hills, alone above the river. Blank green hills, to the normal eye.

When Kennerly had studied, he said "That graveyard?"

Forrest said, "Yes. My mother's in there. Her family's graves. The house is gone."

"Who was she?" Kennerly said. "No Mayfield, was she?"

"A Goodwin," Forrest said. "Anna Goodwin."

Kennerly still stared out across the river.

So Forrest looked too. He squinted and strained but could not see the graves, though his eyes were famous with his students for keenness.

Then Kennerly turned. "What's yours?" he said.

Forrest smiled and said "Pardon?"

Kennerly gestured again at the view. "What's yours in all this?"

Forrest could see the house at least, the black roof in sunlight—the spot on the eaves beneath which, now, Eva folded and stowed, obliterating her traces, her touch. She had brought to it nothing but the clothes on her back—and her whole live body droning like a hive with her hope and purpose. She was packing it all round the core of the child to take with her now, leaving what? *What?* He could only think of the mattress-ticking on their mutual bed—the side turned down, still dark with her dried blood, stiff with its salt. *That much*, he thought. But he said to Kennerly, "Your sister and your nephew. A few books and papers. A change of clothes."

Kennerly smiled for the first time since stepping from the train the night before. "Good thing you're such a big reader then." He climbed past Forrest on up the green hill.

Forrest said, "You have got three-quarters of an hour. Go alone. I am heading to the house. Eva'll need me."

Kennerly said "She won't."

"Still—" Forrest said, already walking down, eyes downward to navigate the rocky ground. So he did not see what was freely offered, even to him— Eva dressed and ready at the bedroom window, untouched by the heat which the black roof soaked, her eyes raised higher and set on Kennerly, his on her (both steady, all but smiling), Rob swaddled thickly, suckled and sleeping, cocooned in his mother's arms, making his own life in every cell, waiting to blossom solely for her.

3

In the night Hatt dreamed of her dead husband James—a calm visit from him, rare as it was real, and like many of her dreams, a simple memory. She lay, in the dream, in their bed but alone. She was young, sixteen. He was older, thirty. They had just been married, her mother having died three weeks before and she needing company and care for herself and her brother Forrest. The bed where she waited was in James's house and had been shared by him and his first wife who'd died eight months ago. What Hatt waited for, she wasn't certain. She had heard tales, rumors from schoolmates, Negroes; and half-hoped that all of them were true except that she could not imagine performing such complicated work with her own lean body, dense as iron-wood. Or that James would be any sort of good teacher. He did not have children (the house was empty of all but Forrest in the attic room); and his wife had died with cancer of the breast—both sides eaten like bread toward her heart, then that eaten too. Still she was there and warm and trusted that she was safe—her whole life had not made her suspect the world of secret intent to take and dissolve her: not her vanished father, her broke-down mother, her lonely brother. He was polishing shoes—James, by the one lamp. His first, then hers. No use to clean hers; they were cracked past saving. But she did not tell him. Let him work all night—it was nine o'clock. Let him work till day. Then she would stand and fry his breakfast and send him to the depot. He was freight agent there. But he finished, stopped, folded his soft rag carefully, laid it in his shine-box and looked up toward her. When he found her eyes, he said "Go to Forrest." He'd said it kindly and she'd flinched with pleasure at the chance to leave, but she did not understand his reason. "Why?" she said. "He is crying," James said. She strained to hear—nothing, silence. "He's not," she said but thought "I will ruin my chance to go." —"I think you will find me right," James said, standing and beginning to unbutton his shirt. So she rose and went in her nightgown—no robe; she didn't own a robe. In the dream she traveled the distance in darkness—the long hall, the steep narrow stairs to the attic—but even unlighted and in a strange house, she went surefooted because of her destination: Forrest, all she had. Surefooted, barefooted (she also had no bed-shoes). *To no use at all.* Forrest was not there, neither crying nor quiet. She walked to his narrow bed, felt it along its whole length—unused. She had made it for him with clean sheets that day; and he'd gone without touching them—tired, abandoned and abandoning.

Hatt waked herself then with the lingering certainty that her actual hands had searched her own bed for her young brother. She listened—only sounds of James's old house breaking up; and through her open window a single whippoorwill volleying: for what? She stood; found her shoes; and still with no robe, made her way toward Eva and Forrest's room (her own boys were in the attic now, asleep as the dead). The door was open, to Hatt's surprise—even as a boy Forrest slept shut-in, could not be persuaded in the hottest August to open his door and catch chance breezes. His secrets to save. She had come again in darkness, and she waited on the sill for her eyes to search him out in the great bed. But they wouldn't—pitch black. So she spoke his name clearly, her daytime voice. No answer. She moved toward the bed and reached and met cold bedsprings. No cover, no body, no mattress—stripped.

She rose and shuddered in the power of a fear that had not come near her for twenty years, the fear of her dream; and in her struggle to suck air for antidote, she caught the first rank smell of burning. It entered the back window, propped half-open. Hatt stood on Eva's rag rug by the bed and thought, "I have never done one thing to help him. Not once in his life. He has barely asked but wherever he's at, whatever he's doing, is punishment on me—deserved and righteous." Then she walked to the window and bent to its crack and saw, by firelight, Forrest in his good clothes, a pole in his hand with which he was struggling to force the remains of a goosedown mattress to vanish in smoke. The air that struck Hatt was strong as a flat hand, as harsh with burning feathers as with fear, as the face she imagined and set on her brother there, dark and abandoned.

But when she moved, it was toward retreat, her own room and bed. If he chose to burn house and her to the ground, James's sleeping sons, she would not stop him now.

He did not of course. At dawn when she went down (she'd slept again, lightly but dreamlessly), he was waiting in the kitchen, washed and hungry though generally silent; and in all the years that remained of her life, Hatt never alluded to her knowledge of the night or the loss she'd suffered but bore them as penalty, imposed and paid.

4

After supper on her second night at home, refusing Rena's help, Eva took Sylvie upstairs and showed her how to arrange the room, to hold the crib and her own small trunk (Hatt's, James Shorter's really). The room was the back room, shared by her and Rena through their whole childhood. It had been Rena's idea that they would share it now; and they'd tried the first night, but nobody slept—Rob from exhaustion, Rena from the strangeness rising in her, Eva from relief. So Eva had suggested in the morning that she move to the downstairs parlor, set up a bed there for temporary quarters (the parlor was only used at Christmas). But Rena had said "No"; and when Eva pressed her for a reason, turned and said, "All right. Call Sylvie; we'll air it for you. But it's where Mother's body lay two days waiting till the ground thawed enough for a hole. Call Sylvie now." Eva had only held her tongue and gone to the shared room and nursed the baby; and in half an hour, Rena had come and said, "You and Rob stay here. It's yours. I'll move in with Kennerly awhile." Eva had thanked her.

Now when Sylvie had done all Eva asked and was turning to leave, Eva said, "Couldn't you two stop her, Sylvie?"

Sylvie stared at the floor. "No ma'm."

Eva said, "You didn't know what she was planning to do?"

"Yes, ma'm, I knew. Been knowing two days since I brought her your letter."

"The letter was from Forrest—Mr. Mayfield, Sylvie."

"Yes ma'm. I knew."

"How?"

"I knowed her all my life. I could watch her."

"And you never told a soul?"

Sylvie faced her. "No ma'm."

"Explain me that, Sylvie."

"She got her right, Eva. You ought to know that. You took your right and walked off with it; she was thanking you."

"How do you know that? Did she tell you something?"

Sylvie waited. "No ma'm. I could watch her. I knew."

Eva sat on the foot of the bed. Rob was snoring three feet away.

Sylvie said "I hadn't thanked you."

Eva thought and said "What?"

"For my goldpiece you sent me."

Eva nodded. "You save it. There'll be no more."

Sylvie said, "I spent it, getting me some teeth." She spread back her full purple lips on teeth that, even in the light of dusk, flashed gold. One canine tooth in solid gold. She held the pose, even stepped a foot nearer for Eva's inspection; but wide as the lips gaped, they did not smile.

Rena stood in the door. "You got what you need?"

Eva oared with a hand at Sylvie's presence. "Everything."

Rena said, "Then Sylvie go and wash Father's feet."

"Yes'm." Sylvie went.

Rena went to the crib and, not bending, looked down at Rob asleep, darkening. "No question who his father is," she said.

"No there's not," Eva said. She had still not risen. "Please don't wake him, Rena. Anything but that."

Rena turned and said, full voice, "Why not? He has just got a little while to learn half his family. He shouldn't sleep through it."

"He won't," Eva said. "He has got time enough." She lay back flat across the bed.

Rena walked to the table and lit the lamp—the plain glass lamp they had always had, whose chimney they had each cleaned thousands of times and never broken, even as girls. She ran the wick up just short of smoking and turned toward Eva and drew from the pocket in her black work-dress an envelope.

Eva tried to see Rena's eyes, thinking quickly "She has gone past me. She has seen worse than me. She has earned Father now"; but the light only struck Rena's strong wrists and fingers, extending to Eva.

"I swear before God I have not read this. It was never sealed but I've saved it for you." Rena's hand was out but she did not move nearer. Eva must meet her in this, must accept.

Eva rose and looked. Even standing and the light blocked, she could read the lines of her mother's tall and mannish script on the face of the envelope.

Rena offered it that way, refusable. *Rena. In the event I succeed, put this directly into Eva's hands.*

It was in them now.

Rena said, "Please remember; that was my duty, Eva."

"I'll try," Eva said. It was in her hand but extended from her at her farthest reach as though she had aged and her eyes contracted farsightedly.

"She doesn't say when you should read it," Rena said. "Maybe wait till you're stronger."

"I may not ever get stronger," Eva said. "Especially if I wait." She sat again, the paper still with her, touching only her hand.

Rena reached toward her sister. "Let me keep it awhile. I'll keep it safe. I've come too soon."

"No," Eva said. She was fixed on Rena, her face a target. "You've come when you wanted to come, to ruin me. Have the plain grace at least not to lie."

"It may just be a goodbye," Rena said.

Eva said "Please go."

Rena went down silently.

Eva sat awhile, revolving in her head the chances of being spared this next. She could light the dry paper at the lamp and hold it till it took full flame, then fling it out the window to the black tin roof to finish there. She could save it, as Rena had said, till she strengthened. She could go to her father now, hand it to him, ask him to decide. No. It bore her name. For all she had seized that was rightfully her mother's, she could give this at least—simple attention. She set down the paper on the edge of the bed and stood and went to the crib and leaned—drowned asleep, his head pressing left away from her, fists clenched shoulder-high, mouth slack and open as if swept by wind, as if he flew or were drawn through air toward some destination different from this. His father all in him. She knew that to touch him now was a risk—to have him awake and howling for hours—but with both hands round his thickening trunk she lifted him, not to her, not against her own warmth but into the air; then quickly across to her bed, laid him there in the center in his cotton summer blanket. She stood back above him and waited—sleep. He had not only lasted the move but clearly had stopped the journey of his previous dream. He was here, enduring his infancy. She took up the envelope; drew out the paper, folded once, and opened it. Then she ran her spare hand under the blanket, found Rob's foot, stripped off its knitted boot and held it while she read.

Eva, I assume that you are alive and will go on living. And if so, I know that should I succeed awhile from now in my aim to die, then I'll never know your fate for certain. I will be in darkness and you may be elsewhere. Or may go elsewhere, if you last this crisis and have a life. But I wonder, will you? Will there be another place that can bear the soul you've made yourself? Even now, it is not for me to say; and everyone will tell you that I died wild or crazy. I have never been clearer, in my mind or my acts; and so it is my final wish to tell you what I see this morning, at the brink of death. Nobody else I knew needs or wants it; and as I have said, I may be wasting time—you may have gone already, may even be awaiting me, calling me to you. I may see you yet, and will say it to you there.

But, here, what I know is—I do not want to live in a world that will harbor and succor a heart like yours. Or that, in my lifetime, has held two such. You

*do not know the history of your grandfather—my father Thad Watson (if you
live, and care, ask your own poor father)—but in short he killed my mother,
then himself; and joined with you now, is crushing me. Because you have both
torn the lives of others by seeking the sole satisfaction of body. That fleeting food
is only found—or only hunted—in other bodies: my mother, Forrest Mayfield.
And those who offer themselves as scenes for that foul catch richly earn their
fate. I would not reverse it. My mother, your pitiful cheated husband. My one
regret for what I do now is the hurt with which I endow your father. Of all the
humans that I have known, he is so far the strongest, most courteous, as to brook
no rival in life or story. He knows my gratitude. I've taken that care through
all these years, to thank him each day for that day's goodness. So he will stand,
despite this blow. He will know its target, know it is not him. He can proudly
recall that once he had got the children his tender heart required, he asked me
my wishes and I said, "May we live as brother and sister?" and though he did
not answer then or later by actual word, he answered by deed, by a loving neg-
ligence which, if I could wish one blessing on you, would be my choice—that
you understand. We have lived untouching for fifteen years in pure devotion—and are paid by you with the sight of your life, the public sight of your
inflamed flesh tracking down its assuagement in a heart as simple as the one
you seized. I cannot bear it. Or will not at least, despite your demand for my
constant witness. My father had the goodness to leave before I could raise my
head to see his face. You have not, or had not two days ago; but wait at the door
of our lives and beg entry. So, Eva, I precede you with something like pride, the
scent in my nostrils—the first time in years, in maybe my life—of something
like what other people have told me was actual gladness.*

Show this to no one.

*Your only
Mother*

Eva knew she had suffered unmeasured assault. The questions that followed now in her silence were not of her mother's clarity or sickness or the
justice of the wounds she had surely inflicted—those could be answered in
calmer times—but of the nature and depth of those wounds, of the damage
to herself, its site in her body, the hope of repair. What felt most endangered
was the center of her chest, the flat breastbone through which her breath
seemed rapidly howling. She took her hand quickly from Rob's warm foot—
it did not occur to her to drop the paper—and thumbed that plane of gristle fiercely.

Blood had almost come when Sylvie spoke. "You can't stop him?" She
was tall in the door again.

Eva looked up, then heard Rob's wailing and turned to him.

He was red and sweating. He had cried for minutes. His foot pumped wildly in the blanket, caught.

Eva said "What's wrong?"—to Sylvie as much as Rob.

Sylvie said, "We heard him downstairs. Sound mad."

With her free right hand, Eva reached again for his rapid foot; but he kicked in her grasp and his crying deepened.

"Hold him up," Sylvie said. "He hungry, ain't he?"

"No," Eva said. "I fed him at six."

Sylvie said, "Eight o'clock now. He starving."

Eva folded the letter, laid it beside her, found Rob's body in his hot hive of cover, and raised him to her. When he did not calm and Sylvie stood on, Eva said, "I won't have a spoonful to give him."

Sylvie said "I have" and moved forward three steps into the light.

Eva looked up at her as though she now, after all this day, were the sizable mystery, demanding reply.

Sylvie said "I got it" and raised one hand to her own full breast, touched the left breast once. On her tan cotton dress above her clear nipple was the ring of a stain.

Rob had stopped; only reached for air in little sobs, a finger in the soft pit of Eva's throat.

Eva said, "What are you telling me?"

Sylvie pointed to Rob. "I can help you nurse him if you running short."

"How?"

"I had me a baby. Two weeks last Sunday."

"You? What is it?" All Eva's fear seemed a steady piece, an infinite shaft being forced through her chest by relays of hands. Sylvie's now.

"A boy. Come early. Never drew breath."

Eva waited, then said, "You are telling me it died? You had a baby two weeks ago and it died?"

"Born dead," Sylvie said.

"And already buried?"

Sylvie nodded.

"You know the father?"

"He give me some money."

"Are you all right? Did you lose much blood?"

"I guess I'm all right. Got this milk." She touched her breast again.

Eva said at Sylvie what she could have said to the whole long day— "How can I stand that?"

Sylvie said, "You can't feed him, Eva? You pay me to?"

5

That same night Forrest took her in his head. The first time he'd touched her entirely since March, first time in his head since before their marriage. He had dreaded such a seizure, and despite his not sleeping the night before, had tried to work, to train his mind to solitude again, however brief. When Hatt had fixed his breakfast and watched him eat it, she had said, "There's a mattress in the attic, old but good if the rats haven't got it. Bring it down and I'll air it today. It's sunny." He had said, "Is it that one I peed on for years?" — "No the goat ate that." She had laughed and he'd climbed to the attic and found it, dusty but whole. Then he'd laid it on the front porch in sun, drawn water, gone to his room and shut himself in; and surrounded by the morning sounds of the boys, had washed and shaved and dressed in worn clothes and worked by main force for more than an hour to transcribe the lines that had formed in his head through the previous night.

TO HADES AS YOU ENTER HIS DOOR
to be placed in your hand
This was called Eva with our Mother's name
Whom here on Earth, through three quick years, I loved.
Deal with her gently in your endless night
And let, from age to age, one shaft of light
Fall down the brown, unmoving air
To plow rich furrows in her hair.
Then leave her to her myriad sleep
And in the dark and make it deep,
For what are you but Death and young
As love songs sung by golden boys to unseen girls
And raging for her silent curls?
The vineyards of her flesh were mine,
Where I have fed and pressed the wine,
And sought the rain to heal the drouth,
And will abide no second mouth.

Finished, he'd destroyed his working drafts and hid the fair copy in the pages of his Horace—a poem for her death, now or later, in whatever form that death should seize her. Or had already seized her, from his life at least. Then he had gone down and joined his nephews who struggled with the mule to plow a garden. They'd worked together in full hot sun till dinner, eaten in silence, then worked on into late afternoon. Then he'd come in and washed and changed to good clothes and headed toward town to meet the last post. No chance of word unless she had wired, which she would not do and he had not asked.

Still when he'd found no mail for anyone—nothing even from Hatt's crazy sister-in-law who wrote three or four times a week, inquiring indirectly after James's money (of which there was none)—he'd walked across the road to the depot and asked Mr. Rochelle if there was a wire.

No, none.

As he'd turned to leave, the electric chatter of the black key had started. He'd waited, listening as closely to the code as if the impulses were freely repeating a simple sentence of devotion and promise intended for him should he know its language.

Mr. Rochelle had tapped out a burst of response, then had written for a while and folded the paper.

Forrest had said "Still nothing for me?"

"Not a word," Mr. Rochelle had said and turned, grinning for the first time in Forrest's long memory. "You tell me what you want to hear and pay me a quarter, and I'll send out an all-stations call for an answer. I'll get you something if it's nothing but news of a bridge out in Georgia."

Forrest had also smiled and said "I'm broke" and had gone out the door and past the bunch of waiters on the platform (waiting for Jesus or Judgment Day, no actual train) and half-down the steps to the station yard when a voice said "Mr. Forrest"—a woman's, black. He had turned and searched the dozen faces—Veenie, who'd belonged to his mother's family and who through his childhood had come to help his mother when she could. Or when she came, no more loyal than most.

She had stood to meet him—tall, thin as a slat but straight and her loose dress covered with safety pins (not to hold it together; it was not in rags) so she'd seemed in the sun to stand in armor, all her wealth on her, an ounce of nickel. She had said "You grown."

"You too."

"I'm dead." She had laughed. She was somewhere near ninety. She recalled passing fifty before Appomattox, said her nature had dried up before freedom came. "But they ain't come to get me."

"They won't," he had said.

"Better not." She had laughed. "Who you come for?"

"Nobody, fresh air."

"You ain't still lonesome? I heard you was *fixed*."

"I am," he had said.

"Little young girl?"

"Small," he'd said, "but old enough."

"Them's the best kind, ain't they? Teach em while they blind." She had not laughed then—a serious truth—and her eyes, opalescent with cataracts, had held fast on him. "Where you been?"

"What you mean?"

"When have I seen you?"

"Two, three years maybe. I've been back here since May. Where've you been?"

"State of Maine," she'd said.

"Why on earth Maine? You'd freeze to death."

"Did. Why I'm back. No, Rover's in Maine. Augusta, Maine—building boats. Called me to him, to die in comfort. I stayed one winter and froze both feets and never spoke to one soul that won't my kin. So I'll die here."

"Who you come for today?" he'd said. He had felt surprise at not wanting to leave her—old bore, old rascal. She would find a way to beg money if he stayed.

"Not a soul today. But tomorrow this time if I be live, my great-grand-baby-boy coming to see me." She pointed down at the glistening rails. "I'm here checking tracks to see he come safe."

"Rover's boy?"

"Rover's," she had said; then had stopped and thought. "Lord Jesus, my great-great-*great*-grandson." She'd laughed again. "I started early like your little girl."

He had smiled. "A boy."

"And named for your father?"

"Yes."

She had waited. "He can live that down if he want to."

"I don't know. Maybe my father is happy."

"May be," she had said. "You his mirror anyhow. If he come, you want me to bring him to see you? Tell me is he smart as I think he is."

He had slowly realized she meant Rover's boy. "All right. I'm at Hatt's."

"I know that. If he don't come I'm coming anyhow, to see your girl."

"Then wait. She's down at her home right now."

"When she here, she treat you right?"

"Yes," he'd said.

"Them young ones know how now."

"Yes."

She had laughed.

That night he took her—Eva, consciously, awake in his bed. It had not been his purpose. He had meant to respect her absence entirely—"If she chooses to go, for whatever reason or term, I must let her"—but once the house was black and silent and only he awake, he had found himself considering a question: "Could I live if Eva is gone for good? If so, what was it she gave me when here that made me believe we had grown into one?"

At first the answers came as words—*loveliness, kindliness, need*: her whole offer—but as they passed, they drew pictures with them, illustrative scenes. And soon, though he dreaded it, the picture of their union—borne upward, forward from the rear of his mind like an army veiled, their faces muffled but their hands stocked with power. He let it come. He abandoned himself to the effort to know the name and objective, the diet, of this power. And the effort demanded enactment of the rite—his entering her, her welcoming him. Or abiding him. Demanded its picture, image of the—what?—some seventy times they'd agreed to explore their mutual offer, their dedication to a single life.

Her small body, finely joined at its bends like a skillful garment, which after the first day had always been bare, completely naked—Eva's own choice, executed by her, which he had since followed: proud of the long-boned strength of his own limbs. Her hair spread behind her like a half-lost net in perpetual process of blowing away, of revelation—perpetually held in place round its treasure, her secret head, the shoulders, chest, trunk that flowed down from that vault. More rooms, more guards. To which her round knees, opening like the covers of a heavy book, slowly offered entrance.

Entrance, not knowledge, even explanation. That had been his chore—not the simple taking and giving of pleasure (natural to them both as the leafing of trees) but the study of what was exchanged and why, the weighing of damage versus repair, wounds versus healing.

It had seemed to him, all year, only healing. But now, in his head, he accepted her offer; and kneeling above, bent to hunt with his mouth—in her dry hair, across the waiting planes of her face, her placid neck, the close breasts (looseheld fistsful of nurture), the high flat belly, the core beneath (barely garlanded) rank with the fragrance of its own demand. By then the instrument of his own search was ready; and again, as generally from the first, with strong hands she pressed him quickly in and, with strong heels crossed in the small of his back, locked him in place.

He thrust. She yielded. And in those minutes—whole minutes!—their act seemed game or dance, solemn, silent, and productive of the minimum joys of a game: the pride in one's self, in the mind's own picture of its body's grace (bowing, ducking, in air), the eye's true image of the all but unacceptable fact of one's partner's *presence*, not to speak of her courteous obedience, her unison. Unacceptable because incredible, unearned, bestowed by a god whose kindness is crushing, unrestrained, not adjusted for mortal capacities. Then the game seemed the oldest memory of all—with Mother and truly wanted there, at last, no rival; no rush to wean, grow, leave. Implored by her to stay forever. He could think that calmly, knowing its truth.

Then she met his thrusts with her own strong heaving—at first, in what seemed a struggle to dislodge him; a cry to which he had all but acceded (there were cries, hers) when he knew his joy had mounted by double. Knew it by seeing her body as his mirror—her face as open as a mine at work: her eyes on his, her haunches approaching his, meeting not retreating. Little cries of his own came antiphonal to hers. No words, no words—he could think of none; she offered none.

So he strained for words through the final miles—words to speak, not his thanks (thanks would come at the end, in the peaceful trough: "Thank you." —"You were welcome") but his present *meaning*, which would be his true purpose and his only chance at knowing her meaning, their use to each other, the omens for their life.

The shock of his loins began its fast climb through his belly, chest, throat, to his crowded skull with, as ever, its threat to kill as it came. Or to burn its bridges, leave the route closed to further passage forever. It arrived. His brain struck like a great bell tolled, the noise poured through him, shuddered on into her; and he knew five words, which he did not speak but would always know—*It is only for me.*

Forrest lay back, ruined, on the bed still musty despite its sunning. Nothing was shared. Nothing gained that could not be gained elsewhere. Nothing lost but the atoms of strife and cry, the sparse clots of joy now cooling on his chest. He touched them respectfully, the second or third time only in his life he had dabbled in his own seed without revulsion. Only months ago, eleven months, Eva's body had consumed precisely this; then ruminant had slowly built it into the fresh body of the child he had not yet known, and might never, though it bore—at his wish—his own father's name. His famished destroying father—still wandering? She would not change that; could not stop the working of his own life in the boy, yeast in the loaf.

6

The two days after that, Forrest worked in the garden—at first with the boys, who were funny enough to ease his mind; then alone once they'd begged off to go up the hill and help the Palmer boys with their summer plan (the building from scratch of a steam-piano). By then—with the sun, the clearing air all flushed through his body, the message of his solitude two nights before, and the customary toughness of his mind (returning now in answer to need)—he was better, firmer on his feet, only the edges of his mind in danger, the pales beyond which lay both past and future. He saw them in place there and honored their presence, their evident power; but he also trusted from his whole life's experience that they would act when they would, not in response to his bruises or dreads. Today they were waiting.

And so he had worked through the axis of the day—the afternoon train, final mail—absorbed in labor, self-contained. When he'd heard the train, he had paused and thought "What's there will wait; what's not will come" and had planted on to the end of his row, a row of gourds. Then his job was finished. He put up his tools and went to the well and drew cold water and climbed to his room and washed and dressed. It was when he had laced his shoes and stood that he thought for no reason of Aunt Veenie's remark—"You his mirror," his father's mirror. No one had ever said it before; and since no pictures of his father survived except in his memory (and Hatt's no doubt), he walked to the dresser mirror and faced himself. He'd shaved that morning but without really looking. Now he needed to look—past the few things of Eva's he'd left there neatly (a hair-receiver Hatt had given her for Christmas, the ribbon she'd worn the night of their marriage, an arrowhead the boys had given Rob). It yielded him nothing, though he smiled, frowned, even worked at producing now with his own face the memory of his father's that distant morning, pressing closer toward him in secret or incommunicable hunger. Nothing—his own familiar face, ready, open as a plate, slightly reddened from his work in the sun. He smiled again—another relief, one more brace—and went down and called toward Hatt in the kitchen "Do you need anything?" and when she said "No but hurry back," he stepped out the front door and down the steps and was trotting down the walk when he heard the gate hinges and looked up—a man, a Negro, serious. Forrest stopped in his tracks, swaying from speed; and the man stopped too in the open gate.

"Mr. Forrest?"

He nodded.

"I'm Grainger," he said. A boy not a man, tall, a light quick voice.

"Grainger *who?*" Forrest said.

"My grandmama sent me," he said. "Miss Veenie." He stood in place but extended his hand. A letter was in it.

Sun was on the envelope. The writing was face-down though. So Forrest searched the boy's face for who he truly was and what was his message. He was maybe twelve—long-boned, long-necked but still on the calm near-side of manhood (in his face and voice; the dry unfulfilled skin of his chest that showed in the open neck of his white shirt, the color of well-used laundry soap or cocoa butter). No visible trace of Veenie's iron roughness. Instead a steady kind of exhalation from the eyes and lips that seemed more urgently his message than the letter. *Hermes, son of Maia and the God, eloquent herald, conductor of souls.* Forrest held his own ground. "What is it?" he said, knowing Veenie could not write.

The boy's hand was firm on the air as a statue's—offering the letter not giving it. But the question released him. He smiled on perfect teeth, stepped forward. "Good news," he said.

Forrest said "You read it?"

"No sir," he said but quickly held it to the sun as if to remedy the failure. His smile bloomed wider. "*Feels* good," he said.

Forrest took the letter from his hand in midair. Eva's script postmarked two days ago; the boy was one step away still smiling, his empty hand slowly returning to his side, no intention of leaving. Forrest said "Wait" and rummaged for his pocketknife and cut the envelope and read the message there, the boy's warmth reaching him across the space—warmth and the clean bitter smell of child sweat.

May 17, 1904

Dear Forrest,

We got here day before yesterday. It seems like a month of years already. We both stood the journey and have been allowed to rest; no visitors yet, though with this house containing so much sadness old and new, I have not found it possible to draw free breath. I had hoped otherwise. Father is kind and caring but broken. Everyone else has been stunned by Mother into states quite foreign to their general lives, as we knew them at least.

So as you will imagine, I am laying plans now for an early return. Three weeks more are unthinkable. The plans however are all in my heart. Do not put them in writing in your next to me—they would be read and used harmfully—but when the time comes, when I can see Father is strong enough, I'll signal you somehow and you come for us. Whatever the greeting, we can stand it together.

Our boy looks steadily at the sights around him (has slept very little, though has barely cried) and permits the attentions of his relatives but apparently like me is reserving his smiles, the gift of his heart, for his absent father. Can what I suspect be the actual case?—that he searches my face (his only source) for your whereabouts? Or as though my face were a cloudy mirror in which he receives a memory of you? That last is no wife's dream, I think; for your face—the mem-

ory of each hair and line, its various odors — is worn into me as profoundly as
the memory of water in stone. But happily, gratefully, *and in expectation of*
imminent reunion.

Your promised
Eva

Forrest looked up.

The boy had waited in place; and his face maintained its smile —
unfixed, fresh as in his moment of giving but confirmed now, fulfilled. "I
was right," he said.

"Yes," Forrest said.

"Do you thank me now?"

"Yes," Forrest said and reached into his pocket for a suitable coin.

When money jingled, the boy shook his head. "Just thank me," he said.

Forrest tested the last dam against his joy. He held out the letter. "Why
did you have this?"

"My Grandmama Veenie was bringing me to see you, but she stopped at
the office first and asked for your mail; and when you had that — and the
lady give it to her, and I read her the postmark — she said she would wait at
the depot for me, to go on alone and watch you reading and help what I
could if you needed help."

The dam fell; joy inundated Forrest. He could not know that, pressed
almost past bearing, Eva had lied. Or had told the weaker half of the
truth. "You told me your name," Forrest said. "I forgot."

"Grainger," the boy said.

"Thank you," Forrest said as best he could. "Thank you, Grainger," he
said. And in Eva's absence, with the hand that had reached for money for
the boy, he touched the forehead an arm's reach from him. Warm, dry.
With all five fingers he read at the dome of smooth bone and skin, con-
verting the simple unquestioning presence of a strange brown boy into tender memory — the feel on these same hands of Eva's body awhile before
dawn when, awake himself, he would turn to her and gently lure her up
from sleep, the aqueous sounds of her dark interior as she'd bear once
again the rescue of day.

The boy's smile vanished while he waited through that — or appeared to
vanish. What it did was retreat like water through sand toward a center as
dry as Forrest's own. Grainger tried but could not think when he had been
touched — any hand on his skin (a wanted hand; Veenie had touched him
the day before). He was twelve years old, his own caretaker for seven, eight

years. He was happy here, in these tracks, by this man. He thought that clearly, knew he had never felt happy till now. "I love him," Grainger thought. "He will love me for this. He will always love me because of this. This is the place my life will happen."

AUGUST 1904

Forrest rose into darkness on straight arms above her. By careful study he could see her face in moonlight that came on a breeze through the window he'd opened—August night—once the lamp was doused. She was gratified. Her full calm pleasure, even lacking light, reflected his own. Flood tide again. And again they were freely volunteering the sight of their separate naked joy to one another—one another only. The almost fatal pitch of their pleasure had been ample warrant of mutual abstinence, a mutual wait. She was not wholly silent; above the gentle sounds of subsidence sent up by her body, her dim smile spoke its own firm word. Forrest read it as "Now we are back again, where our fates intend us. It is happy here." And himself—what he wanted to say was "Thank you"; but knowing he had said it to the point of foolery, he said the next thing that rose to his mouth: "All promises intact." Eva appeared to nod, in her nimbus of hair—all part of the night, growing into night—though she moved so slightly Forrest thought the mere breeze might have rocked her.

"I'll meet you in Heaven if not before"—a strange man's voice.

"Heaven or beyond"—a younger man. Then two doors closing, the turn of locks.

Eva laughed one clear note.

"Drummers," Forrest said. "I saw them at supper—one in shoes, one in corsets."

"The young one in corsets, I bet," she said and laughed again.

They were lying in a second-story room of the Fontaine Hotel and Dining Room. It was ten o'clock (the courthouse had struck as they struggled toward joy). They had been together exactly an hour, the first sight of one another since May; and for all but three or four minutes at the start, they had been bare to one another, vulnerable. So no practical questions had been answered yet (no questions had been raised, practical or not, whatever Forrest fancied).

He climbed gently off her and walked to the washstand. Still in the dark, he felt for one of the two waterglasses and poured one glass full of tepid water and returned to the bed. At the edge he held it out to her.

She clearly shook her head.

So he sat on the edge and drank the glass dry, then set it on the floor and lay flat beside her. "How did Sylvie tell you?"

"Plain as always. I was upstairs with Rob. He had had a whooping spell in the late afternoon—the first in a week and it scared him badly—so I was beside him, just touching his back. Sylvie stopped in the door and said 'Mr. Forrest here.' My hand jerked hard. I was scared I'd waked Rob, so I sat still a moment to help him sleep. Sylvie thought I'd forgot. She took a step in and said, 'Eva, Mr. Forrest your husband is here.' Rob seemed safe. I motioned her over to the farthest corner and asked her where."

"Were you shocked?" he said.

"No."

They waited. Then Forrest said "Tell the rest."

"Sylvie said she had just stepped out of the store—I'd sent her for Father's cereal; we were out—and you stepped toward her, grip in hand." Eva seemed to have finished.

Forrest said "After that?"

Eva lay on, silent.

"Did you ask what I said?"

"Yes."

"What I said *first?*"

Eva rose on her elbows, still looking forward. "She said you asked how strong Rob was."

"I did," he said. "You had not written me for nearly two weeks. I was wild with thinking he was dead and you gone."

"Sylvie said she told you he was coming along. He is. It's a very slow sickness, Forrest. You're lucky he's living; it took all I had in time and strength. I couldn't write too."

"You could have sent for me; sent a wire by Sylvie, any Negro in the road."

Eva faced him in the dark. "I am living in a house where your name is not mentioned."

"Mention it and see what will happen," he said. "I am your one husband, your child's one father. The world is real; they have got to accept it."

"It would just hurt people that are down already."

"Hurt them," he said. "It is not their son. You are not their wife."

"I won't," she said.

"But you've crucified *me* with loneliness, waiting, uncertainty."

"I know I have."

"Then why?" he said.

She sat up fully, hands in her lap, and faced out again—the dark room, silence. Beyond the door, silence. Through the window, silence more strongly than the breeze. She did not know.

"Tell the rest then," he said, "—what happened when you knew I was down here waiting."

"When Sylvie had told me you'd wait till dark for a word, then you'd come, I went straight to Father. He was on the porch waiting for supper. Brother was with him. I asked him to step inside with me—we went to his room—and I said you were down at the hotel expecting word from me. He said, 'All right. Do you want to see him?' I said 'Yes sir' and he said, 'Then go. Get your baby to sleep and Rena will watch him. Sylvie or Brother will see you downtown.' I thanked him and turned to go upstairs; and he said, 'If you plan to take any luggage, I'll harness the buggy.' So I thanked him again."

"You had not thought of it?"

"No," she said. "Not at first." She looked down to Forrest. "Is that painful to you?"

He rolled over quickly and stood, his back to Eva. Then he walked to the window and brushed back the curtain and stared at the dark street.

Eva could see him outlined in moonlight and knew any passer below, looking up, would see his whole body; but she did not warn him. She thought, "He is trying to believe this. He understands; now he needs to believe."

He turned and came back, stopping at the bed, his knees on the side rails. "Yes," he said. "It is all more painful than my whole life till now."

"I'm sorry," she said. She knew he had stated the simple truth. "I did not aim at that. I am here after all. I came to meet you."

"For how long?" he said.

"Till somebody comes to say Rob is whooping or, if not, till dawn."

"Then what?" he said.

"Then whatever you want."

"You know what I want. I wanted you not to leave in May. I wanted you to come back the way you said. I wanted to see you and Rob my son. I wanted to keep my promise to you. I wanted you to let me keep my promise."

"What promise?" she said.

"In the springhouse," he said. "A year ago. Remember that far?"

"Yes," she said. "A year and a half. We were keeping it, I thought."

He had meant to laugh; it came as a moan. "You have broke it to Hell."

Eva waited and thought. "Listen to what I have done," she said. "I have had time in these three months to think; so I know what I say is true for me and will stay true always. I made you a promise a year ago—for far more reasons than I knew then or still, though I think of them nightly; far more reasons than you can ever know, you not having had my sixteen years. I kept that promise to the letter, Forrest; I married you. I left my family in cruelty and followed you. I don't blame you. I thought it was my wish. I took a baby from you and nursed it inside me through nine long months till it tried to kill me. I made a human like you'd make a shed, a good tight shed that will turn wind and water. I killed my mother. I came back here to visit the remnants of my family for pardon. The boy got sick, nearly died; and I've stayed—to nurse him with help; he could not be moved. You know all this."

"Yes," he said. He sat on the edge, quite separate from her. "All but one thing—I know you had reasons; I never understood them. I doubt you do, whatever you say. I doubt any human since Adam understands any full true reason."

"I do," she said.

"And another thing—you talk as if you've done all that in pain. I have never forced you, Eva; not in one single thing. I have thought of that carefully each moment we've had—'She must do this freely, do it from need; *her* need, not mine or anyone else's.'" He paused and sat watching her; she'd faced him through that. He expected reward.

"May I speak?" she said. "You stopped me just now."

"I've begged you to speak for months now, Eva."

"Stop begging and listen. Or ask me questions; don't tell me what you don't know and then say *I* don't. I *know* some answers." She had said it through calmly, the vehemence contained in the words themselves as they rose to her mouth. She stopped and waited for the answers to come. They came but she only said "Forrest, excuse me" and touched his flank.

He bore the touch—her hand stayed there—and he said "For what?"

"For meanness," she said.

"Excused," he said. "Entirely forgiven. But tell me, for God's sake, anything you know about what we've had, Eva; what we can have."

Her hand stayed on him. "I know what *I* had—the fact that you wanted me. The fact that you looked at me across classrooms or the porch at home—your face in a work to hide your meaning but plain to me—as if I were one last crust of bread after long lean years."

"You were," he said. "I told you that."

"That's wrong," she said. "There was nothing scary. You never once made me think you meant to consume me." She thought again. "—As if I were golden, some beautiful work you'd stumbled on and had the grace to recognize: the first person ever. I was very grateful."

"That's all?" he said.

"It's the part I'm sure of."

"Are you grateful still?"

"Yes," she said calmly, though she did not move toward him and he did not draw her. Then she said "Yes" again. "But I also know I was wrong, wrong to think you were all that watched me or joyed in me. There were others, from the start. I didn't know or just didn't see—I've been good at blindness and have suffered for that. I've made them suffer. Some of them still do; need me and suffer, both."

"Who?" he said.

"Father."

Forrest touched her cooling hand that had lain unused by either of them—clasped it; she let him. "I can come here and teach," he said. "They might well let me now that things have calmed, now they see we were serious. Or near here at least, near enough you could see your people every week."

"Just Father," she said. "The others can vanish."

"I'll see Mr. Cooper tomorrow morning. He always liked me. He'll have me back."

"Never," she said. "Too late anyhow. School starts in three weeks. You're promised in Bracey."

"I could try. Eva, Bracey can live without me."

"So can you without me. So have I without you."

"What does that mean in terms of our future?"

"Nothing much, I guess. It is just one more thing I'm certain I know after this past year."

"Then when are you coming back home?" Forrest said.

"I am home," she said. She withdrew her hand and waved gently round her, the local darkness. "Wherever you or I might happen to camp, *home* is here. I'm as sorry as you."

"I believe it," he said. He made no move to reclaim her touch. But he faced her through darkness with scrutiny as fervent as any touch. "What day will you be back in Bracey with Rob, in Hatt Shorter's house, in our own room?"

"When Rob is well."

"What day will that be?"

"A month, six weeks. Forrest, I'm no prophet. You are lucky the boy is alive at all. I know of three babies that have died since June, and of plain whooping cough—Sylvie's nephew for one, Mag's grandson."

"I'll ask the doctor tomorrow morning," he said. "The air in the hills would be better for him, cooler and drier. We could break the trip if necessary. He'd be with the people that love him, Eva."

"My family love him; Rena worships his shadow. Mag and Sylvie love him."

"*We* made him. I want him to be with us."

"Any dogs in a ditch can make a baby. Forrest, you are ruining people's plans again. Don't you see all the trouble of the past long year has sprung from you?—the question you asked me that day at the spring?"

"You answered," he said.

"But I never would have asked."

"You'd have let us die?—our feeling, unspoken?"

"It was not for me to speak," she said.

"Why not?" he said.

"The feeling was yours."

His entire body, the roots of his hair, then knew he had lost; said it clearly in his head—*Your oldest home.* But he did not speak another audible word. He stood and walked to the window again, pulled down the shade against early day. Then he went back and lay down quietly—on his back but economically, drawn to his minimum size, the least bother.

When Eva had seen his eyes shut firmly, she lay back also—on her right side toward him, her natural posture.

They slept till dawn.

Then they hardly spoke—in neither case from coldness or anger but numbness: Forrest numb from loss, the fresh return of his oldest companion; Eva from what seemed the chance she was free, that these chains at least had proved rotten or weak, not chains at all but silk cords cast in luxury and pity, a girl's quick foolish generosity. Forrest stayed on his back when she rose to wash (he had not moved once in five hours of sleep, despite his dreams). His eyes were open but they studied the ceiling—a sepia stain in the form of a sea lion plunging through waves—leaving Eva to dress, unwatched and private as the girl he had first seen, three years before, at the head of his class, poised to recite a perfect lesson, then laugh. He did not even think he was waiting—for her voice saying whatever sleep had brought her (*Goodbye* or *Soon*), least of all for her touch. If he'd thought, he'd have thought, "I'll never need touching. I have had all of that."

She did speak finally. She came to his side of the bed and stood. His right arm could have reached her. She said, "Rob will be awake soon and hungry." She was dressed and ready. Having brought no grip, she could walk out clean. But she waited in place for an answer from Forrest.

He put his right hand back and raised his head with it, enough to face her. "May I see him somehow?"

She genuinely tried to think of a way. There were ways of course, but none came to her. "Please wait," she said. "Make people's lives easy."

That instantly drew "Goodbye" to his lips, but he did not say it. She must say it herself. He had asked the first question sixteen months ago; she must speak the end.

She smiled, shut her eyes once tightly in pleasure, looked again still smiling and turned and went.

When she'd shut the door, he thanked her.

2

He had luckily beat both the drummers and the heat of day downstairs and so ate cool and nearly alone, only the pad of Negroes behind him, the tired wail of flies, the sounds through open windows of the waking town—harness, hooves, a distant man's voice raised to say "Bless your heart" which Forrest strained to recognize and failed. As no one had seemed to recognize him. He had entered a town of eight hundred people in broad August daylight—a town in which he had lived for three years, teaching several hundred children, whose parents he had finally scandalized—and no one had known him except his wife, for whom he had sent. (Mrs. Dameron, the hotel-owner, was away on a visit to Raleigh; he had stayed with her his first month in Fontaine; she'd have known him or would she have turned him away? The clerk anyhow, a strange country boy, had barely read Forrest's name on the register; and when he had said "I expect my wife," had only said, "Good. Room Six. Real clean.") He turned now to ask for a third cup of coffee and saw, behind him, not the coal-black boy who had waited before but a small yellow girl—three feet away, smiling. "Can you get me some coffee?" he said, to her eyes that willed to hold him.

She had it in her hand, having waited for this; and her smile spread full as she stepped forward to him and filled his cup.

He thanked her and leaned to take the sugar.

"I know you," she said.

She was too near for him to study closely (her high odor ringed him). He pushed back his chair. No. "From where?" he said.

"You never seen me. I know about you. Sylvie my cousin."

"Sylvie knows me," he thought—one more human witness. But this girl was offering more than second-hand witness. He drew himself back to the table. "Thank you." She was meant to leave.

"I seen your boy."

"What boy do you mean?"

She pointed the right way. "Up at the Kendals'. Little white boy. Eva's."

He knew it was the only further chance he'd be given. He asked this grinning slut, "When did you see him?"

"Every three, four days. I go see Sylvie when I get off here; I got to breathe *air.*" She laughed, set the coffee pot down on the table, and fanned the still air before her face.

"How is he now?"

"He making it now." She moved back two steps and searched Forrest's face. "Do he favor you?"

Helpless, Forrest smiled. "Does he? At all?"

She seriously worked to know the truth. With a beautiful hand she traced one slow sweep across her eyes. "Some little," she said. "Some little through the eyes." She was no longer smiling. "You looking for a place to stay?" she said.

"What?"

"You from up North, ain't you? You looking for a place?"

He stood. His napkin fell to the floor. "Who are you?" he said.

"Flora."

"Flora who?"

"You ask anybody in Fontaine. They tell you."

"I won't though," he said.

3

In the room he packed quickly in his mother's small grip, used by her twice—on her single trip to Old Point Comfort before the war and the final trip on a stretcher in the baggage car to Richmond to die, crowded to death by a growth in her womb the size of a head. He had brought only one change of underclothes, a cake of soap, his shaving utensils—not even his piddling summer work. Though all his life he had flung himself on work in times of misery, work had never received him, never consoled. Still he'd worked—drilling uses for the Dative of Reference, the Subjunctive of Purpose, into wall-eyed children who would spend short lives selling harness leather or lard or plowing, or spreading lean thighs every year on the wet head of one more baby (toothless draining mouth)—and all this summer since Eva's departure, he'd tinkered at English versions of things he loved in Latin. Most of them things he could not show his students—alas: they were poems to galvanize corpses. On his table at Hatt's he had left his latest raid on the start of the sixty-third poem of Catullus, *Super alta vectus Attis*. With well over half his usable goods beneath his hands now, load the size of a baby, and no destination but back to the train, the long ride, his home—his sister's home, sister with whom he could talk of nothing but greens and beets, the growth of her sons, not even their mutual vanished parents of whom Hatt's memories were richer than his—his own pale memory of Catullus' fury came to his mouth; and he spoke it softly, for no reason then apparent to him.

> Borne on swift ship through deep seas, Attis
> Hastened on yearning feet to Phrygia,
> Came to the Grove—dark, crowned by trees,
> Haunt of the Goddess—where rabid fury,
> Wandering mind, forced him with sharp flint
> To cast down the heavy burden of his groin;
> Then knowing all manhood gone from her limbs,
> Fresh blood spotting the face of Earth,
> She seized the light timbrel in hands of snow—
> Your timbrel, Cybele; your mysteries, Mother—
> And ringing soft fingers on hollow oxhide, sang
> To her sisters tremulous, "Up! Go, Gallae,
> Together to mountain forests of Cybele." . . .

He had a destination; how could he not have known it? He set his grip from the bed to the floor, quickly stripped the stained lower sheet, carefully folded it to minimum size, went to the large white china washbowl, and put it to soak in all that was left of his shaving water. It was barely covered—enough though to leave it unfit for whatever searching eyes would come—Flora's, whosoever. Enough to leech out the evidence and memory—if not from the cloth then his own mind anyhow (the memory's one home) and for this one morning, this moment at least—of what he knew in every cell to have been an ending, what every day of his life till now had promised and constantly, clearly, whispered to his deaf ears, dumb heart: *Alone. Love that. Love only that. Beyond you is harm, betrayal, theft.* He stood now with wet hands in the rented room, hearing the voice, believing it, and waiting for the prize of consolation—the descent on his head of the dense balsam wreath of patience, detachment. It did not descend. Young as he was, he knew it would never. With his long life behind him—thirty-odd years of hours entrenched in his total memory, not one forgot—he knew it would never. He took his grip and left. No one saw him go.

4

He scared the old Negro, not by intention but because the path was wet and silent from the hard rain shower toward four o'clock and because, soaked himself and tired from the long walk, he looked more harmful than in fact he was.

The old man dropped the plank he had loudly wrenched from the shed (there were three more at his feet, good dry heart-pine) and said "Who you after?"

Forrest smiled—"Nobody"—and knew it was the first lie he'd told in months.

"They ain't here then. They ain't been here. I'm the man here and the white man give me permission for this." He pointed to the shed's south wall, half-stripped of siding, the uprights exposed to day. Green light slotted to the dry earth floor.

Forrest looked to the floor. The white flint circles of masonry were there, apparently unchanged. He walked forward to them and found the center of the room to be dark.

Again the old man said "Who are you?"

Forrest bent to see. Both springs were there far down in the shade, clogged with the trash of years, spider silk, but visibly running, their over-flow absorbed by buried piping that, miraculously open, carried the water outdoors, downhill. A chained enamel cup stood on the rim of the closer spring. Forrest reached to take it (seeing, as he reached, that its mate was gone, ripped from its chain and nowhere in sight).

"Drink a drop of that, you'll die before night."

Forrest looked up, still smiling. "I may anyhow."

"You sick?"

Forrest nodded and extended his soaked arms. "Pneumonia."

"Not in August," the Negro said.

"Then exhaustion. I have walked fourteen miles since breakfast. I have not eaten since. I am tired, wet, hungry; and my wife and boy have left me. I'm a lonesome ghost." He intended fun.

"You a man. What your name?"

"Forrest Mayfield."

"Where from?"

"Up north. Near Bracey, Virginia."

"That's a *hundred* miles."

"You been there?" Forrest said.

The Negro said "Near it."

"Who are you?" Forrest said.

"Eighty-some years old."

"How long you lived here?"

"Most of my life, last forty years." The old eyes, yellow as piano keys, met Forrest's unblinking.

"Where were you in April a year ago then?"

The Negro thought. "Bound to been here," he said.

"You were hiding then."

"What you aiming at?"

"I was here that April with twenty schoolchildren, a dozen mothers, three or four teachers besides myself, buggies and horses; there was nobody here."

The man said, "What's the name of this place?"

"Panacea Springs."

He pointed at the springs with a black hand folded and dry as Forrest's grip. "You think that's one of them healing springs?"

Forrest said, "The old folks did awhile back." He squatted by the circles.

"They all dead, ain't they?"

"Who?"

"Them folks and what they thought."

Forrest looked at the old face. It was almost surely smiling. "Dead and gone," he said.

The Negro said, "I know what I'm talking about. I worked at one of them places in Virginia when I was a boy. Won't nothing but water. Make your pecker work. Like anybody's water." He stood while the words worked over to Forrest through cool damp dimness. Then he also squatted and faced Forrest eye-level, eight feet away. Then he broke into high continuous laughter, a boy's voice, young.

Helpless, Forrest joined him.

5

By seven o'clock they had cooked a supper of sidemeat and hominy and kettle-coffee on the smallest stove in the kitchen of the abandoned Springs

Hotel, using the boards from the springhouse as fuel. Then—the Negro leading—they climbed the backstairs and walked the long hall to the front of the
house, the second-story porch. The old man carried the hot iron pan with
their mutual food; Forrest carried the kettle and the two spring cups, having
wrenched off the last one at the Negro's instructions. The porch floor was
thick with branches, dead leaves, fallen hornets' nests, a child's shoe; but a
space had been cleared at the north breezy end. The Negro headed there
and, with his free hand, motioned Forrest to sit in the better place—on the
floor with his back to the wall of the house, looking out at the tops of thick
undergrowth which had reached that high. The man himself sat as easy as
a boy with his back to the posts of the lovely railing; and once he had
brought out his long folding knife and halved the meat, he pushed the pan
toward Forrest. "Half of it yours."

"Thank you," Forrest said and reached out his hand.

"Forgot your spoon." The Negro felt himself on both breast pockets,
reached into one and drew out a tin spoon and held it to Forrest.

"Where's yours?" Forrest said.

"Just one," he said. "Just one for company. I got good fingers." He flexed
his long fingers, the spoon still in them.

So Forrest took the spoon; and they ate in silence, each consuming
exactly half of all the pan held and hot cups of coffee. By then with the thickness of leaves around them, they were nearly in darkness. Lightning bugs had
started their signaling. The old man searched himself again, found a plug of
tobacco, and again with his knife cut two equal chews and offered one to Forrest. He took it, though he did not normally chew; and the silence continued while they both made starts on the rich dark cud. The quiet, the general
peace, was so heavy—despite the presence three feet away of a strange old
Negro, maybe wild, with a knife—that it calmed whatever of pain or fear
had survived Forrest's day, the long hot walk. Or not so much calmed as
pressed it down by a greater force—his need for rest having found perfect harbor in this place like a happy afterworld for heroes destroyed in the war of
love, an Elysium promised in no religion but palpably here, tonight, and his.

At last the Negro rose, spat over the rail and said, "Mayfield—that your
truthful name?"

"Yes," Forrest said.

"That name I told you; that won't my truthful name."

Forrest was certain he had heard no name—its absence was part of the
peace he'd felt—but he said "All right."

"I don't tell my truthful name to nobody."

"That's all right with me. I'm obliged to you for kindness. I'll be leaving at daylight."

"What you doing here?" the Negro said.

"You invited me to supper."

"In that shed, I mean; by them dirty springs." He spat again.

Forrest also stood and quietly turned out the contents of his mouth to the dark leaves below. Then he swallowed two mouthfuls of bitter spit in the effort to cleanse his tongue and teeth. His back was turned to both the Negro and the springhouse, but his voice was clear and firm. "This is where a young lady and I made a promise some time ago. I came back to see it."

"You seen it, ain't you?"

"What was left of it," Forrest said. "The little you had left." He wanted to laugh but his head turned instead; and he begged the Negro, "Who are you? What are you doing here?"

"Don't blame me," the Negro said. "I never knew you, never heard you was coming. All I thought was, nobody here for thirty, forty years; nobody coming; I'm keeping me warm." Though the heat of the day had barely lifted, he cradled his arms on himself, rubbed his shoulders.

Calm again, Forrest said, "Tell me something to call you."

The Negro thought. "You need to call me, you call me Zack."

"Thank you," Forrest said. Then he sat again by the cold iron pan and looked up to meet the Negro's eyes, hardly possible now with the progress of evening. "Beg your pardon," he said. "I'd have blamed whoever I spoke to today. I'm in serious trouble."

Zack nodded. "Who you kill?"

"That girl that loved me." Forrest felt that his answer was in fact the truth, though he also knew it would throw this old man into some incalculable response. He knew he wanted that—strike, counter-strike.

"And you come back here to the place you found her?"

"Yes."

"They looking for you?"

"No," Forrest said.

"They starting tomorrow?"

"No," Forrest said.

"They already found her?—and they ain't hunting you?"

"They got her. They don't care where I go."

"She white?"

"Yes," Forrest said.

"You crazy, ain't you?"

Forrest laughed a little and nodded—"But safe."

"Where you going tomorrow?"

"Back home. Virginia."

"Who waiting for you?"

"Kin-people, my job."

"That's one more something than waits on me."

"What's that?" Forrest said.

"Dying. Sickness—that do make two." He was smiling apparently; his voice seemed filtered through a broad smile.

"No people at all?" Forrest said. "On earth?"

"Oh I've got people, I'm fairly sure—two questions about them: where they at? they waiting for *me?*"

Forrest said "Who are you?" He waited a little. "I'm perfectly safe. Never hurt a fly. That's half my problem."

"Just killed your woman?"

Forrest nodded. The lie seemed a handsome gift, return for shelter.

"Bankey Patterson," the Negro said, "born what they called a slave round here, somewhere around here some eighty years past. A good while past, least-ways anyhow—this place won't built when I was born, not as I recall. What I recall—you seen I'm in my good mind, ain't you?"

Forrest nodded, all dark.

"What I recall—my mama belonged to a man named Fitts that owned this land through here, three hundred acres. His own house stood where we at now—we on his foundation; his house done burned—and my mama had a little place near your springs. They was there same as now, no shed to roof them but dirty as now. Everybody round here cleaned them out once at least as a child and drank a cold handful—bitter as alum, tasted like a fart, a month-old egg—but nobody ever took a second drink and, sure God, nobody ever thought the world would *pay* to drink it. They did for a while—so it look like, don't it?; so word got to me—but I never had to watch it: dances and sick folks, sick folks dancing. I got out of here." He stopped as if at the sudden end of a stock of generosity he'd thought was large.

"When was that?" Forrest said.

"You tell me," he said. "That's most of my study—when things happen; how they got away from me." He stopped again and waited. "You can read. You tell me—if I'm eighty-some now, what was I at the freedom?"

Forrest calculated with his finger on the dark floor. "Forty-some, I guess."

"Seem like to me I was older than that, *feel* like it anyhow. But maybe not. All my children were born after freedom, so I was still plenty good when it come. I never had married in slavery times. I waited it out. I knew I was waiting."

"For what?" Forrest said.

"A fair chance to see my way to the end. The Fittses was good but the Fittses was humans. They didn't own many niggers, didn't need to—rich as they was, little as they farmed—so they sold they surplus off every year or give them away to they children and kin. I had good eyes; I looked and saw; and when I got to twelve and they kept me on—twelve was when they weeded, before breeding time—I said to myself, 'You hold your own. Tend your own heart, else they break it to Hell.' "

"Why did they keep you?" Forrest said.

"My mama fought for me. Some people say I was kin to the Fittses; and they kept they own (I used to be brighter in the skin than now; bright niggers darken—you notice that?). I always aimed, when I got grown, to ask Mama what was the truth of that; but I never did and now I reckon it's past too late." It was nearly full night; he extended his hand though to search it again. "Her husband was Dolfus, lived some miles from here on another place; and when he come to see her once a month on a pass from his master, she make me sleep in the yard if it's summer. But that don't make me call him Father and I still ain't. The thing I *know* is, Mama fought for me. I never heard her do it; but Zack Fitts told me, they youngest boy that I played with. He say my mama come in one evening to where they all set talking in the parlor and tell the master she need to talk. He rise up and go to meet her in the hall and ask what's troubling her (she they head cook, they jewel); and she say 'Bankey.' —'What Bankey done?' he say. —'Nothing,' she say, 'but you want to kill me, you send him off. I dead in two months. My heart dry in me.' Any nigger say that but Mama be beat; good as Master was, he won't stand that. But Zack tell me his papa say, 'Julia, go home and sleep'; and she know she won. So I had me two debts, to Mama and Master; and I paid on them for all them years till freedom come, a good blacksmith. I'm still strong as iron. And like I tell you, I had me a lesson—hold to your black heart else they ruin it. I ain't saying I turned into no steer—too many heifers around for that, and they coming at me—but I tell you what's truth, white man, once I done humped and groveled my way through the two, three years I was getting my nature, I found out that stuff won't all they claiming. You can buy it and sell it or get it free; but it ain't going to cure one trouble you got, not the least boil rising on your black ass."

Forrest said "Why?"

"You tell me," he said. "I big a fool as you. By time freedom come, my mama was crazy; had lost every bit of the sense she had. Times was hard—niggers all turning wild, white folks turning mean, white trash taking over, our master dead, Zack killed in the war, Mistress and her two girls setting out here just staring at the woods like the woods could help. So I'm at the age you say I am—full-growed man—and leave her, leave Mama with Dip her onliest sister and strike out north. Three reasons why—no work round here, nothing I can do for Mama but watch her eat dirt from the road-bank and pick at herself; and some Yankee pass through holding a paper saying iron-workers wanted in Baltimore, a dollar a day. So I walk to Maryland—Baltimore. No such thing. They ain't hiring niggers. I ought to come home; but what I eat if I come here?—old honeysuckle? So I walk down on the map a little and penetrate all round the state of Virginia, doing nigger jobs—a little blacksmithing, a whole lot of digging; everybody back then always digging holes."

"Were you still by yourself? Traveling alone?"

"I left that out. But to answer your question—yes I traveled alone, light as rabbit fur. But a whole lot of time I was standing still or laying down, and then I had company. Two or three wives; three, four sets of children. All named for me."

"Where are they now?"

He looked round slowly, both sides and behind, as though they all might have gathered while he talked, as though by speaking he had summoned not only their memory but their faces, their palpable accusing bodies. "They ain't with me. I ain't with them."

"You've come here hunting them?"

"No indeed. They never heard of here. I never used to tell present folks my past."

Forrest said, "Is the story you're telling me true?" He felt that an answer was urgent to him now; he didn't know why.

"Pretty nearly, pretty nearly—the way I recall it."

"Then go on. Tell the rest, to now."

The Negro waited. "Nothing else," he said. "What you expect? Eighty years of getting up, working, laying down. You want to hear all that, you need eighty years which I ain't got."

"Please. Why are you here, in this old place?"

"Same reason as you—looking."

Forrest said "For what?"

"My mama."

Forrest gave a little chuff through his nose—laugh, wonder.

"She be in her hundreds if you counting right. Nothing but a girl when

I was born. She always say I parted her ways while they still was green; I her live first-born. I looking for her."

Forrest said "Why?"

"To see her again, see do she know me, did she ever get well, get her right mind back, let her blame me some."

"Blame you for what?"

"Not fighting no harder for her, when I could."

Forrest said "How could you?"

"Sat and watched her, talked to her, answered her questions. All the stuff I thought was vain."

Forrest said, "Did you fight for anybody?"

"Me," he said quickly and struck at himself, palm on his chest twice, dry hollow thumps. Then he waited and thought and said, "Who the Hell you?—all time doubting me, all time asking *why?* I'm telling you *what*, the *what* I recall, what I need to find. If you here to listen, you listen to *what*. It's all I giving."

Forrest also waited. Then he said "Beg your pardon."

"I don't beg yours. Who you anyhow?"

Forrest told him again—his name, age, home, his work.

"And you killed your woman?"

"What she felt for me, yes."

"But she still living?"

Forrest nodded in the dark.

"And you hunting her?"

The answer reached Forrest from wherever it had waited or freshly burgeoned. In total dark it caused him no pain to give it to this rank old madman, powerless to use its news, powerless to hurt. "No I'm not," he said. "I am heading home."

Bankey said, "I'm there. And I'm ready to sleep. You welcome to sleep in my poor home." He waited, then cackled with laughter awhile, then bowed from the waist toward where Forrest sat, then entered the black house.

6

There were two large rooms on the front of the house, the old public rooms. When Forrest stood and followed Bankey indoors, he found him waiting in the hall, hand extended; found him with his own hand in the unrelieved dark. The dry old skin gave a rustle at his touch—hide of a rattler, dragon, hermit; the skin of all Negroes he had ever touched, the tough loving cooks (spiteful and tender) of his own childhood—but he did not refuse it; and Bankey said "You ready?" Forrest nodded which no human eye could have seen and felt himself drawn off to the right, the center of that room, till his toes were stumped by a low soft obstacle. "This your bed." Bankey left him.

Forrest squatted and felt at the mass on the floor. It seemed a pallet made of carpets or draperies; *dirt, vermin*, he thought but didn't care. Again a huge weight, greater than fatigue, was pressing him earthward. So great even he did not struggle to see it, name it, discern its need or diet. He loosened his high shoes and lay and sank. No fear. Surrender.

After hours of pure sleep and lesser dreams, he came to this. He had walked for days, in familiar country, southern Virginia (pine woods, rolling pastures, the trees and the air one enormous bell ceaselessly rung by millions of thirteen-year cicadas); and now tired but calm, he had come to a small town, a boarding house. He had signed his name in the book which the lady kept by the door (the house was her home, small but cool; she was beautiful, a widow in her early forties, well-spoken, fighting with lovely and effortless grace to feed her children, herself, her servants, by the hard expedient of opening her doors to a streaming world—he felt that in the dream). She led him to a room on the back of the house, far from noise; and once she had shown him the wardrobe and basin, she turned to go, then stopped and said "This bed is yours." There were two iron beds, one large, one small; she had shown him the small. He did not ask why, only set down his grip (which by now he had rigged with rope as a pack); but she smiled and said, "You have paid for a room that holds two people. Now we'll wait for the other." Then she turned and left; and he did not see her, had in fact no life at all till evening when from far at the other side of the house a bell rang supper and he washed and went. And had eaten a full meal—steak, pan gravy, corn, greenbeans, tomatoes—when the lady appeared in the dining-room door and, grave as a sibyl, searched the faces of his fellow feeders. It was him she wanted. Forrest knew that at once—there was someone behind her in the darkening hall—but he did not speak. A fellow guest, a young man at his right, was asking him the purpose of his journey. As he offered his face to the lady's search, he was also trying to answer the question, to remember the answer. Just when he knew and was ready to speak, the lady spoke also but not to him. She turned to the person waiting behind her and clearly said, "Mayfield—take the seat by Mr. Mayfield." An elderly man—white hair in clean long locks to his shoulders, the clothes of a wanderer (more nearly a tramp)—stepped slowly forward. As he came he studied only the floor, his shuffling feet; a careful mover forced into care by age and exhaustion. Forrest thought he should rise to help the man; but the young man beside him again asked the purpose of his lengthy trip; so Forrest turned and said, "My health, for my health"; and by then the old man was seated beside him. Silently. Breathing hard from his effort, the latest leg of his own long journey, but no word of greeting and no look, no smile. The old man faced only his plate, empty, white; and when Forrest passed the cooling food to him, he served himself in silence, staring down. The young man beside Forrest asked what was wrong—"You look quite well"—but Forrest was openly watching the old man and knew, though he couldn't look up now to check, that the lady stood on in the doorway, watching also. She was watching two—Forrest, the old man—and still she was grave, not from puzzlement but fear: that something would not happen. It did. Then. The old man separated a biscuit into halves. He was Forrest's father. Forrest saw it; no question of doubt or error. He sensed that the lady was also smiling. Forrest spoke the name—"Robinson. Father." The old man ate the biscuit slowly, still watching his plate. He did not seem hungry. He was eating because he had been led there where eating was expected. Yet when he had chewed it all and swallowed, he turned to Forrest waiting with eyes from the morning which Forrest remembered; but with this crushing difference—their gaze was no longer needy or searching, merely polite. He was trying to think of an answer for this stranger smiling beside him. No one but Forrest was waiting now. All the others were eating blackberry roll (it was mid-July); the lady had gone. The old man—Robinson Mayfield undoubtedly, the father Forrest had not seen for twenty-eight years, for whom he now yearned—that old man carefully said "Forgive me," then smiled. "Maybe so. You may very well be right. I am too tired to say. Too tired, too far." Forrest did not wonder *Too far* from what or why his heart yearned so fiercely tonight for the simple sound of his own name spoken in that old voice. He said "Forgiven" and turned to the food congealed on his plate.

In the midst of that, at the point where Forrest heard the dinner bell, black Bankey came to the door of the room and stood—no light. Since leaving Forrest here, he had been to the kitchen to deposit their pan, then into the breezeway to wash his feet, then back to the front room opposite Forrest's. He had sat in an armchair and tried to sleep (he had not slept flat on his back for years—danger of death) but had failed and succeeded only in thinking: memory, faces he had hoped to see only in Heaven (he was certain of Heaven, though afraid to go). So he'd crossed the hall and listened for the sounds that would locate Forrest and, more, tell his nature—the secret signals of kindness or cruelty which, all his life, Bankey had detected in darkness or light, near or far.

He stood and listened till the end of the dream. There seemed to be sounds of quicker breath, two muffled blows of a fist on the floor; but age had dulled the special keenness of his organ of knowledge (that film of skin on his palms, in his nostrils, across his eyes that received from the world—or had for eight decades—the urgent news: early warning or, rarely, confirmation of clear path ahead, invitation to safety, pleasure, rest); and silence had taken the room again.

So Bankey moved slowly to enter the space, sliding each foot forward with fear and care so as not to touch the body somewhere there asleep, afloat in its secret life, castaway. Bankey thought some of that—and felt it all—and when he knew that his right foot had come to the edge of the body, he stopped and waited a little, thinking. The white man covered in dark beneath him—in reach of all his organs of touch, his harmful instruments—seemed quiet again, entirely quiet. Bankey slowly reached to his own hip pocket, no fumbling now, and found his knife. He opened it silently and in one move, fluid and quiet as a snake—no cracking of joints—he knelt to the floor.

His knees touched Forrest's warm right hand where, abandoned in the dream, it lay open, empty. The knife was in Bankey's own right hand. He extended his left and with perfect aim inserted his forefinger, dry, and touched Forrest lightly on the palm. Misery poured from the hand into Bankey like the jolting current he had known thirty years before when lightning struck a mule he had just finished plowing fifty yards away and slammed through the damp earth to burn his feet. His finger moved on still accurately and stopped at the crest of the sleeping wrist where a pulse thudded up to meet him like cries, deep wide-spaced bellowing. He had not felt active pity for years, maybe since his mother lost her mind and raved; but he felt it now and knew its name and also thought he knew its demand.

He drew back his probing hand, extended the other—the right hand armed with the open knife—and with no need to gauge his force or feel for his target, he pulled the sharp edge once across the wrist. Lightly though, a dry rehearsal. He felt again. The wrist was dry and in that instant of touch, Bankey knew he could not help this man, not give him the peace that lay in his power to render now. He drew back his knife, folded and hid it in his pocket again.

Then knowing there was no chance that he would sleep and die unawares, he lay slowly back on the hard floor. Forrest was just beyond his reach, ten inches more than the length of his arm; and to ease the morning, the strange awakening, Bankey's head was laid at Forrest's feet. At first light Forrest would not have to wake to immediate sight of Bankey's eyes, open and waiting.

                              *   *   *

He woke a good two hours past dawn, not from any external sound or movement or Bankey's nearness or the light full on him through the tall east window but from satiation, a rest so deep and venturesome as to give him the
sense, as his eyes broke open, of lightness and cleanness, of a life unburdened
by past or future, all an open *present* like a cleared field in sunlight. A sense
of healing that bore in its heart no threat to end. His dream had sunk
beneath conscious memory, and the turbulence that rose from its plummet
was hope. He could live his life; he knew the way. And so he was happy for
twenty, thirty seconds. He had waked on his back; and all he had seen till then
was ceiling, the strangely intact unstained white plaster twelve feet above.

But Bankey had waited as long as he could. When he heard the final
sounds of waking, he quickly rose to his knees again and was there over
Forrest. "I'm going with you."

Forrest looked. All the causes of misery stood in him, large and genuine,
his respite ended. "Where am I going?" he said.

Bankey smiled, the first time. "You say. I'm following."

Forrest said "Why?"

"You by yourself now. You need some help, need somebody. I'm free
and ready."

Forrest said, "You are looking for your mother."

"Did I tell you that?" Bankey said. "I was. When I came back down here,
I thought I was—two, three weeks ago. First day, I come straight here, found
this. I knew it was the place; somebody told me years ago the Fittses had sold
out to some poor trash that had built this hotel and then gone broke. But
before they left, they tore down all that was in my memory except your springs
and a tree or two I recognized. All the quarters was gone—my mama's
house, Dip her sister's, the shop I forged in. Trees and foul water. So I
walked on to Micro—I knew that good, ain't barely changed—and asked this
old white man in the store if he heard of Julia Patterson. He told me, 'Sure.
Old crazy Julia. Lived back yonder with all them dogs.' I ask was she live. He
say he ain't seen her for twenty years; but he say, 'Don't trust me. Heap of folks
I ain't seen ain't dead, and some of em come back and cheat me.' I ask him
who must I trust; and he say, 'Won't she a Fitts nigger? Miss Caroline Fitts still
living up the road.' He tell me where; so I go and there she, old as me and
meaner and three-fourths blind. But she knew me the minute she see my face.
'You're too late, Bankey,' she say first thing; 'I'm poor as you' (it looked like
she was, but she a big liar). I say to her I ain't here for money, but can she tell
me where Mama is? She say to me 'No' as quick as that. —'When she die?'
I say. Miss Caroline say, 'Who say she dead? Maybe she living in the Washington White House, cooking angel-food cakes for Teddy Roosevelt. Maybe

she living in a shack near here with fourteen hounds, eating dirt and scratching. Either way, you're no good to her now. Too late, Bankey; too late again.' She always been the bitch in the crowd, Miss Caroline; but she tell what her mouth think is so; so I didn't backtalk none at all. I say to her 'True.' Then she say 'Where you living?' and I ask her do she have a suggestion? She say 'No' again; she quick as ever. I ask her, 'Who own that old piece of hotel where the house used to be?' She say 'I do.' I told her I heard the Fittses lost it. —'Did,' she say, 'but the trash that bought it couldn't sit there and work long enough to pay the mortgage so it's mine again.' Then she study me hard, then say 'You want it?' I say 'Yes' to see what she mean. —'Take it,' she say. 'It's mine to give. Take it, use it and when you done, burn it. But don't come asking me for Julia again or money or food. Don't bring me your face another time.' Then she shut the door. I swear to God—two weeks ago."

Forrest nodded. "I believe you. You've got a grand home." He smiled, waved round at the big bright room.

Bankey said, "This don't mean birdshit to me."

Forrest said "It does to me." He had heard all that, half-risen, arms propped behind him. Now he reached for his shoes and laced them on carefully. Then he stood and walked four steps toward the door (nearer to the door than Bankey, still kneeling); then he turned and said, "I'm sorry, Bankey, and I thank you for kindness. I am going home myself—eventually, I hope." As Forrest spoke, he knew he had said that last night; but it came entirely differently now like the mention of a gate, a goal not a terminus. "And, the way I'll live, I cannot use you. I would be no help on earth to you."

"Help won't what I needed," Bankey said. "I *helping* myself." He rose, faced Forrest and extended his arms to demonstrate his truthfulness—his strength well-tended for a man any age, the knowledge of his years intact, unhardened, offered for use.

Though he did not know it and never would, Forrest had taken the thing he could use—the message imparted by Bankey's example, inserted in his sleep: the dream still buried beneath his memory; his own lost father, burnt-out, abandoned. He felt in his coat, withdrew his wallet and extended a paper dollar toward Bankey. "For your trouble," he said.

Bankey shook his head and held his place, his eyes full open, unblinking on Forrest, who said again "Thank you" and turned and, finding his grip in the hall, went quickly out.

7

By the middle of the morning he had got to Micro, a crossroads—two stores, post office, a depot, six or eight squatty houses in sight. A train was in the station, northbound and ready. Two Negro girls in white clothes were boarding. He could be home by evening. But he knew his purpose, or his plan if not its purpose; and he walked past the train with his grip in hand and waved at the sweating conductor to show they could leave without him, which they slowly did.

Then he went in the first of the stores and waited till a game of backgammon had played itself out. Then he bought a tablet of paper and a pencil and asked the clerk, "Ever heard of a Negro named Julia Patterson?"

"Never hear of nobody else, looks like." The clerk was a hunchback five feet high with snow-white hair and eyebrows the black of fresh hot pitch—no smile, no chance of one. "Why you need to know?"

Forrest said, "I don't need to know; I wondered. I heard she was old and pitiful."

"Old all right. Last time I saw her—ten, twenty years ago—she was pushing eighty. But save your pity. I've been at this counter all my life; what I don't see is known but to God. She went crazy right after niggers ran free. They all went crazy, don't you know, but her worse. That didn't stop her though from her main business—way into her fifties, when most women dry up, she went on dropping babies every nine months. Bred em like maggots. Eight or ten head at her shack any time, and her raving round like a hoot owl at harvest. Then she did dry up or—maybe; let me see; yes, I know I'm right—the Klan took a hand. Younguns scattered like tumbleturds in the breeze; some old as twenty, breeding their own. So she just had dogs from there on out, lived alone with dogs, her the mangiest one. Save your pity, friend. Put it on *my* back. I'm a working cripple." He showed his back. "Born with this."

"I'm sorry," Forrest said. "You've earned your keep." And before the man could question him further, he took up his purchase and went into daylight, knowing as it struck him that he needed food, knowing more strongly that he needed to leave.

8

By early afternoon he had walked eight miles; and hunger was gathering behind his eyes, a small clenched fist. But he'd walked on narrow roads in deepening country—no town, only two or three far poor houses, no wild thing to eat (though vines were heavy with hard green grapes, due in late September)—so when his path descended once more to a sandy creek-crossing, he told himself he must stop here and wash. Then he'd be fit at least to ask for food at the next likely house. There was no house in sight, no sense of one near; still he turned off the path and entered the dense woods that banked the creek and walked till the path was well-hid behind him and, in the green dark, there was no sound of bird or squirrel or snake. Only his own loud feet on ground that might well not have been touched till then.

A tight tall clearing—open half-circle with the creek on one side, thicket all behind, and a shaft of green air rising through the hole in high beech trees toward sky, sunlight (which only reached this depth, slowed and cooled as though it had fallen through miles of seawater, millions of tons). Forrest stopped in the center and listened closely for human sounds—none, only water. So he went to the thicket side, set down his grip, untied his shoes, then stripped off the clothes that were now fine nets retaining the dirt and secreted misery of two full days. In fact as he peeled down his underdrawers and caught their stench, he wanted above all to wash every thread in the quick clear water—and had leaned to gather them for that purpose when calm thought told him they would not dry in this light in less than a day. A measure of both his need and his calm, the curious peace that had numbed him all day, was the fact that he stood whole moments and thought, "I will wash them and wait—a whole day, two, in this one spot" and did not see the wait as intolerable. What decided him against it was merely the will for physical motion—to be out of this place and into another, no conscious thought of his movement as either *flight* or *hunt*; *for* or *from* anyone, anything.

He spread each piece of his clothing to air on clean low bushes (the ground was dry to his tender feet, but there'd been no rain; road dust could not sift in this deep). Then he walked to the edge of the water and studied it. A simple bank of sand, brown gravel; no holes for snakes. Two feet or so of water over sand, round rocks—cold and with strong eddies threading his calves as he stepped to the middle. He looked to the bottom for crawfish, minnows.

Waste. Shameful waste, the shame of which was only his. Sinful waste, an offense in the nostrils of whatever powers witnessed or intended his stopped dry life. The sight of his sex, hung dark from the dark hair of his whiter groin, roped with the veins that (however vulnerable) still bore the blood that could swell him to ready strength in a moment should there be an object, be a present need—that daily sight, familiar as his hands, brought down the frail but roofing shed he had nailed above him in the months since Eva and Rob's departure, a roof made of pride in his gift for solitude (the main gift offered by his whole past life), patches of work, messages from Eva, patches of hope, the thought of (at last) a life companioned, the sight of a son taking form before him, short kindnesses from passers. *Rotten scantlings.* The screened light of day, the eyes of his own mind, had full sight now of his white huddled life — a thirty-three-year-old orphan boy who could teach Latin verbs to country children, whose dick would work in the presence of friction (give pleasure, strow seed), whose hand could chop wood, weed a garden, tinker out a milksop line of verse; but who could not extend that same plain hand (competent, ready) and seize the only food he desired. Seize and *hold* — hold by becoming, in deed and word, pleasant himself to whomever he needed, then deeply delightful, then vital for life. He had never been that to anyone — oh vital to his son in the sense of providing the first warm clot but now (when the boy was six months old and, however weakened, increasingly aware of the passing world and smiling surely) not even so much as pleasant to him. To Eva, what? — a recollection, memory from which all force had leaked.

He stood in the water, swayed by its mild hands, staring at his life, unable to weep but retching from the sour pit of his belly, hacking at the young firm cords of his trunk as though his error were a gorging hookworm, a fluke encysted, a suckfish fastened to the base of his heart which violence could now dislodge and kill.

As though he were not already standing in the life he wanted, the life he required — palpable as this water around him, clean and cleansing.

9

August 4, 1904

Dear Sister,

I am all right and hope that you and the boys are bearing the heat and having cool nights. I have talked to Eva. I have not seen Rob, though I am told he is coming along better now and has a fair chance. Otherwise I now know that your fears were justified. I do not think we shall see Eva again.

Again, as I said, I am all right. I am coming home slowly. So look for me when you see me.

Your grateful brother,
Forrest Mayfield

August 4, 1904

Dear Grainger,

I hope very much that this message finds you. If so, I am pretty sure you are surprised. You would be a lot more surprised if you could see where and how I am writing it. I am about twenty miles northwest of Fontaine, North Carolina, propped against a beech tree beside a creek in which I have just bathed myself. Now I am waiting for my traveling clothes to air before I commence my trip again. My trip is eventually toward home; but I have decided to walk for my health and since, with the heat, that may take four or five more days, I am writing this to mail at the next depot. You will have it tomorrow evening, if Aunt Veenie passes anywhere near the post office.

It is to say that if you still mean what you told me last month, then I am ready to accept. I am also glad. You can help me, Grainger. In the fall I will be moving out of my sister's into some place private to me if I can, and there I will need somebody's help.

If you are ready to leave your people and live in Bracey or wherever I go and if you will work as hard as you promised and grow up clean and honest and loyal, then I will be faithful to tend your needs.

Read this message to Veenie and ask her to guide your choice. If you answer Yes, you must stay with her till I get back and find some suitable quarters. Or maybe in the weeks before school opens, I will need to travel and you can come with me.

Be serious, Grainger, and give me your word as soon as you can. I will send to know when I reach home. I will also hope to hear you have read the books I lent you and can answer questions.

> Very truly,
> Forrest Mayfield

AUGUST 1904

There was no word from Grainger at home when he got there—Hatt's home strange to him now as a hostel, with an air that repelled him, a literal odor of death in his nostrils, the brown dry odor of generations of choking and throes. The walk had stretched into five full days, more than time for the letter to precede him; but when he asked Hatt for mail or messages, she said "Not a word" with, he thought, a harsh pleasure—he was hers again. She had thought he was hanging on news from Eva; he did not correct her. He went out within an hour of arriving, having only taken time to wash and change, and walked to the post office (still open at six) and checked for his own mail; then asked Miss Lula if she had any mail for old Aunt Veenie—he was headed to see her.

"Nothing since that one you sent her boy, three, four days ago. First they've got in years." There was good-natured triumph on her face; she'd known his hand.

But he would not rally. "He got it then?"

"I gave it to her personally, told her I'd read it to her."

"It was Grainger's," he said.

Miss Lula smiled. "She said that herself, said he could read; if his name was on it, she'd take it to him. I told her it was, with *Master* in front of it and in your writing. So it got here, yes. Or as near here as Veenie. She may have forgotten it and have it in her bosom still. If you don't remind her, it'll stay there till October 1st, her fall bath."

Forrest nodded and left and walked ten yards, meaning to go straight to Veenie's and check; then he stopped and wondered where Veenie lived. He had not been there in twenty years; now that he thought, he had never been there—never had any reason or wish to go. Veenie had simply materialized throughout his youth when his mother needed help. He did remember

going with Hatt to the funeral of one of Veenie's daughters and cringing at
the spectacle of wild grief and rage which issued from the generally solemn
Veenie like the voice and fury of a hurtful spirit, a demon entrenched. But
her house, no. It would be on Clay Hill, the north end of town, where loose
strings of cabins rode the pitching tumult of red slick earth.

So he headed there and met no one he had ever seen—children born in
his years away, in rags that could not conceal their laughter—but he did not
need to ask directions. She was in the yard of the third place he passed, in a
straight-backed chair that seemed made from cast-up pieces of the Ark, in the
shade of a low umbrella tree—though all was in virtual shade by now—and
she watched him come up the hill, cross the gulley, with no sign of recognition or welcome. Yet she seemed alone—no one else in sight, no dog or
chickens—and in need of company. He charged it to her cataracts and
came to within two feet of the chair before he stopped and squatted below
her.

She faced him squarely, still no flicker of greeting.

He said "What you doing?"—his voice would name him.

"You really asking," she said, "or passing time?"

"Asking," he said.

"Then what I'm doing is waiting on you, what I been doing four or five
days."

"Grainger got my message then?"

"No," she said.

He pointed behind them back toward town. "Miss Lula said she gave
the letter to you."

Veenie nodded. "She did."

"Then what?" Forrest said.

"I got it," she said.

"Does Grainger know?"

She shook her head.

"Is he still here?"

She nodded. "Out somewhere playing with some little girl."

Forrest stood—her eyes didn't follow him—and looked in a circle: no
other humans. "Aunt Veenie," he said, "kindly tell me why."

Her eyes had found him. "Sparing *him*," she said.

"Sparing him what?"

"You trying to harm him."

He thought she had yielded to age, confusion; so he waited awhile, then
went on calmly. "Harm is the last thing I intend. Veenie, you sent him to meet
me, remember?—three months ago. He took to me. We worked together

those weeks at Hatt's, painting her roof, building new steps. He's a good worker and, like I say, he took to me—"

She nodded. "He did."

"—So when I quit to go south for my wife and boy, he said he would like to serve me for good. I told him thank you but that I was expecting my own folks back and would not be able to pay his keep. Now I can. The letter says that. It offers him work."

"What else?" Veenie said.

"Just that—good care as long as I live. You know my people keep their word."

She made a snorting sound, high in her head as if from her eyes. "I ain't studying that—your people's word; *I* know your people some sixty years before you born. What I'm asking you is, what else you tell him in that letter yonder?" She pointed to her house, its whereabouts.

Forrest tried to recall, tried to guess her concern. "Not another thing that I remember; oh I said I hoped he had read my books."

"Read em all fore you got to the edge of town." She laughed at that, the incredible memory, a picture before her. Forrest joined her briefly; then when she'd calmed she said, "Forrest, listen. Will you give your oath?" She had whispered it, a confidence in an empty world.

"I will if I understand," he said. "Veenie, I do not understand."

But as he spoke, she was rising and going toward the house—six or eight steps, tottering slowly in an arc as grand as a ship underway, before she stopped and waited, listening; then turned and said "You said you would." She paused no longer, going on, climbing steps, vanishing inward.

Forrest waited. He did not want to follow her—her general air of harsh mystery, the edge of harm which even at her age she pressed against him, and (easier to face, his conscious reason) the promised heat and stink of her house. Two other reasons urged him though—the chance of light on her curious claims and, stronger, the chance of Grainger's help in whatever lay ahead for his own remaining life. So he went toward her or at least in her tracks. For all he knew of what lay ahead, the dark low doorway open on darkness might hold behind it a wall of solvent that had just taken Veenie and waited now to take him also, reduce him to essence in punishment. But he went and quickly. And stopped on the sill to let his eyes open.

The room seemed also a relic of the Flood, survivor of many floods beached here Except for the tin stove painted silver, it all was wood—wood scoured with sand or ashes or lye to a blond near-white so that what his eyes adjusted to from the waning day was not the promised darkness but an excess of light. Veenie herself was the darkest thing—she and the low trunk she knelt before, a black horsehair lady's trunk with brass studs, its rolled lid open. He watched only her, unable to search elsewhere in the room for signs of Grainger, hints of other lives; and hers was the only odor that reached him—not fetid but strong, proud metal of age, an exhalation of the core of force that had brought her this far in a life as low to the earth as a weed, untrammeled and rank. And the posture she held now (kneeling, straight-backed) was clearly no bow but a purposeful, calmly considered self-service. He stared on, silent through her rummaging.

Finally she turned. "Come here to me." It was not the mock-hard voice Negroes kept for laggard children; it was feral but still contained by a purpose.

Forrest felt he was summoned to retribution but also felt, whatever his crime, the justice of the summons; so he went through the bright room (it seemed to take hours) and stopped three feet from Veenie by a bed. A small bed, wooden, short and narrow, cleanly made and spread in August with a quilt—Grainger's surely, his length and width.

Veenie's eyes found him, held onto him. "I had a Bible your grandma give me right at the freedom, saying I would need it; but I never needed it. I kept it in here locked up from niggers and now it's gone." She waited and thought. "You swear anyhow."

"All right," he said. "Tell me what."

She waited again, then turned and reached back into her trunk, searched under more quilts and folded skirts till she found a parcel wrapped in white tissue. With her back still to Forrest, though he could see, she unwrapped it slowly with her careful utterly inhuman fingers—the brown prehensile tentacles of sea-life, blind but infallible. What she had was a picture.

Forrest caught a glimpse before she took it to her chest and rubbed it there—cleaning it? greeting it?—faded and sepia, apparently a man. Was she finally crazy? Should he turn and go?

She rounded on him. "This good enough. Swear on this." She offered the picture on both flat palms.

A man, yes. More nearly a boy—sixteen, seventeen. His dark fine hair parted sharply on the left and pulled back high on a broad smooth forehead. Deep-set eyes that seemed blue or gray—startlingly bright in their recessed sockets, in the picture's pallor, and immensely sad. A long straight nose, a long straight line of mouth slightly down. What seemed the beginnings of a mustache and goatee, more fur than hair, that soft and defensive. A dark coat and vest, light shirt and stock, a watch chain and fob. Short arms—wrists showed at the bottom edge, but the hands were omitted. No visible sign of resemblance to Veenie. If the boy were black, it was just a taint; long lines to Britain stretched back of the eyes. Forrest brought the fingers of his right hand together and laid the five tips on the boy's sad face. Then he nodded his head.

"Say it," Veenie said.

He said "I swear."

"All right," she said. She turned at once to wrapping the picture.

Forrest stood encased in the heat of the room, feeling it for the first time—an element in which all will to movement seemed idle, ludicrous. So he did not move, but he said to Veenie "What have I sworn?"

She went on wrapping. "To never tell Rover, Jess, Gardn—" She broke off the roll of her scattered kin. "What's my baby name?"

"Grainger."

"To never tell Grainger his rightful story."

"Who did I swear on?"

Her hands stopped work. She turned and studied him. "Your daddy, fool. Your Mr. Rob."

His hand flew out. "Show me."

She balked.

"Please. I don't know him."

She gripped the covered picture. "Your own blood daddy."

"I was five when he left."

"Other people was young when he done other things, not young enough though."

Stunned, baffled as he was, Forrest knew his only hope—here with her—was to take one thread of the tangle and hold it; refuse to drop it till it led to help or proof of her lunacy, proof of malice. He chose the face, asked for it again.

She handed him the parcel.

He opened it, careful as she; and tilting the face toward the small side window, pressed the image with his own good eyes for recognition, response, reward. Nothing came. He worked at the eyes especially—the strongest trace left in his own mind—but while he could see again their beauty, their faded lament, he did not feel the stock of images joining: his memory to this. "Where did you get it?" His own voice shocked him far more than the face, a steely tone of insatiable demand.

"He gave it to me."

"I don't believe you." The fat of his right thumb rubbed the face, still no knowledge. "When did he give it?"

"You right. I stole it."

"Who from?"

"Your mama's stuff, when she dead."

"How come?"

"It mine just much as hers," Veenie said. Her own force flowed back into her voice.

"The Hell you say. I've gone these long years with no face for him."

"You got it now."

"Have I?" Forrest said. "How will I know? You may be lying again, again."

Veenie said "I ain't. You his picture, Forrest." She pointed behind him, a fragment of looking-glass propped on a table beside a basin.

But he knew his own face. He studied the picture, touching it over and over, Braille. He was; and for reasons he did not now consider, he had failed to see it—the live present image of this vanished boy, give or take some grief, whoever the boy. A clamor of something—hunger? devotion? the new chance of joy?—poured out of his heart, an uprush of birds. "Where is he?" he said, his voice low but firm.

"Richmond City last I heard."

Forrest said "When was that?"

"Oh Jesus. Don't ask me."

"Since Mother died?"

Veenie thought that out and nodded Yes. By now her eyes had dropped from his. She watched the legs of the nearest table.

"Since I left home?"

She thought again. "How old is Grainger?"

"Twelve, I think."

"Twelve," she said. "Twelve years ago then; that's the last." She pressed with her thin arms, palms flat as stovelids, to rise and stand.

"Goddammit, Veenie, stay still and *tell* me." He touched her forehead, bald as an old man's—not with pressure but to stress his urgency, the three middle fingers of his left hand: she was cold.

She had borne, fairly often in her life, physical trials harder than this—a beating for theft at seventeen; the hackings of various careless men (no care but for their own hunger), the procession through her tight dry narrows of eleven children; the deaths of nine (death, for her, being physical trial)—but she could not remember, now where she knelt, the last time she'd cried. When was the last death?—she couldn't think: Cassie's? Anica's? ten, twenty years ago? Her face was wet, both dull eyes streaming; and though she struggled to hold herself, before this boy with no claim on her, the rails of her chest could not hold the noise—her mouth and nose gave off high bellows. *A broke-down cow lost far from the herd*; she thought it that way. But she did not think of the boy above her, knowing in her tough heart that he (little he) was not a cause of her present affliction, only a trigger, the blind slewfoot that kicked down the first grit that tripped the rockslide.

Forrest saw her and said in an easier voice, "Remember. I don't understand anything. You're the one that can tell me."

It took her awhile (his hand stayed on her); but she calmed herself enough to say, "Mr. Forrest, I figured you knew all this. I beg your pardon. I ought to been dead thirty years ago."

"You won't die," he said.

"You right," she said. "I pray for it some. Lord good to me when I ask Him right."

"I've asked *you* something."

She stood up slowly; he let her rise. "I know you have. Let me set down here. My knees give out." She shuffled past him to the near small bed and sat on the edge. Then she motioned him over to the second bed, ten feet away, a broad marriage bed. "Sit yonder and rest where I can see you."

He kept his place.

"Sit down. It's clean as your right hand—Grainger's bed. He love to stretch."

Forrest went and sat and bore her direct gaze for the time it took her to find whatever of him she could see and focus on. When she started speaking, he looked to the floor, imagining at least that it was cooler, that the ground beneath (visible in cracks) was cooler still.

"Start with me," Veenie said. "Start with Veenie Goodwin. I one of your mama's folks' favorite niggers cause I breed so good; your mama's granddaddy call me 'Mean But Quick.' First baby I drop, I was still a child—twelve years old, I guess. First baby to live come later though, three years later when I learned how to have em and keep em, both together—come a big fat girl named Mary Lucretia. Your great-grandmammy name her that; I was too weak to study no names, I tell you. Good like I was, I was always weak; took the bed for the best part of two weeks every time. Say I'm lazy; go on and say it. Too late—it's done. Good sleeping rest!" She laughed for herself, not expecting response. Once started now, this was all for herself. He was only the room in which she said it, excuse for reeling it out aloud. "All I call her was Mary Lu, and she the next in what I'm telling. She young as me, maybe younger still, when she have her first, another bitch. Your mama's great-uncle say womens in my line has a bitch first to open the track; then the race is for dogs. He mean men-babies and he near bout right. Mary Lu's was Anica. Then Anica waited till she near dead, seventeen years old; and *she* drop a girl, Elvira Jane. I go on having em all this time; ain't studying being no great-grandmammy at forty-five years old, give or take; but what I'm telling now stop right there. On Anica's girl, Elvira Jane. My old head say she born fore freedom; but she big enough to run and talk when it come, cause it's her that brought it to me and Trim. We sitting in the dark, cooling off from day—March, early planting—and she come running and say the news: 'Miss Pattie say we free. Start moaning.' Miss Pattie—she your mama's own grandmammy; she foreman, overseer, everything else while mens at war—Miss Pattie she think we due to moan. Some did, some didn't. Elvira didn't. She don't remember no hard time at all, but she take to freedom like it got her name wrote on it in ink. So it stop with her." Veenie stopped—a clear end, no pause.

Forrest looked. She still watched him or the space he filled. To give her a moment more of grace, he looked aside—an old wicker fern-stand beside the bed; the socket intended for plants had been lined with flannel, and his books were there, Grainger's cache: *Gayley's Classic Myths of Greece and Rome*; a McGuffey he himself had used as a boy; *The Boy's Life of Washington*; *The Indian Princess* (a life of Pocahontas); Mrs. Ashmore's *History of the Commonwealth of Virginia*; *Tom Sawyer, Detective*. Rob his own son—he thought of Rob, first time in hours. These were rightfully Rob's, should be stored up for him. Some of them bore inscriptions in his mother's bold hand—always *Forrest from his mother, to help him on* and the date, never more.

"They Grainger's," Veenie said. She could see him after all.

Forrest said, "I'm glad to let him use them."

"He'll use em *up*," Veenie said and waited. Then she said, "Where he at once he know every bit of that foolishness by heart? Where that take him he ain't at now?—under some fig bush rubbing some nigger girl's flat little titties?"

Forrest stood and took two steps toward her. "Where is my father? And why do you know? Give me his picture."

She gave him more, dead at his face, her own eyes not blinking once as she finished the tale she knew and had sworn him to keep. "He Elvira's white man, he Rover's daddy. Why I know he in Richmond some years back—when Rover had his first child in Maine and it was a boy, this boy here Grainger, he wrote your daddy a letter to tell him; and your daddy sent back a five-dollar goldpiece. Rover still got it. Rover always knowed. Elvira told him, told him everything down to where your daddy was boarding at. Worst thing she done; that's saying a mouthful. I told her when she died, God never forgive her. She my own great-grandbaby-daughter; but I stood right yonder"—Veenie pointed to the floor before the big bed where he had just sat, the spot his feet had touched—"and said as she sucked her last cold breath, 'Nobody love you no more. Go on.' "

It was Elvira's funeral he and Hatt had attended. "Does my sister know?"

"Don't ask her," Veenie said. "Don't ask nobody. You swore to me you stop it *here*." She pointed again to the floor between them. "I may be the meanest nigger left, but you swore to me."

Forrest nodded. "I did."

In the yard, filtered to them through knot-pierced walls, a dog spoke once in pleasure.

A Negro girl said "Come back here."

A Negro boy said, "Go your way. I'm heading home"—Grainger on the steps.

Within, both Forrest and Veenie smiled—he fully; she barely, weak from her story, the backward trek he had forced on a life that aimed only forward: death, rest.

2

That evening Forrest had pled exhaustion to Hatt and taken three syrup biscuits upstairs where the trapped heat of day was no added burden to his head and chest that seemed now either released from failure—a shaft onto hope—or permanently stove, past remorse or repair. He had opened the window on the hills behind, no lamp for bugs, and eaten one biscuit and stripped and washed; then had turned back the blankets Hatt offered year round and slid in between rough sheets—a welcome. His hands had risen and dropped by his ears, fingers closed but unclenched (he had sought sleep thus each night of his life there was no one to hold, literal surrender). Sleep had accepted and he'd sunk for an hour through peaceful depths.

Then Hatt stood over him. No reason to knock now, she'd listened at the door; then opened it quietly and entered and looked for a long time (the boys were back on the hill, playing late). Then silent she set her lamp on the table and touched the covered blade of his left shin and learned he was bare. His nearness reached her, stirred the silt of her own loneliness. So she thought he was also desperate and with fresher reason—one more desertion and no indication that this was the last for Forrest or her. Her James was gone (but at least into death), and the voices of her boys came fading through the window. She would never have more of them than now. Gid had noticed girls; Whitby would soon endure the need. She and Forrest were back where they'd started at their mother's death, each other's. Safe. Hatt knew that suddenly—a team of orphans, ground and gouged for thirty-odd years by the force of others till now they fitted each other only, stone and socket, anvil and mallet, trapped rocks in a backwater carved through ages into perfect contingency (she felt that, not thought it). She sat on the near edge; and when he did not wake, she touched him again, his complicated knee.

He slowly woke and, though by the candle he could see his sister, he said "Yes ma'm?"

Hatt smiled. "I am just your elder," she said.

He took the time to wake up fully; she waited, quiet. Then he said, "You are. Do you know more than me?"

"I think so," she said.

"What?"

"You've give up on Eva."

"I may have," he said. "She has on me. But I knew that."

"Then we're even," Hatt said. "You hungry now?"

Forrest moved his calf against her spread hip—a juncture; he also felt their congruence. "Where is Father?" he said.

"Dead, to us anyhow." She waited. "Why?"

"He would be old now. He might want to see us."

Dark as it was, Hatt faced him squarely. "You want to see him. But he left you."

"And you and Mother."

"And I've let him go, you notice," she said. "I think he's dead."

"Truly?"

She thought. "He would be the first to say he deserved to be."

"But you aren't certain?"

Hatt shook her head. "You've been talking to Veenie."

He nodded Yes. "When did she tell you?"

Hatt said, "She never did and I'll never let her. No, through the years I have heard people say Veenie knew a good deal. But I heard it from Mother, so I never troubled Veenie."

Forrest said "When?"

"The year she died."

"Why would she tell you?"

"I was old enough," Hatt said in defense. Then she waited and the harshness settled into puzzlement. "I used to wonder myself, now you mention it—why she would tell an ignorant child. It sure never helped me. But I've been busy so I never dwelt on it; and now when I do, I know she didn't intend it for help."

"What?" Forrest said.

"—One more anchor she was dropping for herself, in hopes of striking bottom. She was trying not to die. She had held it long years. She told who she could."

"You were sixteen," Forrest said.

"I know I was." Hatt thought it ended there; that now she could turn and clarify the present, the news from Forrest. But the old story stood in her throat, alive and claiming its toll, sporadic but great (she was beautiful to Forrest by the one weak light). "I was sewing for you, mending some blouse. She had taught me of course; and she liked to watch me at it, long after I needed supervision. It meant you were safe—me sewing for you; she knew she was dead; you were in skilled hands. And so I asked her some trifling question, to let her share—would the patch be stronger on the slant or straight?—and she gave it to me like a normal answer: 'Hattie, why your father abandoned us was I asked him politely to honor his vow and love just me. His reply was to vanish by night awhile later when he'd let me almost believe I'd won.' Well, I just sewed on, never questioned again; and she died soon."

Forrest waited; then said, "You were too young to ask."

"No," she said. "I understood. I'd had good eyes and ears all along; what are names and dates? No I just didn't care and still don't; I'm busy. I've been kept busy."

Forrest said "Thank you" to turn the rebuke. But then he said, "I'm going to move out of here, find my own place, let Grainger work for me; then hunt Father down and offer him home here again if he'll come."

Hatt frowned deeply in response to pain, not a sign of disgust. "Why?" she said.

But he did not answer. He was trusting as always in dream, dim warning, the urgent promises of sleep.

Hatt actually smiled. "You are grown and free. It'll occupy your mind. It may be best. You were all he loved the time I knew him."

Forrest smiled in return. He could not be sure she saw him at all. The light ran to her.

3

August 12, 1904

Dear Rover,

I am a voice from the past, the one you used to say played baseball worse than you crocheted. I gave up trying after you moved north—nobody to rag me—and spent most of those years right up to now teaching school at home and in Carolina. Aunt Veenie or someone may have posted you on my life. Suffice to say I've often thought that you had picked a perfect job, just you and some timbers and tar and the sea. Mingling with children and hoping to aid them is old-maid's work, people life has refused.

Anyhow I am back here in Bracey now, plan to teach here next month, and will be moving out of my sister's house as soon as Grainger helps me fix the old Brame place so I can live there. I will be by myself.

That is one of my reasons for writing now. I would like to keep Grainger down here with me. He would be a great asset in my new quarters, and I would respond by teaching him privately six days a week. I could guarantee him kindness, wholesome food, schooling, enough work to train him for a future life, and sufficient rest. He would also be near Aunt Veenie and could watch her, though as you know she takes less watching than most people half her age and puts up with less. I could guarantee you and his mother he'd be safe, barring acts of God. There is no one here to harm him; his goodness wins all.

My second reason is to ask if you know where Father lives now or whether he's living and, if not, where he lies? My sister and I have had no word for twenty-eight years, and I at least am hopeful now of meeting him again if he's on this earth. Veenie said you might know his whereabouts. I wish him only well—which of course I wish you, Rover; you and all yours. Bring them back someday for a look at their seedbed, a chance to thaw out! I would like to shake your hand, maybe fan a few pitches while we both can still move.

Yours in good memory,
Forrest Mayfield

P.S. When I spoke as a "voice from the past," I only meant your past and mine together. I have no intention, and have sworn so to Veenie, of burdening your boy with the old wrongs of others.

August 21, 1904

Dear Grainger,

I will write to Mr. Forrest and say you can work there for him if he really want you. I am sending this to you first in care of Miss Veenie so you keep it to yourself, my last word to you about this anyhow. You had a real easy life up here with us, everybody good to you, so you don't know yet what they holding back to hit you with. Count on it coming though and pretty soon now and not letting up. Never failed yet, Virginia or Maine. When it come and I can't tell you how it will look you remember you got a dry place up here and a job I will teach you, nothing all that good but a fair day's trade. Forrest was a good boy when I used to know him but he didn't know nothing then that he could teach a flea

*that the flea could use and anyhow he living in a hole right now till his peo-
ple come back or he get new people so you watch out for Grainger and leave
fore they tell you to. You still got us here like I told you before and you got Miss
Veenie and kin people there so don't stay any place they can't use you and do
right by you and give you plenty rest. We doing all right. Your mama say hey
and we see you someday, any day you ready.*

Your father,
Rover Walters

NOVEMBER–DECEMBER 1904

Thanksgiving night, 1904

Dear Forrest,

No word of you since August, but now I am writing to honor your birthday on Monday next. All good things for you, is my genuine wish; and Rob would join me if he understood. Maybe he does. At least I have told him. He seems to know more every day, although he is still held back by his ordeal— thin and pale and has a spell of whooping every two or three days yet, by which I am much more scared than he: he threatens to leave, and even in his hardest throes of gasping, with his eyes on me (me begging him to stay), something in him seems calm, seems ready for the journey if that is demanded.

Forrest, I am sure that is you working in him—that and his face. You are all in his face whenever I watch him, which is every two or three minutes of the day. No sign of me or any of my people.

An early hard frost here last night. All day we have barely moved from the stove. We hope you are warm and spared affliction and, again, that your birthday brings you your wishes.

Love from,
Eva

Forrest waited three weeks till he knew his intent, that his wish was his need. Then he spent the best part of a Friday evening writing her this.

December 16, 1904

Dear Eva,

Thank you both for your hopes. I have taken what you said as honest and kind, in purpose at least—though I cannot imagine living long enough to acquire understanding of how, over eight months, you go on extending me an open hand yet withhold all the rest: heart and presence, the sight of my son. Maybe this was all you ever intended—to smile at a distance, in my direction, and witness my answer. Maybe the only error was mine—to breach that purpose, seek to close that gap.

You cannot witness me at this distance though, so here is my news since you left me last.

We have found my father, or his whereabouts. A long chain of circumstances, too long to tell, has led us to his door; and I think I am hoping to see him some-how during the Christmas.

Then I will let you know more about me, for Rob's future use if nothing more, though one of my hopes is—whatever our fate—that you will understand more fully and forgive what you seem to feel I have wreaked on your life.

For now, suffice that I live alone in the old Brame house on the hill back of Hatt's. It is small, four rooms, but is fully mine for as long as I wish. Some meals I take with Hatt, some here. A Negro boy is working for me—young, from a fam-ily we know of old—and he is rapidly learning to cook; so I have health and care and the sound at least of another animal, near in my space.

More word soon, I trust.

Ever,
Forrest Mayfield

December 19, 1904

My dear Forrest,

I have just read your letter and am in my room, one hand on Rob awake beside me, inspecting his own hand with grave amazement (he found it last week and is still amazed). It is only the strength of his great discovery—he is late in this, having been so weak—that keeps him from sensing my load of sadness.

I want to see you. I was hoping you had some Christmas plan for us but now you don't.

I know I should say I am glad you are healthy and have a new house and have found your father, but I feel only lonesome misery. I know I should kneel and beg your pardon for my childish meanness in these past months. I do that now and only ask that, in thinking of me, you recall what a child I actually am. Or was till now—a feeble plea but the only one I make and true. Also the fact that, once I was home, there were awful circumstances holding me here which I did not mention to you last August—a message from Mother that hurt, being true, a letter she left me, delivered by Rena who spares me nothing, my personal hound.

All of that though is not an excuse but the start of a partial explanation, the rest of which will require whole years of my life to come. Whatever your feeling and whatever your answer, I vow to change.

More love from,
Eva

December 21, 1904

Dear Eva,

Your second letter was here when I came home yesterday evening from school. Grainger, my help, had fetched it and propped it in the midst of my desk; so I read it at once — and many more times before going to bed, where I did not sleep.

What I must say is this. You are now stranger to me than an animal would be, and what you say in this latest letter is a stroke more cruel than any human being has ever dealt me (with no claim at all to a martyr's crown, still I think I can say I have had strokes enough in thirty-odd years to give me some title to accuracy in the recognition and gauging of harm; you know my past well enough, you cannot object).

I was all but repaired. Have you no plain mercy?

That calls for an answer, an answer which might well need your life; but so then have you called for more from me. I thought I had given that once for all, the day we promised ourselves last year. I meant quite literally all I said, how- ever quickly put. Now recall how I put it. Surely you can.

Yet because — for whatever reason — you ask, I say it again. Not in words this time. Words failed before. But in something you can see and touch and wear, something weighty and not forgettable. It is in the smaller of the parcels in this crate — my mother's ring which, despite her sadness (or whatever she felt), she wore to the end of her life. And would have worn to her grave for good if Hatt had not gone in an hour before her burial and reached in the coffin and worked it from her finger and brought it to me. It has since been mine. Now I give it to you, whatever your meaning.

If you take it and wear it — on your own left hand, above our own — it will signify our reforged bond and, for me at least, my triumph (with your help) over whatever blight struck my parents' union. If you will not wear it, please keep it in some safe place for Rob till the day he needs it or gives some sign of the adult strength to understand its total meaning in our own lives, yours and mine, and the previous lives of his father's family. I trust you to let me know of your choice.

Taking it, you take me. If that is your wish, I will come for you on New Year's Eve, whatever the weather. My Christmas is now involved with my father.

The other parcel is for Rob, the nicest express wagon I could buy here, a thing

*my father gave me very early which I also remember—him hauling me around
the house and laughing, saying, "Forrest and I are bound for bliss!" I don't know
if it will have meaning for him yet; but whatever your own need and choice may
be, I trust you will help me in seeing that the boy has something from me on
his first conscious Christmas.*

So, Eva, I'm waiting. But you never doubted that.

Love ever from
Forrest

The initials in the ring stand for Robinson Mayfield to Anna Goodwin.

He placed that letter in an envelope and addressed it to *Mrs. Eva Mayfield, In the Care of Kendal, Fontaine, North Carolina.* Then he took the
sturdy gun-shell crate which Grainger had got for the purpose in town
and—padding with newsprint, clean rags, and straw—he carefully packed his
three solid gifts: the wagon for Rob (red with removable wooden sides and
rubber tires), the ring for Eva (in the small jeweler's box it had come in some
forty years before), and his letter at the top. Then he laid on a final thickness
of padding (a clean white shirt of his own, slightly worn) and nailed down
the top with broadheaded dark-blue roofing nails—the blue, as he recalled,
of the Atlantic Ocean (his father had carried them once to Norfolk). Then
with Grainger's help he carried it out to the woodshed in back and hauled
out an ancient two-wheeled goat-cart, some old playtoy of the dead Brame
children, and with Grainger in the staves (prancing, laughing), he saw it
downhill to the depot, the train.

2

In Fontaine the next day, eleven o'clock, Sylvie was coming out the post-office
door, no mail for the Kendals. The morning was bright and the ground was
stiff-frozen; but she wore no shawl or scarf, just her dress and apron, the rag
on her head, the shoes that had been her brother Doc's. So her step was fast,
aimed back toward warmth; and in time to her feet, her mind worked
quickly on happy pictures—Christmas, the end of a hard bad year, the
sense pouring through her (just now this morning, the first time in months,
since her baby's death) that what stretched ahead promised better than the
past. She was also in love.

"You. Sylvie"—a man's voice off to her left. A white man.

She looked but did not break step. Old Mr. Rooker on the depot porch, waving her toward him. She stopped and rubbed her arms against cold but did not go nearer.

He tried to come to her—an old man, gimp-legged, blue-faced and bald with whom she had purposely had no dealings in her whole life till now; somebody who paid a nickel to touch you. So her sisters had said. He came down the stairs and took four or five lame steps toward her, collapsing on himself like a complicated mechanical toy; then he gave up the effort and said, "*Come* on. I'm ruined, you see."

She went and he turned and climbed back up and waited for her at the top of the stairs. She stopped at the bottom.

"You're Sylvie, ain't you? Mag's Sylvie?"

"*Sylvie's* Sylvie."

Mr. Rooker grinned. "You want a job?"

"Not yours," she said and took a step to go.

"Hold on." He laughed and reached down a short arm toward her; hopeless, it dropped.

But Sylvie stepped again as if in one more try he could touch her.

"Too early in the morning, too cold," he said.

Sylvie turned back, smiling.

Mr. Rooker whispered, "Just a little message; just carry a message."

She took back the two steps to hear his message, but she crossed her arms on her chest as a shield.

"Come on up here. You got to see it. Warm-up a minute." He turned and stumped through the freightroom door.

She followed him in and shut the door behind her. It was warm—hot, stifling, and dry. The big room held two other men—old Mr. Mitchell who wore ladies' silk stockings under his clothes (wool trousers on his skin gave him open sores) and black Harry Brown, bent halfway double from fifty years of hauling.

"You know Bedford Kendal? You know him, don't you?" Mr. Rooker was standing four feet away. "You know that much?"

"Yes."

"Yes *what?*"

"Yes sir," she said. She had stopped the smile.

"Then look at this." He pointed beside him to a crate on a dolly. "This here's for him. Go home and tell him."

"Harry'll bring it." She pointed to Harry, who was studying her.

Mr. Rooker shook his head. "My instructions was different. You going to deliver my message or not?"

Sylvie came a step closer and looked at the crate.

Mr. Rooker moved on her and managed to lay a quick hand on her chest before she could drop back and reach for the door—Mr. Mitchell grinning, Harry Brown laughing with Mr. Rooker. Mr. Rooker said "That won't the message!"

Sylvie stood—door open, neither nodding nor smiling yet holding her ground, having seen enough to raise her curiosity.

Mr. Rooker said "Repeat it."

"You say, 'Tell Mr. Bedford he got him a box. Come down here and get it.'" She paused. "Is it heavy?"

"N'mind how heavy. Just tell him that—nobody but him, no other soul."

She nodded and turned again to go.

"You got your reward already," Mr. Rooker said, alluding to the spotty dry hand that had brushed her.

Harry Brown laughed again.

But she had slammed the door and was down the stairs, stepping faster than ever and huddled inward now on more than her cold assaulted breasts, on the certain knowledge that the box was for Eva from Eva's husband. She could not read—Sylvie—but she knew two or three words by size and shape: *baby* and *spoon* and *train* and *Eva*.

3

After supper that night they had all adjourned to the sitting room and poked up the fire. The room was actually Rena's now (when Rob had come down with whooping cough, she had silently resigned her own room to Eva—her share of hers and Eva's room—and set up a cot in the sitting-room corner, so short and narrow as to make it easy to conceal her traces each morning early: her few clothes were hid in various corners around the house); but they still sat there because of the warmth, the lack of a better place to go, the weight of the memory of the dead in the parlor. Eva sat till everyone else was settled—her father reading, Kennerly doing the accounts on his knee, Rena talking to Rob. Then she stood and asked Rena, "Will you watch him awhile?" Rena's contented answer was Yes. Eva climbed to her room, with no explanation to anyone and questioned by none. She knew that they knew; it pertained to Forrest, her other life.

She was making a Christmas gift for Forrest by lamplight in these few minutes of evening (daylight hours being taken by Rob and her gradual share of the household duties). She had had no money to spend since June when the three dollars Forrest had given her exhausted themselves in things for Rob;

so she'd cut up a fine dresser-scarf of her mother's and for three weeks now had been making the gift, a single big linen handkerchief which she'd hem-stitched and edged and was embroidering in silk, *F. M.* There was only the last downward leg of the *M*; and she strained forward now at the delicate stitching (she was good at small work, her mother's instruction). Tomorrow she'd manage to post it off. Or she'd hear by then and deliver it some other way, direct.

Sylvie's step on the stairs. No need or reason for Sylvie this late. Eva did not hide the handkerchief though; Sylvie had seen it (in silence, no questions). She looked up to meet her and found her already in the door, dark, waiting empty-handed.

"You working," Sylvie said, plain statement, a fact reported to no one but them.

Eva nodded and bent to the light again.

"You be done soon?"

"Tonight I hope."

Sylvie said "You better."

Eva looked up but did not ask her meaning.

Sylvie entered and walked past the bed to the dresser. She felt in the dark and found an object which she carefully brought to the foot of the bed, the edge of the light—a silver mirror. She tilted it, studied it, traced on its back with her index finger the confirmation of her earlier knowledge—*Eva*, engraved in lavish script. Then she carefully set it back in its place, never having sought her own reflection.

Eva laughed one note. "What is that meant to mean?"

"That you better get that job done tonight."

Eva said, "I know. Time's bearing down." But her voice was puzzled.

Sylvie was still by the dresser, dim. She whispered from there. "What you get? From him?"

"It's not Christmas yet."

"In the box, today."

Eva said, "I don't know what you mean."

"Can't fool me," Sylvie said. "I seen it."

Eva turned up the lamp to the verge of smoking. "What?" she said.

"The box you got today from your husband."

Eva shook her head slowly.

"It sure God come here. I seen it and touched it." Sylvie pointed to her own eyes; then outward through walls toward the depot, Mr. Rooker.

Eva only waited.

"I coming back this morning, no mail, and that old *feeling* Mr. Rooker, all hands, called me in to the depot and showed me—a gunshell box. He say it for your father, for me to tell him and nobody else. So I told him when he come in the backdoor for dinner, and he just thanked me and set down and ate. I step home this afternoon for a while—Mama still right weak—so I won't here when they brought it up." Her smile was visible. "What you get from him?"

Eva strained for accuracy. "Sylvie, to my knowledge, no box has come. When it does, it will be for Father like you say."

Sylvie shook her head, still smiling. "For you," she said aloud, triumphant. She reached behind her for the mirror again, reckless this time, endangering it. But she got it across to Eva safely, held its back to the light, traced the name for Eva. "Your name on it. I *seen* it, Eva."

Eva kept to her chair but studied upward—Sylvie's face. No sign of harm, intended or accomplished. No readable sign. "You're sure?" Eva said.

Sylvie knocked with her knuckles on the mirror, the name. "If this your name like you said it was, then that box for you." Again she pointed toward the distant spot where she'd witnessed this morning her present chance. "I *know* your name."

4

When she'd sent Sylvie down and had stood by her bed, asking herself for a stretch of minutes "What do I want to do with this?", then she went to the top of the stairs and listened—the crack of the fire, Rena babbling to Rob. Then she spoke out. "Father."

Mr. Kendal was asleep.

"Father?" again more urgently.

Kennerly said "Eva's after you." Then louder, "Answer Eva, please sir."

The sounds that reached her were—her father waking, slowly rising, walking slowly to the foot of the stairs, his patient voice saying "Darling, what?"

She waited for him there at the landing; but when he had climbed up and stood two steps below her face, waiting, she could not speak. Her mouth refused, the muscles of her chest. So she turned—they were in all but total dark—and led the way toward her open room from which the only light crept coldly.

He hesitated in place a moment, then followed her and shut the heavy door behind them.

She had gone to her work-chair and stood beside it. The lamp was below her face and light reached it. Her work—the linen, the silk, the frame—were on the lamp-table, unconcealed. She was looking toward him.

He waited, looking; and when she stayed silent, he said, "There are not many more climbs in me—this rheumatism." He was fifty-four. "Say something to make it worth my trip." He smiled.

Eva could see it. She even tried to match it and speak at once, but her face contorted round her eyes like a fist; and her voice broke, guttural and dry in her neck.

He kept his place. "What has Sylvie told you?"

Again she worked for calm and speech, and failed though silently. So slowly she shook her head side to side—her lifelong means of restoring calm, as if some reeling or winching were done: her voice drawn gradually up from its well. "A box that came today—my name."

He nodded. "It did."

"Where is it now?"

He came as far forward as the foot of the bed, then drew out his watch, tilted it to light, read it carefully, then looked up smiling. "Twenty, thirty miles south of Bracey, Virginia if the night train's on time. The north-bound train."

"You sent it back?"

"Refused it," he said.

"Tell me why. Every reason. It bore my name." She'd found her voice and, with each word, acquired firmer grip on her mettle.

Her father did not quickly alter expression. His smile survived half through her question; then it began a slow descent into gravity. When she'd finished, he was grave but utterly calm. He let the air settle; then said, "Your reasons. Entirely for you. What I do is for you. You make it plain that your life is here. Since you came back to this house that morning in August—I never asked a word of what passed that night; I know you sent him away, that's all—since that day, Eva, I determined to help you defend your own will. All I needed was one sign from you, of your purpose. You gave me that."

Again she began to shake her head, involuntarily this time; and what came was tears, full, hot and silent. She had not wept, she knew, in a year; since her opposite misery the previous Christmas in Hatt's bare house.

He came no nearer but he said "*My* reasons." He was forced to pause. When he spoke again, it was with his hands straight down at his sides, palms flat and outward.

Eva watched those, dim as they were—his gentle hands—and thought that she could not remember a time when he'd whispered before.

"I have had all the leaving I can bear this year. I am asking you, politely as I can, to stay."

His face—stroked by the light from beneath—seemed young and lifting, a hopeful boy's, long life ahead but requiring help. Entirely helpless. Eva nodded toward him, though she could not smile.

5

Hours later far into night, Eva lay awake in her bed alone, the bed she had occupied all her life except for a year from the age of four. The bed was in place in its own room—hers, empty tonight of all but her and borne cold but safe on the silent depths of the separate sleep of all her truest family beneath her. The element, her rightful harbor, the socket in which her life was made and which held it again after brief dislocation. Even Rob had been sheered away, tonight at least; when her father had taken her silent nod as answer to his plea, he had turned and gone back down to the others and seated himself and said to Rena (Eva heard it from her room), "Go see if Eva wants Robinson with her." Rena had come and knocked on the doorframe— the door was open—and then stepped forward and searched Eva's face (Eva was standing still by the lamp) and said, "I am keeping Rob downstairs with me. He is already asleep in his basket; don't worry." Eva had said "I thank you" and sat; and Rena had gone out, shutting the door. Eva had sat on, the room chilling round her, the wick in the lamp thumping drily for a while in its struggle to burn on vanishing oil. Then the light had extinguished, and she'd sat on longer through the sounds of her family working beneath her to end the day. Then when they'd quieted and seemed asleep, she'd stood in the dark and reached to the table beside her for her work and had gone to the bottom drawer of her chest and, kneeling there, had stored it deep. Then she'd risen and quickly stripped to bare skin and walked to the window and had drawn back the curtain in hopes of moonlight to show herself the nakedness she'd hardly seen since leaving Virginia—none, black night. She had not touched herself; and in all that time since her father had left, she had not had anything approaching a thought. Her mind had been, not asleep but struck or like a hand suddenly sliced by a blade, recoiling in numbness to wait till the quantity of blood that sprang would announce and measure the wound sustained, the hope of cure. And so she had entered her bed, still naked, and fallen on sleep like a plummet, depth-bound.

In her sleep she had dreamed. Dreams were uncommon to her; and when they came were mostly credible amusing stories made from the lumber of her daily life (she'd forgot the dream of her wedding night, though it also was hardly total invention). But this had been strange and entirely new, a discovery. *Light*—the main sensation was light, a clear warm sun filtered in and gentled by tall broad windows. The windows were set in a large building. The building was neither a house nor a store. *Have I ever,* she actually asked in the dream, *been in a building which is not intended for sleeping or selling?* She could not remember but went on wandering through many floors of light-washed rooms, past silent happy people at tables working or reading or looking out windows. No one spoke to her; but she did not mind, did not feel unwelcome or invisible. All that troubled her nearly perfect sense of peace was a straining forward of her whole clear mind; she felt it in the dream, probing forward to a point, straining to discover the use of this place, the purpose of all these quiet workers, the name of their work. The strain had all but brought her to grief—her steps had quickened, her face gathered tight—when she saw one man at a distant table poured over by sun, watching neither his work nor the sun but her. He was nearly her age, more nearly a boy; so it did not occur to her to ask him the meaning. And he was not smiling. Yet as she took the last step past him, he stood in place and said to her "What?" She stopped and turned and, in the effort to recognize him (he now seemed familiar, maybe kin), she also did not smile. No more name would come for him than the place, so she said "Where am I?" He said "In the school." She said "Which one?" — "The only one." — "How did I get here?" — "By needing to come." She stood and thought. Then she nodded and said "What must I learn?" He could finally smile— "You must learn that too." He put out his hands, personal bafflement; the hunt would be hers. In the instant, she accepted and was flooded with joy like the room with sun. Her smile asked it for her of its own accord— "Then tell me your name and I'll begin." His faded to gravity, his hands dropped down, his head shook twice. "That is part of what you have lost and must learn."

That woke her abruptly on her back in the dark, uncovered to the waist and cold in the frozen air of the room. But her pleasure, the joy toward the end of the dream, survived her waking and the man's last question, his own grave face. Survived too the earlier question of her dream—who was the man? Why had she felt she had known him always? That question had already sunk to oblivion through the fragile net of nocturnal memory. So she lay on awhile, having covered herself with quilts and comforts, and thought of all she remembered from the dream. Alone as she was and was likely to be, it seemed sufficient program for years to come—the learning of what she required to know. Required *in secret* apparently; for though she knew, knew above all else, that she had great needs for knowledge and understanding and help, she also knew—lying here now warming—that the question she remembered from her dream was just: she did not know the names of her needs. Did anyone else? The ones who had tried, who had offered her answers—Forrest, her mother, gloomy Hatt, the silent answer proffered by Rob, forty feet away now through plaster walls—had failed her as fully as she herself. The names then were neither *love* nor *hatred*, *heat* nor *cold*. And her father, pitiful in loneliness. What more did he offer than versions of love— *need* and *shelter*? She'd take the shelter. It was natural to her—his house, her room, her dark deep bed. The few things she'd learned, she'd learned in these walls, dim as they were, oiled with bad memory. They'd serve awhile longer.

She did not feel that as a sizable choice. It slid through her mind like smooth waxed thread. Behind it though it drew a question, again the man's first question from the dream but now in her own voice silently—*What do I know?*

She actually waited. Still no answer came, not even the old lies offered by others. She waited for the truth. Silence, night, cocoon of warmth in the old house cracking with bitter cold, the burden of its freight—her father, Rob, Kennerly, Rena, and Sylvie; her vanished mother, heavier still.

Then she'd wait on here. There was no other chance to learn what she must know, the name she would need to launch her own life. Simple as that. She knew she was smiling, at nothing but the ceiling lost above her. Slowly with her hand she sought herself.

DECEMBER 1904–FEBRUARY 1905

The man was young and knew him at once. He did not smile but he said "Well, Forrest."

Forrest said "Yes sir" and knew that his own face, tilted up, was helplessly smiling. He'd have known this man in a chance encounter on the farthest star. The face was his own—as Veenie had said, his living mirror, shockingly unchanged since the one dim picture and his own clear memory. The fur on his upper lip had stiffened into mannish wire and was shot with gray, as his temples were; but the eyes, while they did not fix on Forrest, had lasted perfect in depth and sadness, clear of whatever these twenty-eight years had pressed against them. How old could he be? Forrest never had known and had not realized it till now here below him, the least of the questions that clamored for answer.

"How you coming?" his father said, not moving. He had not extended his hand for shaking, his arms for embrace, and had not stepped forward across the worn sill.

"Cold," Forrest said and shuddered, still grinning. He meant the day, the still gray morning cracking with frost even now at ten. Christmas eve.

"Where's your overcoat?—that little Prince Albert I bought you: when was it? black with velvet piping all round. Waste. Your mother never forgave me."

"No sir. She did." Forrest shook again, all over, helpless. He was in his only suit, a worn serge, no coat or hat.

His father said, "You asking to come in?"

"I've come this far."

"How far?"

"From Bracey." Forrest pointed.

And his father looked. Then he smiled the first smile Forrest could remember on him; it came on him suddenly as if pushed at him against his will. But he kept his teeth covered and, still looking toward Bracey, said, "That's nowhere. Nowhere to speak of. Now *I've* come a distance."

"Same distance," Forrest said.

His father laughed on teeth that at once aged him twenty years—an old sick man still propped round the hole in the midst of his heart which years ago he'd asked even a five-year-old boy to fill. At the end his nose dripped. He wiped it with his hand and hacked his throat clear and said, "I took a few detours. Never travel in a line if you want an education."

"Yes sir," Forrest said. "Please let me in."

His father faced him for the first time fully, eyes on eyes. "I ain't got a penny." With both hands he patted his trouser pockets. Empty, the cloth fell in on stick legs.

Forrest said "I knew that."

"Then how come you're here, in Richmond at Christmas, a hundred miles from home on a sick old fool's doorstep in the cold?"

"To see you. Ask you a thing or two. A little help."

His father's hands stayed loose at his sides, palms outward now, bare as bread troughs. "I couldn't help a mad dog swallow his slaver. I know I've had some part in you—my eyes still work—but I don't even know I can call your name."

"You already have—Forrest," he said.

His father nodded. "I'd have guessed you was him." But he did not move to unblock the door.

Forrest reached into his own breast pocket and withdrew a small oblong package tied with string. He offered it up. "Christmas cheer."

His father thought awhile, then accepted. He turned it several times in his hands, probing with hard brown spatulate thumbs.

"Cigars," Forrest said. "I remember you smoked them."

The old man looked down, actually studied him. "You're definitely Forrest?" It was clearly put as a genuine question.

Forrest nodded. "The one thing I'm certain of."

"You can come in," he said, "but it's warmer outside. I'm by myself, not a lump of coal."

Forrest said, "I could go and find you some."

"Don't worry yourself." He stood aside and waved Forrest in.

"There's no sense freezing, with Richmond full of coal."

His father said, "Don't worry. The Lord'll provide." He gestured up, the cold hard sky, with both empty hands—Elijah and ravens. Then he looked down to Forrest. He was smiling again, the broad closed smile that pulled Forrest inward—had pulled him, he now saw, through all these years; the single question to which these years had been a set of answers offered by him in addled desperation to people who never had asked the question.

Forrest also smiled and followed his father—a final chance, though he thought of it happily with warming hope.

The hall down which they went was dim and bare as a mine. The single traces of human presence, at some past date, were wild curls of white dust which dogged their steps and stirred in their wake. Four dark doors, all shut. Mr. Mayfield stopped by the last one and said again, "This'll be freezing"; but Forrest nodded so he turned the knob and led on in. A bedroom—bright (light fell through two windows) and warmer than promised. And on the light and heat, a third surprise—the high dry smell of burnt hemp leaves, asthma cigarettes (which Forrest had smelled only once before, visiting a pupil whose father smoked them in his bouts of strangulation, slim relief). His father had gone on toward the bed; so he shut the door behind them and said "No it's warm."

Mr. Mayfield sat in the unmade covers and said "Just wait." He did not gesture to the single chair, a dark oak rocker.

But Forrest went to it and carefully sat.

Mr. Mayfield pointed to the rusty iron stove. "Woman that helps me, made a fire just before she left. Used all my coal."

Forrest saw the battered empty scuttle on its bed of black dust beside the hearth. Between it and where he sat was a woodbox. For something to do, he rocked forward and leaned to see in—more than a few scraps of dark pinebark, sufficient for a half-hour more of warmth. "Let me throw these scraps on for you," Forrest said; he moved to rise.

His father said "No" more quickly and firmly than he'd said anything else in Forrest's presence.

Forrest stopped in midair and turned back to see.

The old man was still in his stale yellow sheets, green and pink quilt Forrest smelled through the hemp. His neck, now revealed by his slumping shoulders, was dry and ropey. But his eyes had lighted again and were urgent; he'd given an order not a request.

Forrest obeyed, though with obvious puzzlement, almost fear. "I thought it was wood."

"It is. My collection," Mr. Mayfield said. "The things I make." He offered no more but was calm again.

So Forrest leaned to look. The huddle of scraps in the bottom of the crate were in fact crude figures, dim memories of human form; hacked out by one whose senses or sympathies were failing or had failed, as quick reminders of what had been lost or ceded or, worse, never known. Already knowing, Forrest said, "For what? Make them for what, sir?"

His father thought awhile; then stood with some trouble and went to the box and leaned and rummaged and came up with two figures, one in each hand. Then he went back and sat and studied them, rubbing their powdery surfaces with slow thumbs, inquiring. "Well," he said, "*time.* For time, I guess, if you want a true reason." He waited again, looked up and smiled. "How old are you?"

"Thirty-four," Forrest said.

"You know what I mean then, though years from now you'll know a lot better. The problem in life is getting through time—all the time they give you and, Jesus, they give it. I'm sixty-five my last birthday, which I'll guarantee is a good many days to wake up and walk through and stay out of harm in." He still was talking to the dolls in his hands. "So these are for that, just foolishness to paddle me on through a few more days. I'm not strong, you see— tell the truth, I never was, though till recently nobody knew it but me." He looked up at Forrest. "When did you know me?"

"Thirty-four years ago. For five years and seven months."

His father nodded. "I was sick even then. Bad rheumatism in all my joints, so sore it was like teeth aching all over me. Night after night, I'd lie on my back by whoever happened to be there beside me—them sleeping and breathing slow and rested, me alive and hurting. Nobody believed me; I was too good at loving!" For the second time, he laughed; and again the firm plain beauty of his face fell in on his mouth—ruined teeth, black holes.

Forrest looked to the dolls in his father's hands. "Who are they?" he said.

At the end of his laugh, Mr. Mayfield turned the dolls toward Forrest. "My mother and father." Then he offered them out insistently.

Forrest accepted. A savage could have made them or an idle boy. He had never known his Mayfield kin, never seen any other likeness of them; but these dolls—four, five inches long; square-necked, box-shouldered, slew-foot—were hardly more than schemes for people. Both had round eyes and slashed smiling mouths. The lady distinguished herself by a low relief of breasts; the rest of her body was finished smooth, no crease or fold. The man bore no marks but a face and a navel, a swell in the left groin. Both had been handled long and hard; the usual dust and gum of pinebark had been rubbed to smoothness. Forrest also rubbed them, found his own thumbs helplessly stroking their chests while he asked himself, "Have I come too late? Is he too far gone?" But before he could think of a public remark, his father stood again.

In place by the bed, Mr. Mayfield searched the room for something hid—stove, woodbox, scuttle, a mantel with two glass jars (one filled with buttons), a two-doored wardrobe painted apple green, a white china slopjar lidded with a rag, Forrest in the rocker, a straw floormat, the bed itself. Nothing else visible. He said, "Somewhere here I got a little dress." He reached down and took one doll from Forrest. "Little dress for Mama." He was stroking her belly again, both thumbs. "Woman that helps me made her a dress. I told her how, one I remembered. It's here somewhere. I'm arranging my things. Things are failing me."

"Where am *I?*" Forrest said.

His father understood. He took the three steps to the box of dolls and looked down at it. "No children," he said. "No children here." He smiled. "No *room.* Yet here I'm alone. Dying by myself, strangling in spit, and not a soul beside me." The smile had curiously lasted through that, though nothing in his eyes or the tone of his voice permitted any thought that he was not utterly earnest, even desperate.

Forrest said "*Me.* I've volunteered."

His father studied him; then nodded slowly, the nearest he had come to gratitude. Then he handed back the doll as though she mattered, as though she were an urgent counter in a game. Then he said, "But why come here alone, come empty-handed bringing nothing but your grin? Hell, cats can grin."

"I brought those cigars—"

"—Which I'll have to throw away. They'd ruin my chest." Mr. Mayfield rubbed at his own breastbone with the heel of his hand as though scouring it.

Forrest stood.

"Where you headed?"

"Home," Forrest said.

"You quit easy, don't you?"

"Yes," Forrest said, "whenever I'm not needed."

"Who else but me don't need you then?" Mr. Mayfield was smiling. He took a step toward Forrest.

So Forrest smiled. "That would be my life-story."

His father went quickly to the bed and sat. "Tell it," he said.

"Don't mock me, please sir."

"I'm not. I'm not. You've come this long way at Christmas to tell it. I got nothing but time. I'd be glad to hear." He motioned to the rocker.

Forrest obeyed and sat. He said "It takes a minute."

His father nodded.

"The first five years, I guess you know. Then you had gone and we watched Mother try to stand up from that. She tried oh six years and then gave up."

"Who is *we?*" his father said. "You say '*We* watched.' "

"Hatt and I. Hattie, my sister."

His father nodded.

"She is still in Bracey—a widow, two sons."

"Just tell *your* story. That's what I bargained for."

"I lived with Hattie. When Mother died I was just twelve; so Hatt got married to make us a home with old James Shorter, a whole lot older."

"Good," Mr. Mayfield said. "James is good."

"He's dead too," Forrest said. "I told you."

"Most people are," Mr. Mayfield said. "You ain't. Keep telling."

"I grew up, is all. I stayed there in Bracey in James Shorter's house and ate his food and took his orders and waited for you. I knew you were living and were somewhere near, though nobody told me. I tried to think you were hunting for me and would someday find me."

"I knew where you were. I knew very well. And I knew you were far better off without me."

"Why, please sir?" Forrest said. "We didn't agree."

"That's part of my story. You're telling yours."

Forrest waited to think. "Well, what?" he said. "I had the same trouble you just mentioned, time to endure. Stuck off up in the eaves at James Shorter's— broiling in summer, blue in winter—I had to get through my life till you'd come. It never dawned on me that children could die; so there I was in the attic, reading." Forrest raised both hands from his knees to point, whatever attic this present house possessed; and saw that he held the two dolls still, his father's parents. Pitiful faceless images of two lives whose actual blood composed his own, channeled his own, hacked out of pine by a sick man lonely as a hawk in heaven who—for all Forrest knew, by the lights he had—had never been capable of lasting love for any live object with more face than these, more vulnerable limbs, and who sat here now three feet away, reeling his own painful story from him as entertainment, an hour killed. He lowered the dolls to his lap again, then laid them in their box. Where could he go when he stood now and left, as he surely must? He had come for the first time in memory to a terminus.

His father said "What sort of reading?"

That came for Forrest like a break in the frown of some final judge, a threat of mercy. And with it came a long-postponed recognition, shaft of light thrown backward at his childhood, at all his life till now—all his aims which he now saw were single. "Anything about people getting along, stories of families, stories of friends, people older than any I'd known (give or take some Negroes). The only books children ever want to read."

His father nodded but he said, "Not so. All I read was the Bible—all we had to read except medicine labels—and nobody gets along in the Bible. Not one happy pair, not one that lasts long enough to watch and learn *how* from. So I gave up reading and took up holding onto people. You know how that lasted me." He gestured round the room, his witness, bare of love as the ocean floor. His sweep included Forrest.

So Forrest smiled. "Sir, I had no choice. Nobody to hold but Hatt or James."

"Hell, you hunt people down," his father said.

"If you've got time and strength."

"What's kept you so busy then, to be here alone?"

Forrest said, "Teaching. Teaching Latin in school."

"Good God," his father said. "*Ego amo te.* What caused that?"

Forrest laughed a little. "The reading, I guess. One book led to another book; and one or two teachers were good to me, encouraged me onward. Everything seemed to be promising what I wanted to hear—every book, every teacher: that by working and learning I would make myself the kind of person other people would come to, and some would love. I couldn't go to college—" He stopped to wonder if any of this were really true, if it were the *case* or only the plea which his voice was making for this old man.

His father said, "Don't look like to me a man teaching school would have much trouble drawing friendly company. You teach in the school there in Bracey, you say?"

"I do now, yes sir."

"Boys *and* girls?"

"Yes sir."

"What age mostly?"

"Twelve up to sixteen."

Mr. Mayfield beamed and waved with both hands, a problem solved. "There you go." But when Forrest did not join his fun, he said, "I guess that could land you in trouble?—last train out of town?"

Forrest nodded Yes.

"You'd probably meet me on it!" he said. "I've rode it enough times to own shares in it."

Forrest said, "Let me go now and buy you some coal, a Christmas present."

His father said, "Say what you will, send me anywhere you want in convict-chains; but if I was teaching roomfuls of girls that age, sooner than later I'd be slapping one of ems little nubbin if it harelipped every Baptist preacher in the county!"

Forrest sat in the noise of his father's laughter and planned this latest retreat, perhaps the last. He would stand and, if urged, say he'd come back this evening; but would go instead to the nearest coal merchant, have a cart sent out for his father's warmth a few days longer, then make his own way to the dark depot, find Grainger on a bench, and take the home train. When he'd seen his way clear, he stood and worked to smile.

His father said "You're quitting me."

"I've got some quick business in town," Forrest said.

"No," his father said. "You're quitting me too." He stayed in his nest of sour covers, hands on his knees; but his face assumed in the instant of speech a flat finality of comprehension. This grinning gap-toothed dying satyr knew the facts of the case and the truth they concealed and not only knew but would speak his knowledge now.

Forrest neither wished to stop him nor had the power. He sat on and heard.

"You let a young pretty girl slip right by you and never reached out to grab her. You let her take your boy, that you'll never get back. You've left your sister and her wild boys and camped out alone with a little nigger waiter in a shack on a hill with a leaking roof. Christ Jesus, Son, who you want to *be?* Be yourself, not *me.* If all the years you've grown up thinking I was something to copy—well, now you know. Now you know different. This is—what?— Christmas, ain't it?"

"Day before," Forrest said, "the twenty-fourth."

"That's near enough," he said. "This is Christmas Eve and Robinson Mayfield—which is me if you're wondering—has washed up here in Richmond, Virginia (a place as ugly as you'd hope to find) in these old rooms as empty as his heart and far more lonesome than before he was born: *he* being *me,* you understand. You're half my age and here you sit, bad off as me and thirty years to go. Change it. Change it now if you can. I doubt you can."

From that, to his own surprise, Forrest drew the strength to say, "Who told you please? How long have you known?"

His father studied him as if for worthiness; then drew breath to speak, answer or refusal.

A distant noise far down the hall—the street door opening, entering steps, the door shut, a wait, then those same steps shuffling nearer toward them.

Forrest spoke again, "Who is it?"—as much to the door behind which the steps had stopped now, listening, as to his father.

His father was smiling past him at the door. He said clearly "Yes—" like the rising plea of a happy greedy child.

It opened on a girl wrapped tight against cold, her clear pale skin all lit to red life by whatever trek she'd made to be here. She also smiled—also past Forrest—and standing in place in the open door, set down two large canvas bags she'd brought and began to unwrap herself, her head. She was lovely and had shown her auburn hair, her tall brow, to the grim chilled room like gifts for the season to whoever was needy, whoever would take them, before she had strayed enough from her smile to catch the presence of a waiting stranger. "I'm sorry," she said but to Mr. Mayfield.

It was Forrest who stood though and said "I was leaving."

She studied him, his face, for the time it took to read his past; then a slow shock rose from deep in her chest and stilled her smile. She put a hand toward him but not in greeting—to force him back—and said, "Oh don't. I have just brought coal. Then I got to go cook his dinner; he's starving. Let me make up a fire."

So Forrest sat.

And the girl slid her bags across the sill and shut the door and then brought them forward to the stove and knelt.

Forrest said to his father, "How far did she come?" He intended by that to discover the coalyard.

But his father recalled their first exchange. "She's *from* here," he said. "Richmond's her home." He was staring at her.

She had set one bag of the coal aside, far back on the hearth; now she worked with quiet uncomplicated grace, with hands surprisingly white and small, to build them a fire in the ashes of the last. She wore no rings. She was twenty maybe. Maybe less, eighteen. The silent economy of her competence, the absence from her face and sturdy wrists of any trace of childish fullness or petulance—all suggested a woman well on in pain and knowledge, not the unseamed girl she appeared to be. The two men, seated and quiet as she, watched her do her task.

Through that, Forrest really only saw her. His mind was stilled. He briefly wondered one thing—"How does he pay her?"—but afterward he watched. A neighbor maybe, the landlord's daughter? He knew he was lulled, even now while the room was still stark cold; but he did not resist or question why. He was ministered to; if he'd summoned his feeling and named it aloud, he'd have said some such.

The girl turned then, still kneeling and her hands now black in midair. "You light it please," she said to Mr. Mayfield.

"It's safe," he said. "Just slow wet coal."

"Please," she said again. She was not smiling.

Forrest rocked forward slightly and said "Let me."

His father stood. "She's scared," he said. "She was burnt bad recently; lamp exploded. I try to convince her the world's half-safe; but it's early yet—early, ain't it, honey?" He paused above her a moment for balance and rested a hand on the crown of her head.

"*I* believe you," she said, "but I want you to help me." He lifted his hand and went to the mantel for a tin matchbox; and she looked to Forrest and gave a short laugh, soft but happy.

Forrest suspected he was in secret trouble, had already been damaged past hope of repair (she had not been, clearly—not the visible parts of her body at least: her face, neck, hands were free of burns; no trace of scars). He said to the girl, "I am Forrest Mayfield."

She nodded. "His son. Have to be blind not to see that much."

Forrest could not stop there with the compliment she intended. His sense of danger was growing.

The girl though was watching his father approach the stove with fire, no longer afraid, entrusted to him.

Forrest said "Who are you?"

His father stopped; a short cone of newspaper burned in his hand. He said, "My help. She's the one person helps me."

The girl said "Polly—"

Mr. Mayfield told her, "You go cook dinner."

She stood and said again firmly "Polly"—to Forrest, still smiling. Then she left apparently in glad obedience, though with no glance back.

Forrest thought that she trusted one thing at least—Robinson Mayfield, that Robinson Mayfield would wait out her absence, be here at her call or call her when needed—and he felt strongly drawn to follow her, to learn plain trust from her plain clear pattern, rarer than happiness.

But his father had lighted the fire by then; and as he stood near its cracking heart, he took quick strength—from what? simple fire?—and looked to Forrest with steady eyes. "What you come here for?"

Forrest found he had also drawn new force from his cornered state; he was battling now. He stood and took three steps back from his father and said, "I'm the one who has come this far. You answer me." Then he waited; his father's eyes never flickered. "Please sir, *you* answer. Do that much for me."

His father slowly nodded.

"Will it be the truth?"

"Far as I know it."

"I can't stay for less," Forrest said.

"What you want first?"

"—How you knew about me? My wife and boy."

Mr. Mayfield half-smiled. "My nigger kin." Then he went to the bed again and sat.

Forrest stayed on his feet, alone in the warming air.

"You better sit down." His father pointed.

Forrest accepted and went to the rocker and faced his father.

"You ain't here to harm me?" Mr. Mayfield said.

Forrest thought that through. "I don't believe so."

"And you see I'm broke, in money and health, and nobody near me?"

"Yes sir. I do."

That freed Mr. Mayfield to start. "You want to know everything. I'll tell you what counts—don't say I don't know; I've had time to think. The fourth job I had was fireman on the railroad. You don't remember but back then Bracey amounted to something—a fresh-air resort; people came from all over just to breathe the air—so of course it was something of a railroad junction. We'd change crews there; get in late at night after running ten hours, black and stinking, and go to the big old Assembly Hall and take a hot bath and eat a big supper and sleep till day. Then we'd start out again. But that's where you come in—the supper. Your mother's mother ran the dining room. They had been good people, a monied family; but the nigger war had knocked em down—killed their father, your Grandfather Goodwin, and eat up their money and (before I got to town) their land. And old Mrs. Goodwin was cooking for trash. Like me, as she never missed a chance to let me know. Hell, what did I care? I was scum and I knew it (scum is what *rises*) and didn't mind at all, enjoyed it in fact since I noticed I was grinning with my belly full while the Goodwins and all their kind were moaning. Moaning and empty. Well, one of em didn't stay empty long. Your pitiful mama. They had lost their place, that house on the hill where the Goodwins are buried; and they lived in the loft of that old Hall. One ratty room. Rats racing in the wall, gnawing hats in the cupboards. But the old lady worked half the night as I said, hollering at niggers over hot cookstoves; so I made me a number of visits to the rats. Anna Goodwin—she was eighteen years old and dying on the vine. But I brought her new life. That was in my line—don't you see?—back then. It was what I could do, though I've long since lost it. I could make people happy. Make em *want* me at least, make em think they was in Hog Heaven with me. And I never cheated. I never abused em. I was happy as they were, just offering my service, my one little gift. I'm not telling you your mother was a strumpet. I'm not saying I ever put her to bed till the night we were married. I don't think I did, don't recall I did. I'm saying that somehow I made

her happy, made her think she was happy by thinking she loved me. I've wondered *how* many times through the years. How does one person—sorry as me,
no education, the morals of a housefly—cause people to move? I think I
know. It is some people's talent, some rare few people, to make other folks
(mostly women) think this—'There's a poor ruined soul that I can help.'
What most women thought I needed was *rest*, a place to lie down in and rest.
Trouble is, the best place to rest is *bed*; and beds got to have roofs to keep out
rain, and roofs need walls; and next thing you know, you've laid down to
snooze and some woman's built a two-story house round you and stocked it
with babies and is back in the kitchen frying your dinner—and you won't
even hungry. Course, a further trouble with me back then was—bed was the
last place I could rest, specially if some little body was beside me; but you
understand what I'm driving at? I got it figured early—*Don't never stand still*,
which is why I arrived in Bracey, Virginia at twenty-seven years old with no
home ties. And I left it with none, as you know I guess, a little later—just cut
em clean (that's the one kind way: cut clean and quick; then the wound'll
stanch itself). But what you are asking me is why I lingered, why I stood still
long as I did. I've asked myself; and here's the true answer—I'm a gentle soul.
I saw your mother as a heart in need, saw it the first evening I ever laid eyes
on her; and since pretty soon she saw me as what *she* needed, I volunteered
to go on and be it for her. And whatever you may think, it never harmed her.
I guess you just recall her as sad, the years between when I had to leave and
she finally died. I'm sorry you can't recall her early picture. She was sweet
to look at, provided you didn't dwell long on her eyes. Her eyes were scary;
lot of women's are. Comes from them having to wait so much. Waiting will
eat your heart plumb out. She waited very little for *me*, I'd say. The grief she'd
had before I got there was caused by others, no fault of her own—her family's losses, the burdens her mother had to lay on her back when she'd been
trained to expect nothing heavier than shot-silk or swan's down—and she'd
borne up brave and healthy, laughed a lot. Still when I walked into that dining room on an April evening, having just scrubbed clean in a big copper tub
in her mama's cellar, and laid eyes on her for the first time ever and she on
me—well, she thought right away she'd been badly abused by, what do you
call it?, the winds of Fate. Hell, she'd barely had a ringlet blown out of place;
but have you noticed this?—when people fall in love (women, I mean), they
decide on the spot that their lives to that instant have been blank torment;
and *you* are the single straw on the sea, their last hope of floating? I've
noticed that. I'd noticed it before your mama came along—my own, for
instance. My mama looked at me from the day I was born as if I was moon
and stars and hot food; but I also noticed that when I left home at fourteen

to work, she took it about as hard as a fleabite. She lived and was fat till two years ago. You never saw her; pity on you. Your mama was different. She couldn't turn loose. In the ten-odd years I stayed there with her, she never blinked once from gazing at me. I was meant to be God and the angels for her—so she believed, in her honest heart—and for some damned reason, I halfway tried. Course, I still traveled; went right on working as a railroad fireman spite of your Grandmother Goodwin sneering. She wanted me to stop too and stand stock-still, not so she could love me but to better her name. I told her that the Mayfields were building good fires for the happiness of man when the Goodwins was still hauling pigshit for pennies. That shut her up. It also killed her; she passed not a year after we got married. No I went on traveling for two main reasons—to halfway wean your mother, give her strength; and for my own health, just good fresh air. I was not only trash but also a tramp, my true vocation. I always had—back then, I mean—a lot more life stored up in me than any one woman or house could use; so I spent it on the wind, spreading happiness where your mama couldn't see it to worry over, coming back to her—and you and Hatt—at the end of each turn. And I honestly think I'd be there now; I honestly think if anybody'd asked me, up to a week before I left, I'd have said 'Oh yes, I'm here for life; when I'm *here*, that is.' But then I changed all in a night, had to leave and left. You were fast asleep." The slow voice had stopped. Its certain flow had come in those minutes to seem so entirely the contents of the room that now with silence the space was shockingly empty, imperiled.

Forrest said to fill it, "I was, yes."

His father took no encouragement from that but stood and walked again to the stove—which was burning well; the ear could hear—and opened its door and bent to look. Satisfied, he rose and went to the mantel and found a piece of mirror which he held to the light; then he studied his face.

Forrest also studied. His chair was placed so that he could see all the mirror saw.

His father half-smiled.

The story is ended, Forrest thought, amazed. *He thinks that is all. He thinks I have come to hear that much, and am now fully answered. Perhaps I am?* Forrest waited to see if that last were credible. No and would never be. He said, "Sir, how? How did you change?"

His father continued to watch himself; but he said, "Like I told you, I had to go."

Forrest said "Why?"

His father looked up, hot-eyed and sudden. "I am not your pupil. Don't examine me."

"Forgive me," Forrest said but sat on, expectant.

Mr. Mayfield said, "I thought you were mine. You favor me."

Forrest said, "I am, which is why I am here."

His father's eyes had calmed but his head shook No. "Any son of mine would have stayed away—Hell, *run* to the opposite side of the world once he heard where I was. You're hers all right. She'd have tracked me down and broke me like this." With one hand he drew a half-circle round him in the empty air, the precincts of his body, the scene of damage.

Forrest said "I do not understand."

His father said, "Don't claim you forgot. You're bound to recall—how she hunted me out of that house and your lives."

Forrest nodded, a lie extended for bait. He remembered his mother as stricken prey, silent and seated.

"She built her whole long picture of me, of what she imagined I'd been at first and was now changing into under her guiding hand; and then when after ten long years some pieces of truth, of the real plain me, swum up to view, she all but lost her mind at the sight; went cutting around at crazy random like a circular saw broke loose from socket and wheeling in air. So I left—if you really want to know—for protection, for plain damn safety."

Forrest said, "What pieces? What pieces of the truth?"

His father said, "Niggering. I was niggering around. You knew that surely."

Forrest said, "I've heard Veenie, her long old tale. She's got your picture; she knew you were here."

His father nodded. "Her tale is true—or I guess it is. It ought to be. She knows it all. Or knew it once."

Forrest said "Elvira. Elvira's boy."

His father nodded, still solemn from the story Forrest forced him to give. But then, standing on in place by the stove, his face spread open and one dry laugh husked up from his chest. "Imagine being washed up here for that, being run from your home and children for that. Hell, every good boy with a pecker that worked was niggering round me—you could hardly walk on a weekday night (not to mention Saturday) without stepping smack on a bare white ass pumping joy on black—but she had to think I invented it all. She went to Veenie. Hell, went to the *preacher!*—had him praying for me. Then she came to me—at night as always; she'd wait till I was tired—and what she asked me, all she could think to ask me after thirteen years of moving in each other's shadow, was 'Rob, do you want to kill me dead?' I asked her what she meant—it was all news to me—and she talked for an hour and I said No. One word *No*. But I thought a few more and made my plans; and when I had told you and Hatt goodbye, I went on off. She killed herself, was who did the killing." He waited a little. "Now she's killing me, all this much later, these miles away."

Forrest stood but did not approach his father. He knew he had heard a sad stream of lies—a mind so confused by age and sickness or by years of flight as to be incapable of knowing the truth, the whole just truth; or else in clear full possession of the past but rigging it shamelessly for self-service, mercy—yet he also knew that when his own lips opened, he would make the farthest offer he'd considered in the weeks before coming here. He did not smile but he said, "I am willing to carry you home. Willing and glad. I've got my own house and a boy to help me. Or Hatt and her boys would be more than glad—plenty room, steady company, good steady food." Forrest looked round the room again. It seemed the merest camp that could be stowed and moved in half an hour. "We can be home for supper. Tomorrow's Christmas."

His father said "Thank you," but he shook his head slowly. He still faced Forrest though. His eyes never dropped.

"It would give me a great deal of satisfaction," Forrest said. "You are what I have got."

"It would kill her," his father said. "This is her home."

Forrest didn't speak but silence put the question.

His father said "Polly" and pointed quickly through the wall toward the kitchen. "She helps me a lot, and I'm grateful to her."

Forrest said, "You'll have all the help you can use." He was smiling now.

His father did not need to wait to think. "No," he said. He had also grown pleasant, though his firmness held. He was young again, face clear and ready, all but hopeful.

"What kin is she to you?" Forrest said.

"Not a bit in the world."

Again Forrest did not speak; but his head gave a little twist forward, incredulous—*Then you're coming with me.*

His father said "I want her."

Still silent, Forrest also pointed to the wall behind which occasional sounds of metal had ignited like distant approaching war.

His father said "Yes."

"Is she your wife?"

His father said, "No. Your mother was that. I've tried to respect her claim to that, wherever she sits in Heaven or Hell. No. I've had other help—I've had to have it; so will you in time—but just one wife, one set of children: Hatt and you."

Forrest said "Elvira had a boy."

His father nodded.

Forrest said, "I'm here. Nobody else is. I'm here and I'm Forrest, and Forrest is offering to carry you home and tend you well as long as you need him. Just you. Just you."

His father looked slowly again toward the kitchen and listened as though its sounds were a steady message, unheeded till now. Then he turned back to Forrest and opened his mouth, and a rush of bright blood flooded his chin. But he stood on, calm; and when he could speak, what he said in moving blood was "Her. Call her please. Now."

2

A half hour later Forrest sat at a bare pine table in the kitchen and waited for the dinner which Polly was serving. She had asked him to stay. Once she had answered his call and come and quickly but calmly had helped his father to bed and had sat till the blood slowed, darkened and stopped and his father had slept, then she'd looked up to Forrest and silently nodded and beckoned him gravely to follow her. He had done so and when they were in the warm kitchen, she had not said a word but had walked to the small stove and recommenced work. Forrest had gone to the table and sat and then had said "What's wrong with him?" She had worked on awhile, then had turned and said "He calls it asthma"; then had smiled and said, "*I* call it the way to keep me here." Then she'd gone grave again and had said, "I'm not leaving. I promised him that. Why don't he believe me?" Forrest had said, "I can't help you there"; and then they had both stayed silent till she'd brought him a full plate of food and he'd thanked her; and then she'd said, "Can I eat now with you? Is that all right?" and he'd told her Yes.

That nearness—she sat two feet from his hand, had chosen that nearness—gave him the courage to ask her more. "You want to stay here?"

She took two mouthfuls—of turnips, yams, and boiled sidemeat—and worked and swallowed slowly and neatly; and then she looked up at Forrest. "You want me to leave?"

"I don't know," he said. "Please answer me first."

She waited again, though she did not eat. It was clear that, however hungry or cold, her throat could not now handle food. Words alone were sufficient struggle and, when they came, bore the signs of their coming, ragged and spent. But she gave them to Forrest, straight at his eyes. "Yes sir, I've thought about it a lot. I'm staying by him as long as he lets me."

"He's dying. You're young."

"That's all right," she said.

"He's leaving you. He's left everybody that ever loved him."

"I know that, yes sir. He's taking his time though, with me at least." Polly sat and waited for an answer from Forrest, some word or move; and when neither came, she broke into smiling, the natural product of what she had said and was presently thinking. It lifted her small face—the smile, her thoughts of a man who had just now hemorrhaged freely—and she took on the color of warmth and welcome. Her high flat cheekbones were bright with their own blood, young and durable and waiting to serve. Her blue eyes opened, backward endless, into views of honest fidelity—the world that existed in her head and chest, her whole easy body, quiet but ample and incapable of lying or of truth withheld. Her hair was chestnut and had somehow been washed in the recent cold days; and though it was parted and drawn back tightly, it also bore the flood of her happiness, another channel of her total life, her permanent promise. In the dim light it burned, no threat of exhaustion.

Forrest saw all that, bore it through his own eyes helpless to refuse. He tried to evade her by turning to his food; but after one swallow his throat balked and closed. He was forced to look up.

She was eating now, slow but untroubled; and she watched her plate only, her present duty, present delight.

She had staked Forrest's heart. He knew, his mouth plugged with cold pork fat, that now this moment at an old wood table in a Richmond slum, he was at the worst; the bottom of his life. A step from here was appallingly simple, certain as night—a self-made end or a miracle of grace; some rope lowered to him for rescue, haulage. He thought quite clearly with the cold and fearless abandon of despair, "I will let her choose."

He set down his fork and forced down the cud and said "What shall I do?"

"For who?" she said.

Her question with its crushing load of expectation—*to do* was to do for *someone* simply—fell fully on him; but he also saw that, with all its pain, it still offered rescue. He could do for her, her few plain needs. He slowly constructed a mask of pleasantness behind his face and offered it toward her and ate a little and then said, "Tell me please who you are. Are we any kin?"

She genuinely laughed; the remaining corners of her beauty lighted. "No more than usual—through Adam and Eve, I mean," she said.

"Then is this your home?" He touched the table with his index finger; he meant this house.

"No sir. I'm a city girl." She laughed again. "Washington, D.C."

"He said you were born in Richmond, a native."

"He lies about me. No I'm capital-bred." She stopped there though.

She wants to be lured, Forrest thought; wants attention. "Then why are you here?"

"I'm grown," she said, "and I want to be." The firmness of her thought and speech did not have time to color her face before she had gone on to something she felt to be gentler. "It's a story," she said. "Eighteen years long. You still want to hear it?"

Forrest nodded.

"Don't worry. The first part goes quick—seventeen years of work, hard work. I was my dad's woman. My mother had died right after I came; Dad said I killed her. She turned all septic from some blood poison; and her last cries were weaker than mine—I was five days old—so I guess I did, though I didn't intend it. Dad understood that; he was telling the truth, not blaming me; and I've always took it as truth, just the news. I've pitied her memory and dressed her grave most years on my birthday, but I never gave up growing or smiling because of her. I never *knew* her. Dad was all my kin; and with God looking on, I can say Dad tried but he didn't strain. The War had completely wore him out. He was from Virginia and fought with General Jackson on foot, and he said he had walked the equal of from here to Jerusalem and back *uphill* (they fought in the mountains). So from when I remember, he would barely move. He had walked home from up around Natural Bridge at the end, to Arlington really; and sold what little his mama still owned and moved over to Washington, saying he meant to live on the winning side. They rented some rooms and he set to thinking of things to do. He had just turned twenty and before the War had worked at tanning leather; but he said he could never do that again, smell an old hide rotting; so he settled finally on tortoiseshell. His mother, who was Irish, had somewhere learned to work tortoiseshell. So he settled on that—well, really on *her*; she of course did the work; he was just the boss—and they made combs for ladies, in tortoiseshell and ivory, which he would take out and peddle round town. A little comb factory. And you know it succeeded. At first, plain combs in various sizes; but you know what Washington is—people looking—so he got his mama to invent souvenirs: little watchfobs carved like Lincoln or Lee, little pictures on the combs (sunset at sea), helpful lines of verse ("May you never know sorrow"). And they were thriving; made enough to rent a whole house near the Capitol, small but dry, and then she died. His mother wore out. And there he was with a houseful of tusks and great turtle shells. Well, according to him, he barely missed step. A museum was what came to him at once. So he married the girl that would be my mother—a small girl named Lillian—and set her to keeping his old museum: selling tickets and guarding the junk from thieves while he went back out to the battlefields and gathered up souvenirs for his show. Guns and balls and bayonets, poor soggy boots. He even had a mummified Rebel leg that a lady sold him till some men came by a year or so later and made him burn it and bury the ashes. See, what he had set his heart to have was the first and only Confederate museum in Washington City; and you know, he got it. Or halfway got it. He could never do anything perfectly pure—he kept all his tusks and shells lying round and eventually he got an old nigger with eczema and straightened his hair and dressed him like an Indian brave. I remember that. I had come by then, laying Mother under as I just now said; and that's how I grew up. I liked it. I really did. It mostly was happy."

Forrest had managed to eat while listening; and he felt appreciable strength rising in him, though he thought it came from the warm heavy food; he gave her no credit. She herself had reached a pause and begun to eat; so he said, "Then why are you here with him?"

"That's the rest of the story," she said. "You want it?"

"Please," he said.

"Well, it fell on me, by the time I could talk, to run the place—Dad never remarried. It seemed like he had all of that he needed. Of course I didn't watch him (he was gone a lot); but I have the impression I was all he had in the female line; and I was his daughter, you understand. He hired in a woman to get me started; but once I was up hip-high, it was mine. And run it I did; it was run it or starve. He was drinking by then and had lost all interest in new exhibits; and of course I was too young to travel or buy, but every now and then some old pal of his would send us a treasure to put in the cases (that's how we got the big finger-ring made from Traveller's hair and the stuffed mascot of the 32nd Rifles). And people kept coming, that's the funny part; people will pay to see a dead dog that they wouldn't glance at in the road for free. Funnier still, it was mostly Yankees; I guess few Rebels could afford the outing or maybe they just didn't want to remember. No, Yankees would come with their wives and boys and brag out-loud how they'd saved the earth for God and progress; they'd tell the old dressed-up nigger Indian how lucky he was the redskins had been brought civilization before Jesus came to judge their evil. That actual thing had happened, I swear, the first day I ever saw your father. So when he came I was more than ready for what he offered, smiling eyes and a voice from Virginia."

Forrest said, "What words did he say to you first?"

She did not know at once but waited to think. Then she smiled. " 'How serious is your need for a nickel?' "

Forrest said "Meaning what?"

"—Could he get in free. A nickel was what we charged for admission. I sat at the front door and sold nickel-tickets, children two cents. It was early fall, the first chilly day; so I was not just mad but cold. I was busy crocheting when he walked in, and he got close on me before I saw him. I was sitting down; he was standing over me two feet away; and that was his plea—could he get in free? I said, 'No sir, my dad would kill me.' He said, 'What if I was to kill him first? There's sufficient means' (he meant in the museum, the guns and knives). I said, 'Then you'd have one orphan to raise'; and he said 'Suits me.' I said, 'Wait a minute; you don't know the orphan.' He said 'It's you' and I nodded it was. 'I accept,' he said, 'I still accept.' So I let him in. And was happy to."

Forrest said, "Then what did he do?"

"Started bleeding. I indicated to him how busy I was; so he'd gone on in and started looking, and it wasn't two minutes till the nigger yelled. I ran through the first two rooms before I found him. He was standing by the case full of eating equipment—tin plates and spoons, long knives and forks, leather waterbottles. Your dad was standing there staring down, and the blood was streaking his chin like now." She pointed to the bedroom, the place in time.

Forrest said "What caused it?"

Her eyes searched him thoroughly. "You really don't know? Same thing as always."

"His asthma then?"

She shook her head No and, by moving, pulled up the start of a smile— a game, another round of her happy game.

Forrest chose to play. "Tell me."

"Shame," she said. "It's always shame. I notice that every time he bleeds." Forrest said "For what?"

"The war," she said. "The poor old war. He was twenty-one or two when it cranked up, but he has his weak chest and didn't go. All those souvenirs brought it back to him, what he'd wanted to do so long before."

Forrest said, "He has done most of what he wanted; you and I are the leavings, two of his leavings."

But she smiled, "I *will* be, after he's dead. I'm here till then. You speak for you."

So he did. He suddenly knew his intention. It seemed his final mission here, a rite that would free him to leave, walk clean away into his own life at last. He pushed back his chair and stood in place and reached deep into his left hand pocket. He drew out a plush box the size of a small egg and offered it to Polly.

She set down her fork and wiped her right hand on the thigh of her dress and took the box, flicking one finger back and forth on its velvet—a pale rose color, worn and stained—but she showed no sign of opening it, no sign that she'd also been given permission to open it.

"It's yours," Forrest said. "For Christmas. You've won it."

She wiped her hand again and looked up smiling and opened the box. A gold ring, wide and heavy and plain. She lifted it gently from its satin socket and turned it carefully, then saw the writing. She tilted it all ways in the dim light. Then she looked back to Forrest. "This is somebody else's. I can't see whose in this poor light."

He waited awhile to see if she would see. Then he thought "She can't read." So he said it, not needing to take the ring—*"Robinson Mayfield to Anna Goodwin.* My mother's ring. She is long past needing it. My sister has her own. I've got no use for it now or likely ever. And it's mine to give. God knows you've won it."

She quickly turned serious but held the ring. "God knows very little about me," she said, "since I came here."

He ignored that, smiling. "Please wear it," he said.

She examined the ring once more, though not to read it—not the valuing eye of a jeweler or bride but the calm sad face of a judge, a mother. "No," she said. "Oh no. I couldn't."

"Why?" Forrest said.

She set it down carefully on the bare wood between them, nearer him than her. "It may be yours to give; but see, it's not mine to take while he's there alive. He explained that to me."

Forrest said "How?"

"The day he asked me to leave with him. That first day of course I led him back to our quarters and got him eased, and then I fed him; and within an hour, he knew more about me than my own dad, knew more than any other human ever had—just because he asked. Weak as he was, he asked me *questions.* Jesus in the air on Judgment Day won't dare to ask anybody half of what your father asked me, strange as we were to each other that day."

Forrest said "What?"

She looked to see if he'd use her well. "My age and weight, my health and the names of my favorite foods. The colors I liked. My full entire name—Margaret Jane Drewry. Was I happy then? *'This minute; tell me quick!'* I told him 'Yes sir' and then he asked 'Why?' "

Forrest said, "You knew. I'll bet you knew."

She nodded. "And told him. I'm as bold and truthful as he is curious; you've noticed that. It took me a minute that day to know. But he waited on the couch, Dad's old leather couch; and finally I said, 'I'm happy to have helped you.' He said "Tell the truth"; and I said, 'That's it, though I'm naturally happy, as you'd know if you knew me.'—'When will I?' he said; and since I had seen how close he had watched me, I said, 'You *do*. You know me right now, much as you ever will. I'm the most open heart on the whole east coast as far as I know (I've barely traveled). What you see is what's *here!* So he said he'd take it, and I slapped his hand and said it wasn't for sale. He begged my pardon which I freely gave; and then he laughed and said, 'A good thing since I'm broke as Judas. Would you have me for nothing?' Well, sir, I ask you—what would you do if a total stranger walked into your house and had a small hemorrhage and then both insulted you and asked for your hand? You'd throw him out or at least call for help; I still had the nigger, two rooms away. You'd do that, I know. But I'm another story and have always been. I told him 'Yes.' Oh it took me another minute and some looking—at his eyes, just his eyes—but I knew my true answer; so I went on and said it. And here we sit in Richmond, Virginia."

"Why here?" Forrest said.

"His home," she said. "You know, his home." Her hand waved slowly round in the air.

He did not know but waited till she told him.

"This was the Mayfield place, his daddy's. His mother had lived here till just a few weeks before I saw him. He had nursed her a long time—years, I guess—and she had just died well on in her eighties, leaving this to him and all her furniture. He had sold most of that but what's in the bedroom and this cooking stuff and taken the money and given himself the trip as reward. Rest for his mind; his body was rested—he hadn't worked a day in many a year except tending her, boiling oatmeal and rice, telling her all the tales he had lived through or dreamed. Well, he got it, I think—a rested mind except for the hemorrhage—and I have to say he got it from me. I told you how quick he made his offer. I've always taken that to be the sign; he *saw* me and loved me. I understand that; I live by *my* eyes. I chose to trust him, though he told me about you and your poor mother, and here we sit. It will be yours soon." Again she waved round, the Mayfield place.

But Forrest ignored that. He said, "You're here. Where did that leave your father?"

"On his own," she said. "Where he'd just as soon be."

"Not needing you?"

"He never did; never said he did. You can see that all in the story I've told. He liked somebody around him to joke with—cooking and sewing he learned at war—and he needed one person to stand at the door and take in money; but mostly he was independent as a snake: that clean and lonely without being lonesome. He liked me though; I don't mean he didn't. He genuinely liked me. We had laughed a lot."

"He's dead?" Forrest said—she spoke in past tenses.

"Not to my knowledge, no." She waited awhile. "I am to him." This was painful for her, the first hard thing she had met so far. "When I went to him, nine days to the day after meeting your father, and asked his permission to leave home finally, he of course said 'With who?' and I told the truth; he had met your dad one afternoon briefly. He said, 'You are asking to marry the dead; that fellow is dead, plus he's older than me.' I said, 'There is no plan to marry nobody; he's had one wife and children that he's true to, though he hasn't seen them in thirty years.'—'Go then,' he said. 'But go for good. Take anything here that's yours or your mother's and vanish please.' He smiled all through it, but of course he was earnest so here I am. I keep saying that."

Forrest nodded. "Keep the ring." He moved it back toward her.

But she shook her head. "It's not necessary, understand. I've promised. I'm here till the end."

Forrest said "After that?"

She had thought of that also. She faced him smiling, her hands palm-up on the table before her, small for her strength. "I'm young," she said. "Nobody here knows me. I can start a life."

Forrest said "You will."

3

In the bedroom again he took three steps toward his sleeping father, quietly, to wake him gently.

His father's eyes stayed shut, but a hand flicked up and across his face as though at a gnat.

He stopped at the foot of the bed. "It's Forrest."

"I know it is. Write down this letter." He had still not looked or raised his head.

Forrest searched round for paper. "Sir, there's nothing to write on."

His father waited. "Remember it then. Write it down when you're able."

Forrest said "All right."

Then his father lined it out on the air with a finger. "Lay in a large supply of goods." His voice was firm, the tone calm and sane.

"Yes sir," Forrest said.

"Apples," his father said, the finger still urging. "Also cheese."

Forrest said "Yes sir" but then he said "Why?"

His father looked; his head raised slightly. "You got a cook?"

Forrest nodded Yes (Grainger was learning).

His father said, "Please start her cooking for me."

Forrest wondered as always in the presence of age, "Is his mind really broken or am I being tested? And if so, how; tested for what?" He said, "You have got Polly yonder now, cooking Christmas dinner." He pointed to the kitchen, a better sanctuary than any he'd found in his own years of hunting. Cruel to tear any man from that, whatever the needs of past or future, of present duty.

His father glanced there. "Are you going to take her?"

"No sir," Forrest said. "She'll stay here with you. She wants that, has promised that just now to me. I'll send what little help I can."

"I know that," his father said—of Polly's promise. He ignored Forrest's money and laid his head back deep in the pillow. But then he said, "Is anything here that you want?"

Forrest tried to think, all this time and distance; but nothing would come. "No sir," he said.

Mr. Mayfield nodded. "It will be yours directly. You're the one that would want it. You come here and get it. You'll hear when I die. You come here and claim it."

"Yes sir," Forrest said. He did not ask what was here to claim—a bed; a cookstove; a woodbox of pine bark; a bare house no doubt burdened with taxes; remains of people he had never known (who yet steered his life), the oil and dead cast scales of their flesh in the grain of the wood, immovable. *There is nothing to claim.* He suddenly saw that. *There has never been.* He was happy at the sight, the freeing knowledge. A life seemed possible. Only one last barrier. He walked to his father's right side and, still standing, said "This is yours." He extended the small ringbox again.

Mr. Mayfield looked and knew it. "No it ain't," he said. "Who took it off her?"

Forrest said, "Hatt. Just before she was buried."

"I never took it off her; who the Hell was Hattie?"

"A girl," Forrest said. "A sixteen-year-old girl that you left the job to."

His father made a deep sound of hate in his throat. "Girls have caused four-fifths of the pain on earth."

Forrest continued to offer the ring. "I don't want this."

"Then give it to your boy. He's got the name; he is yours, ain't he?"

"His mother refused it. Here, you pawn it. Let Polly pawn it." He set it beside his father's hand on the quilt.

The hand drew back. "Polly won't touch it."

Forrest waited; then turned to go for good, the ring in his hand. His own new life, whatever that would be—at least not this, free at least of this.

He had taken three steps when his father said, "Give it to the little nigger then."

Forrest looked—the face was deathbound but smiling—then was able to laugh, the first time in months: an issue of fresh sweet blood from his own heart, the promise of more.

4

At four in the morning—Christmas morning—Forrest dreamed this dream in a boarding-house bed (trains to Bracey had been stopped by ice, all switches frozen): he was sleeping well in his bed at home, restorative sleep through which he sank like a stone in the sea, no fear of bottom, no fear of morning or the duties of day; but then he was stopped and dredged toward light, gently, slowly but against his will. Wakened by his father who stretched above him, full weight on his body and rode there calmly as if on that deep water or a dream, a dream of his own. Yet his face seemed needful, open eyes and lips. So Forrest said, "Father, what are you after?" But his father stayed on him, still as gall on an oak; and at last said, "I've taken it. Never you mind. I take what I need."

Forrest spoke aloud then, though still deep asleep—"All yours anyhow." He never again recalled the words; but they ended the dream, permitted his further plunge through night. He sank toward morning.

They woke Grainger though. He had slept on a pallet on the cold floor by Forrest; and despite the hard day (the blank hours of waiting on a depot bench, then Forrest's return and the long afternoon of Richmond's sights—the Capitol, the church where Patrick Henry spoke, the tomb of Poe's mother), he had slept very lightly as though set to run at some unknown signal: to run for life. Now the words had waked him, the signal at last. He heard sounds only, not their meaning; but he sat up quickly—he was fully dressed except for shoes—and looked toward the bed where Forrest was still and silent again. Grainger listened for breathing—soft but steady; he counted three breaths. *Safe*, he thought—or felt in all his chilly body. *Christmas*, he knew—by the high hard moonlight of early morning that poured through curtains of their single window. He looked to the window but could see only light, no shapes of trees or buildings yet. So he rose to his knees in the neat warm covers and looked again to Forrest. By the moon he could now see the face all surrendered to rest. The eyes seemed sunk past rising in their sockets, and the mouth that obeyed instantaneously every need of the mind (it was Grainger's vane for detecting the weather of any moment) was slack and half-open. Grainger's was smiling, broad and helpless. *I have had my Christmas*, he thought so strongly and happily as to draw him to his feet, upright but silent. He looked back again. He had not waked Forrest; so being up anyhow (however cold), he stepped to the window and parted the curtains with both dark hands and spread them in moonlight.

The left hand shone with the ring, his Christmas, which Forrest had given him six hours ago before darkening the room for their try at sleep. He had said, "You have been a good help to me, Grainger. Take this as my thanks" and extended the box. When Grainger had seen it and smiled at the shine, he said, "Mr. Forrest, this come from you?" — "It does now," Forrest said; "See if it fits." The right hand was too large; the left slipped in easily, room to grow. "Wear it," Forrest had said, "as long as you can and remember when you see it, it stands for the good help you gave me this year; and it hopes for more." Grainger had said, "I'll die in this. You count on that. I'll die thanking you." Then Forrest had simply said "Good night" and blown out the lamp; but once they had quieted, though Grainger's blood still raced with pleasure, Forrest spoke again—"Never tell a soul." Grainger had promised.

Now freezing in sockfeet by the frosted pane, he made it again, silent— his promise. He shut his lips tight to prove they were sealed, but pleasure and thanks broke them quickly open. He smiled again. *I am set for life.* He had never before imagined a life but had waited in the endless present of childhood. Now he could go back and lie in his covers, find the remains of his vanishing warmth and wait for day. His twelfth Christmas, the start of his life, three hours away.

5

February 21, 1905

Dear Mr. Forrest,

I made you two promises—to stick by your dad and to let you know when the news got bad. I have already kept the first one, I'm proud. He died sometime this morning in his sleep so peaceful as not to disturb my own rest. I had woke up just after light and roused myself to start the fire so he could have warm air to stand up in. He had been a little under but nothing too low and the blood spells had not come no more than normal. I tried to work quiet but he heard me and looked and said "Margaret Jane Drewry." That is my full name. He was in his right mind. I said "Yes sir" but I won't say I laughed since nobody hates rising cold worse than me. So he said "Margaret Jane Drewry" again—voice strong as yours and looking young as you, all rested and clean—and then he said "I don't see how you stand this." I'm sorry to say I answered him true. I said "Rob, I won't lie and say it's easy." You knew already that I used his first name so you won't think hard and anyhow I promised to send you the news, that is part of my news. The rest of it is that I dozed back to rest for maybe half an hour while the stove was cracking and when heat woke me finally he was some while gone. Not a teaspoon of blood, no rigor nor cry, and his last word to me had been to beg pardon. Well he has it now as I hope he knows. And that is my news. Both promises kept.

I know you are busy with your own life there and anyhow he left me his burial wishes which are simple enough for even me to follow and he has sufficient money of his mother's to cover. I could understand and would not think hard if you or your sister didn't feel drawn to come. He gave you little cause for duty I know. But this is all yours now. He kept saying that so as not to fool me and I was not fooled. The little that's here is yours and your sister's. If you send me word you can come here soon. I will wait till then and give you my keys and tell you what few little things I know that you may not. I have laid him out clean in his own cold bed and have moved myself to a cot in the kitchen. I will wait three days for instructions from you and then if none come I will do his wishes and shut up the place good and mail you the key for your convenience.

Awaiting your plan, I am
Truly,
Margaret Jane Drewry

T W O

THE HEART IN DREAMS

MAY 1921

Sylvie stood at the hot sink, straight and firm. The window to her left still let in daylight, but she'd already lit the hanging lamp; so she worked in two lights, day and oil, washing in silence.

Rob came up behind her in sockfeet, silent, and stood two feet away and said, half-whispering, "This is my night. Now. My night's coming on."

He had not surprised her and she didn't turn. She washed a gravy boat and said in her normal voice, "A whole lot of nights here lately been yours."

"But now I'm grown." He moved a step nearer — just into the edge of Sylvie's odor, clean and her own but harsh, guarding, thrown out around her in defense of a center of precious life.

She still didn't turn, though she'd finished the dishes. She kept her hands in the thick dark water and said, "Just sliding through school to the end on grinning and singing — that makes you grown?"

"No," Rob said. "But something else does." He'd kept his voice low, but now there was laughter all under it. "Look here," he said. He stepped back a little to give her room to see.

Sylvie turned. What seemed refusal and anger in her face (the blue-black skin, the yellow eye-whites) was plain exhaustion. She was thirty-four; what she'd laid out by day for this one family for twenty-odd years had not been replaced elsewhere by night. She had lived alone a good while now, since her mother's death; and her company was brief. What was offered her this evening after twelve hours' work was a white boy just past seventeen in white shirt, white trousers, white sockfeet, grinning wide — he'd pulled a starched end of his shirttail through his fly; and it stuck out, a waggling prow beneath his laughing. She had watched him prance through similar jokes all the years she'd known him, had bathed the flesh behind the cloth dummy hundreds of times. Sylvie wanted to smile but she closed her eyes and turned her back on him and sidestepped away to dry her hands.

Rob was left with no witness. "This needs pressing," he said.

Sylvie looked again and laughed. "No such thing," she said. "It need a rest." She had always liked him; he had not yet harmed a living soul; the sleeves of his clean shirt were wet to the elbow. "Fool, you don't put *on* your shirt till you finished shaving. Talking about grown! I done the last rescue I'm doing on you till you learn manners."

"Please, Sylvie," he said. They both were still smiling.

She shook her head No.

Rena called "Oh Rob" from the front of the house.

Sylvie pointed to the voice and lowered her own. "There's your presser," she said. "I'm leaving here." Still smiling, she stripped off her apron and hung it; took up her bucket of old bread and scraps and went out the backdoor before Rob could slow her.

He knew he had lightened the end of her day—she had left like a girl— and he cared enough for her to be glad of that; but he wished she had left him good luck for tonight (she had luck to give, though none of her own). He adjusted his shirttail and buttons to follow her; he'd force her to stand and confer a grudging blessing through the mocking smile that knew him as well, as long, as any.

But his aunt stood behind him. "Let me see you," she said.

Rob turned.

Rena's round face crouched. "You're not ready." She was—her one hat, her one good dress (in which, as always, she looked as offended as a dressed-up terrier, surprised and comic).

Rob said, "No but I never claimed to be. I'm ready for nothing the earth's offered yet!" He shook his bright face in smiling refusal but was serious.

Rena looked to the loud clock on the kitchen mantel. "We have to leave here in fifteen minutes." She saw his shirt. "You have ruined your shirt."

"It's water," he said. "Is Mother coming?"

She came forward to him and felt the damp sleeves. "You'll get rheumatism; this has got to be pressed. Sylvie's not gone, is she?"

"Yes ma'm," Rob said. "Is my mother coming?"

Rena's hand was still on him, the flesh of his full wrist. "You know she can't."

"You could stay with Papa." Rob had stepped back from her. The daylight had failed; he was mostly dark.

Rena tried to see him, a hunt in spring dusk for the one face she loved but had never allowed herself to trust, knowing it must leave; now she knew she'd been right. "Rob, Eva has asked me to go for her. I'll represent her. People understand."

"I don't," he said.

"You will," Rena said. "Time'll see to that." She took off her light coat and went to the cookstove and laid a hand on it. "Good," she said. "Hot. I can press that in no time. Hand it to me, quick." Hard as her hands were, she'd burned herself.

Rob obeyed and waited on the back stoop quietly, accepting her service, determined to refuse her present offer of which this was only the millionth earnest—the whole remainder of her life, time, strength. He would thank her and leave. Or endure this evening, a last hostage to her, his silly commencement—songs, speeches. Commencement truly, of flight toward his life from this dark web of feeders. Soon, soon. His whole body, beautiful and rank with the power of his father and mother, burned to go with a rising roar. He could not believe the house did not hear him—his dying grandfather, his trapped happy mother, Uncle Kennerly and his feist-wife two houses down the street, his desperate aunt ironing twelve feet behind: *I do not thank you, and I will not stay.*

2

But by half-past ten he had drunk enough lightning to ease the pressure (he had chipped in two dollars the day before, and they'd sent Bip Rollins out the Raleigh road to the best bootlegger south of Petersburg; Bip had hauled back a gallon); so his chief aim now was to fulfill the claim he had made to Sylvie—that the night was his. The object of the aim was completion of his body, use of it all; the means at hand was the girl beside him, Min Tharrington. It was not that simple to Rob now though. He imagined he loved her, that he'd plan on her when the day came to plan. Min had asked him the question for more than a year—was he serious toward her? what was his plan?—but tonight with the force of his life behind him (seventeen years and two months, lived out minute by minute), the aching needs of all his grand faculties, the freedom of drink, he felt he was ready to answer Yes: he planned on Min. "Let's breathe," he said. He meant fresh air. They were at a dance by Stallings Mill Pond, a squat little barn of a house thick with smoke and two girls' sick.

Min nodded consent, would have nodded consent to inhale torchfire; and they went out through cheerful drunks and glazed chaperones, past a few cars ringed with still harder drinkers to the edge of the pond. She knew they were young; that marriage, at best—what she thought of as *life*—was some years off, after Rob had grounded himself in money. And she also knew he had never said one word to feed her hope. All the kissing she'd yielded had been yielded to his honesty—his frank unspoken requirement for warmth, lip on lip, which he took or accepted with laughing courtesy, stopping always at the bounds beyond which, however she wanted him, he'd have broken her trust, entered rooms within her which she still well knew were not habitable safely. He had never made her say any kind of No. All of which made her feel thanks and longing but chiefly worship. He seemed to her simply, as he'd grown all his life in her presence and sight, a piece of the one precious heart of things, the satisfied whole toward which parts yearned, requiring and utterly worthy of homage but covered and secret, easy to miss (a born Presbyterian, still Min felt that, and much of her life moved round it; but she could not have thought it out in order or said it). She thought they would stand now and mention the few stars, then move to the usual rock nearby and sit and kiss.

Rob said, "Do you want me to say I love you?"

"I never asked that."

He wanted to say, "You sing it like birdsong"; but he said "Please answer."

Min did not try to see him; she needed calm. She looked at the pond. A fish jumped once or a small comet fell—the dark was that thick. She could not see at all. She said, "Any person likes to hear that, sure. I can be set up by meeting old stinking Aunt Cat in the road and hearing her say she's loved me forever."

"I'm white," Rob said, "and I bathed this evening."

The words seemed to come through a smile so she laughed. Then she turned and touched him, her hand on his arm.

"Don't do that," he said, "till you've answered me." He pulled back from her.

"You're enjoying this, Rob—too much, I think; your own private part. Well, I'll leave you to it." She took a step back toward the other drunks.

"You leave now, Min, and you're gone for good."

She turned and said "Yes."

"Yes what?"

"My answer. My answer is Yes."

Rob stood awhile, accepting that. Then he said "Come on."

By then Min could look. He faced the pavilion and carlights struck him. He bore, all on him, the promise of harm. He was rushing now. She could not see the reason (being younger than he, not living in his home); so she thought what, two minutes before, would have seemed beyond her power—

This is for him. I am not in this. She also thought that drink was the cause, but she did not believe it enough to obey him. Nothing in his voice or his outline on the dark gave her anything to trust. "I'm leaving," she said.

"For good, remember."

Min gave a little laugh, immensely expensive, and said "So be it" and walked toward the lights. She believed him entirely. His only lie had been just now, the offer to say what could not be forgiven—deceit, for a purpose. All the way uphill she tried to imagine another day, this night survived; but every small hope that rose was stunned by knowledge.

3

Sylvie's dog didn't rise, too late for that, but gave a formal display of threat from her hole in the dirt.

Rob went up to her, to the sound in darkness, and knelt and put out his hand to find her, the snarling muzzle. Then he thought of her name and said it—"Rowboat"—and ringed her mouth with his fingers tightly.

She had not smelled him for maybe twelve years (then Sylvie had been sleeping in the kitchen at the Kendals'—Mr. Kendal's first seizure—and had brought Rowboat with her, a neat year-old); but she bore him now and, when he released his grip to stroke her throat, she consumed his odor with quick old gasps but never licked him. Hot, dry.

"What you guarding?" he said.

The sound of a door, a silent wait, no trace of light. A man's voice said, "You Rowboat. Who you got?"

Rob said "Me" and stood.

"Shit on you."

Rob laughed and came forward. "Rob Mayfield, Slick."

"Well, Jesus," Slick said.

"No, Rob," he laughed. "Not even a Christian." He had reached the foot of the four steps and bumped them but waited there.

"What you after?" Slick said. "It's Friday night."

Rob said, "I was after Sylvie's place. I thought this was hers."

Slick waited. "Is."

Rob said "Where is she?"

"Right behind him," Sylvie said.

A fourth voice—behind them all: dark, a woman—laughed once.

Rob said "Hey, Sylvie."

"You done graduated?"

"Yes," he said. "Finished school forever."

"What else you finished," Sylvie said and also laughed.

"Not a goddamned thing," Rob said.

She said "Shame."

The voice that had laughed first came nearer to Sylvie. "Who you hollering at?"

Rob sat on the bottom step to hear himself named. He was suddenly tired.

Sylvie said, "My baby. My darling boy" but she laughed again.

The woman said, "Let me see him; come here, boy."

Rob could hear they were slightly less drunk than he, but he stood and waited for word from Sylvie.

Silence. Nothing but all their breathing, snoring from Rowboat, a chuckling bird they'd managed to waken.

So he said "Can I come in?"

The woman said "I told you."

"Shut up," Slick said. "None of this yours." Then he said to Sylvie, "I thought you was off work."

But Sylvie said "Sure" to Rob. No offer of a light to help him up.

Rob thought of his Uncle Kennerly's saying—"They're blind to a tumble-turd crawling cross your dinner but can see your britches swell in pitch-black night"—and began to climb, one step at a time, the thin planks swaying treacherous beneath him; the sound up ahead of bodies retreating inward to wait. His hands out, blind-man, struck the dry doorframe. He hauled himself up onto what seemed the sill; then he wished he had gone on home, safe bed, or had laughed off Min's highhorse. Failed and sick.

"Step in," Sylvie said.

There was a light, low and sooty in a corner. It showed a small table and two women standing by the table—or their dresses: there were two dresses surely; the shoulders and heads rose well into darkness. No sign of a third—Slick's voice; where was he? Rob thought, "I'm dead. I have walked into murder."

The woman said "He hungry."

Sylvie said, "Been hungry since he born. Too late now though. Stove cold as me; Rowboat eat my scraps."

Rob said "I'm fine." He still held the doorframe. "Where you hiding Slick?"

"You sick," Sylvie said. "Grown man and you sick."

Rob nodded. "Dying."

"Don't be sick in here."

"Sit down," the woman said and reached behind her, drew a straight chair to light.

"Can I, Sylvie?" he said.

"You behaving?" Sylvie said.

He extended his arms to the side, palm out as though good intentions, helplessness in fact, were visible.

"Come on," Sylvie said.

Rob thought he would never cross the twelve feet of floor; it multiplied beneath him. He wanted to find Slick or the hole at least through which Slick had vanished but needed all his vision and balance for the journey to the chair—rest, however threatened. So he chose something round on Sylvie's table, mysterious but shining enough for a beacon, and swam toward it. He was in the chair, his hands on the table; the shining thing was a glass bowl. He leaned. A fishbowl. He waited. The fish waved by—glinting, gold. *Mine*, he thought, *Money*. He looked back for Sylvie. "Is this Money?" he said (he had given her a goldfish years ago—seven? eight? for Christmas maybe?—and had named it at the time).

Sylvie seemed to nod.

He leaned still nearer. It seemed worth tears. The old fish endlessly rounding its world; a gift from his childhood when all outward gifts had been clear signals, smilingly flown, for *visits* in the midst of the busy absence of Father (gone, all questions muffled), Mother (in total service to her father). The floor of the bowl was white creek-sand from which rose various dark arms of color—shards of glass, bottlenecks; a wilderness he'd made for Money and long since forgot: a fragile gift, perfectly intact. He turned again. "Sylvie, I still give you this." He meant it as the one good deed of his day.

The woman said, "He Money but he don't buy me." Her laugh was a powerful promise of harm.

Rob searched round for Sylvie—vanished like Slick. He looked to the woman, who had come no closer but was clearer now that his eyes had settled to the light in the room. "You know me?" he said.

"All your life," she said.

He studied her for age. When he first had entered, she'd seemed as tall as Sylvie. Now she seemed a girl, small and breakable, maybe younger than he—light unlined skin that stretched on her bones like seamless cloth. At the end of one bare arm, her hand worked steadily—opening outward, then silently clamping and knocking her thigh. "How you know me?" he said.

"Your daddy," she said.

"What?"

"I seen your daddy." For an instant her hand stopped its valving and pointed vaguely toward town.

"Where is he?" Rob said.

"Your eyes," she said. Again her hand stopped and passed across her own eyes, smiling now.

"That's all you mean?"

She studied him, unanswering.

"Who are you then?"

"Sylvie's cousin. Flora."

"How come I don't know you?"

"I left this place before you could see good. Leaving it again tomorrow too. Baltimore." The name renewed her fading smile.

"Then why are you here?"

"My son. He live out with Mama in the country. Making him a visit."

"How old is he?"

"Fourteen," she said. "Bo Parker. You know him?"

"Never did," Rob said.

"He growing," she said.

"I'm grown," Rob said. "Me and Money here full-grown, ain't we, Sylvie?" He asked Sylvie, both in the bafflement of drink and the hope that he'd make her appear now to help him. He did not search round but no answer came. So he had to face Flora again. "Get Sylvie."

"She busy."

"What doing?"

"*Her* business."

"I'm sick. Please get Sylvie now."

Flora frowned and said "Don't puke in here," but she turned to the far dark corner and said "You Slick. Get Sylvie."

A dim narrow bed, a black shape rising, Slick's voice rusty with stupor and anger—"Who need her?"

"This boy."

"Shit on him," Slick said and fell back down. The bed again vanished.

But when Rob's eyes opened again, it was round him—a deep clean feather-bed piled up around him. He put out slow hands and felt at his sides. Iron rails, no Slick, no Sylvie, still dark. He strained to hear—silence, eventually a weak snort filtered up from Rowboat. The rafters above him were still oiled with lamplight. He looked no farther, not from fear now or sickness (they both had passed; how long ago?) but from peace. Sad peace. He only thought of time, his familiar sadness since the age of five when he first saw clearly that he'd been left alone (or with Rena and Sylvie, the same as alone since he neither wanted nor needed them or any of their offerings, though he'd learned to thank them and laugh in their presence). *All this time I have got to get through.* His life (it would never occur to him to stop it; his gifts for joy were natural and large). He could not know he was still child enough to be desperate, no sense of the hope of change or reward, only the iron conviction of entrapment. *Here I am, and will stay. How? How?* He thought, as he'd thought for four years now, that the means of escape—or if not the means then at least an ointment—was the touch of bodies other than his own, the right to search particular bodies that swam up toward him in the barren days, bodies he'd endowed with the power to save him, should he touch them entirely, know them at their own extremes of need. He had still not tried—Min had faced him beautifully; he honored her choice but would keep his word and quit her—and now he could only think of rest. Sleep. Home. He could not sleep here; Aunt Rena would be wild with worry already. Could he rise and stand and find his grandfather's car and crank it and see it safely home, for however short a time (he remembered, and intended his promise to leave)? He made a first try. His right hand gripped the side rail again and he pulled once upward. Too weakly; he fell back. A squealing of iron.

A face bent over him—Flora's, her teeth; was she grinning or grinding them? He felt her breath before he heard words, clean and wet. The smell was from elsewhere on her, high and raw.

"You kicking?" she said.

"Still."

"But not high, huh?"

"I didn't say that."

"I needs my fare back to Baltimore then."

"You'll get it," Rob said. "Woods full of money."

It was a grin, broad. "You couldn't, could you?"

"How much?"

"Two dollars."

"Can't help you," he said. By then he was smiling, the first time in hours, since taking his diploma.

"Well," Flora said. Her hand was still working at its little chore. She took a step forward till her thighs touched the rails; then she sat beside him, not right against his body but near, by his knees. "Forget about the money; you still couldn't, could you?"

Rob thought that he couldn't but found in the long slow following time that he could, very well.

4

Eva had waited for him, nodding in a chair in the dining room, dressed; and as he came through the kitchen quietly, she opened her eyes to the pale dawn light and waited till his steps reached the door of the hall. Then she stopped him. "Son."

"Are you all right?" he said.

"Sit down a minute please." She was whispering but clearly.

"What's wrong?" he said. Her back was to him, though her head was half-turned; he did not move toward her.

"Not a thing with me. How about you?" she said.

"I'm dirty," Rob said, "and I was a little drunk and all; but otherwise fine—I'm getting tired now."

"Not yet," Eva said. "Sit down with me please." (In recent years, with the family smaller, they had made a little sitting corner by the table.)

"Yes ma'm," he said and quickly checked his clothes—only wrinkles, sweat, a little red dirt. He went to the straight chair across from his mother, eight feet away. Then he sat and looked.

She bore his looking quietly. She was perfectly well, her eyes clear of worry, only slightly drowsy. Her father had lasted one more of his spells.

In spite of his night, its hard new expenses, the full force of all the love Rob had ever felt, ever longed to offer, rushed up in him now. Could he say it, finally? Had she waited for that? He whispered "Good morning," which he meant as the start of his whole grand gift if she wanted or would take it.

She watched him awhile.

Rob thought she was weighing his offer slowly, to keep or return, when what she was doing was struggling to say no more than the truth, a truth that could neither harm this child she'd neglected (a fine man before her now, no help from her) nor be turned back by him in justice against her.

"Well," she said, "I love you."

It shocked him, the last thing he'd planned to hear, and stopped his own helpless offer in its tracks. Still he smiled and said "Thank you."

She nodded acceptance. "Have you always known that?"

Rob studied her face. Thirty-four years old (the age, though he did not know it now, at which his father had first loved her), finer in hair and lines of bone, clarity of skin, the sad depth of eyes, than on any previous day of her life—a beauty fed by time and hunger to what now shone as a lovely firm-footed needlessness: *I am mine, and happy.* Yet all Rob saw or would ever see was the simple goal of every longing he could presently remember, encased in a girl three steps away.

"Don't answer," she said. "All the time in the world." Then she reached down beside her and under the cushion and brought out an envelope and held it toward him. "All happiness, Son." She meant him to come to her and take it.

Gravely he did—money? a handkerchief?—then went back and sat and studied it: a letter. An old letter, hand-delivered, *To Eva*, unsealed but safe, kept carefully for years. "What is it?" he said.

"From your father to me after you were born."

"Why?"

"Oh it's time. It's all of him I've got, and I want you to have it."

"Why please?" he said.

She knew and could say. "Because I have thought a good deal just lately, and I see I have done two serious things. I damaged my mother, who had no shields; and I kept you and Forrest apart when you needed him."

So he said it finally, still low-voiced at dawn. "It was you I needed."

Eva laughed. "You've *had* me every day for seventeen years, give or take your few little trips with friends."

Rob saw that she simply believed herself. He could not challenge that, too late anyhow. He looked to the letter again—no feeling, though he wanted hot blood to slam through his head. Not looking up, he said, "Do I read it now?"

"Soon," she said. "When you've slept and eaten."

"Yes ma'm," Rob said. "I'll do the sleeping now." He gently shook the letter. "It's waited these years; it'll last out a nap."

"Good night then," she said.

"Have you slept any?"

She said, "Enough. I'll wait on for Sylvie, fix Papa's tray."

"Is he all right?"

She nodded. "Resting. So is Rena, praise God. Walk easy past their doors."

He moved on beyond her. "I will," he said. "So easy they'll think I'm already gone."

If Eva heard him, she did not turn. The crown of her head topped the back of the chair with the same rich brown she had always offered, lit now by morning, a memory from the literal start of his life.

5

The door to his grandfather's room was open (no one but Rena slept behind closed doors); and he tried to reach the stairs in silence, another promise kept.

But his grandfather called out clearly—"Darling?"

"Rob, sir," he said.

A wait, then "Oh." Then "Where would Eva be?"

"In the dining room, resting."

"Oh." A sizable wait.

Rob climbed two steps.

"Robinson?"

"Yes sir."

"Step here if you would." The voice half-strangled.

"Suppose he died with me," Rob thought. "I will not call Mother. Mine, mine." He went down the steps and across to the door more quietly than he'd ever done anything. When he stopped two feet from the foot of the bed, he whispered "All right."

"Pour me some water please. My arm won't move." It had not moved for twelve years, two strokes and angina pectoris.

Rob went to the nightstand and filled a glass from the cool white pitcher, then supported the white dry head while it drank.

"Prop me up please," he said.

"Shouldn't you be resting?"

Mr. Kendal studied him; the eyes worked perfectly, a scary light blue. "Yes I should," he said. "I should be dead too. You'd do me a favor if you brought me a pistol." The left hand lifted and pointed to the mantel, the old Colt revolver yielding to rust but still fully loaded, actively waiting.

Rob smiled. "I'd have to go clean it first. It won't hurt a fly."

"It'd kill me though."

"Just sleep instead. Let me sleep too."

"Prop me up."

So Rob propped him a little roughly on pillows; then stood back and said, "What else do you want?" He was mostly fond of his grandfather, but now he was tired.

"Did you finish school?"

"Last night," Rob said. "I just got back."

Mr. Kendal checked the window for light. "From where?"

"A dance out at Stallings', some crazy drinking, telling Min Tharrington to go on off, a while at Sylvie's." Though it seemed impossible—here, now—not to tell the rest (the narrow bed, Flora—tired, vague as he was, it seemed a good memory, partial confirmation that his hopes as to others were not in vain, a rank quick flickering of what he might yet discover in the world: steady help), he stopped with that much. No lie at least. *I'm not going to lie to any-body ever, for whatever reason they ask me to.*

Mr. Kendal said, "You really ready for me to die?"

Rob smiled. "You take all the time you want."

"No, answer me."

"Ready for what, sir?"

"To grow on up in five damn seconds; you won't have much more than that, once I'm gone. Mainly to take on Eva's life."

"I'm grown," Rob said. "Everything I've got's in tip-top shape, working beautifully. And what does Mother need? She's stronger than all of us."

Mr. Kendal said, "When I pull out, she'll cave in like a shed." With his good hand he made a little show of falling; heavy fingers plunged down, splayed on the sheet.

Rob looked at the hand.

"You got to take over."

Rob suddenly nodded. "I can. Just rest." He believed himself. He suspected he was happy. The air around him—shared with a sick man, sweetish with death—the brown papered walls, the roof overhead, seemed a bearable shell that could hold his life a good while longer.

6

Rob slept without dreaming till ten o'clock. Then Rena could not wait and came in and went to his wardrobe and opened it and rummaged around on the pretense of hunting up laundry to boil. He knew she was nearing the end of her patience (having borne her dry kiss of congratulation, he had left her at nine to walk home from school with old Mrs. Bradley; she'd assured him she needed the air and the stretching, that he should go on with Min to his fun); so he said into his pillow now, "Get out of here. My clothes are clean as me. If you bang one more door, I'll go strip-naked the rest of my life."

"Who do you think that would please?" Rena said.

He waited; she worked on. "A number," he said, "a sizable number."

Rena had her bundle now, barely two handsful. She stood and walked to the edge of the bed and seized Rob's heel through the thickness of cloth (he was laid on his belly) and said "But not Min."

No answer from Rob. He was feigning and imploring sleep simultaneously.

Rena shook the hard heel. "But not Minnie Tharrington."

Rob kicked free and said from the depths of feathers, "Correct. You've seen her mother. Good work."

"Thank you," Rena said. "She all but slapped my face while I was sweeping the walk—lurked since day and once I showed a hair, came streaking right to me and lowrated you for abandoning Minnie. Left her torn all to pieces, her nerves in ribbons, to find a ride home with Sim Brasher drunk."

Rob said, "Correct. But soberer than me. Sim upchucks a lot."

"Hush," Rena said. "You are nothing but a child."

"Ask Min about that."

"Hush again," Rena said.

"Ask a number of others. Sizable number."

"Get up from there," she said.

"It would shock you to death."

Rena laughed. "Stuck-up."

"Simple fact," Rob said. "The shock would kill you."

"I'll spare myself then. Try the shock on Sylvie. She's waiting to fry your breakfast, grumbling hard."

"She's paid to," he said. His head burrowed deeper.

Rena walked to the door. "Get on up please. Everything's waiting on you."

"I'm coming," Rob said.

"Good work," Rena whispered. "She was never good for you, never fit to wash your socks."

"She wouldn't have had to, would she?" Rob said.

7

He had half-finished shaving when he saw the old letter in his scabby mirror, across on the bureau where he'd left it unread when at dawn he'd collapsed. If Rena had seen it, she'd asked no questions (if she had, she'd be planning her questions now, careful long-term strategies to uncover every trace of motive, purpose, effect of the gift, with a minimum of realization by Rob or Eva that they'd been sacked as thoroughly as Jericho); and his mother never would. It would be her way—as he'd come to understand her—to wait all night, not sleeping, in a chair to make her strange gift doubly impressive; then proceed to pretend she'd forgot it entirely till, holding the actual thing in your hand, you wondered if it had in fact come from her or had merely been summoned from empty air by your own long need to make her act, make her reach out toward you if only in dream. The last thing you'd guess at with any assurance was her secret intent or whether she'd had one or whether she was inwardly pleased now at winning or bitter at the one more failed plea for help. Or had she ever pled? Was she ever less than happy? As he laced his shoes, Rob carefully thought, "I am nobody's fool but I do not know if my mother has asked me for anything ever."

He stood to read the letter by the bed he had slept in for fourteen years, alone and lonely.

March 18, 1904

My darling Eva,

A week ago today you met what I pray is the worst test life will ever offer you. Since the ordeal was largely of my making, I want to write down now (for your eyes only, when you're able to read) two fervent things—all the pardon my heart can beg for handing you on toward this abyss and my solemn promise to honor in the future any course your mind and body choose to follow. Your presence in my life, at whatever distance, is the cause of thanks that only deepen as I watch you grow and encounter the trials I have forced upon you.

And now this boy—fresh thanks for him. He strengthens daily as you do, only quicker (having struggled less and lost no blood at all, save in severing from you). My strong feeling is that he rushes toward a station of safe health at which he can wait for your own safe arrival. My solace in these bad days has been only that if you both live and grow together, then when I must leave, he will last and be my care for you, you for him. If you see him as clearly as you seem to do when Hatt holds him to you, you have surely registered his loving impatience, his readiness, and will come back to him as soon as your sojourn in dream and sleep relents.

Come also to me please,

Your loving,
Forrest

I write this now while I still have the force to make the necessary promise above. It will be in my Bible when you're able to read.

Rob thought, "It has never relented yet. But three of us now know it must, and soon—her, Papa, me. She is telling me she knows. She has kept me from her for sixteen years; but I grew inside her beneath her heart, and I know it better than anyone alive. She sees that finally. It's not too late." The suspicion of happiness he'd felt in his grandfather's room at daybreak was certainty now. He folded the letter and went to the drawer of his own washstand and took out the Bible that had been his Grandmother Kendal's, now his. It fell open naturally to the book of Micah as it had since long before he owned it— "Therefore night shall be unto you, that ye shall not have a vision; and it shall be dark unto you, that ye shall not divine; and the sun shall go down over the prophets, and the day shall be dark over them. Then shall the seers be ashamed, and the diviners confounded: yea, they shall all cover their lips; for there is no answer of God."

Rob hid the letter there and went toward the stairs—the kitchen, food—young again and ready.

8

Sylvie walked from the stove to the kitchen table with his second set of pancakes on the palm of her hand—no napkin, no plate—and held them out to him.

Rob looked from her hand to her face. "Who they for?"

"For you. You ordered them." She slid them to his plate. "Now go on and eat. My hand clean as yours. Cleaner, cleaner."

He reached for the butter. "No doubt," he said, recalling his intention to take a morning shower (three summers before with full manhood on him, he had built a little stall for a shower in the yard, watered by a cistern, used only by him; Rena called it "a coffin with waterworks").

"Shame on you," Sylvie said.

"*I'm* happy," he said.

"Makes one," she said.

"What's ailing you?"

"You know good as me—fools keeping me wake."

"I'm sorry," he said. "I was bad off though."

She turned and faced him, took a sassafras-stick toothbrush from her mouth and said in a voice that reached Rob with full flat power but went no farther. "Don't never come to Sylvie's for that kind of *bad* again; plenty other folks handle that kind of *bad*."

Rob nodded. "That wasn't the trouble I meant. That was Flora's doing."

"Well, Flora long-gone so don't come looking."

"You left me," he said. "You didn't have to watch."

"Thank Jesus," she said. She turned to the sink. "My house had to watch."

"I said I was sorry." His face had composed into earnest regret.

Sylvie hissed a high stream of contempt through her teeth, but she did not look.

Rob swallowed awhile, then he said "Where'd you go?"

Silence.

"Slick find you?"

Still silence. She was standing not working.

"I asked you a question."

"I heard it," she said. "I ain't his to find. No part of me his."

Rob said, "All right. I was just being pleasant."

Sylvie faced him again. "No you won't," she said. "I'll tell you what you being—hateful. Hateful. No piece of me belong to Slick or you or old Mr. Bedford in yonder now griping." She pointed to the front of the house. She was serious.

Rob saw he, or someone, had lanced a rising in her; and he saw he had two choices—to shut her up hard (would she take that from him?) or to let it drain clean. He nodded. "All right." She had known him all his life; she had punished him before and never without cause.

Then her pointing hand moved another way. "I went in the woods down back of my place and puked up the whole fish sandwich I paid for, and then I set my tail in the dirt and drank my lightning and cried till day. Then I went home and give Rowboat some bread and woke Flora up out of my good bed and give her the train fare and told her I'd cut her if she won't gone on number eight—and gone for good till I changed my spirit—and then I walk on over to here for the twenty-ninth year. Here I'm standing, ready to wash your slops."

"She had her fare," Rob said, "but thank you." Sylvie seemed spent, eased.

But she shook her head slowly, no stage refusal. "You keep all the thanks you got, you hear? You'll need em for some of these folks you belongs to."

He could take her gaze, take it steady as she poured it like lye toward his eyes. "Who does my mother belong to?" he said.

Her eyes burned higher, then calmed into wary questioning. "You know all that."

"I don't," he said. "That's the trouble I'm in, the trouble I mentioned."

Her face closed, she shook her head. "Can't help you."

"Yes you can."

Sylvie listened to the house—no sounds but its settling: Rena was shopping, Eva asleep, Mr. Kendal silent. She reached behind her for a towel, dried her hands (that were dry as drumheads). Then she went to a corner and sat on the high stool, twelve feet from Rob. "Get this plain—I'm doing this for you."

Rob nodded acceptance.

"None of them others."

"Thank you," he said. Then he waited for her.

Considerable wait. "Ask your question," she said.

"Is Mother still married?"

"She wearing that ring."

"Widows do that. He may be dead."

"May be, may be. But Miss Eva don't know it."

"Did you ever ask her?"

"No, God," Sylvie said. "She ain't mentioned him since you lived through the whooping cough. Nobody else neither."

"He might have sent letters."

Sylvie pointed to the roof. "By pigeon-back then. I bring in the mail here for twenty-nine years."

"Who was he then?"

"You swear you don't know? She ain't never told you?"

"She nor nobody else. When I was maybe four, I asked her about him. She said, 'He is gone on a very long trip he may never finish. I'll tell you if he does. Till then he has begged us not to talk about him.' "

"Rena ain't said nothing?"

"She explained my name. I asked her who was I named *Robinson* for, and she said 'Your father's father' and I stopped there."

Sylvie said, "I never knew that much. I know what I saw eighteen years ago."

"Tell that," Rob said. "That would be news to me."

"Nothing new about people acting like dogs. Eva couldn't stand her mama, see—and good enough reason—so she took the first train ticket out of town, which was her school teacher, Mr. Mayfield, your daddy. They run to Virginia and she had you and Miss Charlotte killed herself, so Eva turned back up here. And here she sit."

"Why?" Rob said.

"What she wanted to do. Miss Eva never done one thing she didn't want to. She loved Mr. Bedford and she had him all this time."

"He's going any day. He knows that himself."

"Eva know it too."

"Then what?" Rob said.

"Then if she got sense, she'll buy her a page in every newspaper between here and Hell and beg that poor man's pardon she left."

"You said she wanted to go," Rob said.

"You see for how long, don't you?"

"Is he live?" Rob said.

Sylvie nodded. "Ought to be. He won't so old. He be about fifty, wherever he at."

"Was he good?"

"Good at what?" Sylvie smiled for the first time that morning. "No I never knew him. He come here to supper a time or two before Miss Charlotte seen

he sweet on Eva; even used to come here and help her with her lessons—
sit yonder in the dining room and work at the table, and Miss Charlotte keep
sending Rena back here to get her drinks of water just so she could spy. Rena
never told nothing, to her mama nohow; told me 'Sylvie, they passing notes.'
He took her from her people; that's how good he was. Not good enough to
keep her though. You look some like him, got his eyes and hands."

Rob's hands were hidden on his knees. They moved together, rubbed
dry palms silently. The eyes stayed on Sylvie, conscious of effort.

Sylvie stood; time to work. "How come you ain't asked all this before?—
asked Eva; she know."

"Never wanted to." Rob smiled; another day ruined, killed dead in its
tracks. "Never did and still don't." He stood, dropped his napkin, stooped
for it, folded it. Then he went toward the door.

Sylvie said "You forgetting—"

He turned. "Many thanks."

She demanded thanks, a frugal diet. She nodded, unsmiling.

9

Rob went from the kitchen door straight through the yard, past wellhouse and
woodshed to the old green stable where he'd left the car. If he'd asked himself he'd have said that he went to check it for safety; had he got it back
unmarked from his night? Would it pass his grandfather's fierce inspection
(if Papa ever should rise again; nobody else cared, least of all Rob himself—
young as he was, he could not love *things*: a car was precisely a means
toward motion). But when he had circled it and found it clean, he opened
the door and raised the toolbox and took out the fruitjar still half-full of lightning and thought he must stow it in a gentler place. The ledge in his bathhouse. He unscrewed the lid and sucked two long raw mouthfuls down,
thinking nothing at all, neither shame nor pride, a gesture as pure as a deep
breath in sleep. Then he shut it again and held it to his chest and went out
the back stable door toward the bathhouse.

His Uncle Kennerly met him, walking up through weeds at the end of
the yard but in plain view and looking, apparently smiling.

Neither of them slackened but when they were near enough for audible
whispering, Rob said, "Where's the best hiding place?" and stopped.

Kennerly came on to within twelve inches of Rob's bright face and said,
normal voice, "What you got to hide?"

"My fun," Rob said.

His uncle said "I can handle that" and reached out quickly and took Rob's jar and, all in one move, brought it down hard on a twenty-penny nail in the top of a low cedar post beside them. The dry white wood drank all the clear liquor; not a drop reached ground.

"Much obliged," Rob said. His smile survived.

So had his uncle's. "Glad to help," he said.

"How else do you plan to help me?" Rob said. They were still no more than a foot apart. He bore the cool breath of Kennerly's cud all over his face—the second or third small chew of the day, honey-flavored tobacco.

Kennerly said, "I'll offer you work. That's the best help there is. Now I've got the freight office, I'm easing old Rooker out soon as I can—real softening of the brain. He's felt his last girl up, on my time at least. I'll make you freight agent any week you say and get him to train you. Work right here at home—free room and board, fresh well, good garden, good niggers, your people. Ought to kneel here and thank me." He smiled very slightly.

Rob nodded. "I've thought of another way. You wire me a salary once a month, and I'll stay out of your sight forever."

Kennerly thought, then offered his hand. "A *deal*," he said.

Rob put his own right hand behind him, refusal.

Kennerly said "You're bluffing. I ain't."

"I know it," Rob said. "Got jokes in my blood."

"What blood?"

"The Mayfield."

Kennerly's smile had still not faded. It burned some clearly abundant fuel, pure and secret. "The Mayfield I knew—I just knew one—was sure no comedian. More like a dried Presbyterian preacher that would steal you blind while you fed him fried chicken."

"Is that so?" Rob said. "At least you saw him, so I won't contradict you; but it looks like to me the joke was on Mother."

Kennerly thought again, then nodded. "It was. Don't tell her."

"She knows. She knows."

"Has she told you so?"

"Not in so many words."

"And she won't either," Kennerly said. "I'll bet you money. Eva knows one thing—"

"—Papa's dying," Rob said.

"That's it. That's all."

Rob said, "No she knows she will last past that, a good while past. She knows she's young. She wants me to help her."

Kennerly smiled and his head fell back, mouth silently open, his standard indication of pleasure. "What job you got for her? You firing Sylvie and nig-gering Eva? You planning a stroke? You planning to blow off a leg or two, lit-tle dynamite accident?"

Rob thought. "That's what you recommend?"

"You said you wanted to help my sister. I was thinking of ways."

Rob nodded. "You planning to live awhile longer too?"

"—The Lord be willing."

"Who's going to help *you*?"

Kennerly smiled again. "The old reliable—me, me, me."

"Lucky three," Rob said.

Kennerly struck him flat-handed on his left cheek, a measured blow, no pain, all threat.

Rob took a step backward. "You're breaking up things this morning, ain't you?" He worked to grin and managed it.

"Got to," his uncle said. "Need one in every family; keep the undergrowth cleared." He walked past Rob—four, five steps—then turned and said, "Son, get you a bucket and pick up that glass. Somebody'll get hurt."

"Yes sir," Rob said. "You going in to Papa?"

"Going to see can I help him, yes." Again he did his silent act of pleasure and walked on that way till Rob stopped watching and bent to collect shattered glass in his hands, saying clearly to himself, "Help him on his way."

10

God-knows-where, near Fayetteville
May 22, 1921

Dear Mother,

I hope you are well and all happy at home. This will show I am well despite the mosquitoes (the one on my forehead right now feels shod). Happy I will not claim to be. Was it you that made me go on this party or was I really fool enough to come, free-will? Anyhow I'm here and will stay, if I live, for the whole promised week; but you may not know me on my return—swollen past recognition with bites or wasted to nothing with chills and fever. Get the chill tonic out!

No, calm down now. I am really all right, just a few pounds lighter; but here's the gruesome tale. We all got here in one piece generally, although the trip took over six hours, till long past dark, since Coley's car boiled most of the way—the girls look stewed—and we had two punctures and hit a pig. More damage to the pig than the Ford anyhow. Ever hit a pig?—like a good brick wall about four feet thick. We stopped (!) and surveyed the mutual ruins — *the pig was panting her last in the road — and Christine looked up and said "Here it comes." It was the owner of the pig, slightly thinner (but only a shade) in nothing but "overhalls" and a knife. No shirt or hat. From a distance, the knife looked about a foot long. Up close, it was fourteen inches maybe; and Christine and Fanny and Niles and I — and Min, Mamie, Theo, and Coley behind us; they were still in their car — thought Time was up. Killing-Time in the Country. Well, it was — for the pig. He said not a word but went straight to the fallen and cut her throat one good swipe and then stood up and looked at Christine and said, "Thank you,* lady. *I been wanting to kill her ever since Mama died. She was Mama's favorite and mean as a snake." And there were we, thinking we would have to buy her at least if not fight off a crazed, armed pig-farmer. He offered us some meat! — said, "When you all head back home next week, stop by. I'll salt her down; I'll save you the chine." So get ready for that too.*

Then we rolled into Fayetteville and ate some cold supper at Christine's uncle's and found out we had to drive another hour on to his fishing camp, way up the Cape Fear, eating dust all the way — his and the cook's.

That's the main hitch in the whole operation. Uncle Pepp is a bachelor. We knew that ahead but what we didn't know is he won't hire a woman for any purpose — cooking, cleaning, nothing. So the girls are tickled not to be chaperoned; and the boys are choking on cobwebs and dust — you ought to see our sheets! — *and the food of course. Old Tump's fried food. He brags on it, starting at four in the morning — his good catfish, little light cornbread, little light pancakes. Light — good night! — I expect the house to sink. It is also doing that, being built on swamp.*

But seriously, I am doing good and enjoying the river and most of the company and Uncle Pepp's rubs. He is one of those massagers, does a good deal of kneading on everybody. The girls are black and blue; I have got a charley-horse. He's alone a lot so we understand and bear it — good exercise.

I wander out by myself a good bit or go fishing with Tump, who shuts up outdoors; and thus I am getting plenty of time to think about my future that Aunt Rena is always preaching about. What I think is this. I will come on back at the end of this party and take the depot job with Uncle Kennerly. Who knows, I may own the railroad eventually — all ladders have bottoms — but in any event I can live there at home and help you out any way needed. You may recall that I have thought a long time about going off for a little at least and testing myself elsewhere, anywhere away. You know too I guess that the point of that plan was hoping to force you to ask me to stay. For a while there it looked bad! But what you gave me the morning after commencement turned the tide.

Now Mother, you can rest assured that whatever the next months and years hold for any of us in the way of trouble and loss, Rob will be on hand to offer his service for what it's worth.

Maybe it will not just be worth nothing *as it's been up to now. As years go by, I will show you I love you and ease your way.*

Thank you for asking,

Your own son,
Rob

Love also to all.

APRIL 1925

Dear Rob,

I have given myself a month since the morning you left. I am not, as you well know, a powerful thinker; so I have given myself that time to think over all you laid in my path before taking your own way out of here. I have needed almost all those days, but I think I have some answers for you now. What will take a great deal longer will be to forget both your questions and my answers, both our awful voices—and above all for me, the shock of coming in to wish you "Happy Birthday" on your day of manhood and finding you ready to go with no warning. I know that people leave, both willing and forced, and you must surely know I have made my own share of sudden departures; but admission of guilt permits me to say one thing I know that you didn't ask for—abandonment of any soul that loves or trusts you is never pardoned, in Heaven or here. (I have also been left, by my own mother, once; and though I choose to believe you in saying that you would have come in to tell me "Goodbye," I still need to say: you should thank God above that I found you and spoke, that you could not be even so much as tempted to flee and then spend a lifetime paying on a debt impossible for you to pay or me to cancel.)

Enough of that though. I am not here to blame; and I trust you will not, when you hear my answers. They are explanations and I think they are true.

That I have not loved you. *I have, I think. I have always enjoyed and honored your presence; and more than a few of my grateful memories were gifts from you—the day you looked up from your book on the sea, that Rena gave you (you were four years old), and told me your plan for making friends with a shark (you had had sharks very much in mind for days, had drawn pictures of them with men in their jaws): "First, you catch him. Then you don't cook him." —*

The time you hid my luggage strap in hopes I would cancel my outing to Richmond. There are also however, as you're old enough to know, a few dark spots that have never bleached out—the simple fact that your birth tried to kill me; and though I fought for and won new life, I still and will always suffer that damage in mind and organs. I was torn for you. There is also the fact of your father in you. But no, I repeat I have honored you, liked you, and taken much pleasure from the years you were here. If I spent less time on your daily care than some mothers would have, you need to recall that I had prior claims— Father's sadness and need, the pain I had caused him—and that there was ample care at hand, your aunt, Mag, Sylvie, a whole loving house of which you were one of the actual centers. To say you were not loved here, and by me among the others, is only to say you have small notion of what love is or entails and exacts. Never say it again.

That I held you back from your father and his people. *I did; I agree. For these two reasons—first, I thought I had harmed you enough in advance by bringing you into the life I could offer, without splitting you into further pieces. My own life has taught me the Kendals are very poor at trouble; we generally run. So were the Watsons, my mother's people, and so—to my certain knowledge—were the Mayfields, all except Hattie your father's sister. Why would I flag you onward then into trouble I knew you would surely not face but flee and thus deepen? Second, your father has not asked for you since Christmas of 1904. Not a word nor a cent.*

That I kept you in ignorance of half your family. *Again I did—and again I did it out of what I intended as kindness to us both. I never knew the past to be of help to anybody. Far from it. I have seen it ruin my own mother and paralyze your father as surely as a stroke, though young and strong and with much to lose—namely you and me. My aim is generally to live for the day, or the day after; but all around me I have always had, and felt smothered by, people who live for a past as dead as Didymus. Please don't you, which brings me to the most hurtful question of all—*that I want your care, demand your presence as a means of protection for my own future life.

I honestly do not. Again two reasons—I am permanently cared for (you well know) by Father; he has seen to that and explained all the business to Kennerly and me. When he goes there will be no trouble at least; not riches but life as always, I guess. Even if he hadn't though and I were alone, I am sure I could live. I am strong enough to work. I could teach school, nurse, sew for people, paint flowers, bake, scrub if need be, pick cotton, hoe corn. What pride I possess is not the lady kind. I know ways to fight, and some ways to win. You are witness to that, one of the chief.

Those are the answers which, again, I obviously think are true. I offer them anyhow, this serious and full, because you asked so seriously. You will use them your way but—however, wherever, need it or not—always with my love.

My love then,
Mother

Everyone else here would send love too if they knew I was writing. Father asks after you several times a day. Rena has no doubt written you that, and all the other news. Sylvie may miss you worst of all. She is poorly and cross but keeps your room like a bandbox, ready. Come when you will and know you are wanted. I trust this will find you, since I do not think I could write it out again. I will use the only address you gave and hope that the Shenandoah Valley knows your name.

Again,
E.K.M.

2

The letter reached Rob in Bracey, Virginia—his Aunt Hatt's kitchen—in the hand of Grainger, a clear Saturday noon in the middle of April. He had wandered a month after leaving home in the third-hand Chevrolet bought with the four-year savings of his job at the depot under Kennerly. He had left accompanied by Niles Fitzhugh, his oldest friend. They'd intended to sightsee awhile at first—Petersburg, Richmond, Lynchburg, Lexington—then on up the Valley to Staunton where Niles had an older half-brother in hardware who had offered them jobs and room-and-board till they got on their feet. The trip went well in spite of the roads, fourteen punctures in the first three days. They saw any number of battlefields, pocketed a good many scrap souvenirs (bullets, balls), talked with two fairly addled retired Confederates, seen the tomb of Lee (and Traveller's bones) and gone to a whorehouse in Buena Vista called Roller's Retreat (they'd retreated more than once with girls much older than they'd hoped to find yet grinning and ready, cheap and restful). But Staunton was a washout—ugly and all brick, tall pointed houses hung on the sides of hills like red shirts on pegs—and Niles's brother had the jobs all right but also a wife like a bandsaw spinning and three children under the age of five. So Rob worked there a week in misery till a mountain farmer built like a wharf rat accused him of cheating (a subtraction error), and he packed and left. The one week's wages and the rest of his savings would fuel a little more looking round.

So he drove across with some difficulty to Warm Springs Baths; and finding it much too rich for his blood (girls dying for husbands, mothers hoarse with urging), he slipped on down to Goshen Pass and stayed in a wild old widow's boarding house and drank the strong waters (more for fun than in hope; he had drunk no liquor since leaving home with the single exception of some beer while retreating, to ease the sights) and learned that a foreman was due there soon to hire on a crew to widen a road through the pass by the river once the spring weather settled. He would wait for that.

In all those days he had thought very little of home or his mother, their hard last meeting. He had not left in quite as much anger as she'd thought—more restlessness than anger, so he honestly believed; she had forced their farewell to its cruel pitch—and the trip itself (he had traveled so little) had been specific to whatever sadness lingered. But once his chances of work seemed good (his landlady said, "They'll have to hire you; not two other men in this whole county would know a road by sight if it ran in their front door and out the back and killed their wife, much less how to lay one"), he could take time to stop long mornings in bed, long evenings on porches; and then he began to think of his life—all he did not know, had been denied. Three days of that, and the rusty alum water he drank from the springs, and he'd sunk himself back dangerously near to the paralyzed misery he fled at home; the four years of thankless loveless work in the thick immortal shadows of his family. Half his family.

He dreamed of the other half one Thursday night, having eaten his landlady's leaden supper and answered her questions for an hour on the porch ("You told me you're saved? Do I recollect that?" — "You do, yes ma'm. I was barely lost") and taken a lonely walk to the river with the town all asleep. Then oddly he dreamed not of his father but his father's sister. He'd had a face for her for some years now. Shortly after commencement, he had asked his Aunt Rena a single question one morning early while his mother was asleep—"Can you put your hands on a picture of my father?" She had waited awhile—they were in the kitchen and Sylvie was present—then she'd said flat "No." But Sylvie had said, "Step yonder to the mirror" and pointed to her own piece of glass on the mantel. He had kept his seat, would not walk an inch to see his own face; and Rena had gone out and come back soon and walked straight to him and held out a picture, a good-faced woman plain as a board, two plain boys beside her. Rob had said, "Which one is he, then?" — "Neither," Rena had said. "They're your cousins. She's your aunt—Hattie Mayfield, married a Shorter, who died." "Does she favor my father?" " 'Not a bit, thank God, and neither do you. You're a Watson to the ground; Mother's all over you." Sylvie had shaken her head No, smiling. Rob had said to Rena, "Why do you have this?" She had gently taken it from him then. "Because she sent it to me. When Mother died I wrote to her a time or two, knowing Eva was so weak from having you but wanting all the same to pass on the news, to punish everybody. I was great on punishment then; girls are. But Hattie took it all with kindness and pity and wrote me long letters about the good weather and spring in the hills and of how you were strengthening, so I asked her for this and she sent it down. When Eva came back, I broke off writing." Rob had asked one other thing, "Where is she now?" — "In Heaven maybe. Or Bracey, Virginia. She lived near there."

Alone in the mountains then, Rob dreamed of Hatt, a simple dream with no clear demands—she was doing man's work, shoveling a stable clean. The stable was dim, lit by the open door toward which she worked and a far clouded window. Beneath the window on their haunches and hunkers were numbers of children, all boys, pale, their heads shaved. Their eyes were brighter than either source of light, and they watched the open door. They were waiting to run, past her and gone.

The next morning Rob inquired again in town about the road-man—due in five days, a week if it rained—so he asked his landlady if she'd hold his room through a long weekend while he visited family (there was no other guest, slim chance of one till summer deepened; he asked to be kind). She said "Not a chance"—alone as a rock—which forced him to pay her and leave with her grudge, one more set of eyes aimed cursing at his back (he asked her to forward any letter that came in the next two days—*Bracey, General Delivery*—and, going out the door, he tried to say "See you Tuesday maybe"; but she said "Don't never try again").

He drove the whole rough seventy miles under heavy clouds, a piss-ant drizzle, occasional fog; and when he'd reached Bracey, he was so low and fearful as to make him think he would pass through toward anywhere—home even, any company. But he stopped of necessity at the one gas pump; and when the storekeeper had filled the tank and was bringing his change—it was past six o'clock, little daylight left—he stared up at Rob and said, "You a Mayfield, ain't you?" Rob said "What told you?" The man kept staring, searching Rob's face as though for some sort of goods that could be converted to use, quick cash. "Know all the Mayfields," he said, "or knew them. You got to watch close to see a Mayfield at all—big runners. Whose are you?" Rob said "Hattie's" for no clear reason; "Where is she living?" The man said, "You the oldest or what?" Rob said, "The youngest, by a long shot the youngest"— a game by then, more dangerous than most he had ever played. The man's whole face and body said *fool* or *simpleton* or *scoundrel*; but finally he pointed, "She's out there in that same old piece of house where you boys left her, lonesome as an angel." —"I heard they came in choirs," Rob said and tipped his cap and drove on in the general direction.

Two miles by the gauge till he saw a dark solitary house to the right and turned in there. He drove to the empty backyard, searching for lights; and when he saw none, he still got down and headed toward the back steps. If anyone was there, they would be in the kitchen.

She was on the steps though, waiting for him trustingly—Hatt alone in darkness, saying "Yes" as he touched the bottom step. Startled, really scared, Rob jumped back down but quickly recovered and laughed and said "Yes to *what?*" She also laughed—did she have a gun, an axe?—and said "Yes who are you?" He paused over that and then said politely, "Excuse me asking but if you'll go first, I'll know if I'm wasting your time or not." —"Hatt Shorter," she said. "The widow Shorter. Helpless as a girl." She laughed again, a deep-fed laugh—"Which I'm far from being." —"Then I'm Robinson," he said. "Forrest's boy." They both waited then; she must say the next. "Oh Jesus," she said but it came through a smile, the sounds of welcome.

She rushed him indoors to her strongest lamp and fed him enormously and asked him only the gentlest questions before suggesting he was tired and should sleep and leading him up to the small high room that had been his father's when his father was a boy, though she didn't mention that till the following morning after heavy breakfast in clear spring light—late: he had slept past ten, deep, untroubled.

3

Hatt cleared the last dishes—the platter of steak and gravy, the last fresh biscuits—poured him more coffee; then sat for the first time and said "You slept."

"I did, yes ma'm. Like the peaceful dead."

"They don't sleep," she said.

Rob looked up slowly to check her fervor. Was he stuck with a Christer?

She was smiling though, no zealot's rictus. "I meant they were happy and never tired. Their search is ended."

He took a long draft of the strong tinny coffee. "So is mine," he said. "Let me just say this—I'm here out of nothing but polite curiosity. I don't bear a grudge or a past-due bill for money or service, or a writ or nothing. I was just up in Coshen, waiting as I said for a job to start; and dumb as it sounds, I dreamed about you, knowing your face from my Aunt Rena's picture."

"Nothing dumb in that. I've wondered if she ever showed you that picture, only good one ever made of me. And I've dreamed about you for twenty-one years."

"Thank you," Rob said. "I hope they were fun. No I'm here on a visit, not a hunt or a raid."

Hatt said, "I knew that. Your name's Mayfield. All the Mayfields but me are short-term guests—travel light, take no toll but gray hair and wrinkles on their poor fool hosts. I've got them already so I'm safe at last." She stroked at her clean bare face with her hands, combed back through her hair—seamy skin, gray hair. But the large eyes were happy, more nearly at rest. "You were in your father's bed," she said.

Rob said "Is he dead?"

Hatt studied him closely. "You really don't know?"

"No ma'm. Not a word."

"Doesn't Eva?"

"She claims not. I have to believe her."

"He's alive," Hatt said. "Fifty-four years old." She stopped and knocked her front teeth with a knuckle, then bit herself hard. Her wrists and shoulders, her hair, neck, face were a legible receipt of the tolls she had mentioned, all taken on her and no return (her father, James Shorter, Forrest, her sons; this nephew fresh-burgeoned at her table, demanding). The same knuckle knocked the table twice gently; her eyes had never let go of Rob's. "Will you use this right?"

He nodded. "Yes ma'm."

"Won't hurt nobody with it?"

"No ma'm, I'm kindly." He smiled at her broadly, a bid to break the tone.

"You're a Mayfield," she said, "—*Robinson* at that. My father's all in you. He'd have hurt Baby Jesus if he needed to."

"Not me," Rob said. "I promise, not me."

Hatt knew he was wrong—not that he lied, only spoke in young ignorance—but she said anyhow, "He is living in Richmond in our grandparents' house."

Rob said "They're dead?"

"Yes God," she said. "Before you were born. Our own father too, Robinson your namesake."

"Is Father alone?"

"No," she said. "He could never stand that. I'm the hermit in the family. So it's turned out at least—the best-natured one of all, the one that loves noise: here you see me on a windy hill, an old crow-roost!" She had made herself smile; it drained off slowly. "No he has a housekeeper; been with him some years, ever since he moved there. She's made him a home. I can thank her for that."

Rob waited to see if she'd come to an end. Then he said "So can I." It cost him nothing.

"You won't be needing to see him though." Hatt did not stay for an answer to that—it was not a question—but stood and went to the stove for the kettle which had boiled through their talk (she would wash his dishes). It held a gallon and was heavy even for her strong arms; but she stopped halfway between stove and sink and said, "You don't hate him, do you?"

Rob laughed at once, the oddity of it. Did he hate squirrels in trees, grapes on vines? They pertained more nearly. Yet he wanted to answer both truly and quickly; she would hold the hot kettle there suspended till she heard. So he said "No surely," which freed her to go on at least and pour the water.

She poured it slowly and refilled the kettle from the bucket he'd drawn her and set it on the stove and came back to sit again, a different chair, farther from him, opposite. She was waiting for more.

"I'm speaking only for me," Rob said. "Nobody at home ever mentioned him."

"I'd have guessed that," Hatt said. "I always liked Eva. She had a hard time here. I knew she'd never abuse your father's name, whyever she left him."

He said "Why did she?"

Again Hatt waited; she had not thought of this for a number of years. "I never thought she did. Of course about some things I know less than you—they were neither one *talkers*—but unless you convince me different today, I'll go to my grave (which won't be long) claiming Eva Mayfield is waiting on him still."

"No ma'm, she's not."

"How come?" Hatt said. "What else has she got?" She answered herself—"You, to be sure."

"No ma'm," Rob said.

Hatt thought and decided to let that stand. "Me either," she said. "I repeat, here I am. I have raised a brother, kept a husband clean and fed, brought his two sons to life and trained them. And here I am—I am fifty-seven years old; I'm not even tired and all that's left me is to scrub this old house that I still hate (it was never mine: the Shorter place)." She waited, solemn awhile; then she said "Well, I'm naturally happy."

"Where are your boys?"

"Not here, God knows. The baby is buried in Flanders, I think—gassed,

twenty-five, *Whitby Shorter*. Gid's in Danville selling silk stockings, married
to a woman that can't stand the country. I don't much blame her; she was
raised on a hog farm a mile from here. I see them at Christmas when they
ask me down, no pride at all." Her whole face smiled, raw as a flayed dog.

Rob said "You'll live."

"I'm *living*, thank you." She nodded and stood and went to the sink. She
turned her back and began to wash. "When have you seen your mother?"
she said.

"A month or so."

"You don't know exactly?"

"Yes. Thirty-four days."

"How was she doing then?"

"The same," Rob said. "She is always the same."

"That don't tell me much," Hatt said. "It's been some time."

"You'd know her."

"Is she pretty? She was pretty as a girl."

Rob stood, reached into the pocket of his coat and found an oval velvet
case. He opened it, looked a moment, then stepped toward Hatt and offered
it to her.

"I'd ruin it; I'm wet."

So he held it for her—Eva, a girl, the miniature made from a picture taken
just before her commencement, ordered by her father before the marriage
but kept through the bad times and given by him to Rob on his twenty-first
a month ago. She was turned to her right and showed only one eye; but all
her hair was drawn round and fell down her visible shoulder, bare and full
for her age. She wore a gold chain that had been her mother's (never worn
since by anyone). Rob studied it again as carefully as Hatt. Despite his life,
what he felt was pride—in the chance to carry and show such a likeness of
what had once been alive and available, even in this house, for actual witness; what was still (only hours from here) as grand in its darker less promising way.

"That's her," Hatt said. "And she's lasted, you say?"

"Very well," he said. "If you'd never seen her, you'd know her from this.
It was given to me just recently."

Still looking, Hatt said, "She would last, wouldn't she? She wouldn't
take wear; she would not *take* it. You can choose that, you know—oh up to
a point. I'm worn to the socket; and still I'll live, maybe thirty more years." Hatt
turned back to work. "Is she happy at all?"

"Yes ma'm. Quite a lot."

"Doing what?" Hatt said.

"Her father, tending him. He takes a lot of care."

"He's still alive? Lord God, he's a hundred."

"Oh no," Rob said. "It just seems long. He has strokes regularly; spells with his heart."

Hatt said, "Well, a job's a job."

"I don't know," Rob said. "There's all grades of jobs."

"What's yours?" Hatt said. "You told me; I forgot." She was almost finished; she was scouring the pans.

"No ma'm, I didn't. I've made two or three little messes since school, but I'm out of work now. Plan to be back Monday; money's running out!"

"Down at home?"

"No in Goshen."

"Dipping water? Bathing ladies?" She glanced back, laughing. "They like good rubs, the old ones specially. You'd be just the ticket, strong hands and back!"

"I would," he said, "if my heart didn't fail. The Kendals have bad hearts."

"Don't worry," Hatt said. "You're pure Mayfield, to look at at least—my father, God help you." She had not stopped smiling. "But you were talking jobs."

"Road-building," he said. "Through Goshen Pass soon as spring really settles. Dynamite and rockslides; I may not live! I'm signing-on Monday."

Her smile didn't vanish but underwent a stiffening, the flush of pain behind it; her teeth looked dry. "You're leaving me then?"

Rob thought it was banter, mock family-pleading. "Afraid so," he said. "I never promised more."

"And you're not going home to Eva either?"

He saw she was earnest; had she broken a little, out here scot-alone? "No ma'm, least of all. I'm not needed there."

"Who are you trying to kill?" Hatt said. Her skin had tightened with the force of her anger.

He tried smiling; felt its uselessness and took two steps back, pocketing the picture. "Maybe me," he said. It seemed fresh knowledge but undoubtable.

Hatt said "I could help you."

"By keeping me?"

"Yes."

"Here on this hill?"

"I'll close this tomorrow and bury the key if you'll say the word. Goshen or Lynchburg, Fontaine even. I'm a well-known cook and I'm neat as a bird, eat practically nothing, sew like a spider." Flat in abjection, she was cheering herself. It all was true but she offered it as fun.

Rob smiled to help her, but he also weighed her offer. To his conscious surprise, he felt himself standing at the edge of a choice he had not made before—to ask for a life or to take the life offered (they'd been offered before).

"I mean it," Hatt said.

"I know you do."

"What have you got better?"

He tried to think.

"I knew the minute you drove up last night, you were bad off as me— once I seen your face."

"I am," he said.

"Do something about it."

"I want to," he said.

"Eva won't—"

He raised a hand; his eyes crouched inward. He intended to stop her. And she saw her mistake, flushed hot with regret. But his gesture held on, a warning, *listen.*

Steps on the backporch, the door, the hall. "Miss Hattie?" A boy's voice. She said "All right."

A young Negro man—light-skinned, tall, lean—opened slowly, took a step toward them and stopped. "I saw you had company, car out yonder." He pointed through the wall.

"I do," she said. "It's Forrest's boy."

The man nodded to her; he had not looked to Rob. "I knew that," he said. He brought his hand up, a clean letter in it, and crossed the space between him and Rob. "This just come for you. They ask me to bring it." He pointed again—toward town, the mail.

Hatt said, "This is Grainger, Rob. He helps me on Saturdays."

Rob nodded half-smiling and took the letter—his mother's script, forwarded from Goshen. Grainger's empty hand stayed out so he shook it.

"They didn't know who you was at the Mail; thought you was your granddaddy. I told them better. I figured you was here."

Rob said "A little visit," but his eyes and attention were all on the letter.

"Yes sir," Grainger said. "We been waiting on you." He saw he was ignored and understood the reason; but he said to Hatt, "Ain't we waiting, Miss Hatt?" He was not ready yet to leave for the yard.

"We were," she said. "Fools forever! He's leaving any minute. Look at him while you can."

Grainger looked, frankly, gravely.

But Rob said to Hatt, "I can stay through Monday if you've got room for me."

"*Room?*" she said. "I could put up the veterans of the Rainbow Division, no two in a bed; and Grainger could cook—he's a good *egg* cook."

"Yes ma'm," Grainger said.

"Then I'll go shave," Rob said. "The day looks bright. Maybe I can help Grainger some, outdoors." He was smiling but the sealed letter chilled his hand.

Grainger said "Yes sir."

Hatt said "Take your water." She moved toward the steaming spitting kettle, a service planned in advance, now rendered.

4

When he'd read the letter a single time, standing by his bed, he carefully returned it to its envelope and opened his small grip and buried it carefully— its edges straight, right angles to the grip—beneath his clean linen (washed in Goshen by his landlady, free). Then he went to the washstand and felt the kettle with the palms of both hands, not gingerly but reckless. It still was scalding so he poured it out, threw off his coat, fished out his razor, his badger-brush, the bar of castile soap worn to a coin, and lathered as best he could and shaved. An action as unpleasant as any in his life, though it gave him the silent minutes of thought in which he considered his mother's refusals and generated his own reply. Finished, wiped clean, he slapped on cold raw alcohol and, every pore howling, emptied the water in the china slopjar.

Then he wiped the basin entirely clean of stubble and poured in the last two inches of water, smoking still, and went to his coat and found the velvet picture case, opened it and carefully slipped out the porcelain on which the image lay, had lain these years. Eva as he all but remembered her—she'd been this nearly, in his earliest memories; this grand at least.

He took it to the basin and with both hands gently laid it in the water; let it rest for a minute—the face survived. Then he reached in again and scrubbed it with his thumbs till the water was pale brown, the porcelain white. He emptied that water too and dried the plate thoroughly, returned it to its case—a picture of nothing, a sheet of white china polished and ready—and put it into his pocket.

Then he hooked on his collar and knotted his tie and went to the window and searched the view, a far round hill crowned with trees that were starting the annual revival. New yellow leaves hung like fume on black limbs; some scrubby pasture with a scrubby cow, udder shrunk and slack as an empty glove; a single dead tree at the edge of the yard, long dead, stripped of bark by years of weather till it stood in naked simplicity more nearly like a man-made thing than a former life (a giant machine for lifting loads, a multiple gallows); a few outbuildings all standing by little more than faith and grace, rotten at the ground, rotted halfway up; and Grainger in a small patch of garden, plowing with an old one-wheeled push-plow whose squeak Rob could hear, even high as he was and protected by glass. The sight of Grainger's strength—in wrists, neck, shoulders—the speed of his gait as he scored hard dirt produced in Rob the one plain fact he had known all day, the one thing known which brought him hope, a chance of pleasure, rest: "That nigger can show me where to buy cheap liquor."

Among the many facts which this room offered for use and help, unknown to Rob, was the glass he looked through, the bubbled pane. His mother had held him to that same glass a thousand times in three long months as she waited for strength after his hard assault, strength to bear him away (or draw him behind her in her own fast wake). His father had seen him through that same glass on the day Eva left this house for good and changed many lives.

Rob repeated what he knew, a saving kernel in general famine—"Hatt's man will help me."

5

April 22, 1925

Dear Mother,

I would thank you for your careful letter except that I don't feel thanks are in order. I know that I asked—and hurt you by leaving (why else would I leave?)—and I know you took pains to speak your full mind. But also you gave pain and gave it so strong that I'm just now coming up for breath and light, to see can I breathe and is it still day. You should be more careful—I speak from respect and long years' experience—because you are fitted with terrible weapons; and as I should have known, the worst is your voice: the things you know and can say, and will. Well, the worst is your face—my memories of hard times I've caused your face—but your voice, on paper, can still cut rock. Not that I'm any rock—fewer words would have worked to silence me, very nicely too—but I split anyhow into numerous pieces for several days. I want you to know.

The letter found me in Bracey at Aunt Hatt's. I had driven down there, not to harm anybody, least of all you (barring your letter, I never would have told you I went at all), but out of curiosity and time on my hands. Was anybody still there? Had anybody ever been? Would any of them know me?

Two of them did—Aunt Hatt, who said I was pure Mayfield (old Robinson
my namesake), and a colored boy who helps her out (Grainger, who said he
never saw you but worked for my father and so knew me on sight at once). And
I was hoping to have a day or two to talk to them about various things—they
were welcoming me; the weather was dry—when your letter came, in Grainger's
hand, sent up the hill to that house by him, the house you knew, where I was
born; you are still all in it, especially upstairs; you didn't need to speak, not
while I was there anyhow. I was in the process of coming to understand a thing
or two—one of them was you as a girl—and I hadn't intended to stay long; but
you took care of that.

The letter got to me about noon; and by six I was well on my way to forgetting it, and you. I had to wait till then because Grainger was plowing and
couldn't stop to lead me to the nigger bootlegger; and since I had to fill that
time somehow—I was already hurting—I called Aunt Hatt to come upstairs
and said would she kindly help me out? She had already offered help numerous times—she is all alone—though surely she never planned to have her seriousness tested so soon and in such a hard way, but anyhow she said "Yes" of
course; so I said, "Whether you know it or not, two of my ancestors killed themselves; and I'm wondering—what's your advice for me?" I handed her your letter. She took it and saw your hand and put her big hand across my lips and
said "God shut him up" with a broad deep smile. Did she smile all the time
when you lived there? Is she maybe a little simple by now? Simple or not, she
sat down by me on the edge of the bed where she said I was born and read it
through slowly, tracing lines with her finger; and then when she finished, she
couldn't look up—just would not face me—but stared on down at your sig-
nature and finally said "That's your decision, Son."

I decided to live, not that minute though. I don't think she meant to scare
me but she did. She meant to tell the truth like you; and she did (will I ever
have the luck to meet a lady that can lie; tell me just what I need, not what I
ask?). No it took a little while to make up my mind; and I spent the time hearing Aunt Hatt tell all she thought I should know. She said at the end it was
all she knew. It may not have been. But it surely was enough to help me around
some of what has lain across my path since I heard there was a path and that
I must take it. I mean you mostly, and Father (though he has not been a sizable worry, ever for me—anyhow now I know a lot more about him; Hatt says
he is happy and, as I've said before, I don't think she knows any ways to lie. Of
course she hasn't seen him for several years now since her younger boy Whitby
was killed in Belgium and Father came down to stay a few days and see her
through or so she says). She helped me to recognize you both as children; and
since I am likely to stay one myself, I can greet both of you—as you were then,

before me—and wish you the luck you will not have. The luck that would have left you safe enough, free enough, to allow you to love not honor me—your freezing offer, honor. I never was honorable and never want to be.

So the child got drunk by dark as I said and did a good deal of raving around in the local hills—some dangerous driving, mechanical damage (cost me fourteen dollars); and I cut myself, not in very much earnest as I already hinted but enough to scare Grainger who was with me (sober) and made him half-haul and half-persuade me to go home to Hatt's and try to sleep. So he drove me there after mending a puncture in night thick as grease; and what I discovered in no time at all was that whatever Aunt Hatt is good at, and she claims wide skills, she is what I would call a piss-poor nurse for a drunk. Pardon French.

This is all meant to be fairly painful, you see—just a boy, make allowance.

The first thing she did was to start warming milk—I should drink hot milk; you know you're in trouble when they start heating milk—so I waited for that, laid down on the old leather couch in the hall outside the kitchen and waited in peace (peaceful to onlookers; different within, though easier by then); and what did I hear in the next five minutes?—her whispering to Grainger, him going outside and coming back in, then some more low talking, then the awful sound of pouring. She had given Grainger orders to bring her my liquor and was pouring it out in her old slop-pail. Her idea of help. Poured the last pure drop, and I lay there and listened. I didn't say a thing. I waited till she said, "Can you come drink your milk?" Then I kind of walked in and sat at her table. She had made a bowl of milktoast; and someway, I ate it. She and Grainger watched me awhile; then she told him to bring her some wood—to get him out. When she had us alone she of course said "Why?" and I think I told her. You already know and I thought she did, though another thing I'm coming to know about women is that none of them understands forgetfulness, that a sane strong man might need to forget a thing or two (temporarily of course)—no women I've met. Why is that, do you think? Are they scared the thing you'll forget is them, and permanently? Why have they ever doubted their strength?

Then she and Grainger got me upstairs and put me to bed—I was able by then; but I let them do it: most fun they'd had since the big ice storm—and scared as I was being there on that hill just started on my comfort and it all wasted in with Hatt's hogslops, I went on to sleep and slept like a great long trip to whatever's in the heart of the ground: not a sound, not a sight, not a soul trying either to harm or help.

Of course I came-to around four o'clock. She'd left a lamp lighted in the corner of my room, dark as Hell outside; and I looked at the little flame and prayed

*a good while. I just kept praying all you told me to pray—"Thy will be done"—
oh for maybe half an hour. So apparently what happened next was God's perfect will. I got out and dressed and made it downstairs without waking Hatt
up; and what I figured was—I thought I was sober—I could get out the back
way and crank my car and find that bootlegger one more time. Hatt sleeps like
a chain on the ocean floor. But Grainger was awake. What hadn't dawned on
me was that I'd been so bad off that evening that Grainger volunteered to sleep
in the downstairs hall on the couch. Do you recall the couch? It must have been
there (must have been at the circumcision of Moses, the making of the hills).
A rock couldn't rest on it, much less Grainger; so when I tipped past him, he
just said "What?" and I said, "You know. You let her ruin me." He said, "I did.
I asked her to stop. I knew what you felt." —"No you don't," I said; "I'm going
back for more." —"And I'm coming," he said. Someway we got out without waking Hatt—maybe she has gone a little deaf too with years—and Grainger did
the driving plus saving my life.*

*He's here with me now. How that worked out was that after we had waked
up the poor bootlegger and bought what he had left (he'd had a big Saturday)—a quart of brandy buried out in a shed—Grainger drove me on to his
place. I've been in worse, been drunk in worse; so we sat down there and before
day broke or I got scared again, Grainger talked to me about his life and I truly
listened. We are half first-cousins according to him—old Robinson grandfa-
thered both him and me. Said he never did know it till my father told him. He
worked for my father from the time we left for a year or so; had grown up in
Maine but came down to Bracey to visit some ancestor named Aunt Veenie and
met his Uncle Forrest Mayfield, your husband, and lived with Forrest as long
as he could; then lived with his Bracey ancestor till she died at past a hundred,
plus serving a year in the army in France—"Digging trenches for white boys
to climb out of into sheets of fire; I stayed low, digging, and here I sit alive as
you"—then came back here and had a dark wife (who is now long-gone up
north somewhere, though he says he expects her eventually) and worked as janitor in the school and some churches. He also reported that my father is happy,
though he has not seen him for some years either and only speaks of him in the
distant past. He has a few books that belonged to Father, just children's books.
He can still read in them. He read me the story of Pocahontas when he'd finished with his own—"She died of a broken heart beneath foreign skies with
memories of the green woods of east Virginia, the swarming streams, from whose
sweet shallows she is still divided by the thousands of leagues of rolling salt deep
by which she sleeps her longing sleep." I think he recited, though he looked at
the pages and turned them at times. At the end he offered the book to me, saying I might want some part of my father, that he knew it by now; but I left it*

with him since he seemed to care, and anyhow he has been on that rolling deep which I never have.

By then it was light and, all things together (the brandy half-gone), I was feeling pretty firm on my feet again—well, able to stand—so I said would he drive me to Aunt Hatt's again and I'd eat and rest and then head for Goshen? He said was I ready to face her yet? I said "Meaning what?" and he said, "She'll have to abuse you some before she lets go." I said that I had to get my grip someway—it contained a few objects of sentimental value not to mention my drawers—and he said if I'd just wait a little while longer, she'd be at Sunday school and I could get in safe and out unseen. I said "Fair enough" but that I needed something to eat and some air. The house we were in was his old ancestor's and still smelled like her, though it looked clean as Sylvie's or ours for that matter. I ought to have known there was no cafe for twenty miles round, that he'd offer to cook. He did—"Miss Hatt say I cook good eggs"— and I didn't want to harm one more damned soul; so I said I'd be grateful, and he went out and squeezed his old Dominecker hen and cooked me up a breakfast as good as I've seen. I couldn't eat much so I told him to finish, but he said he was not a big eater and didn't. Then he said did I still want to take a walk? I had mentioned air—I was thinking of a ride—but I said "All right," thinking he might have some famed local beautyspot he wanted to show. (Nature has never done much for me. Of course I've never done much for her.)

It was nothing but a little house—one-story, three rooms, painted yellow once, a front porch, a johnny—where he and Father had lived for a while after you and I vanished. He said it had been empty more than a year. Some local boy came home from teaching piano at Johns Hopkins, Baltimore, and moved in to spend a summer for his nerves and wound up shooting himself on the porch in sight of his mother's house across the valley early one morning. She may not have watched—Grainger didn't know that—but he lay there with what was left of his head till way after noon when some passer found him. No takers since then. We walked right in and Grainger took me round it, telling where things had stood, where little things happened. He had been twelve, thirteen years old and had slept on a little cot back in the kitchen. Father taught him to cook. He was naturally neat. He would stay home and clean while Father taught school, go to see his ancestor, help her get around, come back and study in the afternoon (Father made him recite a lesson every night—reading and simple figures, household management, a little agriculture, mythology: "Ladies changing to trees; being stole by bulls, great birds, swans, eagles!"); then he'd start their dinner and Father would come. He showed me Father's room. The bed was still there—they had got it all furnished—a narrow child's bed with side-rails Grainger had lengthened for Father so his legs could stretch.

It was Grainger's site, see? He wanted to show it. He was still proud of it. So I let him talk on and listened politely but didn't really calculate where he would end. He said, "Listen, you've left the only home you got. You hurting all over. You could rent this place, get a job around here—teach school, clerk store—and I'd move in here and keep it nice for you. Or I could still stay at Miss Veenie's where I am and walk over here—it ain't any ways. That'd help you a lot."

I am in demand. Mother, understand this—there are numerous people by now, none crazy, who have asked to spend full time with me. I am not bragging now; I am hoping to show you—they recognize something, and in me. I've asked myself what in God's name it is—Aunt Rena, Min, Hatt, even Sylvie, now Grainger—and I think I know: they see me in need and they see I am loyal which means to them that I've got gold to give. I have. They are right. But not for them. I must choose my own and already have.

I thanked him and said someday I might need a set-up like that and would call on him then. He said "You need it now," a little harder than he should have; so I thought it was time to conclude the tour and dodge Aunt Hatt and head for Goshen. I could drive by then—I was clear as the day, which was already perfect—but I let Grainger do it so as not to hurt him too far; and since my hands were idle awhile, they occupied themselves with the rest of the brandy. Grainger never said "No"—a true drunkard's friend—and by the time we pulled up in Hatt's poor yard, I had fallen into something like the Sleep of the Just (Just couldn't stand up!).

When I knew myself again, we were three-fourths to Goshen. It was midafternoon and Grainger was driving like he had good sense and knew my will. Maybe he does. I sat up as best I could and looked out (try that after sleeping several hours in a Chevrolet on mountain roads and you full of homemade-brandy and eggs). I said "What's this?" and Grainger said, "It's help. Going where you said." So I laid back and he got us on in to the edge of Goshen and then stopped and said, "Can you drive on from here?" I could but I said "What about you?" of course. He said, "I'll head on back if you're ready." — "How?" I said; "It'll be dark soon. These are mountains, boy. You fall and you're gone." He said that was all right; so I had to say, "No, come on with me and stay till tomorrow; and I'll get you over to the downhill train." He nodded to that and rolled ahead and left me with something like half a mile to decide two things— a place that would take a man looking and smelling like me, plus a bed for a Negro in a county where Negroes are scarce as smiles. I knew my old widow had meant what she said; and at first I thought we should just move on to the country beyond and sleep on the ground (I had that afghan you gave me years ago); but then I remembered a place I'd passed on the far side of town, rundown

but big, an old-time resort. I'd seen a Negro girl out sweeping the yard there,
so at least I knew Grainger wouldn't scare them dead. I guided him to it; and
when we pulled up in front he said, "You don't care nothing about yourself. You
ain't staying here." —"We got to," I said.

And three days later, we're still staying here—me in the main building,
him in some old quarters left out back. I'm waiting on the foreman of the
roadbuilding gang and so now is Grainger. A true Mayfield. He has got a job
already and decided to stay. A number of reasons, all of them simple.

This whole thing is simple. What I'm saying in all the above is this—all
this is very simple: what is wrong with me. I am just twenty-one. I have just
started this. I can be turned around. It could easily be helped.

Help then,
Love,
Rob

6

Rob mailed his letter in the late afternoon; then walked awhile to clear his
head and hands; then ate a light supper in the hotel dining room, empty but
for him and the owner Mr. Hutchins and Grainger who, as one of his jobs,
helped Della serve what little there was (Della being the girl Rob had seen
in the yard, the cook and maid). Then he sat on the porch and listened again
to Mr. Hutchins' plans to rejuvenate his property in hopes of a new influx
of guests provided by the road that was coming through—"There are people
right now all over Virginia just as sick as dogs and no way to get here for this
good air and this stinking water but that mountain track that's killed more
dozens than I'd care to admit. Not even counting Maryland and Washington and your poor state. You build that road and I'll be here ready."

Rob said, "Will you have a doctor by then? You'll need a doctor." He
referred to the fact that Mr. Hutchins' wife had been in Lynchburg six
weeks apparently to keep a sick daughter under doctor's care.

Mr. Hutchins said, "*They'll* be here, have to beat them back with sticks
when they see that traffic all green with money. They follow the color *green*
if you notice. That's been my experience. You may have doctors in your family that are saints."

Rob said, "No sir, we are sick as dogs too. Why you think I'm here?"

Mr. Hutchins said, "*Smart* but you're several months early."

Rob said "Do or die" and excused himself and went to his room. There he
lit his lamp and tried to write again—a note to his Aunt Hatt: apology and an

explanation of Grainger's disappearance, a promise to come back later that summer in perfect shape and make it up to her and be a loyal nephew—but after two starts, there seemed no need. She would either forgive him in the weeks of silence or add him to the roll of those who'd left her and could never earn pardon. Then he stood to undress and was down to his skin when a voice said "Rob?" beyond his door—Grainger, whispering. Rob half-opened on him and saw he was alone and said, "Step in. Make yourself at home. I'm bound for the arms of Morpheus" (Grainger had been coming to his room each night with the stated intent of discussing the day, their chances for life here, but really—Rob knew—to check on his health, the state of his mind). Rob went to the bed and entered it deftly as though this were winter, not warming April.

Grainger came in and shut the heavy door behind him and sat in the one straight chair by the lamp and said, "I have got something serious to ask you. I'm older than you and have wasted enough of my time on liars; so please tell me true—you honest in saying you mean to stay here?"

"All depends," Rob said.

"On what please?"

"On whether I get a decent job tomorrow, whether I can do the work once it begins (I've never built nothing), whether anybody back home should need me. Hell, Grainger, I could die in my sleep tonight."

Grainger studied him hard by the warm steady light—the wide chest propped dark against the dark walnut, muscled as though he had hauled great burdens in heavy harness since the day he could walk, not swum through a life like warm bathwater; the face with its calm breadths on which you could lay your whole flat hand if the skin itself didn't threaten to burn with a fierce life flickering out from the eyes which could watch you as steady as a picture of Jesus, as full as Jesus of the promise to speak and stay at hand till all wounds healed, perfect peace arrived. Grainger smiled. "You not dying no night soon, less some girl kill you."

"Then I'm safe," Rob said. "Don't know but one girl from here to Buena Vista and she works nights."

"Mine too," Grainger said.

"You getting into Della? You're moving, boy."

Grainger laughed a little, nodding; but then he said, "Listen, I'm lying again. Della's nice to me but I ain't touched her once and may not never."

"You've got *my* permission," Rob said. "Go to it."

Grainger nodded again. "If I need to go."

"You'll need to," Rob said, "in this good air."

Grainger thought; then said, "It puts the stiffening in you all right; but I'm waiting, I guess."

"What on?" Rob said. "Della's hot as a pistol. I had to just leave this room this morning—she was spreading my bed and giving off power."

Grainger said "On Gracie."

"If she's ever coming back, you taking a little fun here won't stop her."

"Yes it would," Grainger said. "I feel like it would."

Rob said "Is she worth it?"

Grainger said, "Nobody asked me that before."

Rob wanted to ask his pardon but couldn't.

"She used to be anyhow—to me, just me. Everybody else but me called her trash—Miss Veenie, your daddy."

"What did you call her?"

Grainger visibly retired into memory, pictures. Then he said, "Nice. She was just the nicest somebody I ever knew." He seemed prepared to stop.

"What way?" Rob said.

"Every way you can mention—at the stove, in the bed, at church; she could sing. Lot of other women got Gracie beat for looks but she suited me. I could watch her all evening. I could sit here right now and watch her till morning, if she was where you are, just to see her wake up and take first light—an easy riser; she can speak right off, don't have to go dragging around till noon. First time she pass a whole night by me, after Miss Veenie die, I'm lying there watching her and day creeping in; and she breathe deep once (her eyes still shut) and say out loud, 'I am certainly pleased.' " Grainger stopped again. "So I'm waiting on her."

Rob said, "Go to it. But my father—what did he have against her?"

"Same thing everybody did. '*She after your money.*' So what if she is? Ain't nothing but money. Nobody but me dug trenches to get it; let me give it where I please. No, money scares people. Scared em terrible in 1919, I tell you—colored boys coming home from the U.S. Army, shovels in one hand and money in the other. Scared people to death; thought we'd buy up land, you see, and own the damn world. Two or three did, little poor piece of dirt; but you want to know the truth?"

"Yes."

"You want to know who saved the world from niggerboys?"

"Sure."

"Mr. Henry Ford."

"How?"

"Model T. Every nigger had to have one, poured his money down it, saved the land for white folks." Grainger ended smiling.

"Good thing," Rob said, smiling also. But tired as he was, he would not be derailed by a joke, even true. "Why did my father care either way?" he said. "You had left him by then."

"He wanted me to get some more education. Wanted me to buy it with my army pay. I was twenty-seven years old and hadn't been to school since I left home in Maine—1904—except what he taught me when I lived with him and those little children's books I read through the years. When the Armistice was over, he got my address in France from Miss Veenie; hadn't heard from him once in all that digging, and him about the only one I knew that could write. He wrote to me then and said was I still alive and, if so, take my money and come to this school he was teaching at in Richmond; said I wasn't too old and could better myself for the time Miss Veenie died and I was alone; said he would help me again, all he could. He was teaching niggers how to write their name, read about old gods."

"You turned him down."

Grainger nodded. "Right flat. I didn't tell myself I was going to though. I got home that April on a boat to Norfolk; and I headed straight to Bracey to know was she dead—Miss Veenie, a hundred and four years old. She was picking cotton! Or claimed she was; her mind came and went. She could walk in the yard, kick the chickens some; but she hadn't picked cotton in eight or ten years. Picked *me* was what—picked on me terrible: buy her this or that, warm her up, knock her up (said she wanted a baby). I knew it was age and wouldn't last long; and I knew she had been good to me as anybody—three times better—but she wore me down those first weeks at home (I was long out of practice); so I was half-thinking about your daddy's suggestion. Hadn't written to him though. Then I come on Gracie, at the church, spring meeting. Hadn't told Miss Veenie I was going even or I'd have had to tote her, and she couldn't hear a cannon (just gave her a big drink of liquor with her supper and laid her in bed); but I headed on down there to listen to some noise. Missed the biggest noise though; she had finally shouted just before I got in, Gracie had. Been on the mourner's bench two whole days, not eating once, just to get religion. See, she was seventeen and time was getting late—you want to get religion as soon as you can, get your habits all set. Well, Gracie got it late (and I never got it); but they said she made up for lost time, shouting. Said she climbed over six rows of heart-pine benches yelling 'Safe, Jesus, safe!' When I walked up though, they had her in the yard—her auntie, old Sandra (her folks were gone, turned out to be dead)— and were giving her little drinks of water from the well. I didn't know what she'd been through, you see; so I stopped right beside her and said 'Where you been?' Back then I thought I was nigger-number-one that had *been* somewhere (I had known her since a baby; she had stayed right in Bracey), and I meant it just for fun; but she looked me dead-straight and said 'Near to Heaven' and I said 'I believe you'—her expression, I mean: she was light as a blaze. I had known her forever; but I hadn't never seen her lit-up like that— nobody else had—so what I told myself (in my head, standing there) was, love at first sight."

"And believed it," Rob said.

"Had to," Grainger said. "Never felt it before, first sight or fiftieth."

"What?" Rob said.

"—That I wanted her company from then on out everywhere I would go."

"Did you tell her that night?"

"No, God," Grainger said. "My first mistake. I ought to said, 'Sandra, I'm taking her now' and carried her with me back to Miss Veenie's then and next morning said to Miss Veenie, 'Here she *is*. She is something I want, first thing in years; so don't say one word that sounds like No.'"

"But you did what?" Rob said.

"Tried to be nice like everybody taught me. See, I hadn't never wanted nobody before—little fun now and then but fun is easy—so I thought you went after people you wanted the same way you went after money or din- ner: smiling and asking. It worked for a while; she had never been asked, just told, and she answered."

"What did she say?"

"Various things; we had three years. At first it was mostly just 'Lead and I'll follow.' And since I was fresh from the U.S. Army, I knew how to lead!— straight into the woods. We didn't come out but to eat and sleep. What I'm telling you is, it was new to me. I had been kept back by different ones—your daddy, Miss Veenie. Not all the way back but far enough so what she was offering was new ground to me. I felt like the white men seeing Pocahontas, first time of all. I don't think she minded—she knew more than me; several ways to Heaven and she'd tried them all. So it wasn't too long till the tune started changing to 'Come here to me; eat out of my hand.' I heard her changing and I came right on. What I am—you know it—is obedient. To people I love. No other way to thank em."

Rob nodded and said, "Please blow out the lamp—mosquitoes, I think." When Grainger had done that and sat back down and they were dark, Rob said, "Her hand, the one she was holding out—what was she offering in it to eat?"

Grainger thought awhile. "That was just my way of putting it," he said.

"Putting what though?"

It took him even longer. "I have already told you. You already know. Every member of your family know it by now—Grainger got a good heart. He like to help."

"Thank you," Rob said. "But why is that?"

"That's something I know, worked it out in France. See, all the army gives you is time to think (last thing *you* need to be is a soldier). Reason is, I had such a happy life. Till I got down in them trenches and mud, hadn't nobody done one mean thing to me that I could remember. Good mama and daddy, Miss Veenie good as gold till she got crazy, your daddy, Miss Hatt. Not to say I hadn't heard some hard words now; I'd learned trench-digging in Camp Dix, New Jersey. I'm speaking of deeds; they'd all been kind. And even the Germans weren't aiming at *me*. Nothing personal, you see. So I been good myself, tried to please. Simple as that. Niggers been telling me all my life—you a sapsucking *fool*. I'm the nigger that's warm though, good roof on my head."

"But you didn't please Gracie? Is that why you're waiting?"

In the dark Grainger couldn't test Rob's face for cruelty. The voice seemed only curious though, a further need. "I wouldn't say that. And I don't think if you could find Gracie, she'd say that either. She'd say Grainger done a lot better by her than any other man before him or since. She say that in every message she send me (I taught her to write a few words and she writes em— *Needing to see you, Coming home soon, Cold up here*; I didn't never show her how to spell *cash money*, but I send it to her anyhow; it might be her fare). No I've worked on that a whole lot too, her going to Newark. *Curiosity.* Curiosity is all. I'd lived in Maine and traveled back and forth on Seaboard trains and been to France, been to east New Jersey; so I know what she don't yet—it's all one place; there are just different people. She learning that in Newark, put it in her last message—*Nobody nice as you north of you.*"

"When is she coming then?"

"When she get ready."

"How will she find you, off in the mountains?"

"I already wrote her my new address. Told her my plans."

"What are they?" Rob said.

"To stay by you long as I'm helping out or till she need me worse." Grainger said it as fact, expecting no reward now or ever, only the chance to pass what time still stretched before him in ways he understood and had been good at.

And no reward came from Rob. Silence. Then the sound of him sliding down flat on the bed, a deep sigh addressed to sleep, hopeful greeting.

The dry sound of skin on cloth, all dark, came over Grainger like word of refusal, a bad long minute of possible death. He worked to survive. In a low voice, low enough to leave Rob asleep if he'd already gone, he said "You believe me?"

Considerable silence; then Rob's voice, normal. "I believe you," he said. Exhausted as he was from his own hard day, his effort to tell a whole truth to his mother and endure the tale, Rob thought he believed what Grainger had offered, a pitiful fool's life story to now, and thought he could bear Grainger's gamble on him. Even fully awake and his mind at ease, Rob would not have thought to search farther in, would not have believed that a search through Grainger's omissions and lies would have yielded the real help Grainger could give, the lifelines extending toward a center of rest in the scattered heart of his hurtful family—the dream Grainger dreamt that night for instance.

7

A boy again, Grainger was seated on a train that moved through successions of day and night as he stared out the window at fields and towns in the gradual process of undergoing spring—leaves, blossoms, grass. There were several more passengers; but he was alone, a small wicker satchel in the rack overhead (his father's, containing his change of clothes). He thought as he rode through the various days that he had no baggage or worry but the satchel—young as he was he could handle that—and he thought he was headed to his great-great-great-grandmother's, Veenie's in Virginia. Simple destination. She would be there to meet him, give him all he lacked. So he thought he was happy and smiled at himself in the window-pane whenever they passed through tunnels or darkness. He thought that he only needed to wait; his trip would *happen* like spring to the land. Then the train stopped awhile—no town, open country—and the whitehaired Seaboard conductor came to him and smiled and said, "I have got you a new place to sit. Good place. You follow me." The conductor reached up and brought down the satchel and said "Is that all?" When Grainger said "Yes sir," then he led the way on back through cars—white cars, black cars—to a final car with a single seat. He pointed Grainger to it and stowed the satchel gently in the single rack and then, still smiling, the conductor said, "Now you're sure you've got your message?" Grainger said "Yes sir" and the old man left. Alone, he was miserable. He did not have a message and did not understand, could not even think what a *message* was or who one would be for if it blossomed now in the palm of his hand (Miss Veenie needed nothing; she was well-off in life as his father said). He stood on the plush seat and searched through his satchel—two union suits, two pants, two shirts, a pocketknife, and a bar of soap. Nothing new or useful to anyone but him. So he rode on in misery another long while till the old man came back and said "You're there" and took down the satchel and said again "You've got it?" and led him to the steps down. The train was in Bracey, stopping at the station. The old man said, "You've been a good rider" and went down first with his satchel; then lifted him slowly through warm air to the ground and said "Goodbye" and climbed back and vanished. No Veenie in sight, no other soul. *They know I have let them down and are gone. I am left here forever, nobody but me.* Then a man stood above him—white, the age of a father—and promised kindness, though he did not smile. He held out a big hand and said, "Please. You've brought it. It's meant for me." Grainger said, "No sir. I am just what you see." The man's face clouded, sadness not meanness; and he said, "You're sure? Try hard to recall." Then Grainger knew, sudden and whole, and said it out quickly, "Forget all that please. All that's over. They say tend to me." The man, whom he saw then as Forrest, smiled and reached for his hand. No thought of Veenie or the long trip behind him.

In his sleep on his back in cold mountain air, Grainger also smiled, though alone and dark, stretched his long legs and rolled to his belly. Long hours of rest.

8

Rob also dreamt—after Grainger, toward morning—a dream which brought him no news or rest, only further pictures of a knowledge he was powerless to use or abandon. He stood in the door of an army barracks—French, in Flanders. He thought he was searching for his Cousin Whitby Shorter, had been sent by his Aunt Hatt to rescue Whitby. The room was huge—a low room of rough dark lumber, unpainted—and seemed entirely empty of all but its furniture: many rows of beds. So his search must consist of walking down the rows, each separate bed. They were oddly built; same wood as the walls, crudely nailed into long deep flatbottomed boxes like coffins or mangers. One by one they were empty of all but bedding. Each contained an identical wad of bedding, a brown cocoon of quilted cloth thrown back by the rudely awakened sleeper to show his leavings, dried plaques of stain—some colorless, some bloody, some excremental. No single exception; all were fouled, though none gave clues to the occupant's name or whether he meant to return here at night—whether rest were possible in this dry filth—or had left in revulsion or spilled all his wastes through a wound on the field. So why was he hunting a cousin here? No hope of his presence. He would be underground, returning to dirt, or fighting above it. Rob thought he would give up and turned to leave, head back out the door. The last row he walked down was like all the others except that on one bed midway down its length a person was seated, lap covered by quilting, toward whom Rob walked—his mother, a girl, long-haired, in tears. She did not see him. The search was for her.

MAY–SEPTEMBER 1925

May 27, 1925

Dear Alice,

I feel awful not to have written you till now. But since it is really the only thing I feel awful about at present and since I am devoting an hour of my twentieth birthday to you—today: you forgot but how could you remember? I never told you—I trust you will forgive me and reply very soon and set a firm date for your promised visit here. Set it late in June though or early July—come for the Fourth and maybe I will explode—since Father said, when Mother showed him Dr. Matthews' letter, that I must rest on for at least two months, just sitting and staring. Two months will be over on June 29th if I live till then. Oh my chest is strong—I doubt it was ever weak—but my nerves may be hanging in strips by then from all this stillness. It has always just been nerves from the start.

No actually, they are strong now too; and when I have told you the news that follows, I think you will guess the remedy that's worked when nothing else seemed to—your father's medicines, your mother's good food, even your own high spirits and jokes.

You remember that a strange Negro turned up to get us in a strange Chevrolet? That was only the first two surprising links in a chain that ends, I think, in a heart—a large heart containing a wonderful face, strange to me till now but likely to heal, I fervently hope. You remember also that Father never wrote us more than duty demanded, so how could we know that he'd done a good deal of moving in our absence? The Negro again was just the first hint. He'd been hired in April to help Father put the old place here in shape for what Father guesses is a golden wave of guests heading toward us on a new east-west road running through the mountains which is just now beginning to be widened from this end (the previous quick way to get here from eastward was to make prior plans to be born on the spot).

One of the builders is Robinson Mayfield. He is the face contained in the heart toward which all the recent surprises lead. Twenty-one years old and not well himself; with him also it is nothing but nerves.

From the start of it though. The trip home was rough. I was weak from all the resting; and the new Negro—Grainger—told us nothing substantial of the changes at home, only that he'd been hired shortly before and that the Chevrolet belonged to a man who was boarding with us while he worked on the road. Father's old car was laid up as usual, so he'd offered the man a bargain on a week's rent if we could use the Chevy. It got us here at least; but I won't be needing Grainger to drive me again—Donner and Blitzen! And what was waiting at first was just Father. He may not have written much; but he has been worried (I told you he lost his own mother and a sister with galloping consumption, though long years ago). The signs of that were that he met us in the yard, kissed Mother and me (he is not a big kisser), tipped Grainger a dollar in the presence of us all (my father and dollars are magnet-and-iron), and then said Della would show me my room. I told him I remembered quite well where it was—it had been mine forever—but he said "No you don't"; and he and Della led me (Della is the maid). He had changed my room—every stick, every picture—and set me up in what used to be the old Bridal Suite on the southeast corner: not a suite, to be sure, and no bridal couple ever crossed the doorsill in my recollection, but a big high room with good exposure to cross-ventilation. All for my chest, when all my chest needs is just a little padding! Well, it was very thoughtful and I did appreciate it, even if I noticed he'd neglected to paint the old walls (the chest may fail; no need to splurge yet!). But when they all went out and left me to rest for the hour before supper, I was low as a mole. And because of Father. In spite of your father's long letter explaining that now I was largely out of danger and could live my life, here he was intending to shore me up in a run-down resort that if he poured thousands of dollars into would not draw flies, much less rich Virginians if he offered to bring them here in his arms over that new road (and all he intends to pour is a trickle—ten dollars here, thirty-five dollars there). And if I am rushing toward death, what a place to die!—a hotel swarming with loud old ladies.

I am not going to die, but I prayed to then. I'll admit it to you. I lay on my bed on April 30th and prayed to God to strike me with everything they thought I had—failed lungs, failed mind—but make it quick please. I meant it so much that I said it out loud, some part of it anyhow—I was in the Bridal Suite; nobody was near.

Or so I thought (my mind is weak).

Somebody knocked in the midst of a groan. I thought it was Father or Mother at least; so I had to say "All right," still lying down. And there stood this strange man looking concerned. I sat straight up and said "You're in the wrong pew" (I was fully dressed). He said, "I was hoping to save a life—heard a soul in distress." I said "Not me." He said, "Give a groan; let me hear you groan." I gave a little groan and he said, "You're lying; that was you just now." Well, in spite of his looks, he was dirty as a clam (he had just come from work—blasting rock since dawn—but I didn't know that); so I said, "So what please? And who are you?" He said "I'm the groom." I must have looked baffled; so he said, "The bridegroom. I live in the other half of the Bridal Suite." (It turned out he did—our new paying guest; Father had given him the other room; mine was second-best.) I said, "What's the groom's name then, please sir?"; and he said, "Rob Mayfield the Second, and willing." I decided not to go a step farther that way but said, "I am Rachel Hutchins, just back." He said, "I know. Know all about that." — "Tell me then," I said; "I sure God don't." He waited a whole minute, staring hard at me. "You're better," he said. "In fact, you're well." I said "Who says?" He said "My eyes" and touched his eyes. — "Are they truthful?" I said. He said "You decide" and walked forward to me. So I sat to the edge of the bed for that, my feet on the floor in case Father came—he'd have shot Rob dead. They were brown. I can never tell about brown eyes. "What's the verdict?" he said. I said, "They go very well with your hair; that's as much as I know." — "Or ever will," he said.

I was ready to get mad, but Della walked up to the open door and asked did I want a tray or would I come down? I found I'd decided to trust the eyes. I said I'd join everybody downstairs as soon as I'd washed; and since everybody was nothing but my parents plus Rob Mayfield, I've hardly been back upstairs since then. That was almost a month ago; and more things have grown than just the flowers, mainly my care for Rob.

To tell the pure truth, I will have to say that my care has grown both higher and deeper than Rob's for me. Apparently at least. He often doesn't get back till long past dark and then is tired and eats in the kitchen and is something of a night walker (easing his nerves), and Father watches me like a hawk; so until last weekend I knew little more than the thing I felt, which was happiness to know he was in the world or that I was in a world which offered him— when these recent months I've suspected much worse.

He came in on Saturday evening from work and washed in his room and stretched out to rest on his bed before supper; I knew because I've learned to read his life through walls. I was also "resting," as per Father's orders, though what I was actually doing was straining in every nerve to hear when he'd rise and which way he'd walk. I was testing my strength; could I cause him to come to my door and knock and say something hopeful (the previous two nights he had either been exhausted and had barely spoken or had gone out riding *with some boys on his crew). I was thinking, "Now get up and help me please. Nobody else can need you like me." I was also working against the clock—the dinner bell. Della would be ringing it at six.*

Then with four minutes left, he stood to the floor and waited a little on the rug by his bed and opened his door and walked down to mine and knocked once so lightly as to be heard only by the nearest hound or by Rachel waiting.

To stay still myself, I went to the door and opened it on him; and he said—no greeting, never calling my name—"I know you've got a birthday coming next week. I'll be working of course, and you've got your family; but I'd like to help you celebrate tomorrow afternoon. A picnic maybe."

I said the next three things in backward order—Yes; who had told him?; I would have to ask Father. He said he did not remember, maybe Grainger, and that if I wanted he would speak to Father and assure him of his wish not to tire me out. I thanked him and said No, I'd better handle that; and he said again, "I just want to help you celebrate."

It came true. Nobody ever helped me more. After supper that night— nobody left at table but Father and me, and Della clearing—I said, "Could I ride out with Rob tomorrow and breathe a little hill air and eat a good lunch?" He stared down awhile and then just said "Whose idea is it?" — "Rob's," I said. "He is trying to help me." He stared awhile longer and gave no sign of answer- ing; so I said, "Do you want me to go on and die?" He looked up and checked me for seriousness and said, "That is not my intention, no." Then he said he'd speak to Rob and, whatever got said, it all came true.

And no lies told. It was just what Rob promised and what I told Father—a smooth ride and fresh air down by the river and Della's cold chicken, a help- ful celebration (I did leave out the celebration part in all my descriptions, before and after, since excitement is supposed to be rat-bane for me). But it was a cel- ebration and as calm as the day. I was weaker than I knew from being cooped- up; and though Rob never once asked was I tired, he used me all day as if he knew what there was to know about my condition and was gauging every move- ment, every question he asked, to strengthen not abuse. In fact there were very few questions at all and none about my life. My guess is he'd heard from Della, through Grainger, some version of the past—Della knows all you know, likely more—and I hope that he has. The last thing I'd want is to be deceitful about my life or the little meager offerings I can make to his needs.

That's what we talked about finally, his life. He thinks it has been poor; it sounds good to me—a father that left them when he was a baby, a mother who watched him as little as possible. When he finished his story (longer than Leviticus and he's just twenty-one) and turned to me, expecting an answer, I said, "Is that a complaint or what?" He thought it over by looking at the moun-

tain (when you come here I'll ask you to draw that mountain; I want it framed near me for the rest of my life); and that gave me a close chance to study him — a long oval face with a high clear forehead, great wide cheekbones like wings laid back from a firm inquisitive nose, a broad mouth that flares (almost shocking in a man). Brown eyes as I said — beautiful but shut to me; by his choice, I think. Strong coarse brown hair, lightening with the long days of work in the sun — his skin of course darkening. (What good is all that to you, you wonder? — none, I guess. You could not construct him from a ream of words; but I have no other likeness to send you except all this letter which is testimony to him. You might well find him an ordinary sight. Mother does.) Anyhow when he had thought, he said, "No I figured you would see. It's an invitation." I had to ask "To what?" though I feared the whole day would collapse right there, and he nearly died laughing. I joined him, confused, but stopped before he did; and when he recovered he said, "You are cured. *Nothing wrong with you." I said, "I agree. Now answer my question." — "To be good to me," he said.*

I'd been doing that! — though it was a relief to have his permission — but being me, I just said "Thank you" (I am bad under pressure as you well know). And he left it there. He didn't say "Thank you Yes or No," but nodded and smiled and ate the last shortleg. So I relaxed too — as far as I could with a satisfied heart! — and after we had talked on some about his road job (which he's flabbergasted to find he enjoys) and Father's grand plans for a tourist magnet (which we both think are crazy), he calmly said, "It's time you were home. That was part of my promise."

So home we went and happy it's been. We have not been off the premises since — together, I mean. Rob's worked, to be sure; but two of the last four evenings we have sat by ourselves on the sideporch and talked. He has still not asked me an unkind question, and I don't think he will. With me he seems determined to live in the present, and you'll know how grand I think that is.

It does of course raise thoughts of the future; but all I can do is hope and be calm, try to get myself into good working-order and accept his simple invitation to be good (to keep you calm let me just explain that the most touching we've done so far is his hand now and then to help me through a door). He plans to board here another few months, at least till the road pushes so far away that the crew can't make it back here in the evening (two more of them are staying here now — young boys and quiet — on Rob's recommendation, which greatly pleases Father and feeds his hopes). Beyond that he says he won't think. But you'll know I do. All I know about love — all I know about simply being good to the needy — is that such contracts are sworn forever. I'm nothing if not lasting.

Certainly this letter has lasted forever. I beg your pardon. But you helped me so much in those weeks at your home; and now I've been silent so long, and apparently ungrateful, that I had to tell you at some full length of the new help, the new chance, that's been offered to me. I am trying to take it this time, for good. But calmly as I said. Another month of calm enforced by Father—another good thing, I begin to suspect.

So make your plans now to come in late June and really visit. By then I hope to be unrecognizable—stronger, a better friend; by then someone you can confide to, not just listen to day after day.

Write me all your news. Warm regards to your parents—don't show this to your Father (in fact burn it), but tell him I am better! Thanks and love to you,

> *Happy birthday to me,*
> *As always,*
> *Rachel*

June 14, 1925

Dear Niles,

Aunt Rena has forwarded your letter; and I take this first chance, my one day off, to tell you that Yes I'm alive and all right. Matter of fact, I am also close by. After leaving you in Staunton with the cowchain and slopjars, I wandered a little and drank a lot and wound up begging a job with Lassiter Construction Company. We are building a road going east through the mountains from Goshen to Roller's Retreat (remember?), and I'm not sure if I can wait to get there.

I am sure, to tell you the pure-God truth. I can wait here forever, the way it feels now. I'm well taken care of on all sides here and the job—third foreman in charge of moving rock (with dynamite; I learned blasting quick)—pays better than I've ever got before and has the added virtue of wearing me down to a nub every evening.

Unfortunately, as various Baptist deacons might say, the nub still works. And the nub is what's getting all the good care (not all, but a good part; one joy at a time though). The nub's care is coming, on the strict Q.T., from a girl that works at the place I'm boarding. Snuff-brown, age nineteen (she thinks), the cook and general-help at this place. I'm whipped a good many nights as I said; but when I'm not and can creep out back where she has her room without being seen by the various watches, then it's all I need; then it's perfect proof of what I have told you these past five years—there are remedies, boy. The world is a doctor if you know who to ask.

Otherwise I spend what hours are left—oh precious few!—being good to another girl. White this time, daughter to the manager of this old dump of a watering hole. Good *in her case mainly means* listening. *She has just turned twenty, been in poor health for years (just home in fact from a stay at a chest place over near Lynchburg, apparently safe now but weak on her pins) and talks a good deal; but tired as I am by the time she gets to me, she does have the power to command attention. My attention anyhow. Partly her looks—she is almost as tall as me and thin, but the main thing about her is hair and eyes. Black horse hair that, old as she is, she still wears long so that, when she starts talking to me at night, it swags round her face and hides her neck like two dense stranglers; and then her face (pale from the months indoors) just hangs on the dark and carries her eyes—the steady thing. They are dark as her hair and hold dead on me. I am the rescue; I know that clearly. She has made me that; chose me from thin air—her name is Rachel Hutchins—and so far I've let her and listened as I said.*

Certainly I'm flattered and since the "staples," so to speak, are coming from another quarter (and no questions asked, no answers expected), I seem to be liking her and looking forward to her. She is by the way no fool at all—no show-off either but a good tough wit, a hard little scrapper (if she's stronger now, it's her own mind that's done it—her parents would make General Pershing nervous, and her Lynchburg doctor sounds like a loud quack); and most of the talk anyhow concerns your old friend and mine, Rob Mayfield the Second.

—Who is as I say doing tolerably well, though sinking right now toward the bed (alone). If the work eases up in a month or so, maybe I can take a Saturday afternoon off and drive down to meet you in the feed-and-seed; and we could tour the churches of Staunton on Sunday. Will I know you at all? Do you wear sleeve garters yet? An isinglass eyeshade?

You won't know me. I am handsome again. Keep me posted please (assuming, that is, that you know something more than the current price of nails; how's your own nub, for instance?). Have you been home yet? Any real news from there?

Ever,
Rob

June 23, 1925

Dearest Rob,

You know me. Others may keep an infinite silence, and God knows I try at appropriate times but finally I burst. So here are the burstings.

Very little has changed. You'd recognize us all if you walked in tonight which of course I frequently pray that you will. Three and a half months is one hundred days, a very hard diet to ask us to eat after twenty-one years.

Well, we eat it is all *and are grateful, I guess, to be all healthy and sham-*

bling along day to day. You'll know what the news has been since you left—barring deaths or the sudden descent of Jesus, you'll know the news here wherever you go, however long you stay. We are dedicated to the way things are, which you also know.

For something to say though, here's how they are. Father has been stronger with the good warm weather. No hot sieges yet so Sylvie and Eva have managed to get him out in the yard several bright mornings. He can stump along between them and sit in the shade in the old wicker rocker (but still as a stone; rocking just sets him wild). What most concerns him now is the palm tree. Slick got it back outdoors the same time as Father; and he likes to watch it and call passers over and tell them its age, which is going on forty, and the whole thrilling story of how Uncle Deward brought it up in his lap (a six-inch seedling) from Gainesville, Florida; a Christmas gift to Eva just after she was born, well before me! It is eight feet tall now—was when you left—and gives every sign of being in the best health of any creature present. Father runs it a close second.

Not that anybody else is really down. I have had the eczema all over my hands since right after you left. Has driven me all but crazy this time—in fact I can't imagine why I haven't gone. Dr. Turner has me wearing thick mittens at night so I won't gouge myself all raw in my sleep. Sleep!—slim chance. If I've slept a solid hour in the last four months, it has gone undetected by me at least. Still I trust to recover. When or how is a secret (can you shed any light?).

Eva's all right—busy of course. I saw the letter you wrote her, Son, unbeknownst to her. I trust you'll excuse me when I tell you why. Sylvie told me you'd written, right after she delivered it (she had been waiting as worried as I); so I didn't say a word but watched Eva closely, from desperate curiosity to hear about you and also because, as you may not know, letters have been the cause of disaster in this house before. I watched but there was nothing to see, nothing I hadn't seen every day of the years since she came back. By suppertime, I was quite upset but held my tongue; and when Eva came in to get Father's tray, Sylvie said, "How is Mister Rob getting on?" Eva turned, as calm as sunrise at sea, and said, "Everybody can rest in peace. He is safe and sound in Goshen, Virginia; has a job all but promised and sends his love." Well, I haven't known her all this time for nothing (Sylvie either). Both of us just said "Good, good" and let her go on. When she got out of earshot, Sylvie said, "Miss Rena, she lying. That was the biggest letter I ever brought here." I told her to hush, but I went on watching. Eva sat with Father extra late that night and to my surprise read to him from the Bible—Mother's Bible that she took from your room (you know roughly how much the Bible means to Eva), gentle parts from the prophets, those promises of help that have been inexplicably delayed. When she left him though, I gave her a while; then went in to her and said, "Is there anything you need me for?" She smiled and tried to say "Such as what?" but her tongue seized on her. I had not seen Eva at a loss in something like twenty years; so I went and touched her, just took her by the wrists and offered to kiss them. She didn't draw back but she shook her head. I walked her to the bed and sat down beside her, still holding one hand. I didn't speak again. If I've learned anything in my life it's to wait. Eva also waited, dry and cold, and finally she looked square at me and said, "He is trying to finish me. Maybe I should let him." I just said "Rob?" She nodded Yes but then said, "Please don't ask any more. I'll talk when I can." I said, "Just this — were you truthful? Is he safe?" She said, "For now. Yes you can sleep easy." I said, "Would you like me to sleep in here? I could make a pallet." She smiled — "No thank you. I am not Mother anyhow. You get your sleep."

Curiously I did. I could barely get through my prayers awake, worn out from waiting; but I got my mittens on and plunged to the depths where I dreamt for what I honestly believe is the first time since Mother died. It concerned you and me being chased through snowy woods by men. I was happy all through it and happiest at the end, that I crawled through to safety for both of us. I was bearing you. You were going to be free. So the next morning I was unusually rested, and Eva had managed to seal herself over. She gave no sign of even remembering our previous words; and I didn't press, warned Sylvie not to. But when more days passed with nothing else from you and Eva never offered me a chance to ask what had struck her so hard, I was forced to act and went for the letter. I have since read it twice (she keeps it on her bureau, plain to all).

I can't say that much of it was news exactly (except your movements and the tales of drinking; you can stop that tomorrow as you say and you must — there have been all sorts of weak minds among the Kendals but never a drunk, so don't be the first one; and even if the Mayfields are sots back to Noah, you break the chain); so it didn't affect me as heavily as Eva. I also know it wasn't meant for me. You are one of the few occasions in my life which I do not regret. I would stand before God Almighty tonight and dare him to name one sin I did you; one time I failed in the work I saw laid down for me the moment you entered this house, a helpless babe. I confess a billion other grave faults, but in you I succeeded.

What failed, Son, was you. Eva won't tell you that because she does not see it and because, above all, you love her so and she can't risk losing that, however she's ignored it — especially now when the years have left her all but alone and will leave her that soon. But I know it with the knowledge of a loving witness who has gone unloved (this is no plea now; you are too far gone; there is noth-

ing you could give me now which I could use; nothing which I could believe in, even). I can and will tell you—you accept gifts badly. You abuse the generous. Children do that and are pardoned for their youth. You are fully a man now and are not forgiven—and will not be, not by me or Father (whose money you've eaten since before you could stand) or your own strange mother (who has loved you, I see now, as best she could in view of her life—and of your cold nature), not even by Sylvie who has told me more than I wanted to hear. People like you who have won heaven's grace bear the largest burden of all, I believe; and bear it you must—learn to take the world's praise, its helpless thanks—or spoil in the way you're spoiling now. You complain of lacks, of long neglect. I cannot in all my admittedly narrow experience recall another human who has been so continuously attended. Most men are solitary marchers, by you; not to speak of women.

Leave us then. By all means, go. And for the sake of mercy, stop begging your mother for what she does not have to give. For your strange reasons, some of which I grant are no fault of yours, you have made us your poison. Have the sense—and simple dignity, Rob—to stop licking at us. Find something that is actually food you can eat, that will offer itself; then eat till it's gone.

Will it seem crazy of me at the end here to reaffirm what you've known for years—you're the love of my life? Simple as that. And I could not be turned around tomorrow—too old, too accustomed, nowhere else to go. So you know you are always welcome here. Anything I have said elsewhere above should not be construed as "banishment," only as the long-thought-out advice, painful for me as you, of one who has at least watched you more steadily these twenty-odd years than any other human breathing air at present.

Everybody sends love or would if I asked them. Don't mention me or any of this in your next to us; but do write soon with calmer news—and remember to include a greeting for Sylvie. She literally pines. She said this week, "This place like a engine without no gas." I told her, "I didn't know you could drive." — *"Can't," she said, "but I sure can* ride."

So can I,
Rena Kendal

July 4, 1925

Dear Mr. Forrest,

Here is Grainger finally. I guess you think it has been a long time but I have kept busy since I come from the war and have not had other reason to write. Thank you for your letter that got to me in France with promise of help. I planned to accept but went home awhile and found duty there. Also decided I better not try a second time and put everybody in misery again like I did before.

I was still young then and had high notions. Miss Polly knew that so I guess she excused me in her heart by now. Tell her please that I feel different now and am truly sorry if she is still there nearby to hear you. I learned right much in my own dealings in these past twenty years trying to keep Miss Veenie and fight the war and live with a wife who has gone off now.

What I am writing you about though is not me but Rob your boy. He turned up in Bracey three months ago to see Miss Hatt. I guess she told you. Curiosity mostly. He got upset and she asked me to watch him. Wasn't much left for me around there and he seem to want me so that landed me with him up here in the high mountains, Goshen. He is building a road and I am helping out at the same hotel where he stay and eat. He has been fair to me, don't notice me much as you did at first, and you know how young he is but here just lately he gone off the track more times than one, drinking heavy and leaning on women, one colored.

Much as I watch him I can't do all, trying to save a little money for my own family all scattered, and you know how much he listen to me, just laugh and leave and do his next wish. Already been in a wreck and a fight, that much known to me, and somebody else bound to get hurt soon, mostly one of his women.

What I'm asking is, you speak to him and find out his trouble and see can you stop him while he still in safety and nobody ruined.

Just thought you would want to know this in time, after all this time. Wishing you the best and to see your face,

Your old friend,
Grainger

Write Rob Mayfield, Hutchins Hotel, Goshen.

July 21, 1925

My dear Robinson,

I am or was your father. Though you can surely have no memories of me, my images of you are clear and correct despite these years; and though you will have grown past knowing, I still hope strongly to see you soon and match valued thoughts against the reality worked by time.

What this constitutes then is an invitation. Will you come here soon and visit me freely for as long as you wish or your job permits? I am myself in vacation now, so am mostly open as to time and duty but have learned from my sister of your whereabouts and work.

I could come there to you if you wish it at all (the mountains have always been good to me, and I have not seen them for many years); but my own hope is that you could find time to come here long enough to meet and talk.

There's a great deal to say, which you might care to hear or need to know; and the house I have is my dead father's house, the Mayfield place. It would be part yours, if I ever die.

You have some cause to blame me, Son—may I call you that? It at least is simple fact, never challenged by any. There are also long due debts to me, never paid or acknowledged—which I've long since canceled. If you find it in your heart to discard a past so long and heavy, the lies and failures made mostly by others (who, whatever their errors, meant you no harm), you will find me ready—even eager now—to begin a friendship, an explanation, a try at amends. Please speak up soon.

Yours ever,
Forrest Mayfield

care of The James Normal Institute
Richmond, Virginia
P.S. You would have a private room here. No lack of space.

July 29, 1925

My dear Rob,

Again I have waited a long time to answer word from you. Waited and listened in the hope I would hear somehow in my empty head a useful answer that would ease my failure and fill your need, punish you and help you. I have even called on God for the words, a course which you know I seldom take, feeling He has enough to trouble His depths without the annoyance of what little gravel you or I pitch in to stir His shallows.

I'm sorry to say though, nothing has come. You picked the wrong mother.

Is that the answer? Could well be, it strikes me now. In which case, in any case, the next thing to do is have your life. I've had mine, you see—am having it daily and for years to come, I trust—and whatever others think about my accidents and choices, I can say in full truth—here in roughly midstream—that I do not, cannot, regret or condemn it. I accuse myself of hurting some feelings, through the ignorance of youth or the need to preserve my sanity and health in the face of another person's claims on me—my mother, your father—but the acts of others were theirs not mine; and I have not tortured myself for them and never intend to. I have paid however. But I've had much pleasure, some deep satisfactions—I've given some—and hope to have more. The surest blight I could fall to now would be the belief that love was the best thing life could give. After years, and the sights I've seen and lived, such a fall is unlikely.

You suffer that blight though, I honestly believe—in relation to me—and now *Rena tells me you have written to say there's a girl up there who has cheered you up in recent weeks and that you are considering a life in harness. Consider it* hard; *let me urge that on you. You have numerous blessings. I can see them all on you—a man, young, bound to no parent (never likely to be; I've told you I'm safe), graced with the open face and manner which the world seeks out and gladly rewards, with a keen able mind (if you'll keep it clear and straight) and a body which can be its own solace alone far more than you'll guess till you've yoked it to the mercy of another body's needs. Forgive me but I'm telling you the little I know.*

I'm not asking here that you care for no one or hoard your gifts so they wither and choke you, just that you give much thought to two things—your family history (mine and *your father's; every day I breathe I believe more strongly that your home is your fate, all laid down and waiting) and your own long future with the few little scraps of freedom you possess. I also suggest that your home is here. I cannot guess where else it might be.*

So bait hook and fish for your own life, by all means. But be sure you cast into water not air and that what you catch will be what you can use.

We are all right here, blessed by lovely weather—bright days but bearable and short cool nights. Father sits out a good deal as Rena may have told you and profits by the passers who stop to talk. A day or two ago I left him for a minute (I mostly sit with him and work at the mending; I'm brown as a field hand, which maybe I'll become); and when I rejoined him, he was entertaining Min Tharrington. She's back with her diploma. Plans to spend the summer here, then has a job teaching in the country near Raleigh. God help her in that; she still seems a good deal too gentle for the world, especially children. But then she's got Tharringtons and Spencers behind her, stretching to Adam (a lot of grit!); and maybe they will gather in her craw soon now and toughen her more. Her looks are already settling down—a good calm face; her eyes are relaxing. She was hoping for you though. I knew that at once so spared her the shame of having to ask by telling her you had a laborer's job, were making good money, and keeping your own close counsel as to news or the promise of a visit. She said "Good, good," though I saw that her view of the summer was marred; but Father broke in and said "Fool, fool." No more nor less. Min or I neither one asked Who? *I gave her your address; she never would have asked.*

Nobody wants to see you more than I. But that in no way cancels what I've said all above here about your own life. Trouble with me always is that I mean everything I say—and I say so much in various directions. I'm not to be trusted, I guess is the moral. But I know I am. Believe me and keep me posted.

Love,
Mother

August 15, 1925

Dear Alice,

We all got your kind letters of thanks earlier this week. I will let Father and Mother speak for themselves (Mother anyhow; Father wouldn't answer an auto-graphed letter from Jesus, in English); but all I can say now—a worn out record!—is thank you, my dear. For your own good company, a tonic in itself (you're the only female I have ever really liked, not to mention trusted—you're the only one worthy who's crossed my path) but maybe most of all for your understanding Rob or my view of Rob. The trick about friends, my few friends at least, is to like their *friends; not to finally decide they are fools or crazy to fall for some crook or crank that they cherish. Not to mention require.*

I think it is now safe to call it that, on both sides. Despite the fact that Rob took to you and arranged those outings, he seemed to me more than a little set back *the whole time you were here and, as you noticed, practically invisible the last few days. So much so that, once you were gone, I asked him about it and he said, grinning widely as he always does when serious, "I know it is wrong but what I believe is, I am the only person alive who can love two people or more at once. Anybody else who tries is a cheat; and I have to leave them, can't stand to watch." I thought and said, "Oh no you are right. Alice is a friend, the first I've had; but Alice would be the first to know I would leave her for you if you said the word." He waited a good while—dark on the porch, Mother ten steps away, Della clearing off supper through the window behind us—and then he said, "What word would it be?" I said, "That's unfortunately for you to discover. I'll know if I hear it." He nodded then—"All right. Give me time. I'll rummage around. You may hear it yet." I said "Please hurry." He said, "I will. I'm ready as you." I asked him "For what?" and he said, "That's more of what I got to find." So I sat on and then said "Hurry" again. He said "What's your rush?" and I laughed and said, "The little time left; I may not last!" He said, "You'll be living ninety years from now." I said, "Not long enough by far." He sat a few minutes more, pleasant quiet; then got up and whispered he needed a walk. I'd walk to Asia of course with him, but Mother was still on duty nearby, and I'm not supposed to breathe deep at night; so I kept my place and have hardly seen him since; he has been so busy, day and dark.*

But late last night he knocked on my door. I was nine-tenths dressed and brushing my hair. I went as I was, barefoot for silence, and opened on him, not certain it was him. I have not seen more than two or three drunks (Father won't let them stay); but I think he was drunk—all oily with sweat, his face unstrung, his eyes skimmed over. He stood straight though and kept his hands down. I said "Good evening." He said "No, bad." I said "I'm sorry" but he said, "Don't be. Just answer one thing; are you still waiting?" I said I was; for a number of things — a place in glory chiefly. I honestly thought he was going to strike me. I still think he was. But I quickly said, "Don't. Please what do you mean?" He said, "For the word that would bring you to me." I said, "Oh that. Lord God, I am there." He said, "No you're not. But wait till Monday. I may know then." I was whispering; he was not — I expected Father's presence momentarily — so I didn't risk asking why Monday was special but just said, "Rob, are you sure you're all right?" He said, "Hell no. Are you waiting or not?" I said I was and he left again.

That was Friday night. This is Saturday noon. Somehow I haven't worried but have been mostly calm — the surest sign yet that, for whatever reason, I am more nearly back to my best true self than in many dark years. Alice, you bear a part of the blame for that rescue! (you and your parents); and whoever commands me in whatever words, whoever I follow or if I stay here and wither alone, I'll remember that always as a gift barely second to any I've received (whatever Rob offers will not be a gift but a serious burden). I hope I have given you more than just care. You laughed a lot here; so I'll treasure that at least — that I caused kind laughter for two good weeks toward the end of a summer which I'd neither hoped nor intended to survive.

Let me hear by return please more news of your return and, if you will, your considered opinion of all you saw here. I need it in writing, so to speak. Renew my grateful greetings to your parents and to anyone left in the Weak-Chest Wards who remembers

Your
Rachel

P.S. I had just closed this and was washing my face to walk down to mail it when a knock at my door, which was Grainger, standing. Did I know where Mr. Rob was today? I said "No why?" He said, "That's all right. I just needed to find him" and thanked me and left before I thought to quiz him further. So now I'm afraid I'm a little shaken. What Grainger doesn't know about Rob will be strange. What Grainger doesn't know about anything — Well, Rob said to wait. Monday's two days off. I wait, I wait. Ever, R.H.

2

The woman who answered Rob's single knock stood silent, carefully looking, and then said "Morning" in a voice with no trace of question or fear, more nearly the calm spontaneous answer to a question posed long years before, considered ever since. She smiled very slightly and looked maybe thirty—Rob judged age poorly like all young men: there were two stripes of gray in auburn hair that seemed fluid with satisfied life of its own, one at each temple. She was middle-sized and met Rob's eyes dead-level (he was one step down).

"Forrest Mayfield," he said. "Is he living here?"

"He's been here twenty-one years," she said. "But right this minute he has stepped out to buy him a black shoelace." She touched the back of her own neck gently; she liked herself.

Rob scrubbed his chin with the heel of his left hand. He said, "I'm sorry to look so scrappy." He pointed to his muddy car at the curb. "But I drove through the night from back in the mountains."

She nodded. "That's easy to mend. You can wash. You can use his razor." But she stood in the door still, not waving him in.

"I'm *Rob* Mayfield."

"The Second," she said. "I was figuring that." She touched both eyes. "I'm not a big reader, but I've trained my eyes fairly well through the years." She looked on, still standing, as if there were more than a name to figure, a face to see. "I'm your father's help."

"I heard that," he said.

"Who from?"

"Aunt Hatt."

"What word did she use?"

Rob thought. "*Help*, I think—that you'd helped him a lot."

She nodded. "That was kind. It's been my wish anyhow, God knows. He needed it. I am Margaret Jane Drewry." She stepped back, smiling again. "Come in."

Rob thanked her and entered the long hall behind her. The back of the hall, a wide door, was open; and the clear sun of early afternoon boiled slowly in the space, on clean cream walls hung with wide brown photos of ancient Rome in dark oak frames—*The Temple of Virile Fortune, of the Magna Mater, of Venus Genetrix.* Rob passed them, not looking, aiming only toward the woman who waited near the end by another open door (every school he had known owned similar sets, supremely unnoticed except by the spinsters who now and then pointed to one with startling passion).

But she said, "Those were left to your father last year by an old-maid teacher that believed in him. I think she was hoping to drive him back to Latin."

So Rob paused and stared at the *Virile Fortune*, glum tan rubble. "I see why he left." Then he faced her. "*Did* he leave?"

"No," she said quickly. "Oh no he was left." Even finished and silent, she rang like a bell with the force of her peal.

He smiled. "I just meant Latin," he said and gestured to the pictures.

She nodded, relieved. "He had to leave that. It's a colored school—teaching them how to live: machine work and all. He teaches just reading and a few little poems—John Greenleaf Whittier, all they can take."

"Well, I'm sorry," Rob said.

Quick and urgent again, she said "Don't be"; then stopped herself and deeply blushed—embarrassed revelation—then recovered conviction. "He's happy, I mean."

Rob said, "I'm glad. Hatt said to thank you."

She stood still and looked down, listening to that, cradling it side to side in her mind, one spoon of water on a parching tongue. Then she swallowed it slowly; and when she looked up, she said, "Wait for him in here. This is where he works."

Rob moved to obey—he'd made her forget that he needed to wash; he would not tell her now—but before he had walked three steps toward the light, she said, "If you sit in that black leather chair and lie back and rest, I'll come in and give you a painless shave and never even interrupt your pleasant dreams." Rob nodded and went on, accepting her offer, and not only rested but slept—no dreams. Too tired for dreams.

He had driven all night and half of today, starting in bad shape and worsening steadily. The sights and messages of recent days had mounted and pressed; and he'd started drinking at work on Friday—his first turn to drink, with serious intent, since the bout in Bracey with his Aunt Hatt and Grainger (the other times had served the purpose of fun, nights with his work-mates; so he told himself). He thought he had got through till quitting time without his boss's notice; but when he'd stepped up to collect his pay, Mr. Lassiter had said, "Mayfield, are you coming down sick?" There was nobody near and Mr. Lassiter had seemed to like him since the day he'd started; so Rob said, "Could be. I've been under pressure." Mr. Lassiter said "The Hutchins girl?" Rob had said "No sir, home"; and Mr. Lassiter said, "Take till Monday morning and get the pressure off. If you aren't here Monday morning fit to work at six, I'll hire a new man." Rob had thanked him and passed up a ride back to town on the little gang-truck, saying honestly he felt like taking a walk. There had been a lot of laughter—who was waiting for him where? would she take him all dusty as he was, unshaved? But they'd gone off without him, and he'd walked on behind.

The walk was five miles, some three hours long since he stopped several times to suck on his bottle and mull on his worries in various spots by the loud white river in shades of dying light. When he'd got near the hotel, it was well past nine—supper over and cleared—so he'd walked a long arc and approached from the back in hopes of finding either Grainger or Della off-duty in their quarters.

Grainger had gone off with Mr. Hutchins to talk to a carpenter back on the mountain about rebuilding the springhouse cheap; but Della was sitting barefoot in the dark at the end of her cot, singing hymns to herself. He had walked in on her in total silence and waited till she said, "You early. What you mean?" He had said, "I mean I am in bad trouble." —"What you want me to do?" (she had said it gently, an offer not a spurning); so to give her a task, to give himself a little more quiet time, he asked her to go back and pack his dinner pail—he was taking a trip. She had asked him to where and was he coming back? He had said, "I'm thinking. Just get me some dinner" (no trip had crossed his mind till then). She had smelled his harsh breath, known food was the last thing he really wanted but had gone on and rummaged by a single candle to find him enough food to keep him alive; then had come back and, finding him waiting in her chair, had said, "Here it is but you leaving here stinking." Rob had said, "I'll be crossing a number of rivers. I can wash—Hell, drown." She had said, "I got all your pressing right here" (she washed his work clothes), so he'd let her find him a clean shirt and pants; and then he'd turned and left without another word, though he'd laid a silver dollar on her bureau as he passed. He'd stowed the food and clothes on the seat of the car, checked the tool box for the pint of whisky wedged there, then had felt his dark way round to crank the engine. He'd seen Rachel's light and, not really waiting a moment to think, had climbed the stairs to her—unheard by anyone—and made his vague promise with no conscious prior intention behind him, no serious pledge. Then he'd driven away and run all night over miserable roads—down the mountains, fording creeks that were swollen to torrents, stopping twice for punctures, and one time to contemplate his death.

He had brought himself to that, let himself be brought. He was in grave earnest fifty miles west of Richmond, the last of the hills above the James River, eight in the morning. He had seen from the road that the hill made a clean hundred-foot drop to water, sufficient wet rocks; so he'd pulled over there and stopped the car, thinking, "Rest your eyes for a little anyhow and maybe end it now—the whole damn relay race you've been in for twenty-one years, no choice of your own, running hell-for-leather with a baton passed by the dead or the useless and no one to take it." He had sat on a flat rock the size of a pillow and watched the moiling water for ten full minutes, not thinking especially but listening in calm pain to all that his body or mind volunteered, neither news nor hope. And his head was clear, his body cleaned out. He had not had a drink since leaving Goshen or eaten the dinner. His access to liquor was still in his own grip. What he'd told his mother in the spring held true—he could stop it at will; it was not yet a necessary substance of his blood but an easy comfort. By the river, in slant early Saturday light, the question had come to: *what thing to stop, of the stoppable things?*

Then he'd heard from far down young high voices and hunted till he saw two boys, ten or twelve, on the opposite bank with a single rifle. They quieted soon and studied the water as if it withheld some urgent unit of their own further lives. Rob had strained to find it with them; feared he'd found it before them—a snapping turtle the size of a galvanized tub treading calmly in a still center pool, a great floating melon, a gray precursor who fiercely promised to survive brief man if granted this space (Rob felt that, never brought it to conscious thought; like men of any age, much less of his youth and degree of training, Rob thought very little). Then the younger boy had seen it and yelled "Yonder, yonder!" and the older boy had shot, reloaded, shot—four quick times. His aim had seemed fine; the turtle had sunk (dead, hurt, or fleeing); both boys had sat down then and waited for the river to offer up news of death or another escape.

Rob had said to himself with no further waiting, "I will give them something"—the sight of his body in air, a sure end. That became his huge wish, the one known feeling subduing all others, the job at hand—"I can show them what they've done" (intending by *them*, at first, ranks of people from his parents forward but finally these boys). "*They* need me at least, my message to them."

He had stood up slowly so as not to draw their gaze too soon and had gone to the car to unload his pockets of his wages and the case with the porcelain which had borne the picture of his mother, now canceled. As he'd bent above the seat, he had smelled the food ripening in the dinner pail and had known he was hungry, not a solid bite swallowed in twenty hours. He would eat something first, fall better for the breakfast, leave the empty pail. The boys below would wait, showed no sign of leaving; and word would reach Della that at least he'd finished what she'd bothered to fix: that much of a message to one person likely to regret his leaving. Nothing to Rachel, which he briefly regretted; but she'd given him nothing. Nothing to Grainger.

So he'd gone to the rock again and sat and eaten two pieces of chicken and two cold biscuits; and when he'd reached again for maybe something sweet, had found not a layer of slick waxed paper but a folded page from a cheap school tablet. He'd opened it and seen, sprawled in dim pencil letters, *"Rob, hoping you like this stuff from Della, think about Della in the city, keep smiling, so long for now."* Rob had wadded it tightly and flung it toward the river and had noticed then that the boys were gone, no word from the snapper. Then he'd eaten the remains of the food—wilted celery, good pound cake—and gone to the car and in broad daylight changed his filthy clothes; then had driven on to Richmond, an arbitrary goal.

3

When Polly had shaved him and dried his face, she saw he was dozing; so she tried to go silently and leave him unshaken. He spoke though, eyes closed, "You going far?"

"The cookstove," she said, half-whispering, "—twenty feet from here. Dinner's at one. Speak if you need me."

Rob said "Thank you, ma'm."

She stood and waited; then she said it full voice—"I'm just Polly Drewry. Call me Polly please."

Rob still did not look but he nodded. "All right."

Then a force in her—held twenty years by locks of gratitude, safety, steady reward—rocked; then spilled. She came back a step toward Rob and said, "You've come for yourself, just yourself? Is that it?"

Rob looked. She was older by ten years or so. Her skin had thinned down and paled in these minutes. She was on some cliff of her own, alone. He smiled and whispered as if she were the sleeper, "Oh yes ma'm, for me. I'm a free-will agent. You can cook in peace."

She also smiled but could not rush the fullness and calm to her face. Her top teeth showed through the paper of her lip, and she did not risk another speech till the door. There she stopped and said it again, not turning, "Say Polly please." Then she left and shut the door firmly behind her.

Rob said "Polly" once aloud and tried to settle back to rest, his exhaustion so great that he did not object to the thought of being found asleep and helpless by a father he had not seen for twenty years, of whom he had no physical picture or knowledge of intent. He slept for an hour in the room that offered no threat to his peace, though after forty minutes the door opened quietly and Forrest stood silent on the sill looking in. When Rob slept on, Forrest stepped forward to him and waited four feet from the chair, looking down; then when that didn't stir him, Forrest went to his own desk, bright by the windows; and turned one picture face-down and went out.

4

It was Polly who woke him. She softly whistled a two-note phrase as introduction, more wind than music; then she said "Dinner please."

Rob had gone deeper down than a casual nap, and he came up slowly
against his mind's will. When his eyes broke open, they were fixed on the
room not on Polly at the door; and since he did not know either at first, he
studied the room before facing her—one wall of books, lined square and neat,
faded and used; three bare cream walls (a fireplace in one with a plain brown
mantel, its shelf populated with souvenirs; in another, two windows and
between them a desk, papers laid on its top at strict right angles). Rob was
still unconfirmed in his whereabouts, still half-asleep. He turned to the
woman.

"I know you are tired," she said, "but it's ready."

Rob stood. She stepped aside in the door and waved him through. In
the light hall again, he looked back to her, awaiting guidance.

So she said "Just here," and walked on before him through an opposite
door by the picture of *The Altar of Augustan Peace.*

Rob touched his uncombed head with both flat palms; then followed
her in—another light room, a small round table set plentifully. A man on
the far side, standing, turned to Rob. A sizable wait.

She said, "Take the seat by Mr. Mayfield. There."

The man said "Robinson. Please" and bowed slightly.

There were three places laid. Forrest stood by the farthest one, near the
window; and though his face and voice were pleasant, he did not move forward to greet Rob directly. So Rob said "Thank you, sir" and aimed for the
middle chair, four feet from his father's. After two steps he thought, "I am on
the bottom of the James after all"; he seemed to be struggling upright to walk
through millions of tons of fast dark water. He stopped short of goal and said,
"Excuse me. I'm dirty from work. I came here from work." He looked round
for Polly to mention the shave. She was gone, just his father.

Forrest said, "I'll take that as a compliment then."

"How so?" Rob said.

Forrest smiled. "That you hurried."

It seemed necessary here to tell pure truth—new room, new chance. Rob
also smiled, a hard expense. "Ran," he said, "—more *from* than *to.*"

Forrest waited as if he were also submerged and must turn dim echoes into
usable words; then he actually laughed. "That's the purpose of legs." He
stepped to the middle chair and offered it to Rob. "They've run you to this."
Then he turned to the open door on his right. "Polly, *food.* We're sinking."

"Rescue," she said, appearing at once, both hands full and steaming. Rob found he could cross the rest of the space.

5

They had eaten calmly with sparse but easy talk—Rob's trip, his job, the quality of the day after undue rains. Any silence that had threatened had been promptly filled by Polly, not with chatter but funny memories—a recent letter from her aging father on his year-long attempt to sell his museum to the federal government, then the state of Virginia, then (rejected by those) to the other Confederate States in order of secession till finally he had given it to a Baptist boy's school in north Alabama and wound up paying for the crating and freight, and no invitation to come and caretake it—which had been half his plan. When she'd brought them the hot rice pudding though, she'd left—pleading work upstairs—and Forrest had said in the first moment's quiet, "One thing first: will you spend the night?"

Rob had said "Yes" at once, mildly pleased to say it.

"Then you'll want to continue your nap now, won't you? We'll have all evening to talk, when you're rested."

Rob had thought, "Maybe my main trouble is I'm tired." He had said, "Yes sir. I am no good now, the shape I'm in."

So Forrest had led him to the study again, a cot draped fully in a paisley shawl; and said, "I have got to go to school for a while. Polly will be here if you need help. Meanwhile you can die-to-the-world in peace." Then he'd shut him in; and for a second time, the room gave Rob an oblivion as simple as any in a cradle, as bare of demanding memory or image, as untouched by knives of past or present, the future blank.

He woke in the light of late afternoon on his back, eyes open on the high wide ceiling. Its unbroken stretch seemed an emblem, an earnest, of plainer life; a field on which he might outline now—with no threat of veto or external change—a life he could walk through with pleasure and generosity, not only having skills and gifts to give but easily finding the hands to receive them, hands behind which would lie faces he could honor, faces he would need. He began, as he had so often when a boy on summer mornings before the house woke, to write with his mind on the patient plaster surface—imaginary words inscribed by his eyes but clear and straight in his customary script: *Robinson Mayfield, twenty-one years old; a one-story home under old oak trees never struck by lightning, Sylvie in the kitchen, three miles in the country from a crossroads town where his two parents live in their own large house which he and his older brother and sister visit on Sundays and holidays for dinner; a wife two years his junior, dark-haired and a whole head shorter when standing before him, though her eyes greet his eyes four inches away as she turns each morning in early light and wakes him slowly to welcome his body in the secret leisure of their own house and time, no further drafts on his energy except some job that will yield to the arcs his body must make as it swings toward happiness and finally rest.* Rob saw it, as legible as Moses' law; held it for long healing moments there above him. No visible reason why he couldn't enact it, obey its claims. He heard a dry rustling; his eyes cut left.

His father was seated at the desk also writing (having come back from school at four o'clock and waited awhile for sounds from Rob, then entered to work beside him in silence). He had not seen that the boy was now conscious.

So Rob watched him secretly—at first as an image, a proximate stranger, a man maybe fifty whose skull had refused to acknowledge time. No skin-slides or ruts at the jaw or neck, not a cell of fat to conspire with the downward haul of the earth. The one dark eye which was visible to Rob seemed never to have rested but always studied and not been dimmed by the sights but fueled, made hungrier minute by minute yet *fed*. There was none of the low wail of vacancy in him—the woman's assertion of grievance, desertion, offense endured, deliverance begged.

Rob then looked in the effort to settle some blame on the man for his own stagnant misery, encirclement. He was not by nature an accuser or a judge; but here in this room after so much time, he saw that his life had been *made* after all; that one of the makers was near him now, revealed in the total shape of his guilt—a young girl abandoned, an infant boy, thrust back to a nest which had proved a cage, a magnet attracting to its famished self all human impulse before it could rush to other poles. Rob actually narrowed his eyes, crouched them inward to draw from the face ten feet away a silent acknowledgment of damage done, penalties owed, fines offered (the man had spoken first and had mentioned amends). But nothing would come either out of Forrest or from Rob toward him. No charge, no conviction.

Then he tried affection. Would it have been good as a young boy to wake from hot summer naps on musty sofas to find this man in the same room working, light on this same face (but younger, gentler, still useful for years)? Rob relaxed his eyes, the cords of his own face, and waited whole minutes. Nothing again. He had never wanted this man, could not now, would not ever. He spoke to be speaking, no intent but sound. "This is a pretty good house you've got" (he'd forgot Forrest saying it would be his in time).

If Forrest was startled, he gave no sign. He answered while writing a final phrase — "For ninety years old, it's doing all right. Your great-grandfather, who was Forrest before me, built it hand-over-hand — just himself and two slaves — in 1835. A gift for his bride, whatever bride he'd get. And with such a dry house, he found one quick — Amelia Collins, somewhat his inferior. They moved in in '36 — sold one slave, both were single men — and had my father (your grandfather Rob) in March '39. Then old Forrest fell dead — a master carpenter, on a roof — and she lived on here, a seamstress and candy-maker, sixty some years: most of them alone. Kept the Yankees out though, kept the roof and walls standing when most of Richmond fell. Just pure force of will; she wouldn't be buried."

Rob said "Did you know her?"

"I didn't, no, I'm sorry to say. In the years my own father lived with us, she wouldn't speak to him, wouldn't meet his wife, wouldn't even so much as acknowledge our births — mine and Hatt's."

Rob said "He had left her." It was not a question.

"That may have been. He never spoke a word about it to me. I thought she was dead. But then I was five years old when he vanished, just saw him one more day before he died. He explained it to Polly. He came back and lived here with her, you see — his mother Amelia till she died in her eighties. He went shortly after."

Rob passed up the questions of what explanation and why to Polly. He looked round the space again. "Whose room was this?"

Forrest thought awhile. "Grainger's," he said. "That's where I come in. Before that, I think it was some kind of pantry. When my father died it was cram-full of junk. Then when I moved here, we cleared it for Grainger. He slept where you are — why the cot's so small: he left at thirteen."

Rob nodded but had no question to ask.

His father said "How is he?"

"Waiting," Rob said.

"For what?"

"He says *Gracie*; she's still in Philadelphia, sucking money like a funnel."

Forrest said, "Oh no; on us, on us. He is waiting on us, the Mayfields, his people. You know who he is?"

Rob said, "He told me; old Rob's grandson."

Forrest said, "Apparently. No reason to doubt it. No doubt we've got kin, all shades and grades, scattered broadcast all along the eastern seaboard; my father needed frequent company." He smiled.

Rob responded. "I suspected that; may run in the family."

Still smiling, Forrest said "It skipped a generation."

Rob showed pleasant doubt.

Forrest shrugged. "Not entirely." He paused long enough to reassume seriousness. "What else has he told you?—Grainger, I mean."

"That you taught him a lot; that he lived with you as long as he could; that then he went back to Bracey, kept his old grandmother; went to war in France; that you asked him to come on here to school but he found a girl, the Gracie I mentioned."

Forrest said, "Go back. Did he say why he left me?" His face showed the matter was calmly urgent.

Rob worked to recall. "No sir, he didn't; just why he didn't come here to school from the war."

Forrest said "The girl."

Rob said, "Well, her and the fact you didn't write to him till the war was over. He had missed hearing from you."

Forrest shook his head once. "He hadn't heard from me in thirteen years. He left *me*, you see. Most people have. I had offered him a life well past his own hopes. But he ran back to Bracey; should have gone to Maine at least."

Rob saw he was in the presence of a pain which had not yet decided it could bear exploration. He said to himself "For once I'll wait"; so he didn't speak but sat upright to the edge of the cot, then leaned against the wall.

Forrest said "You've seen Bracey."

"Through something of a haze as you probably heard; but yes sir, I have."

"How was my sister?"

Rob said, "Friendly but baffled a little"; he meant by his visit, his own behavior.

His father said "Crazy. Solitary desolation."

"You left her," Rob said.

"Everybody did. It was leave her or *be* her, turn into her ghost. She was far too kind, our mother's child. I had to work, you see—work or strangle in misery—and the work was here."

Rob said, "I thought you were teaching in Bracey. Grainger showed me your little private house on the hill, where the man shot himself."

Forrest studied the boy for malice, found none—if anything, a courteous puzzlement: *He's accepted my dinner, my cot for tonight; he thinks he owes me attention now.* Forrest said, "Awhile back, you spoke of running." He stopped at that.

Rob nodded. "Yes sir, running *from* not *to.*"

Forrest smiled. "I was doing both," he said, "twice as hard as you and some years older."

"The *to* part was just teaching poems to Negroes?"

Anger stood up in Forrest's throat—he thought it was anger and felt he must down it; but waiting, he knew it was memory. "I forgot your mother was a Kendal," he said, "—Kendal and Watson, mean streaks on both sides." Then he felt he had no right to blame, having passed on the Mayfield and Goodwin hungers (the victim's eyes) but not stayed around to help forge the polar strains into one working man, both true and merciful. Yet he begged no pardon. He said in his normal voice, "The *to* part was Margaret Jane Drewry, called Polly. I thought you'd seen that and would understand, thought you were old enough to honor that."

"I am," Rob said.

But Forrest had more. "I've had two accounts of your own recent troubles—troubles or mischief: please help me distinguish. Hatt sent a rather high-strung tale of your visit; and Grainger broke a fifteen-year-long silence and swallowed much pride to write me that you had gone past him and his power to help. Don't tell him I told you; he's a generous heart and acts by his lights, no easy lights to follow; but he's why I spoke up and asked you here. Nobody's said what your trouble is. I thought I would show you what I had to give though and hope that would help."

Rob thought and then smiled. "The dinner was good; the nap was needed."

Forrest said, "I meant a good deal more than that."

"I'm sorry," Rob said, "and I'm here to watch."

Forrest said, "You've seen it, the best part anyhow—she shaved you and fed you. The other parts are this house, a good still place, and the work I do both here and at school."

Rob said, "Sir, pardon me. I *am* half-Kendal (you chose a Kendal, no fault of mine); and I can be hard—you're not the first human to tell me that—but I don't mean to be one thing more than honest in saying: how on God's earth can you help me by showing me pictures from your life here when you barely know more of me than my name? You don't even know what's troubling me, what one damned day of my life is like."

Forrest nodded. "I'm free. I'm ready to hear."

Rob waited in silence for a reason to tell it, a reason for being here at all. It came—*There is nobody else to listen; nobody with the patience to hear it out or the calm not to panic, not to use it against me, or the good sense to guess what festers all in it, the guts to pick it out*—so he said, "I wake up at six in the morning to a bell that sounds like Jesus at Judgment. I go to my wash bowl and clear up my eyes and brush my teeth. Then I lie back down and say my prayers; I like to be halfway clean for that. I just say the names of the ones I love or am worried about and 'Thy will be done.' Then I may have a little quick fun with my body: you asked for this now; and you're getting it straight (not every morning certainly—sometimes I've had that seen to otherwise the previous night—but morning is of course when I'm not worn out). Then I put on my trousers and my undershirt and go downstairs to the hotel kitchen—I live in a rundown springs hotel—and get some hot water from the cook and shave on the backporch and look at the mountain standing up there before me. I'm not that much of a nature lover, but a full-sized mountain with a falls and laurel does help me get started if I wake up low. Then I put on my shirt which I bring down with me and sit at a table on the same long porch and eat a big breakfast cooked by that same girl. There are other people present—other men on the crew, the hotel owner (checking up on the portions, though he never says 'Stop'), and Grainger waiting table—but I say very little that early in the day: my head's still frozen. And nobody there's got a claim on me anyhow. Grainger maybe; I'm friendly to him. By the time we are finished, Grainger's brought out our dinners all packed in buckets by the cook (ten cents); and we head out to the crossroads and wait a few minutes for the crew truck. That's half of my day. The other half is evening. The eleven hours in between, I widen the old road down through the pass, eastward toward money—slowest work known and dangerous and dirty but it pays fairly well, and I've learned it fast. Then evening as I said. It generally comes."

Forrest said, "Wait. Do you like the work?"

Rob thought it half-through and laughed. "Wouldn't everybody like to blow up rocks? Of course the novelty wears off." He waited. "No sir, *like* is not part of it. It's what I'm doing to wear me out till something harder comes; and you see, I'm young with a good deal of strength; so it doesn't even tire me more than half of the time." He laughed again; he had talked himself through another narrow passage—his father's face agreed. "I get to the hotel and wash off the dust and go downstairs at just about dark and eat my supper in the dining room, whatever time it is. Me and two Roberts boys from Jennings' Ordinary who work on the crew are the only three regular paying guests, plus a dogeared drummer every week or so; so they hold supper for us, and we all eat together—Mr. and Mrs. Hutchins and Rachel their daughter, the Roberts boys, me, and Grainger serving every good thing Della cooks (she's the girl I mentioned—till Grainger came, the only black face in sight around there). That's generally pleasant. Mr. Hutchins has some pretty grand ideas about the amount of money that's going to stream toward him down our new road—he's sixty-some and remembers the time when his mother had twenty guests a night from May through August—so he's got

Grainger also working on repairs: some whitewashing, changing a board here and there. His main aim now is to get the spring covered, new shingles on the springhouse, lattice on the sides. But far as I'm concerned, he's been decent to me. He trusts me with Rachel, who has not been well; but he's right to trust me. I've been decent to her, clean as a pin. Most evenings after supper I sit down with Rachel on the dark sideporch. It helps her to talk—she talks, I listen. She's been a nervous girl all her life it seems, which is twenty years; but her father decided after this past Christmas that she had T. B. or the warning signs and sent her off to some little chest place in Lynchburg, her mother in tow. She's strengthening now and talks a lot about her future which I'm afraid she thinks means me; she counts on me, I think. I've tried not to fail her so far as I'm able—which hasn't been easy, considering that two or three nights a week, once Rachel has gone upstairs to bed (at ten, Father's orders), I get to stroll out and visit the colored: Grainger if he's up, which usually he isn't since he turns in soon as he's finished supper dishes, but mostly Della. She's younger than Grainger, younger than me, and a restless sleeper; so I pay her little calls, and she lets me in."

Forrest said, "That's being friendly to Grainger?" He smiled slightly, falsely, so as not to stop Rob.

Rob nodded at once. "No doubt about it. I waited till I saw he had passed up the chance, even asked him about it before I moved. I'm keeping her out of his way, you see, so he can go on waiting Gracie in peace."

Forrest said, "I told you what he's waiting for"; but he motioned Rob on.

"If Grainger is waiting on me, you mean, to bring him happiness from God on a tray, he's simpler than he looks. I let him trail me, I listen to him talk (he'll talk you dead if you just sit still), I waited till I saw he had no intention of visiting Della in the same building with him; then I lived my life. I enjoy human company; I take it when offered if it warms my eye and comes bearing no due-bills or claims." Rob had stumbled, in that, on a door he had really not known to exist; a door concealed near the pit of his throat—he felt it now as keenly as though it had locus and heft and hinges. It opened inward on a small low room, white, utterly bare. He stared at the sight and said, "Father, please listen. I was twenty-one years old five months ago. That may seem the wink of an eye to you; it has been my life. And if you've sat here those twenty-one years, eating good hot meals from a white housekeeper and thinking your son down in Fontaine, N. C. was laughing non-stop at his little happy life, I can tell you he wasn't. Right now, today, let me guarantee it to you—Hell, look at me, sir. I was raised in her spare time by my Aunt Rena and black lonesome Sylvie while my own mother, that I loved like the world, was tending her father who was due to die but is still to my knowledge

as healthy as most fieldhands at harvest, barring strokes and pain (I mean he
won't die)."

Forrest said, "Most mothers have to nurse somebody—you never had to
fight a brother or sister—but a day's a long time, lot of chances in a day. I'm
sure Eva gave you more than you grant."

"She didn't," Rob said.

"What did you want?"

"What you wanted, I guess."

"But she married me."

"And bore me all bloody." Rob had said that quietly, no trace of pride or
pity. Then he stared at the small green rug at his feet and scuffed it slowly.
When he looked up again, his face (his whole body) wore the silent still radiance which he'd previously shown to only three people—Rena, Min Tharrington, Rachel Hutchins. Helpless he turned to his father with it now, not
knowing it had passed through his father to him from vanished ranks of Mayfields.

Forrest failed at first to see it. He said, "She never wanted either one of
us—me because I was me, you because you were mine. You are dreadfully
mine, my father's and mine—the way we were at least. Now you have
come this long way to show me. I'm grateful." Forrest stopped as if at an
end. He thought he had finished, seen the sight to be seen. But the boy
held still; so he looked on at him and saw him at last, grand in his face as
the young Alexander horned like Ammon, in all his form like Aeneas at
Carthage (*ante alios pulcherrimus omnis*, before all others most beautiful);
and made by Forrest, the sole remains of his old unhappiness—those famished dreams of an aging boy, corrosive hungers but potent and eating at
this boy now. Forrest leaned out and pled in a gentle whisper, "Oh Jesus,
Son, change. Change now while you can. Find someone to help you and
start your life."

"Yes sir," Rob said and intended to obey, ignoring the live working presence of Eva in all his fibers (as Forrest had forgot it through happiness and
years).

6

That evening when she'd fed them a second time and seen them rush off
in Rob's car so Forrest could show him the school while daylight lasted and
then to the last night of Pola Negri in *Shadows of Paris*, Polly put fresh sheets
on the study cot and turned in early, puzzled by tiredness (she was seldom

tired), and slept at once. No fear or grudge of which she would have spoken or privately thought—awake by day.

In her sleep she walked through a large busy town, strange from the first and increasingly frightening as she lost her way, whatever way she'd had, and was finally forced to stop one stranger after another and ask directions to the Drewrys', her father's. She was clearly herself, a full-grown woman with her present skills and knowledge, not a child or senile; but the strangers all treated her as shameful, repulsive. All of them were men, no woman in sight, and would either turn from her in scorning silence or give her some scrap of direction so brief as to lead her farther into loss and confusion. She knew less of where she was with every step till she'd come to the gloomy heart of the town where dark old houses of the poor leaned together, propping one another in a useless struggle against decay. She stood at the junction of two narrow streets in stinking mud and was desperate. A Negro boy came from an opposite alley, walked too close on her, and stopped and said, "You never going to find it. You want me to show you?" She could not speak but nodded, and he took her hand. She thought, "At least he is not shamed by me," though her own hot wrist (which he ringed with dry fingers) was pained by his touch. He led her a long way till she understood that where she had met him had been no heart of misery but a limb, a pale extremity. They walked through streets past houses so poor she could feel their odor, the scent of offense, like a scalding poultice across her mouth and eyes. Then she realized that the boy had left her, vanished in silence; but she found that she now knew her way somehow—the Negro's grip had conveyed it like grease through her skin. She went another fifty feet and stopped at a house right down in the street, no sidewalk or steps. She knew she was there. Dry curls of the dark brown paint on the door fell at her knock, and more as it opened. An old woman—white, straight, clean for the place, stiff white hair like foam round her head, a long face strong as a flagstone slab, as blank and unknowing. Polly said, "Where is Mr. Drewry please?" The old woman dried both hands on her worn skirt, working to recall. At last her voice was older than her face—"With Jesus in Glory, I hope, but dead." Polly said, "I have come here to stay with him." The old woman stood on, now blocking the door. Polly said, "I'm his daughter. He expected me." The old woman nodded. "No he didn't," she said, "and I know who you are. You are Margaret Jane. But you can't stay here; the young man is here." Polly looked past the woman and could see in the dark room a single man, dark-haired, seated at a table examining his hands as if they were one thing in all this filth that bore close study, might yet prove precious. He did not look up, so he had no face; but the old woman said, "You can stand in this room a minute and rest"; and

Polly saw that the woman was her mother, secretly survived but ancient and ruined. Undoubtedly her. Polly took the offer, entered and stood one stifling minute in the room crammed with heat, the odor of rancid lard in the walls; then was led out silently and shut in the street.

She was wakened by the front door opening downstairs. She half-sat up and—stunned, pulling for breath—listened for voices: Forrest's first, low, "I'll see you to bed and leave you to sleep; I know you're exhausted"; then Rob's young and clear, "No sir. I could talk if you want to talk." Their steps down the hall to Grainger's old room, its door shut behind them, their laughter and talk stripped of words by the thick walls, the oak door, but not of their meaning. Their glad relay of muffled exchanges came at her like the lucid sentences of blame, announcement of desertion. Her life discarded.

She lay back and waited in thick hot darkness for the sound of Forrest leaving, coming upstairs to bed. After nearly two hours by the chime of the station clock, a half-mile away, she heard him on the stairs—quiet not to wake her. He passed her open door (no pause, no audible thought); went on to his own room, poured a glass of stale water, drank it, undressed, breathed the regular rhythms of sleep at once. The downstairs was silent.

Polly said to herself, "Sleep, goose. Just a dream." And later she slept, though a wading in shallows, no cleansing fall. She had had no previous such dream or threat in the thirty-nine years since killing her mother.

7

When Forrest had left him, Rob did not try to sleep. His afternoon nap and the unexpected curious excitements of the trip, transfusions of life, had him wide awake and more nearly on the edge of the sense of a *turn* than at any time since March—the chance at least of continuance and change, departure from childhood. So he stripped to his underpants and studied the room, books first since books were the main thing in sight. He passed them quickly. Almost half were in Latin or Greek, and the half in English was mostly verse. Few stories, no accounts of animals or travels, no life of Jesus telling more than the Gospels, no medical texts of the sort he had always hoped to find and knew to exist—his body's resources all clearly explained, his needs both acknowledged and briskly forgiven, calm guidance given to chances he had never yet taken (or heard of) for sanity and pleasure. Then he went to the mantel where he'd seen what he took to be souvenirs—the cast dried skin of a red rat snake, which Rob could not touch; a small polished disc of petrified wood; the skull of a bird (the size of a bird egg and paper-thin but intri-

cate as gears, also untouchable); an old bronze coin (some fat man's profile—
a Caesar, Rob guessed); a small gold medal on a faded ribbon (*The Orator's
Medal to Forrest Mayfield, April 1887—Vox Humana, Vox Divina*); and two
rough carvings the size of a hand in soft pinebark, old and polished by
touch.

Rob reached for one and remembered at once his own crude carvings at
six or eight, when a whole afternoon spent carving some horse or bird or girl
was not so much an effort at skill as at simple courage, the struggle to fight
down the scary feel of pinebark; the dry rind of trees whose hearts were
streaming rosin, skin scaly as a lizard's and slightly feverish. A little square
man—bullet head, gouged eyes, club-footed, legs wide. Down the man's
right leg hung the equally rough indication of genitals. For no reason known
to him, other than the need to conquer fear, Rob cradled the man in his large
right hand and stroked the bark. Safe, no fear—the bark's own polish, the
hardness of his hands after months on the road. He put him down gently
beside his mate, a breasted woman, and stood a moment thinking.

He would write his postcards (they had stopped at a drugstore before the
picture, and he'd bought three cards of the Richmond sights)—to Della and
Sylvie, no thought of consequences for them or himself, only of their pleasure in a distant thought. He would see Della well before the card could
reach her, but he owed her that much. Sylvie would use hers as she saw fit,
secret or public; there was no predicting (she would sometimes keep letters
days or weeks till she found some person she could trust to read them to her).

He went to the desk where he'd laid them and sat, expecting to find a pen
or indelible pencil at least. None in sight, only mail of his father's and the
stack of school papers on which his father had worked that afternoon. Rob
reached for the top one—*Jonathan Simpkin, Last Composition, My Thought
Upon 'Laus Deo' by Whittier*, "This poem says Mr. Whittier is glad to hear
about the freedom. He is living up north and word come to him. He think
about God first thing in Latin." Rob put it back thinking that, so far at least,
it matched his own Last Composition except for the errors which his father
had patiently corrected in red (Aunt Rena'd checked all Rob's work and saved
him often); but who could spend a life knocking s's off the verbs of future
masons, farmers; stuffing words into mouths incapable of holding them?
(hungry for a damned sight more than words).

Rob remembered what his father had said of Aunt Hatt—"Crazy: loss and
loneliness." Was it also the verdict on all known Mayfields?—his father,
Grainger, his own moaning self? He would not think that through—thought
had done enough already to ruin his trip—but it did cross his mind that, whatever Forrest Mayfield's past or present pains, he had given a first-rate imita-

tion of contentment today: a life in harness to round greased wheels, the wheels rolling quiet and smooth, level ground.

No pen in sight though. Rob opened the one long drawer to hunt, silently; he knew he was now out of bounds (drawers of the Kendal house were private as toilets). Two cheap steel pens, a bottle of red ink, a neat further lot of school work, gradebooks, a small picture-frame face down toward the back. Rob naturally took it, raised it out to the dim hot gooseneck lamp, and looked. His mother and himself, no question of either, though he'd never seen the picture and (despite his age in it—four, maybe five) did not remember the day or the sitting. His mother was gazing dead-level at the camera, her dark hair lustrous and straight as an Indian's rising from a high smooth forehead to a height half that of her face, her full lips pale and entirely closed, though drawn slightly back as if ready to answer or to tell the man No, the darks of her eyes enormously deep and lit by real light, her right brow raised not in anger or question but as if to throw one single line askew. Her right hand was hid in the lap of a fine light summer dress; her left lay free on the arm of the chair. Rob himself stood by that, his own eyes down, as grave as some leader at the end of a life—a white sailor suit, blue-trimmed; a wood whistle on an oddly knotted cord round his neck, untouched. Eva seemed to have borne all the weight of the world, to be bearing it *then* with unquestioned competence, no hint of complaint, only the firm reservation of her eyes as they spoke their sentence, *I am bearing it. I can. I cannot stop you watching.*

Rob touched his dry lips to the cool glass above her. Then he carefully returned the frame to its place and wrote his two cards.

Dear Sylvie, Rob thought about you in Richmond.

Dear Della, Safe trip, much obliged for help, I trust to see you before you see this.

R.M.

Then he wiped the pen clean with paper from the grate, turned out the one light, raised the two windows higher, stripped himself entirely, and lay down to sleep on top of the cover. His troubles though real were as old as he, as natural as his hair or the eggs of his groin and older in power and need than they. His body had learned to live in their presence if he'd only trust his body, surrender his mind. He trusted it now, made a quick sweet resort to its offer of pleasure (no image before him of any living creature: himself a closed engine, adequate and lovely); then he slept. Plain rest.

8

He woke in clear light to a cool house, still silent. For the fifteen minutes that he lay slowly surfacing, he thought it was only a little past dawn and that he had waked first and must wait for the others. He had started another experiment—that this was his home, this room his room; that his parents were overhead sleeping still or silently conducting the secret rites which parents require, rites which did not exclude him but in fact had summoned his existence and now by repetition insured his continuance, his own eventual manhood. He could bear the thought easily and began to expand it to include the pictured bodies of his father and Polly, their faces in the spreading rictus of joy, both younger than now, unmarked by their lives. Rob had had no prior occasion in his life for such a soothing game and would have run on to the vivid end of his present vision; but through windows the station clock started its chime. He counted ten strokes and thought it was wrong (outside the town was as still as the house); but he jumped up and went to his watch on the desk and found it was ten. Naked, he stood by the windows in dry sun and listened to the house again, straining for news. A child's blank fears—*They are gone or dead.* There seemed to be rare muffled knocks from the kitchen.

Unwashed, Rob scrambled into his clothes; opened the door; stepped into the hall and listened. He was barefoot. The kitchen door was shut. No speaking voices but there were sounds of work with water and metal, so he went there and knocked. A considerable wait.

Polly said "Is it you?"

"—Rob if that's who you mean."

"I did," she said.

He opened. She turned from the sink, not smiling. He saw his bare toes, ugly as most. "Excuse me," he said and pointed to his feet, "I was scared."

"What of?"

"The house sounded empty."

"Your father has gone." She had not yet smiled, and she turned back to scouring a deep black pan.

Rob suddenly laughed. In place on the doorsill, he laughed so long that Polly turned to watch him and, despite her seriousness, was forced to join.

She stopped before him though and said "What's the joke?"

"That he's gone," Rob said. "Lady, he was never here."

She smiled but she said, "I am Polly, again; and yes he was here. He's been here twenty years, wherever else he hadn't been, and will be back by two p.m., I know, if he lives that long." She paused till it reached him. "Are you ready for breakfast?"

Rob remembered. His father had told him last night—he must leave at eight-thirty to teach Bible-class at school, then be monitor at chapel; then preside at dinner for the hundred summer students, his duty once a month. Rob nodded he was ready. "I'll put on my shoes."

"Not for me," Polly said. "Stay cool while you can. Sit down and start your coffee." She went to the icebox and took out four eggs; and Rob moved on to the table by the window, a long narrow table painted red. Polly set the brown eggs in a bowl by the sink, took a thick white mug, and filled it with coffee from a blue enamel pot. She brought it to the table, set it by Rob's hand.

He noticed again her youth in her hands; and when she returned to the stove to cook, he fixed on them in their quick neat work—frying bacon slowly with the gravest care; cracking eggs, whipping, scrambling. Bare of rings, her hands were also unmarked by age or damage, only the intricate cords of her strength obeying her will which was also her wish. Rob's throat was rushed by a hot contentment he had not felt for years, since childhood surely (he recognized the flood but could not remember or pause to recover the rare occasions; they would all involve Eva). He sat and welcomed it, not even so much as worrying to name its cause or end. Polly never looked toward him. His first clear thought was "She likes this work"; then its valid extension, "She is working for me." He had seldom been served in a safe calm room by a young white woman who was not simultaneously pleading for rescue, the chance to accompany his life from that moment. He took a long draft of the hot black coffee and said, "You're a very happy lady; am I right?"

She was spooning the eggs from the pan to a platter. She did not look round; but she said "Well—"; then stopped, clearly searching for an answer. Rob waited and she brought the food over to him—the eggs and meat, then a plate of fresh biscuits. He thanked her and she went to the opposite chair and stood straight behind it, her hands holding firm on the thick side-rails. Her face was serious though not deeply troubled. She said again "Well" and smiled. "Half-yes, I guess. I don't have to answer to 'Lady' every day. Many don't think I'm that, but many are meaner than mad dogs in August. I think I've been happy though—by nature, I mean. I have to be, don't I?"

Rob said "Why?"

Polly studied him carefully; then pulled out the chair and sat upright, not leaning toward the table. "Your eyes look strong. You can see good, can't you?"

Rob nodded (he was eating).

"And you're twenty-one years old?"

"Yes ma'm," he said.

"Then you ought not to ask." With one hand she stirred a large circle of air before her chest, by which she meant her life, her surroundings.

Rob said, "I'm sorry. I'm not the brightest Mayfield."

Polly studied again. "You may be," she said, "and don't all the time be begging for pardon that you don't need. You haven't harmed me but some-day you might, so you don't want to wear out my pardons now." She had brought herself to smile.

Rob nodded. "Sure. *Damn* me."

"That's not called for either yet," she said. They both paused then—Rob eating, Polly watching. At last she leaned forward and offered him a glass dish of fig preserves; she stayed that much closer (just her hands on the table edge) and said, "Could you tell me why he asked you to come? I mean, I'm glad to meet you—"

"He didn't," Rob said. "It was my idea. He heard from Grainger that I was in trouble and wrote me to offer what help he could; but coming after twenty-one years of silence, it didn't exactly thrill me, you know. I figured I had got by that long without him."

"Your mother left *him*."

"So they tell me," Rob said, "so he told me last night. But why does he have that picture of Mother and me as a boy?"

Polly said, "It appeared on his birthday one year. I think he asked for it. You better ask him."

"No matter," Rob said.

"Oh it may be," she said, "to you and him." She paused. "You were telling me about your visit."

Rob faced her, eye-level. "You want me to leave. I'm leaving once I eat." His face could have been read as angry or joking.

She worked at reading him, decided on anger. Her own eyes suddenly filled with tears. She struck the table gently with both flat palms. "*Yes*," she said.

Rob laid down his fork. "How have I harmed you please?" he said.

It took her awhile before she could speak; but she never looked down or hid her face, never loosened the grip of her hands on the table. Finally she could say, "I am not sure it's harm. All I know is I'm scared. I had the worst night of my life last night, saw things I never really hoped to see. I take what is offered to me in sleep as serious, maybe more so than what comes in day-light, but that's just me. You surprised me, you see—whyever you're here. I have answered that same door for more than twenty years; and I don't remember ever letting in one soul that meant me harm—ever answering to one (Grainger came in the back door and left that way). I was brought here by your Granddad Rob; and I tended to him till he died in his sleep—sleep is just as real as day. I was left just a young woman, nowhere to go but back to my funny old dad I mentioned. Then your father came here to see to the funeral; and since he was also at the end of his rope, he asked me would I stay on here and cook; take care of the place. It turned out he'd already got his present job and needed a home. The house of course was his (and his sister's, I guess); and he treated me as decently as anybody ever had in nineteen years. Much more so really; he's a gentleman of God, whatever else he is. If you don't think a nineteen-year-old girl who has grown up in cities and kept a museum of Confederate junk has met a lot of treatment that was far less than decent, then you don't know girls or cities either. Not to mention museums. But you probably do. Anyhow I accepted. He had his job in Bracey till the end of April; so I cleaned around here good and then locked up and went to Washington till May—on the train, one bag. I'm a Washington girl. I had left my dad there a good while before with his museum to tend, when I came down here. He had said to me then, very pleasant but firm, that if I left him not to ever come back. And I nine-tenths believed him (he will change his mind thirty times an hour about himself, but he's set like lockjaw in what he thinks of others); so when I walked up to his Washington door, I didn't know whether he would spit or kiss me. He managed both. At first he pretended he didn't recognize me. I stepped in the open door, bag in hand, and went to the table where he sat selling tickets. He glanced up briefly and then back down and said 'Ladies five cents.' I went along with him. I fished out a nickel, of which there were few, and pushed it toward him. He actually took it, put it in his tin box, pointed to the rooms where his old stuff was and said 'Take your time.' I had to stop it there—I am happy by nature but bad at jokes; they always scare me. I said 'Dad, it's Margaret Jane.' —'I know that,' he said. He was reading the memoirs of P. T. Barnum for the eight-hundredth time and went back to them, really read on awhile; I could see his eyes flicking. I was young enough to figure he was asking me to beg. Well, I've never minded begging; that's all prayer is, except for the few little compliments to God which I'm sure He ignores. I said, 'I have got a two-month vacation till my next job starts; and I've come home to help you.' He still looked down—'What help would that be?' I said, 'I doubt it'll be any help, now you mention it (I'll cook you some meals); but it might be fun. I'm good-natured, remember?' He thought that over and apparently remembered and pointed to the stairs and said, 'Your bed's where it was, not used since

you left.' So I took my satchel and climbed upstairs and found my cubbyhole
the way I had left it. The sheets I had slept in my last night at home were still
on the bed with my wrinkles in them, my hair on the pillow (I hemstitched
the pillowslip at age eleven; I'd know it on the moon). Strangest old bear in
the woods, my dad; but from that minute on, he acted like I'd never been
gone ten minutes; and we did have fun. We always had, nothing out of the
ordinary—talking and teasing. I stayed two months and cooked and cleaned
and sold people tickets to see his poor show (by then he had bought a little
railroad stock and was halfway solvent); and then your dad wrote me toward
the end of April and said everything was straight on the rails and would I beat
him there and air-out the house? I washed my few duds and, that night at supper, said 'Tomorrow's the day'; and Dad said 'About time.' I cooked his next
breakfast and packed and combed my hair. He was not downstairs when I
went to say goodbye, so I caught the streetcar to the 12:20 train and have not
been back. I've written of course and he answers now and then if he's got
some funny news. I've been right here in the Mayfield house; and excepting the last few weeks of Grainger's stay, I have generally been happy." Polly
stopped and sat a moment; then again touched the table with her beautiful
hands, this time more nearly caressing than striking. She was smiling mildly.

Rob had eaten throughout her story. Now he set down his fork and said,
"Why did you tell me all that please?" His tone and face were pleasant.

She had not lost her way. She knew at once. "To show why I wanted you
to leave," she said.

"Then you failed, I'm afraid; or maybe I just failed to understand."

"That's it," she said, still smiling. "I was clear as a bell. *This is all I've got,
and I hate for you to take it.*"

"This house, you mean? You can have my share when the great day
comes; of course I don't know who else has claims. Maybe Mayfields abound;
I suspect they do."

She was grave again and, firm in her purpose, she neglected to offer Rob
fresh hot coffee. "Not the house," she said, "though it is a good house; and
I'm rightly grateful to it. No you're making me say it when I hoped you
would *see*. I mean Forrest Mayfield. He is what I have."

Hearing that, Rob discovered in himself a hardness he had not used in
months, more likely in years. He actually thought of Min Tharrington's
face as she turned from his meanness four years ago. But again he accepted
its demands and said, "Could you live without him?"

"Of course I could; people live blind and dumb with no arms or legs and
their backs raw with sores. But I wouldn't want to; I would pray not to—and
I'm not a church-goer."

"Me either," Rob said.

Polly thrust to the rank tender center of her fear. "Didn't Eva send you here?" She stopped and flushed deeply, from embarrassment not pain. "Your mother, I mean. He still calls her Eva when he mentions her at all; I've never seen her face."

Rob said "Yes she did," the coldness still in him, though he knew he hadn't lied.

Polly said, "I knew that. I knew she'd try again."

Rob nodded but was silent.

"That picture you saw on Forrest's desk?"

"In his drawer," Rob said.

"Then he hid it from you; it's always been out. She sent him that picture from a clear blue sky on his birthday five years after she'd left him, five years without one word or sign when he'd walked through coals of white fire just to live and forget you both."

Rob said "With you helping."

"So *right*," Polly said. "I was helping like fury. I had met the postman that day, like I said; and here was a little square package for Forrest. I didn't know the writing; but I knew the postmark and knew anything sent from Fontaine, N. C. was bound to harm him. So I hid it at first in the hall-table drawer; he was here eating breakfast, set to leave for school. I didn't know whether I would open it first or burn it; but I lied to him then, just gave him a bill and a card from his sister and said that was all. Then once he was gone, I tried to work and think. The Christian thing was to wait till evening and say it had come in the afternoon mail; he'd at least have evening and night to recover in, whatever the damage. But by noon I was wild and mad and scared; and I brought it back here and opened it as secret as if I was some hateful enemy at night, not his help at noon. I was sick as I did it—the knots in the string— but nothing like as sick as I got to be when I saw those faces: Eva Mayfield and Rob. I stood up to burn it. Who on earth would know? Strings of *pearls* are lost in the mail every day, not to mention pictures of people who left you to struggle alone."

Rob said "What stopped you?"

"The fact I wasn't *sure*. I was nine-tenths certain—I had the postmark— but, see, I had never seen Eva or you. He'd denied to me that he owned any pictures—said he had her living presence so why take pictures?—and I don't think he lied. You were too young to resemble him yet; he hadn't taken charge of your eyes and mouth the way he has since. I stood at the stove and told myself there was one slim chance that woman and child were somebody else and were safe to us both (there was no note or card in the package, just faces; the letter came the next day, delayed somehow); so I wrapped it back up and put it on his desk with the afternoon mail, and he never gave me one hint of getting it. He was a little quiet at supper, I thought; but that could have just been tiredness from school. Then the next day, the letter in the morning mail. He took it off with him unopened on the streetcar; and still not a word to me, not a flicker. I was sick all through it; but again if he noticed, he kept his own counsel. I knew he was thinking. And I knew very well my life was before him in some kind of balance with you and your mother. Every day when he'd leave, I'd hunt for the letter; I guess it was at school. I am telling you this, though it's my hot shame after sixteen years."

Rob said, "You could leave. You are not chained down."

But she nodded. "I was."

"A baby?" he said.

She shut her eyes, shook her head. "Never. No." She waited and swallowed as if at a knot of dry cloth in her throat. Then she looked again. "I understand a lot from you being here—his past, I mean; what your mother put him through. You are hers all right."

"I am," Rob said. "I'm sorry to be."

"Too late now," she said.

Rob said, "Maybe not. She left me as sure as she left Forrest Mayfield."

Polly shook her head again. "She never left Forrest, not for good, still hasn't. I found the letter. After nearly three weeks, I went in to clean his study one morning; and there stood the picture on his desk. He had framed it. I sat down and tried to study it calmly. I was cold as Christmas. You've seen it yourself; you know what it says even now after years—*Is there some way back?*"

Rob said "I doubt that," though he didn't doubt it.

Polly said, "You wouldn't if you'd read the letter. I found it in his desk drawer; he'd brought it home the same day. It disappeared later and I guess he may have burned it or I'd show it to you now. But I sure God read it three times that day. She started out by asking how he liked his work (she had got some news from Hattie and his Richmond address); then she went on with news from you and her (funny things you were saying, little jobs she was doing—hooking rugs, crocheting for various friends); then she said everything there was going on as ever except that her brother had got married recently and come home to stay with his new little wife till their own house was built some while in the future and that seams were bursting, not to mention people's patience."

"They were," Rob said. "I was sleeping in her room. That was just the true news she was telling him, no begging in that."

"Oh there was," Polly said. "Forrest knew it well. The picture was the begging, and it shook him to the sockets."

"You said he never spoke."

"I can *see*," she said, "and I watched him for days as close as I could; he kept shy of me. In his study always writing, little notebooks he'd take back to school every morning. Then he gradually eased and talked to me more; and one night I went in to where he was working to tell him good night and found him so calm that I got nerve to say 'Is that Eva and Rob?' —'Aren't they lovely?' he said; and I had to agree, looking through his eyes, though for all those weeks (looking just through my own) I had felt like wiping you both off the earth and had prayed for the power." She managed to smile at the end of that; it was clearly an end, a fistula drained.

Rob touched his white cup. "I would give a good deal for some coffee," he said.

"Such as what?" She was playing.

Rob was thoroughly grave. "This much for certain, which I won't take back—I came here purely on my own. I was hurting. He can tell you how. It is not to do with him, not directly. I have not blamed him for anything ever; and I didn't come here with messages or claims from me or anybody. I was down, far down; he asked me to come here, and here I've been. I'm leaving as I said." He began to fold his napkin.

"Your coffee," Polly said and moved toward the stove where the blue pot was steaming. She touched it with the flat of her hand, satisfaction; and brought it to his cup, poured it carefully. On her way to the stove again (her face turned from him), she said, "You've been sick lately, you mean?"

Rob laughed a dry chuff. "—As a dog," he said. "Maybe past curing."

Polly turned to face him and touched her own breastbone with her strong right thumb. "Your chest? Is it that?"

Rob mimicked her gesture in the center of his forehead. "My empty head."

Polly came back and sat while he sweetened his coffee. "Empty of what?"

"Don't make me," Rob said. "He made me last night, and it didn't help at all."

She nodded. "I'm sorry." She waited, Rob drank. Then tracing a delicate curve on the table (over and over, precise and perfect; her eyes on the curve), she said, "I am going to tell you the truth. I am thirty-nine years old so no need to lie. I have loved three people in all that time. My mother died when I was born, so Dad was the first. He never needed me; I've shown you that. The second was Rob Mayfield, long dead. I came here with him and eased his death; he died right beside me, and I never even stirred (and I as light a sleeper as a bird on a bough). The third was your dad—and I trust will be the last." Her tracing finger lifted and her eyes met Rob's. Again she had reached some end of her own.

Rob waited till he saw she had finished her message. It had not reached him, but he first said "Thank you."

Polly nodded. "Very welcome."

Then he said, "How is that meant to help me please?"

She knew he was earnest. "It means I have told you all I know."

"Did you marry my grandfather?"

"No. We spoke about it but he didn't want that. He had run from his children; he had to save them something."

"This house?"

"This house and the few things in it."

"One of which was you?" Rob intended it kindly as plain description.

Polly read his intent. "You could say that." She smiled. "You wouldn't be the first. I was part of his leavings, but I wanted to be."

"Did you marry my father?"

She shook her head slowly. "He is married," she said. "He's also married. You know, your mother. He won't change that, wouldn't change it if he could; and I don't know the law, haven't tried to learn. He has not ever spoken about it to me except that one day I mentioned your picture and he asked weren't you lovely? That broke me from questions." She was smiling still.

"You said a few minutes ago you were happy."

"By nature, I said." She paused, thought it through. "And also by *luck*. They were three kind men, Rob and Forrest especially. I call that luck."

"—That they kept you a servant?"

Again she tested his face for malice, the edge of his voice. "That they cherished me." She had said it gently; but the words drew behind them a flock of feelings—pride, secret joy, continuing hope (however assailed)—that decked her face and shoulders all fresh with a greater beauty of light and depth, victory and promise, than Rob had witnessed on any other form except his own mother's the dawn he had crept home stinking from Flora after high-school commencement and found his mother awake and extending what she never meant to give. Lacked the will to give, lacked the knowledge of how.

"They love you," he said.

"Thank you," Polly said. "That is all my hope. I love them surely. And I've told them, many ways. I can beg for you that you'll have such a life." She waved round her slightly with one slow hand as if all her time and luck were gathered in this warm room and were visible—witness and proof.

Half-smiling, Rob looked. Then he said "Beg who?"

"Well, I pray some," she said. "I mentioned that."

Rob said "Wait please," even held out a staying hand. "I doubt I could bear it."

"Me praying?"

"—Such a life."

"Then you'll die young," she said, "or dry at the heart before your time. No Mayfield has, not in my sight at least."

He waited a good while; his question wasn't idle. "Say what I must do."

"Do you love anybody?"

"My mother," he said.

"Anybody with a chance of lasting you for life?"

"No ma'm," Rob said. "One or two love me."

"Pick the strong one," Polly said.

9

When Rob drove up by the dark hotel, his own frail headlamps were the only light. He cut them; cut the harassed engine; and hands on the wheel still, slumped round a sudden hole in his chest through which the gains of the past two days, gains that had fueled him in calm elation through the long trip back, seemed unstanchably flowing. For the past three hours, he had only thought of sleep (he had no watch but the fact of darkness in Mr. Hutchins' room meant eleven at least, maybe twelve or one); and as he was now, sleep seemed not only desirable but urgent. His strength had measured itself with utter economy, had lasted him to this dark yard precisely.

Yet when he moved, it was not toward the side stairs (the second-floor porch, the hall, his room) but back toward Grainger's and Della's rooms. The end of his strength was taking him there in no light at all; there was no moon or stars.

He opened their front door and entered the trapped warm air of their hall. The door on the left was Grainger's. Rob stroked it twice with his knuckles. No answer. More firmly, two knocks. No voice or move. He felt down the ribbed pine of the door to the china knob and turned it and pushed.

Grainger's close black air—every window chinked shut—stood to meet him, a solid element neither foul nor harsh but such as no white man could lay down around him or breathe for long, a separate diet. Rob took a step inward and said once "Grainger—" Nothing, though Grainger slept lightly as a rule. He took a second step, raised his voice and called again. When only silence answered, Rob felt so strongly that he needed Grainger now that he walked all the way through the foreign air till his hands found the edge of Grainger's bed, then blindly searched it. The covers were thrown back, the thin pillow crumpled; and though they were hotter than the room—freshly used—they were empty of Grainger. Rob stood and tried once more, whispering "Grainger?"

Then he went out quickly to the hall—Della's door, stood and strained to hear. Nothing again. Or was there a single whimper, smothered? Rob did not knock but found the knob easily and opened full. The same thick element; the dry sounds of movement, skin on cloth.

"Something wrong?"

"Della?"

A stupified wait, more movement. "Something wrong?"

"May be. Della?"

"You back," Della said.

Rob could not speak, for gratitude.

"You hungry?" she said.

He knew that he was, that likely she had some cold bread on her bureau, that what he wanted first was to ask after Grainger; but he said "You alone?"

Della laughed. "Is a rock?"

He said "Yes" as if she'd intended an answer, then began at the buttons of his shirt and was naked in fifteen seconds. He stood in the pile of shed clothes and said "Where is Grainger now?"

"In Heaven if the Lord be merciful to *me*."

"He's not in his room, but his bed is warm."

"You go on back and wait for him then and keep it warm, not waking me up when I need rest to talk about a fool that I hadn't seen since dark tonight."

Rob regretted his bareness, however concealed, and knew he should quietly dress and leave—Della to the few hours' sleep before dawn when she'd rise to cook; himself to ruinous solitary night, his heart still draining.

"You going or staying?" Her voice was as harsh as in dealing with Grainger and bore to his nose a pure raw gust of the metal deep in her, the actual high smell of fingered brass, the shock of tin on his own back teeth.

But he went on toward her and met her silent welcome—her thin white gown shucked quickly; her short close bones and hot dense skin extended as an unseen harbor, a bed, in which he could hunt again the consolation of permitted triumph. Hunt and, as always, find. Even as he hooked his bristling chin on the hinge of Della's shoulder (he had never touched her mouth) and felt for her hipbones to haul her upward (she never moved at first of her own accord, only toward the end), he knew he would win this time as always. One good thing which had never yet refused him. It didn't now.

Exhausted as he was from the trip, the real *journey*, the whole elaborate net of his senses poised itself slowly (no haste, no fear); cast itself surely and caught its small prey- -a spot on his forebrain the size of a child's hand in which his total body met a rest so perfect, reward so sufficient, that he did not resent Della's own private seizure, her hoarse employment of what seemed now a distant county of a country at peace. Nor the cries she stifled in the heel of her hand, a blind fed puppy.

"You all right?" she said.

"Now," he said.

"Well, you back like I said." She touched the knob at the back of his neck, the crest of his spine beneath which his powers of movement lay bound in a simple cord.

"Not for long" Rob said.

"Where you headed?"

"Out of *here*."

"When you leaving?"

"Not sure."

"Who you taking?"

Rob paused, uncertain of her meaning.

"You come here with Grainger. Who you taking when you leave?"

Rob thought that he knew. For the first time today, in all his life, he thought that he knew who would leave with him; go with him toward a life he could live. He could not tell Della, not now in her arms—rank, wet with her gift.

10

Ten minutes later, threading rocks and roots in the yard, he passed his car on the way to sleep; and Grainger's voice whispered "You all right, Rob?"

Rob was too tired for fear, but he stopped and searched the dark before answering. He thought he detected some signs that Grainger was sitting on the nearside runningboard, so he said "Where you been?"

Grainger said "You the traveler."

Rob came closer to him, stopped five feet away. It was Grainger; Grainger's heat reached him even through the cool air of mountain night. He could not now remember why he'd sought Grainger first half an hour ago or what he might have said if Grainger had been waiting; but he knew he must not cheat

him now and leave without some greeting. Rob went to the car and sat beside
him on the hard runningboard and finally said, "You have been to New Jersey and Maine and France."

Grainger waited awhile. "You been to Richmond?"

Rob also waited. "Yes thank you," he said.

"See your daddy?"

"Yes."

"Miss Polly?"

"Yes."

"They doing all right?"

"Good as anybody else," Rob said.

"They treat you nice?"

"Very nice," Rob said. "Good food, good bed."

"You like your daddy?"

"All right," Rob said. "Too early to know."

"He going to help you?"

Rob said "He tried."

"Talked to you a lot?"

Rob laughed. "He's a talker. Nothing wrong with that Polly's public-
speaking either."

"Never was," Grainger said. He laughed, then waited. "He get you a
job?"

"He said he would try. I didn't promise nothing."

"If you were a nigger, he could send you to school."

Rob said, "That might be a good idea."

"—Being nigger or smart?"

"Some of both, I guess."

"Too late," Grainger said.

"Could be," Rob said, "but I may keep trying. I just now came from rubbing on black." He pointed toward the quarters, dark as it was.

Grainger said "I seen you."

"Where were you then?"

"Out here. I mean I heard you coming out."

Rob said, "Where were you before that? I went to your room."

"I been looking for you."

"You'll get yourself shot, poking round at night. These mountaineers
don't give you time to explain, specially if you're dark."

Grainger said, "You the one been poking, not me. More people shot for
poking than looking."

"Where the Hell you think I was hiding round here? Didn't Della tell you I had gone on a trip?"

"Wouldn't ask Della for moisture in a drouth. I knew where you were. I was waiting not looking. I couldn't get to sleep. I was down by the spring— worked there all day; got the new shingles on. Start cleaning it tomorrow."

Rob hauled himself to his numbing feet and walked a step. "Stop waiting," he said. "For God's sake, stop. I'm back. Day's coming."

"I'll see," Grainger said. He also stood, came toward Rob, and easily found Rob's wrist with his fingers. He ringed the wrist tightly and twisted three times before Rob pulled free. "If day come," he said (he was whispering again) "you look at that good; see did dark rub off. Did—it come off Grainger. Grainger give you your wish."

11

At the hint of day five hours later, in Richmond not Goshen, Forrest Mayfield's eyes opened fully from sleep, awake in the instant, though he'd slept only five hours since turning in at one after finishing a letter to Rob in the study. He had stayed on at school till three on Sunday; then had come home to find Polly gone, no note. He had read until five—a search in Vergil—when he'd heard her come in, climb straight to her room, and shut her door quietly. She often took walks; he knew she was low from Robinson's visit, a state which he counted on time to repair; so he'd read on till six; then despite their having late supper on Sundays, he wondered at her silence and went to the foot of the steps and listened. Nothing at all. He'd called out mildly, "Are you starving me from home?" and after a while, she opened her door (her face webbed with sleep) and said "No it's yours." — "Please feed me then," he'd said and waited smiling as she went back to wash her face. He helped her in the kitchen; and they ate with few words on the smallest subjects (Polly ate very little). He had tried to crystallize in his mind one thing he could say to satisfy her, to acknowledge his thanks and the size of her care, to honor her fears but belittle them gently. Nothing useful would come, only lines with multiple edges, all keen—"Did you take to him?" "Can we help him at all?" "Should we try now or have we already done enough?" So while she cleared the table, Forrest sat and watched her face till at last he could say, "Is there anything you need to ask me, Polly?" She had drawn a pan of water and begun to wash dishes before she said (her face still to Forrest), "I need to know how much is changed." — "Nothing" rushed to his lips; but he'd held it in, suspecting a lie; and when he'd stood to go do Monday's preparations, he'd said, "I will tell you as soon as I know." She had nodded, not turning; and he'd worked on his lessons till he heard her turn in, then had started the necessary letter to Rob. When he'd finished and climbed to bed at one, he had not paused at Polly's open door, though he'd noticed the darkness and silence beyond it and felt the intensity of baffled waiting.

Now at dawn, a little startled to be thoroughly rested by so little sleep, Forrest lay in cool sheets on his narrow bed and consulted his body with the flats of his own broad hands under cloth. He did not often touch himself at leisure and, though he had never despised the offers of pleasure (even transport), he lacked the voluptuary's constant wonder in the constant resources of self, simple meat. But what pleased his hands now was firm lean health—the fact that, with no conscious effort by him of exercise or diet, he had withstood years; his body had ignored these fifty-four years (or, say, the past fifteen: he looked a man of thirty-eight and felt it), though he knew there were millions of ambushes gathering, suicides planned in every cell. With his hands on the hot dry stripes of his groin, where his long legs became his high full balls (the balls of a boy in the first rush of power, the embarrassed crest of male generosity), Forrest said to himself what he suddenly knew and had not known before, "I have chosen this." It was something that he might have guessed long before—twenty-one years before, naked in a stream near Panacea Springs, having seen Eva leave him the final time. He had waited till now— a gift from Rob? his letter to Rob? Polly's separate fear one room away? He was roused as always by real news, by knowledge—roused in spirit.

So he rose, poured water in his china bowl (running water was piped no higher than the kitchen), washed his mouth and eyes, and walked to Polly's doorway.

Her eyes were open; she was facing him. She lay on her right side and faced him unsmiling; her left arm splayed back behind her grotesquely, boneless or wrenched.

Forrest wanted to speak. If he'd been fully dressed or covered by darkness, he could have stood ground on the sill and said, "Very little is changed. Maybe nothing at all. Whatever may flow from these two days will not move you." But he stood in pale daylight in the crumpled absurdity of underwear at the end of her gaze; so he did what he seldom did at all, maybe ten times a year, and never till now without her permission. He walked quickly in and sat at the foot of Polly's bed. They were silent awhile; then he said "Have you slept?"

"I think so," she said. She looked to her window; the green shade was down. "What time is it now?"

With his hand Forrest sought her shin through cloth, a muffled blade. "Five-thirty," he said.

Polly did not move her leg from his grip.

He took that to be her latest permission; and waiting a moment to allow her denial, he touched the sheet on the crest of her shoulder and drew it down enough to allow his entry into space that was neat as if she'd made it freshly to greet his arrival and cool as the coolest hour of the night which had left him so ready—the night through which, he now understood, she could not have slept. He stayed on his back in the narrow place, touching Polly nowhere, and fixed on the single black light-cord that hung from the spotted ceiling like a plumb. It seemed to promise that the answer he would give—must give in a moment—would be true and just, merciful and grateful. He waited for words.

Polly touched his arm, with one left finger. Then she raised herself very slightly from the waist and removed her gown—drew it over her head; her hair was loose—then dropped it on the clean floor and lay flat herself.

Forrest took that as his best hope of answer. Years of contiguous restraint had given their bodies a gift of speech more lucid than words; their rare full meetings had therefore preserved the power to delight, deepen mystery, appall, but chiefly to confirm in plain detail with a logic as bare as the figures of Euclid their mutual love. They confirmed it now in mutual silence. The sounds around them were the sounds of objects—cloth, wood, iron, the approving air.

Done and rested and the room filling quickly with Monday through gaps at the edge of the shade, Forrest only said, "I must leave in an hour."

"All right," Polly said. "You dress; I'll cook." She raised herself again and fished for her gown. "What you teaching them today?"

"The names of God in fourteen tongues."

She laughed and he joined her.

12

By six-thirty, Rachel in her bed in Goshen had sunk to the lowest shelf of sleep. She had gone to bed early in search of refuge from the speculations of her mother and the Roberts boys, the dumb pain of Grainger, her own fear and hope; and of course she'd pitched restless through the next three hours till the whole house was quiet. Then she'd paddled through a long stretch of what seemed no more than harassed darkness (a cruel taunting) but was actually sleep, hectic and frail yet deep enough to shield her from the various sounds of Rob's return. Some ear in her mind perceived that though—his arrival in his room, his quiet undressing, not his visit with Della or talk with Grainger—and freed her then to begin the oblivion she'd wanted since Friday when he'd left with his curious promise to come back bearing the word that would win her or to hunt it at least. So she'd roamed through a number of levels of rest on her slow descent—the quick bright chatter that she often so easily delivered in sleep (little poems, long volleys of witty exchange, neat but lethal retorts: all gone before day), a tale in which she was learning from Lucy (Della's long-dead mother) how to carve up dirt into squares like candy that would please her father who did not like sweets, a perfect list of the names of the children she had known in school from the age of seven till nine years later when she'd finished with honors—but no trace of Rob. Her mind thought of that, the peculiar omission, tried to force itself to imagine his face and rig a tale round it, to sort through the language in search of a word which by day she could give him, the necessary word.

No use. She was flat on the bottom of rest, all voices appeased, when at six-thirty Monday, a hand on her door. Or a long warning maybe. She wrenched herself conscious with the thought that the hotel was far-gone in flames, one hand struggling to wake her. She sat up, said "Yes?", checked the windows for safety—clear morning, no smoke. But no voice answered. Then again gentle knocking. "Father?"

"No. Rob."

She reached for her robe and was almost at the door when he opened it a little. "Good morning," she said.

He nodded. "I'm back."

"You are; I see. I've thought about you."

"I've thought some myself."

"About what?" she said.

"Living my life or not."

Against her will, she smiled. "You're white and twenty-one. Did you reach a conclusion?"

"I hope so," he said, "but first, have you?"

Even torn from sleep, Rachel could not hedge or lie. "Not yet," she said.

Rob said, "Then listen. If I was planning to live out a life, some decent sort of life, would you live it with me?"

Rachel thought, "If someone had said to me 'Compose the speech you would most need to hear from a person you love,' could I have guessed this?—guessed anything half as close as this?"

"You don't have to answer this minute," he said. He must leave for work or forfeit the job.

"Are you *planning* that?" she said.

"It depends, I guess." Rob had not smiled yet.

"On me?"

"Yes ma'm." He smiled and ducked a little bow. As his head reached its low point and saw her bare feet, white as tallow and dry, he knew he had lied, though he did not know he'd forget that knowledge, remember it only long months from now.

"Then thank you," she said.

"You will?"

"Yes thank you."

Smiling still, Rob clamped his eyes shut and nodded. Then he looked again and said, "I'll see you this evening."

"See Father," Rachel said. "He has got some say."

13

Rob had worked late on Monday, been exhausted and gone to bed once he'd eaten, barely speaking to Rachel and not even seeing her father or mother. On Tuesday when he reached the hotel at seven, this letter was waiting on the dark hall-table. He went to his room and read it before washing.

August 16, 1925

Dear Robinson,

I had hoped that somehow you could hold off leaving till I got back from school, but I well understand how you had to leave. What a cruel distance, and twice in two days. I only hope you are safely there and will rest tonight for your new week tomorrow. It is strange for me that after long years of having you out of my cares entirely (though not from my griefs, however buried), I now find I've worried all evening about you; guessed at your whereabouts, pictured your condition.

I suppose you have felt, if you've felt at all, that I let your mother leave with very little struggle, which would also mean little struggle for you. That is less than half-true. I wrote strong letters, sent valuable gifts returned by Mr. Kendal, and made a last trip to Fontaine in August (you were five months old; I was not allowed to see you). Then I pled on by mail till I saw, was profoundly made to know, two related facts—Eva and me. We were separate and strange to one another as a cat and a dog, though without that enmity. We never once fought, however hard we spoke in the effort not to lie. A cat can be made to adopt a puppy if his mother dies; she will even nurse him if she has milk to give; but however grateful and needful he becomes, she will walk off and leave him when he's big enough to wean. Claw him blind if need be; I've seen it happen. And the puppy will imagine desperation and death. But he'll live of course and find he enjoys it and seek his own kind. You know all that. What a puppy cannot do or a full-grown dog is imagine and feel the weight and value of a fellow creature as I've imagined yours this afternoon and evening (it is past midnight), to my deep surprise. It has been my observation in fifty years of watching that few men are capable of close attention over long spans of time to another human being. That is woman's great gift and her steadiest pain, to gaze at another for years on years and care each moment as much as for herself, occasionally more. My sister Hattie, Rena Kendal (from what you tell me), Polly Drewry, maybe Grainger. Of the men I have watched—maybe Grainger, now me (or me again: I felt this with Eva, but it had to fade).

Is it also your burden?—too great an attention? From the two talks we had, I suspect it may be; and because I have spent a large part of my life in the company of books (by no means the safe flight or warm consolation so often charged) and because I believe from my own experience and that of men far my superiors in life that the wisdom of a few books carefully studied will prove more useful and slightly less wearing than the raw fray of life—because of those things, I have searched this evening for a passage in Vergil which began to pull at the edge of my mind through all you told me of your own life and worries. You said that you read Book Four of the Aeneid *under Thorne Bradley in school; I do not know that you read other parts or encountered this passage, so I write it out for you. (I'll confess that my own work has kept me from Vergil so long that I did indeed have to hunt for the lines.) But first will you grant me, a lifelong teacher, a little preamble to set the stage?*

Aeneas has fled the ruins of Troy and is borne on a storm of Juno's hatred to the shores of Africa, confused and despairing, having lost his wife, his father and home. There on Libyan sands his mother comes to him. She is Venus but disguised from his recognition as a huntress, armed. He sees her divinity, though not her name, and tells her his plight. She urges him onward to the palace in Carthage, the seat of Dido. Her parting words are,

> Perge modo et, qua te ducit via, derige gressum.
> *Only proceed and walk with the road.*

From there, in light of your claim to bad Latin, may I translate for you?

She spoke and, turning, her rose neck shone.
From the crown ambrosial hair breathed fragrance;
Raiment fell round her feet and in gait she was shown
An actual god. He knew her as mother
And chased her vanishing with words—
"You cruel too? Why tempt your son
So often with false games? Why may
My right hand not greet yours and why
Not hear true words and answer truthfully?"

—Well, I offer you those for whatever good they hold, restraining myself from comment but for this: remember her last words,

> Only proceed and walk with the road,

and that, despite the cries of Aeneas, it is she who is godly and sees his fate, not miserable he. His fate is not her.

I certainly don't claim special powers of foresight or wisdom as to where your road must lead or what the road is; but I can say this much now with some assurance. You can have a job here on January 1st in the business office. As I told you last night, the bursar's clerk is retiring at seventy (and none too soon; no two columns of figures have balanced in the past five years). I went in to see the superintendent this afternoon and mentioned that you were in hopes of bettering your outlook, and could he help out? He thought awhile and said he'd intended to put a young Negro in the job, a graduate if possible; but had recently had second thoughts on the subject (the job calls for some little traveling in the state and into Carolina, some meeting the public—bankers, preachers, etc.). So in short if you are inclined to take it, he would lean your way, I am virtually certain. He hinted as much, being heavy on hints and light on decisions; but you must act fairly soon. First, tell me if you are interested. Then I'll send you the outline of what he would want by way of application and references (would Thorne recommend you? who else in Fontaine? would your present boss?).

Please give this good, but not slow, thought. You need to act soon. And if you should ask, as you very well may, why Forrest Mayfield comes now after twenty years of silence and absence, seeking company, I would answer you or Eva or anyone else something close to this. It is not for personal gain or even pleasure (though I'd hope to take pleasure in your nearness, to be sure) but in the strong and natural hope of recompense; of showing you something, after years with the Kendals, which one Mayfield at least has learned—in fact all the Mayfields I've known before you: how simply to proceed. Any of the others could show you as well as I, I'm sure—my father, were he here, or Hattie

_or Grainger—but I at least am willing and probably have less desperation of
heart than they, which is my commendation._

_Thank you for coming here and hearing me out—well, hardly out. I have
nothing if not a long stream of words, but we are after all amending the faults
and omissions of decades. Many still yawn; some will never bear filling. If you
come back and stay—this home is ready for you; it is yours as much as mine—
I will work more quietly at a stronger repairing: by act, by deed._

In any case, proceed, Son, and answer me please.

Your hopeful,
Father

14

When Rob had washed and eaten and sat on the sideporch with Rachel till
dark, talking only of what didn't matter a hair to anyone alive (they were both
a little rigid with the effort to avoid spoken recollection of yesterday's promise;
and they separately wondered if they'd dreamt the meeting, the contract
made) and when Mrs. Hutchins had said her good nights and gone indoors,
pulling Rachel in her wake, Rob went to the corner where Mr. Hutchins sat
every night till eleven and said, "May I sit here awhile, Mr. Hutchins?"

Mr. Hutchins said, "You've paid for it. Sit anywhere."

Rob sat on the railing, his back to the night, feet hooked in the posts. He
was six feet from Mr. Hutchins but eye-level to him. Rob sat awhile in
silence (Mr. Hutchins had started his final cigar). Then he said, "Have you
known me long enough?" He was smiling, though at air; Mr. Hutchins
wasn't looking.

"Long enough for what?"

"To judge my nature."

A sizable wait. "I think so, yes."

"Then tell me please."

Mr. Hutchins laughed. "Haven't known you that long."

Rob said "How's that?"

"I mean I have my own clear opinion, but I don't know you well enough
to say if you could take it."

Rob said "It's that bad?"

"It has some rough edges." He did not laugh again, but his words were
colored by the smile they slid through. He sucked at his cigar; then he said,
"Which one are you after?"

Rob said "Sir?"—caught and chilled.

"There are two women roughly your age around here."

Rob had honestly assumed himself to be invisible to the man. His plan, the speech he'd relied on to come, was paralyzed.

Mr. Hutchins said, "Have you been down to the spring since Grainger fixed the roof?"

Rob said, "He told me but, no sir, I haven't."

"You're thirsty, I trust?"

"Yes sir," Rob said with no conception of what would follow (he had not passed a hundred words alone with Mr. Hutchins since moving here).

Mr. Hutchins stood—"I'll show you"—and was half-down the steps to the yard when Rob joined him. They had gone ten yards in the cooling thick darkness before Mr. Hutchins said, "I've killed two rattlers right here since spring" and proceeded from there with slow high steps.

Rob said "Grainger told me" and also stepped higher.

Mr. Hutchins said, "Yes but Grainger didn't *kill* them, came calling for me"; and neither spoke again (they were flanking the quarters) till they reached the springhouse, an open-sided octagon twelve feet across, lattice work all round maybe three feet high. Mr. Hutchins paused at the entrance side and reached up to touch the edge of the sloping roof, stroked it like the neck of a dog three times. Without looking back, in a studious voice, he said, "Now this is one thing will outlast you, a red cedar roof."

Rob came up beside him and also reached. He was shorter by a head, so only the tips of his fingers could touch the dry fragrant verge of Grainger's work. Yet it seemed important to touch what he could of the substance which would silver through the next ten years, then begin to moss over but still turn water maybe fifty years from now when Rob Mayfield would be sodden or vanished; to touch it not only to please Mr. Hutchins who was watching but to search in himself for the small coal of serious hope uncovered by Polly and his father or put there by them. Rob found the coal and warmed it; he would not lose it now. He lowered his arm and entered the springhouse before Mr. Hutchins, passed the round central font, and sat on the railing of the dark far side.

Mr. Hutchins stayed out.

Rob said, "I am after Rachel, Mr. Hutchins. It's Rachel I want."

Mr. Hutchins reached up again and patted his roof. Then he stepped inside and came on as far as the spring itself and stood behind that. "The roof before this one was put on in eighteen and seventy-three by my grandfather once he'd figured the war was actually over and that people might start getting sick again. My mother was the main one he had in mind. She was his youngest daughter and had married my father, young Raven Hutchins, the previous year; and

they'd moved here to live and help with what few guests still came. The worst
guest was me. I came in the late fall of '72 — November rains — and just about
tore my mother to pieces. She was short and narrow. I was big from the start
like my father's people, and she stayed down in bed the rest of that winter.
Then in spring when it looked like she still couldn't strengthen (and all my
father could do was grieve — sweet man, helpless fool), my grandfather
thought this water might help her, make her think she'd live. It had been
boarded up since during the war when a young girl that refugeed here from
Richmond caught the typhoid and died and her mother blamed the water;
she may have been right. I've never claimed that it had anything to recommend it but wetness and sulphur; if you're dry or have got the itch or mange,
it may help you some. Otherwise you're better off drinking whatever you were
drinking the Sunday you came here. Anyhow my grandfather had it cleaned
out and tore down the old shed and built this new one, twice the size. And
she did improve — my mother, strange to say. In a matter of weeks, she was out
on the porch; and by the time my clear memories begin, she was strong as you
or me and stronger than my father. They worked on here to run the hotel. I
grew up here; only place I know, only place I'd ask the Lord to spare. It was
always a one-horse operation, never more than ten rooms. We never doubted
that — Warm Springs and Rockbridge Baths were right down the road — but
we had a small number of elderly people who came every summer and rocked
and talked, even drank a dipperful of this stinking water once or twice a day.
Good for their bowels; we had four johnnies. What they mainly came for was
Mother's good meals three times a day. Cooked and served by Mother — great
tubs of fresh food, fresh bread and cakes — with nothing to help her but my
sister Lou, and me to chop wood, and Della's black mother (the mountains
were not strong on Negroes then). But they did have to struggle to get here
like I said — catch the train to Hot Springs; I'd meet them in the wagon and
haul them to here on that little road: it has stopped several hearts and no water
would start them — and people these days aren't looking for struggles; so gradually the business thinned out to nothing. A widow or two, some mean old
maids. I was grown by then and clerking dry goods for Wilson Hamlett.
Grandpa had died. My own sorry father just sat on the porch and prayed for
money; what little we had was squeezed by Mother and me from odd drummers and the few summer guests. (I helped her at night when I got home from
work. We'd sometimes scramble till one in the morning, turning mattresses
or cooking. I'd help her put up great bushels of food; we worked smooth
together.) This spring here had come down to nothing but spiders, lizards all
in it, big healthy snakes. And then I got married; you know to who. She had
grown up in Goshen way out by the river (her people had come here to teach

from east Virginia—Isle of Wight, near Suffolk; good stock, big readers); but we planned to move out of here when we could. I was planning to take any job God offered just to leave this hole. Well, God wasn't offering—not in 1894, not through the mails (which is what I was trying: writing off for jobs)—so finally I decided to hunt in person. That meant telling Mother. I came down early one Saturday morning (I had begged the day off), and she fixed my breakfast (my wife was upstairs). She thought I was just going off to Hamlett's, and I had decided to let her think it; I told my wife, 'If you come down and tell Mother where I've gone, I'll leave you flat.' But then she touched me— my mother, I mean. She was not a great toucher; I don't think she'd touched me in oh nine years; but she came up behind me that Saturday morning— nobody was with us—and carefully touched my head with her hands, parted my hair with her long tough fingers. It almost killed me; food seized in my throat. I thought, 'I am Peter and the cock's crowed thrice.' But I kept my own counsel and prayed she would just go on with her cooking. Well, she finished my hair and moved her hands down to rest on my shoulders; then still there behind me which didn't help a bit, she said, 'You feel like you're leaving me.' —'I'm warm,' I said; 'Is that what you mean?' (it was early June). 'No it's not,' she said. Then we both were quiet and still as old logs. Then somebody's feet started coming downstairs—a lady named Simpson from South Carolina; from Mullins, I think. Mother said 'Tell me quick.' So I swallowed my cold cud and told her, not looking, 'Yes ma'm. We are hoping to move to Lynch-burg.' And back quick as voltage, she said 'Then damn you.' But I went to Lynchburg."

Rob, in the dark behind the spring, thought Mr. Hutchins had only paused for breath; so he did not speak through a sizable wait, though he saw Mr. Hutchins was looking to him. Finally Rob said, "You went and she died?"

Mr. Hutchins stepped up and under the roof and came as far forward as the edge of the spring. "You figured that out or did Della tell you?"

"Rachel," Rob said.

"It's true anyhow."

"Right away?" Rob said.

"No a year and a half. She waited that long. I got a job in Lynchburg, clerk-ing again; and we moved there in August. She never tried to stop me after that first time—wrote me letters every Sunday, sent me little gifts of food—and we came back here to visit at Christmas. Everything seemed the same. It wasn't; she was hiding, not her sickness maybe (it may not have started) but her mis-ery surely. She was left alone. Father was there and Lou and the help, but it turned out they didn't matter to her. I had almost killed her one time before; so she gave me the power to do it again, to finish what I started twenty-five years before. I finished it. We went back to Lynchburg, my wife and I; and the following November when I came up here one Sunday for my birthday, I found her just about dead. No warning except that one little time like I said when she damned me. Advanced T.B.—really galloping consumption as the old people called it. Everybody knows, or knew back then before doctors ruled the world, that consumption was something you wished on yourself or at least welcomed-in. She had made everybody else promise not to tell me; so I walked in cold on the sight of her wasting. What it did was make me mad, at her and the others. I think I kept it from her; but I felt it like gall in my mouth all that day, just pure damned mad that she'd used me like that when all I'd done was start my life: she pretended I'd loved her and had gone back on that; it was her loved me. And I left again to prove it. It killed her by Christmas, six days before. The last thing she told me when I left that Sunday (my birthday visit) was 'You can come back now, just a few more days.' I told myself I never would; but after the funeral I could see my father was all caved in and would follow her soon. He had not known he loved her. He was left like a pissed-out bladder, that empty. I thought I would move back long enough to close this dump down and see Father through to his end—he was older than Mother, well on in his fifties and had a bad heart—and then sell all this and strike out again on my own plans. So back we came and here we are. It was Lou that died; she had caught it from Mother. Father lived on till just before Rachel got sick, two years ago; and sometime in there after those two deaths, I just gave up. You've seen me here." Mr. Hutchins waved round himself with both hands mildly. "I guess I stayed for Rachel. It is all she knew, she was always frail, I hated to move her. Now it's harming her."

Rob said, "Then I offer to take her away."

"To where?"

"Maybe Richmond. I can get a job there much better than this one. My father will help me."

"—Teaching Negroes *what?* What else do you know that Negroes can use?" Mr. Hutchins was calm but his voice meant to damage.

Rob laughed. "I thought you slept better than that."

"No I don't. I've heard every time—you creeping back here. Thank Jesus I haven't heard more than the creeping."

"Yes sir," Rob said. Silence extended. Then he said, "I never heard you tell me to stop."

Mr. Hutchins said, "And won't. I offered her to you, still offer her now."

"To keep me off Rachel? I have not touched Rachel."

"I know that too."

"How please sir?" Rob said.

"Because Rachel's happy. Rachel's stronger every day."

Rob waited again, then was forced to say "I don't understand you."

Mr. Hutchins said, "She really hasn't told you?"

"No sir. I mean, she has mentioned Lynchburg, that doctor's place. She says it was never her chest, just nerves."

"She was sick all over," Mr. Hutchins said. "See, nobody claimed that place in Lynchburg was just for T.B. It's a real hospital. I thought she had it; and Dr. James here did, for what he's worth—which is less than he charges (he tended my mother and also Lou, watched them strangle). But everybody knew her nerves were involved."

Rob said, "I'm no doctor but, as women's health goes, she seems well to me."

Mr. Hutchins waited, then bent where he stood and lifted the round wood lid that covered the mouth of the spring. He reached above in the peak of the ceiling and found the great dipper—a yard long, copper—and stooped and carefully filled it with water. Then he walked to Rob and, still holding the handle, offered the drink.

Rob accepted, set lips to the strong-tasting metal, and held the first draft from this spring on his tongue. A frightening presence within his own gates, old with minerals and rank with gas—poison or balm? He could still spit it out and refuse its effects.

But Mr. Hutchins stood above him, watching as keenly as if it were day and Rob were a message he could read with effort.

Rob swallowed twice.

Mr. Hutchins raised the dipper to his own face but stopped. He turned slightly sideward and threw out the few drinks Rob had left. Then he hung the dipper in the dark again and said, "I can thank you for saving her life."

Rob said, "Not I. I have just cheered her some. She has helped me as much."

Mr. Hutchins said, "And you swear Della hasn't told you?"

"Della's never said her name."

Mr. Hutchins sat on the edge of the spring. "Rachel lost her mind. Two years ago. She got the idea she was having a baby. Don't ask me how. The doctors that looked said no man had gone near her; she swore so herself. But she showed many signs of carrying a child for more than six months—the curse stopped in her; she was violently sick but gained flesh steadily. To see her, you would think you had met a soul in torment, though she never claimed that. She would barely speak, and then just a word to Della or her mother. I went in one morning after maybe four months and tried to be pleasant, tried to pass a little time (which hung heavy on her—she had finished school; she didn't have friends). I said did she have all the clothes she needed, meaning we could order her something nice. She nodded Yes three times and walked to the mantel and took up a tape measure, measured her waist right in front of me. Then she came close on me and said—fierce as you would say '*Die!*' or '*Kneel!*'—'This baby is coming here day by day and not one stitch in the whole house for it. It will perish bare.' I said to her, 'Rachel, there is not any baby. You are tired and confused. But you're also young—just relax now and rest; don't press on your mind. Then you'll be yourself again and can get on with starting your life with those you love.'"

Rob said "Who were they?"

"Her mother and me, the whole place here. She was partial to Della's mother, Lucy."

Rob said, "She was bound to be in love with somebody."

Mr. Hutchins thought it through. "She had had some school friends, a boy or two that came to see her, take her up on the mountain with a big crowd—picnics. But no love, no. I'd have been the first to know. She's a mystery to her mother, but to me she's plain as print. We are hopeless close-kindred."

Rob said, smiling slightly, "Then she knew I was coming."

Mr. Hutchins said, "She may have. I sure to God did." He stopped as if regretting it, then bowed to explaining. "I knew the night you got here she would love you soon."

Rob said, "She was still in Lynchburg then."

"She was. But I knew."

"How please?"

"I've told you. She and me are close-kindred. She's all I've cared about in all my life and I'm fifty-two. My mother worshipped me and I killed her for it, but I can't say I loved her. I had hurt her too much, from right at the first when I tore her so badly—you can't forgive that: that you tried to kill a woman and she lasted and loves you. My wife—well, you've seen her; she does what's needed, does it quietly and well. But Rachel is a daughter. You can understand the rest—you were born, I trust; and I know you've had women—but you've never had a daughter; so you can't know till then. She is something you make in absolute pleasure with no work at all; and she comes into life bearing half your nature—in some cases, more. Treat her gently and decently, she'll turn to you like leaves to light before she can talk and tell you her care. By the time she's a child—say, seven or eight—you will find, if you're lucky (though I wonder is it luck or one more burden?), she has turned *into* you. You and her are one thing. So back last April, I saw you coming up my yard with Grainger; and I knew you were hers."

Rob said "Can she have me?"

"When?"

"Oh end of summer."

Mr. Hutchins stood and closed down the lid of the spring. "Might as well," he said. He turned, walked three steps toward the entrance; then said, not looking back, "But kill her and I'll find you wherever you are, make you pray to die."

Rob said "Yes sir."

15

August 23, 1925

Dear Father,

Yes, Mr. Bradley did take us through that part of the Aeneid. *I could have told you about the meeting with Venus; but as you suspected, I'd mislaid the advice or never really heard it (the way we were hauled through Vergil—kicking, bleeding—would have deafened a deer). Walk with the road—I'm doing that, I guess, since I'm building the road; and it seems to aim at Richmond, eastward at least.*

I didn't plan on that. It was planned by the Commonwealth of Virginia. Looking back over my twenty-one years, I can't see that I have planned anything much. I hoped some things would happen—a life of long content—but until I was forced to pull up stakes in Fontaine this spring, I don't think I did much to help them happen, unless it was to reach out and take somebody (nobody I had hoped for anyhow). Even that pull-up was forced by Mother, as I tried to explain, and by Kennerly Kendal's meanness of heart. Even my visit to you and Polly was planned by Grainger and urged by you which is not to say that I didn't enjoy it (I did and am grateful; please pass that to her).

But now after five little months of misery—three of them spent pulverizing hills that God intended to last till Judgment—in a job just two notches better than what any barebacked rockheaded fieldhand black as a stove could ask for and get (and better me at): now I have done one thing on my own, Rob Mayfield has. I plan to be married. Nobody but me and the girl involved; and the idea was mine, though I know it had crossed her mind once or twice.

She is who I mentioned to you last Saturday when we had got back from the show and you'd said, "Then who on earth will accompany you?" Remember I named Aunt Rena and Sylvie and Grainger maybe. I was smiling, I think, to show I was joking; but you didn't see that. You said, "Think, Robinson. They are all your seniors; they will die and leave you"; and I'd said "All right." But once you'd asked who would go with me, this name came to mind—Rachel Hutchins, remember? I'd known her three months and had felt drawn to her by needs of her own; I had even made some curious promises to her. So she didn't rise up from the blue that night just to answer you. But I did come straight back here Sunday evening, my mind made up, and asked her Monday morning and her father Tuesday night.

We plan on being married here this coming Thanksgiving. My job lasts till then and Rachel needs the time (she has been a little sick but is much improved; three more months should do the trick). I invite you herewith to be present then. I also mean to ask Mother and Rena. I hope you will come.

Then after that I hope to accept the job you mention in Richmond. You say it would be in the business office. I am pretty good at figures as I think I told you, so I guess I can do it or learn quick enough. Would you please let me know what letter I should write to whom saying what? And will you make any deeper search you can into whether I will really get the job or not?

If I don't maybe Grainger can. He would be the right shade and is no doubt as good at figures as me. In fact now I mention it, I spoke to Grainger on all these developments this afternoon, the November wedding and the Richmond job. He listened at first and wished me well; but later on when I was asleep (Sunday nap), he came to my room and let himself in when I didn't answer and woke me up and said would I need him once I'd made those changes? As I told you, he came here with me last April on the spur of the moment when I was bad off and in need of help: just shut up his house and came, clean and bare (once he got the job here, he went back for two days and got a few belongings— the books you gave him—and moved some old woman cousin of his in to hold down his floor till he came home, if ever). So in short I said I would. Need him, I mean. He said, "Then you're asking me to come with you?" I said I was, providing I went; and he said "Does Mr. Forrest know?" I said no you didn't but that I planned to write you a letter tonight. "Then ask him," he said; "ask him can I come." My own quick plan was that we could use him—that is, Rachel and I. He is good in the house, and she will need help. So I told him that though you had kindly said that I could move in at the Mayfield place, I had tripled my numbers without warning you and thus would intend to find a small place of my own, room for him. He thought about that but still said again, "You ask Mr. Forrest does he want me to come. Then show me his answer." I promised I would—and I have, so please answer. I thought I noticed some reservation on Polly's part when I spoke of Grainger; if there is, tell me now. And kindly answer soon.

I am trying—do you see?—just to proceed. I am making these plans now entirely on my own. If others can't bless them, then I'll go on alone; or Rachel and I will. Clearly I hope you can bless and welcome this latest Mayfield who has only now started to learn what you promise my elders know.

Thanks again to Miss Polly. I'm waiting to hear.

Your loving son,
Rob

August 23, 1925

Dear Mother,

No word from down there for ten days now. Has the heat laid you out or has Rena's hand withered? I trust you are all there and upright and breathing or someone would have wired me.

I think I am better than I've been for some time; and I hope that an explanation of why will give you maternal satisfaction if not joy.

I invite you to my wedding in Goshen, Virginia sometime in late fall, most likely Thanksgiving. You can get here by train in under eight hours; the days will be cool and the mountains in their beauty; so I'd like to see you here if your work at home permits. It goes without saying that the rest are invited if they all care to come—Kennerly and Blunt, Sylvie of course. I will write a special note to Rena after this. You would have a good seat, the clearest view available of Rob starting life—his life as you've urged.

The bride is Rachel Hutchins. I have mentioned her in past letters to you, I think. I know I have to Rena; she expressed her pleasure and her usual warnings.

In any case, her family own the hotel in Goshen where I have lived since April. They are people you could honor, have held this spot for years (there's a little mineral spring, not famous, not healing; but it won't stop running, so they built next to it some hundred years ago and have stayed right on). Rachel is in certain ways a likeness of you—not in looks or size but in having, like you, a death-grip on one single vision of life and of what she wants in it, and the courage and strength to seize out and hold it. Like you too she's strained herself in the effort; but she's young, just twenty, and is in careful hands (her parents' lavish care); and she thinks I am what life intends for her. I want to agree. She may be right.

Once the wedding is over, my job here will end. After that I am planning to move to Richmond. I have hopes of bettering my outlook there—more money, cleaner work. It would be at the school where Father teaches. I have now met him, and he has offered to help me onto my feet. Of course I asked him to be at the wedding. There is no other way. That doesn't harm you, anything you have meant to me in the past or will go on meaning. Please understand that. You, if anybody, can. You are back of this.

I had hoped to be able to beg a day off and get down to spend a weekend with you all; but now with these plans, I will need to stay here. We are also pushing the road extra hours to get our stretch finished before the fall rains.

Please write to me soon, give me news of all, give love from me to all that would want it.

Your effortful son,
Rob Mayfield II

16

Two mornings later when they'd finished breakfast and Eva had washed her father and shaved him, Sylvie helped her to walk him out into the yard and seat him in the shade; then she went for the mail. Eva asked him a question or two about his comfort. Then he nodded off and she got to work on the last of the cutwork napkins she was making for a distant cousin who had finished school in May. She was months late as always; but the girl should be grateful to get, any time, eight handmade napkins from kin she barely knew and cared less about. She was thinking that through—had almost decided to put them in a drawer and save them till someone she actually liked graduated or married: they would keep forever; the cousin was ugly and would never use them—when her father spoke clearly.

"I wonder where she went."

He frequently talked in half-dreams or stupors, and Eva seldom answered unless it was plain that he'd asked her to. She worked on in silence, and he lapsed into what seemed certain sleep.

But in less than a minute his chin kicked the air; he fixed his eyes on her—she still had not noticed—and watched with a fierce intensity of waiting. His blue eyes never blinked. When she did not look, he said, "I begged you to tell me."

Eva turned and was startled but pretended calm and said, "Please ask me again. The heat's blocked my hearing."

He worked to remember, then said with slow pain and the urgency of morning, "I asked you to tell me where she went. An easy question. You did not answer."

"Who, Father?—Sylvie? She's gone for the mail and will no doubt take her time coming back. Rena's indoors waxing the dining-room floor."

He sat awhile, eyes shut, as though that were his answer; as though his need were as simple as that—had been purified by age and apoplexy to a dog's need, a baby's. Then he begged again. "Charlotte Kendal, my wife. Charlotte Watson, she was." He had turned again on Eva.

Eva felt she should touch his hand that was gripped to the arm of the chair, but his eyes refused her. She looked at her work and said "In Heaven, I trust."

He said, "You don't believe a word of that."

"I do, yes sir."

"Did you ever know her?—a Watson child, an orphan?"

Eva said, "Years later, well after she was grown."

"Too late," he said, "long years too late."

"How is that?"

"I ruined her. I got to her early."

Eva said, "You loved her. Everybody knew that."

"*She* knew it," he said. "All Hell knows she knew it; if she's anywhere, she's there. But she also knows I harmed her."

"Her mother and father did that, Thad and Katherine."

Mr. Kendal's face could no longer show feelings more various than rage, exhaustion or boredom; so he watched her with what seemed sustained fury still, though in fact it was honest surprise. "You knew them, did you?"

"No, Father, they were dead. You told us the story."

"Never," he said. "I never told a soul."

It had been Eva's observation since her father had suffered two strokes that no good came of humoring his confusions—he would fly too far afield—so she said, "Sir, you did. I remember distinctly. You told it to Rena and Kennerly and me the night I went off with Forrest to Virginia." Her voice had stayed calm; she'd worked at the napkin. She had not mentioned Forrest's name to her father for maybe twenty years, eighteen at least. He had made it easy for her.

"You are lying again."

"No sir. I haven't lied to you since that same night."

Two mentions of the night, blunt shocks to his chest, set him back on whatever narrow rails he possessed. He waited awhile. Then he said, "Well, thank you. I can thank you at least."

She was able to touch him, her right hand on his wrist, though she did not meet his eyes.

With great difficulty he turned his stiff hand palm-up on the chair.

The move left her fingers on the crest of his pulse—a strong life, regular and harsh as cries. She bore it long moments; then she reached farther down, and his fingers gripped hers. They sat like that all the time it took Sylvie to come from her laughing meeting at the corner, with Nan the Bradleys' cook, up the walk to them. Eva took back her hand to accept the mail.

Sylvie stood beyond her reach and said, "You got you one from Rob."

Eva said, "I am glad you're not all that he remembers." She was smiling but, as Sylvie knew, the card that came from Richmond a few days before (first word from Rob in August) had gone down badly—intended for Sylvie.

Sylvie stepped a little forward and surrendered the letter, then stood as Eva opened it. "Did he get back from Richmond?"

Eva read a few lines, then folded the sheets. "Thank you, Sylvie. You'll want to get those squash on for dinner."

Sylvie stood on awhile to show that she could (Eva straightened the neck of her father's robe). Then she said, "He telling you he ain't coming back" and headed for the kitchen, muttering as she went—"Some people got sense."

Eva opened the letter and read it through quickly in the late morning sun that was finding its way through their thin screen of leaves.

Her father didn't watch her, clamped his eyes and suffered the creeping glare; but when he heard paper folding again, he said "When's he coming?"

"Sylvie's right; he's not."

"Need money?"

"No, Father. He is paid every week. He needs a wife apparently. This says he's getting married."

Mr. Kendal didn't turn. Eyes shut, bare crown of his head assaulted by glare, he said "Read it to me."

Eva read it through clearly in a low voice which many good ears could not have understood; she knew her father could. When she finished, they sat in silence a moment; then she said, "You are broiling, Father. Let me go call Rena and help you in."

He shook his head. "Sit still." She sat and they waited another little while till he turned his eyes and slowly looked toward her.

She bore his gaze as he searched her, merciless.

Finally he turned back and faced the street again and said, "You were who I meant."

Eva needed to stop him now; she couldn't let him wander. She said "I'm grateful" and moved to stand.

"Sit still please," he said. "Just obey me once more. I have meant to say this for some years; but it slips my mind—you know my mind." He paused, staring out as though the street held his message. "You were who I meant." He looked to Eva, smiling the disastrous smile which his age would permit.

"Sir, I don't understand."

He scratched at the air with one long finger, writing it for her. "—Who I meant just now. The one I ruined."

Eva smiled but did not speak, still plainly puzzled.

"Your mother was responsible for all she did. She killed two people before herself. I loved her just the same. It was you I harmed."

Eva shook her head slowly.

"I am begging your pardon."

She said, "Father, Mother was nothing but a child; a baby just born."

"But she paid. Don't you see?"

"She was unhappy, yes; through no fault of yours. She explained that to me. Put her out of your mind."

"She's out," he said. "It's you I'm begging."

"I've been happy," Eva said. "I've had a good life, and I hope to have more." Her father said "Liar."

Eva said "Please don't."

"All right," he said.

She stood and laid her work on the chair and called loudly, "Rena—"

Quick, strong as a boy, Mr. Kendal reached out, ringed her wrist, pulled her toward him (she managed not to stumble, to stand straight before him). He whispered now—"But you know my meaning?"

Eva said "I do" and knew that she did, saw clearly for the first time that he'd given her her due and would leave now soon. She called again for Rena, pleading.

17

Five hours later Eva sat on the porch alone, slowly swinging. Her father was asleep; Rena had gone in search of a load of manure for her fall garden; Sylvie was at home for her own short rest before cooking supper. At such a time Eva would normally have gone to her quiet room and shut the door—at her father's first stroke, she had moved downstairs to the room behind his; Rob had taken her room—but two things had forced her out to the porch: the heat indoors, stifling by four, and the need for a space between her and her father. Breathing space, to settle her mind and prepare her answers for the questions that would rush her from every side by tomorrow at the latest when Rena would get her own announcing letter from Rob (she had so far told no one except her father and had managed, last moment, in the yard to warn him—"Don't mention Rob's marriage. It would ruin Rena's day").

But alone and quiet in the hot little wind she could raise by swinging, she found that her old devices for calm had also left her—she could not shut her eyes and by force of will flush her mind clean and blank, she could not pray that Jesus stand by her with strength, could not say a poem to herself, hum a song. She could think one thing. It seemed total knowledge, the sum of her life, both pitifully meager and pressingly huge, crowding all else aside—*You are being abandoned.* Father miserable and dying; Rob gone in condemnation but heaping coals of kind fire now on her head; Forrest barely present in her memory even, much less in her hope (she had no picture of him, had never had; only Rob's growing image, an innocent mimic). She was left with Rena and Sylvie, coal-black. It seemed to her—for the first time now (she had never considered the blame till now, having never been alone)—entirely her fault.

What the present weight of omen saved her thinking or recalling (she'd dreamt it clearly twenty years before) was the fact that she'd willed the choices of her life, the company she'd had, and had lived in what any sober witness might have called unusual happiness. The life she had wanted. It was quitting her now with the suddenness of death, of all catastrophe.

She stood and went down the steps, down the stone walk, aware that for the first time in sixteen years she had left her father entirely unattended. A cry would reach her though; she was walking nowhere, only stirring the heat. She stopped at the end of the walk, at the road, and crouched and began to weed Rena's bed of zinnias. It had been a wet August, and Rena had been busy in the back with her vegetables. As Eva worked she knew that Rena would notice ("Some rabbit was down at my flowers today"); but she worked on delicately, harming nothing. When she finished she had a little stack of hay beside her. She'd walk to the sideyard and put it round the roses; but rising quickly in the heavy sun, she tottered. Dizzy blood flooded her sight. She sat backward hard, to keep from falling. She was in plain view of the road—any passer—with her dress caught high on her folded calves, her hair matted wet on her forehead, mouth gasping; but she did not look out to check for passers: she did not care. She cared for herself, the small dry room in the front of her skull where her bare self lived; had happily lived these thirty-eight years, give or take a bad hour and the year with Forrest. The room had been light; and though the one door opened outward only, it had let her move freely to the few destinations she required and loved. *Vanishing* and no substitutes in sight. The room itself darkened, the air brown and close, the one door sealed.

Eva thought she would weep; tears were all in her throat, at the backs of her eyes. While she waited for tears, she searched for when she had really wept last. Mag's funeral maybe, six years before?—not that Mag had ever quite welcomed her back when she'd come home with Rob or in all the years after; but she couldn't remember a later time. And she didn't weep now. No pressure relented but no release came. Still unsure of standing, she looked down and saw she had landed on the name-stone, a small granite wheel from a disused mill on her father's river place. He had hauled it here when Eva was seven or eight and sunk it in the walk among smaller stones. It had been late summer—school had still not begun—and Kennerly had come out next morning with a chisel and hammered *K.K.* very neatly in the granite, on the edge of the hole. It had taken him till noon; she and Rena had watched him. When he'd shaped the last serif, he'd moved round and started on an R for Rena, who was youngest and could barely make her letters on paper, much less in stone. Eva had watched till he started on the curve that proved it an R, not an E. Then she'd said, "I am going in the back to play with Sylvie. When you finish with Rena, I want to do my own." Kennerly had laughed, "Good luck! This is granite." Still he'd called when he finished; and once they'd eaten dinner, she had chiseled at her own *E.K.* for hours. Smaller than the others and listing to the right but there in its proper place beside the great socket.

And there still. She traced it with a finger now. The simple touch, rough and dry, proved the channel she'd needed. But no tears came; only a retching in her throat which she did not try to strangle. She yielded to all its awfulness. A shameful release in August glare not three yards short of the public road. She did not hear the steps behind her, would still not have cared.

"Mrs. Mayfield?"

Eva turned—Min Tharrington, frightened above her.

Eva nodded. "You caught me."

"Not soon enough. Are you hurt anywhere?"

"Yes," Eva said. "But nothing you can help." Her vertigo had calmed; she stood up easily and smiled at Min. "Can I help *you?*"

"I just came to say goodbye."

"That's no help at all. Anybody can leave." Eva stroked back her hair with both hands blindly. "Your school hasn't started. Why leave so early?"

"Brother's taking me to Raleigh this Saturday. My principal has found me a room near the school with a satisfactory widow; but Mother has insisted that Brother go and check so Saturday's the day."

"Luck to you, Min. You've earned it at least." Stronger each moment, Eva made no move toward the house or porch.

Min waited a moment for an invitation; then said, "Could we sit down a minute, if you have a minute?"

"To be sure," Eva said. "Just let me check on Father."

They climbed up and Min sat while Eva went in (her father still asleep) and combed her hair. When she came back, she brought two glasses of water which they drank in silence before they spoke.

At last Eva said, "This has been hard on you. I can see it has." She looked to the brown-haired girl beside her, calm in a yellow dress—a grown woman leaving.

"Not really," Min said. "I was scared you had fallen."

"Oh that," Eva said. "I sat to *keep* from falling, sun on my brain. No I meant your plans."

"Well, I've got this degree, four years in the galleys. I might as well use it."

Eva nodded. "So right." Then she finished her water. "But you had to fight your mother. I meant that part."

"Did Mother tell you that?"

Eva smiled. "Several times. I was on your side and I told Kate so."

"Thank you," Min said. "I suspected as much. She never said a word to me against it—didn't dare after Father's deathbed wish that I *train* for something—but of course I felt her grudging every step of the way."

"She's a mother," Eva said. "Don't blame her too much. You've made little things in your life too, all those good grades, your clothes, your pictures. Someday you'll make a child."

"Maybe not," Min said.

"With that hair of yours and deep green eyes? Try to stop it," Eva said. "And when you've made it and seen it through the years, not days or weeks, when you honestly wanted to push it out the window or prayed it would melt like a salted snail, then you'll understand."

"I understand now; I've loved somebody."

"I know you have, know it very well. But it's not love I mean, though it may include love. It's ownership. You want what you've made; it's familiar easy company."

Min waited awhile. "How is Rob? Have you heard?"

"This morning," Eva said. She decided that instant—she would keep her own counsel; she would not risk telling. "He is doing very well, working hard, sounds healthy."

"Will they work up there in the mountains through winter?"

"I doubt it," Eva said.

"Will he come back here?"

"To visit at least. He misses Sylvie!"

"But he'll keep the road job?"

Eva searched Min's face; then laughed, "You ask him. *You're* his friend. I'm his mother; boys tell their mothers very little."

Min said, "In that case we'll neither one know."

"I thought you two were in regular touch."

"No ma'm. I have not touched Rob in four years."

Eva laughed. "He wouldn't mind."

Min nodded firmly. "He would. He knows I want him."

Eva waited. "For what?"

"For life."

"How do you know, Min?" Any edge on Eva's voice, of harm or raillery, had yielded now to real curiosity.

Min heard that, agreed to answer the truth. "I've thought about very little else for four years. He's all I want."

"Did you ever tell him?"

"He knew," Min said.

With a quick flood of pleasure, Eva thought *Me in him.* But she held back the smile that would naturally have followed. "God help you," she said.

Min waited. "I don't understand, Mrs. Mayfield."

Eva said, "I'm not sure I do myself. Maybe something like this—it is built into him, in the *mortar* joints, to run from being held. He came by it rightly."

"How so?"

"From his mother." Eva did smile now. "I'm a runner. I have run all my life. No doubt you've heard."

"No ma'm, I haven't."

"My marriage, Min. I'm sure you've heard. It was quite the topic."

"But before I was born. I've heard a few stories. I didn't pay attention."

"*Do,*" Eva said. "They are worth your time, I honestly believe."

Min waited as though the stories would follow.

Eva said, "When I was sixteen and had just finished school, the night before commencement, I got up off that stoop right there and walked through this house and out the back door to marry in secret a man almost twenty years older than me, who had been my teacher. For two reasons only, as far as I can see, and I've looked for reasons—I thought I was unhappy living with my mother (I was far from her favorite; we were too much alike); and I thought that no honor would ever come to me like the honor of that kind gentle man asking me to be his: for life as you say." Eva stopped as if that were the story, told.

Min said "Were you right?"

Eva looked to her, baffled.

"Did a better honor come?"

She had never thought it out. She did, quickly now. Then she shook her head. "Never." It made her smile. "Of course I have only lived half my life. I've barely begun. Earth lies all before me!"

"But you're sorry for the past?"

Eva saw that Min pressed her from need not malice; so she said, "What part? There are terrible parts—my mother, Rob's birth."

"—That you came home here. Never saw your husband. Mother said you have never seen him again."

Eva nodded. "Never. August the third, nineteen hundred and four. The length of your life, and a little more." She paused to think. "What did you ask me?"

"Are you sorry?" Min said.

"What right do you have?" Eva said it as calmly as "Another glass of water?"

"—That you started to tell me, that you've known me all my life, that you see as clear as anybody why I need to know."

Eva shut her eyes. "All right." She leaned her head back on the chair's white wicker and spoke from there as if from a distance or the wisdom of sleep. "I was not sorry then; there was too much to do, the turmoil here after Mother's death, Rob's case of whooping cough, Father's pitiful state. Then when they began to ease, I found I believed one thing above all—Mr. May-field had picked me for reasons of his own which he didn't understand (and God knew I didn't). He thought of my reasons no more than you'd think of the wishes of a warm egg you take from the nest. Does a thing have wishes? Very likely it does. So sitting here in that first year or two, I thought that at least my wish was not *him*, not Forrest Mayfield. I thought that I just wanted something to do—the kitchen was held down by Mag and Sylvie, the house (and more than half of Rob) by Rena; Father was active at his farms and in timber. So I gave voice lessons. I had a sweet voice and knew how to use it. I thought I could pass time in that useful way—please God, make some money, and beautify the air; but the pupils didn't care. Nothing on earth is worse than bad singing; I'd rather hear tin scrape tin any day. I stopped in a year and sat here awhile. Then I wrote to my husband—or sent him our pic-ture, Rob's and mine. A stone would have wept. Not a word of reply. He was living in Richmond by then, teaching Negroes. I had ruined his reputation. His sister had told me; we exchanged Christmas greetings for several years, the sister and I. He had a housekeeper that had worked for his father. Their family home. That was eighteen years ago. He's still there, I think. I have been to Richmond twice in that time—once with your mother shopping (up at dawn, back at dark); once with Sylvie to look into me taking courses from a correspondence college to teach grade school—but he never crossed my path, and I wasn't out to hunt him. I was leaving it to fate, and fate left me here!" Eva waited, smiling. She had seen Sylvie far down the road; coming onward in the heat, no hat, no shade. She would grumble all evening.

Min said, "What happened to your plan to teach school?"

Eva turned. "—Father. He had his first stroke. He was all I could do. Has been ever since." She stopped again; she had told the story.

But Min said, "The answer is, you're sorry for it all?"

"I wasn't, no. But I may be soon."

"Then please," Min said—she leaned to say it—"Please tell me why you thought I should hear that."

Eva said, "I suspected it was not in your books, not taught in college. Postgraduate instruction. No charge at all." She smiled and waved to Sylvie, who did not wave back.

"Do you think I'm a fool?"

"In what?" Eva said.

"Leaving home. That job."

"No," Eva said. "You have got to pass time. Your family live forever; you're a babe in the womb."

Min said "Forget Rob."

Eva laughed. "Please explain."

"You are telling me, 'Forget about Rob; go your way.'"

Knowing all she knew, with no intent to harm, Eva said, "No never. Hold him any way you can." Her left hand had reached through the heat toward Min; Min had not reached to take it.

Sylvie called from the end of the porch by the palm, "What Rob say today?—that letter I brought you."

"Said he's happy," Eva said. "Sent his love to you."

18

Dear Alice,

I've held off answering till I knew what I felt and if that was what I meant and then whether I would be able to say it.

What I mainly feel is puzzlement that you step forward now with objections to Rob—you say reservations *but* objections *is the word—when you liked him here and wrote me to say so. I trusted that you had been telling the truth, and I really continue to think that you were. I can only explain your turn in this way—in your first letter after your visit here, you were praising a surface. He was making it lovely; he wanted you to like him. And I think that's a natural thing to praise. I surely don't deny that he has lures and snares all over him. The first time I mentioned him to you, I seem to recall waxing big on his face. He still has the face; and now you warn me against it—"Those eyes will go on inviting people in, and the people will come . . . He is not looking outward any farther than his lashes . . . He is built for harm."*

No doubt he is (I know I am. I have kept two people in misery for years, and I may not stop; I may add more); but if what I honestly believe I know about why human beings choose to follow each other is true at all, then whether he is hateful as a Hun on horseback or gentle as a pastry cook is no concern of yours *or even of* mine *and* his.

This is what I believe, seems all I believe these recent weeks; and it's what I have to tell you. Two people who are grown in good control of their bodies and minds, who are not being forced by parents or a baby or either party's money or anything other than their own heart's speaking, will contemplate spending the whole of their two lives beneath one roof (whatever time holds for them and the roof) for one reason only—they want each other. They also suspect and may even believe that want *is* need *and will always be, but here as in other ways the mercy of time is their only hope.*

Rob thinks he needs me. He has said so directly on numbers of occasions to me and to others—my father for instance (my father trusts him). I have every reason to believe he is in fair control of his faculties (Jesus drank at times).

I deeply believe I am in control of mine—partly through your help, your father's, partly Rob's. I also believe, and I've thought it through as sternly as a judge thinks a sentence, that the troubles I've had and have visited on others were not true diseases but symptoms of an illness in no book known to me or your father—some strange starvation in the core of the heart for which no one but time can prescribe, if time ever does. I believe it has for me. I would be the one to know, the heart being mine.

Of course he has faults. I know them better than you, better than any other woman in Virginia. I know he's needed pieces off of other human beings (with him, needing is taking)—I know more there than he thinks I know, having good night-vision—but I'm the only person that he's asked for all of; and I'm giving it all two months from now. He knows my faults in honest detail; Father told him in advance. I'm giving it for three very simple reasons that are both entirely scary and *the sole consolation I have found to date—he's asked, I wanted him to ask, and I've answered. It may ruin us both—or him or me or some unborn, unthought-of, consequence—but so might the beefsteak we ate for supper, the breath I'm drawing as I write this line.*

I asked you to bless us as my Maid of Honor, and I ask you again. If you wish us well, can stand there behind us and watch the joining and wish it well, come. *I say* well *in every sense—good luck, good healing, fresh water in our deeps. If you don't, if anything in you says stay, then for God's sake* stay. *Whichever you choose, be always certain that my present hard feelings will in no way cancel my grateful memory of the strong warm care you offered me before when I was prone to die. My memory has always been my perfect trait.*

> *Till I hear then,*
> *Love from*
> *Rachel*

NOVEMBER 1925

Mr. Hutchins rose at the head of the table, leaned far forward, and turned up the wick of the hanging brass lamp. Lamps burned on the sideboard, the mantel behind him; so now the whole room was brighter than warm (the iron stove beside him was stoked but barely drawing, and the evening was cold). Then he stood in his own place and thumped his water-glass for attention. It rang, high and pure, and everyone turned. He said, "As the proud host of all of this, I get the first word. But since I'm a mountaineer and paying for the oil"—he gestured to the five lamps—"I'll make it just a word; everybody please copy. The word is *glad*. I am yielding a daughter that I love like myself to a boy that I trust will know her needs and struggle to tend them. He's a worker; the Robertses can swear to that, their job being finished here a week ahead of schedule—"

The two Roberts boys, twelve feet away toward the foot of the table, nodded smiling. They were too dark to see.

"—She also, even if she is my child (mine and her mother's and all her strong ancestors'), has big gifts to give. A feeling heart. Miss Kendal, Mr. Mayfield, I think I can say with no fear of lying, and no intention surely, that all our families have made a good swap and stand to show a profit from what we're here to do." Mr. Hutchins stopped, thought a moment, had said his full say. "Mr. Mayfield," he said, "the boy's proud father—I take it you're proud—your good word please."

Also dark at the far end, at Rachel's mother's right, Forrest half-rose long enough to say, "Mr. Chairman, yes, *proud*. I defer to Miss Rena. She has done all the work." He looked up to Rena, met her firm clear eyes. Neither of them smiled but they both nodded grave and mutual acknowledgment of parts played, honors earned.

Rena kept her seat but took a long drink of the water before her;

and when she spoke, she spoke of course to Rob. "*Thank* you," she said.

Rob was opposite her, four feet away. He kissed the back of his own right hand and turned it to her slowly. Another gift. Everyone sat in silence till she took it—the gift not his hand. She threw her head back and laughed a high short cry; it came down smiling and everybody clapped.

Mr. Hutchins said, "Are you done, Miss Kendal?"

"I've said my word."

"You can have several more since you've come such a way."

Rena shook her head, then thought, then looked to Mr. Hutchins. "I'll speak for his mother."

"Please do."

She looked to Rob. "Eva sends you a world of luck and her love."

Rob said, "She could have brought it." His voice sounded happy but he'd said it all the same.

"But she didn't," Rena said. She looked at once to Forrest. "Please say a little more."

Rachel sat in front of Forrest, so he said it to Rachel. "You know this boy at least as well as I do—this man, he is. You've really known him longer, though I saw him for a while at the very beginning of his life. *Yesterday!* It has brought me tremendous happiness since summer, that he hunted me down and offered me a bond where I had no right to expect anything but continuous parting. He has also found you. From your eyes and joy, I can guess you believe you have found him too. I am trusting you have, and I'll offer such prayers as I pray to that end. It would be a great victory, for our family at least and—and if I might have your permission, Miss Rena—for his mother's as well."

Rena's eyes never flickered off Forrest's face, however far away; but she gave no sign of permission or refusal.

Forrest went on, to Rachel. "You will have the harder job. He's half-Mayfield and will not like pain. But he's also half-Kendal; and as all here can see at this table tonight in good lamplight, the Kendals are lovely and invite us to follow." He nodded toward Rena.

"The *Watsons*," Rena said. She smiled at Rob, then returned to Forrest. "My mother was a Watson; it was them that people followed—my father, you. I'm a Kendal. Kendals *follow*; here I am today."

Forrest laughed—all did—and concluded for Rachel, "There's part of your job—sort out who he is. And you'll likely find he's many. Then love all you find." He found his eyes were filling and turned to Rachel's father. "If this were drinking country, we could drink to their health."

Mr. Hutchins said "We can." He looked to his wife. "We are all friends here." He turned to Rena. "Miss Kendal, would you drink a glass of old mountain brandy?"

"Very gladly," Rena said.

Mr. Hutchins nodded to his wife, who rang a bell. Everybody sat silently as if on a train and heard steps come quickly toward them from the kitchen— Grainger at the door, smiling like a guest. Mr. Hutchins said, "Go down in the cellar past all the preserves. You'll find a gray jug that says *Raven* in blue— my given name, my father's before me" (that was offered to Rena). "Bring me that and ten glasses."

Grainger said "Yes sir. Everything else fine?"

"Very nice, yes thank you."

"Mr. Rob, you holding up?" Grainger pointed to Rob.

"Sinking fast," Rob laughed. "Bring the jug here quick."

Grainger said "On the way" and turned to go.

Mrs. Hutchins said, "Grainger, while you do that ask Gracie to pass the ham and the rolls."

"And a pitcher of water," Rob said. "From the spring. Could we please have that?"

Grainger looked to Mr. Hutchins.

Mr. Hutchins laughed and nodded.

But Rachel said, "Don't. Well-water please. You'd kill the guests."

Mr. Hutchins said, "Well-water then for all, but do your errand first."

Grainger said "A gray jug" and went to find it.

Forrest watched him out of sight and listened to his steps; then he turned to Alice by him and said, "I believe you have known Rob awhile?"

Alice said, "Since summer. Just three, four months."

Forrest said, "As I told you, that's longer than I."

Alice said, "Then you have a lot to look forward to."

Forrest said, "I hope I do. You really think I do?" Alice sat on his right; he had spoken to her softly, requesting an answer.

She looked to Rob quickly, six feet past her beyond Wirt Roberts, who was still eating loudly. "They'll be living near you. I meant you'd be close and would have time to know him."

"Would you trust him?" Forrest said.

"With what?"

"Your life, something serious as that."

Alice said, "I am trusting him with Rachel's at least."

"That's easy," Forrest said.

Alice said, "I doubt that. I'm her Maid of Honor. I will march down tomorrow in the presence of the Lord and say I approve what the Lord is asked to bless."

Forrest shook his head. "You won't have to speak a word."

"I will *be* there though; speech enough for me."

A tall dark girl had entered during that and came first to Forrest's left and stood—the plate of ham. All the previous serving had been done by Grainger; and since Forrest had got here only an hour before supper (the last train from Richmond), he had not had a chance to visit the kitchen. He looked up at the girl now and said "You're Grainger's Gracie."

"*Gracie*," she said and shook the dish slightly, a final offer.

He served himself a slice. "We'll be seeing you in Richmond."

"If you seeing quick," she said.

Forrest tried to search her face, as fine as a hand in its power and concealment, the eyes huge but narrowed, the mouth smiling inward.

"Serve Miss Alice, Gracie." Mrs. Hutchins moved her on.

Then Grainger was back with a large round tray, the jug and the glasses. He set it on the sideboard behind Mr. Hutchins and said, "You going to pour it or me?"

Mr. Hutchins said "You" and went on talking to Rena and Rob. Only the two Roberts boys were silent and Forrest who had pushed his chair back a little to watch Grainger work, five yards away, pouring thick amber brandy into small waterglasses as carefully as if he had transmuted water itself for these guests (empowered by the day, his part in its slow and happy unfolding), these few strangers held by a brief common purpose in their contrary lives, and would offer it now with grace sufficient to the night, the coming day.

Mrs. Hutchins asked a question. But Grainger held Forrest; he did not even face her.

Then half his job done, Grainger lifted his tray again and went straight to Rena, who accepted her glass and smiled and told him "Thank you," her only words to Grainger.

Grainger chose to answer, whispered in the midst of six conversations; but Forrest heard him clearly. He said "I'm glad" and moved on to Niles Fitzhugh beyond Rena, Rob's best man tomorrow.

Forrest stood where he was and said, "My heart is very full. Mr. Hutchins, before I drink your brandy, may I say a word more while my head is still clear?"

Rob said, "Yes sir, you'd better. This stuff looks mighty."

Rachel said, "Very mighty. Mr. Mayfield, speak."

Mr. Hutchins said "Quick."

Rena clapped; the others followed.

Grainger rounded the table.

Forrest said, "I am fifty-five years old this month. Never say 'Time flies'; it has seemed like forever. But things have come at intervals to lure me on, make me still yearn to last; things I now trust were *sent*, not accidents of time. This evening and the morning that awaits us are such things—of a beauty and hope which nobody present (this is bald presumption but I'll wager its truth) had any right to plan for, dream for, expect. Not Miss Rena, if I may, whose own good home has been troubled for decades by onslaughts of anguish as hard as any on mine or me. Not Robinson my son or Rachel his bride, whose beauty of form and spirit and laughter were no guarantee that life would prove yielding—the opposite, in fact: grace has often drawn nothing but the envy of fate, its sour grim grin. If I were the genius I once pined to be, I could paint you in words the face of my father, of Miss Rena's mother (Rob's Kendal grandmother), both lovely as daylight, both wrecked by time—"

Through that, Grainger quietly served all the others; then came back and stood five feet behind Forrest with the one last glass. In the pause he offered the tray, not looking at Forrest's eyes (because of Forrest's lateness, they had still said no more than ten words of greeting over platters of food; their first real meeting in twenty whole years was before them, if ever—the drawn scars of love and rupture untested).

Forrest reached for the full glass, let Grainger step back and turn toward the door; then continued, "—Not Grainger who has been with my people, been one of my people, since his early boyhood: since before his birth."

Grainger waited and looked.

Forrest faced him at last. "You did not plan this, did not even dream it, that first day in June twenty-one years ago when you brought me good news of Rob and his mother that proved bitter lies—surely not. Am I right?"

Grainger said, "No sir. I thought it would end some way like this."

"You were twelve years old—"

Grainger laughed. "N'mind. I still wanted things. Course, I doubted them since. No more. Not tonight." He stood quiet a moment, then knew he must go. He reached for the gray jug and set it on the floor by Mr. Hutchins' feet.

Mr. Hutchins said, "Go back, get three more glasses, and come in here with Della and Gracie."

Grainger said "Yes sir."

As he went, Forrest sat and, after brief silence, talk began again—the hum of waiting.

Rachel leaned toward Forrest. "I'm on Grainger's side. He knew, he said. God knows, I didn't; didn't know day from night for weeks on end. But I always hoped. I've thought just lately that hope was my trouble. I wanted all this, all Rob is giving; and I strained so hard to hope it into being that I almost ruined it. I thought I couldn't wait. Most children are hopeless; they think they are trapped and will always live in whatever misery they feel that instant. I was living for this." She smiled a little fiercely and looked to Alice. "Tell Mr. Mayfield I'm really not lying."

Alice said "No she's not."

Forrest said, "I believe you. The failure was mine."

Mrs. Hutchins touched Rachel on the back of her long hand. "Eat your supper, darling. What you still need is strength."

Rachel said, "I am stronger than anybody here. I've lived through my life."

"It's not over yet," Mrs. Hutchins said and tapped Rachel's plate—chicken, ham, corn pudding, green beans, stewed tomatoes, chow-chow, a buttered roll.

Grainger entered again with the same large tray—three glasses, the same kind—and Della and Gracie. Della still gave off the heat of cooking; her brick-red dress was wet in great splotches shaped like countries on maps or the organs of animals, dark livers, lungs.

Mr. Hutchins bent down and brought up the jug and looked to Grainger. All the talking stopped, though Wirt Roberts ate.

Grainger offered the tray and Mr. Hutchins poured three-quarters of an inch of brandy for the Negroes. Grainger passed it to the women—Gracie first, then Della.

Mr. Hutchins took his own glass and warmed it in his hand, looking down toward his wife and Rachel and Forrest. Then he said, "Who's the one to pronounce this blessing? I'm about talked-out."

"So is Father," Rob said.

Forrest laughed with the others and nodded and said, "Since Grainger has planned this whole happy evening for twenty-some years now, I nominate him." He took his own glass.

Gracie's eyes turned on Grainger, the side of his face, like a pair of matched hunters who had never yet failed to rout and cover any chosen quarry.

Della tried to see Rachel.

Rachel only watched Rob.

Rob was rocking his glass.

Grainger waited, not smiling.

Mr. Hutchins said "Grainger."

Grainger said "Yes sir."

Mr. Hutchins said "Bless it."

"Bless what, sir?"

"This crowd, everybody present here. This union tomorrow."

Grainger said, "I have said what I know to say."

Rob said "Say it again."

Grainger smiled toward Rob. "I knew this was coming. I knew you people would end up happy and doing me right. Me and Gracie look forward to helping you in Richmond. Mr. Forrest, I told you long years ago it would end up like this if you be patient."

Forrest nodded. "You did."

Rena led the others.

Gracie wiped her wet mouth with the back of her wrist and turned back to Della, who was two steps behind her. "Nothing finished, is it, Della?"

Only Della could hear her, and Della bent to laugh.

Gracie rolled her head back and licked the sweet hot rim of her glass.

Only Forrest saw the broad gold ring on Gracie's left hand—his mother's, waiting there in dull lamplight on its permanent journey through a melting world. "Content there," he thought. He smiled and, seated though he was, bowed deeply to Rachel (lit with surety, her eyes bright as any two lamps around her).

2

At ten-thirty Rob left Niles and the Robertses laughing in the parlor and climbed upstairs in the chilling dark to his Aunt Rena's door (her room flanked Rachel's on the other side from his). She had come to him shortly after supper and asked if he'd find a good lamp and lead her to her room; she was tired from her trip and had mending to do. He had led her and seen her in and fed her stove; and when she had thanked him and offered, like her best gift, a simple goodnight (a quick kiss, no speeches), Rob had said, "I will come back up in an hour and see that you're safe." She had said, "I'm safe. I will not let you down. Unlike some people, I have not come all this way by train to show-off such wounds as I have to a houseful of strange mountaineers. I'm a house-broken guest." Then she'd laughed to prevent his reading her too closely and had pushed him toward the door.

He leaned to it now and listened. Silence from Rena, though the voices of Rachel and her mother, muffled, leaked from Rachel's room. He stepped back and crouched and strained to see beneath. A frail warm draft blew against his mouth, but he saw no sign of light or glow. He had waited too long; Rena was dead asleep. Though he'd borne the weight of her love all his life, it did not occur to him that pure morphine could not have made her sleep while she waited for him to keep another promise or break another. Kneeling in the dark hall, he felt he must keep it—this last time at least—and felt he must keep it for Rena's sake, not permitting himself to see his own need: obeisance to the actual servant of his life. He stood and brushed the knees of his suit, rubbed his palms. Then he turned the cold doorknob and gently pressed—open. Dark and heat. He opened it another few inches and listened—nothing but the stove. He could not speak; he was dumb with sudden shame. *She is tired as a dog, and from nothing but me, her only work (my childish show); and here I stand to wake her, to pull more from her when the whole house and yard are live with other offers—awake and ready, more usable to me.* He was more than half-sober too (they'd finished the gray jug among the six men and a second glass for Grainger, a harmless division); but still he stood waiting. Long moments that seemed as empty as childhood of purpose or hope or even impatience. Given cover of dark, he could stand so forever.

At last Rena said, "I am trying to see." Her voice seemed to come from the chair not the bed.

"It's me," Rob said.

"I was trusting that."

"You were right again."

"You can come in," she said. "You're wasting the heat."

Rob stepped fully in and shut the door behind him. "How come it's so dark?"

"I had given up," she said. "I am in my nightgown. I figured those boys had you tied up till dawn."

"Oh no ma'm," he said. "They are just telling tales. I could leave them easy. They were trying to scare me."

"How was that?" Rena said.

"You know," Rob said, "—all the terrors of a wife, the sweetness of freedom."

Rena made a short sound in the pit of her mouth which Rob knew at once she had learned from her brother—Kennerly's glee at the gall of life. "Was your father joining in?" She was tense with power.

"Oh no ma'm," Rob said. "He is visiting Grainger."

"That's something then," she said. Her force was still gathering.

Rob heard but couldn't name it.

Then she launched it calmly. "I didn't mean to offer you a word of advice. I have gritted my teeth for long months now since that letter I sent you in—what was it?—June. But let me say this much and shut up forever.

I have worshipped you, you know. You gave me nine-tenths of the pleasure I've had in the past twenty years, in all my life to now—you and flowers. But I never once doubted that a far greater thing for me as for most would have been a good marriage. From the depths and the heights of my spinster state, I can still see that—the greatest good. I've known what there is to know about solitude, for all that busy house. It has handled me kindly on balance, I guess. I am in strong health, I've kept my mind clear, I am not an old crank, I wish the world well. I've also known, through the kindness of my kin—my own parents, yours—how most sets of two people scrape themselves raw or, worse still, *smooth* through blindness or meanness or maybe just idleness: time enough to kill in; chickens in a coop pecking each other bald, then bloody, then dead. I've witnessed that closely. But I still swear to you on my gravest honor that the thing I know most surely of all, the thing *Jesus* knew (and knows this night, wherever He sits) is nothing but this—a single journey is a dry rag to suck. A single life. It was my given lot. I've often asked why but I never blamed a soul, just gnawed at the rag till it turned into food, a thin steady diet. But never say again that you spit on marriage, never laugh with any fool who peddles freedom to you. Son, *spiders* are free. Freedom's one more rag."

Rob waited till he knew she'd poured it all. Then he said, "I knew that and I haven't been laughing. Those boys are my guests; I was just being friendly."

Rena also waited. "Are you serious?" she said.

"Yes ma'm."

"About Rachel?"

"About what I'm doing."

"Which is what?" Rena said.

"Taking something life has thrown me."

Rena waited. "God help you. God help Rachel Hutchins." She did not sound desperate, was not imprecating or begging for help but calmly praying.

Rob said "Where is your lamp?" He needed now to see her, confirmation through his eyes that the flood of thanks he felt should run toward her.

"Please don't," Rena said.

"Why?"

"You need to leave."

Rob said "Why?"

Rena laughed. "You need your strength."

"I've got it," he said. "I'll have it tomorrow."

"No doubt," she said. "No doubt about that." She waited awhile; he did not move to go. So she stood in place. "I'll need *mine*," she said. "Son, I'll need all of mine."

"Yes ma'm," he said at last. Then he felt his way forward through air that grew hotter as he neared the stove till he found her cool face, her cold left hand. With his own right hand—warm, soft as he could make it—he felt for her brow and bent and kissed her once. Then he turned and quickly left.

3

Yet he paused at the foot of the stairs and listened for sounds of his friends; they had quieted but were there. Niles' voice had dropped to give them the story of his and Rob's visit to Roller's Retreat, a lengthy triumph (mainly for Niles). Rob hoped his father was still out with Grainger; he knew Mr. Hutchins had gone to his own room an hour before to give them this freedom, part of his welcome.

There was nowhere else Rob wanted to go and nowhere he needed, not reachable from here anyhow, not by morning (he felt morning coming). There was no human being he wanted to see. In fact, now he stood and plotted a course, there were several he dreaded to meet at all. A word in their voices, a thrust of their hands might rupture the paper walls he'd propped round the cube of space at the core of his chest, walls he'd shown to Rachel as permanent ramparts, worthy of trust, offered for life. Grainger and Della—powerful enemies, terrible friends. He'd go to them (he had not thought of bed; bed was hours from now, with Rachel twenty feet away merely hidden by lathing and plaster, merely postponed).

There was no light from Grainger's window or Della's; but he went on anyhow, strengthened by the cold (it had already frosted; his feet bit drily into brittle icing, parchment leaves); and as he passed the springhouse, Forrest said "Rob?" He turned and went there, stopping in the entrance, and saw by the starlight that his father was seated on the far-side railing, no overcoat or hat. Rob said "This'll kill you."

"It's advertised to *heal.*"

Rob said, "I meant the night air."

"It won't," Forrest said, "and if it does, I die happy. I need to cool off. Been with Grainger and Gracie; they've got it hot as August, hot enough to cure tobacco."

"Old as they are?" Rob laughed.

"With their woodstove, I meant. They were just sitting talking, when I left anyhow."

Rob said, "What did Grainger tell you?"

"Nothing," Forrest said, "Did he have a thing to tell me?"

Rob said, "So I thought. He's been worried about you, that you'd come here and shun him."

Forrest said, "That was useless. I wrote him a letter oh a month ago to say any feelings that had backed up between us in the past twenty years could scatter now in peace; that as far as I intended, he was welcome back in Richmond as a help to you and Rachel—I would help him how I could."

Rob said "Maybe I should know—"

"What?"

"The cause of hard feelings, why you sent him home to Bracey."

Forrest paused. "That's over. Don't worry. That's past; he told me just now."

Rob said "All right" and stepped into the springhouse; went and sat on the railing, two feet from his father. He had no intention but patience, time to pass.

But Forrest said "Maybe you should," then stopped. "—If you're going to live with him. You may have him forever—Gracie won't stay long; I can see that even by oil-light in darkness." Then he stopped again and felt he was too near Rob, the presence like a live field of steady repulsion. Forrest stood and went over to the lid of the spring and sat down there. "He's told you who he is; you said that, didn't you?"

"Yes sir, he did."

"I told him that, my worst mistake."

Rob said "You sure it's true?"

Forrest said, "Father said so, the last time I saw him. It was right after Eva had taken you and gone. I had begged her back by sending her a Christmas box—a wagon for you and my mother's ring for Eva, Mother's wedding ring. Mr. Kendal sent it all back to me, next train; and when I found Father a little while later, I offered him the ring. He was with Polly in the Mayfield house in Richmond—Polly'd come there to nurse him—and I thought he might want to give the ring to Polly then. It was rightfully his since Mother was dead; he'd bought it years before. But he wouldn't hear of taking it or letting Polly wear it; she also refused. I was near-desperate then; and Grainger was with me (though he hadn't come to Father's, waited at the boarding house). It seemed like I couldn't give anything away. It was drowning my heart—my hands were full; nobody would take me. So I gave it to Grainger; Father told me to. Grainger's Christmas present—Gracie's wearing it tonight; says she's never had it off since Grainger gave it to her. The sights it's seen. And some months later just before we packed up and moved to Richmond, Grainger asked me why I had given him the ring (Hatt never forgave me, though she didn't blame Grainger); and I told him what I knew, what Aunt Veenie had told me and sworn me to keep. She knew it would ruin him. I thought she was wrong.

I had lived with your mother for the previous year; and I thought I had learned one good thing from her, that telling every scrap of truth your mind might hold was the answer to trouble. So I told it to Grainger; and it ruined him slowly, heightened his hopes far beyond my power to satisfy. (Eva went on winning in my life, you see, long after she left.) If I'd just held my tongue, he'd have loved me anyhow. He was well on the way. And I treasured him."

Rob said "Where'd he go?"

"Not a single step. I mean, he came to Richmond and helped me settle there. I didn't go till May when my teaching had finished—except in February, two days to bury Father and to do right by Polly. I thought he would like to live in Richmond—he had grown up in Maine with people teeming round him; Bracey must have been a desert—and he did pitch in like he meant to help. We stripped that house from attic to cellar, he and I alone with Polly watching; took every stick of furniture out in the yard to let the sun clean it. Then we scrubbed every inch of the inside with brushes and carbolic acid; then we painted it white and varnished the floors. I sold some furniture, gave some away—it had Father all in it—and then we moved in. A little bare at first. I got a few pieces we needed later on, but it looked then very much the way it looks now."

"Grainger slept in your study."

"It was his room then, entirely his. I had promised him that too."

"You sent him to school?"

"No I trained him at home. I hadn't gone to work at the Institute then; that was two years later. I was still dragging white children downward through Latin till my past caught up, as pasts will do—a cradle-robber was the general impression. Not easy to deny, being more than half-true. Anyhow I trained him in the evenings as I said. In the days he went on fixing up the house—he knew a lot of carpentry; his father built boats in Augusta, Maine—and he'd try to help Polly, with the cooking especially."

Rob said "Polly was the trouble."

"Did she tell you that? I know she talked to you."

"No sir, but she let me know she lost no love on Grainger."

Dark as it was, Forrest tried to see Rob. He wanted to see that his meanings were clear; that they registered clearly in the one living person for whom they now had urgency, a possible use in the matters of life—simple peace and continuance—which Rob was now volunteering to master: four sizable lives. But against the sky, Rob was dark, a shape. So rather than stand and go to him again, Forrest said, "Let me say this now once for all; and you please use it like the burdened man you are—Polly's never had love to lose anywhere. She has always been *at mercy*—of her father, then my father."

Rob said, "Polly chose that. She told me she was happy just three months ago." He pointed as if Polly's heart were a place, however far off.

Forrest said, "Only partly. No woman I've known, except your own mother, chose all of her life. They are dreadful to watch — women, I mean. I say that with knowledge; I have watched two of them living minute by minute through the life I gave them."

Rob said "Mother and who?"

"You know already. But I mean to confirm it so there'll never be a doubt once you've come to Richmond, so you'll know above all whenever I die — Margaret Jane Drewry has made my life. If you value me at all, help me repay her for it."

Rob nodded. "I knew. She told me that morning; but the other way around — she said her life there with you had been good."

"She was mainly being brave. She was scaring you off. It has been hard for her. She lives in a private cupboard of my life. She knows the space is small (because I am *me*) and always in danger, from me and the world; so she fights for her corner."

"She fought-off Grainger?"

"He tried to fight her."

"How?"

"By worshipping me."

Rob laughed.

"No I mean it; not that I was any statue of God. Don't forget he was a child six hundred miles from home; his father turned him loose as easy as a pet. And he thought we were kin. That again was the worst. He'd lived in Maine — Negroes scarce as palm trees till Rover at least (now I guess there are Mayfields all over New England in shades of beige, called Walters for their grandmother Elvira Jane — my father's strong life still pumping through faces you and I will never see, the most of our kin). And he'd been treated well by his own people there; so he got it in his head he was nearly my son. I'm responsible for that. He was what I had in the awful months after Eva had gone — he and some little poems I was trying to write, pitiful trash. Hatt was no good to me (for all her kindness, she was nothing I needed); but Grainger filled in for a good many things that were suddenly absent or had always been — a son, a brother, another kind animal weaker than me and therefore safe and (while kin) strange enough to be always of interest, a little scary but invariably gentle to me. For me."

"It was Polly he fought?"

"Yes."

"She sent him away?"

"No she had no right to. I sent him away."

Rob waited awhile, then said, "Better tell me. You said yourself that I might need to know."

Forrest said, "He and I moved to Richmond in June. The next November—Thanksgiving in fact, eleven months exactly since I laid eyes on her—I went in to Polly and asked her to take me: as a wife would, I mean. I promised her nothing but the care she'd need while she chose to stay. She seemed to understand and has never asked for more, though she's had much more—twenty years' faith from me if that matters to her."

"She said it did."

"I'll choose to believe you. She's a very poor liar. Anyhow by Christmas, Grainger understood. I've never known how."

Rob said, "*I* knew the minute I saw her, when she answered the door."

"That was after long years; it had marked her face. Grainger knew in a week."

Rob said, "It's not a mansion and he's got good ears."

"But I tried to protect him."

Rob laughed again. "From what, please tell me?—a Negro boy with his own nature growing?"

"Oh the news," Forrest said, "—that I'd used him, compelled his love by claiming kinship, then discarded him already. Understand, I didn't think I had discarded him. I thought he could live there the rest of his life—it was fine by me; there was work to do. But he knew I'd ruined it; and the one thing he is is purer than Christ, in his purpose, his meaning. He means what he says—every word, every move—and will act it all out in the face of white coals of blinding fire."

"He will," Rob said. At last he yielded to the cold and shuddered from his belly upward to his chest, throat, teeth. He could not stop himself; what had started as a chill surrendered to some other force within him, a deeper fever that must have its way.

Forrest saw through the dark and patiently watched.

In a minute it had passed or shrunk into hiding again, pleased for now. Rob bound his coat tighter about him, hugged himself. "So will I," he said.

Forrest waited. "What, Son?"

Rob quietly drew all the breath he would need, seamless through his teeth. "I will do what I promise. I have always said I would, all my life. No person has asked me, not till now. Now I will."

Forrest said "God help you" and stood and came forward. With Rob still seated, Forrest was taller by a head; so he leaned and carefully kissed his son at the crest of the brow where cold flesh rose into colder hair.

4

In the little hall between Grainger's door and Della's, Rob stood to listen. He had come to see Grainger, delayed by his father but strengthened in the need; and he silently tilted his head toward the door for signs of life. At first he heard none. Then because he was urgent enough to consider waking a man who had just finished seventeen hours of work and must start again in five more hours (and whose long-gone wife was with him again after nearly four years), Rob went on listening till finally he could hear what at first seemed the life of the pine door itself, some peaceful exchange of life in its heart. Tired as he was and the brandy still in him like a soft bass line, Rob was primed for comfort in any shape; so his left ear pressed to the ribbed wood, his eyes shut. The life continued. Their struggling of course—Grainger's and Gracie's, their bodies joining, their wordless swapping of welcome and hate, thanks and blame, in the voices of children: helpless but accurate, utterly precise as they dug and worked in one another to find that childhood of perfect assurance one step beyond which lay endless peril, a lifetime of danger, abandonment. More silent than ever, Rob begged them not to stop, yearned somehow to join them.

But Gracie stopped—four cries of loss, maybe also of gain (some private gain of strength or knowledge she could take away with her).

Grainger dug awhile longer—Gracie's voice clearly said "You getting anywhere?"—then his own stop came: blunt stop, no sound. Then long silence from them both. No noise from the bed or the dry floor beneath them or the stove that would surely be roaring high—as if they had spent not only their little savings of force and want but their lives as well, total being, and had left the bed empty, the room, the house.

Rob turned toward Della's, first time in three months, the last intention he had had for tonight. He did not listen but quietly knocked and stood back to hope. He could not hear steps or Della listening or her hand on the knob, but after a minute the door slowly opened.

Her one lamp was lit, not bright enough to show through her window shade but enough for her work (a collar for the dress she would wear to the wedding) and to outline her now as she stood, looking out.

Rob said, "You ought to been asleep long ago."

Della said, "I ought to been an angel with wings and long yellow curls."

"Well, you weren't."

"What you doing about it?"

"Praying," Rob said. He could smile by then.

Della stood on in the door, the heat running past her like a breath against Rob.

"Can I step in?" he said.

She thought it through slowly. Then she stepped back a step. "You used to know the way."

"Still do," he said. He entered in one move and shut the door behind him, then looked first to see that her shade was truly down. It was—he was instantly safer, calm: a ship, a sealed ship plowing the night, unsuspected, unseen.

Della went to her bed again and sat where she'd been, in a narrow nest by her pineboard table where the lamp burned steady. She reached to turn it up.

Rob said "Leave it please."

She studied him a good while. "You hiding again?"

He smiled and nodded and started toward her one chair.

"You come to the wrong place then," Della said. She picked up her sewing.

Rob stopped at the chair, held the tops of its back. "Why is that?"

"You know." She did not look up but took three stitches, small and neat as a nun's.

"I don't," he said. "You have been good to me."

"I done finished that."

"How come?"

Della looked. She could hardly see him for the dark, but her mind supplied what her eyes were denied. "You know; that's all." She stared on a moment. "Anyhow I'm busy."

"What at?"

"My plans."

Rob laughed once. "What are they?"

"*My* business," she said.

At that he sat down. Della showed no response. "You planning to die?" he said (the dress on her lap was a dark shade of green and seemed nearly black in the dark).

"Be good to me," she said.

"I was joking," Rob said. "I'm tired and crazy. Are you going somewhere?"

"Yes sir," Della said. "Tomorrow morning I'm going in the front room to see you and Rachel get married together. Then I'm running out here to this little piece of house to get out of this good dress in a hurry. Then I'm going to the kitchen and cook my black titties off all day so Grainger and Gracie can put on aprons and serve all the company."

Rob said "You're paid." He offered it gently, a mild reminder of a fact forgotten (he intended to leave her ten dollars tomorrow, had saved it for the purpose; but he didn't tell her now, a final surprise).

Della nodded. "So right. And I saved four pennies out of every five."

"For me?" Rob said. "You making me a present?"

"You got the last present you getting out of me." Her face was calm as wood. But her voice was earnest; she would not be mistaken.

"—And I came here to thank you. You've helped me keep going."

"I'll carry that with me then."

"Not tomorrow," Rob said. "Just enjoy tomorrow. But after I'm gone, you remember I'm grateful."

She turned up her lamp to the edge of smoking. Rob was clear to her now. "Shit *on* you," she said.

Rob said, "Don't, Della. I need a lot of goodness."

"More than goodness," she said.

"What?"

"You marrying Rachel?—Rachel's your bride, ain't she?"

"Tomorrow morning."

"Well, it be morning soon if it ain't already; and when you get Rachel, you got you a job make road-building look like stuffing feather beds."

"You sure?" Rob said. He had not spoken Rachel's name in this room before.

"Rachel always been a job."

"How long have you known her?"

"Lot longer than you. But you the one getting her."

"How long?" Rob said.

"Born with Rachel." Della stopped again. She genuinely did not want to speak of Rachel—delicacy, hatred.

Rob said, "Please tell me what you know. I may need to use it."

"My life or Rachel's?"

"Rachel."

"Too late. You *in* her."

"Tomorrow," Rob said.

"And from then on out."

It was part of the slender power Rob possessed, that he did not guess the cause of Della's edge. He suspected it came from her being a servant with years of time to witness Rachel's case and now a final judgment of despisal. He did not think in any part of his mind that he himself—in all his different shapes, the air he bore around him—had poisoned one more thing by his presence. He saw Della now as a generous friend who had helped him in need—the morning when he'd stood above the river and intended to die, the nights on her body—and of whom he knew more than of any other human besides perhaps his mother (he had shared their bodies in various ways; lived in his mother's, visited Della's). He thought she could help him again, and should. He tried to persuade her. "You were born around here?"

"This room," Della said.

"Your people lived here?"

"Worked here—my mama did; my papa was gone."

"How did she get here?"

"Her mama worked here—my grandmama Julia. *Her* mama belonged to Mr. Raven's people; and my great-grandaddy was a man that come through after the freedom—so few niggers round here, he settled on her; but he passed on off when Julia come. Same as my daddy. Nothing round here for men to do less they want to turn woman and wait on people. No land to farm. So anyhow I was born right in this bed; some hot summer nights I can still smell blood. I come after Rachel, just ten months later; but she use that to try bossing me. She want me to dress her up and plait her hair and pull her round the yard in a old goat cart. I won't studying Rachel. I played by myself when I won't helping Mama; and sometime some little white children would come to stay in the rooms, and Mr. Raven pay me a nickel a week to tend to em. Then Rachel got to like me. I didn't change a bit, but she grew up enough to stop being mean or to see it won't getting her nowhere but ugly. And for five or six years we was close as two sisters. I would sleep in her room when Mama would let me—little cot she had—and we used to teach each other what we knew." Della stopped at that and rethreaded her needle as quickly as in daylight and worked on in silence.

Rob said "What did she know?"

"School stuff. How to read. She was funny then too, knew a lot of funny stuff. She could take-off people till you fell down laughing or were scared to death—sometimes she would change into some other person, some girl that had spent the summer here or a boy that was dead, and stay that way for an hour, all night. I slept right with her, more nights than one, when I couldn't swear I knew who she be in the morning when daylight strike her. It was just fun then."

"What did you teach her?"

Della waited awhile. "Nothing dirty if that's what you aiming at. She knew all that; she the one went to school and saw other children. No I guess I didn't show her nothing but care. I liked her by then—she was bigger than me—and I always told her. I never held back; didn't lay down my head in her room *one* night till I ask her, 'Rachel, you still staying here, ain't you?'

or 'Rachel, you want me to call you in the morning?' (she outslept me; I was up with the roosters and would lay down beside her on top of the cover till she finished her dream, then I'd tell her 'You late'). Nobody love her but me and Mr. Raven, back then anyhow. And she loved us, acted like she did—us and my mama."

"Where is your mother?"

"In Heaven."

"How long ago?"

"Two years this Christmas. While Rachel was sick."

"Tell me what that was like."

"Mama dying or Rachel?"

"Rachel please."

Della smiled for the first time, long, straight at him. "You going to have a whole life to hear about Rachel in."

"I know it," Rob said.

"I'm the one that *know* though."

"What?" Rob said.

"Her dream that caused it." Della pointed to her table. "I got my book."

Rob stood to see. In all his visits here, he'd never had light; so the things he knew, he knew by touch. He had thought it was a Bible—*Thompson's Egyptian Secrets Unveiled: The Book of Dreams*, bound in something like blue oilcloth, heavily used. He did not want to touch it but sat down again and said "Tell me then," no request, an order.

Della went on as calmly as if it were her wish—by now it was; it would show her power, the rest of the story. "One morning I woke up and was lying down by Rachel; and she started shivering in fast little snatches, hard as pneumonia. I thought she was teasing—she was out on her back—so I leaned over close to study her eyes. They were shut down tight but shivering like her. She was suffering something, so I let her do it. Then finally she slowed down and rested too deep—too much like her corpse—so I woke her up; and she said to me 'Thank you.' I told her, 'You been somewhere; where was it?' She say, 'I been hunting my boy that was drowning.' I say, 'I saw you. Look like you found him.' —'Did,' she say, 'but I couldn't get him out.' I ask her 'Where is he?' So she lie there—it's early; nobody up but us, not even Mr. Raven—and tell me, 'Della, I had this boy that was close to me as skin; but I woke up one night, and he won't there with me. I stripped down the bed to see where he hiding, right down to the slats, or maybe in my sleep I had smothered his face. I was having to feel; the whole thing was dark. But I still couldn't find him; so I ran outside in my thin nightgown—it was summer and hot—and went to some woods and called round there till he answered his name, way off, real weak. Then I kept on calling, and he answer his name, and I finally get to him. I still can't see him, but I hear him speak his name, and he's struggling to float. It seem like a pond and him at the edge. I try to reach out; fall down on my stomach and stretch way toward him. And I do get to touch him—brush his fingers: so weak they can't hold me now—but he go on sinking, and I run back home.' That was when she could rest again, when I saw her resting."

Rob said "What was his name?"

"She never said that."

"Then what did it mean?"

Della said, "It *still* mean. Dreams always true, true all your life; that's the trouble with dreams. But I hadn't paid all that much mind to dreams, not up till then. The book belonged to Mama; she kept it for years, all she could read. So that morning, laying there, I thought it meant a sweetheart, some boy Rachel was loving and couldn't get to. She had quit school by then; but some boys hung around—she won't that shy. I told her right then, 'It mean you getting married.' Rachel stare back at me like she planning to cut me. She say, 'My baby. That boy was my baby.'"

"Who was right?" Rob said.

"Rachel, part right."

"What part?"

"The baby. Later on that morning after I cooked breakfast and helped Mama sweep (I was cook by then; Mama had what killed her), I come out here and read in the book. Trouble is, you got to know what to look for, where the seed of the dream is really at. So I picked *drowning*; it was what Rachel said when she first woke up. And *drowning* in the book mean 'A healthy baby coming.'"

"Did you tell Rachel that?"

"I told Mama first and she say 'Don't.'"

"Then what did it cause? You said the dream caused something."

"You bound to know that." She had finished her work and began to fold the dress as carefully as though for perpetual storage, no hope of use.

"I talked to Mr. Hutchins. I know what he told me."

"He tell you she spent the best part of a year working on a baby?"

Rob said, "He told me she imagined a baby."

Della looked up and nodded. "Imagined it, started it growing inside her, and nearly let it kill her. She not well yet."

"But she didn't have a sweetheart?"

Della smiled. "You."

"—Before her sickness."

"Nobody ever touched her deep, I know, if that's what you asking."

"So why did it happen?"

Della said, "Ask Miss Alice; her daddy was the doctor."

"I'm asking you."

Della searched his face slowly for seriousness. "Punishment," she said.

Rob could not ask *for what?* He knew enough answers.

"Mama thought so too."

"Where is she?"

"In the ground; I already told you. While Rachel was crazy. Mama knew Rachel even better than me; so when Rachel got bad, couldn't nobody else but Mama make her eat—couldn't nobody else get near her half the time. She hated her daddy, turned against him like he was dog turds. Things I heard her say to Mr. Raven would stop most hearts: *'You asking me to kill this baby I love. I'll kill you first.'* And he never done nothing on earth to Rachel but cherish her, give her all she need. But she stayed good to Mama—and me too really; still I couldn't make her eat. She was trying to starve that baby out; but Mama would sit with her hour on end and talk to her gentle and get her to swallow three mouthfuls of something, then take out her slops. Mama never told her once that she didn't believe her, that the baby won't there. She just say, 'Let him go on and *come*, Rachel. We ready to love him.' And Rachel got better."

"At the clinic?" Rob said, "—Alice's father's?"

"Right here," Della said. "My mama talked her round in under a year. Got her out and talking sense and facing people; and then died herself, Mama did. Fell dead out yonder on the way to the spring. I saw her out the window and flew straight to her, but by then she didn't know me. Doctor say her brain split right down to the core like a twisted apple; say it pressed her to death, just drowned her in blood. And Rachel ain't mentioned her since to this day, hurt her too much when she still so weak. That hospital business in Lynchburg was something else, just resting up and eating and making new friends after Lucy my mama worked herself dead to bring her back to life." Della put both hands in the cover at her sides, buried them deep as if protecting some precious part from what might come. Then she said, "Rob, how come you taking her on?"

He was not offended. He knew an answer which he thought was true, and he knew nobody who deserved it more than Della. "She's the person who has asked me."

Della smiled a little and looked at the floor. "More ways than one to ask somebody. More than one thing to ask him."

Rob studied her then—what little he could see, folded on herself in the dark as she was. He had never seen all of her, however much he'd held or delved in for solace. It seemed to him now a necessity to see her; to honor her entirely by a grateful searching of her only gift, this small strong body that would last a few years at the rate it was burning (less than years if she went now to Philly or Richmond even), an image of help. It was nothing he had planned; it would not be for him—for Della finally, a clean farewell they could both understand. He felt no constraint from the idea of Rachel or his duties tomorrow but stood and stepped forward quietly, no hurry.

She did not look up.

He reached for her chin—his hands had not touched her face before— and tilted her skull (a bird's skull) upward.

She was managing to smile.

Rob said, "More ways than one to answer too."

She did not understand but, still in his hand as a polished stone, she took time to think. "N'mind about that. I was thinking to myself." She lifted her face very neatly from his hold and stared toward a ceiling which, for all they could see, might have been the bare sky—a night to fly through, in dream, from here. "You go," Della said. Her face never looked back down to watch him—his quick obedience, his simple "Thank you"—and long after he had gone out the door and shut her behind him with no sound at all, she was still looking up, recalling the sight of her mother struck dumb in wet cold dirt, not knowing her, not caring, refusing even to clasp Della's finger which was all that was left her as she rushed toward whatever peace she had won, what secret reward.

5

In his own room once he had lighted the lamp, Rob found two things, both waiting on his bed, both in white envelopes, one on the other. He turned the lamp higher and examined them. The top one said *Rob* in a strange script elaborate with flourishes. The other said *Robinson* with Rena's manly economy. Hers was the thicker so he sat on the bed by the light and opened it— a picture and a note. The picture was clearly Rena but a girl, no Rena he remembered, just the bud of her present face behind a wild laugh. A girl at the stable door, fifteen or sixteen, a heavy wood rake like a banner in one hand, a child in her other hand (its fingers held loosely), Rena faced the camera and was laughing for that; the child faced her—a long look up; the child was maybe three—and laughed for her so gladly that its face was a fading ghost. The note said,

Rob,

This is you and I nineteen years ago. I was cleaning out the stable, much against Eva's will. She had tried to argue me out of it all morning, saying if I couldn't stand a little manure underfoot, Father had good strapping men for the job. I told her "None better than me" and went. So she had the grace to leave me alone two hours, when I'd almost finished. Then she woke you up from your nap and dressed you—Eva made the sailor-suit—and taught you a sentence to say to me. Then you both came to get me. Eva brought her Kodak. You were meant to stay with her, well back from the stable, and call out to me "Your beau is here." Then Eva would snap my picture as I came to the door all embarrassed (I never knew at what; there was surely no beau, in the yard or on the moon). She had just got her camera as a gift from Father; took her five years to stop catching people off balance. Anyhow you said your piece and I heard you; but I thought you said "Your boy is here," and I still think you did (what did you know of beaux?). So I trudged to the door with my dirty rake to see you—me dirty as the rake—and you ran toward me while Eva was sighting. Sylvie was behind her, laughing too. You were meant to stay clean and save your little suit.

Well, I thought you were mine from then on out. I had prized you before, since the day she brought you home after Mother's death. But I took this as proof, and you never let me doubt it in all the years since. It is one of the few things I'm glad have lasted; and I hope you will take it now this night as not just the record of a child's laughing choice (in the picture I am looking at Eva to see if she knows it yet—she does, she does) or even as my cheap wedding present to you but as further proof of my outburst tonight: that two of anything are better than one, dirtier no doubt but likelier to laugh.

Sleep well, dear boy. I will watch you tomorrow.

> *Your satisfied,*
> *Rena*

He laid those two things carefully on the table—he would put them in his bag, take them with him tomorrow—and studied the other envelope. Still strange, and he knew every script in the house except Gracie's. It was firmly sealed so he tore it open. *Dear Rob* . . . signed *Rachel* but not in Rachel's hand. Dictated—to whom? Suddenly colder than the unheated room, Rob strained to read it.

Dear Rob,

Before I can go to sleep, I want to give you one real chance to stop—to think it through again now, with hours still left, and see if you thoroughly

want to do what you'll promise tomorrow. If not, I can swear to you now and
for always that I *will* understand *and will not blame you long.*

You are packed. You can take your grip now and go, letting absence be
your answer.

Or else you can come to my room and tell me. I will not be asleep; that's
the one sure thing.

If I see you tomorrow I will take that as sign that you mean *all we do and*
will always mean it.

> *In grateful honesty,*
> *Rachel Hutchins*

The hand was Niles'—Rob was almost certain (Niles disguised by a powerful effort that caught Rachel's voice but missed her plain headlong script).
Almost certainly Niles. Rob had waited two days for the wedding jokes to
start—from Niles, the Robertses, even Grainger—but nothing till this. He
tried to summon anger—they were still awake downstairs in the parlor; an
occasional laugh filtered up, a happy word: all smeared with ignorance, ignorant fear, of the simple pains and duties of love which Rob had yearned since
childhood to shoulder and was shouldering now.

Yet he read it again; and despite the fraud, was shaken deeply by Niles'
understanding of the life at stake; more deeply than at any time since August
when he'd run toward his father, a random goal almost not reached, and settled the course he'd begin tomorrow. He did not doubt what the fake letter
doubted—his own strength of purpose, the durability of present intentions.
He doubted, feared, Rachel's own capacity to bear his purpose, his loyalty.
In his whole life till now, only Rena had borne him; and he'd chosen her
early, a laughing girl cleaning out a stable. Maybe Sylvie. Maybe Grainger—
though with Gracie back, Rob hoped that Grainger could stare at her awhile,
spare the Mayfields a little of his expectations. But Rachel. What had Rachel
ever borne but herself?—her own fears, the murderous wildness of her
heart. Why had he thought she could ever support a thing as crushing as con-
stancy?

He listened to the house. Sounds still came up from Niles in the parlor,
and oddly still caused no anger in Rob. He had spent his whole life being
understood. What he gambled on now, or would tomorrow, was blind and
dumb—permanent welcome, permanent thanks. He was listening for
Rachel. He sat in the thickening cold of his room, having doused his lamp,
and listened in total stillness for minutes. No creak or breath. When he knew
she was sleeping or gone or dead, he rose and groped through the dark to find
her.

6

Rachel was sleeping lightly and so heard his one knock as merely an innocent noise of the old house yielding to frost. He was at her bed and sitting on
the edge before she knew she was not alone. The room was black but she felt
no alarm—Rob, by his smell: the thread of brandy on the broad deep mass
of his nature, clean, dry. She lay in place and looked toward his presence.
"Everybody else asleep?" she said.

"I don't think so."

"Who saw you come in?"

"How much does it matter?" Rob spoke normally, not whispering.

"It all depends."

"On what?"

Rachel waited in the hope that day would break or her eyes adjust to see
his face and test it for gravity, cruelty, drunkenness maybe (no, he smelled
too sane). Then she said, "It depends on how many people you want to
hurt before tomorrow comes."

"None of them," Rob said. "If me coming in here to talk to you hurts a
living soul, then it's that soul's problem. This is not their business."

"Is it mine?" Rachel said.

"You are Rachel, aren't you?"

"Yes."

"You plan to marry me?"

"At eleven o'clock tomorrow."

"Then it's sure *God* your business." His voice stayed steady as a glove
reaching toward her with a still hand inside it, powerful, cold, and urgent to
seize or harm or save.

Rachel waited again in hopes Rob would offer more explanation, but
after a while she said "Don't scare me."

"Why not?"

"I think you know. I've been scared too long."

"No I don't know," he said.

"You talked to Father. He told me he talked to you very fully. Rob, they
know everything I know," Rachel said, "—everything but the terrible ways I
felt. And I thought you knew that. You promised you did; your kindness
promised you knew my feelings."

"I do," Rob said. "I've thought I did. But I wonder now."

"What?"

He lay down beside her, his head on the vacant pillow but his body outside the cover, fully clothed. "I wonder what the story of all this is."

Rachel turned toward his nearness, but they did not touch. "What if I told you the truth?" she said.

"I'd marry you tomorrow."

"What if I lied?"

"I'd marry you still."

"Tomorrow?"

"Yes."

Rachel stayed on her back but raised both arms toward the distant ceiling. "Then I'll tell you the truth. It's just a story; there's no explanation. But the story happened, and happened to me." Her hands came down and, with perfect accuracy, her left hand lighted on Rob's own right—her hand, herself, the survivor of her story. Rob turned his palm toward her, and her fingers stayed there. "I lived in misery all of my life till you came here—the honest truth. I had what I needed of clothes and food and Father's goodness, constant care. I know that the world is mostly people who are naked and starved and crusty with sores and alone as mules, but I also know my misery was real and strong enough to wrench up a mind like a tree. Not that I was any white oak, but anyhow I went."

"What was wrong? What misery?"

"That's the hard part," she said, "—where I sound spoiled and whining. But I think the fact is this—by the time I was four or five years old, I had looked around enough (at Father and Mother, my poor grandfather, the few guests here, Della and Lucy) to figure out that what waited for me was *time*. Not punishment or age but simple time. Tens of thousands of days, all waiting ahead, requiring me to live them."

Rob said "You could have quit."

"I didn't know that. Children don't kill themselves; they don't know they can."

"I did," Rob said. "I knew the very gun on my grandfather's mantel that would do the trick. I used to get a footstool and climb up and watch it, watch it for signs that it wanted to serve."

"But watching was all?"

"I stroked it occasionally," he said, "—never gripped it though. I was in love; I had some hope."

"Who with?" Rachel said.

"I told you. I loved my mother. She kept dropping promises like notes in my path that she'd turn to me soon and let me tell her, stand still and let me show her."

Rachel said "You were lucky."

"I was miserable as you."

She pressed his palm hard. "You were so deeply lucky you should fall on this cold floor now and thank Jesus. I was bare as a bone."

Rob said "What was the difference?"

"I've already told you."

"Again please," he said. "It's late and I'm worried."

"Several people loved me but I couldn't love them."

"Boys?" Rob said.

"Oh no, just my family. You had your mother which taught you a lot, proved to you anyhow that people existed—one person at least—who could pull you through all the time ahead."

"Your father told me he worshipped you."

"That was just what he did; it was part of my trouble—he worshipped the likeness of his mother in me. I'm her likeness, they say (I've startled old ladies that have stayed here for years by walking out onto the porch in the morning, and they'd think it was Grandmother fifty years ago). He had hurt her, you see, by trying to leave here and then she died; so all my life, he's been recompensing me."

"He said he understood you."

Rachel said, "I think he did. I still think he does. I think most men understand most women if they just stop to think—men were made by women; every man ever born lived inside a woman's body, the whole safe world, for almost a year before she turned him out. What my father knew though was mainly this—there was nobody near me, nor any sure hope of anybody ever, that my heart could move toward. He'd known his mother and he'd been himself. He knew there were people who must live their lives with not one object they can sacrifice to, no room they can dress with the gifts they have." She turned her head to Rob, to try again to see him. Nothing still. So she lay on in silence.

He said, "That's the story? That's all the story?"

"It's the part I'm sure I can bear to tell tonight."

He took his hands from her and said "Tell the rest."

Rachel waited till she knew he was serious—he did not return his hand. Then she waited till she knew she would not refuse him. Then she searched for his hand and found it on his thigh.

He accepted her touch, returned a slight pressure.

She said, "By the time I had finished school, I still knew my one thing—the world was empty for me. I could read and cook, I could make people listen when I talked in a room, I could even make them watch me and smile when I passed (I had strong teeth that are naturally white); but I hadn't found a soul that made me want to draw the next two breaths."

"Was it simple as that?"

"That simple," she said. "I've had a simple life like everybody else."

"So then you lost hold." Rob gave it as a fact to ease her onward.

"I tried to *take* hold. The whole thing that got everybody so scared just started by me trying to change my luck."

"How was that?"

"That child; you knew about that?"

"The one you dreamed about?"

"Della told you?"

"I asked her," Rob said.

Rachel weighed that a little—a bearable burden? Then she said, "All right. Della knows as much as any other body, excepting Father. She was in at the first; she was cut off like me, only she never cared."

"She does," Rob said.

"You asked her that too?"

"Yes." He pressed her hand again.

It was not enough to go on. She was suddenly famished of fuel to continue. She took back her hand and rolled slowly toward him, to her own left side, stopping so near him that the breath from her nostrils was still damp and warm when it struck his right cheek and returned to her.

Rob turned also and accepted her nearness. They swapped breath silently but did not touch.

Then Rachel could say, "Della thought I was actually carrying a child that would grow and be born. So did Lucy her mother. I'd given all the signs; they had every right. I believed it myself, eventually at least, once Mother and the doctors had said I was crazy. It was Father that knew and never really doubted. When I had got bad and turned on them all and stayed in my room, trying hard to live in the face of them saying I was sick and must die—when I was like that, Father came in one morning and I wouldn't speak (he had tried a few days before to say I was only imagining and should face plain truth; I was Rachel, alone). I was lying full-dressed on my bed—not this one; then I lived downstairs—and he said 'Can I sit?' I said, 'You can sit or jump or swim; I will not listen to you.' So he sat there awhile quite a way from the bed in a white cane rocker; and then he started in just easy and quiet, that good voice of his I could no more refuse than a crown from angels. He said, 'Rachel, I have come to beg your pardon for yesterday, for doubting you. I have thought all night, and I know I was wrong. I not only doubted you but also myself, my own heart's knowledge, the one kind that matters. I know what I've known since before you could talk—you are trying to make your-self a life you can bear to live; you are craving this child. If you'll come back

to us, if you'll live here with us again and wait awhile longer, I will promise
you this; I can give it like a gift—the world will open and let you in; there
will be somebody to meet you when you enter.' I decided to believe him.
There was nothing else to do but rot here in hatred or bafflement. So I said
to him, 'Tell me how to come back'; and he said 'Let me think'—I had caught
him off guard; he had just not expected me to answer him then. He didn't
know the powers he had earned through the years, to calm me and ease me.
He sat on awhile. We didn't speak again but late that evening he came back
in and said he had thought and would I make a short visit to Lynchburg for
strength and rest? I knew what he meant, but I said yes I would (he had
already wired to see if they'd take me); and two days later Mother, Della, and
I went down on the train—Della just for the trip, to help Mother out if I broke
my promise. I never did, though I had some bad days, and Father didn't
either. After all those weeks with Alice's father, I came back home; and you
know it from there. I was helped several ways." Her face was still toward him.
They still had not touched.

Rob said "That's the story?"

"Till now," Rachel said.

"And it's true?"

"I swear."

"You know mine," he said, "—why I'm here, why we're going."

She found his face, his jaw, with her fingers. "One question," she said.
"Why am I going with you?"

"You just told me that."

"No. Why have you asked *me?* Why do you want me?"

Rob knew that he didn't. For the first time clearly he saw, as a picture, the
enduring future of this small choice—years of days with a poor child he knew
he was bound to harm, as he had been harmed by his own mother's choice
so soon regretted. A future to which he was bound now by honor, natural
courtesy, because this thin girl stretched here beside him, stroking his face,
had asked for his life; no one else had. But they *had*—Rena, Grainger, his
wild Aunt Hatt. He also saw them now; they seemed welcome refuge compared with this—generous calmers whom he'd cruelly abandoned tonight,
tomorrow, in a quick resort to remedies as harsh as any his mother had seized
as a girl, his mother's mother self-poisoned on the floor. Della, Sylvie, his
father, Polly—he was generally loved: Min Tharrington. But he'd now chosen something lonelier than solitude despite the plain fact that, all his life,
he had liked laughing company, the nearness of others. The thing he did not
consider at all was refusal, this moment—clean quick flight, the lesson of old
Robinson his father's father. He did not take the fingers that warmed his

cheek, but he yielded to the gentle endless plea. By slow degrees his face pressed forward—the growing of a vine, the progress of a hand on the face of a clock—till his mouth met hers.

She welcomed him fiercely with both her hands.

Rob gave what he could with mouth and head. Nothing else of his body wanted to serve or offered to. It had not reneged, for four years now, such a fervent chance. After two long minutes he drew back and lay staring up, not breathing. Then he breathed out in one long silent flushing.

Rachel said, "Everything I have told you is true. It is all I know."

Rob laughed, the loudest sound either had made. "Well, I thank you," he said. "It's more than *I* know, more than anybody else ever told me before. I believe you though and I swear to use it every way I can." He stood and left quietly; not touching her again. He would trust time for that; tired as he was, he was young and learning. Time would teach him to take her.

7

November 28, 1925

Dear Mother,

It is just about three in the morning. My clock has run down; so I'm guess- ing by the state of my brain and eyes—very poor but I'll live till tomorrow, I guess. It is tomorrow. Rob's wedding day and Forrest Mayfield's birthday (had you remembered that? Of course I never knew it; but Grainger said at supper, "Mr. Forrest, you're celebrating two things tomorrow," and I asked what he meant—fifty-five years old). He looks very strong and well—Father, I mean— and is here by himself and has asked after you. He has never said one word against you ever. So you could have come, you see; I told you you could. Even if he'd stood here with Polly his help on the steps to meet you, pouring out con- tempt; even if I'd let him, you still could have come. You have faced worse than that. I am your only child, all on earth that will love you once Papa dies. Sylvie could have nursed him there as well as you, for one day and night. Anyhow you aren't here for the curious to watch (they all need to see you, having heard me for months); but you're here for me. Very much here and running the whole strange show, driving it—the engine.

All's quiet right now. Even the groomsmen are long since asleep or dead or in comas (Mr. Hutchins broached a jug of mountain brandy; we may all die by dawn or be blind for the service, an all-blind wedding! It's that anyhow). No one but me seems to be awake, and I won't be any longer than it takes me to tell you this. What I mean by calling you the engine of this is—I do it for you, as

a gift and as obedience. The gift is that now I take my weight off you. The obe-
dience is that you urged me toward life, and this looks like life. You of all liv-
ing creatures should be here to bless me.

   I will just have to guess what you mean when you say in the note with the
gift (we thank you for that; Rachel will write you)—Long lives together. That
will occupy my mind quite sufficiently, I think, through a whole wedding day.
I am scared you are right; all your wishes are granted or have been till now.

   So you'll know where to reach me in case of trouble, we are going to Wash-
ington tomorrow evening and will be at the Hotel Hamilton there for four or
five days till we run out of monuments, museums, and money. Then we'll be
at the Richmond address, which you have. Grainger and his wife (who is back
for now) will go on ahead and get the house open and well dried out. It
should be in good running order by Christmas, and you are invited to spend
that with us. There is plenty of room, and I won't go to work before January sec-
ond. You would do Rachel Mayfield an honor and a favor if you make the trip.
She may well be shaky on her pins for a while, having never left home except
for treatment; and you, I know, could show her a lot about steadiness. It's what
you've shown me.

Thanks for it,
Love,
Rob

8

Two hours after that, just before she must wake in the cold damp dark and
head for the kitchen, well before day, Della made this dream from the
trapped reservoirs of her mind, heart, body, and not only watched it in sleep
like a hemorrhage streaming up from her but wished it on all the sleepers
around her in quarters and house, a permanent hurt.

   She had gone in and started the stoves and was baking six brown-sugar pies
for the wedding dinner (Grainger puttered behind her but she took no
notice) when the door from the dining room opened and through it her
mother walked, young as when Della could first remember her and strong,
though not smiling. Della thought to herself, "Mama dead and gone; why
she coming here?" and she went cold with fright; but she could not speak or
move for joy. She was still young herself—young as her mother, well and
strong—and now the one deep grief of her life was canceled, healing. Her
mother spoke quietly to Grainger; then laughed and said, "Della, get busy.
They coming." Then the house was full for the rest of the dream—loud

rooms of people all eating food as if food were new, not simply free. Della cooked it, not stopping—deep skillets of chicken, two turkeys, a beef roast, hot biscuits and rolls, whole tubs of corn pudding, a fresh set of pies—and her young mother served it with Grainger ducking round her like a pigeon in heat. But Della was happy, did not mind the work—no sign of the Hutchins—because of this luck, this piece of repair. She said to herself, "I could cook night and day—no rest, no water—for a yard of hounddogs and still be glad." But she had not yet said a word to her mother and seldom dared to look, though her mother went on throwing jokes at Della (little peaceful flowers that Della took, smiling, and strained to remember like prayers for help or the meanings of dreams). Then the day was dark but the house was still full, and Della began to know she was tired. Yet her mother came at her every minute or two with hands extended for fresh plates of food till finally she knew that her mother was real, had strengthened in death and was really come back and was planning to stay here, their home again; so Della said finally "Mama, let's *breathe*," meaning pause and rest. Her mother thought quickly and said, "Sit down. Every mouth fed now and the bellies can wait." Della sat by a table at the side of the room and leaned on her hand. Her mother stood on in the empty middle beneath the hanging lamp; and Della could watch her now steadily, no fear of her wasting. She even said, "Mama, come sit down here" (there was just one chair; the place was her lap). Her mother gave a laugh and said *"I'm* staying; n'mind me." Then the hall door opened—Mr. Hutchins, one arm stretched down, leading something. A pale naked baby all arms and legs, too young to walk but standing anyhow on shriveled white feet and pulling at Mr. Hutchins' hand like the tits of an udder. Della's mother didn't look; she was still facing Della. Mr. Hutchins said, "This thing has got to be fed." Della looked round for Grainger— nowhere, gone. She knew that she had nothing to give it. She was tired and resting. Again she didn't speak. The baby came forward; left Mr. Hutchins and lurched forward fast on its spidery toes and went to Della's mother and (with no help from her, no notice even) began to clutch and climb her, fist over fist, as if she were a rope. She never touched it, never reached out to help it climb; but when it reached her waist she opened her dress and gave it her breast, the full left breast which Della still knew as well as her own: the dry purple nipple pleated once through the middle to give warm milk, all a child could need. This child climbed to it and reached well round her and gripped her loose dress tightly at the sides and ate her slowly, small quiet mouthfuls like the chews of a cat, which gave it new life and color and strength while beneath it Della's mother shrank slowly and was gone.

*   *   *

When she woke it was too dark to hunt in her book for wisdom or warning. She thought but decided not to light her lamp; she knew all she wanted to know now or ever. Quickly she dressed to beat Grainger there (she could hear Gracie stirring) and walked out silent toward the high black house. She slowed only once at the spring a minute to rinse her mouth three times with water, foul with sulphur but sweeter than her own taste, the rags of the dream still strewn in her mind. Then she went on to work.

DECEMBER 1925–MARCH 1927

December 3, 1925

Dear Rachel and Robinson,

You were good to let me know about your wedding and job and plans. I am trusting that a new bride and groom could use some help in the cooking department so have packed you a case of the vegetables and fruits I put up this summer and will ship it on to you soon as somebody passes that can haul it to the depot. Or you could come get it. Rob, you know the way and remember you promised you would come back and sit for a better visit when you got on your feet. That last one was nothing; didn't get my eyes focused before you were gone. I know you will have your hands full getting settled in the next week or two but how about Christmas? Gid has asked me to come to Danville and celebrate with them; but after last year I made up my mind it was more celebration in my house alone—just me and the wind—than down there with him and his wife, an ill-wisher. So I will be here. I will be here so far as I know till I die and a good while after if nobody finds me. You are welcome both, Christmas or anytime. No need to warn me, though it might help an old heart to weather the shock if you drop me a postal card and say you are coming. I am always ready, nothing else to be. House clean as your hand, pantry sagging with food.

Is Grainger still with you? I saw old Elba who is living in his house about two weeks ago; and she said he sent her a message to say he was happy again and for her to stay put, he was not coming back. Elba took it to mean that Gracie was back or had promised one more time to be back soon. If he's there and Gracie with him—Rob, I hope you will watch her. She has never been no use to anybody—well, you know the one use. She pulled the wool over poor Grainger's eyes the first time he saw her, and he's never seen clearly from that day to this. He is yours to guide now as I guess your daddy told you. I took him from Forrest when Forrest let him go, you took him from me. God's watching it all so do right by him. He's a gentle soul. I would welcome him tomorrow if Gracie would vanish. Tell him anyhow that Elba said the stove has cracked and draws very poorly but otherwise things are still waiting safely for him. (If stoves were just the only things cracked!)

And how is Forrest? I have not had a word from him in over a month. Tell him if Miss Drewry is going home for Christmas, he should come on and join us. This house knows him well; he could still breathe in it.

Let me hear you are coming. I need to know you both, and the day may come when you need to know me (Rachel, I'm a far better cook than Grainger, much neater than Gracie)—don't wait too late! I am fifty-eight now and will need glasses soon.

Your hopeful,
Aunt Hatt

February 12, 1926

Dear Mother,

Happy birthday. I'm sorry to be a little late; but as you can imagine, since I tend so many fires now, I sometimes leave one awhile too long. No smoke, I trust? There is smoke enough elsewhere. I hope you had a good day; it was bright here and warmer after all the recent ice. I thought about you that night and wished you—backward (and forward of course)—more years of happy time.

Things are pretty happy here as a matter of fact. Rachel has stood up to all the newness and, with Gracie and Grainger, has made this house a good place already. She says she has told you the household details, so I won't repeat them; but all we really lack is a little more room. When Father got it for us, we planned on being three—two Mayfields and Grainger—but then he told Gracie he was moving to Richmond, and she volunteered to join him after years of empty promising (or so Grainger says; I suspect he begged her). We're got enough beds at least and doors to hide behind, though sometimes the moving space gets a little full—not too full to fit you comfortably in when you make your first visit that I still count on.

My job is all right. For now I mostly just sit in my office and try to learn to bookkeep by checking back through my old predecessor's records. Highway robbery! To my certain knowledge, he made off with well over four thousand dollars in his thirty years here. They vanished anyhow and his books admit it as bald as day. Nobody's looked before so I guess they didn't miss it, and I don't plan to tell them. He's retired to a nice little house near Jamestown with wife and new Plymouth (his first car ever—he is seventy-five); I'll try to keep his secret.

My secret is simple and I'll tell it to you. I think I am finally learning to take what the world provides and call it my need and believe it will nourish me adequately. You can learn to live on air; you've been telling me that for some years, I see now, but trying is believing. Why couldn't I see it? Why couldn't I just look at you in your health and understand? Well, I guess you know; I was looking steadily but for the wrong message. Belated thanks.

This is not to say, Mother, that I'm living on nothing or just on the pleasures, however tremendous, of light bookkeeping for a Negro trade school—no, on the contrary. I find little pieces of food everyday, little pieces of life that (a month ago even) I'd have stepped on or over but which stop me now and hold me and make a contribution to the deep empty coffer I've been for so long. I was talking today to William, the Negro that sweeps our building. He was stirring round behind me; but I kept working—if he speaks and you answer, he's got you for a talk or a very lengthy listen. Anyhow I worked and he finished his dusting and was at the door to leave when something pressed him harder than he knew how to bear. He said, "Mr. Mayfield, did you fight in the war?" I told him I was fourteen at the Armistice, but yes I did my duty and manned the Belgian trenches and killed twelve men. He was thinking that over, so I said "Didn't you?" (he is in his late fifties best I can tell). He said no he didn't. So I said, "Why not? Don't you love your country?" and he said, "Mr. Rob, I'll tell you a fact; I've lived in town so many years now that I don't care nothing bout the country no more." I told him neither did I, and I almost meant it. —That's a contribution (he knew it was and meant it to be; he's laughing still), and Rachel makes her share. Last Sunday morning she told me she hadn't known the world had doors, real doors you could enter and, just as important, walk back through. I said I hadn't either. Grainger came out the other night to where I was buffing up a scratch on the car and said he thanked me. I said he was welcome and then said "For what?" He said, "You getting Gracie back here with me"; and I saw later on that I had got her back—that I give them the room and the chance to last—but also that Grainger has saved me twice and may do so again. I owe him more than room. And I mean to try to give it.

Rachel's gone on to bed. I am mighty tired myself and badly need to join her. Wish me sleep and rest. Come to see us.

Love,
Rob

P.S. Remember me also to Rena and Papa and Sylvie. Tell Uncle Kennerly that even he could pass on my neatness at work. My books are clean as saucers and I steal not a penny—not needing to, now.

April 11, 1926

Dear Miss Hattie,

I got what you sent me for my birthday. I sat here tonight and thought you never had forgot me in all this time, twenty-one years. I will remember you. I am going to save it and once I get a chance, I am going to buy me a good Sunday shirt. You can get real nice ones for two dollars here and I need something nice when I go to the school some days with Mr. Forrest. I sit in his classroom and listen to him talk about stories and poems and how to write letters. He has come a long way like all the rest of us and I hope he is helping these boys and girls like he thinks he is. They all dress up anyhow and be quiet so I guess they are listening. I haven't gone but four times since Miss Rachel needs a lot of help in the house and Gracie can't do it all and I am trying to get the outside going, planting grass and some bushes. But that's all right. Grainger knows most of what Grainger going to know. One big thing is, you wrong about Gracie, Miss Hatt. I'm sorry. She was young when she left but she got good eyes and she learned a whole lot. She like living here and I think she like me. Think she always did, just needed to travel. I had been to France, see.

Rob says he going to bring all of us down to Bracey soon to spend a few days. I can see to my house and visit you then. Then see do you think I been lying to you all along about Gracie. See don't you believe me.

Your friend,
Grainger

June 17, 1926

Dear Rob,

Thank you for being so loyal with letters. Your latest cheerful word arrived this morning; and I'm glad for you that, after only six months at the job, you are getting a week's vacation now and the hope of another in August. You are obviously pleasing someone in power! (I trust though that you haven't had to expose your predecessor's sins in your own march to virtue; let him die in that new Plymouth, cooling-off.)

And thank you warmly for the new invitation to visit you there. I really never thought that sixteen months of my life would pass with no sight of you — none of us here ever dreamt such an absence and are saddened as it lengthens — but I've thought this out, Son, and have to say it now since I gather you do not understand my repeated declining to come. A good many of my reasons do pertain to Father as you always suggest. After all these years of his kindness to me — after he fed and clothed and fostered you and me both when Forrest had taken up another life that prevented his sending us an ounce of help — after such devotion, I am hardly going to risk leaving here now he's weak and may

go anytime. I've managed to forgive myself several things; but I couldn't face
that down, however long I lasted—having him die in pain and calling for Eva,
and Eva not there. You understand that, I am almost certain; that is love, pure
and simple, and gratitude. What I've known for almost a year is this (since you
first went to Forrest)—you don't understand much of self-respect or fear, not as
they pertain to me at least. I won't speak for you. For me though the main
impediments to coming are those two things.

You deserve an explanation and as I have thought a great deal since you left
here and warned me of your marriage, I think I can explain. I have not tried
before because it's still painful, and I didn't think you cared; but I guess by now
you'll have had other versions from other onlookers, so you'd better have the
truth from the one who bore it.

Despite what you think, you didn't have the first unhappy childhood. I was
paralyzed in woe from twelve years old, when I turned into a woman, through
all the years of school. No very strong reasons now I look back on it, except that
I thought Mother had it in for me (she did love Kennerly but Father loved me).
It turned out later in her awful death that she cared a good deal about me and
my life. I had never really known it. She had never tried to tell me, yet I pressed
her to death; and she let me do it in absolute silence, though she left me a message that made a lot plain. Your father walked into that misery of mine; and
because I was honestly a lovely girl and smart in school and because he had
had short rations himself (for longer than I), he saw me as what life was offering him—as food, as reward—and he reached out to seize me. Very gently at
first so that I quickly came to believe what he said, that I would be simply obeying time's will in joining with him and nursing his need. I also saw him in my
smart little head as a gate that would lead me out of a place which I blamed
for my misery. What he led to though was deeper trouble. He turned out to need
much more than I could give—to him anyhow and at my age then. He was full-
grown, a man; and I think he loved me—wanted me there at hand forever. We
were in a place he had always known (his sister's house in Bracey); he could
show his happiness to onlookers daily, his old friends and family. I was a child
as I soon came to know who had never left home and who now realized that,
of the places offered, I preferred Father's house and that, of the offered people,
I most wanted family—Rena, Father, Mag and Sylvie, even Mother finally.
Simple as that, I honestly believe—a homesick girl. And if Forrest had sent me
home that Christmas and let me make my peace with the family, I still think
I'd be living with him today. But from hunger and fear, he held on to me; and
then you came—and that was too late. Too late to save our life. I was so weakened then that it forced Mother's hand—she felt she was responsible, had
driven me from home, and had kept them from forgiving me. So once you and

I were strong enough to travel in early spring, we came here to make a solemn visit of grief and reconciliation. You got sick with whooping cough (brought to you by Sylvie); and during those hard weeks, I settled far back into my old life—a daughter, home. Too far—your father came to get us that August, and I turned on him badly. He was easy to turn on, easy to punish for all his deep hungers with my bright eyes and tongue. Right tonight I remember most of what I said to him, much of it true but crueler still. God may have excused me—I've asked Him to—but I blame myself and will die in regret. Anyhow by November I understood my failures, and I wrote and asked him to send for us by Christmas. What I knew I felt then was unhappiness at home—my old deep sense that this house loathed me and was forcing me out. Again I was thinking of Forrest as a gate. But by then I was wrong. Through my love of you—a little hot creature with no speech or gifts to give—I understood in secret what I only now begin to see in broad day: I can go many places. My heart can, I mean—or could have gone then. If anyone had showed me, I would gladly have believed that love is by no means a hard thing to get and surely not to give. Forrest learned that soon enough, I gather, once I'd turned him back again—well, not I but Father. I wrote him as I said and told him we were ready to join him for Christmas. He didn't come to get us or send any word; but he sent a large box—gifts, I've always supposed—and Father refused it, never let it be delivered. When Sylvie let me know (she had seen it at the depot), I broke and blamed Father; and that night in this room, he asked my pardon and begged us to stay. Mother's wounds were very fresh in all our breasts, and I'd loved Father longer than any other human; so for then I stayed—we stayed, you with me—and the time slid by.

You may know all that, as I've said, in some form—my form is honest to memories as hard as the days I bore them. What you may not know (Forrest may not have told you; it may be his shame) is that four years later, I broke long silence. There had been not a word, a check or a coin, passed between us those years. Silence feeds on silence. Then I sent him our picture, a sudden decision. I had not planned to do it; but a man named Nepper from Raleigh came through, and people around us were going to pose. All I had of you were little blurred snapshots I'd taken myself—just you and Rena, you and Sylvie. So I asked Father could I; and he put up the money. It was very expensive. We looked our best, both of us, if I do say; and when the finished product came, it almost broke my heart. We looked so lovely and so deeply unloved, dreadfully wasted hanging there in brown air like unreachable ghosts not knowing we were dead. I had ordered four prints—for Father, Rena, Sylvie, and me. Rena didn't like hers (you can surely guess why—I was in it beside you); and two mornings later I wrapped it myself and walked down the street and mailed it to Forrest. The end, the end. I'm certain he got it; Hattie had kept me posted on his whereabouts. He just never answered. I had to assume it arrived too late, that he'd already learned what I secretly knew—you can eat anything; you can live anywhere. I waited the best part of two months for an answer. Then I sat back and started my life again, this girl's life I've led and will no doubt lead to my nearly-virgin grave. It was also your life. I apologize for that but I had little choice as I hope you see now. Where could we have gone? We were honored here at least.

Please visit here then. I would meet you in some third place except for Father and the silly expense of renting "neutral ground." You have seen Rachel's home. She needs to see yours. It is different from hers, by Rena's account, and will tell her things she may need to know in the long years I hope she has with you.

So I'll turn the tables on you and ask you here for that second week of vacation coming in August. It will be no hotter in Fontaine, I'm sure, than the pavements of Richmond. We will keep the trees standing to shade your brows; and anyhow Father, as I know you remember, always strengthens in heat (being tempered he says) and can welcome you better. If you want to bring Gracie and Grainger for the ride, Sylvie knows several places where they could stay. She'd be glad of the help since (like others I know, including myself) all her old good faculties are slowing down now—all, that is, but the grumbling: that's picking up speed.

Two months to wait then. I'll possess my soul in patience and start airing beds. Say yes.

Love,
Mother

August 27, 1926

Dear Alice,

Please excuse me. This is the first time in six weeks that I've had a truly sustained free moment to sit down and undertake answering your last. I am in Carolina, Rob's home, Fontaine. We are spending the last week of his vacation with his mother's family. I had not met her of course so dreaded the trip, though her few letters to me were funny and kind; but this is the fifth day, and all has gone well. They are just a family very much like all in their loyal jostling and scraping, thicker than hops could ever grow (no crowbar could part them much less a new inlaw if she had the mind, which you know I don't). They appear to have liked me, even Rob's Aunt Rena who as you remember from the wedding party had rights of resentment against me but refused them. What puzzles me is only what must puzzle any bystander lonely in the midst of people holding hands— the question Why? Why do they choose each other so steadily? Why can they bear it?—these unbroken gazes through whole lives of years, these permanent burdens of weight and demand. Why don't they see they are just simple humans?—replaceable at any moment's notice by thousands more worthy than they of such love and more needy. I confide those to you, no need to answer; rest assured I will not be asking them here, though I really think the Kendals are a family that might answer. They strike me as people who know what they mean—every word, every hand moved from here to there. Even Sylvie their cook has the dark heavy air of intending her actions and silences (she is silent to me; but knows me by heart, every pore of my skin—she watches me).

The real news for me of course is Mrs. Mayfield. Rob had told me last spring of her part in his then unhappiness; and while I never said it, I thought more than once of the oddness of a young man's still volunteering his peace and his plans to the mercies of a figure so far in his past, so safely survived (my own desperations were caused by the future as you well know—a fear that the present would simply endure). But after four days in her presence and shadow, I understand more. She has genuine size, not of form (though she's tall and bears a grand head on a round firm neck not yielded to age) but, well, of merit. She has done what I beg God I'll someday do, earned her space and the air she drinks. She has earned it by keeping her face intact through decades that must have been all but bone-dry (she left Mr. Mayfield when Rob was just born). Miss Rena looks hungry as a stoat, hot-eyed; Mrs. Mayfield is fed, though on what is her secret. She is straight as a maple and smiles like one; she is funny and leaves rooms laughing behind her; she quietly tends to a crippled old father (bedpans, bedsores, the stench of dry skin) as if that were a privilege and pleasure to do. She makes me welcome with the ease she'd have shown some school friend Rob had brought home for supper, though she doesn't look down. She sees my needs and lets me fill them; never hoards back from me or shames my little graspings (of Rob, just Rob). I think I may hate her, but there's time till then. Rob is freer than he was. I think I can free him entirely and soon, give him better refuge.

I am happy, you see. The literal truth. You can tell your father. My father said I would be if I could hold out and lo!—I am. The thanks go to Rob. He has quietly borne all I needed to give; and since he bears it with such pleasant patience, I think he is finding me more than a burden. I work at that all the time anyhow—to be a help, an answer, not a set of heavy questions when he's had a life of those. I think I am winning; there are no bad times, not for me, not yet, though I'm told they will come. Rob has these burdens—his father and Polly, his mother, his job at the school—and it's part of his nature, I know, to plunge low about every fourth day when some fool sets a small rock in his path—Grainger's feelings get hurt, Gracie goes for a night (she did that the first time a month ago; but he stayed out till morning driving Grainger, and they found her—a natural cat; they'd better let her be, though she works like a sawmill hand when she's there and not pouting and I value her spirit). I seem to have no burdens whatsoever. Euphoria *you'll say and no doubt it is, but give me my head for a while. I'll slow. I only hope I can stand it when I do.*

The house here is roughly the size of ours, with more people in it; so we whisper a lot. But Rob is clearly enjoying the rest and is showing me sides of himself hid till now. He is better than I knew—plain kindness, I mean. He likes to please people. His idea of rest *yesterday was to strike out in the broiling heat and drive Mrs. Tharrington, a lifelong neighbor, to a dentist thirty miles away. Miss Rena managed to tell me in the middle of his absence—I stayed here in the shade—that Mrs. Tharrington's daughter was along for the ride (and with perfect teeth). In any case he was back here before dark which at present is as much as my mind seems to ask. If his need is bigger than mine, so's his gift.*

You'll snort at that, to which the true *answer is also cruel. You do not yet know what strangeness is involved. You will not till you live day and night in small rooms with someone you cherish, and with no thought of living otherwise now or ever. I say that not to hurt but in explanation of the distance between us which I hope you can close soon by sharing your life with something more yielding than a houseful of pale and querulous sick, your mother and father however good and grateful. You are lovelier than I, and I've seen men see it—Niles Fitzhugh for one, at the wedding parties. Let your heart face the purpose of all that beauty and open doors other than the one marked* Friend. *There are several other doors as you must know by now. Anyone who has stared at the world as intently as you with pencil in hand has seen that, Alice, and long before me. I've seen it in drawings that you threw aside, of just my face when I was near bottom. You could see I was hunting to live and would* find, *see it and set it down in lines. See yourself now and notice the doors all opening out.*

I am hoping to open the one marked Mother. *I have asked for a child. Please do not tell your father or either of my parents if you're in touch with them. I have just told Rob, just now this week. Till now he has not raised the question but has gone on and done what was needed to protect me. Now I've asked him to stop, to let me truly risk what I played at before—simple creation. He has asked me to give him a few days to think; he says he may really not be willing yet. His* mind *may not but the rest of him is. His body yearns toward me.*

Pray for us.

> *Love,*
> *Rachel*

December 22, 1926

Dear Eva,

Robinson has asked me to send you a wire; but since years ago I conveyed one quick mortal shock to your home and since he tells me your father is low, I take it on myself to tell you in a letter what cannot be gently told. Rachel and Rob are alive and in hope. Threats have retreated, though not yet gone.

At five this morning Rachel lost her child. She had had a good night of untroubled sleep, it seems; and was only wakened by a painless rush of blood. She lay in dark awhile to be sure she wasn't dreaming and even then made no real try at waking Rob. He told me he was wakened by the quiet sound of grief; again her only pain has been mental, wounded hopes. He turned on their light and was badly frightened but called the doctor quickly, who came at once. He was there in twenty minutes, and the issue had stopped. Still he recommended taking her to Barnes Hospital; and on the way, with Grainger at the wheel and Rob in back beside her, Rachel quietly delivered a well-formed son—a boy it would have been, the doctor told Rob, four months underway; never drew breath or moved. The doctor told me when I saw him this evening that, barring infection, Rachel's chances are good. Rob of course is with her and will sleep there tonight, which is why I write this.

It is ten-fifteen and now I must hurry to post this on the last train so you will know tomorrow. I can't resist saying though that part of my sadness, and no small part, in today's mischance is the fact that again, after all this waiting, you and I are foiled. At a distance to be sure and in a first try at a living "posterity" which may yet live in a later child (doctor sees no reason that she could not try again); but still I feel saddened more deeply than I planned, and I wanted you to know.

Rob will no doubt write tomorrow. We have him at least, proud man and strengthening daily. Tonight when I left him—grieved as he was, transparent with fatigue—he was lit with the firm light of your own early strength. I told him that I hoped this would not set them back or lock them in the fears of life that halted his parents in their tracks too early. He thought it out slowly and faced me and said, not a trace of a smile, "I don't think the suit of clothes has been invented yet that will hold my body back from doing its will if she lives and still wants me"—the voice of my father, old Robinson. He is in better hands then than yours and mine.

In haste with Christmas hopes for Eva
from Forrest

February 23, 1927

Dear Miss Hattie,

 I'm sorry you haven't heard from us in so long. Everybody got your good Christmas box and Rob and Miss Rachel got your last two letters but couldn't answer right then so I'll tell you now. Things here have been going downhill since Christmas, three days before Christmas. Miss Rachel woke up bleeding in the night and lost her baby she was expecting in May, a little boy she named Raven for her daddy, saying he never wanted her to have any that lived. She told Rob that and he told Gracie. Told Gracie if Miss Rachel feel like that he won't going to help her with no second chance at a live one. So since then he has been very gentle with Miss Rachel but that's all. Her mother was here to nurse her till a week ago and almost half the time then Rob was out late, coming home drinking sometime but always gentle and laying down in their bed the same as before but not helping Rachel. She told Gracie that.

 We been having bad weather which has not helped either. Everybody low and damp. I spend so much time downstairs stoking coal that I don't get to watch Rob as much as he need me and if I leave at night to find where he's roaming then Gracie's here by herself with Miss Rachel, a bad idea. You'd be proud of Gracie now, Miss Hatt. She's holding ground and helping. I'd be bad off without her. Don't wish me that again.

 I hope you got better news in Bracey than us. Maybe if spring ever come Miss Rachel can go to her home in the mountains and rest some there and Gracie and me could come up to Bracey and see everybody. Rob say he would like to come when I mentioned it to him. He took to you. Don't worry too much. I have seen him worse than this and so have you and he say Miss Rachel been a lot worse than this. Everybody just down like I say and damp, *just waiting for some sunshine. Keep well and I'll tell you when the news here change.*

Your friend,
Grainger

February 28, 1927

Dear Father,

 Your letter came in the first mail this morning; and I hasten to say how sorry I am that Mother told you as much as she did or in the way that she did. I can see she has misunderstood and misled you. I am a good bit stronger than she thinks. She has never believed in my fiber—I guess I've given her reasons not to—but you know it's there, woven strong right through me (I mean to live and like it); and since you have promised me a better time, I plan just to hang on and have it when it comes. It is already better than it's been before—my days, I mean—and the doctor here says I am not badly damaged but can hope for more chances once I rest my resources and heal the ripped edges of various things.

So I read a lot and help what I can with the house; and three bright days in a row this week, I went to work with Rob and attended English class under Mr. Mayfield. He taught me and twenty-eight Negro boys something I at least had never heard before (the dark ones seemed to know it; at least they didn't flinch)—God wants us to understand life as a comedy. He thinks it is funny since He knows the outcome, has planned it fully and knows we'll enjoy it when we get there at least (the trip seems longer to us than to Him but that's not important). Mr. Mayfield has got them studying Milton!—Paradise Lost—and they sit there like ebony angels (in their twenties, some of them men with families) and listen to him lecture on and on. God's plan and man's pranks—what on earth can they think? Well, nobody cracks a smile as I said. I come home and ponder. I can't speak for them; but maybe they are learning as much as I, in and out of class.

Rob is all right, Father. Calm down about him please. In a way what has happened was hardest on him. I mean, I could have died and all; but stay or go, he feels he's responsible for aiding me in this, that he volunteered too quickly to help me forward on a dangerous path. So he's had some bad nights, two of which Mother witnessed. Bad only to himself though; I trust she told you that. To me he is nothing but kind and caring, quietly needful. That helps me, Father—some real work to do. You will understand that, as Mother never will, if you just think back to the poisonous idleness of all my years till now.

Not entirely idle. I loved you in them and have every plan to persist in that. So uncrease your brow now, clean up the place, get the spring dredged out; in the second half of March, I hope to come visit. Rob will be on the road awhile, scaring up scholars for the Milton classes. Keep laughing. It's a play!

Love for now,
Rachel

March 10, 1927

Dear Robinson,

I mean this to reach you on your twenty-third birthday. I have never spent any of your birthdays with you; but I watched your birth and helped what I could to save your life and your mother's, that were doubtful. Several of us helped hard, so I guess you owe us a really good job of it—live on proudly.

Grainger wrote me your news two weeks ago. He is not my spy so don't turn on him, but I hadn't heard from you or Rachel either one since awhile before Christmas and nothing from Grainger, and I was brooding on you—I have lots of worry-time. You know I'm deeply saddened. I've had fair experience with loss myself—Father, Mother, James, Whitby in Flanders, even Forrest (he's gone just as far as if he'd died, to me anyhow)—so I hope you won't take it hard of me when I say there are worse things than losing another. I say this to you; never tell Rachel however strong she gets.

One worse thing, I know, is losing yourself—losing that place inside your own chest where you honor yourself and can bear your own company in the face of pure solitude. I'm lonely as a chicken hawk—you saw that in person—but I'm pretty good company too, for myself. I enjoy myself, though of course I welcome the faces I love, a very rare welcome as the years run on. Worse still is losing your courtesy to others if there are any others, just bathing in yourself as if you were single on the whole blank earth and could rear and pitch at will.

Our father did that. Forrest doesn't remember—he was far too young—and since he just saw Father at the end, all weak in Richmond with Miss Drewry there to tame him, he may have told you things that are not really so. If Robinson Mayfield ever thought once, not to mention twice, of his wife and children's feelings—the sights they must carry in their memory to the grave—well, he never told me or gave me any sign. I liked him a lot. Everybody likes a good-looking tall laugher that smells as good as he did after he had scrubbed. But I watched him ruin several and never ask pardon, never know what he'd ruined. I was not one of them—I decided not to be, the week Mama died; I would not be her—but behind me, Forrest was. He surrendered to Father at the age of five and is still in defeat, hauling poor Miss Drewry like Father's old washing and teaching poor Negroes useless poems all because Rob Mayfield had a few mulatto children. One for certain.

Son, please don't you be another meal for him, his strong empty cravings—my sweet killing dreadful father. Don't be him either. One was more than a plenty. Grainger says you are worried. I guess you have been; you've had real cause. But I trust that the causes are fading out now and that any need for running toward doors (that are never really there) is gone. I hope to see a man in this family just once stand and take what he's chosen, take it and all its secrets and hang on till judgment. Several women have already.

Give Rachel my greetings and best prayers please. I'd send her my love; but since she hadn't seen me yet, she might not want raw love from a stranger. You've seen me though so whether you want it or not,

Love from
Hattie

You are still wanted here whenever you can come. And I'll go anywhere you say if you need me. Aging but ready,

Ever,
H.S.

JULY 1929

Rob woke at a loud long shudder of the axles and looked out quickly—safe, a deep hole behind them in the road.

Grainger said, "Didn't see it. You can go back to sleep."

Rob put his head back to try again, thinking, "I will need every minute I can get"; but the heat and light pressed steadily at him, so he rolled his eyes right and watched the sliding country. At first he was lost; this could be any one of a hundred roads he'd traveled before—narrow through scrub pine and parched wastes of corn, cotton, weeds, and rough as a cob. Not a human in sight—three starved black cows posted out in an open furnace of a field, still and bony as a doctor's office furniture. Then as Grainger slowed for another rut, a shack swam by and an old man before it, black as any cow they'd passed and dressed to the neck in a snow-white Spanish-American Navy uniform—Deepwater Pritchard, drunk at nine in the morning. Rob looked back and waved.

They were twelve miles from home, his home at least. Fontaine, the Kendals, his grandfather maybe dying at last, maybe already dead (the call had come at three in the night—his worst stroke yet; he was speechless, still and staring—they had dressed and eaten and left by four, leaving Rachel alone for the hour till dawn). Rob had seen none of it since the previous Christmas when they'd come down from Richmond for three fair days; so he felt its power now, not a power to hurt (that was long since dead, he could tell himself) nor even a power to rake old memory (he thought of nothing older than this morning as they rode) but the force of attraction. Rob was held on this road as on magnetic rails by the place's desire that he rush on through it to its waiting heart—a deathbed postponed for twenty wasteful years, the lodestone (still potent) of his grandfather's life, still arranging, requiring the lives of others. He turned left to Grainger. "You tired as me?"

Grainger looked over quickly. "Tireder," he said.

"I apologize."

"For what?" Grainger said, not looking again.

"Taking you away now."

"What's wrong with now?"

"You were waiting for Gracie."

No answer from Grainger.

"She'll be back," Rob said, "and Rachel can hold her."

Grainger watched the narrow road. "I thought myself I was waiting on Gracie, waiting all this week; but just last night I was sitting in the room still dressed in the dark, and I knew to my soul two things quick as lightning—one, Gracie was gone; and two, I was glad. I won't even studying waiting on Gracie."

Rob waited and then said, "You don't still want her?"

Grainger knew at once. "No sir, I don't."

Rob was genuinely startled—the nights he had spent hearing Grainger extol her, implore her return; the nights of hunting her down when she'd run (Rob waiting at the wheel of the car by some cafe, miserable as pigshit, in deep Niggertown while Grainger went in and, finding her, begged). He studied the right half of Grainger's face, blank as new calfskin and age thirty-seven. What had ever moved him, ever hooked deep enough in that fine hide to hold or hurt?

Grainger bore the gaze awhile; then turned, smiling fully, and said in a rich mock-Rastus voice, "I tell you what's a fact. I lived in town so long, Mr. Rob, I don't care nothing bout country girls now."

Rob smiled but said "Why not?"

"I meant just Gracie. I don't want Gracie." Grainger stopped with that—what seemed a full reply. Then something more rose, more knowledge than Grainger had known he'd earned and could face and describe. "Not so," he said. "I mean everybody. Don't need any of em."

"I doubt you know everybody," Rob said. They rode a mile in silence.

Then Grainger said, "Maybe I just know Grainger. I thought I knew you."

Rob said "Lucky if you do" and faced Grainger, grinning.

"How's that?" Grainger said.

"—You know a happy man. Anybody knows me today knows a happy man." Rob touched his wet breastbone with the pad of his thumb through the damp white cloth.

Grainger said, "We headed to a funeral, I thought."

"Most likely, yes. I didn't mean that, though I'm not the only soul that's waited for the day."

Grainger nodded, not looking, and asked no more. Tired and possessed by his own new knowledge, he did not want more.

Rob went on and gave it. "I mean I'm lucky too. It's nothing I've won for being sweet-me; but just these last few months, few weeks—Hell, just last night—I've noticed I'm happy."

Grainger said "All right."

"And it's her. Rachel."

Grainger turned full to Rob. "She giving you all the stuff you can use?" He held his eyes off the road, unblinking as if he had no further intention of guarding their lives, reaching their goal.

Rob bore the whole moment—the speech, the eyes—like a lash on his mouth. Stunned, scared, angered, he said "You drive."

Grainger looked back, a smooth empty stretch of road; and drove a little faster, his face all clear and blank as the tan dirt that drew them on.

Rob waited till he found a tolerable answer—he had misunderstood; no harm had been meant. Grainger only meant love, Rachel's patient gifts. Then he could go on, calm again, to explain his new life. "You saw me marry her. You know why I did it—misery and meanness, and she asked for help. Nobody else asked."

"Not so," Grainger said.

"Who else?"

"You think."

"—You *got* it," Rob said. "Didn't you get help?"

Grainger said "All right."

Rob said, "You have worked every day since you knew me."

Grainger said "I have."

"And you're guaranteed." With his gentle fist, Rob stamped Grainger's knee. "Long as I'm able, and I *mean* to be, you are guaranteed."

Grainger said, "I thank you and I hope you last."

Rob said, "I said I mean to. I have to now—you, Rachel, Mother soon as this old man dies, Aunt Rena, all them. And like I said, I want to."

Grainger nodded, not turning.

But Rob had to tell him again. "Because of Rachel."

"Then pray she last," Grainger said.

"I will."

By then they were passing through a long stand of woods that was Kendal land, a cool dense island of walnut and oak, old pine and poplar that had lasted the gradual selling-off of the draining years of Bedford Kendal's illness, still-standing money not yet redeemed—because they contained, deeper in from the road, the old Kendal house, Bedford's own birthplace.

It would be Rob's soon, had been given to him or promised at least a year ago. He had been down with Rachel for a week's vacation; his grandfather had been weaker than ever and confused for most of the week; but the day before they were planning to leave, he had sent Sylvie upstairs to wake Rob at seven. When Rob had come down in his bathrobe, groggy, his grandfather said, "Get Sylvie to feed you and come on with me." Rob said "Where to?" and his grandfather said "Wherever I lead." So Rob ate quickly and dressed without shaving and went to obey. By then his mother was awake and with her father, combing his hair. When Mr. Kendal saw Rob walk in, he seized Eva's wrist with his one good hand and said, "You go on. He's come back to get me." Oddly Eva had accepted dismissal and left, simply saying to Rob, "Don't leave him in sunlight"; and Rob had dressed the milk-blue body, the sick scarce hairs, to his grandfather's orders and then leaned over and said "Where to?" again. His grandfather said, "Have you got a gentle horse?" Rob said "What for?" —"For me to ride. I'm a little weak today." Rob said, "Yes sir, I've got a sweet old plug"; and Mr. Kendal said, "Then lead me out to her." Rob, with no sure sense of where they would end, had bent and lifted the heavy body and carried it through hall, kitchen, yard to his car. Then he'd said "I'm ready"; and his grandfather said, "Ride out of here first."

When they'd passed through the center of town—August Saturday, the streets chocked with Negroes already at eight—Mr. Kendal turned toward him and said, "Listen here. I don't recognize one thing in all this" (he had not seen town for three or four years since Kennerly last bothered to give him an outing). "If you know anything at all, take me home." Rob had nodded and slowly boxed a block to go back; but as they stopped to cross the old Essex road, his grandfather said "Thank Jesus. Turn here." Rob said, "I thought we were heading home" (sun fell in the far side, all down Mr. Kendal); "I'm a little hot myself." His grandfather said, "I am asking you for rescue" and pointed right again; so Rob turned carefully and drove two miles down the rough Essex road, thinking, "Any minute now he'll forget and I can turn." But at the fork to Richmond, his grandfather pointed again to the right. Rob obeyed but said "Sir, rescue from what?" The flat eyes worked to remember—and remembered; they cleared and deepened—but he only said, "I want to see if my home is safe" and pointed onward.

Rob had understood then—the old Kendal place. He had seen it a time or two as a boy when they'd gone out for visits with a spinster half great-aunt and two distant cousins (old men, deaf as slate); but they had all died and the place had been rented to a man named Weaver who had once been a drunkard and killed his own son but had come round nicely and run the farm on half-shares and, old as he was (Rob remembered him as ancient), had started new children on a new young wife (the old one having left him at the killed boy's grave). Then he'd died and it passed through a slew of other hands, each sorrier than the last; and Rob had not seen it for oh twelve years.

It was safe when they got there—a high frame house nearly twice as tall as broad, on brick pillars high enough to let a school child walk upright beneath it, not a flake of paint left on roof or sides, every door and window open and a goat in the yard on a rusty chain. When they'd stopped and sat a moment and cut the engine, it meant nothing to Rob—the place, another millstone for some other neck—though he worked a whole moment at making it matter: one of the cradles of his life, one of the causes. Dead boards and bricks. He had turned to his grandfather then and found the old face feeding on the sight, through buggy plate glass, as if at a tit full of final joy. To break the long meal, Rob said at last "It's safe all right." Not turning, his grandfather nodded and made awful efforts to smile. Then the smile screwed downward into bafflement. Rob looked to the house. In the doorway— scared, big-eyed and staring—was a wedge of Negro children, four or five in view and the shadows of more, taller, behind them.

Rob had understood then; remembered in fact (Rena had mentioned it some months before)—Kennerly had brought in a Negro named Jarrel, a better deal. These were all his. Rob had assumed that his grandfather knew. He said, "They are keeping it very clean." His grandfather waited a sizable while; then only said, "Thank the goat for that." Rob said, "Do you want me to find somebody?" Another long wait; a tall woman stood in the doorway now, snuff-stick in her mouth. Rob said, "Do you want to speak to Jarrel's wife?" His grandfather watched her, not blinking once; but said to Rob, "I just want this—when I die soon, you take this place and fix it right and bring Eva here and look out for her." Rob had said, "She's happy in Fontaine, Papa." Mr. Kendal shook his head—"She won't be then. She'll need some place. Are you promising me or must I die in misery?" Rob had promised him simply to break his stare, then had waved to the woman and turned and gone home where his grandfather never once mentioned the trip. Neither had Rob, and forgot it till now.

Now he said to Grainger, "What about us living here?"

"In the road?—mighty dusty."

"In these woods, fool. I may own a farm back of here very soon, may own it already if my grandfather's died."

"I told you I didn't care much about the country."

Rob said, "I may be serious. Would you come here and help me?"

"You got a good job. What you know about farming?"

"More than you," Rob said. "No I'd get a good tenant. That job at the school is just to please Father. I wouldn't care if I never looked at a ledger-book in all my future life."

"What you want to look at?"

Rob said, "I don't know. I could sit still though till I'd thought it out good—maybe just at my children."

Grainger said "Where they coming from?" but gently now with real concern.

With his right hand, Rob cupped his own full groin. "From here," he said, also quietly. "Out from here into Rachel and out of her again." Then he looked up to Grainger.

"Is it time?" Grainger said. "Is she ready for that?"

Rob said, "The doctor told her six months ago she could try again. I asked her to wait; I still wasn't ready."

"How come?"

"Just scared. Scared to risk her again now I valued her truly. Scared to ask any child to bear me as father."

Grainger said "You ready now?"

Rob said "Since last night."

Grainger nodded. "I heard you" (his room was under theirs).

Rob said "You didn't *see*."

"No sir, I didn't. I was sitting in the dark."

"We were dark too," Rob said. "I was fixing to love her, rolling it on. She was flat there before me. I was up on my knees. She waited till I was full-dressed in the rubber, and then she said 'No.' I begged her 'Please'—I was that far ready—and she said, 'Surely. I meant *don't spare me.*' I said, 'You will have to let me decide that.' She said 'It's *my* life'; and I said, 'But you halved it; you handed me half.' She said, 'I did once and I will again; but you have got to give—you are hoarding back. All I promised was love; I never promised safety.' So I laid on her and went in her, bareback, first time in three years. It makes some difference. I had truly forgotten."

Rob had said it to Grainger, though not really for him. Grainger gave no sign of accepting, even hearing; but he took it as personal, intended to reach him with taunting and triumph. He drove as carefully as if they were lost in desperation—not three miles from town, their easy goal.

Rob said "Do you blame me?"

Grainger said, "You're rushing me. Give me time to think." He threatened to smile but in honesty he didn't, and he did not meet Rob's eyes again till they reached the Kendals' and stopped in the yard. Then Grainger said "I got you here" and extended his right hand as if for reward.

Grateful and needful (Rena rushed toward them now), Rob touched the hand, held it a long full moment. Faced with this day, this death and its duties, the risks of the night, Grainger's offered life—he had not been happier, would not be for years. He thought that now.

Then Rena was on him, begging "Hurry. Quick."

2

Though Rena tried to pull him, Rob stopped in the door of his grandfather's room. It was full—the big bed, the wardrobe, the washstand, the black leather couch, Rena, Kennerly and Blunt, Min's mother Kate Tharrington, the doctor at the bedside holding a wrist. The arm was dead, the uncovered neck—violet and drier than any crisp paper, plainly dead. The blue lips were open on yellow peg teeth, the shut eyes had quickly rounded in their sockets to perfect little globes the size of great marbles. It seemed entirely permanent, a state that had lasted days or weeks; but Rob saw at once on every face but the knowing doctor's that he'd got here precisely at the instant of death. A killing presence.

The doctor said to Rena, "Where is Eva? Get Eva."

Rena said, "In the kitchen crushing ice. She's coming."

He said "Go meet her" and laid the wrist down.

Rena looked down at it, never got to the face. She shut her eyes hard once, then went past Rob up the hall toward the kitchen.

The doctor turned to Kennerly and Blunt and nodded. They sat on the couch in unison, axed. Then he saw Rob, two steps inside the room. He stayed by the bed but spoke at Rob clearly—"You are too late for him. Get ready for Eva."

Rob nodded. Quick steps were coming up the hall.

Eva rushed in past him, no notice of his presence, though her right hand brushed him like a strong bird's wing on his damp left sleeve as she oared to the foot of the bed and stopped. She studied what was left for a sizable moment—ten, fifteen seconds. Then she looked to the doctor and said "Where is he?"

He half-whispered "Gone" and offered her a hand.

If she saw it she scorned it. She stepped round quickly to the rag mat she'd hooked just the previous March for his feet when he stood (she hooked rugs in March, too hot a job for summer). In one move she dropped to her knees, touched the bed with both flat hands; and looking at her father, said low but plain, "Let me speak to him. I have got to speak to him."

Rob had never heard her pray before or speak of prayer (the few times he'd seen her at church through the years, she'd sat open-eyed through prayers and benedictions). He looked at the others; all but Kennerly's Blunt were fixed first on Eva, then (once she'd begged) on Mr. Kendal's face. Blunt was crying, had been crying since the first sign of death.

The lips moved first, a slow jerk to free themselves from drying teeth as if they would speak. Then the eyes were open, not focused on Eva but upward, dazed.

Eva smiled and half-rose, bent close above him to be in his stare. "I just went to get you some ice," she said. "Eva's back now. You rest."

Rob reached the foot of the bed in two steps. This was maybe for him, some word to warn or bless him, some hunt for his face. None of that, no. He was only in time to be all but sure that he saw a knowing nod, for his mother alone. Then the eyes clamped down again; and whatever last life had glowed up to answer that summons, take that message, guttered silently and fast.

Rena went to Eva's back and touched her bent spine.

Kennerly stood and opened a window eight inches and propped it. The first breath of air in the room for years. Blunt was still weeping, little puppydog yips.

The doctor moved up by the standing sisters and touched Mr. Kendal's wrist again, a mute wait of five seconds; Rob counted each. Then he nodded to Rena.

Rena held Eva tighter, one hand round her waist, and said "He saw you."

Eva stood only then. She said "I know he did." Then she looked to Rena; but Rob could see her plainly, lit by her triumph, dreadful and strong, her face young and lifting. He could not move toward her; she had not seen him.

She said to Rena, "I need a little walk, just a minute in the air." She faced the door, seeing it only.

Rena said to the doctor, "We'll be back shortly"; then to Kennerly, "Take over." Still holding Eva, who was straight and steady, she led them on a neat narrow path to the door, not pausing or speaking to anyone.

Rob watched them go.

Min's mother came to him and touched his left hand which was braced on the dark high foot of the bed. Her own round face, normally as boneless as a handful of veal, was firm and lustrous with the sights it had witnessed, the duties it must do now. "Thank God you made it in time," she said. "Min is coming, I know."

"Yes I made it," Rob said and answered her smile, sparing her the weight of his own recent sights, fresh harrowing up of his own oldest grief. Then he went to speak to Blunt and Kennerly, the only place to go.

3

When the doctor had finished arranging the body (the washing and dressing were Eva's job) and packed his satchel, he left for the yard to find the sisters. Blunt and Min's mother left for the kitchen, so Rob and Kennerly
were there with Mr. Kendal. They both were standing and had done no more
than shake hands, speak names when they saw they were together alone, first
time in years. Rob said, "I got here as soon as I could."

Kennerly said, "It was soon enough. He saw you."

Rob said "I doubt it."

Kennerly said "I doubt it matters." He stepped from the window to the
spool-legged table by the head of the bed. Its top was empty of all but a glass
lamp, an old corked bottle of codeine syrup, and the comb Eva kept there.
He opened the drawer and brought out a gold stemwinder watch. Then he
looked back to Rob. "This is mine," he said. "This is the only thing here that
is mine."

Rob nodded as if his permission mattered.

"He gave it to me when I left home; I tried to leave here right after your
mother. They called us both back. He gave it to me then in the depot, waiting—said, 'If anything happens to me while you're gone, ask your mother for
this; say I wanted you always to know what mattered: just time, killing time.'
I've had to kill a mighty lot of time to get it, ain't I?" He weighed its solemn
roundness on his hard flat palm. Then he smiled at Rob.

"He had his own time, I guess," Rob said.

"Yes I noticed that too." Kennerly pressed the watch stem and opened the
cover—six-twenty, it said, and had said all the years since his father's second
stroke. "I will have to get it cleaned." Then he worked with his thumbnail
at a small raised lip on the back; and it opened, a private compartment. He
studied it quietly, then held it out to Rob. "Who is that?" he said.

Rob stepped up to see—an old photograph half the size of a stamp. A boy
maybe four or five years old in a Wild-West hat, bandanna round his neck,
smiling slightly. Some Kendal cast in the features but who?—the brother who
had vanished to Missouri long since? Bedford himself? As a clear peace offering, Rob said "Is it you?"

"Eighteen and eighty-nine," Kennerly said. "Mother brought me the hat
from a trip to Raleigh; and old Mrs. Bradley made a whole set of pictures—
she'd got a big camera once she passed the change of life. I'd forgot all
about it."

"He hadn't," Rob said.

Kennerly didn't smile again but he looked down pleasantly and touched the face with the tip of a finger. The spot of glue that held it to the gold flaked off, and the picture fell slowly to the mat at their feet. Rob bent to retrieve it but Kennerly stopped him. "I'll get it," he said. When he had it safe again, he put it in the watch-back and snapped down the lid. "He just kept it there. He'd forgotten it, I guess. Mother must have made him save it. I never knew it, see." He put the watch gently in the pocket of his cotton coat. "It's all that's mine here."

Rob said, "Can I have his pistol then?" and nodded toward the mantel.

"Ask your mother," Kennerly said. "Ask Eva and Rena. All this is theirs."

"Did he leave a will?"

"No he told me his wishes early last spring. The house and contents are Eva and Rena's, and all the cash from cotton and corn. The timber is mine and all the land except the Kendal homeplace. He said that was yours."

Rob said, "So he told me. He just told me once. I didn't know he meant it; I doubted he'd remember."

"He did. He said you had always wanted it."

Rob smiled. "Never. It means far less to me than this dusty rug" (he meant the mat beneath them). "What am I meant to do with a firewood house that Negroes have ruined and all those trees?" He had seen a good deal since his morning talk with Grainger, their ride through the cool stretch of woods now his—sights that made Richmond seem his feasible home or some place farther from here than Richmond.

But Kennerly answered. "You could kill time in it. He meant that by handing it on to you. Move your tenants out this winter, fix the house up a little, move Rachel in this spring, and you and Grainger farm it. You can also watch your mother. You owe her something better than worry, twenty-odd years of worry. She'll want you closer now."

"No she won't," Rob said.

"She'll need you anyhow."

Rob looked to his grandfather, no longer purple with the strain to live but lucid as a porcelain cup in daylight with the first short minutes of infinite rest. Who could blame him now? Rob found that he could. "Yes she may," he said. "She'll find it's too late."

Kennerly's face took receipt of that clearly but thrust it inward against future need. He didn't reply, didn't speak another word. He turned from Rob to his dead cold father; and not pausing once to study or fix his final picture, he bent quickly, neatly, and kissed the high forehead. Then he left the room.

Rob could hear Rena meet him halfway down the hall. "Eva's resting," she said. "She'll fix him when she can. You make all the plans, notify everybody."

"Does that suit Eva?"

"Those are Eva's instructions."

"All right. I will"—and he took two steps farther on toward the kitchen. Rena said "Where is Rob?"

Kennerly stopped. "He was still there with Father thirty seconds ago, but he may be gone. He is planning to go, always a great leaver."

"Hush," Rena said and moved toward the bedroom.

Rob seized the last free moment he would have and also bent to the face, hard as plaster, and kissed the cool mouth. It seemed a kiss of gratitude; this man had freed him, not in death but in life—by twenty-five years of forcing starvation on a needy child till the child went elsewhere and nursed other dugs and stood now, free. Rob could see that at last.

Rena saw and heard nothing.

4

She came up beside him and took his hand, having not yet greeted him properly. "I never should have rushed you in here," she said. "Forgive me please. I thought there was some chance you might mean something to him. Nobody else did. He didn't know a soul after three o'clock this morning."

Rob said "He knew Mother."

Rena studied her father. "Let her think he did. Let her think that much. It was nothing but muscles though, settling round death. You've seen things die. It takes them awhile."

Rob said "Where is she?"

Rena pointed overhead. "I sent her upstairs. Down here will be bedlam in another ten minutes. Kate Tharrington is already sounding the call—and I made a caramel cake last night. There'll be six brought here by dark and you know it; I'll never be able to touch one again. Haven't touched a piece of bacon since Mother died." Then she pulled on Rob's hand and pointed to the door and whispered, "I need five words with you." She led him quickly across the hall, the old front parlor which had held Eva's bed for twenty years; and shut the door behind them. When she'd got them to the center of the old rose rug, she said in a firm voice one tone above a whisper, "Remember one thing and hold it tight through all that's coming. You are the only hope of this crowd, and I mean to see that you get the right share of whatever Father had. Hold tight to that now. Till blood springs out of your nails if need be." She had never turned him loose; she gripped him harder now.

Rob nodded and continued to take her steady gaze as locked as an ermine's, but he said "Hope for what?"

She did not understand.

"You said I was the hope—the hope of what though?"

Rena thought a long time, even lowered her eyes. Then she found that she knew. "Oh Jesus," she said, "just *rest*, my darling." Tears brimmed her eyes. She had not looked up again; they fell, a clean drop, small spots on the rug.

Rob had never seen that. He tried to remember when he'd last seen tears in the walls of this house. There'd surely been tears (since his own childhood storms); he could think of none—or had they all been hidden, choked back behind doors? Whatever, they had found a free channel in Rena, who let them run. When he saw they had spent their urgent flood, he said, "You can rest. You have got years to rest. Once we get through the funeral, you have got a long calm. You hold to that." He touched her at the shoulders, small handsful of strength (lean muscle, firm bone).

By then she could smile. "I didn't mean that."

"Tell me then please."

It was harder to say than any other thing, any speech she had dared in forty years of ready speech. But she partly knew, for the first time ever, what she'd meant to say (had meant for years); and though her eyes had dried, her brow and chin showed the reckless effort. "I mean that nobody in this house, nobody that ever slept one night here, has ever got the thing they wanted from life. I just mean that." What she did not say was what she did not know, not consciously—that she spoke for herself, that her hope was for him: his total return here, body and spirit, return to her own steady gaze and care. She could not admit, even far beneath consciousness, that this one strong boy could not put a whole hungry household to rest.

Rob nodded. "How can I hope to remedy that?"

"Did Kennerly tell you about the will?"

He said "No ma'm," a complicated lie, part sly child's wish to give her the chance to bring him fresh news, part canny man's scheme to check two accounts for consistency.

But she knew very little. "You ask him," she said. "Father told him last spring. It's in his head."

Rob was caught, shamed. "He did tell me this much—I get the home-place."

Rena waited to think. "You mean this house." She pointed to the floor.

"The Kendal place."

She shook her head hard once and puffed a breath of disgust. "A ready-made bonfire. One match would send it up."

Rob said, "He loved it. He wanted me to have it."

That turned her at once. The brief flight of yearning and anticipation which had borne her so high was wrenched down flat. "He wanted you to *die*—to sit in the country and die in the tracks of people whose names you never even heard, I never even knew: old selfish Kendals. You listen to me—" She checked her heat. "*Please* listen to me; drive out there this evening and beg that Negro to farm that place for the rest of his life and not bother you for any more than prayer. Beg him that if it means kneeling down in the dirt and scrubbing his feet."

Rob smiled. "Calm down. I'm staying put."

"In Richmond," she said.

"Yes ma'm. For the time. We have started being happy."

"Who is *we?*"

"Me and Rachel; you remember my wedding?" He smiled again, touched her shoulders again.

Rena stepped backward gently but out of his reach. "I remember very well. Can you remember *me*, what I told you that night?"

"Yes ma'm, I do. I have taken it to heart."

"I told you the life that I've had here, the life Eva's had, has been gristle and bone."

Rob said "She had Papa."

"And I had you as I said, twenty years."

Rob said, "Cheer up—Papa's all that's gone."

Rena laughed, a strip of sound like an issue of blood. "Not so," she said. She went to the door. But she stopped on the worn sill and faced him again. "Did it really matter?"

"What please?"

"What I told you—find another life and hold it, hold it; don't ever go single?"

"More than anything I think I've ever seen," Rob said. He had meant to say *heard*; but he'd seen Rena's life, all the lives of this house. The long sights had mattered. He let the word stand.

"Well, Jesus," she said. She was somehow grinning. "At least I touched bottom." She moved again to leave.

Rob was moved to stop her—one final offer, though he neither understood his need to say it nor the fact that he meant it as his largest gift. "I am going to have a child," he said.

Rena took it, nodded "Thank you" and was gone.

5

By ten that night all the callers had left except for Thorne Bradley who stayed on the front porch with Kennerly and Eva (Rena had excused herself for the first time in memory and gone to bed at nine); so Rob went back to the kitchen where Sylvie was finishing and took a slice of cake and a glass of milk and sat at the big worktable in the center, too tired to think. He chewed on slowly while Sylvie moved round him, moaning now and then in her own exhaustion, addressing herself or the empty air with snatches of talk which Rob ignored.

Finally she stopped far from him by the sink and watched Rob, meaning him to look her way. When she'd failed to turn him, she said, "Look here. When they going to bed?"

Rob looked. Her eyes were heavy, mouth slack. "Go on," he said. "You've done a gracious plenty."

"She asked me to stay."

"Who?"

"Miss Eva."

"Stay where?"

"Where you think? In here. I'll lay down a pallet once they go to bed."

Rob had thought that the old arrangement would pertain; Grainger and Gracie had always slept at Sylvie's. "Is Grainger at your place already then?"

"You know," Sylvie said.

"I know very little about this place." He smiled but meant it.

"He gone in your car to meet Miss Min."

He'd forgotten entirely. Kate Tharrington had asked him early in the evening if Grainger might drive her the six miles over to meet the Raleigh train (she had phoned Min the news, and oddly Min was coming). He smiled toward Sylvie. "Guess she needed the rest" (Min had taken a job when school term ended at the State Library, searching family trees).

Sylvie also smiled. "*Rest* nothing," she said, "—she be busy struggling to watch you, Rob."

"Then I'll hold real still, make it easy on her."

Sylvie laughed but said, "If you smart you'll run. She get you yet."

"I'm *got*," Rob said.

Sylvie waited. "Miss Rachel?"

Rob searched her face quickly, no sign of mockery. "Yes."

Sylvie took a damp rag and scrubbed down the lip of the sink another time. She alone had rubbed it to rust through the years. Then she spread the rag carefully to dry and said, "How she going to hold you?" Still her face for all its tiredness was blank as basalt.

Half or more of what Rob had learned of his body—its growing and power, its offers of solace—had come from Sylvie. (The baths she had given him, stroking and laughter; the shards of her own life-story she would slip him when his mother and Rena had left a room—some fool that had sought her; some visitor she'd borne for the whole night before, to exhaustion and rest. *Vicellars Hargrove*—Rob remembered the name now: a short dark man who would wait for Sylvie at the kitchen door fifteen years ago. Gone like all her company. The night of his own high-school commencement—Sylvie's deep bed, old gold Money swimming, the dangerous darkness, dark Flora above him astraddle his horn more ready than ever in all nights since, more grandly assuaged.) But now tonight Rob could not read her meaning; was it kind curiosity or tired joke or a search for weapons to press against him? He gambled on hurting her. "Pussy," he said. "Simple as pussy. You know what that is."

Struck, Sylvie nodded before she really heard. When it reached her, she sat in her chair by the sink, no thought of leaving. While Rob drained his milk, she waited and thought. When he looked up and wiped his mouth, she said "Who taught you that?"

"What?"

"—That Rachel?"

Rob said "Who taught me what?"

Sylvie said, "Meanness. Never learned it from me."

Rob said "Excuse me."

She faced him level. "Too late," she said.

He waited awhile, then looked around. "Any more of that cake?"

"You get it," she said. "You just now told me I done a plenty."

Rob tried again. "Please, Sylvie. I'm dead."

"I'm *buried*," she said. "You sit there and wait till your nigger come back here with Minnie; they'll serve you, one of em."

Eva said "Something wrong?"

Both looked. She was straight in the door, one hand on the frame. Rob said, "No ma'm. We're resting our feet. Sit down; it's cooler."

She came forward quickly and sat.

Sylvie stood. "Miss Eva, you hungry?"

Eva thought for a moment. "I believe I am."

So Sylvie went to work—the clean blue plate that Eva favored, a large breast of chicken, half a fresh tomato, cold potato salad, rolls still warm from where she'd kept them nested, buttered and closed.

But before she had brought the plate to his mother, Rob said, "Are you going to be all right?"

Eva thought again. "For when?" she said.

He decided to tell her. "From now on. For good."

"The funeral is tomorrow afternoon at three; we just settled that after you left the porch. I can last through that, I honestly think. After that—" She stopped and turned back to Sylvie, "We'll see, won't we, Sylvie?"

Sylvie said, "Nothing but. What you want me to pour you?"

"Any buttermilk left?"

"A gallon."

"One glass please."

Sylvie went to the icebox, poured the thick milk, and set it with the full plate between Eva's hands, flat before her on the table. Eva thanked her and said, "You are staying with us, aren't you?"

"I told you not to worry," Sylvie said and sat again.

Eva ate two mouthfuls, swallowed with effort; and said to Rob, "If I've worried you, you can start calming down. I was tired just now. I'll certainly live." She took a taste of milk. "I can't say *how*—what I'll do, I mean."

"Come to Richmond," Rob said and touched her cool wrist. "Come visit me and Rachel."

Eva gave that a moment. "I may," she said.

"Come back with me Sunday. No need to stay here. Rena and Sylvie can hold down the fort till you draw breath—can't you, Sylvie?"

"Yes ma'm. Take Rena on with you. I do it by myself."

Eva faced him and studied. "Don't rush me," she said. "This is where I can breathe or *have* been breathing. I may strangle elsewhere."

"I'd be there," Rob said.

"I thought you were coming back here anyhow."

"No ma'm," Rob said. "Who told you that?"

"Father, last summer. After you and Rachel left, he told me you had asked him for the old Kendal place; so he said you should have it."

"No ma'm," Rob said. "It was his idea."

"But you promised him," she said.

He'd forgot the promise, his lie that morning to calm the old man. Could his mother know of it? "What?" Rob said.

She knew precisely. "To move there and clean it up and take care of me."

He felt cold fear for the first time since childhood (he was not a fearful person and had known it for years, no special virtue but a trait like his hair). He thought, "She is giving it now at last."

Before he could move on to ask if he wanted it, could use it any longer,

Sylvie spoke. "God help him." She cast it as a mumble, but it rang clear as oratory.

Eva met his eyes, held on them a searching moment, then broke out laughing.

Sylvie followed higher.

Before they had finished, Rob managed a smile but a pale one, pinched.

Eva chewed a biscuit, swallowed it; then still smiling said, "What's so good about Richmond?"

He needed to harm her. All in him, a hot need to strike stood up. He tried to let it cool; but he lost and said, "You are not there mainly."

Eva's smile deepened, broadened. Before him again she was flying back to girlhood—his oldest sight of her, bent above him, baffled, genuinely searching him for answers and help. But she said, "No I'm not. You're safe; I never will be."

Sylvie clucked twice—"Shamed." She did not say of whom, knowing neither of them cared.

Rob said, "I'm sorry. It's been a long day. I'm too tired to talk."

Eva said, "Some people have been tired for years but have held their tongues." She was still pleasant-faced.

So he smiled in answer. "I'm working at that; that's what is in Richmond. I'm learning several things."

"Name us some," Eva said.

Sylvie said, "Same fool I've known from a baby."

Rob said, "All the stuff I had not known before. I am learning to love my wife and hope for children. I am—"

Eva's face had darkened and gathered through that. She stopped him with a hand. "Won't somebody *quit*?" She was white with the wish.

Sylvie said "Quit what?"

Rob waited only.

Eva's force had drained in the words themselves. She was left high, beached, ashamed of explaining. "I said I was tired. But I'm tireder than I knew. Sylvie, I have been tired for twenty years exactly."

"I know you have." Sylvie stood to check the plate.

Eva looked back to Rob. Her hand was still on him, his wrist; she flicked it lightly, hair lighter than hers, diluted by Forrest. "No reason for me to force others to rest though."

He waited till she knew he'd accepted the apology, then withdrew his wrist and covered her hand with his whole palm entirely. "There's not. You're right. No reason at all." He met her dry eyes that were working to hold him. For the first time in all his life, he merely liked her.

"Every reason on God's green earth," Sylvie said. "Get out of here and let me rest my tail."

The three laughed together.

6

Rob waited on the porch alone for Grainger. His mother had gone from the kitchen to bed; he had told her he'd sit with his grandfather awhile, then turn in himself. The oil lamp burned low and hot by his bed (Mr. Kendal had never let his own room be wired); and Rob had stood a minute by the still tallow corpse—composed, dressed, and combed by his mother this morning while some warmth remained in the neck, arms, legs. He'd known that a farewell of sorts was due; seemed expected even by the head, propped and waiting on the bolster from which it had fueled this house, these lives, for twenty years. But not Rob's, he saw then. He'd been unable to feel so much as simple relief at this final absence; not to mention hate or the various triumphs which might have been just, had surely been earned. He'd clenched his hands a time or two, nails deep into palms, to rouse some flare of pain or pleasure. Nothing came but the steady peaceful sight of an old man resting on his lifelong bed in his good black suit; so he'd turned down the lamp to the barest shine that would represent light—a watch till morning—then he'd gone to the porch and sat on the left in the old green swing, the place he'd stretched for so many empty hours, his head in Rena's lap, her long fingers scratching in his short hot hair.

It was cooler now, almost eleven; and he'd swung himself nearly to rest again when the lights of his car turned down beside the house and into the yard—Grainger. He must meet him, keep him out of the kitchen where Sylvie had already spread her pallet.

It was Grainger and Min. Min waited by the car till he'd got nearly to her; then she said, "It's later than I knew, Rob. I'm sorry. We let Mother out but I asked Grainger please just to run me by here; I meant to see your mother."

"She's gone on to bed."

"Is she all right, Rob?"

"I think so," he said. "Nobody knows yet, me least of all. I never have known her."

"Oh you have," Min said.

Rob laughed. "Still arguing. I hoped you'd outgrow it."

"I didn't," Min said. She looked back to Grainger, who was dark there behind them, awaiting his duty. "Thank you, Grainger. I'll walk on home now. It's cool."

Rob said, "Wait a minute, Min. —Grainger, Sylvie's in the kitchen; Mother asked her to stay. She said you could go on to her place tonight, said the little bed was clean and for you to use that. Take the car—just lock it—and be back by seven: a busy day tomorrow."

Grainger stood, no answer.

"Something wrong?" Rob said.

Grainger beckoned with his shoulder—"Let me talk to you please"—and turned to walk off.

Rob said, "Min, I will walk with you home, just a second."

Min said "I'd be grateful" and stepped on the running board and sat on the fender, dusty as it was.

Rob went after Grainger to the stand he'd taken far over by the hedge, past the reach of the one weak backdoor light. He stopped two steps short of touching him and said, "Are you tired as me?"

Grainger said "No I'm not."

"You need any money?"

"I'm all right, thank you."

Rob said, "Then I'll see you at seven in the morning."

Grainger came forward one of the steps between them. His clean high odor, cured hay in a loft, was firm as a wall. "You talk to Miss Rachel?"

"Three hours ago. I thought I told you."

"You didn't. I was waiting."

"She'll get here on the noon train tomorrow. You can meet her."

"—Miss Rachel," Grainger said. "You mean Miss Rachel?"

Rob remembered then. "So far as I know. She was still by herself at eight o'clock tonight."

"No sign of Gracie?"

"Grainger, I didn't ask but surely she'd have told me."

Grainger stood in place another long moment; then stepped back, forced by the ignorance that poured out of Rob in a sickening torrent. "Maybe not," he said, "if she thinking like you."

Rob said, "Well, she's not. She's better than me. I said I was tired; you know all the reasons."

Grainger nodded. "I've heard em."

Rob waited, hoping to outlast the anger. He searched to see Grainger's face—some chance that he'd misheard or misread the last two minutes; that Grainger was not now trying, as it seemed, to cut loose and flail with all his long hoarding of witness and knowledge, a dreadful weapon; then leave for good. But though Grainger faced the house and the light, Rob could still not read the face held level before him, a mirror which fiercely declined to reflect. So he said the beginnings of what was just—"I will beg your pardon, Grainger."

Grainger said "Now or when?"

"Now. This minute." Then Rob said in his own head silently, "I have saved my life." He meant his spirit, his chance of peace; and for now he was right.

Grainger also knew, had the grace not to thank him or mention the moment which neither would forget in all their lives to come. He said, "I'll see you in the morning like I said." Then he reclaimed the single step he'd retreated and whispered the rest with a half-edge of laughter. "You take Miss Minnie straight home, no pausing."

Rob said "That's the plan."

"She tending to pause."

Rob said "Ease your mind" and punched him once lightly in the belly with the tips of his straight right fingers.

Grainger would have said *"Eased"*—it came to his mind—had he not had troubles that lay beyond this white boy in his path. He said "I'm working on it."

Rob turned and they went back in Indian file.

Min slid down to meet them.

Grainger said, "Good night, Miss Min. Sleep good."

"Thank you, Grainger," she said.

7

In sight of Min's house, Rob slowed and said, "You didn't have to come all the way home for this. People prayed for this death; nobody's bereft."

"Just your mother," Min said. "I came to watch her."

Rob said, "Then you've wasted a good train ticket. You won't see a tear; she's calm as my hand." In the warm dark he held out a steady hand.

Min said, "I can see tears on any street corner. I came to watch calm."

"For what?" Rob said.

"Education," Min said. "I'm a scholar, remember?"

Rob said, "I do. What's your present subject?"

"*Calm* as I said."

"You writing a book?" He stopped and faced her smiling.

Min also stopped but could barely see him. "No I'm living my life."

"And that's hard?" Rob said.

She nodded. "Part of it."

"What part?" Rob said.

"Are you really asking or passing time?"

"Does it matter?" Rob said.

"This much," Min said, "—if you're asking, I'll *tell* you. If you're stirring a breeze, I'll say goodnight." They had almost reached the walk to her house. A porch light was shining and some dimness upstairs.

"Your mother's gone up."

"We can sit on the porch," Min said, "—if you're asking. Otherwise I'm tired." She was also smiling and Rob could see her.

"All right," he said.

So she led them up the walk and quietly onto the porch—the old green rockers. Rob sat in the far one; but Min stood on at the top of the steps till she heard her mother's presence at the upstairs window. "It's Rob and me, Mother. We're down on the porch. I'll see you at breakfast." Kate Tharrington agreed and Min reached inside and turned off the light and came and sat an arm's reach from Rob, though he did not reach; did not think of reaching. He gave her silent time to recall his question and plan her answer. Finally she said, "The hard part is solitude. I never asked for that; but I've got it, big supply."

Rob said, "You asked for it. I was present and heard you." His tone was pleasant.

"When was that?"

"Our commencement, the party at the lake, you and me by the water."

"I did," Min said. "I suspected you'd forgot."

Rob said, "I remembered and I honored your wish. I could see you meant it."

"I did," Min said, "but just for that minute. You were awful that minute."

"I was honest at least."

"Honest in what?"

"In saying I needed you to help me then."

"You needed help about as much as Jesus in glory. Rob, you were the victor through all those years."

"If that's all you know, you were blind and dumb. I was worse off than most."

"From your mother?" Min said.

"Then you understood something."

"No I didn't," Min said. "I was thinking of me, a full-time job. No your mother sat me down four summers ago and told me her story, right before your wedding."

"Her marriage?—all that?"

"All that."

"She mentioned me?"

"In passing," Min said. "That was how I knew; you were just in passing. You were worse off than me and had always been." She guarded in silence the rest of her memory. Eva's plea that she take Rob and hold him however.

"I'm better now," he said. "I am all but cured." His tone was joking but a joker would have thumped his chest then to show soundness. Rob extended straight arms to the darkness before him as if it would care for the last of his needs. He held there a moment, then withdrew them to his lap again and rocked on slowly.

There was just enough light from one hall lamp and the far street corner for Min to see him. She took the chance. He was facing outward, calm, a little tired. He had meant no harm, only simple truth—he seemed better now: this boy (twenty-five, no better than dozens within two miles of here and oiled as he was with the seizures he'd made from other human lives, the tolls he'd taken for his own selfish need); this boy was her wish. Her single wish, alive after eight years of earnest stifling and flight. She would have to speak or sit till he turned and found her. She said "You like your work," a fact not a question, though she didn't know the answer.

Rob considered that slowly, surprised as always to find that he did—at the edge of his mind where he might have liked a dog or a clerk in a store. "It helps some," he said. He regretted that at once; she could plunge on and force him to bruise her again. He'd allowed her to steer it her own old way.

She proceeded. "What else?"

He faced her in dread which he tried to wear as puzzlement.

"What other help?" she said. "You claimed you were well."

"Just better, I said. You knew me at the low point."

"Something's helped you though."

"More than one thing, Min."

"I'm asking you to tell me."

Rob studied her. Till now she'd seemed grave as she was when a girl, every instant a sum to be teased till solved, the solutions presented with laughing surprise (however brief). Now he saw she was wild—denied and baffled. It seemed a new sight, a fresh message shown by a dying fire. He would not receive it. But in silence and exhaustion and because Min still faced him, he went on watching till he knew that her offer was common as bread in his own short life—the only word he had ever had from women: Rena, even Sylvie, Hatt Shorter, Rachel. Polly at the daily will of his father. Della in her black room, her deep dry bed. The Hell they stood in and beckoned from (all but

Eva sufficient in her own full place, arms down, or Gracie taunting Grainger). He had answered only Rachel, was trying to answer; had tried last night in their slow embrace, bare and dangerous. He did not know why and was not a man to ask; he felt now simply that he'd chosen rightly to put his lean strength into one strange socket—a girl named Rachel, as wild as any—that he had no strength remaining for others: Rena or Grainger or (a wonder) Eva. Or Min here now. He smiled and said, "Min, the answer is I'm loved."

"You were always that."

"Maybe so," Rob said. "Now I'm happy to be."

Min gave herself time; then she said, "Do you mind me watching you?"

"Help yourself," he said. But then he said, "Now or for years to come?"

"The years," she said.

"Yes I do. Yes ma'm. It's bad for us both."

She waited again; then laughed, amazed to find a laugh natural. "Then I'll stop," she said.

Rob said, "You'll feel a lot better" and joined her. "You'll be a new woman."

"Praise Jesus!" Min said. That calmed them a little.

8

Tired from the day (four hours on a hot train, a funeral, the crowd), Rachel went up before Rob and slept and dreamt before he joined her—she was on this bed on her back as now; but the bed was under heavy fathoms of water, and a dark girl (Gracie? she could not see a face) was far up above her bending over the surface of whatever pool this was and calling down to her, the words all muffled. Rachel thought in the dream, "I am safe from whatever that girl foretells"; and she did seem safe. She could breathe underwater, she could hold her breath and rest for long black hours, the dark girl would vanish. She was happy in the dream as she all but was in life, as life had begun to promise her she'd be. Soon. Through Rob.

He came up at ten-thirty, moving so lightly that Rachel didn't wake till he tried to raise a window. Then she surfaced from sleep and dream and saw him by the various dim lights that reached the window—streetlamp and moonlight, the odd passing car (he stood that long looking out, his side to Rachel): a boy a little shorter than she'd ever realized, his right hand hung on his sloped left shoulder, his weight on the left side, entirely bare. Since he seemed bemused and locked there, staring up the street, she took the chance to study him, a chance she'd seldom had since whenever he was naked he was generally in motion. A good while passed; he still stood on. Rachel fed on the offering he did not know he made. She understood nothing and was happy in the mystery; one portion of life encased in one form (particular, with all its own grandeurs and failures) had come through the dense world and stood here now apparently for her when she'd feared to the blank lip of certainty and farther that no one would come, not for her, not in time. She whispered "Good evening."

He did not turn.

"Good evening."

Still there, no flicker of notice.

She knew him well enough by now to stay calm. *He has not departed, he is cooling off, who's he here for but me?* But the calm was frail and raveled by the moment. *He'll turn now and tell me to go back without him. Go where? Away.* She clenched both hands—*Crazy; call his name.* She said "Rob" aloud.

His body stayed firm; his head turned slightly.

"Good evening," she said again.

He shook his head. "It hasn't been all that good so far."

"Your mother?"

"Everybody."

"That's why I came from Richmond."

"Why?"

"I thought you'd be down."

"You were right that far." Still looking toward her through the dark, Rob waited. Then he said, "Tell me how you thought you could help by being here."

She knew he'd been the fulcrum of the whole heavy day; so in spite of the chance that he'd taken some turn since touching her last, she said, "Relief. Maybe comic relief. I knew all the locals would be very solemn."

"Tell a joke," Rob said.

She was silent.

"Quick."

So she said, "All right—all I have is with me, my warm open skin. It was waiting for you. It will bear you to bliss."

He said "Please whisper"—she had spoken aloud.

She whispered *"Bliss"* and laughed once.

He turned.

By the light she could see he'd been ready awhile, for her apparently (who else was here?); for what she had brought, the little she'd brought. She felt it like that as he moved down on her and finally joined her. It seemed all she knew, all she'd needed to know through the bad time behind her or would ever need. She thought now of futures, a whole life ahead. What she didn't know—despite her plea of two nights before, despite Rob's second bareness as he came to port within her—was her other deep readiness: her body's fresh offer to accept his total gift and change it to a child, an actual child, that dangerous surrender, a long delight or death.

When they'd calmed and Rachel had drawn the sheet up to cover them, Rob said, "Tell me your idea of what comes now."

"Dreamless sleep."

"No from here on out, the rest of the time."

Rachel turned to her back—she had been facing toward him—and looked to the ceiling as he was doing. "Oh natural lives."

"What are they?"

"What we have, what we've had just lately—two people passing time, close and careful; eventually children, giving them room."

Rob said nothing.

"What's wrong with that?"

"It's harder than that. Two of anything is hard, not to mention fours and sixes—my mother, your father, any children that come. How on earth can we learn how to care for all that?" He still watched the ceiling, the string of the center light, a pale rope to nowhere.

Rachel said, "I think—and I think you will think if you look back a little—that Rachel knows at least as much of hardness as you."

He weighed that carefully as if it were urgent to know exact figures for burdens borne, payments earned—a rigorous fairness. Then he turned to his right side and faced her dark profile. "I think she does."

Rachel also turned—their breaths met and mingled, both clean and hot. "*She is me*," she said, "—Rachel Mayfield born Hutchins. I have given you my life. You can trust me forever. Nobody you have ever known could touch me for strength or for love of you. The rest of the time you can rest on me. I am more than you knew, ever dreamt I would be."

Rob could no longer see her; the moon had moved, all cars had passed. He tried—total darkness, though he knew she was there. Her breath brushed his face every five or six seconds; the voice had been hers, pitched upward by a fervor he'd imagined in her past but had not heard before—the lip-edge of wildness which till now only Della had recognized as *sight*, the visitation upon one girl in Goshen, Virginia of the gift of knowledge of present and future; the gift of *certainty* awarded for whole years of unbroken gaze toward cores of the world he'd barely glanced over, from weakness and fear. Suffi-

cient home for heart and body, room in that home for whatever product of
love might issue through its bloody gates (some risky child); the patience to
plead those gifts from life, seize them if need be, honor them always—natural lives.

A hand touched his chin, stroked down to his throat, then the nape of
his neck; then slowly downward.

He fully surrendered and slowly she brought him to readiness again.
What he did not know of course as now he rolled on her—what she would
not have turned back from had she known—was the near cold future: nine
months from now this child's birth would kill her, this child started now in
this lovely juncture.

9

Well before day Grainger woke on his back in Sylvie's extra bed—a little corner off her big main room, no door, no air, not reached by the low lamp she
burned by her own bed. He had slept untroubled since his head touched the
pillow before midnight, but he knew the instant his eyes opened now that
his rest was over. He must wait for day and Sylvie; she breathed on slowly ten
yards away. He was fully dressed—just his shoes untied, his collar unbuttoned—so his watch was in his pocket. He quietly withdrew it in the small
hope of gauging the time he must wait (it felt about five, the weight of the
air); and though its steel ticking was the loudest noise for miles, he couldn't
see hands; couldn't even see the face. He brought it to within five inches of
his best eye and tilted both the watch and his head all ways to catch any loose
light passing in the air. Not a trace, full-dark. It could be two o'clock; he could
have to lie here on his back four hours and breathe Sylvie's used air (she
wouldn't crack a window) and face his own facts.

It wouldn't be the first time—he had that at least; he'd had a fair number
of wakings in recent years. And in the first minute or so of any waking, he
would mention to himself what Mr. Forrest told him long years ago—
"Never dwell on any grave matter in the dark and flat of your back. If you
wake up worried or scared by a dream, take the bull by the horns and use your
precious mind; use the knowledge you've gained, try to name all the states
or the chief exports of the world by country or say all your poems. But don't
ever pray, not dead in the night; you'll think you are desperate in fifteen seconds, not to mention rousing God." For years that had worked; he'd obeyed
and profited—the names of the tongues of the Indian nations of North and
South America, the battles of the Civil War in order by date and by casual-

ties—but increasing years had brought him to this: all his recent knowledge, precious or trash, was hard and harmful. And now at thirty-seven, his older knowledge—what he'd heard from Miss Veenie, Mr. Forrest, Miss Hatt, his captain in France—began to seem in danger, not so much of being lies but of having been always a grinning cheat, the meanest joke. What had they all ever told him but this?—*If you mind your step, stay clean and pretty, stay well and on-time, you can be our pet; we will see you through.* He'd liked them and listened; and they had seen him through—to this, this night: a middle-aged man in a hot nigger shack forced to wait till day till an ignorant woman, much darker than he, had slept out her stupor and woke (hacking, hawking) to feed her old dog and ride with him back to a kitchen where he'd help her make biscuits and breakfast for a table of the ones who were seeing him through, then drive two of them (the youngest two and best) up the roadmap to Richmond where his own little clean room would swallow him in dumb dry silence, glad to have him.

Grainger went through that in the first ten minutes or so of his wait.

What saved him was this—*who had got any more?* The one voice that ever said another thing was Gracie (he'd known for some time now that that was why he'd sought her); and what she had said through all her going and coming, pitching and cutting; what she bellowed out clear in this latest last absence, what she'd said (he saw now) in her heat and light that first day he'd seen her in the churchyard in Bracey was no less than this—*I will have my life. Anybody that can help me, I will stay with awhile; I will lie underneath you long as you help. When you stop, I leave; when you run out of whatever I call help, that day, that minute. What I won't do is lie—I am hunting just this: what will use me up, what will burn me down (however quick it work) till nothing's left to touch, no spot of my grease, no rusty black hair, no slick bone to bury.*

Maybe Gracie had won, had got more than anybody else he'd watched. More what?—good life, good speed toward home. What was home?—well, rest. Who was headed elsewhere? Grainger thought for the first time in four, five years of the end of the story of the dark Pocahontas. He tested could he say it in his head in silence but working his lips—"She died of a broken heart beneath foreign skies with memories of the green woods of east Virginia, the swarming streams from whose sweet shallows she is still divided by the thousands of leagues of rolling salt deep by which she sleeps her longing sleep."

He wished Gracie speed on her way, long sleep; and by then felt the chance of dozing again, calm again anyhow.

But Sylvie spoke some hoarse quick sentence, clearly in her sleep.

Grainger rose to his elbows to hear if she repeated; he still had faith in the wisdom of sleep.

She said "Come here," low but urgently.

The last thing he wanted. He lay still and small.

She called out louder—"Here," in genuine pain.

Grainger said "Sylvie?"

A long wait. "What?"

"You sick or something?"

"No, fool," she said and scuffled with her quilt to return to sleep.

"You were hollering out."

Another long wait. "I got plenty reason."

He knew he'd been wrong. "You said come yonder."

"Won't talking to you."

"I know that," he said. Then he said "Who was it?"

"Seen a little baby in trouble," she said. She wanted to sleep.

"You catch it?" he said.

Sylvie lay back and told him. "I'm not sure I did. I was in this crowd lined up by the road, everybody watching something. Must have been a parade; you seen a parade?"

"Right often," he said.

"Where at?"

"Richmond. France. I saw more parades between here and France than I hope to see again."

"This was bad too," she said, "—everybody watching nothing but cars passing by. I was back from the road, lot of people around me; and I seen this baby crawl down in the gully and start for the road. Cars were still coming and I look around; nobody noticing so I leg out in the mud and catch him just before one big wheel grind him down. He not even dirty and grinning at me, not a year old yet. I bring him back over to the shoulder of the road, and there stand his mama. So I hand him to her, and she don't even thank me. I go on back to my place in the crowd; and next time I look, that baby on the ground again and that woman kicking him out in the road and cars still coming."

"You were hollering at him."

"I guess so," she said.

"But you woke up then."

"You called me," she said. "But he looked at me. He was looking up at me; he knew where I was."

"You'd have caught him," Grainger said.

Sylvie waited till he thought she had sunk back under; then she said, "I'd have tried. I'd have sure God tried."

Grainger said, "You'll catch him. You still got time. Go on back to sleep."

In a minute she was gone.

But her story stayed and worked on Grainger slowly. For reasons no stranger than necessity and patience, he lay and let it work—the harsh dream littered with hatred and hunger, not even his own. Yet it chose him as its object—he'd felt its arrival like a hand on his body—and bore in on him; and once it found home in his empty chest, it spread like streams and filled him with, of all things, happiness: a happiness that nothing else had brought him in weeks. Maybe months. No, years—twenty-five years nearly: a boy in a cold dark room in Richmond, Christmas, a gold ring, the promise of a life. He knew he was sane. He knew what those years had brought had been mostly pigshit and not of his making. He knew there was very slim chance of a change. Still he was happy. And could not think why.

But he didn't strain to know; he was glad to let it flood him, cool grace in the night. A grown half-black houseboy now abandoned by his field-nigger wife, a burdensome pet of the two white men who were now all he had (his actual kin), a man who could do nothing stronger than make flowers grow anywhere or keep a car clean or drive it neatly and say a few poems, who had made no children in ten years of trying—that seemed all he knew, this one night in August.

Yet he did not feel it. He believed in blessing. This clearly was a blessing at work in him now, Sylvie's dark dream intended for Grainger. The dense dry earth was promising to bless him, as it planned to kill Rachel and devastate Rob. It had saved him before; he would trust it again. He had earned his keep and would not be refused.

Grainger smiled, a gesture as hidden as the work of the hands of his watch, then raised his long legs and tied his loose shoes (a new gift from Rob) and waited for day, rested and ready, his long life to come. After half an hour, he thought of a question he should have asked Sylvie—was the boy white or colored?—but her breathing was slow again, her welcome stupor. She'd tell him tomorrow if he thought to ask her; if she still remembered the message she'd borne him, the chance moving toward him through time, time's amends.

T H R E E

PARTIAL AMENDS

JUNE 5–7, 1944

They had slept four hours when the dream began, ran its slow course, and woke them—Rob, then Min. Rob woke in fact well before the end, to stop it. Naked on his back on the soaked narrow mattress, he had managed to refuse to endure the end again and he opened his eyes. But he didn't touch Min or turn in the dark to find her. He lay flat, waiting for the fan's next swing, and watched the low ceiling while she saw it through beside him eight inches away, suffering little yips and moans toward the end as she struggled to surface and took the first breath of consciousness, hot for early June. Then they both lay quiet, still separate though bare, testing in the rate and depth of breath how ready each was to speak, start a day.

Finally Min said "Have you been asleep?"

"Long as you, two minutes less."

"What got you?" she said.

He said "You know."

"But tell me." She turned—in place, no nearer—and saw him by the street-light filtered through shades: the line of his features like a map for the road of the rest of her life (she saw it that way, had seen it for years despite his refusal).

Rob understood both her turn and what she saw; and neither from cruelty nor fear, he turned away—the need to focus on the story he'd seen and learn its demands. Then he put one finger longway between his teeth, a bridle should he need one; and said, "I was a boy. Fourteen, fifteen. We lived in the country and a war was on, around us but not near us. We were in the foothills, unharmed and green; and I had a sickness—my chest, my breath— though I felt well and safe and ready for my life. My father walked with me to the nearest town; and the doctor said—smiling, everybody was smiling, clear beautiful day—'T.B., very grave' and that, owing to the war, I must walk on up in the mountains to the springs. The good air, the waters. I left from there, not even going home—Father just vanished, no kiss, no wave—and I walked west for days through emptiness. Little towns in the distance, churches, trains; but not a living soul and I wasn't lonesome or hungry either. I just had the clothes on my back—a blue poplin shirt with the collar gone, big brown pants, old brogans—and a silver dollar to pay for my treatments at the end of the line. But I never ate a mouthful on the whole long trip, never felt the need. I was happy. All the way, every step of the way—all steep uphill—I was smiling to myself, needing nothing but me. Oh I touched a deer and saw most other kinds of harmless creatures; and every now and then I would hear the war, guns behind me muttering away. All the men were there, I guess; but old folks and children—where had they gone? And I never slept once. It was that far to go; and I wanted it that bad—the place, the springs, and not just my health but something beneath it, better than health: a magnet in the ground." Rob waited, the finger still in his teeth, still turned away.

Min said, "Are you telling me all that is true?"

He began an answer but only exhaled.

"Are you saying that happened?"

"It seemed to be," he said.

"But not to you."

"Maybe not," he said. "I'd have to think back."

"Think forward," she said. "Tell on to the end."

"I didn't let it end." Both their voices were as clear and clean as if they had never slept in their lives but had watched at doors steadily for arrivals.

"Tell as far as you went." Min watched him still, just the side of his head. He was beautiful and seemed calm now, which was why she urged him on— to learn all she could in the spaces of calm.

"The final night of the trip, all night, I walked through a storm like Hell on the rise. Night bright as day with lightning, trees crashing, rocks big as sheds falling at my feet—tame as dogs, sparing me."

"You were scared though."

"Was I? I don't remember."

"Yes."

"But I didn't stop, did I? That wasn't what it meant anyhow, the storm. It was not for me. I just went on—one foot, then the other, steeper up—into calm and morning which came together. And the first sight of people in all those days. I had come round a curve near the top of the mountain; and the road stretched straight before me, half a mile. At the far end were people all turned toward me—they'd been turned when I came into sight; they were waiting—so I went on toward them and knew I was there, my destination.

Still I asked the first man—tall, old as my father—'Is this the springs?' He said, 'It was and it was mine.' Everybody else nodded—men and women, all grown but a girl a little younger than me, all sad but not hard. I said to him '*Was?* I've walked days to drink. I'm dying, mister.' And he said, 'Well, die. The springs is gone.' I looked round at everybody there, all nodding, and said to them 'Help!' "

"You were scared."

"I remember—and honest, in earnest. Not a human moved. So I said it again; and the one girl stepped forward, just beyond being a child, a month or two beyond. And she said, 'Listen. We had the storm too, and it flooded our river and buried our springs.' I said 'Under what?' She said 'Six feet of dirt'; and I said, 'Hell, I'm dying. Let's *dig.*' The girl said 'Yes' but the first man said, 'How much do you cost?' I said, 'I'm free if you'll save my life.' The girl said 'No.' I said, 'You want me to die?' She said, 'No not that. But nothing's free. I just meant that; don't give away anything except for *return.*' So I said, 'Fair enough. I'll take you then'; and knew I was cured, healed down to the sockets and the springs still buried. The man didn't like it, frowned a lot; but all the rest grinned, and the girl led the way toward a little springhouse, white lattice work that was half under mud. And we dug forever. Days. Weeks more nearly. Every man but that one, who was my girl's father; and the women would cook us things and stand round and hum."

"This is much too pretty," Min said. "You're lying."

"I said it was a dream."

"—That you said was true."

"True the way dreams are, good stories that could happen."

Min waited. "My dreams have been literally true for thirty-nine years."

"I was coming to the true part next."

"That you were healed? That's never been the truth."

"—That I thought I was, felt truly that I was. Hell, I *was* then and there. The sight of that one girl had made me feel it, her voice saying 'Don't give except for return!' Hell, sight and sound, just plain human words, have cured old lepers and lighted the blind. Who was I to fail? I was just weak-chested."

"In the dream," Min said, "—weak-chested in the dream. What would that be in life?"

Rob said, "I thought you were volunteering help. I can find mean bitches in any bus station."

She touched him, her left hand firmly on his belly

He took it and moved it to her own side gently. "That's another thing available at every streetlight."

"Mine was free," Min said. She smiled toward his turned face.

He answered it fully as if smiles were as easy in his life as they'd been in the years she first knew him. "Nothing's free," he said, "like the young lady said."

"What else did she say?"

"She didn't speak again through all that digging. Not to me anyhow. I'd see her at a distance tell her father to smile; it was him we were saving more than me. I could read it on her lips. But all she'd do to me was grin and feed me and listen to my chest when we'd quit at night. I'd ask her 'What you hear?'—meaning *death?* or *what?* (I could still hear the war *every* day or so, no nearer but there)—and she wouldn't say so much as 'Hush' but just smile. I knew she was right, though I'd never told her I was sound as a dollar from the hour I met her—*because* I'd met her—and that all my digging in mud for a spring was just work for her, to earn my gift. She wouldn't have known a lung from a kidney anyhow; she was real in the dream, no magic girl. Real and waiting. So was I."

"For what?" Min said.

"Ma'm?"

"Waiting for what?"

"I told you once; this is nothing but a dream. Don't press it so hard. Just a story I made to pass one night."

Min waited. "But you know what you wanted from her."

"I do," Rob said, "—to love her, the girl."

"—For her to love *you.*"

"I might have hoped for that in time; but no, the way I said it—I wanted her to stand there and bear my love."

"To sleep inside her?"

He thought it out as slowly as if it still mattered; it was still dark enough to take the question gravely. "I don't think I knew people entered each other or wanted to, even."

"Didn't know in the dream or in actual life?"

"They're the same, I told you. I was fourteen, fifteen; I lived in the country surrounded by animals. I still didn't know human beings needed that, to rub little tits of themselves on each other. But I knew there was something called love in the world. Most children do; it is God's main gift, once He's given blood and breath. It may be His last if you don't take and work it. I *knew* as I say not from hearing folks praise it or do it in my sight but from parts of my heart that had always been with me. A loving heart."

Min had waited for that; but she didn't try to touch him again, didn't smile.

Rob smiled and looked toward her quickly, then back.

"So you loved her," she said.

"Not yet, not at once. I'd made a deal. Her father stood there to keep me to it if I'd wanted to quit. So days, weeks later I found the first spring, a little ring round it of white flint rock. Everybody clapped but her father, and then we stood quiet till the water ran clean. I offered it to him, the first pure drink; and he came forward to me still frowning and said 'It's yours' so I drank. He said 'It's all yours' and showed with his hand the whole place, the people, the spring, the girl. It was his to give. I said 'Yes' and stopped."

"Stopped the dream?" Min said.

"Yes."

"You could stop it that easy?"

"By waking up, yes. I was happy enough."

Min said, "Mine lasted. Mine went on from there."

"I knew it would." Rob lay on silent through the pass of the fan, then silent in its absence.

"Ask me how," she said. "Ask me what I dreamt."

He said "All right."

"—That I was the one smiling girl and you killed me."

He turned to her slowly, to within four inches of her breathing face; then rose to his elbow, then to his knees, straddled her flanks, studied her face still dim and vague, then struck her in the mouth.

She gave no sound, never flinched or turned, never broke her own stare at his dim face above her.

He rode on another minute, bearing her look; then dismantled himself and lay down again, flat on his back.

No sound from Min. No move of response once her face had settled.

They both lay prostrate, staring up through the minutes till dawn—summer dawn, early. Then when daylight had clearly begun to replace the lamp outside and the dead-heavy weight of heat above them gave the first signs of new life, active pressure, Min turned to her side and faced Rob again. After half a minute, he accepted the gaze; and she said very quietly, "Listen to this. Please listen to this. I haven't ever dreamt it; but it's all I know, a story that could not only happen but did. I have used you in every way I could, every way you'd let me since I got old enough to have needs other than food and a roof and a few kind words. I have always known it was second-best—God, *fourteenth*-best. I've stood, don't forget, and watched you sucking on the ones you needed; that fed your craving. I could have turned and left. Well, no I *couldn't*; maybe even shouldn't. Where would we be, either one, right now if I'd kept my pride?" She paused, not specifically waiting for an answer.

But Rob said, "Dead. I at least would be dead. You'd be far better off, a real home, some rest."

"I might be," she said. Then helpless she smiled. "I also might be Eleanor Roosevelt and saving the world. I might be a high-yellow girl in heels at a Saturday dance in some shaky hall with my bosoms on fire and my razor fresh-honed—"

"You might have been some people's decent wife and mother."

"—Not a whore pushing forty with a poor drunk friend, school-teaching by day?" She had not intended to strike so soon or with so blunt a sledge. She hadn't intended to strike at all but to state the true past and plead one last time to have a true future, honest lives.

"*You* said that," he said. "But if that's what you think, if that's all it's been, I would still say thank you."

There was more to the story she'd meant to tell—the demand she had meant to make at the end: that at last Rob take her or leave her completely—but now he had stopped her with guileless thanks. She knew or had always chosen to believe that what she had loved and served in him through years of disorder, refusal, and shame was that one piece of the heart of the world—the precious meaning of life and pain, both cause and reward—which had been held toward her very early in her life (a small quiet life), the one chance for service and meaning and use which life had extended her. She half-rose now on her right elbow and looked all down him. Softened as he was, encased in his years, even a little rank from the heat, it was still buried in him—a perfect core which she'd once seen clearly in both their youths and reachable now in one last try. She knew of no other way to reach it but this—she silently climbed to the posture he'd taken: straddled him, kneeling but lower down, her knees at his calves. She rose there above him a long silent moment, her own surrenders to wear and gravity honestly shown; then her face sank toward him, and she brushed back her short hair with both hands carefully as if it were long and would hinder them.

He didn't touch her but he said "Please don't."

She shook her head No and loosened a forelock that hid her eyes. Then she used him as if he were nourishment; as if feeding on him would not exhaust any store he possessed but would honor, replenish.

So he didn't withhold but when she had roused him (his body which had never been all of him), he set both hands on the crown of her head and let them ride out her long careful act (too tired to ask was she giving or taking, healing or harming) till he'd given himself, again not all but a little hot clot that cut its way out more like death than pleasure.

Her face still hid, Min said her own thanks and rolled—never rising to his face—and slowly lay beside him, asking nothing more.

Rob waited to be sure, even offered her his own large hand to use any way she needed.

But she only pressed his fingers once more in thanks, then half-turned away and shut her eyes calmly as if headed for sleep.

Rob knew they mustn't rest; light was well underway. In another half hour he would hear his landlady cough herself out of bed, and then he and Min would be trapped here till eight when she might take her old scottie out for his walk. He must get Min out now and back to her place, get himself finally on the road he had planned and dreaded all spring.

He sat up quietly and propped himself to look round and let the room reel him up the last few fathoms into day and duty—a good-sized room, fifteen by twenty; all he had here at least, twelve dollars a month from a widow so lonely she made him feel lucky. But the room was still hers despite his long presence, going on nine years. One deep breath proved her ownership. It was drowned in the smell of her life not his, not to mention poor Min's—the dense dry smell of her dead kin, vanished children, as if in his absence at school or at meals she'd slip in to clean and, helpless, would grease every inch of floor and wall with glandular musk from the depths of her body. Even his clothes—two suits in a wardrobe, four shirts in a drawer—his worn hairbrushes, his pocketknife, gold watch, each day's small change: all conquered by her, it seemed to him now. Maybe even the pictures, unframed and curling by the dresser mirror. He stood and went to them and bent to see.

A girl fifteen, not smiling, long curls, staring fearless at the camera as if it might save her. A boy not twelve yet, still safe in childhood, brown-haired, smiling freely out from ample stores, the eyes a little crouched. The one of the boy was newer by years, raw and glossy, a school picture—Hutch his one child. The girl's was precious, though bare and unprotected—his picture of Rachel, the one she'd given him. Rob reached for them both; put them face to face and held them at his side, not studying them. They were still his at least. He looked to the bed.

Min lay jackknifed on her side; but her hair was well back and half her face showed. The eyes were still shut; and the good full line of her leg, hip, side was pulled overhill by her calm loose belly—"the abandoned melon," Min called it when he cupped her unawares at night.

Rob smiled and thought, "At my mercy. Offered. Unprotected, ruin or take." Then he went to the wardrobe and took out an old black Gladstone bag which had been his father's. He carefully laid the two pictures in the bot-

tom; then covered them with two suits of underwear, black socks, two shirts.
Then he dressed himself in his summer suit and shoes, tied his tie, combed
his hair, drank a glass of stale water from the china pitcher. Then he went
to his side of the bed and stood, trusting the force of his wait to wake her. In
a minute it hadn't; out the open window a cardinal burst on its bossy song.
Rob said "Time's up" pleasantly.

She turned at once; she had not been asleep but waiting for this. When
she saw him all dressed, shielded against her, she knew she could say it after
twenty-three years. She covered her breasts with folded arms, raised her knees
toward her waist to hide her slit, nodded slowly, and said "It is. Sure is."

Rob also nodded. "Let me take you home, a working girl."

"Working woman," Min said. "Where are you going then?"

He still could smile. "To the moon, thereabouts."

"You don't understand what I just said, do you?"

"I thought I did, yes ma'm. I—"

She shook her head. "The *time* part, the part about time being up."

He didn't speak but sat, straight and neat, to listen.

"My waiting-time," she said. "I cannot wait on. You have got to find out
soon and let me know. In words I can hear and understand—final words,
Rob, soon."

"It's a bad time," he said. "Let me go see the boy; I've promised him a trip.
Let me get some things settled. I plan to see the principal in Fontaine
tomorrow; Mother thinks he may hire me. Let me check the old house; I
doubt you could stand it."

"I'm too old," she said.

"It's dry," he said. "I could halfway heat it if it's not too ruined."

She shook her head again. "Not the house, Rob," she said. "I could live
in the tomb of Cheops tomorrow. I am what's too old."

"For what?" Rob said.

"For waiting on you one extra week." She reached down and hauled the
crushed sheet to her chin. "If you can't tell me Yes by a week from today,
don't ever speak again, not to me. I'll be gone."

"Next Monday," he said. "I may well be in Richmond or Jamestown
even."

"They have telephones and wires. Send me one cheap wire— *Minnie
Tharrington, Raleigh. I accept. Come on.* Signed *Robinson, always.*" She had
counted the words on her fingers as she spoke. "Nine words," she said. "A
whole word to spare. You could even say *love.*"

Rob sat still awhile. Then he said "You mean that?"

"I do. I'm sorry. I know it's a bad time for you—no job and all your scattered families—but what you haven't seen is, it's gotten bad for me. Too bad to keep bearing."

"You told me you were strong. I asked you that—remember?—when we started this at all."

"I still am," she said. "I think I still am. But I'm also older and I want to be kind to me and to you. Another round of this and we'll both be worse, much worse by the minute. All the tides are going out."

Rob nodded. "Right now. I'm bad off now." He held out his right hand halfway toward her.

Min didn't take it but watched as he intended.

It shuddered in the air with a movement as delicate, as hard to see, as a struck bell's rigor or a bird's hot breathing and as hard to stop.

"Meaning what?" she said.

"Meaning *help*, I guess." He dropped it to the sheet.

She sat up, no effort to keep the sheet on her. "Rob," she said, "try to comprehend this. I am saying one thing and very little else—Min has not got any help left to give. Not in this situation. Not another day of this."

He let it all land, arrive deep in him; she meant it at least. He'd outlasted worse, he'd maybe last this, he could not think how—except for the boy. He thought of his son, who seemed a real goal. "I've got to go," he said. "Please get up now."

"You're not shaved," she said.

"You've seen beard before."

"For your trip, I mean."

He thumbed toward his landlady's room downstairs. "If we draw water now, we'll have her up, the damn dog howling. I'll take you and come back. I need to see her anyhow, explain about the rent. I need to write a letter. I'll leave by ten maybe."

Min nodded and wiped at her eyes with dry hands. Then she stood up and, not glancing once at the mirror, she quickly dressed. Then she took up her own handbag and went toward him, stopping two feet away so he could choose—precede her out the door or wish her goodbye.

Rob wished it but he said it; he could no longer touch her. "I think I'll be back. I think you can believe me. Let me just see Hutch and Mother and some others; I'll try to get us right. Believe that; believe *me*. And still try to help."

Min faced him clearly, calm in the knowledge that settled heavy on her—he must take or leave—but she lied again to save him a few days longer. "I'll try," she said. "I'll hunt for ways, no promise though to find them."

"I know that," he said. "I won't expect much. I just said it anyhow for old time's sake." He felt a smile and showed it; it spread up his throat and across his stale face like a slow show of broad firm wings from his youth, opened to morning. "I won't sink now. Men forty years old don't sink in broad day with the waters calm beneath them just because they've lost a job through a little weak whisky; just because they can't make up their mind to have a life, take the people who are present, and ignore the poor dead." The smile had survived. "They seldom sink, do they?"

"Every day," Min said. "Every day on every street." But she also smiled.

For the moment they stood there as willing mirrors, they seemed themselves again, their early selves, savable. Rob led her out quietly and safely down the stairs.

2

June 5, 1944

Dear Polly,

Are you well? You know that I hope so, though how would you know except on faith in light of my silence? I meant to write to you long before now. I've meant to do a lot of things since Father's funeral, but I've been much lower than I'd thought I would be. Not that I doubted I would be sad awhile, regretting the way he left so fast and regretting your loneliness; but you know as well as anyone alive how sizable people can leave your life and you stride on, not deeply struck (you and your father, all the tales you told me).

This has struck me deeply. I let him down so badly, from the day Rachel died; and since you called me with word of his death and I stood by you and watched him buried next to Robinson Senior, I have not once shaken the heavy thought that I've lost another last chance to recompense a person who only wished me happiness and worked to help me get it — worked to show me what it looked like, his life there with you.

Now because of that sadness and the drinking it caused and the anguish after that, I have been told here that I'd better go my way. You can teach something upward of a thousand children in nine straight years how to do long division and what life requires and still be shown to the back door fast if your own life skips any single requirement they've got for more than one day (I was absent six days spread over two weeks and paid my replacement; but I cried one day in the midst of explaining how you calculate the quantity of plaster needed to cover the ceiling of a hotel ballroom so big by so, and since thirty seventh-graders looked a little puzzled, I explained that too — what was needed by me:

you won't need to hear, same old old story you heard years ago and answered so truly.

So now I'm fired, the last man but one in the Raleigh school system—all old maids now and one 4-F'er, an old maid too).

That brings me up one more time again to the starting line of a race I never even volunteered to enter. I know by now you are thinking "Boohoo"— you've sure God earned the right—but I trust you'll also know that I am lining up and will lurch off again once I draw four breaths, which is why I'm writing now.

I am leaving here this morning and will go to Fontaine for a day or so with them. I will also be seeing if the school board there can consider hiring me for their one vacant job, "shop" teacher. Picture that; I have seldom nailed a nail that didn't bend double. I will also be seeing if I think I could bear moving home after years. They are all healthy there so have never had the need to understand the poorly. Whatever happens anyhow I plan to strike out by the middle of the week and give Hutch the trip I've been promising him. Mother's brother Kennerly is on the country ration board and promised me the gas once I told him I would have to see you on Father's business. We will go up to Norfolk for a day at the beach, then to Jamestown and thereabouts as mileage permits. Then if you are agreeable, we'll come on to you by Saturday evening. Hutch can look around Richmond or go to the show for as long as it takes you and me to sort the papers and settle the estate.

I know you are not looking forward to that anymore than I am. My own impulse is to build a bonfire; but others are involved as you well know, mainly Hutch and Aunt Hattie and her one living son. Let me say this though in advance of our meeting—I said it at the funeral; but here it is in writing: as far as my part goes, I mean you to have it and will throw every ounce of strength I have, which is roughly one ounce, into seeing that the other Mayfields follow suit. They have all got lives of long ample standing; there is nobody starving; if they don't already know the years of debt we all owe to you (two generations' worth), they will when I've finished, if I can keep afloat. Maybe floating's not the word. Anyhow I think I can with Hutch along to watch me. And you have always helped.

I hope to be in Fontaine by suppertime tonight unless I'm wrecked and dead (I have slept very little), so please drop a line by return mail to say whether this plan fits in with your own convenience. You know I hope it does since I feel the need to talk—far beyond the Mayfield business. Soon, I pray.

Love,
Rob

3

After mailing the letter he stopped around town, paying all his May bills. Then at once because he had never thought of breakfast, he went to the Green Grill and ate a big lunch. He had not been there in the weeks since Forrest's death; but his old waitress Luna was ready for him, smiling—a short woman maybe four or five years his elder with the kind of permanent good-spiritedness that bespoke in her either a mild feeble-mind or the grace of God (Rob could never say which).

Once she got through the questions and regrets about his father, she said, "Do you notice I am acting any different?" and stepped back to stand and let him size up the change.

He looked a long moment and said "Well, *act*."

She paused awhile thinking, then crossed her large arms on her low breasts. "I'm a mother," she said.

Rob said "Who's the lucky boy?"

She shook her head. "No sir. This is serious," she said. "They called us from the Welfare five weeks ago and said they had a girl and to come down and see her. I cried all the way, begging Jesus for help—*Let her answer our prayers; let me and Jess love her.* I've had this love all blocked in my chest since Jess wouldn't use it, nowhere else to send it. So we got to the place, and the case-worker brought out a three-months' baby. I took her right then in my arms and deeper; and I knew the whole time of waiting was over. She is named Rosalee; I let Jess name her—Rosalee was his aunt. That was five weeks ago. Jess has not touched a drop—five weeks dry as dust; four weeks was his record more than twenty years ago. You come here next week and eat you a dinner; and if I'm not here and they tell you I'm dead, you stand up and say 'Luna Wall died laughing.'" She laughed full-eyed.

Rob said "God help him," meaning Jess her husband.

4

It was past two o'clock when he drove off for home, and the day was baking. He had gone three miles and was just past the final fringes of town when his old dread of lonely trips fell on him. *Places* in his life, his various houses, had been hard enough; but *roads* had been harder because so chancy, so glad to oblige. You could die on a road in utter privacy, secrecy of means; a road would conceal you, agree to your vanishing and yield no trace. Yet it would not guarantee your destination; if you took its offers, would you land in oblivion or punishment or just a cheap wallpapered room in a town big enough not to notice your face? *Imagine it's a tunnel*, Rob told himself—*a tunnel long enough to get you to Hutch the one living human that still needs to see you, still truly depends; the one human you have vowed God to live for. No windows in the tunnel but Hutch at the end.* He knew he was wrong and to this extent—there were windows for every regret of his life, and he had two solitary hours now to sit and stare through them at scenes he had made but could no longer mend.

He saw a Negro thumbing fifty yards up the road in an army uniform with a small canvas bag in the dirt by his feet. Negroes seldom thumbed white men in strange territory but stood as they passed, watching and ready. Nearer, Rob could see that this was no young boy—a short heavyset man, coal-black and glossy, great shoulders and neck but smiling frankly. He slowed the car and stopped precisely at the man, not forcing him to trot in the naked sun. All the windows were open. Rob said "Can you drive?"

"Yes sir."

"Got a license?"

"Yes sir." He reached to his khaki hip to fish out a wallet.

Rob said, "I believe you. Will you drive me to Fontaine, N.C. in guaranteed safety?"

The Negro smiled broader. "You lying," he said.

"Pure truth," Rob said. "I need a little help; been sick here lately."

"You got it," the Negro said. "I'm headed there myself. Didn't think nobody else in *this* world was going." He took up his satchel and came round the car. Rob slid to the passenger seat and watched as the man climbed in, set his bag on the back floor, and turned to check quickly for his benefactor's motives. When he saw he was safe, the man said, "Fontaine? You come from Fontaine?"

"My mother's people do," Rob said. "I lived there some."

"I lived there all my life," the man said, "till the army sent for me."

"Who are you?" Rob said.

"A Parker, Bowles Parker. I live in the country six miles out from town near what they call Beechleaf."

Rob nodded. "I know there're some Parkers out there. But Bowles, let's roll. This sun's out to kill us."

"Yes sir," Parker said and released the hand brake. They rode on a mile or so in silence while Parker got the feel of the '39 Hudson.

Rob wanted most to sleep. He had slept only minutes in the nights since his firing and would hardly sleep tonight after all his mother's questions and the supper they would give him. And he did feel drowsy; but he also felt the need to perform two duties now—be pleasant for a while and question his driver a little more closely before lapsing into unconsciousness beside him. So he said "How's the war?"

Parker said, "I ain't seen it, not yet noway."

"How long you been in?"

"Two years and two weeks."

"The infantry?"

"Yes sir. But my feet flat as pans, so they letting me cook. I can sit down and cook."

"You down at Fort Bragg?"

"Right now I am, yes sir. I been down at Fort Benning for more than a year, but they moved us up here three weeks ago. Said they giving us a change; but we know what it is—they fattening us up. They throwing us on overseas just as soon as they make that invasion." He smiled at the road.

"You still going to cook?—over yonder, I mean?"

"They still going to eat. So I'll be frying and the shells be dropping."

"You scared?" Rob said.

"No sir."

"How come?"

"I'm *certain*."

"What of?"

"Dying early. No pain."

Rob said "Where?"

"In Germany."

Rob studied the black face—calm as a table, though not smiling now. "How are you so certain?"

"Jesus told me in the night."

"How? What did He say?"

"Said, 'You going to die in Germany easy, shot through the head, so tell em goodbye.' "

"You going home to tell them?"

"*See* em," Parker said. "I ain't telling nothing."

"Told *me*."

"You a stranger."

"How old are you, Bowles?"

"Thirty-seven last month."

"Who you got left at home?"

"My wife and three children; one of em is hers, oldest boy. He can keep her. Some cousins. My mama."

"Who is she?"

"Flora Parker. She just come back, been living up north since I was a baby."

Rob looked; searched the profile—smooth as pasture, nose and forehead. *Is he somehow my son?* was his first clear thought. No way, too old. Relief and disappointment. *It could have helped me now,* he thought, *to find I made a strong man my first night trying—a second good deed, one strapping black cook.* Still looking Rob said "Any brothers or sisters?"

"I wouldn't be surprised. Mama had a big life, but I never asked her much when she come home to visit—she come on my birthday every year but one. I didn't want to know; didn't want to crowd my mind, just think about her for the time I had (I lived with my uncle). And now she don't know. Her mind is affected."

"By what?"

"That life I told you she had. Doctor said her mind dead and will keep on dying, so she back home now."

Rob said "She's still young."

"No sir, she pushing fifty."

"I recall her as young."

"So do I," Parker said before he really heard. Then he heard and took his eyes off the road a long moment. "How you know her?" he said.

"Through Sylvie our cook. She used to visit Sylvie."

"Her and Sylvie fell out way back," Parker said.

"Will she know you?"

"Who? Sylvie? I ain't studying Sylvie. Sylvie come up to me one Saturday night when I was a boy in town just to look—big dance at the Hall—and she say 'You Bo?' I tell her 'Yes ma'm.' She step back and look and say, 'You ever see a orphan?' I tell her 'No ma'm.' I never heard the word; I was fourteen, fifteen. She step back to me and raise this little mirror right to my face—she been combing her hair—and laugh like a fool, 'You seeing one now.'"

"She was drinking," Rob said.

"I know it," Parker said, "—knowed it then; know it now. And I still don't excuse her. Anyhow she was wrong." He stopped as if exhausted.

So Rob thought he'd rest now; he leaned his head back.

"Still Mama won't know me."

Rob shut his eyes and waited; then he said "So you're dying."

"Yes sir," Parker said. "That ain't all the reason."

"For your country?" Rob said, no smile in his voice, though he waited to smile.

Parker said "No sir."

Rob decided not to press him—he seemed so earnest—and worked to clear his own mind for a doze. But Parker's great dignity, the weight of his voice announcing a doom as calmly as breakfast, would not let him rest. A genuine question formed in his head and seemed more urgent each moment he held it; he held it back though till he'd got it formed truly. Then he asked Parker quietly, "Tell me your reasons. I don't mean to drag you through anything painful, but I'm a man in trouble too. I'm looking for help." His eyes had stayed shut.

Parker said "You Miss Eva's boy?"

"Yes."

"Rob Kendal?"

"Mayfield," Rob said. "Mother married a Mayfield."

"I never heard of him."

"He lasted twenty minutes or so," Rob said, "—left before you were born."

Parker said, "That's the trouble?—the trouble you in?"

"Oh no," Rob said. "He got over that. I grew up and met him, and knew him till he died. He died this spring, had a very happy life. He found a good woman."

Parker said "You got one?"

Rob thought "He's turned the tables"; but tired as he was, he recognized a chance. A black army cook, a little cracked maybe, was holding out a welcome to the news of his life. Rob wanted to give it. He raised his head, opened his eyes on the road—deep country now: blank fields, black woods—and said "I had one." He didn't face Parker, afraid to see a simple fool or spite or abject courtesy. He focused on a hawk high above them up the road.

"She gone?" Parker said.

"Fourteen years ago."

"She dead?"

"All that time."

"You got anybody left?"

"A boy, fourteen."

"He kill her?" Parker said.

Rob considered that slowly, then said "No your friend Jesus."

"He'll do it," Parker said, "if it be His will."

Rob looked to him now, and Parker met the look for a quick close instant. "Listen to me," Rob said. "Listen here to what happened; and tell me why He did it, what your Friend was aiming at."

Parker nodded and listened.

"I had a good girl that really wanted me; really wanted to help me and knew a lot of ways, didn't just dream about me. She was also nervous and had had a little trouble with her mind before I met her. And she'd lost the first baby that I tried to give her which weakened her awhile and scared me off her; but when she felt strong enough, she begged me back on. So I started her again, summer 1929—"

"You speaking of a baby?" Parker said. "Just a baby?"

Rob nodded, looking forward. "It meant a lot to her. That had been her early trouble, wanting some child to love. Then she'd had me awhile till she saw I was a man and could not stand still but just so long for service, for her to decorate me like a tree with kindness, all she needed to give me." He turned to see Parker. "You know what I mean?"

"No I don't," Parker said. "I could stand still till Judgment, anybody want to touch me."

Rob smiled but thought it through. "So could I but years before, long years before my wife. By the time I met her, I was doing the touching."

Parker said, "All right. That didn't kill her, did it?"

"No I told you, the baby."

Parker said, "That used to happen a lot. I've known several die, couldn't nobody save em. My own wife drop em as easy as kittens; but I seen my auntie that was so good to me when Mama had left—I stood and seen her perish with the baby half in her. It died a minute later. I was right by her, watching; took the last look she gave. She say to me, 'Bo, help me back; help me back.' She thought she was slipping, thought she was falling. She thought I could reach her. I was fifteen years old." Parker waited.

Rob made no sound of consolation.

So Parker said, "Seventeen. She lived to be seventeen, just older than me. We all knew the daddy. He didn't aim to harm her; she let him in, smiling. Nobody blame a poor man for what Jesus do."

Rob said, "I'm to blame. Don't haul in Jesus. I caused her to die just as sure as you're causing this car not to wreck; you could kill us this minute, save yourself a trip to Europe if you just wanted to."

"I don't," Parker said, though he swung the wheel once to confirm his real power.

Rob leaned back his head and swallowed twice at nothing. "No I didn't either." He stopped and shut his eyes.

Parker said, "You telling me or asking me to guess?"

Still back, Rob said, "I'm telling you. Listen." Then he changed. "Please listen. Please drive and just listen. I once knew your mother."

Parker nodded again, knowing Rob could not see him.

"We were living in Richmond. I had a fair job at the James Institute; had a good solid house, a good man helping in the kitchen and yard. We nursed her through the months like a porcelain rose, barely let her cut butter, never let her touch a broom. We were giving her a chance; we were clearing the whole world to give her safe room so she could make her baby and walk on forward through the rest of her life. Nobody we knew till then had had much life."

"You mentioning *we*," Parker said, "—you and who?"

"The colored man that helped us. Lives in Fontaine now—Grainger Walters; you know him?"

"I've seen him from a distance. He wouldn't talk to me. I'm a little too brown."

Rob did not stop for that. "It mattered to us all, and for just the cause I told you; we were hoping for better, in various ways. And we almost got it. Everything was moving right, through the fall and winter. Wall Street failed of course, and word of that reached us; but nobody guessed for some months to come that half the world had ended, not at James Institute anyhow among people that had barely held a dollar much less lost one. So we got into spring—late April, green weather—and my wife's doctor said both heartbeats were strong, the baby's and hers, and that three weeks from then if our luck held out, we could thank God for blessings." Rob paused to wet his lips. "This is how much luck; this is what blessing came—I had an old friend I had grown up with. She was teaching school in Raleigh and came up to Richmond, chaperoning some children that had won a school prize to see patriotic shrines. Just a quick spring trip while a little money lasted. She never even warned me. I ran into her on Broad Street at noon; I had gone to buy a straw hat—I looked good then."

"You do right now."

"You ought to seen me then."

"I did," Parker said. "I remember you now. I seen you way back. You were standing on the street and telling some story to an old white man. You were waving your arms."

"And I'm telling *you* one."

Parker said "I guessed it."

"—That I met her that evening and did what I did? In a hotel room with two rooms of children on either side of us, listening like rabbits."

"And then your wife smelled it on you and hollered."

Rob waited. "No she didn't. I came home and told her I should wash before supper—it had been a hot day—and slow as she was by then with the baby, she came up and laid out my clean clothes for me. She liked to watch me dress; and until that day, I liked to have her watch me. It was something I could give her for all she'd offered; she had genuinely helped by just being present near the middle of my life. See, I've always been easy to help;

wanted little, and most of that at home. But that one night like I said, she was watching; and I felt so scalded by her eyes that I rushed and was reaching for my pants still wet as a rat when she said 'Slow down.' I said 'I'm cold.' She said 'No you're not,' and I stood and faced her plainly. She looked for a minute, not smiling but careful as if I was teaching her facts she could use in a long hard life. Then she said, 'I doubt I will ever believe it.' I had to say 'What?' and she said, 'What's here—this room, us in it.' It was just a plain room, small and too bright for me; but I knew what she meant, and it burned on through me like terrible acid till it got to my chest. It settled there and stayed."

"You tried to swamp it, didn't you?"

"If *drunk* is what you're saying, I was drunk in two days—I stood it two days—and stayed drunk the best part of two weeks to come. Nobody knew why. They tried to protect me; told my boss I was sick, told my mother-in-law not to come down yet (she was coming from the mountains to help with the child). I'm a nice quiet drunk; I don't leave home. So at least they don't have to run me down; and I held my tongue—I never told them why, though she couldn't help asking: my wife, I mean. They always ask and I always know, but generally I spare them. Anyhow she stopped her mother; and my own father moved in with us for a while in the evenings after work to see me through the nights and to look out for Rachel—" Rob stopped, chilled and sick. He had meant to hold her name back at least from his tale. But because Parker drove on in large waiting silence, Rob could think of going on. He looked to the calm face, harmless as a child's, and believed now in Parker's own private dream—*This boy's bound to die, is sailing already toward a death as sure as evening. I'm telling a spirit.*

"You know when she died?"

"Very clearly. Very clearly."

"That sobered you up."

"No I'd done that myself. She understood me well enough to let me run my course. She would let Grainger go out and buy what it took to taper me off; and then she'd give it to me when I asked her for it or when she saw me trembling, just a taste in a ruby-red glass we had bought on our honeymoon four years before, my name etched in it and hers and the date. Then five days before her time to come due, she was reading beside me in late afternoon—I was down on a couch, feeling weak but cured for the time being anyhow—and she looked up and took my eyes and said 'Are you ready now?' I asked her 'For what?' and she said 'This child.' I thought and said, 'I think we should ask another question—is he ready for me?' Right off, she said 'Yes.' I said, 'If you know what you're doing, bring him on.' That was late on a Saturday. I'd gauged myself to be well for work on Monday (they believed I was sick; I had not missed before in my whole four years). She had told Grainger he could take the evening off; and when Father came by after supper to check, we sat and talked a little. Then I told him he could leave; he had a friend at home. I thought I was safe as I said. We'd cleared the house. I thought I could bear her again, full strength. What I didn't understand—it was her in danger; she was gone by breakfast."

"And left you the baby."

"Strong and happy," Rob said. "He had smiled before evening."

Parker said, "I seen him. I spoke to him once. Named Hutch."

"—For her father in the mountains, Raven Hutchins Mayfield; I gave her that at least. She didn't live to see him, but she knew his full name."

Parker said "Good."

5

They had lost two hours at a crossroads garage while an old man hunted them a used fuel pump in his acre of wrecks, well-hid in honeysuckle; then installed it as carefully as if it would last and earn him praise long years from now. That had put them past supper as they came to Fontaine; and since he had given Hutch no definite schedule and since all afternoon Parker had borne more weight than he'd bargained for, Rob told him just to drive straight through to Beechleaf, a ride to his door; and Parker accepted.

The house was old, not a flake of paint on it; but it stood two stories with a broad side-chimney of rose-colored brick as lovely as a human hand, in craft and service—big as the old Kendal place, which was Rob's, and as nearly ruined. The yard was all children, not a whole suit of clothes among the eight or ten, and all in quick motion despite the thick heat that hung on heavy, though the light was pale now and rapidly dying. They froze and watched the car, seeing Rob's face first. Rob said "Will they know you?"

"Some of em, yes. All of em ain't mine." Parker looked to Rob, not smiling. "You need a drink of water?—anything like that?"

Rob said "No but thank you."

"I thank *you*," Parker said. "I hope you do better."

Rob smiled. "So do I."

The children saw their father and bolted for the house; poured themselves through the open door, a single dog behind them, clean Eskimo spitz.

Parker said, "Step in here please and speak to Mama."

Rob thought a short moment. "It's been too long."

Parker looked to his own hands, still hung on the wheel; then back to

Rob, begging. "Help me see em, Mr. Rob. Help me ease on in. God knows I hate to see em."

"Why?"

"—Me going like I am."

Rob nodded, touched the handle of his door, and looked out. A girl was in the door or a strong young woman. For a while it seemed Flora till he saw what she lacked—Flora's harsh thrust into unlived life and of course Flora's age. This girl hung back and children clung to her; she bore their grasp as calmly as a breeze. Rob said "That your wife?"

"Lena. Yes sir."

Rob stood to the ground and smiled to Lena. "I brought him home safe."

She nodded—silent, still—and one boy laughed and ran as far out as the top of the steps; then stopped and stared.

Parker reached back and found his bag and got out and stood. He put on his hat and said "Who you, boy?"

"*Your* boy," the child said.

"You talking," Parker said. Then he said "Hey" to Lena.

She said "All right" and smiled.

"Everybody doing good?"

"Pretty good," Lena said.

Parker said, "Where Mama? This man come to see her; he Sylvie's Rob."

Lena swept the big yard with solemn eyes. "I don't know," she said. "Ain't seen her since morning."

The boy at the top of the steps said "Yonder" and pointed to the woods. "She lying back yonder."

"Go call her," Parker said.

Rob said, "Bo, leave her. She's found her some shade. I better get home."

But the boy had run to call her. With silent speed he had run down the steps, bare feet in deep dust, and over to a big rusty bell on the ground, an old farm bell long rotted off its post. He took up a stick and beat the bell four, five times. It gave a sound, more moan than ring. Then he looked to his father. "She be here now. She think we eating."

Parker said, "Sit down on the porch, Mr. Rob. Cool off a minute. She be right here." There was one straight chair on the porch, bottom sagging.

Rob walked to the steps and sat down there, his feet on the ground, his back to Lena and the shy clot of children.

Parker came forward too and when he'd reached the steps and climbed halfway, the boy who'd rung the bell raised the same stick of wood and fired it like a gun, a single *Pow!* Parker dropped his bag and fell to his knees on the step above Rob, both hands at his chest. He groaned "Bull's eye."

The boy laughed and ran a straight streak toward the woods; then stopped a little short and watched the big woman come out and past him, heavy and barefoot and in a blue cotton dress pinned at every tear.

When she got to the steps she stopped at the bottom and looked up to Lena. "What you giving me now?"

Lena said "Not me" and pointed to Parker.

Flora didn't face him but he stood up and said "Hey Mama. It's Bo."

She looked to Rob instead, still seated on his step eye-level to her.

There was nothing here for him. He would never have known her, and he had a fine memory for faces once seen. She was padded in fat like Chinese quilting, a final fortress. He tried to smile but couldn't.

She said, "Did you ever see your little boy again?"

He said, "Not lately but I'm going to him now."

Flora shook her great head. "She won't let you have him."

Rob smiled, though it ached. "She will; she'd better."

She shut her eyes and shook again. "She need him too bad. She told me herself—'He won't never touch him, Flora. All this is mine.'"

Rob thought it out clearly. "She thinks I am Forrest. She saw him that once. I have got to get home." He stood up quickly but she blocked his way down, not by trying but by presence. She had swollen that large in twenty-three years; he had shrunk that much.

Parker said "Look, Mama." He had reached in his bag and brought out her present, a comb-and-brush-set in a celluloid box. She took it—not speaking, never facing him once—and climbed up between them through Lena and the children, out of sight in the house.

They came forward finally in hopes of their gifts.

6

At the car Parker said, "She knew you at least."

Rob said, "No she didn't. She thought I was my father."

"She got the right crowd anyhow," Parker said.

Rob said, "What's the matter? She's not that old."

"Wore out," Parker said.

"Will she speak to you later?"

"—May. May not. She know I'm dying; she known for years. How come she left me—didn't want to watch, didn't want that grief."

Rob nodded, half-believing; opened the door and sat behind the wheel.

Parker came a step closer, ten inches from his ear; and half-whispered clearly, "You never let me tell you."

"What?"

"The reason I'm glad to be going toward my dream."

"Don't I know?" Rob said. "I know by now." He cranked the slow engine. But Parker stayed on, his hands on the window ledge, his face still near. So Rob said, "Luck to you. Take care anyhow. He may change his mind."

Parker smiled. "That's another thing you didn't let me tell me—why He done this to you?" Parker spread both his huge hands and gestured wide to include the car as if it were Rob's history, pressed down and portable.

"Is it short?" Rob said. "I'm long overdue."

"Yes sir. He love you. He calling you to Him."

Rob thought a moment, thanked him; then fished up two dollars from his own scarce funds and said, "Buy Flora some little thing she needs."

"She need a new life," Parker said and stepped back; but he took the money.

"Then something she wants," Rob said and rolled off.

The one boy ran behind him far as the gate.

7

By the time Rob had got back to Fontaine again, what he'd thought was the point of his hours with Parker (company and calm at the sight of others' trouble) had turned full against him. Bo and Flora had thrust deep fingers into flesh he had not known was tender. As he passed the first shacks on the black edge of town, he felt not exhaustion and despair as with Min but fear, hot fright as if a vein had been lanced in the soft of his heel or the back of his knee and was rushing to drain him before he could know or find helpful care. Eva, Rena, Hutch, Grainger—they did not seem this instant a possible goal: more hooking hands to grapple at a body now as fragile as a lidless eye. He could not head back to Raleigh—Min abiding his answer. He could not go to Richmond—his promise to Hutch.

He saw a light at Sylvie's, far back on his left. He slewed to the left shoulder, stopped and tried to see toward her. Two hundred yards through thick new leaves; he caught only light, no sign of her, no sound. (She had had lights a year now, having said one morning, "Miss Rena, I am scared now to live in the dark. I either got to get the wires or move in here." Since Grainger occupied the only quarters at the Kendals', there had been no choice for

Rena but to take the news to Kennerly. He had got her house wired before the week was out and given her a radio; and that had helped to ease her, though she'd recently announced she'd be going home at six. Walking home too late, she said, made her realize her state—"Make me think I'm dying lonesome." So they served their own supper now, and Grainger washed the dishes.) Rob thought "I'll go to Sylvie" and cranked the car again; he had killed it in the sudden swerve.

He couldn't move though, not forward. He shook. In place on the dry dirt shoulder of a road a mile from the house which contained his living kin, all upright and strong, none contingent on him—the house in which he had known his first happiness, still whole in his mind and available for visits— he shook with a dry grief that rose from the deepest sink of his belly as if it were birth, the throes of expulsion, and rushed his chest, throat, mouth, skull, so broadly that he thought one clear thought—"Thank Jesus I'm *going*"— then fell to its power.

When it passed, he looked first to see if he were watched—no Negro in sight; he had lasted alone. He worked his dry lips loose from dry teeth, put his hands to the wheel and found they would grip, and felt a clear space at the front of his mind—a small patch, palm-sized, but clear and light.

With it, he saw his life and knew this much; could say it to himself—he had asked for one thing since he first heard of gifts, forty years ago; nothing far beyond any soul's just expectance: an ordinary home containing no more than an ordinary home. A decent grown man with clean work to push against ten hours a day that would leave him with the strength to come back at dark in courtesy and patience to the people who had waited—a woman he had chosen for their mutual want (who went on wanting and receiving as he did: courteous, patient) and the child they made (he had never wanted two, never trusted his own stores to stretch over two). Human beings had that, never millions but enough—in his sight too—to make it seem a plain hope, not howling at a beacon burning well beyond earth in the deep hole of night. He hadn't asked permanence, a set of frozen smiles; he'd granted grief and age long before most men. He had asked twenty, thirty years at most in the midst of a life which could water all the rest and firm it for death.

And if earning mattered, hadn't he earned it? What had he done in forty years worse than rub a small portion of his secret body on the secret of one woman not his wife? Nothing, he knew. If the rules of life were visibly posted (and he trusted they were; despite his not darkening a church for twenty years, he'd never once doubted that the rules were given, were just and plain and were followable), he'd done nothing worse than betray his promise to love Rachel only—betrayed it half an hour.

No, never. Not a moment. He had *loved* only Rachel; what he'd done with Min was rub at a starved little knot in his brain, starved by weeks of simple deprivation, his care for Rachel. Any hand could have rubbed it; Min was simply familiar, a willing friend, keen to oblige.

So keen she'd rubbed him now to blood and nerve and asked for his life. He might give it to her. No one else was asking; it had to go somewhere. Death was a place. He thought of his morning high above the James River, though he didn't remember the boys or the turtle. The trip was still easy. No, he wanted to stay.

Why?—Hutch and Grainger; he had shaken them enough. Eva and Rena—they had maybe earned their mother's foaming death (he had never weighed that) but surely not his; they had meant him well. Min so tangled in his own roots now that she couldn't tear free whatever she threatened— or promised (it seemed a promise: freedom, space).

None of them, no. They were not the brakes on him. He could grant that now; but he didn't understand what was deep under that, that he had a gift for pleasure, a true seed within him from Robinson his grandfather. That had grown once and for twenty-five years of its own strong accord till he'd cut it back to earth, let it be packed down. There were still live roots with their own patient will.

He went to see Sylvie.

8

"You got anything here to eat?" he said.

"They waiting for you down yonder," Sylvie said and pointed to the Kendals'. "I fried chicken all this afternoon, cooked butterbeans and squash. Hutch turning ice cream—"

Rob shook his head. "I can't." He was on her middle step.

She was broad in the door behind her new screen that had come with the lights (the lights had drawn bugs). She studied him well. "What you telling me, Rob?"

"I'm hungry like I said."

"No you ain't. What you done?"

"Lost my job," he said.

"Again?"

"Nine years."

"You drinking?"

"I was."

"Well, God—" Sylvie said.

"Can I sit down?" he said.

"You sure you sober? Don't come here drunk."

"Yes, Sylvie," he said. "When did you get religion?"

"Ain't," she said. "Just worn out with drunks."

"So am I," Rob said. "This one anyhow." He touched himself on the covered breastbone.

She searched him again as if she'd never known him or as if she'd known him well these whole forty years and was only now totaling the sum of the days. "No you ain't," she said. But she unhooked the screen and stepped back inward and waved him in.

The room was hot and bright; two naked bulbs pumped heat like hearts. The radio was on, some news of the war. Sylvie went back toward it and sat in her chair and leaned to listen. Rob had not been here in twenty-three years—his time with Flora—and since Sylvie hadn't invited him to sit, he stood and looked round. The real change was light and the radio's rattle. The two main absences, her dog and her fish, were filled by pictures in dime-store frames propped on every flat surface. No one they knew—moviestars and generals, all white and all smiling: Deanna Durbin, Maureen O'Hara, Kay Francis, Gary Cooper, Mark Clark, Eisenhower, Mrs. Roosevelt. Rob had given her his own picture some years before, one he'd had made for Rachel just after the wedding; it was nowhere in sight. Her news had turned into a singing ad for soap; so he said, "Where am I? Not pretty enough? My teeth beat Eleanor's." He gestured to the frames.

Sylvie turned down the volume. "You here but I hid you."

"I'm honored," he said.

"You know why," she said.

He didn't at all—he had been her choice—but he spared himself and didn't ask.

"Sit down there," she said, "if you ain't going home."

He knew he was not, not for hours anyhow while anyone was up who could question him. He'd face them at breakfast; they wouldn't probe in daylight. Sylvie's other chair was straight and against the far wall. He brought it over toward her, six feet from her own, and sat on the hard cane. "You doing all right?"

"I'm the same," she said.

"I like your new lights."

"Draw bugs," she said, "but they help keep it warm."

It was eighty degrees this minute, he knew. "That's company," he said and nodded to the radio, a mystery play now.

"Is," Sylvie said.

She did not want him here. Rob felt it like power. "You're mad with me."

"Just sick."

"With me?"

She gave it some time. "You the one turned up this evening," she said.

"How have I hurt you?"

"Every breath you draw." She had fiddled with her knee till then. She faced him. Then she laughed a little. "What you want to eat?"

"What you got?"

"Eggs and lightbread."

"Good," Rob said.

Sylvie heaved herself up and left him with the softspoken mystery on the air, an old man trapped in a shed by a stranger who smiles but never speaks.

She fried two slices of bread in bacon grease, scrambled four eggs with crumbs of cheese, poured him a glass of water from the bucket, and set it on the table which was now against the wall (no longer in the center; she had cleared the center years ago). Then she said "Help yourself" and went to her chair again.

Rob went to her basin and washed his hands quickly, pulled his chair up, swallowed two bites, and said "Fine." Then he ate on in silence through half the food while Sylvie seemed to listen, her eyes narrowed downward.

Finally though she said, "I ain't studying this mess. Talk to me if you want to." She snapped off the mystery with the stranger still strange.

Rob said, "Guess who drove me all the way here from Raleigh?—Bo Parker, hitchhiking."

"You lucky you alive."

"How's that?" Rob said.

"He been half-crazy ever since he a baby."

"How come?"

"Being Flora's. Watching Flora till she run."

Rob said, "She's back now; I took him by his house."

"You see her?"

"For a second."

"She *all*, crazy, ain't she?" Sylvie smiled, first time.

"Seems confused anyhow. And she's put on flesh."

"Lost her mind," Sylvie said.

Rob said "What's the trouble?"

Sylvie freshened her smile. "No trouble," she said, "—she collecting her pension."

"She old enough for welfare?"

"Oh no," Sylvie said, "I'm talking about her *pension*, what she been storing up. It coming to her now."

Rob chewed that through; then he also smiled. "Yours coming in yet?"

She paused an instant to test his edge for power; then she nodded. "Come in torrents." She gestured all round her—her room, bed, life—but she went on grinning and said, "Like yours. Yours coming in early."

"What is mine?" Rob said. He believed her and waited.

"You told me just now," she said, "—the time you having."

"Will it get any worse?"

"May do," she said. "You got a lot of time."

"What way?" Rob said.

She actually laughed. "I'm joking you, Rob. I don't know nothing."

"I'm serious," he said. "You know me good as anybody, better than most—maybe all but Mother."

"Then go ask Eva. She waiting down the road with a freezer of cream going soft right now."

"I've asked," Rob said, "and God knows she's told me. She'll tell me again."

"Tell you what?"

"That I still have to learn to stand alone," Rob said.

"Like her—"

He nodded.

"She lying," Sylvie said, "—been lying forty years. Nobody lean harder than Eva, let me tell you—Mr. Forrest, Mr. Bedford, Rena, poor Hutch." She stopped and stared again at Rob as if she couldn't harm him. "You standing," she said. "You alone as me."

He saw she believed it, knew he had to correct her. "No I'm not. Wish I was."

"What you leaning on but liquor?"

"Min Tharrington," he said. "You know about that."

"I know what I see; I can't see to Raleigh. But seem like to me if she your leaning-post, you falling through space."

Rob smiled. "I am."

"And Min ain't," she said.

"She's stuck by me though."

"—What she wanted to do since she three years old."

"She did it anyhow," Rob said. "Wasn't easy."

"Eating *supper* ain't easy," Sylvie said. "What you want?"

"This is plenty," he said, "gracious plenty. Many thanks."

"—In your life, I mean, fool. You eat all my *food*."

"—What you and I and Grainger and Mother and Rena haven't got and never had."

"That's nothing but company," she said.

"No it's not; not *nothing but*, Sylvie, and you know it. Here you sit in this house—"

"On a happy tail," she said. "Got all this room, screen wire, new lights. This radio the best friend I ever had—cheap, clean, ever-ready, on all through the night."

"You'll die here at night by yourself," Rob said and loathed his sudden harshness, the last thing he'd meant.

She had lived her life with Eva; she decided not to blame him. "Suits me," she said. "Everybody I ever watched die died single."

"But we got years to go."

"May do," Sylvie said. "I'm ready for em now. You get yourself ready."

"How? I'm here to ask that."

"You seen it," Sylvie said, "—seen all I got to tell you. A satisfied mind." She showed the room again with one slow hand, then laid it on her knee. "Live in what you got. Too late to change."

Rob nodded. "How are they?"

"At the house, you mean?"

"The people we know."

"I know a hundred people," Sylvie said. "*Yours* all right. Hutch and Grainger waiting on you."

"Just them?"

"Well, you know—Miss Eva and Rena got they own fish to fry."

Rob smiled. "Such as what?"

"They business, big business; stay busier than you. Eva got Hutch, doing everything for him but sleeping and breathing. Rena got the garden and arguing with Kennerly."

Rob said "Grainger?"

"Grainger got Hutch. Everybody got Hutch—you got him; *all* you got."

"Does he love me?" Rob said.

"Don't matter," Sylvie said. "He yours anyhow."

"But does he?"

She considered it. "Somehow," she said. "He got a loving heart. Don't hate a human soul. Don't grudge nobody."

Rob said "He's fourteen."

"Shame on you," Sylvie said. "He had his life; good because he want to be. God love him that much."

"Thought you hadn't got religion." Rob smiled.

Sylvie didn't. "Still ain't," she said. "Who I'm speaking of is Hutch—your boy and Miss Rachel's, Eva's, Mr. Forrest's, Mr. Bedford's, Miss Charlotte's. Had to get his help from somewhere."

9

Hutch slept on, though the room had filled with morning and the house was awake—Eva, Rena, Grainger all muffled in the kitchen. With school just out, they were letting him sleep; and despite his worry of the night before (Rob never appearing), he lay on his back on the white iron bed and bore a last dream. He was still too young and drowned too deeply to end it by will; and in fact he was held by the story, not hurt. He had seen it many times.

He was walking in the pine woods behind this house. He was simply himself—fourteen, his present age—and he walked with no purpose, no dog or gun, no friend, no secret. When he'd gone in as far as he generally went, through the woods and his uncle's field of early cotton, he stopped on the bank of the creek, the sandbar, and saw it was late. He would be late for breakfast (it was morning in the dream; this morning, clear and hot). So he went the last steps to the creek to touch water—that now seemed his goal—and saw the girl. She stood on the far bank eight feet away, his own age (maybe a year or so older) with hair to her shoulders, facing him not smiling. He said "Rachel" and was rushed by powerful pleasure; he had never called her Mother. She nodded, though there'd never been a shadow of doubt; they were standing mirrors of one another. He stood his ground on his side, not crossing, happy enough there. He only thought, "She has been dead but isn't. She's back for good." But he did not tell her to wade over toward him, and he did not think of going to get her. He did not think of taking her home. But he said, "Wait here. I'll get the others." Then he ran to the house which was empty of all but Grainger in the kitchen. Hutch told him she was back; and Grainger believed it and put on his hat and followed—Hutch running, Grainger stumbling with his morning rheumatism—and of course she was gone. Just the empty pillar of air where she'd stood, uncrossed by a leaf or branch or insect. He stared at the space and said "It was true." Grainger said "I believe you"; and with Grainger looking, Hutch knelt to the sand, rolled onto his back, opened his mouth to release the plug of grief. But the day, the morning sky through trees, poured in like water and lodged it in place, its permanent place. He had caused her to leave a second time.

Rob saw none of that, though he'd come through the door and walked without stealth to the foot of the bed and stood, watching his son. The boy's face was turned, but his neck and cheek seemed peaceful. His long bare chest was still, his breath slow and regular. Only in the gapped fly of his blue pajama pants was there visible sign of a fierce hidden act—the horn stood full as it ever would be, stronger than its bearer who would not grow to match it for eight or nine years. But Rob read that as a sign of his age, the stoked sleep of boys on the balked edge of manhood. He said the name "Hutch."

No move.

He spoke again. "Hutch Mayfield, arise."

The face rolled toward him, but the eyes stayed shut; and in three more seconds the breath was the slow breath of sleep again (deceitful peace—in the dream Hutch was plunging past Grainger toward the girl, his living mother).

So Rob slowly took off his jacket and tie, unbuttoned his collar, stepped out of his shoes, and took the last steps till his legs touched the bed. Then he laid himself—full-length, dead-weight—on Hutch's body, the bristles of his chin at the boy's warm ear (he had washed his face at Sylvie's but had waited to shave). He didn't speak again.

Hutch halted at the threshold, swapping the familiar misery of sleep for this scarce pleasure that waited all down the length of his body, joy that also threatened to kill him. The strongest, strangest memory of his childhood, four or five, when this same great body would enter at dawn and lie as now without mercy till he'd gasp in fear and happiness for air. Now he could throw himself free with one roll of his own strong hips; but he lay and bore the weight for thirty, forty seconds till the old desperation broke loose in his chest. With what air he held, he laughed and said "Help!"

Rob lay a moment longer, then kissed the boy's ear and rolled rightward onto the bed beside him (the bed in which he and Rachel had made him, though he'd never told Hutch and did not remember now).

Hutch rose to his elbows—he wore no shirt—and looked down, grinning. It was in his mouth to say "You came in time" (he was still in the dream); but he said, "You missed some Hutch-made banana ice cream. We waited till dark."

"I had a bad fuel pump. Took till ten to fix it, and I was dog-tired; so I stayed in a tourist court the other side of Wilton but woke up at dawn." (When he'd finally said to Sylvie, "Can I sleep here tonight?", she had thought a good while before saying "Dead-secret?")

Hutch said, "Ought to saved your money."

"Why?"

"Case we take our trip."

"Where to?" Rob said.

"Well, the stars would suit me but you mentioned Richmond. Are we leaving today?" Hutch noticed the gap in his pants and quickly closed it; he had lost the dream's force anyhow, a boy again.

"No, tomorrow; maybe Wednesday. I've got some chores here."

"Who with?"

"Mind your business." Rob smiled as he said it but too late; Hutch had seen—the old yellow teeth of his father's shame and flight. "About a job," Rob said. "What if I move home, back to Fontaine at least?"

"Or you could move to Richmond, and I could come with you."

"What's good about Richmond?"

"I was born there," Hutch said.

"Your mother died there."

Hutch hunted his father for blame, the final refusal he'd awaited all his life—*You killed her and must pay.* Not in sight, not now. "She's buried in Goshen," he said.

"So right."

"And I've never seen the grave."

Rob could smile and say it—"It's waiting, sweetheart."

Eva called from downstairs. "Breakfast served in two minutes."

Hutch was watching his father, no move to rise. He knew he was waiting for an urgent choice to be made on his life; he knew his father was the one who could make it—that his own strong body, for all its rush to fullness, was in the hands of others and would be for years yet. Might always be (he had had no taste of freedom in life or dreams).

Rob said "Invite me home." He was whispering now.

"Sir?"

"Invite me here to live."

"This house?" Hutch said.

"Just at first. We could move to the Kendal place by fall."

"We and who?" Hutch said.

"Grainger maybe. Maybe Min."

Hutch met his eyes, asking. They were genuinely asking Hutch for some gift at last. But he knew he couldn't give it. It was not his to give; it had not grown in him yet. Still he didn't say that; didn't say, "I'm still a boy. Nothing in me understands you." He shook his head. "No sir." Then he stood and went to the chair where his clothes lay and turned his back to Rob.

"I thought you were happy here."

"No sir, I'm not," Hutch said. He dropped his pants, stood naked with his back still turned.

"Son, I've got to feed us, understand."

"I'm *fed* here," Hutch said. "You could bring me to you. Feed me there." He faced round. "You've promised that forever."

Rob said, "Mother needs you. You're the thing she's got."

"I'm all *you've* got," Hutch said, still grave. He believed it as fact, as some children do—that he was both axle and wheel for his father—and was righter than most.

Rob wanted to say it out now for good—"No you're not; now listen"—but seeing the boy (his own eyes set in Rachel's face and hair), he said "Then never leave me."

"I haven't," Hutch said. "It was you left me. My mother, then you."

"None of us could help that. One day you'll understand."

Hutch had listened and made no move to dress. "I'm old enough, sir. I'm old enough to die. Boys die every day—drown, fall, run-over. Boys sixteen are dying in Italy this minute, babies being starved over most of the earth. I may not have *time* is what scares me. Tell me now; I'll understand." He believed himself again and felt he was desperate, though he'd gone to bed with expectations of pleasure, the sight of his father.

Rob saw more than heard, saw he'd made what was now in most ways a man (the ways nature honored). But he lied a second time. "There's nothing else to tell, Son. What I mean is just that you'll feel other ways when you're grown and look back—about a good many things, things you've always known but in part, Son, in *part.*"

"I don't even know I can get through today much less thirty more years."

Rob said "*Hope.*"

Hutch stood on a moment, then reached for his drawers and raised a foot; but he stopped and said "No."

"No what?"

"I can't wait. You owe me a lot. Pay me that little bit."

"Of what, Son?"

"—The story, why you left me with these women and still won't have me; why you still won't forgive me for Mother: I was young." He had stayed calm, unpetulant as a tree and as alien to any adult witness. And he'd won, just the face and body he had earned for himself in fourteen years had won for him now.

His father said, "I'll try. We have got our trip. All this time ahead."

Hutch said "Then you promise."

Rob nodded "I do," having no sense how, not knowing himself any single true answer or a whole true story.

Hutch proceeded to dress—his drawers, khaki shorts, a white short-sleeved shirt.

Eva called up again. "Hutch, you're failing. Bring your daddy."

"I'm bringing him," Hutch said.

10

Miss Hilah Spencer was at her old percolator, watching it pump, when Rob knocked once on the open door. She wheeled as if caught in something worse than office-coffee—a pencil flew out of her wild white hair—but she said, "A pleasure! I dreamed about you."

"Good, I hope?"

"Too good to tell." She laughed, the freest tongue in town. "Come on drink some coffee." She reached for another mug.

"Coffeed *up*," Rob said. "I'm nervous as a cat."

"Then you're in the wrong pew; this is Crazy House today. He's adding attendance figures from six county schools, and he may lose a teacher. Children stayed home in droves—the radio, I told him. Too much thrilling news." Hilah thumbed toward a shut door, the superintendent's office.

"I need to see him though."

She had filled her mug by now, disconnected the pot, and gone to her desk. She took a long black drink and searched Rob mercilessly. "Step through the door please."

He came to the desk, touched his legs up against it.

"You want to come home?" She had never mastered whispering.

"May need to," he said.

"That's not what I asked. Several may need *you*. What I said was *want*."

"I hope I do," he said.

Hilah held another long moment on him; then smiled so suddenly, fully, as to shock him. "Wait a second," she said. She stalked to the shut door, knocked once, and opened. "Cheer up, Mr. Bradley; a stranger to see you."

"What about?"

She turned to Rob. "The waters of life."

Thorne Bradley said, "Hilah, don't trifle with me"; but he stood and came out to his door and looked. He knew Rob at once, had known him from the age of four, five months; but he only said "Stranger—"

Rob said, "Mr. Bradley, I see you're busy. I can come back later."

Bradley drew out his watch and studied it thoroughly. "No, step on in." He smiled a smile as neat as the click of a boxlid.

Rob followed, smiling at Hilah when he passed (she said "Come home"), and entered the office he'd never seen before. A big bright room with a big desk and two chairs, a leather nap-couch, heavy wood filing cases, book-shelves on every wall and, above them, dark pictures of the ruins of Rome. As Bradley moved on to his own swivel chair, Rob stopped at one scene— *Venus Genetrix*: a titled piece of pavement, the brown stumps of pillars.

"Take a chair please, Rob."

He looked to Bradley pleasantly. "My father had this"; he touched the oak frame, the wavy glass.

"I imagine he did."

"It's still in Richmond. I'm going up this week; may get it for Hutch. He had a whole set—Father, I mean—that a school teacher gave him."

Bradley sat. "Don't burden Hutch with Forrest's leavings, Rob. *You* be his last bearer."

Rob recalled his father as the kindest of men; had studied Latin under Thorne Bradley three years, years dry as desert sand. He wanted to say now, "We both bear him gladly"; but he came as a beggar and went to the free chair, six feet from Bradley. "I may need your help."

"What help have I got?"

"A job this fall."

Bradley shook his head. "Sorry."

"Teaching shop," Rob said. "I heard that was vacant."

"And may stay so," Bradley said. "I never thought it mattered one dry hill of beans, teaching good future farmers how to make fancy bookends for books that don't and won't exist."

Rob said, "Furniture maybe. I used to make furniture."

"Where? In High Point?"

"James Institute in Richmond. When my wife died I cast round for peace-ful things to do, evening hours, days off. They had a shop there—old tools but they worked—and I'd go down and sometimes work till dawn. I made several tables, a big corner cupboard. I could do it again."

"What happened in Raleigh?"

"Sir?"

Bradley's face was clear, no sign of special knowledge. "You seemed well-fixed there. Eva told me recently she couldn't pry you loose."

Rob knew he'd gain nothing by partial concealment. He said "They've let me go."

Bradley sat forward slowly, knowing kindness was required. "Do you want to say why?"

"I will," Rob said. "I know you blame my father for what happened years ago, but I don't remember that. Once I grew up and found him, he did a lot for me."

"What?"

Rob had thought it out. Not *a lot* but one thing, a plain clear example, one kind of decent life in the face of difficulties. Love and generosity, sufficient patience for the slow stream of days. He could not say that here; and before he could frame some harmless answer, Thorne Bradley broke in.

"Was it drinking?"

"Sir?"

"Your trouble, why they let you go in Raleigh?"

"My father died in May. I doubt you know about it. They had let him go on teaching after seventy; they owed him more than they could ever pay and they knew it. They let him keep an office, and he was down there marking his examination papers; said he'd be home for supper. When he wasn't home by eight, his housekeeper took the bus and went down to see; she said she didn't phone for fear of learning at a distance. So she learned first hand. It was already night but his office light was out. She said she stood outside and tried to see through frosted glass till students passed and stared. Then she had to go in, switch the light on herself. He had turned his chair over as he fell but somehow had got himself composed and was over by the radiator, calm on his back. He had graded all the papers but three, the three best. He'd saved them to draw him onward, always did that. Once she'd felt he was gone, she set his chair up and sat at the desk to calm her own self. Then she marked the three papers, just the grade, all A (she had helped in the past and could imitate his hand). Then she went to get assistance."

Bradley had turned to his window through that. He stayed looking out but he said, "Tell me this—why come here and tell me this?"

Rob had not planned to tell it. "I guess because I've known all these years how hard you judged him. I wanted you to see he earned himself a pleasant death."

Bradley faced him. "I see it. So have many black hearts; Tiberius Caesar died grinning like a baby. But you've misunderstood me. I never judged him, Rob, whatever words I used. I *missed* him, understand. Understand I loved him deeply, and loved him several ways. He was older than me, eleven years older; and when I came home from Trinity to find him rooming at Mother's, ten feet from me, and working beside me at school every day, I loved him in a week, as friend and father. *Worshipped* him in time; I'm not ashamed to say it. Even now it seems right, seems a just response to him. He had lacked my luck in going to college; but he'd read more deeply than anyone I'd known— read because he needed to, fell on it like food, and turned it to strength and generous warmth. He wrote poems also—you may not know—and while they were heavy with standard young sorrows, I thought he was happy. We would teach all day till I was fit to slaughter; then Mother would feed us and we'd walk awhile out the old Green road; then we'd do our preparations in separate rooms; and sometimes after I had blown out the light (so dead I could groan), he would open my door and sit on the foot of my bed in the dark and read what he'd written—

Can what I hope in dream prove, waking, true?—
The long road of my life find rest in you?

I was totally deceived. I know I should have seen his secret rushing toward me—he proposed to Eva with me just yards away, the class picnic—but it was a sort of virtue after all that I didn't, that I bore more shock than anyone except your grandfather when they ran off at last: I had buried my attention in my own love of Forrest, that 'meeting of souls.'" Bradley stopped to smile in irony, to show a smile was possible; and found he had finished—that story at least. He said straight at Rob, "I'm glad he died happy, glad the living know he did." Then he fished in his pocket, drew out a key; and opened the bottom drawer of his desk, a careful hunt through a black tin box, the right letter found. He leaned toward Rob. "I've waited for you, see." He offered the letter.

Still calm from Bradley's story, Rob took it. Addressed to Thorne in his father's hand, postmarked *Bracey* two months ago. The sight of the script was still more painful than pictures or tales, a clear strong trail secreted by a life now far past reach (but at rest, rest surely). "Did you hear from him often?"

"Once in these forty years. *That* once," Thorne said and pointed to the letter.

"Do you mean me to read it?"

"I think I do, yes. I think you'd better."

Rob opened it carefully.

Easter Sunday, 1944

Dear Thorne,

A long silence. Please let me break it now; please read this through. I break it because I honestly think I am soon to enter a much longer silence, and I want to speak out to you on two matters that require some speech.

The first thing is pardon. I ask your full pardon after all this time for deceiving you, young as you were, with my marriage. All I showed you was true—I returned your full friendship; I wish I'd seen you daily for the past forty years—but I had an older need that Eva seemed to fulfill; so I flew toward that. You will understand by now. I was wrong about her of course and harmed her by my error; but she had the mind and strength to throw me off in time, and I landed (by a curious grace) in satisfaction. I have had a good life. It has felt good to me, I mean, with three main exceptions—the years till 1905, my lying to you, my part in Rob. You can help me twice over, it occurs to me now—say you've canceled my old debt, and help me with Rob.

Let me say what I mean in that second request. I have little sense of how well you know my son; but you knew me and know of my dumb power to harm, a power I neither intended nor learned of till far too late. My chief failure there was acceding to Eva's clean wish to leave me. By the time she'd convinced me of her firm resolve, I had moved on in my life to duties and dangers which made it unthinkable to claim a share in Rob (I was claiming my life, what had been kept from me). So he grew up with access to only a half of his natural rights, the less loving half. The Kendals have strengths that I crave even now— they have learned solitude—but they have sealed hearts. Maybe sealed because full—they have filled one another and require no one else—but firmly sealed: no home for a boy with the Mayfield doors in his heart flung open in welcome and positive hunger.

I found him too late; the damage was done. He married the first girl who showed she loved him, a choice in its own way more ruinous than mine—the one girl in all the world, no doubt, less fitted by health and her own legacies to make the belated amends. The strange thing is, he was perfect for her; he gave her all she'd dreamt of, including early death, though he's never seen that. And so since her death, he has been in confusion that nothing seems to clear. As you know, he left a good job here to take his child to Eva when I'd shown him that the best care was ready in my home with my own tried companion volunteering to serve. Then when that too failed him—Eva again, the whole shut house, the shameful job that Kennerly found him—he moved on to Raleigh and has taught there till now, a sad job with children who don't seem to prize him. I've urged him back here, but he says Richmond's ruined by his old bad luck.

Now I feel I won't be there myself much longer. They have kept me on kindly past the age of retirement at James Institute and seem quite prepared to give me a desk and some faces to polish till I pitch over cold.

That is what's coming soon. No doctor has told me; I know it too deeply. A bad siege of headaches some three months ago and a sudden loss of vision in both my eyes which is permanent it seems, though I still can read. Then the headaches eased, leaving one strong scar, a small globe of numbness in the midst of my brow just under the skull. No pain but a presence, something ripening there that will either spread or burst. I have taken pains in Richmond to order my affairs. I am spending Easter here in my boyhood home with my one sister Hattie who is older than me but will long outlast me—an open soul still, though occasionally addled from years on a hill alone, talking to her dog. She doesn't need me; I am saying goodbye but she doesn't know that.

What I think will happen when I die is this—Rob will suffer more than any-one, thinking he has failed me. To tell him that he hasn't would make him suf-fer more; I would have to tell him that he came too late, into my life, I mean. I had answered my questions or had them answered when he found me in Rich-mond. He became a young friend that I cherished, delighted in often, and regretted. But while his life in these fourteen years has saddened me often, it has not cut me deeply; so I couldn't tell him that, despite what I fear he will go through once I'm gone—a long bout of drinking and maybe unemployment (he has been warned in Raleigh, is on probation). If I'm right, he'll come to you. He has mentioned it before when he's felt pulled to Hutch, and has told me that you are the superintendent and may lean his way.

I ask you to refuse him. Not because he isn't good—he's a very fair teacher, and he shows them signs of life which they've never seen before—but because he will die, really die from the heart out, if he gives up and comes to Eva again. She would welcome him now, is my own distant guess. There are other places for him more genuinely his—my own house in Richmond, the Mayfield home, and almost surely a job at James Institute (he left a good memory, and I've spo-ken to the principal) or his aunt's place here (this was my mother's home—Bracey, I mean—and he was born here in the room where I'm writing) or even in the mountains, his wife's home Goshen (he has in-laws there with a small hotel). He can make himself a life for another thirty years if he wants to now and is not folded back into flight and ease—his mother and Rena, Sylvie and Grainger. He will make it hard on you if he does come asking; he was always lovable, a fact he's never known. All I'm asking you to do is urge him back outward into something more yielding, more likely to save, than his own old cradle.

You may think I am wrong as I guess you've done for years. And I may well be. But I've said my say with the gravity and hope of a man near the close; and I've called for the hand, over space and years, of an old friend who seems now a permanent creditor.

With thanks for your time and still in expectation

Yours as once,
Forrest Mayfield

Rob was calmer than before. He laid the letter unfolded on the desk and looked up to Bradley. "I'm begging still. He didn't understand."

"What?"

Rob said, "A good deal. All that's happened since I left him. He never could see that I'd made my peace with Mother, had truly left home. He didn't want to see it, so I didn't force it on him. He thought he had saved me. Then the other main thing, I kept from him too—for some years now I have leaned on Min Tharrington. She's given me a lot, and I have to thank her now."

Bradley nodded; the news was no news at all. "What way?" he said.

"Well, a life together."

"You seem to have that."

"A home," Rob said. "She has asked for that."

"You've *waited*," Bradley said. "I can hardly urge caution on either of you, can I?"

"*I* waited," Rob said. "Min was ready long since. I was held back by things."

Bradley reached for Forrest's letter and folded it slowly. "You're telling me you want to marry Min and bring her back, teach shop—and live where?"

"Some place of our own. The old Kendal place has been mine since Papa died."

"Ruined as Rome," Bradley said.

"No more so than us. We could all rise together from our own cool ashes." Rob laughed once, no strain.

Bradley said, "You're here now? You've moved out of Raleigh?"

"No I'm here to see you, see what my chances are. Then I'm taking Hutch with me to clear up things in Richmond—Father's papers to sort. Min is still at her job. I haven't told her anything sure enough to move her."

Bradley took up the folded letter again, inserted it into its envelope. "Then tell her," he said.

"Sir?"

"Tell her something sure."

"How can I?"

"Because I said so. If a job is what you need—a job here, teaching—and if you will give me solemn word that the drinking is behind you, then you've got what you need. I can almost guarantee it; I have to poll the schoolboard, but I think they'll concur."

Rob said "When will they meet?"

"Two weeks from tomorrow. But I'll see them all before then; I can let you know the drift."

Rob intended to thank him and give his solemn word (he'd given it before, always solemnly); but he said, "You are going against Father's wishes."

Bradley nodded. "I am."

"Why?"

"Because he was wrong. I knew before you told me, though I didn't know how. He was wrong all his life, Rob, in every big way; but he made his own home or so people tell me. Now you've got to make yours."

"Or what?" Rob said. He smiled. "What if I don't?"

Bradley thought it through awhile, then also smiled. "Nothing much," he said. "One more drowned life. But let me ask this favor on behalf of your people"—he leaned forward, grinning excessively—"Leave here. Get *gone*. Drown well out of sight. Don't ask Hutch and Eva and Rena to watch. Nothing's less amusing, less instructive than a drunk—a drunk never moves, never learns a thing; and he takes so long to drown. Don't ask Min Tharrington to stand on the shore and throw straws at you for thirty more years. Me, I don't really care. I am being polite."

Rob said "I know." It seemed all he knew and would ever know.

11

At four o'clock when Hutch had gone to his piano lesson and the early heat had eased, Rob and Grainger went out to the old Kendal place, first time in a year (it was still farmed by Jarrel, who reported to Kennerly, who passed Rob his share of whatever came in). Rob chose the hour on purpose—to be alone with Grainger, whom he needed to question, and to see the place while Jarrel was still in the field, not wanting to scare them with the threat of eviction till he'd seen if the house were livable for Min. Grainger drove and when they had cleared the last edge of town, Rob turned to see him closely, the first chance since Christmas (he had been away at Easter in Bracey with the cousin who still lived in Veenie's house). Nineteen years since Rob had met him; he had aged profoundly without looking older—the skin drawn closer to the bones like varnish, uncrazed and clear; the straight nose sharper, the nostrils larger; the line of the broad lips more like a graven boundary (the mouth a foreign organ swollen with threat in the milder face); the black eyes slightly purple in the late sun now, opalescent in their depths as if in hopes of clouding into senile blindness. Rob wanted to ask his age, early fifties somewhere; but he knew Grainger had strong feelings on that (he'd worn his hair clipped to the skull for ten years since it first showed gray). So after they had praised a few things about Hutch—his school marks, his growth—Rob moved to the question he had held for two days: "Are you here now for good?"

"Here *where*?"

"Fontaine. Mother's house; you know."

"Why you needing to know?"

Rob said, "I've got to move, got to make new plans. I'm wondering if I can count on you?"

"For what?"

Rob waited. "Steady help, I guess. I know you've got your place in Bracey still. I know you've got Gracie when she turns back up, but you've been here seven years."

"You moving here, you saying?"

"I asked you first." Rob also smiled, entirely earnest.

Grainger drove half a mile (they were on dirt now, already thick dust); then he said, "I got Miss Veenie's place in Bracey; saw it this Easter, still in one piece. Gracie wrote me a letter eight months ago Wednesday; I sent her ten dollars for bus fare to here. No sign of her yet and no more word. She don't need me and I never needed her. I thought I did; people said I did. I'm here because of Hutch, like to watch him moving up. He been good to me, Miss Eva been good, Miss Rena good as gold, Sylvie don't bother me. You moving Hutch from here?" He faced Rob a moment.

Rob said, "He wants to go. He thinks he wants to go; thinks we'd have a good chance—him and me somewhere, you with us of course. But I'm caught again, Grainger. They've turned me loose in Raleigh; I may have to come here."

"What you going to use for money?"

"I can teach here, I think. I checked that this morning."

"And live with Miss Eva?"

"No with you and Hutch, I hope."

"Who's cooking?"

"Min."

"Miss Min? Minnie Tharrington? You giving in to her?"

Rob said, "I may have to; she's told me to decide. And Grainger, I was forty years old last winter. I'm not as good at loneliness as I used to be."

Grainger nodded and waited. "When have you been alone?"

"A good part of my life. It's got worse lately; you get tired of it, want somebody in your room."

Grainger said, "I saw you alone one time—the first day I saw you, in Bracey, Miss Hattie's. Every time since then you *swimming* in people."

"People aren't what I'm after."

"Young Della was people; you fed off of her. What did she get back? Miss Rachel was people. Mr. Forrest, Miss Polly, them children at school. Miss Rena, Miss Eva, Hutch and me. What we got to show?" He continued to grin.

Rob said, "I've tried to thank you. I've tried the ways I know."

Grainger said, "How much candy your thanks going to buy us when we walk in the store and show a handful of thanks?"

Rob said, "Not a piece. I never said it would."

"You sorry for that?"

"That's the main thing I am. You know that well. My main trouble always."

"Then change it," Grainger said. "Change it while we got time. You lost two of us already; too late."

"I've told you," Rob said. "I'm trying now."

"Marry Miss Min and come out here and live in a house too sorry for niggers and teach wild children—and think Hutch and me be glad of that? You telling me that? You pull Hutch out, you kill Miss Eva; that's the start of your change."

Rob said "All right," which he did not mean. Then he looked to Grainger, turned firmly to the road, and said "Have mercy."

Grainger waited again. He was grave by now. He said in a voice barely more than a whisper, "Mercy all I had for nineteen years, mercy all my life. Now I mean to *cut* some. Listen here what I done. I watched your mess through all this time and cleaned it behind you. I let your daddy treat me worse than a dog when I was a child he promised to raise. Now he dead—God help him—but you still in sight with long years to go; and you ask am I staying? I tell you this, Rob—you come here and strow your old mess again round Hutch and Miss Eva, Miss Rena and me, I'll make you wish I had gone to the stars on a one-mule wagon." He finished, laughing. The separate mouth so odd in his face contorted in long, nearly silent laughter; but his eyes never changed—they had meant every word and would always mean them, would find strength not only to mean but do.

Rob said "Go tomorrow."

"I work for Miss Eva. You get her to tell me."

12

The yard was empty when they pulled up and stopped—no dogs, no goat— and the house had the tall solemnity of abandonment (a good deal less paint than when Rob had first seen it thirty-seven years ago, the porch steps sway-backed and two windows blocked with paper; but the whole shape unaltered, abiding this present, a minor pause). Rob leaned and touched the horn once. A wait—still no one. Then a black bantam rooster strolled out from the well. Rob said "Are you sure?"

"Unless they're dead," Grainger said. "Hutch was out here last Sunday, Mr. Kennerly and him."

Rob leaned for the horn again.

Grainger took his wrist. "Leave em alone," he said. "Your house; walk in."

Rob said "Come with me" and opened his door. Grainger followed him out and walked well behind him. Halfway up the steps Rob stopped and said clearly "Anybody living here?" A wait.

Grainger said "A whole family."

"Where are they now then?"

"In the field, your field."

Rob climbed on up, knocked twice at the shut door; then reached for the knob. It turned, no lock. He entered the long center hall and looked to Grainger. "Step in," he said.

"I'll wait out here."

It was his all right. He turned to the left through a half-open door—an empty room, entirely empty: the good white plaster ivoried with age but bound by pighair and barely cracked. His great-aunt's bedroom, scene of a third of her life at least. Shut windows, damp heat. He walked through the room to its own inner door and opened that. The old dining room; the old table still there, eight feet of oval walnut, black and coated with age. But clean, wiped clean, no crumb in the cracks. The windows here were shut too, no screens on them ever; and late sun was pounding this side of the house. Rob went to the old glass to raise it a little. Lovely old iron lock, elaborate as a child's toy, some penny bank that did a short stunt to thank a child. The window cried hoarsely.

A woman said "*Who?*"

Cold with fright, Rob turned.

On a narrow cot against the far wall, a black girl craning up, face wild with sleep.

He said, "I'm Mr. Mayfield. Let me give you some air."

"Flies," she said. She waved a hand across her eyes, drew her long legs slowly off the cot to the floor; and sat up slowly round a sizable belly— seven, eight months pregnant.

Rob said "Where's your daddy?"

"New York last Christmas, the last I heard."

"I mean Sam Jarrel; I thought you were his."

She was waking by then. "No sir," she said. "His wife my auntie. They somewhere working."

"You live here?" he said.

"I have right lately. I been kind of low."

"When's your baby?" he said.

"I don't know exactly."

"You haven't seen a doctor?"

"I didn't want to ask em for the money, no sir."

"So you just sit and sweat?"

"Sir?" she said.

Rob didn't answer. He was studying her room (the cot seemed her bed—two pairs of shoes were under it; a round mirror framed in green celluloid stood above it on the molding with a nail-polish bottle). They had given her this, in the midst of their eating; why not his aunt's room or a place upstairs? He remembered now Kennerly saying that Jarrel stored his hay upstairs since the old barn fell—a great tinder box over all their heads, no other dry storage. And so she was kept here, her dry hot place. "What's your name?" Rob said.

"Persilla," she said.

"Will you have your baby here?"

"I hope so," she said, "if Sam let me stay. He want me to leave; say I'm a bad example."

Rob wondered *Of what?*

Coal-black as she was, she was bright with the force of her hope and dread. She turned it on Rob. "You kin to Mr. Kennerly?"

"My uncle, yes."

She attempted to smile. "You tell him for me? You tell him, 'Tell Sam be good to Persilla. He all she got.'" Her smile dawned broadly like the pain of a thrust on her meager face.

Rob nodded. "This is mine."

13

After supper and a slow hour of talk on the porch with his mother, Hutch and Rena, Rob excused himself and climbed to his old room—Hutch's room; there were two beds now. He sat at the table, switched on the student's lamp (an instant furnace), found a tablet of Hutch's, and started a letter as a pool to take the rush of the knowledge and chances that had boiled up today, the two past days.

June 6, 1944

Dear Min,

I got here safely, though I did stop at Sylvie's last night to brace myself and wound up sleeping there which no one here knows. I pled car trouble. They are all as ever except maybe Hutch who is showing his age, the worst age of all. When I was fourteen I used to ask God every morning and night to give me some sign that He wanted me to go on enduring such days. They were very mild days; I can see that now—just the total absence of nourishment and hope, no sense

that I'd ever be of use to any soul (I could not notice Rena standing quietly wait-
ing). I have had worse since—you have watched me have them: worse in the
sense of causing real harm and knowing I'd caused it and could never repay—
but always since manhood with the awful grace of hope, the knowledge of a
future, that my body if nothing else at least meant to live and deliver me gen-
erally intact to tomorrow. Hutch is doubting that now and rightly so; he has
no evidence which he can believe that says otherwise. And the hard question
is, can anyone help him? Can I or Mother or Grainger or you say a word, do
a deed, that will give him the chance you and I craved then, the word of
hope?—the absence of which, when we needed it most, has brought us to where
we were yesterday, two mornings ago, my dream, your demand. That is what
I want to try—helping Hutch, my own last chance to make partial payment
on some aging debts: among them debts to you. Can you grant me that,
maybe wait awhile for that?

It had taken him a half hour to say that much. He had paused and switched
off the hot light to sit in a little dark and think when he heard the front
screen open, steps in the hall, then slowly up the stairs—Hutch. Rob
stayed dark and waited.

Hutch stopped on the sill, tried to see into the room; but the downstairs
light didn't reach the table. He said "Where are you?"

No answer.

"Rob?" (Hutch rarely called him Father; he'd seen him too seldom. He
saw him as Rena and Sylvie did, a brief young visitor.)

Rob still didn't answer, though his chair gave creaks and the sounds of
his body were a hum above Eva's voice, rising through the window. He was
not out to tease or scare his son; he was frozen, waiting for some better
word than "Here" or "Telling Min *No.*"

Hutch came on forward through the long warm dark, though Rob
had known him to be scared of dark. He paused near the foot of his own bed
and touched it, the familiar cool iron; then moved on again till his hand
touched his father. "You should speak to me," he said, his hand still resting
on Rob's folded arm, his voice grave but friendly.

Rob said, "Well, good evening. Tell me who you are."

Hutch stood in his place, no closer, no farther (Rob could see him
slightly now against the dim window). He said "I was yours." He had not
planned to say it.

Rob's right hand opened, an inch from Hutch's, and moved to take him.
"I've counted on that. I was still counting on it. If I'm wrong, tell me now."

"What difference would it make?"

Rob waited and tried to think it would matter. This boy might vanish now, and what? *Very little*—provided he vanished in silence, no pain, in darkness as now. The words surged up in his throat, claiming knowledge, claiming simple truth of the sort Eva'd strewn in her wake all his life. But he forced them down unspoken, partly true yet much less than whole. Hutch had asked a whole question; Rob owed a full answer. He sat another long moment, holding two fingers of a hand as invisible as Rachel's when he'd met her in this room to start this. Then he said, "This difference. I doubt you know this unless Grainger's told you; he's the other one who knows, because he was there. Before you were born, when your mother still had you and we were both waiting, I let down and hurt her and was so shamed by that that I went back to something I had done as a boy—drinking as a way to excuse myself. But just to myself; I'd excuse myself. I was hurting all the others more every night—your mother and Grainger, your grandfather, you. Then a month or so passed, and it seemed I had killed you. Your mother tried to bring you into the world, for nearly two days, a terrible struggle. You were turned all crooked; you were trapped and strangling. I was out in the hall; but I heard your mother, weak as she was. A nurse came to me and said the doctor said you were both of you *going* and that I could come in the delivery room and say a last word. My father was with me, and I looked at him. He said 'Better go.' But I went outside. I just turned and left him. It was right before daylight and cold for May. I went to the car; my liquor was there. I had in my head to take one long drink and then go back where your mother was. But Grainger was waiting; I'd forgotten him. He had come down with us but couldn't sit inside; so he'd gone back out and was on the back seat, trying to sleep. I scared him, I guess; I opened the door and he sat up and said, 'You've had all you get.' I had caught him in a dream. I sat on the front seat and opened the glove box; and Grainger said, 'What are you the father of?' I told him 'They're dying.' He said 'And you're here?' I opened my bottle and took one swallow and said 'I'm going back.' Grainger said, 'Tell me this—Miss Rachel still conscious?' I told him she was when I left; I meant her moans. He said, 'Do this. You lean down and tell her, tell her slow so she hear—"You come back and live and bring a strong baby back with you, I'll *change*."' I asked him 'Change how?' Grainger said, 'Pay your debts to everybody round you, every soul you *invited*.' I asked him who gave him the right to say that, and he said 'Jesus Christ.' Then he laughed one time. I turned and meant to strike him; but I couldn't, then or since." Rob waited for breath and released the hot fingers.

Hutch moved to his bed, sat there on the edge ten feet from his father. His father stayed silent till Hutch said finally, "You were telling me the difference."

Rob said, "Still am. It's more than I thought."

Hutch said "Did you tell her?"

"What?"

"The speech Grainger gave you."

"Oh no."

"Why sir?"

"She was gone."

"I was there," Hutch said. "You could have told me."

"You were there," Rob said. "They had pulled you through. You had never even cried, just came free and breathed, all weak from the hours, your head all torn (they had pulled you with forceps when they once got you turned); but yes you were there."

"And I'm here," Hutch said. "You can still tell me now."

Rob said "Son, I'm telling you."

"Not the difference," Hutch said. "You've told that already. Tell me what Grainger said you should tell my mother."

Rob thought that through; then sat forward slowly and felt for his letter; he had just now said it after all, but to Min. He could say it to Hutch. "All right."

"*Say* it please, sir."

"I will pay you every debt I know how to pay."

"Starting when?" Hutch said.

Rob stood and went forward to the boy and touched his head, the warm crown rank with the clean dried sweat of another long day. Then he kissed where he'd touched; the answer was *now*.

14

When he got to the porch, they were both still waiting—Eva in the swing, Rena in the chair that was nearest the stoop and the old tubbed palm. They both said gladly "Sit down and rest"; Rob took the chair between them and sank. It was cooler and still, no car on the street for the first few minutes; so he did rest a little. (Hutch was in bed and sleeping; Rob had waited upstairs at the foot of the bed till he heard slow breathing, the safety of peace. Then he'd gone to the table and reached for the lamp to finish his letter but had heard Rena's laugh and decided to pursue it.) For all its withholdings, this house—porch, yard—had offered him as much calm as any other place. *More* it seemed now as he rocked here silently between his aunt and mother, his first and longest lover, his first beloved. Old forces had leeched away in time, old hungers been fed or starved into weakness too feeble to stand; they sat like a family in a child's dream of home. He could live here at last. He turned to Rena. "What was funny just now?"

He caught her half-dozing. She said "Very little."

"No you laughed. We heard you all the way upstairs."

Eva said, "At me—when you laughed at me, when you asked for the moon."

Rena said, "Oh the moon. Yes I'd been sitting here much admiring the moon. Hutch and I had discussed it; it keeps us awake. Then he went upstairs, and we sat on awhile; and when I next looked, it was nowhere in sight. So I said to Eva, 'Eva, where is the moon?' and she said, 'Don't ask me. I'm a stranger here.'"

They all laughed again and Rob turned to see her as they quieted slowly—his mother, not by moonlight (it was gone) but a lamp in the parlor, Eva's bedroom for years, that reached her right profile as she swung her little arc. No one on God's earth was less a stranger anywhere than Eva was here, this precise small axle rotating through space these fifty-seven years—a few boards and plaster, four dozen panes of glass. A life at home; had that been her whole triumph and the source of her power? It seemed so now (her face in the half-light, unyielding as ever, prepared as the marshal of an armored division for what lay in the woods—the ambush of age, failed mind, racked body or unchallenged march into harvest fields and river encampment, a slow drift to sleep).

She was watching the road not him or Rena, but she said "Where is Hutch?" in a whisper not to wake him if he'd already slept.

Rob also faced the road—nothing, still empty. One distant tired Negro. "Asleep, ten minutes. He seemed very tired."

"He was," Rena said. "We waited last night."

Eva pushed past the claim. "How long is your trip?"

"Oh long as my business and our little sightseeing." Rob had not spoken to her of the business till now. He had written Hutch a note just before his father's funeral, and he'd laid out his plans to Kennerly fully when he asked for the gas; so he guessed she knew of the death and the duties that faced him now.

But she didn't ask for more. "Less than two weeks?" she said.

"Yes ma'm. It's for him"—Rob pointed upstairs—"I have got to get back."

"To where?" Rena said. She had faced him all along, though he sat in full dark.

He offered it to Rena then. "What about to here? Can you find room for me?"

Rena said, "I did once. I'd try to again." She thought he meant the sum-

mer months from now till September. He had not told her or Eva of his firing or his morning talk with Thorne, and they clearly hadn't guessed. Rena
said, "Plenty weeds waiting for you right now" and thumbed behind her,
her half-acre vegetable garden just beginning. "Grainger's griping already;
saw a black snake this morning. I'll get your hoe ready."

Eva said, "Hutch can move down and sleep in my room, give you space
upstairs."

Rob still spoke to Rena. "I may mean for good. How would that sit with
you?"

Eva swung on in silence.

Rena turned to the road, but her voice had the old rich puzzlement of
hope. "Like sherbet," she said. She drew a long breath. "Lemon sherbet in
the shade."

Eva said "Come here."

Rob looked over toward her.

She had moved to the dark street-end of the swing and was touching the
vacant space. "Sit here a minute, Son."

Rob stood and obeyed.

But she spoke first to Rena. "Sister, what about your herring?" (Rena
had bought salt herring to cook for Rob's breakfast; they would have to be
soaked overnight, starting now.)

"What about them?" Rena said. "They were dead last I looked." But she
sprang up in a moment and entered the house.

Rob said "Coming back?"

"When I've found the moon," she said and never broke step.

Eva said "And she *may.*"

Rob gave a strong thrust with his heel to swing them. Eva said "Good!"
and they watched one another, both smiling broadly as their cool arcs slackened and left them still again, the warm air close. The house was silent—
Hutch asleep, Rena buried far back in the kitchen, Grainger in his own place
fifty feet to the rear.

Rob said "How are you?"

"As I've always been."

"Then happy," he said.

Eva laughed once, high. "Has it seemed that to you?"

"To me, yes," he said. "I can't speak for others."

"You're the one who would know."

"Why me?"

"You've loved me. You're the last one who's loved me." She was smiling
still but he saw she was earnest.

Rob couldn't deny her, not tonight anyhow. Any earlier night in the past ten years, he'd have said, "No, Hutch. You are leaving Hutch out." But after this morning and Hutch's plea to leave, he could only allow her claim unchallenged. He nodded. "I've enjoyed it, however much I moaned." Then he went on to tell her what he suddenly knew. "You are happy and have been ever since I knew you clearly."

"How is that?" Eva said. "It has never seemed easy."

"No I'm sure," Rob said.

"—I abandoned loving parents for a man I could please. I bore you in danger, and my mother killed herself. I left my husband, came here and nursed a dying father, leaving you to yourself—and rightly won your grudge."

"But you wanted it all."

"Why?"

"I truly think you did. Mother, that was what hurt me—that you had left me willingly to Rena and Sylvie. You left Father easily as stepping from a room. You had the best of Hutch, all his plain child's love. You have never been refused, I honestly believe. Very few humans are ever deeply refused, barring cruelty or sickness. Most people die smiling or are happy till the last. Most people get the lives they asked life to give; their needs get filled."

Eva seemed to smile again (she had faced forward now; he could not see her fully). "I have noticed through the years how good you are at inventing explanations for everybody else on earth but you."

"Maybe so," Rob said.

"No maybe about it," Eva said and touched his knee. "Here, answer me this—since most of us humans are happy tonight, how are *you*, sweet love?"

Rob waited awhile; they were still swinging gently enough to cool them. "Tonight I'm resting and am glad to be. Many days I'm not, most days here lately."

"What need have you got that is not being fed?" She had taken back her hand and had moved away slightly, just beyond the reach of light.

Rob did not think he knew. What came as his answer was the recent sad past. "I have not mentioned this by mail, understand. I've waited for the chance to sit here and tell you. But I've lost my job in Raleigh and am loose again."

Eva waited. "Son, why?"

"Father's death," he said. "It caught me so suddenly when other things were low. I stayed home and drank some and missed a little work. They said they'd had enough."

"When was this?"

"A week ago."

"Are you drinking now?" she said.

"No ma'm," Rob said.

"You and Hutch shouldn't go—"

"No, Mother," he said. "I have got myself together."

She faced him for proof and studied him as if there were plentiful light to show the degree of control in a man, the strength in his eyes. "I have never comprehended—what is drinking for?" she said; she herself had never drunk more than sherry at Christmas.

"Oh for ease, from shame."

"Shame of what please, Son?"

"Different things in different people."

"You're the one I know," she said.

"I've failed so many; Father's death showed me that."

"Any death shows that. That's the purpose of death. What did you owe Forrest?"

"What I've owed all of you, a useful life."

"Useful to what?" Eva said, deeply curious but almost whispering.

Rob knew at once. "God and all my family."

"Useful how?" she said.

"Just the usual ways—kindness, care, dependability. If nothing else, to furnish one rare lovely sight for others' eyes to rest on."

"You've done that," she said. "You have been more loved than anyone I've known—Sister, Sylvie, Grainger, Rachel, your father apparently, Min Tharrington, your son. *Me*—believe that at last. I've loved the best I could. Don't forget. I was half-wild from *my* mother's blood, all the fleeing killing Watsons. I had to feed myself. Once I had, I loved you." She reached for his hand; it was cool there beside her, palm-down on the swing. She traced a figure-eight in the curls of its back as if a slow figure would complete her message, detained forty years. The hand moved a little but stayed flat down.

Rob spoke though. "I believe you."

Eva kept her hand in place, riding his very lightly. In a while she said, still softly, "What now?"

"Sleep, I hope."

"No your future, your plans."

"I mentioned coming here," Rob said.

"To do what?"

"Teach school, teach shop. I saw Thorne this morning; he seems quite hopeful."

"Starting when?"

"This fall. I would come back sooner; get well settled in once we finish our trip, once I clear out in Raleigh—the rent's paid for June."

"You were not teasing Sister; I thought you were."

"No ma'm. I have had to keep it quiet like this till I thought my way through, till I knew if I was welcome."

"Who else have you told?"

"Min and Hutch, Thorne and Grainger. You now—"

Eva said "And you know?"

"Ma'm?"

"You know that you're welcome?"

"Are you telling me I am?"

Eva said, "I am asking if you are sure. You are too old to blunder here one more time."

"What would blundering be?"

"Failing again in sight of your family."

"You said it wouldn't matter, hadn't mattered all along."

"Not to us," Eva said. "I spoke for us—well, Rena and me; I can't speak for Hutch. No, to *you*. You would care; caring's ruined your life. I just meant that; can you welcome yourself? You are at home now; can you sit here and take it the way we have?"

Rob said, "No ma'm, not in this house here. I wouldn't try here. I would find my own place—the old Kendal place; I might go there—and take my own family: Hutch and Grainger, maybe Min. I may need to marry Min."

Eva faced the empty street and touched the swing's chain, old rusted cow chain. She carefully felt her way with thumb and finger up eight or ten links; she would smell of rust till morning. "Are you sure Hutch would go?"

"Yes."

"You already asked him?"

"Told him, yes ma'm."

"He would follow you out to that wreck of the past?"

"He'd like to go farther. He's growing up now."

"How did he tell you that?" Eva said.

Rob had never held a genuine weapon against her, never had one to hold. And because she faced the road and could not be seen, he was not sure he held one now, not sure she cared. Had Hutch been more than her latest job of nursing, ending soon and gladly? He did not wait to know; either way, he spared her. "Our trip," he said. "I just meant our trip. Hutch wants it to last, wants to go on to Goshen and see his mother's home."

"Will you go?"

"I doubt it. We've got the gas for Richmond, a day at the beach, maybe Jamestown at most."

"Let him go," Eva said. "Let him see his mother's home. Rachel earned that much."

He'd invented the lie—Hutch had not asked for Goshen—but she forced him on now. "Please say what you mean."

"I mean he asks about her, just lately, not before. For long years he never spoke her name. Then he started on Sylvie, oh a year ago. She told me one evening, 'Miss Eva, Hutch ask me how old is his mama.' I told her to send him to me next time, that I'd fill him in; but he somehow knew and didn't ask her again. I think he's asked Rena, but she'd never tell me."

Rob said, "I can tell him what there is to tell."

"But gently," Eva said. "Children suffer from blame."

"Yes ma'm," Rob said. "I've heard that, I think." He was suddenly exhausted—the restless night at Sylvie's, the tides of this day towing various ways, the thought of tomorrow and the hot drive north. He stood and said, "Excuse me please. I've just given out."

"Too early," Eva said. "You won't sleep, you know."

"I'll lie quiet though," he said, "and rest my eyes. Can I help you lock up?"

"Oh no. I'll sit here and wait for Sister. She's still in the kitchen. Those herring must have *fought* her."

"She'll win," Rob said.

"Little doubt," Eva said.

He did not lean to kiss her but faced her, raised his right hand; and gave a slow greeting—palm held shoulder-level and broad in the dark—as though to a stranger met high in dense mountains after long search in thin air on vanishing food.

Or as though at the bar, vowing truth with God's help. Eva read it that way. "Swearing what?" she said.

He held the pose, baffled.

"You are poised there to swear."

"—Amends," Rob said. "Even partial amends."

"You never harmed me. Come back," Eva said.

He could say no more, would never feel more certain that he had a claim on life, could continue and mend. He dropped his hand as slowly as he'd raised it and turned and went in and climbed toward his sleeping son, his chief good deed. He stripped and slept quickly, rest in a hot flood, palpable balm.

15

He woke in early light awhile before six—no sound but birds, the downstairs quiet, Rena's room still shut, Hutch so silent that Rob craned up to check on his life. He was there on the near edge of his own tangled bed, hands clenched by his open lips which gave no sign of breath; but the rails of his lean sides swelled and sank every eight or nine seconds, so he'd also lasted. With his eyes on Hutch, Rob said the old prayer he had always said—"*Your will, Yours*"—then stood in his cotton shorts and top and went to the table and, not reading through what he'd written last night, continued his letter.

You have waited long years, I know very well—remember; so have I—and you've taken what few rewards I could give in strangling secrecy. Precious few. But I beg you for one last stretch of patience. Then I hope I can offer the best I have, a final answer. It will be one of two things you've asked me to say, firm Yes or No.

If Yes it will be for the simplest reasons—that most of our lives we have stuck together for what must be natural inclinations to mutual care, that now I can turn myself from old bonds and ask you clearly to take me openly for better or worse in what time is left us (for better will surely be my intention; you've had enough worse to hold you nicely), that I miss your company when you are not with me and always will. Lastly, that I'm much more grateful to you than you've ever believed. I could make you believe or could die trying hard.

If No the reason will also be simple—that I can't find a way to do both justices, to Hutch and you. Remember that I drove off nine years ago and left him age five in a house that nurtured my own miseries and have seen him since only as a brief Santa Claus (a poor one at that and occasionally shaky). I will try to know now on our coming trip how much I can give—what he needs and I have—and how much is too late. Or was never really wanted, just imagined by me.

You said one week. I will write you by then or maybe try to phone; but I won't have a whole sure answer in a week, maybe not for some weeks. Maybe not before fall when he and I have moved out of here and fit together in a separate place. So if that is too late, you can let me know now (care of Polly in Richmond); and if we should never meet in privacy again, I can say now I'll thank you well beyond my grave, not excluding here and now. You have been the best help. My continuing troubles were not your fault and without you would have drowned me. Maybe we should have let them. Hope we won't.

Ever,
Rob

16

By the time he had got that sealed and addressed, he heard the single cough that began Rena's day; then the quick sounds of dressing—his one chance to see her. He quickly stepped into his own trousers, took his shaving bag, and entered the hall. Her door was still shut; but he stepped up and listened—perfect silence. Had she slipped out somehow? Or dropped in her tracks ungreeted, unthanked? He opened the door. Her bed was made; he couldn't find her. He drew a deep breath.

Rena whispered "Step in." She was over by the window in her caneback chair, her back to the door.

Rob stepped in and shut the door behind him. "I was headed down to shave; I thought I heard you. Then your room was quiet."

She turned her chair toward him. "Come sit down," she said. She leaned and touched the foot of her bed.

Rob went there and sat. "Are my herring ready?"

"They will be," she said. She had her Bible open on her lap; she let him see it (he had never seen her go near a Bible before). "This is yours," she said. It was—his grandmother's, given to him by his grandfather thirty-odd years ago as soon as he could read. "I borrowed it last year. It was in your room."

"Should have been with me, shouldn't it? I'd have been better off."

"Maybe so," she said.

"Is it saving *you?*"

Rena looked down at it, the book of Romans. "From what?" she said.

He remembered her father's death, their meeting in the parlor. "You once mentioned rest. I was hoping you had found it."

She weighed that a moment, then looked up smiling. "Oh no," she said. "But you don't have to find it. It comes; it comes." She looked to her book and said him a verse—" 'For I reckon that the sufferings of this present time are not worthy to be compared with the glory which shall be revealed in us. For the earnest expectation of the creature waiteth for the manifestation of the sons of God.' "

Rob said "Are you suffering?"

She thought again. "I'm hoping mainly. Hoping still."

"For what?"

"The sons of God, I guess. I don't expect much!"

"No really," Rob said.

"You know," Rena said. "Simple courtesy would serve till glory be revealed. You abused me last night—*Could you come back home?*"

"I was honestly asking."

"I honestly answered." She closed her book.

He reached out to touch her. She was just beyond reach, so he did not lean. "You left too soon; I didn't explain. I have got to go somewhere soon, a new job."

"What happened in Raleigh?"

"I broke down a little when Father died. They couldn't stand the sight."

Rena nodded. "He deserved it. He earned every tear."

Rob remembered her coldness to Forrest at the wedding, the cool smiling distance of her few meetings with him when she visited Richmond after Rachel's death. "From me, you mean?"

"From us," Rena said. "We ruined his plans. We all owed him something—the Kendals, I mean."

"I paid it," Rob said. "Too late of course."

"Maybe not," Rena said. "Anyhow wait and see. People sometimes cancel debts long after death; I know that for certain. Mother freed me through you."

"What way?" Rob said.

"From blame, real blame. I knew she was wild, and I went off and left her."

"The day she died? I thought you were here."

"In school," Rena said, "—and I hated school. She had asked me to stay, but I turned her down. The night before she died, she came to my room and knelt down before me to pin up the hem in a dress she was making for my school commencement (still six weeks off; she knew she was rushing). I had not cleaned my lamp; she had trouble seeing and worked very slowly till I finally said, 'Mother, I have got to *study*.' She rocked back then, sat flat on the floor, and wept bitter tears. I stood and let her weep them—never moved, never touched her (she was one foot away), never once said 'Why?' or what did she need? In a while she said, 'Stay home please tomorrow. Let's finish this thing.' I didn't say 'Why?' I knew she was nervous; we had heard of your birth the day before and Eva's weakness. I thought it was normal and that she would calm down. I was also too young to think I could matter; nobody had told me. So I said 'For what?' That was what she couldn't answer. At last she said, 'I thought you might enjoy it.' I said 'No ma'm' and you know the rest."

"It was not your doing."

"You were not here," Rena said. "It was mine all right. Anything you can help and don't is your doing."

"Who said?"

"Just God."

"And I helped you?" Rob said.

"You *freed* me, I said. You were Mother's way to free me."

"How?"

"I rescued you. When Eva turned to Father, I turned to you—with open arms; yours were open to take me. You'd have sunk otherwise."

"Are you sure I didn't after all?" Rob said.

Rena searched his eyes. "Not yet," she said. "Of course you still can. You have got years of chances. Even strong old boats have been known to plummet on calm summer days in clear sight of shore."

"You're telling me that I have got a chance of freedom."

Rena said, "I am not telling *nothing*, sweetheart. I was thinking my morning thoughts and you broke it."

Rob said "I'm sorry" and stood to leave.

She did not try to stop him; but she said, "Oh no. I was glad to see you. I hope to see you every day the rest of my life."

Beneath them, through the floor, they could hear Eva singing, softly but pure enough to penetrate walls—no tune they had heard, the product of a long night of tranquil dreaming.

17

Once he'd shaved in the bathroom, Rob passed through the kitchen—Sylvie rolling biscuit dough, no sign of his mother—and through the wet grass of the yard to his bathhouse, still the only shower in this end of town, though used now only by himself on visits. The once-mossy lattice of the floor was dry; and the few old threats—black widows, snakes—were represented only by a token dead spider in the low south corner, translucent from starvation. But the old pipes worked; and once he'd hung his pants on the single nail, the cold water rushed him—panic and pain. He bore it as always by a long high yell; then he wet the yellow soap and shut off the water and lathered his body from face to toes with serious care. All winter he had washed in his landlady's tub, quick shallow splashes to avoid a long stewing in his own scum and bristles, but now he lingered. Despite the shock of cold, he felt himself slowly; and was slowly pleased. This body which had borne him through some fifteen thousand days, through ninety percent of the pleasure he'd had; which had suffered the blame of Rachel's death, all the subsequent gifts to and punishments of Min, seemed young in his hands again, fresh and ready.

For what?—himself. Why not himself? Wasn't forty years of leaning on various others—rubbing on others—enough for one life? Hadn't Eva urged it on him twenty years ago in telling him the body had its own private solace if he'd only accept it? *A strong closed world*—he seemed that to himself now, the first time in his life. He could dress, walk out of here, crank his car and leave—no word of goodbye, no prayer for pardon. He could get a job in Norfolk at the shipyards or Baltimore. A plain rented room with one single key. Who would suffer from that?—Min for maybe a month till she'd raise up and know she was blessedly free; Hutch for sometime longer, for some years maybe till he bowed to the fact of his own composition (the potent bloods in him—Watson, Kendal, Goodwin, Mayfield: all commanding his life, *demanding* it really); Rena forever but she planned on that (how would she greet a true son of God if he came to her now with a pledge of loyal presence?—she'd head for her garden, leaving him in the swing). *Old Robinson*; whom had old Robinson harmed in a lifetime of flight? Fewer souls surely than Eva in her one place, Bedford Kendal in his, than Forrest even with his need to change lives (fieldhands reading Ovid).

His sex had stood in his soapy hand, first time in two days. Rob studied it, smiling. For all its hungers and humiliations, it had served him kindly for thirty years. And never better than in solitude as now, the uninvaded joy of self-dependence, perfect self-service. He could be his own solace, had been the sole solace of his own life to now.

Cold and wet, upright in his bathhouse with slightly bent knees, Rob honored himself. And his whole body thanked him with a pure flood of pleasure that cleaned him more deeply than soap and cold water, than long years of waiting on others (hunting them) in the hope of purgation, eventual rest. He reached for the faucet to rinse himself.

Grainger said "Who is that?" and tapped on the wall outside behind Rob.

"Your oldest friend."

"Is he clean?"

"Not yet."

Grainger opened the door as the water struck Rob. Rob's back was turned. Grainger said, "Step to my house please when you're clean."

Rob turned in the freezing water to face him. "That may be years."

Grainger nodded. "I'll wait."

18

Dried and dressed, Rob walked on to Grainger's beyond the bathhouse on the edge of the garden—the old cook's house built for Sylvie's grandmother Panthea Ann when she was a young girl brought from the Kendal farm, barely just free. The door was closed. Rob knocked once and stood. The hyacinth leaves by the step had died, a dense mat of yellow.

"Step in."

Rob opened the door and looked, the one dark room. He was blinded by the sun but was searching for Grainger.

"Step into the shade." He was in the far corner, squatting by his small trunk and locking it.

Rob entered the cool. "Am I clean enough?"

Grainger pointed to his one chair, a slat-bottomed rocker. "Rest yourself a minute."

Rob took a step toward it; then stopped, looking down. "You leaving today?" He knew he was not; his belongings were still in their old rigid places—on top of the small pine table by his bed, a battery radio, a Barlow knife, a dollar watch, the Irish potato Grainger normally carried for rheumatism (exchanging each one as it shriveled with poison drawn from his joints). No drawer in the table. Across the tan floor—boards scrubbed once a month—and against the back wall was a second larger table with a little stack of clothes (shirts, pants, underwear, all folded precisely), a graniteware pitcher and bowl, a bar of soap, a shaving brush worn to a stubble of fuzz, a shut straight-razor (its strop on a hook at the end of the table), a pocket mirror laid flat, a pair of nail clippers. The walls were bare as always—no calendar, thermometer, no nail or peg, no pictures of dogs, no human face.

Grainger stood and came toward him, no smile, no answer. He held a small box. "I need to talk to you; sit down here please." He went to his narrow bed and sat on the edge.

So Rob took the chair. "You've recovered?" he said.

"What from?"

"Yesterday. I thought you'd got rabies. I see you're better."

Grainger waited, watching Rob; then began on an answer. "I slept all night, first time in three months. Yes I'm—" He stopped there and held out the box, white cardboard tied with a cord.

"This a snake?" Rob said.

"You open it and see."

"Sing 'Happy Birthday.'"

"Your birthday's in March. This ain't for you anyhow." But he offered it still.

Rob took it and weighed it on his palm, feather-light. He loosened the cord and opened the lid on a bed of white cotton which he didn't move to touch.

"Lift it up, fool, please."

A gold coin, smaller than a quarter. Rob took it, strummed the thin milled edge, turned it over—Five Dollars, 1839. He looked up, grinning. "You're under arrest. Gold money's illegal for the past ten years."

"For Hutch." Grainger pointed. "That's for you to give Hutch."

Rob set it in its cotton and offered it back. "You give it to him then; he'll be up in a little."

Grainger shook his head twice. "That would force him," he said. "I don't mean to force him; he'll love me or not. You just change it, secret; and buy him some present, some thing he see on his trip and want."

Rob nodded and took it, closed the box, retied it. Then he moved to rise — breakfast, the day.

Grainger spread his right hand like a fan, meaning *wait*. "You wonder where I got it?"

"I *didn't*," Rob said. "People used to have gold."

Grainger said, "Mr. Rob your dead grandaddy. At the time I was born. He sent it to Papa in that same box to the state of Maine; said, 'Give it to Grainger to bring him luck.'"

Rob rose, stuffed the box into his deep hip-pocket. "Would you say it had worked?"

Grainger thought. "Off and on, like it did for him. He had got it at his birth; some cousin give it to him. It was made that year. Mr. Forrest used to tell me he made a good death."

Rob took two steps, then turned again. "You thinking of death?"

"Not much," Grainger said.

Rob came back toward him, all the way to the bed, and stood there above him not a foot away. "I am," he said, "—more and more here lately."

Grainger said, "You're a boy; you barely cut your teeth."

Rob showed his teeth fully in earnest, not joking, an unbroken set. "When He was my age, Jesus Christ had been dead seven years and some months."

"If He died."

"He died. Question is, did He rise?"

Grainger said, "Question is, what you mean about *you?*—thinking death."

Rob bent even closer. "We're leaving today; Hutch and I, this trip. If anything happens, if you get the word to come and help, tell me now if you'll answer."

Grainger said "What help?" They were whispering. "What thing might happen?"

"I might start drinking when I get to Richmond. I may fail there. God knows, I could die."

"On purpose, you mean?"

"I don't plan it, no; but you see where I'm headed—to tunnel through all Forrest Mayfield's leavings."

"You're coming back here. You're setting up house. I'm helping you out if Miss Eva spare me."

Rob nodded. "But answer; will you come when you're called?"

"If you're *live*," Grainger said. He laid his flat palm on Rob's breastbone and felt the heart adjacent. "You're live this morning; I'll swear to that. If they send here and say you're dead, I'll wait. Miss Rena can fetch you."

Rob covered the hard dry hand with his own; he smiled—"Breakfast served"—and made a waiter's bow.

19

After breakfast while Eva was packing for Hutch, Rob walked the quarter-mile to Kennerly's house. His Aunt Blunt's car was already gone (the single woman in the family who could drive); Kennerly's truck was nowhere in sight; and when Rob knocked twice on the front screen and entered, no one rose to meet him—the cool dark hall: Blunt's paintings of dogwood, an Indian praying, the Angel Gabriel descending with lilies. Rob called out "Aurelia?" (the cook—he could hear her far back in the kitchen, already humming hymns).

No answer.

"*Anybody?*"

"Would your old uncle do?" —Kennerly in the parlor. He had said he'd be gone by daylight, cruising pulpwood.

Rob went forward to him; he was seated with the paper. "I thought you'd be covered with ticks by now."

"I thought so last night, but I waited for you."

Rob laughed. "I've never drunk a drop of your blood."

Kennerly offered his wrist. "Help yourself," he said. "Everybody else does. You may need it yet."

Rob sat on a footstool, a yard from his uncle. "I'm sorry if I held up your business," he said. "I thought you'd just leave the gas stamps with Blunt."

"I said I would; then I ran into Thorne and thought I'd better see you, hear the tale from you."

Rob nodded—"All right, sir"—but offered no tale.

"You mean to come home?"

"I mean to make a living; I'm out of a job."

"Why is that?" Kennerly said.

"Thorne told you."

"No he didn't and I didn't press him."

"Then don't press me please either," Rob said. "It's been a bad month, but I've not harmed a soul, and I'm looking for work near my own baby-cradle."

Kennerly nodded. "Just tell me one thing; you haven't been tampering with any child, have you?"

Rob smiled. "That was Forrest, Forrest Mayfield; I'm *Rob.*"

"His boy."

"His boy, yes sir, who was grieving for him. I missed a little school from grieving for him. Us colored boys grieves worse than you white folks; we feels things harder, things cuts us deeper; we takes the occasion to grieve when we can."

The joking stopped Kennerly. "You're settling his estate?"

"No estate," Rob said, "—just a house near niggertown and several bales of paper."

"Did he leave it to you?"

"No will, no sir."

"Then it's partly your mother's. She's his sole legal widow. What's Virginia law on that?"

"Does she need it?" Rob said. "Tell me clearly right now; would a few thousand dollars mean a thing to her now?"

Kennerly shook his head. "She's fixed. Father left her well-fixed. What's fairly hers though ought to come her way."

"Then it won't," Rob said. "Nothing fair in her having one red cent of his. You watched that story; she chose her own life."

"Father chose."

"And she accepted, with a deep lasting smile. What's left should go to Hattie—it was her father's house—and to my father's helper: she's the one worked for this over forty long years."

"Give it to her," Kennerly said. "Eva wouldn't go near it. Then you're coming back here?"

"Did Thorne say I could?"

"Yes."

"Do you think I should?"

"Rob, you've never taken one piece of warning from me. I've stopped wasting breath."

"No, tell me," Rob said. "You've watched me close as any. Tell me what you know now."

"You're a very small part of what I know," Kennerly said. "I've watched you, sure, but not because of you. You were in my line of sight; I have watched all my people."

"Tell me that small part."

"Will you use it?"

"If I can."

"Come to life," Kennerly said. He had known it at once, had not paused to breathe.

"Sir?"

"Come-to-life."

Rob waited to think, then shut his eyes tightly, extended his hands; then looked again brightly. "Lo! I am," he said. "Feel my hands and see."

"No you're dreaming," Kennerly said, "—flat in bed still dreaming for the forty-first year."

Rob said "Dreaming what?"

"Perfect peace. You expect a happy life. You can dream that forever."

Rob waited till he knew he could speak without heat. "When did you wake up?"

Again no pause. "When Mother fell dead; I was eighteen by then."

"What had been your dream?"

"Same as yours. They all are, only dream people have. It's a way of dying young."

"So you woke up and saw?—"

"—That it's just a long wait, that your life is this wait."

"What for?" Rob said.

Kennerly hadn't thought. He had held his newspaper on his knees through that; he raised it now and looked, a random inner page. Then he put it down. "Oh peace."

"Have you got it?" Rob said.

"Don't expect to any more. That's the thing I mean to tell you."

"You could die," Rob said.

"That would get it," Kennerly said. He was smiling again. He folded his paper and laid it on the floor. "I appreciate your counsel. I'll give it sober thought." He moved to rise.

Rob stopped him with a hand. "If I come back here, would you call that a life?"

"Could be," Kennerly said. "You could have a life in Raleigh—Hell, in Boston, Massachusetts if you'd set your mind to have it."

"Should I marry Minnie now?"

Kennerly sat back to think.

"Should we move to the country, fix the old place up?"

"You set to drown some niggers?"

"Sir?"

"You dispossess Tom Jarrel, you'll need to drown his children or watch them starve before you. Drown a teen-age girl with a little nigger *in* her."

"Can't we find him a place close by? Tom could keep on working for us."

"*You* tell him," Kennerly said. "*You* find him the house. I quit right now if that's your main plan." He grasped the leather chair-arms and stood in one thrust, as strong as a boy. "I'll get your gas-stamps, and you get out of town." But he stopped at the door. "Let me tell you this story that you don't understand. You'd have known it all your life if you'd ever woke up. We are very plain people. We're the history of the world; nothing one bit unusual in any of our lives. You are just one of us; you have not been singled out for special mistreatment. Let me tell you my life; I can tell it in a minute, and it's sadder far than yours. I worshipped my mother—she was something very rare, she could charm the birds silent, she'd have set you straight in minutes—and she seemed to care for me, since I was the boy and she was partial to boys. But I was dreaming, see—how to get myself calm. I had hated school badly, Eva had all of Father, he could barely *see* me. So I took a little job, little bird-shit job jobbing brogan shoes two counties away, to help me keep dreaming. I had a little rented room where I could get my things straight. I had my combs and brushes laid as parallel as tracks on the bureau top; and thought that was perfect, that I'd found still harbor. Then Mother went under, was driven down simply by your two parents and their selfish meanness. They'd have never succeeded if I had been here (Eva didn't need Father by then, and Rena never); but I was hunting peace, and my mother died in absolute misery—without so much as a last word to me. I woke up as I said and came back home, thinking Father would need me. He didn't, never had. But he'd taught me one skill—how to estimate timber—so I did that for him, for myself (to keep awake). Eva came home by then; and the first night she got there, I knew she'd never leave. *She* was needed, all right, and wanted to be. She had her a skill that would keep her calm forever—how to please one precious human soul entirely, how to live on the interest of that once he'd gone. I watched that for two years and decided to leave, just to here, a quarter-mile. Leaving meant you got a wife. I had known the Powell sisters since I'd known anybody; so I settled on them—both of them, couldn't choose. One day I asked Mag which one must I take. She stood and thought a minute; then she said, 'The high one's pretty but the squatty one's the *worker.*' The high one was Sally; I settled on Blunt, and she's worked fairly well. We have not raised our voices more than half a dozen times in thirty-six years. She'd have liked to have children, but one of us couldn't which didn't bother me. I've kept my eyes open, since Mother tore them open; and let me ask you this—can you name me three children that have brought their parents pleasure? I mean long-standing pleasure, not a picnic here and there."

Rob said "Mother—"

"I said *parents,* two people. She breathed just for Father."

Rob said, "No I can't, no sir."

"You've had Hutch these years, you and Eva and Grainger; but he's gathering to leave. I can see it in him more every day that passes over—*I am aimed out of here; God help the one that blocks me.*"

Rob nodded. "Why is that? He's had what I lacked."

Kennerly grinned broadly, walked halfway back. "I told you," he said. "You didn't understand. That's the point of my story, mine and Eva's—Hell, *Sylvie's:* nobody lacks nothing. Nothing special, I mean, barring rank starvation and external torture. Everybody gets the same if you add it all up; some a little more here but a little less there. It's a flat damn tittie everybody gets to gum. You are luckier than most. You are luckier than me; no you killed a woman too. So we're even. Come to life. Forty's just about time. Most men wake up very naturally at forty. Few are called like me, few as fortunate as me—Charlotte Watson foaming blood."

Rob also stood. "I do understand and I'll try to believe you."

Kennerly's grin reignited. "Don't matter," he said. "Don't let it get you down. The truth is something separate from you—pretty you!—and it won't lose a minute's rest, a particle of its power, to spit you in flames if Rob Mayfield can't believe at middle age." He left to get the gas-stamps.

20

Hutch was seated in the car (they had told him goodbye); and Rob was standing at the open driver's door with Eva and Rena and Grainger around him when Sylvie came out the kitchen door, heading toward them with two paper bags.

She went round to Hutch's side and gave them to him. "Here's your lunch. Don't waste it; people begging for food."

Rob said "What's the news?"

Sylvie stayed at Hutch's window and spoke across him. "They killing em now; they killing by hundreds." It was just after ten. She had heard the war news on her kitchen radio, heard it all day through as each hour struck. France had been breached on Tuesday by a hundred thousand men, the final invasion.

Rena said, "Not killing them fast enough."

Sylvie said, "Plenty fast. Plenty of em to kill."

Rob leaned to face Sylvie. "Don't you want it to end?"

"I won't the one started it. *You* go help it stop." She had found ways before to deplore his freedom, though she well knew his age exempted him nicely (her one nephew Albert had been shipped to England, maybe on to France now).

Rob laughed. "Shall I swim? We could strike out from Norfolk; Hutch could tow me when I failed."

Sylvie searched Hutch closely all down his length—a blue polo shirt, khaki shorts, new sandals.

On the far side Eva said once firmly "Sylvie."

Sylvie touched Hutch's ear with her thick forefinger, gently on the top rim. "You leave Hutch safe on the beach; I'll come get him." She had said it to Rob, but Hutch took her wrist (he could still barely ring it). She wrenched free easily and went toward the house. After six or eight steps, she stopped and faced Rob; but at first she didn't speak. Everybody turned to watch her.

Rob said, "I'll pray, Sylvie; for Albert, this evening."

She nodded. "You pray. Then see do that save him."

Eva said again "Sylvie," milder now, and moved to Rob.

Rob said, "We'll see you, Sylvie. Anything you want?"

"Not a thing," Sylvie said. "Not a thing they got that you can buy." She went in slowly.

Hutch said "Let's go please," an audible whisper.

Eva said "She's worried," not wanting to expand in Grainger's presence (he and Sylvie had lived in armed truce for some years).

Rob touched his mother's shoulder. "We'll phone you tonight when we're settled at the beach."

Eva nodded. "I'll wait." Then she offered her face.

Rob was struck by the change. What had seemed, last night on the porch in darkness, a map of contentment—perfect and glazed—seemed suddenly the flayed drying head of a girl gravely assaulted and utterly puzzled but still uncondemning, a silent beggar. With his hand still on her, his wish was to flee; to pull back simply to the car behind him and drive till night, long nights from now where this face would be hid if not vanished, forgot. She had always loved him; he had failed her entirely. He bent and brushed his lips on hers—his carefully dry, hers wet as a wound. Then he turned and sat.

Rena held her ground three yards from the car; but she spoke up from there, having waited her turn. "We'll expect you," she said. With her big right hand, she managed a wave that was like a little spooning at the air, three times.

Grainger said "Let me know—"
Hutch again said "Please."

21

Rob had driven two hours—fifty miles north of that—and knew he must stop
to buy Hutch a drink, let him eat Sylvie's lunch; but the deep chill of flight
was still on his forehead, the five cold bits still cutting his mouth (Min,
Hutch, Eva, Rena, Grainger straining to turn him five separate ways). At last
he touched Hutch's leg. "Son, eat what Sylvie fixed you. I am not hungry yet;
let me just push us on."

Hutch ate a dry sandwich and rode on gladly.

JUNE 7, 1944

They had got to Virginia Beach in late afternoon and found a room at a cheap clean cottage called Abbotsford—two white iron beds like the room at home. Rob's headlong force had brought him this far, then abandoned him quickly; so he'd told Hutch to sit on the porch or walk while he himself napped. Then they'd find a fish supper.

Hutch walked half an hour toward the north sparse end, barefoot in wet sand, his own heart gradually lifting in solitude—the element he'd always suspected was his (both hoped and dreaded), though he'd known real loneliness of this sort only in half-hour scraps of wandering from home or behind a shut door. What he did not know from his fourteen years, and needed to know before all else, was a simple answer—could he live in the world, this world he'd had, the only world shown him by others in daylight, where grown men and women chose (apparently *chose*) to bind their own strong selves to others till they withered together and propped one another in permanent yokes? Could he live like that for sixty more years?

He had felt the substance not the words of such thoughts for nearly ten years. He had come to them slowly by witnessing the life of his grandmother's house, by guessing at the secrets of his father's life, and now through the sight of his friends whose bodies like his had burst into growth (loud with puzzlement and pleasure, new demands). The pleasure he'd accepted almost daily for two years, alone in his room or behind the house in woods. The puzzle of how such a large pure joy could be shared with another (the actual *method*—who would move how?—and stranger still, the *motive* for sharing an act so easeful, so healing and scarce): that puzzle he'd held deep in him, but by force and with shame; its demands were its own law and knew no place or time.

The fierce intermittence of hunger and surfeit had brought a new fear

Hutch had not known in childhood. In the long years of being at the mercy of others for care and kindness, he had treasured some hope that once his body firmed (*if* his body firmed; he had seen his naked father and older boys swimming, which were no guarantees that the process was general), he would gain calm control of his world and his choices. He would have his own way. Now the process had all but run its course in him—and delivered him over to a far harsher power than any he'd faced. (All the others had been people—his dead mother, Rob, his grandmother, Grainger. This was in himself and wild.)

Then he came to a long clean empty stretch of beach and had walked toward the middle of that, an old jetty. No human in sight, no houses either way for two hundred yards. He had not seen the ocean for three summers now; and though it was no large part of his wishes (he had lived far from it), it seemed here this evening a possible mate, companion by which he could pass through a whole good life alone, unwatched, his body unchallenged except by itself beside this predictable wordless water. Behind him far back was a low grassy dune. He went there to sit while this new calm lasted, to test it for good sense and possible endurance (he'd never been sure any goodness would recur).

It had lasted whole minutes, and toward the end he had wished for his father to walk here and find him and silently sit. No thought of the dream of his mother's return.

Then he saw he'd been accompanied. Sixty yards to his left just beyond the reach of water in a gray wool blanket, a man and a woman. Only their hair and slick faces showed; the rest was covered which was partly why he'd missed them. They'd also been still as a beached log or shark. When he saw them he crouched, his chin on his knees. The move had been soundless, he was downwind from them; but at that the man looked, looked up toward Hutch, seemed to meet Hutch's eyes.

No man but a boy—seventeen, eighteen, short-haired, plain-faced. Was his nod a greeting? He smiled very broadly, then faced her again, then moved above her. He was lying all on her, though he held up slightly; their heads didn't touch.

Hutch thought he should leave but had he been seen? The smile was uncertain; could have been the rush of pleasure, not intended for Hutch. The girl had never looked. She was just the boy's mirror. To stand now and go would be to make a speech they could not fail to hear—*I've seen you, can leave you.* This was offered to him; they gave it to him—he chose to believe that. So he rolled to his elbows, extended his legs in dry sand behind him. Flat down in the sand, hopeful and dreading, Hutch watched them closely.

They moved in their gray cloth like sleeping breath—steady, unstopping, all but past detecting—and they moved so long that Hutch established rhythms: the great joint heart made by their two bodies beat six times for each slap of water on sand. And that never changed; that was what reached Hutch as sweet confirmation—*This is simple as breath, a new rate of breath that will come to you soon in its own natural time like the hair on your groin, strong sweat in your hollows.* His pleasure in the thought and the sight that had made it did not call on him to seek their same goal; his own sex was calm. But he mimicked their beating with his narrow hips in the cool dry dune.

Then the boy laughed clearly, three high sounds quick but separate as beads, and looked up again to where Hutch had been. With Hutch flat down, their eyes failed to meet; and the boy then covered the girl completely—faces vanished. Their body was still. They might never move again, might never need breath.

Hutch went toward his father, searching some way to tell him and ask for more.

2

But Rob had still seemed exhausted through supper, asking Hutch only easy things about school and Sylvie and Grainger. Hutch had answered politely with part of his mind, a thin forward part. The deeper core still focused on the beach, the gift he'd been offered by two covered strangers hardly older than he. He had eaten his scallops and settled on secrecy—tomorrow maybe when Rob had rested—and the simple freedom of new air around him, new public food unburdened by Sylvie's visible labor, prevented impatience or mute regret. Then Rob had said, "Ready for a picture show?" Hutch said "—And willing"; and they'd walked a short way to an old brick building to sit through the last half of *Young Mr. Pitt.*

When it ended Hutch waited for lights to come on, the gap between pictures; but they darkened even further and from somewhere in front came the nasal whine of electric guitars, not Hawaiian or South Seas but generally eastern, maybe Japanese. Some collection for the war?—dead Japanese children? Hutch tried to see his father; he was sealed off in dark. So when the music went on and no announcement came, Hutch said "What is this?" A man on his right said "Shhh" and Rob was silent. Then the music built on toward a faster louder end. A spotlight struck the curtain; and a man's Yankee voice said, "Ladies and gentlemen, for your evening entertainment and patriotic pleasure, we proudly present—from across the salt Pacific and our grand ally China—the famous Ming-Toy to dance her nation's dances." The music

came again, slow and soft. The spotlight widened. The curtain spread
quickly on a short figure, swallowed neck to sole in purple cloth, hands flared
to hide a face.

The hands oared slowly sideward. The face was round and pale, white as
warm fish flesh. The mouth was straight and solemn; the eyes were black,
tip-ended, and stared out more fiercely than any Hutch had seen—how did
this dark room offend her? Who were all these hidden watchers? (Hutch himself had entered darkly and had still not seen around him; what was on his
father's face?)

She began to tremble gently at her own veiled center, no relation to the
music. That grew to deep shaking which began to sway her arms. Her legs
began to buckle. She was finally all in motion on the net of the music
before Hutch could realize that this commenced a dance, that the girl herself was willing.

For a while she danced in place, only raised hands and feet at the edges
of her purple-gold slits in a tent. Then she worked toward a fury which
involved long lopings and high straight kicks. Still her face never broke its
white glare at the room, never joined her body's turmoil.

Then her hair poured downward. It had been bound tight on the crown
of her still head; she'd loosed it someway. It reached to the waist of her robe,
lank black. She held still again, her head turned down, the hair swung forward. When it covered her face, her hands moved inward to work at the four
gold frogs on her robe. She shuddered one time and the robe fell off; a small
white foot kicked it firmly behind her. The music had stopped. She was in
a gold halter and small gold pants, both tasseled with gold. She was smaller
than before, than the robe had made her seem; and frozen as she now stood
(her head down, hid), it did seem to Hutch that she'd come to the end of her
nation's dance—China starved and shamed since before he could remember, a billion baffled children. She bore a long look from all the dark faces,
all silent as she.

Hutch again looked for Rob—still concealed but there: their arms pressed
together on the common armrest. Was clapping now in order or was it too
solemn? Would she just walk off?

A voice said "I'm waiting," a man behind Hutch.

There were two seconds more. Then her hands sought her halter, slowly
climbing her belly; and it fell too—she had hardly seemed to touch it.
Another kick backward, her head lifted slowly. In hiding, her mouth had
smiled very slightly, and it stayed smiling now. Her breasts were bare.

Hutch had never seen breasts in actual life. Since his own mother's
death, he had lived with old women who concealed themselves; so his

knowledge was confined to magazine pictures and the plaster casts at school of Venus and Victory. Yet he hadn't deeply wondered; they were so much a pendulous fact of his elders, denied still to all but a few girls his age. He studied now though with wide-eyed quickness, certain that Rob would lead him out any moment. They were perfectly round and while they quivered with her—she was moving again to softer music—they defied the earth as firm as white bowls held by magic to her chest and stained at dead-center with brown aureoles the size of great flowers. What had made her want to bare them? Why were people here watching? What secret was shielded by such plain bulwarks that people would be drawn to pay and sit staring? Was another gift involved, his second today? A gift to use how, now that he could feed himself, had never fed here? What good was being done?

The lights began to swell, the music quick again. She accepted both changes and was starting to whirl, her arms milling wild. Hutch knew that if he turned he could see his father now; other men were forming round him. But now he didn't look—for fear a deeper puzzle would stare back, grinning: another secret offered, exposed without warning and no explanation. Had Rob known of this?—that they would see this, much more than a show? Hutch had noticed no sign out front, no word from Rob.

The girl was all naked. In the last gyrations she'd torn herself finally free of all cover and had stopped, back turned. A high flat behind like any boy's swimming. To the loudest music yet, she spread her arms straight like wings and faced them quickly. At the fork of her clamped legs, the short fold of flesh—as hairless as her mouth—was lined with bright stones that glistened three seconds. Then every light blackened.

Rob clapped with the others.

3

In their room an hour later after seeing all the picture and eating ice cream and deciding they were tired, Hutch was in bed already with a light sheet on him, face turned to the pine wall, his mind still grinding.

Rob entered from the bathroom in his shorts and sockfeet and sat on his bed. The boy turned away. Rob tried by kind staring to force him to look. Or was he asleep? He was not old enough to have lost the child's gift of total surrender. "Did you say your prayers, Son?"

"Yes sir."

"Pray for Albert?"

A sizable wait. "I have now, yes sir." He didn't plan to turn.

"Are you mad at me?"

"No sir. What about?"

Rob had peeled off his socks and was kneading his feet. "Any number of things—the vaudeville show."

"No sir."

"Did you like it?"

Another long wait. "I don't understand it."

"What part?" Rob said.

"The whole thing."

"Do you want me to tell you?"

"Yes."

"You've got to look at me then; I don't talk to walls."

Hutch rolled over slowly as if it were work. He faced his father vaguely, no trace of a smile but entirely awake.

Rob said, "I didn't know it was going to be that. I thought she'd be an acrobat or some hula dancer. She was just pleasing men, just selling quick fun."

Rob nodded. "What was fun?"

"—That she showed herself naked, things people want to touch."

"Men, you mean?"

"Men and boys. You are not getting younger. It'll come to you soon."

Hutch had met his father's eyes through all that; now he flinched. He looked down and flushed in great splotches, neck and chest.

Rob saw that clearly and felt the cold burning of a child's shamed refusal to face the settled fact that he's left one room and walked deep into another, that doors have shut behind him. He had his own knowledge of Hutch's new body; his own fresh memories of the same in himself twenty-six years ago, the cold spit of torment. He knew Hutch prayed for the room to darken now, for them both to part and sleep. But he also felt as strongly the need to give a gift—what he'd never had in childhood; had scrounged from long years of waste, harm, and punishment: a partial shield composed of battered scraps but true at least. What old Robinson had known and refused to pass to Forrest. What Forrest also scrounged but hoarded till too late. He began his painful offer. "In a short while from now, Hutch, you'll need all of that. All she showed and all that's under."

Hutch rolled full over now and lay on his belly, face half-hid in pillow. Then he said "For what?"

"Your ease. So you'll think. See, you'll soon get to where you'll be twisted up with what will seem like desperate starvation. What you'll really be is *curious*; but you'll think you're dead with need and that what we saw will feed you—what was under that purple, what she'd stuck cheap diamonds on."

Hutch thought, then said "I doubt it."

"No you will. You're mine and Rachel's. You could not escape by trying. You could jump up now and start in your light cotton drawers and run like deer forever; and it would tap your shoulder in a year or so and seize you. You are mine and Rachel's child."

Hutch said, "Can we go to Goshen?"

"No."

"We'd skip the trip to Jamestown and go on to the mountains. I've read Pocahontas."

Rob said "Why?"

"To see Mother's place."

"I can tell you all you need. We would not be welcome, Son."

"Then tell me," Hutch said.

"What?"

"All I need." He rose to his elbows and met his father clearly.

Rob bore the look a moment, then walked to the door and switched off the light. Then he came back and spread down his own top covers and lay flat on them. He spoke to the ceiling but strongly enough to carry on the din of surf that pumped through their two open windows, mild but constant. "I've thought about this for some years now. I think this is all you will need or can use; I honestly do. When I was twenty-one years old at home, I thought I was unhappy. I had thought it long before but had not known I could act. I thought I'd been neglected by my mother, who was busy; and of course I'd never seen Forrest Mayfield to remember. I was hot after that, after all I'd been denied; so I struck out to find it, which meant to find another. I thought it lay in others and could be mined out, that streams could be dug which would fill me forever. Just by touching others, young girls my age, the size of that poor girl tonight. They were all hid from me; so I thought it was there, the ease I mentioned. I still think it is, but that's a later story. Well, girls grow on trees as you may have seen already; and quite a gratifying quantity of them thought the same thing as me and were ready to try. It *does* help—don't ever let a Christian say it doesn't; even Jesus never said it—but it helps very briefly, the length of two aspirin. Or until you wash yourself and the feel begins to fade in your mind with the picture and the words you and her said to bait each other out of hiding and look. So when I got to Goshen after wandering a little, I had had several little spells of ease as I said; but what had made me leave home was still far beyond me. Then I saw Rachel Hutchins, who lived where I slept; and she above every other human I've known believed what I did."

"What was that?"

"That you could live. That no power in heaven had ever intended for people to want one day of their lives, not for calm human kindness; that people could furnish each other all the needs of a good useful life if they'd set their minds to it; that some people's minds were already set and waiting."

"Rachel, you mean?"

"Rachel. Your mother. She was younger than me; but she'd run well past me in the hunt for her hope, had all but given up when I crossed her path."

Hutch said, "You are telling all that about bodies?—just bodies together? You still believe that? I thought it killed Mother."

Rob rolled to see Hutch. A window was behind him; and by the dim black-out lights of town, Rob could only see the compact ridge of his side—he was turned Rob's way anyhow and seemed to wait. So Rob said "It did" but could not follow that—no tears, plain blankness. He'd exhausted his knowledge, his pitiful gift that had meant to stretch miles. A fourteen-year-old child had dried him up in less than five minutes. He sat up quickly, no sense of destination. A little walk maybe.

Hutch said "Nobody blames you."

"Thank them for me," Rob said. He went to the chair and felt for his clothes, stepped into his trousers.

"Are you leaving?" Hutch said.

"For a while," Rob said.

"Want me to stay here?"

"You wait."

"For how long?"

"Till I tell you to stop." Rob had kept his voice calm, but the spine showed in it. He walked to the bathroom and shut the thin door.

Hutch rose and found the light and also dressed. When his father came out, Hutch was opening his bag.

"*You* leaving?" Rob said.

"Yes sir."

"Where to?"

"To the bus station first." Hutch had kept his back turned. He was taking out a light jacket; packing his book, *Swiss Family Robinson*.

"Have you got any money?"

"Grandmother gave me some."

"Would you go back to her?"

"To Goshen first maybe."

Rob walked nearer to him, two steps from his back. "There is nothing in Goshen but one girl dissolving six feet underground."

Hutch nodded. "Maybe not." Then he shut his bag and turned, his face white with purpose, taut with revulsion. "That's more than is here."

Rob struck him, not gently, on his left ear and neck; and even before the shocked face responded, Rob said to himself "A *second time*." He meant the second irreparable harm he'd done in his life—Rachel, now her son. He was accurate.

But Hutch, when he'd swallowed astonishment and pain, said "You promised to stay."

"Where?"

"With me. Rob, I've *waited*. I've waited for you since I was five years old—to come back and take me to live with you, to find us a place. You said that to me plainly the day you went to Raleigh. Grainger heard you say it; I didn't dream it up: 'You stay here with Eva and Rena just awhile till you get school-age. Then we'll be back together and can hear ourselves think.' So I've lived with old ladies picking at me nine years, and you've had a good time. Now you say you'll come back to Fontaine and drop there. I won't be there to catch you."

Rob smiled. "Where can I find you?—just for Christmas cards and funerals." He touched the hot shoulder which stiffened in his grip, then pulled free and turned.

Hutch opened his bag again and reached deep in it. He found a short envelope and handed it to Rob. Then he went to the window and tried to see out.

Rob handled it slowly, the postmark *Goshen*, May of this year. To *Master Raven Hutchins Mayfield, Fontaine, N.C.* Inside, a single sheet of lined tablet paper.

May 18, 1944

Dear Raven

I know you had a birthday a day or so ago; and since I saw awhile back in one of my papers that your other grandfather had passed to his grave, I thought you might be interested to have your last male forebear rise and wish you happy days.

Happy Days.

Come to see me if the spirit ever moves you;
I am here all but alone,

Rachel's father,
Raven Hutchins

Rob said "What did Eva say?"

Hutch had gone to the edge of his bed and sat. "She never knew about it. Sylvie brought it straight to me."

"Did you show it to Sylvie?"

"No."

"Or Grainger?"

"No sir. I was waiting for our trip."

Rob went to the bag, laid the letter in on top. "Did he write to you before?"

"The Christmas I was five, Rachel's mother wrote to me — just a card saying *Love*. Eva showed me that. But him, no sir. I remember him though."

"How?"

"He's all I remember. Was I three or four? — anyhow that time you took me up there before we moved to Fontaine."

"We were pulling out of Richmond; I had given up there and was hunting a place. 1933, you had just turned three; can you really remember?" Rob lay across the foot of his own tangled bed.

Hutch said, "A drink of water in a strong-tasting cup, that much anyhow. And that he seemed old. You were not with us, were you? I don't remember you."

"I may not have been. We stayed several days. I was looking for a job, and he used to keep you with him."

Hutch nodded. "'*Stay here.*' He asked me to stay. We had had the drink of water and walked out into sunshine. Then he picked me up and faced me and said, 'You can stay. You are Rachel to the ground.' I think he said that much; I'm sure he said *Stay*. I'm sure about the water. Was my grandmother there? I can't see her at all."

"Oh yes," Rob said. "She was very little noticed. Very kind and obliging, very ready to forgive; but she liked to fade back, till she faded completely. Rena heard that she died of some blood weakness the year the war started — Rena'd swapped notes with her; they had met at our wedding. Mr. Hutchins notified her."

Hutch said, "Why are you not welcome then?"

Rob waited awhile, working back through it. "I doubt you want to know."

"I do, yes sir."

"It's more of what you wouldn't listen to just now, what you cut me about."

Hutch said, "But tell me. I promise to listen."

Rob knew that the start lay a good way back. He could not tell it in another rented room. He sat up and said, "Come with me to walk."

4

They went down a block to the ocean in silence, Rob a little in the lead. He had kept his feet bare and walked to the extreme edge of the calm surf before breaking step. Hutch came up beside him. There was no real light—the town mostly black; no moon or stars, though the sky seemed clear. No bomber could have found them. Looking out Rob said, "Shall we swim on for Sylvie and join Albert fighting?" He pointed straight out to the unseen horizon. "Just three thousand miles; think we could find him?"

"Where?"

"In France. I'm guessing he's in the invasion if he's not dead by now."

Hutch said, "Sir, you're pointing at the Straits of Gibraltar; but sure, I'm ready."

Rob laughed. "Walk north first. Walk north to Nova Scotia; we'll need to aim for France."

So Hutch led them left the way he'd gone alone before in late afternoon. He walked on damp sand but beyond the reach of water; his father on the ragged edge of its fling, his ankles now and then phosphorescent with foam. When they'd walked some distance and Rob had not spoken, Hutch said, "About welcome—you were telling me that: why you can't take me there."

Rob said, "All right. I was still thinking back. It maybe starts here; anyhow this was early in the story. I first went to Goshen when your mother was away. She had had a nervous breakdown and gone off for treatment; so when she came home, I was already there—her father's hotel with a job of my own and Grainger in the kitchen and the form of help I mentioned (also in the kitchen: a colored girl who lived on the place, named Della). *She* welcomed me right off. I had gone to her most of the nights I was there till Rachel came back; she lived on the place, next to Grainger in the quarters. She bore me up through whole weeks when, Son, I planned to die—just by letting me in. You don't understand that now—you won't ever; I sure God don't—but you might start believing it and honoring it now just on your father's word. It is some kind of bridge, to bear you through life; and it bore me to Rachel. I have to tell you now; I didn't love Rachel till after we were married. We were natural mates though, as I said awhile back; we were both that reckless to have our own will, the same goal in life. But even after I had met Rachel and chosen her, I still went to Della. She was still helping out." Rob paused and, not stopping, walked rightward till the surf reached half to his knees (he had rolled up his trousers).

Hutch said, "And Grandfather objected to that?"

"Not at all. Not then. I didn't think he knew—Rachel never did at least—but it turned out he did and had helped us along, hoping I would be eased and could pass Rachel up. That wasn't Rachel's plan."

"What did Grainger think of her?"

"Very little, I guess. He was waiting for Gracie—she had already left him—so he'd taken me on as a spare-time job, but I never let him stop me."

"You just said he did."

"When?"

"The morning I was born. You said Grainger stopped you and sent you in to Rachel to tell her you'd changed."

"That once," Rob said. "And he's helped at times; of course he has—it has been half his life, thinking he saved us. It was Della that saved me, without even knowing."

"And Grandfather blamed you?—for lasting on Della, for getting through to Rachel?"

"I don't think he did. He'd given up on Rachel himself, I think; he saw he couldn't ease her however hard he tried, and he'd seen enough of me to think I might. No your grandfather only spoke hard to me twice—the night I asked him for Rachel's hand, he promised to harm me if I harmed her (he never knew I did, never blamed me for you) and the time you remember, 1933. After Rachel died I tried to stay in Richmond, keep my job at the colored school (I was head bookkeeper and by then was teaching a little mathematics). The first few weeks my Aunt Hatt came and nursed you along; and your Grandmother Hutchins and Rena paid visits, and Polly was always nearby to help; but after you were oh maybe six months old, you were just mine and Grainger's—we were what you had. And we did right by you. God never made a better baby anywhere than you. You would only cry for hunger or for actual pain. I could wake you up any hour of the night I needed to see you, and you'd wake up grinning. You sobered up later when you understood more, but you did a life's share of bellylaughing as a baby. I could talk like a duck and you'd answer somehow; that could last us an hour almost any night. And Grainger would read to you out of his book or play his mouth-organ, and you would dance circles. You slept in my bed from the time you could walk; and I'd lie down beside you in some dim light and watch you for minutes. You would always breathe through your mouth, wide-open, breath fresh as new milk. I'd let it wash my face, same smell as your mother. I never once blamed you; you were innocent as any clear pane of glass. I loved you till it drew great tears down my cheeks, and I stayed good for you—I'd made God the promise Grainger said to make Rachel. I had tried to change. I would lie some nights after you were deep asleep and whisper you questions up against your ear. One night after you had moved to my bed, as I put you to sleep, I said, 'When I come to bed will you wake up nicely and take a little leak?' and you said, 'Ask me. I'll answer you.' So for some time I asked you did you want to go pee, and you'd always answer in your sleep Yes or No; and were always right, never wet me again. That gave me the idea to ask other things. At first child's questions—'Hutch, growl like a tiger.' You'd growl in your sleep. Then I'd ask did you love me? You'd generally nod and once you grinned, but you never said Yes. And once after two years, I asked did you mean me to keep my promise? I don't think you knew what a promise was, not to mention *my* promise (unless Grainger told you); but you said Yes as clear as day."

Hutch said, "What was the promise?—just to change your life?" They had passed all lights now and walked in pure darkness, guided by waves and the faint earthshine; their feet bare to shells, rocks, rotting fish but safe so far.

"To stop harming people in the ways I had, by not touching one human body again (not for my old reasons), by not drinking liquor; I had drunk a lot of that since I was your age."

"Why?"

"A form of ether, deadens the pain."

Hutch said, "But you promised that *if* we two lived, Rachel *and* I. You got just half."

"That was why I asked you; you were all that was left. I thought you should say. I thought you might be taken if I broke it."

"And I told you Yes?"

"In your sleep, age three."

"Did you listen?" Hutch said.

"Obey, you mean?" Rob stopped in his tracks.

Since Hutch could not see him and was one step ahead, he walked on a few yards and came to a block. His foot struck a low wall; he bent and groped at it. This afternoon's jetty. He looked back for Rob.

"No I didn't," Rob said.

"Step here," Hutch said.

"We'd better head back."

"We can sleep late tomorrow. Step here please, Rob."

Rob went toward the voice and blundered into Hutch.

Hutch took his father's left arm and pulled him one way. "We can sit up here. There's good dry place. I was here this afternoon."

Rob accepted the lead and they went up the beach to the low dry dune—the sharp dune grass—till they stood still, touching, in what seemed a bowl. Hutch pulled Rob down and they both lay flat on their backs looking up, both hunting lights in a sky that seemed cloudless but was also unbroken.

Hutch said "Why not?"

Rob was lost. "Not what?"

"Your promise, why you broke it."

Rob lay still awhile. "You are changing tack. I was telling something else, the story of Goshen."

Hutch said "All right."

Rob thought, then laughed. "It's all one story. It'll answer all your questions. I broke my promise from the time you were two, long before I asked you, by needing human touch and finding it in places that shamed me to drink. I was drunk when I asked you, more than half-gone beside you. You weren't enough, Son, though you tried to be. I had a taste for human touch, had it from the night I finished high school; and no young child, even one as kind as you, could help me ease that. This is nothing very strange or scarce at least, common as trees. You'll come to see that."

Hutch said "I don't yet"; but he also laughed and recited Rena's universal answer to *common*—Acts 10:15, " 'What God hath cleansed, *that* call not thou common.' "

"I don't," Rob said. "They were mostly good people, a girl at the school, an old friend of mine, the odd cheerful stranger. But I'd made that promise; and there you were to prove it, to warn me and shame me. So I shunted back and forth for a year or so between weeks of honoring you and Rachel's memory and backsliding weekends of gorging and puking. Grainger kept it from you very well, I think. I would stay out until I could come home calm; he would say I was working and take you to Forrest's, and Polly would feed you."

Hutch said "I don't remember."

"Oh somewhere you do; I knew you would and I still couldn't stop. Then I lost my job."

"Did they punish the girl?"

"She wasn't the cause; they never knew about her. No I started missing work—Mondays, Mondays and Tuesdays. It nearly killed Forrest or so I thought then. I guess it just embarrassed him; he'd spoken of me highly. He'd worked so neatly to keep his own life well out of their reach; and here I'd gone on show—I would drink on the job. So he didn't fight for me—I never could blame him—and we sold out in Richmond, took Grainger back to Bracey, and went on to Goshen: 1933."

"The time he said *Stay*, my Grandfather Hutchins."

"Yes. To you, not me."

"—The story you're telling."

"You and I went to Goshen in May. We'd been invited. Your Grandmother

Hutchins had asked us for the summer ever since Rachel died, or for my vacation, and we'd never accepted. So when I was let go at James Institute, I wrote her and said we could come if she liked. I had made a new start in the mountains once before, my *only* start; I thought I might again. I hadn't been up there since Rachel's funeral and you'd never been. They might help; I was ready to slave, empty slopjars, anything. 1933 was miserable times for more men than me, even after Roosevelt—several dozen million men. We had two hundred dollars after selling all our stuff; everything but clothes and toys, a few souvenirs nobody else would want (though I tried to sell them, even pictures of Rachel), an electric fan. Well, we rested a day or two, eating and sleeping—the little I could sleep—and then I told your grandfather what our plight was. Half-told anyhow. I didn't give the reasons for me being fired but blamed it on the times. He said he was sorry and to let him know if you were ever in need, but he didn't offer any direct help or job. And I understood why; he was near-broke himself. Not a whole lot of people were seeking out a rest spot in Goshen, Virginia in those years then. He had cut back, no help in the kitchen but his wife and a white girl that came in to make beds and sweep; he did his own upkeep. And of course he dreaded us. We were signs of Rachel when he'd almost got her hidden. Dreaded me at least; you say he wanted you. Fair enough—I'd been the cause. But somehow I felt there was no place left; that if we couldn't stay there, we might as well die."

"Kill us, you mean?"

"No. Yes maybe I did. I'm pretty sure I did, just driving those roads that I'd helped build and knew like my body; one swing of my hand, we'd have plunged a quarter-mile over sharp rocks and laurel. But that was no plan, no big intention. I still planned to live, and I saw you did. So I asked him point-blank if he knew of any work in the county nearby. He could have said No and sent us on then; but he gave me a list of three or four slim chances—a dry-goods store, the local welldigger, the local high school. And I set off to beg, though I skipped the school, knowing they would want references. A beautiful day; I can feel it right now, air cool and dry as powder, miles of yellow leaf light. I left you with him and checked all his leads and a few of my own. They can't even say No with grace in the mountains. The welldigger said, 'For eight dollars a month you can stand and watch me piss; that's as much contact with running water as I've had since Herbert Hoover dried up the world.' He meant I could pay *him*. By late that evening, I was dismal as a blind dog. I knew I was expected—suppertime was bearing down—but I walked half a mile to the west side of town and stopped by the river. There are bad rapids there, rocks the size of whole houses. I was not thinking clearly, though I hadn't drunk for days. I could think of rest though; and it seemed a simple reach, just to grasp out and hold it. Or to fall down and cut myself to ragged pieces. You'd have never had to see me, they'd have raised you well as I, you were just as much theirs. Then I saw a colored boy walking slowly toward me, maybe younger than you are now, maybe twelve. He was barefoot and wearing the rags of rags, and he didn't want to cross the little bridge with me on it. He just stood and waited on the far side, looking. So I told him, 'Come on. I won't throw you in'; and he came on past me. I thought I recognized him, not him but something in him. I said—he was moving—'Have you got a name?' and he said 'Fitts Simmons.' I said, 'Do you know a colored girl named Della Simmons?'—'My auntie,' he said. I asked him did he know where she was that day."

Hutch said "Your old friend?"

"From my first time in Goshen."

"Was she there?"

"Slow down. The boy said 'No sir.' I said 'What about yesterday?'—'No sir' again. I said, 'I'm her oldest friend; I've come here to see her.' The boy said 'Too late.'"

"She was dead," Hutch said.

"So I thought. And I thought if Della was dead that would just about do it—clear my own way to go (not that I'd thought of her twice in eight years). But I asked him and he said she had been there to visit just a few days before and had gone back to Philly; he made it sound like Heaven not the tailside of torment. So I asked him was he heading to his house right then and could I come with him? He said, 'Who you know at my house but me and Della?' I said 'Nobody' so he said 'Come on.' It was just a short distance."

"Was she really not there?"

"If she was, they had her hid. No she'd gone to Philadelphia the day we came to Goshen."

"Running from us?" Hutch said.

"I doubt it; even asked in a roundabout way. It seemed she'd intended from the first to leave then, though the boy's mother did say she'd heard we were in town. She was some distant cousin of Della's, strange to me. Said she'd seen me years before; said she served at our wedding which I think was a lie. Anyhow she was ready to sit and answer questions; so we sat on her shaky porch and talked past dark. She was older than Della; the boy was her grandchild. She seemed to have memories of Della and me, little hints Della gave her; but she used them very gently, just suggested Della might come and work for us now since we were alone. She had known Rachel well, said she pitied you and me. Said Della was a day-maid in cold Pennsylvania, had still never married or had any children but claimed she was happy. Asked how happy was I. I told her fairly plainly—"

"And she gave you some liquor."

Rob stopped and rolled over to his side, toward Hutch. By then his eyes had widened or some light had risen; he could see the boy's shape. He bent over the face; it seemed to be smiling. "Are you smiling?" Rob said.

"Not to speak of, no sir."

"Well, don't yet," Rob said. "It'd be a little early; this gets even sadder."

"Tell on," Hutch said. "I'm ready as ever."

Rob also grinned. "It helped me a lot. It has always helped me to sit down with Negroes and smell their strangeness, let them bleed me with questions. They are either much worse off or so much better—I've never known which—that they soothe me at once."

"They are spirits," Hutch said, "—like angels here to guard us."

"I didn't claim *that*."

"Grainger does," Hutch said.

"When?"

"A week or so ago. We were listening to the news in his house late at night; and the man read a piece about Negroes in the war—how many had enlisted and what they were doing: building bridges, cooking meals. Grainger shut the man off in the midst of a sentence and said, 'You remember'—and pointed at me—'They are guarding people's lives, which is God's plan for em. They are spirits bringing word. You listen to a nigger if he ever bring you word.'"

Rob waited. "Grainger's aging, going hard like Sylvie. But that one in Goshen, Della's cousin, soothed me down. And I went to the Hutchins' after dark, still alive and sober as tonight, still jobless and broke but intending to live and to stay on there as long as they'd have us till I found us a place."

Hutch said, "I don't remember; I must have been asleep."

"You were watching," Rob said. "It happened in the kitchen. When I got there your grandmother met me, distraught. It was later than I knew, nearly half past nine; and you had been crying for me ever since dark, kept asking was I dead? (you had heard the word from Grainger—that was some of his *word*; had you scared you were orphaned). They had tried everything they knew and failed to calm you; so your grandfather had gone out, hunting me down. I calmed you, no trouble; and told Mrs. Hutchins that I'd been in the country and had had a flat tire. We three were eating supper in the kitchen when he came. He had found my car parked in town and asked questions; somebody told him they had seen me on the bridge before dark with Fitts Simmons, and he'd gone there to check. Must have passed me walking back, but neither of us noticed. He had known of Della's visit and thought that I had; thought I'd come there to see her and had met her several times in the previous days (he had just asked her cousin if she'd seen me at all, not for any details). So with you in the high chair, all spotty at my elbow, he let us both have it. I was nothing but a nigger-loving, ass-sniffing drunk who with your help had killed all he loved in the world. I didn't want to scare you two times in a day; so I asked him if I could just finish my supper—he had not said to leave; I doubt he meant us to. He walked out in silence and sat on the porch. She apologized to us, said she hoped I understood what Rachel meant to him and how sad he'd been. I told her I understood every single feeling any human ever had (I had had it before him); what troubled me was not under-standing but excusing."

"How soon did we leave?"

"Soon as I got us packed. I finished my supper and took you upstairs and put you in pajamas and folded our things. When we got back down to the foot of the steps, she was waiting there for us with food in one hand and a lamp in the other; they didn't have lights. She whispered 'Step here' and led us back a little to the foot of the hall, the shut door of his room. I said, 'No ma'm, I won't speak to him'; and she whispered again, 'He is still on the porch.' Then she opened the door and pulled us in. He had moved in there alone before I knew Rachel, but I'd never passed the door. It was big and pitch-dark except for her lamp. She went toward a corner; and we followed her over through a smell thick as grease—old cloth, old medicine, all clean and dry as sand. Where she stopped was a dresser with a dark high mirror and a brown marble top. He had made a little shrine—several pictures of Rachel, her ivory comb, a petrified flower (most likely from her grave), a book she had used (*Evangeline*, her favorite). Mrs. Hutchins never spoke, never touched a single object but held the lamp steady. So I turned and got us out."

"Did we tell him goodbye?" Hutch said.

"Just the word. He was on the porch as she'd said, at the corner; so he saw us coming out. She was helping with the luggage; he didn't lift a finger. When I'd got us all ready and told her goodbye—she was dry-eyed but wor-ried; she said she would write and that things would calm down—I called out to him, 'We thank you, Mr. Hutchins' and he said 'Goodbye.' I think you may have waved; you were very strong on waving."

Hutch waited awhile, then said "I don't remember."

"What?"

"None of it really. But his room—that's funny. You'd think I'd have kept that, remembered that much."

"You do," Rob said. "You did once at least."

"When?"

"A year or two later. I was still in Fontaine, still working for Kennerly, eating his meanness. I came home one evening from estimating timber. I was studded with ticks—always fascinated you; I would strip and let you count them, but you'd never touch one—and Rena had gone down to get the scalding water (I would sit in the tub, she would pour water on me, ticks would float like corks). I was still upstairs and you were still with me, counting—thirty-some was the record—and then you said, 'Rob, I need a picture of Rachel.' You'd never asked to see her; of course I had pictures, but I kept them wrapped up—they were still too painful. I said 'Why, Son?' and you said, 'For a show. I can make a penny-show like the one we saw of Rachel!' Somebody had made you a penny-show that spring, Sylvie maybe; dug a cradle in the ground and lined it with flowers, put a toy or two in it, laid a pane of glass on it, and hid it under dirt. For a penny you would sweep it clean and show your little treasure. You'd remembered pretty clearly up till then at least."

Hutch was silent.

"There are several pictures of her—Rena's got some, even Grainger; I have got one in our room in my grip right now. You can have it any time. I was trying just to spare you."

Hutch said, "All right, sir. Thank you. No real hurry though." Then he sat up slowly to face the black water. It was in a brief trough of calm, quiet as a pond; but it still gave a steady glow of light to eyes as open to the night as Hutch's now. Its horizon showed, a line curved downward at the ends like brooding wings. Day was far ahead though, still six or seven hours (Albert fighting now in daylight or dead or buried). Rob had stayed flat beside him; they had not touched since lying here. Hutch clasped his own hands. "You mentioned a bridge."

"When?"

"In speaking of Della. You called her a bridge."

Rob thought back to there. "Not Della herself but the welcome she offered."

"Letting you touch her?"

"It's a good deal more than that; it's all in your mind or eighty percent." He tried to see Hutch. "You know that by now."

"Maybe so," Hutch said. But he held the reins closely. "You also broke the promise after I was born and lived."

"I said I did, yes."

"Even after asking me."

"Hutch, by then I was a grown man scrambling to live. You were still a plain infant."

"I'm not blaming," Hutch said, "—not now, just asking. This is my first chance."

Rob knew that it was and waited in place.

"I mainly need to see how you've lasted; lasting worries *me* now. You've mentioned these bridges. They're years ahead of me if I want them at all."

"Son, I said they were bridges; not the only road."

"Name some others."

"People's jobs; many people live to work—my father, Rena's garden, Sylvie standing at the stove. That has been my great lack; I can see that now, twenty years too late. Or protecting a home with your wife and children in it and a good tin roof. Or comforting your parents when they get toward the end. Or hunting fat quail."

"You've lacked all of those."

Rob waited. "Yes I have."

"I thought you had *me*," Hutch said. "All this time. I thought I was standing in my room like a magnet, or reading at school or back in the woods, to hold you true and draw you to me. I thought you wanted that, thought you told me you did when you left me at Eva's."

Rob said, "I did. Son, it's taken this long. Raleigh seems close to you, two hours away; but I've had ten years of my life to wade through. I may be ready now; I told you that and you turned it down flat."

"No sir," Hutch said. "You are not being fair. You didn't say *me*; you said Fontaine, a house holding Grainger and Min Tharrington. If I've been the bridge to that, it wasn't what I meant—not to mention what I hoped."

Rob said, "I know that. But you've been a child, Hutch. What you hoped were child's hopes, you and me on a kind of safe boat in warm water. I've had my share of child's hopes all my life. I've tried to tell you that; they have damn nearly choked me. They're the only hopes that *are*. So I've tried to root them out. Now I'm trying just to live, one foot before the other. And I've asked you to help me. I've asked to help you."

"But with Min looking on. She has been the main bridge."

"Far from it," Rob said. "More the other way round. I have borne Min up since she was your age. She chose to love me when we were both children just for reasons of her own. I used her like dirt; she was none of my need. She tried to go her own way; I went off with Rachel. You know all that. Then when we were back at Mother's—'33, '34—and me a cowed dog, Min took her last hope and kept me close company the whole of both summers. I was very grateful to her—thanks will bind you to people more strongly than love— and I got used to her, her gentle steady help."

"Like Della? Della's help?"

Rob waited that out. "Min is still living, Hutch. We could hurt her past healing, just by talking here tonight. I can say this much; we never harmed a soul, Min and I, in anything."

Hutch said, "I think there were souls you never asked."

Rob could not answer that.

And Hutch had nothing else, no question, no blame. He lay back again in the sand and was still; and in three or four minutes, the long weight of day had pressed him to sleep. He breathed, slow and high, mouth open to the world (another Mayfield trait).

Rob also was still and nearly exhausted but calmer than he'd been since before Forrest's death. His only conscious worry, no worry at all, was that now they must stand and walk all the dark way back to their beds. Something brushed his right arm, surely Hutch. He raised slightly and bent toward Hutch—no, sleep: the slow pendulum of rest devoured with the urgency of hunger. Rob brushed his touched arm. A sand crab maybe? They were buried in night, as native to here as any blind crawler; but one another's own, one another's only mate in the swarm of strange feeders. Rob bent farther down till Hutch's breath brushed him, their only touch; and he said, half-whisper, "I am asking you now."

Hutch gave no response.

"I'm asking you to tell me."

The warm breath paused an instant, caught like a cough. Then with no other sign that he'd waked, he said "I will."

"What now?—you and me."

A sizable wait with no sound of breathing. Then Hutch, clear and natural—"We would go on from here, never go back home; but we'd let them know. We would stop first in Goshen. You could keep yourself hid; but I would see my grandfather, see Rachel's grave. I owe myself that; I owe her that. I could pay what I owe or show I meant to try—a good kind life. Then I'd come back to you; and we would go on farther up in the mountains till we came to a town that we'd neither one seen and where nobody knew us. We could change these names. You could get a job there; why would you need a job? We could sell what we brought and rent an old house and grow our own garden. We could watch each other, really watch all day. I would learn a good deal."

Rob said "What about night?"

"First, we'd be tired by night. But with any strength left, we could take long walks, steep climbs over rocks high up to clear air. There are more planets

there; you can see more planets, make guesses about them. We would sleep
out a lot." Hutch stopped and thought. "It would be like that whole years at
a time."

"War and sickness?" Rob said.

"We'd take them if they came; but we'd both be healthy, and I doubt
there'd be a war, not after this one's over, maybe fifty more years. We could
both die there."

"Our people?" Rob said.

"They've lasted through worse. They would barely miss a day, Grandmother and Rena. I know Sylvie wouldn't; she would feel simplified. Grainger
might miss us; but then he might not—Gracie might come back, and he'd
have her to tend." That seemed the whole vision; Hutch offered no more.

And Rob knew of no questions. He lay back for one last time before rising, the forced walk to bed. But he said "What for?"

"Sir?"

"What would it be for? Why would we do that? What would we be winning?"

Hutch waited through the break of three slow waves. "The thing we
want."

Rob quickly thought "What?" again but held it, didn't say it. He knew
that he knew. He said "Yes sir."

Hutch was uphill from him by maybe a foot. He rolled down silently and
stopped against Rob. Then he raised himself on straight arms and moved
above Rob. Then he lay down on him full-length, full-weight, the way Rob
had lain on him many times—most recently a day ago at Eva's in their room:
the room where Rachel and Rob had made him, in which he had learned
(been given by them, warm funnels of the past) what he knew so clearly of
hunt and capture, hunger and food, work and sleep.

Rob bore him gladly for longer than he knew—not thinking of Hutch,
who seemed all safe, or of Min still waiting for simple word, or of Eva, Rena,
Grainger, his dead father, Polly, his own vague future or of mute helpful
Della with her accurate dreams but of Sylvie's Albert in the cold Norman
dawn (maybe colder himself, all word now delivered) and of Flora's Bo still
poised in Beechleaf for the death Jesus willed him. They did seem spirits,
though stout, dark, and glistening with earthly sweat, emerging toward him
and his growing son with word of strength, sufficient pardon, the promise of
hope. Rob prayed his prayer for them.

The long way back, they were all but silent, knowing nothing was cured—
nothing planned or settled—but already partly rested and pleased.

JUNE 10–13, 1944

Against Polly's protests, Rob had helped her clear supper and sat in the hot kitchen now while she scraped up and drew her dishwater. It was well past nine. He and Hutch had come at seven from their two days of looking (Yorktown, Williamsburg, Jamestown); and Hutch had gone straight up from table to bed, suddenly exhausted from newness and the sun. Rob was also tired—hours of poking round ruins and reconstructions, dead-weight on his feet—but as often in the past, the air off Polly trimmed his strength to attention, curiosity. Still he waited in silence, not wanting to quiz her on their multitude of problems. Let her find their way and show it.

She washed all the glasses before she spoke. "I hadn't heard that much about Pocahontas since Grainger was young. He was hipped on her somehow; and we never heard the end, till he left at least."

Rob said, "He still is and has passed it on to Hutch; Hutch can tell you everything about her down to her height."

Polly washed on awhile. Then she said, "Wonder why. I've always kind of blamed her."

"How's that?"

"For her life. Here she was, this pretty child—great king for a father, woods as far as you could walk, deer as tame as house plants—and she left her own people and sold it all away to a crowd of English crooks that turned it into this." She gestured round widely with her wet left hand—the space beside her.

Rob smiled. "But for *love*. It was love, Miss Polly. We were founded on love."

Again she took her time. "Then we ought to beg pardon and give it all back, call the deer in and say 'Graze here in peace' and go drown in the James."

"The James wouldn't hold us."

"Then the blue ocean would. It's a few miles east."

Rob studied her back, then laughed. "Good night!"

She looked round to face him. "I'm serious," she said. "It *must* have been for love, some pale white fool; and see where it got her (homesick in cold England, smallpox at twenty)—see where it got us." She waved round a second time as if this kitchen where she'd lived since a girl, a room only some one hundred years old, were the ruined world.

Rob did not try to answer.

So she turned to work. "I'm sorry," she said. "I meant to be cheerful; I promised myself I would meet you, all smiles. It's just that I've had time to study here lately—oh I've had it all my life; any woman minus children has a good deal of time—and all I can see is what a waste people make, choosing up like they do."

"Pocahontas or me? Are you speaking of me?" Rob spoke in earnest now.

"Yes both," Polly said, "but mainly Polly Drewry, Miss Margaret Jane Drewry."

"Why?"

She didn't turn again but she said, "You've got eyes. I had my own place that my mother died to give me; I could have stayed there."

Rob barely understood. "Washington, you mean?"

Polly nodded. "But I sold it, gave it up that easy"; she snapped a wet thumb.

"Now you've got this place."

"I haven't, no."

"I wrote you, Polly, and I told you in April; nothing I or Hattie or Hutch could ever do will half-repay all your goodness to Father."

"I came here before him."

Rob said, "I know that. It's part of our debt."

"How much do you know?"

"Ma'm?"

"You say 'I know that.' Just say what you know."

"—That you worked here for Grandfather, nursed him at the end; that you made a home for Forrest when Mother turned on him, helped him have his good life."

She had turned to hear that, her washing half-done. Now she drew her hands from water, carefully dried them, came to the table, and sat beside him. Through all that followed she cupped a salt cellar in her long red hands and made little swirls in the salt with a finger, eating the white grains in moments of pause. "Is that what you know? Be honest now."

Rob said "Yes"—it virtually was; all else had been guess. "You told me that first time I ever came here."

"There's a little more," she said. She watched her own hands, did not face him (he watched the clean crown of her head, still chestnut though striped with gray). "I started years ago, well before you were born. I came here from home for what I figured was love. It may have been that. You never saw Rob. Even sick, he was a magnet—to me anyhow (and a good many others; all before me, I can brag). And he may have loved me. He died there beside me in the old store room"; she pointed behind her. "That was our bedroom. Well, for what *that* meant; you can die in the street. What I'm sure of—he was grateful. Then your father came to get him, take care of the funeral. I mentioned that to you, as you say, the first time. I think I told you Forrest had his job here already; that wasn't quite true. He got it right then, morning after the funeral, February twenty-fourth, 1905. I had been here with Rob by myself three days— him lying in his bed; I kept the fire low—so you can imagine I was nearly worn out when Forrest turned up and made the arrangements. A very small funeral, just us and the preacher and one old stranger. Forrest had wanted to put it in the paper; but I warned him against it, knowing Rob had debts and a few ill-wishers who might seize the chance. Still this fellow turned up, short and red as a stove (and the grave all but frozen). We didn't speak to him, but he stood through the service; then he came up to me and smiled and was crying. He said 'Do you know me?' I said 'No sir.' He said, 'I am Willie Ayscue, Rob's fireman from the railroad days when we used to come to Bracey, your mother's hotel. I knew you from the start, same time as he did; I knew you would last him.' I didn't understand, I honestly didn't; but Forrest did and took over then, thanked the old fellow kindly (he'd been asked by the preacher as Rob's oldest friend; they had been boys together). He had thought I was Anna, Rob's wife, your grandmother; she'd been dead something like twenty years by then. I was eighteen myself, though I did look older. When we got back here, I cooked Forrest a meal; and right at this table, he looked up and said, 'If I come here for good, how long could you stay?'—'Well, for good,' I said; and it turned out I did. Till now anyway."

"No for good," Rob said.

Polly looked up at last and managed to smile. "I thank you," she said. "You've been more than kind. In all these years you've treated me like I was right to be here. But Rob, I'm not begging a roof for my age."

"I know that," he said. "You've got it, always had it. Hatt will say that too once I've had a chance to see her."

Polly nodded. "I have no doubt she will, and I'm grateful to all, but I doubt I can stay."

"Why?"

She searched his face. "Have you thought about this? Rob, think about this—I was here forty years with two men who saw that, however I *felt*, I never once *lacked*. I've taken in sewing sometime to stay busy, a lot since April; but I've never spent three seconds worrying for money. Now that has to start."

"No it doesn't."

"It does." She was smiling but firm. "I'm fifty-eight now; I could live thirty years. I could outlive you and Hutch and Grainger; my dad lived to eighty-six, and I'm much like him. These are hard times, I know, for you and most men; and even if they weren't, I couldn't draw on you—not yet anyhow, not till I'm blind and down."

Rob said, "It's my pleasure to do what I can."

"Don't tell yourself that till you've done it for years. I know what I'm saying, and you don't yet; *pleasure*'s not the word. No if I'm lucky I'll keep my strength for fifteen years or so, my working strength. So I plan to be a nurse, just a practical nurse, somebody's companion. People still need those and it answers my needs, but it also means I won't need a house. I'll either live in with the people I nurse or get a small place—one room suits me nicely; I like walls close round me."

Rob said "What's left in Washington?"

"Nothing, not a hair. The U.S. Government. By the time Dad died, he was on public pension (and the check Forrest sent him, fifteen dollars a month) so no that's out."

"Come to me and Hutch." Rob had not planned to say it and at once chilled slightly but kept it from showing.

Polly laughed. "Three of us in one room in Raleigh?"

"I've got to leave Raleigh. I wrote you that."

"Can you go to Fontaine? You mentioned work there."

"I can *go* there, I guess. I looked into that; the shop job was open." He was starting to tell her of Forrest's plea to Throne but wondered if the premonition of death had issued in similar precautions for Polly, plans for her future. No sign it had, not to Rob anyhow; so he held that back. "Can I stay there though? Mother's there in full sail, Aunt Rena gazing at me, Grainger grudging me breath. Hutch is begging to leave, says I dumped him down there and left for my fun. You know how much fun—"

"Where is Min in this?" Polly said, "—anywhere?"

"Very much in the middle." Then he knew that was wrong. Min was out at the rim where he'd posted her, to wait his call. "That's another thing," he said. "I've got to decide. Min has been good to me through thick and thin, mainly thin; and I've used what she had. It's eased me at times; but it's harmed me too, and now I must tell her to come for good or go."

"How has she harmed you? I can't picture that."

"She has kept Rachel's memory raw, never healed."

"How? I thought Min was gentle the time I met her."

"She is," Rob said. "She's as good a soul as you." In fourteen years he had told only Grainger of his meeting with Min in a Richmond hotel just before Rachel's death—Grainger and, this week, Flora's cracked Bo. He could tell Polly now, of all living women, and bear her quick pardon; she would pardon it surely, brush it off with a hand that had brushed things as heavy a far safe distance. When he looked up to tell her, she was facing him though, upright, waiting calmly. Her broad worn face—still damp from work, still burning in her flat seamed cheeks with the life that had forced her this far through the shames she had eaten and would haul her far onward—her face crushed his heart. She was still here waiting, still ready to serve. How could any man have borne to share space with her, to see each day—and offend— that face, with its grave health and hopes as fragile as shell (but daily reborn)? He said, "Polly, listen. I was not made for life, not the life people want."

Polly smiled. "You fooled me."

"Really. Listen. I wasn't. I may have known it always, but now I can see it."

"What life do people want?"

Rob laughed in protection. "The one you've had; you and Forrest, forty years."

Her smile survived but she said "God help them." When Rob didn't answer she said, "No I guess it was some above average; I try to think that. What do you mean you don't want it?"

"I want it, yes Jesus. No I meant I couldn't take it. Something's set wrong somewhere in my training or blood; it *costs* me too much. I can sit here with you, see you lonely and strong, know you've had a full life; but you know what I feel?—like running forever, like standing up here and bolting through that door and running through night and day till somewhere I reach a place as bare as my hand, not a person left to face me. You and Hutch, my mother's kin, Aunt Hatt, Grainger, Gracie—Hell, children in the road: I can hardly bear to see you. I have got a heart as tender as a baby's blue eye—"

"No you're scared," Polly said.

"—It must have come from Forrest; Eva's still as strong as you."

"No it didn't," Polly said. "He could bear anything. He bore, as you say, living here forty years and letting me serve him. He bore his own death—knowing of it far ahead; the doctor said so—and never warned me, never made one arrangement to see me through this. He was strong all right."

"And he knew you were. He didn't want to grieve you with maybe false warnings. He knew you could stand anything that happened, and he knew I would see you were honored and thanked."

"By being left high and dry alone in this house? I know you mean well, Rob; but that is plain torture. You can kill me tonight if that's your plan."

"No'm, it's not." He smiled.

"Well, I've told you mine. Once you've gone through his papers and made your arrangements, for the house and all—I'll gladly help with that—then I mean to start over. A little place, a job. I may have a life yet." She stood at the end of that and went to the sink. She was well into finishing her dishes before Rob spoke again.

"You didn't find a will then or any instructions?" At the funeral he had been so stunned by regret that when Polly had said, "Will you look through his papers?" he had said, "Please let me just wait till June; it will wait till then." But seeing her face, he had opened Forrest's desk and checked the obvious places—a great many rollbooks, a notebook of his poems, a lifetime of letters (or the ones he had saved, none of them from Eva); no sign of a will or a letter of wishes.

Polly said, "You saw the desk. I haven't opened that; that was his one place. I have checked his bureau, since I always stacked his clothes, and the shelf in his wardrobe. I searched my own room from ceiling to floor; he would sometimes leave me notes I would find days later, little gratitudes for things. But no not a word." She dried the last skillet; then she turned in place. "He didn't write to you?—any warning, I mean."

"No ma'm, just the news, the present daily news."

"I've wondered this," she said. "I may be foolish. Do you think he wrote to Grainger?"

"I doubt it," Rob said. "He never wrote to Grainger, maybe sometimes at Christmas. Why would you think that?"

"Forrest loved him," Polly said. "He thought he was responsible for Grainger somehow. He encouraged Grainger as you well know; then because of me, he dropped him. So he brooded ever after."

"I never really knew the whole story of that—Grainger came here with Forrest in 1905?"

"And stayed six months, helping fix up the house. He had his own room, your grandfather's room. Forrest wouldn't sleep there but stayed in the study then and moved me upstairs. He got a little spending money, bought himself books; and when fall came and Forrest started teaching Negro classes, Grainger'd go out and sit through every word he said. But he never liked me—Grainger, I mean. I had addled his dream. He thought he had found a real gold mine in Forrest, a kind white father or brother or something that would need him forever and give him a home."

"I doubt he wanted money."

"I don't mean he did. By *gold* I meant care, just care. All *I* wanted. Before long he saw I was cared for too, and he turned on me."

Rob said "How?"

"Oh at Christmas. I have always dreaded Christmas. You get too expectant; it never lives up or *you* never do. Anyhow it was Forrest's first Christmas here, my first since Rob died; we were both a little sad and felt we needed calm (he had told your Aunt Hatt he would come there for New Year). So well ahead of time, he called Grainger in and said he knew Grainger was missing his people and should see them for Christmas—either make the trip to Bracey to his old ancestor or all the way to Maine. Forrest offered him the ticket; he refused it right off, saying he had a home and Maine was too cold. Forrest meant to stop there, but I guess I must have pressed him. He had been rude to me since the day he came; treated *me* like the brown one (I washed his underclothes the first week or so till I said I just couldn't, and Forrest took them out to a woman at the school). He barely spoke to me, but he showed what he thought—they are first-rate *show-ers*—sitting round with that ring. You know about that?"

"Grainger's ring?"

"*Your* ring by all natural rights. Yours and Hutch's beyond you. It was your Grandmother Mayfield's wedding band. She had left it to Forrest. When Forrest found his father, he brought him the ring—some idea of his he had dreamed in a poem—but Rob wouldn't have it; said give it to Grainger. You know he was joking; but never trust Forrest to recognize a joke. He gave it to Grainger, who wore it like a leech. Anyhow Forrest told him he would have to leave for Christmas, that I needed a rest; so Grainger chose Bracey (he would never go to Maine; once he left he couldn't bear to think he had a real father who was not Forrest Mayfield). I packed him a lunch, and Forrest took him to the station. When they got to the colored cars and Forrest said goodbye, Grainger wouldn't shake his hand. He stepped back and took off the ring and held it out. Forrest asked him why was that. He said, 'For Miss Polly. She think it's hers.' I had never said one word about that ring to Grainger—or God. Forrest said, 'It's not hers'—he told me all this (his famous soft heart)—'I gave it to you.' Grainger still held it out; so Forrest said, 'Just throw it on the tracks yonder then.' That brought him to his senses, and he put it in his pocket. If he wore it after that, I at least never saw it; never saw him though. I never saw him again till you brought him back; he stayed in Bracey, pouting. When I saw that ring, it was on Gracie's hand. I guessed it at once, but I didn't ask Forrest. I waited till a day when I was over helping Rachel upholster a stool, and Gracie stepped in once when Rachel stepped out. I said to her, 'Gracie, I admire your ring.'—'Me too,' she said.—'It looks like an old one' (it was broad and thick, heavy). Gracie said, 'Bound to be. It come from Old Misery,' which I knew meant Grainger. She left that month, ring and all, last time."

Rob said, "There are lots of broad bands in the world."

Polly said, "I know that." She smiled. "I've noticed that. But if you ever see Gracie Walters again, you tell her to let you see hers. Engraved inside it will say 'Anna Goodwin from Rob Mayfield' not 'Gracie from Grainger.'"

Rob was exhausted; the day fell on him. He pushed back his chair and braced himself to rise. "I won't ever see her, and Grainger won't either."

Polly came to the table and wiped it with a rag. "I saw her last week."

"Where?"

"Here. This room. I see her every year or so. She comes back to Richmond; some kin of hers here over past the old icehouse, a cousin, Gladys Fishel. She begs a day's work, and I try to give it to her if Forrest is at school." Polly spread her rag before her and pressed it with her palms, then folded it neatly as dry Irish linen. She'd done it ten thousand times in this house. "It helps with her wine. I tell her the news, what little I know. She never mentions Grainger—just Rachel, you, Hutch. She asks for all of you."

Rob said, "Did you tell her we'd be here now?"

"No I didn't, didn't know."

Rob nodded. "Thank God."

Polly said, "You're dropping. Let me turn down your bed."

Rob said "Oh yes."

2

Rob stood at Forrest's desk while Polly turned back the fresh sheets of the cot.

"Rob, you're welcome to *my* room. I can sleep here fine; this is good for my back." She thumped the felt mattress.

"No ma'm," Rob said. "This will be old times. I slept here the first time I found this house." He saw in the quick assurance of her hands, folding, smoothing—even now this late—the willing skills of a life at work in its only home, in actual harness. To what? And why? He said, "Polly, why are you doing this?"

She didn't look back. "Doing what?"

"Caring for me; big supper, this bed."

"I work here," she said; but her voice was pleasant.

"I'm serious," he said.

She stood and looked toward him. "Rob, are you drinking?"

"No ma'm."

"Are you sick?"

"No I'm curious," he said.

"What about?"

"What I asked you," he said. "Do you really care if I live or die?"

She sat on the edge of the bed, at the foot. "I don't understand what you're after, Rob."

He sat on the desk by the picture of Eva and himself age five. "Just this," he said. "I would really like to know. Why would any grown human, any crawling child, spend a minute on me? Don't answer with praise; I can't use that. Say truthfully why you can sit here with me."

"I've known you twenty years. Why not?" Polly said.

"Because I only amount to this"—he rubbed his chest with his flat right hand—"a nice-hearted former boy (except if you cross him) who had a good face till his nature showed through it some ten years ago, whose mind and talents are little over average, who has never propped any other human ten yards on their way through life since he can't be leaned on (he drinks under pressure, so has lost three jobs of the four he has held, not counting family handouts) and has come up now at forty years old with less good credit on *anybody's* books, Lord Jesus included, than most drunk Negroes with a long razor scar laid out in the road come Sunday dawn."

Polly smiled quite broadly.

"That's true," Rob said. "A fair description."

"Maybe so," she said. "I won't dispute you." Her smile didn't fade.

"What's funny?"

"Not much."

"You're grinning," Rob said.

"No I'm answering you."

"Then say it," Rob said. "I won't guess right."

She said it to the white summer quilt she sat on, unable to face him. "You're the thing that's left of what I had."

3

The next morning, Sunday, Rob and Hutch slept late; ate a big long breakfast; then in early afternoon set out to see Richmond, ending up downriver at James Institute. School was out for the summer; so they saw nobody whom Rob remembered but went to Forrest's office (Rob had always had a key) and checked his desk there—only neat piles of good student-work from past years and more class-rolls back to 1905 (several hundred Negro boys, some now old men whom he'd read poems at—had they called him a fool; and if so, did they still? had he known or cared?). There were some good books, one box full maybe, and his white bust of Byron. They would come for them later, give the rest to the school. Hutch asked for the Byron.

Then they went back to Polly, ate a light early supper, and took her downtown to see *Cabin in the Sky*. Then they bought ice-cream cones and window-shopped awhile before heading home to help Polly wash the cold dishes which she'd dreaded to leave. They listened to the nine o'clock radio news—Germans claimed to have captured fifteen hundred Allies—and turned in early. Rob would start his chores on Monday.

It rained about eleven which cooled the house nicely; and Rob was able to slide under then, a deeper sleep than any he'd been given in months, a slow dark stroking through cool thick waters. Toward dawn he dreamed this. He was walking through a field near the ocean in France. There was high summer grass that reached to his waist and made him feel safe, though the day was still and the war itself seemed a distant dream from which he'd escaped by skill and strength. He had a destination or his body did. It bore him straight forward; he didn't think to *where?* He was not hungry, not thirsty; clothes were clean; he did not need sleep. A woods loomed ahead, cool shade. He went toward it. A girl came out and started to him through the grass. At first he'd never seen her; then her skin and hair resolved—Della, still coming toward him. He stopped; Della stopped maybe six feet away. He told her her name; she nodded agreement. "You safe here?" he said. She nodded she was, then held up her left hand—"I got my protection. My ring you give me." He saw the gold band, freshly cleaned, on her finger and felt that it had some right to be there; but he said to himself, "I gave you nothing; you'll die before night." The war was all round them.

4

At ten, after breakfast, he saw Hutch to the bus stop for a day in town—the Confederate museum, Hollywood cemetery, another show, the stores. Then he came back and shaved and was ready to work through Forrest's desk when Polly brought the mail, one for Hutch from Grainger, one for Rob from Min. He let Polly go, then sat at the desk to read it.

June 10, 1944

Dear Rob,

You didn't believe me. I knew you wouldn't. You were wrong not to, this time anyway. I meant every word and have meant them some months now, longer than I realized. I can't wait, no (and it's can't not *won't). I won't lie either; there is no other person or thing in the wings. There is just my long-delayed understanding that what I've been to you has been hardly unique and that, however much I believe you when you thank me, I know that any number of women could have done the same service and got the same pay.*

I'm humiliated, Rob. Or I've seen this spring, more clearly each day since your father's death and our trip to the funeral, that I've been humiliated most of my life. I'm not blaming you; I volunteered for it. (If you want a little blame, take thirty percent.) All I hope you can do now is try to understand that it's fairly bleak for a woman near forty to look back and see that the force of her life has been pressed against someone who really didn't want that force at all, however he took it. I also feel foolish. Just understand that please.

I understand it all. That is my worst trait; I see all sides. I know that your own life has had its troubles, not all of your making; and I well comprehend your present resolve to concentrate on Hutch and see him through the slow woes of adolescence. But I also know how Hutch resents me, and I see why clearly. He would not let us be, even if you were ready.

Someday you may be; you are still saying that. But remember, Min's not. And honor that please. Just leave Min alone for a long time to come. Maybe years from now we could sit on a porch and talk it through again—weigh it one more time, find it wanting once more—but for now I mean to rest, just do my job and eat well, sleep long nights, and forget what a small part I played after all in this story you seem to be telling yourself called Rob Mayfield.

We will no doubt collide in Fontaine or Raleigh; I don't plan to dodge you. If you grin so will I.

> *Strongest good hopes, Rob, and thanks for what there was,*
>> *Min*

Regards to Miss Polly.

Rob thought he was relieved, consciously thought that he had not had such a great weight lifted since his Grandfather Kendal's death years before. He would answer her tonight, warm thanks and parting; then honor her plea for silence and absence. A *simplification*, whatever else. He laid Min's letter in the top of his suitcase, stood Hutch's on the mantel (and recalled he'd forgot to give him Grainger's gift, the goldpiece—well, something for tonight). Then he sat at Forrest's desk and began to search the drawers.

The letters had been carefully weeded and sorted into neat tied bundles, by correspondent. None from anyone in Fontaine; even Hutch's thank-you notes at Christmas and birthdays had been discarded, not a trace of Grainger. A few from Rob which he could not bear to read but identified by dates—the announcement of his wedding-plans, a note from his honeymoon, the long tale of shame and promised reparation which he'd written from Goshen when he and Hutch had gone there in 1933, two or three from Raleigh in 1939 begging small loans when Hutch was suffering asthma (the loans had come on payday by telegraph, but Eva had paid the doctor), a card in '42 saying only "Cheer up! I am too old to draft. Happy Father's Day from Rob." Then three sets from students—one a dentist in Portsmouth, a Bristol undertaker, an insurance man from Chatham: mostly writing once a year with their stiff news of births and deaths, their rising incomes, their formulas of thanks (script and grammar sliding steeply downhill with each year). Four large stacks from Hatt—surely none was missing: every penciled note pleading company, covering gifts (iced cakes mailed in tins, beaten biscuits, a ham once that streamed grease from Bracey to here). Only three from Polly—single thin letters: one to Forrest in Bracey in 1905, one to Goshen in November '25 (Rob's wedding), one c/o Stevens' Hotel in Asbury Park where he'd gone to a four-day Negro teachers' convention in August '29.

Rob could hear her overhead, the treadle of her sewing. He would take these to her; but lulled by her steady work and curious of her needs, he read the one to Goshen, nineteen years before.

November 27, 1925

Dear Forrest,

I doubt this will have time to even reach you but you said write so here I am. I am safe of course like I said I'd be but there was a little excitement this morning once you left. It was bright and dry still so about ten o'clock once I finished the sweeping, I rinsed a few clothes and was hanging them out when the Pittman girl came running down her steps and through your yard to ask could I come quick, her baby was going. You know he has had those hard convulsions, three in a year. I thought he was gone. He was laid out flat on the bare kitchen table with the cook holding on. Blue as indigo and twitching with his eyes rolled back. She had fed him some egg. Egg is poison to him. I guessed that before when he had the last one after eating pound cake. He was hot as a kettle. I said call the doctor and she said they had tried but couldn't get to him. They use Dr. Macon. So I said I know a good clean Negro doctor at James

Institute, do you want to call him? So she called Dr. Otis at the school and got him. Meantime all I knew was we had to break the fever. His head was scalding. I told the cook to draw me a sink of cold water and I stripped the baby right out of his suit like undressing a tree, he had gone that stiff, and commenced to plunge him in and out of that bath. In three or four minutes he was limbering up and his eyes were showing. I could see him sucking breaths. By the time Dr. Otis got there he was crying so I thought he would live. He said I did right, Otis I mean. He was giving him an enema when Dr. Macon came. I wish you could have seen Dr. Macon's face but he spoke to him nicely and called him Dr. Anyway they worked together and I came on home. I tried to eat my dinner. Then I tried to clean the stove. Then I broke down and boohooed for something like an hour. I thought it was for him being helpless and young and some of it was but it mostly was for me, I guess, and for joy. It was somebody else's trouble. I don't have to bear it and never will. Then I took my little nap and walked to the store and fixed a trash supper, a can of corned beef, and ate more than half! Now it's cooling off fast but I won't light a fire.

I hope you are fine. Before the excitement I worried all morning that I used mayonnaise in those sandwiches and that it would spoil on you and leave you in trouble. I trust you ate them early though and got through alive. If you did I know you'll have a big spread tonight. You are greatly missed here and will be till you're back.

Remember what you see and save it up for me. I have never seen a wedding. I hope you've told Rob my message already, a life of good help to each other forever as long as they last. He told me last summer the first time I saw him that he had two girls and who must he pick? I told him the strong one. Do you think he has? He will need that I know like the rest of the world.

This will not even reach you if you come back tomorrow. Till you do rest yourself, have a good birthday,

Very truly,
Polly Drewry

It reached Rob at least. He took up the envelope and saw what he'd missed; the Goshen address had been struck through once and, in Mr. Hutchins' hand, returned to Richmond. Forrest had been safely back here, surrounded, when this had come to him—a luxury of patient care so large as to stand like a picture of heart's desire, clear and attainable. Attained in this house for days at least, whole human days.

The noise of Polly's work went on above. Rob stood and walked to the study door and shut it. Then he sat again and tied Polly's letter in its bundle and reached for the picture of Eva and himself.

Surely they'd been a sad joke to Forrest, their pale last offer to wind his life again in numb coils of anxious perpetual need.

He laid them, still framed, in the bottom of Forrest's dry wicker wastebasket and buried them with two generations of letters—the Negroes', the family's, sparing only Polly's. He would keep those himself unless she should ask.

Rob worked through the morning on his father's business papers, old bills, paid checks, tax assessments on the house, five thousand dollars' worth of lapsed life insurance, a postal-savings account (sixty dollars). When he heard Polly come down to start a cooked dinner, he went in to ask her just to bring him a sandwich and a glass of tea. She brought it, no questions; and he worked on till four in the gathering heat. He searched the volumes his father read most (Vergil, the Psalms, Emerson, Browning, Woodrow Wilson's history of America). He even read quickly through the notebook of verse—some Latin translations, a few old laments for Eva and Rob (1904), musings about the purpose of teaching, a memory of his mother, a birth-poem for Hutch, a dozen clean limericks, but no clear word of care or concern for any survivor. No burdens either; the largest bill was for eighteen dollars, the early spring coal. Forrest Mayfield had had his life and had known it was ending; aside from the letter to Thorne Bradley, he'd departed in silence.

As Rob laid more dense bales of waste in the pile, this much came to him—*That is his last intention*. A perfect silence after long years of talk.

Yet he'd also intended that *someone* speak, had surely known that silence would force choice and action on his leavings. Polly and Rob. They had already spoken, to opposite purposes—Polly's aim to leave and work, Rob's easy munificence (a useless house).

Must he speak again now? There were two more choices—make her some further offer or accept her aim, move her out, lock the house, and hope to sell it. With any luck (as was, with no repairs), it would bring three thousand dollars. He could give Hutch a third, a third to Hatt, the rest to Polly—a nest egg to start her on the life she planned. She would never accept it. Then what?—abandon her at her present age to the mercy of life: a string of old cripples with bedsores and money enough to keep her in rented rooms for fifteen years till her own self failed her, then a charity home?

He'd asked her to live with Hutch and him, the rush of impulse two nights ago. She had not forced it on him; and he'd dropped it gladly, a load he wouldn't even have to shoulder, much less unload. But two days had held the proof of Forrest's silence and Min's final letter. He could stand now and find her (on the backporch, shelling peas) and say, "Miss Polly, I am begging this of you—come to me and Hutch." Hutch loved the long tales of a life which, however plain, she made seem crusty with vigor and riot; Rob bore her only gratitude. She'd simplify their lives.

But where? Not Fontaine. Even granting that he'd repossess the old Kendal place, he could not bring her there—Eva's nearness, Rena's spite, Grainger watching from the yard.

They could come to her, Richmond. He could hunt a job here, even beg again out at James Institute; say he'd sworn a new life since 1933, come back as a teacher. Failing that, a salesman, a clerk—anything. Men as young as he were scarce, and the war would last awhile. He would have this at least— a house that was his, his growing son in it, a woman who had known him for half his life and who might ease the rest.

Would she want that at all? Would she want more than that?—and wanting, would she ask? Could he find some human way to say that her needs were as useless to him now as the needs of a good horse, a good yard dog that has served for years? Where would he take what Min had given for a steady eight years?—what no child or woman near sixty could give but his own blind clamor would go on requiring?

She'd moved to the kitchen by then and was filling pans. Rob did a little sum—the fifteen-thousandth-odd supper she'd started in that one room. She was working alone but she'd always done that. Since old Rob's death, she had spent the best part of each day here alone, no real friend but Forrest. It was one of her elements; solitude and quiet, as strange a part of her strength as any other.

The front bell rang. Rob kept his place and let her go but listened through the door.

Polly said, "Was it locked? That's just my habit; old hermits love locks!"

Hutch said "So do I."

"Was the world still there?"

"Ma'm?"

"How was the world?" she said. "You've been out in it."

"Oh I liked it," he said.

"Come tell me then," she said. "I'm getting supper on." She started down the hall.

Hutch seemed to stay put. "Where is Rob?"

Polly said, "Still working in the study. You come help me. He'll be out directly."

So Hutch went with her, not pausing at the study.

And Rob sat to listen. Though the kitchen door was open, they were ten yards away; and their words came to Rob as no more than smoothed sounds, worn counters in a long cool game of contentment they were offering each other—flat rocks in a gully, slow bubbles in a pond. What had it been for?—the whole of Rob's life, all that this house had held (and the Kendal house and the Hutchins' hotel)—if not to have this and to go on having it? The far rounded voices of a woman and a child who wanted your presence and wished you well.

Rob admitted to himself that Forrest had no will, that tomorrow he must go to the clerk of court and investigate the handling of intestate remains—would he need to be bonded? would they bond a jobless man? would the final disbursement after all be his? He named the questions over as a gray bottom harmony to Hutch and Polly's chatter, but the questions rode him lightly. He stood from the desk and walked to Forrest's cot and fell asleep with ease.

5

Rob waited at the dining-room table for dessert while Hutch took dishes out to Polly in the kitchen. There had been a quick storm while he had his nap, and the windows bore in light cool air. Through the open door he heard Polly—"What did Grainger say?"

Hutch's voice was puzzled. "Ma'm?"

"Your letter from Grainger."

Rob had not thought to tell him. When Hutch had come in to wake Rob for supper, they had talked a few minutes (Rob groggy with sleep); then gone straight to eat. He called toward the kitchen now, "It's on the study mantel, Son. It slipped my mind."

Hutch came to the door and looked at him closely. "Did you read it?"

"No sir. That's a federal offense." Rob smiled.

Hutch didn't but continued to face his father, then turned and went through the kitchen to the study.

Polly came with lime gelatin and cold whipped cream, served it out in three bowls. She raised her voice—"Hutch?"

Rob said, "Let him be. He'll come when he's ready. Very touchy about mail. Eva's kept some from him; now he thinks I've started."

Polly said, "I'm sorry if I stirred up trouble."

"You didn't. Give him time."

But they ate on in silence and Hutch didn't come. When Polly offered more, Rob stood. "I'll go get him."

6

The study door was closed. Rob opened it, no knock. Hutch was over by the window, back turned, staring down. Rob stood in the door. "Grainger living?" he said.

Hutch nodded, not looking, and folded the letter.

Rob said, "Son, it's simple. I was dazed from my nap; I forgot you had a letter."

Hutch nodded again but still didn't turn.

"How are Mother and Rena?"

Hutch began to say "Fine"; then his throat stopped on him.

Rob thought "He's tired" and walked over to him, gripped both of his shoulders, and buried his own broad chin in the strong hair of Hutch's skull. Though the letter was folded, Rob could see it was Min's. Grainger's lay spread flat on the desk at their left, a neat half-page. Rob raised his chin and reached round and took the folded sheet, Min's ribbed blue paper. He took a step back, stuffed it into a pocket, and said "Are you glad?"

Hutch nodded.

Rob said "Answer."

"Yes sir," Hutch said.

"Glad of what?" Rob said. He was filling like a narrow pipe with anger; it reached his throat, a cold sour cud.

Hutch turned. "—That now you're alone." He'd recovered the strength of his voice and was calm. Or hidden at least; all feeling was blanked from his features by the force of his hidden purpose—harm or spite or plain embarrassment or, again, balked care?

Rob thought of all that but asked nothing further, afraid to know. He said to himself what he seldom remembered—"He's mostly Rachel's. She works deep in him."

Hutch said, "Can I have my money please?"

"What money?"

He pointed to Grainger's letter, touched a line near the end.

Rob was genuinely puzzled and bent to read Grainger's upright hand. *"You can either spend your money on something you like or bring it back and save it. Rob will tell you what it is and why I passed it to you. Then you can decide. Anyhow now you got it. If you meaning to save it let Rob keep it for you in his safe place. It is too old to lose."*

Hutch said "What money?"

Rob went to his bag and found the small box. He gave it to Hutch and said, "Can I read the rest of his letter?"

Hutch nodded. "All right."

Rob sat in Forrest's chair; Hutch sat on the cot to open his gift. Grainger said,

Dear Hutch,

Everybody here is fine and wanting you back but glad you got a chance to see the world. Remember it and tell me but I don't guess it changed much since last time I saw it.

Miss Rena was painting the yard chairs this morning and I was weeding round and when she got done she said did I want her to paint my house, she had some left. I said "You hadn't got nothing like enough" but she said she could paint the south side at least and cool it from the sun. So I told her yes and she painted it white. It's after supper now and it does seem cooler. Still smell it though. Miss Rena is a case.

No more news I guess. You write me a postal card and say how you doing and anything go wrong along the way, you sit down where you are and call Miss Eva and I will come get you. Night or day, count on it. Tell Rob the same thing. But have a good time.

You can either spend your money—

Rob faced Hutch, who'd quietly thumbed the coin.

"Is it gold?" Hutch said.

Rob said "Five dollars' worth" and held out his hand.

Hutch hesitated, then passed Rob the coin.

"Grainger gave this to me last Wednesday morning as we were leaving home. He wouldn't give it to you directly himself since, or so he said then, he didn't want to press you for thanks or returns. In fact he told me not to tell you but to change it and buy you something you wanted. I was planning on that."

Hutch said "Something changed his mind." His face had resolved to its usual transparency; a boy was behind it.

Rob said, "Me taking you away, that's what. Grainger knows you might like it; he's scared you might stay."

"In Richmond, you mean?"

"We own a house here."

"You mean this house?"

Rob smiled. "I didn't mean the state capitol." He rubbed his right shoe on the floor as a touch. "This was built by your Great-Great-Grandfather Mayfield—the first Forrest, anyhow the first known to me—in 1835, just him and two slaves. Then he found a wife for it."

Hutch had listened and nodded. Now he stood, reached out, and took back the coin. He sat on the cot again and said "Whose is this?"

"Yours, from Grainger."

"Whose was it back then?—1839?"

"It was given to Grainger by my father's father when Grainger was born, a good-luck piece."

Hutch calculated back. "That was 1892."

"People saved gold."

"Wonder where it had been all those years."

"In somebody's sock."

Hutch rubbed it for answers. "When was old Rob born?"

"Oh I don't really know. We could check on his grave. Or ask Miss Polly." He recalled Forrest's story of twenty years ago. "I know it was after this house was built; he was born in this house."

Hutch nodded. "That's it. This was his, don't you guess? Somebody gave it to him when he was just born, and he kept it for luck."

"Maybe so," Rob said.

"Why'd he give it to Grainger? Grainger lived in Maine."

"He knew Grainger's daddy and kept up with him." Hutch was facing him plainly, no sign of knowledge or pressure to know, though ready for a story if there were a story. So Rob started telling it. "Grainger was his grandson."

"Whose?"

"Rob Mayfield's."

"How did that happen?"

Rob smiled. "The way it always does; somebody laid down on somebody else. I don't know all that many facts about it; Forrest told me what I know. My Grandfather Rob moved from here up to Bracey and married a Goodwin; she had Hatt and Forrest. Then he messed with a Negro girl and she had Rover. When Rover got grown, he moved north to Maine and married up there and he had Grainger."

Hutch said "Why?"

"Why Maine?"

"No, messing with the girl. Why did he do that?"

"His nature. It seems he was a wheelhorse till T.B. curbed him."

"Was his wife still living?"

"Oh yes, lived for years."

Hutch said "Is that a sin?"

"A very common sin, Moses' seventh commandment."

Hutch said, "I don't understand. What you told me at the beach, that grown men want a girl who'll ease their life. Why would he want two?"

"More than two," Rob said, "—must have had a lot to ease." But he saw Hutch was earnest, still waiting on the numb puzzled far side of manhood. "Men and women are as separate as rabbits and cats. Just because we bear some resemblance to women—two eyes, two ears—and because women bear us, we think they are like us and have our needs. They don't, really don't—which is part of their beauty and most of their trouble. They know they're alone which men never learn (or way too late), and they set out as early as they can to hide—in a husband and children. They try to duck under, but men try to fight it. Once the woman is buried in all her work (and can barely see him), then he starts all over to hunt a way out. Or a way *through* at least."

"—Through to ease?" Hutch said. "Is it always ease?"

"No it's sometimes to harm her, to punish her for failing you, but yes mostly ease."

"And you never get to it?"

"For minutes, just minutes. I'm speaking for myself. And for my grandfather; maybe some have done better."

"Who?"

"Forrest—here maybe."

Hutch nodded, no question.

"Even old Rob maybe toward the end of his life."

"Did he ever see Grainger?"

"No."

"Does Grainger know this story?"

"Yes—or so Forrest told me. But in all these years with me, he never let on."

Hutch had repacked his coin in the box, retied it. "I think Grainger's eased. How is Grainger so peaceful?"

"What makes you think he is?"

"He just has his life out there in the yard. Never sees Gracie or anybody else very much but us. Never tries to harm people."

Rob had never thought it through. He took awhile now; then said, "Listen, Hutch, you'll never figure Grainger; do and you'll be a wiser man than me or Forrest. Father took him up, then dropped him—cut him to the quick—but never understood him no more than that doll." Rob pointed to the old bark doll on the mantel which he'd stood upright in a pause this morning. "*I* came along and Grainger took *me* up, really helped me out of misery for a while with genuine care; and I really meant to thank him, to give him a good home as long as I lived. But he'd married Gracie before I turned up and she changed things."

Hutch said "How?"

"She came back to him. She had run off once already when I met him. I never even saw her till the time I was married. He was with me in Goshen, and he'd begged and begged her back, and she came for the wedding."

"Why?"

"She always liked a big crowd, but that may not be why. I never knew her reasons, never gave them much thought. Anyhow there was Gracie, serving ham at the wedding—a good-looking tall girl with hair straight as yours—and she stayed two years. Came with us to Richmond and lived with Grainger and worked like a Trojan, was a big help to Rachel (who couldn't cool milk on her own at first). Then something broke in her or broke loose again, and she started drinking and vanishing nights."

Hutch said "Was it you?"

Rob said "Sir?" quickly before he really heard. Then he went hot in anticipation of anger but decided on patience. "Was it me *how* please?"

"Was it you broke Gracie?" Hutch's eyes were grave but curious not condemning.

Rob said "No sir."

"You didn't even touch her?"

"Not once." Then he smiled. "She touched me a time or two; she had strong hands and could work out a crick in your neck, a sore muscle. But no that was all and Rachel watched that."

"You didn't want to touch her?"

"I had Rachel, Son."

"You said men were different and would hunt other ways."

"Some men, I said. I didn't speak for all. I didn't speak for Grainger. He's lived minus women, minus anything but you and work for fourteen years. He's got his own strength."

Hutch said, "No but *you*; did you stay just with Rachel?"

Rob knew they were near the place he dreaded. Must they push on now?—arrive and see it clear, the tan square room where he'd failed once for all on Min, clenched and damp—or could he detour them, wait till Hutch had grown further toward his own needs and mercies? Eva, Rena, Min, Grainger, Rachel long dried to leather—they had all left him now, *had no further use*. Hutch was simply what he had; Hutch needed him awhile yet. He mustn't lie at least. Rob said, "All but once. One day in four years, part of one afternoon."

"But not with Gracie?"

"No." Rob was braced to answer the next and explain, to ask a child for the clean forgiveness no one else had given or ever could.

But Hutch said, "Then why has Grainger turned against you?"

Rob said, "Has he turned? I didn't think so."

"I do."

"Say why. Has he told you something?"

"One thing, several times in the past month or so—that some people leave you and some people stay, and that you should know which and lean on the stayers."

"Did he say I'd left?"

"No he never mentioned names."

"He could have meant Gracie."

Hutch nodded. "You and Gracie and Grandfather Mayfield; all his stories are about you, you and France in the war."

"Most of mine include him," Rob said. "We know each other. It's you he loves though. He has to love you; you have been there with him, and you're worthy of love. Now he's struggling for you; he sees you are leaving, sees he'll wind up with Sylvie grouching at him at breakfast and Rena whitewashing his south wall for coolness."

Hutch said, "He's a man. Why can't he change that?"

Rob said, "It's too late. Son, he bet on us; on Forrest, then me, and now on you."

"Bet us what?"

"What I've told you ever since we left Eva's, all I've really got to tell you about anybody—that we'd give him his home place, the few things he needed; that we'd do it all his life and that he would help us."

Hutch said "How?"

"The work he does, the company he gives us."

"Then he's won," Hutch said. "He's got what he wanted."

Rob nodded. "He's had it for three short spells—the few months with Forrest in a little house in Bracey when he was a boy, awhile with me in Goshen, this longer spell with you. Now he knows that's ending. You'll be leaving him soon, four years at the most."

"*You're* coming back, aren't you? Everybody wants you back."

Rob said "You don't."

Hutch smiled. "Now I do. It was Min I didn't want. Nobody wanted Min." He stood, the coin box in his closed left hand, and went to the mantel and reached for the bark doll.

Rob watched him—he seemed to have grown an inch today, a frightening speed in his size and knowledge—and waited for a new string of questions to come: who had made the doll and why? He tried to think ahead through what Forrest had told him—old Rob's last days, his family of dolls (and with Polly at hand, young, ready to serve) all burnt by Forrest but this one sample—yet his mind was stopped. The sight of that one boy's strong right hand making touch with an old man's desperate effort at help, the model of a father long powdered to dust, raised a panic of fear. A high wall of sadness, that he'd thought past coming, rushed toward him and fell. As Hutch turned to face him, Rob said, "*I* did. I still wanted Min. She helped me for years. None of you ever will." He took up his light coat and left the room, the house.

7

In the kitchen Polly overheard the end of Rob's speech and the front door slamming. She worked on a little and waited for Hutch; but when he didn't come, she dried her hands and went to the study door and looked.

Hutch was flat on the cot, eyes open, looking up. He didn't turn to face her.

"War over?" she said.

Hutch shook his head No.

Polly came to the desk and stood by Forrest's chair. Hutch's eyes were dry but his cheeks were pale. "You forgot your dessert. Looks like to me you need it."

"No ma'm," he said.

She was tired and should sit, but she'd never sat at Forrest's desk since that hard morning when Eva sent the picture of herself and Rob, and she'd opened it here and sat a quarter of an hour considering the depth of the wound sustained and her chances of continuance in this one place that was home to her then. She went to the foot of the cot and sat. Hutch drew in his bare feet to give her room; but she sat all the way back against the wall, then lifted his ankles and laid them on her lap. She hadn't borne his weight, any part of his weight, for eleven years. She had not, she knew now, borne the weight of a boy in all her life. Two full-grown men but never a boy; she had missed knowing boys. Her hands were beside her, not touching him now; and she didn't look up at his face at first but studied the smooth knees, the blades of the calves slowly furring with brown, to find more signs of the men she'd known in the boy they'd made. Nothing, none. A lean neat boy whose joints gave promise of height and grace (six, seven years from now) but no marks of old Rob or Forrest in sight—all Rachel's maybe? (she recalled Rachel's face but no other part). Finally she laid one palm on his dry skin. "You're growing while I watch you."

Hutch said "I hope so."

"Growing up to what?" she said.

"Ma'm?"

"You'll grow up to something if you live and keep eating. Have you planned on *to what?*"

Hutch waited a good while; then reached up above him, both hands overhead, as if to find and pull down a firm destination. Then he offered it to Polly. "Yes ma'm, an artist."

"Well, you'll need you a smock. I can make one tomorrow." His eyes cut to her, and she realized her error. "No I'm glad," she said. "My father was an artist."

"Did he make a good living?"

Polly said, "Pretty decent till Herbert Hoover struck."

"Have you got any pictures he painted?"

"Oh no he kept everything. It was part of his living. When I left him, he had his museum still; and the pictures were for that—soldiers dying, an Indian cutting a baby, a white woman screaming. They went with the museum when he gave that to an Alabama college. He learned it from his mother; she was Irish and smart—I descend from her! Have you got one of yours?"

"No ma'm, they're at home" (they were with him but secret).

"This is one of your homes. You could draw me right now."

Hutch raised his head and looked at her profile awhile. "You would be hard," he said.

Polly laughed. "All the wrinkles? You could leave them out. Imagine me a girl. I used to be one. Wrinkles didn't use to be here when you first saw me anyhow."

Hutch said "I don't remember then."

Polly waited. "I do. I do clear as light. I kept you whole weeks at a time when you were little. We were good friends then."

Hutch said, "I don't remember much before I was three."

Polly said, "You will. I mean it's there in you. You saw it all happen; it will rise up in time."

"When it does, will I like it?"

She laughed. "Oh a lot. We had good times. When your Grandmother Hutchins and Miss Rena had left, Rob would bring you by here as he went to work; and I'd keep you till evening."

"I thought I stayed with Grainger."

"You did sometimes. But Grainger had his hands full watching out for Rob—he stuck by Rob like a guard that year—so you came to me."

"Would I talk to you ever?"

"At first you were a baby, three, four months old. But eventually you did;

I taught you all you know! Really—Grainger and I. It used to worry Forrest that you talked like us. We were all in the kitchen one evening drying dishes (Rob had gone somewhere), and Forrest dropped a lid. You said 'God-dammit!' and Forrest nearly keeled over. But that came from Grainger; I only *praise* God." She squeezed his ankle, laughing.

And Hutch turned to smile. "What else would I say?"

"Oh a lot like that till Forrest set you straight (he brought you in here and read you a sermon on good words and bad). You liked for me to sing; you were always calling out from two rooms away, 'Polly, sing all you know,' meaning all my many songs—I could make up songs. I'd sing till I parched or you fell asleep." She stopped there and waited as if he might sleep again now and leave her.

He was watching her calmly, his head propped slightly on Forrest's felt pillow from Asbury Park.

"We weren't just jokers though; it wasn't all laughing. I thought it was my duty to remind you of Rachel. Nobody else would—Rob, Forrest, Grainger. They sealed her off from you and I understood why. But I'd come the same narrow road as you, lost my mother before I could see; so I made it my part to tell you little things about her when I could, when we were alone."

"Like what?"

"Her expressions, the words she'd use, the color of her hair; just a lot of little things."

"You'd think I would remember," Hutch said, "but I don't."

"Don't worry; it's in you. You could start running now and run sixty years; she would still be in you, controlling your feet."

Hutch said "Is that bad?"

Polly hadn't thought of that, but she did and answered truly. "Part *no*, part *yes*. Rachel was more full of hope than any other girl, worked harder than any other human I've known to make her hopes happen; to hold and please Rob, to bring you to life. Which was also her main fault—she hoped too much. She couldn't understand that the best people get is a few peaceful breaks; they don't get their wants. So she died from pure wanting. You will have to fight that."

Hutch nodded. "Rob's in me," meaning Rob worked in him as surely as Rachel.

Polly said "Where is he?"

"All through me, I guess."

Polly smiled. "No *now*. Where's he gone right now?"

At first Hutch seemed not to hear her at all; but since he lay flat, he stood no chance of concealing the water that pooled in his eyes. Still he tried not to blink and flush it down his temples. Polly watched him though; so at last he confessed his misery, blinked, and said "I'm afraid."

"What of?"

"That he is gone."

"Where?" Polly said.

"Anywhere, but for good."

Polly said, "I doubt it. What happened in here? What did Grainger say?"

Hutch said, "Not Grainger—Min Tharrington. Rob heard from her today that she wouldn't wait for him any more, so not to ask her. I saw the letter yonder on the desk and read it and told Rob I was glad."

"Glad of what?"

"That she'd left him alone."

Polly said, "I would think that you'd wish your father well."

"I do."

"But he's lonesome. He's drying up, Hutch."

"He's got me now; I'm old enough to help him. He's got you too; we could come here with you."

Polly sat on awhile; then she lifted Hutch's ankles and stood from beneath them. She went to Forrest's chair and sat and faced him. "No you couldn't," she said.

"Why? I want to; Rob has mentioned it."

"He's young," Polly said. "Forty's still too young to settle for this."

Hutch said "What is this?"

"A house with nothing but a young boy in it and a woman fifty-eight years old, played-out."

"We would love him," Hutch said.

"Not the right way," she said.

"What would be the right way?"

"Maybe Min's," Polly said. "I liked her when I saw her; she has surely stuck by him."

"So have I," Hutch said, "except when he left me."

"It takes touching, see. Every grown man I've ever known, except my funny daddy, needs some amount of that."

"I touch him."

"So could I"—Polly smiled at her hands—"but I won't. We're the wrong beasts, Hutch; too old, too young, misshaped to his purpose." Hutch was flat on his back again, facing the ceiling with his arms straight beside him; so she rose and took the one step and picked up the bark doll that lay by his hip. Then she sat and studied quietly, then said "You understand this?"

"—That it's Grandfather Mayfield's?"

"Great-grandfather's," Polly said, "—old Robinson's. He used to have several. When I came here to help him, he had a box full that he'd made in the months while he watched his mother die. He had names for them; said they stood for his people, different ones in his life—some white, some not, but all brown as bark. He wanted me to dress them, make suits of real clothes (I could sew then as good as I ever have since; I'm Singer's best friend). I told him that was crazy; that I had better work—this house was a buzzard's nest when I came here—but he said, 'Then just dress Mam and Pap.'" Polly shook the one she held—"He called this one Pap, the man that built this house. I said I'd dress his Mam, but I wouldn't touch this one. He said, 'Pap's the one needs dressing.' He'd made this doll of his Pap with a thing, a man's thing also carved out of bark and set on a little wire axle in the crotch so it could raise and lower. He thought that was funny, said it favored his Pap in every small way. I said it was the *big* way that I wouldn't touch; and he unwired the moving part, just carved this notch here to show it was a man; and I made him some breeches and a coat, long lost." Polly stood again and laid it on the cot by Hutch. "You keep it," she said. "When you get to be an artist, you can try to do better."

"It's Rob's," Hutch said.

"No it's not. It was Polly's; now it's yours till you lose it. Everything that was old Rob's, Forrest gave me—all his little souvenirs that Forrest didn't burn (he burned every doll but this one, even Mam). I've got them upstairs, what was left—razors, Bible, a picture or two. I left this down here because Forrest liked it."

"Did he give you the house?"

"Sir?"

"Grandfather Mayfield," Hutch said, "—this house; did he give it to you? It was old Rob's, wasn't it?"

"It was. And yes Forrest said it was mine. On the way to the funeral, Forrest said to me plainly that they thanked me for the care I had spent on his father and they wanted me to have everything that was his. Rob had abused him and Hattie by leaving; and they wanted none of him now he couldn't keep running. That was before Forrest knew he would move here, an hour before; he never brought it up again."

"But he never said different, did he?"

"No," Polly said. "Oh no, not a word. We just passed the time for all those years."

"Then it's yours," Hutch said. "You could ask me here." He sat up slowly and faced her, still grave.

Polly smiled. "I *would.*"

"No, ask me," he said.

Polly said "All right." She spread both hands on the flats of her thighs, looked again at her fingers not withered or dry. Then she gave a short laugh to show they were joking, that she must stand now and finish her work.

Hutch said "Where has Rob gone?"

"To Heaven I hope but I very much doubt it."

Hutch waited awhile. "No *my* Rob," he said.

"Oh." She thought, then rose. "He has gone to find liquor. He'll be back late. We'll see plenty then but we have to wait here. You come help me."

Hutch stood to obey.

8

Rob found her well after dark, not knowing at first that he'd set out to find her. At first he had driven out to James Institute and parked and walked up to Forrest's office door before he remembered he didn't have the key (it was on the study mantel). He hadn't had a real purpose there anyhow, had brought no cartons to pack the books; so he'd gone back out and was nearly at his car when he saw an old Negro standing twenty feet away, staring at him through the late clear dusk, dressed neatly with a bamboo cane. Rob stopped and called out, "You love your country yet?"

The man took two slow steps and said "Sir?"

"I said I hope you have learned to love your country, with a new war on."

The man came all the way forward and studied. "Mr. Rob?"

"Hey, William," Rob said and extended his hand.

The old serpent took it in his cool horny palm and squeezed it, laughing. "You ain't lost nothing; remember *too* good!"

"Well, I never knew a better janitor, William. Haven't been really clean since I left here."

"You back?"

"Just to visit, just to pack my daddy's things."

William nodded. "Mr. Rob, nobody told me nothing. They retired me here June two years ago, seventy-five years old. Took my broom and give me this." He stirred a little maelstrom in the air with his cane. "Last time I saw Mr. Forrest, he was *standing*, strong and straight as ever; I come by to see him on Christmas like he told me. He give me my cigars and say, 'Look, William, you shining your wings?' I tell him, 'Yes sir, my wings is ready; but I'll be climbing and circling like a chicken long before you—you young as ever.' He looked real solemn and say, 'I doubt it. Place I'm going they don't let you fly.' — 'What you done?' I say, and he say 'Failed my people.' I told him, 'Mr. Forrest, you talking about white folks, I can't speak for them; but you see I'm dark so let me just tell you, you sure God saved black niggers by the dozen.' Mr. Forrest say 'From what?' " William stopped there and stood, looking off toward a squad of wild dogs by the statue of Robert Burns (a Carnegie gift).

Rob said "Did you say?"

William came back slowly. "Say what?"

" — From what? Saved them from what?"

"No sir," William said. Then he faced the dogs again. They had cornered a bitch; and the big male was mounting her or struggling to — she'd agreed to take him, but his haunches humped drily in the air between them. When William turned he said, "That light girl told me." His own face (the color of a good tan glove) was fierce with anger, suddenly young.

Rob was honestly puzzled.

" — Girl used to be married to that fool of yours."

"Grainger? He was Father's. It was Father spoiled Grainger."

"Yours when I knew him, hanging round to watch *you.*"

Rob hoped to derail him and calm him at once. "You run into Gracie? I hear she's back."

But the eyes still glared. "Gracie, that's her. She run into me. I minding my business, heading toward the ice plant one evening last week; and she yell out at me, 'Mr. William, come help me.' She was setting in a slat chair right down in the road; I never would have known her, she aged so bad. But I went over to her to help *any* creature and saw she was drinking — Mr. Rob, she was drunk. I said 'Who are you?' and she told me to guess. I said, 'I'm too old to stand here guessing'; and she asked me what else was I too old for?"

Rob said, "You mean she was smack in the road?"

"In front of a house but right in the street, two feet from the cars."

"Did you tell her you were young enough to handle her still?"

William studied; then smiled, easing as he went. "No sir, cause I ain't. Old as she look, she could grind me dead!"

Rob smiled. "Maybe so. I'm tired myself." The need to stop William, to move onward now had stood strong in him.

William said, "No such a thing. You ain't even started."

Rob said, "Then God save me. Can I carry you home?"

William thought a moment slowly, checked the sky for light. "No sir, thank you no. Old woman's still awake. I'm walking till she tired, at least her *tongue* tired." He laughed; Rob joined him. Then he pointed with his cane "I'm just over yonder where I always been, behind the old smithy. Little house still holding; they ain't made me move. I'm praying they don't; being real good—don't you know?—so they don't think about me. Come see me fore you go."

Rob said "I'll do it."

"You need any help?"

"All kinds; what you giving?"

"Packing up, cleaning out. My knees still good; I just carry this—give me something to do." William waved his cane again, a grinning flourish.

Rob followed its point to the feverish dogs who had somehow calmed and were spaced on the grass as flat and separate as folded bats, staring his way.

9

So it was full dark before he found the icehouse and bought a small melon and asked for directions to Gracie's cousin's house. As he turned into the steep dirt street, he saw a straight chair twenty yards ahead, almost in the road—Gracie's but empty (there was one streetlight at the far dead-end). He drove there and parked half into a ditch and walked through the tin cans of flowers toward the dark house and called through the screen door—"Gracie? Gracie Walters?"

"Nobody named that." The voice was from nearby and clearly was Gracie's.

He just said, "Gracie, it's Rob out here."

A sizable silence, some fumbling with metal; then a flashlight lit at the end of the front room and searched for his face at the screen.

He gave it, stood still with his face almost at the wire and smiled in the beam. "I used to work for you."

"Oh God," she said and rose from the bed she'd lain across and came to the door, bare feet on planks. She still held the light, still fixed on Rob. Then she said, "You sure did. Step in here and rest."

"I stopped at the icehouse to ask where you were and bought a little melon; it's in the car cold."

"You get it," Gracie said. "We cut it on the porch, but it give me the headache. What else you brought?"

Rob had not really seen her; she was still behind the screen. "What you see," he said, "—my last remains."

"You shaping up," she said. "Ain't you got no nip?" She threw her light down to his hips and pockets.

"Not a drop. I remembered that was your department."

She thought a long moment. Rob could not see her nod, but she did once quickly. "You got to pay for it."

"What is it?"

"Mean wine," Gracie said.

"How much you got?"

"Best part of a quart."

Rob grinned. "Not enough."

Gracie lit his face again. "Maybe not," she said.

"Your cousin here with you?"

"She work all night; nurse a old white lady."

"And you're by yourself?"

"Way I like it," she said. She turned half-away, half-intending to leave (he'd waked her from a deep sleep which pulled her back).

But he needed to see her. "I got a little money for you; sit down and talk."

Gracie halted. "Who from? You ain't still trying to find me for Grainger?"

"No I'm not. That's your business. The money's from Father; he asked me to give you a little when I saw you so you'd think kindly of him."

Gracie said "How much?"

"A five-dollar bill."

She was back at the screen; then she opened it enough to hold out her hand. "I'll remember just that kindly," she said.

Rob stepped back enough to see the one streetlight and took out his wallet, tried to see five dollars. (He thought he had only wanted to see her, hear her talk of the past, ask her one or two questions. But she'd caught him in his lie; now he'd tip her and go.) He could not really see. "Come here with your light."

Gracie unhooked the screen and brought the beam toward him. She moved fast and straight; and once she got to him, he could smell her slow breath, damp and warm but fresh. She had not drunk for hours at least, he knew. She stood in deep silence, aiming her light at his thin sheaf of cash.

He found five dollars, drew it out, began to fold it. "Can we sit down a minute?" There were rockers beside them on the porch and a swing.

Gracie switched off the beam. "What you want me to talk about? I'm low as a well."

Rob said, "Nothing special, thought I'd tell you the news; Polly said you were asking. You could tell me yours."

She thought it out. "Who you telling what I told you?"

He did not understand.

"I sit down here and tell you my story, who you carry it to?"

"Nobody you tell me not to," he said.

"Grainger Walters," she said. "You keep it from him." She went to the far chair and sat, sighing.

Rob took the other chair. He still held the money in his right hand, wadded. She had not reached again. They sat a good while, Rob rocking, Gracie still. It had been a mild day, and the evening was cool; so the breeze that suddenly rose on their right was almost chilling.

It started Gracie. "No *news*," she said. "Nothing you don't know or ain't seen me do; had a whole lot of jobs, a lot of good times, a lot of bad lately. Been drinking for my health. But you know that too." She stopped and asked nothing, didn't turn toward Rob but faced his car.

He tried to see her now, the damage William mentioned; but could only see the line of her features and throat. It perfectly matched his memories of her nineteen years before—silent, sullen at his wedding; a laughing help to Rachel their first year in Richmond; then the slack hurtful drunk whom he'd tracked down with Grainger so many weekends till she vanished entirely. She was still all those, in this light at least. For the first time he knew what he'd come here to ask (not for drink or the use of any piece of her body). He said "Gracie, what was wrong?"

"Wrong with what?"

"—That you left us, that you ran so far and tired yourself out. Did I harm you anyway? Did Rachel ever harm you?"

"Won't running," she said. "Nobody scared *me*."

"You left though."

"A lot of times. And came back a lot."

"For what? Was it us?"

She waited till he thought she was silently refusing or had dropped off to sleep or chosen at last not to hurt anybody else by word or deed. Then she raised her left hand, brought it down on the chair arm announcing a fact; and said, "I was pleasing my mind. That simple." She waited again; then gave a low chuckle, the liquid burble of a drowsy bird.

Rob said "Are you still?"

She was sure. "Nothing but."

"So you don't blame us?"

"I didn't say that." She waited a little. "Not *you*," she said.

"What was wrong with Grainger?"

Again she was sure, had known it for years and not been asked. "Not enough white blood."

Rob said "Meaning what?"

"Meaning Grainger couldn't ease his mind no way on earth. I was too much nigger to ever satisfy him. Oh he come back from France all hot from the sights and men blowing up round him; and I eased him awhile, thought he was easing me. But once I showed him every trick I knew—he didn't know *nothing*—he figured he'd got to the dead-end of Gracie; so he struck up, you know, to *staring at the wind*: hoping two suits of white skin would blow in the door and him and me be real kin to your dead daddy. Or *one* suit of skin; it was him he dreamed for, dreamed Gracie right on out of his life. You thought I was running; I was looking for home—some warm dry place with a black nigger in it that could use my butt when he come home tired from a hard day's hauling, not gazing at wind like the wind would blow in because you were pretty and bank blessings on you."

Rob said "He's still waiting."

"Not for *me*?"

"Not you. No I don't really know."

Gracie said, "*I* do—nobody but you. I told Miss Polly last Wednesday when I seen her and she asked me was I ever going back to the fool—'He don't want me no more and ain't for fifteen years since Mr. Rob walked in and halfway adopted him. He just want the rest of that.'"

"Of what?"

"The whole adoption, to be your whole brother. Rob, you all he waiting on. You the one can do the trick."

"What's the trick?"

"Where's he at? At your mama's place?"

"Still in her backyard listening to the war news, making her garden, watching Hutch grow up and leave him like us all."

"Then you go out to him when you go back home—that coffin he live in, two feet square—and you hold out your clean hand and say, 'Mr. Grainger, I know you at last.'"

"Know what?" Rob said.

"Whose people he is, what's rightfully his. He don't know you know, or didn't when I left him."

Rob said "How do *you* know?"

Gracie said, "Two things to know—how did I know he's white? how did I know you knew? Grainger told me the first part, the first time I left him—'You leaving a good man that's nearly half-white.' I threw oil at him (I was filling his lamp so he'd have light to read by when I was long gone, them dream books that ruined him—Pocahontas eating grief till it choked her heart because she was two shades too dark to know Jesus). Mr. Forrest told me you knew."

"When?"

"Years ago." She offered no more.

So Rob let her sit and rocked on another minute, telling himself that he'd come for nothing but the air, the change, and should stand now and tip her and go back to Hutch and Polly, face them. As heavy as they were, they were after all walls holding back deeper waters that were ready to pour. He sat to the edge of the chair and faced her. She still refused to meet his look but gazed on outward at his car, the road, her old chair beside it. Only her hands moved—long thin hands on the broad chair arms, still silently flapping in rhythm as steady as any fine clock. She was telling time. She wore the gold ring; Rob could catch its dull presence. Rising, he tapped it once with his finger—"You haven't lost that." Then he held out the money packed down through their talk to a hot wet bullet.

Gracie didn't reach to take it. "That's a lie," she said.

"Pardon me then. I thought I saw a ring, thought I recognized it."

"—What I said: Mr. Forrest. He told me you knew who Grainger was the same day he died, early that afternoon. Miss Polly don't know it; you tell her and I'll kill you. I had come down here from Newark, New Jersey to see my cousin; see would she let me live here with her. She say I could if I help with her bills, ten dollars a month, first payment due *then*. I didn't have nothing but a bus-ticket back to pigshit Newark (I hate that hole; freeze you inside and out) and was getting real nervous with no wine to help me; so I took my chances and went to James Institute and found Mr. Forrest. He give me fifteen dollars, no hesitation, all he had in his pocket. I told him once I moved back down here for good, I'd work it out for him; and he said all right, not to worry about it. Then he ask after Grainger; didn't try to make me feel bad for leaving or nothing, just wanted to know if I understood his troubles. I say, 'Yes sir, Grainger told me years back'; and he say nobody was to blame but his father for starting it off, not watching hisself; and nobody could help it now unless *you* knew a way. He said he'd told you."

"Help what?"

"Just Grainger. I guess he meant Grainger."

"I don't," Rob said, "—no way on God's earth."

"That's it then," Gracie said. "I told him it would be."

Rob said, "That last day—he seemed all right?"

"Same as ever but old, marking his little nigger papers like old times. He did seem sad but that was old times too, saddest soul I ever seen. I offered him this"—she raised her left hand. "You know what it is?"

"Yes."

"You know everything; can't nobody help you." But she chuckled again. "I told him he could take it for the fifteen dollars. He say, 'I lost my chance at that ring. It's having its life; I can't stop it now.'"

Rob stood a long moment; then stepped up to her, laid the money in her lap. "Will you sell it to me?"

"This ring or my monkey?" (in the dark he'd brushed her more deeply than he meant).

Rob said, "Well, thanks all the same — but the ring."

"What you want to do with it?"

"Keep it. Maybe Hutch —"

"You want to get married? Where your Miss Minnie?"

"Wore her out," Rob said. "She gave up waiting."

Gracie tapped the broad ring on the wood of the chair. "You show her this thing, she come back snappy."

"You didn't," Rob said. "You took it and went."

Gracie said, "I'm different; I told you how different. I just wanted one thing men had to give; that's easy to get if you look good as me, good as I used to look — had em standing thick as pulpwood. Miss Minnie wanted *you*, that thing and all the rest — wet breath from your nostrils, white gristle in your heart."

Rob said, "She can have it. I planned to tell her soon; then she called time on me. Got a letter this morning saying she was past reach now, to leave her alone."

"She playing," Gracie said.

"No she's not. I've abused her."

"What she *want* you to do." Gracie sat forward quickly and struggled with her hands in the dark of her shadow. "Give her this," she said. With the hand that held his money, she offered the ring.

Rob weighed it on his palm. "How much would I owe you? I'm a little hard up now, out of work myself."

Gracie said "You been drinking?"

"Enough to get fired."

She thought awhile. "You keep it. Got your name in it anyhow; never had mine, fool Grainger's neither."

"You ought not to give it."

"It was give to me. I never worked for it. When time come to work was when I left."

Rob suddenly brought it to his lips and touched it. "*I* sure God have."

"You ever get a little bit ahead," Gracie said, "you send me a buck or so."

"How will I find you?"

"Miss Polly; she'll know me."

"She says she's leaving too," Rob said, "—to nurse. I feel bad about it, but she won't let me help her."

Gracie passed over that if she heard it at all. "Then send it to Jesus; He keep up with me." She gave a long laugh like a seam of fresh water she'd found in her chest, unsuspected till now.

Rob said, "I'll do it. He knows me too." Then he walked to the steps. "If you're over our way tomorrow, stop by. You haven't seen Hutch; he's two-thirds grown."

Gracie stood in place. "All right. I hadn't seen him—Lord—six years." Her flashlight lay on the floor by her chair; but she came on without it, stopped one step from Rob. "I ain't," she said, "so don't wait for me. Ain't coming nowhere where that child is."

Baffled, Rob said, "He's good. He won't tell Grainger."

"I know he's good," she said, "and he welcome to tell Grainger anything he see. No I'm sparing myself. I started doing that; you ought to try it too. I don't see children if there's any way to help it. Children break me down worse than anything else."

Rob touched her on the elbow, the flesh hot and dense in its slick dry rind. "Keep us posted someway. Try to keep up with Polly; you can help her a lot."

Gracie nodded—"She'll make it"—and gently freed her arm.

Rob went down the steps and straight to his car. At the shut door he looked up and said "I thank you."

"Glad somebody do."

He could no longer see her—she was shaded by the porch posts, her cousin's tubbed ferns—but he thought of one thing he'd forgot till now. "How about this melon? It'll still be cool; you could take you an aspirin."

"Can't do it," she said, "—give me dreams this late." Then she turned and went in; just the sound of the rusty screen opened, shut, hooked.

So Rob leaned in and drew the light melon out—still cool as he'd promised, striped with snakes of dark green—and set it in the straight slat chair by the street. She could face it tomorrow, maybe swap it for a drink; or her cousin coming home in the dawn could find it, or some early child—a gift from grace itself, the sky.

10

Polly went up to bed at seven o'clock, telling Hutch there was no use in ruining themselves in a wait that might well last till noon (she recalled such waits by Forrest and Grainger after Rachel's death). Hutch had said he would stay in the study and read till he felt really tired, and he read till one in his grandfather's copy of *Martin Eden*. He was still not tired enough to face a dark bed; but by then he suspected there might be worse sights to face if he stayed to meet his father, so he quietly switched off all but the porch light and climbed to his room.

He didn't think he slept; but he did fairly soon, a frail speeding through half-formed visions of fear, assault, the chasms of final abandonment. He had raced himself to a deeper unhappiness than any he'd known—still faceless, embryonic, drawn from his own mind—when Rob's key woke him as it grated in the street door. Rob or someone Rob had sent or someone who'd killed Rob and come straight here—Hutch added all those to the chances around him. He raised to his elbows and strained to hear. The door had not shut.

At first there was only the breathing from Polly's room—her door was half-open; she slept on through even this, another abandonment. Hutch tried to see his watch—too dark: at the window there were no signs of day. Then downstairs the door shut firmly at last, then steps down the hall (not certainly Rob's; they were quick and heavy), then the brass light-switch clicked loudly in the study.

Hutch's arms went numb as wool from the weight of his urgent body as it waited for news. For a long time he took no notice at all of their lack of blood. Then when minutes on minutes of unstirred silence continued to pump from below like a flood, he fell back and let the cold blood pour through him, sour and scalding. He had heard all his life of his father's failures—in mumbled scraps from Sylvie and Grainger, a friend or two—but he'd never seen one. Till now something spared him; now he knew it had stopped. He must stand now and find his way downstairs to see—whoever, whatever, was offered and waiting. Nothing in his whole life had readied him for this; not his mother's absence or the warnings of Negroes that this lay ahead or the war that had run in Europe and Asia since he had been nine, consuming in hordes (as its food and fuel) the bodies of children as good as he, as worthy of mercy.

He stood in his cotton pajamas, barefoot, and felt his way like a blind boy down.

11

The study was a blank plane of hot white glare from the ceiling light and showed no sign of containing more than when Hutch had left it two hours ago—furniture and light, the rank summer mold on yards of books. The one man here was his great-grandfather's bark doll on the cot. So he went there to sit and wait again.

Another man was huddled in the dark square yard of space between desk and cot—buck-naked, curled on his side like a fetus and silent as bread.

Hutch was stunned and scared but held his place, standing one step from the legs. Then questions poured on him—was it Rob? was he dead? was it Rob or a stranger waiting to spring? He said "Rob," whispering so as not to wake Polly (though what could wake her now?). No answer, no stir. He took the last step and crouched by the body, hoping it was anyone on earth but his father. The man had wet the clothes he lay on.

They were Rob's tan trousers; the legs were his, strong calves still thickly haired with brown when most men his age had worn their legs bald.

Hutch bent forward, holding his breath against the piss; and shook the flat hip—"Rob."

The waist was moving slightly to breathe, no other move.

Hutch pressed the hip hard, forced the body flat to face him.

Rob's eyes were half-open, though in fact he was dreaming. He'd started to dream before he lay here, had lain down only to ease its progress through his mind and eyes.

Hutch said, "Wait here. I'll go get Grainger." In his own shock and fear, he thought they were at home; that he and Grainger hauling together could lift him.

Rob said, "Understand. I want this rest," a speech from his dream. His sex was half-standing, still bore a yellow drop.

Hutch thought he understood. He rose and left.

12

In his room again, he shut the door quietly and turned on the one lamp beside the bed. Then he sat on the edge and tore with his nails at the rims of summer callus on both his heels. When he had a pile of dead skin the size of a quarter on the sheet beside him—his left heel was bleeding—he knew his course. He went to his open bag and found his drawing tablet. Near the back on the clean sheet that followed his portraits of Chopin and Liszt, he wrote this quickly.

June 13, 1944

Dear Grainger,

It is now three-thirty in the morning, and I am still in Richmond. I got your letter last night after supper. Till then I didn't know about the goldpiece or I would have already thanked you for it. Rob forgot to tell me. I blamed him for that, and he went out and got what I guess is drunk and is lying downstairs on the study floor now, naked asleep. He wouldn't let me help him.

So I'm leaving right now. Where I'm going is to see my Grandfather Hutchins before he dies. He wrote me on my birthday and said he'd like to see me. Also I want to see some things near there. I will try to ride the bus. I have twelve dollars from my savings and from Grandmother. If that runs out, I have now got the goldpiece and can cash that in. I will leave in five minutes, meaning sometime tonight I hope to be in Goshen if you need to send me word. This is not any secret. From Rob, I mean. I will leave him a note. But don't tell anybody else in Fontaine.

Do you want to come join me? You could take a few days off and ride the bus yourself and show me the things you remember in Goshen. We could head home together when we had our visit. Anyhow think about it. I will try to stay till Sunday at least if Grandfather seems well and knows who I am and wants me that long. So come before Sunday if you're coming at all.

I am doing all right but really feel bad. I guess you know how.

Thanks again, I hope to see you.

> *Sincerely,*
> *Raven "Hutch"*

Then he took a last sheet and wrote

Dear Miss Polly,

You are fast asleep so this is to thank you for my visit here. I enjoyed your part of it and am sorry to leave early, but after our talk tonight I guess you understand why.

I'm going down now to try to get a bus to Goshen where my mother is buried. I have got enough money and will be all right. Boys younger than me around the whole world except here are fighting.

Rob is back downstairs, and since you have known him so much longer than me you will know what to do. He told me to leave him alone and I will. You can tell him where I am and that I will go to Fontaine as soon as I have finished.

I hope you will have a good time from now on. I would like to give you anything here that is mine, and I hope I will see you again some day when I know as much as you and can sit down to talk.

> *Your friend,*
> *Hutch Mayfield*

Then he packed his few things and, carrying his bag and his sandals, went out and left the note for Polly on the doorsill of her room. All the way downstairs he kept his eyes from the open study where the light still burned; but once he reached the hall he knew of three things that he could and must do. He set down the bag and entered the room; pulled the spread off the cot and covered his father, sparing Polly the sight. He took the bark doll, despite his gift to Polly in the note he'd left (she had never wanted this), and turned off the light. Then in pure hot darkness he found his way out.

JUNE 13–14, 1944

She saw him take the first step at the bottom of the hill, two hundred yards off; and she paused only long enough to prove to herself that he climbed toward her. Then she bent again to chopping weeds between her rows of corn (corn she knew she'd never eat; she planted it for company). It would be time wasted to strain to know him yet, to look up again till he stood within arm's reach. She'd enter her seventy-eighth year next week and had long since surrendered curiosity and safety to the thickening veil of twin cataracts. She could still see the weeds.

And then she forgot him, thinking calmly but with dread fresh as warm milk of Whitby, her younger, in Belgium now at the mercy of nothing more visible than God—twenty-five years old, her favorite and her hope. If they killed him, she'd die. She had stood all the rest; she wouldn't stand that.

Hutch came to the edge of the garden and stopped; set his bag in the dirt and said, "Have I got to the Mayfield place?"

She rose and looked; still only a slim clot of color beyond her in the tan light of evening. "No the *Shorter* place," she said, "but I'm no Shorter. My husband was, my boys are. No Mayfield either but that's by choice."

Hutch said "Miss Hattie?" (he had never called her *Aunt*; never seen her to remember, not since 1933).

"Yes, Hattie," she said. She was straight as the hoe-handle upright beside her and could hear his short breaths, quick from the climb; but she would not say she could not see his face.

"I'm your nephew," he said. "I was trying to find you."

She smiled but said "From where?"

"Richmond last night. I'm headed on west but my bus stopped here, so I thought I'd try to find you."

Hatt spread her free arm, one bare bone wing. "You found what's left! What you want to do with it?"

"Good evening," Hutch said.

2

They had said very little through supper or before (when they'd gone to the house, Hatt had said, "You climb on up to your room. Wash your face, lie down, I'll call you when I'm ready"; so he'd climbed the strange stairs and found the bare open room that seemed not hers and washed with the pitcher of warm water ready by a white china bowl and then had fallen back on the bed in which his father was conceived and slept off an hour of the debt he'd acquired in the past hard night before Hatt called, "You can eat if you're ready"); but once they had got near the end of the baked eggs, four vegetables, and biscuits, Hatt said, "Now tell me how your whole trip went."

Hutch had not said Rob's name once till then—she had not asked for it—and he could not now. He said, "Everything was crowded, lot of soldiers; and I had to stand up a good part of the way, but it was all right. I'm glad to rest here."

Hatt said "I know you are." Despite her silences she'd smiled often freely, especially when he'd looked up and caught her in a squinting gaze at his face. She was smiling now. "The walk did you good."

Hutch thought she referred to his climb up the hill. "Yes ma'm," he said. "I'm used to flat country."

"No you're not," she said.

From that moment Hutch knew she had him wrong. He hadn't said more than that he was her nephew; he knew she had no other—her great-nephew really. So she thought he was Rob. Was she really that far gone? She looked clean and kept, no trace of the burning odor of age, the singed-chicken-feather stench of unwashed bewilderment which rose (he knew already) from a number of souls with years yet to live. He surely couldn't ask her, stop now and set her right—"I am younger than that; I am *Hutchins* Mayfield." What he'd seen last night could not be worsened. No news of the war, no one photograph of the hundreds he'd seen of children in torment had rushed on him stronger. He knew in his deep heart that then he had passed a trial which would never come at him again, that he'd earned a permanent safety from fear. He could wait and listen. He smiled at Hatt and said, "Well, it taught me some things—the walk, I mean."

"Like what?"

"Like nothing will hurt me, from now till I die."

"What tried?" Hatt said.

"Different people, things they said."

"Saying you were an orphan?"

"Alone, yes ma'm."

Hatt was opposite him at the big square table, four feet away. She leaned over suddenly and took his left wrist that lay on the clean cloth.

"You know the word *liar?*" Her face was pressed blank of its lines by the force of her question, nearly young.

"Yes ma'm, but I haven't—"

"Then use it," she said. She settled back again. "Words are meant to be used; they'll stand you in good stead when all else fails—eyes and hands'll *fail*. Words are what I mostly have now."

"Use it how?" Hutch said.

"In the teeth of any human tries to say you aren't cared for, loved as close as any blood-child that draws breath. Call em *liar*, plain *liar*." She was still lit and lifted by faith in her words, but she sat unmoving with her palms down before her like guards by her plate (she had barely eaten half).

"By who?" Hutch said, "—cared for by who?" He felt for the first clear time in his life that he played two games, both serious and funny, his aunt's and his. She thought he was someone he knew he was not; he deceived her in that. But himself, he was bent now on knowing her error; hungry to know could he wear her error as a useful disguise in this new life he'd started, today at dawn.

Hatt waited a good while, upright and still, no longer facing him. Hutch thought she was lost in confusion again; she was not. She was straining to bear his question, the fact he could ask it. Then she said, "Try Hattie. Try guessing it's Hattie. See how does that feel." She had not looked up.

He nodded "I'll try" but was faintly smiling.

And though she couldn't see it, she smiled again; let it open on a laugh to show how certain she was of her claim. She loved him enough; one human was safe. She thought he was Forrest her brother, age twelve, who for lack of a dollar had been unable to ride with his school-class excursion to Danville, two hours by train, so had walked there ahead and met them at the station and walked back alone, arriving just now. That had actually happened sixty-one years ago after their mother's death and had been a main cause of Hatt's own rush to marry James Shorter and bear him the two sons who'd left her entirely in the past two hours; left her memory, her worry. Soon she'd never be forced to shame Forrest again. They would be past shame.

She went on smiling. But something remained to block full pleasure and darken her hope. She stayed in her seat, and her hands stayed still; but she faced him again—his face one vague white globe among globes—and said, "Forrest, what I'm asking for now is pardon."

Before Hutch could know should he laugh or leave or ask *For what?* or tell her all the fresh truth in one quick stream, he said "That's easy" and touched the broad top of her right wrist with fingers that wanted to calm and were sixty years younger yet were cool as new sheets on her hot dry skin, the fervent meeting of utter strangers.

3

Before it turned dark, Hatt had told him he should go on to bed; so with no more questions or answers, he had climbed to the bare room again and stripped to his underwear (the room was still hot) and looked out the window toward the dense black crest of the hill they were on. He settled his eyes on a nearer dead tree (stripped of leaves, branches, bark; of all the fittings and intentions of a tree but its need to stand) and thought of the string of new chances which spun from his choices today.

He had chosen to leave his father, huddled naked on a floor. (Or had he been *sent*, as he'd felt at first? He'd puzzled that all day, what Rob's speech had meant—"Understand. I need this.") At the station, when he'd found a bus to Goshen wouldn't leave before mid-afternoon, he had gone in to breakfast at the station cafe to consider if the wait would be fatal to his plan, whether Rob would recover enough to come and find him and, if so, what answer he would give to that. As he'd started on his peach pie, a loudspeaker called out a bus to Bracey, Danville, and points southwest; and though he barely noticed the name at all, the old waitress writing out his check before him had said, "There you go. Want your pie in a sack?" and he'd said "Please ma'm," taking that as his next choice, offered by luck—a step on, at least. Once in Bracey he'd asked for directions to his aunt; then had let her build her own confusions round him, let her suffer for that (unless the easy pardon he'd laid across the table had actually reached her and sealed some cut which his voice had reopened). He'd chosen in fact to be her dead brother, his dead grandfather, for an hour or so.

Could he go on from there? What would morning bring? Would her mind have cleared so she knew him as himself? If so would she probe where he couldn't bear probing?—Rob's whereabouts, his own unlikely future? Would she beg him for all she so clearly lacked? Could he say No and leave? Should he dress and leave now?—creep past her down the stairs and walk toward Goshen or the next bus station or lie here and wait till she slept and leave then? (she was still in the kitchen; a radio was on).

Or could he *be* Forrest, become Hatt's dream?—not just to ease her for the time she had left (surely he was safe here; they'd hunt him in Goshen, never think to look here—they'd all dodged Hattie since before he could remember) but to help himself, save himself from the coming life which flew toward him now: Rob and all his power to hurt, power to raise love and hope by his simple words and presence and crush them each evening.

Standing there all but stripped at a window which had framed his grandfather's face for years—then his desperate grandmother's, then his newborn father's—Hutch thought he could sleep here and rise and be new, be Forrest Mayfield and live a life free of choices that would bring down pain on himself and nine others. He knew (from Sylvie, Grainger) enough facts of past years—Forrest running off with Eva and the main aftermaths—to think that ten lives were bent crooked by the choice: Eva, Forrest, Eva's parents, Rena, Hatt, Grainger, Rob, then Rachel and Hutch. He could choose to spare them all, save Charlotte Kendal's life, save Robinson and Hutchins from having lives at all. What would flow out from him would be calm satisfaction—his Aunt Hatt's old age accompanied and tended, his own great longing for freedom from others (from love *or* pain) quenched daily by life in this bare room, bare house: hoeing beans, climbing that hill there to its top, looking back on a dead tree, the peaceful empty house, the road in the bottom, the far hill beyond, reducing each in order to a picture in his tablet. Lasting, useful, safe, harmless.

Knowing again that he played two games—only with himself now—he thought he could stay here, be that. Could and would. He would be here tomorrow and as long after that as his life moved safely.

The hill had darkened, the bare tree melted into dark grass behind it. Hutch went to his suitcase, took out his tablet, turned on the one bright overhead light; and sitting on the stiff bed before the old mirror, began for the first time to draw his own face—an excellent likeness and a first firm memorial of what he was leaving for this new life.

4

Well into night, ten minutes past twelve when the last news had finished, Hatt shut off the last light and climbed in black dark to the top of the stairs, no need to feel her way. She stood still there till she heard steady breath from Forrest's room. Then with no attempt at silence, she walked to that door—

half-shut—and pushed it open. What moonlight there was reached her only as a thick screen of glow between her and her goal, the boy she could hear and must touch now freely before she could sleep. She hardly knew this room, had avoided it for years, only swept it spring and fall; so she put out her arms and shuffled to the rag rug, struck the bed with her knees. The boy's breath stopped awhile; then started, safe and deep. She sat on the edge of the mattress and waited. She was not sure for what—the comfort of a living animal in reach, entrusted to her, or for some further answer. Yes a question remained.

At last she remembered. Sure in the dark now, she found his broad hip with one reach of her hand and let it ride there till the breath stilled again. Through the cotton spread and sheet, she pressed the flat bone. The breath had stayed silent; he would be awake or nearly. She was sorry to have roused him, but she had to ask now while she held it all clearly together in her mind. "This Normandy," she said, "—is it anywhere near Flanders?" She knew he loved maps.

He said "Yes ma'm."

They stayed like that for a good while, quiet. He could see her above him, her face as young in moonlight as it had been with fervor at the table over supper when she swore how loved he was.

"That's it then," she said. "That's it. He's gone."

He was dazed from deep sleep, but he thought she meant the war. "You been listening to the news?" He could see her nod slowly.

"—Said the Germans pushed them back today right up against the water: Cherbourg, around there. Said they suffered pretty bad."

He thought he understood. He said, "Albert?—he's safe. He's never looked up."

"Whitby," she said. "I seem to know he's gone."

He thought he remembered she had lost a son; hadn't Rena told him something the day of Pearl Harbor when he'd asked, if it lasted, would he have to die in it? "Not likely," she'd said. "God seldom takes two, only rarely and for necessary reasons of His own. Your cousin died in Flanders. Makes you all but safe, however long it lasts." But he wasn't sure *Whitby* was the name, so he only touched the hand that was still on his hip.

Hatt bore the touch but did not try to hold it or press on it any dumb message or thanks. She stayed on beside him though, the hand on hers, and remained so silent in her certainty of loss that he soon slept again, this time beyond waking, if there'd been a cause to wake him.

After some long time she began to feel cold and thought she must go to her own room for warmth. Her down quilt was there at the foot of her bed, her mother's quilt really. She could wait under that. Since 1918 she'd slept very little and, until her sight had failed, had often spent night after night downstairs mending clothes, writing mail, making perfect preserves to send whoever — contentedly enough. Since her blindness the only thing to do was hear news, five years of war news — all the late bursts of shortwave news in all tongues, any one as sad as English — so she'd started lying down again in James's old bed, the one she'd shared with him where she'd never felt easy.

She would feel this child first. As hard as he slept now, and with his long day, he might be feverish. She found his face again in one sure reach — his brow dry and cool, his breath on her palm still regular and moist. Then her fingers stayed to search him for any other threats, any trace of shame or fear brought back from his trip and concealed in daylight.

No the whole face was calm, entirely surrendered — brow, eyelids, mouth, chin. But it wasn't any face she had ever touched before; a whole new country lay beneath her light hand, young and eased and trusting but new.

5

At seven Hutch woke, clear sun through the window; and said his prayers and dressed. He thought he could smell bread baking downstairs and the smoke from bacon. They were only his hope; when he passed his aunt's door, heading straight for the stairs, he saw her upright in a black Morris chair against the far wall, wearing last night's clothes, her eyes on him. He walked to her doorsill and said, "Good morning. Have you been up long?"

She nodded, not smiling.

"I didn't hear a sound; dead to all, I guess. I needed to be." He took a step inward.

"Please wait," she said. She held out the hand which had studied him by night.

He waited, baffled.

"No it's all right," she said. "Just answer me this — have you ever known me?"

"I'm your nephew, yes ma'm. I said that, remember?"

"Not Rob," she said.

"No'm, Hutchins."

No light. She looked every instant of her age, spared nothing.

"Rob's —" he said; that burned him too deep. "Rachel's Hutch," he said;

and knew he must leave now—his old life again, guarded round by the thickets which called themselves love but were hunger and fright.

Hatt understood nothing, remembered no Rachel; but she stood without effort and grinned and came toward him. "You can still stay," she said.

JUNE 14–17, 1944

June 14, 1944

Dear Min,

It's early Wednesday here, a little past six. Your letter came Monday and was one of the last straws the old camel bore before buckling under. You told me not to write, and you may just burn this without ever looking; but I've lain through the night, seldom closing my eyes, and Polly's still asleep; so I'll tell it toward you, hoping truly that it reaches.

In the week since I wrote, these main things have happened. The "shop" job at home had not been filled, and Thorne Bradley seemed inclined to give it to me if I'd sign The Pledge in blood. Mother, Rena, Sylvie, Grainger are each far gone at the ends of their tethers—no thought of coming back; they can barely hear each other and are happy as fleas—so I can't stay there. But with some fumigation and a week of whitewashing, the old Kendal place would be habitable once I locate the nerve to turn eight Negroes flat out in the road (one is not yet with us—the oldest girl is pregnant—but is well on the way). Hutch would not live with me if you were in sight and may well have gone for good now in any case. More about that. The sand and water of the Atlantic Ocean are holding up well, all recent things considered (two world wars etc., all the drowned young men, their effect on sharks). The shrines of colonial Virginia stand firm, as do all Virginians I have met so far—Miss Polly among them. She is Hellbent on moving her duds out of here as soon as I leave and taking up practical nursing, age fifty-eight (she is rightly mad and puzzled that Father left no will or instructions for her welfare, so has chosen me to punish in his unquestioned absence). I have offered her the house here and every stick in it; she still says No, which means I have to sell it all at auction or burn it or come here and live—using what for money? eating leaves from Father's Vergil, his deathless lines to Eva at sixteen? Also Grainger's Gracie; she's here and I've seen *her, what's left anyhow. And I took some of* that, *her wedding ring which really was my Grandmother Mayfield's. Father gave it to Grainger. I can wear it in my nose, but no one wants to lead me. Or sell it if I have to—twenty dollars if I'm lucky (it is far out of style, wide and flat, just gold). Hutch accused me of stealing five dollars from him, a story in itself which you won't need to hear. And no doubt half a dozen boys I have known, maybe some I have taught (maybe Sylvie's nephew Albert), have died in France in fouled underdrawers shot square through the brains while I bore my week.*

As I said, I didn't bear it. Once I got the ring from Gracie, I found a boot-legger and drank myself under but not far enough. I got back here alive and lay down to rest on the floor in my skin—my floor, my skin—and my son found me and fled the whole scene. That was yesterday morning. He left a note saying he had pushed on to Goshen to see Rachel's father and would head home from there. I have not gone in hot pursuit as you see. He is fourteen years old, could father a child; so I guess he can cross the state of Virginia without great risk. If he can't—well, I've hurt people weaker than him and as dear to me.

In my last to you, I said I was trying to do Hutch justice alongside of you. Maybe now I have, to him at least. I've shown him two things I never could have told him—the stock he comes from, or half of the stock, and how little he has actually meant to me. He's all I ever made that was half-worth making, that stands some chance of redeeming the backed-up debts of my life, Forrest's, Eva's, old Rob's. And I made God a vow on the morning he was born that I'd turn and be a man, a decent man you could lean on, if he and Rachel lived. God did half His part; I've never done mine. If I'd loved that boy, I'd have done it, Min, you know—not to mention God or you or Rena, Grainger, Sylvie.

So he knows he's on his own—age fourteen years, long before I knew—and he's given up hope, of me anyhow. If there's anyone on earth I should truly leave alone, I guess it's him now. My grandfather left my father, age five; and Forrest died happy or gave that appearance, not seriously troubled by his failure of Mother or leaving me, age one, or leaving Polly now as abrupt as a sneeze. We have all chugged on, some with more smoke than others but no stopped hearts.

Will you marry me on Monday or as soon thereafter as law permits? You have asked to go free and I understand why; but I'm also as sober as the day I was born (woke at noon yesterday and have needed nothing since, nothing sold in bottles); and I know I must beg you to come back and stay now from here till the end, whoever ends first (and I just mean death, for my part anyhow). I've known it long years, Min; but shame has held me back—shame and my promise to be a good man, with Hutch as God's hostage. God has taken him and gone, so I'm free to beg you. Take please the man that's left. It is who you've

*always known, minus any sane reasons for further shame or hope or Pledge—
except the hope to meet you soon; the pledge to stay by you, such as I am, for
all the time left (maybe thirty more years if I'm like my ancestors in body as in
heart).*

*What I hope to do is this—finish up here by Friday (start the no doubt slow
process of getting myself named executor of Father's intestate estate and, failing any chance of Polly staying in the house, help her move; lock the door; and
think awhile of how to sell it, rent it, burn it, or come back); then drive on to
see Aunt Hatt who has rights in this, I guess; then to Goshen very briefly to see
if Hutch is there safe and wants a ride home. I must do that for Mother if
nobody else. And of course I wish him well. If you write or wire Yes c/o Hutchins
Hotel, I will drive down to Raleigh by Sunday evening if my gas stamps hold
out; and we can work from there—though there's nothing else to say, as you've
already said, except Yes or No.*

*You've tried to say No, and I'll never doubt you felt it with more than good
cause and meant it in your bones, but I'm begging you to change. You have
understood Yes all your life; keep on. I think I have also; it is my single
virtue—how few I've refused. I've damaged six or eight and killed one girl; but
who up to now have I ever refused but you? Pardon please. Let me work at pardon. I may last your life.*

*Will you tell me by Saturday, Sunday morning at the latest? If Yes, then
we'll have other questions to face—do we stay on in Raleigh, you keeping your
job while I hunt for something (my rent there is paid through July 1st and, with
marriage license, I'd let you in)? do we go back to Fontaine for me to teach there,
assuming that's settled? do we head for the moon in a '39 Hudson whose tires
are badly showing their age?—*

> *Though no worse than*
> *Rob*

2

Hutch had asked no directions but walked from the bus toward the west end
of town, past shut stores and houses and the bridge Rob had mentioned into
sudden thick pines and high banks of laurel dark as wet snakeskin and the
sight of one mountain still catching the sunset, well after eight. He thought
he was lost and knew he was weak from not having eaten more than five
cents' worth of peanuts since leaving his aunt's (he was holding his money
back against the unknowns of himself and Goshen—how he'd face his
grandfather, his mother's grave). But he felt no need to turn and ask. If he'd

come the wrong road, he would lie down at dark and sleep till light and find his way then. He had worked through to calm in the past two days, a calm which he recognized and thought he had earned by his courage in making his own life at last, not knowing that it came more than half as a gift from the lives buried in him and the lonely day and whatever cared for him in the hidden world.

So he came up first on the servant's house and saw a light there (the main house was dark), but he knew he was right. It was all in his memory and rose now to match what stood here before him—the house, the springhouse, the broke-down quarters. The light showed dim at the one small window; and since he thought he'd seen a body moving there, he set down his bag and, barely raising his voice, said "Is somebody here?" He knew the walls were thin, two thicknesses of pine; but he heard no steps and no voice answered.

Then a face looked out—Negro, a woman, black as oiled slate.

Hutch only smiled.

And at first the woman answered—the start of her own smile, canceled at once by eyes as refusing as any his mother turned toward him in dreams.

He said "This is Hutchins," meaning his name.

She shook her head No, shut her eyes and was gone.

By then it was nearly dark where he stood. The main house was darker; he could not go there. Yet he knew he had come to the place he expected, that somewhere in this he would find his mother's father. The woman hadn't heard him; maybe he had scared her (she seemed all alone and might have thought he looked like his mother, a spirit). He went to the front door and knocked three times.

Finally she came, switching on a hall light—a tall woman wearing a navy-blue dress, two strings of white beads; her skin as dark as field hands', though she seemed above work.

Hutch said, "I'm looking for Mr. Raven Hutchins."

She shook her head again.

"This is Hutchins Hotel?" He pointed to the house. "I'm not lost, am I?"

"It was," she said.

"He's my grandfather."

She shook her head.

"I'm Rachel's son—"

"*Rob's*," she said.

"—Raven Hutchins," he said, to clarify his name.

"Too late," she said. "He passed in May."

"Is anybody here?" He pointed again.

"Two ladies from Roanoke, on the far side, guests."

"No Hutchins though?"

"*You* if you telling the truth." She reached out as if to touch his right cheekbone, a test of his claim; but even in the new dark, her sight had confirmed him. "You tired?" she said.

"More hungry, I guess."

"Step in here," she said.

Hutch stooped for his bag but thought and stood. "Are you Della?" he said.

"I was," she said. "Step in and let's see." By then she had smiled, if only for herself, at the patience of years.

3

Hutch had asked no more questions and Della had volunteered no answers through the next twenty minutes but had worked at eating. She had brought food out from the kitchen when she'd finished there—enough for her supper and something in the night—and she'd put off eating till she sat and heard the news; so she was hungry also and had enough to share and a spare plate to hold it: cold ham, macaroni and cheese, rolls and water. She had sat on her bed, Hutch in her one chair; they'd swallowed in silence but had studied each other in quick deep glances by the one hanging light—Della searching him for all the signs of his parents, the chance that their old claims on her and her life continued in him; Hutch picturing her younger and helping his father countless nights in this room.

She held on his eyes at last and said "How you know me?"

Hutch had cleaned his plate. He set it by his feet and said "Rob."

"You call him Rob?"

He nodded. "My father."

"I know him. What he tell you?"

"That you used to help him out."

"Out of what?"

"Oh trouble. He said he'd been very unhappy when he got here, and you were a bridge for him."

Della laughed. "To what?"

"My mother, I guess."

"And that made him happy? Well, Jesus be praised; I can die satisfied."

Two days before this, he'd have stood and walked out, proud of one more chance to refuse such a world. Now he was tired and, deeper than tired, knew he also needed help bad as Rob ever had (he was wrong, being safer than Rob at any time; but the two past days had made him doubt every landmark he'd relied on for fourteen years—people, houses, trees). He could not ask directly, not knowing what help or what she would give; so he said, "He thanks you. Rob does; he just told me."

"Where is he?"

"In Richmond."

"They let him back in Richmond?"

"No my grandfather died. Rob's there to settle things."

"Your Mayfield grandpa?—you're losing em, ain't you?"

Hutch saw she spoke earnestly, no taunt on her face. "I'm used to that," he said. "Rob said you knew my mother."

"Good as anybody did. She liked to be secret, but I grew up with her—she couldn't hide long."

Hutch said "She did from me."

Della said "What you remember?"

"Don't you know I never saw her?"

Della said, "I was gone. Excuse me; I was gone, left here when they married. I thought she lasted long enough for you to know her some."

Hutch shook his head. "No. I've seen pictures of her. I've had dreams about her."

Della nodded. "What she do?"

"In the dreams?—she leaves. I find her by accident, standing in the woods; and I ask her to wait so I can call Rob, but she always leaves then."

"You go to get Rob?"

"He's back at the house." Hutch pointed behind him, out of the dream.

"You leave her then; you leave Rachel *first*. That was what she was scared of; nobody would stay. She worked against that so hard it killed her."

Hutch said "I killed her."

Della thought a good while, then stood with her plate, and went to the bureau and set it there. She studied herself in the cloudy mirror, not reaching for her comb or touching herself but as long and closely as if all she knew lay in sight on her face, printed deep in the dark skin, eventually legible. She knew about Rachel what she knew about Della. So she went to the bed again, the far side now, and sat facing Hutch. "Somebody lied to you; I ain't asking who but I *ain't* lying. You hang on to this; I know it's God's truth—Rachel died doing all Rachel ever tried to do. She had her deep faults—I was one that suffered from em—but she wanted one thing in her life: to *have* something. To have it for good. And she wanted it *living*—no clothes or shoes, no ring you could turn. She wanted it *talking*—no dog or cat. She thought it was various ones that it wasn't—her daddy, little friends. They all cut her deep;

no shame on them. Then here come Rob, with the same idea; and she thought it was him. Must have turned out it wasn't—I was gone like I say. So she dreamed it was you."

"Did she tell you that?"

"No, Son, I never saw her once she left that house. I cooked her wedding dinner, and she came in and give me the flowers she had carried and told me I knowed her and to come if she call. I told her I would, and I guess I was lying (I was aiming for Philly). She never did test me though so maybe I wasn't. But no, she dreamed all her life about you; you were something she knew she could truly have, make and keep by her. She died by accident or God cut her string. You stuck with her, ain't you?—you got her deep eyes; you back here now."

"But they're gone," Hutch said. Neither he nor Della had mentioned his grandfather once since she first spoke.

She smiled. "We ain't."

Hutch smiled, agreeing, but he needed more now. "Was he sick a long time?"

"Mr. Raven? Not long. I lived up north from the time I left him, but he'd been good to my mother long as she lived (I used to not think so, but now I see better); and every year he'd think of my birthday, never failed. Here would come a little check wherever I lived, no news, just the money. So when I would come back every two or three years to see my cousin, I would step here to see him; and he'd ask me this (after Miss Carrie died)—'Della, what will you do when I call you to nurse me?' I'd laugh and tell him, 'Mr. Raven, I'll be calling *you*.' I liked it up north and had some good jobs; but the weather didn't suit me, gave me arthritis so bad I got *crippled*, thought I'd sure have to wash up here soon and die. I come down this Easter at the end of a long spell, out of work since Christmas and broke as a honest man. I stayed at my cousin's for the first week or so, just drawing my strength up; didn't go to see him; so he finally come to me. Drove up in the yard and climbed out slow. I saw him out the window and knew he was sick—the way he lifted his legs too high, trying too hard, and once I could see him close, the back of his hands: yellow as gourds and shriveling fast. My cousin was gone and Fitts her boy; so I stood there alone and said 'Della, here it come.' I knew he had called me; and I had to answer—he buried my mother, paid every last penny when pennies round here were thinner than now. And I said, 'All you need now is one more dying'; a friend of mine had died on me back in the fall. But I went to the door and sat with him on the porch. He talked about business, never mentioned the past (only man I know didn't care for the past); said he had a good crowd due in July and August—people give up going to the beach, scared of Germans. Then he said would I come there and help him in the kitchen. I told him I won't what I used to be, that you couldn't lean on me like you used to could. He bent over then—we were setting in rockers—and said it to the ground: 'You everything I got. I got to lean on you.' So I asked him was he poorly. Said he guessed he was. He reached over then and took my hand that was still bad swollen and brought it to his left side and said 'What's that?' My mother used to rub his neck for him sometime (her right hand was healing), so I pressed on him gentle. He said 'Go deeper.' I probed down then and this tumor was waiting, the size of a near-born baby's foot but streaming roots. I tried to laugh and told him 'Feel like you expecting.' — 'Am,' he said, 'so I'm begging you back.'" Della stopped there and looked toward the one window—pure night. She offered no more, thinking that was sufficient or that now Hutch must ask whatever else he wondered.

He said "Were you glad?" —last word she'd expected.

She knew now she had been, an order to rest; but she held that back. That would mean telling this child more than he needed or ever could use. She said, "I was holding the truth in my hand. I told him I would, and you see I did. I'm even still here."

"You said it was May?"

"Three weeks yesterday."

"Nobody had told me."

Della said, "He wrote you. I well know he wrote you; I mailed it myself."

Hutch said, "My birthday—to wish me happy birthday."

"To beg *you* too. He was begging you to come." He voice was low but powerful within, firm with knowledge and her long need to judge.

"He never said that; he said *sometime*." Hutch pointed to his bag and half-rose to open it, prove his excuse.

Della waved him back. "You how old, you tell me?"

"Fourteen in May."

"You old enough to have two children of your own, old enough to die shot if you lie to the army like a lot of good boys; and you saying you thought that was birthday wishes?"

Hutch nodded. "Yes ma'm. I read it that way."

"Let me teach you something then—how to read between lines; that's the best book there is. He was here, going fast, no other kin but you. He didn't talk about you—you were part of the past—but he knew your birthday and wrote that letter and told me to mail it and made me swear I did when I got back to him. He wanted you present, you to *be* the present and all that come after."

Hutch went to his bag then and found the letter. He read it through slowly;

then folded it back, no offer to Della. "Not there," he said. "Nothing there but good wishes, 'Come to see me sometime.' " He was still on his feet.

"All right," Della said, still gentle, still firm, "—sit down and answer this."

Hutch obeyed and faced her.

"How come he give me this?" Looking only at him, she touched the bed with her index finger.

Hutch smiled. "You were tired."

Her high laugh surprised her, a scared-dog yip. "Tired as God," she said. "Tired as waves in the water, but I mean the whole thing. He give me this place." She waved slowly round her with the hand that had pointed. "The hotel, the springhouse, the nigger house, all."

Hutch said "He did right."

Della nodded. "Thank you. I stayed to the real end. We put off the guests that were due to come in May, and Fitts and me saw him through best we could. I never saw him suffer; he could swallow all that, swallowed that all his life. And he wouldn't let me call no doctor for nothing, said doctors were the suckingest leeches on feet; had watched his mama, my mama, and Rachel die in their own blood and still sent him bills just for watching up close. 'They can guess about *me*,' he told me, '—no charge.' So I cooked what he'd eat—bread pudding, boiled custard—and Fitts bathed and shaved him when he couldn't raise his hands. Toward the end I offered to sleep in his room, but he told me '*Too late*' and laughed long minutes. The last time he laughed. After that it froze his tongue, and he could barely talk; so the little he said, he said dead-earnest. He thought I was Mama for two long days and begged my pardon. I never told him better, but he cleared up finally; and when I brought his supper on the evening he died, he said, 'Della, we've seen the whole story of the world.' I told him 'Yes sir'—he had had his own life; and I'd told him some parts of my own little business up north, up yonder." She pointed to the ceiling as if that were north—Philadelphia, Glenolden, tile kitchens she'd kept like the skin of her face, steam-heated dry rooms she'd slept stone-alone in, the men who had found her. "Then he said 'What you know?' —'Know I'm tired, Mr. Raven.' —'Then rest here,' he said. I thought he meant his room; he had his old couch he used to nap on. I told him, 'I'm going to go soak my feet and hit my old bed like a sack of dead birds.' He didn't say no more till I had finished feeding him and picked up the tray. I was heading to the door and he said 'Say thank you.' I said, 'All right. Now tell me what for.' He knew I hadn't understood—'I give you this place,' he said. I said 'You mean the house?' and he said 'All I'm leaving.' So I told him 'Thank you' and went on out, thinking he was just talking and would be there in the morning still waiting for you. He was there, cold as Christmas. Fitts went up and found him—God spared me that much—and we buried him next morning. Preacher asked me 'Where his people?' and I told him we had wrote you, and you never had answered—you nor Rob neither one. He said he'd notify you, but I guess he never did."

"Not me," Hutch said. "I was coming just to see him. It had been eleven years."

"Going to be a lot more." She smiled; trusting fifty, sixty years lay before him.

But he said "Maybe not."

"You sick yourself?"

"No, tired like you."

"I'm pushing forty hard," Della said. "I earned it. What you tired of?—candy? little girls coming at you?"

Hutch knew. "No. Waiting."

"Child, you talk about waiting; you ain't started yet—something else I can teach you."

"What you waiting for?" he said.

She started to tell him—she also knew—but she said "I talked enough."

Hutch said, "My father. I've waited for him going on eight years."

"For him to do what?"

"Find a place for us."

"You ain't got a home? I thought his mama had you."

"She's kept me," he said, "and she's been good to me; I can love her for that. But I wanted Rob—"

"Lot of people wanted Rob—"

"—I didn't have a mother; so I turned to him: he drew me to him, said he wanted me there. At least he showed me that, five years—three years in Richmond till he lost out there; then we tried to come here (Grandfather wouldn't have us, not Rob anyhow); then two years in Fontaine at my grandmother's. Then he left for Raleigh."

"Didn't take you with him?"

"He promised he would. He hadn't even told me he was going till he went. One late August morning I was in the backyard out behind Grainger's house, digging by myself; and Rob came to me and said, 'Sweetheart, I am going for a while to be in Raleigh. I've found a better chance for both of us and will come and get you and Grainger both by New Year's.' So I didn't cry then, but I might as well have and got him behind me. The chance was for just him; he never kept his word."

"What job he have?"

"Teaching school, high school."

"What's Rob know enough about to teach anybody? The stuff he was learning when he lived here, you can't teach children."

Hutch heard that and understood but saw no way to follow it on into her life, the memories she clearly theatened to show. He took up his own story, nearly as hard. "He has this woman in Raleigh that he needs. He's stayed there for her."

Della said "Who is she?"

"Min Tharrington, a teacher. He's known her all his life, since long before Rachel."

"You say they ain't married?"

"He says not, no. They spend time together—"

Della nodded. "All right. You grudging him that?"

"Yes ma'm."

"All right. Then you want him to die. Or grieve himself sick."

Hutch had studied her room through all of that. It was all but bare of the signs of a person—at the foot of the bed, a pair of white shoes, high-heeled and broken; a book on the shelf by the head of the bed, old, crudely covered in new blue cloth; a black alarm clock that had ticked on beneath them, loud in their silence. Otherwise a hotel or a hospital room, where people could twist in torment or die and then be wheeled out and leave no speck. He said "*You've* lived; you are sitting here smiling."

Before she had fully understood him, Della said "I'm smiling at you."

And Hutch said "I'm funny—"

Then she saw he had rushed in and weighed her life and registered it wrong. The force of her feeling for his mother and father, rubbed raw now by their signs in Hutch, longed to slam forward here and tell him precisely *how* she had lived and with what little help from the world—strangers, kin, even those who had promised to pay her with care for the use of her kindness, her quick lean butt. With what little baggage she had come back to Goshen, to what meager welcome (her mother's sunk grave, a helpless ignorant cousin, a dead white man's house she knew she couldn't keep)—still smiling, sucking breath. But the sight of Rachel's eyes, reset in this face ten feet from her bed, recalled what her own dead mother had said when Rachel was wild and pouring abuse—"Remember that child don't mean to cut you, don't know you are here. You can't see it yet, but she's struggling to live *in the same world as you*—new clothes, big house, plenty coal in the shed; but the same hail of fire that'll scald you too is licking her now. She walked out early; your day'll come soon." So Della rose and came round the bed and stood at the foot, Hutch an arm's length away, though she did not touch him.

She said, "It hadn't seemed that hard to me." It had seemed hard as pigiron.

Hutch nodded. "You're lonesome."

"A little, right now. But not for much longer; I'm heading north in June once those ladies leave. They just come Sunday, saying they didn't know; Mr. Raven wrote the others telling them it was over—somehow forgot those. They got another ten days; then I'm heading out."

"And leaving your stuff?"

"I can carry my stuff, one good handful."

"The place," he said.

"Place *yours*," Della said.

"He gave it to you."

"It won't his to give."

Hutch said "Why not?"

"Oh don't get me wrong; it's the Hutchins place and *been* that. I guess what I mean is, it won't mine to take even if the law let me and I could pay taxes— Rachel all over it (and all over you), your daddy's memory, old high-hat Grainger, my mama dropping dead out there by the spring and all us watching. It's yours, Son. *Take it.* You got your place now." She touched him finally, the first time ever, on his right ear and jaw. He was also Rob's; same good skin seamless as a pressed linen sheet, as warm and dry.

Hutch stood, took his bag, and walked to the door. Then he said, "Have you got any sort of flashlight?"

"Where you going?"

"To the house. I remember it now. I'll find a spare bed."

Della shook her head. "Nothing, no flashlight or candle. You go stumbling round over yonder tonight, you'll kill those ladies; two hearts'll stop. They already bolted in tight like they beautiful. Mr. Grainger's room right here next to me; you sleep here tonight, do your looking tomorrow."

He was tired to the sockets so he nodded acceptance.

Della went to a bureau drawer and found clean sheets and stood to come toward him; but again the sight stopped her—his active face, worked as surely by Rachel as if she were in him, still waiting her life. Della spoke to break the lock. "Say thank you," she said.

Hutch said "All right."

"For the place, I mean." She was smiling, dead-earnest.

Hutch nodded. "I knew. I thanked you for that."

4

Tired as he was once she'd made his bed, Hutch had lain three minutes in close concentration on the name of his mother, his version of her face, in the hope of guiding himself into whatever corridor of sleep held the dream of his mother by the creek. He would wait this time till she spoke or called him.

But he failed entirely. For hours, it seemed, his mind only moved through lists of words, no people or scenes. The words were names of things he had wanted all his life, all actual things that could somewhere be got but had never come to him—a Noah's ark like the ones in child's books (two of everything living, the family of Noah, and the great houseboat with its loading ramp), a four-foot hollow stick for use as a blowgun, a set of real photographs of men's and women's bodies from which he could draw and imagine possibilities still beyond him (how the bodies could join and what would be proved or gained in their meeting), an accurate likeness of Joan of Arc, a book explaining what was not told of Jesus in the King James Bible, Hitler's autograph. Then after more hours of deep blank peace, he made a full dream which lasted till dawn, not the story he wanted but the one he got.

He was walking on a flat dark field in France through hills of corpses, not a live soul in sight, no sound but his own feet and distant thunder which was sure to be guns. He was hunting for Rob, but he had no light. That forced him to crouch over man after man and feel cold faces for the traits of his father. The wet stumps of necks. Chests pierced more deeply than any girl. Boys smaller than himself. But no trace of Rob. Then he noticed a brown glow some way ahead and hurried to that—a good-sized tent with a light inside but all flaps laced. He scratched with his nails at the drumhead canvas till he started a tear which he slowly lengthened till he had a straight slit the length of a door. He slid through and found himself warm in kerosene light which showed two men, Sylvie's nephew Albert on a low pine stool and a man on a cot. The man was Rob and, though he was dressed in a clean uniform, Hutch knew he was dead. He took two steps forward into the light—not to touch, only study the resting face (calm as water in a bowl)—but Albert spoke low: "I found him, I'll guard him, you head on back."

He woke then, the first news of day at the window; still dark but the total silence of dawn. He did not remember the facts of his dreams but knew he had failed to reach his mother and though he might well have lain and thought of Grainger (his bed; this room that had held him, hopeful) or of Rob in Richmond (if he'd stayed in Richmond, had not gone to Min or called her to him), he returned to his mother whom sleep would not give him.

But now, even waking, he had lost her face. No memory would come. He stood to the cold floor and felt through the dark for the one light string, found it, scalded the room with sudden glare. He had wanted a mirror—Rachel's face in his—but the pine walls were bare: a long-dead thermometer stuck at 28. In his thin underclothes, Hutch held himself, shivering. The morning before, he had risen at his Aunt Hatt's, planning a new life to spare himself the debts of his kin, their designs to own him outside and in. Here—freezing on a dirty floor, miles from what he wanted, refused by his mother this final time (his sex half-hard still from dreams she avoided)—he saw he'd found nothing new and would never. The world was *made.* It had offered him space and a section of years, a full set of harness to which any number of people held reins, some of them stone-dead. At any moment, unannounced, the offer would vanish and his be a life like Rob's—unwashable shame, permanent flight. Fourteen years old. Children much younger this morning, this instant, were forced into harness as heavy though brief—unrescued death.

Hutch chose to wear it. No sound from Della. He crept to his clothes and quietly dressed. Then he turned out the light again and stopped for his prayers, the Lord's prayer quickly and the names of his kin, adding Grainger and Della. By the end of that, there was some daylight in the room, thin as mist but sufficient for movement. He turned the old doorknob, a rusty cry; if he woke Della now, he would simply explain. He waited on the sill but could only hear her turn once and settle into snoring. So he entered the hall and passed out the main door with no further sound.

The dawn air was colder than the quarters had been, but Hutch stopped and stood in the hope of finding memories to guide him on now through the scarce tan light. They came at him slowly and in the form of buildings—on his right the springhouse, cedar roof pale as pewter. He had drunk there once in his grandfather's arms eleven years ago. He could still taste the cup.

It was waiting there still—a long-handled copper cup, poison-green from its years of use in strong water. Hutch took it down and opened the lid of the spring and bent far down where no light had seeped yet before he found water. Then he drank a slow swallow, far warmer than expected. His Grandfather Hutchins had held it up to him and said, "Son, drink. You ever drink this, you'll need to stay here. It has cured some pain." Hutch found that now like a stone in his mind, covered but patient, ready to serve. He took more water and poured it on his hands and rubbed his face and eyes. Then he hung the dipper back by the working nest of two red wasps and went toward the main house to find the next thing Rob had promised he'd know.

5

He did, though slowly. The big dark kitchen was strange in itself, but there seemed a path through it to an opposite door; and once he had eaten a biscuit from the bread box that stood on a cupboard, he went to the door and (silently again) opened on the central hall of the house, still all but dark. Its only light, through the transom window of the far front door, showed ranks of black doors in whitewashed walls, all closed but the two farthest from him—parlor, dining room. The path seemed to go to the nearest, beyond him. Hutch stood a moment, downing his last dry crumbs and thinking that the door might hide sleeping women or worse—Rob dead on a cot, Albert guarding. Then he took the four steps and opened it quickly and found that he knew—not only that he'd come here with Rob, led secretly, but earlier and freely with his Grandfather Hutchins. It was his bedroom. The shades were up and a window faced the sun.

There was one wide bed with a high carved back—little turrets and pill-boxes, spindles and domes—and below at the foot, a smaller cot like a white dog resting. Both were smoothly made with fresh linen, not a crease in sight. But the path went on to the far wall, a dresser—tall mirror, marble top (a streaked liver-brown). He followed to that. It had been the goal of coming here at all, the source of dreams. It had been where his grandfather kept his mother; Hutch remembered he'd thought of it that way for years. Why? The marble was bare now of all but a yellowing crocheted mat and a pair of men's brushes, bristling dead white hair.

He had been brought here, direct from the springhouse still in his grand-father's arms, to this dresser. He recalled independently of Rob's own story two pictures of a lady, young with dark hair and eyes; his grandfather raising one picture with his free hand for Hutch to see—"This is what we lost. They take it all, Son. Come here and I'll help you." Now he was here. It all was his. Where was the help?

At least there was a mirror. He leaned toward that and searched his face. Though he'd drawn it two nights ago, it seemed strange as ever, unknowable. It had been two years since his Aunt Rena first said he had Rachel's eyes. Till then he'd assumed, when he thought at all, that he'd been and would always be a new thing, a fresh attempt by his parents and God at a thing which would *work* (as the whole world hadn't). But they'd been near the end of Sunday dinner two summers ago, the anniversary of Bedford Kendal's death; and Eva had picked at Rena all morning for having no decent flowers for the grave. Rena as always had waited her time, only saying she was sorry and blaming late frosts; then she had stared long at Hutch and said, "You're turning to

Rachel before our eyes." Eva had said, "There are several eyes present; you speak for your own"; and they'd dropped it there. But Hutch had asked Grainger a few days later and Grainger agreed—"Plain as day; her eyes, for the past year or so." After that Hutch had studied himself with new hope— that the half of his life which had gone at his birth had in fact only slept and was waking inside him, molding his face in silence from within, offering the gift he had never had: absolute certainty of love and safety, a permanent shadow.

Now he leaned till his breath fogged the glass. Still strange. He recalled Della's speech—"She wanted to have one thing in her life: something living, for good. Something talking."

So he spoke. His dry lips brushing cold glass, he said, "You have got it, Mother. You could come back." He drew back then and saw reflected a woman in the open door, tall in a nightgown, a green bathrobe. Calm as at no other time in his life, he turned to meet her.

She said "Who are you?" but before he had answered, she saw and said "Hutchins."

"Yes ma'm. Do I know you?"

It took her awhile. "No you don't, I guess. I was your mother's friend, Alice Matthews." She pointed to her left. "I sleep next door and I heard footsteps. I thought it was Della."

"No ma'm," he said. "How did you recognize me?"

Alice waited again. "Your mother," she said. "You're hers all right."

Hutch said "Tell me how."

"Your face, I meant."

"Do you have her picture?"

"Not with me," she said. "I'm in Roanoke now. There are pictures here though." She came forward then the length of the room and knelt and opened a dresser drawer. "These were your grandfather's. Della put them away just yesterday morning; I was helping her clean." She held out two framed pictures to Hutch.

He suddenly dreaded to take them but did.

Alice rose and stood beside him while he looked.

Rachel, laughing broadly in both. One was blurred by her moving; she leaned far forward with her elbows propped on a high white railing and held her own chin in two long hands. Just the face was blurred; the body was still as a tree in August. It seemed to Hutch that some strange girl was pressing a happy mask to her own face, hidden and safe. But the same girl laughed clear as ice in the other (same dress, same day); the camera had seized her, though not her hair—it burned out round her and mixed with the dark leaves that pressed from behind. She was in the same springhouse that he had just left and beside her, four feet away, another girl stood and watched her closely. Hutch looked up and said, "What was funny, I wonder?"

"So did I," Alice said. "I'm the onlooker there."

Since Rachel faced outward, intent on the camera, Hutch said "Who took it?"

"Rob Mayfield," Alice said. "Is he here with you?" She looked to the door as if Rob might wait there.

"I'm alone," Hutch said. "I'm here on my own."

Alice nodded. "I'm sorry—" She meant his grandfather.

Hutch thought she meant his loneliness. "I am too," he said. Then he studied the second picture again. "What was happening here?"

Alice reached out to take it.

Hutch said, "I think these are mine now please."

Alice flushed and wanted to turn and leave. But twenty years of teaching art to children his age (and a childhood of living in her father's sanitarium) had taught her one thing at least—all children are desperate: boys more so than girls since boys seldom know it; girls taste it from birth. She looked at her watch and said, "Quarter to six. No Della for an hour. Come help me fix coffee. That's a story; I'll tell you." She pointed to the picture, but she did not touch it.

6

When she'd poured their coffee and set it on the table, Alice said, "I would scramble you an egg but Della'd kill me." Then she sat at the far end from Hutch and drank, scalding hot, no cream. Then she said, "November 1925, the day before her wedding. I had come up from Lynchburg on the early train; and her mother had given a small lunch party, her piano teacher and two local girls (Rachel didn't have many friends; she kept them too busy). That was over by three; and her mother ordered naps all round, to protect her. I was frankly delighted, having woke before day; but as soon as I stretched out, Rachel came knocking and wanted to talk. I knew she was wrought up and I understood why, but my father had been her doctor and I'd nursed her; so I said, 'Talk to me for five minutes straight, and then lie here and rest'—all the beds then were double; anybody slept alone was thought to be odd if not in worse trouble. Rachel sat on the edge of the bed and laughed and said, 'Five minutes? I will need one second.' Your mother was a well-practiced talker, Hutchins; she could go on for minutes, hours if Rob was the theme. So I said, 'Praise

God, take two and then rest.' Rachel said 'I'm going to die.' I said 'Says who?'
(my father had seen her through serious trouble, though nothing too mortal).
She lay back beside me then and showed no intention of explaining herself.
I assumed she was joking and dropped off to sleep. We were under a down
quilt—the upstairs was cold—and she lay there as still as a field beside me for
more than an hour till I'd got my strength back and woke up and looked. Her
eyes were open, just watching the ceiling. It was well past four, and the light
was failing. I had already put her joke from my mind; I said 'Did you rest?'
She said 'No ma'm' (I am one year her senior); and I said, 'You missed your
last good chance.' Rob had already gone to meet his Aunt Rena; his father
would get here at six-fifteen; wedding supper was at seven. Rachel said 'Stop
there' and turned her face to see me. Then she said, 'Every string of my being
knows this—*I will not last*. I have been too lucky. I will rest much sooner than
anybody knows. Let me have my way.' I watched her through that and knew
she was right. Some message had reached her; I've never known who from.
Till then, young as I was, I'd really tried to help her, not humor her along as
her poor parents did. I loved her that much, and I thought she could change
(children think people change). But seeing her eyes then, I knew I was wrong.
I said, 'All right. Say what I must do.' She laughed again and said 'Oh nothing.' But she sat up and thought awhile and said, 'Do this. Take some pictures
of me. There are not any good ones.' I said, 'All right but it's getting late.' I had
brought my father's antique Kodak which required blinding light. She
jumped up and combed her hair. I slipped on my dress and shoes, and down
we went. She wanted me to take her in the chair on the porch where she
always sat. I said she would have to lean forward on the railing to catch a little sun, and that explains this one." Alice pointed to a picture.

Hutch said, "What explains the laugh if she knew she was dying?"

"My foolishness," Alice said. "I told her something funny."

Hutch studied the face again, then smiled at Alice. "Tell me," he said.

She flushed again, embarrassed but glad to recall. "I had got my first job
two months before, teaching in South Hill; and I lived in the house of a
widow named Key who had four roomers and one bathroom and severe con-
stipation as her personal cross. The trick every morning was to beat her to the
bathroom or we'd be late for school. The trick seldom worked; the general
sign that the day had started was the sound of her bolting the bathroom door
and running warm water for her enema bag. It was bright red and hung on
the back of the door like an object of pride. By a week before the wedding,
we were fed up with *that*; and the one male roomer—the coach, Peg
Pittman—had planned a revenge and warned me in advance. He went to the
bathroom late that night and poured a full tablespoon of pure turpentine in

her enema bag. So morning came and she bolted the door, and we all lay and listened. Running water, long silence; then cries of '*Mozelle!*' (Mozelle was the maid), 'Mozelle, oh Jesus!' I was telling Rachel that."

Hutch also laughed and said, "Did she live?—your lady, I mean."

"Lived and was cured." Alice rose and poured her cool coffee down the drain and took a hot cup. "You ready for more?"

"No ma'm," he said, taking up the other picture, the one in the spring-house. "You say this is you?"

Alice came and looked again. "I regret to say. Don't I look like a witch?"

"Yes ma'm," Hutch said. "Who was holding the Kodak?"

"Guess."

"Della maybe?"

"Rob," Alice said. "I had taken four or five pictures there on the porch. Rachel said we had enough and took me to the spring. I had been here to visit just once before; and then she had warned me off the spring—it was old and dirty and, if I'm not mistaken, had given her Grandmother Hutchins the ailment that finally killed her. But this day she said, 'Have you tasted the spring?' and I said I hadn't. She said, 'That's part of what I want then'; so we walked over there, and I set down the Kodak on one of the railings. It had been cleaned up quite a lot since I saw it; swept out, new roof, the scrollwork painted. I didn't mention how she'd described it before but drank when she held that dipper out to me. As I swallowed I thought, 'This is all still a joke. Rachel won't drink now and will tell me *I'm* dying.' But she took the cup from me—I had drunk just a swallow—and downed what was left; and we sat on the steps of the far side in sunshine. She asked me to tell her what my life was like. I'd known her some months; she never had asked me; and I started to tell her, the serious part, no more turpentine jokes. Then a man's voice said, 'Now the world can *proceed.*' It was Rob, back from meeting Miss Rena's train. I was square in the middle of what she had asked for, my thrilling life; but she touched my knee and said 'Alice, please wait.' Then she stood and went toward him; and of course I did too, though a good way back. He had seen my Kodak and was aiming it at us; so he caught what was there, caught it clear as you see. I never knew how. All mine were blurred but his was clear—and Rachel vibrated in every cell from the moment he spoke. Miss Rena was behind him, not approving at all."

Hutch said, "Grandfather kept it. But he didn't like Rob."

"Who told you that?"

"Rob."

Alice took a long draught of her coffee, then faced him. "You're four-teen, aren't you?"

"Yes ma'm."

"Live with Rob?"

"No ma'm, with his mother."

"May I tell you my feelings?"

"Yes ma'm," Hutch said.

Alice hooked her own short hair behind her ears and showed her full face, her permission to speak plain, the license she'd earned. A fine calm face with whole long planes like warm ground in light, room to rest, little used. "Mr. Hutchins liked Rob well enough. So did I. What worried us all was the knowledge that he was as needy as Rachel in his own different way, as Hell-bent on food; that they couldn't feed each other for long without one finishing the other off. They were not big feasts; they were country children. Hutch, they could have been Albert Einstein and Madame Curie and still been in danger."

"Why?"

Alice thought she knew, had known for years. "They thought they had *rights*."

"To what?"

"Their wishes. Their wishes fulfilled."

"What's wrong about that?" Hutch said.

"Very little—provided people know that wishes are dreams, stories people tell themselves; that wishes aren't orders which the world will obey. Rob and Rachel didn't know that one simple fact. Rob may have changed since. Rachel never did, I know; never could have, however many years she got."

Hutch said, "Were you old enough to know what they wished?—this day, I mean." He still held the frame with the springhouse picture.

Alice said, "Son, I knew it from birth. So have you. I know it is all any human dreams of, no secret at all." She stopped there and watched him, smiling over her cup.

He also smiled. "You aren't going to tell me?"

"Tell *me*," she said.

Hutch knew she was a teacher and must work like this. At the same time he knew the old school-pleasure of the one right answer on his tongue, held ready. He said, "To be still next to someone you want in a place where there's no extra people in sight."

Alice laughed. She had not planned to hear it that way. She had thought he would somehow speak, like most, of courteous lasting mutual love.

"Then what is it?" Hutch said, a serious question.

She opened her mouth to say it her way, then could not. He had learned a truer wish—or one half-truer than hers at least. If nothing else had come of Rachel and Rob, this had; this lean boy five feet beyond her, waiting silently for what he already knew better than she. So she said, "No, *still*. To be still. Just the *still* part, I think. Other people come later and are mostly mistakes."

Hutch said, "Then Rachel's happy. I did her a favor."

"How's that?"

"That she died. That sounds still to me."

Alice laughed again but cut it down in midair.

"I don't believe you though."

"About what?"

"About people, not for me anyhow. I've wanted Rob with me since before I remember. Nobody else."

Alice said "Where is he?"

"In Richmond two days ago when I left there. But he was drunk then, so he could have moved on. He could be on the moon or in Normandy dead, but he's not wishing Raven Mayfield was there."

"That's you?"

"Yes ma'm."

Alice said "I believe you" and flushed with regret, to have told a child more truth than he required.

But Hutch only looked to the window behind her and said, "Can you say if you've got your wish?"

She could. "Yes I have."

"Will you tell me how?"

She thought awhile. "It has been very simple. Nobody tried to stop me! I've lived in a single room for nineteen years, a good single bed not as wide as this table."

"And you really wanted that?"

Alice waited again till she had the truth. "When I was a child, yes. And more and more lately. My father ran a private sanitarium in Lynchburg— at first for weak chests, then for weak nerves and dopers of various sorts—and I grew up in a house next door, a plain quiet girl who was no good at anything but watercolor drawings; so maybe you will know that all I prayed for till I was, say, your age was *me in a room* with a one-way lock and a window that would see *out* but not show me. I thought I could sit there and spy on the world, which was mostly Father's patients, till I'd understood its beauty—I was told it had a beauty, by God's design—and could draw that pattern down in color on paper so clearly and plainly that I could walk out then and people would love me as naturally as dogs had. I thought it would be pictures of people—the pattern, people clustered like plants in their proper native spheres—and that they would recognize themselves and thank me for it. And they did seem to praise me, when I was a child and walked out occasionally to where people were. Then I got your age and began to think I'd understood wrongly—that the world came *paired,* that the pattern was simple: one here, one there, the line between. And misery began. I thought I'd been bad off before! I'd been *blessed.*"

Hutch said, "Who was it? Did you know who it was?"

Alice nodded. "Clear as a needle through the eye, clearer than anything else I've known. Named Marion Thomas, a tall boy with eyes such a pale light blue that from ten feet away they seemed all-white; and he seemed a statue in warm tan marble. Ten feet was near as I ever got to him, and in Latin class. He was very good at it and smiled a lot but always toward the front (I was three seats behind in the next row over). I kept a full record for one entire year of what he wore to school—gray trousers, blue shirt, a stretched gray sweater; that sort of simple thing. It seemed a path into his secret heart. I still have the list and, you know, it worked. I grew to understand him deep down to the ground. I could wake up and look out my window at the day and know how he'd dress, the socks he'd choose. I could almost guess what he'd smile at in class. He said about eighty-five words to me in the course of that year. Then his father died and he had to work—at a general store on the outskirts of town where I never went. I hurt for two years; I would sit and draw the memory of his face by the hour."

"Did he know?"

Alice traced a peaked vertical line on the table; then repeated it twice as if summoning memory and hardening it, the line of a face. "I used to think not. As I said, all he ever asked about was homework; but then two years ago when my mother died, he came to the funeral. I saw him in the small crowd behind the grave; and it struck me like a great hand, harder than the death. He had barely known Mother, and I hadn't seen him in twenty-four years; so all I could think there, with Mother cold before me, was 'What can he say?' Well, the first thing he said after 'Alice, I'm sorry' was 'Meet my wife'—a thin woman plainer than I'd ever been, with several times more teeth than most humans have. Then he took my hand back and said 'See, I never forgot.'"

Hutch said "What did that mean?"

"I have no idea."

"And you didn't ask him?"

"No. He might have said something like he'd known and was grateful; and then I'd have seen we were both great fools, mooning down the years (though he'd had her standing by to fill in)."

Hutch said, "You were by yourself till then? He was all you wanted?"

Alice smiled and did a whole crowd of quick profiles around her cup, lost on the wood. "Oh no. Several others; I was seldom not pining. Or wishing at least. I was never really pining. They were all real chances, all possible people; no moviestars or princes, none already spoke for."

"Did you ever speak?"

"For one of them? Yes. I learned to do that once Marion was over clerking dried beans and rope. Never lose in silence. Speak up and then wait. I have told three people, in words more or less, that I wanted their lives near mine for good. One of them was Rachel. They all said No, politely but No."

"Who's here with you now?"

"My father's pet sister. I've given her this trip for three years now since your grandfather wrote and invited me up. She suffers from asthma and the mountains help. But I guess this ends it."

Hutch only said, "When did you change your mind?"

"To what?"

"To your old thought of just being still. You said you had come back to wanting that again."

Alice said, "I never really left it altogether. In my deepest longing, sitting two feet away from a human person that I had made God, I would hear the buried core of my mind say, 'Alice, you're lying and you know it.' No I tell you, Hutch, I guess I could forget again tomorrow and fix on some face, magnetize some perfectly plain human face and rush helpless to it; but I have long stretches now of what seems peace."

"When mostly?" Hutch said.

Alice laughed. "Good night! J. Edgar Hoover!"

Hutch smiled. "I'm sorry. But I really need to know."

She studied him again and saw that he did. "Are you busy this morning?"

"No ma'm."

"Then I'll show you. I've talked too much."

Hutch nodded. "What time?"

"An hour after breakfast; let the sun get up." She stood and went to the sink again.

Hutch said, "Please say what was wrong with my mother."

Alice kept her back to him. "In what way?" she said.

"Everything people say makes her sound too strange."

"What way?" Alice said.

"Every way she could go—wanting me, wanting Rob, wanting death that young, not wanting you when you spoke out for her life."

Alice emptied her cup, rinsed the brown dregs down; then turned, grinning broadly. "That was pure good sense. Every one of those," she said. She honestly did not think she lied.

The porch door opened and Della looked in; looked slowly round the whole room, then gravely at Hutch. She said, "Well, it wasn't mine long but I *enjoyed* it. Anybody need a cook? I'm a good bacon cook. Can't everybody cook good bacon, I tell you." She laughed and they joined her.

7

By noon Hutch was thinking he'd finished his picture. It was clear lines drawn with his best hard pencil, no smearing, no shadows. It was what he could see from the flat bare ledge on the rocky slope where he'd sat for two hours — the rest of the slope, the back and head of Alice who was twenty feet down on her own ledge under a big bent cedar, the distant bottom with the quick brown river, the opposite walls of sheer tan rock which (with laurel and some strange yellow flowers) bore the bright green mountain. He clamped the pencil between his teeth and studied the whole sight against his picture. It was not what he'd seen or was seeing now. Nothing he had ever attempted was that. It was what he could make, on this one morning (having driven out to here with his mother's old friend to sit in pure silence — only nesting birds, the fierce hot ringing of bugs in weeds: no word from Alice since she'd chosen her own place and settled to work). Not *could* make, even.

It was one thing he *had* made this morning, unaided, from what the earth offered of its visible skin — the surface it flaunted in dazzling stillness, in the glaze of rest, to beg us to watch; then grope for its heart. (He knew that much now, had known it some weeks; but would not have said it or felt it in words.)

The hard part as always was trees, not their trunks which were easy as human legs and as frank in their purpose but leaves — their hanging gardens in tiers. He had done those badly. The opposite rocks, the back of the mountain, the line of Alice's back and head, her farmer's hat — they were right and true, his own gift offered to the world in return. A peaceful likeness of a peaceful sight. The promise or the strong hope of long years of swapping, with mutual aim — a common stillness, common provisions.

Alice moved, stretched her arms but did not look back. "Want to show me now?"

Hutch looked again. The leaves were worse. "No ma'm," he said.

She returned to work.

If he'd left them out — assumed it was fall (there were days good as this in mid-November) and drawn plain trunks and a few stripped limbs. He reached for his new eraser to strip them. If he'd been on the porch in Fontaine now,

Aunt Rena behind him might have said "No, stop." She had said that the Sunday after his birthday when he'd sat down to use his new tablet and pencils on the yard-trees, the millstone, her shrubs, the road. He had done it in clear lines, then started to shade. She had sat six feet away and watched twenty minutes without a sound. He'd learned to forget her—till his thumb scrubbed-in the first shadow (farthest first). Then she'd rocked forward firmly and said, "May I tell you? The whole world is waiting to see what you're ruining." He had stopped and said, "Ma'm? I'm not that good"; and Rena said, "Not you— the secrets of God. The whole world is waiting in expectation for the revelation of the secrets of God. You've just now drawn their excellent likeness and are ruining it." Hutch had said "It's the yard" but had stopped there and sat, not touching his paper, not asking her more, till she stood and went in.

So he spared the trees now. He trusted to wait till the secret of leaves, if nothing more, came into his power. First the power to watch one green leaf in stillness; then the dark banked branches in all their intricate shifting concealment—concealed good news (that under the face of the earth lay care, a loving heart, though maybe asleep: a giant in a cave who was dreaming the world, a tale for his long night) or concealed news of hatred embellished with green (that a sight like this or a shape like Rob's was only the jeering mask of a demon who knew men's souls and guided their steps). It seemed, now at least, that any such power would come here if anywhere. This place was an entrance. He'd need to wait here.

How nearly alone though? Della would stay, had already offered. They'd have to go on taking odd guests for money. Della and Fitts could see to that. And would Grainger respond to his letter and come and want to stay? Would he be too many, not wishing them well? Hutch knew he was dreaming Alice's dream—not his own or Rob's, surely not Rachel's—but he felt what Alice had promised to show, plain peace. She had not lied. Whoever else in all his life had not lied? He looked down toward her.

She was no longer painting but still looked over toward the mountain, not moving.

He said, "Miss Matthews, could Rachel have sat here?"

"With us, you mean?" She didn't look back.

"Yes ma'm."

"Not really." She waited awhile, then said "Not at all."

"Have you had a good time?"

"This morning? Still am." She hadn't turned yet.

"You teach in Roanoke?"

"September sixth."

"Stay on till then."

Alice looked to the sky. "I might get wet."

Hutch laughed but after a while said "I mean it."

"And I'm grateful," she said.

"Look here please," he said.

Slowly Alice looked round. The sun was behind him but oh what was left of Rachel was clear, the hair and the eyes and behind them the passion for absolute pleasure, the soul's reward. She shaded her eyes then and saw him more clearly, a long-boned boy, young-faced for his age. She thought she could stay here by him for good. A person had asked. The chance was now. It would not come again. Rewards came in *their* time, undreamed-of forms. She thought she was going to say "All right." But Hutch looked away, down at his tablet.

He had taken his pencil and was signing the picture—one name, *Mayfield*. Then he stood and, not looking to the rough ground for safety, he half-ran toward her.

8

Rob said, "Excuse me for knocking this late but the hotel was dark, and I saw your light."

She nodded. "I was listening to the radio." It was on behind her, some grainy music from Cuba or Mexico, hoarse from its journey.

He said, "I just drove up here from Richmond. My name is Mayfield. I'm meeting my son Hutch Mayfield; is he here?"

She pointed toward the dark house. "Yonder asleep."

"Mr. Hutchins asleep?"

"Mr. Hutchins been dead three weeks, Rob," she said.

The only light was her overhead bulb which struck him fully but barely touched her. Still he searched at her face. "You know me?" he said.

"I used to, a little."

He still couldn't see and the voice was strange. "Is it Della Simmons' cousin?"

She waited in silence a good five seconds, then bent down laughing, then stood and took two steps back into light. "It used to be *Della*," she said, "—last I looked."

Rob followed her in but kept the same distance while he studied the face. Even in the white light, he didn't know her—an older sister who had had a harder life but no, not Della. Yet she'd known him on sight, and why would she lie? He looked round for some firm piece of the past. The bed, the table, the dresser were the same; but they were Mr. Hutchins'. He said, "Have you got your dream book still?"

"You dreaming too?" She pointed to the shelf beside the bed, the yellow edges of an old book wrapped in fresh blue cloth.

"Can I sit down?" he said.

"You didn't use to ask." She was no longer smiling, but she showed him the chair. While he sat, she stayed on her feet to watch him. Then she said "You sick?"

"I have been," he said. "No I'm mainly tired—old thin recaps, had to drive so slow the car boiled over. Had to wait two hours by the side of the road."

"You want you a shot?"

Rob faced her again. Was she really Della? "You keeping that now?"

"I got me a pint, case a snake crawl on me." She stepped toward the bureau.

"Is Hutch really here?"

"I told you he was sleep. Mr. Raven's room."

"And Mr. Raven's dead?"

"The cancer. In May."

She had found her pint, a little more than half-full. With pure concentration she took her one waterglass and poured in an inch of whisky, knocked it back in a single swallow. Then a pause, then again. Then she turned to Rob. "Speak now or hold your peace."

He shook his head No. "What is that for?" he said. It could have been cold tea; she hadn't winced once.

Della capped her bottle carefully and laid it away. "I heard you were some kind of expert on that."

"From Hutch?"

"N'mind who."

Rob smiled. "I am. Maybe not an expert but pretty well-trained. And you know why, you know every reason, you've known a long time. I was asking about you."

Della went to the radio and turned it down so the music was ghostly under what came after. Then she sat on the foot of her bed, facing Rob. "What you want?" she said. "You want me to tell you I died-off for you?—just rolled over sick when Rachel grabbed you, just started sucking bottles? You come to hear that?"

He still smiled. "No."

"Good thing," Della said. "You'd have wasted good gas."

"I came to get Hutch."

"You wasted it then."

Rob said "What are you saying?"

"I'm saying that child ain't letting you get him. He got what he say he always wanted, a place; and he plan on sticking with it."

"This place?"

Della nodded. "From me. I give it to him. Mr. Raven left it to me, and I passed it on to Hutch."

"And Hutch plans to run it?—fourteen years old, poorest hotel in Virginia?"

"We got two paying guests in yonder right now and more on the way once he tell em 'Come on' (Mr. Raven stopped a lot of folks by mail when he was dying). People like this place, old people anyhow—my age, don't you know." She seemed entirely earnest.

Rob said, "You staying here with him then?"

"He asked me to, this morning first thing. Come out here and woke me up at quarter to six—said he couldn't sleep for thinking—and told me he was wanting to live on here and us run the place and him go to school here and Miss Alice come back next summer and help him. Said old Grainger might come."

"Miss Alice who?" Rob said.

"Matthews. Rachel's friend."

"She's the one here now?"

"With her old aunt from Lynchburg."

Rob said, "She's in on this dream too? She putting up some money?"

Della wiped her dry lips with the back of her hand. "I told you too much. He swore me not to tell. I was all he had told till I told you. You go mock him now, I'll kill you, Rob."

She seemed half to smile but her face was so changed from his memory that he saw no firm landmarks for judging her now—not fat but a thick inward padding deep round her, held forward like a shield of air or feathers. Finally he said "You never liked Rachel."

"I never liked you."

Rob nodded. "All right. I meant something else."

"Say it then."

"You're helping Hutch."

"I never claimed that." She shook her head firmly.

"You talk about staying here with him," Rob said, "—that foolishness."

Della looked to her lap. "I'm helping *me* and about-damn-time."

Rob said, "I already asked you what was wrong."

She studied him a long time; then faced her bureau mirror—tried to cut down through meat to the old face he'd known, that had helped bring him here those eighteen nights in the summer and fall of '25: a girl all pointed with

the will to *leave*, hot to the touch with the steady banked coals of denial and
silence and famishment, eyes like a fox. She found her easily, then offered her
to Rob. "I left here two days after you and Rachel; didn't give no word of notice
or nothing, just walked out and went. Straight north to Philadelphia and my
Cousin Tee. She was my mother's best niece, and I hadn't seen her since I
was a child; but she sent me a message when Mama died, saying, 'Come on
to Heaven and live with me.' Heaven was a cafe named The Delicate
Teacup that she owned part of. I went straight to it from the depot by asking,
and she hadn't got my letter. But she knew me by sight (I hadn't changed then;
you'd have still recognized me) and started in hollering when I stepped
through the door—'O Jesus, *Lucy.*' I said I was Della; and she said 'Can you
work?'—it was Saturday night. Well, the hollering stopped. I cooked right on
through Christmas and New Year, cooked three years without looking up.
Same way I cook here. They didn't seem to mind; ate it all anyhow and paid
good money—colored people, understand. Then Tee got married. She
had had one husband that melted away but never no baby (and that had half-
killed her), so I had lived with her and managed all right. But here come the
new man, a whole lot younger; and here come a baby. She picked her a baby
right out of that man like a splinter from your finger. Forty-four years old. I
told her 'Be ashamed'; and she told me, 'All right but you can't watch'; she
meant 'Get out.' I was glad by then. I had a fellow my age been asking for me,
named Newmarket Watters. He come in The Teacup on Saturday nights and
wait till I finish, which would be near morning, and carry me to ride or something like that. He worked out from Philly on a rich man's place, gardener and
chauffeur; and they let him take they car on his night off. That meant they
trusted him—ought to: they raised him (his mama was their cook, and he grew
up beside em; she died before he saw me). I trusted him too; first person I
trusted since I was a child. Trusted him and started thinking my time had
come, my *luck* had come. So when Tee's baby started and I ruined my welcome, he asked me did I want a job with his white folks; they were needing
a maid, already had a cook. I told him 'All right'; and he said I was hired—
they trusted him to hire me. Well, he moved me out there the week before
Christmas; and I *knew* I was blessed. Had a good warm room to myself in the
quarters (Newmarket next door) and never touched a stove; they had a man-
cook from overseas. I just swept up and polished floors. They were gone
half the winter—in Georgia, staying warm—and when they were there, they
didn't barely know you. I mean, they could smile if they bumped into you;
but they didn't want nothing they hadn't paid for, a good-smelling house.
Didn't want your whole life. I gave it to em, the sweet-smelling house; the rest
I was giving to Newmarket Watters." Della stopped and looked to the mirror

again. She could see her old face; it still seemed a gift. She turned back to Rob. "You believe me, don't you? You know what I got."

Rob nodded he did.

Then she said, "No you don't. You don't know half. I was opening up all grades of flowers down in me that you never got near and sure never *touched*. Newmarket was four shades darker than me (I darkened since then); and I thought he could last me; thought time would come when he'd tell me by day, and in presence of company, what he told me by night. So a year of that passed; and I thought it was Heaven, like Tee had promised. I still think it was, ain't never spit on it, nothing ever been as good. Then here come Hoover and his depression. My folks lost they money or the best part of it; and four months later he keeled over dead, heart split down the middle. But the lady was living. She still had the house, and I was still waxing floors; and Newmarket still come visiting me, no sign he had changed. Thing was, he hadn't. It was me had been the change; little temporary change, little snack of home cooking before he went back where he wanted to be. Two months after that old man's heart broke, Newmarket come in to me one evening extra early. We just talked awhile; then I rose up to touch him (he made touching him seem part of your duty; he was that fine to see), and he said 'Wait a minute.' I waited while he told how hard-up the lady was, how hard she had to save, how she had to let me and the foreigner go. I said 'What about you?' and he said 'She need me.' I said '*I* need you' (I wish I'd bit my tongue out); and he said, 'I've been here all my life. I can't leave now.' Then he reached out to feel me, and I struck him like a snake. He had told me to wait. I said, 'You can wait till the hills yawn open and show you Hell, you ain't even *smelling* Della Simmons again.' He never did neither. I was packed up and gone out of there in a hour, never got my last pay."

"That was 1929?"

"1930, May 1930."

Rob said, "Rachel died the same month."

"I heard it," Della said, "—people down here wrote me." She waited awhile; then she said straight at him, "I was telling *you*. You asked me the reason. If you want to tell your troubles, let me sleep. Go wake up Hutch or Miss Alice; they'll listen."

He said again "You know mine" and managed to smile.

She said "I know everybody's," then surprised herself by easy laughter.

Rob waited till she finished. Then when she didn't speak again but pleated her bedspread, he said "What's your joke?"

"*Everybody* know," she said. "Everybody know everybody's troubles; all the same. What am *I* telling *you*?"

"A story," Rob said.

"What about?"

"Why you're back here. Why you want to stay."

Della shook her head silently, still pinching the spread. She fell back heavily against the one pillow. Her eyes were clamped shut. Then she said "Wrong again."

Tired as he was, Rob thought he understood. With her story as a trowel she had dug back not only to her first young face, the face that had drawn him, but to feelings he'd tasted in her nineteen years ago—a girl's first craving to float a man's weight on what she has guessed is a great deep of water, the untested secret of her nature and strength. Aching and dazed, he found she'd uncovered his own old need—to ride such a deep and to probe its dark, its constant promise that the skin of a body, of maybe the earth, was only the veil of a better place where the soul would be *borne*. A sheltered bay.

He stood and went to the edge of her bed and sat on the small square of pleats she'd made, not quite touching her. He was speechless with thanks— for old help renewed with no prior claim of sacrifice or debt. He was not so much young and starting again as *himself* again. He felt what he'd always been in his depths (however long buried, drowned, assaulted, ignored)—a strong gentle boy named Robinson Mayfield, who meant only good to the world and himself and would live to achieve it as trees do leaves, in silent perfection, the absence of doubt, a natural skill. The back of his right hand touched her right arm.

Della's eyes stayed shut but she breathed on calmly, awake and permitting his nearness again.

So in that dream of faith, he was free to move gradually; dream farther onward, this minute sustained. He could live on here, with Hutch again. There was one school in town, four county schools; men scarce in the mountains as Negroes or flat fields, all broke-down or fighting. They could ask Polly here. It was Hutch's not Forrest's; she'd come for Hutch. She'd take to Della, another strong orphan with the courage of oak. He would last out his life now, forgiven and freed, his intended self.

Della moved her arm, separate from Rob, and laid it on her stomach.

It did not jar his calm or hope. He said, "You're sure this will all go to Hutch?"

She nodded, not looking. "*Gone,*" she said. "Already gone to him. Nobody else want it. Rachel getting him back here to keep like she planned."

Rob said "And you're staying?"

"Not for Rachel," she said.

"No for you."

Della chuckled. Then she looked up at him. "I'm staying in the hope I die soon in peace and can lie by my mother."

Rob could not speak to that; he silently believed her.

Her smile endured but with such a strong light as to show both her gravity and some hidden joy which even she had only guessed, the hope of rest. She said, "I've got a little burial savings. Not nearly enough. Will you see me buried right?—good waterproof box?"

Rob nodded. "Are you sick?"

"No strong as a bear. Just tired, tired out. But you done promised—Della buried in style." She laughed again and shut her eyes; crossed her thick hands on her puddled breasts, her picture of peace.

So Rob laughed also and took her right wrist and raised it in the air. "Look here," he said.

Della looked at his asking eyes and understood. "I couldn't. Not now. These bones wouldn't bear you."

He waited, their hands joined, suspended between them. "They have," he said. "We have not really changed." Then he said "I'm begging."

9

Hutch did not wake till he heard the sound of running water. He had been deep asleep, not dreaming or hoping to but genuinely healing in every cell. Then he came awake cleanly, not shocked or scared. The room that opened off the far bedroom-wall was a small bath made from a closed sideporch. The light was on there, and the door was closed; but someone was filling the basin slowly, then slowly washing—Hutch could hear soap-on-rag, rag slapping skin, a toweling-down, a mouth rinsed twice. There was some faint light from the moon through blinds, enough to see there were clothes on a rocker which were not his own (too crumpled to know) but no sign of a bag. He knew it was Rob, no question at all—the rhythms of washing (Rob could never wash quickly; he'd rather go dirty than speed through a rite as solemn as any), the sound from the rinsed throat of grateful relief. Rob had come now and found him.

Hutch at first wondered why and what he would say to whatever came next, anger and orders or the old numb apologies, pledges, amends. He'd moved so far from Rob in these four days—Hatt, Della, and Alice; the chances of real life—that he'd planned no replies for what was now on him. Still he was not worried; and the hard revulsion of the last night in Richmond, though remembered, was distant. It occurred to him, waiting, that he must have wanted this. A man had come through his door and, whatever else, had undressed ten feet from his sleeping body; and he had not stirred. He liked to think he woke at the slightest change round him and generally he did. He thought now he'd known in the pit of his sleep who the change represented—his father—and had welcomed him by love's homeliest gift, the adjacent trust of untroubled sleep. Hutch also knew Rob had never surprised him, even drunk and naked on his own father's floor. He saw now how children learn the terrors of the world—by watching their parents, suspecting them of infinite power to turn in an instant into monsters, then confirming that suspicion. *And surviving it.*

Hutch knew, lying in the great black room that had been a recent temple to his vanished mother, that he had not vanished and would not soon, barring accident. He had had a life already, fourteen years of life, one-fifth of his seventy. At fourteen most dumb animals were long dead or blind with age; fourteen-year-old automobiles were relics. He smiled to the air.

The light went out in the bath; the door opened. In the new sudden dark, Rob could not see to move. He stood still to wait while his eyes responded.

Hutch could not see him. He was naked, still holding a small hand towel. He seemed to have thinned down, drawn himself inward to some firmer core that was Hutch's oldest memory—his father young beside him, asking questions through the night: all the years before them. Which now they'd survived—both, alive and here again, one another's goal (of all human destinations either one could see, that walked above ground). Yet Hutch couldn't speak, not from fear or uncertainty of how he'd be met—Rob was standing bare, free to be harmed or ignored—but because he could not think of what to say first. What had he said last? He could take up from there; but he couldn't remember—Rob had begged to be left alone; had he answered that in words? No he'd left. Could he say he was sorry then? He wasn't. He had walked straight forward into this, the socket for his life. Could he simply say, "Lie down. You are back with me now. This is mine and I've asked you"? Rob would say it wasn't possible, list a dozen reasons why the plan would never work, why they couldn't stay here—bills, taxes, rusted roofing, youth, age, the hurt feelings of a squad of bystanders.

He could say that he'd gone into Goshen that morning at Alice's prompting and seen an old lawyer who had known his grandfather and said that if no will actually existed, and the lawyer knew of none, then the hotel was Hutch's for what it was worth, which had been next to nothing since the early depression; that the Hutchins had lived on the income from timber Mrs. Hutchins owned near Suffolk, sold stand by stand (it had been her mother's); that some of it was left, he was almost sure, and might be Hutch's if there were no great outstanding debts, which of course there might be, and if Mrs. Hutchins had no kin in Isle of Wight who would file family claims. So he buried his head half-down in the pillow and said, "You are going to catch cold in your peter. Then where will you be?"

Rob jerked a little, startled; then laughed—"Better off." Then he came forward slowly through the dark to the cot, still there at Hutch's foot, right-angled to the bed (who had it been for?). He sat on the center edge and faced toward the boy; he could only see his outline. "I tried not to wake you up."

Hutch said, "I doubt you did; I wake up all night. Did you just get here?"

"I stopped and saw Della."

"Did she tell you what's happened?"

"Since your grandfather's death?—yes it sounds like a lot for you to have to deal with."

Hutch said, "It is. Did you get Richmond settled?"

"No I have to go back soon. Polly said she'd pack all the stuff we were keeping. She'll stay that long; then she'll go her own way. I can't even get her to consider staying on. She's had her pride hurt; first time in her life and it came too late. She refuses to take it."

"She could come here," Hutch said.

Rob waited awhile. "You can ask her—go to it—but I think you'd have better luck asking Mussolini. He's a man anyhow."

"Did you see your telegram? It's there on the dresser."

Rob said "What does it say?"

Hutch waited, then laughed once. "It says 'No please.'"

"Min, you mean?"

"Yes sir."

"Just those two words?"

"And her name, yes sir. I was going to mail it to Fontaine tomorrow."

Rob raised his legs and slowly lay flat on the cot, his face upward.

When he didn't speak for minutes, Hutch strained to see his father's eyes—open or shut? It seemed a piece of news necessary to proceeding; but he couldn't, just the clear line of head, chest, legs (both hands cupped his groin). Finally he said "Is that bad?"

"Yes. You'll live to understand."

Hutch said, "I do now. Don't forget I left Richmond."

"No I won't. Never fear. I'll live a long time—Kendals, Mayfields, both do—and I won't forget that."

Hutch said, "Might as well. I'm forgetting it soon."

"You've scheduled it, have you?"

June 14–17, 1944   *533*

"Yes sir. I'll be working so I won't dwell on things."

"Hotelling? Son, you won't have ten guests a year. You and Della'll be crazy as owls by Labor Day."

"—My drawing," Hutch said. "Rachel's friend Alice helps me. She thinks I'm worth the time." Hutch laughed but thought. He could tell her story now (Alice lonely and peaceful); Rob would like her better when they met in the morning. Might like her too much though. Hutch kept his silence.

Rob said, "I guess you have seen Rachel's grave."

"No sir." Hutch waited, then told the truth which caused him no shame. "I forgot to, really. I saw her picture, the one where you surprised her right before your wedding."

"All I did was surprise her. She never once believed me—that I meant to be with her, that I was truly *there* when I sat down beside her or touched her at night, that I would come back any time I left the house. She expected me to vanish, doubted I was ever there. I surprised her to death; I could never see why."

Hutch sat up quietly to prop himself on pillows. "I can," he said. "I can see very well. It's why I need to leave you."

"Still?"

"I think so, yes sir."

"I was thinking you could hire me in your enterprise here; might need a good yard-man."

Hutch said "I've written Grainger."

"Oh well, I withdraw then. He outclasses me." Rob had kept his tone light, but he rallied no further.

They were silent a good while. It seemed Rob might have dozed off, no sound of his breath; and Hutch thought of getting up and covering him with quilts (there were two at his own feet; he still could see Rob's nakedness, the hands at the ears now).

But Rob said "You sleepy?"

"No sir, wide awake."

"Can I tell you one thing while it's clear in my mind?—it might fade again."

"Yes sir," Hutch said.

So Rob thought awhile. "You mentioned that wedding, your mother's and mine. It happened in the morning up the hall in the parlor; and then there was a big feed for everybody here, Della cooking and Grainger and Gracie serving. Then Alice and a friend of mine that died shortly after (Niles Fitzhugh from home) drove the two of us to Lynchburg to catch the train

to Washington, our honeymoon trip. There had been an early snow somewhere in West Virginia; and the train was hours late, maybe wouldn't even
come till some time the next morning. We sat in the depot with Alice and
Niles till way after dark—Niles had to head on; Alice lived in Lynchburg, her
people did—so I paid a Negro porter to come round and warn us when they
got final word on when we would leave; and your mother and I walked across
the street and got a bedroom in an old hotel, old drummer's hotel, old railroad boys (all about my present age, I guess, looking back). It had been a
pretty tiring two days for us both, and Rachel had never been all that strong;
so we turned on in, not a morsel to eat—"

Hutch said "Rob—"

"Yes?"

"Listen—" Then he held a good while. "Am I meant to hear this?"

"Meaning what?" Rob said.

"Do I really need to hear this? Things worry me a lot."

Rob said "I know they do." He was silent a minute. Then he said, "Yes
you do. I really think you do. You've suffered not knowing."

Hutch said "All right, sir."

"We were tired as I said, and you always had to guard Rachel from exhaustion (she would rush straight to it; it was home to her); but I also didn't much
trust that porter to give us fair warning, and I meant us to leave; so I said we
would just kick off our shoes and lie in our clothes in the dark, all ready. She
agreed to that and pulled up a thin blue blanket that was folded at the foot
of the bed and lay right down in her traveling suit. I darkened us and joined
her. She kissed me like a sister; and in under twenty seconds, I was rowing
through sleep like I hadn't ever slept. We'd lived in neighboring rooms for
some months, right overhead here; but I'd never slept beside her, barely
touched her. The funny thing to me was, I knew I was resting. Far down as
I sank, some eye in my mind could still see and register that I was being
washed, being truly refreshed."

"Was Rachel?"

Rob waited. "I very much doubt it."

"What dream did you have?"

"None I remember, too far to remember."

Hutch said, "You generally dream. I just wondered."

"How do you know that?"

"You talk in your sleep."

Rob laughed once, then waited again a long time. "I did then too," he
said. "Rachel had to wake me. I had almost scared her."

"Must have had a nightmare."

"Oh no," Rob said with the speed of certainty. Then it came back to him through the nineteen years like a spirit called up from the patient earth, bearing freight that the caller had not foreseen. When he'd seen its shape, though not its full load, Rob told it to Hutch. "I was sleeping in a bed like the hotel bed; and Rachel was beside me, only we had undressed and were naked under sheets."

"In the dream?" Hutch said.

Rob nodded in the dark. "I could see us stretched out. Day seemed to be breaking (light was rising round us); and I was in two places, resting in my body and watching overhead. Then the light woke Rachel, and she saw the tall man standing in the door. The light was from him. She didn't understand so she started shaking me, begging me to wake up. I struggled against her and said 'I *need* this,' but she kept on till finally I opened and looked. I knew right away. The man was an angel. He was dressed like a real man in common street clothes, but I knew what he was. Every really grand thing I ever encountered was wearing street clothes; but I don't fail to know them—I'm a student of eyes. This man had *eyes.* He was watching us calmly; and though he didn't speak, I understood clearly. It was Judgment; he had been sent to tell us that message direct. I wondered *why us?* out of all the world's souls; but I said, 'Not now. I need this please.' Then Rachel really shook me— in real life, I mean—and I woke up scared, thinking numbers of things: mainly that the train was leaving and we'd missed it. The room was dark and we hadn't missed anything as it turned out. She said I had been dreaming hard for some time (my arms and legs twitching); but that she had had to wake me when I called out twice, me begging the man. Whether she'd ever slept, she had us both awake then. The only light was from out in the hall, seeping round the doorframe; but I could see enough of her to want to proceed then, before any message, to thank her for her gift to me and show her she'd been right—I was all she had dreamt and would always be. I undressed us both as gently as babies; and though she had never even kissed a man but me, I managed to show her and thank her both and leave her not hurt or confused or sorry but smiling and ready. It was dawning by then, by the time I was through; and I could see her face. Till then I had had a lot of worries about her and whether I was right in taking her on, whether I would harm her—God knows I've had them since—but that one morning I could *see* I was right. Could have been right for years if I'd kept that sight foremost in my mind and worked to preserve it. Then the porter came to tell us the train was there, due out in five minutes; so we dressed and ran. First mistake we made and the worst; my mistake not hers. Should have lain right there in that old hotel till I really understood what my dreams had said for twenty-one years, what Rachel's face meant. Then angels could have come by troops with swords; they'd have found no mortal fault in me, no fault they could judge." Rob paused there to think, then knew he had finished.

But Hutch said "Finish."

"That's all, just some sightseeing up and down Washington. The story was over once that Negro knocked."

"No the meaning," Hutch said. "What you claim to understand—all your dreams, Mother's face."

Rob said, "I claimed that I would have understood if I'd gone on watching Rachel closely as that. Or any other person that I wanted to watch and who held still for me."

Hutch said "Min."

"Min wanted *me* so she never held still. And now she's stopped."

They were quiet a short while; the house was still settling from the heat of the past day, groans that could easily have come from humans, any person from the hundreds who had stopped here briefly or lived out lives. Hutch said, "Why did you think I had to hear that?"

"Did it bother you?"

"No not yet anyhow but you need to explain."

Rob understood then. He said, "I was happy. I was happy that once. I could have kept on. I wanted you to know. People get what they need if they stand still and watch till the earth sends it up, most people I've known—Mother, Forrest, Rachel. What they need, not want."

Hutch said "I knew that."

"How?"

"It's happened to me."

"Already?" Rob said.

"Yes sir."

"Here lately?"

"Yes sir."

"Want to tell me about it?"

Hutch waited. "Not now."

Rob said, "Well, it's late. Got to rest for tomorrow."

"What happens tomorrow?"

"I'll drive down to Bracey."

"Aunt Hatt won't know you. I was there Tuesday night."

"She never has known me," Rob said, "—nothing new. Can she still sign a paper? That's all I need."

"What paper?"

"Just a form saying I can live in Richmond at Forrest's, that she won't claim it for her living son."

"She might want to live with you."

"Might let her," Rob said. "—little old-folks' home. Might be just the trick. I'm not moving backward through time, sure thing."

"Then you're staying in Richmond?"

"I think I may try it, beg Polly to stay. She could sew and support me!"

"When did you plan that?"

"Just now," Rob said.

"Have you looked for a job?"

"I'll start Monday morning. It's a big enough place. I could change my name, start a whole new life—pick a name from the air: be Newmarket Watters, a model of trust, credit to all my loved ones and friends." Rob was too tired to laugh. He reached behind him and molded the thin child's pillow to his head. Then he said "Say your prayers."

"Long since," Hutch said.

They lay without moving again for ten minutes, Rob bare on his back, Hutch propped in the midst of a bed his arms could not yet span. They were both too tired to think or plan, regret or hope; too tired to sleep, at least as they were—their bodies a great T-square in the dark room, but four feet from meeting.

Hutch could see more of Rob now; the moon had moved round. He tried to imagine his own life starting in that groin there, yearning out into Rachel fifteen years ago. Had it been as good a night as the first in Lynchburg? What room, what bed?—surrounded by what? (what house, what dreams?). He must think to ask at the next good chance. Ask who?—this boy stretched here at his feet? In the pale glare his father seemed nothing else but young and already cold (the mountain night was cold). He'd chosen that—Rob had; he'd just said as much. And Hutch had chosen his now, a gift from Rachel through his Grandfather Hutchins and Alice Matthews (all he had of his Grandfather Mayfield was a bark doll, and that was made by old Rob and passed on through Polly); a place to stand in till the world showed its core, its secret news, its reward to his patient watch on its skin.

Rob moved, stood huddled on the floor to turn his covers down; then slowly climbed back in and lay on his left side away from Hutch. But in five more minutes, his breath hadn't settled to the calm of sleep. He was silently awake.

So Hutch said, "Why don't you sleep with the master?"

Rob said "Where is that?"

"Isn't this the master bedroom?"

"Yes."

"Well, here's the master bed." Hutch slid to the right half, a cold plain of cloth.

Rob came to join him.

They did not touch at first, of their own volition; but quickly slept in the warming depths of Raven Hutchins' bed, not thinking of his death.

In an hour Rob woke in new dense dark—the moon was gone—and found that he'd worked his way to Hutch's turned back. He had not slept a whole night beside his son since they'd first left Richmond eleven years ago and passed through this room (Mrs. Hutchins leading) on their sad way to Fontaine, Raleigh, all the time since. The mutual warmth of their bodies had stoked a feverish sweat down the length of their juncture. Rob's left side was damp against Hutch's damp back and pants. He flapped the top edge of the covers twice to draw in cold air and moved to turn back to his own empty half.

But the bedsprings were ancient and had puddled in the center. They lay in a trough; any turn was uphill. So Rob lay another moment, touching the boy, planning a gentle heave to free himself. The moment stretched till the touch seemed a graft, a natural bond. Hot as he was, Rob remembered a question he had not asked in years, since they'd last slept close—*should he keep his promise?* The promise Grainger told him to offer Rachel dying—that he'd change, starting then; take his present life and honor it, love it when he could (if never, then never: half the world had had that) but honor it daily. The actual present.

Supposing he planned to renew that promise, what was present now to honor? What had ever been present these fourteen years but this one child he'd volunteered to start on a girl frail as paper?—a child not sufficient to have held him true. Clearly not sufficient but present here now.

And clearly too these last few days—*the child had his own life;* was struggling free into plans of his own, however doomed and childish. Leaving, aimed outward, no backward glance. But still here tonight. Here, anywhere in the breadth of the world, all he had was this child. Absolutely nothing else but a body that worked fairly well for its age.

Or so he thought now, and he knew he thought clearly. Della's deep welcome, as if they'd never parted but had gentled through long years of daily meeting, and the one hour of sleep had cleaned Rob's mind to a freshness as familiar as rare—once before. He had once seen, as now, with this perfect clarity; a quick space of knowledge, prophetic and true. Still against his back, Rob searched for that time. His first meeting with Grainger, Grainger quoting from his books as though books might serve a drunk boy bound for death? The meeting with Min in a Richmond hotel, the bleak aftermath of hunger and food when they'd still lain together, comprehending their future, their whole lives till now? His first morning with Rachel—Lynchburg, his dream of judgment? No, true as they were, something truer lay behind them.

Hutch shifted his back, spooned deeper into Rob.

It came to him, whole and clear as at its birth—May 1921, seventeen years old, his high-school commencement, creeping home in the morning from his drunk sleep at Sylvie's (the meeting with Flora) to find Eva, beautiful, waiting for him calmly to speak her own love and to prove his father's, despite barren years, whatever her reasons. That had been his life's height, Rob realized now—not the happiest time or the one he'd repeat but the literal height, the precipice from which he'd surveyed all his chances and seen them as good, subject only to his own will, the world's permission. A boy loved at last by the girl who had borne him, who swore to go with him through whatever might rise. A girl as needy as he'd ever been, and begging him.

He had never believed her. If he'd only confided in her offer that morning and bent his life to it—a job, their own place—what would he be now? An aging boy maybe, as dry as Thorne Bradley. He was that anyhow. For all his scraping, cutting, through the life of a man, what lay round him now— round his unchanged heart—but a middle-aged child's loose arms, legs, belly: an abandoned melon? He smiled to himself and saw Eva's face as he'd left her last week in the yard, a lost girl, still straining to grow toward a prop that would hold her.

Rob decided to believe her now at last—both Eva and Forrest, however untrue. Decided to believe they'd intended his life; that they met in him, only place on earth. That last at least could never be a lie. Had he not nearly killed Eva proving he was her need, proving Forrest's need to love and renew her? He could *let* them meet in him, even now this late; let them come to the restful harbor they'd sought, a son made from their lives but stronger—to perfect their purpose and transmit it. He'd refused them too long, and they'd torn him for it.

As they met in and tore this hot child sighing against him now. So did he and Rachel, both big-eyed with fear and hunger and flight. Bedford Kendal and Charlotte Watson, both wild. Anna Goodwin and old Rob, more famished than any. The child needed help.

What help on earth could Rob Mayfield give any living soul, much less his own son whom he'd left nine years ago to grow unwatched? Supposing he believed Eva's old claim now, Eva's and Forrest's—that they'd met above all to start his life, that their separate dreams had been the world's means of driving them together to start a further life (*his*, beating in him now in the close cold dark). Supposing that then and supposing they had loved the one life they made and wished it well, hung their main hopes on it, and supposing he could trust them through all remaining years—then how must he change and, once changed firmly, what help could he bring to his own child?

He could come back at least, starting now tonight, wherever *back* would be—Richmond, Fontaine, Goshen, or some fresh chance. He could stay in place wherever they landed and watch Hutch closely till Hutch said *Stop*, one still human face that had asked him to watch, that remained to be known. He could watch it at least. That might be help someway in time, for one child anyhow, the one he'd started. All the rest were beyond him or behind him, past help—Forrest vanished, alone. Polly bound for lone age, no child, no kin. Hatt addled by abandonment, too loving for comfort.

He saw for the first time in all his life how, though he'd been started (been aimed) by his parents, he had been steered and saved (so far as he was saved) by the single and barren—Rena, Sylvie, Grainger, Polly, Della, even Kennerly. They passed through his sight now like old Bible figures, tall forms in dark pictures on whom the sky leans—but sufficient to bear it. Any dog could start a litter; they had shivered alone. He honored their strength now and prayed for them, that they die in God's care.

His whelp was here now, a twin to his flesh. With his lips on the bone of the boy's left shoulder, Rob promised again, though he did not speak or forget as he promised how he'd failed other times after fervors of hope. Then he turned away and slept in a minute, a rest like warm blood, no scrap of dream. Rob did not know—no one alive knew, though his father had known till his dying day—that this same night forty-one years ago Eva Kendal, still mainly believing she was happy, was doing her own will, insuring her life, had borne Forrest Mayfield over her again and drawn from his joy the seed and permission to grow her one child.

Hutch dreamt of children, real children a little smaller than he, seated far apart in a bare Norman field, consumed by real flames—no man in sight or hearing, no woman. Real agony.

10

At eight in the morning, they were still asleep. The muffled sounds of Alice and Della in the kitchen since seven had not disturbed them, but now Rob woke as the hall door opened slowly. Dazed and scared he sat up to see— Mr. Hutchins, alive? Some boy on the doorsill—Negro boy, well-dressed in a dark blue summer suit, a clean white shirt buttoned neatly at the throat. No smile, no recognition; he was not seeing Rob but was fixed on Hutch. Some kin of Della's?

Then the boy looked to Rob and beckoned him once with a long left hand, no words but a call to follow him.

Naked as he was, Rob almost obeyed; but the gesture, hand slow as if air were liquid, had waked him fully—Grainger, Grainger Walters in Sunday clothes, always younger in the morning before a day's toll (surely though he'd traveled through the night to be here?). Rob said "You can come in," half-whispering to spare Hutch. Then he propped on his pillow against the high headboard.

Grainger stepped in, shut the door, and walked to the cot. He stopped there and stood, then nodded toward Hutch. "He all right now?"

Hutch sprawled on his stomach, covered to the ears, his face toward Rob, mouth slack, no sound of breath.

Rob said "Fine, last night anyhow. I got in late but he woke up and met me. He's dead-out now."

"Della told me what happened."

"Mr. Hutchins?"

Grainger nodded, leaned to the cot, spread up the covers, and sat on the edge. "You mean to stay with him?"

"Della tell you his plan?"

Grainger said "I knew it."

Rob said, "We'll have to see. We may not can eat here, may have to eat leaves."

"He won't mind that." Grainger grinned toward Hutch.

Rob said, "Of course not. Little minor detail like life wouldn't stop him; he banks on the Lord. But I'll have to check round. I just came for one day to see was he safe; he left me in Richmond. I got to finish there."

"He told me you were drinking."

"I was. One night though, not a drop since. I had a partial reason; I killed that nerve. Or numbed it awhile."

Grainger pointed behind him through the wall, outdoors. "Ought to stay here and force yourself to drink from that spring; that'll cure all your nerves or break you from wanting any beverage again. Rinsed my mouth while ago when I got here—tell you, I'd forgot." He showed his clamped teeth still edgy from the water. "My roof lasted good."

Rob said, "Knew it would. It'll outlast you."

"You too," Grainger said. "Say you heading back to Richmond?"

"Today, maybe Sunday. Still clearing-up there. Polly means to move out. I searched high and low through all Father's stuff; no will after all. Her pride took a beating."

Grainger nodded. "She'll make it. You need me with you?"

"Thank you, no," Rob said. "She's packing things now. I'll sell all the rest if I don't stay here."

"Anything there for me?"

Rob did not understand. "No. I said no will."

Grainger shook his head once. "See Gracie anywhere?"

"In Richmond? She's there."

"Somebody said she was. I got word from Bracey."

"I saw her one evening. She lives with her cousin."

"She doing all right?"

"Drinking," Rob said, "but all right, I guess—little shaky but walking. Good as most of your friends."

Grainger nodded twice. "Send me any message?"

Rob shook his head quickly, then knew that she had; knew he was her messenger, duty bound. Not waiting to think what the full message said or from whom it had passed to miserable Gracie, Rob raised his left hand and pulled the wide ring from his little finger. He held it toward Grainger.

Grainger studied it a moment in the dim air, then leaned; then shut it in his long palm, hid from them both. He looked to the floor and understood it all, understood all its senders.

It hurt Rob to have done it—late, too late. But he honored his act and said, "Everybody all right at home?"

"Same as ever. Missing Hutch. Sylvie grieving all week."

"Over Hutch?"

"Kin people. Some kin of hers dead."

"Not Albert?"

"Flora's boy."

"The one in the army?"

Grainger nodded. "Car wreck. He was thumbing back to camp. Old man picked him up, let the boy take the wheel. They were dead in ten miles; dodged a mule, rolled over. Sylvie grieving all week."

Rob laughed, full voice.

Hutch raised up—"What?"—face stiff with confusion.

"Good morning," Rob said.

Hutch scrubbed at his eyes. "What's funny?" he said.

"Sylvie," Rob said. Then he said "Look there" and pointed to the cot.

Still flat, Hutch craned round and, once the sight reached him, grinned slow and broad. "How did you get here?"

Grainger smiled. "My wings." He stroked one shoulder with his shut right hand.

"Dressed *up*," Hutch said. "You brought your work clothes? Got work here to do."

Grainger nodded he had.

They all held a moment; something crashed in the kitchen.

Then Grainger leaned forward, half-over the bed. "What I brought—" he said. He held his arm to Hutch, far enough to make him rise.

Bare to the waist, skin creased by the stiff pure linen beneath him, Hutch sat up slowly and turned and looked—Grainger, Grainger reaching. So he met Grainger's hand with his own, slightly cupped. Hutch had never seen the ring, never known of its life; but it fit his left hand.

THE
SOURCE
OF
LIGHT

FOR

DAVID CECIL

AND

STEPHEN SPENDER

That angelic language has nothing in common
with human languages is shown by this—
that angels cannot utter one word of human language.
They have tried but could not, for they cannot
utter anything that is not in
perfect agreement with their nature.

SWEDENBORG, *Heaven and Its Wonders and Hell*, 237

O N E

THE PRINCIPLE OF
PERTURBATIONS

MAY–AUGUST 1955

Hutchins Mayfield had stripped and faced the water, intending to enter before his father and stage the drowned-man act to greet him. But turning in the half-dark cubicle, he was stopped by sight of another man, naked also, close there beside him. He took two quick steps to leave, then knew—a dressing mirror he'd failed to notice hung on the pine wall. He went back and looked, not having seen himself for a while—not alone and startled, fresh for study. (In fact, except for negligent shaves, it had been two weeks—his twenty-fifth birthday. He'd been in Richmond that night with Ann; his grandmother tracked him down by phone to wish him luck. He'd borne her rambling a little impatiently; so she closed by saying, "Have you checked your looks now you're over the hill?—twenty-five is the downside in our family, Hutch, whatever doctors say. Twenty-five, we're *grown*." He'd checked in Ann's bureau mirror and confirmed it.) Now he studied his groin, full in the warm day, and thought how little it had caused but pleasure—a grown man's first means of work hung on him, an aging toy. But he smiled and reached a hand toward the cool glass, stroked the dim image. It bobbed in gratitude—pony, pet turtle—and Hutch laughed once, then heard his father's voice at the pool.

"What things will this cure?" Rob Mayfield said.

"Sir?"—the Negro attendant.

Now an exchange was promised in the earliest consoling sound of Hutch's life—a white voice, a black voice twined and teasing. He stood to wait it out.

"Which one of all my many troubles will this spring cure?"

"They tell us not to make big claims no more. Used to say kidneys, liver, eczema, the worst kind of blues, warts, falling hair. Whatever they tell me, it cured my feet. I was born flat-footed."

Rob said "Bathing fixed them?"

"No, never. I drink it. But it sure God jacked these feet off the ground. Born glued to the floor; now my kids play under em—run in and out, hide all in the shade. This your first time here?"

Rob said, "Yes. Thirty years ago I lived in Goshen, but I never got over the mountain somehow."

"Shame on you then," the Negro said. "Goshen ain't nothing but sand and cold river. Warm Springs would have helped you, just twenty minutes west."

"It seemed farther then. The road was bad."

"Beautiful now. Go on; step in—never too late."

Rob laughed but said "Oh it is." Then he moved.

Hutch came to the door of the cubicle to look—Rob Mayfield's back. His father stripped was something he really hadn't seen, not for years.

Fifty-one years old but still white and firm in waist and hams, Rob stooped to grip the rails of the stairs and descended slowly into eight feet of clear water bubbling from the earth, precisely the heat of a well human body. Then he swam four strokes to the center of the pool; embraced the ridgepole and looked back, smiling, to his only child. "I should have found this thirty years ago. Might have changed some things."

Hutch also gripped the rails but paused at the top. "What things?"

Rob continued smiling and paddled his hair back, still barely gray, but said no more.

Hutch looked for the Negro. He was back out of sight with his radio; so Hutch could say, "You might not have had me." He grinned but was earnest.

"I didn't say that."

"I've been the main trouble for most of those years."

"Never said that either."

Hutch nodded—it was true—but he stood on, dry in the thick warm air of late afternoon, and looked at what seemed the only block in his path: this middle-sized man, drenched and curling. The main thing he'd loved, that might yet stop him.

Rob clapped his hands once. "Were you ever baptized?"

"Not in my recollection."

"Then descend," Rob said and raised his right arm. The smile never broke, but he said "Father. Son—"

Hutch slowly descended. They laughed together as Hutch's head sank. But he didn't rise. He went straight into the drowning tableau—emptied his lungs so he fell to the smooth rocks that paved the spring and sprawled there, lit by green light that pierced the water.

It worked. Rob saw him as dead, that quickly—dead limbs gently flapped by currents, the long hair snaky. Yet he didn't move; he called the Negro. "Sam, step here."

The man was named Franklin, but he came at a trot.

Rob pointed down.

Franklin nodded. "Dead again." He stared a long moment. "Looks real, don't it? He do that a lot, every time he come—like to scared his young friend to death last week."

Hutch jerked to life and thrust toward the surface. He broke out, streaming; faced his father, and said "—Holy Ghost."

Rob said "Welcome."

They swam, sank, floated for the hour they'd purchased. No other bather joined them, and Franklin stayed off in his own little room. Within three minutes of the drowning, they had calmed. The water's constant match of their own body-heat soon made it a companion—gentle, promising of perfect fidelity: the craving of both men, in different ways. To Hutch it seemed a large faceless woman—spread and open, inescapable—into which he inserted his whole free body; four times in the hour he stiffened and fell. To Rob it finally seemed a place—the original lake in which he had formed, which he'd left insanely but had now found again, and in which he'd dissolve. They scarcely spoke, only fragments of pleasure. They felt no need, for the first time ever in one another's presence. When the hour was up and Franklin came, they were deep in separate dreams of safety.

Franklin said "You shriveling yet?"

Rob looked to Hutch.

Hutch looked at his own right hand. "A little."

"Then time to get out. Hour's all you can stand." Franklin held white towels like gifts more tempting than the spring itself.

Hutch swam the strokes that put him by his father. That whole charged body was covered with beads of air like an armor. He reached out and wiped his hand down Rob's chest, clearing a space.

Rob took the wrist and, not releasing it, swam back an arm's length to focus the face. "I'll try not ever to forget this," he said. "You please try the same."

"I can promise," Hutch said.

"No, just try."

Hutch nodded and they swam together toward the stairs.

In the safe dreamy hour, Rob had found no way to tell his son what he'd had confirmed two days ago—that Rob Mayfield, early as it was, would be dead by winter; that the body which had served him unfailingly till now had conceived and was feeding in a lobe of its right lung a life that would need nothing less than all. At the stairs he said "You first. You're slower." He wanted that instant of sight to decide.

Hutch gave it. He climbed out strongly but paused on the top step, not looking back; then he cupped his face in both large hands and shuddered hard—only once but enough.

Rob saw that to tell him now before the end would be to stop the trip he'd planned, that he'd leaned his life on mysteriously. Or, if he should still leave in face of the news, to show him as the final demon of dreams— faithless after decades of smooth deceit. Rob took the rails also. Against the lovely pull of the spring—its promise of care—he hauled himself and his fresh partner up.

2

They ate a good supper at the Warm Springs Inn (mountain trout, new lettuce) and set out at eight in clear cool darkness to drive the pickup on to Hutch's near Edom—some sixty miles north through mountains and valleys, and they both were tired. Rob had started up from North Carolina at noon to meet Hutch at five. Hutch had thumbed down from Edom; the bath was his idea. So Hutch drove now and—through the first mountain, cross the Cowpasture River—they said very little. Past the river Hutch realized his whole idea would force Goshen on them—on his father at least, who had not been there in eight or nine years. They had already passed two signs naming Goshen, but it still lay a quarter-hour ahead, and Rob had not mentioned it since talking to Franklin. So Hutch said, "Tell me what you want me to do" (meaning, stop at the grave or drive on past).

Rob said, "Be a better man than me at least."

Hutch started to explain but accepted the delay. "Tell me how to go about it."

"I expect you know. You've lived a quarter-century; you've hurt nobody, not that I know of."

Hutch said "I killed my mother."

"You couldn't help that. I couldn't keep you from her. Rachel pulled you out of me by main force, Son; and she held on to you, but you had to come out. Rachel died of bad luck. Your luck was better—and my luck, to have you."

"Thank you," Hutch said, "but still tell me how."

Rob turned to the dim profile beside him. "I was answering politely, just words to say. I couldn't tell a dog how to bury a bone, much less a grown man how to live. I don't even understand your plan."

Hutch glanced across. "The trip?"

"Well, no. I did a little wandering myself—sooner than you, on a smaller map: a few whistle-stops in southwest Virginia. Europe was torn up all through my freedom. No I meant what comes once you've seen the world and are back here, ticking through the numerous years. You're counting on the ravens to feed you apparently; they often renege."

Hutch smiled at the road. "I can do two things that'll tide me over if the ravens fail—teach children English and make women think they've been rushed to Heaven before their time." Since he was grown he had hardly mentioned love to his father.

Rob remembered that and waited. Then he said, "How many would you estimate you'd rushed?"

"Sir?"

"Women, to Heaven—how many have you sent?"

Hutch said "I was joking."

Rob said, "I'm not. I'd like to know. It would help me to know what women mean to you. It's a danger that runs in your family, you've noticed—the Mayfield side."

Hutch also waited. His window was open on the loud spring night; it spoke at their silence—incessant jangle of small life *signaling*, no one creature mute in solitude, even the fox that crossed before them musky with lure. He thought that awhile; then said, "It would help me too. I doubt I know. I've liked two or three women more than anybody—Alice Matthews, Polly. I may need Ann Gatlin—she hopes I do; I hope I do."

"But you haven't asked Ann to marry you yet?"

Hutch said, "Worse—I've asked her not to visit me in Europe. She'd started on plans to join me for Christmas."

"What made you do that?"

Hutch waited again, then tried the answer he'd offered Ann. "I think I need air."

"To do what in?"

"—Need stillness around me."

Rob said, "Nine-tenths of the world's population works eight or ten hours a day more than you. You've rested, Son. Lie back and be grateful."

Hutch laughed. "You hit it. I'm so well-rested my mind is souring but *grateful* I'm not. I'm an aging boy, as you point out. I need to work and I think I'm going toward it."

"Ann Gatlin sounds like a nice job to me, a fine evening shift—the one shift that pays."

Hutch said "She'd like that."

"What's wrong with that?"

"I didn't know you rated Ann very high."

Rob said, "Now I do. She wants you around. She means to last."

Hutch said "I think you're right."

"But you're holding her off?"

"For now. No choice."

Rob said "There you're wrong."

"I can't take her with me."

"Then ask her to wait. Hell, beg her." Rob looked away.

They let another patch of silence spread. By now the river was steady beside them in the unseen gorge. Its chilly clatter blanked all other sounds; and when the patch had lasted three minutes and Hutch had thought of nothing but fear—fear of failing his kin, fear of finally knowing no work to do, fear of solitude—he said, "You can see I have brought you to Goshen." The meanness was instant filth on his tongue.

But Rob answered calmly. "I noticed you had. I figured you would." He leaned forward, opened the glove compartment, drew out a flashlight, and shone it on Hutch. "So I came prepared. Stop by Rachel's grave."

Hutch nodded. "Two miles."

Rob said, "Time enough to tell you this story. May prove useful someday. It's named 'Little Hubert.' Little Hubert used to like the girls in kindergarten. One day the teacher sent his mother a note—*Hubert runs his hand up all the girls' dresses. Please tell him to quit*—so his mother said, 'Son, do you know what girls have under their dresses?' Hubert said 'No ma'm.' She said, 'A pink mouth with a lot of sharp teeth. Remember that.' Hubert said, 'Yes ma'm. Thank *you* for the tip.' And he acted on it—never touched a girl, though he did a lot of dreaming and a lot of self-service. Twenty-five years of good behavior passed. Then a woman named Charlene chased him down—flat wouldn't let Hubert say No, even Maybe—and they got married. Went to Tampa on their honeymoon, palm trees and moonlight; danced till near-dawn when Charlene asked him if it wasn't time for bed. Hubert said 'O.K.' and they went upstairs. It took her about an hour, but finally Charlene came out of the bathroom all sweet and ready in a peach satin gown. Hubert was long since under the covers in flannel pajamas, more than half-asleep. But she slid in beside him and commenced to stroke his arm till Hubert said, 'I thought you were *tired*.' She said, 'But Sugar, you haven't even touched me' and pulled his hand toward you-know-where. He jerked back fast and said

'No you don't!' She said, 'What do you mean? This is my first night!' Hubert said, 'Go to it. But count me out. *I* know what you're hiding down there.' She said 'Just what's *normal*, silly.' He said, 'So right!—the normal set of teeth. I'm not risking my good fingers on you.' And he was about to head back into sleep when she said, 'Sugar, you're out of your mind—my teeth are in my head. Look here.' She threw back the sheets and raised that gown. So Hubert sat up and bent over gradually and took a long look. Then he said, 'No wonder! Good night, Charlene! Just look at the condition of those poor *gums!'*"

Hutch laughed; he'd never heard it.

Rob sat like a stuffed Baptist preacher through the laughter; but when Hutch subsided, he said, "Don't forget it, especially in Europe. The gums over there make ours look healthy." Then he switched the flashlight on, at his own face, and turned to his son—a wide bright grin. "You know he was wrong, little Hubert—don't you?"

Hutch smiled. "Yes sir—"

"Very sadly wrong."

Hutch said, "Yes sir, I have reason to know."

"You're not afraid, are you?"

"Not of that," Hutch said. Then he slowed to turn left.

In a Stepin Fetchit voice, Rob said, "You mean you scared of dead folks, cap'n?"

Hutch said "I may be."

"And you may be right."

They had stopped at a pair of shut iron gates. The headlights showed the nearest stones, which were also the oldest—marble tree-trunks, lambs, the locally famous seated-boy-with-birddog (an only son, self-shot while hunting). Hutch doused the lights but made no move, though the plan had been his.

At last Rob opened the door in darkness and stepped to the ground. He stood a minute while his eyes adjusted; when Hutch didn't move, he took a long leak. Then he looked back once at the truck—only outlines—and went on to climb the easy gates. On the other side he lit his flashlight and walked a knowing path forward, fairly straight.

Hutch sat and watched him, held in place by feelings that had waylaid him unexpected—reluctance to pay this farewell homage to his mother by night; a small seed of dread to visit at night a mother he'd never seen alive, whom his own life had canceled; and worse, to visit her this last time with Rob who had cared so little for her memory as not to have been here in nearly a decade. Rob's light had vanished. *Well, let it. Let him bear full-force what he'd tried to deny—the physical locus of his own worst damage: the strip of earth which held in solution all that remained of a lovely girl gone twenty-five years, kept from her son.* The darkness continued, no further light. Then shame replaced the harsher knowledge, and Hutch was freed to go. He cranked the engine, switched on the headlights (which didn't reach Rob); and climbed out to find his father, wherever. He had been here often in recent years; so he had no trouble finding the way, though he entered black dark within fifty feet, and still there was no sign or sound but the river. His feet had struck the low rock-border of the Hutchins plot before he saw pale wavering light and heard what seemed an animal scrabbling. The one large tombstone blocked his way; Hutch stepped round it slowly.

The flashlight was propped at the base of the stone, rapidly failing. Rob was kneeling on the head of Rachel's grave, digging with his nails in the ground above her face. Or filling a hole the size of a softball with what seemed fresh dirt. Rob didn't look up or speak but finished the little job, replacing a lid of turf at the end. Then still not looking, he reached for the light and slammed it once on the stone—pure black. Then the sounds of him rising, stepping toward Hutch; a hand that found Hutch's shoulder, no fumbling, and gripped it hard. His calm voice said, "You've chosen this, have you?"

Hutch said "Sir?"

"Home—you think of this place as home?"

Hutch had not thought that. He'd spent no more than an hour here in short rare visits, no more than two or three weeks in the town. But now he said, "I may, yes sir. I think I may."

"Then once you decide—if you ever decide, decide soon enough—bury me here. Bury me wherever you think is your home."

Hutch said, "Yes sir. But by then I'll surely be senile myself; you'd do well to leave some written instructions for somebody younger than both of us."

Rob said "You'll do." His hand came down from shoulder to wrist; he gripped Hutch's wrist.

So Hutch raised the joined hands—a sizable weight—and searched over Rob's dark face with dry fingers. They found tears of course.

3

Though they'd been nearly midnight reaching Hutch's in Edom, they both woke easily at dawn—a bright sky but cool still. Under compulsion Rob had slept in the bed; Hutch had slept on the ample davenport. Each knew the other was awake by silence (mouth-breathers both, they slept like seals—steadily announcing their vulnerability); but for twenty minutes neither one spoke. Hutch was thinking of ways to get Rob out of the house for the morning; he needed calm for his final packing. It didn't occur to him, huddled on himself, that his father was colder and thinking too. Despite his age Hutch rested in the standard child's assumption that a parent's mind is a marble wall, uncut by a single urgent requirement or even impatience.

But in those minutes Rob firmly decided his answer to the question he'd faced all yesterday. He wouldn't tell Hutch. He would not ask himself to bear the boy's response, whatever—the man's; he could seldom believe he had made at least half of what was now a man. Today he would help the man load his boxes of books and records, his desk, in the truck; then he'd leave as cheerfully as he could manage. The man would be in England in a week, for at least a year. Rob would be underground before that ended. Now for the first time, it seemed desirable—sleep as blank as the heart of a potato or some unimaginable form of reward. Whatever his sins, none of which he'd forgot, Rob Mayfield didn't anticipate punishment. But he found he was hungry. Having always been a famished riser, he saw no reason to abandon the habit; so without sitting up he suddenly spoke. "Have you got your pencil handy?"

Hutch also stayed down and said "No sir."

"Then listen carefully, remember perfectly, and execute at once—"

Hutch said "I'll try."

"—A small glass of sweetmilk, three eggs scrambled in butter (keep them soft), country sausage, hot biscuits, fig preserves, and strong coffee."

Hutch said "Coming up" but made no move.

Rob recalled he'd neglected to say any prayer; so he said to himself what, a boy of twelve, he'd seen was the heart of Jesus' prayer (the only one that didn't seem a showoff, and even that could be trimmed to two words—"Your will"). Then he sat up in the cold air and looked.

Hutch was still drawn tight beneath his quilt, head turned away.

For a moment Rob felt a strong desire to be served for once, to lie back and let this child start the day—warm the space, cook the food, soothe the sick, earn the keep. He even fell back on his elbows and beamed the wish toward Hutch—*Stand up and take over. Do everything for me. You'll be amazed how little that will be, how soon I won't need anything at all.* But he thought of the end the doctor had outlined three days ago—"You'll begin to cough; no syrup will help. Then you'll have trouble breathing, worse and worse till your lungs fill steadily with fluid and drown you. No pain." He'd asked if the doctor was promising no pain. Humorless as Moses, the doctor said, "No. If it spreads into bone, then we'll have real pain" (Rob had let the *we* pass). That would no doubt come to more than a little service before the end. He would ask nobody but his mother to give it. Though he still hadn't told her, there was no chance of doubt that Eva Mayfield would say any word but Yes—and mean it, have the full strength to mean it. So he stood to the cold bare floor in his underpants, walked to the front room, and lit the oil heater. Then he parted the curtains and looked to the woods. In a high black pine, a young owl sat on a limb near the trunk, beginning its rest. A gang of blue jays quarreled at it with no effect, then flew on their way. Then the only sound was the tin stove warming, cracks and booms.

From the quilt Hutch said a muffled "Blessings on your head."

Rob said, "I accept them and will use them in your name. Now haul your precious white ass to the ground and feed this hollow old man you invited."

Hutch said, "Back to sleep. I've packed all the food."

"Unpack me an egg."

"I'm leaving, remember?"

Rob said "Goodbye."

4

By nine Hutch had managed to get Rob out. He'd given him a choice of the local sights—a self-conducted tour of the school or the New Market battle-field twelve miles north or Endless Caverns. Rob had said, "The caverns sound more like me. I'll be back at noon and we can load up—if I don't get lost; I'll try to get lost." He'd laughed and gone. Hutch had sat and drunk a third cup of coffee, consuming the quiet as if it were a suddenly discovered vein of some scarce mineral his bones required. (That he'd been with his father only sixteen hours, six of them asleep, and still craved solitude shamed him a little; but it came as no news. He was coming to see that all his con-scious life—from four or five on—he had moved to a law which required him to take equal time alone for every hour of company, however amusing.) Then unwashed he started the last packing in a small footlocker, the final choice of what would accompany him on the trip. The rooms were already lined with boxes of the clearly expendable things, for storage in Fontaine. It was part of his purpose to go as nearly clean as he could, stripped of all but the vital minimum of the thicket of props he'd set round himself. Clothes were simple (he owned very few and they meant nothing to him, though he kept them neat). He laid out two changes of winter and summer clothes, then turned to hard choices.

Music—he would have no phonograph, but he chose two records he felt he might need when he got near anyone else's machine: Brahms's *Alto Rhapsody* by Marian Anderson, Purcell's *Dido and Aeneas* with Flagstad.

Books—a Bible, which Rob had given him (it had been his Great-grand-mother Kendal's); *The Diary of a Country Priest* by Bernanos; *Anna Karenina* (World's Classics edition, four inches by six, miraculous compression); a tattered pamphlet of pornographic photographs he'd found in a garbage can at college (a beautiful, and beautifully joined, young couple); his notebook and the daily log he kept.

Pictures—his mother and father, young together; his Grandmother May-field, Alice Matthews, Ann Gatlin, a postcard view of the marble head of a girl from Chios (Boston Museum).

Objects—the five-inch marble torso of a boy he'd bought in New York for fifty dollars three summers ago (sold for Greek but more likely Roman, though gentled by elegance); a box of drawing pencils, pen points, erasers; a box of watercolors; a pad of drawing paper; a pinebark carving of a human body which had once been a man but was now finished smooth.

It took him two hours to make the choices, stow the rest, set the boxes on the porch; but when he had thrown the last food to the birds, the house was effectively free of him. The three years he'd lived here—mostly happy—had altered it only by a few extra nailholes, a few strands of hair in unswept corners (he'd paid a woman to clean it tomorrow). He walked to the center of the house—the short hall—and stood in the emptiness for maybe two minutes, regretting and fearing. Then he stripped off his work clothes, folded them into a box bound for storage, walked to the shower, and bathed very carefully. Only then did he see that the wide gold band—tight on his left hand—was the main thing he carried, except for his pleasant and pleasing body.

5

To fill the half-hour till Rob was back, Hutch drove the four green miles in to school. He had said his farewells two days ago—and received the Head-master's valedictory sermon—but there might be some mail; and whatever the woes of teaching three years in a rural Episcopal Virginia boys' school, he was nudged already by a sudden posthumous love of the place; nostalgia for a time which had been (he hoped) the end of childhood, delayed but calm. He passed no visible human on the drive; and even as he swung through the campus gates and parked by The Office, he could see nobody, though he actively searched—no colleague or town-boy, no yardman mowing. Monday's commencement had emptied the space as thoroughly as war; so he sat a moment, accepting the favor. Little as he'd moved in his life till now, he already knew the shock of returning to find loud strangers bang-ing on the sets of his former life. Then he entered the dim cool hall of The Office. On his way to the pigeonholes, he passed the Master's open outer room and Fairfax Wilson there, fervently typing. She hadn't seen him—good. He could go out the back and miss her completely, no need to hear-out today's diatribe. But his name was already gone from the slot. Competent to organize vast migrations of nations cross oceans or nuclear blitzkrieg, Fair-fax had done her duty by the school (and by herself; she resented his leav-ing)—the quitter was effaced. She would have any mail that had come today. When he stopped in her door, ten feet from her, she didn't look up but pounded on. So he tried to turn her, concentrated in silence on her rapt profile—lean sister to a class of moviestar (Kay Francis, Barbara Stanwyck) who had shaped her looks twenty years ago, then moved beyond her into fleshy surrender while Fairfax had kept her virgin strength: a little withered but still a banner, proud flag of choice and loyalty-to-choice.

Finally she cut her big dark eyes toward him, no more smiling than a stork. "I thought you were strolling on the Left Bank by now."

"No ma'm, England. And not for eight days—I've got five days on the water first."

She hiked a black brow. "Water? I thought anybody rich as you would be flying first-class."

He'd explained it fully some months ago; but in the slack time, he was will-ing to rally with her awhile (if you let her discharge her excess life in keen exchange, you might be spared a monologue on the fools she dealt with, the dog's road she trod). "No ma'm, I told you I'd be eating rat cheese and soda crackers."

"They may not even have cheese and crackers—they don't have *heat*—and what's this *ma'm?* I just age a year at a time like you. My friends call me Fair." She smiled at last, broad smile that drew real beauty to her face.

As always Hutch was a little startled by the urgent beauty and by his own quick but reluctant sense that they'd missed a chance at one another. Twenty years between them seemed a flimsy screen. He'd have given her something she'd maybe never had; she'd at least have taught him how to burn on *high* for forty-five years and show no scorching. He said, "Miss Wilson, are you say-ing I'm a friend?"

She swiveled the chair to face him, then looked to the Headmaster's door. "He's not here today—in Lynchburg buying a new ballplayer; some eight-foot child that can't write his name." She'd whispered that much but straight at his eyes, her own eyes burning. Then she raised her voice to its normal power—a carrying richness—and said, "Hutchins Mayfield, I consider you the finest young man now residing in the Old Dominion; and you know how stuck I am on Virginia."

Hutch smiled and nodded but said, "I'm leaving in an hour, sad to say. Will Virginia survive?"

She refused the fun. "You'd better go now. An hour wouldn't give me time to say how far above the run you are. There are plenty people here who think you're crazy as a duck-in-love to be throwing yourself on fate like this, but you know what I tell them?—I tell them 'Lucky fate!' "

As always half-convinced by her force, Hutch could only thank her.

"Don't thank me. Just send me a Christmas card from some famous spot—nothing naked please—and in your first book put a lunatic maiden-lady from Virginia who types to perfection and knows what's what."

Hutch laughed. "A promise."

6

He returned with his trifling mail to the car, looking down in hopes of seeing no one; so he'd reached for the door before he saw a man lying back on the hood. A boy—Strawson Stuart, long for his age, Hutch's pupil for two years. He lived in town; his eyes were shut. Hutch said, "I heard you had died Monday night at Morse Mitchell's party, but I didn't know I'd get the body for disposal."

Straw sat up solemn. "Well, you have." He extended his arms cruciform and held the pose. Then he smiled, the second dazzler of the day. "No I've risen and come by to help you load. Saw the note to your father; he's still not back."

"He may never be. He went to Endless Caverns."

Straw said, "Then carry me to Warm Springs quick."

Hutch said, "I scared you so bad last time, I doubted you'd ever want to go again" (he had drowned for Straw; even more than Rob, it had shaken the boy who'd seemed unshakable).

Straw said "But I do."

Hutch studied him long enough to know a true answer. "So do I, very much. There's no chance at all. I've got to load the truck, see Father off, then drive on to Richmond by suppertime. You said you'd see me in England."

"I will."

Though Straw had graduated and Hutch resigned, the place itself—the campus in sunlight, its order—had kept Hutch from thinking of the hours that followed their bath in the spring. Now the different place which Straw constituted, in power and need, demanded homage. The sight of the stripped boy asleep in his arms last Saturday dawn stood clear in Hutch's mind. He watched it gladly with no regret. "We'll drive down to Cornwall—Tristan, Tintagel. You liked that in class."

Straw nodded—"I liked it"—still grave as an arbiter.

Or a god—young god of Want and Use, no more kind or cruel than electric current. Hutch thought that also, then said "Let's pack."

7

The three-hour silence of the drive to Richmond—across the Shenandoah and the last line of mountains in afternoon light—had come over Hutch like total sleep, an apparently endless depth of rest into which he could dig with easy hands, no dreams to meet. Welcome as food, though he hadn't thought of the past few days as trial or punishment. He accepted the rest, drove his old Chrysler gently but fast, and managed an almost perfect exercise of his kindest skill—life in the present. The future vanished before him, no trace— his father's life without him; the choices Ann would face, the bid she awaited; the thousand accidents of setting in a strange place; the cold fear that soon his promise to work would uncover only empty shafts in himself and in plain view of the friends and kin who held his promise, a tangible note. The past existed only as happiness, snatches of memory of childhood peace—whole summer hours in the swing by his grandmother, hearing her life; carving bark with Grainger, drawing hills with Alice. No agonized mother; no father drunk and stripped on a bare floor, dribbling piss; no need to choose one person from the world and love only that. The present was all—his serviceable self borne on through evening and country peaceful as a child asleep, its own reward, toward nothing at all.

Yet of course toward Ann. When he entered her door at half-past six, there were no lights on; and he couldn't hear her. He set down his small bag and stood to listen—still nothing. Was she gone on an errand? Gone for good? How much would he care? He waited to know but no news came, no feeling at least. He only hoped for the quiet to continue, and without conscious stealth he managed to walk the length of the hall with no board creaking. Then he stopped just short of the open kitchen door; there were small sounds there—scraping, small splashes. He leaned out to see.

Ann was at the sink, looking west through the window, scraping potatoes. The light that was left fell in around her and lit her at the boundaries—the line of her head and hair, her shoulders. She seemed to burn, very hot at the core; sunlight was only the breeze that fanned her and heightened her flare.

Hutch felt that he should be responding to her action, her work for him—this living Vermeer unconsciously staged for no one but him; a loving and lovely woman in daylight, worked by love as by coal or steam. And he did feel grateful; but much more strongly, he felt the pity of the line she made— the deceptive stillness of a human body which seems enduring when of course it is swept by time like a wind. He thought again that what set him off from others his age—here at least; would it be true in Europe?—was the fact he'd always believed in death, his mother's main gift. He'd always known that individual people *leave* apparently forever; that the hope of knowing, really knowing, any single person must be exercised *now*. And the only means of knowledge was touch. Rob had taught him that. Right or wrong, it was one more conviction which set Hutch firmly off from ninety-five percent of the people he met. They saw their bodies as hoards of treasure to be guarded unsleepingly; Hutch saw his as a nearly bare room, doors ajar.

Ann turned and made a few signs in the air with one empty hand.

Hutch said "Meaning what?"

She smiled. "—Meaning I thought you had gone deaf and dumb, standing there so long."

"You heard me?"

"Yes."

"Why didn't you look?"

She said, "I couldn't think of anything to say."

"That's a new problem, right?"

A born narrator, she laughed once. "Right. But it's also new being left four thousand miles behind, typing letters for a lawyer and peeling potatoes for just myself."

The depth of the room—twelve feet—was still between them; and in those few words, the sun had set, blue dusk had risen. Hutch felt a powerful need to leave; to say a plain "Sorry," then turn and go.

But Ann made another set of signs, both hands.

He recalled she'd learned sign language as a girl—Girl Scouts or school. "Are you really spelling words?"

"Yes." She made the phrase again.

"Still lost," he said.

So she came on toward him, a finger to her lips. One step away she stopped and said, "The young lady said, 'Leave me something to remember.' You got anything you could spare to leave her?"

Hutch smiled. "Tell her yes."

She led on past him through the darkened hall.

He followed. She shared his trust in touch, the body's hunt for ease and honor.

In a speechless half-hour, they each found both—the ease that follows successful grounding of a long day's chagrin, the mutual honor two satisfied bodies award one another for candor and nerve. Then Hutch fell asleep in the dark beside Ann, and her arm on his chest became in three minutes the dream of the tunnel. He'd endured the dream from early childhood, though not for some years. Not a story but a trial—far underground he must dig for his life through a tunnel no bigger than his own clothed body, inching forward only with the strength of his nails which he knew to be bleeding, though he couldn't see.

When he'd spasmed and whimpered more than once, Ann shook him. She knew the dangers of stopping a dream, and she shook too gently.

So he dug on awhile.

Ann let him go but pressed her mouth forward till she brushed his ear; then whispered her menu, "New potatoes, Swiss steak, snap beans—"

Hutch was still.

Ann said "Banana pudding."

Hutch said, "Let me leave you this one green banana for future use." His hand found her fingers and set them on his crotch. It was simple to turn and meet her lips.

She said, "I accept it and will name it for you," though the sense she had in her warming palm was of sleeping birds, blind and bare but close in a nest and shielded by her.

8

The whole last hour of the long drive home, Rob pushed for speed to make it by dark. But even the light load of Hutch's belongings strained the old engine and defeated the plan. When he saw he couldn't be there much before eight, he concentrated on a second small chance—that Grainger had come out as promised to check, feed Thal, and leave a few lights on (she still dreaded dark). So he made that his aim—the lighted house; the nine-year-old Boston bulldog, fed and gassy. And it drew him on successfully, hardly thinking; only seeing those two modest hopes, both likely. He got to the mail box at ten to eight—just the paper and a bill from the freezer-locker plant—then geared down to climb the half-mile of drive, still rutted from winter. But at the bend, past the last stand of pines, the house was black as the sky behind it. Rob actually stopped in disbelief and tried to recall the last time Grainger failed him—never before. Was he sick or was Eva? Was he in there dead (Grainger was sixty-three, with high blood-pressure)? It took main force to start up again and finish the trip.

The flashlight was also dead, from last night. Rob stepped to the ground in thick dark and hurled it far as he could; if it crashed, he never heard it. He felt his way slowly, feet low to the ground, through the yard to the steps. Then he climbed carefully. On the porch he waited in final hope someone was inside—Grainger or a drunk or an angel of death. Not even the scrape of Thal's claws at the door. He called once "Grainger." Then "Thal." Then he whistled. Still as slate.

So he went to the door. The knob turned freely; warmer air rushed to meet him but nothing else. He could hear Thal though, her disastrous lopped-snout struggle to breathe now quickened by fright. He knew she was sitting in her gunshell box at the back of the hall, shuddering hard; but he didn't try the light. He stood on the sill and said, "Thal, please explain why it's dark like this."

Thal snorted and sneezed but held in place.

"Are you starving?" Rob was hoping she knew him by now (she wouldn't have barked at a stranger with an axe unless he struck Hutch).

But she stayed and her shivers had the rabies tag jingling at her neck like a midget dancer—terrified or glad?

Rob took a step in and reached to his left for the light switch. Nothing. He flipped it three times, then felt his way to the low hall-table and found the lamp. Nothing. He said, "Miss Thalia, have you eaten the wires?"

She was suddenly still.

He found the table drawer where he kept his only matches safe from mice, then cupped his groin against bumps and groped with the free hand for the oil lamp waiting on his bedroom mantel. He hoped there was oil. His hand found the pistol—his Grandfather Kendal's loaded revolver now fired just six times a year, on Christmas day, to prove it worked. It had never failed but had never been needed, not in Rob's recollection. Now he read it like a blind man, from the scored wood butt to the cooler barrel, tamping the open bore—too small for a finger to probe, though he tried it calmly. Then he found the lamp and only then struck a match—yes, half-full. He lit it. Quick white flame, the hot smell of coal oil, yellow light as loving as any one hand that had ever touched him. He faced the door. "Thal, we're safe now. Light."

Silence still.

"*Light*, old lady. Come here and see." He even slapped his thigh. Nothing. Was she gone?

He took the lamp and, cradling the chimney, entered the hall again and took enough slow steps to let the glow reach her.

At its touch she snorted, stood up fully, and did the little horizontal welcome-home shimmy with her wide spayed rear.

Rob wanted her to meet him. "Step *here*," he said and whistled through his teeth.

Gradually she came, still a-dance but looking down, no longer afraid but not yet clear of the doze and dream of two days alone.

When she got up near him, he squatted and set down the lamp and scratched her throat—vigorous digs. "Has Grainger been here?"

She loved it, threw her head back as if plunged into some serious bliss more welcome than rest, and peed a small puddle in token of thanks.

"I see you're not perishing for water at least." He stood and went to the screen to let her out. As he passed the table, he could now see enough to notice a white sheet of paper he'd missed, propped against the phone. Thal took her time debating the wisdom of going, then went; and Rob brought the lamp back to read the note.

Rob, I was out here at 5 o'clock. Fed Thal and left you and her some lights on. Miss Eva expecting you for dinner tomorrow at 12:30. Then I'll come out with you and unload Hutch's stuff. Hope he was well and you gave him a kick in the tail from

Grainger

He needs it.

Rob lifted the receiver of the phone; it hummed. So he found the number and called the power company. A young woman answered, a girl's voice really. He told her he had got home to find his lights out.

"All over?"

"Yes ma'm."

"You checked your fuses?"

"No but it's failed on at least two circuits, and I don't want to play with a house old as this."

"How old?" she said.

"A hundred-ten years and dry as east Egypt." Then he laughed. "What the hell has that got to do with anything?"

She said, "Let it burn. And you take pictures—make lovely Christmas cards."

Rob laughed again. "Have I got the power company?"

"No the firebug-ward at the State Hospital."

"Who are you?"

"Matilda Blackley."

"When are visiting hours?"

"Every Sunday all day. I wear pink and wait." Then she laughed at last. "*I'm* sorry," she said. "It's been a hard evening and you sounded nice. No, power is off all out your way. Lightning hit a substation."

"Has there been a storm?"

"Lord, where have you been? Thought the world was *over*."

"—In Virginia," he said. "Just now drove in. It doesn't even seem to have rained out here."

"You out near Essex?"

"Yes."

"No wonder," she said. "You all are deprived in general out there."

"Would you like to help?" In the pause that followed, Rob gave no thought to whether he'd angered her; he spent some seconds realizing that he was actually killing himself—this racing tumor—out of pure need for help: the help of close company, lacking ten years. He was building a little partner in his chest, which would stop when he did.

The girl said, "Shoot, I'm worse off than you. You know what a girl makes, starting down here on the weekend switchboard?"

She'd chosen not to freeze; Rob felt thankful but afraid he'd lost her now. Not that he thought any meeting was likely, only that her bright voice had propped him when he'd had no hope of a prop.

"You got you a lantern?"

"A kerosene lamp as old as the house; but it works, yes ma'm. Nice gentle light. Worst mistake ever made, bulb-light on human faces."

"You're older than you sound. You must date back." There was still the tug of interest in her voice, beyond politeness.

"Old enough to have sense," he said.

"Then tell me something true to see me through the night. I've got four calls blinking at me right now."

Rob didn't need to think but gave it to her truly the moment she asked. "You've helped one deprived soul out near Essex."

"No charge," she said. "I'm glad to have talked to a courteous voice."

"My name is Rob."

"Thank you, Mr. Mayfield. I was Tilda King. I knew you at school—never took your class but watched you from a distance. You'll have light soon." She winked out quick as a fallen star.

By then Thal had drained and was back at the screen door, yipping for entry.

The lights stayed out while he ate a cold supper of cheese and white bread. He tried to read the paper; but kind as it was, the oil light strained his eyes before he got far. He read a last sentence on the lower front page—"Mistaken for a turkey, Roscoe Bobbitt was shot in the face Tuesday evening at his home"—then thought he might phone his mother to confirm he'd see her tomorrow. She didn't need a call; she knew he'd be there. For all the nearly seventy years of reasons life had offered her for doubting a future, she went on trusting that her plans would unfold—and if not, she'd survive. Or Hutch—he doubted he could bear to hear Hutch this soon again (when Hutch had said he'd phone from New York Sunday, Rob had said, "We've made a nice personal goodbye. Let's don't string it out down the seaboard on wires"); he was anyhow with Ann now, hardly waiting for his father. Or sleep—could he sleep? He sat at the kitchen table and wondered—testing his body for sufficient exhaustion; its agreement to acquiesce in a few hours, prone and not dreaming.

It did seem weary but it made him no promise. What else was there though?—to go out with Thal and walk them both senseless in an evening still warm and close as a loft, to drive in to Fontaine and see his mother early or chance finding Grainger awake at his radio; or step ten feet to the pantry and take the pint of bourbon he kept there, sealed, as test and proof of his vow not to drink; then drink himself out. He weighed each of them; wanted no single one more than sleep, if that would come.

He wanted his son here with him to the end. He wanted his wife, dead twenty-five years. He wanted Min Tharrington, who'd wanted him for years; then had left him when he chose to rear his son here. He wanted not to die—well-behaved so long, still young as men went in his dogged family, still lonely as he'd been from the day he was born (excepting odd stretches which, counted end to end, might make a few weeks from a life of—what?—two thousand-six hundred weeks). He bedded Thal down in her box, let her lick the last salt from his thumb; then fumbled toward his own room, stripped, slept at once—no substantial dream, only moments of gratitude in which he tasted the grainy brown blankness of the rest and managed to think *If where I'm headed is the least like this, I can gladly go.*

Hours later—2:40 by the clock—he was waked by Thal at the edge of his bed. She couldn't reach high enough to see him fully; but she hadn't jumped or barked, only propped on the side rail and watched till he turned. They were scalded in light. The naked bulb suspended over Rob was burning. He sat up. "You scared?"

She wasn't; she'd only been waked herself and had come to show him. Ears back, grinning with the excess joy which seized her several times a day and would long since have worn a human flat-down, she strained to kiss him.

He rolled near to let her, not touching with his hands but repeating her whole name—"Thalia" (Hutch had named her as a puppy for the muse of comedy, in honor of the ease with which simple pleasures exalted her). When she'd had her fill, he said, "Hours till day. Please turn out the lights and go back to bed."

She considered it.

Then Rob hauled himself from the damp sheets and stepped to the hall. Grainger at least had kept his promise—there was light from the kitchen, the front bedroom, the porch, the hall. It was not till he moved toward the porch and caught himself in a mirror that he saw his dick wagging solid before him, half-gorged with the sham immunities of sleep. He stopped and turned full-face to the glass. He could hardly remember using it before (mirrors were quick resorts for shaving; this big one hung here because, when his mother was furnishing the house, she said, "Any man teaching schoolchildren needs to check at least his buttons as he runs out the door"). Despite the lights and the unshaded windows by the door, he took himself in hand and stroked till he crested hard again above his curly navel—the bare head as eager as ever and sleek with the same purple blood, same hope. The belly and chest it pointed to were still lean and white, the nipples high and flat. Thal had gone to her box, but he spoke to her now. "I'm grateful to you, Thal—never say I'm not—but keep this in mind when you outlast me: it was some kind of shame and disgrace to life that Rob Mayfield was left here with you. He refuses the blame."

She didn't look up.

He took the phone again, dialed the operator, and placed a call to Min Tharrington in Raleigh. They hadn't met since Christmas, hadn't spoken since he called to thank her for a birthday card in March; but late as it was, he had no question of his right to wake her. Four rings—she was gone, never took more than two (she lived in three rooms). In an instant he felt what he hadn't felt till now—*I will not bear this.*

But she answered, her voice drugged with something—surely sleep.

"I woke you up."

"No you didn't."

"You're lying." He was already smiling—some chance of reprieve, his old delight in her lifelong refusal to admit anybody had ever caught her sleeping when mostly after ten she would answer like a mummy or a child waked to pee.

"I was stretched out reading"; she paused as though gone. "Even if I wasn't you could say you were sorry."

"But I'm not," Rob said.

"That's nothing new."

By then she was clearing; he could hear little puffs as she propped up in bed. "There is something new," he said.

"Can I stand to hear it?"

"You'll have to judge that. Will you be there Sunday?"

"I'll be here, Rob, till they wheel me out."

"Sunday then about four o'clock?"

"Is that the new thing?—you paying me a visit?"

He knew that it was. He didn't want to tell her anything, only see her, touch her if she'd let him after so long. "Yes," he said.

"Come at five. I might even fix us a meal."

"Too hot," Rob said.

"Might change by then."

There was nothing else to say—not now, this late—but the sweetness of having one familiar voice answer when he spoke (even sixty miles off) was almost sufficient to rescue this day, the day that had passed. "Will it be just you?" he said.

"What's that meant to mean?"

"On Sunday. Will there be anybody there with us?"

"Just the ferns." Min laughed. "You remember the ferns; they've multiplied. Glad something here has."

"Only checking," Rob said. "Now go back to sleep. See you Sunday at five."

"No, wait," she said quickly; then stopped a moment. "Let me say just this—I'm here alone now, I will be Sunday and every day after. We chose that, remember?"

"I remember *you* chose it."

"Rob, it's too late to fight. You know what I mean."

He nodded.

"*You* sleep." She hung up then.

Even dropped that suddenly, he still felt reprieved. He stood with the dead receiver at his chest as if to broadcast a set of heartbeats to whoever might listen—strong, a little fast. Then he said again "Sunday," louder than before.

Thal looked up, jingling. She took his rising inflection to be some sort of invitation; and game as ever, she jumped to the floor, shook once, sneezed, watched him—more closely than anything else had watched him except his young wife and Min as a girl.

He said, "I'm sorry. False alarm—for you anyhow, old lady. Back to bed."

She held her place and shook again, happy.

"You feel like a ride to Raleigh on Sunday?"

She felt like anything but pain or fright.

"You'd wait in the car though—you understand that? Couldn't have you, at your age, witnessing what I hope to witness. Might finish you off."

She was losing interest; she turned to gnaw a flea.

Rob smiled. "May very well finish *me* off, finish all involved." He doused all the lights and slept again easily.

9

That morning—Friday—Hutch breakfasted with Ann, drove her to work; then headed south on the turnpike for Petersburg, twenty-five miles in full hot sun. By quarter to ten he had found the building, a 1920s brick apartment-house with limestone Chinese lions at the entrance and dragon rainspouts. He'd never been here before but climbed to the third floor and found with no trouble the bell labeled *Matthews*. He heard its dim ring and the quick response—sharp steps forward from several rooms back—and felt the delight of hope.

She had felt the same and opened smiling—Alice Matthews, his mother's friend. She studied him a moment; then said, "Dear God, when have I seen you?"

He said, "Labor Day, almost nine months."

"You're grown," Alice said. With both long hands she stroked her own cheekbones, to show him the site of the change in himself. "What happened?"

Hutch laughed. "Is it that bad?"

She waited. "Oh no. It's fine; you're gorgeous. I was just surprised."

"You're always surprised."

"So I am," Alice said. "It keeps me young." She stood back finally to beckon him in. "You haven't seen this."

He hadn't. She had moved in January (her father having died at ninety-three and left her well-off, she'd quit her teaching after thirty years and improved her quarters). The first room was long and light with high arched ceilings, rough rabbit-gray walls on which squads of pictures hung; the old davenport and chairs were freshly covered in umber velvet and stood on a deep wine-colored rug. The lean new grandeur was startling after years of the crowded teacher's-rooms she'd camped in—wardrobes and hotplates.

Alice said, "You hate it. You think it's wrong."

Hutch went to the sofa and sat by the table, which bore only one book— *Etchings of Rembrandt.* Then he said "No it's right" and knew he was honest. She'd earned the space surely as if it had waited here, a visible goal through all the years but sealed till now.

She smiled. "It is. I hoped you'd see it. Everybody else of course thinks I'm flat crazy—'You'll die if you quit; you've been teaching too long.' *I'll* say I have. In thirty-odd years of public-school art, I taught some sweet children—a few of them beauties so stunning you longed to freeze them on the spot in their one perfect day—but I never taught a single one that wanted what I knew, the little I knew, and thanked me for it."

Hutch said, "Not so. I've been thanking you steadily since I was fourteen."

Alice nodded. "You have. You shame me, fairly. But I never taught you."

"Just everything I know."

"What's that?" Alice said. She still hadn't sat but stood before him, straight and attentive as though this were more than a courtesy call—some final chance to break through screens and see truth plain. The money and ease had not cooled her fervor.

"The thing I know now is, I'd like a cup of coffee."

She balked a moment, loath to stop in her search. Then she grinned. "It's ready. Sit still and I'll bring it."

He sat, to give her a pause for calm, and looked round the walls—mostly familiar. At his left a few old reproductions—Giorgione's cave "Nativity," Henner's "Fabiola," a big Gainsborough girl's head, the Kritios boy. On the broad wall opposite, landscape drawings and watercolors by Alice and her friends—among them, his own laborious copy of a mountain and trees in the country near Goshen, done the day he'd met Alice eleven years ago. At his right something new—eight portrait photographs, men and women, different ages, some smiling, some sober (he recognized only himself and his mother). He walked toward those. The older man and woman would be her parents; they showed bits of her. But the other three—two men and a woman, all young, in their twenties. Kin or friends? He knew Alice had one long-lost brother, but neither of these boys was like her at all. The younger in fact was younger than he'd first thought, seventeen maybe. The girl was fine, her shoulder to the camera with the sideways glance so popular thirty years before and so likely to show any face at its best—the line from forehead to chin that mimicked the line of a straight back and good high buttocks. He straightened her frame.

Alice entered with a tray. "Do they break your heart?"

"Ma'm?"

"They still break mine. That's why they're in here." She set down the coffee and stood beside him. "I carried them round in a folder for years, thinking someday I'd have space to hang them. So when all this space opened wondrously, I framed them and hung them by my bed back there." She pointed behind her, then studied the pictures a moment. "Couldn't *take* it." She sat to pour coffee.

Hutch joined her. "Take what?"

She shook her head, looking down, as though she wouldn't speak. But when she gave him his cup, she said, "—The fact that they're gone."

"Not me."

"Sure you are."

"I'll be back."

"No you won't, not for me. You left me when you were fifteen years old."

Hutch smiled. "I really don't see it that way."

And by then she was smiling. "Doesn't matter how you *see* it. I know how it *is*. We spent a good part of two summers together when you were a boy. Then you'd got all I had and were grown and went elsewhere."

"I thought I'd been taking from you right on; I know I have. But I had Rob to see to and my Grandmother Mayfield."

Alice shook her head again.

"Did you want me to stay?"

When she looked up her face was clear and young, taut with deprivation. "I wanted every one of you to stay and you knew it. I asked you all daily, every day you knew me." She drank a long draft of very hot coffee.

Hutch could see two choices—to stand at once and leave without speaking (what his father might do, half the men in his family) or to deal calm hands and play them out. The first was his preference, but he looked to the pictures again and was held. "Who are they?" he said, "—the ones I don't know."

She waited awhile, then decided to tell him. "My mother and father, then Rachel Hutchins Mayfield, Hutchins Mayfield, Marion Thomas, York Henly, Callie Majors."

"How many are dead?"

"My parents and your mother. The rest are no more than three hours from here, in a well-tuned car—which my car is."

"You know where they are?"

"Sure. They're all three chained-up to glum or dumb mates."

Hutch remembered her speaking of Marion Thomas the morning

they'd met—a boy she loved in high school and never told. So he said, "You told me who Marion was a long time ago. Which one is he?"

"On the lower left there."

Hutch saw it was the young one—a foursquare face looking gravely out, clipped straight hair, a celluloid collar, Scotch-plaid tie. "If he never knew, how did you get the picture?"

"From the paper at home. He had won a trip to Washington for selling the *Grit*, and our paper ran his picture. I saw my chance. I wrote in and asked to buy the original, not thinking that it surely belonged to his mother and would be retrieved; and you know they sent it to me—next day, free, not a word of comment. Just as if it was my due." She took another draft. "For once they were right."

Hutch said "York and Callie?"

"Callie's the girl who's not your mother; York is the boy who's neither you nor Marion."

"They were friends?" Hutch said.

Alice laughed. "Oh *enough!*—too much about me. Yes sir, they were friends I worshiped and loved (two different things); but they're no longer active in my present, shall we say? Now tell me what matters. Tell me all your plans."

Hutch said, "I can't remember what I've written you."

Alice laughed again. "Precious little, dear bean. Your letters are as generous as a Christmas box from Hetty Green."

He nodded. "I'm sorry. I'll do better in England."

"That's a promise?"

"Yes ma'm." She had slipped off her shoes and curled in the chair; Hutch could see she meant to hear him out. They'd always had this right over one another—permission to ask any question and be answered. Despite the twenty-six years between them, they'd never lied or bent or held back. He suddenly knew he'd tell her now—anything; she must only ask.

She started. "So it's Oxford?"

He nodded. "Has to be. When we sold that timber of Mother's last fall, I thought I could take my part of the money and buy at least a year in Europe—to roam round; then settle maybe, start my work finally."

"Writing?"

"Whatever. I'm still scared to say. In any case the Draft Board said No to that. With a teacher's deferment they can't let me off—there's a risk I might enjoy it—but they said if I planned to do further study (a little guaranteed pain), they'd back me to the moon. So I sent a few letters and found to my surprise that any American smart enough to tie his shoes and willing to pay can get into Oxford or Cambridge in a minute. And in fact they're cheap, cost a lot less than here."

"So you'll study what?"

"As little as possible; I'm not sure yet. Their letters are sublimely uninformative—little handwritten notes: *Dear Mayfield, You'll be assigned rooms in college. No need to seek digs.* I like the *Mayfield*; makes me feel I'm a soldier in the desert campaign with Rommel bearing down."

"Is it Magdalen College?"

"No they didn't want me for some secret reason, maybe not rich enough; they're famous snobs. Merton did and it's oldest; and Eliot was there, hiding out from the *First* War, so that's a good omen. Far as I can see, once you get past their looks, all the colleges have the same good and bad points. The good is—they leave you very much to yourself. The bad is—they all have pleistocene plumbing, no heat, and hog food."

"Have you got your long johns?"

"Grandmother bought those the day I was accepted."

Alice nodded. "Fine. I bought you a chain."

Hutch smiled but plainly didn't understand.

"—To chain yourself down."

"Will I need that? Why?"

She shook her head. "I'm sorry. Is your coffee too cold?"

"No, tell me what you meant."

"Just jealous," she said.

"No you aren't. I need to know."

She sat up, extended her feet to the floor, and faced him straight. She looked her age again, not tired but worn from unrewarded waiting. "This is not fair," she said. "I know we've been friends. I know you were glad as a child to find someone who'd read a book or two and could halfway draw and was lonely as you. You've gone past that and I really don't mind—I'm a small-town spinster with appropriate resources; never once thought I was Rosa Bonheur or wanted to be. So you were not mine, and I made very few claims on you through the years. But here now lately, with your mother's face near me, I see I was wrong. Or wrong not to state what I knew all along—you're mine as much as Rob's, more than anyone else's. I'll tell you how. I loved your mother before you were born. When she came to Lynchburg to Father's sanitarium, nineteen years old and out of her mind—wild as a panther, thinking she had a growing child in her womb and had never touched a man—I loved her on sight. I was one year older and had already winnowed through a big hill of evidence that I'd live life out alone as a waterhole in deepest Death Valley. Poor Marion there was my main indication—barely knowing

I existed, he showed me I was cursed to choose every time, from any room I entered, the person who possessed two distinguishing traits: some odd startling beauty which many would miss *and* the utter inability to love Alice Matthews. I sound self-pitying. I'm not. I'm honest. And I know I'm a fool, a fool the size of the Gobi Desert—I've tried to change; they've tried to bleach Negroes—but here was your mother, grand as a spring storm, and she loved me back. For more than a month in the spring of 1925, when she was nearly well, she loved only me. Or clung to me; I called it love—still do, since the ways she found to cling to me (whole nights) were the final ways we ever love." Alice stopped and waited a moment, still facing him. "You still want to know?"

"Yes."

"I'm not upsetting you? You don't think I'm crazy?"

"No."

She said, "I'm not lying anyway. Count on that."

"I do," Hutch said. "I have for years."

She nodded. "Fine. You're what we made." She stopped again, then thought she had finished and stood to take the cups.

He touched her arm, bare and cool. "I don't understand."

So she sat on the edge of the chair, looking down, and said, "I didn't know how odd it would sound—worse, *crazy*: a cracked old maid inventing life backward."

"It's the only kind of life there is."

Alice laughed. "O Diogenes, praise to thy wisdom!" Then she looked, saw him shamed in his innocence, was sorry, and laid out the rest of what mattered. "What's hard to say but true is this—I loved your mother before you were born. For some weeks I gave her the care and attention she'd craved and lacked. I was too young to ask her to stay with me, too young to know we would never find better—or half as good. Rob stepped in and asked. In the silence round her, she answered Yes. But through the four years they had together, she still turned to me for all he couldn't give—steady care, I mean (I could watch her, not blinking, for days on end and never be tired); we never touched again except to greet and part, with Rob looking on. Then you were born, which ended her. Half-ended me too. I saw you when I came to her funeral of course; but after that, not till we met again in Goshen. You were what?—fourteen. Within six hours I knew you were mine—the thing that was left of your mother and me, mine at least as much as Rob Mayfield's, *made* out of me sure as mountains are made out of hot blind rock." She waited, then held out her hands as if for shackles. "Lead me to the madhouse." She laughed again.

Hutch closed her wrists in his own dry fingers, then kissed her forehead.
"Don't fail us," she said.

"What would failing be?"

"Not honoring us, the courage we had—your mother and I as girls,
dumb girls—to take what food the world provided and make life from it."

"I won't," Hutch said, knowing he meant it and grateful for the order but
warned by the heat of her solitude, the speed and spin of her self-intoxica-
tion. He'd come here the way he came as a boy, to tell one sane unshock-
able soul his clattering secrets of need and fear and fevered hope. She'd asked
him nothing more serious than where he'd sleep for the next twelve months.
Well, he'd answered that—on a no doubt narrow cot in south-central England. He could head toward that now, clean, unencumbered, also callow and
cruel.

10

Rob's mother said *"Summer"* as she opened for him; as usual she was right.
Here two-thirds through spring was a broad summer day; and though the yard
oaks were already full-leaved and shaded the porch, enough of the dry light
reached down to show her unchanged in her ease—Eva Mayfield, born
Kendal in this same house sixty-eight years ago, gone from here only the
twelve months it took her to marry, bear Rob, and learn that her own life
required this place and service to her father long as he lived (with young Rob
a watcher at the rim of the work). In all that mattered—the line, eyes,
smile—she was still the girl he had first known and needed. Only the brown
hair was pure white; the skin slightly thinner, more porous to sun.

"Yes beautiful," he said.

She waved him in and reached up to kiss him in the notch of his jaw.
"You're twenty minutes late. Sylvie may want to kill you."

Rob said, "About time—no I'm sorry. Had to stop by the superintendent's
office." (He'd stopped by to say that, barring intervention of a personal
nature by the right hand of God, they should not count on Rob Mayfield
teaching school again—September or ever.)

"You're done at least." She had already turned and stepped toward the
dining room.

He could not help a laugh.

Eva didn't stop but said, "All your paper-work in? Every grade on every
dummy?"

"Yes ma'm."

"Then you're all set to help me now."

She meant the list of chores she always gathered through the winter to lay straight on him the day school closed (she feared few things; Rob-at-leisure was one). Yet what he thought as he followed her back was not how high the ironies were stacking but that so far she hadn't mentioned Hutch, the satisfactory object of her gaze for twenty years. And he thought of explanations—she was jealous that Rob had had last sight of Hutch as he wandered off, or Hutch had phoned her last night or today and fed her curiosity; or now Hutch was gone, she was forcing herself to relearn the strokes of a solitary swim in cold water otherwise empty of life. It didn't matter which, maybe some of each. Let her ask for Hutch then if she wanted news. Behind the short tale of Warm Springs, Goshen, the Caverns, the packing, stood Rob's own news—the first real freshness he'd brought her in years, since he claimed he'd finished drinking. It was only a question—would she see him through? He wanted to know today, no later (Monday Hutch would be past recall). He wanted to stop in his tracks in the hall and say, "Mother, help *me*. I strongly suspect I can finally show you a need even you won't wave off, smiling." But he went on, begged pardon of Sylvie in the kitchen, then sat to let them gorge him again.

11

And afterward, cooling on the porch by Eva, he'd still found no way to start and tell it. Never having mentioned the early signs or his visits to the doctor, whatever he said now must be total news—nothing gentler than "Watch me. One more man is leaving," though it hadn't escaped him that the shock might also be a kind of gift, another stripping-off from her life that had sought simplicity avidly as ships' hulls or wings. Leaving only Hutch—and he nearly launched, wherever he landed. So against his vow, he started with Hutch. "Don't forget to tell Grainger to come before dark. Got to unload the truck before another rain, and I don't feel up to doing it alone."

Eva nodded. "He promised he'd be back by three. I can't fathom why he's starting rabbits again" (he'd gone thirty miles in her car to buy a pair of rabbits).

Rob said "Hutch has left him."

She studied his face, the first time today, but could see no wish to harm in his eyes. Then she looked to the street, now softening in glare. "Hutch left every one of us three years ago. Grainger knew it good as me."

Rob smiled. "Many thanks for keeping it from me. I guess I thought he was mine till now, till yesterday anyhow at 2:15."

Still facing out she said, "He has been. I'm sorry. You were what he hung onto, harder than he knew. He set down the rest of us gentle as birds; he's holding you still."

Rob saw it was the only defeat she'd conceded in a life of wins, only one he'd witnessed. He knew what it cost her; and though he doubted her accuracy (he'd ceased understanding Hutch a long way back), he also saw his chance and took it. "Now he'll have to let go, even me."

"He won't. You made him."

"I did. I remember—upstairs in this house. But Mother, his wishes in this don't count."

Eva searched him again and found nothing new. "He'll be back; you watch."

"*You* watch." He half-smiled.

"Then you had a falling-out?"

"No." Rob was stopped by a bubble of laughter. "You could say that."

"You say it. You're the cryptic clown today."

"Yes ma'm. I'm the one; I'm the fall-out, Mother."

"Have you taken a drink?"

"Would to God I had. I'm dying instead."

"*All* are, darling."

"Look, please ma'm."

She looked. There was something new, just now—a fullness that pressed on his face from within, excess power. She thought it was early sorrow for Hutch; it left him anyway younger than she'd seen him since Rachel's death, an odd rebirth in the impeded light. So she smiled. "Look fine."

"Thank you," Rob said, "but it's not the case."

Eva said, "Let's end the little mystery-hour. What's happened please?"

"I'm pretty bad off." With flat palms he struck both knees twice silently and breathed out hard. With the breath went a sizable quantity of pleasure, to be giving her at last the bedrock demand. His face dulled and shrank.

She saw it and believed him. "What can I do to help?"—the simplest offer she'd ever made.

He couldn't say it straight but said it to the nearest tree, the maple that still showed rusty nailheads by which his Aunt Rena had measured his growth every birthday for twenty years. "I'm very much afraid that by fall I'll have to ask you to tend to me."

Eva nodded. "I can start today. Say the word."

"The word is my lungs. I've got extensive tumors, nothing left but to wait."

"Dr. Simkin says so?"

"—And the best men at Duke; he sent them the X rays. It's in my spit."

"Do they want to operate?"

"No ma'm, it's scattered—little shadows all over." He scrubbed his upper chest and then looked toward her.

"Get Grainger to move you in here today."

"Thank you, not yet—six to nine months, they say. Let me do a few things."

"You didn't tell Hutch?"

"I wanted to but No."

"That was right," Eva said. "Tell him when it's time."

Rob could smile again. "When will that be, Mother?"

"I'll tell you," she said.

Rob nodded.

Eva stood.

12

The fan belt had broken in Delaware, so they got to New York on Saturday evening too late to use their tickets to *Bus Stop* (twelve dollars wasted); but their rooms at the Taft were ready, side by side. Neither of them had much experience driving north of Washington, and they both were flat and glazed by heat and the hours of rudeness that stretched like yellow unbreathable fog north from the Susquehanna. They washed and agreed on separate naps; then supper, a walk, a late movie maybe.

Hutch had slept an hour when he woke in the close dark—a noise at his door. Someone repeatedly turned the locked doorknob and rattled the frame. He was naked but sat up and called out "Ann?"

No answer; then the door was still.

Could he have dreamt it? He found a wet towel in the blackness, draped it round him, walked to the door, and said again "Ann?" Nothing. So he opened it. Nothing. He leaned out. No one in sight on the long dim hall. A dream then or possibly the house detective (from previous trips he remembered them checking on trusting out-of-towners who left rooms open to the whole five boroughs). He shut it quietly and, awake by now, could see red light straining through the thin curtains. He went to the window and looked down the twelve floors to Seventh Avenue, surprisingly empty. Its emptiness always surprised and pleased him—pockets of vacancy every few yards through the crammed blistered city. The first time he'd come here alone, four years ago, he'd walked everywhere and especially late at night with a growing exultation as he saw what was new and vital for a child reared in family webs—that you truly could live among human people but not live with them; that endless swarms of unthinkable variety would pour from the ground and grant you license to study them forever, provided you never addressed or touched them. He wanted to dress and go straight down and walk till morning, but he went to the phone and asked for Ann's room. In a moment through the wall, he could hear the bell. Again and again.

The operator came on—a chromium voice—and said "No reply."

He said, "Please try again, 1232; must have got the wrong room," though he knew they hadn't—in the bathroom maybe.

After nine more rings the operator said, "Your party's out, sir."

He said "No she's not"; but he hung up, chilled. Who was leaving who? Not lighting the room, he found his traveling clothes and dressed quickly, stepped to Ann's door, knocked, and called her name. No reply. Again. He tried the knob—locked.

Far down the hall a man in his undershirt looked out and went on looking.

Hutch returned to his room, sat on his bed, turned on the reading lamp—his mouth foul with bafflement about to be fear—and said to himself as plainly as at school, "Something has started which you can't stop, and you are the cause." Then he took hold and tried to consider chances. She had waked up, tried to rouse him at the door, then gone down for coffee. She had left for home (why?—he'd refused to let her wear his ring and register for one room as man and wife). She was still in the room, angry or dead. Having laid those out—pieces on his board—he gained the genuine competence of dread. He knocked once more and said "Ann, I'm worried." Then he phoned the operator and gambled on candor—he was worried; could she help?

"Certainly," she said, her voice still hard. "Hang up and I'll call you back in five minutes."

He propped himself on the wooden headboard, shut his eyes, and tried not to think. But in twenty seconds he'd gone again through the list of chances, deepening the dangers. So he tried to seize control by asking, "Suppose each has happened—then so what?" If she'd gone downstairs a page would find her. If she'd gone outside she'd be back soon. Independent as she was, she didn't court trouble; not from strangers at least. If she had died (strokes ran in her family but not this young), then the trip was off for another month maybe; an elegant stickhouse of plans would tumble. "*Jesus*," he thought. He meant his own blank monstrosity—his amazement at that—but it made him see that he'd asked no help from anything stronger than a telephone voice. He said his father's prayer and opened a drawer on a Gideon Bible. Then he shut his eyes again, opened the book at random, blindly ran a finger down the page, and stopped— "Therefore night shall be unto you, that ye shall not have a vision; and it shall be dark unto you, that ye shall not divine." Her safety, her life close up by his seemed suddenly the urgent need of the world. For another two minutes, still stretched on the bed, he felt nothing else.

The telephone rang. "Sir, I get no response to a page in the lobby or the coffee shop. Any news up there?" With the last her voice was assuming life.

"Nothing. No."

A long wait passed in which it seemed she had no other hope or had disconnected. Then she said, "I could put you through to Mr. Amsler, the night assistant-manager—"

Hutch said "All right" but as the ring started, he thought how helpless and absurd he'd sound. After two more rings he'd hang up and wait.

"Leonard Amsler speaking."

Hutch paused an instant with the sense that a broad wheel, oiled and poised, was waiting only for the sound of his voice to turn and plunge on a course it had already chosen and yearned toward. He said, "Mr. Amsler, this is Hutchins Mayfield, room 1230. I may have a problem. Miss Ann Gatlin and I checked in here at eight this evening—she's in 1232. We were tired and agreed to nap for an hour, then meet for supper. I've had my nap but I can't contact her. Her phone doesn't answer. I've knocked on her door. We've paged downstairs."

"Then she must have gone out."

"Not without me, no."

Another long wait, then Amsler's voice descended in pitch and volume and slowed—the professional clerk's preparation for trespass. "You seem to be worried. Any reason to think she'd behave untypically?"

Reasons flew up like bats; but Hutch said, "She'd been a little blue, yes."

He'd thrown the right switch, yielded crucial ground. Amsler jerked into gear, a galvanized frog. "I'll come right up and check her room. You're in 1230?"

"Yes, I'll wait for you here."

By then Hutch was more than half-sure they'd find her dead—natural causes, murder, suicide. Once listed, the means of death didn't concern him, only the need to settle the fact and free in his locked throat the years of feeling—tenderness, thanks—he'd stored for this girl. He combed his hair, repaired his quick dressing, stepped into the hall. He didn't knock again but waited at his own door and, working his mind, tried to separate strands of the odor that filled all hotel corridors—talcum, cold cigars, drying rubber goods, wallpaper glue.

The elevator opened; two men stepped out—one in business clothes, the other a bellhop with a brass hoop of keys. When they reached Hutch, Amsler extended a hand—"Len Amsler, Mr. Maitland"—and the bellhop grinned.

"This is standard," Hutch thought. "They do this hourly." So he didn't delay them to hear his right name.

Amsler said, "Let's see what we have in the room. Mike, open the door."

Mike found his passkey, advanced on the lock with a hunched squinting stealth, and labored to turn it. "Sometimes these things take awhile to work"—Irish as cold rain.

Hutch stepped toward the door. "I'd better look first."

Amsler said in his solemn telephone voice, "Mr. Maitland, you may be glad to have witnesses."

Hutch barely allowed himself to understand. What he suddenly felt was the laughter of trust; he trusted in some easy answer to this. And he actually smiled as he nodded to Amsler.

Mike opened the door on hot solid dark.

Amsler leaned in far enough to switch on a light. The room took a left turn; the bed was hidden. All they could see was Ann's open suitcase, her scuffed-off shoes. Amsler stepped back and said to Hutch, "We'll be right behind you."

Hutch tried once more to forestall discovery. He called "Ann Gatlin."

Amsler laid a firm hand against his back.

She was there on the bed, stretched on her stomach in a blue quilted robe, no other cover—feet and calves bare. Her face was averted, hands palm-down at the sides of her head as if in surrender to whatever she'd met or was meeting now.

Hutch stood at the edge, in the hope of seeing breath.

Amsler stood beside him.

Mike, at the end of the bed, reached out and held her foot a moment. "She's warm, O.K."

Too late, Amsler waved to restrain him.

But Ann extended the touched foot farther, paddled it twice.

Mike giggled.

Hutch bent and took her shoulder; rocked it gently, calling her back.

She said, "I'm sorry. I thought I locked my door." Then she craned her neck and looked round, wincing in the raw yellow light. Her face was latticed with the damask of the covers, the muscles slack in the chaos of sleep. She was still too dazed to be puzzled by strangers.

Hutch said "Are you all right?"

She nodded and smiled, then noticed Mike and Amsler.

Hutch said, "We've been trying to rouse you half an hour. Thought maybe you were dead."

She nodded again. "I was." Then she smiled again. "Needed to be."

Hutch saw the men out, explaining she'd never done this before. He was dazed himself, by anger and thanks.

13

They ate downstairs— club sandwiches and French fries—then walked out into the warm damp night and laughed their way through a tour of Times Square. Once the scare had receded, Hutch was tired again; but Ann was ready to look till dawn (they'd agreed a movie was a waste of time). So he trudged on with her through open-fronted jazz bars, Ripley's *Believe It Or Not!* Museum, pinball arcades, bookshops, junk shops. Finally she insisted on paying three dollars to have Hutch photographed alone at a baize table playing out a hand of poker, chips stacked before him. In the finished print, ten minutes later, he was shown at play with three solid partners, all wearing his face at appropriate angles—accomplished with mirrors and surprisingly good. They laughed and he ordered a second print to mail to Rob, but he knew something crucial had been stumbled on, and he knew Ann knew. He also knew he could ask her now to head back in. The sight of his four faces bluffing each other had drawn a firm line to the tawdry hour. Ann was suddenly quiet. Hutch was gray with exhaustion and the picture's news—an unlosable game—but also ringing in every cell like summer woods with the need to lay his skin on hers, to risk a partner.

14

Ann welcomed him in, but in her own room—her one condition, that they be in her bed. And once he agreed and came back to join her, they didn't speak again for more than an hour. As they worked through the dark time, Hutch realized the splendor—that they'd built this much in seven years together: the mutual right and total competence to please one another through measurable and surely memorable spaces as empty of words as the pith of a tree. And better than *please*—the mitigation they could press from one another by the simple motions which practice had taught them, practice in the deepest courtesy of all.

When they'd each come to that at separate speeds, Hutch kissed her eyes, lay flat beside her, and slept at once.

As Ann heard his breathing shift to the helpless rate of surrender—his daily change into what she dreamed all their days might be—she rolled to her left side, huddled against him, burrowed her head in the curve of his arm, and laid her right hand flat on his belly.

In the dream Hutch was having—he'd dreamt in a moment—he was still free to move his hand to cover hers.

She accepted that awhile, then questioned her right. *If someone you've spent seven years of your life steadily learning like a hard foreign language—learning to use, serve, honor, protect and three-fourths succeeding—if that someone can one day decide to walk flat away and give no reason, having asked for you every day of those years or at least never told you to haul-ass home, and you can't stop him—don't know another way, have all but forgot everything you knew before him—what right do you have to lie in a hot room high in the black air of New York City, the biggest collection of quitters and leavers ever gathered on one slim spit of land since land began, and bear the dead weight of your own private quitter's five resting fingers? To hell with* right—*why be* fool *enough?* She drew her hand out, spread it at her lips, and quietly puffed cool air across it. It seemed the first service she'd done herself in weeks, maybe months. Slowly not to wake him, she turned back apart till her body touched him nowhere. She would surely not sleep; she could lie alone though. In another two minutes he felt as far as Burma.

Hutch had waked when she claimed her hand. He'd understood at once and honored the withdrawal. He didn't move or speak. He had hoped to go—and maybe return—without ever trapping the act in words. He'd thought they could both resume, or forget, much easier without the nets of apology, blame, analysis, and hope that he (and all his kin) spun naturally as spider silk. But the evening's skirmish with possible disaster or comic abandonment had shown him he owed her as full an explanation as he knew and could give. He lay there till he knew it. Then he listened for her sounds. Silent as wax—she was surely awake. He said, "May I talk for just two minutes?"

Ann paused long enough to give him doubts. "You can talk till noon, Demosthenes; but I don't guarantee Miss Gatlin will hear more than fifteen words."

"Tired?"

"Amen."

"After that last nap I thought you wouldn't need sleep for weeks."

"Yes, well—stop a moment in your rush toward progress and think how hard Miss Gatlin has *lived* in recent weeks. She should go underground and curl-up till Groundhog Day at least."

"Two minutes—I promise."

She slid still farther away, then propped her head on the pillow but looked only up at the vanished ceiling. "Sure. Deal," she said, though she sounded gentle.

Hutch turned to face her, keeping the distance she'd set between them. He said it to the edge of her profile, where it caught the last of the light pumped toward them from the street. "I'm not leaving now because of any wish to lose you. I'm as grateful to you as to anyone alive, except maybe my father, and you understand that. But I'm twenty-five years old—the way I figure it, more than a third of a normal lifespan—and the trouble for us comes out of that. I've known you for only a part of that time, seven mostly good years. There were long years before you, and several more people; and what you and I've made cannot cancel that. I never meant us to; I never felt cursed or really burdened by, you know, all the layers of May-fields and Kendals and Hutchins piled on me. What I have felt is full, *crowded* even. I'm the place where a good deal of time comes to bear, and several lives—the only place on earth. You remember in the war they were always telling us not to waste a crumb or an atom of steel. I took them seriously then and still do. My people abandoned so much on my doorstep— or had it snatched from them and set down here. There's no one but me left to use it at all, consume it, convert it, redeem back all my people pawned away—their generous starved hearts." He paused, not feeling he'd lied or bragged but sure that his words built the statue of a fool, sure as Tar built the Baby. So he thought he'd finished.

Ann seemed to agree. She lay quiet a good while, though still propped and breathing attentively. Then she said, "You've got one whole minute left."

Hutch laughed. "I yield it."

"Then the question-and-answer period can start?"

"Yes ma'm—one minute."

"Thank you, sir. I may need two of my own." She faced toward him slightly but kept her limbs clear. "This plan of redemption—just how will that run?"

He laughed again as he felt himself slam down, wing-shot. "Slow as Christmas, I'll bet, with backfire and smoke. No, you know what I mean— the work I'm planning." He saw her nod.

"You're stopping your own life to sit in a cold room with only yourself and chew on the little you know or have dreamt about a dozen dead people who mostly never saw you, surely never wished you harm—that's as much as I know."

"And it makes us even—it's as much as I know."

"Then I beat you," she said. "I know something else."

"What?"

She faced him finally. "You're crazy."

Hutch laughed. "May very well be. It would be quite appropriate, another family custom."

"I was serious," she said.

"It's crazy to want to be a grown man at work? Ann, grown cattle *work*."

"Making milk"—she nodded—"for calves they've made. Bulls just eat and screw and have temper tantrums."

"In Spain they work."

"To get killed."

"Or free." He could see that her right hand lay extended on the crest of her thigh. It had offered—he well knew—to hold no one but him. He knew that the natural thing on earth would be to reach toward it, accept, take her with him. And the wish to touch her flooded him now, this soon again—but *touch* not *hold*. He'd surrendered the right; only Ann could renew it.

Ann lay very still, transmitting nothing but the single dim line—shoulder, arm, legs (her head was all dark, her feet in the linen).

It seemed again a sensible goal, near and possible but endless in promise. Hutch quivered with want but kept his place and studied what was visible, all it might mean. It was clearly the best chance offered anyone in his family for years to have what, with all his marginal hopes, he had never doubted was the central aim—a well-paired life. But the aim for *whom?* Well, the animal world and, within it, that part of the human race that was not somehow lame or scared. Or *designated* by whatever hand of God, Fate, The Past to stand on the edge alone and stare inward steadily. Was he designated? For ten years at least he'd suspected so; and for all his native buoyancy, his huge but sporadic needs for the time and touch of others, he had more than half hoped so. In his own childhood he'd often felt like the low but well-built cooking fire round which, at distances carefully gauged, the members of his own blood-family wheeled—for the sight and warmth, with occasional startling forays toward him (where he lay alone also). But when his own manhood flared up in him, it consumed his fuel and, though his family had never understood it, changed him to a member in their own ring of prowlers, impelled by hunger. He'd made his own forays, seized his own food—none of which had lasted long, most of which had left him burned. Ann had been the exception. For almost a third of his life—patient, funny, and as nearly inexhaustible as anyone he'd known or heard of ever—she'd volunteered to want him and to want more of him than any other asker. Surely her knowledge was as usual right; he was crazy to go, to risk her absence whenever he returned. And risk it for what?—for clear space and time in which to prove he was either a born outrider capable of calling in useful reports or a driven scout on solitary missions of value to groups huddled nearer the fire or a wheyfaced fool fed on flakes of his own dry skin and nails: an ordinary Mayfield, the latest of hundreds.

Ann sat up and fished for her half of the sheet, pulled it to cover her, then lay back and settled into what was her usual posture for sleep—flat on her back, face rightward; hands laddered on her belly, which was calm now.

In a minute she'd be gone. Hutch slipped from his left hand the ring that had started as his great-grandmother's. He'd had it stretched when he reached his full growth; so he knew it would swallow any finger of Ann's, strong as she was. He closed it in his palm; then laid that fist on Ann's right hand, opened it slowly, and left the ring. It was warm as the air; he doubted she could feel it.

And she didn't move or speak for a while. Then she slid her left hand down to cover her right. "What does this change?" she said.

Hutch knew he didn't know. He had mainly acted to forestall her sleep—feeling that tomorrow would be a new thing, that one night's sleep might build the last courses of a final wall between them. So he said "Nothing really."

"Then it's just a gold string."

"Ma'm?"

"—The string to keep me on till you know your plans."

"I think you know the ring means more to me than that."

"I know it's some heirloom."

They'd talked enough; he wouldn't tell her now. "It has a little history attached to it, yes. But for now what it means is, come to Rome at Christmas." They'd discussed a Christmas meeting when he first planned to leave; last month he'd told her No.

Ann stayed in place, quiet. Then slowly she found the proper finger on his hand and replaced the ring.

Hutch said "What does this change?"

"Nothing really," she said. "It means I am still on a string, my own string. I plan to stay on it till Thanksgiving Day, which gives us six months. If the transatlantic postal system pulls the string hard and steady between now and then, I'll come to Rome at Christmas and hope for you there."

Hutch laughed once. "I *fold*."

They kissed, cool as cousins.

15

Sunday morning Sylvie showed up an hour late—eight o'clock. She opened the back screen on Eva, fully dressed, drinking coffee at the table. But before she could comment on the oddness of that, she had to ask the question that had bothered her all night. She stood on the threshold with good sun behind her and said, "Miss Eva, how old am I?"

"The same age as me nearly, twelve days younger."

Sylvie stepped on in and set down the bag of ginger snaps she would eat through the day. Then she turned her back, took off her sun hat (a man's, wide-brimmed), and slipped on the red knitted skullcap that covered her gray hair entirely. Then she ran the cold faucet to clear the pipes—she hated pipe water—and said, "That don't help me one bit."

"You know my age. You fixed my last cake."

"I fixed every cake you had but one—or watched Mama fix it. I've still forgot."

"I'm three score and ten minus two; so are you. Why is that so important?"

Sylvie didn't answer. Now the water was pure, she filled the percolator and plugged it in.

Eva said, "I've had all the coffee I need."

"That instant mess—eat your stomach right out. You ain't the only one; Mr. Grainger got to eat. He ain't eat, is he?"

"Not that I know of. Haven't seen him since he left here for Rob's yesterday."

"The car is back. He'll come pulling soon." She sliced thick bacon and laid it in a cold pan, careful as a nurse. Then she turned to cracking eggs.

Eva said "You didn't answer."

"Must be I didn't want to. I may be making plans."

"What plans?"

"To leave *here*. I ain't sticking round here for this integration, plan to save my skin for a lovely funeral."

"You know something I don't? You heard of any trouble?"

"Ain't saying what I heard. Don't need ears though to know mean white folks making *they* plans."

"Name two white people that were ever mean to you."

"If I gave you the list, I'd ruin this bacon—you want some bacon, don't you?"

"And where would you go that didn't have trash of all shades, with their meanness?"

"New York," Sylvie said.

"Great Jonah! New York is the sink of the earth; they use colored people for *sausage* meat."

"May do," Sylvie said, "but they settled this integration long ago."

"Yes. You know what it means in New York City? It means that, for money, they'll let you sit your poor tired tail by a rich white woman on the bus for six blocks till she gets off at her air-conditioned house, leaving you to ride to Harlem and sleep with rats running cross your body big as dogs in the heat."

Sylvie turned her bacon. "Sound safer than it going to be down here when *cutting* start." She knew she was teasing, and fairly near the quick, but it suited her this morning; Miss Eva understood.

Eva didn't answer though.

And when Sylvie turned she saw what she hadn't seen for twenty-six years, since Eva's father died.

Eva faced the door, the warm sun, her eyes cupping water. It spilled down her cheeks, and she said "Be good to me."

"What's wrong with you?" But Sylvie stood her ground—never go to Eva till Eva called you.

She didn't call. She dried her face and waited and then said, "I've got another dying to manage. I doubt I can do it."

"*I* don't," Sylvie said. She laid the perfect bacon on a brown bag to drain. When she poured in the eggs, she would ask for the name. But she heard Grainger's door open back in the yard, so she quickly said "Who sick?"

"Rob. Cancer. By Christmas."

Sylvie couldn't turn again. She said "Oh Jesus" for herself, for Rob. Then she said "Grainger know?"

"I doubt it. Rob just told me yesterday—after lunch; you'd left."

Sylvie stirred seven eggs into flecked bacon grease and said "We'll do it." When Grainger stepped in and Eva stood to set his place, Sylvie said, "Radio saying peace coming soon."

Eva said, "Good morning, Grainger. Peace coming where, Sylvie?"

"All over. Any day."

Grainger said "Who said?"

"Some preacher," Sylvie said. "Big smart man, raking in money by the peck. Count on him to be telling it straight."

16

From the moment Min met him at the door, Rob had worked at reclaiming her—his sense of her; whatever within her had held him six or seven years and had sent her to him since her own girlhood. Was it in her at all, a radiance, or simply a route his own desolation found and took? And the same for himself—what had he shown her that made him a goal? Why had she found the means, after years of waiting, to wait no longer? Had they been plain fools? Or had they been right, till time canceled whatever signals they'd flown at one another? Were the signals gone forever? He felt no urgency to answer the questions; only to uncover from the debris of years enough of the girl he had sometimes wanted, then to want her again and ask for the chance—just once, tonight, first time in ten years.

And though she'd disguised her former body in a uniform fifteen pounds of flesh, she did throw occasional messages of promise that time had not passed but had drifted like snow round one standing obstacle—the first Min he'd known. In the dim alcove she used for a kitchen, Rob had stood three steps back and watched her assemble their supper—chicken salad, lettuce, crackers, canned snaps barely warmed on her doll-house stove. When she'd got it on the tray, she'd turned and said, "You can take this in please and lay it out prettier than it deserves. I thought a cold feast was called for to damp such raging hearts." Then she'd laughed for the first time, eyes flaring wide—her perfect feature, now mostly hooded. And when she'd offered him the second slice of icebox lime pie and he'd accepted, she'd returned with an equal second for herself—"You're only middle-aged once; never waste an instant's chance at help. Food's the surest consolation, in a plentiful land." Yet after they'd finished and had sat back to rest, what Rob still hunted was some trace Min might want him after so long a gap for more than talk—a slow Sunday killed.

She talked about work though. In recent years she'd lived as an independent genealogical researcher, mostly at the State Library and Archives in the interests of mainly northern women in their sixties and seventies who were either demonstrating to husbands and children that the family's roots plunged south for water or were rushing to plait some net against age—made of dates, blank names, wills conveying mules and bedticks. She sat at the far end of her ruined sofa and said, "I've been working for a New Jersey lady with a Carolina past or so she hoped; it's turned out poorly so far, Baptist preachers stretching back toward *Palestine.* But anyway she's put endless money behind me, so I drove up last week around Mount Airy to look for graves. I was lost in short order and stopped for directions on the far edge of town at a low white four-room house with forsythia piled to the eaves. As I got to the porch, a tan dog ran right at me from the bushes, silent as cotton. I stopped of course to let him decide on mangling or welcome. But he never had time; he was still smelling ankles when an odd voice said, 'You come to get him?'—not quite a cleft palate but something badly wrong in the roof of her mouth. A squat woman not much older than me, in a wash dress and sweater, was at the screen, smiling. I thought she meant the dog; and since he still was silent, I wondered whether everything on the place had voice trouble. But I said, 'Oh no I've come for directions. I'm afraid I'm lost.' The woman stamped her foot, drummed hard on the tight screen; and the dog flew off—he'd dug a deep hole beneath a crepe myrtle, so he hid in that and watched me. Then she unhooked the screen and opened it to me and said, 'No ma'm. You're at the *place.*' A wonderful smell—gingerbread, I still think—was pouring out round her, which was why I went in. I was half-scared of her—her eyes were such a light gray they seemed all but white, and her hair was fine as fur—but the fact she was clean and the comforting smell made me go in. When I'd got in the living room and rearranged my eyes—unpainted pine walls, hard chairs, not a picture—I said, 'I'm looking for the homeplace of Stilby Warren or his family graves.' She went on smiling and pointed to the rocker and said, 'I'll find him for you. Just rest.' She'd seen I was tired; and peculiar as it all was, I actually rested—ten minutes maybe. Not a sound from her. I don't think I slept, but I did shut my eyes. I know that for sure because, when I opened them, they'd adjusted even further to the cool dark air; and I saw that the far wall was papered, top to floor, with magazine pictures of children, trimmed neatly and glued without wrinkles. Every size and color—the children, I mean (black as grapes, pink, yellow)—though none were just babies, none too young to walk. Then she reappeared, quick and quiet as the dog. She had put on white anklet socks but was otherwise the same. 'He was almost packed,' she said. 'I just helped him some.' I noticed she was carrying a little tan suitcase, a child's case really with brass stud-nails and a curious lock." Min stopped and looked up; had she carried Rob with her this far?

He said, "You were scared at that point."

She waited to consider. "Funny thing is, no. She was too kind-looking, and I was still hoping her gingerbread was ready and would be my reward."

"For what?"

"Being there, having found her somehow. I'd already figured I was her only company since the war at least."

"What made you think that?" Rob said.

"The bareness, I guess—the age of the pictures: every child but one was dressed in '30s clothes." Min moved to stand.

Rob saw his chance failing. "No, finish," he said.

So she sat back, laughed, and said, "I saw I had to stop her. I told her, 'I'm sorry but you misunderstood. The man I'm hunting died ninety years ago.' I stood but she stepped toward me and opened the valise. Laid in it was a doll—a brown-headed boy—dressed neatly in a handmade blue chambray shirt and black felt overalls with big pearl buttons. He was packed in tight with wads of what looked like baby underclothes and socks, a child's yellow toothbrush."

Rob said "You ran."

"No I didn't."

"—Crazy as her. I'd have been halfway back to Raleigh by then."

Min nodded. "You would have."

He saw he'd offended. *Good*—he had the power still. *Bad*—she'd close against him. She'd started this, laughing, but she'd struck something more as she dug through the story in his presence and for him. He must take the small gift or be ready to leave. He said, "Any signs of a man on the place?"

She said "I wasn't looking." But she thought it through. "No I don't think there were. Signs of nobody really but I told you that."

"Were you dreaming?"

Min laughed. "Oh no I touched the boy. She raised up his hand."

"Was the lady a dummy?"

"A moron, you mean?"

"They keep dolls sometimes when they've got nothing else. I've seen morons sixty years old with dolls."

Min smiled. "Well, this one was just my age. No she looked all right. She was giving it to me."

"Why?"

"I didn't ask."

"Can I see him?" Rob said.

"If you want to drive to Mount Airy, sure. You don't think I took it?"

"Might have been the right thing—polite anyhow: don't refuse a kind giver."

She said, "I didn't. I held the open case and asked his name. She said she hadn't named him, so I named him then and asked her to go on keeping him for me till I had a real place of my own to take him. She had to think a minute but finally agreed. The last thing she said was, 'He'll wait happy here.' I said I didn't doubt it and then I left. The dog made another mute run at my heels, but I got out intact. She was standing at the door still waving, last I looked."

Rob said "What's the name?"

"Sir?"

"—The name you gave him."

She smiled. "That's the secret. I have to save something."

He made a little ring with his thumb and middle finger to signal O.K., then he saw her through the ring and brought it to his eye as if it were a lens. She was looking down, yawning; and though her smile survived, Rob saw for the first time how much worse her luck was than his. In a good many things, they were fairly even—the central people they'd loved had vanished; their daily work had mostly been *jobs*, little handfuls of money their only reward. But Rob saw himself as continuing. Despite Hutch's leaving now in grinning indifference, he was leaving alive with whole tracts of Rob's face copied in his. For all the big differences which Rob hardly fathomed, he knew he'd made one thing that had its own chances—and made it on a girl he'd finally loved. Min was stopped; she ended here, in her own four walls, her thickened body. Kind as she'd been at her best—and even now—nothing would survive her but a mixed crate of knickknacks, the muffled gratitudes of a few aging schoolchildren and her old-lady clients. He was partly responsible, he'd always known—unable as a boy to bear her worship, unable after Rachel's death to pardon himself long enough to marry Min, then bound to Hutch so closely as to ease and gradually cancel the separate will of a ravenous body which had sent him to her. By then—thankful, pitiful, hoping to bless—he wanted her again. So he made the long reach, through air that seemed numb, to take her right hand.

Her hand was palm-down on the cushion beside her. She turned it to accept him, wove her fingers with his. But she didn't face him. Being tired and calm, she laid her head back and shut her eyes.

"Name it Rob," he said. "—A dressed-up baby still waiting in a box."

"For what? *I'm* the waiter."

"You quit," Rob said. "You told me you were tired."

"I was, when I told you. You never checked again."

"Hutch needed me," he said.

"He's gone now surely." She said it so gently as to leave it half a question.

Rob conceded her rightness. "He thinks so, yes."

"How long will he stay?"

"That won't concern me." It was literally true and he'd said it quickly to end this tack. In the few little meetings they'd had since parting eleven years ago, he and Min had silently agreed to ration all reference to Hutch severely. Though Hutch stood between them thoroughly as a mountain, they'd chosen to ignore him—in respect, fear; and maybe on the chance he'd someday vanish, leaving them free again for one another. To ease the warning Rob raised their joined hands and turned them in the light. But they didn't bear looking at, not this late. The lamp was at his shoulder; he switched it off. Then he sat back and waited for his eyes to open to whatever flow seeped up from the street through Min's gauze curtains. Considerable—in a while she was back there beside him. Were they some kind of tragedy, linked like this but with no time before them? He couldn't feel that. Was it some unforgivable waste, to be punished, that they'd lost ten years they might have spent together? Here just now, he couldn't think that, though he carefully tried. He could only want to reach her entirely again, down all their length (he had asked the doctor if he was dangerous to others—none at all, at last). He began, as always at their best, with her face—exploring it lightly.

When he reached her dry mouth, her lips moved silently once to greet him. Then she said, "Do you think we are starting anything?"

"No ma'm—confirming."

Min nodded. "That's better."

"So it's fine by you?"

She waited. "Not fine exactly but friendly."

Rob laughed and, though they continued then more closely by the moment, Min never felt his few glad tears—never mentioned them at least.

17

When he'd thanked her and told her goodbye (but no more), Rob went down to the street at half-past eleven and found both Grainger and Thalia dozing in the car at the curb. The air was still close, and the windows were down. Thal heard him first and sat up grinning, but he had to speak to Grainger. He leaned in and said in a disguised voice, "Would you be kind enough to tell me the way to the local White Citizens' Council Office?"

Grainger's head stayed back, his eyes stayed closed; but he said, "Step in. I'll drive you to the door. I work for them."

"Doing what?"

"Mailing colored babies back to Africa, fast as they cry. Driving white gentlemen round for little visits to old ladyfriends."

Rob opened the door, slid in, reached to Thal.

Grainger sat up and reached for the starter.

"You tired?" Rob said. "I'll be glad to drive."

Grainger cranked the engine. "No me and Thal are fine. I been to two shows, she snored and pooted for six good hours." Before he drove off he glanced to Rob. "You rejuvenated?"

Rob smiled ahead. "Very nicely, thank you." Then he knew he was thoroughly drained of strength, though he felt no pain or desperation. "But I may need a few minutes' sleep myself."

"Sleep on," Grainger said. "This old man's awake."

He slept to within ten miles of home, another peaceful hour (was the tumor consuming his dreams as well?—when he woke he couldn't think when he'd dreamt last). He looked to Grainger, calm as a post. Thal was buried on the floor in the back, hardly breathing. For a mile he was happy—having left an old friend in perfect understanding; being driven safely toward his own good place by a Negro who was not just his half first-cousin but the one wholly trustworthy human he'd known, and for thirty years. Then like an inspiration, he felt in his upper right chest not a pain but a sudden sense of *white*, a knobbed patch of whiteness blank as his nap and the size of a monkey's hand. He lay back and waited; the hand stayed in place, extended, still, nerveless. He could not know it would never close again or stay still long—it was now a declared component of his time—but he felt stunned enough to say, "You made your summer plans?" (Grainger spent a month or six weeks, most summers lately, at the house he owned in Bracey, Virginia).

Grainger nodded. "Yesterday."

"About the first of July?"

Grainger waited a space. "Staying here this summer."

Rob recalled Eva saying he'd gone to buy rabbits two days ago. "I'll watch your rabbits for you."

"Scared Sylvie might kill em."

"She might," Rob said. "I'll watch her too, been watching her forever."

Grainger nodded. "I'm staying."

That came as another assurance, whyever, that the weeks ahead were a crossable distance. Rob said "You got some project?"

"Guess so."

"What is it?"

Grainger faced him finally. "You going to make me tell you?"

Rob laughed once. "Not if it's against your religion."

Grainger said, "I'm moving out to stay with you, long as you stay there."

Rob said "Not long." Then he waited and looked. "You know what I mean?"

Grainger seemed to nod.

"Mother told you?"

"This morning—me and Sylvie, at breakfast."

"What did Sylvie say?"

Grainger said, "She heard it before I came in. By the time I got there, she won't saying nothing."

"What did you say?"

"You're the one love to talk."

Rob laughed (Grainger with him). "You can rest your ears by New Year though."

Grainger said "I can wait." Then he said, "How long you be keeping your strength?"

"To move around?"

"Yes."

"Doctor didn't say. I'm counting on another four or five months at most."

"Let's take us a trip."

Rob said "How far?"

"Our old places, not far—just round Virginia."

"Hutch took me by Goshen."

"I didn't mean there—maybe Bracey, Richmond. Haven't seen Miss Polly in a good while; have you?"

Rob thought and said "Two years, maybe three."

"She still alive, ain't she?"

"Was at Christmas; I heard from her then."

"Me too," Grainger said. "Sent me that dollar bill she sends every year. Me and her live long enough, I'll be a rich man."

Rob said, "She'll live. She may never die. She likes it too much."

Grainger said "Good." Then he said "You disagree?"

Rob didn't know at once. He looked to his right. By their glare he could see they were coming to the turn-off for Stallings Mill Pond, the site of numerous early drunks and of his first serious quarrel with Min when she'd been strong enough to walk off rather than beg him for care (he'd asked her to beg). She'd thought he was taunting; he'd thought he was taunting—but if thirty-four years had shown one thing, they'd shown he was earnest. All he'd ever wanted was care not control, not strength but safety. Little stretches of that had come in his youth from his Aunt Rena, Sylvie, his father, Polly, Grainger. Only Hutch, in the four close years they'd had, built real walls for him. Tomorrow by noon Hutch would have sailed, the gate of the first wall floated away. Rob looked back to see if the pond showed at all in the thin moonlight. No the woods were too dense. So he said "Not really."

Grainger said "Beg your pardon?"

Rob laughed, "I'm not really head over heels in love with the world, if that's what you mean. I never really was. I loved a few people. I wish Hutch was here."

"He'll be back in time."

"How?"

"We'll call him back in time."

Rob said, "Oh no. He's left it to us."

18

Hutch dreamt. In his own room alone at four (that stretch, not quite an hour long, when New York is silent enough for thought), he saw himself enter a sizable building the walls of which were solid glass. He felt it was England, but the indoors was warm; and the man who came down a hall to meet him was certainly Rob, by look and voice. He said a short welcome, though he gave no sign of recognition or special relation. Then he led Hutch forward on inspection of numerous rooms and yards—all empty as robbed graves, flooded with light; no picture on the walls, no place to sit. More and more, as the man named off the rooms, Hutch wondered if he'd somehow changed past knowing; and he hoped for a mirror but no mirror came. Finally as they rounded back to the entrance, Hutch thought he would call the man *Father* when he left. But he wasn't leaving. The man put his hand out, smiled very broadly, and said, "I'd worried that you wouldn't show up. More than one said you wouldn't. But you kept your word. You're here and I'm thankful. It's safe in your hands." When he'd pressed Hutch's right hand warmly and firmly, he walked out the door into light even brighter than the prismatic rooms. Hutch stayed in place and watched him out of sight.

Then on the street below, garbage men sounded Monday—his departure.

He woke and lay still, cool and afraid, for half an hour till natural light first stroked at the curtains. Then he stood, stepped into his underpants, opened the curtains on grimy glass, went back to his bed, and knelt beside it. Facing the window and the straining dawn, he asked for strength to do what he should—this day and later—and he named every person he remembered loving and commended them to care. He mentioned no regrets and asked no pardon. It took him ten minutes. Then he stood again, washed his face and teeth, dressed lightly, and went next door to join Ann. By then there were six hours left till he sailed.

19

May 28, 1955

Dear Hutchins,

I think you said the Queen Mary. *If it's the* Elizabeth *I hope they'll somehow read my addled brain and get this to you on your sailing day—to say "Fare well," also that I'm sorry I talked so much yesterday and listened so little. It's been one of the permanent intentions of my life not to finish as the kind of bore I knew so many of when young—old crocodiles utterly trapped in their leather, satisfied as fed babies, pouring out the sweet songs of Self Self Self or the Dreadful World (I've never liked myself but have treasured the world).*

No, two things were working. One I see so few people that, when one turns up, I forget I'm susceptible, imbibe too fast, am drunk with company in under ten minutes and raving like a parrot on Spanish rum; Two in sight of your eyes, which are your mother's eyes, I suddenly felt I should tell you the last things you didn't know—how I wanted your mother, how nearly you are mine. Hence my curious outburst, not quite uncontrolled as I hope you know.

I listened to you at the right time to listen—that summer you were fourteen and we stayed in Goshen. That was when you knew all you needed to know, with no contradictions—who had loved you, who you thanked, who you missed and needed, what you meant to make in the long time you had. The first day you and I were ever together, standing up to walk back from drawing the mountain, I asked you how you felt about the morning (meaning what we had done, our separate pictures); and you said, "Well, objects seem to have a lot of patience." I recall I laughed. You took no offense and even joined in. Now I see that was what you needed to know and are acting on now.

Go to it, dear bean; look all you can, and the best luck ever. May I add only one small qualification, which you already know?—people are objects surely as hills but they last a bit less and are thus less patient. Be as true to them as you've been to the ground and to various trees—and gentler, Hutch.

Send any reports you care to show. I'll respond or not, as you tell me to. Whatever—I'm here, patient as bread.

Love from
Alice

May 28, 1955

Dear Hutch,

You were sweet to call me up and tell me goodbye. It would have also been good to see your face one more time at least, but I know you were busy as a demon at Judgment. Men in your family have been telling me goodbye for over fifty years so by now I ought to be grateful for the distance—don't you think? We had our good visit at Easter anyway. I went back to the cemetery two weeks later and know you'll be as surprised as I was to know that your azalea was blooming right on at your grandfather's headstone—and your great-grandfather's—in spite of a hard late frost and much wind. They were always warmers *though in very different ways as your own father is and I trust you will be.*

England is a place I can't picture well. I hope you will have a roof for your head since I read they haven't rebuilt from the war and I hope you like hot tea better than me. If you don't and if they sell any coffee, I am sending five dollars. Buy some on me and when it keeps you up in the late cold night, wing a thought my way. I will no doubt be right here sewing some lace tent for a rich stout lady with a daughter altar-bound but I'll feel the compliment and bless your name. My blessings work.

Blessings on you, son,
Your friend,
Polly Drewry

6:10 AM MAY 30 1955

AWAKE ALL NIGHT HUNTING RIGHT FIFTY WORDS TO SAY WHAT I THINK. ALL I FIND IS FOURTEEN. SPEND EVERYTHING YOU TAKE. BRING HOME NEW LUGGAGE. YOU WILL ONLY REGRET YOUR ECONOMIES.

LOVE AS LONG AS I LIVE
GRANDMOTHER

June 1, 1955

Dear Rob,

Three days on the water now, and none of it has been quite what I expected—which is good, I guess. Especially since nothing has been bad but the heat, and that only lasted through one long night. The day we left New York was hot—nearly ninety by noon—and this old boat was hot as a locked-up Buick in Texas by the time we backed out and breasted the sea. Since nothing English is air-conditioned, we carried the heat—a pocket of Hell—for eighteen hours. My cabin did at least. Cabin is a serious exaggeration—this one makes Abe Lincoln's look like Pennsylvania Station—and mine it's not; I share it with two men. One is a German Jew who seems to have lived in Buffalo for ten years and learned no English (won't answer me anyhow); he's going back to Frankfurt where he'll be understood. The other—Lew Davis—is a fellow my age who grew up in Wales but has been in Canada traveling with a circus in recent years. He'll be visiting his family "to see if I can stick it for more than two weeks without falling down dead from laughter or tears" and has asked me to join him. I may once I've got my bearings and a car. I think he's a gypsy, but he swears he's not.

He and I walked the deck that first night in search of air (the German stewed downstairs in flannel pajamas). Then by dawn things cooled off, and ever since I've given my famous imitation of the Great Tree Sloth—long bouts of hard sleep and overtime dreaming, interrupted briefly by mammoth British meals. I met a London surgeon in the bar last night and eventually told him I'd been mostly unconscious for seventy-two hours; was anything wrong? He said, "Nothing worse than carbohydrate shock." I laughed but he said, "A very real condition, prevalent on sudden contact with British food. Many prisoners of war, brought home to pure starch, were felled like poplars. Lost two myself." So time may be short; remember me in prayers. In another half-hour I'll be summoned by a gong to eat mushroom tarts, well-done roast beef, Yorkshire pudding, roast potatoes, Brussels sprouts, white bread, boiled pudding, and a toasted cheese savory to finish. Finish! is the word.*

Otherwise the threats consist of fellow passengers. I boarded in hope of high-toned couples in evening dress with sunset breeze in their hair as they sauntered the polished timbers, faintly smiling at the herds in steerage. So far all I've seen is twenty-odd Congressional secretaries, traveling together at budget rate and famished as yuccas. They're all thirty-eight, all single at present. They've run through assorted legislators, pages, colonels—or been run through like sieves—and see no objection to trying on a Fledgling Southern Writer (I slipped and told them the first night out; they all read Thomas Wolfe in junior high school and pray I'm his ghost). But I cling to the memory of Little Hubert's wisdom and guard my digits, something T. Wolfe neglected.

Next morning. *Read over, that seems too dumb to mail. But I'll mail it to show you how hard I've been huffing and puffing to cheer myself up in this odd high leap I find myself taking. What we didn't discuss last week were the things I am scared of. The main thing is me—that once I've paid for and found this famous stillness around me, filled my fountain pen, and faced the window, then there'll be no work: not a thing I know that'll prove big enough to hold any human eye but mine and no words to say even small things in. With all my need to get space and air, get away from friends and home, I neglected to see how thoroughly all of you screened me from the chance that stares at me now on the east Atlantic in a tacky old hotel that happens to float—I may be a fraud. Last night Lew Davis said "Say me a poem." We were up at the bow—clear sky, many stars. I said him Hopkins' "Starlight Night," a favorite of mine; pretty hard, no doubt. He nodded and said "Good work," maybe thinking the poem was a sample of me. I held back from giving him a speech on Hopkins and said nothing at all. Then he said,*

> *"Assuming those stars are holes*
> *Punched through a high tent*
> *Onto some brand of light*
> *That heals most pain,*
> *Assuming I could swim my arms*
> *Three times and pass through a hole*
> *Into nothing but light—*
> *I'd stand on here."*

I asked him who wrote it. He laughed—"Nobody. I said it. Now it's gone" (wrong—*I learned it as he went). I'm not standing Lew Davis up by Father Hopkins, but see what I mean? Lew had a thing to say, a little odd but plain. I had this funny* performance *to give, of another man's dare. And I never told him better, though I will today.*

So scared, yes. But hoping.

We're due in Southampton tomorrow afternoon about four o'clock. Assuming I'm not detained as a hoax by H. M. Immigration, I'll take the train to Oxford and be there by bedtime—if I find a bed. I'll look the place over, store my trunk in college, take delivery of my car, and hit the road to wander for the month of June; then back to Merton and down to work.

I'll mail this on landing and write again soon as I've breathed English air. Write me c/o Merton; they'll know my stopping points and will forward news, I trust. The fact that I'm gone doesn't mean I'm gone. Soon please.

Love,
Hutch

June 3, 1955

Dearest Ann,

We passed Land's End—my landfall on England, on anything but home—at sunrise this morning. I was up to see it in surprising clear light with only a handful of old British stalwarts on deck beside me. They drank up the sight with ravenous reserve. It scared me a little, the low brown rocks seeing me as plainly as I saw them and stating their case—Why the hell are you here? I'll postpone my answer a year at least. You'd have had one ready, right?—He's running. Not at all sure you'd have been wrong either.

The coastline has gentled at least since then, the celebrated green hills and occasional chalk. We'll be called to our last vast meal shortly now, then wait off the Isle of Wight for a good tide to lift us in. Once landed and rested I'll write in detail (with two roommates rest has been pretty scarce—not sleep but rest; with two strangers near I don't dream much, and dreams equal rest for me).

I did want to say I dreamt of you once—in a deck chair, chilly, two after-noons back. I went to a party and you were there, happily talking to a ring of other people. I walked straight up and gave a little bow. You flat didn't know me. I thought you were kidding. I told the strange man on your right your name; you looked at me blank as a square of tile and said, "I'm sorry but I know I've never seen you." I said, "You've hardly seen anybody else for some years now." The stranger took your elbow and said to me "Prove it." So I told you a joke— "A young nun died and arrived at Heaven's gate. St. Peter stopped her there, examined her record, and saw she'd had little time to do good. But he liked her looks, so he set her a test—if she passed she was in. He'd ask her three ques-tions; she must get all three. 'Name the first man.' —'Adam.' —'The first woman?'—'Eve' —'All right, now tell me Eve's first words to Adam.' The lit-tle nun broke out in beads of ice. She racked her memory and found not a trace; so she bowed her head and said, 'Oh that's a hard one.' Three hundred gongs sounded, the gates swung open, young angels ran to greet her." The strange man dropped you; your other friends vanished. I burst out laughing and you knew me at once. We were both still laughing when the deck steward came round and offered me tea. If I'd had any place to be alone (better than a two-foot-square saltwater shower), I'd have taken the dream on forward—conscious—and studied again my best memory of you: ten days ago, Richmond, late afternoon light, you astride and posting solemn as a saint toward the last gates of grace, me half-dead with thanks to be the road you traveled and to have my own reward poured through me in my own good time. With any luck at all, I'll have a place tonight—a room and just me—and if I have six kilowatts of strength left, I'll study you.

More after that then. And till then remember the best you've seen; *keep it clear till Christmas. And write.*

Love,
Hutch

An hour later. *If you hate anything in this, please tell me. I count on you to keep me told when I change for the worse—though the way I've felt in recent weeks, I suspect any change will be for the better. Even jackasses get a little dignity with age.*

June 3, 1955

My dear Hutch,

I had meant to get a letter off to meet you on your landing, but the old sum-mer slow-down crept up on me, and the days have gone by. I can't even think of three things I have done since leaving you, and neither one of them is worth writing down and shipping cross the second-biggest ocean on the planet Earth. I remember lots of naps and that we have been blessed so far by the weather— not a day above 75, evening showers, and cool nights for catching up on my thinking time. Everybody else is fine and await first news that the Family Hope is safe on his pins and dry and not treading water off the Greenland coast. If you are, keep treading and send word soon. I'll be there somehow or Grainger will at least.

I didn't mean to sound sarcastic just then by mentioning Hope. I was being honest. I was never really much of a hope to anyone but Rena (who hoped I was God) and your mother (the same), so I've felt no jealousy and know what it means. It means three people now alive—Eva, Grainger, me, and maybe some dead—would be grateful if anyone looked back on us (not down) and saw that we'd made anything like a diagram in these fifty years, anything more than harum-scarum tracks in the dirt as a handful of scared souls scuttled for cover. My dictionary tells me a diagram is "a writing in lines." I can't recall seeing an ugly diagram; so that's the hope, Son—that we make some figure. If we do you'd be the one to know (though it may take awhile to know you know).

Why should I think that? No doubt you're the smartest since my father at least or have read the most books. But the real reason's this—somehow you're the one named Kendal-Hutchins-Mayfield that escaped having whatever worm gnawed us. I have spent some time lately guessing what its name was or what it was after as it ate through us all; and I think what it wanted was happiness—from other humans, here and now. Of course it never got it. Oh minutes here and there. I have had in my life a total of maybe forty-five minutes when I rose up to clear air and felt satisfied; the rest was various stages of want. You escaped that, didn't you? Something spared you that. Even as a young child (three or four), you were safe to yourself. I can't recall you crying for anyone or anything but pain, real physical pain. Maybe you hid more from me than I knew; but until that bad last time I was drunk at Polly's and you left me, I sometimes wondered if your nerves were normal or if you were slightly numb. You had good reason. The thing, passed on to you through me and Rachel, may have just been exhausted or somehow fed. Or all of us may have earned a kind of peace in you, earned it for you. I hope so. Please enjoy it. And if all that is crazy, if you've been in torment of your own from the start and were keeping it from me, better not tell me now. I doubt I could handle the news this late!

At least have fun if not happiness. I wish one person had told me that when I was your age or a few years younger (but remember that your father didn't use bottled fun very admirably). And once you get your car, don't let any Limey corrupt your good habits. You drive to the right whatever they say. Damned fools—no wonder they lost the world.

Let me hear.

Love,
Rob

June 4, 1955

Dear Mr. Mayfield,

You said to let you know when I had plans and now I do. My brother and I will be getting to London on July 10th. I should take a week or ten days to be with him. Then he will go to Paris, and I could come to you wherever you say for maybe a week till I join up with him again and head east. He wants to see Germany which—since he is more like Hitler than anybody else I know—is fitting. I'll go to hold him down.

Anything though will be an improvement on Edom, Virginia in June. I have been drunk in a few bat caves. I have done some painting on the house for my father. I have come pretty close to screwing a doctor's wife who shall be nameless—and may report total success when I see you. I have read every book in the house and county. But now I've had it and am hitching down to Wilmington in your trash state to visit Morse Mitchell and snake hunt with him. He has already made more than two hundred dollars catching cottonmouth moccasins to sell for the venom. I'll help him out till time to fly.

Write to me soon at my home address. I may be dead or a triple amputee by then and need someone to open the letter for me. Wouldn't want to miss your news or seeing you in your new better life.

Till I do,
Strawson Stuart

June 6, 1955

Dear Alice,

Your letter got to me in time. It was waiting on my narrow chaste cot in my cabin in the—yes—Queen Mary, and thank you for it. But you didn't need to worry after our visit. You never need to worry, not about anything I may ever feel when I'm with you or later. After all you've given me (and you gave the main pattern), it would take much more than an hour's high spirits—it would take bleeding real wounds to reach the deep veins of thanks that run in me and have run since we met.

—And surely long before, as you've now helped me see. You'll understand, I trust, that I was so full of my trip when I saw you as to be a poor listener or a slow responder. I stored what you said though and thought through it often

in the slow days at sea. Nothing in it surprised me *is the first thing to say. I'd known, from Rob and old things you told me, that you'd helped Mother in her really bad time; and since the only kind of help I ever want comes through actual touch, I guess I should have known how you reached her then. And in light of my instant attraction to you, I should also have known the chief way I was yours—not just through shared needs. I want to think about that a good deal more (what, if anything, it means for me to have you as a parent); and I may be asking you some questions later. For now though just thanks and some recent news.*

The voyage wasn't much but food and sleep and dodging old doctors from Cleveland or Nyack and their monologous wives. If the Mary's any omen, the Empire is finished, though may take awhile to die. Still the crew (who were callused and grinningly roguish) gave a fair exhibition in sunset glow of the broad backs that bore the Union Jack round the world.

The first impression of England was of course rain. Owing to some delay in the tide—!—we docked two hours late; and by the time I cleared immigration, it was dark as Egypt. Rain began about an hour from Oxford; so I reached that alarmingly famous station (the size of your apartment—used by Ruskin, Newman, Arnold, Wilde, Dodgson, Hopkins, Verlaine, Housman, Eliot, Graham Greene, Auden, Spender, et al.) in an earnest downpour and was drenched when the taxi abandoned me at Merton in a seersucker suit at 9:15 with trunk and grip. I stumbled through the low black wooden gate and was in a short arcade with a clutch of young men, all furiously talking, none noticing me. An open door on my left so I entered; in a glassed-off space in a dark suit and tie, a plump bald man about fifty was eating what seemed to be salad in thick white dressing on a broad white plate. The sight of raw greens, after five days of Mary's *stewed sprouts and cabbage, gave me courage to knock. He was Victor the porter; and through he sized me up as stringently as if I were volunteering atom bombs at bargain rates, he said "Yes you're expected." Then he took a ring of keys straight from* Les Misérables, *a huge umbrella from* Robinson Crusoe; *and led me out, saying "Simpson will bring your bags along, sir." We walked thirty yards through a big quad, an arch, another arcade, and were in a small quad—through a door, up a flight of worn wood stairs, to a room maybe twenty by fifteen feet: a big bay window facing the dark, stuffed sofa and chairs, a desk, long table, an oak bookcase. Off that was a cubicle twelve by seven—a swaybacked bed, a wardrobe, a brand-new basin with running hot water. The surprise was, it's mine. I'd understood they'd put me up for a few days in a guestroom, then expect me to leave till the students clear out in two or three weeks. But Victor departed and Simpson arrived, my grip in hand, with the news that "The chap who had these rooms came down with dreadful jaundice*

*a few days ago and was sent to High Wycombe" (his home, I hope). Simpson —
a wiry man who seems fifty, may be thirty, and bears not one whole atom of
fat — proves to be my "scout." He will wake me for breakfast, make my bed, clean
up, and wash my teacups. He had saved me some supper in a tin warming-lid
and made my bed with college linen while I ate the regulation two pounds of
starch. Anyhow it was nice not to lay my tired head on hepatitic sheets, and
lay it I did. In spite of a short round of bibulous song from somewhere below,
I was out of my soaked clothes and dead by ten. With my last conscious
breath, I thought, "Rise! Dress! Your first night in Oxford! — you should be
prowling lonesome through the dark haunts of Sidney, Raleigh, Donne, the
Scholar Gypsy! Thomas Wolfe would be up embracing the rain, licking the holy
scurf from the stones." Then I slept nine hours till Jack Simpson came in at 7:30,
threw back my curtains, and said "Morning, sir."*

*It was, actually — a square of deep turquoise sky at the window. When I stood
and looked out, I knew (from my reading) where I'd spent my first night — in
Mob, the oldest quad in Oxford, built 1306, a small near-square of two-story
buildings in ruinous stone, with a mat of healthy grass the size of your new rug
and the Chapel tower rising just to the north. That seemed more than even I
bargained for — celebrated by a great throat-lump that's recurred more than
once in the past two days as I've wandered the surprisingly busy town, the central meadows by the Thames where silence is deep as a well and the town as
distant-seeming as home (the windows in my sitting room look south over the
same meadows toward the river, hidden in trees).*

*But lest I melt too soon in careless ecstasy, I'll list a few drawbacks noted
already. The nearest toilet is downstairs, outdoors, fifty feet away leaned
up against the Chapel; and toilet-paper holders, containing tiny sheets of what
is apparently waxed paper, were just installed a week ago after nearly seven hundred years (a note today in the student complaint-book takes account of them
and adds, "Let it not be forgot that the French Revolution was precipitated by
a slight alleviation in the plight of the Third Estate. . . ."). The baths — tubs only,
circa 1880 (very tall, very deep, and so far very scummy with the last man's leavings) — are outside, fifty feet in the other direction, in a peaked dark hovel. Proximity to locals in confined spaces does not yet suggest that bathing ranks high
on the young gentlemen's priorities — we're having warm days, mid70s now. They
are all still in green tweeds and oatmeal trousers that would adequately clothe
a polar expedition; the effect is quite memorable (horses in a closet? brown bears
in a car? — not fetid but, well, piquant). I went to the corner chemist's today and
asked for deodorant. The clerk produced one small spray bottle of Odor-O-No,
wreathed in spring flowers. I said, "Don't you have any roll-on for men?" She
said, "But it's not for men, now is it?" Apparently not.*

It's not the effluvium though that's kept me from meeting any students. And it's not the fabled English chilliness—no one has been unkind, no trace of the plentiful harshness of the American northeast, just the sense till now that I'm invisible. I've been here the best part of three days now and have been addressed only when I was the man seated nearest some bowl of food that was needed—by members of the Middle Class, that is; lower orders have been warm and helpful from the start. I don't much mind. In fact I welcome the chance to watch from a distance just now—learn the rules from the shoulder of the road before driving (I only hope they are watching me too; if so, they're perfect spies).

Speaking of driving—at the end of this week, I'm to pick up my new black Volkswagen, straight off the boat from Germany. I had some qualms about commerce-with-the-enemy, but the cars are so plainly superior to similarly priced English efforts (as were their torture and death machines too—well, Americans worship competence, right?). Then I'll strike out to see as much as I can hold—maybe Scotland, Wales, Cornwall—before coming back in a month or six weeks to sit. Or to turn on myself—in this room, at this desk—and hunt for tangible evidence that I'm here as more than an aging drifter, a light-weight skater on ponds and backwaters, safely alone. I'll forward any evidence I manage to find.

Till then, just some postcards from the heaths and hedges. Please write me a letter at least this long and with no single word of apology in it. Unless you stop me, I would like to think of you as the willing receptor of as near to a journal as I can bear to keep. I've always avoided the rapt mirror-gazing that diaries invite; but if I talk on to you through this, then there'll be some sort of archive at least—a drawer full of time that I could ask to search when these present sights, clear as water, have clouded or sunk.

The best love from,
Hutch

June 7, 1955

Dear Hutch,

Well I told you what I looked for here, to be bored shit blind in under a week. It has been four days and I can't see daylight, just a uniform brown haze on everything. My mother has fed me every half-hour sharp and all her old girl-friends have come round to see me like the lad with the two-pronged cock in the fair. I'll have to check that in point of fact. Maybe mine has split up to search for ways out of this box it's in. Otherwise I haven't really seen it since Canada. Youngest girl anywhere near is well over fifty. That may not be any obstacle soon.

Hope you are doing better, not so good however that you cancel your plan to rescue me. I told my muvver an American poet would be paying me to give him a tour round Cornwall. She said "You wouldn't know Cornwall from Spain and if he's a poet you'll be wanting to paint a scarey face on your arse." So I have done that with iodine and am ready when you are. For the trip I mean. I checked and found I can use my Canadian license to help you along with the driving. Let me know when. *You could come here and spend a night just to see how the working class live, then we could start. I have always meant to see the Scilly Isles. How does that sound to you? If I don't hear in another few days I shall strike off alone.*

Hoping then,

Your cabin mate,
Lew

June 9, 1955

Dear Lew,

Sorry you've had such a bleak homecoming. I won't say that my home-leaving has threatened me with high blood-pressure yet. But I have had several nice moments in the past week, all alone and looking *though. Your countrymen—upper middle-class division—still haven't thrown any welcoming parties, and in any case I'm planning to wander a little before work begins. So sure let's merge our forces for that. If it's O.K. with you, I'll leave here three days from now—Sunday morning—take my time driving down through Burford and Gloucester, and spend the night somewhere near Tintern Abbey (maybe flat on the ground in the ruins themselves). Expect a possibly rheumatic old groaner then sometime Monday, by noon I should guess. I'd like to see as much of your native spot as you can bear to show, and I feel some need to assure your mother of the relative safety of* unproved *poets, so you decide when we push off for Cornwall. I mainly want to see the King Arthur country round Tintagel and Fowey; otherwise I'm game for the Scillies or whatever, provided they're cheap and not cold or hostile.*

You may not have time to answer by mail. If not you can either send a telegram or phone and leave me a message at the Lodge. If I haven't heard No by Sunday morning, I'll strike out after the dazzling breakfast I'm sure to get and see you Monday noon.

Yours,
Hutch

P.S. I'm to pick up my car after lunch today, a German bargain with American drive. The above assumes that it works and that I do (under local conditions, I mean of course).

WILL WAIT BESIDE TURNING FOR OXWICH CASTLE NOON MONDAY. HURRY.

LEW DAVIS

June 11, 1955

Dear Hutch,

This is my first day off since I got your letter. I had to stay late last night typing stuff since, on Monday morning, Mr. Tidd goes to court to defend Lily Quarles, the fifty-five-year-old lilac-haired lady I told you about who stabbed her husband in fourteen places above the waist, bathed the body, put fourteen separate bandaids on the holes, got him into clean pajamas, then phoned Mr. Tidd at 1 a.m., and said she had something curious to show him. Now he thinks he can save her. I plan to stay in all weekend and pray!

In fact I've just spent the morning washing hair—mine. It was still feeling filthy from old New York, so I scrubbed myself half-bald and am drying my new clean pate in the sun out back. The gent next door has been out to check his birdbath three times in an hour—and no bird for miles—which I hope means I look a lot better than I did. The third time I caught him looking and he smiled. I nodded, serious as the Widow Quarles; but to tell the truth, was glad for confirmation that I'm visible again and no bandersnatch. Think he'll ask me to lunch? He cooks a lot.

Later. Took a little nap there apparently. Now awake and finding myself intact, I read your letter again. Here goes. No I don't hate anything you say. Or anything you're doing, that I know of at least. If I put up any kind of fight before you left—and I see I did—it was not from hate, God knows. Puzzlement, I honestly think. Twelve years of public school and four of college did their damndest to find some ambition in me and warm it to life. Forget it—none there. I'm a woman as old-style as anything painted on the walls of caves. I don't much doubt I could do quite well at a number of jobs outside in the world if I set my sights and tucked my chin (I'm well-stocked with chin). I hope that won't be necessary ever. And the reason is this—the brand of applause you can get from the world means as much to me as a plate of well-warmed vanilla ice cream. Not that the world has hung around clapping at the sight of me, but I've had little bursts here and there for chores done. Forget it, again. What I want is to work inside at home, making life easy (or easier) for two-to-four people in whom I'm involved and who want me to be.

So there. I never thought it right through before and surely never said it all out loud, though you heard pieces of it more times than you liked. I don't know why—why would anybody want any sort of homelife after what my parents dis-

played as a sample?—but from age eleven it was my idea. At first I slouched around, trying to hang it on boys in books or in the movies—I've had more to do in my mind with Toby Tyler and Johnny Sheffield than with anybody since. Then the Great Spring Hormone Freshet swept through me; and soon I was choosing a boy a week, sometimes several a day—real boys in school. Not that they ever knew it, not that one ever touched me much below the neck. But though you never asked me, you surely know since, along with that ancestral wedding-band, you wear at least one more ring—my pink maidenhood.

Don't get me wrong. I'm glad you have it, even if I never see you again. I picked you for it, I hope you know. The day you were called on in freshman English to come up and read your first theme to us as a model of virtue, and you stood to read five hundred words about a grown woman asking for you in a dark hotel room and you saying Yes—I picked you then. I also thought you were dying, which helped. You were so pale and lean. We could get it over fast; then you would be gone. I would be your relic through several generations, telling tales of you.

I got over that, the sudden-death part. By the time we'd gone to two or three movies and talked till midnight behind the dorm, I knew you were roughly as sick as the Matterhorn in morning light. You were going to make it. So I settled in to last long as you did, beside you. You didn't seem to mind. And once we had managed to make real love, that got your attention! You said your best mental picture of me was recent—me on you last month—and you told me to study my best one of you. Since I don't have an album mind like yours (I recall words better), I had to hunt awhile. But I have it finally and can tell you what it is. After our first time you stayed gone a week. I thought I'd failed you some terrible way. Then you called up and asked me to Myrtle Beach. I accepted before I realized the string of lies I'd have to spin to get permission, but I spun like a jenny, and off we went in Jack Hagen's car. The rest you know, up to my favorite part. You slept through that so you can't have known. It was just before sunrise. I had waked up somehow, thinking you had spoken. But you were breathing slowly and were turned away. I moved in against your back, not touching. Then I touched your shoulder and just said "What?" You waited awhile and I didn't move. You had to be asleep, but you said "Wait here"—as clear as urgent. I wondered "For what?" but decided not to ask. Then when light started working through the rusty blinds—Mrs. Benson's Guest House—you rolled to face me and slept in my sight for three hours more. Except for short snoozes I lay there and looked. You looked very fine. I chose to wait.

That's the best part I've got, of us at least. And if you really want us to meet at Christmas—Rome or wherever—I'll save my pennies while studying that. Not full-time, don't worry, but enough to keep it true. Meanwhile I'll struggle in the cause of mercy for Lily Quarles (justice would chain her to oars in a hulk off the coast of Guatemala) and of keeping my own chin up and pointing east, though prepared to tack if that signal comes. One way or another I hope to have more and longer life than the nun in your nautical dream about me. I was glad to be featured in a dream, understand. I just want to have more fun than most nuns—while working like them for the Love of Another.

It's getting pure hot and my neighbor's approaching with what looks like an axe and a glass of lemonade. I could write a lot of questions about your first days—where, when, what, who? I'll trust you instead to tell me all I need or can use to my profit and personal uplift. Speaking of which, my bosoms are lonesome. Remember them too.

Love,
Ann

June 11, 1955

Dear Polly,

The best thing waiting for me on that boat was your kind letter. I've kicked myself every day since then that I didn't set eyes on you before leaving. You probably guessed I came through Richmond to pick up Ann; but I felt so tired from loading my life's goods one more time in Rob's old truck that I went straight to sleep, then had to get on my way to New York. I'm saving the five-dollar bill you sent, to remember your goodness and to keep me from ever forgetting again a thing you told me when I was fifteen and visiting you. You asked me to walk downtown with you to a nine o'clock show, That Hamilton Woman. *I had been out all afternoon drawing the State Capitol in August sun and said I believed I needed to sleep. You said, "Not me. I plan to make up for all lost sleep the first two days after I'm stone-dead." I've still never seen* That Hamilton Woman, *though I do hope to see both Vivien Leigh and Laurence Olivier soon in the flesh. They're doing three Shakespeare plays at Stratford, forty miles north of here; and once the tourists thin in September, I'll try to get tickets (if it means missing sleep). Till then I mean to hide out on the edges of Wales and Cornwall and in my six-hundred-year-old rooms here.*

I'll write you in more detail about those and a good deal else at the end of the month when I'm back from the first trip and settled in here. Meanwhile let me close by telling you one thing and asking another.

I hadn't realized there were still so many American servicemen in England; but Oxford alone has several big bases within twenty miles, all manned with tall chunky fellows from Ohio (and one base graced with atomic bombs poised to fly just a short leg east to Berlin or farther on). Anyhow last night I was feeling mildly homesick, nothing terminal, so walked the three blocks from this Altar of Learning to the place where I'd seen flocks of airmen heading last weekend—White's Bar, High Street (just so you understand, I had two beers; you needn't tell Rob). I was wearing my best Young American disguise—cotton coat, khaki trousers, white socks, brown loafers—but I guess my hair was three inches too long or I wasn't wearing anything powder-blue: that seems the big color in P.X. men's wear. In an hour nobody volunteered a word my way, though I overheard a lot and was near the center of more than one fight. I was ready to leave, feeling much less homesick, when a woman came over and took the chair beside me—young herself, maybe twenty-one. She was ready to talk, over fairly swift glasses of warm pink gin (no ice in the building—in the town, I gather). Well, to boil down what took her another hour—she was Marleen Pickett, born in London and raised there except for the years of the Blitz which she spent with an uncle in the country near here. That was when she acquired her love of Oxford—"Lovely chaps, like bats in their gowns; I'm the only girl I've met who likes bats"—and when she had grown up and chosen her career, she decided to spend her weekends in Oxford. Keeps a little apartment in Beaumont Street—"All books. I dream of the day I'll read; have the time, I mean. I barely sit down." No doubt but I'd seen well before she spoke that she spent many waking hours prone (or is it supine?). In short she's a fine individual example of American aid. She brings peace and welcome to lost young Yanks; and they pay her rent, her little food bill ("I eat once a day, a big tea at six"), her mother's expenses, and the storage on her dog (he stays in London, spared the sight of her work). Business didn't seem good last evening, so I asked if she liked my compatriots—or the local sample. She gave me a slow examining look; then said, "I can tell you want the truth. When they're sober, yes—which is rare as bright days. When they're not, it's 'Look at these snaps of my girl—or Mum or wife'; and then they dig in. No insult, mind you; but your chaps got better food than ours for ten years there—milk, cheese, fat oranges. It all went to one place—they're giants, believe me—and I have to bear it, night after night. What I've always really fancied is students—thin, white, built normal (but their dreadful socks!)." I told her I wore fresh socks every day before I realized that I was a student again or would soon be. She didn't even smile. She said, "These airmen are stuffed with money. I know most students scrape by on grants so I make adjustments. Rhodes or Fulbright—which are you on?" I admired her homework but told her I'd tried for a Rhodes and washed-out twice as not really promising sufficient public service. Before she could ask for my private-service record, I also told her I was something of an heir (concealing that my hoard of capital amounts to ten thousand dollars worth of pines crushed to paper). She gave that a whole minute's thought, drained her glass, then stood—"Oh well in that case, go buy a duchess. Their need is far more desperate than mine, these

*days at least." She walked a chalk line to a tall loud boy from Camden, New
Jersey; and they'd made a deal before I could laugh. So I didn't that night—
laugh, I mean—and I've wondered today: would you say that incident dis-
qualifies me as a* warmer *in your view? Think and let me know please. I'm only
half-joking.*

*And if you're not busy, try to get Rob to pay you a visit soon. I don't mean
to say I think my leaving has him drooping on the vine; but I do think he'd got
a little stymied lately, no one to do for and Grandmother still strong as Boul-
der Dam. Please think of some way to say you need to see him; otherwise he'll
sit there all summer swatting flies. Haven't seen an insect of any description
here yet or a snake—there are no poisonous snakes, only one viper almost never
encountered that causes mild swelling. Other problems will no doubt rise to
attention. But I'm here for that.*

Answer soon.

Love,
Hutch

*P.S. In fact I mean to spend your money tonight. There's a half-good imita-
tion French place round the corner called Café de Paris—low stocky English
waiters in black bow ties (and fingernails to match) mispronouncing French
dishes. I'll have steak and eggs to brace me for the road.*

20

The boy came back from inside the garage, leaned into Grainger's window,
and spoke across him to Rob. "Says if you mean the old James Shorter
place, he thinks niggers took it three or four years ago. It was empty till then.
You could drive on up there. Wouldn't nobody mind."

Rob nodded. "Thank you."

Grainger spoke to the windshield but firmly. "Care to join us, brother?"

"What?" The boy stepped back—fifteen, sixteen, black-haired, dark-eyed.

Grainger looked and smiled. "No, sorry, my mistake. Up close I thought
I could smell nigger blood. Sorry, captain. Many thanks." He moved Rob's
truck slowly into the road.

Rob waited half a mile; then said, "It doesn't much matter to me—
might even be a blessing, nice bullet through the eye—but I didn't know
you meant to die right yet."

Grainger shook his head. "Don't."

"Then let me drive. You've lost your mind."

"Why?—kidding that child?"

Rob nodded. "—In *Virginia*. They don't have the sweet sense of humor about Negroes you're used to at home."

Grainger laughed. "Maine's my home. You're the one from Virginia."

Rob looked to his right—a long low hill bare of all but grass, with the sweet swell and tuck of a young girl's side; a mule staring toward him as if its whole mission through years of cold nights had been to wait here for this moment as proof that one living thing was loyal and still; a clear stream talking its slow way east, no house, no person. He said, "You lived here longer than I did."

Grainger said, "Don't mean a pig's ass-hole to me. I left this place. You were born here though; *born* is what counts."

"Counts how?" Rob said.

Grainger pointed. "Look yonder." They'd turned the last curve; and up the hill before them was the Shorter place, its charred remains. "Niggers got it and *gone*." Grainger took the narrow drive, now two deep ditches.

Through the hard jolts Rob sat and wondered if he *felt*—no question they'd found the first destination on their little last tour. The place James Shorter had brought Hattie Mayfield, his young second wife; the place Hatt's brother Forrest brought his own new wife (Eva Kendal, sixteen and happy in the first days); the place where Eva conceived and made Rob, in growing desperation, and brought him forth—herself nearly killed. They'd found the site at least. Once up the drive and stopped, Grainger's guess was confirmed; whoever had lived here last burned the house. Or hunters, boys, lightning. Gone—just the chimney, front and back steps, tin sheets from the roof. Rob wondered if it mattered. He turned to Grainger. "When was Hutch here last?"

"Ten years ago maybe. He come with us to Miss Hatt's funeral; when was that?"

Rob nodded. "Ten years." Then he faced the pile again, surprisingly large for an eight-room two-story house plain as anything drawn by a child with a ruler. "Shall we get out?" he said.

Grainger said, "This is your trip, Rob. You say."

Rob opened his door.

21

Rob had eaten the big cold supper Polly gave him and helped her stack dishes before he had a real chance to study her. But once she'd refused his help at the sink, he sat at the clear pine table and watched her—her back straight as ever, her left profile in the white bulb-light. He knew she was only a year short of seventy. She'd thrown in her young lot with Rob's dying grandfather and moved with him here—this house in Richmond—the year Rob was born. Still she seemed much younger. Or if you dimmed your eyes enough to soften the two strong cords in her throat, she seemed no age—foolish to calculate. The fine auburn hair was maybe half-white, the eyes slightly veiled when she looked down as now; but her long hands were white and unspotted, quick as ever as they scrubbed at plates and knives they'd scrubbed in that same spot more than fifty years. He thought, "All the women who've mattered to me refuse to age." He meant Eva, Polly, Min, his dead Aunt Rena, Rachel dead in her fresh youth; he himself felt worn as any felled column in his father's old photographs of Rome, still hanging. *Dissolved*—who'd have thought there were scraps enough left to draw cancer on him? Was it why, after all, *all* women had mattered (barring eight or ten mean-mouthed bitches)? More than any other man he'd known or heard of, he'd valued women; really loved them for themselves—creatures separate from his own wants and needs—and craved their nearness. Other men wanted them for humping, cooking, children; Rob had wanted them simply as the crown of creation, the last best work. That Eve had made the first mistake gave him no cause for grudge, nor that his mother had been unable to love only him when he most wanted that. He steadily forgave them as they'd forgiven him—though any harm he'd done was harm they requested. If his own fifty-one years had ever broken through the lovely sad crust of this present world onto glimpses of permanence, constant reward, they had always come in the company of women (mostly bare but not always). Or was that soft whining from a dying brain? Had there been a single glimpse? If so, why was he now commanded to pass through pain and suffocation to reach full sight?

Polly looked back, shuddered, then burst out laughing. "Old fool!—me, I mean. You scared me, sitting there. So quiet I forgot you were anywhere near. I was thinking great thoughts."

Rob smiled. "What about?"

She paused to consider, then actually blushed. "Not about *sewing*. I'm caught up on work and no more promised; may never make another cent that way, wouldn't mind."

Rob saw she was dodging and wanted to stop her. He smiled again. "Tell me one great thought. I could use inspiration."

By then she'd finished work. She untied her apron, stroked her hair twice with the flats of her hands. "You want to sit on here? Aren't you too warm?"

"No."

She came to the table, held the back of her chair. "Inspiration was what I was thinking about."

"Reach any conclusion?"

Polly's face tightened quickly. She took the salt cellar and packed the grains down. "No I didn't. If I had I'd keep it inside. I'm no missionary."

"Didn't mean to say you were." He sat forward then; she was three feet away, still watching the salt. To win back her eyes seemed the urgent job. "I'm lying," he said.

She looked.

"You *have* brought a lot of help, to me and many others."

She shook her head. "To two—your father, his father."

Rob said "And me."

Polly said, "Not so. You never needed me."

"Sure I did, when Rachel died."

"I cooked you a few meals, kept Hutch awhile. Any kind colored woman could have done that much. You needed somebody all right but not me."

He accepted that. "I may now though."

"You're lonesome for Hutch."

Rob nodded. "Part of it."

"What's the rest?"

He laughed. He couldn't tell her now. "Tell *me*."

"I *know*," Polly said. "It was my great thought just now." She laughed and touched him, one finger briefly on the back of his hand. "A surprising lot of people, not all of them dark, are born to be servants."

Rob said, "Good night!—the children of Ham."

She paused. "I don't know them. I meant you and me."

"Please tell me."

"All we ever wanted was to work day and night for somebody we loved—time off for naps."

"Naps *with* them," Rob said.

Polly smiled but said "You speak for you."

He waited a little to let that pass; then said, "Why are you sitting here out of work?"

"Everybody died or left."

"We could find other jobs."

"Too old," she said. "People looking for help want young agile smilers."

Rob said, "My turn to say 'You speak for *you*'—I don't feel old."

Polly took that with sudden surprising force, shaking her grand head in fierce affirmation. "Whole days, even now, I don't feel ten minutes older than the girl who stepped through this door fifty-two years ago with your grandfather—my duds in a bundle the size of a lapdog and happy as one, a strong spotted feist. I'd been requested. I knew Rob Mayfield was old and sick—nothing to it; I could cure him."

"You almost did."

"You were not even born. No I eased him some—let him talk, fed him well, bumped against him enough to let him know I stood here and planned to last him out."

Rob said, "What did he talk about?"

"*Plans*. What was coming. See, he believed too that I'd get him right again. Since he left your grandmother many years before, he'd had no permanent woman near him but his own old mother; and she had just died. I know there had been some temporary people—he had been big on roaming—and I know he'd been hunting just what I seemed to offer: steady service, no running, lot of jokes and smiles. He'd believed in women the way most people believe in money; so when Margaret Jane Drewry packed her grip in Washington and followed him here—I was seventeen years old, pretty as a green leaf and far longer-lasting—he thought his prayer was answered at last. He would drag round all day by the stove—coughing, losing blood—then at night get his strength back and lie there and tell me the future by the hour, our future. Different plans every night but with two steady parts—he was moving; I was with him. He had never been west of Louisville, Kentucky; so mostly we would be pushing on past there toward San Francisco. That was always his aim, however we journeyed; and since he died a good year before the quake, the aim was never spoiled. He had all the details in black and white. If he woke up strong, he'd be down at the station searching every timetable from here to California, all the rules, exact fares. Then he'd come back and, that night, lay it out for me—lower berths from here to Denver, a week of rest there (the Brown Palace Hotel; is there really such a place?), then on through mountains and deserts to the ocean. *Hills by water*—they were big in his plans. I'd say, 'There are hills by the James River, Rob, that cost less to see.' He wouldn't even hear me, just take my hand and go on reading his lists. Made more lists than anybody alive; for him to make a list was good as doing something. Funny thing was, they were realistic—the money part at least. His mother had left him a little nest-egg that would see us there, and back if necessary. But he generally planned on us staying gone for good—never said what he'd do about the house here." She paused and looked up, half-surprised to find it round her.

Rob said, "Maybe he meant to contact his children and give it to them."

Polly smiled but shook her head. "They were never mentioned, no more than God's name, even after your father tracked him down that last Christmas and offered to tend him."

"I thought he asked you to notify Father once he died."

"No never. He died in his sleep; and all he ever said after your father's visit was, 'Forrest will be needing help long after me.' "

"He knew he was dying?"

Polly nodded. "One night that February I was doing my last little chore—I used to rub his chest with camphorated balm and pin flannel round him before he went to sleep—when he took my wrists and held them tight a minute. Then he said, 'Lay your hands please flat on my nipples and ask God to save me.' As I mentioned, he hadn't ever spoken of God. I said, 'It may be a little late for Him. If God is any kind of churchgoing Christian, we're both in bad trouble.' I think he grinned—the lamp was down low—but he stayed quiet awhile and I rubbed on. Then he said, 'Please do it anyhow on your own.' So I pressed my palms down hard on his chest—there was no more fat than this table's got—and looked him in the eyes (what I could see of them) and said, 'If any power wants to help you and will use me to do it, let that happen now. Or if me being by you is a harmful sin, let me be sent somewhere I can hurt nobody.' I hadn't really known I felt that way till I'd said it out loud; and once I had, I hoped Rob would say he wanted me by him—whatever the harm, whoever it offended. I waited but somehow he slipped off without me seeing. To sleep, I mean. In a week he had slipped off for good, dead beside me in that same bed, still bound in my flannel—all the help that did him." She'd said her say for now.

And Rob let the quiet spread round them while he thought of what he could offer or beg from her now. He took the salt cellar she'd smoothed and the pepper; and with them and the two clean unused knives, he made a little foursided house—no roof. Then not looking up he said "You still know how?"

Polly laughed. "To do what?"

"Little healing jobs."

She tried to wait till he looked up; he didn't. "No meanness," she said, "—too late for that."

Rob nodded. "No meanness." Then he met her eyes and attempted to smile.

She saw what till now he'd hid so well, what she'd seen in two men's faces before (his grandfather, father)—the worst sight of all: surrender to death. Rob was ready to die. His eyes were glad. She pressed back slightly in her chair. "What is it?"

"What terms are you on with the powers you mentioned?"

"Better now than before."

Rob said, "Then why do they want us all so early?"

"*I'm* old."

He shook his head. "The Mayfield men—not one of us got his three-score-and-ten."

Polly said "You're young" and regretted it at once. He was old as the others. Or as oddly nimble on the lip of extinction.

Rob said, "I have done almost all I can think to do." He hadn't planned to say it, hadn't known he knew it; the plain fact stopped him.

Polly thought he was speaking of desperation. She said, "I know you've got your mother and Grainger, but I'll help any way you ask me to."

He could only think to thank her.

But far in the night as he slept upstairs in his dead father's room, Rob lived through this—pleasure and news. He was traveling in his car, alone and strong. A hot June day but dry as fall, longest day of the year. He had started at dawn; by one he was hungry and stopped at a low white house by the road to buy a meal. There was no sign saying *Cafe* or *Food*, but he thought he was right; he'd be welcome here (and for very little money). The wood door was shut, but he opened and entered—a normal front-room: sofa, chairs, pictures, one small table spread with a white cloth and on it a bowl of broad red poppies. He tried to remember when he'd seen poppies last and wondered if it really was safe to be shut indoors with a living odor as strong as theirs. While he was thinking a woman walked in—or moved in so quietly he heard no sound till she said "Can I help you?" But he was not startled. He turned and looked. At once he knew that—in every particular of face, color, size—she was what his own whole body had wanted since becoming a man. She seemed a woman made from the line of vacant space that hugged his own profile, head to foot; a creature made to be set up against him, to stay there forever in place, not abrading, and who'd waited here till he found and claimed her. Yet she also seemed a feasible woman, as credible as perfect. So he answered her question by moving straight to her and taking her hand. She accepted that, though she didn't meet his eyes. He led her from the room down a short dim hall till an open door showed him one room with a bed—another entirely possible room: throw-rugs, a dresser, an aging mirror. When they stopped in the center of the room, he turned and carefully but quickly began to undress her. She still didn't face him, but she let him work with no resistance; and when he had her entirely bare in unflawed beauty, she set her own small hands on his wrists and drew him to the bed, neatly opening the covers. Rob opened her. Once bare himself against her—she did fill all his adjacent emptiness—he found that he wanted to open and eat her. He left her face and arms and slowly made way down the length of her body, honoring the skin itself with the only tribute he could offer—silent kisses on her firm pooled breasts, the trough between, her flat belly plush with fine blond hair that took the light from a single window, the patient powerful bone of her left hip. He kneaded that with his stubbled chin, her legs moved apart, he thought he could hear her say "Rob. Now." He wondered how she could know his name, but he wouldn't speak to ask. He obeyed both her voice and his own delight in a hunger on the verge of perfect food. He rose to his knees and slid to the small space she'd offered in her fork. His hands went under her knees, her legs lifted, he bent to the gift. In long laps he spread the tiers of leaves that covered his goal, led by the clean salt stench of her blood and her welcoming oils. Then he devoured her. Or thought he devoured. He licked down easily through layers of happiness, each of which seemed a further dream in the longer dream and each one better (he knew he was dreaming). Yet his eyes were shut, and strong in the midst of all was this knowledge—*She dries and shrinks below me as I eat; all the others have.* He consumed her youth unavoidably, speeded her death. She never said "Stop" and he never relented till at last she gripped at his hair like reins, endured the short by-product of his meal, and could speak again—"Good." Still blind he laid his head where he'd worked, knowing he must open his eyes in a moment and see his chief fear—one more woman ruined, who had offered help. She gripped again, rocked him, and he looked up. The same girl faced him, damp but changed only by the smile she gave. She had not smiled till then. He had only made her happy. He would never have to leave.

At the end of the dream—still asleep—Rob began to speak to the girl but also aloud in the room, the door open in hope of a breeze. Muffled sounds but audible.

Polly heard them and woke. At first she thought he was in some distress, and she sat up to go. But while she felt in the dark for her robe, she noticed the sounds were peaceful—little greetings. By the time she was up and had tied the belt, Rob was quiet again. Her eyes however had opened to the seepage of light from the one burning bulb downstairs; the news of his illness gathered weight in her head as she stood there alone. In a minute it seemed intolerable. She'd borne the consecutive years of assaults—her own mother's death, death of the two men who'd valued her, long isolation—with the calm and resilience that had been natural to her as thick hair, a free tongue. No longer. That Rob Mayfield should be asked to strangle in broad mid-life, his beauty still on him, was the thing she'd refuse. She'd earned a choice. So she sat again on the edge of her bed and said one sentence to a God she knew of but seldom consulted—"Not him, not now" (the codicil to which was implied not spoken: *If there's crying need for a sacrifice, I volunteer*). She sat on awhile to catch any answer. There was no rejection; no acceptance either but rejection was what she'd listened for. A decision on the codicil was of no interest to her. She was still here alive, for now at least. And while she lasted she would try to tell Rob. In the warm dark she fully believed herself. So she walked barefoot on clean boards to his door. The light didn't reach there. She waited to hear any sign of his waking.

Easy sighs, deep sleep.

She extended her hands and made her way toward him, landing at the foot of the bed—an island. She pulled herself round, felt carefully, and established that he lay on the far side from her. Gently she sat on the vacant edge. His breath didn't alter.

She reached out again—it seemed as far as England—and found his chest, bare, cooler than she'd planned. Her palm was narrow but the fingers were long. She found she was able to cover one breast with the heel of her hand, the other with her fingers.

He'd grown entirely silent.

She said, "You are going to be all right."

He covered her hand. "Thank you," he said. "I won't doubt that."

Polly sat in place another whole minute, glad to be by him and glad of the thick dark—that Rob couldn't see her. Then the spell weakened slightly; she wondered if he thought she'd broken with age. She moved to leave.

But Rob held her firmly by the hand. "Stay on. It'll be day soon."

It would. Polly stayed—at first upright, Rob's hand strong on hers. Then when he turned away and gave signs of sleep, she carefully lay outside the covers. Her left hand rested in the small of his back, sheet and spread between them; and her eyes stayed shut, but she didn't sleep again. She knew the length of every moment till dawn when she rose.

22

The first light woke Grainger. When he'd left Rob at Polly's the previous evening, he'd driven a mile to a house he remembered on a Negro street where an old lady rented occasional rooms. A young woman answered. He asked for Mrs. Adams.

She said, "Mrs. Adams been dead ten years, night Roosevelt died." He'd turned to go but she said, "If you needing somewhere to stay, I could find room, I guess."

Grainger waited; then said, "A whole room?—private? For just one night."

She nodded. "With a hook on the door. Course, children might wake you up before day."

He'd paid her two dollars, and she'd led him to a small swept room at the back. The only other thing she required was his name, which she wrote in his presence with plain difficulty. Then she'd given him hers—Lela—and left him alone. He'd locked the truck carefully, walked till he found a clean place to eat fish; then gone to the Booker T. and watched *East of Eden*, remarking how much the young boy favored Rob—Rob thirty-one years ago when Grainger first saw him. He'd walked slowly back, not looking for friends but thinking he might encounter one or two from the years he lived in Richmond. Not a single face in hundreds, so he got back to Lela's at a little past nine. On her porch there were two men and two other women to whom she introduced him—"Sit down and drink beer; I'll send for you one." He excused himself on grounds of fatigue, wondering as he left who she'd send for beer (the children she mentioned had still not appeared).

In the room he latched the door, took off his new shoes, lay down with his head at the end of the cot to catch the center light, read two chapters in *Robinson Crusoe*—"I am Very Ill and Frighted" and "I Take a Survey of the Island" —then was tired and stood to undress for sleep. He heard something crying, put his ear to the door—a child, almost surely, and close to his room. He waited for the sound of Lela to ease it; but no sound came and when he was stripped to his underwear and the crying went on, he switched off the light and cracked the door open. The crying wasn't frantic, just a steady thread of pleading; no other children spoke to help it or join it. Grainger took two steps out into the dark hall—no sounds from the porch. He was here with the child or whatever was here; they'd left him the guard. He went back, put his trousers on, and—in the dark—went toward the noise. The next room was open; it came from there. He stood in the door, waited for a pause, and said "Who is this howling?"

The pause drew out; then the child said "Tossy."

"You by yourself?"

"Yes."

"Where your brothers and sisters?"

No answer to that.

"Where your mama?"

No answer.

Grainger said, "You got you a light in here?"

"In the air, in the middle. Too high for me."

He felt his way forward and found the hanging bulb. "Here it comes," he said. "Shut your eyes a minute."

The child had obeyed. She lay in a big iron bed—a girl maybe five in white underpants, on top of patched sheets, both eyes shut but calm.

Grainger walked over to her. "Let em come open slow now and see who's with you."

She obeyed again, screening her raw eyes till they opened; then she studied him gravely.

"I'm the man paid your mama to sleep next door." He pointed to his room.

Tossy nodded twice, took her left thumb, and sucked it.

Grainger said, "I'll be nearby. You sleep."

She shook her head No.

He smiled. "You cry, you'll keep me wake. I'll want my money back."

The thumb popped out. "Lie down here, else I'll dream again and holler."

"You dream a lot?"

Tossy said "When they leave me."

Grainger said "They coming back."

She thought that through. "If they don't, you staying?"

The answer surprised him. *Yes* rose in his head like a cork on a pond. All the things that had left him (and most things had but his health and strength) seemed small by this—he'd never had a child. Even in the days before Gracie left, when she'd welcomed him in most nights of the week, she had begged for no child. He'd respected her, thinking there was time ahead. Now there was nothing his body had made or nothing more responsive than the shrubs he'd planted, the roofs he'd mended, the three white men (Forrest, Rob, Hutch) he'd stayed near and watched. He kept the Yes silent though. He said, "Let's turn this hot light off. I'll wait here with you."

She'd never smiled. She slid to her right to give him space and took her thumb again.

Grainger reached for the light, then took the three steps, and lay straight beside her.

Tossy lay where she'd landed, not moving to touch him. When he'd settled she said "You kin to me?"

"May be."

"Hope so." She was out in an instant.

Grainger followed her easily, exploring as he sank unbroken spreads of rolling field ankle-deep in grass—his unchallenged new home, empty as summer air. In an hour of sleep, he still found nothing. Then he woke and felt a quiet path to his own room through the silent house. Lela had left him a pitcher of water by a clean washbowl and a clean slop-jar.

23

When the first light woke him, he could hear other people—three voices, he thought: man, woman, child. It was quarter to six; Rob expected him by nine ("Don't let me down please; Polly may have talked me out"). He rose, washed himself; dressed in clean underwear, the same shirt and trousers. He hoped he could leave unseen, find some breakfast, and maybe drive past Gracie's old cousin's house, give her his thanks. She had sent him a sympathy card when Gracie died nearly two years ago, the first word he had. He'd forgot her street but could poke round and find it; it was not far from here. When he opened his door, the voices were louder and came from a room at the back of the house.

He had taken three steps to go when Tossy ran forward and said "Breakfast ready." She was in a blue dress.

He said, "Got to run. Somebody waiting for me."

"You'll die," she said.

He laughed. "Who'll kill me?"

"Not eating no breakfast."

Lela called from the kitchen, "Getting cold, Mr. Walters."

He followed the child to the good-smelling kitchen.

Lela stood at the stove. At a big center table, a young man was eating fried bread and bacon—maybe seventeen, eighteen. He looked up, unsmiling. Lela turned and grinned, fresh as if she'd slept ten hours underground.

"How many eggs you want?"

"Thank you, none, Miss Lela. My man's looking for me."

She reached for a pot. "Drink some coffee anyway. Tossy say she kept you wake."

"I enjoyed it," Grainger said.

"She been begging to go in your room all morning."

Tossy sat by the young man but still watched Grainger.

He told her, "You could have. I'm too old to sleep."

Tossy pointed to a chair. "That's yours. I wiped it."

So he sat two feet from the young man's left; and before he'd drawn his chair up, Lela set down a plate of neat eggs and bacon. "Mr. Walters, this boy say he known you forever." She touched the boy's left ear with the towel she carried.

The boy looked down.

Grainger studied him a moment—never seen him surely. But there was a band of deep ease across his eyes and nose, a memory of someone.

"Name Eric," Lela said.

Grainger offered his hand across the full table.

Tossy leaned out and took it.

The boy looked up and said, "Your wife was my cousin. My name's Eric Fishel." His bright eyes were Gracie's.

"You live here?" Grainger said.

"No sir, Mama sent me. Somebody come by the house last night, told Mama you were here. She down in the back, so she told me to stop here this morning on my way to work."

Lela said, "You were sleep. I made him eat and wait."

It seemed to Grainger he'd been slowly led here to stand this trial, that this strange house had worked all night behind a screen of welcome to charge him at daybreak with unanswerable wrong. Again he thought of standing, trying to leave. He looked over dishes and salt to Tossy.

She said, "I don't have no more dreams."

So he saw no way but to sit on and meet whatever was waiting. He chewed and swallowed a mouthful of eggs. Then he said straight to Eric, "Where was Gracie when she died?"

"Mama's kitchen."

"Who was with her?"

"Eric Fishel." With their ease his eyes also had Gracie's speed; they were cold now with offense. "I was all she knew, all she wanted to see."

"What killed her?"

Eric ate again, carefully swabbing his plate.

Lela said "Dollar-wine." She'd never sat down but stood by Tossy, drinking coffee from a glass.

Eric said, "Wanted to—died wanting to die."

Lela said, "Her mind been eat up for years."

Tossy said, "I don't like no kind of wine."

Eric said, "She was crazy but she knew my face. She cooked my supper every night and watched me eat it. Any money she had, she give me half. Thought Mama meant to hurt her."

Grainger said, "I hadn't seen her since early in the war."

"She knew you too. Talked about you anyhow."

"Don't guess it was very sweet music," Grainger said.

Eric shook his head. "She was giving you things, all the time walking round giving you things. She wouldn't sit down except to sleep. She would touch little things that were Mama's or mine and make up a wild tale of where she got them. Then she'd tell me, 'Eric, you see this gets back to Grainger Walters, Fontaine, N.C., care of Rob Mayfield.' "

Grainger smiled. "You never reached me."

But Eric insisted. "Wasn't nothing to send—old clothes, empty bottles. She did keep one old suitcase locked. When she passed, Mama told me to bust it open—two hundred paperbags all folded like fans and one little box. Mama said that was yours. She saved it till you came." He reached to the floor and brought up a narrow box, three inches deep and shut with rubber bands.

Tossy said "Can I have it?"

Lela thumped her on the head.

Eric set it by Grainger's right hand on the table.

Grainger said "What is it?"

"Swear to God I don't know. Didn't want to know. Mama kept it. I'd forgot it. Then she heard you were here."

Tossy said "Whose is it?"

Grainger still hadn't touched it. He told her gently. "Belonged to my wife."

"Where she?"

"Long gone."

24

He drove up the dirt street from Lela's four blocks to the main paved road. He turned left there toward Miss Polly's and Rob but, in two more blocks, remembered it was early—twenty minutes to seven. There was no traffic yet—some old men walking. He pulled to the curb by a dry-cleaning plant and listened to the news. Then when he'd heard that the weather promised well, he took up the box from the warm seat beside him and slid off the bands; they were oozing with age. The first sight was cotton, a strip of batting old as the bands. He lifted that. Lying on its back, gazing up and all but smiling, was a five-inch-long Negro doll—a girl dressed in what seemed to be a handmade nightgown, drawstring at the neck. He raised the hem and touched the stiff leg, still cooler than the morning round them. If she'd had this when he knew her, she'd kept it hid. Well, he'd seen it now. He covered it carefully, wished he could go back and leave it with Tossy; but he cranked the car again, and went on for Rob—a last rescue.

25

By nine that evening Ann Gatlin had finished an hour's nap and a solitary supper and was reading Moravia, *The Fancy Dress Party.* She was waiting for a visit from Linda Tripp, the new girl at her office who was hunting a room. Ann had offered to share, which she hadn't done in all the years Hutch was near. She'd read for forty-five minutes on her porch in dry slant light when the telephone rang—Linda, postponing? But when she stood to answer, she surprised herself by thinking, "I haven't thought of Hutch Mayfield in two hours."

Polly Drewry said, "Ann, I'm ashamed to call you this late in the evening; but I've worried all day, and I have to speak."

Ann assured her she was welcome to phone anytime.

Polly thanked her, promised she would not abuse the privilege; then said, "I don't know an easy way to tell it—Rob Mayfield was just here visiting me. He's sick to death."

Ann at first felt relief. Hutch was safe anyway. Mr. Mayfield had never really liked her from the start. When she'd heard what was wrong and the expectations, she said, "You just found out today?"

"Last night. Grainger drove Rob up here to see me; they left this morning. I've worried ever since. He'd have called you, I know; but you were at work. He had to get home."

"When did Hutch find out?"

"That's the thing," Polly said. "Rob still hasn't told him and says he never will. He's sworn me and everybody else to keep quiet."

"Why on earth?"

"You know."

Ann said "I'm not sure."

"Hutch would come straight back."

Ann said "He might."

"No *might* about it. He'd be on the first plane."

"Hutch has changed, Miss Drewry."

Polly paused for that. "You've seen him more than me, in recent years at least. You may've seen something I've failed to see. I've known him since the day he was born though, Ann; and the main thing I seem to have noticed in life is that people change about as much as children change rocks by hopping across them. When Hutch Mayfield hears Rob is going, he'll be back with him. If I'm wrong I'm crazy and have lived in vain."

Ann thought *She has and she's bats too at last.* But she said, "Mr. Mayfield doesn't want that, it seems."

"Of course he does." Then silence extended, humming like a kite-string.

So Ann spoke to end it, having seen her own chance. "Can I be any help?"

"None at all. No none."

"Then Miss Drewry, let me ask you politely why you're calling."

Polly paused again, then loosened. "I'm asking if you think I should do anything?"

"Such as what, please ma'm?"

"Such as take it on myself to write Hutch now. Or ask you to do it."

"And bring him back?"

"I've said that, yes."

The chance was a sudden door opened in what had been a seamless wall. Ann sat in the ladderback chair; the hall was dark now. "What reason could he give?"

"The reason of being all Rob's ever had."

Ann said, "Hutch couldn't say that. He may know it's true, but it's half of what he's left."

"Is the other half you?"

Ann laughed once. "Oh I'm fifteen percent, maybe twenty-one or two."

Then Polly could laugh. "That runs in the family. They've been fairly fast off the mark through the years, when it came to bolting for their own nerves' sake—all but Rob; Rob would *stay*."

Ann said, "Does Mr. Mayfield's mother know?"

"We never speak of her; Rob spares me that."

Ann said, "If she does, she may have written Hutch."

"Never," Polly said.

"Why? She wants Hutch too."

Polly said, "Ann, Eva Mayfield is a stranger to me; but I've known at close quarters three men she changed. I lived with Rob's father, as you may well have heard, from the year she left him till the year he died—all but forty years. I've known Rob himself since he turned twenty-one and tracked down his father; known him good and bad, thick and thin—and frankly a long strip of it was *thin*: drinking and women and other useless misery. Hutch I held in my arms the day he was born and his mother died; and he's come to me for what Eva couldn't give, though she's loved him like a limpet. What I've guessed from those men is, she'll want this to herself; want the whole of Rob's death, not even Hutch to share it. When Rob left here at ten this morning, I knew I'd never see him above ground again."

The fervor of that had left Ann calmer. It had shown her, in a way Hutch himself had never managed, why he'd left and must stay—till he'd cleared his legs at least from the webs spun at him by housefuls of faces, her own among them. Fairness was no more natural to her than to anyone with needs; but she said, "Miss Drewry, you say Mr. Mayfield left—going where?"

"Back home, Grainger driving."

"Then since you've asked me, let's let him just *go*. Let his mother have it all; she hasn't had much."

Polly said quietly, "She's had a fine life. From where I sit—and I've mostly *stood*—I haven't heard her do any one thing she hated."

Ann said, "Oh she has—her marriage, her mother's suicide, her father's death. She's suffered a lot. Or so Hutch says."

"Don't believe it," Polly said. "Watch her closer than you have, if she'll let you close. Learn happiness from her. She could give good lessons."

Ann said "I like you better."

Polly laughed. "Several have! I'm outliving them." But she also said thanks.

26

Late in the night Ann was waked by a dream that came as a single sentence not a story. So clear that, as she lay in the dark, she thought she must have spoken it aloud—*Done now.* She first thought it meant Mr. Mayfield's fate, that she'd helped him in his wish to leave Hutch free. But she rose and walked with no light to the toilet; as the cold seat ringed her warm butt and thighs, she saw she'd meant Hutch. She had cut Hutch loose as she hadn't before, even thrust him away when a chance had been offered to hold him again. Hard regret and fear of solitude seized her then and shook her. She bent to her own bare knees and embraced them, crying quite silently.

27

June 15, 1955

Dear Ann,

   Polly Drewry called me late last night to say she'd talked to you and said more than I asked her to. I thought about calling you but, in view of the hour and my new inclination to cast myself on the Mercy of Fate, I decided to hold off till morning and a letter.

   Polly says she pledged you to keep her trust—of course I'd pledged her. I don't mind you knowing; there's nothing unusually precious to me in having this new twist all to myself. But I have two reasons for the choice I made. First, I want Hutch to have this distance for now. It's the main thing he's lacked; and he'll be better for it, maybe better for you. He's suffered, as I did till well past his age, from thinking our people were more than normally hard on each other—hard in what they expect or who they ignore (we aren't, I'm sure; just run of the draw, though scarey as hell). Second, this next strip of my own road is of uncertain length. I really don't think I want or could stand him back here watching. He couldn't not *watch and there's already days when I'm not up to giving my old imitations of joy and peace.*

If you've already told him, don't dive off a wall. If you haven't, please think of my reasons and don't. He's had more of my life than anyone else. We can spare him this.

I've always liked you. I hope you'll be a Mayfield (a mingled boon!). You seem to have the grit.

Till whenever,
Rob Mayfield

June 15, 1955

Dear Hutchins,

It's a cool evening here, and the radio promises cool through the weekend. So I'll take the omen and sit down and start a letter to you. It may be long and I won't mail it soon, maybe not for some months. Or it may just wait here for you in your room. I'll go on sending little separate dispatches to keep you up on the little events; this will be about a bigger one, big for me anyhow. When and if you ever read it, you will already know its first piece of news—I will be out of sight—so I'll give the few details I have on that, then pass to what I've been thinking of lately and want you to have.

Grainger and I got back last night from a two-day circle up to Bracey and Richmond. I hadn't seen Polly since New Year's, as you know; and I had an unaccustomed curiosity to see what was left of Hatt's house in Bracey, my birthplace after all. Polly was fine, absolutely herself (which means that, with Rena, she's been one of the two most selfless people I've happened to know). Bracey was worse—or the inexplicably still-unmarked Historic Site of Rob Mayfield's birth is a pile of ashes, a small pile at that. Burned down after Negroes took it four years ago. I don't say they did it, but my point is it happened and in gorgeous Virginia. Wouldn't you have thought that a state which puts up a two-ton silver sign to mark every dead spot left in the weeds where General Lee peed would have taken protective measures round the cradle of Robinson Mayfield, the Last Rose of Bracey? Well, they somehow didn't.

God-Above hasn't either—or if what's underway is protective, then He's got me buffaloed again.

See, two days before I came up to get your stuff from Edom, I got the results of two weeks of tests. In April when I really believed you were going, I figured it was time to change my insurance—revalue my life at a little higher rate and leave you enough to bury me at least with the usual modest ten-thousand-dollar rites. In a man my age, the company insisted on a physical check; so I went to Sam Simkin, and everything slid along fine till I stepped behind the fluoroscope—he seemed to see a shadow the size of a quarter on one of my lungs.

To simplify the next two weeks of the tale, he made valiant efforts to prove it was anything but what it is—had me spitting from caverns I never knew were down there. We couldn't get a sign of trouble that way, just the normal jillion flora and fauna. So three days before I came up to you, he made a last try—highly diverting little episode in which a tube the size of a European sausage with lights and mirrors was slowly inserted down my throat to my lungs for the luxury tour. What was seen was a sizable lesion, as they call it in their euphemistic code, and little lesionettes (or lesionnaires) all up in the bronchials and on into darkness. Sarcoma, which is cancer. They could operate, haul the whole lung out; but Sam says at best that would give me two years. So I've chosen to preserve my beauty intact, my uncut hide. It has maybe six months of its seamless pride left, eight if I'm unlucky.

I'm here at my home. Grainger, Mother, and Sylvie are taking good care. There is no sufficient cause—I searched—to call you back from a trip you need. We said a good farewell. There've been very few points, now I think about it, in all our time together when a sudden final parting would have left either one of us with much unsaid. In recent years at least we've done pretty well at acting our feelings. I feel that I've watched a whole show, start to finish. I wouldn't want to claim it was Buster Keaton, but it surely had speed and curves and hills, and it rolled to a good warm destination.

If there's memory after death (I suspect there is, though the local Christians doubt I remember Jesus' last name or his winter-hat size), I'll hope to remember the view I had of you in the mirror of my truck as I left you in Edom. You watched me out of sight—highest marks in my book. Almost no human friend will stand to watch you go or turn back one last time when they leave you. They are too expectant, too ready for change. I liked you not waving, just standing still—but standing. Of course I'd like to see you. I'd like to see you every other day left in history, but that would be for me. There's nothing here now for you that you can't learn from reading this letter, and it may be long. I'll try to work on it a little every few days—another family author, a tad late as ever. My Life and What It Showed Me *or* What I Think I Saw.

June 16

   Looking for a way to start this that will keep it going. I know you don't need an autobiography of me, long or short. I know I don't plan to preserve my Great Thoughts on Time and Space for babes yet unborn who'll have the punk luck not to hear me in person. I suspect an account of my circumscribed movements would be barbiturate. I could write out all the jokes I remember, but I don't remember many (why would somebody loving to laugh as much as me live a life and not make up one joke or remember three?). I could finally entrust my famous recipes—hoecake and popcorn. But I read last week in a good biography of Count Tolstoy that he said any fool could write a novel if he'd put down all one person did and thought in one whole day. He ought to know.

   My present days are mostly pretty calm however. I'm still sleeping out here alone with Thal. Grainger wants to move out. Mother wants me to move in. I plan to stay put as long as I can. Far as symptoms go, that could nearly be forever—I cough a few times a day, a dry feather down beneath my breast bone; and my joints are stiffer than usual in the morning (but as the old lady said, "It's good to have something stiff around the house"). So I live my usual summer days—up early for a walk, a big hot breakfast, a piddling morning with the paper and books, then a drive into town for the mail, lunch with Mother, a long afternoon-nap in my old room there, then back out here for the evening and night. Mother thinks I'm taking too much time alone, but I seem to like it. There were years when I wanted somebody nearby every minute of the day—Mother, Min, Rachel, you—but now this solitude seems like a wonderful food I've ignored at serious peril. It well might have saved me if I'd found it in time, even short strips of it. Till now I can't remember ten happy minutes alone, but I'm working to have one whole happy day with nobody but Thal before I quit. I'll let you know.

June 17

   That kept me thinking a good deal of last night. I was trying to remember happy time alone—before now, I mean. All I could come up with was the hours spent jacking off. Nobody ever told me it was dangerous or wrong, so I took to that with serious application at about age four. I know that because I recall going over behind a big laundry basket that Rena had painted green and giving myself that neat reward. Then Rena decided she didn't like the color— goose-turd—and gave the basket to old Mag. Mag died well before I started school, which is how I date my first lonely pleasures. I was wrong yesterday— I've had some very nice lonely minutes but all before the age of twelve. After that, however alone I was, I was always working to the close accompaniment of one or another of the many mental pictures from my gallery of hopes, little packs of girls like baseball cards. Or Con DeBerry when I was fourteen (he and I stayed steamed up about each other through that whole summer, all fumbling hands in hot barns and sheds). Nice minutes, as I said, but pretty sad memories—love thrown to the wind.

To cheer myself up for discovering that, I lay on awake and tried to select much longer good stretches. I decided to hunt for the three best days of my fifty-one years. Ever tried that, with your twenty-five? You're a trained hand at memory, and you probably have the best at your fingertips; but I've never kept any diaries or records, so I just lay still in the dark and asked for my three best days to come back as visions. Nothing came at first. To help myself I divided the available years by three; I've lived exactly three times seventeen years. So I dwelt on age one to seventeen and then this came—

The August I was six—1910—my Aunt Rena said at the table one morning, "You'll be starting school soon, and that ends freedom for good and all. I'm going to take us to Raleigh for a last fling." I of course hollered. Mother was sitting there but spoke not a word. Grandfather said, "No such of a thing—never see either of you alive again." But three mornings later Rena spoke up again, "Rob and I are leaving on the first train tomorrow. We'll be spending two nights at the Yarborough Hotel. I've never been anywhere and neither has he; we've earned the right." Grandfather said, "Then Sylvie's going with you." Sylvie stood there with pancakes, nodding agreement. Rena said, "Thank you, no. Rob and I have worked for this. You mustn't keep it from us." I was speechless with joy and flat with amazement, never having heard anybody go against him. He finished his breakfast in silence thick as custard; and I never heard another word of discussion, though there may have been some.

Next morning at seven he walked us to the station, holding Rena's grip (I carried my own, that midget doctor's-satchel you used to play with). The only thing he told us was "Don't speak to anybody younger than fifty; and if you get lost, find a Methodist Church and ask for the preacher." From there on I barely remember the first day—so near a dream that I've lost all of it but the fact that our room had two big beds with white summer counterpanes and one tall wardrobe that we took turns hiding in to scare each other (Rena was still a child herself, not quite twenty-two). The second day is what I remember entirely.

We both woke up a little while before light and could hear each other breathing normally. There was some good distance between our beds. I turned to try to see her, but she was still dark and still hadn't moved, so finally I said "You ready for company?" She thought about that and, for her own reasons, eventually said, "Let's keep our own places, so dry and cool." Then she said "Say your prayers." I did that in a hurry. Rena took a little longer, having more time behind her; and we had a long breakfast in the bright dining-room—beefsteak and *gravy, corn muffins and butter in hard ribbed curls. I asked for coffee. The old Negro waiter shook his head—"Stunt your growth." Rena said, "That's the idea. Bring him black coffee." I drank three cups, was pied as Ben Turpin the rest of the morning, and happier for it—my fatal first hint that ease came in liquid state, readily procured. Then we walked downtown. I remember dim hours in the old museum—mastodon leg-bones the size of Negro houses, some Indian teeth from Roanoke Island, a live snapping-turtle that had taken two joints of a little boy's finger in Perquimans County, and a male diamondback rattler thick as my leg that had been on a fast ever since they caught it five months before. That morning in our presence they tried again—set a month-old squirrel in beside his bronze eye. I wanted to leave; Rena said "Pay attention." In under thirty seconds he drew back and struck, and we stayed to watch him swallow all but the tail. I remember eating two banana sandwiches (where did we get them?) in the shadow of the statue to Confederate women (whose idea was that? anyhow Rena liked it). I remember she took me to Briggs Hardware and said, "Buy anything that costs a dollar." I bought a full-sized ball peen hammer; still have it—you can hang pictures with it when it comes your way.*

Then in late afternoon when even I was tired of the blistering day, Rena found a church standing open—First Baptist, unfortunately. She said "Let's rest." We were near the hotel. I said, "You've paid for those two cool beds." Even then I could see there was something she'd expected and not found yet. I thought it was hiding somewhere in the town. She pulled me behind her, and we went in and sat way over on the side in half-dark. The Kendals, as you know, were not big churchgoers, though Rena read St. Paul more than was healthy. Still I knew when to sit quiet and draw in my horns. Right off, she shut her eyes. I figured she was praying, so I watched her and tried to guess what she wanted. Pretty soon I decided she wanted this to last—us alone off together. I still loved Mother so much there was small room left for Rena even, so I couldn't share the wish, but I did keep watching till I thought she was beautiful. You well know she wasn't, not to see at least—plain as any rake handle. But I saw otherwise that one afternoon. I thought she was something like Pharaoh's daughter in Tales From the Bible. *And maybe I was right. Children are dead-right about so many things they later get wrong or mislay completely; maybe looks is one. I tried to imagine getting back to the hotel and finding a wire saying Mother was dead. It ruined me of course, and my eyes watered some. But I do recall thinking, "There will be Rena left, who is pretty too." I went on thinking that from then on out and leaning on it—didn't every one of us?—till you found her that morning, cold by the steps. At least she missed this. By then she'd finished praying or stopped. She faced me. I said, "Do you really hear Him talk back?" She shook her head, solemn—"Not always, no."*

By the time we had had our naps and supper, it was well on to dark. She asked if I wanted another short walk. I was tired to the bone but couldn't say that. I said I would rather she read to me. So after we talked to a gentleman well past fifty in the lobby, we went up and lay in our clothes on the beds; and she read a chapter of My Poor Dick—*I swear to God, a novel she'd brought; all we had but the Bible. It was set in England, and it put me under—a hero named Dick that everybody loved.*

But before I had gone completely, Rena said, "Let me rub those tired legs with cold witch-hazel." It had happened before, more than once for chiggers and growing pains. I knew the procedure. I stripped to my under-britches, lay on my belly, and she rubbed me nicely. What was new was she finally said "Slip down your drawers." I did and she said, "Now lie on your back." I knew we were wading into deeper water but liked the prospect. I don't think I'd ever felt naked before, not for anyone but mirrors. I remember hoping my thing wouldn't stand; it had already started playing me tricks. Well, she kept to my legs as she had before—not much above the knee—and I kept my eyes shut. I was thinking any minute I would be afraid or have to answer questions I didn't understand. But witch-hazel is one of life's cheaper blessings, and its clean odor just steadily soothed any worry that rose. They were all that rose and finally they stopped; and then—somewhere on the near side of sleep—I found myself praying what I'd guessed was Rena's prayer, that this not end. She and I here for good.

As she'd foretold earlier, I heard no answer. But by then I was deeper down into sleep. She woke me with a thump on the navel, laughing. I looked. She was corking the bottle and standing. She said, "Now I've seen one. Thought I might never. Not much to live for!" I didn't understand the words themselves. But gone as I was, I knew we'd come through some narrow alley back into free space; and I knew she'd led me. So before I slept again—eight or ten seconds— I tasted, pure tasted, the thought I will not be happier than this. *I may have thought* safer, *the same thing really.*

Let that be recalled then, by you if no one else, as one of your father's best stretches of time. Notice too—in that tale, like all the rest, he is not the hero and didn't try to be. He waits for a woman to lead him to daylight. You may think he's wrong and will pay ever after but sometimes they can. So can rocks though maybe, ponds in the shade or one standing pine. My wisdom, you've noticed, tends to vanish when fingered.

I'll keep to stories then, as I vowed at the start. Next time I'm horizontal and calm as last night, I'll try to discover the next good day—seventeen to thirty-four. You were born in there. Cross your fingers and hope.

Where are you this minute?—five hours on past me, at the very least. You were always ahead. Anyhow, whatever I said right above, I trust your fingers are better employed than crossed and waiting. That was my poor line.

28

As promised Lew had met Hutch at Oxwich Castle. They'd spent twenty minutes in its modest ruins—Lew inventing sagas of Roman attack, Hutch looking down to fields and parallel hedges and a clutch of white houses all stroked with damp sun, "in country sleep." Less than two years before, Dylan Thomas had died in a New York November too far from here, his native place. Hutch had thought they'd go on to Lew's for lunch, meet his mother at least, and maybe spend a night. But Lew had called out from a turret "Flee! Flee!" and, when he'd run down, had actually meant it—they must push on at once; he'd had home for now. So they spent three days in the west of Wales—Milford Haven, St. David's, Cardigan, Aberystwyth; then down through the Brecon Beacons and the coal towns to Bristol, Bath, Wells, Glastonbury. They stayed in Glastonbury through a fine afternoon, exploring the probably spurious but powerful traces of Joseph of Arimathea's English visit—the haven of the Grail, the thorn that had grown from his planted staff; the site of the grave of Arthur himself, entombed in a hollow oak, Guinevere at his feet (whose gold hair had powdered at a greedy monk's touch when the bones were discovered). They'd been flushed from the grounds at sunset by a guard, and treated themselves to a long dinner at the Copper Beech; then decided, on wine, to drive through the night into Cornwall—Tintagel.

And till then they had travcled easily together. Lew's appetite was mainly for the road, onward motion; but he'd seemed quite ready to hear Hutch lay out the various stories of Arthur and his woes. He'd even read aloud as Hutch drove, the entire text of Bédier's *Romance of Tristan and Iseult*; it took him two days with his interpolation of oddly convincing passages of photographic *eros*, mostly centered on Iseult's resourcefulness in bed or bower. So when they arrived in early morning mist at Trevena, the dismal village behind Tintagel Head, Hutch pulled up beside the Round Table Cafe and said, "Shall we have a little cold grease and mead before we take the next castle?"

Lew consulted a furry mouth with his tongue, then turned and smiled. "Tell you what—I'm beat and my arse thinks it's dead. Let's find a nice widow with a bed for rent. I'll doss down while you eat. Take all day to look; come wake me when you're done."

Hutch said, "I can drive to Castle Dore now. I'll wait till you're up to see Tintagel."

Lew nodded. "Drive anywhere. Enjoy the day, nice Cornish day"—it was still dim and dense. "Then if you want to take me to see anything, find a whacking color-picture with Marilyn Monroe. Or any kind of show starring anybody naked."

Hutch laughed and agreed.

Lew opened his door and stepped to the street. An old man was passing with a slow camel gait. "Beg your pardon," Lew said. "Do you know a nice widow with a lovely daughter rents rooms by the day?"

The man said "Please?" and stopped with difficulty, still rolling his knees.

"Two gents need rest. Know a cheap dry place?"

The man pointed through the Lancelot News Agency as if it were air. "Next road. Mrs. Mason. Little card in her window. Daughter's fat but blind."

Mrs. Mason was fat—two hundred pounds of red-haired cheer, exactly the color of her asthmatic spaniel. The daughter Jill was half a head taller, pleasant-looking brunette with excellent eyes. They were washing breakfast dishes when Hutch and Lew knocked; and yes they had one room, ten shillings. It faced a yard of hens, all mired in black mud; but the wide oak bed seemed dry and clean. Lew insisted on paying and changed his mind far enough to eat the big breakfast the women offered. Then he did turn in and Hutch set off.

29

The wet gray walls of Arthur's Tintagel struck Hutch as the first perfect site he'd seen. He knew that the visible ruins of the castle were some six centuries younger than any historical Arthur. Still its unroofed walls coiled tense as a snake on the high sea-crag, precisely as advertised by poets, sufficiently grand to have witnessed all the legends bestowed—the deceitful conception of Arthur and his birth by Uther on Ygrain through the arts of Merlin. But though Hutch had been the morning's first visitor and had the whole thing to himself half an hour with mist and gulls and cold salt gusts, he had not responded to more than the sights. Why?—Arthur had been his childhood favorite, with Pocahontas and Alexander. He poked round an hour taking photographs, staring out to sea and back at the Saxon church set alone on the next cliff, as open to gales. By then he'd decided—the place, with all its

grandeur, was a *set*; the show was long over. He was wrong of course, knowing nothing of the two millennia of men who'd held this rock before any
Arthur (if Arthur ever was) and their sturdy successors. What still bound him
in like skin on his eyes was the distance from home, the newness of his break.
Even grass here was unlike any grass he'd known; in its rank health it caught
at his ankles, soaked and slowed him.

But two hours later, twenty-five miles south, he began to feel freed—or
opening slowly. He'd driven the width of the county and come to his next
planned stop. A little above Fowey on the spine of its peninsula at a country
junction with no human being or animal in sight, he came on two things.
A seven-foot stone plinth of obvious age stood in weeds and flowers. Hutch
pulled to the shoulder of the narrow road, stepped across, and waited for the
sun to take cover. Then he traced with his finger the much-disputed Latin.
To him it seemed clearly to say what he'd hoped—DRUSTANUS HIC IACIT
CUNOMORI FILIUS. "Here lies Drustan son of Cunomorus." *Drustan* was the
Celtic spelling of *Tristan*. *Cunomorus* was another of King Mark's names. In
all the stories Tristan was Mark's nephew. Did the inscription signify "son of
his loins" or "adopted son"? Had the poets made a hard tale softer?—incest,
real or legal, smoothed to household adultery?

Hutch walked through tall dry grass and more flowers (he seldom noticed
flowers) toward a huge earthwork maybe ten feet high and easy to climb. At
the top he was standing on the mound of Castle Dore—the undoubted hill-
fort and palace of Mark, local king of the fields here surveyed, dated early
sixth century by recent excavation. He could still see no one and nothing
man-made but the green ridge he stood on. Within its small ring the most
famous love of the modern world, since Antony and Cleopatra at least, had
blossomed and spread—there was real chance of that. The sun cleared
again. Hutch squatted to the ground and probed its softness.

He remembered—not Iseult from his *Boy's King Arthur*, slender, low-
belted—but Kirsten Flagstad four years before, her last Isolde at the Metro-
politan. He'd watched her from the side of the Family Circle, a
fifty-four-year-old Norwegian matron whose two hundred pounds were not
concealed by the white negligée of Act Two (*the night*) till she rose to the first
great crest and poured—

> Have you not known . . .
> The mighty Queen
> Of boldest hearts,

> Mistress of Earth's ways?
> Life and Death
> Are under Her.
> Them she weaves of joy and pain.

He'd taken the question personally then and later in his single room at the Taft. *Had he known Her at all? And was the claim true?* What came with birth and trebled at puberty, he'd known right along. He'd always suspected himself of enjoying his body more than anyone else he'd known. Alone or with others it had simply never failed him, and he'd used it daily at least for twelve years. But had he ever known a constant need only one could fill?— from all reports, that seemed to be love. He believed he hadn't. He thought that such a need must be taught, almost surely by a mother. His mother had died the day of his birth. He'd been set the example by Rob, Polly, Grainger, Eva, Alice, now Ann. At various times one or more of those had aimed at his eyes an offer of love, a plea for love, that had now proved blinding. Dazzling at least. He'd run from that—and first stopped here. This hour seemed the first still hour he'd had in months, maybe years. And it came at Castle Dore, surely one of the earth's main ganglia of love and its famished cry.

What he felt though was ease, a simple light pleasure to be loose in a warm day, splotched by sun, hunched down in sweet grass and digging idly. *Home*, he thought; then knew that home had never meant ease. His nail scraped a rock. He gouged it up and rubbed it clean—a palm-sized parallelogram of gray shale with streaks of sea-green and, on its long edge, jagged stains brown as old blood. With the sun hid again, the rock had its own sheen, lunar but steady. He was not a skilled judge, but it didn't seem shaped by human work. Still it might have been walked on by Iseult or Mark. There were no signs forbidding the theft of a rock; he'd take this one then.

He stood and was instantly hit by the rise. His sight swam; he laughed once aloud and half-spun. Then he waited to calm. His natural compass told him he was facing southwest; that one sense never failed him. A true line grounded here, extended four thousand-four hundred miles, would touch— what? Rob anyhow—Ann, Eva, all the others nested there. *Looking homeward* then, angel or not. Milton's angel had stood on the hill in Penzance harbor forty miles from here, staring out toward Spain in protection and defiance. Hutch said the lines, richer in loss than any other—

> Look homeward Angel now, and melt with ruth.
> And, O ye Dolphins, waft the hapless youth.

Well, he'd work that out—who was who, where was *homeward.* That was why he was here. Rob had asked for a diagram. If one was there he'd find it—from here, sufficient distance. Sufficient *time*—this year, maybe more, stretched before him clear as Roman road. He'd bought himself time.

Then why, at that, did a shudder seize him and cold tears start? They held him another whole minute there high on the green midden raised over Europe's great love and foul deceit.

30

That evening they'd bought a can of corned beef, tomatoes, cheese, a Hovis loaf, cider, and plums and driven five miles to lie in a pasture by a small stone bridge that crossed a river barely wider than a creek. They'd asked—nearest cinema with anything bearable was an hour away; so they'd eat here, find a pub, and turn in fairly early. Hutch was tired from his day, Lew still groggy from his nap; and they mostly ate in silence, watching six cows slowly graze toward the river. The smallest would stop every minute or so and throw a long soulful look their way. Finally she moved out boldly from the others and sauntered forward, stopping only at the water, her feet in muck. Hutch and Lew were sprawled ten feet apart. She turned her muzzle distinctly to Hutch and gave a slow bellow.

Lew said, "Are you wearing your bull scent again?"

Hutch said, "I haven't bathed if that's what you mean."

"Oh lovely. That's one thing wrong with your country—people wash too much. You can barely tell they're people when you rub up against them. I like a good whiff when I'm in the mood."

Hutch nodded and smiled. "Me too, to a point."

Lew still faced the heifer; she was drinking now. "Can't recall ever having anything so pongy I couldn't lick it clean enough." He'd spoken as earnestly as if it were a finding of some importance, and he seemed to weigh it. Then he turned to Hutch, grinning. "I had this mate in the army—from Oxford; you should look him up: little low-built chap with deep-set black eyes. He was just eighteen and pure as new cream; but soon as I saw him, I said, 'Stand clear. That one's wound tight as wire. Whoever cuts *his* string had better be seated and gripping iron rails!' He was straight from square-bashing. Anyhow first weekend I took him into Salisbury—me and two others—and this old girl that I'd known some time gave us each ten minutes in a shed. Him first, as the baby—name was Gary; still is, I daresay and hope. He said it went nicely and so did the girl, though she prided herself on professional ethics—didn't blab on her trade, but she thanked me for Gary. Well, *ethics*—poor dear, she'd slipped that week. There were Irish Guards in town; I blame them—worst dogs of all. On schedule my knob popped a nice red blister. I went in for tests and a pint of penicillin. So did one of the others. And I warned young Gary, but he said he was clear—shy as foxes, he was; always washed in a corner with his arse to us. Still in three more days, he woke with this sore at the side of his mouth; he had full lips, another good sign. I asked him who'd chewed on his lip in the night. He flushed red as Christmas and said 'Nobody.' But next day the thing had spread and looked hot. I said he should have it seen to at once before his looks were marred for good. That night I found him, stood over in the dark, rubbing salve on his sore. It really hadn't crossed my mind what he had. I said, 'Got you back on the road to fame, have they?' (we always told him he was made for pictures). He turned to the light and was redder than ever, struggling with whether to knock me flat. I said 'No harm,' meaning I was his mate. He said, 'Bloody right. I'll be fit in a month. Then I'll taste it again—sweet as sherbet, it was.' He'd managed it upright in that stinking shed. Well, peace to his wounds!—a hero of love, through filth and flame."

During that the heifer had returned to her grazing. The sky was suddenly three shades dimmer; it was nearly nine. The mist that had burned off by noon was returning, lying in the middle distance beyond them and extending gradual arms their way, two feet from the ground. The light had gone violet and gave a low hum as far as Hutch could hear. He rolled to his belly facing Lew and pointed to the half-dark bridge. "Guess what happened here."

"Your eighth-great-grandmother passed a kidney stone at age ninety-nine."

"No the Mayfields were from Sussex."

Lew said, "I'm sure you'd know, Master Hutch." But he still watched the bridge. "George Washington crossed it as a lad of ten on his way west to steal Paradise from the Limeys."

Hutch laughed. "George Washington never touched England."

"Lucky sod."

"Or Wales."

"Lucky sod."

Hutch said, "It's called Slaughter Bridge. King Arthur's bastard son Modred met him here, hand to hand, and stabbed him in the head. They took him upstream—there's a rock marks the spot—and he died there at sundown."

Lew said "Lucky sod," still watching the bridge. Then he suddenly turned and faced Hutch fully, his small fine-boned skull clear in the dusk. "Might have known," he said harshly.

"What?"

"—You'd pull this on me." He was plainly not joking.

Hutch swallowed his mouthful of bread. "I'm lost."

"You're *not*. That's just it. You're hauling me round these spots dead as Egypt. I hate all this." He thumbed toward the bridge. "I told you this morning I'd had it with this."

"You said you were sleepy."

Lew laughed, which drained a little of his steam. "So sleepy I'd like to go dead right here, be nailed in a box, and not resurrected till the box reaches New York—Miami at least. Never Canada again."

"Why?"

"You've not seen it, right?"

"Right," Hutch said.

"Don't waste dollars then. It's good for a laugh in the first few weeks—grown men standing round, heads bowed in prayer that they'll turn into Yanks; but all drinking tea and debating if they'll get a nice visit this year from the Queen and her docked-cock husband. After that it's Hell."

"Go to New York then."

"You proposing marriage? That would be my one hope with your bloody immigration."

Hutch said "Sure."

They both laughed and lay back in place on the thick grass. Light was all but gone. The cows had melted off. The mist was nearly on them. Lew said, "Ever had piles or rheumatism?"

"No. Why?"

"You do now."

"Why?"

"Lying out here. Any fool who lies on British soil at night gets piles and rheumatism, dead or crippled in a week."

"How did ancient Britons fuck?"

"In trees. On stones. That's the well-kept secret of Stonehenge, mate—no temple at all, just a great knocking-shop, lovely stones big as beds. All from Wales, by the way."

Hutch laughed. "I know."

They waited another minute. Lew said, "Anything you *don't* know, Nostradamus?"

Hutch laughed but saw Lew had struck something hard. He did know the future, had always known it—what others would do. What stopped him was the past—what had been done and why, where it pressed on him. He said, "I don't know what's happened to me—in my life, I mean."

"Lucky sod," Lew said; "*I* do" and stood to go.

They walked, in faith, through total dark past the slaughter of Arthur—
a bridge as fitting for a Mother Goose jingle:

> As I was going to St. Ives,
> I met a man with seven wives. . . .

They were halfway back to their lodging, driving slow in earnest fog, when
Hutch said, "You claimed you knew what had happened—to me or you?"

Lew took a little time, then spoke to the road. "Oh both. You've had it very
easy, all you wanted—iced lollies in the sun and more on the way. I was one
of six children to a drunk stonemason in a four-room cottage on the Gower
Peninsula of poor old Wales. Postcard views of Heaven. To me it meant a shit-
hole out in the yard with sick chickens staring in the cold and mud while I
sat breathing poison from my family's bowels with my blue knees knocking.
I had the misfortune to be my mum's pet and to have a schoolmaster who
thought I was special—maybe had a brain cell or two to bear me away:
Richard Burton at the Vic; Emlyn Williams, you know. What I had was a
smile that would melt Pembroke bluestone. That and words; I could talk. Or
sing—the Welsh chant: *Pardon-would-you-kindly-suck-my-knob?*" He intoned
it, high and sweet.

Hutch said "A lovely sound."

Lew said, "Try to *spend* it. Try to start your life with two strong arms, a
straight white smile, and fulltime opera streaming out of your teeth—how
far would you get?"

"Covent Garden, the Met."

"Very likely. They got me two marvelous years in Her Majesty's forces,
all the birds I could shag; then six months in rural Ontario with my dad's
sister, sweeping warehouse floors and minding her kids; then two whole
seasons with that sorry show."

"Feeding elephants?"

"One elephant, a lion, four bears, three seals—they loved the smile; they
had to."

"What was wrong with that? Every boy wants a circus."

"Nothing actually but the owner's wife. See, he was a Jew and died near
the end of my first season—worn to the quick; he'd come from Poland after
the war. His wife was French-Canadian, a good bit younger. She kept the show
going and summoned me on—to her lonely arse. You ever try touring the
wilds of Saskatchewan and Manitoba with a one-ring show, you'd find yourself climbing on the baboons if they paused long enough. I liked it at first—
she was strong and funny (the seals were hers)—and she ran everything so

smoothly I thought I was set for a while. Thought I was seated by a nice warm grate with my feet on the hob. I was really lost on the autumn sea near the rim of a bloody great storm wheeling at me. Every storm is hollow at the core, you know—Yvonne Taborski was sucking me in as fast as I'd come. Which is why I'm here. I ran, I mean."

"—And landed with a Yank fleeing opposite ways on a historic tour of unhistoric sites."

"Suits me, for now. Sorry I spouted back there. I hate cows."

"We'll just rest tomorrow. You set the pace."

Lew thought and shook his head. "I was whacked this morning, but I can't bear rest—reminds me of Wales."

Hutch grinned. "You decide."

Lew still faced the glass; they'd reached Trevena. It seemed to exist in midair, frail, founded on vapor. He nodded. "All right."

For Hutch, by the low green light from the dash, Lew's profile seemed strong as an Attic head—the Kritios boy on Alice's wall: a still survivor of time, acid fate, marauding hungers, triumphant though scarred and gravely generous, ready to share its patient secret if properly asked, its diamond endurance—simple as coal. He was only half-wrong.

31

Mrs. Mason was taking saffron cake from the oven when they knocked at ten. Jill was out with her young man—"wall-eyed but honest"—so she urged them to sit in the kitchen with her for Ovaltine and slices of the warm splendid cake. They were full and tired but agreed and sat. In a moment she joined them and, with no question asked, commenced a monologue on her husband Les's recent long-drawn death. "They told me his kidneys were solid as puddings when they tried to cut. I'd known his *heart* was solid for years—six months after I married him too—but I didn't have the stomach to ask what they found *there* —they cut him, fork to tit, a two-foot seam. I know; I washed it."

Lew stood at that, begged exhaustion, and left.

Hutch stayed for the tale of funeral and bills and another slice of cake. When he managed to extract himself half an hour later, he said, "I'm praying for very deep sleep."

Mrs. Mason said, "You've got the bed for that, all right. It was our old bed—mine and Les's; *he* could sleep. Slept through most of *my* life at least."

Hutch said, "Sleep has never been my problem either."

"Well, I hope Mr. Davis hasn't taken your half."

"I'll move him if he has."

Mrs. Mason thought a moment; she was rinsing their cups. Then she looked back and grinned. "I had two chaps here early last spring—from Cambridge, doing very much the same as you: nosing round old stones, asking me what I'd heard as a child of King Arthur. I told them nobody I knew had ever known him; he came with the cars, you know—trippers, once the good old war shut down. Can't disappoint trippers. Seemed to ruin their day—my chaps, I mean. I reckon they thought I had private news they could take back with them and win big prizes. Never mind; they recovered." She pointed to the wall that hid Lew from them. "I heard em playing leapfrog for three nights straight!"

Hutch laughed and left.

32

Lew had turned out the light and sounded asleep. Hutch quietly washed at the bowl in the corner. Some moonlight had reached through the one high window; it seemed the source of cold in the room. As he stripped to his shorts, Hutch shook and gripped his shoulders. Then he felt his way to the empty side of Les's bed—the usual English millstone of covers, welcome now. Still he dreaded the first touch of clammy sheets. In just a half-hour Lew had warmed them though. Hutch lay back, grateful, and condensed his body to its most economical bulk for the night. They had not shared a bed till now; good luck. He said a short prayer, then saw Castle Dore again—the shape of a great crab extending claws from a green carapace, to capture what? *Safety* surely. Safety from what? Other men. It had failed. Within the shell itself lay Tristan, a hollow heart.

His knee itched. He carefully reached down to rub it. Something cold struck his calf. He waited, then probed on down to find it. His blind fingers finally were forced to admit they'd found a knife, a dull table-knife. He drew it out quietly and held it to the moon. In its homely bluntness it managed a gleam.

Lew whispered. "'She lay down and Tristan put his naked sword between them. To their good fortune they'd kept on their clothes. So they slept divided in the heart of the wood and were found there, pure by the wretched Mark.'"

Hutch laughed—"A-plus. A fine demonstration of the famous Celtic memory"—and set the knife on the floor by his head.

Neither of them slept at ease all night.

33

But three mornings later they sailed from Penzance in an old island steamer, past St. Michael's Mount (the angel's home) and west thirty-five miles on high seas four hours to the low granite Scillies. Lew spent the time sick in the chilly "lounge," a dim cabin ten feet square with wood benches; Hutch stayed on deck, incapable apparently of that one malaise. They docked on St. Mary's, wandered an hour in gray Hugh Town while Lew's head settled, then caught the mail-launch two miles north to Tresco. It literally beached them in a red shingle cove where an old man waited to take the mail. By then Lew was fit to resume his duties as quartermaster. Mrs. Mason had told them of a cousin of hers, married to a fisherman somewhere on the island, who would take them in; they only knew his name. "Can you tell us where to find Albert Gibbons please?"

The man's face was split—half innocent-islander, half lifelong-seaman. His eyes never met them but consulted the beach or the low hill behind. "You've got a long journey to find Bert Gibbons."

Lew smiled. "I heard Tresco was two miles long."

The man nodded. "Some less—one and three-quarter on a good bright day" (it was suddenly that, all clouds blown clear). Then he shifted the one bag and stepped toward the hill. "Bert ain't on Tresco nor in the world. Drowned maybe two months back; you won't find him."

"But he's got a wife, right?"

The man's back was to them, cresting the rise. From there he turned and looked out to the launch, barely audible, leaving. He gave it a wave. "And two bad children. Walk straight through the Garden, lean right to Lizard Point, ask the first face you see for Kay Gibbons' cottage. If she opens the door, you'll be the first that's seen her."

34

The first face was monstrous. When they'd skirted the weird Abbey Garden— thick with palms and cactus—and followed a rolling path northeast five hundred yards, a boy stood up from a rock on their right. His body seemed eight or nine years old; his face was huge and his eyes blared wildly, but he made no noise. They stopped in their tracks. Then Lew laughed. "How much will you take for that?"

The boy came forward, still holding to his face a big round glass framed stoutly with metal—eight inches broad, some curious nautical magnifier.

He held it out to them. "You can have it," he said. "Just found it by the bay."

Lew took it, held it to his own dark face, and turned to Hutch—a fish-eyed smile and hoggish grunts.

But Hutch was watching the pale thin boy, surprised by his readiness to give up so soon a genuine find any child would have prized. Five minutes before as they'd come through the garden, he'd thought the word *Eden*. He thought it again.

So did Lew, in his way. He gave back the glass. "You'll need this," he said. "It would just scare me mate."

The boy took it slowly, suspecting some part of his life had been abused. He thumbed the brass binding, then looked to Hutch. "You frightened?" he said.

Hutch smiled. "Not of you."

"*You* keep it," he said. "My mother wouldn't like it."

Hutch accepted it with thanks. "I'll remember you behind it."

The boy nodded—"Please"—and gathered to run.

Lew said, "Could you show us where Bert Gibbons lived?"

He nodded. "Why?"

"Mrs. Gibbons' cousin in Trevena said they might put us up."

The boy said "All right" and walked on ahead.

By then their bags were heavy in the sun. The boy was moving at a healthy clip, never looking back. Hutch wondered, "Does he think this is all less than perfect?" To Hutch, with his own life, it seemed perfect so far—sun, a lush garden, no cars, no town, rocks and sea as a permanent guard.

But Lew said "Oy!" to the child and stopped. "I'm an old man. Have mercy."

The boy looked back, said "Sorry," and waited.

Hutch said, "My name is Hutchins. What's yours?"—a very American question, he knew. The British he'd met till now lived happily in ignorance of names; Lew had never said *Hutch* to his face.

The boy said "Archie."

Lew said, "You want to make a shilling?—take this." He set down his bag.

Hutch said, "He's not big enough for that, Lew."

Archie nodded. "I'm not."

Lew said, "At your age I was lifting stones for my dad, twice the weight all day."

Hutch said "—And hated it."

Lew said "*Life*, me boy."

Hutch said "I'll take it." It was heavier than his, Lew's total possessions.

Lew said, "I've been breathing in hope of that." Then he smiled. "Save your strength."

Archie said, "We could all help. We're nearly there."

So Hutch and Lew shared the handle of the heavy bag; Archie took Hutch's. At the top of the next low rise, Archie pointed. Fifty yards ahead at the end of the path in a copse of low trees (some of which were palms) stood a two-story stone cottage, fenced close on all sides.

At the gate Archie said, "I'll tell her you've come."

Hutch said "She's not expecting us."

But the child ran forward, set the bag by the door, and entered shouting. "Mam, there's two big chaps here've come to sleep."

Hutch said "Archie *Gibbons*."

Lew said "I knew that."

"How?"

"Fellow Celt. Celts are magic." He narrowed his eyes at Hutch and bared his teeth as though transmitting power.

"Good. You may have to cast a spell on one crazy widow."

A young woman suddenly stood in the door, twelve feet beyond them. She was medium-sized with strong arms and legs and maybe fifteen extra pounds on her hips; but her face was blond and open as the door, though she hadn't smiled.

Lew said "Mrs. Gibbons?"

She nodded—"Kay"—and pointed behind her. "He says Mary Mason sent you here to me."

Hutch said "She did."

"I really don't know her."

"She said she was kin."

"She is, I believe. I just never saw her."

Lew laughed. "Your eyes have missed a treat. She's four feet tall, weighs fourteen stone, red hair from a bottle, and cooks like a saint."

The woman smiled; her face took it well, fresh gentle light. The boy was clearly hers. "Does that mean she's good? Don't know as I'd care to eat a real saint's cooking; don't they grudge their bodies?"

Lew said "More than me, true."

A small silence then. Lew looked back to Hutch; but before either spoke, Archie reappeared with bread and butter. "Your room will be across from mine," he said.

His mother said, "And you'll have to pipe-down at last."

He grinned and piped three piercing notes, a fine fake whistle.

35

Kay—she invited them to call her that—had given them a scraped-together lunch of eggs, cheese, and creamy milk. She'd spread it in the small sitting-room on the front, which she said would be theirs to read in or warm. Despite the bright sky a low fire had burned in the grate against damp. Once they'd sat they were left entirely alone, though sounds of Archie and maybe two women came in snatches from the kitchen—little questions and cautions. The few things Hutch or Lew said were whispered.

Lew said, "She's done pretty well, I'd say, considering we're the first men she's seen for months." He also said, "Where's the famous bad daughter the old fool mentioned?"

Hutch said, "I think I may just stay here, have my trunk sent from Oxford. I suspect this is Heaven."

Lew said, "It is. I'm the Archangel Maud." Then he said, "Cool your wick. Give it twenty-four hours. I suspect it's *England*." Then he went to their upstairs bedroom for his nap.

Hutch followed him long enough to unpack Bédier's *Tristan* again.

While he was stripping—he took naps seriously—Lew said, "I've read that to you. Branch out. Your face is long as a wet week already. Read something funny now" (he had *Three Men in a Boat* in his bag).

Hutch said, "I think this is funny as they come."

"Suit yourself," Lew said and stepped to the one round window—naked, cupping his balls. He pointed. "Go lie in that boat in the sun with your book. By three you'll be brown as a bus conductor from east Barbados—I quite like them—and I'll come join you. We can bathe before tea."

"Water's cold."

"So are hearts but I've warmed a few."

Hutch stepped up behind him and leaned to see out—a white sand cove like the perfect letter C, no human in sight, the silvered ribs of a fifteen-foot fishing boat abandoned down near the water. "See you there," he said. "I may sleep too."

Lew didn't look back but he nodded. "You need it. Been racing your brain."

"Not at all."

"You have."

"What about?"

Lew turned (they were two feet apart) and searched Hutch's face. At last he covered it with his broad left hand. "We wizards keep a great part of our knowledge hidden. You mortals couldn't bear it."

Hutch stepped back from hiding, grinned, and left. He stopped in the kitchen where Kay was scrubbing the rough stone floor—no sign of Archie and still no daughter. She offered tea; he declined and asked if there was any reason why he shouldn't lie in that beached wreck and read.

She didn't look up. "It won't float if that's what you mean," she said.

"I meant is it private property? Will anyone object?"

"Oh no," she said. "This is Tresco, Mr. Mayfield. People are really quite generous here; nothing else to be. You've heard what they say—nothing else to do in the Scillies, so people take in each other's laundry."

"*Hutchins*," he said. "I answer to Hutch."

She faced him, still kneeling. "As in *rabbit?*"

He laughed.

"You've come home then. We're the rabbit center of the universe. They take everything. Nothing seems to help." She seemed to be ready for a lecture on rabbits, no trace of a smile.

So Hutch turned to go in the momentary pause. At the door he said "Could I bring anything?"

"From where?"

"The shops."

"You haven't seen the shops!" She did smile then, reached up to the table and hoisted herself, held her head with both hands to stop the whirl. "There's a very great deal you could bring but not from there."

36

Lying in the dry boat, Hutch read again the chapter in *Tristan* called "The Wood of Morois"—Tristan and Iseult (fleeing when Mark surrenders Iseult to the lust of a band of mendicant lepers) wander three-quarters of a year in the savage wood, accompanied only by Tristan's man Gorvenal, eating fresh game and missing only "the taste of salt"; for "They loved each other and they did not know that they suffered." It was the part Lew had quoted, with the knife in Tintagel; and like any part of a truthful whole, it seemed to Hutch a sufficient picture of the world in itself—wild hunger generating its own food, rich and nutritious and finally lethal. Then in the sun which had still not clouded, he took off his shirt, lay flat in the hull, spread his arms, and slept.

In his dream he, Ann, and Lew were together on this island in the Garden. They seemed the only people, and they didn't seem in flight from any other place. At least they had managed a calm unquestioned division of labor to fill the days—summer days but they worked against the coming of cold. Hutch wandered the paths and fields and beaches, gathering stones to build a hut. Lew chased down rabbits, choked them with his bare hands, skinned and cured them over smoky fires. Ann softened the dried skins and sewed them neatly, like states on a map, into one growing cover—a broad deep quilt of tan and blue fur under which, with winter, they would sleep together. Till then they slept on pallets of palm leaves, separate but near. Hutch wondered if the others longed for winter like him; but they never spoke of it since *patience* was the element in which they moved, not *time* or *hope*. They were trying silently to teach him patience; he was trying to learn, though his body (strengthening daily with the work) steadily requested other bodies and was steadily balked.

The bow of the boat was long since stove-in, a hole the size of a pony-cart. Toward the end of the dream, Archie Gibbons approached, thrust his head and shoulders in, and stared at Hutch. He could see Hutch was chilly in the rising breeze but fast asleep. He could see in the fork of his legs that his thing was standing hard. He stayed still and silent, wondering if there were any chance in the world this man might stay here and never go. He'd wanted that since morning on the path when the man accepted his gift of the glass. He crawled forward, never shaking the boat, till he knelt compactly between the man's legs; then he touched them, laid both hands on the large knees.

Just before he woke, Hutch thought, "—The first hands to touch me since when?" The answer was "In three weeks, since Ann on the pier"; but he didn't think that. He opened his eyes on the same blue sky; then slowly looked down at Archie, who was solemn as an acolyte. Hutch said "Good morning."

Archie shook his head No.

"Good night?"

Another shake.

"Merry Christmas?"

Archie nodded. "Will you give me what I ask?"

"Is it something I can give?"

"Yes."

"You're sure?"

"It's easy." Archie still hadn't smiled, an earnest transaction.

Hutch said "Better tell me first."

Archie shook his head. "Answer Yes or No—that simple."

Hutch said "I might lie."

"Never lie."

"O.K. No."

Archie waited, then put his hands between his own knees. "You made an awful mistake," he said.

Hutch said "Let me hear."

"I asked you to stay."

"In this boat?—it's chilly." The breeze had stiffened.

Archie said "On the island."

Hutch waited. "I'm sorry. Do I get another chance?"

Archie shook his head.

Hutch said again "I'm sorry," then sat up, put on his shirt, slipped sternward, and lay back down. He said, "Could we talk a little while anyhow?"

"What about?"

"Well, your age—say you're ten?" (Though he'd never had a brother, Hutch knew you must always overestimate age.)

"I didn't tell you, no. I'm eight-and-a-half, nine in January."

"What day?"

"Nineteenth."

"That's also General Lee's."

"Who's he?" Archie said.

"The best American soldier—very handsome, lost all his wars, born on Archie Gibbons' birthday."

"You're American, are you?"

"Till today," Hutch said.

"You changing?"

"I may."

"Why?"

"I've seen Tresco."

Archie shook his head again. "Missed your go at staying here." But he pulled his body through the hole and propped up at right angles to Hutch—below his feet, no longer in contact.

Hutch lay still awhile, then asked what he'd always asked his students for their first short essay. "What's the absolutely first thing you remember in your life?" The students often took several days to decide.

Archie knew at once. "Being in my mother's belly."

"Was it nice?"

"Not half."

"What part was best?"

Archie said, "I liked the way the light looked in there."

"How was that?"

That slowed him and he faced Hutch frankly for the first time since Hutch refused. Then he said, "Do you know what torches are in America?"

"Sticks of wood on fire."

"No, electric with batteries."

Hutch nodded.

"And you press it to your fingers at night, see blood and bones?"

Hutch nodded.

"That was it. Sun shined through my mother and me all day. I could see all her bones."

"And your own?"

"Don't remember. I was looking at her."

"At night?" Hutch said. "It was dark; you were sleeping."

"No I slept afternoons. Nights I touched my dad."

"How was that?"

"In bed. We would lie on our sides. He would press up to Mam. I would feel through her skin; I could feel him all night, till he turned away."

Hutch said, "My mother died the day I was born."

Archie took the connection. "You miss her?"

"Not really. I never had memories as good as yours. I used to dream about her but now I've stopped."

Archie pressed the sole of his shoe to Hutch's ankle.

Hutch said "Miss your father?"

"Most days. Today."

"It'll slowly get better."

"No it won't," Archie said.

They paused on that. Hutch thought it was time for Lew to appear and change the air. He covered his eyes with an arm as a screen.

But Archie said, "There's one I never have missed."

"Who?"

"My sister."

"Where's she?"

"Drowned with Dad."

"Same time?" Hutch said.

"Together." Archie waited; then reached behind and above, seized the boat's rim, hauled himself up, and faced the water. Through the long silence he rapidly aged, revealing the face he would earn years from now—a steady witness of what the world gives, declining to smile. Then he pointed precisely and held the point till Hutch rose to see—blank beach, presumably marked for Archie. "I watched it from there."

Hutch said, "The man just told us about your father."

"He's daft," Archie said. "He hates my mother."

"Why?" (meaning *why hate?*).

Archie said, "Don't know. She stood in the boat, slapped her ear, and fell over. Dad jumped right behind her. They may have come up, but I never saw them. Clear day too like this."

"Was she older than you?"

"She was six, really small but always loud. Never made a sound though the time she fell. Dad neither."

"What was her name?"

"Win."

"What happened?"

"I told you."

Hutch said, "Want to ask me your question again?"

Archie said "Forget that."

When Lew hadn't showed in another silent minute, Hutch checked his watch for the first time since morning—twenty past five. Above them dark gray poured in from the darker west. The Gibbons cottage was still as plain as a model under glass but unreachable from here before the path itself would flood with impassable gray, the air go solid. Hutch said, "Could we walk past the church going home?"

Archie stood, looked down, and nodded. "All right but it's not your home."

The church was nineteenth-century, low and ordinary except for a plaque to the First-War Fallen in the island contingent—

> Lovely and pleasant in their lives,
> And in their death they were not divided.

Archie watched Hutch read it. "Know where that comes from?"

"The stone?"

"The writing."

"From the vicar?" Hutch said.

"The Bible. Guess where."

"Book of Acts?—the disciples?"

"Nothing lovely in Acts," Archie said. "Guess again."

"Nothing lovely in the Bible."

Archie shook his head firmly. "Just this. David's sorry for Saul and Jonathan."

Hutch remembered and agreed. "'The gazelle of Israel is slain on the heights.'" He took Archie's shoulder from behind, tense and bony. "How'd you know?"

"Dad read it every morning at table, one chapter. I hated to hear it."

With no warning creak the logy organ attempted two bars of César Franck. Hutch was game to sit and absorb a basting.

Archie said, "I'm not staying here through music."

Hutch said, "Can I just say one short prayer?"

"I'll wait in the yard."

Hutch stood at the choir steps and asked that his father die soon, no pain. The force of the wish surprised and shocked him. He had no notion of its source or purpose, but he didn't retract it or ask for pardon. When he got to the yard, the boy had vanished—partial punishment in cold wind that rushed his mouth, coarse as dog hair. He strode as if hunted, for the cottage and fire.

37

In the last broad field, well ahead in high grass, three figures stood in a knot, maybe joined. Despite the clouds and wind, it was daylight—would be light three hours—but partly because they were hid to the thighs by a hump of ground, Hutch assumed they were strangers. They stood near the path; there was no way to skirt them, short of striking through low ground that seemed half-marsh. So he told himself it was England not Ireland—Tresco, the navel of the British florist-trade—and went on toward them. He was ten yards away, the rise still between them, when the tallest turned.

It was Lew with Archie and an older boy. They were all in dark heavy sweaters like a team. Lew said "Did he answer?"

"Who?"

"The Lord. Young Archie says you've been on your knees at prayer."

Hutch stopped where he was, six steps away. "I was. No, no answer."

Lew said, "Never mind. Francis here has provided." He took a side step and showed the strange boy.

Fourteen, tall, with cheeks that threatened hemorrhage, Francis cradled something live in the crook of his arm. It jerked once, then fixed on Hutch and watched him closely.

He went to join them.

The boy held what seemed an albino weasel, ivory-haired with pink eyes hard as enamel and hot. Round its thin strong neck was a noose of common twine; the boy held the coiled remainder, many yards. At his feet by the path lay four dead rabbits, all good-sized and still iridescent—dove-gray, streaks of violet, all the browns, white. No sign of a gun.

Hutch said "What happened?"

Archie said, "This is Oliver, Francis's ferret. He runs through the burrows, Francis stands at the other end, rabbits run out, Francis bashes em down."

Lew said, "I told him you'd buy these here for our dinner—lovely stew. I've left my money in the room."

Hutch squatted and probed the hind paw of the biggest—the pads still warm, the claws ice-cold. He worked the leg in its complex socket, fluid as oil. No blood anywhere. Then he stood and said to the boy "You're Francis?"

"Yes."

"How much?"

Archie said "Four bob."

Hutch said "I asked Francis."

Francis said, "Take em all. They're nothing to us."

"You and Oliver?"

Francis said, "He only likes baby chickens. Still a baby himself." He stroked the fine head, fierce and pointed as a bomb.

Hutch said "May I touch him?"

Archie said "He bites."

But Francis said "Yes."

So Hutch took the last two steps, reached out, and stroked the head.

It accepted the touch as a species of food, the skull rising strongly in counterstrokes, the dry nose guessing voraciously at new prey barely seen by the weak eyes. The rough tongue licked Hutch till satisfied.

Francis said "He likes you."

Lew said "They all do."

Hutch bent and took two rabbits by the ears. He said to Archie, "Can Francis eat with us?"

Archie said "No."

Francis nodded agreement.

Lew said "Sorry, mate" and roughed Francis's hair, then tried to touch the ferret.

Oliver drew back and showed his long foreteeth.

Lew saved his hand and for once was silent, but he took up the other pair of rabbits and looked to Hutch.

Hutch said "We're long overdue" and walked on. "Thank you, Francis. Till tomorrow."

Francis watched him go.

Lew fell in behind, Archie well behind Lew.

Through the four hundred steps, wind steadily stronger, Hutch longed to see his father—not the Rob he had left three weeks ago but the grand lost boy who had lain beside him in infancy, seeking in a child (not yet a year old) full answer to questions the size of rock quarries—*Can I stand up from here, work one more day? Will you only smile? Will you never leave?* Hutch wanted to answer Yes to the last and, in that wish, saw nothing beyond him—the big wild garden raked by wind, the deadly sea; the cottage, safe as an iron spike rusting in stone.

38

When they'd finished supper Lew and Archie went into the front room and played card games, each inventing his rules.

Hutch stayed to help Kay wash up, though she protested. As she worked he watched her. After whatever day she'd had, she seemed fully rested and self-possessed as a healthy tree. He might have thought of Ann; there were likenesses. But his mind stayed here, imagining for once the person at hand. How had she weathered the recent loss (one-half of her family) and kept this strength? Or was it some skin over desperation, stretched to tear at one wrong word? Or—given the various stories of the day—was there one final story, truer than all? Had anyone died and, if so, how and why? He started carefully. "Will you be staying here?"

Kay said "I hardly know."

"Any family here?"

"Not really—Bert's father; he met you."

"With the post?"

She nodded but had still not faced him, working intently as if against morning (it was just after nine).

"*Can* you live here?"

"Can we eat, you mean?"

Again he felt caught in idle curiosity and willful benevolence, peculiarly American. "I mean I don't see much heavy industry on Tresco."

Kay smiled. "Not much. There was talk of an anchovy plant but they vanished."

"Who?"

"The anchovies."

Hutch laughed.

"No really, used to catch them by the tubful. We'd have them for tea, mashed in good sweet butter. And crabs—Bert would kill them with a needle through the eye, couldn't bear to boil them live."

Hutch felt she'd drawn a line, a clean stopping-place; so he said no more and dried two bowls.

Then Kay pushed on. "Who told you about it? Did the Masons know?"

"If they did they didn't say—no, the man this morning and Archie on the beach."

"He's the one who knows."

So Hutch said, "It seemed mysterious to me."

"What?"

"The way they went, in Archie's story at least."

She nodded. "It does. No one else saw it though, just their bodies when they came in." Then she'd finished and walked to the door with her pail. She went to the back wall—hens prancing round her—and slowly poured the water on a thick row of tall flowers, redder in the last light than they'd been all day. Then she came on back, dark falling as she walked.

Hutch had sat at the table.

She shut the door silently, threw the black bolt, and said, "What's not mysterious is one small thing—that we've got to find some way to live like this."

"You and Archie?"

"Who'd join us?" She was maybe twenty-eight, facing fifty more years—clearly made to last.

Hutch said, "Any man in his right mind, I guess."

Kay said, "Well, thanks. No there's no one. This is Tresco."

In the front room Lew and Archie cheated and laughed like any human brothers.

39

When the others turned in at half-past ten, Hutch took Archie's torch and walked back out to the beach and the boat. The wind had blown through, and the sky was clear. As a boy he'd wanted to be an astronomer and searched all the books he could find on the subject, making lists of the private terms of a science which he'd thought more poetic than the poems he'd been offered in school (John McCrae, Longfellow, James Russell Lowell)—*Sidereal Day, Universal Attraction, The Principle of Perturbations, The Equation of Time, The Weight of Light.* Still he remembered whole strings of the terms, when his failures at math had long since ended his hopes of understanding and he'd even forgot the names of stars and their seasonal places. He found the Great Bear though and held on her while he thought "*Filamentous Nebula, Zodiacal Light, Stars of Different Magnitudes, The Rotation of Venus* ('which remains unknown')." They slid him into sleep, and there he invented or maybe uncovered a fact from *Tristan*. At the end, after decades of adhesion and tearing, when Mark stands in blessing over Tristan and Iseult—joined, dead as soused herring—the tragic glow falls not on Mark (who fought after all for his grim share) or on Brangien (who served the successful potion) or even on the internationally-famed spent couple but on Gorvenal, Tristan's empty-handed handyman, unworn as a baby after all his long witness. Hutch watched through Gorvenal's eyes awhile and felt the same sense of abandonment that had blown in on him this afternoon. A single figure—young enough and able—who'd thought he was ready for a life of his own, left suddenly with nothing to show but memory. The fact that Memory was mother to the Muses hadn't sunk deep enough in his mind for dreaming. Or had sunk and been refused as harmful or untrue. He saw himself stand by the glamorous dead till all others left, bearing Iseult above them. Then he took up Tristan, surprisingly light, and walked toward the sea.

He woke, cold and damp, recalling what he'd seen and pressed hard by it. The sky was clearer and closer than before; but its lucid figures gave no relief, barely held his eyes. He sat up stiffly, climbed on his knees through Archie's hole, and went toward the cottage—impelled by the dream, still stronger than any wind he'd felt. The torch struck three grown rabbits as it swung; each froze for his passing, then quickly forgot him and leapt into darkness.

40

The ground floor was silent, and no light was on, so Hutch kept the torch and climbed the steps quickly as old boards allowed (only the downstairs was wired for power). When he opened the bedroom door, a smell of kerosene stopped him on the sill. A lamp by the bed burned low and hot. Lew was on the near side, back turned, surely asleep. The window was shut. Hutch went there first and opened it wide. The lamp fumes streamed out, crossed by clean salt breeze. There still was no moon, but he guessed there was starshine enough to undress by. He went to the flame and blew it out with one breath.

Lew said, "I was hoping you'd leave it be."

"The light?"

"Yes."

"Why?"

"I wanted to see you."

Hutch laughed in a whisper, pulled off the sweater, and began his shirt buttons. "Why?" By then his eyes had opened to the shine again.

Lew rolled to his back and looked straight up, an ancient recumbent. "I really feel bad."

"Rabbit fever?"

Lew said "Please."

Hutch sat on the chair to untie his shoes. "Then what?"

"This trap, whole bloody sad trap." Lew covered his face with the crook of his arm.

Hutch thought he understood. "You're out of it though. You're *Canadian*—just a tourist here." He stood, dropped his trousers, and folded them.

Lew said "—In *your* life."

Hutch drew back the cover and entered his half, stretched flat on his back. In a minute he said, "Want to talk about that?"

Lew said "Why bother?" Then after a while he said, "You've been very nice, very Yank about it all. But notice you brought me to the end of the earth. We won't be slogging round Oxford together."

"You'd be welcome any time."

"As a tripper," Lew said, "—hot winkles and chips."

"The Scillies were your idea. I'd never heard of them."

Lew said "Fair enough." Then he said "Know why?"

Hutch knew now he did. Their outward flights could cross only here, in unwatched solitude. He wanted them to and, in the next minute, that chance of intersection became all he'd wanted—or at least a seam worth gambling on to close the tear through which he felt his whole life wasting. He rolled to his left side, facing Lew, and laid his hand on the cool lean belly.

Lew lay still awhile, then turned toward Hutch till the hand rode his hip. "You sure?" he said.

"I'm sure."

"Since when?"

"Since New York, when I saw you."

"You're a great one for *eyes*."

Hutch said "They're my job."

"How new will it be?"

Hutch said "Fairly new."

Lew laughed. "Fairly, eh? There's only one me."

Hutch said "Lucky sod."

"Me?"

"No, me," Hutch said.

So Lew reached out in one accurate line and took him where he was thoroughly ready.

For more than an hour, they met one another in all the ways two bodies can meet—released from time at the west edge of Europe, suspended sweating over Kay and Archie, generous and gentle, happy and used.

41

June 21, 1955

Dear Min,

You and I have talked plainly in the past, so you won't be surprised if I wade right in without waltzing around. I know Rob had supper with you three weeks ago. I know he enjoyed it; but I asked him last night, and he says he hasn't spoken to you since then. So I have good reason to think you don't know his principal news. No one does till now but me, Sylvie, and Grainger. That has been his wish. I am going to fail him one last time though and tell you now, for reasons I'll explain.

Min, he can't be expected to live many months—lung cancer, widespread. Dr. Simkin did not advise surgery, and Rob has refused any radiation. He's known for a month and kept it to himself till Hutch was gone. Then he told us here, after which it has not been mentioned till last night.

Meanwhile he has had a normal summer, staying out there reading and working his garden, making a visit to Bracey and Richmond, dropping in on me every day or two.

Last evening we had a light supper here—he turned up unexpected; Sylvie had left. At first he seemed unchanged from three days before, and he told me about your funny trip to Mount Airy—you ought to have taken that doll; it would have lightened the poor soul's burden—but when we were finished and he tried to stand, he half-fell back. His legs are failing. He sat there, pale, so I sat too and raised a few questions. He didn't want to answer. I had to remind him that a drawn-out death wasn't his sole affair unless he planned to drive west and vanish and be shipped home from some tourist court in Utah, prepaid and ready. I've assisted at two long deaths—Father and Kennerly—and I know. The dead are as selfish as babies.

He told me then that oddly he has no breathing problems but that his legs are steadily weaker, which is the normal course. One thing he has always been is a splendid walker; you know that. I told him again he should move in here. Grainger has offered to move out there. He's kindly told us both to leave him alone.

I've known him too long to disobey. What he wants to have is these little visits and the part at the end when he strangles beside me. I'll take it. What I've wondered all morning though—and why I'm writing—is, short of calling

Hutch (which he'd kill me if I did, I honestly believe), can I give him anything in the way of ease?

You come to mind there. I know he meant a good deal to you once, and I think you did to him. If it hadn't been for Hutch, I think he'd have asked you to stay close by; and I've always regretted he didn't see a way to give Hutch his due and still have a man's life. Well, he didn't. He has never known but one thing at a time; that's the Mayfield in him (not that any Kendals known to me were flibbertygibbets).

So what I'm coming to is, you could ease him. Min, I don't know what has passed between you lately. I don't know much about your own life in Raleigh; but something has told me that if you could turn up and say you'd come for a visit, it would do more for him than all but Hutch could. You know I'm not asking out of any wish to shirk my own clear duties—as I've said, the day will come for those—or out of a wish to burden or hurt you (I know you'd be hurt worse by stumbling on the truth when he's gone past seeing). I simply say what I believe to be true. Rob would welcome you now as never before. If you can bear that, and have any time, come and do what you can.

No one knows I've written this. No one ever will—from me. If you choose not to answer for any earthly reason, you'll never hear a sign of reproach from me. I think I can gauge what I've asked, a solid question. Life offers very few, I seem to have noticed (despite what all the easy groaners contend).

Ever yours affectionately,
Eva Kendal Mayfield

June 21

Hutch, you'll notice I haven't touched this for four days. We had a short set of perfect weather, clear as outer space, steady 80° with perpetual breezes. The birds nearly died of singing, and the leaves are posing for that one great long-awaited Southern landscape painter you used to want to be. Did you ever figure why he's never existed? Has it been too hot to work outside? too humid for the paint to dry? too many bugs landing? Why did you switch to poems? Write me one that explains; I'll probably see it. I say that with something like semi-confidence after this weather. I didn't do much but sit on the steps and feel it and take a few walks back into the woods and try to clear the Kendal graves before the new growth overwhelmed my powers—the legs are still unreliable—but it did give me something I hadn't had for a good many years. That is, a certainty that I matter and don't matter at the same time. I seem to have needed that and hope nothing takes it from me now. I think I can do two things at once—say what I mean about how I feel and tell you the next best day of my life, seventeen to thirty-four. Since it also involved sex, I wonder if I ought to *say in advance that your father has not been hipped on the subject. But that would be a lie. The truth is, I doubt I have lived through a single hour since, say, age eleven without either wanting to use my body for that brand of comfort or regretting I'd done so or playing back some favorite mental home-movie. Same goes for everybody I ever knew with normal good sense, some women excepted. So here is the day. Sorry but you're not in it.*

I left home in March 1925, twenty-one years old—on my birthday, in fact, to hurt Mother's feelings or see if I could. Niles Fitzhugh and I rattled round a week or so in my old Chevy, taking in a few views. You know I have never been much on sightseeing if the sights involve dead folks, which Virginia mostly does. What I mainly remember is Traveller's skeleton at Washington and Lee. Every square inch of bone had some damned piss-ant student's name on it; they signed him for luck. There was General Lee laid out in white marble like Jesus in heaven, battle-flags in a ring and all his dead children (Jesus was what they intended anyhow; I thought he looked more like a dry-goods jobber dead of gastric ulcers and carved in tallow); and down in the basement were the beautiful bones of the noble dumb horse used for self-advertisement by rich adolescents. You know I think the Civil War is the sorriest occasion in history to remember, and I thought those bones put the tin lid on it. So when we left there, I was ready for something live as I could find.

We asked an old Negro to aim us at some girls. He said "White or colored?" We said "Either one." He said, "Tell me they got some in Buena Vista at the Roller's Retreat, but I ain't touched that stuff for twenty years." I asked him why and he said, "My ears. My ears break out every time I get it and itch for a month, so I give it up. My ears doing fine." We drove right on to Buena Vista. The vista then was better than now, though still no peril to sanity. It was Friday evening and the streets were strung with identical rat-faced mountaineers—all each other's half-brothers at least and ready to kill anybody not kin—but we found our own slow way to the Retreat. It was right up near the Ladies' Seminary, young girls patroling in long white dresses and gloves under oak trees. Niles begged to stop there. I told him we'd be lynched. He said "So be it," but I dragged him on.

Roller's Retreat—still wonder what it means—was a decent old house with a Room and Board *sign. You could get a big meal for twenty-five cents, mostly biscuits and gravy with white-girl waiters. When she saw you'd finished, the girl would say, "You're welcome to use our upstairs to rest." And up you went—if you were me. Nothing fancy upstairs, just a wide front-room with sofas and tables and a world of magazines. The first time we went, we were there alone; so we sat down and read. I had finished two issues of* The Literary Digest *before anybody else showed a face.*

Then a woman stepped in, maybe sixty years old and clearly sister to the men on the street. She looked so rough that Niles stood up and said we'd been told we could rest up here. She waited what seemed like a week in December, then said "No you can't." Niles started begging pardon but I stayed still; I was that intent. I said, "Can we spend any more money then?" She said "On what?" — "What you selling?" I said. Plain as any salesman for lightning rods, she said, "Safe liquor, clean pussy. Say which." I said "Both, for me." Niles sat down and nodded. You had to drink first, by yourself in the parlor; girls not allowed to drink or watch you drink. In fact you were not allowed to watch the girls. When we'd had two big snorts, the woman came in again and said "Now follow me." We went down a long hall. She opened one door on dark thick as walnut and waved Niles in; he looked back at me like the Children's Crusade in the hands of pirates but he went ahead. Then she led me right to the end and stopped. She searched me again with her eyes like picks and said, "I'm throwing you a real challenge, son." Thank God I didn't have Niles there to see me. She opened the door. There was dim lamplight and I stepped to my fate. It was not my first time. I started on a cousin of Sylvie's named Flora when I was seventeen and, after that, found several girls in the county. There was one made me take her in her pa's tobacco barn, and the barn was fired. I mean they were killing tobacco in there, late August to boot. I thought I was dying but saw it through, proved at least my heart was good for the race; and so it's been—never missed a beat. I'd never thought of screwing as a challenge though, more like sliding off the slip- periest log on earth into warm clear water that bore me up. At first it seemed the room was empty. Even with the lamp I couldn't see a soul. So I stood very still while my eyes adjusted, thinking every second some six-foot female ape from the hills would fall in on me from the ceiling, all arms. Finally I saw there was this little tuck in the room, a little alcove; I took a step toward it. There by a window was a tall woman in a long blue bathrobe with her back to me. I cleared my throat; she never moved. I said "Good evening." She held still awhile, then half- turned around. She was holding a thick book, open in her hands. There was just a trace of daylight, not enough for me to read. I said, "You must be some kind of cat." She said, "No I'm a very big reader. Let me finish this please. Make your- self at home." I took that to mean Get naked so I did; and she stood there in all but deep night and read four pages of her book, then shut it.

By then I was bare as a willow wand, standing on a throw rug, shivering slightly—mountain air. When she turned I said "Was it good?" She nodded— "Always is. I've read it a lot." I said "What was it?" She said, " 'The Gift of the Magi'—O. Henry." I told her I'd read it, and she set me a test—"Then what's it about?" I said as best I recalled it was about how most gifts people give are unusable but should be given still. She said "That's it" and took her first step, *toward the lamp by the bed. I saw for the first time how old she was—maybe forty-five, not ruined or repulsive but thoroughly seasoned. A big head of brown hair and powerful eyes.*

Then she took off her robe and laid it on the chair. A strong country body as old as her face but very dignified; she didn't touch herself. She held out her hand for me to stay put. Then she studied me slowly, not smiling or frowning. She said to my eyes, "You starting here?" *I had to say* "Ma'm?" *She said, "You starting your love life tonight?" In those days I looked about seventeen. A truthful answer would have been "No ma'm. I've had four girls twelve times, maybe eleven" (I'd tried to keep count). But I grinned and said "Starting." She said, "In that case can I just take over?" I said, "Fine by me. I like everything I ever came across except liver with onions and any kind of pain." She still didn't smile but she said, "Nothing I did ever caused pain." I said "Congratulations." She said "Many thanks."*

I don't know that you'll want a detailed account of the rest of the night— might muddy your memories of dear old Dad—but I want to write it for my own sake now. If it doesn't serve you, there's fire in the world; just burn it up.

She didn't say another word till six a.m., and to this day I don't know her name. She stepped over to me, took me by the elbow, and laid me on the bed. It was clean and turned-down. She stretched out beside me, both flat of our backs. In a minute I tried to roll left toward her. She stopped me with her hand. So we lay still the best part of maybe five minutes. I think I took a nap. Anyhow I was brought to by her rising slowly and parting my legs. She took it from there as she'd asked to do, and I lay and watched. I don't mean to say I only watched. There were two of me present—the one that could see and barely believe, the one that was served in ways he'd only half-dreamed existed.

I said she was dignified; she stayed so right through. She worked at me slowly with hands, mouth, and eyes—she never shut her eyes; most women work blind or did in my day. I'd been used to leading and to leading fast. But she gave me pleasure that was so deep and steady I had time to find what the cause of it was. She was worshiping me. I'd never asked for that from anyone alive (though Rena volunteered it in a different way and I mostly refused). The one that was watching could lie there propped on two goose pillows and see a grown woman honor my one body as if it was all and would always suffice, using nothing but clean-smelling spit as her ointment. I'd tried to worship Mother for twenty-one years; now I saw this was better if it only would last.

It lasted till morning as I already said. The strong part ended in maybe an hour when she straddled me finally and took me in and, slow as before, rode us both to a rest like sleep after good work. I slept at least, not thinking of Niles or home or safety or of how much time two dollars had bought. At dawn she was there beside me, looking calm; so I guess she had stayed. She said, "Son, you're started. Better get you some eggs." That woke me.

I washed and found Niles downstairs, eating eggs. He'd slept on the sofa in the magazine room. I was started all right. I just never finished. That was the challenge. What she hadn't told or shown me was a way to finish, to feed once for all the taste she'd planted—or found; it was there.

Why does that last in my mind then as happy? Because of the worship surely. Looking back I can see I was lovable, and right from the first—a genial baby (once I'd lasted through whooping cough), a thoughtful boy. By the time I washed up at Roller's Retreat, I was something rare as an albino stag with purple rack—a tall healthy man with handsome face, clean wavy hair, strong arms and hands, and a straight round dick with a low brown mole near the end of the shank. I didn't know that or didn't believe it. Nobody but mirrors had told me so, nobody I trusted. I was fool enough not to trust Rena and Min. But I trusted that woman in Buena Vista. I knew she had ample range to compare (college boys came to her, not just mountaineers); but mainly I leaned on the way she had stood there and studied that story to the end once more, then asked me the meaning.

Could I use her gift? Well, could and did. In a month I'd met your mother and believed her. In nine I'd married her and set you in motion. You didn't arrive of course for nearly five years, but you were the main result of the night I've set down above—that your father was licensed to live a whole life, having earned the right.

Have I had it? Let me know.

June 24, 1955

Dear Rob,

I've stood it as long as I want to. June, I mean. Long years out of school, I still think June is when you crawl home, get your clothes clean, sleep late, and stock up on bedrock boredom to see you through the thrilling future. And business conspires—I need to come search through some courthouse records for a swarthy woman from Lansing, Michigan who's praying she's white.

Will you be at all visible, say the midst of next week? I wouldn't be averse to driving up Wednesday morning, doing my work, and seeing you afterward with suitable chaperone—is Grainger there? If not don't call him on my account. The damage is done.

But if you get this tomorrow, please phone sometime this weekend and say. I'll do the work anyway, but it would seem wasteful at our age not to glimpse each other. Especially since glimpses have been our specialty since before man invented the wheel or steam.

Very truly,
Min

June 25, 1955

Dear Min,

Your letter came an hour ago. If I sit down right now, you'll have an answer on Monday—and an original manuscript by Robinson Mayfield, one of the few—and I won't have had to resort to the phone, which I hate worse by the day. At least in letters you could tell people the truth or what you thought was true without the imminent possibility of them bursting into sobs or apoplexy in your hearing. The phone breeds lies.

So here—it's no lie when I say I feel two ways about a meeting next week. Since Hutch left and you gave me that good supper, I've been by myself so much that I'm suspected by Mother and Grainger of taking the veil. They may be right. If so it's because I'm surprised to like it after years of thinking it was man's great curse—loneliness, I mean, or being alone. On the other hand the long days of quiet have given me space to remember a lot (I've been writing down past things that Hutch may need); and what I remember is company, the good and bad. Mostly the good.

You were obviously good. I haven't forgotten our mistake in Richmond. To have cheated on Rachel that once with you is still the main regret in a life which has several real ones. She never guessed at all though, and who did it harm but you and me and the feelings of whatever supernatural traffic happened to fly through the close air of that room that afternoon? The supernaturals are in business to forgive, right?, so they're doing fine. We let it do us in from then on. Or was it just me who loved the load?

Sure, come up Wednesday. I'll wait for you here in the late afternoon with whatever Baptist deacons I can muster as vice patrol.

Your oldest friend above ground (is that correct?),
Rob

June 25, 1955

Dear Hutch,

Your cards from Wales and Cornwall arrived. You sound a little mildewed. Is the weather that depressing or is it your single state? I haven't gone far but solitary travel in a wet land of strangers seems to me a hard way to win Wisdom and Virtue.

There're no easy ways, I at once recall. For instance I have my first roommate *since leaving school, and let me record that the cave of companionship is still as risky as the red sands of hermitage. At least when the two sport the same brand of plumbing or need the same plumbing. I've hardly had one chance to pee at home since Linda Tripp moved in. Have I mentioned her? She was hired at the office two weeks ago and needed a room. She's from up in the mountains—Agricola, Virginia—and at first I thought she was our age or younger. Turns out she is twenty-nine at least, had withered on the vine at a lawyer's office in Lynchburg, and only broke loose to follow her first boyfriend to Richmond—a tall thin lineman for the power company. She met him in Lynchburg; one stroke of the wand and she was set free. Withered in fact is not the word. She is perfectly preserved in rural childhood or was till last week. The peeing is caused by the lineman, it seems—a clear case of honeymoon bladder or is it Virgin's Complaint (Recent-Virgin's Complaint)? But whenever she's visible she's company at least. Much as I've tried to enjoy heroic oneness, I find that I after all prefer to bump fannies with some other creature in the kitchen or hall if nowhere else. And the creature has to be human, no dogs or hamsters—even when her tales of backseat passion recall my own lamented past (I lament that it's past, I mean, or suspended).*

Are you happy as you are, or can you say yet? I'm not but you know that. What neither one of us knows, I guess, is how much you're involved in what I feel and how much of it is just me—the barometric pressure, my bloodsugar level, my whole normal (normally gloomy) past.

In brief then—do I sound enough like a legal secretary?—that's another attempt to say how, much as I want to, I'm not holding you responsible for anything. Whether you chose me or not, I chose you and could learn to withdraw whenever I'm given the back-out flag.

Later — Linda interrupted me there with the lineman. I'd seen him through the window but never met him; he'd told her he thought he'd better look me over. So I sat them down with potato chips and we talked. Well, Linda and I talked. He (his name is Bailey) didn't say three words for the first half-hour but ate every last chip and studied me close enough to see if I was also consumable once the snacks were gone. He has black eyes and I'll have to say I liked it. I was giggling like a girl at her first slumber-party when he finally broke in and, apropos of nothing I could understand, told me the one big story of his life. He was electrocuted last winter, the bad sleet-storm in February. Had to go out with one other man at four in the morning to patch wires broken by ice and trees. The other man was new and stayed on the ground to manage the searchlight. The man dozed off or couldn't aim the light. Bailey by then was icy himself and reached out dark, brushed a bare hot wire, and took (he swears) two thousand pure volts. He fell thirty feet to the ground; the wire lashed him. The other man took his time with rescue. At that point he suddenly pulled up his shirt—in the story, I mean (at that point in the story)—and proved it all. He's as brown and lean as a broad leather belt; but from neck to navel, and points south apparently, he has a white burn-scar straight as a die. Said it fried to the bone. I admired it sufficiently. He said it had taught him all he needed to know. I said, "Not to trust anybody on the ground?" He said, "No ma'm—that from now on I'm free." I asked how was that. He said, "I've died, paid for all my sins, and am now in Heaven." I said, "For an angel, you sure love potato chips"; but he still hasn't smiled. If he's dead though what does that make Linda? What does that make me? And why do I only meet men in love with freedom? I may investigate.

Still later—I've just read the first part of this. Don't it sound noble? Do you think I'll be played by Joan Crawford or Joan Fontaine in the movie of your life? What I'd really prefer is Martha Raye, though her mouth's too small. Let me know your choice in a long letter soon.

Love,
Ann

P.S. I forgot to give you the outcome on Mrs. Quarles, the lady who stabbed her husband fourteen times and bandaged each hole. We got her off, I want you to know. She's walking the streets of Richmond right now, free as you or Bailey. Be sure to contact us in event of your arrest—no crime too awful. Phone collect to Ann Gatlin. She's the mastermind, disguised as secretary.

July 6, 1955

Dear Hutch,

I've already fallen behind, haven't I? Your second letter got here yesterday in the wake of the Fourth (I stayed in at my window all day and watched nearly nonstop parades of Negro Elks and Saints—if they were mad about Virginia White Folks' reaction to the civil-rights challenge, they gave no sign beyond smiles and strong teeth; but oh if they do, there'll be cut throats and burnings). Since it contained the first of those questions you threatened to ask, and I seem to have volunteered for, I feel I must gird up posthaste and answer.

One warning before I do, though I'm sure you know it already—I am not an ideal advisor on matters of the heart, not on the heart-in-the-world at least. What I know (and I do know some things) is spectator's knowledge, acquired from years of fairly steady watching in which I have tried to keep my eyes clean. I may well have failed. I may have seen things the players didn't notice or at least didn't feel or that weren't even there. I may well just be the Dixie Miss Dickinson—but wouldn't you rather ask your questions of Emily than of, say, Hawthorne or Emerson with their wives and babes? Apparently you would.

And in any case I wasn't quite accurate above. I have, as you know, played a few games myself; and if the innings were short or unfinished or finished by the other players drifting away, they certainly went flat-out while they lasted, giving me much cud for lonely rumination (Lord, the scenes my metaphors summon!—a cow at bat: even Disney would quail).

So now to reply. The answer is Yes. Immediate love—"at first sight," I assume you mean—is not only possible, it's the only kind I've known; only kind likely to last as love (slower kinds warm gently, cool back gently into friendship or fairly oblivious matehood). The Bible, all the good poetry—and most of the bad—says nothing but that. What it doesn't often say is the next thing to know and as urgent as the first—find out why the first sight stormed your gates. I don't mean that real love is not mysterious; it is but at the edges not the center. False love—infatuation, the immediate need to rub and be rubbed— is what always comes as high and inscrutable with a clamor of wings. The genuine event however will clarify if you just watch it long enough. And when it does the mystery will mostly turn out to be a name. You've loved the person who either is there for present grasping or the person they promise to be, the one you've perpetually needed. When I was sixteen I loved Marion Thomas because I've always taken beauty pretty seriously and wanted to serve it. Later I loved your mother because, being a healthy woman, I saw I wanted a daughter; and she was ready to be that awhile. Nothing wrong with either case from my side— not that I can make out and, believe me, I've tried. Problem came when Marion and Rachel decided they didn't want to be what they were (not that Marion ever knew).

But aren't you too old to be asking that? Isn't that something most people get settled in the sixth or seventh grade? I seem to remember discussing it with Rachel once; then I took the other side and was wrong. Never mind—I'm right now and there's your answer, however insane. Do you want to say why you tested me with it?—literary curiosity or present concern? Anybody as interested in tales of King Arthur as you seem to be will need clear views on all such questions, no doubt. Glad to help.

Did you cut your trip short? In your first you said you'd tour for six weeks. I was stretched out waiting for a soft rain of postcards from Land's End to Orkney, and here you're back in Oxford. You've sat still before, Hutch. Don't stop and think too soon. Both your parents were lightning leapers-to-conclusions (not merely in love); maybe you should be slower. Let a lot happen first. Don't take quick answers, even mine—least of all!

—Which doesn't mean I won't be eager to see the first installments of your Tristan poem. Like you I've always suspected the servants had the true news on all that unpleasantness; why weren't they interviewed? If I had good sense,

I'd write Brangien's version while you write Gorvenal's. Since I don't I'll await revelation from you.

Lord knows, there's very little here to report. As I said, colored people are keeping present silence in the teeth of Virginia's jackass display of "massive resistance" to school integration. Have you ever wondered—as I do hourly—at what precise moment the state that mainly invented America (on paper anyway) was struck deaf, dumb, blind, and halt as an old dog sprawled in the manager and gnawing at itself? You picked a good time to seek fresh air. I for one hope you find it. Breathe slow deep breaths and keep me posted.

Barely breathing (it's hot) but still your loving,
Alice

July 12, 1955

Dear Mr. Mayfield,

I didn't hear from you before I left home, and there was nothing at American Express when I went there yesterday except a wire from the doctor's wife I told you about. I figure she'll live but she seems to doubt it. Anyhow I'm in London, sleeping at a Polish hotel in Bayswater—cabbage for breakfast—and checking out a few famous ruins with my brother. I thought England won the war, but they don't seem to know it. Can't somebody get them to clean up the place and turn the sun on? Is money all they need? Don't they still own most of Africa and Asia?

I told you my brother is going to Paris, a week from today. I can't get up any enthusiasm for France, not after our trek through Madame Bovary. *So I'm still wondering if you want to join forces for a while. You mentioned Cornwall. Sounds good to me. Only limits on me are ten dollars a day, and I'm finding it hard to spend more than $7.50 plus tax. By the time I see you, I could be rich and we could fly to Pompeii. I always wanted to see that whorehouse they dug up with the peculiar murals.*

Say the word c/o American Express, and I'll meet you anywhere.
Strawson

P.S. Speaking of Africa, which I was in the first paragraph, you might not want to wait till you see me to hear that Waverly Conover from home (you remember, the organ salesman with the withered hand) is starting a fund to export black volunteers back to the Dark Continent. When I left he claimed to have eight hundred dollars and is planning to go nationwide with his plea if Life *magazine will contribute advertising with mail-in coupons. Do you think*

we should warn the English on this or let them be surprised by big boatloads?
It might wake them up. German rockets didn't seem to.

July 14, 1955

Dear Hutch,

Relieved to know you're safely back from the Cornish excursion. My reading assures me Britain has an unnaturally low crime-rate (more murders in
Houston in a month than in Britain all year, Ireland included); so I don't worry
much about your meeting with human violence, but there're always the famous
Acts of God, and I continue to suspect that motor vehicles are not really
understood outside the American three-mile limit and are therefore even more
perilous than here. You can probably use the rest time anyhow. If eleven years
of teaching taught me anything, it's that teaching is roughly as exhausting as
coal mining or perfect attendance at all Southern Baptist conventions of the
past thirty years. Second worst is being a pupil—you've got this pause between
the two; sleep a lot.

I'm still worrying, you see. I was hoping, and I suspect you were, that once
you vanished I'd get some peace—not yet. I still think the world is dangerous
and has a special tendency to try my loved ones. I've even had evidence, you
might say. It's one of the two things that kept me from being the model father
I intended. The other was your mother's vanishing when she did. I'd planned
to be one parent not two. When and if you have a son or children, I hope you
will have the strength—and mercy—to consign them to the world once they
can walk and defend themselves against human threats (by which I mean an
unarmed human of similar size; anything worse is probably Fate). Don't teach
fear as I did to you. No use in it. They won't escape.

But I started this to answer the question about your Welsh friend. I'd like
to help him but see no way. As I understand immigration law, I would have
to provide guaranteed employment and boat-fare home if he's dissatisfied. You
remember the Pole Mrs. Picot took right after the war. He came here elegant
as Lord Halifax, had the place looking like Versailles in a month; then took
up with that trash Pulliam girl, gave her fat blond twins when the Pulliams
hadn't made a blond since Cain set them rolling and vanished north by night,
leaving three empty mouths Mrs. Picot still feeds. Vanished seems to be my big
word this evening, doesn't it? Still as I said, I'd help if I could; but from what
you tell me of his past experience and needs, he doesn't seem custom-built for
these parts. I doubt he'd be happy, and I know for certain that it's past my power
to help him. In any case I gave up—long years back—the attempt to help people by changing their direction. I only caused wrecks except with you, and you

always knew where you were headed and only needed to have your windshield buffed occasionally. Proud to have had my chamois rag handy.

One local thing has changed, and I want to tell you before anybody else. Min Tharrington drove up here to search some courthouse records two weeks ago, ate supper, and has been with me ever since. She can do her genealogies here as well as anywhere with quick trips to Raleigh, and I asked her to stay. The reason is I wanted to and so did she. We figured we were big enough to act on that basis. She has no kin to be startled by the fact, and I hope I don't. You'll have guessed Mother likes it, though she has invented a tale or two as the visit lengthens to explain to friends. My favorite is the one that says Rob has hired Min to track down the Mayfield family for Hutch. Come to think of it, that may be an idea. Shall I set her on the trail? God knows where it ends—in an English jail maybe, some ditch-born baby—but you might like to know, long hence if not now.

Further things you might like to know at once—I'm aware you and I have not discussed Min for ten years at least and that, when we did, you were strongly opposed. I understood why and honored your reasons the best I could while you were nearby. Now you've gone your way, I will go back to mine—or forward to mine. You were my way for years as I trust you recall. So view this rightly wher-ever it leads. It may not last long. What I want is not your blessing but your patience. You're old enough for patience. I'll keep you informed on all you need to know.

What else? Weather's hot but dry as Sahara. Grainger drives out every day and helps Min cook (she is no great chef). Your grandmother, as I implied, is fine. I have to visit her though; she won't come here. I asked her why yesterday. She just smiled and said, "I don't want to be there when Sheriff Wilkes pulls up and hauls you two off in chains for fornication." She's studied the statutes and may well be worried. I'm not. I went to school with Delbert Wilkes and have cause, ten times over and he knows it, to slap a citizen's arrest on him and make it stick.

Keep me in your prayers then but hire no lawyers.

The same loving,
Rob

July 16, 1955

Dear Ann,

My silence is mainly owing to work. I got back here three weeks ago and sat right down to start a poem suggested by the trip. West Britain is all King Arthur country; and though most of the sites are spurious, they look and feel right— if they weren't the scenes, they could have been. One of them anyhow stands at least an even chance of being a witness to real events—the fort of King Mark in the country near Fowey may well be the spot where Tristan and Iseult took the great plunge. So I'm working on them, a maybe long poem. Every morning I wake at seven o'clock, eat a big breakfast in the college Hall (served by friendly dwarfs—grown men who have served teen-agers all their lives, with faces like the archers at Agincourt), then come to my desk and write till noon. Then I walk round town for a couple of hours—the book and junk shops are amazing; today I only just prevented myself from buying a mothy tigerskin complete with snarling teeth and a wastebasket made from an elephant's foot. Then I buy cheese and bread, eat lunch in my rooms, take a nap, read, take a walk in Christ Church Meadow which is right outside my window. In the evening I eat curry at one of the many Indian restaurants (one was closed last week for serving cat) and, if it's fair, drive awhile. You can be in the country in fifteen minutes, any direction you head from here. I mostly go to the north or northwest—almost no one in sight, nobody to mind if you stop by the road and step through a field toward what they call rivers (peaceful creeks) or the few stones left of an abbey or an Iron Age family camp. The light lasts well past nine o'clock. I moon some, then drive on back here to sleep. Sometimes I say whole phrases out loud just to hear a voice, to see if mine works. I've had few chances to talk to anybody.

It seems to suit me so far at least—being on my own like this, a trusted stranger—so I'll follow where it leads. Our first night in New York, I tried to answer your questions honestly. I think I need this now. I may not always. You ask it again and the answer hasn't changed. I don't say it harshly, and my hope to see you at Christmas in Rome is strong as ever. You didn't mention that. Do you still plan to come? If so let's set a date—December 24th. I'll be free till at least January 10th. How much time can you get? Let me know right away, and I'll get us a room. Or do you want two rooms? Since your passport will plainly say Gatlin, we may need two. Do Italians care? I'll ask round and see. I've got the ring. Would you wear it there?

Otherwise—glad to hear you've got Linda and Bailey nearby. He especially sounds like "good value for money," as they say here; so keep him in potato chips. All the evidence on his love life seems to suggest he could use the carbohydrates. When I read about your evening with them, I wished I'd been there. The English have taken me at my word, pretty literally in Oxford at least, and left me alone. I could use a little evening company, but for now I'll hold out and try to wean myself—the trouble being that I want company but only when I want it. I still feel overstocked on being wanted. Part of my plan here is emptying the warehouse, using up the surplus. What's left, if anything, at the end of the clearance is scarey to consider—will anyone want such an empty warehouse? But I've always liked a little scare in my days; stops me sleeping too much, and you know I nap a lot.

Speaking of sleep, in a letter last month you mentioned our first trip to Myrtle Beach—me saying "Wait here" when I seemed asleep and you still waiting. I was asleep and don't recall speaking (aloud at least), but I don't doubt your word. So I wrote this for you by way of thanks. Please keep it if it suits.

No sleeping man is safe. Each volunteers
With baby-calm for any watcher's need.
Most any household implement at hand
Will send him deeper down than he'll have sunk.
Bread-knife, ice-pick, your useless cheap corkscrew
Briefly applied to temple, throat, thigh, groin
Will call his bluff successfully as bombs.
He trusts you won't—trusts kindliness, indifference;
Knows sleeping murder's mainly kept for kings,
Geriatric guests of the Macbeths.

A realer threat bears mentioning however.
The proffered victim may well victimize,
Although unconsciously—spare the dreamer,
Spare the dreamer's dream. This boy for instance—
Age nineteen, no eyesore—sprawls on hotel
Sheets in ocean dawn. Words wake you
(You are curled against his back). You hope
For more, then think you hear "Wait here." You do.
He says the two words clearly, meaning both.
You know he sleeps but take the words one way—

Your way. The other one to know was his.
If you had worked beneath the chilled tan rind,
Ascended knob by knob the fragile spine,
Lain silent in the white dough of his brain,
You would have seen—an orphan, six years old,
Threads underbrush till, standing by a creek,
He sights a girl, tall on the far green bank,
A little older, lovely, turning, leaving.
He knows her in one look and calls "Wait here"—
The girl who bled to death in bearing him.
He wakes and finds you there, prepared to stay,
And joins you long as he can stand your eyes.
Forgive him then for his own distant wait

> *On his green bank, inevitable hunt—*
> *The chance you take, obeying half a dream.*

    It's now nine-ten. The college gates are locked, and I'm pretty well the only human under forty defended by these twelve-foot walls. There is one low wall, facing the meadow. I'll climb over that, walk a dark quarter-mile toward police headquarters, grab a rickety post wrapped with earnest barbed wire, swing myself out and over a deep stagnant ditch, and be free in the nocturnal world of adults. Sounds glamorous, right? Well, no—just Oxford in the Long Vacation. I'll drink a pint of cider called Merrydown in a pub called The Eagle and Child, then reverse my escape route and sleep a long night in my own straw bed (my mattress is actually stuffed with straw; how's that for Olde Worlde?). So your own life there with Linda and Bailey—the Living Dead—and the liberated murderess is thrilling next to mine.

    But I've had thrills a-plenty for twenty-five years. Now I need to sit and watch them, years and thrills.

Love again from,
Hutch

42

When he'd swung himself free of the last barbed wire round Christ Church Meadow, he walked up a thoroughly deserted St. Aldate's past Tom Tower, Pembroke, and the small huddled church where Lawrence of Arabia had taught Sunday school. He stopped in the light by the main post office and carefully checked the letter to Ann, address and postage. Then he made a quick sign of the cross on its face as he always did on important mail; then dropped it in the slot and wished he could fish it back, read it once more to dull harsh edges, blur promises. No chance of course short of dynamite. So he walked up the low hill and crossed Carfax, also curiously empty for Saturday night—were the airmen on maneuvers or sent home at last? Even at the doors of the public dance-hall (opposite The Crown, Shakespeare's customary stop on the London-Stratford route), there were only three would-be Teddy Boys, none over fifteen, and one frizzed girl. On through the Cornmarket, past Beaumont Street where the whores kept flats, past the dark Ashmolean with its Michelangelos hung in back hallways, through half of St. Giles to the Eagle and Child. By the time he saw its sign, Hutch was low as a toad, tasting the thin diet he'd struggled for—abandonment. *This place would ignore you; needn't bother to ask.* He stopped in place and thought of hunting down the whore he'd met in White's Bar in June. She was almost surely in her room not a hundred yards from here (she'd mentioned her address and said she stayed in watching telly till ten on weekend nights). Though the evening was mild, his body seemed hung in a cold vacuum-shaft which no human hand would ever invade. He walked back far as the next street light and opened his wallet—six pounds, enough; she'd said she "made adjustments." But he'd lost her name. Charleen? Doreen? He couldn't ask the landlord for a black-haired girl he'd met a month ago. Why not? Any land-lord would know her trade. Still he set it as a test. He'd walk toward the pub till he got the name; if it didn't come a pint of hard cider might find it.

43

But twenty minutes later in the dim warm pub, the presence of a half-dozen talking strangers had eased the search; Hutch sat calmly in a corner, merely listening. The loudest were a pair of men at the bar—one a parody of the old RAF ace (purple cheeks, fierce mustache, emblematic blazer); the other almost certainly American, though he'd got English clothes and an all-but-perfect accent (his joints were the give-away, the oiled loose-limbs of a peo-ple used to space and reared with Negroes). The ace was challenging the camouflaged Yank to explain how racial integration would not in fact bring America down as it clearly had Rome, Gaul, the whole of Asia (the ace had served in Burma and Malaya). The answer involved rich cultural infusions from the Bantu, Kikuyu, Nubian, etc.—jazz, tap dancing, jokes, sexual san-ity—and as it proceeded, unearthed a complete set of Ohio vowels in the helpless mouth.

Hutch had heard the conversation before from better antagonists. With the last of his cider, the name came finally—Marleen, Marleen Pickens—so he shut his eyes awhile to find her face and body: would she really help at all or would it amount to expensive chatter with a quick hot clot flung out at the end? First he saw Lew Davis in the pasture on Tresco, the ferret refus-ing to take Lew's touch; then Ann in the dark Taft below his own fingers; then Marleen Pickens. He'd only seen her dressed, but she came bare easily and stood clear before him. Like almost every English war-child, she seemed to have two separate bodies. The healthy body she would have got, with suffi-cient fruit and milk in the years of the Blitz, enveloped her actual body like an aura. The actual body was still a little starved, the skin a little taut. Between her nice high breasts with coral nipples, an ugly sternum pressed forward like a face. Above the good calves her knees had knobbed, and webs of purple strung along her thighs and flanks. But a banked unquestionable strength burned in her; she'd warmed herself. She'd help at least.

Hutch had stiffened through that. He smiled to himself. When he'd shrunk enough to stand, he'd go to Marleen. He opened his eyes to quicken the cooling and saw two people at the moment they entered—a girl maybe six or seven, a man maybe twenty. Hutch thought at once that children were not allowed in pubs and awaited an expulsion, but no one behind the bar seemed to mind. And with no discussion the two parted neatly—the man approached the bar; the child approached Hutch, not meeting his eyes, and sat a table away on his right. At once she began to draw small circles on the green linoleum of the table-top, her profile as bent on perfection as Apollo's. She wore a red pullover, nubby at the elbows, with a cross-eyed owl stamped on the front. Hutch said, "Can your owl see to fly with crossed eyes?"

She continued her circles, not looking up. "He never leaves me."

"Why not?"

"I never let him."

"Too young?" Hutch said.

She laid her head on the table, facing him, but didn't answer. She shut her eyes briefly, then looked again straight at him, still silent. At the bar the man was paying for his drinks.

Hutch said "Is he your father?"

She nodded once.

"He's got you out late. Are *you* an owl?"

By then the man was walking carefully toward them with a pint of dark beer and an orange squash. Standing short of the child, he said, "Hop to. We've got hours yet." Then he put the drinks down and sat on her left between her and Hutch, all on the same long window-bench. For three or four minutes, they drank in deep silence; the child was plainly thirsty. Then the man pushed the glasses back and started drawing circles as the child had done. She watched awhile; then joined him, gestures larger than his—circles intersecting delicately, hands never touching.

A game they'd invented? A local child's game? A first means of speech for creatures struck dumb? (they had still not spoken since the man sat)—Hutch listed the questions but kept his own silence, content now to wait. The child had seemed to say the man was her father; could he be? If so she'd been born when he was fourteen, fifteen. Maybe her brother?—he shared the pure line of her features: small, flawless, yet promising somehow to ripen and exceed. Her hair though was light brown, his nearly black. Her skin was ruddy with blood, his pale. Their hands had slowed now, the circles tightened. At last she touched him and both laughed loudly.

"You won!" the man said.

She nodded. "Caught *you*." They returned to their drinks.

Hutch felt them beside him like heaped red coals—a core of energy, harmful but attractive. The man had never looked his way, though their shoulders were only a yard apart. Slowed by a sense that they guarded a secret he'd easily scatter if he did more than watch, he still said, "Could I ask the name of your game?"

The man looked round, slid a little toward the child, then smiled. "Circle-catch. We just made it up." His teeth were the best Hutch had seen since landing—two rows of straight white, rare here as two steady hours of sun.

"She's lovely," Hutch said.

"She's *tired* but she can't sleep yet awhile."

Hutch said "You traveling?"

He thought that over, then turned to the child. "We traveling, Nan?" She nodded, not smiling.

So the man looked back to Hutch and grinned. "Reckon so."

"She your baby sister?"

"I'm her dad."

Hutch said, "You must have been a child-groom then."

"I was," he said quickly; then grinned again. "A child, all right. I was never a groom. I look much older than I am, even now."

Hutch said, "You must be twelve years old."

"Twenty-two," he said. "Been rough just lately."

"How's that?"

He thought again. "How does prison sound?"

Hutch said "Unexpected."

The man laughed. "Me too! The last thing I wanted." He took a long swallow of beer, facing forward and pulling at the sleeves of his jacket—short and worn. His hands were enormous, well-shaped but yellow with callus in the palms.

Hutch thought, "I should leave. He's finished. I'll press him too hard." He raised his own glass and drained the last inch.

But the man said, "It really wasn't all that bad. Played a lot of football."

So Hutch felt permitted. "Where were you?"

"Lewes Prison."

"How long?"

"Eighteen months."

"Then I guess it wasn't murder?"

Nan had listened that far—her head on the table again, eyes open. Now the man, not looking, reached gently to her hair and gathered her in. She came like a sack of down-feathers to his lap, glanced back once at Hutch, then shut her eyes and buried her face. The man stroked her twice; then said, "Not quite—just assault with a dangerous weapon, a bottle. Put the bugger in infirmary for nineteen days, best rest he ever had."

"A friend of yours?"

"—Her mother's," he said. He stroked Nan again; she was sound asleep. Hutch extended his own hand. "I'm Hutchins Mayfield."

The man blushed hard and held back a moment. Then he gave his hand. "James," he said quietly.

In the touch, Hutch remembered Grainger's hand—that smooth and dense, warm worn stone, impermeable. When they parted he said, "Could I ask your work?"

James said, "Mason's helper. Just started that."

"Guess Oxford could offer you plenty of work."

He nodded. "It does. All the colleges are rotten—bloody Headington stone. They're all great sugar cubes melting in rain."

"So you'll stay here awhile?"

James drank the last of his beer, wiped the deep blue cleft of his chin with one finger. "Never been anywhere else but Lewes and Reading."

"Reading Gaol?"

"No, for Nan. Her mother lives there. Or did till last week."

"Where's she now?"

"Search me—well, don't. She's not *here*, is she?"

"You want her to be?"

James quickly said "No," then paused a good while. "You want to hear it out?—it's a sordid lot. I'm hoping to sell it to *News of the World*." He looked up smiling; and as Hutch nodded Yes, James slid out from Nan, stood and took the glasses. "What's your drink?"

"Cider—Merrydown—but let me buy."

James was already moving. "Sit and guard young Nan."

Hutch did. He slipped along the smooth bench till his thighs touched her head. She was now on her back with both hands loosely clenched on her chest. He covered them both with his own right palm. She was cooler than he but warmed in his grip; so he watched her steadily through the wait, calmer than he'd been since when?—Tresco maybe, in the beached boat with Archie or bound to Lew.

James said "You're not Canadian, right?" He stood two steps away with new drinks.

Hutch kept his hand on Nan. "Right—American."

James stayed in place.

"Americans not allowed to drink two pints?" Hutch extended a trembling hand, the comic drunk.

James stepped forward then and set down the mugs. "Most of them shouldn't—the ones I've seen—but you seem safe enough."

Hutch moved to slide back.

But James came round to Nan's feet. "Stay there if you like being there."

"Her hands were cold. I was warming her."

"She's all right," James said. "She's been worse than cold." Then he sat.

So they drank long swallows, Nan between them—now huddled on her side, a short hyphen.

When James had found no way to recommence, Hutch finally said "She seems healthy now."

James ringed her ankle—thin white cotton socks—and studied her. "She looks it, right. So do I; I just saw my own healthy face." He pointed to the distant etched bar-mirror. "We've sort of had it though."

"From what?"

"Her mother."

"That's the sordid part?"

James faced him, grave and searching. "You do want it, don't you?"

Hutch nodded again. "The story at least."

"You aiming to sell it?"

"How?"

"You look like you might be some sort of correspondent."

Hutch laughed. "I'm a poet—apprentice-grade. You can't sell poems, not for money at least."

James waited, then smiled. "I'll give you my address at the end—remind me—and if you make a shilling on any of it, you send her six pence." He was still holding Nan.

Hutch said "A deal" and touched her forehead with one finger, cool from the cider glass. She was warmer now. They both had warmed her.

James said, "It's not much but it's what we were handed. I said we were traveling—to here, I meant. Oxford's my home all my life till prison. I was born in Jericho a quarter-mile from here, and we'll be living there now with my mother. She's serving some whacking great party of dons at New College tonight, so we're waiting for her—won't give me a key till I prove I'm cured of my evil ways!"

"She locks Nan out?"

"She doesn't know Nan's here yet," James said. "I just now took her this afternoon."

"From Reading?"

James nodded. "Her mother's sister's. See, I work with this bloke named Rod. He dances all night. Well, Friday morning—yesterday—he lurched up to me at my first tea and said he'd seen my bird last night. I said, 'My bird is the English robin, sign of spring.' He laughed—'Your Helen. She was down at Carfax dancing last night. I asked was she planning to glimpse your face, and she said she reckoned she'd spare her nerves and was heading to Yorkshire today at dawn.' He also knew about Nan and asked. She said Nan wasn't with her, no, and shut up. So I thought all Friday—buggered up three nice cuts of stone—then thought all night. Then this morning I worked my full half-day, rode my bike home and washed, caught the next train to Reading, went straight to her sister's house, and took Nan."

"The sister didn't stop you?"

"They're scared of me. Anyhow she has asthma and runs from a fight."

Hutch leaned slightly forward—no bags with them: only the clothes on their backs, their circle game. "No question she's yours?"

"Nan?"—James still held her but studied her a moment. "No question at all. I know the night I made her." He looked to Hutch and flushed bright again, not smiling now. "See, Helen was dead-keen on me in French letters. She swept up for this men's hairdresser in Walton Street and every Friday whipped off a few French letters. We'd be on the tow path after the films— some bleeding Anna Neagle tripe; she wolfed that down—and when we'd got steaming, she'd fish out her rubber goods and hand them over in the dark like they were too mean to mention. For months I obeyed and rolled them on, but this one night it was cold as Cape Wrath; and all I could think of was touching her bare, striking real blood-heat. So into the water went three stinking rubbers and me into Helen—just me, first time. She never felt the change, not for weeks. I did   made me like her better; and when she came up, wailing *Baby! baby!*, I said 'Cool your chips. I'll marry you.' I thought she said Yes and I made plans; but she went down to Reading to see her scummy sister (her mum was dead; she stayed up here with her dad, an old drunk) and after a fortnight sent me a letter, saying, 'Dear Mr. Nichols'—I swear to God!—'I have thought a lot and got advice here, and I don't think I want you to be dad to any girl of mine!' (she knew it was a girl; she felt that much). I couldn't understand. She'd bloody sure wanted my cock long enough; started to send it to her in a box with a note saying, 'Feel free to use anytime you need, and show to your girl when she's twelve years old—a warning from Dad.' After that it didn't really bother me much; if she'd ever had a child, I hadn't seen it. I hadn't seen *her* for nearly three years and was going my way very nicely, thank you, packing cases of Cooper's orange marmalade when blimey if she didn't turn back up here with Nan already walking."

"Begging money?" Hutch said.

"Helen?—not her. I'll grant her she never begged a tanner from me. Proud as Lady Docker and just about as kind. I mean, her idea of facing me after two years away—and my daughter half-grown—was to prance up behind me at Carfax one Saturday, cover my eyes, and whisper 'Hullo, James, from a happy mum!' I was hot from dancing, but I went really cold. Couldn't think of anything to say but 'A girl?' and she said 'Named Nan.' Well, you could have floored me with a spoon of cold porridge—Nan's my mother's name. I couldn't speak again. I only thought of bashing her mouth—she seemed alone—but I just stood there like the vicar at a fête. Then she said, 'You can see her at Dad's anytime.' She'd come back to stay with her dad, who was sick. I said 'I may do' and walked away—Christ, walked all night all through Port Meadow. But two days later I washed and went round. I liked her straight off—young Nan, I mean—and she came to me, no gates between us. She could talk very well, and she looked a bit like me. The talking was stranger than the looking though. You step through a door; there's a fast little animal, standing thigh-high with your hair and eyes; and once Helen says 'Nan, come speak to James,' she comes up and holds your knee and says 'What's your name?'—looking up like she hadn't heard Helen. Helen left it to me, so I said it was James. I'm still not clear she knows I'm her father; someone may have told her but never me."

Hutch said, "She knows. She told me first thing."

He nodded. "She calls me James anyway." And by then he seemed exhausted. He asked Hutch the time (the pub clock as always being some minutes fast). It was nearly ten-thirty, closing-time at eleven. He pulled at one stretched cuff of Nan's sweater.

Hutch said, "Will your mother be home by eleven?"

"Quite likely."

"But if not?"

"We'll sit on the step or take a little walk."

Hutch said, "She's surely dead-out now."

James nodded. "She is. She's used to being waked."

"You could come back with me, but we'd have to climb a wall."

"You a don?"

"A student. Or will be in October if I last that long. I'm living in Merton."

James said, "I been there. We're due to work Merton sometime this autumn, lot of patchwork to do. I'll wait till then. Thanks all the same." He drank long swallows and gave no signs of continuing his story. At last though he looked up, entirely earnest. "I'm sorry really. You never asked for that."

"I did," Hutch said.

"Before you knew half."

"I liked it," Hutch said.

James thought through that, then looked up smiling. "Didn't mind it myself, kept thinking I would."

The publican said "Last call please, gentlemen." The RAFer and the transformed Yank were still at the bar, quieter now. Hutch, James, and Nan were the only other patrons. Hutch said, "My go to buy the last round." The winey cider had him high and eased.

James said, "I better not—got to face my mother yet, with an extra mouth to boot."

"She knows Nan surely?"

"A little. But she's sort of had it with kids—bad luck with all hers."

"How many more are there?"

James looked to the clock again. "You want the rest of *me*, there's just time for that."

Hutch said "Good enough."

"They stayed on here. Helen's dad got well enough to work again, so she and Nan lived there and kept up for him the best Helen could; she's an awful mess. She had no objections to me seeing Nan, and I'd come in and see her maybe twice a week, take her out for a walk or to do something new—even took her to St. Giles's Fair, her first fair. Helen came along that day. We were friendly by then, though nothing too close—I was seeing any other girl I fancied; I hadn't touched Helen, didn't need to try; and while Nan and I went to ride the ponies, Helen went to the gypsy and had her palm read. Came back with her face all down round her tits, saying she would be the cause of blood in others. I laughed. Two years before the same ruddy witch had told me and her we'd be happily married in a semidetached house in under six months with a fridge and hot water! But it ruined the fair for her. She left me and Nan to go her way, and that was the day we fell in love—hours together, spending shillings like water. I took her back at dark. There was Helen still moaning while she made her dad's tea, so it came in my head to say 'I'll keep Nan tonight' and Helen said Yes. Nan slept in my bed, right up against me. She sleeps very *still*, no moving at all and dry as my hand. I kept the room dark; but whenever I woke I'd find her face and stroke it awhile, pretending I was blind. I liked it; I'd slept alone since my brother left eight years before and never with a girl. I got a taste for it. Nan did as well. Helen didn't seem to mind, so from then on for six months she stayed every Sunday night with me."

The publican approached them. "Any last orders please?"

They both said No and James looked again to the present Nan between them. He didn't touch her—her shoe touched his thigh—but he watched her calmly as he might have watched a place, an inhuman field in evening light.

Hutch brushed her hair once with the back of his hand but watched her father. He didn't think then of pictures that lay behind this here—Rob and himself twenty years ago, trailing through two states Rob's desperation and his own plain contentment to be with a father who could make old rocks in the road die laughing. But he felt strong pulses of a similar peace, flickering signals which affirmed again that there were real fires outside himself—welcoming, benevolent, worth anyone's tending. Father and child. The longer he watched, the younger James seemed—unguarded, hunted. Even the fixed eyes, older than the skin, were blind to threat. Hutch strained to find one useful word of warning.

But James said, "I still had my Saturday nights. I was seeing a girl from Stanton Harcourt; and this one Saturday I had her at Carfax, dancing again—clean country girl. There was not a big crowd, just a miserable four-piece band from Witney and a few of your countrymen, sucking down vodka by the quart— very generous. There was this black one I'd talked to before—Alfonso-something from Michigan, quite friendly, big high arse and a lot of teeth missing. Always after me to get him 'some white meat free,' not whores. Said he'd never spent a penny for pussy till then and didn't plan to start just because he was homesick. I laughed him off but thought it was awful, wouldn't ever tell him my own girl's name. This night he'd managed to hook one at least—great pale-faced redhead from the pressed-steel works who seemed not to talk—so he was celebrating. I had my own cause to join him too. My girl had just whispered she'd changed her mind; till then it had been set against me working below her ears! It was bloody cold—February—and since what seemed to lie ahead of me was a late trip to Stanton Harcourt on my motorbike and a chance at a frosty shag in the graveyard, I thought I'd better drink as much as he'd give— Alfonso *Masters*. He gave unstinting like I said, and I was pissed when the next bomb landed. There was Helen with a slimy little Welsh tich I also knew, dancing close in a corner. I didn't think I'd care. But since she hated to see me drunk, I went to Alfonso for one more taste; and he gave me the dregs of his bottle, quite a lot. So when I looked round and found my girl gone—she had active kidneys—I sloped up to Helen and her singing midget. Tried to be pleasant enough; and he was willing—gave him the last swallow—but Helen wouldn't hear it, froze over completely and didn't say a word beyond 'Never mind coming for my daughter tomorrow.' That cut really deep, a lot deeper than I'd planned to be cut by her again. First I just walked away four or five steps; then I knew I wouldn't take it. I turned and went back and said all I'd kept up to say for three years. That's the sordid part I warned about; I'll spare you that—guess away, if you like! But it went fast at least. I shoved Helen once; her friend hit me good on the chin (quite strong for such a little newt); I bashed him down with Alfonso's bottle—two times; then it broke and I stopped, not to maul him. Well, of course the first blow had laid his scalp open clean as an orange and earned him weeks of rest like I said." James stopped, touched his glass, decided not to drink. Then he faced Hutch at last. "That enough, you think?" His grin, sudden and white as a flare, surprised them both.

Hutch smiled. "Much obliged." A sweep-up boy was working their way, pausing every few steps to wipe his nose. Hutch lifted the last of his cider toward James. "To a calmer future, you and Nan."

James nodded, took her wrist, and shook it firmly. "But I've liked it, see. I really haven't minded."

Nan was looking straight up, awake as quickly as her father had promised. She looked back to Hutch and studied him a moment, then gave two clear imitations of an owl's lone cry. "Who-ah-oo, who-ah-oo."

Hutch laughed. "Where'd you ever hear an owl, Nan?"

"I didn't," she said.

James stood and lifted her. "Maybe I'll see you this autumn in Merton. Keep your eyes skinned—upward. I'll be on the scaffold."

"Being hanged?" Hutch said.

James laughed. "Just replacing dead stones this time."

44

There was no landlord to face after all. The name on a dignified calling-card was pinned up inside the open door, *Miss Marleen Pickett* with directions in a pale script to *First floor back*. Hutch climbed the long stairs, plunged back through a dark hall, and found only one door with noise behind it—Lehar, the Vilja song, a wiry soprano—so he knocked.

A good wait. The Lehar continued; then its volume throttled down, and a woman's voice said "Yes?" through the wood.

"Miss Pickett please."

"Who's calling?"

He was still not sure it was she, but the cider allowed him to say "Clean Socks."

Another wait; the song died midair. The voice said, "I don't think I heard the name."

"Hutchins Mayfield," he said, "—rich American boy, built normal-size." A laugh. "What's he want?"

"Oh a chance to be better acquainted," he said.

He might have been Orestes with the hungry axe, but she opened then— on a small bed-sitter filled with books as she'd promised and her small self wrapped in a green housecoat, her hair newly washed and lightened like steam from a brief spring snow in the waving gleam of three green candles and a mute television: Anneliese Rothenberger in a grainy bow, troops of violins behind her.

An hour later they'd worked to the closest acquaintance they'd have, though for Hutch it didn't seem negligible. He'd sat while she made them a cup of Horlick's on her new hot-plate (the books by his chair were all war histories— Churchill, Eisenhower, a history of the Greater London Fire Service). They'd watched the still-silent television and drunk the foamy milk, mostly silent themselves—little guesses at the plot of the comedy before them, fat schoolboys apparently drowning an old headmaster in a barrel. When it ended in a muddy cricket match, she'd leaned to switch it off and said, "Now I may have to push off to work—"

Hutch had said, "You're a little late tonight."

"I'm a great opera fan," she'd said. "Never miss it. Anyway it's early by American clocks."

Hutch had said "Not really" and stood to meet her on the small rag-mat she said she'd made.

So they stayed upright in the midst of the candles, their palms pressed together like children in a slow game of push-and-shove. Hutch knew he was still high, knew she was clear, but trusted her to let him choose their speed. She consented and finally he rested on her shoulder, close enough to smell her cleanliness—honest soap, no scent. Then he said "Work here?"

She seemed to nod.

He undressed her carefully as a tired baby who might yet yell.

But she bore all his gentleness—his words of encouragement and praise, the serious unhitching and folding of clothes till she stood mother-naked and hugged herself once in a short chill of thanks. Then he paused, rocking slightly; and she said "Right" and returned the favor.

When he stood bare also, he took a step back and stroked her once from neck to belly, then drew her hand down the same stretch on him. He said, "We're the same age. We look like kin." They did, in dim light—matched in health and frank fineness of workmanship.

But she said, "Mind your manners. I was brought up clean."

Hutch said "You smell it" and knelt before her to graze his fill. A tenor bell in the heart of town began on midnight.

She counted its last three strokes aloud. Then in the same pitch and rhythm and distance, she said "Thanking you" and raised him by his hair.

He searched her eyes, smiling. "Shall we read a good book now and go to sleep?"

She laughed two notes, still mocking the bell; raised a palm to hold him in place, then doused two candles with her fingers. "Yes," she said. "Read me *Poor Old London in Flames Again*. I'm a cold-natured child." She went to the bed and lay flat and neat.

He said, "Once upon a time there was a city child named Marleen Pickett."

"Don't say the name please."

"Why?"

"I don't really feel like her just now."

"Who then?"

A little wait. "You training for police inspector, are you?"

Hutch laughed. "In a way."

"Take a night off then."

So he did—or a long unmeasured space in which they worked with the perfect skill their bodies had promised toward perfect reward, for Hutch at least in the few conscious minutes till she drew a quilt over them and let him sink asleep stretched against her right side. Even sleeping he felt no further need or question, though he dreamed this story. He was in his own bed in his room in Rob's house. He had waked after calm sleep and lay in warm fall light, straining the stillness for some sound of Rob in the kitchen, on the porch. But the stillness was pure and ran through his mind with no residue to stop his own rest and start the day. He sat up naked—he was full grown, his present age—and looked out the window that ran to the floor beside his bed. The yard, clear down to the road, was empty of all but Thalia loping stiffly toward the woods like a black footstool that had managed escape. *From what?* he wondered and stood and called Rob. Still nothing so, naked, he roamed the porch and kitchen, slowly fearful. No Rob—the cookstove cold, table clean. But the truck stood safe in the back by the well. He stopped short of Rob's bedroom door and said "Father." He could hear the hum of something alive but nothing spoke. He went on toward it, feeling only dread. The room was lighter than his own had been. On the bureau Rob's gold watch burned like a lamp. In Rob's broad bed covered only by a sheet lay James and Nan. Nan was facing the door, awake and watchful. When she saw Hutch she smiled. He knew he had not seen her smile till then. His worry dissolved. James slept beyond them; the sound was from him, strong steady breaths.

Marleen laid a hand on his hip and pressed. When he woke she said, "You good for the night?"

"—For sleep if you are."

"I just meant that. I'm tired as you but the rent's due Monday."

"What would my share be?"

She thought awhile, kneading his hip like a nurse. "How would three guineas sound?"

"About right," he said.

She turned toward him then, drew small to his side, touching at every possible point. "Good night, Old Socks."

He thought "Good night" but was not sure he said it before sleep reclaimed him.

45

Hutch and Strawson had a big tea at a cheerful shop near the theatre (a diabetic at the nearest table had insulin trouble, and the manageress uncomplainingly poured sugar-water down him till his pallor cleared). Then they wandered through surprisingly empty streets past the local swans, Shakespeare's timbered birthplace, the garden of his last home, his tomb in the parish church with its bust which Straw said resembled an inflatable Edgar Allan Poe, ten pounds over-filled. Near that a small flowerseller was open. Hutch stopped—"Inspiration."

Straw said "Oh God."

"*Secular* inspiration—Miss Leigh." They went in and found only stalky field flowers, something like carnations, but bought an armload and had them sent backstage at once to Vivien Leigh.

Act One, Scene Five. In the brown wake of Olivier's first meeting with the hags, she strode onstage, the sudden boiled essence of what had till then hung misty and subtle—essence of the blind need of power, the will to seize it, both pure in a small red-haired gorgeous woman in a sea-green dress with barbarous jewels and a phallic belt slung from her crotch. Once she'd invoked in fevered chant the nursing of demons at her round high breasts, she moved straight forward through the midst of the play like a thin asp, far more potent than its length. She forced Macbeth to Duncan's murder, not by volume or stare but by lust—flicking kisses at his neck and ears, quick stings on a soldier deprived many days of bed and wife. The demons clung to her as she took the daggers from him, smeared the drugged grooms with Duncan's gore; then reappeared in a new incandescence, ready at last to yield her body, hot with triumph and salty with blood. Then the strength left her slowly. In the banquet scene she entered as the smiling hostess whose composure barely conceals a knowledge that her husband is steadily passing her in power and secrecy; then as he panicked at Banquo's ghost, she rose with the natural loyalty of a dog, dismissed the guests, and worked to calm him with wifely tenderness. But increasingly certain that he'd now exceeded her in crime and hunger—having used her body as his vaulting horse and cracked her spine— she left, abandoned by all her strengths, desolate and baffled. Thereafter she was only the grizzle-haired child of the sleepwalking scene—singing her dreamy confessions of blood, her last concerns for the peace of a man who'd found her useful to a point awhile back.

Her pale secretary met them downstairs, led them through dim halls to a door, said "Please wait here," and vanished inside. They stood, not speaking, still held by the end—corrosive black glare that streamed from Macbeth in his fight to live—and a little cowed by what now seemed a pointless request: to stare close-up at a beauty who must be drained and shaken. Five yards beyond them another door opened. Olivier stepped out, bare-chested, with a towel—beard and wig off but his eyes still painted. He saw them and smiled and stepped back in.

Straw said "He's smaller than me"—he was.

Hutch laughed and was on the verge of leaving when the nearer door opened on a woman in a tan robe with brown hair pressed down tight round her skull.

She said, "Poor boys. You're frozen. I'm sorry." Then she waved them in. Only inside by better light did they know for certain she was who they'd come for—the famous smile, the green eyes tilted, the voice now raised to its normal cool pitch. She went to a dressing table where their ragged flowers looked fresher in a clear vase beside a framed picture of Olivier, younger, as Romeo. "Mr. Mayfield, Mr. Stuart—thank you *very* much." She made a deep curtsy. "Which is which?" she said.

Hutch looked to Straw.

"I'm the Stuart," Straw said.

"Are you royal?" she said and took a step toward him, her large hand rising.

"Yes ma'm," Straw said, not moving from place. But he took the hand neatly and bent to kiss it, natural as a bird at a still bowl of water.

She accepted, still smiling, then turned to Hutch. "What a lovely name—Mayfield. And you're Southern, your note said. I'm more than an honorary Southerner myself." For a moment her voice took on the plaintive sweetness of Scarlett and Blanche. "The South was kind to me."

Straw said "Then come back."

Her eyes searched him quickly; she laughed. "You don't think I flourished in Scotland tonight?"

"No ma'm," Straw said; then blushed. "*You* were fine. The other Scots didn't seem ready for you though."

She was serious. "Too true." Then the smile again—"Shall we thank God for that?"

Hutch said "Yes alas."

She said, "Carolina—I've seen it from trains: dark green, all pines. Will you go back there?"

Hutch said "I hope I can."

"Together?" she said.

Hutch wondered how she meant it—Lady Macbeth, now a calm matchmaker?

But Straw said, "I'm a Virginian—no ma'm."

They could all laugh at that. Her face scrubbed clean, the lines of midage spreading from her eyes, she had never seemed more beautiful to Hutch—more desperately offered from her frail foothold on the near side of poise. He thought, quick and wild, "I could lead her out of here. She wants to go" (her spells of madness were public knowledge—howlings, clawings). "I could give what she lacks."

But she settled on Straw again. "How long will you stay?"

Straw looked to Hutch.

"You must come for *Twelfth Night*. We do that next. I could save you my seats. I make a nice boy. And *Titus Andronicus*—I lose both hands, my tongue, and my maidenhood but I persevere."

Straw said, "I imagine you do. Thank you, ma'm."

"Kind sir," she said. " 'My Rosenkavalier!' " and dipped to the floor in controlled obeisance, not laughing now.

46

Two hours later they'd scaled Merton wall, picked their way over turning iron-spikes, and walked through the black chilly garden to Hutch's. The sitting room was dank, so Hutch burned both coils of the heater—if this was July, woe betide for winter—and hurried to warm milk for cocoa.

When Straw saw the drift, he said, "I've got a fifth of Scotch. It'd do you more good, ward off T.B."

Hutch laughed. "*You* kissed her. You're the one in danger."

"How's that?"

"She's the world's most noted consumptive."

"I heard she was crazy."

"That too, in spurts." They hadn't talked of her on the drive back to Oxford; Straw had slept the whole way.

"I liked her a lot, offstage more than on."

Hutch said "She liked you."

"Those older women do. I'm the spirit of youth."

Hutch said, "—For ten minutes at the rate you're going."

Straw went to his small bag and fished out the bottle, came back to the sofa, bent over the white cup, and poured a big drink.

Hutch said, "Not for me. Not yet at least."

Straw looked up, solemn as a child on a stele. He thought for a long moment. "So be it," he said, "—plenty others in line." Then he smiled, still standing; drained the cup, and lay back full-length on the sofa.

"This is England. Drink slower."

"Why?"

"You're safe here, aren't you?—no menopausal doctor's wives tracking you down."

"Maybe so, maybe not." He'd shut his eyes again.

Hutch didn't want him to sleep just yet. He himself was awake and gladder than he'd planned—to have Straw here, transplanted intact out of range of home. "You promised to bring me up to date," he said.

"Tomorrow if I live."

"Night's the time to talk trash."

Straw looked out again and studied Hutch. "You're a little low, aren't you?"

"No." His milk was bubbling; he leaned to mix the cocoa.

"—On trash. You look pretty low on trash."

"This *is* a hermit's cell, six hundred years old."

Straw raised up and scanned the long dark room. "Shit," he said. "Bet you young hermits were groveling on each other's butts before the plaster was dry on the walls."

Hutch laughed. "Could be."

Straw was still looking round. "I'm *certain*," he said. "Had to warm up somehow."

Hutch had sat back to drink. "It's July," he said.

"I'm freezing."

"No you're not. Tell the news; that'll toast your toes."

Straw said "Pour me a shot."

Hutch poured two ounces.

"Keep going."

"That's a shot."

"Then make it a torpedo."

Hutch doubled the portion and handed it over.

Straw set it on his breastbone, cradled in his hands. "I lie here before you as a father," he said.

"Of what exactly?"

Again Straw drained the cup in one swallow—no flinch or shudder, though he scrubbed at his mouth. "—Of a pink goldfish about two inches long. I named it for you."

Hutch said, "Many thanks. Do I get him now or later?"

"I said *it*; pay attention. No it's swimming down sewer mains fast as it can toward the Gulf of Mexico. You'd never catch it now."

Hutch said, "You may need to speak plain English. I'm not too good at these dark allegories."

Straw said, "I'm trying to spare you pain."

"Nobody else does. Don't bother; I'm grown."

Straw looked out a moment with utter clarity, the eyes of an instrument collecting evidence for some vast indictment. Then he shut them and set the cup on the floor at Hutch's foot. "I've been fucking Estelle Llewellyn since March, eight times exactly—she's counting not me."

"You wrote me in June that it hadn't happened yet."

"I was lying, to spare you again. You want to hear this or you want to give demerits?"

Against his better judgment Hutch said "Tell on."

"By the time I wrote you, she was already pregnant. She didn't know, didn't tell me anyway—it's not my favorite idea of fun, to poke up a growing baby's ass. But I did, two or three more times; I wouldn't go so far as to say I felt the difference. Then she called me up one evening at home and said I had to meet her at school, nine o'clock—all our meetings had been at school from the start. I wasn't in the mood and told her so as plain as I could with my mother standing four feet away. I'll give her this much—Mrs. Llewellyn, I mean. She never cried a drop or raised her voice. She just said,

'I don't want to lay a hand on you. I want you to know one piece of news.' I knew from that minute, but I went on and met her. She never tried to touch me. I wouldn't have minded; it was *her* idea that she was too old and was cradle-robbing, having dealings with me. I liked how she did most everything she did. We sat in her car, and she told it straight out—she knew it was mine; she was six weeks gone. She'd been down to Staunton to have the test done, false name and all. I knew we were acting in a fairly old movie, but I knew she was hurting under all the big dignity. I said, 'Any doubt that the father's me?' She said there was not; she'd claimed right along she and Dr. Llewellyn had lived like cousins for more than a year, his choice not hers. So I said, 'If you'll have it I'll raise it right.' I meant every word. I could have got a job, found a woman to keep it—my mother would have cut backflips at the chance. Then she told her real news. It was already done. She'd gone to her husband that same afternoon and told him the problem, leaving out my name. He'd solved it right there in his office, twenty minutes. She had cooked their supper and was driving the car. I sat still, glad it was dark at least. I wanted to say some wonderful sentence to end her scene, some noble memory for her to suck on for years. I even ran through all the poems I'd learned. But nothing seemed right. After maybe two minutes I opened the door and stepped out to breathe and here I am." Still blind, he reached down accurately and took the empty cup; licked slowly round the rim.

"You never said a word?"

Straw looked out again, less certainly now. "No I saved it for you. I thought you'd like it."

Hutch felt a yellow surge of nausea in his throat. What he'd honored in this boy for nearly two years was the clear sight of life, a flood of cheerful animal life that had pressed Straw's body and face from within into one more mask of the thing Hutch hunted and worshiped in the world—the same strong grace that still moved the pictures of Rob through his memory. Now supine on ragged cushions in a room that had seen worse surely in six hundred years, Straw seemed nonetheless filthy past cleaning. Hutch licked down deep at the dregs of his cocoa, then bent and poured whiskey in the half-clean cup, then drank a long swallow.

Straw said "I was wrong."

"How?"

"You plain didn't like it."

"What makes you think that?"

Straw propped his head on one hand. "I've done some bad stuff in my time, I agree; but I never to my knowledge made anybody mix good Scotch and cold cocoa."

"It was all right."

"The story?"

"The drink." Hutch drank the rest, walked to his bedroom, pissed in the sink, and ran a little hot water.

As he came slowly back, Straw said, "Anybody that'll piss where he washes his mouth shouldn't blame other people for what they do."

"The john's too far."

"So was love in Virginia."

Hutch sat again. "I was there till June."

Straw watched him steadily. "You were scared."

"Not of you."

"Of what then?"

"Nothing."

"*You're* lying. Don't spare me." Straw sat up finally, gave himself and Hutch drinks, then leaned back upright.

Hutch found no immediate reason to spread out his relics here where they well might be disvalued or abused. "Strawson, I was leaving. What we did was *goodbye.* There was no future for it."

"Did you want there to be?"

"No."

"A lie."

Hutch laughed. "Your lie detector is overheated, son."

Straw shook his head. "I'm a father, remember?"

"Half the world can be that, any man with a minimum of one working ball."

Straw said "Why not you?"

"Give me time."

"We have. World's waiting for your heir; you're aging fast."

Hutch nodded. "That's why I've washed up here. That's the scarey thing."

"—In a hermit museum? With your woman in Richmond, four thousand miles off? You mailing her bottles of your warm white seed?"

"Not yet anyhow. I mailed her a poem."

Straw said, "I know that eased her pain."

Hutch said, "I've retired from the pain-easing business."

"Never knew you had such a long list of patients."

Hutch grinned and drank a little. One or two gates opened. "I don't claim to be Father Damien of the Lepers; but I have been the target, since the day I was born, of a high wall of *hope.* I have more than normal sympathy for instance with poor Baby Jesus and the pre-teen Mozart."

"Nice crowd to run with."

"I'm not claiming kin, just making a point. I was loved as a child; it can be a hard blight."

"You were needed," Straw said. "That's a whole nother story."

"Then tell me the story of love, O mage!"

Straw said, "I just did. It made you piss."

"You and Estelle Llewellyn?—quick bangs in a car?"

Straw nodded. "—Broom closets, wrestling mats in the gym, anywhere I could get her."

"The saints of love are howling," Hutch said. "That was pure goat-need, no offense meant to goats."

"Us goats *are* the saints."

"Please expand," Hutch said.

"I did. For a poet you're pretty damned deaf; never heard of a great deaf poet before."

"First one," Hutch said. "You'll need to speak plain."

Straw said, "How's this? I'm nineteen years old or will be soon. I need to go to college like a mule needs tits. I wanted that baby. Didn't know it at the time. At the time I was getting my wand stroked in company; but from here— lying here in a hermitage, having seen the Oliviers act out a marriage at least as enviable as my own parents', and watching you— I can see I was hoping to really *make* something, the thing that matters."

Hutch laughed well before he saw Straw's tears. "We've had a little too much of this," he said, extending the cup.

"Not enough," Straw said. His eyes indicated there might never be enough, not in all the years.

Soon after that Hutch had brought out a pillow and covers for Strawson to sleep on the sofa. It was past two o'clock; he was worn flat down. Straw had only said he'd sit awhile longer; so Hutch had quickly slept in his own bed, the door between them open. Sometime later he'd waked to hear Straw's feet on the stairs, going down—the john—and he thought he should call him back, give him the flashlight (the chapel johns were blacker than night); but he stayed still for once—let him learn his way—and was out again before Straw reached ground. A sleep so thick and untroubled that he thought in a fragment of dream, *I am being rewarded. For what? For what?* No answer seemed needed and he knew nothing else till a little past four, false dawn at the window.

Straw was standing naked by the sink in the window-end of the bedroom. His head was buried in Hutch's towel; he was mopping at his hair and face, silent and slow.

Hutch tested the chance that the sight was a dream; under the covers he clawed at his own bare thigh and felt the nails. So he whispered, not to startle Straw, "You braved the vile baths?"

Straw looked up but not at Hutch—outward at the first glow.

"You all right?"

"Frozen." The window was open.

"Should have waited till morning. No real hot water till breakfast-time."

"Been swimming," Straw said and went on with his drying.

Hutch said "Good God" and—still half-asleep—imagined the drunk boy climbing out by the low south wall, walking through the otherwise empty meadow to the river, stripping, plunging in over dozing swans, stroking in the cold water, walking back bare with his wadded clothes. All the guesses were right; he knew Straw well. "I've got some flannel pajamas," he said, "in the bottom drawer there beside your feet."

Straw dropped the towel, leaned to fish out the flannels, stood to put on the jacket.

Hutch had slept again by the time he was half-dressed.

So Straw left the pants on the floor, walked forward, and found his own way to the warm narrow trough in Hutch's ruined mattress.

Hutch woke enough to give him a little extra space—the trough they were in had untenable slopes—but he said nothing else. He lay facing Straw and, never quite waking, accepted for what seemed hours the gestures of pure blind service—mouth and hands, anointment and soothing; no word of request, no feeding gaze. The pleasure was strong as any Hutch had known, maybe stronger because of the silence and dark. He climbed through its spaces in a blindness of his own but safe, well-led. No eyes to thank, no debt to pay. Even Lew had begged rescue. He thought of Marleen's kind competence a moment, but gratitude quickly returned him here. He was happy here, one actual room. So, mind and body, he stayed for the rest. At the end he considered asking one thing—*"Have you made something now?"*— but the boy slid straight from his work into sleep. Hutch stayed there facing him till light showed his face, sealed again and young in sobriety. Then he crawled out quietly, went to the sofa, and napped in the shallows till the first morning chime. When Simpson came to wake him, he sat up, pointed to the bedroom; and said, "I've got a guest asleep."

Simpson said "No lady?"

"No *lady*."

Simpson winked.

47

July 24, 1955

Dear Rob,

    Your letter came four days ago while I had company here—Strawson Stuart, my student. You remember he helped us load the truck my last day in Virginia. He's touring with his brother but stopped off alone for three days. We got to see Macbeth *in Stratford on Avon with Laurence Olivier and Vivien Leigh, a really big sight. I still can get chilled, remembering him—so calm at the start and so winning in appearance that you found you'd climbed in the palm of the hand before you noticed that the hand was iron and was closing fast round you with no sound louder than the crunch of your bones. Her voice is better for movies than stage—a microphone catches all grades of her best strengths (poisonous sweetness and serious guile) which are lost in the theatre—but nobody's ever looked or moved any better or half so well. We sent her some flowers and went backstage to see her at the end. On top of the beauty, which is literally incredible (despite her few wrinkles—she's forty-one—I found it hard to talk in her presence; too busy reminding myself she was* there), *she's warm and funny. Or was for five minutes; you've probably read of her mental problems.*

    *Otherwise I'm trying to settle in finally and do three good months of reading and writing before term begins and I'm a schoolboy again. So you can be assured I'm safe as any man in western Europe—*western *civilization. I live in a stone building heavier and older than the combined structures, private and commercial, of the town of Fontaine. My driving will consist of short slow prowls through gentle countryside; and in any case English roads are so narrow and winding, you can seldom exceed forty miles per hour for more than ten seconds (when you can it's a sure sign you're on a Roman road, some arrow-straight stretch laid two thousand years ago and thinly varnished with asphalt now). I'm even learning to pick my way through the breastworks and minefields of English food—mainly by resorting to the Covered Market here where I buy fresh carrots, tomatoes, oranges, dried figs, cheese and maintain the health of my gums if not my soul.*

    It's the soul that's in danger—if anything, Rob. The Mayfield Soul. Or is it a Kendal or Hutchins Soul? All of which is to say that the dangers I smell don't originate in sin. I know I'm a Christian, though I don't go to church (I mean I believe that the Gospel of Mark is a thoroughly trustworthy news-account of actual occurrences some years back but relevant still); yet I honestly doubt I've ever committed a sin of any weight. So far as I understand the Ten Commandments, I've never broken one. I've slept round a little, a relative little, but never *by* force *and never with anybody pledged elsewhere (St. Paul might*

*denounce me, but that was his line; ever notice how little Jesus says about sex?—
at least it didn't give him the fits it gave Paul). I've coveted in snatches but never
stole the thing, the object or person. If I have a prevailing Deadly Sin, it's obviously Pride; but anyone who knows me as well as you knows my pride is external, a transparent glaze. Inside I'm* doubting—*a Mayfield as I said. Or is it just
a human? Since we never really talked about the doubts, maybe I should lay
them out briefly here. Don't bother to brace yourself—no surprises, just the fairly
standard sinking spells of a twenty-year-old in my social class (only I'm twenty-
five).* Can I do anything worth doing for, say, the next forty-five years? If so,
is there any way to do it alone?

*Well, the lay-out was briefer than even I expected; but those two sentences
cover the matter, I'm all but sure. I'm not very sure the second question is as
common as I claimed above, not as early in life as this anyhow (I see nearly
all my contemporaries walking off in matched pairs and issuing small warm
replicas; it's one of the sights I came here to rest from). The first question though
is bound to be widespread—proof: the number of men my age who are drunks
and I understand why. But again no fear—it's one of the last routes I mean to
take. I suspect I might be chemically prone to quick dependence.*

*So—I know I can teach. I could come back now and have three or four decent
jobs by fall, teaching prep or high school. If I stay here long enough to get a
degree—two years' minimum—I'd have a good chance at two or three college
jobs: freshman composition and English Lit. from Adam and Eve to Anthony
Eden. If I start to publish books at a heart-warming rate—anything: poems, stories, a history of feed-and-seed catalogs, so long as they're bound in stiff cloth-
boards and come from a press that the author doesn't own—I could transpire
to some good private university and stay there till dead or too congealed to talk.
The teaching is—is it?—useful in the world. For me it would be the means to
eat while I did what I want and need to do. That, I think, would be writing. And
what use is that to anyone but me, the four or five people who take everything
I do on faith, and God in the skies? Should that be enough? Should I shut
up groaning and* make my items, *even if they finally turn out to be cottage-
industry white-elephants like scale-model copies of the Smithsonian Institute
in toothpicks and glue, admired by the builder's mother and minister?*

What if the answer to all those is No? *I doubt I could jump out the window
just yet; I like too many things. I doubt I could be a bad teacher for long—too
many opportunities for permanent harm. I doubt I could be a good husband-
and-father with no income and time on my hands.* Cable instructions, *as they
say in beleaguered frontier forts. But don't give it too much midnight oil. I'm
a self-winding watch, it begins to appear, though I may lose hours. It also*

begins to come to my notice (something children never see) how very few people ever lie down and quit; how most break the finish-tape some way or other, even creeping or crawling.

Present business, then. I understand your feelings on the question of Lew Davis's immigration. I'd just thought some ready solution might come to mind there at home to start him on his way. He seems to have gone a way at least; I haven't heard from him since we parted in Dorchester a month ago at the home of Thomas Hardy—he was hitching back to Wales or so he said. He has a lot of life which I hope he gets to use.

Understand too your feeling that I might have qualms about Min turning up in your life. I do and don't. Eleven years ago I objected to her strongly on the grounds that I'd missed you so much myself in the years you lived in Raleigh. I wanted you with me, sharing you with no one. Looking back from here, I don't feel shame. Not having a mother and raised by old women, I genuinely craved you—dogs crave grass. I've thanked you more than once for coming to me then, and thank you still. What I guess I haven't done is find a good way to make up to you the sacrifice I caused—leaving you with an adolescent boy through years when you must have been famished as me, for a different food. A big part of what I hope to do here and always is pay that debt in coin you can spend; a further doubt is, what coin would prove good and useful to you. Maybe that would simply be to do what you ask—raise prematurely patriarchal arms and shed warm blessing over you and your choice. But even I balk at some brands of pretension. I used to bless you when I was a boy—in my prayer every night, the years you were gone, and a lot of times silently when you were nearby—but then, like a lot of children, I felt safer than you and responsible for you. The child can be "father to the man" in more senses than Wordsworth meant, and you asked me to be. Or so I thought. It may be one reason I'm a little tired now. I've played more parts—lived them as duties—than a good many men or women age sixty. Thus a short rest now.

So sure, from my rest stop here by the Thames, the strongest blessing I have to send—on you and anyone you want it to land on.

I feel pounds lighter, having passed that miracle; so I'll stop now and take a long walk. It's a fine cool day. Three miles southeast lies apparently the country church where John Milton married his first disastrous wife, Mary Powell. I'll try to get there and back before dark, then work all evening. Let me hear some news on Grandmother, Grainger, and the whole home squad. They are keeping their counsel, but I think of them often—never meant to forget.

Love then from
Hutch

Midnight. *Safe back from the trek to Forest Hill (found the church empty, no Miltonic chords to shake the peace). I reread this, then reread your letter and noticed finally that you asked for patience not benediction. And here I've poured out grams of tortured ethereal ink in the effort to bless! I don't have the heart to copy it over. Also I feel like owning up. Don't hesitate to laugh.*
   Blessings anyhow.

                                                       August 1, 1955
   Hutch, your benediction came this morning and reminded me of several things. The one I can still act on is this letter I laid aside six weeks ago. Min arrived after the last installment; and while we haven't been on any wild scramble, the kind of evening conducive to lengthy retrospect has been a little scarce. Thank God, I guess. The presence of company has also made my hunt for the third good day of my life seem less urgent and a little ridiculous. I mean to finish though. Since you'll be the only one to see it, I'm as ready to have you laugh at me as I was to grin at your letter this morning.
   I've had the day pretty much to myself—Min had to go to Raleigh after breakfast for some work—so I sat down to find that last day for you, age thirty-five till now. I was fairly certain it would center on you; you're right in thinking you've been the hub of this wheel at least for twenty-five years. I even got out my shoebox of pictures. In an hour I'd worked through a lot more memory than I knew I had of you and me—except for my own fears and failures, good memory. I won't say the hour was peaceful though. I seem not to mind the first half of my past—Mother, Father, my jackass behavior for so many years. It's pictures, on paper and in my mind, of Rachel and you that seize me. Not painfully exactly but deeper even now than I like to be seized, in my final quick. Proves there's quick meat in there still—a strip about the size of a laborer's hand to the right of my heart, alive as a year-old bird dog at first frost. Here's the day it pointed, out of all our days.
   It must have been in early June 1944—you took a lot of pictures but neglected to date them. Our famous eventful Virginia trip when we burnt up so much war-rationed gas chasing each other down from seashore to mountains. I'd just been relieved of my job in Raleigh and was facing one more of the blank walls I faced fairly often back then. You must have been fourteen, already enough of a man to throw additional high walls across my path (though not at all blank and generally gated). But you still had the fascination with Jamestown, Pocahontas, and Captain John Smith which Grainger had given you before you could read with all the tales he had manufactured round two normal people.
   By the time we got there, you must have been one of the world's experts on the actual story. On the drive from Virginia Beach, you'd briefed me pretty thor-

oughly—*thoroughly enough for me to know how patiently you listened to the flood of romance that met us in Jamestown, the decrepit couple selling souvenirs who gave us the White-Virgin-Christian-Lady word on Pocahontas, so dear to native Virginia hearts. I left it to you; and your only resistance was to tell the old man that No, we wouldn't need his guidance round the site. He felt the rebuff—can you still see his face?—but stood his ground there beside his junk feathers and tomahawks and let us go.*

Am I right in seeing us there alone from that point on? I believe I am, few people sharing our luck in having an uncle on the local Ration Board. Perfect weather so we wandered on the green slope there above the James, on the actual dirt that had borne all the story and still held the bones of starved and killed colonists, the Indians they killed. I gather they've done some reconstruction since and built a museum for Pocahontas' earrings; but then I remember nothing but the hill itself, a lot of old trees, the ruins of a brick church standing near the site of Pocahontas' marriage, and separate statues of John Smith and her. I liked the one of her in a buckskin dress that fell to her knees, stepping forward with her palms out and looking slightly up. We sat at her feet to eat our lunch. I remember the lunch as something you fixed, but can that be right? We'd stayed in a hotel the night before; where would you have got celery and pimento cheese? Well, however, we ate and picked up our mess; and I told you I had to lie back a minute now and rest my eyes. So you wandered off again. I leaned back under Pocahontas' moccasins and snoozed.

How long was I out?—fifteen, twenty minutes? Long enough at least to have a few dreams of the punishing variety I specialized in. Then a low thumping on the ground woke me up. The sun had moved down and was bright in my eyes. What I saw twenty yards downhill toward the river was a naked child turning cartwheels slower than a normal child could manage. It came to me peacefully that you had just told me two hours before how Pocahontas used to come here as a child, naked as a jay, and turn cartwheels with the white cabinboys round the first English fort. (I just looked it up in your room before I wrote this to confirm I was sane—William Strachey writing in 1612: "Pocahontas, a well-featured but wanton young girl, Powhatan's daughter, sometimes resorting to our fort, of the age then of eleven or twelve years, would get the boys with her forth into the marketplace and make them wheel, falling on their hands, turning their heels upwards, whom she would follow and wheel so—herself naked as she was—all the fort over.") I hoped at first I was still asleep and dreaming, not drunk—you recall I was also in drinking trouble then. It went on another ten seconds or so till I knew I was conscious; then the hope was that I wasn't being entrusted with some revelation from the Womb of Time. I thought something might be calling me on, requiring me to give when I felt about as bankrupt as I'd ever been—of answers to give to God at least or the magic ground.

The child had turned out of sight by then. I shut my eyes and took the sun and put my hands down to feel the grass beside me—the grass had been shivering—and I felt your shirt, a blue summer shirt warm with your sweat. So I looked again and even in the glare I could see you walking up the rise toward me, barechested in your tan shorts, not really a child. But a real revelation that would need acts of care for the rest of my life and maybe beyond. I'd have run if I hadn't known you could outrun me. I pretended I was out still and you walked up. You watched me awhile (I strained you through my lashes), then slid your shirt from my fingers and put it on. You said, "This statue is making me mad. She never wore any dress half as long as that, and her titties should show." That set me free to laugh. I looked up and said what I wanted to say, "Let's make a run for it." You didn't say "To where?" but laughed back and nodded.

I didn't realize we were happy then. I still thought the world was a custom-built millstone with ROB MAYFIELD *sewed neat in its neck like a college boy's sweater. You'll recall also that I acted on my misunderstanding posthaste—the drunk I pulled at Polly's in Richmond, ruining the trip. Well, we got through that and what came after, eleven years. Some of it's been all right, and 85% of the worthwhile enjoyment was owing to you. But it could have been better, which is why I can now see our Jamestown day as the last high point—the last big tree they let me climb. What I saw from there was right. We should somehow have run. Don't ask me to where? There must have been one place left back then where we could have hid out and had a plain life and learned to ignore all the want-lists posted from cradle to grave to train every human into baying at the stars (which do not bay back) till finally we could face each other and say, "I don't want anything alive or dead but you."*

Maybe that makes our Jamestown day the worst day of all. Maybe my mind is affected already, though they don't mention that on my schedule of symptoms. I don't think so. We were happy and knew it. Shame on us for the rest.

T W O

THE ROTATION OF VENUS

DECEMBER 1955–JANUARY 1956

Apacked autobus from the airport left her in Piazza Esedra with her sensible baggage. Three in the afternoon of Christmas eve, warm sun, clean air; and Hutch's map (he was fogbound in London, maybe here by six) showed their rooms only three or four blocks away. So she draped her raincoat over one shoulder, hoisted the bags, and set off briskly southwest toward the light down Via Nazionale. Every five yards one of an unnumbered squad of lounge lizards in pearl-gray suits would glide up and offer lavish assistance, all gallingly in English—"You need a nice room?" "You need a strong boy?" "I get you big room and two Parker fountain pens for three thousand lire." She smiled at each one, firmly refused, and was weak with relief to see the brass plaque for Pensione Pacifica.

When the birdcage elevator bumped down to get her, it unloaded three American boys—soldiers by their haircuts. The safety she felt in their guileless faces and prairie voices was cut by chagrin; like all serious tourists she wished to be unique, the only stranger. They ignored her in beery oblivion. On the fourth floor she stepped through a half-open door with a duplicate plaque—a long dim hall, low music at the far end (Peggy Lee?), not a soul in sight, no sign of a check-in window or desk. She set her bags down and walked slowly forward. Closed doors, a strong presence of international hotel-smell. Finally on the right there was one room open with windows on the sky. A lobby maybe—wicker furniture with worn flowered pillows; one man in U.S. Air Force trousers and a T-shirt, drinking what seemed water from a heavy glass and reading *Paris Match*. When he didn't look up, Ann said "You work here?"

He debated awhile—"No ma'm, in Germany"—then went back to reading.

"*Anybody* work here?"

He didn't look up but halfway smiled. "They're all working *now*."

"How would I check-in?"

He looked up, serious. "Pick a door. Listen good. If nobody's laughing just step on in and make yourself at home." The Appalachians were still in his voice.

"West Virginia?" Ann said.

"Yes ma'm, near Monongah."

"Good luck then." She turned.

A woman stood behind her—tall, a chemical blond, in rose-colored smock and matching scuffs. "*Prego?*" she said in a startling high voice.

Ann spoke very slowly. "I have a reservation, two reservations—Miss Gatlin, Mr. Mayfield."

The high pitch plunged to contralto. "Sure. Where is the man?"

"In England in a fog. He'll be here by night."

"You sure?"

"I'm sure." She was not of course.

"I got fifty chances to rent his room. This is Christmas, understand."

Ann nodded. "I heard. But it's Rome not Bethlehem. Or am I wrong? If he doesn't show up, I'll pay for his room and sleep in two beds."

The woman's mouth accepted the promise with a letterbox click. "You his sister?"

"No."

The woman bent to whisper; but the pitch rose helplessly, winging each word to the farther hills. "I can give you a bargain on one big room."

Ann stepped back and smiled—"No *grazie*; we're rich"—then regretted the joke: overcharges? room-thefts?

The woman thought a moment. "You change your mind, tell me. I'm a sport."

Ann thanked her. "You'll be the very first sport to know."

2

By five o'clock she had walked the length of Via Nazionale in sun that kept its warmth as it sank. She'd paused unavoidably to register her first encounter with the Victor Emmanuel Monument. Then she'd circled the Forum, Colosseum, Circus Maximus, the Palatine Hill—gingerly, not sure of what she passed, not wanting to know before Hutch could join her. The tender gold light and the scarce other walkers made a skimming easy. No one asked for the time, no one winked or pinched her; and only one more Parker fountain-pen salesman had approached with his wares, sallying politely from the Arch of Constantine, retreating politely with a *"Buon Natale"* when she shook her head. It had been the first sign of Christmas since her landing. There were no decorations in sight anywhere; but how decorate Rome, in all its layers of effortful time spread drying in light that seemed little older than the walls themselves? She thought of going back, haggling for a pen. They were probably stolen or Japanese forgeries, but Hutch could use one, and she wanted to speak. A circle of fullness had grown in her chest. She mistook it for joy and thought she could share it—the uncomprehended splendor of the place, her own strong youth, Hutch's slow approach. When she turned though the seller was back by the Arch, a thin brown boy dressed poorer than she'd noticed with his bare arm propped on another boy's shoulder, laughing hard. She'd keep it for Hutch then and pray not to swamp him.

But half an hour later, having skirted the Temple of Virile Fortune and survived the test of thrusting her hand in the frowning lips of the Mouth of Truth, she climbed a long stairs and stood on the crest of the Capitoline Hill in brown old Santa Maria d'Aracoeli at the feet of the famous Santissimo Bambino in his plain birth-crib. She didn't know the church's claim to stand on the spot where the Tiburtine sibyl had foretold to Augustus the imminent birth of God's first son. She didn't know that this small olive-wood Child, crusted with votive jewels like a beetle, was one of Catholic Christendom's main targets of devotion. But waiting in his presence with other happy lookers—fixed by his frozen eyes, his promise to smile or scream in an instant—the globe of her own hope grew and spread to her mouth and arms. Beside her a middle-aged man in business clothes was streaming quiet tears. He faced her and grinned; she hurried out the door.

On the stairs in near-dark, she was stopped by a swarm of living children in white, pressing up toward the Child. She stood and let them brush her like lambs, dazed with their own anticipation and herded by nuns. One girl, maybe six, was singing as she came by; Ann touched her fine hair, but she gave no sign of notice. So the fullness remained and was not desire. When the children had passed her, Ann held on awhile at the summit, looking down on the city—alive now, lighting in its stacked high windows and along the snaky Tiber—and finally asked the question that had poured elation through her: *What do I hope?* There was no quick answer. She'd walk down slowly and know by the time she reached the street. But before she'd descended six steps, music reached her—keen and grievous. She could only hear that through the new cold wind.

On the street three figures were grouped at a lamp—a man, a boy, an older boy. They were dressed alike in black country-clothes and hats, frayed and dusty. The man wore leggings to his knees, sheepskin with the gray wool exposed. The music came from him, a bagpipe made from what seemed like a bladder. The boys stood by him with their hands out mildly, not begging so much as offering; at their feet a good-sized lamb slept, its feet hobbled. Actual shepherds. Well, she'd hoped for them at least without really knowing. One wish was granted. When she laid a hundred lire in the older boy's hand, her joy only grew.

3

Yet back at the Pacifica, unpacked and bathed, she managed to sleep through dinner and a laughing skirmish between a boy from Missouri and a girl from Sorrento. Her dream insisted that she still wasn't here. For nearly three hours she continued east in an open boat that apparently soared without wings through dark. Then she woke in dark or was waked by the sign her dream had awaited. Beneath the tall connecting door to Hutch's room, a slot of light showed—firm footsteps. She was dressed. She sat up and listened for words. A man said "Thank you," not certainly Hutch. She went to the thick door and listened—nothing. Then the sound of running water and footsteps again. The steps came toward the door and stopped. The door seemed to rustle. She pressed her face against it. A hand was scraping at the other side, gently but steadily two inches away. She joined with her own nails, following its path. She felt very calm.

After maybe twenty seconds Hutch said, "Is this a symbol of the tragic plight of modern man?"

Ann laughed. "No it's just a really good French movie. Don't stop. We can wear this away by Easter."

He threw the bolt on his side.

She hesitated, still digging at the wood.

He said, "It's Christmas or will be soon. Take the easy way."

"We never did before."

"We're in Rome," he said. "They invented ease."

Her bolt was stuck but she managed at last.

Hutch opened the door. He looked exhausted but was smiling broadly. "Do you get the feeling we're living in a whorehouse?"

"Positive," she said.

"Shall we leave?"

"Not yet. Might get a few invaluable pointers."

"We didn't use to need them."

"We were *babies*," Ann said. "Wait till you see Rome."

They said the first half of their welcome on the threshold—two clear minutes of unblocked meeting, their eyes open wide. Then Hutch said, "I'm dying. Not a bite to eat since dawn."

Ann suddenly thought that was her problem too. She slumped in his arms. "I'm *dead*. Please administer intravenous glucose."

He lifted her well off the tile by her butt. "I doubt hot pasta will pass through needles. The madam says she'll feed us here gladly."

"They do everything here gladly, you'll notice."

"Then we're where we should always have been," Hutch said.

4

The dining room of the Pacifica was strongly lit by overhead fixtures from the Mussolini years, swollen and featureless. The glare off the apple-green walls threw an undersea haze into every corner; and though Hutch led them to a distant table, they both looked startlingly drowned at first. Ann gurgled loudly like the sinking Ophelia, and the few other eaters turned in astonishment—two large old ladies in perpetual mourning; five more American soldiers together, a young waitress laughing as she cleared their mess. Ann gurgled once more, then laid her head among the knives and napkins.

Hutch touched her scalp. "On guard—girls that doze off here wake in Turkish harems."

She stayed down—"Good"—then slowly rose. "*Not* good. I'm glad to be right here."

Hutch assented, no conditions.

With that commitment they'd silently agreed to raise no serious issue now. The place conspired. The only waitress ignored them entirely, bending all her force on their countrymen who'd now called for more wine and were eating what was plainly a cake baked in Omaha, shipped to Naples or Frankfurt, and hauled here intact.

Hutch said, "If you ask them nicely, they'll give you two pieces—our only chance of a touch of home."

Ann was ready to ask when the blond woman showed in the kitchen door, dressed now. Ann beckoned to her.

She came, smiling broadly on wartime teeth, but spoke to Hutch. "You tell her yet?"

Hutch blushed (Ann had never seen him blush). "Not yet. Could we eat a quick dinner now? We're headed to church."

"San Pietro?—big crowd."

"Santa Maria Maggiore."

The woman said "Better," then stroked Ann's hair. "*Guarda, cara.*"

Ann had studied a Berlitz book for months. She ventured "*Perchè?*"

"Because they show you the bed of Christ. *Molto potente. Guarda* for sure."

Hutch said, "Any power would kill us now. We've got to have food."

The woman said, "*Pronto.* You leave it to me" and went to the kitchen.

Ann reached for the salt, poured some in her hand, and licked it up. "What's the secret you share with our Mother Superior?"

"Nothing. Her American verbs are fuzzy. She wants me to ask you to merge our rooms."

Ann laughed. "Me too. She met me with that. I said we were rich."

Hutch nodded. "True."

5

But at three in the morning—when they'd let themselves in with separate keys, brushed their teeth at separate sinks, and Ann had entered her own broad bed—Hutch came to her side in the chilly dark and said, "Are you sure you were right about *rich?*"

Ann was at least as tired as he. "Oh no I was lying—for me anyway." She stayed where she'd fallen in the midst of the bed.

Hutch shuddered with cold.

She moved to her left. "You're welcome to join your assets to mine. It's too late to count on a discount though."

"They're awake," Hutch said. "They're all awake. I can feel them pulsing in every room from here to the street, international relations— Arkansans, Calabrians, Bantus, nuns."

"No nuns," Ann said. "They're all on their knees."

"—And frozen," Hutch said.

"Then tell em Merry Christmas and avoid pneumonia." She opened the covers.

He told them and joined her, and at once they embraced—quiet, except for the short laughs and groans of perfect depletion, and inevitably chaste (though they made a try). Neither of them minded. They knew they were well past the limits of even their young reserves; they thought there were long restful days ahead. What they hadn't mentioned or acknowledged yet was the actual weight of the mass they'd watched—the actual power announced at dinner, when as they stood in the bronzed smoky dark of the church, four sturdy men had borne straight at them through packed fervent bodies a long gold palanquin with angels and rays whose heart was a crystal box containing the promised fragments of the only Manger: undoubtedly splinters of ancient wood as credible then for Hutch and Ann (for separate reasons) as the laws that suspended a ceiling above them or anchored a floor. It had pressed from each of them their unknown will to start a child, here now in Rome from the simple juncture of bodies adequate as any alive.

That will endured their natural fatigue, and through the night the silent stories they told themselves both nursed its force and explained its reasons. Ann dreamt scattered scenes from a life in which a trustworthy woman, who seemed to be Ann, sat on a straight wood chair in a field and watched steady relays of people walk toward her slightly uphill and in single file. None of them wore recognizable faces, but all seemed as peacefully glad to come as she to receive them, and none of them left. The field filled slowly, though space remained for each newcomer to sit or lie. Hutch mainly saw more scenes from the day when he'd find James Nichols and Nan at the Mayfield house in warm fall light. James never spoke but worked with a trowel as bright as a sword to repoint the stones of the kitchen chimney. Nan stayed by Hutch as he walked wide circles around the yard, also quiet till at last she said "We've made a ditch." They had, with their feet—a shallow trough like the plan for a moat or a dry breastwork against road and trees and eventual passers.

6

Neither of them thought of the dreams when they woke. They woke together at a scratching on Ann's door. Hutch sat up. The scratch became tapping. Ann said "Yes?"

A bass voice half-whispered "Ho-ho-ho!"

Ann mocked it. "Ho yourself."

"Santy Claus is out here. Wake on up." A girl's voice giggled.

Ann said, "Blessings on you, old Santy. Go to bed."

A wait, then the bass again. "We're having Christmas breakfast. Want to join us?—real bacon." It was West Virginia clearly and the all-night waitress.

Ann looked to Hutch.

He smiled but shook his head.

So she said, "Thanks but No. We've had our Christmas." They hadn't, not entirely, but the visitors left them to finish where they'd paused.

Hutch began that (Ann had rolled back to sleep). The room had been hot since well before dawn. He threw back all the covers but a sheet, then

stepped to the window and opened one curtain—a narrow courtyard below
in shadow; a facing wall of identical windows in yellow sun, no faces or noise,
no cars or bells. For a moment the city itself pulled at him—he'd still seen
only the church by night and two sets of shepherds—and seven months of
Britain had taught him to seize any patch of sun. But turning he saw how the
light had reached Ann. He went to her. They woke together slowly—first to
one another's faces, smoothed and ready; then the plentiful remainder. For
more than an hour, the only sounds were the shiftings of cloth and hair and
skin. All questions between them dissolved in what Hutch gradually saw as
perfect work. When they finally lay entirely bare and joined in all their length
like one whole person—even feet and hands—Hutch thought how his other
loves (including Ann till now) had been forms of play, cheerful misunder-
standings. Here now he and Ann seemed finally poised to work at the single
job they'd ignored, a job they could gladly manage forever (or till the shared
body had worn away). The rubbers he'd brought were in his own room; he
remembered them and felt no need or fear. Neither did Ann. A child was
among the last few things they thought they wanted. They didn't start it then
for all their quiet eventual laughter, and again they didn't mind.

7

But later in the day, they each had a full clear sight of the other, which kept
their new will alive and patient. After breakfast they'd exchanged gifts in
Hutch's room (a wool scarf for Hutch, a silk scarf for Ann—the source of
more laughter). Then a little after noon, they'd walked out finally into sun
that gave no threat of ending. Ann had still not mentioned her previous ramble, so Hutch navigated by his Touring Club Italiano guide. And at first they
followed in Ann's footsteps—straight down to the Victor Emmanuel Monument, almost invisible in dead-white glare. So they circled to view it head-
on from Piazza Venezia. Hutch said, "It's undoubtedly the World-Cup
winner in the Carve-Your-Own-Ivory-Soap contest." Ann said, "It's the world's
biggest stone typewriter." Hutch said "You win." Then almost alone—few
cars, few walkers—they climbed the broad ramp of the Capitoline and saw
the bronze she-wolf with sucking boy-twins; Marcus Aurelius in curls on his
horse, fending off vandals and all other foes of mental health with a stiff right
arm. Ann didn't point out the church still above them with the jeweled Child
(on its steps now a single man sat in white shirtsleeves, no shepherds or nuns).
Hutch led them back down. They took off their coats—it was sixty in the
light—and entered three hours of happy silence, broken only by Ann's occa-

sional questions at the next pile of rubble and Hutch's replies verbatim from the guide.

They'd poked through the eastern slope of the Palatine—megalomanic walls and arches on ground that had borne more reason and madness for longer than any other place, on earth at least. By four o'clock they'd worked to the west slope, and Hutch was drowsy (Oxford had trained him for daily naps). He sat on a stump of travertine by what he didn't know was the probable floor of the House of Romulus. He leaned back and watched Ann retreat a few yards to a thicket of tall green ilex trees round a high platform with narrow steps. She climbed and went forward till she halfway vanished. She was facing the sun, which was two-thirds sunk; and its light sought the line of her head and shoulders. Hutch leaned, took a stick from the ground, and copied the line invisibly on the stone beneath him. She held in place while he traced the line again and again as if to gouge one more memorial in this memory dump. *Useless*—the bare line was not the sight, could never produce the sight for anyone more than himself. If the boy he'd been ten years ago were here now with paints and the skills of solitude and adolescent patience—if Ann and the sun would hold their pose—then the sight would survive and repeat itself for any willing watcher. The fact that he'd set those old skills behind him, or watched them depart, still seemed a big loss. No collection of words by anyone could summon this visible instant with its meanings. Words could do anything but make a reader *see*. Try naming this picture—*Young woman in ruins of the Palatine, late afternoon, Christmas Day 1955, as seen by the eyes of a young man who's known her seven years now and begins to love her here*. The picture was better—so much so that when he suspected she'd turn, he almost called "Stay!"

She turned, came back to the top of the steps, and said "Where am I?"

"Lost."

"I know that," she said. "What's the mess underfoot?"

"The Lupercal," he said. He was guessing.

"What's the book say about it?"

"—Site of the cave where the wolf nursed the twins."

"You're guessing; look it up."

Hutch said "Aren't you tired?"

"Not a bit. Look it up please. I like it up here."

He looked up *Lupercal* and read it to her. " 'Sacred grotto where Romulus and Remus were suckled by the wolf. Later site of an altar where was celebrated on February 15th the *Lupercalia*. Priests of the goat-god Lupercus sacrificed goats, daubed two naked youths with blood, bathed them with wool soaked in milk. The youths cut the skins of the victims into whips and ran through the streets, lashing all passers. Women especially sought the encounter, believing it strengthened fertility.' "

Ann looked back a moment, then faced Hutch again. "Wrong," she said.

"Ma'm?"

"There's no cave here, just the statue of a woman—no head but her bosoms resemble my mother."

Hutch said "She's a *goat*" but consulted the map. "Amazing—first mistake of my life! The Lupercal is down the hill there. You're standing in the Temple of the Magna Mater."

"Meaning what?" Ann said.

"Great Mother."

"What else?"

" 'The Sibylline books foretold to the Romans that they should prevail in the Second Punic War if they obtained from Asia Minor and honored a certain silver statue of Cybele, Great Mother of the Gods, giver of life to gods, men, and beasts. The statue, whose head was apparently a black meteorite, secured the promised victory and was installed in a temple here *circa* 191 B.C. Her priests emasculated themselves in imitation of her dead lover Attis; and annually on March 24th, her "Day of Blood," they danced to percussive music at her altar, gashing themselves anew and splashing her with blood.' "

Ann had stayed at the top of the steps to listen. When the last word flew past her toward the Tiber, she said "Good *night!*," then started down. Halfway she stopped, reached out to the wall, and pulled something loose. When she got to Hutch, she handed him a marble shard the size of a biscuit, perfectly white. Then she gave her best imitation of Mae West—"Keep this in your shaving kit, big boy, and remember me when your razor slips." She was already walking, with bumps and grinds, due north toward the Forum.

"They close this an hour before sunset, it says."

"Good," Ann said. "We could sleep in that wolf-cave. Find it and call me."

But he'd followed her down past the generally dormant Farnese Gardens to the House of the Vestals. They'd passed one middle-aged Italian couple taking their time and a uniformed guard who had not mentioned closing (how to close a space that lacked a whole wall?—release wild dogs or famished cutpurses?), so Ann paced off the length of the atrium, and Hutch sat again on the rim of the pool. The guard had vanished. He took out his stolen shard of Cybele and dipped it in water, shockingly colder than the day itself. Submerged, the marble that had seemed pure white showed numerous spots, the brown of old skin. As a boy he'd have got a lot of mileage from the sight— the signs of old blood, loyal stains, actual atoms of a wild priest's life. He rescued it, laid it beside him to dry. If the guard reappeared, it would look quite normal—the millionth scrap.

Ann called from thirty yards behind him, "Read me this please but check the map first."

He'd known it all his life from pictures at his Grandfather Mayfield's in Richmond; but he checked anyway, then faced her and read. "—'Residence of the virgin priestesses of Vesta, who never numbered more than six and were chosen between the ages of six and ten for a term of thirty years at the end of which they were free to marry. Their duties were the maintenance of Vesta's sacred fire and their own virginity. Failure in the former resulted in scourging; in the latter, live burial in the Campus Sceleratus (her lover being flogged to death in the Forum).'"

Ann shook her head, waited, then said a short sentence which didn't reach Hutch.

"Should I hear that?" he said.

"Yes."

He stayed in place, smiling.

"I'll deliver it then." Again she came toward him. He faced her the whole way; and that was how she saw him, the cooler light in her own eyes now, already half-evening. She'd always been a retentive reader, or hearer of anyone else's reading (she still knew the plots and minor players of every story read to her in grade school); so she naturally saw him through what he'd just said. Who would risk live burial—dry dirt in the mouth—for that boy there? Who would risk having his flesh cut from him as he clung to one of these standing columns till the white gristle showed, then the lungs and heart? In five steps she answered herself—*"Ann Gatlin."* Why not? What else? *Why?* Because he'd seemed to ask her at times. How crazy was that? No crazier than all this tonnage round them, this all but endlessly durable wreckage that would easily outwear the race itself to be prowled over by whatever spacelings or angels survived for soul-restoring visits. She reached him silently and stood, looking down at the drying shard.

"I'm waiting," he said.

"Good." She laughed.

"—Your message," he said.

She'd forgot it in the walk. "Is this what I gave you?" She pointed at the shard.

"I gave him a bath."

"It stained him though."

Hutch nodded. "Old blood. From the loins of dead priests."

She laughed again. "I was trusting you to say that."

"Seldom fail," he said.

She remembered her message. "They took it very seriously—the Romans, I mean."

"What's *it?*" Hutch said.

She looked out briefly. "Their poor bodies. Sex."

"They patented the orgy. They loved every minute."

"No they didn't, Dumbo. Your brain's in Oxford." She touched his forehead; he reached for her hand. "This is all sex-magic," Ann said, "every cobble. They were scared to death."

"And they're all dead, notice." Hutch waved wide about them. "Don't see them multiplying." Far as they could see, they were perfectly alone. Behind the last high ruins, the city was silent. He picked up the shard, nearly white again.

"Better leave it," Ann said.

"It's my Christmas gift." He put it in his pocket and stood. It was heavy. He gave a mock stumble as if sinking with the load.

The guard was beside them, having come from nowhere—a tall blond man in a tight uniform. An Ostrogoth?

Hutch assumed there were penalties for palming the antiques—fines or years? He stood and said "Evening."

Ann took a step toward the man, not hinting a smile. "Do you know a good Parker-pen salesman nearby?"

The guard said "*Prego?*"

"My crippled friend here's a poet, overwhelmed by the tides of inspiration."

The guard said, "*Scusi ma adesso è chiuso*" and grimly pointed them out the east gate—Arch of Titus, Arch of Constantine, the Colosseum looking very much like itself. The first motor scooter was the sound of safety. Hutch stopped limping then. They stalled in the midst of the broad hub of streets on the buried base of Nero's colossal statue of himself.

Ann said "This is getting unmanageable."

"What?"

"The layers round here."

He touched her shoulder. "The lay-ees too."

"I mean the *time*, Dumbo—the stacks of time. Any D.A.R. from the Old Dominion would give her best corset for an acre of this, and there's hundreds of acres."

"Five hundred eighty square *miles*, the book says."

"Burn the book," Ann said. "Let's invent it from here." She took him by the wrist and led him toward the Via degli Annibaldi; and though they passed the church with Michelangelo's Moses (and St. Peter's prison-chains), they ignored it, discovering their own better spots in the fast-falling night—Cleopatra's colonic irrigation studio, Michelangelo's model agency and escort service, the site of Roderigo Borgia's Wasserman test, Mussolini's French-tickler purveyor (by appointment). Ann said, "Can't you see him in it now, at attention? It had rabbit ears, translucent and veiny, and pink straps that looped up over his arms like an old tank suit; and at critical moments it would play dance tunes from his mother's native village, up-tempo but softly."

By the time they reached the Pacifica, it seemed a real home. The whole city did, though by then it was cold.

8

After dinner they'd found the one English-language movie and sat through *Doctor at Sea* with Dirk Bogarde, accompanied by only six other scattered bodies—one of whom turned out, when the lights were raised, to be the blond *ingénue* of the plot, a small-boned girl in a tan duffel coat that made her unadorned coarse skin look ill: swamp fever or jaundice. Ann said to Hutch, "I thought they'd drained the Pontine Marshes"; the girl's escort heard, grinned, and nodded. Outside the wind was strong and they took their first taxi. Hutch tried to converse as they roared through empty streets—"Where are the tourists?"—"Just you," the driver said in unaccented English but appeared to smile also.

So they entered the Pacifica again, tired but easy, thinking of nothing but clean teeth and bed (the notion of merging rooms had been shelved with no further discussion). Hutch passed the lobby without looking in, but Ann saw the same West Virginia boy still there as if he'd sat through Christmas. He was not even turning the worn magazines but staring at space with an awful patience. She caught up with Hutch as he opened his door. "Can we go back and cheer up Monongah awhile? He's looking blue."

He said "You go."

She could see he meant it. "What will you do then?"

"Bathe my tired back and read till I sleep."

"What if I wake you?"

He made a loose fist and rapped her belly. "I'll be mad if you don't."

"I'll stay," she said and took a step in.

"Ann, let me read you the first rule of travel"—he lined it on the air—*"Cabin mates will require an absolute minimum of one hour alone for each day together."*

"We're alone all night."

"Not really," Hutch said.

His grin reassured her (and the rule sounded right). She said, "This may not last ten minutes. He may be drunk."

"Or deader than us—he's Santy Claus, remember?"

But she took off her raincoat, gave it to Hutch; and not even stopping to comb her hair, went back to the lobby and stood in the door.

The boy took a minute to sense her and look.

"Merry Christmas," she said.

"You said it was over, way back this morning."

"I'm sorry," she said. "I was fast asleep."

He accepted that. He was neatly dressed now in a purple short-sleeved shirt and gray trousers. He looked under twenty; they'd never swapped names.

"My name is Ann Gatlin."

He stood slowly. "You could sit down, I guess."

"You waiting for somebody?"

"No ma'm," he said.

She sat on a small couch across from his chair; the dry wicker creaked outrageously. She laughed. "This place!"

"It's all right," he said, "—good eats."

"Good company?"

He blushed, then cracked the knuckle of his long middle finger so loudly Ann looked to the ceiling for damage. That was all his answer.

"Where'd you go today?"

"Cross the street," he said, "—that American Bar. It's about as American as Mount-damn-Everest. I ordered a grilled cheese sandwich; ought to *seen* it."

"Just the name makes me hungry."

"The sandwich wouldn't."

"That's all you did?"

"Yes ma'm. I'm not a traveler."

"What you doing here then?"

"I come with two buddies from Germany. They had to see Naples, know a girl near there. I told them, 'Just leave me here to sleep.' They'll pick me up Wednesday; said so anyway."

"If they don't?"

"I'll wait."

"Aren't you in the Army?"

"Air Force—better food."

"And you won't be AWOL?"

"I might, yes ma'm."

"Would you go to jail?"

"Not for long," he said. "They don't call it jail."

"Call me *Ann* please," she said.

He nodded.

"Who are you?"

"Rowlet," he said.

"First name?"

"Rowlet Swanson."

"Why did you leave Monongah?"

For the first time he laughed. His new beauty tore through the space like a ghost and struck her whole face. "You ain't seen Monongah."

Ann knew she should smile, but the sight still held her. "Just pictures," she said. "You plan to go back?"

"When I'm about a hundred years old, in a box."

"It's really that bad?"

He looked off blankly to consider the question, then answered toward the door. "The *place* has got this town beat to hell, but I've got a bunch of brothers." He faced her and laughed again. "You a missionary?"

This time she could join him. "—For *leaving*, yes."

"You got a bad sister?"

"A normal mother."

"Who's your brown-headed friend?" He pointed through the wall.

What to call him? She could only offer "Hutchins Mayfield."

"No kin?"

"Not yet, maybe later."

"Married people aren't kin. That's the point, I thought."

"Then why have babies?"

"I'm a private, lady. You're asking a lot."

"Sorry," Ann said. "I work for a lawyer."

Rowlet said "You could quit," then looked up quickly.

A girl in a green dress stood in the door—black hair, a dense glamor. It took Ann awhile to see it was the waitress, finished in the kitchen (at eleven, Christmas night). She moved to stand.

But Rowlet said, "Rest. I'll be here tomorrow." Then he went to the girl. He could say her difficult name, and did—*Smeralda*, Emerald.

9

Ann didn't switch on the light in her room; but the curtains were open, there was some streetlight, and soon as she entered she saw the bed was empty—carefully made. The door between the two rooms was ajar. She went to the sill and, not looking in, listened quietly. No sure sound of life. So she didn't look in and didn't think why. She undressed, found her nightgown, brushed her teeth; then turned back the covers of her bed and slid on her back to the middle. She oared her arms slowly full-length in the coolness of linen still smelling of iron-scorch. She thought she liked that. She touched her pooled breasts through cloth, smiled, and told them "Just *rest*, doll-babies." She said a short prayer, which was not customary—thanks for the day, that still seemed good; blessings on her mother, who had not tried to phone. Before she had managed to ask for the future, her eyes filled with tears. Even then she thought they were excess pleasure (though she'd always noticed how men wept for pleasure, women for pain). And though they continued for the three or four minutes till she'd sunk to sleep, she didn't suspect they were signs of failure—hers or Hutch's. That came when he joined her.

At five he'd waked to find himself alone. In the dark he couldn't know how long he'd slept—he felt fully rested—and he'd lain still to hear the hall outside. At first there was nothing, then eventually the slow wet slap of a mop—end of night or start of day? He strained for more sound of Ann and the boy—hopeless of course; that was yards away. He didn't once think she was nearby, unconscious. It came on him then, in the crazy accuracy of night, that she'd left with the boy. To where? For how long? He'd heard the table of soldiers last night planning a visit to Bricktop's nightclub. Would that be it? He knew he was still dazed and untrustworthy; but he stood up naked in the cold air, opened the hall door, and looked out gingerly. An old man he'd never seen before was wringing the mop ten feet beyond him. Hutch asked was it morning.

The man said "No."

"*Ma che ora è?*"

"*Cinque ore forse.*"

Hutch didn't know enough words to ask for Ann, but his mind had cleared sufficiently to think of her room. He went there slowly. She'd left the curtains open; and he saw her at once, sprawled neat and alone. The relief he felt seemed out of proportion even as he stood there (he'd already lost the dream that waked him, another prediction of Rob's disappearance). But he went straight forward and entered the bed. Though she'd stayed in the middle, Ann had warmed the whole surface; and at first he lay flat on the edge, still shivering. The relief had settled into gratitude; so once he was warm, he was ready to thank her. She was on her right side, away from him. He turned toward her gently and fitted his front down her warmer back—his hard cock downward in the crack of her legs. He knew she was awake (any falling feather woke her), but she gave no sign of welcome. He tugged at the muscle that thumped his cock like a dog-snout against her—*Attention! Love me!* He'd forgot the Morse code; but he thumped out a spurious stretch of dot-dash meant to greet, thank, beg with his amiable universal greeter-thanker-beggar. Her lean upper leg lifted slightly at last, and he slid into harbor or offshore anchorage. He rubbed his rough chin on the crest of her spine and said "Happy Boxing Day."

She said "What's that?"

"The day after Christmas in Merrie-Olde, when you give gift boxes to servants and tradesmen."

"Which am I?" she said.

She only sounded sleepy; Hutch thought she was volleying. "—The giver," he said. "Lady Bountiful." His left hand moved round her thigh to the slit. She was dry as a child. He worked against that, not harshly but fast.

They'd been in sophomore English together. She said in her street voice, "Patient Griselda."

But he laughed and persisted in the tuning skills which their years had perfected; and in two more minutes (still spooned to her back, licking her neck), he entered the performance he'd never failed at. Through it he constantly watched what he'd seen in the afternoon. *Young woman in ruins of the Palatine*, a nimbus of late light, the clear news he'd waited for longer than he'd known—that he'd go home to her. When he'd calmed again he found Ann's right hand and, after long fumbling, slid his Great-grandmother Mayfield's wedding ring from his own hand and closed it in her palm.

She lay still a long time, discarding many questions. Then she said "What does this say?"

"*'Robinson Mayfield to Anna Goodwin.'*"

"No, *now*. It says something."

He took her middle finger and put the ring on it, still too large.

"You're supposed to use words."

He seized a damp hank of her hair in his teeth and pulled back gently. "—In the morning," he said.

"We talk better at night."

Hutch had gone by then—into sleep like a trapdoor, though still close against her.

Ann wore the ring but never shut her eyes. She lay for an hour, not moving away, in the hope of freeing her body from the net of failure that had fallen across it the moment she woke, the warning that she and Hutch were suddenly parted after one perfect day and would not meet again—not meet, not join. In all her racing through grievances and fears, she never touched the reason.

At ten to seven someone knocked on her door, serious and loud. Ann rose at once, found her robe, and answered.

Rowlet Swanson, still wearing his late-night clothes, stood three feet back. "Is Hutchins Mayfield the name of your friend?"

"Yes."

"I think he's got a call from the States. I'm not sure."

Then she found the reason; the net clung tighter. "Are they waiting?"

"—In the lobby. Smeralda answered it finally. She doesn't know much."

Ann said "He's coming." She shut the door, no mention of thanks.

Hutch was watching by then.

She came halfway. "You're wanted on the phone, they think—in the lobby."

He didn't show fear or bafflement but lay still an instant, then loped to his room and rushed to dress. As he left he called back "Yule greetings from home."

Ann knew he was wrong. When she felt she could move, she washed herself carefully, pinned her hair back, dressed warmly, and sat in her one chair to wait.

10

An Italian operator—sounding worlds away, barely speaking English—established his name and vanished so thoroughly he thought the line was cut.

Then "Hutch? You hear me?"

"Yes"—Grainger as plain as the sun on his bare feet. "Where are you?"

"Sylvie's house. You well?"

"What time is it there?" He could hear Grainger turn and ask Sylvie, hear her answer "One o'clock—black night." They seemed entirely tangible. He might have reached out an actual hand if Rowlet hadn't stood in the door behind him and if cold nodes of fright hadn't formed all through him.

Grainger said "You feeling good?"

"Doing good. Merry Christmas. Did you get my package?"

"Not yet. Thank you though."

The sound of Sylvie coughing.

Hutch saw he'd have to start it, bring it on himself. "Everybody all right?"

"Sylvie's got a bad cold. Miss Eva's pretty good."

"How's Rob?"

"Bad, Hutch. I'm calling to tell you."

"What?"

"They put him in the clinic here two days ago."

"What's the trouble?"

"Can't breathe. They got him in the tent."

"What's the trouble?"

"A cancer."

Sylvie said "Going fast."

"Who's with him?" Hutch said.

"Miss Eva. Miss Min—Miss Min's there now. I left to call you."

"Can I call him?"

"He don't want you to know. Me and Sylvie doing this."

"Then what must I do?"

"Depends," Grainger said.

"What on?"

"You want to see him?"

Sylvie said "Tell him 'Hurry.'"

11

In Ann's room he said, "That was Grainger. Rob's dying."

She said "Where was Grainger?" She'd stood by the chair.

"At Sylvie's, one o'clock in the morning."

"What else did he say?"

Hutch was dry as pressed cloth. He went to her basin, ran water, drank a handful. Then he went to the bed and sat at the foot to face the window. "Please sit there," he said. "It's cancer—his lungs. They can't operate. They've moved him to the clinic in Fontaine for oxygen. Nobody knows how long it'll take. He told them not to tell me."

"Why?" She sat again.

Hutch was watching the bright sky. "—To leave me here."

"Why?"

"He thought I'd asked for it."

"Did Grainger say that?"

Hutch shook his head. "I knew."

Ann said "So did I."

Hutch lay back on his elbows, inspected the ceiling, then faced Ann finally. "Knew what please?"

"I've known about your father since June fourteenth."

"How?"

"Polly—he told her on his trip to Richmond. Swore her to silence but she called me."

"You didn't see Rob then?"

"He never called me, no."

The space between them—eight feet—seemed a moving shaft, lengthening, narrowing. The light in his eyes had almost blanked Ann. "Polly swore you not to tell me?"

"Your father did, Hutch. Polly called him that night to confess what she'd done. He wrote me a letter next morning; *he* swore me."

"Have you got the letter now?"

"Not here. I'm not lying."

"But you have, for six months."

She nodded. "All right." When she breathed after that, she thought she might not breathe again—air was thin and scarce.

Hutch stood. "Let me put on my shoes and wash. We have to eat now."

Between them they ate all the rolls set out, the curls of butter and apricot jam, and drank big basins of cool strong coffee. They said very little and neither asked questions. They knew they were gliding low on declivities neither could see; any glance down might break the frail balance. They could only look forward. Hutch refused more coffee; then said, "Will you let me take a long walk now?"

"Long as you want." Ann nodded, half-smiling.

"It's not what I want."

She nodded again. "I'll wash my hair."

He put his hands forward to the rim of her plate and spoke to its blankness (she'd eaten every crumb). "All I can say now is 'Pardon us please'— Rob and me."

She touched the nail of the finger he'd stripped the ring from at dawn. "I don't have the right but, sure, full pardon."

He looked to the window; the sun was steady. "Don't stay inside. If you want to, walk. I'll be back for lunch."

She nodded. "So will I."

He stopped by the room for his money and guidebook, then set out south-west again down the broad street—no destination for the first ten minutes. But when he pulled up at the Victor Emmanuel, he saw it had grown since yesterday; and he took a hard right through Piazza Venezia and on up the Corso. It was choked with cars, blue with exhaust at barely nine; so he took the first street west in blind hope of steering for the Tiber and air and came out shortly in a small car-park with a marble elephant bearing an obelisk, and a few yards ahead, the rear of what was plainly the Pantheon swathed in cats. He sat on the steps of the nearest church and opened his guide.

He'd landed at one of his few planned targets—or had he been led? (he suspected that). The midget elephant was an early Bernini. The obelisk was left from a temple of Isis that had stood nearby; the church was built on the ruins of a temple to Minerva and contained the tomb of Beato Angelico and Michelangelo's only statue of the grown live Christ, Risen with bronze underpants ("a later addition").

He entered brown dark and went straight forward past chapels and tombs through a haze of incense to the steps of the choir where Risen Christ stood bare, the pants gone. An inch was broken from the end of the penis, but the balls were intact, and their thin-skinned availability measured more terribly than wounds the day of agony He'd borne to stand here, unquestionably risen, His thick hips and haunches an adequate promise He'd suffered for all and would not fail again. Hutch moved up to meet His sideways glance and planned for the first time this morning to ask that his own choice be made, not painless but right. The eyes wouldn't meet him. They wanted no prayers; they knew all outcomes. Nothing was possible but prone adoration—to fall face-down on the steps in thanks. It had surely happened here thousands of times. But thanks were as needless as begging or praise. Hutch looked back once; the nave was still empty. He went through it quietly toward the street and sun and straight through the fierce watchful cats to the doors of the Pantheon.

He knew it also had always been a temple, built to All the Gods by Hadrian, reconsecrated by Boniface IV to Mary the Virgin and twenty-eight wagonloads of martyred bones hauled up from the catacombs to wait here in light. For all its external gloomy mass, the vast inner globe of its heart seemed afloat—a transparent heart loose now in sunlight, slowly ascending; the open eye in its apex peering calm and unblinking at a sure destination: a patient socket in the breast of a sky even clearer, calmer. He walked to the absolute center of the floor, stood on the marble disc still wet from the night (he'd heard no rain) and looked above. Unbroken sky of a blue no painter had matched, never would—no camera, no dream. He spoke to that silently. *Show me now please.* A distant crack reached him. He knew it was knees and looked for the source. An old woman knelt on the stone by a niche containing the Virgin with obese Child. He didn't know that the box beneath contained the dust of Raphael. Unnecessary news. He had the one answer required today—infused through his whole skin as if he were bare as the neighborhood Christ, though with no pain or scar.

He consulted his map, found American Express, found it open and ready, and booked the earliest seat he could get—tomorrow noon: New York, then home. It took all his money but sixty-five dollars.

13

The blond woman helped him place the call to Virginia; then left him alone in the lobby with the old phone, traces of gilt arabesque on its cradle.

Alice was awake as he'd known she'd be, at five in the morning. Neither one mentioned Christmas; and though she seemed farther off than Grainger, she went for the throat. "Who's in trouble?"

"Don't you know?"

"Sure, everybody my age. Which one you mean?"

"Rob. You haven't heard from Rob?"

"Not for years, Hutch. Years. Rob thinks I took you."

She had; he saw now. But he pushed through that. "Grainger just called from home. Rob's going fast—cancer. They knew when I left; he made them keep it from me."

"They were right," Alice said. "Is he conscious still?"

He hadn't asked; he stalled and weighed the omission.

But she said, "Can I meet you? What plane? What time?"

"New York in the morning, then the first plane to Raleigh."

"It's rush-time," she said.

"I'll tell them it's death. They keep space for deaths. Let me call you once I'm home. It may be crowded—Grandmother, Min Tharrington."

"Is she back on?"

"Somehow," Hutch said.

"I'll be here. Always am."

"You can help today."

"I'm dressed," Alice said.

"Find some way to cable me five hundred dollars, care American Express."

"That enough?"

"Should be."

"Is Ann coming with you?"

"Not yet," Hutch said.

When Hutch had finished and stood, there was Rowlet (Ann had told him the name over breakfast). At some point in the call, he'd managed to enter and sit by the door on the deafening wicker couch. Hutch passed him and nodded.

"You got a plane yet?"

Hutch stopped. "Noon tomorrow."

"Want a ride to the field?"

"Thank you. I can take the bus."

"I'll meet you here at ten. Rich buddy left his car when he went to Naples. I got the keys."

Thanks were plainly unwanted. For a moment Hutch thought "Everybody claims a part"; but he did say, "Thanks. Maybe half-past nine? I need to get some money that's being wired to me."

"I could lend you fifty easy."

"It's coming from home. I'll leave some with Ann to pay my bills here."

"You leaving her here?"

Hutch said, "I guess so. She's got two weeks. I can't haul her back to what's waiting for me."

"She'd go," Rowlet said.

Hutch extended his hand. "Hutch Mayfield," he said.

Rowlet gave his long brown hand over like a dog, some young animal in need of slow care. It was solid horn-callus though. He said "I know your name."

"Is Ann back yet?"

Rowlet nodded. "In her room."

Hutch took a step toward him.

"I saw her new ring."

Hutch smiled. "You see all."

"They pay me to. I'm in tower-control."

The voice—dead-flat in its West Virginia vowels—held Hutch in place but with nothing to say. Also the narrow face, steadily offered as any wrecked column in the city. He watched it. After ten seconds it still seemed blank but increasingly strong, for mercy or harm.

Rowlet said "You eat?"

"Not yet."

"Want to eat?"

"I'll check on Ann."

"She's ready. Go call her."

Hutch nodded and took a step.

"After that I'm driving the waitress home. She's got a day off, lives out in the country. Plenty room in the car."

Hutch said "I'll ask Ann."

Rowlet said "She'll come."

14

She did. They piled into the rich buddy's Plymouth; and Smeralda pointed them silently north, Rowlet nosing through streets that were filling again as Christmas ebbed. Up the Via Flaminia, past the Villa Borghese (green core of the city with its weird Caravaggios, which Hutch would not see), cross the Milvian Bridge where Constantine triumphed as promised in his vision; then the traffic thinned suddenly, and after a few miles of gimcrack housing, they were in open country. Hilly pasture with small cows, clumps of gray olives and the huge boles of cork trees, occasional scraps of ancient wall. Smeralda stayed silent, Rowlet only spoke to clarify directions, Ann said "Look" a half-dozen times at fine prospects, Hutch would look and nod.

Otherwise he practiced for thirty minutes his oldest skill—calm witness, all eyes. He saw the beauty of woods and farms. He sensed the unthinkable strata of effort, unbroken relays of human labor, that had gentled the land to this sun-struck peace. But he felt no regret to be leaving tomorrow, and the fact of Rob dying was a sight he'd postponed. It would come in its time late tomorrow—a sight as incalculable as what he now passed through, the land that fed Rome and all her predecessors.

Smeralda said "Stop" at last, and Rowlet stopped hard in the midst of the road. A dwarf tractor crossed fifty yards ahead, led by a black dog. She turned to the back seat and smiled at Hutch. "I'm very sad for your father," she said.

It was many more English words than Hutch had thought she knew. He thanked her.

Then she pointed to Rowlet. "Make him take you to see the old *castello*, Santa Maria di Galéria. Just a few more minutes." She touched Rowlet's shoulder once and was gone, jumping a shallow ditch neatly in her best dress and climbing on strong legs toward a tan house set back in pines with a staring goat. She never looked back.

Hutch almost called to her, thanks again; she seemed that lonely.

Rowlet said "You want to see it?"

Hutch said "Why not?"

"It's not a coal mine, is it?"

Hutch laughed. "No a castle."

"Then aim me. I'm running."

Hutch climbed into the front seat and opened his guide.

Before they moved on, Ann lay back to rest.

15

By the time they'd found the eight-foot-deep track that led like a tunnel to a green river-valley, she was fast asleep. Rowlet stopped at a barbed-wire fence at the foot of a high plateau and faced Hutch for word.

Hutch read out, " 'The ruins of the castle of Galéria stand on the site of Etruscan Careiae. Commanding the wooded valley of the Galera, it served from the ninth to the nineteenth century but was finally abandoned for reasons of health.' "

"Another ghost town," Rowlet said. "You guess it's healthy yet?"

"It's fertile anyhow." Hutch pointed to the thicket of vines on the gateway, the massed bay trees. It seemed an illustration from every child's dream of the gate into strangeness, all laws reversed.

"Want to limber your legs?" Rowlet killed the engine.

Hutch said "Sure" and looked to Ann. Her dry lips had parted, and her teeth were clenched. He turned, put his hand to her mouth, felt her breath—normal heat. Then he touched her forehead, exhaustion not fever. "Shall we wake her?"

"Let her be." Rowlet opened his door.

Hutch wrote her a note on the back of a map of Bavaria—*We are up in those ruins, 4 p.m.* Then he locked Rowlet's door, locked his own; and followed Rowlet up a weedy path toward a fine belltower, no hands on its clock. Sun was strong but a light wind pushed at their backs with a fresh river smell. Hutch turned to face it and take the light for a long quiet minute. Then Rowlet was gone. When he looked up the path again, he saw only shards of tile, naked brambles, and the ash-blond huddles of broken stone walls—roofless warrens hacked open to the sky. No sound at all. Even river and wind moved silently. He pulled on upward, trusting Rowlet would show—maybe jump from hiding in some ghost act. But he reached the arched gate, still alone and silent. The climb had been easy, but his breath came fast; so he stopped by a hole of standing brown water and waited to calm, looking only down. In another long minute a hard rush flooded his mouth and eyes, a fresh sense of having what he'd asked to have—absolute space, the empty world, and time to watch it. For what?—its picture, the figure Rob had missed. For whom?—who but Rob? to reward, win, hold him, protect him from his life. Which had won him now, dissolved him in pain. Leaving Hutch again with memory and no one to hear, an unworn witness in an empty court—an unused fool. He saw no way to laugh, though laughter seemed required.

Rowlet said "Come here." He was hid to the left.

"Where's here?"

Rowlet said "Just follow the voice" and started singing. His speaking voice was deep, but he sang in a strong pure tenor—no words—the tune of "Sweet William."

Hutch found him at the top of a broad staircase in full light; he stopped. "No, finish your song."

"Not mine," Rowlet said. "Don't know it to the end. My sister used to like it."

"Where's she?"

"Jesus knows."

"What killed her?"

"Maybe nothing. She may be alive."

"You don't want to find her?"

"She'll holler if she's hungry."

"Who you looking for now?" Hutch said.

Rowlet faced him, came down a step, and smiled (Hutch had not seen him smile till now). "Your girl," he said.

"Is she still in the car?"

Rowlet came down. "I guess so. I couldn't see more than the roof. Maybe you ought to check."

"You worried about her?"

Rowlet sat on the huge bottom step but spoke to Hutch; concealment seemed as foreign to his nature as lace. "I'm thinking I may ought to worry over you."

Hutch went to him, passed him, climbed three steps above, sat, and touched both his shoulders—he was warmer than the light. "I'll make it," he said.

Rowlet said "Don't doubt it."

"Stop worrying then." His hands stayed in place.

Rowlet bore them like buckets; but he said, "Not till you tell me how I got to act once you're back home and her and me are left together."

Hutch finally laughed. "How old are you?"

"Twenty soon," Rowlet said.

"Age fast then, son. She likes experts."

Rowlet said "Are you one?"

Hutch took back his hands. "She's come here to see me."

"Where do you live?"

"England."

"Why?"

"I'm studying there."

"To be what?" Rowlet said.

"A writer."

"She your subject?"

"Not yet. Too soon."

"How long have you known her?"

"Seven years."

"You engaged?"

"Very likely."

"And you're leaving her here." It was not a question.

But Hutch said "No choice."

"If she asked would you take her?"

"She won't."

Rowlet bent to the ground and took up a scrap of rose-colored brick, dug at it with the nail of his index finger till he'd scored a short line. "That's what you're an expert in?" he said. Not turning, he handed the clay back to Hutch.

Hutch took it—common scrap, the color of brick everywhere on earth. "I haven't given much thought to brick," he said and gouged at the line.

"—*People*," Rowlet said. "You know what people will do in advance, knowing she won't ask to go home with you."

Hutch grinned. "Maybe so."

Rowlet turned just his profile, clear against the dark ground as coastline on maps. "Then foretell me this—what will you do if her and me take up together, two orphans in Rome?" He smiled again downhill toward the car.

That simple line from forehead to chin seemed now to Hutch all he'd ever meant to understand, praise, and save—its brave seal thrust toward the patient fruitful matrix of the world. He leaned, pressed his own mouth against dry hair on the ridge of Rowlet's neck. "I'm the orphan," he said. "Good luck anyhow."

Rowlet stayed a moment, then laughed and stood.

Ann said, "Keep laughing. I'm tracking you down."

Hutch laughed in earnest and threw the scored shard. It cleared a high wall, banked higher on wind, and sailed toward the river.

16

After dinner Ann read in the lobby while he packed (Rowlet had vanished again with the car). At ten he finished and came in to get her. "You tired?"

"Pure dead." She regretted the word.

Hutch was too tired to notice.

They undressed in her room, set her travel-clock to alarm at seven (not counting on Rowlet), and doused the light. After two quiet minutes on his back, Hutch turned and slowly consulted her shoulders, neck, face with a hand as gentle and baffled as a child's. He found no message, though he even pressed a finger through her lips to the teeth and rubbed their warm blankness.

She accepted the prowling long as she could, then spoke to stop him. "Any signs of pyorrhea?"

"No'm, perfect," he said.

"Well damn. I was counting on a full set of dentures, every other tooth gold." She still lay flat.

He tapped her nose, laughed once, ringed her warm throat. Then tears overcame him.

Ann felt them and knew there was cause, but she didn't move or speak.

In a while Hutch said, "Do you want to ask questions?" They had still not discussed his going, her staying.

"Not really," she said. "But I know what you mean."

"That's more than I do."

So she rolled to face him, not seeing but taking his clean breath for presence. "You mean do I understand what's happened here?"

"Do you?"

"How's this? We had a good three days in Rome. You gave me this ring again, and this time I took it."

"Will you keep it?"

"—Till you ask me to stop," she said.

"I haven't."

"I know."

"But I've asked you to stay here."

"I know why," she said.

He waited and then said "You better tell *me*."

"You love your father more than anything else."

"How much do you mind that?"

"I might not at all if I understood why."

Hutch said, "He was what I had from the start. He was lovable."

She laid her right hand on his breastbone and pressed; then spread her fingers and tried to span his nipples, missing by an inch. "Please tell me everything you know about your mother." She'd never asked for that.

"You know what I know. Her name was Rachel; you've seen the few pictures."

"I know she'd had some kind of breakdown before she met your father."

"—Thought she was pregnant; she'd never touched a boy."

"Then she met your father. They had a few years, and she died bearing you."

Hutch covered her hand. "That's the story I know."

"Think harder," Ann said. "You lived in her body—Great God!—nine months."

He laughed once. "I used to remember that. Till the time I was five or six years old, it was all I remembered—all the past I had."

"How was it?"

"Very still. I had time to look."

"At what?"

"Oh light. I'd wake up and hang there for hours, warm in a bath of mild light—the sun through her belly, I guess: rose with blood."

"Maybe you dreamt it."

"Maybe not," he said. "I'd forgot till now." (He'd forgot Archie Gibbons's memory on Tresco.)

She kissed his throat. "Then I'm glad I asked."

"I killed her though."

"Never mind," Ann said. "She volunteered."

"There *is* one dream I've had more than once. I'm a half-grown boy. I find her in the woods and know her on sight. She's the image of me and nearly as young. I ask her to wait while I go for Rob. She's gone when we come. I wrote you that."

"She wanted just you. She'd have stayed for you."

He'd never thought it. "Why?"

"She wanted you before she'd ever seen your father."

"Say why."

"She still wants you."

"Say why though." He kissed her at the edge of her mouth.

"I couldn't. She couldn't. But I'm right; so was she."

Hutch chose to believe her. He lay still, seeing old versions of the dream—Rachel's face, his absent mother. She stood to be watched, gave no sign of flight. She was his present age, a feasible woman.

Ann waited through that, then said "Now me."

Dark as it was, he also saw her—no dream, plain memory, her face in the Forum as she'd brought him her finding: "They were *serious*." He reached out, freed her left ear from hair, and traced its rim. "Dear Dumbo," he said. He was ready by then.

They worked toward it slowly, there on their sides, and slowly arrived—reward for both. When they'd thanked each other, they lay on joined. Ann said, "I'll be in Richmond on the first." She felt him nod but he didn't speak again. Before his head was still, he'd started his sleep. She was calmly awake an hour later when the child began.

17

Rob studied Hutch a moment; then said, "She's gone out to get me a shot."

Hutch smiled. "I leave and here you start drinking."

Rob nodded. "Morphine. White Lightning worked better." When he smiled the teeth that had showed through his translucent lip were the only unchanged things—perfect and white. The hand that lifted the oxygen tent was a long bone rake.

Hutch leaned in, kissed him on the forehead, leaned back. The tent fell between them, fanning out its cool gas and the burnt smell of cancer.

"You're meant to be in Rome."

"I'm not. Here, feel."

Rob took the right hand. "Appears to be you." His voice was familiar but shrunk like the rest, a condensation.

Hutch said, "That sign on your door seems to work—*Absolutely No Visitors*. Grandmother post that?"

"Had to. We were running a menagerie, me the ape in the tent." He pointed to a chair. "Pull that over here."

Hutch sat a yard from him, tasting the oddness of his joy to be back (he'd phoned nobody, come by bus from Raleigh, a taxi to the clinic).

"I sent Min home with Grainger to supper. He'll be back after dark."

Rob took three silent shallow breaths. "They have little arm-wrestling contests to see who gets to sit here through the night and watch me."

Hutch nodded in hopes of slowing the talk.

But Rob turned toward him—"Am I that pretty still?"—and smiled again.

Hutch reached out and covered the hand. "Rest a little. I'll be here now."

The smile survived. Rob looked to the ceiling. "You talk. Tell all."

"Let's rest a few minutes."

"They'll be back by then." Rob shut his eyes and waited.

So Hutch said, "Grainger and Sylvie called me two days ago. I called Alice Matthews; she wired the money. I took the first plane and came straight here. Nobody knows but you."

"Did that woman see you?"

"Mrs. Hayes, at the desk."

"It'll be on the radio by now," Rob said. "There'll be swarms to see you. Ne' mind, ne' mind." He breathed again. "You got any questions?"

Hutch said "Not yet."

"Now is your chance."

"I'm staying, remember?"

Rob nodded.

The door opened wide on a nurse with a small nickel tray and a needle. She stopped on the threshold. "It's *you*. I've lost. I bet Emily Hayes a dollar it was any other human but you. What blew you in?"

Hutch stood—Alta Allen; she'd nursed him through pneumonia nine years ago. "East wind," he said. "Happy New Year."

"Hold your horses," she said, "—four days of this old year left to get through." She walked on to Rob and touched his bare forearm. "You feel like it's time?"

Rob said "Yes ma'm."

She brushed him with alcohol, gave him the drug, and rubbed the arm. Then she looked back to Hutch. "You remember this—Rob Mayfield is four months older than me. He calls me *ma'm* but I know him of old. The tales I could tell!"

Rob tapped on the tent. When she faced him he shook a warning finger slowly, then sank straight to sleep.

Alta smoothed the sheets, checked the oxygen valve, stepped to Hutch, and laid her wide hand on his head. "Nothing bad," she said, "—my tales, I mean. They were mostly funny. He was nobody's enemy but his sweet self's. You got here in time."

Hutch said "Yes ma'm."

She opened the door. "I'll be at the desk."

Hutch stood and whispered, "Did he ask for me?"

Alta faced him plainly. "Not to me, not anywhere in my hearing." She searched his eyes, smiling. "You're past-due to eat. Come eat with me."

"I can't leave yet."

She nodded toward Rob. "He'll rest half an hour, maybe more if God loves him. I'll fix you anything you want in the pantry—provided it's biscuits, bullet-peas, and boiled chicken."

Hutch was suddenly empty and deeply tired. He looked at his watch and knew it was two in the morning in Rome. He could feel Ann awake. Then he followed Alta.

18

They'd finished the tepid food in the pantry under white light when Alta said "You've lost your ring."

Hutch's hand was on the table; he extended the fingers. "This Christmas," he said. "I gave it away."

"Anybody I know?" She lit a cigarette with the calm intensity of addiction.

"Ann Gatlin," he said. "I doubt you've ever seen her."

"Heard her name, heard about her." Alta ate another mouthful of smoke. "Is she worth it?"

"I think so."

"Where is she?"

Hutch checked his watch again. "In Italy asleep, I hope."

"She had to stay on?"

"I asked her to."

Alta stood and took his plate. "You need some lime jello?"

"Not today, no ma'm."

She went to the sink, ran a burst of cold water, then turned in place. "Will you listen to a little unsolicited advice?"

Hutch smiled, cupped an ear.

"Call her up, get her here, this'll get a lot worse." She pointed through a pink wall toward Rob.

"He doesn't seem in pain. Is that the morphine?"

"He just calls it morphine. It's Demerol. Pain won't be the problem. He'll drown in himself. They used to say drowning was a peaceful death, found smiles on their faces when the bodies washed up. But you'll have to watch."

Hutch said "How long?"

Alta walked to the back of her chair and held it. "I'd say two or three more days like this, then a long day to drown. That'll come in late evening. You'd better sleep tonight."

Hutch chose to believe her. He gauged his strength and thought he could walk the mile to his grandmother's. "Tell a tale first."

She thought a long moment. "I was kidding him. They're just child's play, his jokes."

"Remember the best one though, save it till tomorrow."

Alta laughed. "I'll try. My brain's gone to seed."

Grainger said "Well Lord—" He'd seen Hutch's bag by Rob's bed and found them.

Alta said "Is he asleep?"

Grainger nodded.

"Come in then and talk to this refugee a minute. He's sinking too; got to put him to bed if you mean to use him later." She left them quickly.

Hutch saw at once that Grainger had aged, first time since he'd known him. The wide black eyes were skinned over now with a bluish caul. He said, "You could use a month of nights yourself."

Grainger covered the distance and offered his hand. "Who brought you?"

"Bus from Raleigh, Genie's taxi from the station."

"I'd have met you anywhere."

Hutch said, "I know. I was just moving fast." He sat again and motioned Grainger down.

Grainger came to the back of the other chair and stood. "He seen you yet?"

"We talked a few minutes; then he got his shot."

"He understands more when he's sleep than wake."

Hutch said, "Who talked to the doctor last?"

"Miss Min, this morning. He won't estimate."

"Alta Allen says three or four more days."

Grainger nodded. "—Why I called you. Anybody known him long, know he's running now."

"But he didn't ask for me?"

"You well know why."

"What did Min have to say?"

Grainger spread his long fingers on the oak of the chair-back, then leaned forward suddenly and scrubbed Hutch's forehead with his palm. "Quit that. She don't mean much. You the one he was dwelling on, whatever he asked."

Hutch stood. "You well?"

"Don't matter," Grainger said.

"Your rabbits multiplying?"

"Everyone of em gone."

"What happened?"

"The buck. The doe got pregnant. I was busy and missed it. She dropped six babies in the night. He killed em, bit clean through their throats. Just him and the doe were there in the morning. I killed em both. Couldn't give em my time."

19

Cold as it was, Hutch stepped off the walk and stood by the maple, still studded with nailheads that measured his height on each birthday. From there he could see his grandmother's face. She sat in her chair and looked out at what was apparently nothing, clearly unchanged. The dim lamp beside her only stated again what he'd known as his earliest certainty—that time was her element as air is an eagle's, that it fed and sustained her while lashing all others. It still seemed a fact he could stand on safely. He went to the porch, climbed the steps silently, and tapped at the door.

Eva switched on the porch light, then opened fully. She looked for three seconds, indulged half a smile; but said, "You can't have seen everything in Rome."

"It'll wait," he said.

"Rome's a *she*," Eva said. "She's waited all right. Here, step in the warm."

He entered the room where he'd spent his boyhood, directly under the room he was conceived in, and set down his bag. Eva's eyes were dry—kindest sight of the day. He folded her slim body in and held her, his lips on her forehead.

When she stepped back she said, "I knew you'd get here."

He smiled but said, "Who was going to tell me?"

"Anybody—the trees! We were all sworn shut. But I knew you'd know."

He said, "I didn't. I was happy where I was."

"Who told you?—Polly Drewry or Min Tharrington?"

He'd never heard her say Polly's name before. "No, Grainger. He phoned me the day after Christmas."

"That's one cause for thanks," Eva said. "You hungry?"

"Exhausted," Hutch said. "I'm asleep right now."

But an hour later he lay in his old room, dark and awake. He'd run through the possible causes of worry—Rob, Ann, Min, his interrupted work—but now in this house he could face them calmly. He even made a schedule—a week more with Rob, maybe ten days of business, a chance to see Ann and Polly and Alice, then back to Oxford barely late for spring term. The calm was not coldness. He knew it was only a temporary strength. Other strengths would be needed when the eye of this present storm had passed. He tried to plan what he'd need to know and do, how to move on upright in a world swept clean of its prior engine and goal—how to move on at all (he saw now he'd *circled* but felt no regret). Say he'd live a full span; then a third of it spent in circling a center as tall as Rob was surely no waste. He heard his grandmother start upstairs; she'd stayed down to finish *Life* magazine. He counted her steps—sixteen: somehow she'd inserted an extra. She stopped at his shut door and opened it quietly. He'd forgot her hatred of secret space. He saw her stand a moment, then step toward her room. He said "I'm awake."

Eva stopped on the sill and said "You're still in midocean."

"Bring me in then please."

She came to his bed and sat on the edge—old outcry of springs. After a silence she reached for his head and scratched in the coarse hair, slow but earnest. "Shut your eyes; see this—there's a wind from the east. You're a grown corsair with dove-gray wings. Spread them and glide."

Hutch laughed. "The wind's blowing up my tail."

"But it's warm off the Gulf Stream; count your few blessings." She'd found as always the chicken-pox scar in his scalp and picked at it.

For more than a minute, he took her suggestion and skimmed westward fast over mild green water.

But she said, "How much do you know about this?"

"Rob, you mean?—that he'd known he was dying since before I left, that he wanted me to go, that Min's here with him; that he'll stay three or four days more, then drown."

"Who told you that last?"

"Alta Allen, over supper."

Eva said, "Don't depend on any Allen news. She's been wrong all her life."

"She's known him all her life."

Eva said, "I'm the person who's known him all his life, nobody but me."

Hutch gave her her rights. "How long has he got?"

She sat straight to answer. "He told me yesterday he doubted he'd die. Grainger took me over when Min wasn't there; and I was just trying to lift his spirits (Min keeps him *low*), telling things I'd seen, things Sylvie said. I guess I was chattering. He held up his hand and beckoned me over and said, 'No rush. I don't plan to leave.'"

"Is he in his right mind?"

"Clear as you," Eva said, "but he didn't know one thing. Till you walked in that room tonight, he didn't know every good cell in his body was holding out hard for you to get word. He'll go soon now."

Hutch said, "Would you have called me?"

Eva thought a moment; in the shuttered streetlight, he could see her head shake. "I'd given my word. I harmed him at the start by breaking my pledge to live with his father; I'd have kept it this time."

"Are you angry at Grainger?"

"Too sad to be," she said. "Every hair of my head aches with sadness every minute. You wait till you watch a child waste and die. Pray God you die first."

"He doubted you loved him."

"Ne' mind *love*," she said. "I'm speaking of *made*. I made Rob Mayfield sure as Sylvie makes bread. You think that through." She sat a long moment; then said "No, sleep."

20

When he got to the clinic at a little past seven, Grainger was washing Rob's hands with a rag. Rob's eyes stayed shut when Grainger spoke. "Wake early."

Hutch came up beside them. "It's past lunchtime where I was yesterday."

Grainger folded the rag and touched Rob's chin. "I'll shave you tonight."

Rob still didn't look. His whiskers were white, a web round his face, though half his hair was brown.

Grainger said "You walk?"

Hutch nodded. "It's warmer."

"I'll leave the truck here. You might need it later."

Hutch said, "No take it. I'll just be here."

Rob looked then, to Grainger. "Leave the truck. Hutch'll need it."

Grainger took out the keys and set them by the rag on the table. "I'm going—Miss Eva's day to shop. See you after while."

Rob nodded from what seemed enormous distance, unbridgeable, and Grainger left.

Hutch touched the hand again where it lay, the fingers spread.

"You don't have to do that. I may be catching," Rob said but he smiled.

Hutch stayed in place. "I may be. And that would be worse."

"I'll risk it," Rob said and ringed Hutch's wrist; then took his own hand and hid it in the sheets. "You didn't sleep enough."

"I did. I'm fine."

"At Mother's?"

"Yes. She's all right. She'll see you later."

"You haven't talked to Min?"

"I thought I'd see her here."

"I had Alta call her in the night. She's at home."

Hutch said "Whose home?"

Rob faced him harshly. "Mine, where she's welcome."

Hutch nodded, not smiling. "You need anything?"

Rob breathed three long breaths, open-mouthed. Even on the low hiss of oxygen, they grated. Then he grinned. "I'm debating a serious point— would I give all the good screws of thirty-four years for one deep breath?"

Hutch said, "Better not. Where would that leave me?"

Rob said, "That's the next point. I'm coming to that."

Hutch moved toward the chair.

"Stand still," Rob said.

Hutch stood. Pure early light was behind him.

Rob pointed a finger and traced the full shape of his son's right side, a likeness as visible as any while it lasted. Then he said, "I need this—drive out to the house and speak to Min."

"Right now?"

"She's there now."

Hutch sat. "Is there anything I need to know first?"

"Turn the key, put the engine in gear, and ride. Nice views all the way— not Rome, to be sure."

Hutch stood and took the keys.

"—Nothing new since I wrote you. She's not my wife. I just asked her to stay."

Hutch said "I'll be back."

Rob said, "Remember—*right* side of the road. Don't kill anybody you can possibly miss."

Hutch laughed and went.

21

By the time he'd cleared the outskirts of town, he began to wonder how he'd ever left—the place at least, bare of people. The clinging sun threw a white shine as different from its English gray or Italian rose as the tall pines here from the low umbrellas that sheltered Rome. In its truthful light the road, not flattered or pitied by the sky, narrowed to a dirt lane and curved on gently through woods—rolling fields of dry brown stalks with only the odd suspended buzzard to watch his progress. Empty as they were of human life, the woods seemed full of a single waiting presence—some actual messenger in raiment and wings or khaki trousers and faded shirt who would step out into the road at any instant and extend a paper with legible guidance, forward and inward, to the place Hutch craved. What place?—surely here. What had told him otherwise? Where else could he find the stillness and space to hunt out the diagram Rob had requested?—some usable answer to the question set by Rob's balked life and now his gasping grin.

The house on its rise had begun to fade. Hutch hadn't really noticed before he left. The paint he and Rob and Grainger applied ten years ago was all but gone; the timbers were silver and dry again. No rot though; the heartpine was good for longer than anyone alive. It had sheltered four generations of Kendals, two of black tenants, and now Min Tharrington. Her blue Chevrolet was baking in the yard; the kitchen chimney smoked.

He knocked three times and waited a good while.

She spoke through the door first. "Grainger?"

"No, Hutch."

She said "Hutch—" but the door stayed shut.

"Open up, Min. I'm not even armed." He laughed.

She was fully dressed, a pencil in hand; and she smiled at once but searched him with her eyes through the screen a long moment before she could say "I had no idea."

"Rob said Alta called you last night."

"She did—just to say not to come in today before noon, they'd be testing."

Hutch said, "We're the test, I guess—you and me, Min."

She knew she couldn't ask him to enter his own house; she unhooked the screen and stepped well back.

He came in, shut the big door, and glanced round. "You part-Eskimo?" (it was cold in the hall).

"Two-thirds," she said. "But the kitchen's warm."

He followed her there through space that showed few signs of her stay—a knitted cap on a peg in the hall, a brown sweater draped on a dining-room chair, her working papers on the kitchen table.

She gathered them aside.

"Rob said you were climbing the Mayfield family tree. Found any serpents?"

"Not really—a wormy apple or two." She went to the stove and touched the graniteware pot. "Coffee's hotter than the room at least. Get your special cup."

He did have a choice and found it on the top shelf, one lost silverfish squirming in its depths. He drowned it at the sink, rinsed the cup, and held it toward her. When she'd topped it he moved to the table and sat.

Min leaned on the counter and blew at her cup. "Grainger said Christmas Day he might have to call you."

"Did you tell him Yes?"

"He didn't ask for sanction, just wanted your Roman address. I found it."

"You didn't tell Rob?"

"Not a word."

"Why?" Hutch reached for the near chair, pulled it out for Min.

She came but took a different seat, on the other side and down. "You might not have come."

"Why would anybody doubt that?"

"I may have wanted to." She tried then to face him and found that she could.

So he smiled briefly; then thought of a question he needed to ask. Asking it, any way, would grant Min's knowledge of portions of Rob beyond his own reach. Rob had sent him here though; he should walk the whole path. He said, "What reasons did Rob ever give for not telling me?"

Min took the pepper shaker and screwed its lid tight. "I wondered several times but I never could ask; he never brought it up."

"Never swore you to silence?"

She looked off then—the sink window, bare willow. "Before we go one step farther, listen well and believe every word—your name wasn't spoken aloud in this house, unless to a blank wall when I had gone out, from the day I came here in June till this morning."

Hutch heard it and knew he must wait to weigh it. He drank a first swallow. "Where's Thal?" He'd missed her wheezing welcome.

Min smiled. "He and Thal may have had talks about you." Then she sobered her face. "He put Thal to rest, day after Thanksgiving."

"To sleep?"

"—To death. He did it himself."

They'd bought Thal the summer they moved out here. Rob claimed she was needed to collect destitute fleas from Jarrel's hounds (the Negro they'd evicted), but Hutch understood from the first sight of her—her stove-in shimmy—that she came as a mute but attentive witness of their promise to serve one another four years. She'd done that well and neatly, barring flatulence; and once Hutch had left for college, she'd met each vacation visit with an ecstasy no less watchful for its heights, no less retentive (she'd never forgot the first flea she gnawed). Hutch said "Was she sick?"

"Strong as me, just older. No he didn't ask my advice and didn't explain. I saw him take the pistol and walk her out to the nearest woods, and I heard one shot. In a while he walked back with her in his arms and dug a deep grave in the shade by the smokehouse—it took a good hour; he was already weak. When he came in he said 'You understand, don't you?' I had to say Yes."

"Grainger would have kept her."

"She wasn't Grainger's, was she?"

"—Kept her for me."

"Who knew you were coming?"

Hutch said, "Please tell me why you moved in here." He was calm but knew he was hoping to hurt her.

Min knew she could turn the first thrust at least. "The week you left he called me and came down to see me, Sunday supper. He looked tired but well. Then Miss Eva wrote me the news and asked for help. I had to come up here on business and saw him; he still looked well but he asked me to stay."

"How long?"

"He never said. We took it day by day."

"You didn't mind that?"

She wanted to stand but stayed in one place. "Great Jesus, Hutch—I've minded it more than my whole life till now."

"Why please?" he said. The *please* was a truce flag, however small.

Min chose to accept it. "How much do you know about Rob and me?"

"Only what he told me more than ten years ago—that during the time he taught in Raleigh, he was close to you; that you'd thought about marriage but he asked you to wait till he got me started and you said No."

She nodded. "All but true. Two people said No—me and you. Or so Rob told me."

"When?"

"Back then, 1944."

Hutch said, "I did. You must have known why. I'd never known a mother. I'd spent my time with people who loved me and were kind but were women—Polly, Grandmother, Aunt Rena, Sylvie. I was fourteen that summer; I claimed what I needed. It really was mine."

Min said, "I knew that, never tried to deny it. But I knew this too—I had loved Rob Mayfield, not blind but clear-sighted, long before you were born; before he knew your mother existed and well before he had shamed one soul, much less himself. I saw he was large enough to cover us both, a wife *and* a son. Or that you and I were large enough to cover him finally, hide him from himself. I was ready to say you were here and to join you and for all of us to try." As she'd spoken the skin of her face had drawn tight, a memory of the young face Hutch had never known—inexhaustibly ardent. It loosened again in their mutual silence but was still plainly ready for all she'd ever promised.

At last Hutch said, "I couldn't understand that—then, I mean."

Min smiled. "Can you now?"

"I'm trying. Not easy. Rob's dying may help."

Min shook her head once, in surprise not denial. But her smile remained. If his hand had been on the table, she'd have touched it.

He said, "Can I take you to the hospital now?"

22

That night at eleven Alta gave Rob his shot. Hutch turned out the light then and stretched in the chair under a blanket; and with all the day on them, they slept simultaneously though differently—Hutch black and helpless, Rob borne on the drug above his quick panting through an unhurried dream that was one more promise of the total rest he also approached. He knew at the start the dream had a name; the name was *Reward.* But in it, right through, he was his young self—Rob Mayfield, twenty-one, the week he'd left home with Niles Fitzhugh to work in Virginia. Niles was with him in the dream but always silent or grinning at the edge. They reached a small town after long mountain driving and stopped at the obvious eating place—a big white board-inghouse with old men in chairs and swings on the porch under dense maple shade. No one spoke as they came up the steps but all watched; and when they reached the open door, a woman stood waiting—maybe forty, black-haired, in a clean white apron. She didn't smile but said, "We were counting on you. I cooked for three extra." Rob said, "Then charge Niles for two; he eats double." Her eyes stayed grave but she led them to a book on the round hall-table, pointed to a clear space, and asked for their names. Rob wrote his true name; Niles wrote *Jasper Mayhew.* When they looked up from that, the woman had gone; and a young girl, plainly her daughter, stood by them. She was so near the size of a perfect armful that Rob reached both arms slowly to take her. She didn't draw back but his reach failed by inches; and deep in the dim rooms, a bell rang for supper. Old men swarmed past them, the girl swept away, Niles pulled Rob to follow. No one spoke at supper. All the sounds were of eating—knives on chipped plates, drinks of water from glasses heavy as field-stones. The girl and her mother moved silent and quick in opposite circles, replenishing bowls and feeding one man who seemed apoplectic down his whole right side. Then they'd vanished with the brisk convenience of dreams, Niles was off on business of his own, Rob was standing in darkness behind the house by a loud wide creek that hurled through rocks. Yet he heard the girl's steps a good way before she reached him. She still didn't speak but stopped at precisely the length of his arms; and when he had gathered her in and kissed her forehead, he explored her tilted face and found her smiling—her lips were parted upward at least; he touched her dry teeth. He thought this was surely why he'd left home and wandered. He finally said "Where now? You lead." Her hand found his and she led him a long way round toward the house— the front side again, though the porch was empty and every window black. The door let them in on a darkness deeper than the sky outside, but the girl knew a path and took him through sofas, umbrella racks, tables with no sound or brush. They climbed a high stairs, walked the length of a narrow hall; she stopped and Rob heard her open a door, deeper dark. She finally spoke— "Stand here." He stood. She went forward easily, struck a match, lit a lamp. They were in a normal bedroom—wardrobe, washstand, a big iron bed. In the bed a single body was stretched flat, covers to the chin, hands open on the pillow. The girl said "Now step here." Again he obeyed, thinking surely this was Niles; that the room was his and Niles's for the night; that he'd misunderstood and the girl was leaving. But he bent to look, and the boy was Hutch. Even in his youth, Rob knew the face, the rate of its breath. He thought, "It is not time for this—years to wait." When he turned to the girl though, she whispered "No, now"; went past him to the door, and closed it firmly. Then she came back, smiling. The three of them would stay in the room maybe always. He asked her her name; but Hutch moved then, ready to wake. The name of the dream, even there at the end, still seemed *Reward*.

In his chair in the room—Rob's room in the clinic—Hutch dreamt at the same time. His was not a story but a still clear picture, set in no special place. There were only two actors, himself and Ann. Ann stood in the center of a well-lit space in normal street-clothes. He stood just opposite ten feet away. Her belly, though covered by a Scotch-plaid skirt, was clear as washed glass. In the pink convolvulus of sinew and organ, he could see a child hanging by a white cord of flesh. It was still translucent with newness at the edges; but even while he watched, it clouded further—solidifying. He thought of no name for the child or the dream, but it seemed a good promise—no shock or fear—and it did not wake him.

23

While Rob and Hutch slept in the early night, Ann slept in Rome in the Pacifica an hour before dawn. She'd spent the whole day on the far side of Tiber—Castel San Angelo, St. Peter's, the Vatican—and had been left alone. No one spoke to her for more than directions except when a short seminarian from Akron approached as she lay on her back on a bench in the Sistine Chapel and said, "I could read you the canon law on napping here but will just count to ten." So she'd slept since nine like an honest field-hand, unconscious of passers; and it took four bursts of knocking to wake her. She sat up, clanging in her mind, and said "Yes?"

A voice, not whispering, said "This is Rowlet."

Ann stood, found her robe, left the door locked, and said "It's night."

"No, morning."

"What's wrong?"

"I can't tell a *door*. Please open," he said.

She opened. He was fully dressed and soaked to the skin (a cold rain had started at sunset and lasted). He held a windbreaker; his shirt was short-sleeved.

"You're drowned. Is Hutch calling?"

Rowlet shook his head slowly, then grinned and extended his dripping arms. "Just me on the line." He might be drunk—his face was white and slack—but he stood still as rafters.

She said, "Go dry off and get straight to bed."

His arms stayed out and his head shook again.

"Is Smeralda back?"

"Don't know. Don't care." He took a step forward.

Ann didn't back away.

"I need to tell you one secret," Rowlet said. He brought his hands forward, took her shoulders, pressed her inward. He shut the door carefully and faced her plainly, a face any sixteenth-century painter would have walked through Flanders in floodtime to see—scooped bones and kid leather, the eyes of a celibate starveling on the edge of stigmatic grace or the massacre of thousands.

She saw it that way; but she said, "Tell your secret. Then rent your own room."

He marked it on the air with a finger, word by word. "This-is-my-last-day. My-buddies-coming-back. So-bye-bye-me." He dropped the sodden jacket to the floor.

"Where've you been? It's raining."

"—Saving my soul. I'm a Footwashing Baptist. Or my mother is; this is her Christmas present." He began undoing the buttons of his shirt.

Ann said, "I doubt any known brand of Baptist could want you to die of Roman pneumonia."

"Hold still," Rowlet said. "I know what I'm doing."

"Take one more minute and tell me then."

"I remembered my mother showing me an old picture of lions gnawing

Christians. I remembered it had took place somewhere near here; so I slept till afternoon, then went out looking to tell her I had. At dark I found it—big rundown stadium, the one in her picture. Nothing to see but I went on in and climbed through the mess high up as I could and tried to memorize something to tell her—how big it all was, how poor they kept it."

"You're lucky you're alive. Crooks go there at night."

He said, "One old girl touched my ass when I first walked in. She was all I met, but I heard more moaning." He slid from the shirt and dropped it too. "The rain started then and I thought I'd leave; but before I'd gone six steps, I was wet. So I sat back down and stayed till just now."

"Why on earth, Dumbo?"

Rowlet thought a long moment, then grinned again. "I already told you—saving my soul. More ways to be a martyr than nourishing beasts."

"You sat in the cold rain and stared at old stones?"

"Well, all stones are old. I may have took a nap." By then he was opening the belt of his trousers.

Ann didn't speak again but waited in place.

24

Hutch woke at four, eased by his dream (which he didn't recall). Then he heard the oxygen, the wide-spaced gasps, and said "Rob" once. No answer so he sat in the warm dark and felt two things—first, a deep relief that Rob was going and yielding him room; then a deeper fear that the room would be vacant, containing no center round which he could move in the confident swings he'd learned from birth. What would stay?—his grandmother, Grainger, Alice, Polly. But much as he honored and thanked them, he knew they'd never been pivots. Ann—he drew up her image and watched it. After the perfect days in Rome, she seemed more than ever his surest friend, the one with whom he'd shared more pleasures than anyone likely to last for years. But the heights of their meeting—Palatine, Forum, the Pacifica's beds—seemed distant in time as in actual space. The critical gravity they'd both felt at Christmas had weakened for Hutch to a clear line of pictures he could watch with thanks but no strong compulsion. Had he ever felt that toward anyone but Rob? He'd accepted most of the bodies offered him—Ann's, Strawson's, Lew's, Marleen's—in unquestioned readiness and felt no remorse, only a grainier sense of the gifts concealed by common faces, the infinite speaking tenderness of gestures surpassing speech. He'd accept them all again here now, if they'd ask again. Would he ever ask them though, require their presence? Here, a step from the father racing to die in his own proliferating flesh, the answer seemed No. Rob had asked for a diagram; was it maybe this?—out of the intricate toils of a knot comes one strand, single filament, not plaited or paralleled? He watched that a moment, as plain as Ann's face. Like the dream, it eased him. He stood quietly, touched Rob's bed, and entered the hall. Alta was seated at the nurses' desk in blue light, working at charts. He went to the long bench opposite and sat.

She wrote on awhile, then looked up. "How is he?"

"Asleep. Hasn't moved since you saw him at eleven."

Alta said, "Wrong. You're the one never moved. He pressed the button for me at two-thirty."

"You must have talked low."

"Didn't need one word, known each other too long. Just gave him a shot. Doctor says he can have it anytime he calls."

Hutch said, "He doesn't sound worse than before."

"He's moving though. What I told you was right."

Hutch nodded as if she'd predicted rain.

"You go back to sleep."

"Couldn't now," Hutch said. "Once you wake me you've got me."

Alta said, "I never woke you and I've got all I need."

Hutch moved to speak.

"No, stay. I'm lying. You don't know, do you?—Tim died last August."

Hutch said, "I didn't. How, Alta? I'm sorry."

"Everybody in Fontaine was sorry, I tell you—not one cookstove has worked right since or radio; he could evermore make electricity behave. His heart stopped while I was fixing his lunch. He was already waiting in his chair, just slumped. I went on talking a minute or two."

"Where's Jeanette?"

"High Point—good husband, two babies. I'm a double grandmother."

"You stay in your house?"

"Little as possible and never at night. It's why I'm here on the hoot-owl shift. I pray the day comes I can sleep alone, dark. It hasn't come yet."

Hutch said, "Any Mayfield could help you with that. We seek single beds."

Alta tried to see his face, but the far wall was dim. She nodded anyway. "Rob was the one broke the mold."

Hutch said, "I hope that's the story you found."

"I haven't thought back—try to move mainly *on*."

He didn't insist but stayed on the bench.

Alta took a ruler and drew lines awhile. Then not looking up, she said "He was *kind*." She seemed to be claiming it against strong denial.

Hutch had thought of his father many ways but never as kind. He only said "When?"

She looked to both ends of the hall; they were alone. Still she lowered her voice. "You knew about Tim and the Phillips girl—"

He didn't but said "Maxine?"

"No the young one—Martha, God help me."

Martha was Hutch's age, had been in his class from the first grade on—a pale straw-blond with wide-set eyes like open shafts in the ground. He said, "She's in Florida last I heard."

"Heard right," Alta said. "Did you hear of the boy?"

"I knew she was married—in Tampa, round there."

"That came awhile later. The boy was Tim's. He took her down there."

To say he didn't know might stop her now. He said, "How old is the boy?"

"Don't make me count." But she did. "Six, seven. Martha'd finished high school. I knew she had gone to a typing college in Raleigh. I knew Tim was gone a lot most weekends. I never said a word. He wouldn't answer questions; he'd just vanish longer. Finally one Saturday he left in the truck, didn't even take his razor. I was wild by Wednesday; but I still hadn't told a soul, even Jeanette (she was gone too by then). I stayed home and cooked—I canned beans and peaches to feed half of Asia. Then Thursday night Rob knocked on the door. It was blistering hot and I asked him to sit on the porch; but he said, 'Let me come in first.' He had news he didn't want confided to the breeze—the Cokers were next door, ears like mules. So down we sat. Tim had called Rob from Tampa and asked him to see me; he'd loved Rob ever since they wrecked that carload of bootleg liquor on the way back from Weldon—sixteen years old. The message was, he was living down there and could Rob pack his suitcase and ship it? I said, 'He hasn't *got* a suitcase; it's mine.' Rob had to laugh. But later I gave him a cardboard box and showed him Tim's drawer, and he packed a few shirts and underpants. As he left I said, 'I've known you forty years. I never thought you'd end up a messenger-boy for a grown man chasing baby-ass through orange groves.' He looked a little sheepish but left anyway. One week later, same time, he came back. We sat on the porch and talked about childhood; all of us that age had the same childhood, knew each other's whole lives well as our own. Every Wednesday night for two months, he'd turn up—never let me cook him so much as an egg, just drove up at dusk and sat till bedtime. The Cokers were spinning; Rob didn't give a damn and neither did I. I thought he was tending a miserable soul. Well, it turned out he was but in his own way—he was testing me." She stopped, seeming finished.

"For what?" Hutch said.

"—Was I fit to live with?"

"Did he ever decide?" He laughed once for safety.

"Never told me. But after three months Tim rode in at daybreak and didn't leave again till they carried him out in that tacky coffin I paid a leg for."

"Rob had talked him back though?—from Tampa?"

"Tim finally told me. Rob had mailed him his clothes and not said a thing. Then after two months Rob wrote him and said, 'If you don't want her, she's just my speed. Speak now or never holler'—not a word of blame. It took Tim another month to see he'd grabbed something he couldn't hold, but Rob set him thinking and opened his eyes."

"You welcomed him in?"

"*Let* him in," Alta said. "Couldn't stop him if I'd tried; he still had his key. I was in bed asleep when I heard the door move. Tim was standing on the sill. He said, 'Is there room for me to take a long nap? I been driving fifteen hours.' I said, 'There is everything here there always was, plus a pantry full of peaches; but do me this favor—take a hot tub-bath.' I couldn't stand to think there was any Martha on him."

"You said she had a son."

"After Tim was back home. She had some kin down there and stayed with them to have it. Tim sent her monthly checks till she wrote him she was marrying a radio announcer." Alta stood and took a step. "You're bound to be the only one in Fontaine didn't know."

"I must have been in summer school."

She nodded. "Must have been." Then she smiled. "Plan to finish?"

"Ma'm?"

"How many more books can there be you haven't read?"

"Not many," Hutch said. "Now I'm writing my own."

"You'll have a good place."

"Where?"

"Won't Rob's house be yours?"

"Yes."

She nodded—"Green and quiet"—then went to the desk. But before she sat, she whispered "Bring some *company*."

"Why?"

"To live longer. You want to know the truth? Rob Mayfield has killed himself sure as any suicide—plain loneliness."

"Didn't Tim?" Hutch said.

Alta waited, then faced him and found her saving answer. "Oh no. You haven't heard a word I said."

25

When Rob woke at five and had his shot, he seemed much the same, not visibly lower. He told Hutch to go back to Eva's and shave. So when Grainger came at six, Hutch drove back and shaved and sat in the kitchen while Eva and Sylvie cooked and served in a calm intensity of purpose as ceaseless as the gaze of seraphim (when Eva left the room, Sylvie said, "You praying he die today? You ain't, you praying wrong"). Then the force of his dream, which he'd still not recalled, sent him to the hall phone to try to reach Ann. All circuits were busy; they'd call him soon as possible.

His grandmother spoke from the head of the stairs. "I've turned down your bed. Stretch out awhile."

He knew he was tired, though he felt strong and slightly elated—soaring. "I've placed a call to Ann. I'll wait for that."

Eva came down slowly, never looking to her feet. She brushed his hair back. "Thank God she's not here."

Hutch stepped aside. "Why?"

"I doubt I could stand to share it one more way."

"It's not a cake, Grandmother."

She nodded. "—But I think you'll find it's a *meal.* You'll see people grabbing far sooner than you thought."

"For what? He's been broke since before I was born."

"So he thought," Eva said. "He was one big vault people drew and drew on."

"Not you," Hutch said.

"Maybe not, maybe not. But he stopped wanting me." For the first time in Hutch's presence, she was older—a burr on her words. She would also die soon. Still she said, "Make your plans now to go straight to England."

"There'll be a little business."

"Nothing I can't handle—or Grainger and I."

"I may need to get my bearings here, a week or so."

Eva looked round her slowly as if at new sights. "It's good for that—bearings—but it takes your whole life."

Sylvie cleared her throat behind them. "Miss Eva, I can't fry but two of them chickens."

"I just told you four."

"You counting on needing what you don't need yet. You wait till he gone, I'll cook em all then."

The phone rang; Eva waved Sylvie toward the kitchen and followed her.

Two operators, then Ann very clearly.

"I was afraid you'd be out," Hutch said.

"It's raining hard. You left in time."

"Is it lunchtime there?"

"Any minute," she said. "I'm a little late. I was reading in the room."

"Has Rowlet left yet?"

"This afternoon, I think. They'll drive straight to Germany, not stopping to pee."

"Met anybody else?"

"One priest at the Sistine. Italians don't seem to be falling down to know me. The Sistine was worth it."

Hutch said, "Will you fly home and come straight here?" He had not planned to ask it.

"Has he died?"

"No but soon."

"Is it awful?"

"Not yet. Not for me at least."

Ann said, "Does he know you're calling me now?"

"He's past minding anything. He always liked you. I'm asking you to come."

She took two seconds. "I'll call you tonight and tell you what time."

"I won't be here; tell whoever answers. Somebody'll meet you in Raleigh. Need money?"

"I'm pretty sure not. Rowlet's just walked up; he'd like to speak to you."

Before Hutch could speak again, Rowlet said "Hey."

"How are you?"

"All right. I slept most of last night in the Colosseum."

"Ann said it's raining."

"Was then too."

"You drunk?" Hutch said.

"No, sleepy."

Hutch laughed.

"Is the trouble there over?"

"Not yet. He's failing fast."

Rowlet waited. "You tell him I said 'Good luck.'"

"Thank you."

Rowlet said "Listen, I thank you."

"Can I speak to Ann again?"

"She's already gone."

Hutch said, "Give her your address. I may come to Germany."

"She knows it," Rowlet said.

26

Upstairs in his old room, Hutch tried to rest; but his prior sense of glide over distant ground had lasted with no threat to slow or fall. So he went to the bottom drawer of the chest; and there under wilted caps and sweaters from his early childhood, he found what he'd hoped for—a Blue Horse tablet of lined school-paper, the remains of his first try (at ten or eleven) to write a long story: twin brothers on an ocean liner to Europe. Kneeling he read through the six finished pages, tore them off carefully, lay down again, and wrote to the person who'd now come to mind.

December 29, 1955

Dear Strawson,

I'm home unexpectedly. Ann Gatlin and I spent Christmas in Rome and meant to stay on into January, but I was called back here two days ago. My father is dying—lung cancer, which he knew he had before you met him last May in Virginia but kept from me. I still wouldn't know if the Negro man who lives with us hadn't phoned me in Rome. He is conscious and knows me but is now dependent on an oxygen tent and Demerol for pain. The doctor says he could live indefinitely. Grandmother and Grainger and the night nurse (who's known him all his life) say he'll go this week. I'm praying for soon and staying through nights in his room in the clinic. He was what I had for so much of my life—the part that registers—and now I can only stand and watch him fade off. He talks very little but that's all right; we said our say.

I don't know where you are and that's my fault. I meant to write often but got plowed under by the unexpected shock of studying again, plus the Oxford climate which is worse than advertised (and the ads are gruesome), plus trying to start a long poem in the scraps of free time and warmth. Did you go to college finally? If so, did you stay? I'm sending this care of your parents in hopes it will reach you somehow. It says—a good new year and thanks again for your visit in July. I remember it all and still feel glad. I might even have a few new things to answer to the questions you asked me after Macbeth. *Or maybe I should wait till this quake passes and check the main guy-wires before marching out onto any long bridges. I've never left here but I told you that. I'm planning to leave.*

—To England, I mean, in roughly three weeks. Then on from there. On may *mean* back, *since the scene here is shifting.*

Still you could drop me a note to Fontaine—I'm known hereabouts—and give me the news. Despite my silence I do want to hear.

Affectionately,
Hutchins M.

Then he slept for two hours—not hearing a sound, though his door was open. When the phone rang at last and Eva called to him, he still didn't hear.

She climbed the stairs, raised the shades, and shook him.

He surfaced slowly.

She leaned at his side, holding his arm. "Grainger just called here and said you're needed."

"Rob?"

"Must be. What he said was 'Tell Hutch to come back.'"

He sat up—ten-thirty. The soaring he'd felt since dawn thrust its wings for a pull in actual air, the strong light that now filled the room like a substance. He lifted higher.

"Should I go?" Eva said.

He heard her but went to the chest for his keys, not thinking of an answer. Then he folded the letter to Strawson and said "Any envelopes upstairs?"

Eva thought he was weighing her question. She nodded, went quickly out, and came back with stamps and three envelopes.

Hutch addressed one and sealed it. He said, "I'll call you as soon as I know."

She accepted that.

It was only as he came down the post-office steps that he thought, "She's outlived him. She wanted to see." But he went straight to Rob.

27

The room was half-dark; and his sense of smell, refreshed outside, was stunned by the old stench—a low eager burning. Dr. Simkin and Grainger were standing by the bed; there was no sound of breath. Hutch came up beside them. Rob's eyes were shut. His face had gone blue. His dry lips were gaped wide and sucked in a silent irregular nursing.

Grainger said "Here he is."

Rob seemed not to hear.

Simkin said "Let him be" and took Hutch's arm. In the hall he said, "We're in a new phase now. The right lung is gone."

"He seemed the same when I left at six."

"That caused it. Grainger said he thought you were gone."

"Gone where?—I told him."

"We're not dealing here with a healthy mind. He struggled hard till we got him sedated."

The man's face and voice entered Hutch as a taste more offensive than any decay from Rob, but he said "What now?"

"Do a tracheotomy. That'd give him more air. Stop him trying to talk. Min Tharrington is not his wife, far as you know?"

"No."

"Then you'll be the one to sign the permission."

"Never," Hutch said.

"He'll strangle."

"Won't he anyhow?"

Simkin said "In time."

Hutch said "Then today."

Simkin thought it through. "Stay with him."

"—Never left."

28

Rob still seemed asleep. Grainger sat close by him on a straight wood chair. Hutch brushed the covered shin, then drew up his night chair. "Were you here when it happened?"

Grainger nodded.

"What confused him?"

"Don't know, not a dream; he was wake when he started."

"Did he say anything?"

Grainger nodded. "Your name, every time he could breathe. I told him you had just gone to wash your face. Next thing I knew, he had sat bolt upright, pulled out his tubes, and was clawing this tent down. I had to call for help. They give him a big dose; I held him till he dozed."

"No blood?"

"Dry as sand. I don't think he knew me."

Hutch said "Soon now."

Grainger faced him. "Don't rush. This happened before."

"Since I got back?"

"God, no—thirty years ago in Virginia, first time I ever saw him. He was twenty-one years old; he'd just left home and had tracked down his Aunt Hatt, that I used to help. He was born in the house but hadn't been back since Miss Eva took him off when he was a baby. He seemed to enjoy it, and we both liked him (squirrels in the treetops liked him in those days); but second day he stayed there, he heard from his mother—long letter. I brought it from the post office, sealed; never knew what it said. But you know Miss Eva's tongue can slice cold bricks if she see the need. He was far gone in liquor even then, that young; so he had to get drunk. I helped him on his way—old cousin of mine, Slip Dewey, made corn—and once he was high, he wanted to ride: always a big *mover* when anything failed. I rode with him. I was still a fool then, for cars anyway. He did his best to kill us—himself of course but I was along—and finally he managed a little wreck, involving just us. After that and some more mess, I got him to my house and thought I had him calm. I read him that Pocahontas book I gave you and cooked him some eggs. He seemed cold-sober and laid down on the bed soon as I suggested it. I watched him till it looked like he'd sleep a good while; then I went to chop wood. I'd worked half an hour when I heard his voice—didn't know it was him, but it came from the house: deep bellows like a steer. I took the axe with me and went back in. He was sitting upright on the bed, staring wild and making that noise like it hurt him to do it, like lightning down a tree."

"Calling who?" Hutch said. "I was some years off."

"No name, none I could understand at least. Just *calling*."

"You answered."

Grainger said, "Thank you. I did up till now."

But Hutch saw he'd stopped him too soon. "How'd you calm him?"

"First I was mad. I drove that axe two inches in the floor. Didn't faze him a bit; don't think he even heard it. By then he reminded me of boys in the war—they were going trench-crazy by the hour some days. Nothing you could do but throw em down and press em and moan even louder. He let me do that; he was still in two minutes and slept long hours. Then I drove him to Goshen and never left since." He stood to see Rob—silent, unchanged. "You call Miss Min?"

"She'll be here at one; let her just come then."

"Miss Eva want to come?"

"She asked me," Hutch said. "I told her to wait—no way she can help."

Grainger stood a long moment. "*Help* ain't the question. She ought to be here."

Hutch said, "Go eat your lunch and bring her back then."

Grainger quickly lifted the edge of the tent and touched Rob's chin. "I'll shave him when I can."

Hutch saw him out the door, then sat in the straight chair, found Rob's left wrist under the covers, and felt for the pulse—not beats but an almost steady dim signal. He kept his hand there, only listening.

In five minutes Rob's head turned; the eyes opened.

Hutch said, "I went to breakfast. Now I'm back."

Rob pointed to the door. "Lock that."

Hutch stood. There was no lock. He went though and pressed on the handle. Then he sat again and took his father's wrist.

Rob said, "Is it saying anything you can read?" He managed his smile.

"No it's idling now."

"Good news." Rob waited, still looking. "I've left you a lot of reading matter at the house."

Hutch thought he meant the few books. "Thank you, sir."

"Don't thank me till you've swallowed it."

Hutch smiled to stop him.

"—Some days of my life I wrote down for you. They're locked in my desk."

"I've got your keys with me; I'm using the truck."

"No rush," Rob said. "Give yourself enough time."

"I'm already late."

"To what?"—the smile again, appallingly slow.

"My life, I guess."

Rob waited. "You were grown years before I was. I used you for guide."

Hutch laughed. "—And I lost us."

Rob nodded. "Never mind." Then he fished up his hands, lifted the tent back over his face; and whispered quickly, "I don't have a will. Use your own best judgment. Give Min something nice. You and Grainger take the rest. Don't let any sermon be preached over me, just music."

Hutch nodded, then stood and lowered the tent.

Rob said "Can't something be done?"

"Sir?"

"For *me*." The face, drawn taut as a drumhead, was young.

Hutch said "Not now."

Rob waited a good while, staring up; then shut his eyes.

Hutch found the wrist. "One more thing please. You mentioned Goshen, being buried with Rachel."

Rob said "You choose." He didn't speak again. By then it was noon.

29

Hutch sat through the afternoon—holding his father, eating nothing, and standing only to bring in chairs when Min and Eva and Grainger came. They talked on quietly about Hutch's travels, avoiding Rob. Rob heard long stretches of all their voices, though he seemed unconscious of them and the staff that came and went, now spectators too.

At five dark was settling. Eva walked to the bed and called Rob gently.

He heard and answered in his mind but slept.

She tried again firmly. "Son, you want me to stay?"

Still nothing, though he thought "All but one of you, go."

So Eva bent slowly, kissed the covered ridge of his thigh; and said, "Min, you come sleep at home tonight."

Min waited. "Yes ma'm." Then she stood, kissed the same spot, and gripped Hutch's shoulder.

Grainger said, "I'll take them and be back soon."

Rob thought "Stay home."

Hutch nodded, not breaking his hold on the wrist; and when the room was still, he took the first chance to say an urgent thing—"I'm sorry if I ruined it." He meant his father's life, the last half at least; and he spoke it out clearly.

Rob heard but was now in his own free flight and thought of no answer. He believed that he opened and shut his right hand (in greeting not reply), but the hand never moved.

Hutch quietly said their prayer. "Your will."

Rob wondered at the need to ask again. He had reached an old house in the side of a hill. He was neither young nor old but his same steady self, his permanent companion. He was tired but relieved; the house promised harbor, though in late spring evening it showed no lights. On the porch he could make out one object, a lantern. He lit it, knocked twice. No answer so he opened. High deep rooms darker than the open windows warranted. With no sense of trespass, he walked through every cube and hall downstairs—every human need provided for (chairs, beds, a pantry) and all waiting orderly but no sound of people, no trail or scent. He felt no fear, only patient curiosity to see the remainder and peaceful confidence the house had a center which it somehow served in total silence. He climbed the pine stairs in a bell of warm light and again walked slowly through empty rooms—many dozen, each smaller and lower in succession. At last at a closed door, he stopped, doused his light. From the crack at the sill, another light seeped. He knocked. No answer—a normal wood door with a cool china knob. He turned it, took a step—narrow room, high bed, clean lamp on a stand. On the sheets lay a girl (sixteen, seventeen), brown hair flooded round her on huge stacked pillows. Her knees were up and parted, her gown at her waist. From her fork a new child eased into sight. She saw Rob and nodded but continued her work. The child came free—normal crying and flailing, mucus and blood. The girl rose then in her own fresh blood, took the child by the sides, held it slowly to her breast—sounds of feeding. His mother, himself, the room he is born in. Feasible center, discovered in time, revised now and right.

Hutch was blank in the stillness; the pulse stopped then, a flat clean end. He didn't turn loose but stood to see.

The body groaned once, a long low exhaling. The face, purple now, clenched furiously. The head shook hard and flushed a wave downward through chest, arms, legs. The whole shape arched high, shuddered again, fell slowly back. Then the teeth showed white.

Hutch uncovered the head and leaned to the brow—cool and dry. The same dense wave that had drowned his father spread up through his hand and raised him higher than he'd been this whole day of hope, now granted. He stayed in place calmly till Alta walked in, stopped, and saw the smooth face.

"You never deserved one instant of this but you're safe now," she said.

She'd spoken to Rob but Hutch smiled and nodded.

30

At ten Hutch was drinking coffee in the kitchen, Sylvie scrubbing pots behind him. Grainger hadn't come back from the undertaker's where he'd gone to shave Rob, though the coffin would be sealed. Eva and Min were in the front room with straggling callers. Sylvie hadn't mentioned Rob, hadn't mentioned going home but had worked on—manufacturing food for far more friends than anyone here possessed or needed, adding to the excess the visitors had brought since before Rob was cold: deviled eggs, a whole ham, three cakes, chicken salad, jello desserts for a wilderness of children. Hutch said to her back, "Let me take you home now."

"Sit still."

"You're tired."

"—What I'm paid to be."

"We've got enough, Sylvie. Great God, call an orphanage to haul off the surplus."

"I know it," Sylvie said but started dicing celery. When she'd done the first handful, she faced him finally. "Time *you* left though."

Hutch laughed. "Where'm I going?"

"Ain't you staying at Rob's?"

"There's still room here; Min can sleep downstairs."

"Ain't talking about room."

"Then you'd better say what."

She watched her black knife, the same carbon blade she'd used at that table for more than fifty years. "You need to sleep where his spirit be tonight."

"Won't it be here too?"

Sylvie thought and shook her head. "People's spirit seek places they were happy in."

"Was he happy out there?"

"*Act* like it. Sure God wasn't happy much here."

It seemed the right thing. He could phone Alice, Polly; maybe read whatever Rob had left while numbness made a confrontation easy. "Will Grandmother mind?"

"She minded things a-plenty; none of em killed her yet. Just tell her and go."

Hutch waited. "Please step in and call her for me then. I can't get kissed once more tonight."

When Eva came she said, "I forgot your phone message. Ann Gatlin called from Rome. She'll be here Saturday, Raleigh airport at ten. I wish you'd let me know."

"What?"

"That you had asked her here."

Hutch said, "I'm sorry. But she'll cause you no trouble. She'll stay out at Rob's."

"No such a thing—*here*. This town has had long months to fan its gums over Rob and Min; let it rest till he's buried."

Hutch stood, went to her, rubbed the crown of her head with a stubble chin. "Will you be all right if I sleep out there?"

"Tonight?"

"I really ought to."

"Take Grainger with you then."

"No ma'm," Hutch said.

Sylvie said "Go on."

As he moved toward the back stairs to get his suitcase, Eva said, "Polly Drewry—will you be calling her?"

Hutch nodded.

"You know I have never seen her face, but she helped Rob more than once when I couldn't reach him. I'd welcome her here if she thinks she should come."

"I doubt she will."

Sylvie faced him. "*Thank* Miss Eva."

He came all the way back, thanked her, then went.

31

Min had left lights on, upstairs and down; so the house seemed possible at least from the yard. Still he paused by the truck, thought of Sylvie's claim; and silently said, "Come now if you can." Nothing changed in the air, which was bitterly cold; and once inside, he hurried to light all three oilstoves. They boomed with flame as he went to the hall phone, so loudly the operator said "You being shot at?"

Alice said "Alice Matthews."

"—Hutchins Mayfield."

"Where?"

"Rob's house, in the cold."

"I've been standing by," she said.

"So have we. He died this evening."

Alice waited. "Too soon. Are you all right?"

"Tired."

"Is anybody with you?"

"I'm here alone now. Ann's coming for the funeral."

"You got the money then?"

"On time. Please forgive me; things have been moving fast."

"Now they slow," Alice said. "Do you need me—any way? I can leave in ten minutes, be there by one."

Hutch said, "Please wait. I'll need you next week. Let me come up there."

"Any hour you say."

"Do you mind?" Hutch said.

"What?"

"—Not seeing Rob now."

Alice said, "I saw him when he meant to be seen."

Polly seemed hoarse at first but denied she'd been sleeping. Hutch tried to start gently and ask about her Christmas, but she forced his hand. "Are you saying Rob is gone?"

"Yes ma'm, right at dark."

She waited a good while. "I knew it all day. Oh Hutch, be strong. Was he in much pain?"

"Not pain, I don't think."

"When did you get home?"

"Two or three days ago; I'm so tired I lost count."

"And he knew you?"

"Yes ma'm."

"That's something," she said. "Who told you?—Ann Gatlin?"

"No, Grainger."

"Bless his soul. Hutch, I've *choked* since June, being sworn not to tell you."

"I understand that. Will you come to the funeral, Saturday at three?"

"Who wants me?"

"I do. I can send Grainger for you."

"Buses still run," she said. Another firm pause. "Hutch, I've never been there. I can't come now if there's anyone to hurt."

"Grandmother told me you'd be welcome if you could."

"I could *walk*," Polly said. "I miss him that much."

The stoves had quieted; the hall was warmer. Hutch waited by the phone—no one else to tell. And no new presence in the air around him. Empty house. So he went to the dining room and sat at Rob's desk—big oak roll-top, neat now as an airfield, pigeonholes emptied, even the three framed pictures gone (Aunt Rena, young Eva, Hutch himself at Jamestown). Had Rob swept it all away, along with Thal, in a final stripping—a simplification for his own sake and Hutch's? He unlocked the long drawer. No they were there, just stowed out of sight, too hard to watch. Hutch left them. But beside them was an envelope bearing his full name and Oxford address. He took that up and, not knowing why, smelled the edges—only paper and glue. That freed him to open it cleanly with his pocketknife. A thick pack folded once, dead-center. He felt some reluctance to face it ever but recalled his impulse to take it quickly, in the strength of shock. He moved to a better chair, lit the bridge lamp, and read straight through Rob's account of the three days and something he'd added a month ago.

November 27, 1955

I thought I'd finished this in August. Maybe so. But it's pretty plain now that this thing in me is gathering to run, so I've spent a week using my sparse energy to sweep certain decks. I've always pictured myself as moving light, just a toothbrush and comb; but Monday I woke up to the fourth day of rain and realized I hadn't moved anywhere for years. Here I was ending in a warehouse of paper that you or somebody would yet have to clear. I lay still an hour, not praying exactly but hoping fairly hard that one of the stoves would act up at last (as I always thought they would) and send the whole pile off in cinders and smoke—me and Thal included, sparing Min somehow. No such luck of course; so from Monday through Thursday (we skipped Thanksgiving), I sorted paper and Grainger hauled out twenty bushels, I guess, and burnt them in the yard. Then

Friday on my own I put Thal to rest with a single head-shot and buried her neatly. Min can show you where. I know she came here at first as your dog, but she'd been mine lately—right?—and she and I'd discussed the matter more than once. The paper *was old checks, jail-threats from creditors, duplicate class-attendance reports on children who've long since made their own children and noted their absence, plus any letter which didn't seem likely to help you later in whatever questions you choose to ask. What's left—from my father, Eva, Rena, Grainger, Rachel, Min, yourself—is tied up in three shoeboxes in my wardrobe. Yours, with prayers for mercy not judgment.*

Not that I really care, *which is why I'm writing. The surprise in this, Hutch—this funnel of months, now tapering fast—is what I want to tell. I look forward to death. I feel more than ready, not from pain or exhaustion (there is no pain yet, though exhaustion's ever present). I've read enough to know this is not my invention, and I've never been one to understand people who woke up at four a.m. sweating ice at the prospect of turning back to—what is it?— sixty cents of minerals and water, but it seems worth recording: I'm calm as this desk.*

Why is it exactly? Maybe something very natural—the thing could be making, as a normal by-product, some substance that acts as a handy narcotic (how handy I'll presumably know soon now). Or maybe I'm bathed in a light rain of grace. That's the strong hint offered by the two local preachers who've paid recent calls. I can join in the hope, though I haven't asked for it. But if God turns out to be Protestant, I may ask for transfer (I speak of course as one who has known few Catholics and fewer Jews).

I know what it isn't. It's not impatience or boredom with my weakness. Nor any bitter spurning of this damaged world. Nor walleyed eagerness to don harp-and-halo, though I won't underestimate my hope to be somewhere—not as a spy, don't worry; I'd refuse (the idea of dead invisible eyes dancing round the picture molding on down through the ages, watching every nose-picker and driven ass-scratcher, is at least as repugnant as total extinction): assuming I can refuse, that is. I won't make the rules no doubt, there as here. If they send me back on guard, however, I'll try to tip my hand. Listen closely for laughs. Finally, it's not any sense of completeness. There are two things left that I'd planned to enjoy—a second calmer marriage, once you were underway, and the sight of your children.

So it must be hope, some brand strong enough to override smaller hopes— the pure hope of rest? or a child's hope of life? Right now I'd take either, though personally I feel I've had enough rest. Anyhow all I ask is for it to be new; and even if it's rest—just thoughtless sleep—I have some confidence the Patent Holder on Time, Space, and Matter can lay me to rest in a manner that dif-

fers attractively from the eight-hour struggles with feathers and sheeting I've known here below. If it's life, then (despite the days I've recalled and a decent share of others) I'm in no doubt whatever that it's bound to be—well—more imaginative.

Strange postscript, I guess, but I wanted you to know. No further wisdom on past or future, no outstanding mysteries, and no requests but

Love still from
Rob

It had taken half an hour—no real surprises, no apparent assaults (beyond the existence of this perfect record of the voice and its mind). Hutch sat on awhile and listened to the rooms—normal sounds of an old house gripped by cold and dark. No owl, no squirrels in the attic this year. He hadn't been upstairs; he wouldn't go now. His room would be frozen, the sheets stale at best. He stood, laid the letter in the desk, locked the drawer. Then he went to the tall bay window—Rob's nap-cot—climbed under the blanket, and slept at once: not turning, no dream.

When Rob stood over him an hour later, Hutch was on his left side and sensed no presence—his mind a close black bread of rest.

Rob saw the man below him, heard steady breath, smelled a general air of ease in the room—he was almost surely welcome—but though he looked a minute and touched the man's hair (cooler than expected), no name came to him. By the dim lamp the profile seemed familiar like the room—safe, even well-meant, but in no need of Rob and blurring as he watched. In something like respect he leaned once more and laid two fingers at the gap where the lips had parted in sleep. Three warm breaths stroked him, sufficient meeting. Then he went through every other room as slowly, touching every other object that might need care, and was gone by one.

Hutch had still not moved.

32

Grainger woke him at seven—entering with his own key, walking through the dining room lightly toward the kitchen, not noticing the cot. He'd started the coffee and come in to turn out the lamp when Hutch spoke. "If I'd been choosing I'd have asked for you."

Grainger showed no surprise. "Choosing what?"

"One person to see this early today."

"*Late*," Grainger said. "Miss Eva and me been up all night. How many eggs you want?"

"How many I need?"

"Not that many here and they're all Miss Min's. I'll fix what I see." He returned to the kitchen.

Hutch joined him in ten minutes, washed and combed. Lean bacon was already hissing in the pan; sun had reached the window and was taking the floor. He said "I'll make the toast."

"Cooking now," Grainger said, not glancing from the bacon.

So Hutch gathered Min's books and charts to one side, laid two places, and sat at the table—his hands in the light. For two full minutes he watched them as blankly as he'd slept all night. Then he saw they were Rob's. As a boy he'd hoped more than once for just these, his father's long-boned thick-wristed hands. Somehow he'd failed to notice that he had them.

Grainger poured in the eggs. "You lost your ring?"

"You'll see it tomorrow."

"How's that?"

"On Ann."

"You married?" Grainger said.

"Not yet."

"When's your plan?"

Hutch said, "Maybe this summer, maybe next—when I get home from England."

"You heading back there?" Grainger brought the loaded platter now, perfect and plain; the fresh strong coffee. He sat facing Hutch and had still not smiled.

"—When things here are smooth."

Grainger served himself sparsely, then actually laughed.

Hutch bristled but grinned. "What's the joke?"

"No joke. I was thinking you could leave in one minute."

"How?"

"Hutch, things here are smooth as a greased pane of glass—Miss Eva, me, Sylvie all dying with our teeth; plenty money, good car. We're leaving fast and sporty. Don't need you to watch."

"You're all strong as buffaloes. You'll outlast me."

Grainger nodded. "May do." He ate for some while with the disciplined famine Hutch had always admired, like an orphan still only half-convinced of rescue. Then he said, "Stay round long enough for one thing."

"What?"

"Move Rob's grave."

Hutch said, "Where? It's not dug yet."

"Miss Eva said you burying him in town."

Hutch nodded. "That space by Aunt Rena."

"He ask to be there?"

"No he told me to choose, last thing he said. Something wrong with the choice?" He assumed Grainger only meant Goshen, by Rachel.

But Grainger said, "Feels a little off to me."

"Goshen's just too far."

"I'm speaking of here." Grainger pointed to the window—the small Kendal graveyard behind the last shed, not used in decades.

"That's choked out with briars."

"Rob cleaned it this spring right after you left."

"Did he say for what?"

"Not to me. I never asked him."

Hutch said, "I doubt he knew anybody buried there, maybe that last old great-aunt—Carrie."

Grainger said "Don't matter."

"What does?"

"You think. See if this don't matter. He moved here with you when he'd ruined other places. You stayed here with him the whole four years he built back his life."

Hutch said "Then I left."

"Had to. He didn't doubt that."

"You saying he was happy here?—Sylvie said that."

Grainger waited through it carefully and looked up smiling. "Sylvie's wrong about a lot, but he had some good days."

Hutch knew from the letter what Grainger didn't—none of the best days were set on this hill—but he also knew that (for reasons of his own only partly clear) he would stand in a minute now, call the undertaker, and move the grave site. They'd be digging by noon.

33

Saturday night to discourage callers, Eva turned out the lamps in the front of the house and herded them all to the dining room where they sat in candle light—honestly hungry—and made inroads on the hill of food still left in the kitchen, urged on quietly by Grainger and Sylvie. Their first time together round this large table, they sat where Eva had placed them briskly (she and Hutch at the ends; Ann and Min to Hutch's right, Polly Drewry to Eva's); and at first they said little, still hushed from the drive out in cold bright sun, the short grave service in the old Kendal plot—Paul's grand vision of resurrection: "Behold, I shew you a mystery. We shall not all sleep, but we shall all be changed"—and the slow drive back.

Finally Ann, who was somehow not exhausted by her flight from Rome, said, "I haven't seen many but that was the best."

The others nodded but Eva said "What?"

"Mr. Mayfield's funeral."

Eva seemed to accept; then said, "I wish it could have just been music."

Hutch said, "You'd have had to dust your vocal cords off. I wasn't going to put him through a big church service with Miss Mamie Roebuck assaulting the organ."

Eva smiled. "He always enjoyed her efforts."

"Too much," Hutch said. "I didn't want him to laugh."

Grainger stood by Polly with a bowl of glazed yams. He said "I did."

Polly said "So did I." Then even in the dim light, she blushed a hot red.

Eva faced her, registered the blush; and said, "He did laugh better than any other human from the time he was born. I used to brush him with a feather when I bathed him just to hear his laugh; people would run upstairs to hear." She pointed overhead.

Hutch said, "I wish he had had more chances."

Polly nodded.

Min said, "He got a fair share" (despite Eva's frown she'd lit a cigarette).

All but Ann, who'd barely known him, were surprised by the claim. Yet they all thought it out and came on memories that partly agreed. Eva said, "Maybe so—I see him that way—but his expectation was much too high."

Hutch said "What was it?"

Polly had nodded so Eva looked to her. "Am I wrong, Miss Drewry?"

Polly said "No ma'm."

Eva said, "He always planned to be happy." She didn't look to Polly again but Polly smiled.

Hutch said, "I think he made it, right at the end."

Min said "I know he did."

Eva said, "I never saw it. Somebody should have showed me."

Min set down her cigarette and met Eva's eyes. "You could have come out to his place any day these past six months; he asked you many times. You'd have seen him calm as water in a glass." She stroked her own glass.

Eva said, "I'll try to trust you."

Loud knocking at the front door.

Grainger moved to answer.

But Eva said, "Hutch, you go. They'll want you. Please say we're grateful but have all keeled over."

Grainger said, "Some stranger. Never heard such a fist."

When Hutch lit the porch light, Strawson Stuart was leaving—already halfway down the walk. Hutch opened the door, came as far as the steps; and said, "However did you find me here?"

Straw stopped in the farthest edge of light and looked at Hutch closely. "I didn't think I had. A grease monkey told me."

"We're eating in the back. Turned the lights off for peace."

"I'm sorry," Straw said.

Hutch laughed, now warmer than he'd been in days—since Rome, Christmas night. "Come in quick. You're welcome."

Straw said, "I was wondering. I left so fast, got your note this morning."

Hutch said, "Father died right after I mailed it. We buried him today. Ann flew in this morning."

Straw said, "I'm sorry. I can leave right now." But he came a step forward. Since summer the planes of his face had lengthened—leaner, maybe two years older that quickly. He was neatly dressed after four hours' driving.

Hutch said what he thought he suddenly knew. "I'm gladder to see you than anybody else."

Straw accepted that, an honorable wage, and came to the steps.

34

At nine Min left for the country house; Strawson followed her. Hutch kissed his grandmother and Polly and asked Ann to walk him to the truck. Only then did Eva say "You won't forget Sylvie."

He had. Sylvie waited in the kitchen for a ride. He asked Ann to join him for the short breath of air. She found her coat and they went to Sylvie, who was dozing in her chair by the sink. Hutch said "Bedtime."

Sylvie looked. "Way past." She was already wrapped in her thick green coat. She leaned to take up the black purse and hat she'd worn at the funeral.

Hutch said, "Put your hat on. I like that hat."

She held it a moment, then refused. "Bad luck."

Hutch laughed. "Why's that?"

"—My mourning hat. This hat killed people since before you were born." But she smiled at Ann.

※   ※   ※

In the truck Ann said, "Did your family come for Christmas?"

Sylvie waited; then said, "Hutch, you ought to told her my sad old story."

Hutch laughed. "Be ashamed. You're the freest soul I know."

Ann sat in the middle. She turned to Sylvie's profile. "You tell me, Sylvie."

Sylvie looked on ahead but pointed to Hutch. "He told you. I'm all you see; not another living soul want to claim kin with me."

Hutch said "Be glad."

Sylvie first said "Huh." Then she said, "You wait about forty-some years— see how glad you be."

Hutch said, "Your fault. You had plenty of chances. Even I can remember long shoals of boyfriends round your door."

She didn't answer but sat in silence for the next half-mile till he climbed the rutted track and reached her yard, the low dark house. Then she groaned. "Forgot my light. You step in with me."

Hutch said "Sit still." He opened his door, came round, and helped her out (she handed him the hat).

Ann said, "Thank you, Sylvie. I hope you rest."

Sylvie said, "Yes ma'm. It's tomorrow already."

Hutch said, "It's nine-fifteen. Plenty time yet."

But Sylvie was already climbing her steps.

He followed her quickly. "Don't leave your hat."

She entered the main room, switched on a light, walked straight to the midget refrigerator, and put in a small paperbag she'd carried—some predawn snack.

Hutch shut the door behind him. The room was stifling; her stove never stopped. "Safe now?" he said.

Sylvie nodded, watching him closely though. "*You* not," she said.

He smiled. "How's that?"

"Acting so happy all day, tonight. You ain't happy yet."

Hutch saw that his tired efforts at cheer had sat badly with her. "I'm sorry," he said. "I'm at least as sad as you. I've just been trying to skate through today."

Sylvie shook her head. "You falling."

Hutch extended his hand; half the room was between them. "Want to balance me then?"

She shook her head again. "Not in my power."

He waited, then laid the hat on her chair. "I'll see you tomorrow."

"Lord willing." Then as he took the first step to leave, she said, "Don't think I'm evil tonight. I'm tired and aching and I hated to see them new friends of yours making you think you hadn't lost the *world* today."

Hutch nodded. "I did."

"Luck to you then." She took two steps as though to touch him but stopped short and waved.

He smiled. "Sleep good."

"I won't," Sylvie said.

35

Hutch turned the truck, drove them carefully back toward the paved road to Eva's; then pulled to the edge in the last of the woods, and killed the engine. There was heat to last them five minutes maybe. Ann was sitting far enough away to make him move. He slid to touch her, her fine hair first. She faced him and he kissed her—first time since Rome (the airport greeting had been quick and public).

She seemed glad to join, then dissolved it herself and looked straight ahead. "I think I'm scared."

His arm pulled her toward him. "This is Fontaine not Rome. We're safe again."

Ann said, "I think I felt safer in Rome."

"It was fine. I'm sorry I ruined your trip."

"You didn't. I pretty well saw all I wanted."

"You go to the Sistine?"

She nodded on his shoulder. "Better than planned. Only the second thing that ever surprised me, that turned out better than its advertisements."

Hutch laughed. "The first was me?"

"Sorry, Dumbo—the Canyon, the whole Grand Canyon."

"I never knew you saw it."

"I told you; you forgot. The summer my father died we drove out there."

Hutch had never known her father, and she mentioned him so rarely that he'd never been a visible presence in their life. "How did you take that?"

"—Mouth open. It was gorgeous, more reds than Rome."

"His dying, I meant."

Ann waited, then sank her head deeper in his arm. "Just the end of the world."

"You loved him that much?"

"I was fourteen; he was all the men I'd known. He was gone a lot and quiet when there, though he'd talk to me if Mother wasn't near. So *love?*—sure, I guess. But once he was dead, once Mother came in where I was doing home-work at six p.m. on a black card-table and said he'd died in the Pitt Hotel in Bristol, Virginia, having just unloaded more Crosley radios than any other salesman in the district and stretched out to nap—well, the end of the world."

"Why?"

"Who was going to keep us? Every Shirley Temple movie told me orphans were bad off, fair game for all."

"You made it," Hutch said.

She waited. "To where?"

He moved his arm and gripped her neck. "Here, now."

"You aren't staying here."

He had not meant the place but his body, its refuge. Yet she'd showed him that his choice of Rob's grave site was at least the first gesture toward a whole life here. "We could," he said.

"Not with your grandmother still here, not *we*."

"I thought you liked her."

"*Admired* her, I said. I admired the Grand Canyon, but I couldn't live there."

"Where then?"

"You name it, just far from our kin."

Hutch laughed. "Now look who's running for the light."

Ann nodded. "I always was. You never noticed."

"I noticed. I was scared you'd picked me for the light."

"I had. What was scary?"

Hutch said, "I'd been picked before—my father."

She waited. "That's over."

"So far as I can see."

Ann said, "Estimate how far that is."

"Long as I live."

"Then what happens now?"

He said, "I do a few chores on Rob's estate. I visit you in Richmond, and I'll have to thank Alice. I fly back to England, finish my classes, and start my thesis."

"—Which takes you how far?"

"Through a second year, eighteen months away."

"Where do I wait till then?"

Hutch said, "There's no way we could live in Oxford. I'm on a lean budget—even leaner with this trip—and you'd never get permission to work, except maybe something in the country with the air force; and I wouldn't feel too easy with that, too many Rowlets round. So why not Richmond? You don't mind your job; the time'll melt quickly."

Ann seemed to nod—her head dipped slightly—but she didn't speak again. She was finally tired.

So was Hutch. He sat still, her weight pressing heavier each moment on his arm, and knew that a fierce desire was called for—love against death, in poems at least. And he did lean to kiss her again deeply, slowly.

But she met him on his own grounds—courteous greeting at the end of a long day, no further request—and said at last, "You're dealing with a *sleeper.*"

So he said, "You know how grateful I am?"

She took his hand and pressed it.

"Have you got the ring?"

"In my suitcase, buried in talcum powder. Customs never saw it."

"It was legal."

"So I trust."

He stroked the one finger. "Too big to wear?"

She nodded. "Too soon. We can size it when we're ready. I'll dig it out every few days and talk to it."

Hutch drew in his arm and cranked the engine, instant heat. "Give it love from me."

"It knows that," she said.

Half an hour later he was climbing toward Rob's house—the porch light shining—when he knew he'd forgot to wish her happy New Year. It would be New Year in another hour. Well, he'd sleep right through it.

36

But Min and Strawson were awake in the kitchen. Straw had provided a fifth of Jim Beam; and when Hutch walked in, they were seated at the table under raw bulb-light with nearly empty glasses. A third glass stood ready. Straw said "Your ice is melting."

Hutch stopped in the door, startled to be angry. Since Rob had quit drinking the year they moved here, the present sight struck him as a desecration—the body covered only seven hours ago. He said, "We don't dilute it in England."

Straw's eyes were slightly glazed; he looked round the room. "I doubt this is England or will ever be."

Min understood the moment and set her glass down; but she said, "We all need a whole night of sleep."

So for something to do till he calmed again, Hutch went to the sink and washed his hands. Then he sat.

Straw poured four ounces of bourbon and slid it toward him. "You have a flat tire?"

"Had to take Sylvie home. She seems very low."

Min said, "She'd known him second-longest of anybody left alive"—a small true discovery.

Hutch drank a long swallow.

Straw said, "Colored people believe in death."

They rolled that over in silence; Hutch laughed. "It seems to be a fairly universal belief."

Straw shook his head. "Wrong. The minute some white person dies—blam!—flowers, Hammond organs pumping tunes Kate Smith wouldn't touch with a forty-foot pole, preachers grinning like cats. Negroes stand up and yell."

Hutch saw the boy was high and nodded to stop him.

But Min said, "There're various ways to yell. I've wailed fifty years, barely pausing to breathe. Very few people noticed." She smiled at Straw.

Straw said "I'm sorry." He filled her glass and his; then said, "I'm not sure who you are—in all this, I mean." He gestured to the room.

Hutch said, "She was one of my father's oldest friends."

Min said "Still am," straight at Hutch. Then she gave the rest to Straw. "I'm one of the several relicts of the man we buried today. Did you ever meet him?"

"Yes ma'm—once, last May."

"He knew he was sick by then; could you tell?"

Straw said, "No ma'm, he mostly laughed."

She waited awhile, then drew two large figure-eights on the table with a firm forefinger, then faced Straw again. "Let me warn you tonight; leave here knowing this—any human being laughing as much as Rob Mayfield is dying in pain."

Hutch said, "Min's Law?—does it always hold?"

She nodded but to Straw.

Hutch sang the first bar of "*Ridi, pagliaccio.*"

She said, "He asked me to love him way back when we were just children—we grew up together, houses fifty yards apart—and I stayed true for forty damned years."

"He didn't?" Straw said.

Min thought, shut her eyes, and shook her head.

Straw moved his hands toward her, flat on the table, but stopped short of touching. "What does that make you?"

Hutch said "Easy, Straw."

But Min laughed. "I *know*," she said. "I've had time to know. It makes me a fool about the size of east Texas. There used to be lots of old women like me at family reunions. We thought they were freaks but also heroes—some boy they'd loved had been killed or died. They were fresh as wax blossoms at sixty years old, ready for anything—trips to Alaska! No one ever said they were laughable fools."

"They weren't," Hutch said.

She faced him at last. "I know they were."

Straw said "You live here?"

She shook her head. "No sir. I've stayed here since June and Fontaine's my home, but I work in Raleigh."

"Doing what?"

"Family trees. I construct family trees in the State Library for elderly white folks to chin themselves on."

Straw said, "They'll be needing them any day now for more than exercise."

Hutch said "Meaning what?"

Straw looked and grinned for the first time tonight. "—The great tide of blood foretold in The Book. The niggers' revenge, black Jesus with a *blade*. Very few family trees'll be tall enough to save all the scramblers."

Hutch said "Not funny."

Straw said, "Damned right—you're the one with good sense; run to England and hide."

Hutch said, "The sad thing is, nothing's going to change—look at Sylvie and Grainger."

Straw laughed. "They're old. You stay in England."

Min said, "Rob agreed. He talked a lot all fall about what would come when Negroes really noticed the door was thrown open."

Hutch said again "Nothing."

Min locked on his eyes. "You keep thinking that but think it at a distance. Rob said one night, 'Grainger Walters would kill me quick as pass me the salt.'"

Hutch smiled. "Rob was *hoping*—a fast clean end. Grainger loved him more than us."

Min said "Speak for you."

"I am," Hutch said.

Straw said "You're a lie."

Min pushed her glass from her. "This is your table, Hutch—your house overhead—but can I speak freely in it one last time?"

Hutch nodded.

Straw made the first move to rise.

Hutch said "No, stay."

Min said, "While you're measuring people's love, I wonder now if Rob loved you at all. The longer I stayed here—the more we talked—the more I think he selected you as his one halfway acceptable excuse for quitting life, a decent man's life. Then when he saw you'd be vanishing, he planned his death—all secret choices, from himself at least."

Hutch smiled. "That's fairly stale news to me."

"And it makes you smile?"

"No I smiled at you, Min—your big discovery."

"But you left him, knowing what that would cause?"

Hutch said, "I left here seven years ago. I want one of those decent lives you mention."

"He came here for you; you begged him to come."

"—When I was a child eleven years ago, a child he'd made. He knew I'd grow. You wanted him always; I turned out not to."

"You've got him though," she said. "You see that now?"

Hutch said, "I'm very much afraid you're right."

Straw lifted his bottle and poured all round. "This'll stunt everybody. We can still be dwarves."

They sat in silence till Min laughed and drank.

Straw raised a finger and shook his head. "This is serious business. Anybody wants to shrink has to stay grim and *try*."

Min looked to the clock, twenty to twelve. Then she nodded and smiled. "Can it happen by midnight?"

"With luck, yes ma'm."

Hutch said, "Happy New Year—in case we can't talk by then."

Straw hushed him too.

37

Hutch woke at the sound of feet in his room—vague light of dawn. His head stayed down but his eyes opened carefully and looked to the window. Straw had left the other bed and was standing bare at the long east window—his back to Hutch five yards away, sun rising beyond him, no cloud in the sky.

The door was shut and the air was cold; but Straw held firm, not shivering, and looked out steadily. So Hutch watched, never having seen him still before. He was taller since July. The boyish fullness had sunk deeper inward, the back and legs were lean and dense, the right hand clasped the broad left shoulder as if two flat breasts were all that needed hiding. Hutch recalled having seen him last May at school, laid back in sun on the hood of the car, as a permanently youthful god of Need—poised to seize and use his least whim. And in Oxford, cold from his crazy swim, as a child endangered by a world too willing to join his wildness. But here now he seemed a satisfactory image of one of the three kinds of beauty Hutch loved—man, woman, nature. He also recalled Ann in May at her sink, scraping potatoes. Why couldn't both stand still here always—sky and trees beyond them—for him to watch and serve, serve *by* watching? Diagrams of objects as near to perfection as objects came. No touch, no friction, no wear or change. The sun was high enough now to flood Straw.

He turned toward Hutch, saw the open eyes, held another long moment (his heavy sex not shrunk by the chill). Then he said, not whispering, "You all right?"

"I was."

"What stopped you?"

Hutch was silent.

Straw took four steps and paused on the rag rug between the two beds.

Hutch still faced the window. He said "Thank you, Straw."

"For what?"

"Driving down."

Straw said "I'm still here."

Hutch nodded but slowly turned away. "It's still night. Sleep."

Separate as brothers, they slept again in the full cold light. Straw dreamt of a field in which a small child stepped backward from him as he strained to reach it, protect and claim it.

By the time they woke—past ten—Min was gone. They didn't check her room, didn't know she'd packed and cleared all her traces; but they found half a pot of coffee on the stove. Hutch warmed that, toasted bread, found peach jam; and they sat and ate quietly as sun swept round the house and struck the kitchen windows.

Straw stood in place and looked toward the graves. "She may be down there."

Hutch said, "Her car's gone. You want more toast?"

Straw sat. "Has she really got a place to live now?"

Hutch nodded. "Sure, in Raleigh."

"Have you?"

Hutch laughed. "Too many—here, Grandmother's, Ann's, Polly's, Oxford."

"You picked one yet?"

Hutch stood and brought coffee. "I've picked here as home; I buried Rob here. I don't see any way to live here though."

"Why?"

"The trees grow leaves, Straw, not dollar bills."

"The ground grows tobacco. You got an allotment?"

"Eight acres, worked by tenants."

"You ought to be living on the damned Riviera in a forty-foot yacht."

"I won't see two thousand dollars a year, from tobacco anyhow."

"Then you're being robbed blind; better get a new tenant."

Hutch said, "I didn't know you were such a big farm economist. The man we've got has been with us forty years. We put him out of this house when Rob and I moved here; I have to trust him now."

Straw said, "Your grandmother—she's doing all right. Won't she help you along till you're world-renowned?"

"She's doing fine—twenty acres of tobacco and miles of pulpwood."

"Won't that come to you?"

"In the year 3000." Hutch laughed again. "You've seen her; she'll *last.*"

"Then come here and sit. Write your poems and get thin. Let her see your ribs shine. She'll chip in quick."

"What makes you think that?"

"I saw her like you said. She loves your ass."

Hutch smiled. "Well, my *soul.* No I think you're correct. But I wouldn't come alone, and she wouldn't keep two."

"Who you planning to join?"

Hutch studied the face again, quickly but closely—the new broad planes, wide chin, curled mouth. Even now, awake in daylight, it seemed a sane option. Inexhaustible ikon. But he said "You know."

Straw nodded. "Does she?"

"Yes we settled that in Rome."

"Starting when?"

"After Oxford."

Straw said "She'll wait?"

"No choice. People wait. She's got a decent job, decent roof, a safe roommate."

"I like her," Straw said. "She never says much."

"She was tired last night—she says a good deal, no baby talk though.

Don't you be dropping by Richmond to check." Hutch grinned, thrust a slow fist, and bumped Straw's nose.

Straw said "Too old for me."

"I thought you liked ripe ones."

Straw had still not smiled. "I thought so too. They cost too much."

"So you've found a cheap child?"

Straw said, "That's most of what college has to offer."

"I thought they were all gents at Washington and Lee, Christian cavaliers in suede boots and plumes."

Straw nodded. "They are. But they also *smell* and the smell draws Christian maidens in droves from Sweetbriar, Hollins, Buena Vista—maidens for about four minutes once they hit the city limits."

"Then you've had a good fall?"

Straw finally laughed, deep and hoarse. "A *fall* all right. I feel like I fell down a bottomless hole."

"Of girls?"

"No, fools—some of them were girls. I'm not going back."

Hutch said "You flunked out?"

"Hell no—three As, two Bs, and a D. I told them I might come back someday. In my eighties maybe, my *second* childhood. I'm too old now."

"What did your parents say?"

"Not a damned word as always. They're just sitting pale and blank—drinking gin, watching their new rugs, and asking Sweet Jesus what they did to earn me." He turned back and pointed north toward his parents, four hours away; they were palpably stunned.

Hutch said "Where now?"

Straw said "I'm asking you."

"You got any money?"

"Fifteen hundred dollars my great-uncle left me."

Hutch said, "You'll be needing a job pretty fast."

"Want to hire me?"

"For what?"

Straw said, "I was thinking all night while you slept. This house'll be empty. I could caretake it for you—keep the pipes thawed out, paint it up. Houses die if you just lock the door."

Hutch nodded. "They do. I doubt I could afford you."

"I don't cost money."

"You wouldn't burn it down?"

"I don't play with matches," Straw said. "My heart's cool."

"But you drink a lot of bourbon."

"You want me to stop? I can stop this minute. Willpower's my *name*."

Hutch said, "Try to half it—say, two drinks a day."

"—And then I'm hired?"

Hutch said, "You couldn't bring any former maidens from Sweet Briar or Hollins; Grandmother wouldn't stand it."

"That go for locals too?—farm girls now and then?"

Hutch said, "Understand, Straw. This house used to mean the world to me and my father. It may again, to me at least. Anybody who wanted to care-take it now couldn't really change its life."

Straw said, "I know that. I want to stay alone. Any company I need, I can leave and find on quick weekends."

Hutch drained his cup.

Straw said "A deal?"

Hutch looked again slowly. "Is this for me or you?"

Straw smiled. "Don't know. Am I selfish or a saint?"

Hutch said, "Probably neither. The loneliness may kill you; if it doesn't you're a saint."

"I await the outcome with interest then."

Hutch stood and took their plates. "One other thing though—if I ever come back here, I won't come alone." Facing Straw in the sun, it cost more to say than he'd known it would.

Straw nodded. "Yes sir."

Then they walked out silently to see the fresh grave. The night's hard freeze had already thawed, and the red clods were damp. Straw bent and took one and gave it to Hutch, who crushed it in his own palm—dyeing the skin.

38

Hutch had got to Alice's at six in the evening, five days later. The three-hour drive in steady rain had tired him; so after the greetings and a glass of sherry, he'd kicked off his shoes and stretched on her sofa while she worked in the kitchen—not her favorite place. When she'd nearly finished she called "Hungry yet?" No answer. She finished, came to the door, and whispered, "I've done it. Are you game to risk my cooking?" He was deep asleep on his side, facing out, hands clamped in his knees. Well, the food would keep. She lit the two candles on the dining table, switched off the lamp, and sat across from him—sketching on the firm blue wool of her lap the lines of his body with her dry forefinger. He'd always refused to let her draw him—"Wait till I'm grown. I don't like my head." Did he like what he'd got? Even slack now, resting, it was plainly grown. The brow had roughened, the cheeks hollowed out, the neck thickened strongly. Only the wide shut lips had survived from his first young face. She traced them separately, large, on her leg—three times, invisibly but memorably. She thought of the several Picasso etchings in which a sleeper is closely watched by a big-eyed girl—intent on what? Not protection surely (her own size is frail). Not investigation (her gaze is calm). *Memory* then. But to what earthly use? The girl wouldn't know, not for years if ever. Alice knew, here now; she'd always known—for the years of waking movement and absence, movement which always ends in absence. In her own life at least, all the lives she'd seen. She started the long ridgeline of his legs before she saw his eyes.

He watched her, not blinking.

Alice said "Twelfth Night."

"Ma'm?"

"Happy Twelfth Night—I just remembered."

Hutch stood. "I forgot my frankincense."

"No you didn't. Let's eat. My feast awaits."

39

They left next morning at ten and drove west through flat brown fields still soaked from the rain; the sky promised more. The weather and their late night of talk kept them quiet through the first fifty miles, but then near Farmville the sun broke behind them; and thick stands of bare trees took the light as if it were rations, delivered in the nick. Hutch said, "I think I may manage to live" (they'd drunk a lot of wine).

Alice said, "I'm gratified to have that news" and consulted the map. "Ever seen Appomattox?"

"Not in person, just pictures of the house where Lee and Grant met."

"Me either. They rebuilt it not long ago. It's right up the road. Have we got time to stop?"

Hutch said, "You're the guide. I take orders nicely."

"Then turn when I tell you. I think any Southern boy should face up to where the big native doom fell before he goes roaming back through Cornwall and Wales."

Hutch said, "Too late. I've roamed them already."

Alice laughed and folded the map correctly. "The theme of my life, when the sun's out anyway, is 'Never Too Late.'"

"General Lee disagrees."

"General Lee won't be giving us the tour," she said. "He's seated in bliss, playing chess with Hannibal or Antony."

"Or spitted in Hell, barbecued by slave-cooks."

Alice smiled. "Hush and drive."

The surrender house had been rebuilt only five years before on the site of the first house, torn down by speculators after the war and quickly dispersed (though every thirteenth brick in the reconstruction was original). A pleasant middle-sized two-story house perched above a high cellar on the old foundations, it existed now for its left front-room, a small glum parlor packed with bulky chairs and the two small tables where the acts of offer and acceptance had occurred a very slow ninety years ago (the tables were copies; only the iron-maiden sofa had been present in April 1865). That was all told them by a sweet-voiced woman, well-up on her facts and grateful for guests—no one else was in sight. Then they wandered on past the square courthouse, the jail, three old houses, to where the high spine of land dropped away to a wooded valley—the river, no people, no visible building between them and hard cloudless sky. They stood five feet apart and looked out awhile. Hutch said, "Every good place turns out to be empty."

"Who said that?"

"Me."

"We're here."

"We're respectful."

Alice said, "I thought you liked Rome—Rome's full."

"Not of people, not two weeks ago. The places that had seen most were all but deserted."

"Where was your friend Ann?"

"Mostly with me."

Alice said "She's people," then went to a low stone bench and sat. "I knew an old man who had been at Appomattox."

Hutch smiled. "We *are* there now. It's still here."

Alice waited, shook her head. "He was here that day, when it was itself— what it waited through all of history to be. We're just late prowlers in the graveyard, aren't we?"

Hutch laughed. "It was your idea to stop."

Alice said, "He had to line up before dawn—somewhere near here; he said he could hear the river—and then march past a spot and lay down his rifle. He was twenty-one years old; he'd fought the whole war."

Hutch said, "There were none for me to fight. I came between wars."

"Maybe not—I haven't heard of universal peace."

Hutch laughed again. "Right. I'm an old veteran too. Want to see my wound?"

Alice stood and waved a slow hand down his length. "I've seen it, my darling. Let it rest for now."

40

By the time they'd eaten a late lunch in Lexington, bought the flowers, and ascended the narrow pass to Goshen, it was late afternoon. But the sun had lasted on the cliffs and the rapid dangerous stream; and when they reached the cemetery, there was almost a heat above the clustered stones. They were silent again as they found the Hutchins plot. Hutch at once set the yellow high-smelling chrysanthemums at the base of one stone—RACHEL HUTCHINS MAYFIELD, *May 27, 1905–May 12, 1930*: his mother among her parents and kin, dead at twenty-five and buried twenty-five years ago when he'd waited in a Richmond hospital, four days old. He pulled at the tall dead grass, soon harvesting two handsful of hay. Alice bent, joined the work, and dislodged a flap of turf with bare dirt beneath it. She was pressing it back when Hutch crawled closer, took over, and dug. Two inches down he uncovered a coin— a worn fifty-cent piece. Then he recalled Rob here last May, grubbing with his hands by the one flashlight. He held the coin to Alice.

Her glasses were back in the car, but she thrust it to arm's length and said "1948—where on earth?"

"Rob and I stopped here last spring. He must have left it. I saw him dig here."

Alice thumbed at the silver another few times, then set it back in Hutch's palm. "This never was Rachel's."

"Not in '48, no."

She stood with difficulty, dizzy from the squat. "He owed her a lot."

Hutch looked up. "Money? This wouldn't cover much."

But Alice was looking toward the nearest mountain, the one they'd sketched many times years ago. "—Pleasure," she said.

"I didn't think that."

"Why?"

"I thought they hurt each other."

Alice turned back finally. "At the first and the end, there was some pain, yes. Otherwise they were happy; I watched them be." She leaned and touched her chin to the stone, then stepped away.

Hutch buried the coin again, pressed the turf, and stood. His head swam too but he waited to find some message to say. Only "Goodbye" occurred so he said that silently and went, leaving Rob's odd half-dollar gift—as tangible an offering as any Hutch had made in his own life to the unseen girl in whom he'd started.

41

When they'd finished supper—the last two diners—in the Maury Motel, the waitress poured their final coffee; then said, "Excuse me if I'm wrong again, but you've got to be a Hutchins."

Hutch smiled. "Half-right. My mother was a Hutchins."

"Was she Rachel?"

"Yes ma'm. I'm Hutchins Mayfield. This is my friend, Miss Matthews from Petersburg."

The woman—short, stocky, maybe younger than Alice—set the pot on the table and stepped back a little to study his eyes. "I went to the wedding."

Hutch didn't understand.

Alice said "So did I."

The woman glanced toward her but continued to Hutch. "I was Joyce Meadows. I was younger than Rachel, one or two years behind her in school; but I watched her like a hawk from the day I first saw her. I wanted to *be* her; she was that good to see."

Hutch said "Did you tell her?"

The woman thought awhile. "I'm Joyce Neal now. May I sit down a minute? I own this place."

Hutch waved her to a chair.

Only then, when she'd carefully stacked enough dishes to give herself room for her broad elbows, did she really see Alice. "*You're* doing well, aren't you?"

Alice laughed. "For my age."

"No that's what I mean. I knew you first—before I saw his eyes" (she flicked Hutch's brow). "Your name is Alice."

Alice nodded. "Good memory. Did we meet at the wedding?"

Mrs. Neal grinned broadly. "I hated you. Rachel's maid of honor! No I wouldn't come near you! I saved your face though—I knew you right off. You've taken time well."

Alice said, "I can thank you and still think you're wrong. Time has seemed more like a Mack truck, head-on, than anything softer."

"Call me Joyce. Me too, the part about the truck." She turned back to Hutch. "You're the one never saw her."

"I'm sorry to say."

"*Be* sorry; she was fine, for all her troubles. Where's your daddy these days?"

"Dead, last week."

Her face went blank for an instant in respect. Then she grinned. "You people quit early, don't you? You feeling well?"

"Fairly well."

"Don't leave. This mountain air'll save you. Look at me. I thrive." She extended one arm and waved its hanging weight—pink, firm as packed sausage.

Hutch leaned out and stroked her. "My place here is gone."

"The old hotel?—Rachel's daddy's old place? Did you get that?"

"When my grandfather died."

"We were gone in those years; spent the whole war in Norfolk, nailing ships together—my husband anyway. I stayed indoors. Norfolk's wild, all sailors. We got back in '46; the hotel was gone."

Hutch said, "I sold it and they scrapped it for lumber."

Joyce nodded. "Good lumber. We bought a raft of it to finish this place—great heartpine boards; shellacked it myself." She waved to the walls, stained yellow as a jaundice. "You could sleep here tonight, be right back at home. These are Rachel Hutchins' walls."

Alice said, "Her walls were plaster, white as down."

Joyce said, "I never got asked upstairs. The Hutchinses were shy."

"Still are," Hutch said.

She checked him again. "You look bold as bobcats."

Hutch laughed. "Thank you, no—just a sleepy fieldmouse."

"You'll sleep," Joyce said. "This air is a drug. See, I *told* you to stay."

42

They both were tired but, as they walked in the cold toward their rooms, Alice said, "Maybe we ought to see it in the dark."

Hutch knew she meant Rachel's home—the wrecked hotel—though till now they'd silently agreed to bypass it. He said, "I was there last March. Nothing left but scrap."

"Can I borrow the car?"

Hutch paused, rubbed his arms to indicate the chill; but he said, "I don't guess anyone would shoot us."

Alice said, "I'm not too old to dodge."

So they drove out slowly through the shut-up town to the dark far edge. Hutch entered the old drive, narrowed by laurel, and stopped well back to avoid nails and glass. The headlights reached the brick foundations—half-hid in broken lathing, plaster, shingles. He said, "In Italy they'd charge to see this."

"They'd be right." She was watching the high cube of blackness where the rooms had stood, the site of memories hung now in air. She reached for the door. "They must have spared the spring."

"They did," Hutch said, "but it may be dirty. I don't have a flashlight."

She climbed out anyhow and walked ahead.

He gave her the lead she seemed to want, then followed. The air was black—no stars—and spikey with what seemed crystals of ice, but he navigated safely by recollection and soon grasped the springhouse rail. He shook it, still firm as when Grainger restored it years ago. "Any water?"

No answer.

"Alice?" He stepped round and found the narrow entrance. Then he circled the springhead with arms extended, sweeping for Alice. She was not here now. He felt brief fear, then recalled she'd known the place longer than he. He reached above to the ceiling for the dipper—the long copper dipper that had always hung there and was there last March. Gone now—thieving children or an antiques dealer? He squatted and raised the lid from the spring; then gripping the rim with his left hand, he leaned toward the water. Absolutely dark and empty space. Not even the promising echo of water. Did it sink in winter; had it frozen or dried?

Alice said, at some distance, "They left the servants' quarters, solid as ever."

"Can you see me?"

She waited. "Yes sir. You're on your knees."

"Where are you?"

No answer. Then footsteps behind him. "Is it clean?"

"It's gone."

She laughed once. "No. It was here for dinosaurs; it wouldn't leave now." She touched his right shoulder, felt her way down his arm, then knelt beside him.

He could still not see her, but he heard her reach down—her nails scraped the wall, then the crisp quick dabble of fingers in water. "Warm," she said. She drew in her arm. "*Warm.* Taste and see."

His face found her hand, tightly cupped. He licked at the palm—two short swallows, colder than his own lips and throat.

Alice wiped his forehead slowly, then kissed him precisely at the line of his hair.

※   ※   ※

The lock had been pried off the door of the quarters, but the door was shut, so the inside held a little warmth from the bright afternoon. They were back in pure dark though. Hutch led the way down the narrow central hall, both arms out again to brush the walls. His left hand found the door to Grainger's room; but the right found Della's, the hotel maid. He turned toward that, drawing Alice behind (she held his coattail). The door opened silently on what might well have been infinite space—no glow, no sound, none of the stench of a shut airless room. Yet he took two more steps (Alice still with him), trusting his childhood memory to lay a firm floor beneath them, no knives or traps. The floor seemed clear. He said "I wish we smoked."

Alice laughed once. "Why?"

"I'd at least have a match."

"Ask me," she said and fumbled in her bag. "I usually have some, in case I meet a bomb with an unlit fuse." She found them, passed them forward.

Hutch lit four in succession while they saw the room. No whole piece of furniture, empty gunshells, sardine cans, paper—all in corners, oddly neat. Where Della's bed had stood was a low pile of newspapers, spared by the auction. Hutch said "Build a fire," a thought not an order.

But Alice said, "Man's work. You burn, I cook."

Hutch said, "It's a deal—tin-cans-*flambé*-in-dried-squirrel-droppings." He went to the fireplace and probed up the flue. The stove had been ripped out and sold, but the flue seemed open to the sky. He wadded paper.

Alice said, "This all may explode on our heads."

"Ne' mind," Hutch said. "Nobody cares but us." Fire raced through the pages, half of World War II. Then he added the rounds of Della's wrecked chair and went to the yard to hunt more wood.

Alice said, "Now tell me all you want me to know" (the previous night they'd talked of Rob and Rachel, very little of Hutch).

The fire had made the air tenable by now, a fierce success. They were seated on the floor at the ends of the hearth, half-facing one another. Hutch smiled. "My news comes in two forms, long or short."

"I already asked—just the news you brought *me*. Your letters thinned out pretty soon, I recall."

"I was swamped."

"By what?"

"Well, at first by getting what I'd asked to have—bald loneliness. The English will definitely leave you alone if you want to be left. You can feel like a ghost in very short order—hanging round, full-size with hair and teeth more than ready to grin, but invisible to everyone unless you stop and tell them you're in desperate straits: then they're helpful in a tidy way, elbows tucked. That was June through September."

"You had the trip to Cornwall."

"Worse still. That left me alone as any skunk."

Alice said, "Skunks are sociable souls, good pets."

"Once they've been de-smelled. I was still spraying musk."

"So you sat down to work?"

"I sat down, right. Work was hard to live with."

"You said you were starting a King Arthur poem."

Hutch nodded. "Tried hard—Tristan and Iseult from the butler's point of view."

"No luck."

He fed the fire and laughed. "Luck in torrents—thirty pages, each line more depressing than the last."

"Why?"

"Oh the butler was me—the gimp spare-leg, the wheyfaced witness."

"Did you finish?"

"Not yet. Term began in October."

"Did they notice you then?"

"Less, if anything. Oxford education is a swift introduction to utter self-help. After days of waiting to be told what to do, I asked a few questions and by teatime had a message—delivered by a troll—saying call on Mr. Fleishman. He'd been mystically chosen to direct my work. Mr. Fleishman received me in his flat in north Oxford—just across the road from where Lawrence of Arabia's mother still lives, over ninety and blind and oblivious to the fact that her private scandals are now world news. He's middle-aged—Fleishman—and looks like a carefully controlled but crazed Victorian lepidopterist: brown hair and eyes, brown tweed plus-fours, brown stockings, brown jacket, brown kerchief in his sleeve, brown paper on the walls (so help me God), and little rat-mazes through the books on the floor. He heard me out, unsmiling as slate, over raisin cake and sherry—I meant to be a writer but would also have to teach and would need some advanced degree to strengthen my wings for the academic glide. That stoked what was later revealed as a big bed of anti-American coals in his breast. 'You *Americans*' is mostly what he calls me, when he calls—they hate like hell having lost the world to us; I try to assure them we won't keep it long. But I decided to hump my back and bear it, not reminding him that I was twenty-five years old—no Eton choirboy. And by the time I left, he'd vented enough condescending smoke to invite me to his Wednesday-night openhouses (he's a bachelor). I went along to those, shoulders still bowed; and before long he quietly agreed to my plan—I could read for the Bachelor of Letters degree with a thesis on the love and nature poems of Andrew Marvell. He even, the afternoon we reached agreement, read me Marvell's 'Definition of Love'—or recited it. We sat by his window, no light but the sun and it was far down; I could see he'd shifted his eyes from the page to a spot on the hearth and was speaking to that."

Alice leaned toward the fire and said the first lines—

> " 'My Love is of a birth as rare
> As 'tis for object strange and high:
> It was begotten by despair
> Upon Impossibility.' "

She sat back smiling. "None but the Lonely Hearts know *that*." With a finger she wrote on the floor at her feet.

Hutch guessed, from the motion, that she traced her name. He also leaned out and covered her hand.

She paused; then drew it in slowly, not looking. Then she sat back, darker, and said "So you started."

"—Mornings at lectures and in the Bodleian, long afternoon walks, gigantic awful dinners."

Alice waited. "Nights?—they don't have nights?"

"Very long frozen nights."

"You didn't have friends you could see after work?"

"I know a lot of people now; we talk a lot—Oxford's one small chatterbox. But most of the students are younger than me; and even the ones who've spent two years in the army in Suez or Malaya seem boys—broad waxy grins, inattentive as bricks. If the British have truly lost the world, I suspect they've lost it through inattention. They didn't see it leaving, didn't guess it yearned to go."

Alice said "*You* stayed."

"I love it; do I seem to be saying otherwise?"

She laughed. "I couldn't claim you've been singing valentines. You've left out what you love."

He waited. "The place, the green natural place—the way they've let time pile on it like snow, to irrigate. Their big towns are ugly as anybody's—worse: they're awful when they try to be modern—but small as the island is, there's miles of country left. I drive round a lot."

"Will you stay?"

"Long?—no, just to finish the job. Maybe eighteen months more, then back here."

"Where's *here?*"

He laughed. "Wherever in the U.S. wants to pay me to teach."

"You couldn't stay in Fontaine and write for a while?"

"—Not unless my grandmother rings my forehead with crowns of tobacco; Rob left next to nothing except the old house."

"You could stay there surely, a year anyway—grow your food, write your poem."

Hutch nodded. "I could. But it won't be just me."

"Ann?"

"I've asked her to join me soon as I'm home."

"Why?"

He tried to see her face; she was still set back at the dim edge of light. "I can't live alone."

"Sure you can; you haven't tried."

"Do you want that for me?"

"You wanted it, you said."

"When Rob was alive."

"And you think he's not now?" she said.

"I kissed his dead eyes. He was cold as this room."

Alice leaned forward smiling, threw bark on the fire. "We've warmed this room."

43

When they got back to Alice's the next day at two, she offered him lunch; but he said Ann would be expecting him in Richmond and soon drove on. Ann was at her mother's though and would not be in till six. He could stop at Polly's now and clear one more obligation from his list; but before he'd gone a mile, he felt strong need for a lonely stretch—when in the last two weeks had he had a solitary hour, awake and thinking? He stopped in the road and consulted his map. Jamestown was less than an hour away; he could go there and still meet Ann by dark. So for thirty miles he sped through the fields of the James's south bank, then waited at Scotland for the slow old ferry (he'd forgot its slowness).

It was nearly four when he parked at the gates, but the sun was still clear, and the air was only cool. The couple whom Rob had remembered were gone with all their factory-made junk; and the boy who took his money and gave him a pamphlet was plainly an Indian, sealed in calm and saying nothing but "I close up at five."

He skipped the museum, knowing the story; hurried past the recent reconstruction of the first huts (quaint as a Disney elf-village and more vulnerable), and settled at the base of the Pocahontas statue to watch the broad river. He was mostly alone. No more than a half-dozen others poked past, snapped pictures, and vanished. Only one of them spoke.

An old woman came up, studied the statue, then said "You a native?"

He laughed. "Of here?—no ma'm, a paying guest. Do I look that wild?"

She nodded. "Your eyes. You look like you're daring somebody to land."

"Maybe so. I'm tired."

"Well, I'm leaving." She smiled and turned away.

"—Not for me. Take your time. I can rest anywhere."

So she came back and, sighting quickly, took his picture—bronze moccasins above his thick hair. "If it comes out I'll send you a copy," she said but went without asking his name or address.

That left him entirely alone, first time since Rome—the Risen Christ, the Pantheon. He looked from the river to the fading sky, the apex. Now he was the eye, no perfect architect's lens to guide him. He sat a long moment, staring up, to ask the same question—*Show me now*. But he couldn't ask it here. He'd been answered clearly two weeks before in the center of the pavement of Hadrian's temple—*Head home, say an adequate farewell to your father, assume his strength*. He'd obeyed without question, fulfilled the first two; the third would take years. But he'd bent to the task.

His eyes came down on the far brown bank of the James, shadowed now; and his hand reached back to touch the bronze foot. He thought of Pocahontas, her last days in England, her sudden encounter with the man she'd believed dead for nearly eight years—John Smith in her room again, a blond smiling guest. Smith had written, "She turned about, obscured her face, as not seeming well-contented; and in that humor, with divers others, we all left her two or three hours, repenting myself to have writ she could speak English." But then she'd recovered and called Smith "Father." When he'd laughed off the name, she'd insisted gravely, "Were you not afraid to come into my father's country and caused fear in him and all his people (but me) and fear you here I should call you 'Father'? I tell you then I will, and you shall call me 'Child,' and so I will be forever and ever your countryman." She'd died weeks later, bound back here to live with her husband and son.

He knew Rob's absence fully for the first time—the site on the earth round which he'd turned, the single point on which he'd described his own lean figures, father and goal. Could there be another now? Everything his eyes saw, the cold stone behind him, said a firm silent No.

But he stood and found his way on to Richmond.

44

There was no car in Ann's drive, no lights at the front, no answer to his knock. He'd got here before her, and his key was in Oxford at the back of a drawer. Too cold to wait long. He could go on to Polly's; but he didn't want that meeting now, after Alice and the hour in Jamestown. He sat on the stoop—he'd wait till he froze, then drive awhile. In another two minutes he was shuddering and no sign of Ann; he'd trot to the corner. The door cracked behind him.

"Was that you, Hutch?"—a strange woman's voice.

"It was. He's frozen now." He stood and turned—a dim white face—and remembered the roommate.

"I'm Linda, Linda Tripp. I'm cooking in the back. Ann should be here soon. Come on in and thaw."

"That may take a Saint Bernard with brandy."

She nodded. "I've got one."

The brandy was beer and its owner was her friend Bailey Ferguson, seated in kitchen glare. He was maybe a year or two older than Hutch, a little younger than Linda; and when Linda said, "Bailey, this is Ann's Hutch," he stayed in his seat but offered a large hand and said "Linda's Bailey"; then made a sour face that ended in a grin. He stood—well over six feet—brought a can of beer, opened it carefully, and set it near his own. "Hutch's beer," he said.

Linda said, "Behave. I'm slaving for us all. This is meant to be good. Watch in silence and respect."

The two men obeyed awhile—drank and watched her back, a strong narrow back. Then Bailey said, "You the author from England?"

Hutch laughed. "No the fool from Fontaine, N.C."

That silenced him briefly and Linda turned. "We're all very sorry about your dad."

Hutch smiled. "I was sorry to break Ann's trip."

"She wouldn't have had it any other way," Linda said. She was stirring a deep pot that smelled like turnips.

Bailey said, "I saw it in the Navy—Spain, Greece, north Africa. It's all the same hole, just different-colored rats."

Hutch said, "You didn't enjoy your stint?"

Bailey knew at once. "I enjoyed hell out of it, barely shut an eye. No I just said, 'God save the world from most people east of Hatteras.'"

Hutch agreed. "—And west."

Linda said, "I hope Ann warned you I was cooking."

Hutch said, "No but I've had some dangerous meals. I try to be brave."

She actually flushed but laughed. "Well, help! I'm a *famous* cook. I meant I hope you're starved."

Hutch nodded, mouth open.

Bailey said, "Poets starve a lot. Give him small helpings."

Hutch faced him. "I thought you were long since dead."

Bailey paused, then brought his chair down from its tilt. With both hands he thrust back long coarse hair, black as his eyes. "That your latest poem?"

Hutch shook his head. "Ann said you'd been electrocuted."

Bailey waited, then stood in place, and pulled his shirt up to the tight dark nipples.

Linda said, "Stop showing that thing. I hate it."

"You don't," Bailey said but he only watched Hutch.

Hutch's eyes traced the burn—white and satiny—the length of chest and belly to the navel, the trouser waist. "Does it go to the ground?"

Linda laughed but had still not turned from the stove.

Hutch saw she was prettier than Ann had implied, a wide country face with immense blue eyes.

Bailey said, "It knew where to stop, took pity on Linda." With a finger he stroked its trail to his belt and reached beneath. He looked back to Linda.

She said, "I can show *you* pity, Big Boy. Let me sprinkle this Drano on your pork chops, you'll be out of your misery in a New York jiffy."

Bailey nodded. "Go to it. You'd be out of a life."

Linda said, "Stuck-up. There're more where you came from."

"Wrong. I'm my mama's only boy, custom-made."

"—In the world, I meant."

Bailey looked down to Hutch. "Tell her how wrong she is." He lowered his shirt.

Hutch smiled. "She's not."

Bailey said "Pig shit."

Linda said, "That's *his* latest poem, Hutch—applaud."

Hutch laughed, really happy for the first time in days—plumb at the center of what seemed the world. But he didn't applaud; he put out a flat hand and pressed Bailey's chest, the height of the burn. "We're glad you were spared."

"Speak for *you*," Linda said. She had turned now, grinning.

Bailey said "He is" and leaned into the hand.

For a moment Ann watched them from the door, not speaking. Then she said, "I'm here; let the revel begin."

45

In the time since Rome, he'd forgot her body—his eye could hold any other sight for years but not the bare bodies he'd wanted or loved, their lines and shades—so he'd left the dim lamp on and moved in its glow to restore a memory as good as any. Ann had joined him naked; and in the warm air, he'd thrown back the covers. For the first slow minutes, she took his greetings like a courteous child, formally grateful—kisses, cool hands, no audible words. Then he pressed her gently to her back, stroked her whole length with one light hand; then lowered his own length slowly above her—lips on hers, the dry insteps of his feet precisely against her soles, his palms on her flanks. He lay there still for another long minute, trusting she'd warm now and give a sign of welcome. Her head turned left away from the lamp. His chin brushed her ear.

She said, "I am one tired girl tonight."

"Of what?"

"—My mother, three days of her woes. The drive back here. Three hours of Bailey."

"I thought you liked Bailey."

"I used to," she said.

"Want to say why you stopped?"

She waited, shook her head.

"He never tried to harm you?"

"Oh no." She faced him, their eyes all but touching. "Is this *harm*, you think?" Her hands brushed his back, clamped in at the rise of his butt, and stayed there.

"Yes ma'm, in the wrong hands."

"Who says '*right*'?"

"Ma'm?"

"Who gets to choose which hands are right?" she said.

Hutch raised on one arm above her and touched her forehead. "The inmost mind." He rolled his eyes wildly.

Ann didn't smile but nodded.

He saw it as a welcome and again worked slowly down her body, crown to foot, with his lips this time—returning to her dry fork, persisting there with his famished tongue till he'd opened her and freed her odor, fuel in the room. Then he moved up to meet her eyes and take their permission to enter her deeply; but her hands held him down, and her eyes were shut. Baffled and urgent, he waited; then said "Too tired?"

Her head shook No; both hands dug once at the crest of his spine. So he chose to obey. Not pausing to guess at the strangeness, he crouched between her knees and bent to continue the licking service she now required—was it punishment, thanks, or adoration? Quick sights of her shut face gave him no clue. Or gave all clues—she seemed both to suffer and accept boundless praise. It lasted a long time (the shapes they made, the new clear language of yip and moan); and near the end when he tasted her climb toward the quick long glide, he finally set his own hand on himself and fiercely stroked out a parallel leap.

Separate on their backs, they calmed in silence. All Hutch's questions survived unanswered—what had she asked for? what had he given? what had she got?—but he knew not to ask and was half-asleep when Linda's door opened and firm steps passed in the hall.

Ann said "Bailey's gone" and turned out the light.

Hutch said, "He won't be here in the morning?"

"He's never slept here, just hovers and goes."

"That why you don't like him?"

She sat to retrieve the covers, spread them neatly; then lay on her side, facing Hutch.

"All well?" He touched her throat.

She seemed to nod.

But as he felt upward to close her eyes, he found tears—the first he'd known her to shed. "Anything I can help?"

She shook her head.

"Anything I should know?"

"Just sleep now please."

"Yes ma'm. Good night."

She slowly lay flat, a handspan away.

He thought he would thank her—she hadn't thanked him—but he sank straight to sleep.

And Ann followed soon, herself not knowing the one vital thing. Beneath her slack fingers their child grew constantly, still a circular disc in its sac of yolk but safe now and avid.

46

Polly led him down the hall toward her sewing room (the room where she and his great-grandfather had slept when she came here fifty-three years ago). As they passed the sepia pictures of Rome, she waved without looking. "*Please* take these with you. I know them by heart."

Hutch said "When I'm back."

She stopped at the shut door and met his eyes. "You're back now or are my eyes gone at last?" Then she entered, slid the oak rocker into sunlight, and pointed him toward it. Her own straight chair was backed to the window; she took up a pile of white lace and sat.

"If you're making lace your eyes are fine."

Polly smiled. "It was made in Japan, I believe. I'm sewing on six million seed-pearls and sequins so some girl's mother can tack it to her wedding gown and claim full credit." She found a needle and threaded it in one thrust.

"Just swallow your pride," Hutch said.

She swallowed hard and speared up a row of opal sequins from a saucer. "Excuse me."

"For what?" She didn't look up.

"I didn't mean to sound like a wise old man."

"You don't," she said. "I can swallow on my own—swallowed so hard last week, my throat's sore."

"How was that?"

"You know."

"Rob's funeral? Grandmother?"

Polly took four stitches, straight, without glasses (she'd never worn glasses). Then she nodded. "We very nearly liked each other."

"Grandmother liked you."

"Did she say that much?"

Hutch said, "Not in words but I noticed."

"There were quite a few words. The night of Rob's funeral, when you all had left and Ann was asleep, she and I sat on in the front room and talked. I'd started upstairs; she asked me to stay. I could see she was wide awake; I knew I was—it's the only big blessing in old age, Hutch: you never get tired." Polly looked up and offered the gradual smile that had been her most useful gift to friends. Then she speared up ten of the pearls, mere grains.

"Should I know what was said?"

Polly smiled again, downward. "It was not about you."

"Hallelujah, amen."

"She told me her life, just three or four sentences, and asked me mine. Mine took a lot longer!"

"The Kendals were all good *arrows*," Hutch said, "—flew straight to the mark."

Polly nodded and touched her chest with the needle-hand. "I volunteered. I've mostly been the mark."

"It's made you strong."

She thought that out. "Who wants to be strong?"

"Everybody."

"Not me." She shook her head twice, then shrugged in apology. "Maybe I'm peculiar, some ugly exception. I wanted to live in a warm cage, tended."

"You never had that?"

"Ten minutes here and there through the years, no more."

"You told that to Grandmother? That's been your life?"

She faced him again, gravely now. "You didn't know that? Rob never told you that?"

"He told me what I asked. I didn't ask much."

"Tell *me*," Polly said. "Tell me all you know."

"You came here to help my great-grandfather when he was old. You stayed on when he died, and my grandfather moved here after Eva left and stayed till *he* died."

"Was that two sentences or three?" she said.

"Two, I believe."

"And you plan to be an author? Won't you need more skin for the bones than that?"

Hutch laughed. "Yes ma'm, but the skin was what stumped us. Rob hoped they loved you; he never knew for sure."

"That made two of us"—she was working again. "And Miss Polly Drewry is the only one left. I still don't know. I sit here and tell myself the story, hours on end."

"The one you told Grandmother?"

"Longer than that but similar, yes."

Hutch said, "I'm in no hurry at all."

"Sure you are. England's begging you back."

"In four days, four whole days till I leave."

Polly laughed. "It's lasted nearly threescore-and-ten and hasn't ended yet—unless I'm dead and don't know it."

Hutch rose, leaned toward her, and found her pulse. He counted ten strong beats and sat again. "You'll outlast me."

She waited, then said "I truly hope not," then folded the lace.

"Don't ever say that."

She nodded. "I do. I'm meant to be a lesson; you're the last pupil left."

"—And willing," Hutch said.

"I started like you. My own mother died at the time I was born, which wasn't as rare back then as now—Lord no, dead mothers were common as sacks of drowned kittens. So I took that in stride and grew up in Washington beside my dad, who was cracked as a bell but nicer to hear. He'd been in the war as a boy (losing side) and had set up this wondrous Confederate museum, three rooms of wild junk that people paid to watch. You'd have loved it—knives, sabres, a whole box of hair from Rebel boys killed before they were grown, a stuffed dog that walked through the battle of Antietam and was still grinning wide when it died years later. I sold tickets to it and dusted at night and cooked our meals. I thought I was safe. I *was* in a cage. What hadn't dawned on me was, I was the show or a big part of it—for adult men. I was filling out fast. If I had any pictures, I think I could prove I'm telling plain facts not blowing my horn. My eyes and skin were frequently mentioned; I learned to say 'Thank you' and look occupied. I thought I *was*, thought I'd work there for life. The word *unhappiness* had not been invented then. People sat and bore their lives or jumped down the well or left for Oklahoma. Well, to my big surprise—and Dad's, you can guess—I left for Oklahoma. This room, to be exact, but it might as well have been the Sandwich Islands for newness."

"You met old Rob?"

Polly nodded. "Met him, sold him a ticket, heard him start a blood-hemorrhage in the first room of junk—he was full of T.B.—helped him calm down and rest, and accepted his offer: all in one afternoon."

"The offer was what?"

"Come here and share his life."

"You could see he was dying. But you said you wanted safety."

She smiled. "I did. I wanted him too."

"He was older?"

"Much older. Women don't mind that—I didn't. I never really asked other women."

"Is that called love?" Hutch said, "—wanting both: him dying and safety?"

"I seldom say *love* and never tried to name whatever I felt. I guess I figured it would name itself in time."

"And it didn't?" Hutch said.

Polly thought and laughed once. "*Waiting*," she said.

"Ma'm?"

"At your Rob's funeral in that cold sun, I realized the name of what I had was *Waiting*. I waited through nearly a year of old Rob, helping him the best I could. Then his son came—Forrest, when Eva'd left him—and I waited through forty years in this house with him."

"For what? Do you know now?"

"I always did. You said it just now—dying and safety. To protect *and* protection. It's a rare wish maybe, but my mother still wants it."

Hutch said "Where?"

"In my dreams, one dream at least the other night. I've gone long months, maybe years without her—never thinking her name, which was Lillian Drewry. But the night of Rob's funeral (young Rob, your Rob) after your grandmother and I finished talking, I dreamt a whole sensible dream about her. I used to have odd dreams when I was much younger, tracking my mother down through strange awful towns and finding her old or poor or blind, never recognizing me. But that one night at Mrs. Mayfield's, I dreamt she was not much older than me (she wasn't—seventeen the month she died); and we had a smaller house than this with a lot of shade and good friendly noise in the street. We never left that but tended each other in neat succession. Just plain daily care but easy and quiet like a good balanced wheel—spokes in a wheel, just meeting at the hub. I woke up knowing how much I missed her, how much we could do for each other now we're old. My dad always said she could make a snake grin." Polly turned back to face the clean window and laughed. "I sit here waiting for everyone that's gone." She faced Hutch, her eyes bright as when she'd first come here. "They're *gone*. Don't let anybody say they're not." Then she took up the band of lace, rolled it out quickly, draped it round her neck, and stood in place. "They never sent a word back to me anyhow, and I've been quiet enough to hear if they spoke. Let's eat this sweet-potato pie I made." She walked past Hutch and toward the door.

"Won't you ruin your lace?"

Garlanded with all its pearls, Polly turned. "If I do I'll pay."

Hutch said "Is that the lesson?"

"Sir?"

"You said I was the pupil."

She considered that a moment but beckoned with her head. "Eat the pie. I can really make pie." She moved again to go.

He said, "Would you come down and live in Rob's house?"

If she heard she didn't stop.

47

Hutch entered Eva's door and walked through the front room, hall, and dining room with no one in sight. In the kitchen Sylvie stood at the window, back to him, and seemed not to hear—studying the warm noon in progress outside, sudden midwinter spring. The stove cooked beside her obediently. He came up behind her, not trying for stealth; but she didn't look round. So he stopped near enough to lay his hands on her shoulders—stout and firm, though she'd somehow shrunk.

Sylvie still didn't turn.

He kneaded twice. Then he said, "Who you cooking this great spread for?" (it was his farewell lunch; he'd leave tomorrow).

She waited. "Miss Eva. Miss Eva that pays me. I'm keeping her live."

Hutch said, "She's gone. Nowhere to be found."

Sylvie put out her own arm and touched the window, tapped one spot. "I can find her," she said. "I always could. Even when she left here, I knew where she went."

Hutch looked. Back beyond Grainger's house in full sun, his grandmother sat—not reading or working but facing out. The face was in profile, the eyes seemed open, she seemed to look north—the way she'd gone when she left here, a girl, with Hutch's grandfather and the way she'd retraced when she came back single with Rob in her arms: journeys she'd never mentioned to Hutch. He still held Sylvie. "Was she sorry?"

"For what?"

"Coming home so soon, not leaving again."

Sylvie waited, then sank an inch—out of his hands—and stirred at a pan. "You want Miss Eva's secrets, ask Miss Eva." She wouldn't meet his eyes.

"How long till we eat?"

"Twenty minutes, *I'll* be done. You can eat then or not."

"You mad?"

"Always mad."

"Big sin," Hutch said.

She looked round at last, black and solemn as a gorge. "Everybody I used to like is frying in Hell now. I hope to join em."

Hutch laughed—"Happy landing!"—and went toward Eva.

48

"You warm enough?" he said (she wore a light cardigan).

"Yes thank you, most always." Eva gathered to stand.

"Let's sit awhile. Sylvie says she needs twenty minutes."

"That means forty-five."

Hutch squatted, felt the ground—cool but dry—and sat. He flicked her right shoe, a trail in its dust. "What you watching?" There were starlings in a bare oak beyond her, conversing.

"I hope to see England, see what weather you'll have." She looked down smiling at the shoe.

"Wrong way—north*east*." He pointed to England.

Eva followed his hand. "Cold rain." Then she faced him. "Stay here."

Hutch grinned. "We need rain."

"Stay here." She touched his hair. In all his life she'd never begged before; in all her life—no, her father's death: she'd begged him to wait.

He answered her stroking hand with nudges—strong unpredictable thrusts like a horse fed one good morsel—but he said, "You'll be all right and I'll be back."

"When?" She reclaimed her hand and spread it in the light.

"When I'm a certified academic wage-earner of the second class."

"You won't need a job."

Hutch laughed. "I beg to differ. I've spent two weeks—remember?—adding Rob's slim assets. If I really get the full death-benefit from his school insurance and pay his few bills and give Min something, I'll have very little over three thousand dollars. That'll cover these two unexpected plane tickets, some petty cash for Strawson in case of house repairs, and maybe one more eye-opener for me—Florence or Athens."

Eva said, "You'll have every penny of mine."

She had no share in Rob's estate; she had to mean her own solid holdings. He couldn't say "When?"—she sat here, strong and welcome in her place—so he laughed. "When I'm ninety! They'll come up to me in the Old Gents' Home, hand me this check on a silver tray, and I'll be far too feeble to endorse it."

Eva waited, then joined him (his favorite laugh, any laugh of hers). Then she said, "Trains leave when the platform's empty."

"You diesel or steam?"

A broad smile survived. "Oh *steam*," she said, "—big tanks of white steam."

Hutch said "All aboard!", then regretted his rough cheer.

Sylvie said, "Anybody want to eat, wash they hands." On the bright kitchen stoop, she was glossy as the starlings.

Eva whispered, "Please give her five dollars when you go. She's run this whole thing."

Hutch nodded but said "I did my own part."

49

The warmth had survived into late afternoon. Hutch had driven back to Rob's house, packed for the trip, and was at Rob's desk writing memos for Strawson (how to keep the place alive) when he heard a car take the last turn of the drive and stop in the yard. He got to the door in time to see Straw unfold himself and stand by the car doing regulation knee-bends and limber toe-touches to start his blood. He hadn't seen Hutch. As he leaned to the back seat to find his small luggage, Hutch said, "How much would you pay a strong redcap?"

Straw looked and waved. "Not one plugged cent. I never bring more than I can tote in one hand."

"Why's that?"

"Got to have one hand free to fight."

Hutch said, "You're in fairly peaceful country here."

Straw said "Maybe so" and when he came forward, both hands were loaded—an old suitcase and a double-barreled shotgun that looked antique.

"You rob a museum?"

Straw came to the foot of the steps; then extended the gun, barrel-first.

Hutch took it, pulled it to him, sighted past the boy's head toward the low sun, and pulled one trigger—harmless click. "Welcome back," he said. He lowered the weight, examined the mellow walnut stock. "Plan to forage for food?"

"Yes sir, squirrel stew—make me quick and trusty."

Hutch laughed. "I never thought of squirrels as trusty."

"Yes sir," Straw said and took the first step. "You can trust them to thrive and multiply."

Hutch said, "I asked for just *one* caretaker."

"You got him," Straw said and moved toward the door. "—one nineteen-year-old former alcoholic who could guard you if you stayed."

Hutch said, "But I'm leaving at six in the morning."

With his hand on the door, Straw said, "You go. I won't tell a soul."

"Tell what?"

"—You're a fool." Then he entered, confident the place would receive him.

An hour later it plainly had. Hutch had shown him to his room, Rob's old room. They'd drunk hot coffee and then Straw had asked to be shown the bounds of the land itself, his hunting preserve. So they walked out at four into slant yellow light and cooling air. Hutch loped ahead, hands empty at his sides; Straw came behind with the loaded gun. They skirted the graves (Hutch had finished there this morning); then crossed a brief thicket and entered the fields, plowed into one broad fallow whorl. On the far edge as woods began, Straw said "Wait." They'd been silent till then. "This is all tobacco?"

"It will be in April."

"And you still claim you're poor?"

Hutch laughed and turned out both empty pockets of the khaki trousers. "I explained that before—you pay overhead on a colored tenant-family, buy seed and supplies, give the tenant his share of eight strict acres of a crop as delicate as Japanese dancers, you'll be so poor you'll beg God for handouts."

"He gives them," Straw said. He nodded toward the trees.

Hutch looked—the deep acres of hardwood and pine. "I'd rather sell slaves than trees, these trees."

Straw waited. "Can I work with your tenant this spring?"

"I told him you were coming. He'll be by to see you. You ask him yourself if you last till spring."

"I'll last," Straw said.

"On what?"

"Sir?"

"On what? I promised you'd be lonesome."

Straw smiled and tapped his forehead with his free hand. "My mind's a stag movie, cast of thousands, never stops." He brought the gun slowly to his shoulder, aimed, fired. A gray squirrel fell from a tall straight poplar. The echo slapped round them in punishing rings.

Hutch said, "That was mine. You didn't need that." Then he entered the woods.

They walked twenty minutes in Indian file—Hutch leading, both silent. At first they advanced in easy space. The hardwoods were old with thick bare boles and undergrowth was sparse, so the light still reached their faces and chests. Then pines began, with dogwoods and cedars; and the soft dry ground was tangled with scrub. They moved darker there in a green glow, wiping limbs from their eyes and digging their heels in against the downgrade that rushed them on toward the crooked west boundary, the rocky creek. Its far bank was cleared, a field of cornstalks belonging to neighbors; so the sunset was visible across the low stream. Hutch went to a big rock and sat. Straw went to the midst of the water, not pausing, on a fallen willow. They both watched the sun long enough to see movement. Then Hutch said, "I guess I'm a little uneasy."

Straw carefully turned; the gun was his balance. "Over me?"

Hutch nodded. "Come sit down a minute."

Straw came to a separate rock and sat, facing out like Hutch. "Ready," he said.

"For what?"

"Bad news."

Hutch laughed. "Not bad, not yet anyhow." He bent for a handful of washed gravel.

"You're scared I'll burn the place down and run."

Hutch laughed again but waited awhile. "That's more or less the first part."

"The second?"

"—That you won't, that you'll be here in a clean painted house when I return."

Straw said, "I may be. I hope that's more likely than me harming anything." He faced Hutch's profile; Hutch didn't meet the turn. "I'll stand up and walk out of here this minute and grab my duds and be back at my parents' in time for their sleeping pills—just tell me 'Go.'"

Hutch still watched the sun. He wanted to say it—"Thanks. Now go."

But Straw said "Look here. Remember this."

There was nothing to see but the boy's own face, changing from child to man each instant at a rate no slower than the sun's descent but surely as permanent as any other living thing visible and offered. Hutch watched it five seconds, still meaning to say some grateful dismissal.

But a sound arrived from far behind them, long high notes like an animal wail.

Straw said "That a bull?"

Hutch shook his head. "Rob's fox horn. Grainger's calling us in. He's come out to cook us a farewell feast."

Straw said, "I was hoping for something like that."

They stood simultaneously and retraced their steps. At the edge of the fields, Straw claimed his squirrel—cold now and locked in the shape of its fall, only one streak of blood.

50

Near dawn Hutch dreamt the last dream of the night. He was in a dark house and at first seemed alone. But as he felt a path from room to room, he began to know there was someone else; that the other was behind him at varying distances but following. He moved on steadily by groping out objects like milestones or gates—the corners of tables, railings of stairs—and at times he was far ahead in wide empty rooms (his outstretched arms touching nothing as he went). But then he'd enter passages with walls at his ears; and there on his neck he'd feel slow breaths from whatever pursued him, occasional clicks as it swallowed or gaped. He never was frightened; and he wondered at that, thinking as he dreamt "This is meant as a nightmare. Why am I calm?" But he didn't turn and stop, never felt for the lamps that were surely on the frequent tables he passed. He moved through all the last hours of darkness, forward (to him the path seemed forward). Then windows began to appear, faint light. He seemed clear again, no sound behind him; and by the time day had confirmed itself, he'd come to the last room—an ordinary kitchen. There was no door onward. He stood, looking out at an endless bare field, and thought he was no longer safe but trapped. So he went cold with fear and wanted to hide. There was only a table in the midst of the room— long and broad, dark wood. He crawled beneath that and condensed his body to its smallest size, still an awkward mass. Then he waited, trying hard to silence irregular noises—blood and breath. When he'd finally succeeded and was quiet as the air, he heard steps coming and faced the entrance. What entered slowly was a human child, nothing strange or strong. At first it didn't see him and circled the room, also touching walls and corners as though still blind. He knew it was his, that he'd seen it before as it hung in Ann. He thought he would speak any moment to claim it, and he searched for words. But by then it had stopped at the sink and seen him. It extended a hand in the clean early light, no longer translucent but firm and free. On numb cramped legs he began to move toward it. Though the room enlarged, the child waited in place.

He woke in his room, listening for any move that might have waked him—only occasional natural creaks. Strawson was thirty feet away in Rob's room, Grainger downstairs on the dining-room couch. He felt on the table by his bed for the flashlight—ten till four. He could sleep forty minutes; he tried to take it. But his body seemed rested, his mind stayed clear; so he lay and recalled as much of the dream as survived. Just the movement—the strange calm chase through a house that must have been this house (he remembered the feel of objects in the dark, familiar local objects). The end— his discovery on the floor by the child, their silent greeting—had gone or sunk.

The calm continued. He felt no trace of the parting uncertainty he'd felt in May as he woke in New York, no sense that anything here required him more than his postponed work in England. He composed himself flat in the covers—face up, eyes open toward a ceiling that might have been sky for all its tangibility—and again said the prayer he'd said since childhood before any trip: the names of his kin and his few urgent friends, that they'd stay safe in places they chose till he saw them. As he reached Grainger's name, he heard Grainger stand beneath him downstairs and move toward the toilet, beginning the day. After that there was only *Ann* to say. He said it aloud and rolled to his left side, touching his lips to the cold spare pillow.

51

They were twenty minutes from the Raleigh airport with time to spare when Grainger said, "I found out Gracie died too. I didn't tell you that."

They'd said very little but ridden quietly as sun rose reluctant through a mist from the warm night. So Hutch took a moment to think through the sentence—Gracie, Grainger's long-gone wife; he'd never seen her. "I'm sorry. Where was she?"

"Richmond, her cousin's where she'd been since the war."

"Was she sick long?"

"Twenty years. She drank poison wine."

They'd both watched the road through that. Then Hutch faced Grainger. "You see her at the end?"

Grainger was driving; he never glanced over. But he smiled. "I saw her at the end of me."

"When was that?"

"When she left me the last time for good."

Hutch said, "You've done all right, I think."

Grainger said, "I been thinking you're wrong a lot lately." He renewed his smile.

"Want to tell me how? I moved Rob's grave."

Grainger said, "Don't mind me. You know your business."

"Is it Strawson?—you worried about him in the house?"

"Not a bit. Far as I know, he's got good sense."

"Is it me leaving Grandmother?"

Grainger laughed. "If any three other human beings alive were strong as Miss Eva, the world couldn't take it."

Hutch nodded and thought they could leave it at that.

But Grainger said, "I may be leaving soon myself."

"To where?"

"I still got my little piece of house in Virginia, got nieces in Maine."

"What would you do in Maine? You've been warm too long."

"I'd get on the Welfare and rest my tail far as I can go north of this integration mess."

"It won't touch you," Hutch said, "—any place."

Grainger waited. "Too true. Too late to touch me."

"And you haven't got any friends in Virginia."

He faced Hutch quickly—"No friends above ground"—then looked to the road.

"Where does that put me?"

Grainger said, "You're putting *yourself; you* say."

Hutch smiled unseen. "That's the thing I can't do."

"But you're leaving here."

Heard in Grainger's voice, as calm as "Morning," it seemed the decision made and acknowledged. For the length of a mile, Hutch tried to test it against the pine woods that flanked the road, the persistent light that was now winning through and drying the ground. He could see their strong ordinary beauty—had seen it all his life—but they drew at him no more powerfully now than the round Cornish fields, the melting ochre of Roman walls, or the cold heat of Oxford's decay. He turned to Grainger and said, "Nobody will mind for long."

Grainger nodded—"Maybe not"—and seemed to be finished; but once they had both seen the white hut of the airport, he said "Nobody else'll *die* at least."

Hutch had not really known how he'd waited for that, the actual blame. Min's harshness had been easy enough to bear, the fumes from her years of deprivation. But could he accept this verdict from Grainger, who'd shown Rob devotion that was either pure love (unaltered by time) or a force undescribed in the world till now? He said "Thank God."

Grainger laughed. "Thank us. Thank the tough ones, Hutch." Not looking, he put out his wide right hand and blocked Hutch's sight, barely touching the nose. It held there an instant, then returned to the wheel.

When Hutch could see again, he saw clearer light—the air of the landing field swept by engines. He said "Thank you all" and felt its weight as a farewell from which he could hardly return.

52

January 13, 1956

Dear Ann,

I tried hard to spot your chimney as I flew over Richmond two hours ago, but we moved too fast, and you'd already left for work. So the day's one successful accomplishment to now is landing in New York in driving snow and waiting again. I'm at Idlewild with an hour to go till we breast the storm—if we breast it at all — and am stuck in a lounge with a congregation of British nurses bound back from a tour of our native hospitals and still aghast from exposure to U.S. postwar medicine in full bloodless cry. I'd introduce myself and agree if I didn't think they'd all terminate in midAtlantic — each one at this minute is smoking six cigarettes (bargain Yank tobacco) — and leave me friendless.

Maybe that's the other accomplishment today — feeling thoroughly alone, half in England already. The past week has been my second orgy of goodbyes in nine months, and I feel fairly sapped. But also light. I've never felt lighter on my feet in my life. When I shook Grainger's hand in Raleigh just now and walked toward the plane, I knew some hobble was gone from my feet. Or not even a hobble but a band of flesh that had joined my ankles like the Siamese twins, joined me to the ground. I suppose it was Rob. And Rob is removed.

I don't say it flippantly — you understand that — but I sit here now in this dismal lobby where no one has names or precedents or futures and feel vast relief. I loved him all my life and for nearly half of his. I did what I wanted and had to do when I knew he was ill. We had a good parting, and I really think he left. Nothing in the house or the grave or the woods seems to warn that he's stayed, expecting me still. I don't expect him, however much I thank him; and I trust that can last.

What I do expect is you. I expect us together in a short while from now. We can sleep through the interim or maybe even meet in England in the fall. If I get any word that I'm rich on tobacco, I could bring you over and we could repair what I had to ruin in Rome (which is used to ruins). Would your job turn you loose for two or three weeks or does Commonwealth justice require your ceaseless presence?

I'll write again as soon as I've slept off the trip — all the trips (I'd have made a poor pilgrim). I thought you were still a little tired yourself. Let me know when you're rested.

Thanks, thanks forever and love
from Hutch

January 13, 1956

Dear Min,

I'm held up in New York by snow, hoping to leave for England any minute; but the wait gives me time to say what got neglected or swamped when we were there together at Rob's. I don't look back on those meetings with pride, not on my part of them. Whatever my best is, I wasn't at it then. I'd like to plead surprise and exhaustion but I can't. I should have been better prepared. Please forgive. I don't know that you and I will ever wind up again in such close quarters

with such hard parts, but if so I hope to remind you more of Rob than Hutch—
Rob in this last year, strong as he got.

What I didn't say was thank you, not a formal thanks on behalf of Rob
(I'm sure he took care of that himself) but my own and real. The thought of
him enduring those final months without your presence is terrible, and I honestly do not wish I'd shared the burden with you or had it for myself. My hope
now is that you've started to rest and that life can be level soon again. But I
wonder if we're cut much deeper than we know, by a sharper blade?

Grandmother will be writing to you with something Rob wanted you to
have—she's executrix and will always be.

Yours tardily,
Hutch

January 13, 1956

Dear Grainger,

I got as far as New York in one piece, then snow set in. Can't leave till it
stops, which may be April. Why didn't you tell me it was Friday the thirteenth?
Drop by if you head to Maine before spring and see if I'm here. Otherwise I'll
count on seeing you back at the old stand there in eighteen months. Till
when, and beyond, I won't forget your help. It meant most of all to me, especially this morning.

Ever,
Hutch

Dear Rob, I napped twenty minutes just now,
Upright in my vinyl Iron Maiden in
A New York airport blanked by snow
And dreamt you'd made your way underground
From home to here and were butting with what
Was left of your head on the green terrazzo
Like Hamlet Senior ("canst work in the earth
So fast, old mole in the cellarage"?) or Lycidas
Washed to the Hebrides, scouring "the bottom
Of the monstrous world," except that you'd dug
Every inch of your own way with still-sprouting
Nails through mantling rock and that I on
The outer rim of South Queens am stalled
In as monstrous a world as yours
With its dormant grubs and older dead

(Though I grant your last mile, till you nosed out
My shoes, was hardest—the Mafia graves
Of Brooklyn). But the butting was all—
No questions, no orders, just thuds at what
I recall as the rate of your living heart
When calm.
                    So—awake, sentenced to hours
Here before any chance of taking the air,
And trusting you won't breaststroke the Atlantic—
May I now do the talking, the facts and questions
I couldn't advance in the face of your dying
Which lasted the length of my life till now?
(I never believed you meant to stay,
That you wouldn't leave at the sight of one
False move by me. Since no rules were posted,
Which moves were true?)
                    I was mostly a child.
Did you ever see that? Through the years
When you came to me for what the Mother
Goddess herself would have been strapped
To furnish—bedrock beneath you, daily
Reward—I was technically a child: technically and
Really. And though I noticed it as seldom as
You, those treks in which I bore your weight
(A widowered semi-reformed alcoholic
With the density of pitchblende) packed me down—
A dwarf in the mines, a huddled porter
When what my bones requested was height,
The usual chance to rise in makeshift
Scaffolding toward the general view—a life
Of my own.
                    Don't misunderstand. I welcomed
The job, steady child-labor
In the good old Depression
When others my age could barely feed
Their hookworms. Grumpy, Sneezy, Dopey,
Bashful, Happy, Sleepy, Doc
Never took deeper pride in a day with their picks
Than I in our years—you were healing, smiling
Occasionally; I accepted credit. But I wonder now.

Couldn't I have been offered the chance to volunteer
Or renege and join the Cub Scouts and
Prove my merit by looping knots of
Staggering complexity in plain hemp rope,
Not press-ganged at birth by a charm that had long
Since stripped the trees of birds and leaves
Throughout Carolina and the Valley of Virginia?
I assume your answer, now as then, would be
That is what you were for. I assume it is what
Most children are for, but I can't fail to notice
How many decline (and the sky doesn't fall)
Or to ask the next question.

                         What am I for now?
By your terms I seem to be finished, retired —
A twenty-five-year-old pensioner in appallingly
Good health. You left me no answer. All
Your awesome summary letter breathes
No hint, though some months ago you did
Throw a challenge that could last awhile —
Find the figure made by our family's path
(A hundred years of private parabolas,
Beelines, halts, scratched in blood
On the unavoidable public maze!) —
And your actual last words were "You choose."

I've chosen, had chosen before you spoke.
The choice is the answer — I will have your life,
The life you hunted but never caught.
It was not you and I in a house on a low
Hill, a dog, a manservant, your mother
At the moat, all other bridges raised. Whatever I
Planned as a lonely boy or you
As a dying man in that house, we were stopped
By two things — age and body. We were separate
Ages (you were bound to quit before me) but
Identical bodies. What we had was years
Of circling a spot, mules at a mill.
The figure was rings, concentric rings
Round an unseen center (what were we grinding?)
Till I fled and you quit.

Don't misunderstand.
We were first-rate mules;
I wouldn't have missed it. It was my war and peace,
My genuine blaze, while Europe and Asia
Burned out of reach. What I hope I learned
Is the single lesson of any war—
The properties of fire: life and death.

—Which lands me squat in my graybeard
Robes again (the boy-Diogenes, tubby
Wisdom), the son who winged you postal
Blessing when you asked for release.
Well, pardon, Rob. Pardon please
For what I gave prematurely or uselessly
Or never knew to give or flatly
Refused.
              What I have now to offer as recompense
Is memory—a file of memory, my childhood
Hobby, squirreled up in lieu of arrowheads
Or the stamps of Chile and Madagascar.
They aren't yet sorted for Best or Worst,
Improvement, Caution, Terror, Laughter.
I'll wait to sort till the final sight
(Your foaming extinction) has shrunk to size
And trust the shrinkage will come more quickly
On foreign ground—a reason to go.

One sight though insists, here now,
Its natural buoyancy sailing it past
More than once in the recent wakes and dreams.
So here in this frozen port, I watch
It again—nine months ago, you and I in
Warm Springs; the circular pool of fuming
Water (female essence of the heart of the
Ground) accepting your hard white limbs and
Head in farewell grip more total than
Any you'd known in air with prior
Partners (a region of willing girls, my
Famished mother). Seeing, I sink to
The depths in a mock-death (mystery! a sleep

And a change); then rise to your best gift
Again, the sight sustained—a man
Embraced by the killing earth, your potent
Grin as you warn "Remember."
                                        Here's proof
I have, this far at least—the burdened
Last patient American rock
Before the sea.

T H R E E

THE CENTER OF GRAVITY

FEBRUARY–MARCH 1956

After two unbroken hours of driving in cold early dark, Ann crossed the state line. The crossing itself, where rough Virginia road met its well-kept Carolina extension, seemed a question solved. There was help in the world; the car had brought her toward it (refusing every chance to turn west toward her mother's). The first lighted town had a hotel sign in green neon—*Good Coffee Shop*—so she pulled in, calmer than she'd been since Richmond. But when she'd gone halfway across the frozen lawn, she was rushed by the fear that had followed her down. It filled her chest with the milk she'd drunk at noon, hot and cheesy. She stopped. This was crazy; any help was in Richmond or—pray God, not—at her mother's. She turned. She'd go back to Linda, ask Bailey to leave till she'd told her news.

A man had opened the door of her car and was scrounging in the back.

Ann said, "Can I help you? This is my car, sir."

"I know it"—an old head looked up, grinning. "I'm the night clerk—Winston. I was coming on duty and saw you get out. Thought I'd bring your bag for you." He set her small bag on the ground and stood. The inside light from the car showed a face as white as his hair.

Ann said, "I'm not staying here but thanks."

"Better had. We've got rooms that never seen a lady."

Ann laughed. "They'll have to wait awhile longer then. I just need coffee."

"Too late," Winston said. "Coffee closed down at seven." He stood by the bag as though she might change her mind.

She did; he'd forced her. "Is the pay phone closed?"

"That's open all hours and I'll make your change."

"I think I've got change."

He shrugged once. "You won't take assistance, will you?"

Ann said, "Oh I think so, eventually."

Winston smiled. "I'm seventy-two years old. I can't stand out on a freezing Friday night, making useless offers."

"Put my bag back please. That'll be a big favor." He obeyed so slowly that Ann almost thought she'd spend a night here and decide in his shadow, as good as any. But once he'd shut the door and headed toward her, she caught the old smell of his skin and teeth—sweet burnt stagnation. She'd make the call and head on to Raleigh, whatever.

Min answered the first ring loudly—*"Tharrington"*—to discourage a heavy breather who'd called the night before.

Ann deposited coins; then the line seemed dead. She said, "Miss Tharrington, it's Ann. Can you hear me?"

Min waited. "Very clearly. Ann who?"

"—Gatlin. I met you at Mr. Mayfield's funeral."

Another wait, longer. "Of course. Where are you?"

"Norlina, N.C. in a telephone booth."

Min said, "I've been there. It's got a good poem on the wall or it did. Look for it when you're through."

"Yes ma'm. I'm coming on to Raleigh right now. Could I see you this evening?"

Min said, "It'll take you two hours—ten o'clock." Her voice was plainly reluctant with fatigue. "What about tomorrow?"

Ann said "Well, I could"; then stopped and swallowed. "But I guess I'm asking hard to see you tonight."

"Bad news?"

"Not yet."

"From Hutchins?" Min said.

"Maybe so."

Min said, "Ann, I finished with Hutchins at the funeral."

"Yes ma'm, I understand."

"You can leave off the *ma'm*. I still walk unaided." The voice tried to laugh but was seized by coughing.

Ann said, "I am asking for me not Hutch." She had not said the name all week; it surprised her.

Min said, "Have you got a hotel or a friend?"

"Not yet."

"You have now, an old davenport at least. I'll be here beside it."

When Ann had thanked her and shut her purse to go, she remembered the poem and searched the booth. On a stained oak shelf, she could trace these lines—

Alexander Graham Bell, a word of
Thanks from Baxter Conway who spent
Eighty cents here in 1950 to insure
Eternal peace for himself and a friend.
All others forget. I will always recall.

2

Min said, "I guessed you were hungry. Was I right?" She had watched Ann eat three scrambled eggs, a sliver of cured ham, a slice of cold bread, a glass of milk.

Ann nodded. "Apparently. I didn't think so."

Min stood from the table, took the plate and glass; and went to the alcove, the rusty sink. "You want me to tell you what else I know now or wait till morning?"

In the forty-five minutes since arriving, Ann had made no mention of her news. "We could wait. It's past eleven."

Min said, "Maybe you could. I wouldn't sleep a wink." Her back was still turned to Ann—a slow job of washing.

Ann laughed. "You said you already knew."

"I meant I'd known Mayfields all my life, the men anyway. You're here about them."

"The young one at least."

"They don't come separate," Min said. "Deal with both. If you can't, walk away."

"Like you?"

Min waited. "I didn't, not away—just over to the sidelines, in sight."

Ann said, "Are you sorry?"

A longer wait while she polished the glass; then she stowed all she'd washed, came up behind Ann, and said, "We had better sit on easier chairs." They moved farther into the small living room. Ann took the armchair. Min switched off the main light, leaving them dim enough to watch each other with a minimum of pain; then she sat on the davenport. "I'm sorry as hell several times every day—right after I wake up, just before I sleep, more in fall and winter than spring or summer. I'm a living barometer." She raised her right arm, stiffened it, then moved it down slowly like the needle of a gauge—her face clouding over.

Ann said "That's normal."

"The moody part is, sure. The rest is bad, being locked in alone here at my ripe age."

Ann said, "Don't you own the key?"

Min smiled. "I do. I use it all the time. But what they don't tell you—there comes one minute, quiet as wool, when you open; and there's nobody standing on the ledge or landing, nobody in the *streets*. Not for you anyway."

"Then what?" Ann said.

"Then you've got two choices—learn to be a good nun or go nuts fast, start eating your own dry hair and nails."

Ann said "What's a good nun?"

Min laughed. "I was reared Presbyterian so I speak from private speculation only." She paused till she knew. "Oh a watchful well-wisher—equal stress on both. The contemplative life."

"Are you one?"

Min knew at once. "Never. I grudge every *pony* that gets what I lack, not to mention live humans."

"That what keeps you young?"

Min touched both her eyes. "Am I young?"

"Yes ma'm."

"Since Rob died I have felt—what?—every day: not younger but lighter. It's far more relief than I guessed it would be, not to hope anymore. Not that I sat here, keeping vigil by my flame (I'd go weeks, months with no thought of his face); but long as he lived, there were cells deep in me (actual cells) that kept a blank watch without informing me—their sole little duty: would he ever want me again? You may know by now that of course he never did. He needed me though, once Hutchins skipped out. The cells were ready." Her arm came up again, limber now, and waved round slowly as if showing the walls.

Ann looked. There was no more than she'd seen when she entered—a reproduced Winslow Homer of waves, the text of the North Carolina state-song illuminated with pine bough and flag, a coltish Gainsborough girl in pink. No sign of Rob Mayfield, picture or word. She said, "Will you stay on here now?"

Min balked in puzzlement, then said "I live here." Then she grinned. "Whatever others think, I truly *live* here. I'll live better now."

Ann nodded in collusion with the hope.

Min said, "You aren't here on the spur like this to glean the wisdom of my harvest years."

Ann smiled. "Why not? I am, more or less."

Min said "You're pregnant, right?"

"Yes. Heard today; doctor phoned me at four." Ann sat still and cold, holding her knees.

It was Min's eyes that filled. Her whole body shrank to its full age silently. She picked at her skirt.

Ann said "How bad is that?"

Min shook her head, no answer.

But Ann said, "Please. How bad is the news?"

Min leaned forward suddenly and opened a new magazine on the table—a two-page picture of Mamie Eisenhower, all earbobs and bangs. Then she said "I guess it depends."

"On what?"

"Do you want it? Does Hutch?"

"Hutch has no idea."

Min smiled. "Hutch has no idea of a *lot*. You can call him from here."

Ann looked at her watch. "It's four in the morning over there. No phone in his room."

"They'll get him; say it's urgent."

Ann said, "I'm not sure it's his."

"What?"

"The child." Her hands had stayed on her knees. Now they came to her belly and pressed in lightly, first time since she'd known. She felt nothing more than her meal at work; yet for the first time, and for no clear reason, she felt what was true—that the child was Hutch's, that the will of those days in Rome had worked itself.

But Min said, "How many other candidates are there?"

"One—a lonesome boy in Rome after Hutch left me."

"Was he leaving you or just heading home?"

Ann said, "Both, I thought. I may have been wrong."

Min was struck full-face by a surge of indignation—that a possible continuance of Rob had been fouled, that this girl could come here uninvited and tell it as calmly as yesterday's weather. She wanted to stand now and send Ann out—how could she breathe through a whole long night in this hot cube of space (her own space for years) in sound of a stranger who'd fouled half her own hopes—more than half? But something held her tongue, and her legs locked her down. She spread her palms flat on Mrs. Eisenhower's face. Then she said, "Don't you have any feeling whose it is?"

Ann waited but could still say it straight at Min's eyes. "I'm very much afraid it's Hutch's."

Min sat back, took the balsam-stuffed pillow, and smelled its faint cleanness. "I'm not Hutchins' chief defender—never was—but he may grow into something decent yet; his father did."

Ann nodded. "I meant I'm stopping the child. I'm sorry if it's his."

Min stood. "Either way—any way *I* can see—it's yours, mainly yours." She took two steps toward the closet (sheets, blankets). "I'm no help at all."

Ann stayed in her chair. "You are. Now it's mine."

3

By a little past noon, Ann had made her way to the old Kendal place (Hutch had brought her only twice by daylight, but she found she knew the turns). As she drove up the gouged drive, she only thought of Strawson—how to ask him her question. And she saw his car as she cleared the rise, baking in cold sun, Mr. Mayfield's pickup beside it. Smoke from the chimney. She had bet right again. But when she'd knocked three times and waited long minutes, she felt the old fear and went down the steps. She'd rush back to Richmond— Linda would be there, drying her hair; Bailey wouldn't show up till suppertime. The sight of the empty stalled truck stopped her—chalky blue paint, Mr. Mayfield's only means out of here. She could do one right thing at least—see his grave.

At the rear left corner of the house, a row of paint cans. Ann looked toward the eaves. Straw had painted the whole top half of the back, a flat pure white. She liked him for that; everyone else she knew would have started in front, the side toward the world. And the whole backyard seemed cleaner than when they'd threaded through it slowly with the coffin six weeks ago. Piles of old iron and leaves were gone; firewood was stacked by the kitchen door. She tried again, calling *Straw* once at the windows. Nothing still.

The graves were half-turfed. Since the funeral the rough ground had been plowed lightly, and a thick mat of field grass had been laid in neat contiguous rows from the wall toward the graves. The two rows of old stones were already socketed in dim winter greenery; the head of Rob's grave was marked by a stake and was still red dirt—dry, no recent rain. The gate was open but she stopped outside. Maybe twice each year since her own father's death, she'd gone to his grave and tried to talk silently—not always of problems, sometimes just in thanks (she'd felt at least *watched* if not *heard* or *answered*). But now that she'd come here, what could she say to Rob Mayfield still intact in skin and bone?—*You never liked me so I've come to your home to ask a young stranger the simplest way to ease myself of what may be your grandchild?* From all Hutch had said, she knew Rob had ruined enough in his own life to have seas of mercy in his heart by now. *Can you pardon me? Can you see any broader path than I see? Can you aim me toward it?* She thought all the sentences but offered him none. Still her natural courtesy made her step forward, stop at his feet, and bend for a split flint that lay on the surface — oddly warm. When she stood she said *Sorry*, thought it clearly as a speech. If anything watched her, it kept the air adamant. No answer, no pardon, only unruffled light. She replaced the stone carefully and turned to go, then heard a creaking behind the big shed.

A wheelbarrow piled with turf, Grainger behind it. He was twenty feet away before he saw her; and at first he didn't know her but came on and stopped at the gate, unsmiling. He took off his hat, laid it on the turf, then found the name — "Miss Gatlin." More than that, he could only think she brought news of Hutch — sick or dead — so he justified his work. "I'm turfing in here so February doesn't wash it too bad."

"Will it root in the cold?"

"I can do it again. We're well-stocked on grass."

"The paint looks good." Ann pointed to the house.

Grainger smiled and reached for his hat. "—Look better if he'd wake up and work."

"Strawson?"

"You see him?"

"I knocked, no answer."

Grainger said, "He's in there. Sleeps like a crowbar."

"Is he happy here alone?"

Grainger said, "He seems all right when he's *wake*. Like I said, he's sleeping till he get his full growth. I stay out here now myself most nights."

"I was driving back from Raleigh and thought I'd stop by."

"Yes ma'm." He rolled the barrow in through the gate. "The back door's open. Step in there and holler."

"You don't think he'll mind?"

"Somebody got to call him or he'll sleep till spring." He crouched and pressed down a thick plaque of turf. "You see Miss Eva?"

"No."

"She's got a bad cold."

"Hutch seems all right." She'd said it to test herself; it still stung hard.

Grainger didn't look up. "Straw heard from him yesterday. He'll be all right."

Ann said "I don't doubt it."

Grainger faced her, studied her, then pointed to the house. "Make him fix you your lunch. If he doesn't, call me."

Every step through the yard, she felt under broad attack from the day — the bald sky itself.

4

Straw was standing at the range—barefoot on the cold floor, shirt unbuttoned, long hair uncombed. He glanced at her. "Ready for my famous French toast?" He said it to the pan in his slow deep voice.

Ann had seen him only twice before, once when she'd visited Hutch's class at school and once at the funeral. Now she was stopped by his firm air of *residence*; he lived, however he lived, in this house. It had let him in easily. She stood on the sill.

He said, "Come or go. You're wasting my heat" and did a quick shuddering dance in place.

She entered and shut the door. "I thought you were dead. I knocked and yelled."

He looked up. "I heard you. Here I am." Then he took two heated plates from the oven and began to serve the bread, fried neatly.

Ann stepped to the table and sat but said, "I ate eggs for supper and breakfast in Raleigh—any more, I'll sprout tail feathers and a beak."

Straw danced five steps again, cackling now and flapping wings. He brought the two plates, then forks and syrup, then coffee strong as brass. He sat at the far end from her and they ate awhile. Then he said, "You leave something here or what?"

Ann laughed. "I never brought anything here. I've barely been here."

"I like it. I wish to God he'd sell it to me."

Ann said "Make him an offer."

Straw buttoned the top three buttons of his shirt. "I did."

"He trusted you to guard it at least."

Straw thought through that. "*He's* the thing needs guarding."

"Hutch?—from what?" She laughed again. "He's guarded like the Unknown Soldier's Tomb."

"—Used to be. All his guards are dying off." Straw stood, reached for her plate, and went to the stove.

"No more. It was good."

So he put the two final slices on her plate, brought it back, set the plate in his, and chewed a mouthful.

Ann persisted. "From what? What's the danger to Hutch?"

"—Just talking, trying to warm my mouth." He grinned and exercised his lips grotesquely. "He'll grow up now. See, he loved his father."

"Will he come back here?"

Straw said "You a millionaire?"

"No, why?"

"Then you can't live here unless you plan to eat leaves."

Ann said, "I don't think I plan anything for Hutch."

"He plans on you."

"How?"

Straw's large hands spread before him on the table. "I'm not you, you see. You've known him years longer." The sun had swung round and struck his right fingers. He worked them in the warmth like an old man at dawn. When he faced her he saw she was near to breaking, blue-mouthed and taut. He said, "Do you want me to touch you any way?"

Ann shook her head.

Straw said, "Then I don't think I know why you're here."

Low as she was she read that rightly, an unconditioned offer of welcome. So she said, "If I tell you, could it stop here now?"

He nodded. "I keep secrets that *God* wants to know."

She drank a long swallow of the tepid coffee. "You know we went to Rome. I wasn't sure I should. Hutch had left here, singing on about his need for freedom; but his letters kept asking me to meet him in Rome. I dug out pennies from every old sock and turned up on Christmas eve in downtown Rome. He'd been fogged-up in London and was hours late; so I had a whole long afternoon by myself to prowl round the edges, steady warm sun. My mother had said I was crazy to go—crazy and brazen and a blot on the name—and I half-believed her by the time Hutch landed. You ever seen Rome?"

"In *The Sign of the Cross*."

Ann could smile by then. "It's not quite that fierce or that funny either, last month anyway. But if all you've seen is the South and New York and the Colorado Canyon, it's still a big wind. I was knocked right over—or down or onto Hutch. Don't ever meet anybody you feel two ways about in Rome at Christmas; you'll lose your choices."

Straw said "Yes ma'm," wrote himself an invisible memo on the table, then grinned. "Did Hutch?"

"What?"

"Did Hutch take the place hard as you?—he'd practiced in England."

Ann said, "He seemed happy, his old best self; we laughed a lot. But you saw him in England—"

"He was serious there. I gave him a sermon one night—How to Live—from the depths of my wisdom and long hard life."

"Then maybe you're responsible. In Rome he had all his barbed wire cleared; we met more than once. He asked me to wait."

Straw said "Where?"

"In Richmond, till he finished at Oxford and was home."

"But you're down here today." Straw drew his hands back to his lap, out of sight.

Ann nodded.

"Why?"

"To ask you a question."

"I don't know much."

Ann said, "Hutch told me you got an abortion for a girl you knew."

"Hutch was lying," Straw said.

"Or I misunderstood."

"He was lying," Straw said.

"I'm sorry then."

Straw pushed back his chair and stood. "O.K." He stayed in place, staring out the bright window.

Ann stood. "I'm sorry. I'll go on now."

"Yes ma'm," Straw said—not turning back; not conscious of the splendor of the line his face made, pressed on the sun.

Ann saw it but left by the front door quietly.

5

February 11, 1956

Dear Hutch,

This was Saturday but we worked all day. Well, I worked all afternoon. Grainger was up before light as usual. He finished turfing the graves even though he says February will probably kill it. If so that'll give him a reason to live on and do it again in April, he says. My personal guess is he'll turf us all under whenever we die. Don't worry, I don't plan to die here, not now. I stayed on the ladder from two o'clock till sunset and painted a good deal more of the house. It drinks up paint like a dedicated wino, but it looks strong and healthy.

I guess I do too except for the arches of my feet which are ruined from the ladder. Did you know there was a sealed pint of bourbon in the kitchen when you left me? It must have been your father's insurance. It's still here sealed and I haven't brought any of my own in to join it. No other humans either except Mr. Grainger. I call him Mr. Grainger *and he hasn't said* Stop. *He calls me* Straw. *We are straining to integrate one house at least. He seems on the verge of trusting me now but goes on watching about as close as radar. I don't mind much. He is pretty fair company. We even started reading to each other after supper. One night I read us a chapter from* Lord Jim. *The next night he reads from* The Wandering Jew. *He said that would hold us till you got home.*

You sound pretty good. Send us anything you write that wouldn't disrupt our rural daze or harm our morals. As it is we're rolling back the centuries at a swift clip. By spring we may have forgot how to read and be painting deer and foxes on ceilings by the light of fat from the flesh of wild creatures we kill with bare hands.

At noon today Ann Gatlin came by. She'd been down in Raleigh and detoured here on her way to Richmond. I don't know why. I gave her French toast and one cup of coffee. She looked like she missed you and said you'd told her I'd helped my girlfriend dispose of a baby. That made me mad and she left without excess politeness from me. If she writes you about it, you will understand. See, she caught me off guard with a mixed-up version of something I meant you to take as private. If she writes you about it, you can try to see my feelings before you answer. I'd have my child here with me right now if I had my way. And Grainger would like it as much as me. I don't mean to mess in that side of your business, but I promised you a good caretaking job and want you to know my view of what's happened in my own small life. It's nothing I'm proud of—still it happened one way and Ann Gatlin had it wrong.

It's seven o'clock now, pitch-dark outside and cold wind rising. Grainger's just walked in from checking on your grandmother. She's got a cold, he says, but otherwise good. I like her too. He'll cook supper now so I'll stop this and help him. We're having beef hash and waffles, I can smell.

> *Strawson or what's left of*
> *him tonight*

He folded that and rose to set the table, then noticed Grainger was in no hurry—greasing the waffle iron with slow precision. He sat back and said, "Let me read you this one thing I just told Hutch."

Grainger's hands paused a moment but he didn't turn.

So Straw read the sentences about Ann's visit.

Grainger poured the first batter.

Straw said "What you think?"

Grainger still didn't turn. "What you asking?"

"Should I mail it?"

Grainger said "Is it true?"

"Yes."

"She said that about you?"

"Yes."

"And you hadn't hurt her no way at all?"

Straw shook his head firmly, though Grainger hadn't looked.

Grainger's hand had stayed by the waffle iron. He suddenly stepped toward Straw, reached out, and accepted the letter. Then he tore it four times, kneaded the scraps, laid them on the counter, and lifted the lid of the iron—perfect food.

Straw said, "I could just have recopied that page."

Grainger said "She's in trouble" and poured the next batter.

"Can you help her?"

"No sir. She'll find her own help."

"How?"

"I used to live in Richmond," Grainger said. "Richmond's big."

"And we shouldn't tell Hutch?"

"Least of all. Let him rest." His whole right palm lay flat on the hot iron, no sign of pain.

6

Ann got back to Richmond in late afternoon—the house dark and cold, no sound of Linda. When she'd searched upstairs and returned to the living room, she thought she could not stay a minute here alone. She'd turn up the heat, switch on a few lights, go to a movie. Then if Linda wasn't back, the house would at least be ready to take Ann herself. But after ten seconds she knew she was tired; she hadn't slept a whole night in nearly a month. She didn't want to risk her own room though, not alone. She turned up the thermostat, felt the old furnace lurch into flame below her; then she took off her coat and lay on the narrow cot by her landlady's china closet with its souvenirs of years of world's fairs and expositions—squat mugs, pickle dishes, painted pitchers, knife rests. She drew up the afghan Linda's mother had sent them in August. She said four words aloud—"Help me some way"—then plunged into sleep like any child.

In her dream that came quickly, Strawson Stuart stood barefoot in Rob Mayfield's dining room. He was by the tall window in strong winter light, and his back was to Ann. From the door where she waited, she saw that his hands worked swiftly at a task; but she couldn't see what. She said, "We should be out painting the house in this good weather." Her voice was silent; the air refused to sound her words as she gave them, though it calmly consented to warm her skin and fill her lungs. She tried again, just his name—still nothing. So she thought, "I'm not here. I can go anywhere."

She stepped to within a foot of Straw's broad back, then a step to the side. With perfect economy his hands were tending a small tree—recumbent juniper. It was rooted in yard-dirt in a rusty tin can, but it spilled its knots of bluish needles down a watercourse of black limbs shaped by wind—lovely as any pine she'd seen in Rome, lovely as any living thing she'd seen in her life till now. She said "Where'd you find it?"—silence again. So she put out her own hand to touch the highest limb. Not looking, Straw blocked her by ringing her wrist. She stood in his grasp then, watching the tree till beyond it the edge of her sight caught movement. On the couch in the corner, Hutch's father sat, well and strong, signaling to her with a slow wave. She focused on him, nodded. He said, "We thank you and will never forget." Then he rose, walked quickly to Strawson, bent past him, smelled at the needles, and smiled—"Thanks ever." He spoke toward the tree, but Ann knew the offer was aimed at her and bowed her acceptance. She had brought life again to the clean dead house; they would not forget. After that she slept blank.

The front door opened in the Richmond house. Ann didn't hear it. Bailey Ferguson entered from the dusk and stood in the lighted hall, waiting to hear. At first he sensed nothing and moved to stride forward, then paused in the new thought of solitude. He'd never been here alone. But Ann's car was outside. He called her name, normal voice. She'd sunk past hearing. So he stood absolutely still and waited till his body reached its own depth of quiet. Then he cupped his left ear and waited again. Three breaths reached him from the dim room beyond, so slow they seemed inhuman in patience. His own blood slowed. He said again "Gatlin," having always called her that. Then he entered the room and stopped a yard from the cot.

Ann heard him finally, his adjacent stillness. Her eyes didn't know him at first, but she felt no surprise or fear. When his face clarified she said "Linda back?"

Bailey shook his head. "Won't be till Tuesday maybe. I dropped by to tell you."

"Something wrong?"

"Her aunt in Agricola—heart gave out."

"The crazy aunt?"

"No the good one," he said. "You O.K.?"

She waited. She'd been on her back; she turned to her left side now, facing Bailey's knees. "No."

He sat on the cot by her shins, his hands clasped. "I'm sorry."

Ann nodded.

Then he leaned and touched two fingers to her forehead—no fever.

But she laughed. "Ought not to touch live wires; you won't be spared twice."

"I'm a dead man, remember? None of this is really happening. You're in the next world."

"Wonderful." She slowly drew her legs back an inch, not to touch him at all.

Bailey agreed to the distance and sat awhile, watching the china closet—a cut-glass celery dish was handing the absolute last sunlight from facet to facet like a bucket brigade (he saw it that way). At the same time thick blood pooled in his groin; his cock lengthened lazily. He felt no lust but a general magnetized warmth—what he felt when his sister's young daughter would sit in his lap: a will to protect. He said, "Tell me how to help."

Ann shut her eyes and folded both hands beneath her cheek. "Find a place I can stop a baby I've started."

Bailey said, "Got two hundred dollars on hand?"

"In my savings. I can get it Monday at lunch."

"No hurry. I can float you a loan." Bailey stood and went to the china closet; laid his whole hand on the frail arched door, his back to Ann. "You ready right now?"

Ann opened her eyes. "Will I need the cash now?"

"Yes ma'm. I can get it. This town is my friend."

"Can I work Monday morning?"

Bailey said, "Up to you. If you're lucky, I mean."

Ann waited. "I'd hope Linda never has to know."

Bailey still didn't turn. With his dry forefinger he was stroking trails on the glass of the door. But he nodded. "I won't even know, myself."

Ann thanked him. Then she began to sit up.

7

The woman left her alone with a lamp on a clean narrow bed in a room the size of a steamer trunk. Then the house went silent and the street outside—ten on Saturday night. On the stand by the lamp was an old dinner-bell; she was meant to ring that for hard pain or bleeding. So she turned her face toward it. "I will watch just this. I will not think a thought." And for minutes she succeeded. The big dose of paregoric still held her; she only saw the dull lunar flare of the bell and its worn wood handle. Then it slowly shrank. She looked to the walls. The room was receding from her, its center. The single picture was caught in the flight—a foxed mezzotint entitled *Pneumonia*, a bearded white man at the bed of a white girl-child unconscious in the critical hour. Ann thought, "I may be starting to die" and felt at the napkin in her crotch, still cool. Then she slept—that quickly, no panic or prayer. And no trace of dream, no memory of Hutch or her father or the child. She was doing herself a kindness she had lacked all her life; she'd have thought that if she'd thought.

The woman woke her gently, sitting by her knees. "You doing all right?"

"I guess I don't know."

"If you sleeping, you all right."

Ann nodded. "I did. How long?"

"Best part of two hours. He's back to get you now." She pointed to the shut door, her thin arm three shades blacker than her face.

Ann was still half-dazed; the eyes showed puzzlement.

"Your friend that brought you—tall boy, mean eyes." But the woman laughed once.

"He wouldn't hurt a rattler," Ann said.

"—Tried to scotch *you*." The smile continued but the woman drew the quilt down, stood, raised Ann's slip, unpinned the gauze napkin, stepped to a corner, and stood with her back turned for half a minute. Then she rolled the napkin in a sheet of newspaper on a small table there, stepped back, pinned a new napkin quickly in place, and sat again. She took neat pains to smooth the quilt up toward Ann's elbows. Then she looked to the high shaded window. "You all right?"

Ann shut her eyes, then looked to the window herself—mere slot on a world she could not yet imagine, new world she'd made. She faced the woman. "Thank you at least."

The woman nodded. "Most people don't say it."

Ann remembered that she only knew the woman's first name—Bailey had said "Julia." She said, "My name was Ann Gatlin, still is."

The woman looked on at the window awhile, then turned and smiled. "I used to be a Patterson before you were born." She offered no more but picked at a seam.

Ann said "Can I go?"

Julia nodded. "He's waiting in there with my son." She stood in place.

Ann sat up carefully and swung her feet down. When they touched the floor, she knew for certain—she'd changed one part of her life completely, agreed to the change in this small house. She'd never be herself, not the one she'd known. No one else would know her either.

Yet the first thing she said in Bailey's car was, "Please leave me off at Miss Polly Drewry's house."

He accepted her clear directions in silence.

8

February 12, 1956

Dear Hutchins,

It's one day short of a month since you wrote to me. I trust you are not still stuck in New York in an ongoing blizzard and that England received you in the manner you hoped. I've been right here, making feeble attempts to fight back the cobwebs and strange living creatures that took a hold of my luxury apartment while I was with Rob. I've got it about back where it was in June when I left—just near-total chaos. I can't seem to get it much straighter than that, which must be how I want it. If I got really neat, I'd see what I have. And I might die laughing or howling (choose one).

Something that I do have is what you said—that you're glad I was present with Rob toward the end. I'm still not enough of a Scarlet Woman to refuse your thanks. I've also received, from Miss Eva as you warned me, the present from Rob. I walked straight down that morning and banked it, thinking I'd at least earned it. Then I had nights of thinking I must send it back, that you'd need it in Europe. But now I've decided—I'm keeping it to do something on my own that Rob never did. This summer I'm going to pack a small bag and head off to see some place that's not home. *I've never spent more than three nights in a row more than sixty-five miles from my family's house (though I haven't lived there for nearly forty years). I guess that proposal will meet with your approval. I'd bow my head and add "Rob's too" if I hadn't, all my life, gone queasy every time some widow or mother would tremble and say "He of course still sees and knows and is pleased." Rob never watched me, even when I was all that was left to watch (except soda crackers in the cupboard and the dog); so I know he isn't now. I can count on viewing Montana in peace.*

I hope you are peaceful. It can't have been anything but stunning to be called back from Christmas in Rome to see that, helpless. If I spoke hard to you—and I did, I recall—I was stunned myself, though I'd had more time than you to set my dials. Take my genuine regrets then please. But forget them before you have folded this letter, and find ways to clear your mind and life. Your father could never clear one line *from his accounts once he wrote it down. There were whole years when he barely knew there was a present; he was solving the past. But the present killed him. Keep your eyes open then and aimed ahead.*

Maybe we shouldn't correspond anymore now. I need a blank, I guess, like the one you tried.

But love, here, from
Min

February 19, 1956

Dear Hutch,

I've been waiting till I had something good to write, thinking you might be needing it. I certainly have. January always leaves me low as a mole. If only Christ would choose to be born in May, my year would go better. But I've got through, surprised as ever to notice time's main trick — it will not kill you. You can stand what it offers, though you may want to shut yourself in awhile and yell. I didn't have to yell after all this year, which is what I'm here to tell you.

Remember those pearls I was sewing on lace when you stopped here? The dress itself was meant to be made by the mother of the bride. It turns out she has a small problem with liquor, like being dead-drunk for days after Christmas. I understand why, as I said just now, but I wasn't quite set to be faced by the challenge of the bride herself coming in here on me four days before the wedding in serious tears with armloads of uncut satin and veiling. I was prepared if truth be told and glad to be busy. Didn't sleep for two nights but I gave that up eight or ten years ago, just lie down at dark since the air goes quiet. I finished in time and mostly by hand and it looked good on her. Gunny sacks would have looked good on her but I was pleased. So was she — Agnes Butters — and she paid me too much.

What surprised me was the phone ringing well before light on the wedding day. It was Mrs. Butters praising me and saying she wouldn't take No for an answer. She'd send a boy to get me at four o'clock for the candle-light service. I had never been to a wedding in my life and hadn't missed the pleasure but something said "Go" so I said "Thank you." The boy drove up at four as promised in a boiled shirt and swallow tails. He was slightly stiffer than the shirt himself. He said the stag party had never really ended and wouldn't till Monday. He didn't seem to know Richmond all that clearly. We drove through whole quarters I'd never seen before in fifty-odd years here but he finally found the church and we were still early. He turned me over to another dazed boy who was ushering. I whispered my name and he seated me in silence, though he smiled like a spaniel. I noticed I was sitting far forward — second row — but I figured he knew just where I belonged, so I kept in place and the church filled behind me and the music began. I never looked back. After maybe ten minutes they played a tune I knew — "O Danny Boy" — and my left eye seemed to catch a human bearing down. It was my same usher with Celestine Butters, the bride's ailing mother. I was in her pew! Or she was in mine. She greeted me warmly as any sister could have. Her chin was trembling but her breath smelled sober. I whispered "He put me in your pew, I'm sorry." She said "You're where you belong to be" (Mr. Butters is gone) and took my hand.

So we stayed there and looked and listened together. From hearing people talk and the radio, I knew a few words of what would be said. But I wasn't expecting the whole string of promises the old man would make those two children give. Being new to weddings I may have been the one person present who heard him. But I really heard. *Could any two spirits in the safe midst of Heaven say confident Yesses to such good dreams? Well I want you to know Agnes Butters did and Fleetwood Wilmuth. When they turned round to face us at the end, Mrs. Butters said to me "You were born for this night." She was streaming tears. I knew she meant the dress. It would have held its own at a modest coronation if I do say so. But for one hot second I saw another meaning. I should* not *hold my peace. I should rise up and show them from the depths of my knowledge what lies they'd almost certainly told. I didn't, don't worry. I waited till the boy came and led me out—the second to leave after Celestine herself. By then I felt like I'd earned my seat.*

I won't keep you any longer, knowing how you work. But I said I had something to cheer you up and I hope I have. I came home from church that night glad as any child to see my narrow bed and crawl in it single. I still thought as always when the light was out of the ones I've cherished and I thanked their memories. You're the one of them all that's alive so take extra care. There isn't really any other news right now. I won't wait for fire or flood but mail this at once. I can still read, remember, and digest all foods as calm as a goat so send me a word.

> *And take these two—*
> *Long love—from*
> *Polly*

February 25, 1956

Dear Hutch,

I wrote to you awhile back, but the letter disappeared before I could send it. Now Mr. Grainger's big calendar here in the kitchen says you left six weeks ago yesterday. It seems a year longer, we have dug in so deep. Speaking of which, there was snow in the night and all day today. Mr. Grainger and I, being natives of The North, consider it a normal amount for the time; but your grandmother phoned us twice to say it was way past the record for her life here—a good foot everywhere, three feet in drifts. She was home without Sylvie, and

Grainger got stuck when he tried to drive to her, but we knew it was coming and had stocked her with food, so she'll be O.K. Sun's predicted for tomorrow, I'm sorry to say. I wish it could stay like this at least a week. I went out after breakfast and took a long walk back into the woods, mostly the way you and I went last month. Very fine, every step. I can see why you left here when you left. I doubt I'll ever see why if you don't come back when you can and as soon as you can. I remembered when I got in as far as the creek that your father said one private sentence to me the morning I met him. You had stepped back into your empty house in Edom to turn off the power; so he and I were standing by his loaded truck, your life's possessions—I was standing, he was leaning both arms on the side like he couldn't stand alone but watching me close. I can face anybody I've met to date, but I'll grant he was hard. He'd seen that I knew you more than one way. That was as plain as how tired he was. He let me see both. Then when we heard your steps coming through the house, he said, "Will he ever come back, you think?" I looked and saw you forty feet away, and I said "No sir." I thought he meant Edom—would you come back there. I was sad to see you go too so I said No. You must not have seen him in that one minute. He looked like I'd cut him fast, gullet to groin. But he never called me wrong. I wish I'd known enough to lie to him then. Or you can prove me wrong.

I doubt I'll be here to welcome you. The Draft is cranking up to blow my way. It took them awhile to notice I'd dropped out of college and was free to guard South Korea or West Berlin (why do we just get part of a place?). My cousin's on the Draft Board and has staved off action, but he won't hold for long—it's either a second shot at higher learning or they start shooting me. I may choose the latter. The Dean says I'm welcome back at Washington and Lee seven months from now, and I've told my father I'd swallow the pill. But the more I think, I think I'll look into joining the Navy. I've done two sizable unusual things for Americans my age—known you and had one gone child behind me. So I think I'm not ready, and may never be, to join the great Pussy and Grain-Liquor Talking-Club that waits outside. Not that I want to be any monk on a rock, staring out toward perfection; and not that I reckon the U.S. Navy offers a high-toned line of goods. But it might let me move, for three or four years. I'm gambling that if I could spend two or three more nights like that one we spent at Macbeth and after—if I could stand that near the fire again— then I could come back home tame and tuck my chin and find what I think I need and take it.

I think I need what most people need. A place with enough quiet, a good wife and children—not a dozen but two or three to watch so I don't have just me and her to watch or trees. I can only look at trees so long, Shakespeare. I guess I decided that, walking this morning. You'd be welcome to visit anytime you could.

Didn't plan to go that far in when I started this. I mainly meant to say that up till the snow things here were going fine. Mr. Grainger has cleaned up a lot and turfed the graves. I've painted three-fourths of the back of the house. We read to each other at night and watch T.V. Hope you don't mind that, but we bought a used one to keep us in at night — me anyway. It cost thirty dollars and is big as my knee, but Grainger paid for it, and it seems to do the job. I've slept by myself every night, no guests.

I don't know whether that's good luck or bad, so I don't know whether to wish you the same. I'll entrust you to Fate then. I hope Fate thanks me. Let me have all the lowdown — and highdown — when you're free. I'll be here till I tell you.

> Nearly suppertime now,
> Strawson Stuart in person

> March 1, 1956

Dear Famous Author,

Where's the poem you were going to make out of me? It's been all but nine months and I really think it's time. I'm getting quite nervous about my debut in English verse. I've been brushing my hair in case it gets mentioned.

Otherwise I've been knocking about as before. After seeing you I had a job in Swansea in a big wine merchant's. Unfortunately my electric skin drew in the owner's daughter, seventeen and all right. End of future in fortified wines. I'm thinking of getting treatments for the problem. Could they cancel my charge or reverse it or something? You're the one with training. Give a poor sod advice.

Then my mother got married which is quite another tale. Her third time and looks like the best chance yet. I was back for the wedding from Bristol where I'd gone and had many laughs. I told her "It only happens three times, Gwyn." She said "Says who?"

So I donned me bathing knickers, swam back to Canada and greet you from this thrilling spot, your side of the briny. I decided to taste city life for a bit and am serving hot meals at a place in Toronto, not quite the Savoy but I meet funny types and they plaster me with tips. Be wanting any dollars? Let me know right away. This may not last either.

That's all I can tell for now in writing. I doubt I shall ever see England — or Wales — again. I don't know how long I'll stay in these lodgings but I'd like to hear your voice on paper at least and to meet you some day over here where I'm better in control of my mind and words.

> Your freezing mate,
> Lew Davis

P.S. *None of this means to say our summer voyages weren't absolute tops. It was Lew that was low. No regrets, just explaining.*

March 1, 1956

Dear Hutch,

    This card replies to two cards from you. Understand that I'm glad to get colored pictures of ancient stones, but I won't sit down and write lengthy news items or deep meditations to a charmer who tries to plead busyness. I'm glad you're busy. The world is busy. So am I, praise God—I've been painting again. Our trip set me off. The busiest soul has all the time it needs if it just sleeps less. So up with the cuckoo (have you heard the first one yet?) and do yourself justice. Then I'll tell you my story.

Stopgap love,
Alice

March 4, 1956

Dear Hutch,

    A warm Sunday—68°. Just a week ago yesterday, we had calf-deep snow and the usual Three Stooges farce in the streets, us Dixiecrats skidding round like tigers in Finland; but here now it's spring or a blessed sample. No doubt we'll get bonked a time or two more, but I'm planning to live. I've always meant to ask you, Brother Hutchins—in your poring on the Laws of Sky and Land, do you find it's a sin to want to sleep in a hole at the root of an oak tree from December 25th at 10 a.m. till, say, March 21st? If it is I'm finally unredeemable. Bears have got the right idea. But have bears got souls? Let me know when you know.

    That partly explains why my last few missives may have been a little bleak. The other reasons have to do with you and me—no major revelation but the same old gap we've been calling across (or refusing to call). Deep as it always was, I seemed to know the depth. Now your father's going—and all it caused in Rome and Richmond—has dug a new bottom, and I don't see it yet. You must have detected when you were here that I was more or less drowning politely. I mean, I didn't ask for rescue, did I? Or for you to drown with me? Let me claim those two small credits at least, in the face of big debts.

    Am I saying more than that? Maybe just this much. I am trying to stop expecting you. I don't mean to sound like a thin-lipped martyr when I add that I doubt you're expecting me now or that you ever have. Or that either one of us will land in a hermitage if we never see each other again. I'd hate not to see you. I'd miss the eyes and the sides of your neck, though I also know my tendency to stare has been at least part of what sent you away.

You may never come back (partly a statement of possibility and partly per-mission—stay gone if you want). I may not be here. That's as much as I know now or ever knew. Why should that have to mean The End?

Love,
Ann

March 5, 1956

Dear Hutch,

   We are all right and glad to know you are. Straw is working out better than I expected when he gets out of bed. Never saw one person need to sleep that much. I tell him he is going to root to the bed. He says that's the plan. Maybe I should have thought of that sixty years ago. Weather turned off good after a snow and I am thinking about planting us a vegetable garden. Straw talks about joining the Navy at night. Other times he looks like he plans to stay for good. He is a very neat house painter and drinks less than most any painter I know. Miss Eva well again from her cold and feeling mean. She told me today she was glad I moved out. Now she and Sylvie can argue all they want to. She laughed but she meant it.

   Just one more news. Three weeks ago your friend Ann passed through here Saturday afternoon. I saw her five minutes. She was looking for Straw. That evening he told me she asked him did he know where to get a baby fixed. He got mad and she drove off still using your car. So Straw said. I was working on the graves. I write you this because I waited so long about Rob. If I had told you sooner you would be stronger now. Keep your toes warm

From
Grainger

March 8, 1956

Dear Hutch,

   Your letter came yesterday and reminded me how the weeks had slid past, something I seldom expect them to do. Still it's nice to have one thing to prod me this late in my mortal pilgrimage—to where? I hardly thought you'd had time to unpack your socks, and here you are faced with Easter vacation. The English take a very loose view of work, don't they? How on earth did they ever rule the earth? Well, the earth was asleep at the time, I suspect. I'm a witness to that. I was twenty-seven years old—mother to a son more than ten years old—before I ever heard of real shots fired in serious anger, and they were in France and Belgium not here (I don't count the Spanish-American War, a schoolboy's outing though some boys stayed). I've still never heard such a shot with my own ears, never seen anybody struck or cut. But it seems all I'm told of—*such restlessness, especially now that Negroes have got themselves noticed at last. I estimate I've spent a fourth of my life attending to claims on my mind from Negroes, none of whom was brought out of Africa by me or by anyone I've known. I cannot recall an unkind deed I've ever done to one—or one to me from them—but to read the Raleigh paper you'd think I was due to be strangled in bed any evening now. Well, let it come on, whatever's been earned. No stopping it surely, though I personally wish things would doze off again. The world, I mean, and you in its midst.*

Maybe that would put you flat out of work. I'm not the biggest reader in the history of the Kendals—never liked to see other lives that close; that was Rena's choice—but I've gathered that however much peace may be got from reading a poem, the author gets little. Are you sure you've chosen well? In the short years I knew your Grandfather Mayfield, he wrote a number of commendable poems that he said were for me, several ways to say thanks. I knew I was giving him less than nothing; so I knew (even when I'd forgot most else) that the lines were for him, transfusions for his dream that would banish us all. I wish I had them here to show you, but I'm sad to say I burned them when I saw he would not consider taking me and Rob back (I tried to go back, which Rob never knew). What I know is—the reason I'm off on this tack—the poems gave even less comfort than I. But then he found Miss Drewry. I hope she helped him more. I saw in her eyes she had plenty left that nobody had used. I wonder, do I? I've meant to spend it all, in my quiet way here; but it keeps seeping up through my chest at night. I'd thought when you were old, you would wake up aching and stunned by the prospect. My hands are stiff for the first few minutes. In general though I wake up strong as a girl and as full with life to give. This morning after sunup I drifted back to sleep and saw I was standing at my bedroom window, looking down on the yard. The road had become a swift muddy stream; and you were standing on the far side, calculating the current. Or so I guessed—I guessed you were wanting to swim this way. The surface was broken by numerous creatures too fast to name. I knew they were nothing but freshwater fish; and I raised the window to tell you so, but of course I couldn't speak. I can very seldom speak in a dream, however important the news I have.

The waking news is slim, I can tell you. You'll have guessed it before me—a usual winter except for a deep snow and Rob's being absent. I believe he's gone now. For long days I didn't. Two separate times I had picked up the telephone and started on his number before I remembered he could not be there. I've even spoken out to him once or twice at night on the chance he can hear. I don't think he does. That would be the worst punishment God could arrange, to leave dead souls at attention to the world. So I'll say it to you, I loved Rob the best I possibly could. *I think he grew to see that. I live in that hope. When he told me he was sick right after you left, I offered to nurse him from that minute on. He couldn't accept. The air he had finally got between us, that he got from you, wouldn't let him accept. So I wrote to Min. He never knew I'd told her, but she came posthaste and God bless her soul. I know you'd rather not have had her here at the end; blame me not Rob. I was helping finish something, which I haven't always done.*

I have also tended to all your business for you. So far it just consists of paying Rob's bills. He cleaned behind himself the best he could, but a fair amount gathered in his last few weeks that's only now appearing. Dear God, you pay to die. The insurance will cover all but four hundred dollars of his medical expenses. I've paid for the funeral from my own money. I brought him here; I can surely see him off without strapping you. You'll have your own deaths. Please don't try to stop me. I'm going to let you handle the farm. Sam Jarrel stopped here last Saturday to ask did I need any more peanuts. I told him I doubted I could ever look a peanut in the face again. He had such a big crop last year, and Rob couldn't use them, so Sylvie and I did everything with peanuts but paint the walls. He also wanted instructions for planting. I said, "Just do what you've done all your life." He said, "Miss Eva, it ain't yours to say. Hutch may want it different." So I stood corrected and told him to write you (you'll think it's a ransom note if he does; he can barely print his name). If he doesn't and you want to make any changes, such as trimming back the peanuts or planting field daisies instead of tobacco, you know how to reach him. One daughter can read.

Sylvie's heading home now for her afternoon nap. She says it's the only time she sleeps, from three to five. I've offered to put her a cot in the dining room and save her the walk, cold as it is; but she says I'd bother her, "fumbling around." I still don't know if that's meant as a tribute to my afternoon vigor or a judgment of aimless on my present life. I don't plan to ask her to clarify, but she can mail this as she goes so I'll stop.

Whether you travel or stay, let me hear. When you're silent I never doubt you're there (Rena always thought people vanished when they left), but I will say the sight of your hand does help.

> Your last grandmother,
> Eva Kendal Mayfield

9

The sun had survived all through their lunch. Even the breeze that had nudged at the river was gone on north; and when the publican's daughter looked out, the light struck her broadside there on the threshold and pressed one long coo of pleasure from her lips. Then she blushed ferociously to think they'd seen her and came forward primly with her tray to clear dishes. Mr. Fleishman ignored her, rose, crossed the terrace to the low river-wall, and looked across to the ruins of the nunnery lost in briars.

Hutch said to the girl, "More cider for both please."

Mr. Fleishman said "None for me," not turning. He'd finished his pint but had barely touched the pork pie.

The girl met Hutch's eyes at last and frowned conspiratorially.

He laughed. "Isn't this day a miracle?"

She paused to consider, glancing again at the sky—her auburn hair all but molten in the glow. "Not really," she said. "Often we get a few good days in March. May well snow tonight." But she ducked her head once more toward Mr. Fleishman, wrinkled her nose, and grinned as she left.

Hutch loosened his tie, unbuttoned his collar, then stood and went to Mr. Fleishman's side and said, "Fair Rosamond's dust breeds roses" (Henry II's mistress had repented and died in the Godstow nunnery, thirty yards away).

Mr. Fleishman gave no sign of hearing but took the last step till his toes touched the wall. He gazed another minute; then recited as drily as he'd just recited the rules for Hutch's thesis,

> "'A boat beneath a sunny sky
> Lingering onward dreamily
> In an evening of July—'"

It was just past one on the tenth of March; Hutch was mildly baffled. "I can't name it yet."

Mr. Fleishman didn't turn but stood a moment, silent; then pointed his long arm straight at the ruins, the green bank below them.

> "'Children three that nestle near,
> Eager eye and willing ear,
> Pleased a simple tale to hear—'"

Hutch said, "It's not Marvell; Marvell barely mentions children."

Mr. Fleishman turned then and slowly smiled, a labored rearrangement of all his lean face that finally seemed more pained than glad. "—The one great book ever written in Oxford, ninety-odd years ago: I knew men who knew him."

"Newman, Ruskin?" Hutch said. "Early Hopkins maybe?"

Mr. Fleishman's smile continued, rigid now; but his head shook hard, and the oiled hair slid like a wing toward his left eye. He pointed again—

> "'In a Wonderland they lie,
> Dreaming as the days go by,
> Dreaming as the summers die:
>
> Ever drifting down the stream—
> Lingering in the golden gleam—
> Life, what is it but a dream?'"

The girl was back with Hutch's cider and paused, watching both men.

Mr. Fleishman turned. "May I change my mind?—a pint of bitter?"

She nodded, glanced to Hutch, then blushed again but persisted in saying what she knew. "It's *Alice*, that poem—*Through the Looking-Glass*. He wrote it there." She couldn't make herself point but ducked her head twice toward the opposite bank.

Mr. Fleishman said, "Thank you. Might I just have the beer?"

The girl frowned and left.

Mr. Fleishman said "She's half-right" and went to the table.

Hutch followed and sat.

"July 4th, 1862—" Mr. Fleishman said. "Young Mr. Dodgson and his friend from Trinity, Robinson Duckworth, rowed the three Liddell girls— Alice, Ina, and Edith—up the river for tea by the ruins at Godstow. They sat about there, I'm told, on the bank and were not back at Christ Church till half-past eight. It was here and while rowing that he made up the tale— Alice under ground—for the real child, you see."

So Hutch watched the bank and pulled at his drink, held as always by any revelation of the patience of objects (the willingness of grass and dirt and vines to sustain forever the energy of passionate gesture or speech—Tintagel, Castle Dore, Slaughter Bridge, all of Rome, Rob Mayfield's kitchen, the green slope at Godstow). Patient for whom? Waiting for what? He looked to Mr. Fleishman and said what that dry face and voice had stirred. "How old was Alice when she heard the tale?"

"Ten, I think—not older."

"I wonder if the notion of life as a dream could have come from her?"

"I shouldn't think so," Mr. Fleishman said, "—why?"

The girl was in sight again with the beer; but Hutch said, "Because when I was that age, I invented the notion entirely on my own. Nobody told me and I'm sure I hadn't read it."

"You must write to Dr. Jung; you may have an archetype." No sneer was implied.

The girl served in silence, took three steps back into one perfect hoop of direct sun, and said, "My dad says the old lady came back here twenty-five years ago when Dad was a boy."

Mr. Fleishman said "—Lady?"

"Miss Alice," she said, "Mrs. Hargreaves by then. She stopped here for tea, and Dad overheard her name, but he said she never even crossed the bridge."

Hutch said "Is she dead?"

"I should think so," the girl said, "wouldn't you?"

Mr. Fleishman looked to Hutch. "Twenty-odd years ago; she lived till near ninety. You were telling me a story—"

Hutch could see Mr. Fleishman was banishing the girl; she hung a moment, waiting. So he smiled up toward her and, for the first time since Ann's room in Richmond, felt the rush of desire—a thrumming in his ears. If he stood now and asked with an open hand, surely she'd follow him deeper into meadow grass and lend him all her competent body—barely contained in its milky walls, ready to stream. He wanted only that now, his mind a white blank of tender force.

The girl said, "I'm leaving. My dad has your bill." She pointed to the viney door.

"For where?" Hutch said.

She'd somehow won control of her face—no blush—but she looked toward Oxford across the flat pasture. "It's my half-day. I'll go in and buy my birthday present; Dad's given me five pound." She smiled at the scruffy ponies dozing.

Hutch said "What will you buy?"

"No idea really. I'll mooch through the shops till it finds me; it will." She turned to him then, open-faced as the sun itself, and quickly left.

Mr. Fleishman took a short swallow of beer. "You concluded that life was a dream—at what age?"

"Younger than Alice at the picnic at least; before I went to school, five or six years old. I grew up alone, no brothers or sisters, and in a small town with country round me. I spent a good deal of time talking to trees and dogs, whispering to rocks." He paused to check Mr. Fleishman for boredom; but the blue eyes were on him, patient, unblinking.

"Did they whisper back?"

Hutch laughed. "They said 'We're cold and old.'"

But Mr. Fleishman said, "I was not insulting you; don't insult yourself. Young Wordsworth, remember, walking to school would often grasp at a wall or tree to prove to himself the reality of matter."

Hutch nodded. "I never felt realer than the world. I only thought we were all being *dreamt*. We were simultaneous figures in a tale being dreamt by a giant asleep in a cave at the heart of a bare world, otherwise alone."

"Would you vanish if it woke? Did the prospect alarm you?"

Hutch laughed again. "I had a few cold moments, yes—the thought we might *phut* out with no word of warning some clear warm noon."

"—Or one by one," Mr. Fleishman said, "which appears to be the case."

Hutch thought awhile. "I never considered that. He dreamt us all together—my giant was a *he*—and we'd all stop at once if he woke or slept deeper."

Mr. Fleishman blinked, spread his spider fingers on the rusty table, and studied their knobbed length. Then he said "Your father died" (Hutch had told him briefly in January; they'd never discussed it). The fingers came together to form his hands again. "My skin is here in sunlight." He slowly pushed forward across the green iron and tapped Hutch's sleeve. "I am not dreaming you."

Hutch pushed against the finger; then raised his mug and smiled to the riverbank, the cradle of *Alice*, empty but stroked by gorgeous successions of glare and shade. He drained the cider and knew he was safe, suspected he was happy—awake now and free. "Thank you," he said to the whole real place.

Mr. Fleishman waited, then said "Not at all."

10

The happiness lasted through the half-hour it took him to leave Mr. Fleishman back at his flat, drive into town, and park in Beaumont Street. As he walked in pure sun toward St. Giles, he felt the strangeness—that after the shocks of the past three months (and Ann's cool letter had come yesterday), here he'd been lifted by a glimpse of spring, lunch with his bone-dry tutor, and the memory of a childhood certainty. He walked ten steps believing that, then knew the truth—he wanted the girl and was hunting her now, the girl from the pub with her birthday money. Surely he could find her; she'd be in Elliston's or Marks & Sparks or maybe the record shop. He pictured her gravely studying sweaters. She'd be alone or with a girlfriend. He'd appear surprised at finding her, then invite them both for coffee, the girlfriend would dissolve. Or he'd stride up and say no less than the truth—"I'll be twenty-six years old in no time. I've waited too long"—and she'd follow him. He knew he was half-wild with this bright day after two months of work in all the strong wakes of his father's death; but he walked straight on, famished and glad.

She was not to be found. The shops were crowded with grim-jawed dowds still swaddled for winter and couples younger than he with babies, fat as seals and solemn as clocks. But though he combed every aisle, she was missing. He didn't know her name—he'd looked a good while when he realized that. She'd never said her name; and in Mr. Fleishman's presence, he never could have asked. So beside the hills of flannel pajamas in Marks & Sparks, his spiral of expectation collapsed. At first it seemed a small disappointment. He'd head back to college, find a willing friend or two, and drive down into the Vale of the White Horse—a ramble on the chalk, then supper in Wantage or Farringdon.

But once he'd returned to the crowded street, the sun pressed harder than before. He walked a long block, pummeled by shoppers in dense winter clothes now reeking in the warmth; and by the time he'd reached St. Michael's church, with its black Saxon tower, he'd convicted himself of a deeper solitude than he'd known since the night-beach at Tresco. He didn't want to yield though; he felt very strongly that he'd mooned enough in the past year to last any two normal humans a long pair of lives. The steps of the church were bare and in full light. He climbed to the top and sat, vaguely hoping no vicar would shoo him off. None did. No passerby looked his way. So he made himself a speech—"You were never meant for happiness." It tolled like a bell. He actually grinned. His grandmother had trained him, at any low moment, to pause and count his blessings. A well-made body that seemed to work. Four people that unconditionally loved him (Eva, Grainger, Polly, Alice). The power of close attention to things, visible things. The gift of words, not grown yet but growing. Sufficient funds for this year at least, a home to return to. This present bright day. No war to attend. A million smaller credits. *Therefore rejoice*. He smiled again.

But—but, but. There were all the clues (a chain of hints beginning at his birth, with his mother's death) that whatever giant was dreaming his life was dreaming it solo—a solitary journey with skirmishes of company. And any attempts by the characters to change the plot were foiled by the dreamer. The barmaid had vanished in the narrow heart of this one country town. Ann had sent him her letter, bathed in the thin air of distance he'd requested a year ago. Straw was bound for the Navy; Lew was in Canada. He would not hunt them out again, he somehow knew. Never meant for happiness—if happiness was permanent love, mainly calm. But who'd said it was (except ninety-nine percent of Western Man since love was invented in the eleventh century)? He should stand and return to his big dry rooms, stroke out his own calm with an ample hand, then sit at his desk facing Merton Field and the bare elms beyond and haul back the peace he'd known as a boy when any rough water could be stilled by a half-hour of patient sketching—any fraz-zled tree in the yard transferred to the hungry white paper in soothing lines: the happiness of power to see and transform, to dream a whole world in which he could sleep at least peacefully.

The girl passed then—he was almost sure—on the far sidewalk fifty feet away with a taller boy, as fine as she. They were holding hands but facing ahead as if they'd hardly met or were blind and assisted each other in des-perate courtesy.

Hutch let them go. It seemed to cost nothing, no longing at least. He remembered he'd ordered a book from Blackwell's and rose to get it.

11

The shop bore its usual Saturday freight of rural clergymen, embattled dowagers, graduate students in tweeds ripe as Stilton—all more intent on causing no sound and avoiding touch than on any book at hand. Hutch walked past the famous pair of ladies at the cash desk, rigid in their Radclyffe Hall impersonations, and climbed toward the English Lit. shelves at the back—the gnarled youth there who would have his book. As he passed the Art table, he smelled a faint trail of lemon and paused. It came from a small woman four feet beyond him in severe dark blue, her straight back to him. He thought he knew her hair—thin-textured, deep chestnut, half-down her tall neck. So he worked round the table, fingering the luxury of Phaidon folios, till he reached her profile. It was Vivien Leigh, slowly turning through a *Donatello* with spotless white gloves—the line of her own face from fore-head to throat as splendid as any line caught in the book: the hip of the boy David, Judith with the sword. *The Helen of our days*; Hutch secretly fed on the sight for two minutes, preserving it for his own private gallery of perfec-tions. Then she swung full toward him, set the book on its pile, and stared past his shoulder at the high sunny windows. The light showed her worn and too thin for safety, a webbing of shallow lines round her eyes. He knew that she and Olivier kept a house near Thame, ten miles from Oxford; he knew she had a stepson studying at Christ Church and was rumored to be seen dining with him at the George, but here she seemed suspended in an aimlessness as pure as her beauty till the madness smoked upward. He watched her frankly now; and though her eyes avoided him, she bore him calmly. Or was she only gathering the bottled rage of delicate bones to bellow like her Blanche at the end of *Streetcar*?—a hounded doe clawed down in a thicket, demanding aid. He could say, "Miss Leigh, I met you at Stratford last summer—*Macbeth*. Would you have coffee with me?" She seemed the one real chance in this dream-day. He cleared his throat softly.

Her eyes clicked toward him, searched him to the waist, returned to his eyes. Her long lips opened on small clenched teeth. Then she smiled. "Have you lost your glorious friend?"

Hutch was blank with surprise. "Ma'm?"

She laughed once, took two steps, and gave her hand—"Your Virginia gentleman."

He took the hand, nearly as broad as his own; then cupped the two with his free hand. "Yes. He's launched on his life."

She broke the touch easily, retreated a step—"Oh alas"—then took the *Donatello* and left. Her smile endured as far as the desk.

12

It was nearly three when he got back to college. The weather was holding and lunch was long over, so Front Quad was empty and stunned in the unaccustomed glare—no spare friends in sight to lure on a drive. He stopped in the Lodge for the second post—a wrinkled envelope addressed in Grainger's hand, his first from Grainger in more than a year. As he studied the tall script, he felt no conscious apprehension. But deeper he remembered the phone call in Rome, the news of Rob's dying; and he put the letter unopened in his pocket. Then he went toward his rooms. The meeting with Vivien Leigh still held him. He'd made her an offer—coffee at least—and she hadn't refused: turning away was not a firm No. Why hadn't he followed? To say what?— stage-door platitudes, English-teacher questions? When she'd charged her book and vanished through the door, he'd heard in his head but in her rich voice the plea of her Blanche—"I want to *rest!* I want to breathe quietly again!" The plea of a character but plainly her own too. He'd meant to answer that. Why? What rest had he to give, to her or anyone, who had never rested more than eight hours himself (and then in sleep)? As he entered his own quad—old Mob Quad, empty as the moon at full—all the questions found an answer. He had wanted to give the woman some short calm because— in her supreme beauty (fading daily), in the transitory force of an actor's work—she'd become a lucid emblem of his own destination or the long trip there: a life lived for others, though not at their request, ludicrously unneeded by them. No one else in Blackwell's had so much as glanced at a face the frank equal of any face known. He'd have told her that anyhow. Stale painful news to her.

He passed his own staircase, crossed the quad, and entered the Chapel. More vacant space—the vaulted gray belly of a grand whale, beached and drying for a century; a huge life lived out for whom, for what? *Well, for me,* he thought. But when he'd climbed to the choir and sat and faced the bare altar with its crowded but dubious Tintoretto, he could ask for nothing. He said her name silently, "Vivien Leigh." Then he waited and said, "Ann Gatlin. Strawson Stuart. Lew Davis. Hutchins Mayfield." The light in the windows dimmed as he sat. He'd go back and work, no trip today. He recalled Grainger's letter and opened it—the news on Straw's sleepiness, his Navy plans, then Ann's sudden visit, then *"she asked him did he know where to get a baby fixed."* Hutch saw their last night together in Richmond (her pressing him down to nurse at her source); he heard the last words of her letter again—*"You may never come back. . . . I may not be here. . . . Why should that have to mean The End?"* He made a quick calculation of dates. If they'd started a child in Rome and lost it, then she'd written her letter in the aftermath.

He stood to go to the Lodge and call her; it was just ten in the morning at home. He could hope to reach her—to say, God, what? At the door he paused by a swollen jasper urn donated by Czar Alexander I in memory of a visit here in 1814, a year before Waterloo. He looked toward the meadow, in brown shade now, and said what he'd said in the Pantheon—"Show me now please."

13

He waited in the oak-and-glass cage of the Lodge while Victor the porter placed the call on the main college phone, a prewar antiquity massive as a dumbbell. When he finally signaled Hutch to enter the booth, there was thick fur and static on the line (not the unnerving clarity he'd heard in Rome under Grainger's voice). The British operator, a somber man, had reached Ann's house at least. Linda said "Yes."

"I have a call from England for Miss Ann Gatlin."

Linda waited. "Yes sir. She's gone now. I'm sorry."

Hutch said "Gone where?"—the grip of fright.

The man said, "You may not speak yet, Oxford." Then he said, "Is Miss Gatlin expected to return?"

Linda said, "Is it morning there where you are?"

The man paused as if that were also forbidden, a disastrous revelation; then conceded it. "Midafternoon."

"She ought to be back after suppertime Sunday, our suppertime here. Can you figure that out?" She seemed to laugh once. Was Bailey beside her?

The man said, "Oxford, you may try again tomorrow—at midnight perhaps: Greenwich time, of course."

Hutch said, "Can you ask if she's at her mother's please?"

"You could—for the full charge; yes you could."

Hutch said "I'll wait."

Linda said a clear "Yes" and was cut off at once.

Hutch didn't speak again—at her mother's and returning tomorrow for work. She was moving at least, that safe at least. She would not talk freely at her mother's. He must wait. But he had the small satisfaction of breaking the connection on the operator's dogged recital of rules.

14

When he'd thanked the porter and tipped him to book a call for midnight Sunday, he stepped back out into the light, thinking only that he could not imagine any way—any series of harmless conscious actions—to kill the time, thirty-three clock hours. He didn't recall his recent plain prayer. But in those few minutes, the sky had cleared with the disconcerting speed of island weather. Now he'd have that to get through, a glorious day. Though he didn't know it, he strained in every fiber not to think the word *child.* Even his steps on the gritty pavement were gentle, unpercussive. He would sit in the deep musty chair by his window and do what Mr. Fleishman had suggested—read through the whole of Marvell's poems at a stretch. That should take him to dinner, with time for a nap (as always, in trouble, he was already tired). The night—he'd deal with that when it came, though Marleen Pickett's small face lurched up in his mind like a promise.

In the center of the hearthrug of grass in Mob Quad, a single figure stood, looking up toward the Chapel. A young man, middle-size, in clothes that were clearly not student clothes—clean and well-pressed and working-class: a light-blue gabardine suit, cheap and slick; the collar of a soft unbuttoned white shirt. The neck was almost as white, the hair black. The bells played their incomplete quarter-hour tune, which the man completed in a pure hum. Hutch thought he knew the voice but could summon no name; so he said, "You have a great future in music."

The man turned. "That's the first *good* news I've had."

It was James, James Nichols—in the pub last summer with the sleepy child, Nan. Hutch had forgot their quiet meeting and James's forecast of working on the stone here. He'd never recalled the dream he had (in Marleen's room) of finding James asleep at his father's, Nan smiling beside him. But he said, "You planning to restore all this?" He waved to the blistered walls around them.

James nodded. "Right. We're starting in Monday morning—tear it all down, remake it from the ground." He laughed. "You students will be billeted in tents—any luck, we'll have very little more snow. That's how the Americans would do it, right?"

Hutch walked toward him. "Then we'd dress you characters in medieval tights and let you give tours."

"Not me," James said. "Never show my legs."

"Why?"

"Drives the public mad. I learned that in prison." He spoke at normal volume, unashamed of his past, and continued smiling on the perfect teeth.

Hutch said, "We'll put you in monk's robes then."

"My poor feet'll freeze; don't they wear sandals?"

"Barefoot," Hutch said. "You'll need to toughen up."

James paused to think as though the plan were serious. Then he said, "I reckon I've toughened all I mean to. I'm easing down now."

"How's that?"

"Oh I don't know—saving my farthings for a holiday with Nan."

"Is she well?"

"Yes thanks."

"Still with you at your mother's?"

James shook his head once to show surprise. "You retain facts, don't you?"

"It's my trade, storing pictures. I can see her quite clearly."

James shook his head again. "Not the way she is now. She's grown half a foot." He measured her height in the air at his side, then studied the spot and raised his hand an inch. "I haven't seen her either since Boxing Day."

"She's back with her mother?"

"With her aunt in Reading. Her mother's in Yorkshire with a crippled bus-driver. I couldn't keep her here, me and my mum working."

Hutch squatted to the ground and combed in the cool grass. "But you see her when you want?"

James continued standing (he didn't belong here and took no liberties). "Right—well, no. I want to see her every day, but Reading's quite a journey when all you've got's a push-bike."

"You had a motorcycle."

James grinned. "Before prison—my mum sold it then. Just as well, I reckon; I'm dead most nights."

Hutch said, "We could drive down to Reading now."

James thrust both hands in his pockets and was silent.

"If you don't have plans."

"Not really," James said. "I was walking in the Meadow, thought I might find a girl in need on the river. They were all bespoke so I saw the old Chapel here and thought I'd whip over the wall for a look. We'll be in early on Monday like I said."

"Aren't you late? In July you said you'd be here in autumn."

James leaned to the grass and brushed the tips slowly, then stood again. "Maybe so, maybe not. Everything in its time. I go where they tell me."

Hutch rose. "Then to Reading."

15

But they took the long way. Once they'd entered the warm car, James took up the *Guide to Berks. and Oxon.* and said, "Understand—I'm free till dawn Monday. If there's some place you'd rather be than Reading, I'll navigate."

Hutch said, "You'd rather not see Nan today?"

"Oh no. She can still be the goal by dark. She quite liked you—mentioned you more than once, asking her was she an owl. I just meant, if you had the time, we could roam."

Hutch cranked the engine—"I'm free till Sunday midnight"—then faced James's profile: its Italianate simplicity of line and depth (were Roman genes still afloat in British veins?—almost always working-class veins, untapped by Normans).

James accepted the look but still watched the street. "You turn into some kind of pumpkin then?"

Hutch laughed. "I may well. But sure, let's roam."

James opened to the maps in the guide. "Name a place."

"No. You. I'm tired of choosing."

James shut the book. "Inkpen Beacon, due south."

Hutch moved into gear—"What's that?"—and rolled forward.

"Highest chalk down in the British Isles."

"Anything else but chalk? Can we get tea for instance?"

"—Get hung," James said and frowned theatrically and strangled his throat with his broad left hand.

Hutch said, "I'm not sure I deserve that yet."

James looked over then and studied Hutch slowly. "Maybe not, not yet. But they've got a gallows there so mind yourself, eh?"

Hutch turned from Blue Boar Street into St. Aldate's, past Christ Church and Police Headquarters. They'd crossed Folly Bridge and the smooth brown river, when he said, "Keep me posted. I'm a very poor judge." But he felt nearly half-free again, to be rolling.

So they rushed on in steadily warming air, fast patches of cloud, through Frilford with its Romano-British cemetery; then the green eastern end of the Vale of the White Horse and dozing Wantage, the birthplace in 849 A.D. of Alfred the Great (its market-square garnished by Gleicken's white statue of Alfred as a Saxon in a boy's dream of Saxons); then little Great Shefford with its round-towered church ("owing to the prevalence of unworkable flint"), then Hungerford, a fiefdom of John of Gaunt ("who gave his fishing rights to the town; it remains an angling resort today").

They'd stopped nowhere and only slowed for traffic—the occasional Margaret Rutherford twin, heroically cycling in the narrow road. The talk had consisted of James's directions and readings from the guide, Hutch's questions on the story of what they passed. No personal words—only the weather and moderate speed, the consoling wallpaper of the scenes beyond them, the absence of thought.

Then open country, the start of the downs, scattered farms in mucky yards, a road like a path. James led now in silence with pointings and nods. Hutch said, "You know all this like your hand."

James waited. "Never seen any of it before. Never seen anything but Oxford and jail."

"Then you've got second sight."

James said "So I'm told."

Hutch said, "Did you know you'd see me in Merton?" He was watching the road.

"May have."

"What else?"

James waited, then faced him—"Eh?"—blank as paper.

"What else do you know?"

"That I've steered us right." He looked out his window. "That we're actually there." He pointed to a far tall pole on the ridge they were aiming toward. It bore a crossbeam at the top and two braces—cross from a Flemish crucifixion.

Hutch said, "Have you figured what I deserve?"

James said, "A short hike in the sun at least."

So he pulled as far off the lane as he could. James sprang up the bank and spread two strands of wire apart; Hutch crawled through and stood to return the favor. But James poised a moment on the narrow ledge of turf, vaulted the fence in one neat arc; and preceded him through the high grass, still wet despite the sun.

When James reached the gallows, he ringed it with his left arm and stared off south to the lunar downs of Hampshire. Hutch kept a little distance but turned in place, from the bare chalk view toward the greener north. For the first time since Oxford, he thought of his worries. They still seemed powerful—sufficient to end all his orderly plans for work, then life. But here now they seemed unable to find him; he felt he'd been rescued and buried in safety, though the prospect in every direction was endless. He pointed northwest at a distant hill. "What's that?"

James swung round, still hugging the pole, and consulted his guide. "That would be the backside of White Horse Hill."

"Ever seen it?"

James said "I'm seeing it now."

"The horse, I mean."

James said, "I never cared much for horses."

"It's a picture of a horse, prehistoric, cut in chalk."

"That's for you," James said. "You're the picture man."

Hutch grinned—"All right"—and looked to the east, another hill. "And that?"

James read slowly. "'Walbury Hill, the highest chalk elevation in England, on the crest of which (975 feet) lies the Iron Age bastion of Walbury Camp.'"

Hutch nodded, walked past the gallows, looked southwest—Wiltshire, Dorset, Wessex, Hardy country. Then he came back and laid a flat palm on the post above James's arm (James was still facing Walbury, tracing the entrenchment). "Is the verdict in?"

"Eh?"

Hutch laughed. "—On the hanging. Do I hang?"

James said, "What's the worst thing you ever did?"

Hutch said "I refuse to testify."

James said, "I didn't. I sang like a lark. Of course they had a half-dead bloke I'd bashed and a dance hall of witnesses. Take your medicine, mate. You'll feel better for it."

"Do you?" Hutch said.

James waited, then laughed. "A new man—hark!" He turned the pole loose, stepped six feet away, consulted his book. Then he pointed to the gallows and read out clearly in the breeze that had risen—"'The gallows, one of the last in England, is kept in repair as a term of the lease of the nearby farm. The third to stand upon this ridge, its predecessor was struck by lightning. On the first, a couple were hanged in 1676 for drowning the woman's two children in a neighboring dewpond on the downs.'"

Hutch said, "Is all that really in your book?"

James nodded. "Your book."

"You didn't just make it up?"

James shook his head and held the open guide out like a saint on an ikon. "This is England, remember? Everything's got a past as bloody as me." The light was blown across him in scraps by the strengthening wind; and though his hair ruffled and his eyes filled with tears, he stood now clean as any washed child.

Hutch took the largest key from his pocket and quickly scored *H.M.* in the post. There were many other names, carved deeper than his, and one small drawing—a man's profile, the mouth gapped open in laughter or pain.

James said, "You'd need a knife to make that last."

16

The wind stayed behind them on into Reading, and the wall of Irish cloud had clamped evening down on their heads when James said "There, the ugliest house."

Hutch could see no difference. The row of attached houses—two-story, tan brick—was uniformly unredeemed, even by the yellow light of the street lamp which clicked on precisely as he killed the engine.

James turned. "You were thinking of how much time?"

"How much will you need?"

James thought. "Well, I'd estimate ten, twelve years. She'll leave about then." He stroked the steel dash.

"Shall I wait here?"

"For what?" James said, genuinely puzzled.

"Till you break the ice or finish your visit. I wouldn't mind."

James studied him. "You would. You'd die out here—bleeding Scott of the Antarctic! Follow me." He climbed out and knocked three times at the door before Hutch joined him.

Hutch said, "We could take her to dinner."

"She's eaten."

"Whose house is this?"

"Her aunt's, Helen's sister." James knocked again.

The letter slot opened from inside—silence.

James put in his forefinger gradually, smiling.

A child's voice said, "No. I'm here by myself."

James laughed. "You mustn't tell strangers that." He took back his finger. "It's your old dad, Nan. Now give us a look."

Her feet seemed to run away down a hall. Then she stopped and returned. "Say something else."

He said, "I've come a long way to see you."

Nan waited. "We leaving here?"

James squatted slowly and lifted the letter slot. "You turn the key. Ethel won't care. We'll play."

Another long wait as if she were balancing pain in a scale, anticipating loss. Then the sound of her struggle with the key, the bolt slid.

James stood and said "That's it." The door stayed shut. He opened it gently inward on air as dark as the street.

Hutch could see no one, a single dim bulb at the back by a stair.

James stepped forward, beckoning Hutch behind him. When they stood well inside, James shut the door. Nan was pressed in the corner by the hinges, facing out—grave as she'd been in the pub that first night. James said, "Say thanks to this man, eh?"

Nan looked to the worn mat. "Why?"

"He brought me—lovely new car. You remember him."

She shook her head fiercely.

"Course you do. He thought you was an owl, in Oxford the night you come to me."

Her head shook again.

"Where's Ethel gone?"

Nan looked up at Hutch. In the eight months her hair had darkened a little. Her ruddy face was purer now, luminous above her dark green sweater. Her eyes were dry. But every effort of her body, each cell, was aimed at James—to copy his shape.

Hutch squatted and met her gaze. "You had your tea?"

She nodded.

"Could I?"

She said, "I'm not allowed to touch the kettle."

James said "I am."

"You're not," she said. Her face had hardened astonishingly.

There were steps on the pavement, a knock at the door. "Nan, it's me."

James looked to Hutch, whispered "Ethel," and waved him backward down the hall.

Hutch retreated a yard.

James nodded to Nan.

She opened the door—a small woman sealed in a heavy gray coat, a small bundle wrapped in newsprint at her breast.

She saw Hutch first and stopped on the sill as if James were air. What seemed to be anger began in her eyes.

Hutch thought it was fear and smiled. "I'm with James. I drove him down."

That released her to see James; she studied him slowly. "You got a new outfit."

"New to you," he said and stepped from her path. Then he looked to Hutch. "Introduce yourself." He'd forgot Hutch's name.

Hutch said "Hutchins Mayfield."

Nan said "Hutch."

Ethel entered her own house. "She's mentioned you." She set her bundle on the table and hung her coat on a peg. Her face was still taut.

James said, "He's hoping you'll give him his tea." He thumbed toward Hutch.

Ethel picked at a stain on the sleeve of her coat. "Mick's working tonight. Nan's had her tea. I just got some fish and chips for myself. There's nothing else really." But she turned to Hutch. "You driving him back tonight?"

"Yes ma'm."

The *ma'm* surprised her (she was twenty-eight). The eyes half-relented. "You'll need something hot then, won't you?"

"I'm fine."

She waited. "You're not." Then she blushed. "*I'm* sorry—you just seem pale."

James said, "We came by Inkpen, the gallows. He's short on breath."

Ethel said, "James, you could fetch in more fish. I could make the tea." She searched in her coat and brought up a purse.

James looked to Hutch. "That suit you, eh?"

"By all means. But you stay with Nan; I'll go. Where's the nearest shop?"

Ethel forced a ten-shilling note into James's hand. "You know. You go. Bring some beer if you like."

James cupped the crown of Nan's hair but spoke to Hutch. "If I'm not back in twenty minutes, call the Constabulary—they've got me prints." He was gone like a bird, small evening bird.

Ethel said, "Our back room is shocking so brace yourself."

Nan led the way slowly, her arms out straight as if she were walking the thinnest wire.

The room was clean and no more disordered than any used space; but in its mute ugliness, it was mildly shocking—raw overhead light, wallpaper embossed with the ruthless pattern of old pressed-tin, three comfortless chairs, a dust-colored sofa, a chromo of dogs, a rotogravure in acid blues of the Duchess of Kent a-bristle with stones. No papers or books, no television, no sign of a toy. No trace of a child—but Nan herself, who sat on the floor and began to align eight thread-spools in silence.

Ethel lit a gas grate, poked the seat of a chair; and said, "You're welcome to *try* it; don't break a hip." Then she vanished through another door, shut it behind her, and filled a kettle.

Hutch sat to watch Nan—or her shifting spools: he could hardly watch her.

She made neat patterns in a regular order (arrows, stars), proceeding through what seemed a list in her mind of all the permutations of eight. No spool ever toppled and, though she'd clearly moved them many times, they were spotless white. She made a big almond-shape the size of her head, all perfectly placed. Then she looked up at Hutch. "What can you do?"

He laughed. "With what?"

"These," she said. She touched a spool lightly.

"Nothing better than you. You work very well."

She nodded agreement solemnly. "You work with James?"

"Your father?"

"James."

Hutch tried to remember what she'd called James in July; but he said, "Oh no. I'm a student—more boring."

Nan examined him carefully up and down. Then she said, "I never get bored. Ethel asks me but I never do."

"You like school then?"

"I don't go to school yet. One more year." She held up a finger.

"Any playmates about?" There were muffled knocks from the kitchen but still no other sign of children.

Nan shook her head firmly.

"Then what do you do?—besides that game." He bent and moved a spool.

She set it back in place. Then she grinned broadly (James's great sunrise-grin). "Nothing else," she said. "I'm a child, see?" She sprang up and once more held out her arms, balanced now and still as the house.

Hutch sat back and said, "Do you ever miss James?"

Nan bore his look a moment, then quickly faced round—the kitchen door.

Ethel had opened it and stood there broadside. "Run along up, Nan, and put on your trousers—the new little blue ones. James'll like those."

Nan was glad to obey.

Hutch rose. "Did he have far to go?"

Ethel said "Not really." She clasped her hands at her waist like a singer. "Course he may have gone to Zanzibar. On my ten shillings!"

"Not likely," Hutch said. "He's got his job Monday."

"Had a job all his life, ever since he was Nan's age. I knew him then but that never stopped him going his way."

"He loves Nan now."

"*I* love Nan," Ethel said. "I've loved her right through; he drops in on her like bombs, now and then. Mick, my husband, loves her better than James. Mick'd spend every farthing he earned on her if I didn't hold him back."

Hutch said, "There aren't any other children here?"

She shook her head hard. "Can't be. Not with me here. The doctor says I can't." She crouched to the grate and lowered the gas; the room was crackling dry. Then she faced Hutch squarely, pale as he now. "Pardon me asking but aren't you American?"

"Yes."

"You're at college?"

"In Oxford. I met James there."

"You're quite influential with him, I can see."

Hutch smiled. "I've spent all of three hours with him."

Ethel nodded. "He worships Americans. He'd have *swam* there years ago if he could breathe water."

"You needn't worry; I don't own a diving bell."

She waited, then took one step too close and whispered the rest. "No, *take* him—please God. Get him out of Nan's sight."

Hutch eased back slightly. "Won't her mother send for her?"

Ethel laughed, her mouth as sour as if from spew. "Never, never. I'm safe from her."

"How's that?"

"—Men. Her eyes only focus on men."

Hutch said, "She's in Yorkshire now with a man?"

"She was last week. May be with a yak on the moon by now."

The noise of the front door opening—James. Nan calling to him from the top of the stairs. Laughter and some kind of scuffle in the hall.

Ethel said, "If he asks you, say she's better off here. She is and all; anyone can see that." Her eyes stayed on Hutch while she gestured round her, the blistered room.

Hutch nodded "Yes" and tapped her lean shoulder with his cool right hand.

James was on them—his arms full of fish and beer; Nan mounted on his shoulders, smiling fully at last. She had put on her owl sweater, out-grown but clean.

17

They'd eaten, heard Ethel's long rhapsody of trouble, then invented a game with Nan's spools and played it for half an hour on the floor while Ethel washed up. Then Mick returned from the biscuit works, and they talked uneasily with him awhile (he was in his late thirties and had a gimp leg). Then Nan lay by James's knees and fell asleep, sudden and mute as a plummet. James had tested her finally by bending to her eyes, brushing her lashes with his chin, and humming. She was thoroughly gone so he'd stood clear of her (not touching her again) and said, "We might as well go while we can." Mick had tacitly thanked them for going by laughing them off from the curb and standing till they'd vanished at the corner.

They'd ridden quietly the first twenty minutes with only occasional directions from James; but on the near side of Streatley, he said, "I reckon I should ask your pardon for that."

Hutch said, "I can't think of any offense."

James waited, staring off to his right. "Thanks," he said. "I just meant my muck—slogging you blind into all my muck."

"There at Ethel's? It seemed very tidy to me."

James sat through the whole of the town in silence; but when they reached country again, he said, "No—me, my sad little pile of mess."

Hutch said, "All I saw was that Nan has grown but loves you and that Ethel loves her."

James nodded at once but sat another long while, then faced Hutch's profile—"Where does that leave James?"—then quickly looked out his own window again.

Hutch could only think "Here, parallel to me" but he didn't speak. His own mind was aimed at tomorrow night, the chance of finding Ann and knowing what he must know—the size and nature of the muck he'd made.

James said "Well, *here*—eh?" and laughed.

Hutch said "What?"

"*Here*. I'm here in the valley of the Thames, still breathing, under stars as bright as my teeth, being chauffeured by a kind American gent of independent means toward my native heath and my proud profession. Only fifty more years of that—Christ, give me longer!" James laughed again, no bitter note.

Hutch said, "You want to hear where I'm driving *me?*"

James waited. "I don't mind. I said I was free."

"I think I may be too. I'll know tomorrow night."

"What happens then?"

"What I'm driving toward. I have to phone a girl in the States, in Virginia." Hutch stopped there, hoping to be led somehow.

"What will she have to say?"

"Where my child is maybe."

"Your child?" James said.

"One I made with her last Christmas in Rome. She met me there. I'm afraid she took the child."

James counted on his fingers. "It's not born yet."

Hutch nodded. "I'm afraid she's bought an abortion."

"You don't know for certain?"

"No. Her letters haven't said."

"She didn't ask for money?"

"No."

"It's not your baby."

Hutch managed to smile at the quick assumption. "It wouldn't be so simple."

"Is she rich?"

"Not at all—a lawyer's typist."

"Then—begging your pardon, guv—but you ain't the dad: no offense to the lady, who I never saw. At least I assume not."

"You haven't," Hutch said. "She's never been in England." But he pictured a face he hadn't recalled since late December—Rowlet Swanson's mountain vacancies, ready to speak whatever was asked.

James said, "Then she's had that much luck at least. Don't bring her here and wreck it."

Hutch said "I love her."

"Then why—" James quit. "Sorry. It's your life, I'm sure—carry on."

"No, ask any question. I may need to talk."

So again James stroked the dash as if to please it. "I was asking myself why you're here then and she's that far off, cutting out a child."

"Because I planned it."

"You just said you loved her."

Hutch nodded. "Very much."

James said, "I doubt I could understand not being with anybody I ever loved."

"We left Nan asleep."

"I'll go back," James said. "I'll take her when I'm settled."

"That's more or less what I planned," Hutch said. "I'd study here for two years, go home, get a better job, and marry."

"The job'll be what?"

"Teaching college, writing poems."

"Pay you for poems in America, do they?"

Hutch laughed. "No I throw in the poems for free."

James said "I should hope so" and that seemed to stop them.

They were quiet till Wallingford, the lights of its small heart. It was halfway to Oxford, and Hutch thought of pausing at the Lamb or the Feathers to stand James a beer. But when he glanced over, James seemed so embedded in the car's pure privacy—such a safe fair jury—that he drove on and then, in the stretch before Dorchester, said, "Who have you ever loved besides Nan?"

James thought. "Do I love Nan?"

"You said you did."

"When?"

"When I met you and her in the pub last summer. You said you and she fell in love with each other at St. Giles's Fair, the same day the gypsy told Helen she'd be the cause of blood in others."

James said "Christ," astonished; then sat awhile. "Is memory a qualification of authors?"

Hutch laughed. "Yes, the first."

"Then by all rights, mate, you're due to be Shakespeare." He turned to see Hutch for the first time fully. Then he laughed. "Just to show you what *I'm* due to be—I've forgot your name again."

"Hutch Mayfield."

"I like that," James said. "You'll go far with that."

Hutch said, "It's been a long way already. It may be tired."

"You're two hours older than me. Buck up."

"The name, I mean."

James said, "Have I the honor to be hauled by the heir to a noble American line?"

"—A line of deep thinkers and sensitive plants, if that's nobility."

"It's not," James said.

"Wrong again."

"You or me?"

Hutch said "Me."

James sat through a dark mile, the onslaught of wind from the west, the car rocking. Then he said "Never mind" with the same brisk warmth he kept for Nan. He spread both his hands in the panel light and spoke toward them. "The working class has its own slice of fun."

Hutch said, "I've laid a big bet on work."

"Start now."

"On what?"

"Your job," James said. "Make a poem right here." He scrawled in the air with his blunt forefinger.

"Pick a subject then."

James at once said "Me," then wrote on awhile in the chilling air before him. "—Why you've got me here. Why you've bothered with me."

Hutch thought he knew. "I suspect you're my father."

"Is that the poem?"

Hutch laughed once but realized it was, one of the oldest happiest poems—Jacob and Joseph, Odysseus and Telemachus, Lear and Cordelia. He turned to James—"It may well be"—then felt the foolishness.

But James thought it through. "I sort of doubt that. I mean, I've seen a fair number of oddities along my path; and I've known enough girls to be a bit vague—about *this* life, at least—but I doubt you're mine." When he looked round he grinned.

Hutch surprised himself with the confirmation—that something in the boy seemed identical with Rob, of the same good essence. Nothing ghostly or urgent but a gentle palpable return of the oldest presence he'd known and needed—the vulnerable potent needy youth who'd stood at the rim of Hutch's own childhood and asked for help. He faced the road and said, "No my father died a few weeks back. He meant a great deal. You look a little like him." He reached out his right hand and touched James's brow. "The eyes, just the eyes." That was not the case; but it seemed a fair way, on their windy progress up the black Thames valley, to honor the moment and its small consolation.

James looked forward also and nodded slowly. "Glad to help," he said. His strong delicate face, in its stillness, pressed on the night like an adequate prow through whatever waters might wait ahead.

18

The operator was a man again but friendlier. When Ann answered through surges of static, the man said, "Ring off please, America. I'll try again." Then to Hutch, "Sounds like old Roosevelt, don't she? — I quite miss the war."

The second try she came through clear but small. "Am I better now?"

Hutch waited for the operator to speak, then realized he'd vanished. So he quickly said "Yes much better." He paused. "Are you really, Ann?"

"Oh sure." She laughed. "At least all the locals still *call* me Ann. I still recognize me in mirrors I pass."

"I got your letter."

"Good," she said. "Then are you really Hutch?" She laughed again.

"The same. At your service."

She held a long moment. "I'm glad, I guess."

"I also got a few words from Grainger. He said they'd seen you."

"I'd wondered if they did. I felt transparent."

Hutch said "You never are."

"I try," she said. "But I do seem to fade."

"Not for me. I see you every hour at least."

"Thank you," she said. "Is that any help?"

"To me? — a lot. Or it has been till now."

"What would change it now?"

Hutch thought for five expensive seconds. "You wanting me gone."

"Never. I told you."

"You didn't tell all."

Ann said "What's missing?"

"I'm here to ask that. Grainger's note has me worried."

She waited, then saw no way to move but straight. "What did Grainger say?"

"That you asked Straw to help you find an abortion."

"Grainger's more or less right."

"—And that Straw got mad."

"Well, *hurt.* I seemed to hurt him." Her voice still sounded with real regret.

"Did you find it though?"

"Yes."

"Who helped you?"

"Bailey, Linda's Bailey."

"Was Bailey involved?"

"Just in helping," she said, "—finding the woman."

"It was ours, right?"

"I hope not," she said. Hard as it was, she'd never planned to lie.

Hutch said, "Should I know who else was there?"

"Not here—in Rome. After you went—once, for fifteen minutes. I was lost when you left me."

Hutch saw Rowlet's face again, asking his question in the ruins by the river—how to act once he and Ann were alone, "two orphans in Rome." Hutch recalled he'd never answered more than "Good luck." So now he didn't speak Rowlet's name. He suspected he might be fatally cut in some vital part; but he said, "It was not a good time for anybody."

"Awful."

"Are you safe?"

"I hope so," she said.

"Your health, I mean."

"I hope so, yes."

Hutch said, "Was it a real doctor Bailey found?"

"No a colored woman. She was gentle as she could be."

"Have you seen a doctor since?"

Ann said "No."

"When was it?" Then he knew he was multiplying questions in confusion, for balance. "I'm sorry," he said.

"February eleventh, a Saturday night, four weeks ago." Her voice had begun to balk toward the end.

Hutch wondered where he'd been at the actual moment. But then he heard her tears—restrained as they were, still plain through the buried leagues of wire. He said, "Have you managed to work right along?"

"Never missed a day."

"Good."

"I guess so." Her voice had firmed but was suddenly tired.

"Do you want to come here?"

She waited. "For what?"

Hutch laughed. "The sun! The royal palms! No for me, for a rest."

"Have we ever been a rest?" It seemed a dumb riddle, but she didn't revise it.

And Hutch said "Sure," then searched for examples—Rome, Christmas day on the Palatine, the shape of her body laid on the trees at the Great Mother's shrine: a feasible goal. He also saw Lew beside him on Tresco, fervent in loss; Straw bare and cold from his nocturnal swim. Different goals. Or all one center? He said again "Sure."

"Not for me," Ann said.

"That can't be true."

She waited again. "It's true—about *rest*. I've loved more than half our minutes together; but I can't recall resting, not if we were awake."

"Why not?"

"I could never stop wanting you. I could never believe you meant to stay."

Hutch thought "Oh I did" but once more saw the places that had drawn him to their various hearts (the places were people). Could he choose one now? He said, "Is the ring still buried in your powder?"

"I took it home Friday to Mother's. It's safe there, no burglars for years."

"I asked you to wear it." That still seemed his choice, made a year ago nearly.

Ann laughed. "In my nose? We never had it sized."

It fell in on him then, a shoal of regrets that tasted like revulsion. "Ann, the child may have been part mine. Is that much true?"

"Yes."

"And what happened in Rome was a kind of accident?"

"Yes," she said, "a kind of revenge."

"And you still think you want me to stay in your life?"

"Most days, yes. I think it most days."

"Then get back the ring, wear it on a chain till I'm home again, and believe I mean to stay." He believed himself.

Ann said "Let me wait."

"For what?"

"Myself. For me please, Hutch. I've been on a whole long outing of my own—I don't mean Rome—and I wasn't really ready, and I'm not home yet. The main thing I need to believe right now is that I'll get back. When I do I'll know."

"What?"

Her stillness was total but she didn't think. She was locked in the midst of a brown fatigue. Then she said, "I'll hope to know what to want."

Hutch saw no way to ask for more, though the one request that rose in his mind now was *ending*—an honorable mutual walking away. Had he ever felt that with anyone else? Maybe Rob toward the end when the pain of witness exceeded the love. He said, "I'll be here, I guess, when you know."

"I'll write you a letter tomorrow at lunch."

"I live for the mail." He laughed. "Ann, I want to send you the money."

"Please no."

"I owe it."

"You don't," she said. "You've already paid. We're both paid-up."

Hutch thought, hot and fast, "You owe me a life"; but he said "All right." The heavy old receiver in his hand was strong with the scurf of two generations of similar breaths, scattered and gone. He flicked it with his tongue, trying unconsciously to summon her sweetness—the presence against him of skin warm as his with identical intentions: endlessly generous, courteous, conversant through whole long nights.

Ann seemed to say "Thanks."

                                        19

Hutch thanked the porter for managing the call, then entered the dark Front Quad, still raked by wind that had held since Saturday night. High clouds tore past toward what?—White Russia, Mongolia, Alaska. Behind them the sky was uniformly light but starless and no sign of moon. He hoped he'd meet no one but could navigate the fifty yards to his room in silence, then read Rob's posthumous letter again. He'd stored it carefully after the first time, too painful then. Now its memory promised at least counter-pain to the news from Ann—and maybe more. A map toward what he still meant to have, the life Rob missed; a chart-by-omission. A grown man's life, aimed straight toward a goal and proceeding there. A *waking* life, dreamed by no one but his open-eyed self—truthful enough to know its few needs and fill them, if no other body stood to suffer. Even here, Ann's voice five minutes behind him, there seemed no big impediment to that. He felt as stripped as he'd felt in Cornwall or in the wrecked boat on the black beach on Tresco—solitary pilot-and-crew combined—but peaceful now and safe to the end.

No one crossed his path. The glum handful of students who'd lingered to study through Easter were shut in asleep, no light at any window. The dons (surely brandied as Christmas peaches) were snoring in the chill, though his own steps made the sole human sound. The college—five acres of the most fruitful ground ever consecrated to harmless work—was his to roam. But he wanted his own room—the charged souvenirs that mapped his past (the pinebark man carved by old Rob Mayfield, the stones from Castle Dore and Cybele's altar, the magnifying glass from Archie Gibbons, the pages written four thousand miles from here by a man who'd finished eleven years of high school in no blaze of anything brighter than the worship in Min Tharrington's eyes).

His staircase was dark so he started the dozen high steps slowly, boards soft as flannel. In the moments of climb, he discovered this much—that even he had not expected a year mined like this with cuttings and space. He knew it had stunned him and knew he was flat exhausted now; he'd have the whole six weeks of Easter to gauge the damage and feel it deep. And stop it—repair his life and whoever else he'd agreed to hurt. Who else but Ann? Yet Ann had known of Rob's speeding death and kept the secret for her private purpose—to join him, unhindered and smiling, in Rome. A free choice of hers, to lie and face the ends of a lie. What blame should he bear?

His door was half-open. He remembered he'd shut it. Other nights he'd have quickly assumed a flying visit from English friends, with their universal indifference to the warmth he painfully nursed from his two-bar heater. But the friends were gone. He froze two steps below the landing and listened hard. Steps in his bedroom, the low sound of music (jazz from Radio Luxembourg); then steps and radio moved toward the sitting room. Hutch stayed in place. From there in the dark, he could see his desk five yards away, his eyes exactly level with its top. A man came over and stood beside it—back turned, dark clothes, portable radio in hand. He set down the radio and touched an open notebook (Hutch had tried today to revive his Tristan poem—Gorvenal's version, what the butler saw).

The man was James almost certainly—the broad white plane of neck above his back collar, the short black curls. James had known the time of the call to Ann. Hutch had never been robbed, never heard of anyone in college being robbed—no one ever locked a door—so he felt both the standard symptoms of rape (his room, his psychic body, rummaged in) and the second great cave-in of the night. A cheerful likeable acquaintance unmasked as a scheming thief. "*Fool*," Hutch thought. "He told me from the start." He'd also nearly killed a man. Should Hutch go for help?

The radio had stopped—dead batteries? James thumped it gently twice with no success. All his movements were slow as if underwater or in cold oil. He opened the center drawer of the desk. Rob's letter was there.

Of all that had happened today—this year—Hutch could not stand that. He took the last steps loudly, entered the room.

James looked round, smiling calmly. "I found you then. I was scratching about in here to find your name—didn't know your room, picked the one with lights."

Hutch nodded. "It's mine."

"But your wireless is dead." James tapped at the dial again, sudden music. "Hullo, I'm a healer!"

Hutch said "Can I help you?"

James flushed crimson; his eyes crouched incredulous. He took a step back. "I was thinking I might just manage that for *you*."

Hutch frowned a mute question.

"—A bit of help," James said. "I thought you might want it."

"I'm still up and moving."

"—Your call to the States; it sounded like a killer."

"You heard it?"

"Course not—what you told me last night, your girl and that kid."

The desk drawer still hung open. Hutch closed it, closed the notebook and squared it neatly, then switched off the music. "Well, a *maimer*," he said. "I doubt it killed me." He flexed his right hand in the air between them.

James said "I was wrong."

"How?"

"The kid was really yours." He looked to the seat of the chair but stayed upright, an unwelcomed guest.

Hutch had not faced him for two minutes now; he watched the worn carpet and nodded to that. "You were wrong."

"Did you thank her?"

"No."

"You will and all."

"Why?"

"Christ, look at *me*." James struck his own breastbone hard with a fist.

Hutch heard it as an order and looked up then. It had been a sad admission—James's pallor was a firm luminescence in the air, stronger than the lamp and desolate. Rob again, a thousand times in memory. Moth to his own flame, dying and fed. Hutch said, "Send for Nan. I'll take you to get her."

As slowly as he'd moved when Hutch spied on him, James thrust out a flat palm—enough, have mercy. "She's Helen's or Ethel's or Mick's—or the Queen's. Anybody's but mine."

"Where does that leave you?"

"In me skin." James drew back his palm and scrubbed a cheek. Color flooded again, the ready blood. "In your room here."

Hutch said "How'd you get in?"

A sizable gap. "Oh now, mate, *my* little crime was assault. I never stole a tanner."

Hutch nodded. "The porter didn't see you, right?"

James smiled. "No I soared in silent from the river." He pointed out the black uncovered windows. "On me bat-leather wings."

Hutch said "Sit down" and turned to draw the curtains. The big horse-chestnut was loud in the wind.

James sat on the edge of the chair he'd touched.

"I could do up some cocoa."

James said "No thanks."

"I might have a little whiskey left."

James said "No thanks." Then as Hutch knelt to open the battered cupboard, he said "You got any sleep?"

Hutch turned.

"Sleep—you know, what humans do at night." James shut his eyes and snored.

Hutch said "I might." When he stood, empty-handed, he felt a great calm.

20

March 12, 1956

Dear Hutch,

I promised to write you a letter at lunchtime today so here I am. It was not that restful a night, as you can guess; and Monday in the office is always nervous as a jumping bean. And I said, on the phone and in the letter last week, almost everything I know. Please remember that, if you want information on Ann Gatlin still. I like to watch you better than anybody I've known. I like to be with you day after day, even if it keeps me sweating with hope. I'm fairly dry now and I guess you must be after last night, but—well, but what? Nothing right now. I'm trying to curb the prophetess in me; she was so scared of all she thought she saw and was also wrong more than half the time.

Can I stop there for now? Just for now, understand—with this one postscript. In every word I've said since Christmas (I reviewed them all in the dark last night), there was just one lie. I want to correct it. Your ring is not at Mother's house. I had it with me on February 11th; and after the day, I asked Bailey please to take me to Polly's. I told her the story—the only person besides you and Bailey (he hasn't told Linda). She took it the way rocks seem to take rain, so I asked her to hold the ring for safekeeping. It felt like the right thing then and still does. So it's there with her.

I have to go out now and try to find a new dress in thirty-five minutes. Mother made me vow to come home for Easter and gave me a check to refurbish my looks. Did you notice Easter falls on April Fool's Day this year? The Prayer Book says it hasn't done that since 1945 and won't again in the twentieth century. Is that some kind of blessing? Please advise.

Love,
Ann

March 18, 1956
Dear Ann,

I waited till your letter came so as not to babble before you spoke. It came yesterday. I thought a lot of course, this way and that; but like you, I don't have much worth saying. You rein in your sibyl; I'll silence my own tin-horn Jeremiah. That's to say I don't have or feel any trace of blame, and that's not to ask for the year's Big Heart Prize. You must have done all you saw to do. I've been doing the same. My lie was, that doing what I saw to do has included touching several people other than Ann. I'd have told you sooner if I'd known it mattered.

All it means now is, I don't claim pride of place over you and that I'm still open to more of the world than I planned to be. You remember Grandmother telling me last year that, at twenty-five, I was over the hill. In less than two months, I'll be one year farther over—on the skids, by her schedule. And I hoped to be dug in better by now, a hill camp at least from which I could see the line of the route and stock my provisions.

I'm not—dug in, as you well know. So I think I should stop predicting the route. And if I do, don't I stop—like you—knowing who I can ask to share the wait? None of which means I don't remember our numerous best times as grand—long unblemished days—and hope there will, some way, be more of them (well-spaced through whatever lives we get).

Love always,
Hutch

March 20, 1956
Dear Polly,

Isn't this the first day of spring? I ask because I'm a shut-in here—the third straight day of rain, the air's solid water. I wonder how I'm breathing; gills would seem called for. And in fact there were long welts under my jaws when I looked just now—I'm evolving to last in a new world, I trust.

It's Easter vacation, six long weeks of it. After Easter I'll probably spend a *week or so in Cumberland and Scotland; but with the trip home, I got well behind in my work and must scramble. Reading, reading—slow progress, wearing these deep-sea goggles.*

I'm also too far behind with the mail. Your letter, with the word on Agnes Butters' wedding, came three weeks ago and cheered me as intended. But even more so in the past ten days when I read it more than once. I had a note from Grainger, then telephoned Ann and learned her sad news. I'm sorry you had to have one more load of my family's mess left at your door, but I'll always be grateful you were there and ready. She seemed fairly strong when I heard her voice, and I've since had a letter which sounds O.K. She said she would go to her mother's for Easter; but if you have an extra few minutes some evening and could stand the thought, please give her a call and check on her for me. I may have hurt her worse than I've hurt anybody since Rachel died. She won't come here —I asked her plainly—and I can't go there.

I've thought a lot lately of something you said in a letter last summer, that the men in my family had all been warmers. I've wanted to be, God knows, and have worked at it overtime since my eyes focused. But so far I've failed—and over long stretches. I don't know why. Sometimes I think it has to be involved with never having known or even seen my mother. You and Rob and Grainger, Grandmother, Aunt Rena were as kind to me as St. Francis to birds; but I knew about Rachel and wanted her there and kept a place for her that no one else was allowed to fill. Not ten days ago I dreamed her again more or less the way I've always dreamed her. I'm loafing in the woods behind Grandmother's house; and suddenly I see Rachel standing by a creek, on the far side—young and healthy as a straight spring tree. I always tell her "Wait" and run for the others to share my luck. Through the years several roommates have claimed I really called "Wait" in my sleep. The other night a friend was here while I dreamed; and I didn't seem to speak out, didn't wake him at least. I'd lost it when I woke (the end of the dream), but I think she may have stayed, and I crossed over and saw her close at least. Anyhow it's past time to move on from that. What I didn't get from her, I still have to give. And all I know to give is what I seem better at than anything else—the patience to watch things (people mainly) and copy their motions. I hope that will somehow prove a means of love, of finding the place where each thing is still and will no longer leave.

Which brings me to something important at the end. Ann wrote me she'd left the ring with you. I want you not only to keep it but have it. You're the only one left who knew all the men involved in handing it on—old Rob, Forrest, Grainger, young Rob, me. You spoke of Agnes Butters and her groom making outlandish vows at their wedding, just the normal perfect vows. Well, I tremble for them too. But it seems to me you've kept them, out of everyone I've known—steady love for whole lives. I had the ring stretched to fit some years ago; but if you'll wear it, you could have it sized easily. Let me know the cost.

Whatever, now it's yours. When and if I ever need one, please let me start anew. I tried to write a little poem to send with the gift, but poems are in hiding right now. Maybe later.

I'll be here another eighteen months or so. Then who knows where?—but on the same side of the ocean as you. A warming thought. Stay strong and be there always.

Love,
Hutch

March 28, 1956

Dear Hutch,

That ring was offered to me by your grandfather on Christmas eve 1904 for thanks not love. I could not take it then and am honest when I say I have not spent ten seconds wanting it since. But I will take it now and thank you for it here, not wait to see you. It fits my right hand, these knobby old fingers. I won't wear it though. My neighbors would faint then ask fifty questions. I have taped it to the bottom of a slat in the bed your great-grandfather slept and died in. He must have paid for it. Everything in this house is yours in my will. But if I am not here when you get back or have lost these remnants of my great mind, you will know where it is. The ring not my mind.

What means even more is what your letter said, that I kept promises. I hope I did. People just kept asking for things I seemed to have so I can't take any credit for responding. I was lucky there were askers, all men with fine eyes. I still cherish eyes and am glad mine have lasted.

That reminds me to put them back to work now. It is seven a.m. and I have undertaken three Easter dresses that are still lying here in pieces staring at me. One of them is for Ann who seems to be well. She just needs time. So do you, don't worry so much, you're happy. All the men in your family were happy men. Not one of them knew it till I said so. I have said it to you and I know I'm right.

Believe me,
Polly Drewry

THE
PROMISE
OF
REST

FOR

MICHAEL HOWARD RAYMOND JORDAN

FOR
FORTY YEARS

We die with the dying:
See, they depart, and we go with them.
We are born with the dead:
See, they return, and bring us with them.

T. S. ELIOT, *Little Gidding*

O N E

BOUND HOME

APRIL 1993

For thirty-odd years, this white narrow room at the top of a granite building in the midst of Duke University had been one place where Hutchins Mayfield never felt less than alive and useful by the day and the hour. For that long stretch he'd met his seminar students here, and this year's group was gathered for its first meeting of the week. There were fourteen of them, eight men and six women, aged nineteen to twenty-two; and by a pleasant accident, each had a winning face, though two of the men were still in the grip of post-adolescent narcolepsy—frequent short fade-outs.

This noon they all sat, with Hutch at the head, round a long oak table by a wall of windows that opened on dogwoods in early spring riot; and though today was the class's last hour for dealing with Milton's early poems before moving on to Marvell and Herbert, even more students were dazed by the rising heat and the fragrance borne through every window.

In the hope of rousing them for a last twenty minutes, Hutch raised his voice slightly and asked who knew the Latin root of the word *sincere*.

A dozen dead sets of eyes shied from him.

He gave his routine fixed class grin, which meant *I can wait you out till Doom.*

Then the most skittish student of all raised her pale hand and fixed her eyes on Hutch—immense and perfectly focused eyes, bluer than glacial lakes. When Hutch had urged her, months ago, to talk more in class, she'd told him that every time she spoke she was racked by dreams the following night. And still, volunteering, she was ready to bolt at the first sign of pressure from Hutch or the class.

Hutch flinched in the grip of her eyes but called her name. "Karen?"

She said "*Without wax*, from the Latin *sine cere*."

"Right and what does that mean?"

She hadn't quite mustered the breath and daring for a full explanation; but with one long breath, she managed to say "When a careless Roman sculptor botched his marble, he'd fill the blunder with smooth white wax. A sincere statue was one without wax." Once that was out, Karen blushed a dangerous color of red; and her right hand came up to cover her mouth.

Hutch recalled that Karen was the only member of the class who'd studied Latin, three years in high school—an all but vanished yet near-vital skill. He thanked her, then said "The thoroughly dumb but central question that's troubled critics of Milton's 'Lycidas' was stated most famously by pompous Dr. Samuel Johnson late in the eighteenth century. He of course objected mightily, if pointlessly, to the shepherd trappings of a pastoral poem—what would he say about cowboy films today? He even claimed—and I think I can very nearly quote him—that 'He who thus grieves will excite no sympathy; he who thus praises will confer no honor.' I think he's as wrong as a critic can be, which is saying a lot; and I think I can prove it."

Hutch paused to see if their faces could bear what he had in mind; and since the hour was nearly over, most of their eyes had opened wider and were at least faking consciousness again. So he said "I'd like to read the whole poem aloud—again, not because I love my own voice but because any poem is as dead on the page as the notes of a song unless you hear its music performed by a reasonably practiced competent musician. It'll take ten minutes; please wake up and listen." He grinned again.

The narcolepts shook themselves like drowned Labradors. They were oddly both redheads.

One woman with record-long bangs clamped her eyes shut.

Hutch said "Remember now—the most skillful technician in English poetry who lived after Milton was Tennyson, two centuries later. Tennyson was no pushover when it came to praising other poets—very few poets are— but he claimed more than once that 'Lycidas' is the highest touchstone of poetic appreciation in the English language: a touchstone being a device for gauging the gold content of metal. Presumably Tennyson meant that any other English poem, rubbed against 'Lycidas,' will show its gold or base alloy."

Though Hutch had long since memorized the poem, all 193 lines, he looked to his book and started with Milton's prefatory note.

> "In this monody the author bewails a learned friend unfortunately drowned
> in his passage from Chester on the Irish seas, 1637."

Then he braced himself for the steeplechase run-through that had never failed to move him deeply.

"Yet once more, O ye laurels, and once more
Ye myrtles brown, with ivy never sere,
I come to pluck your berries harsh and crude,
And with forced fingers rude,
Shatter your leaves before the mellowing year."

From there on, along the crowded unpredictable way to its visionary end—
with Lycidas rescued and welcomed in Heaven by a glee club of saints and
Christ himself, giving nectar shampoos—Hutch stressed what always felt to
him like the heart of the poem, its authentic cry. It sounded most clearly in
the lines where Milton either feigned or—surely—poured out genuine grief
for the loss of his college friend, Edward King, drowned in a shipwreck at age
twenty-five, converted in the poem to an ancient shepherd named Lycidas
and longed for in this piercing extravagant cry with its keening vowels.

"Thee shepherd, thee the woods, and desert caves,
With wild thyme and the gadding vine o'ergrown,
And all their echoes mourn.
The willows, and the hazel copses green,
Shall now no more be seen,
Fanning their joyous leaves to thy soft lays.
As killing as the canker to the rose,
Or taint-worm to the weanling herds that graze,
Or frost to flowers, that their gay wardrobe wear,
When first the white thorn blows;
Such, Lycidas, thy loss to shepherd's ear."

Ten minutes later at the poem's hushed end—*"Tomorrow to fresh woods,
and pastures new"*—Hutch was even more shaken than he'd meant to be.
Strangely he hadn't quite foreseen a public collusion between Milton's subject and his own ongoing family tragedy. But at least he hadn't wept; so he
sat for five seconds, looking out the window past the creamy white and cruciform blossoms toward the huge water oaks with their new leaves.

Then he faced the class again and repeated from memory the central
lines—"Thee shepherd, thee the woods, and desert caves. . . ." When he
thought they'd sunk as deep as they could into these young television-
devastated brains, he said "Estimate the wax content of those few lines."

Even Karen looked flummoxed again and turned aside.

Hutch tried another way. "—The sincerity quotient. Does Milton truly
miss the sight of young Edward King, King's actual presence before the

poet's eyes; if not, what's he doing in so many carefully laid-down words?" When they all stayed blank as whitewashed walls, Hutch laughed. "Any-body, for ten extra points. Take a flying risk for once in your life." (Through the years, except for the glorious and troubling late 1960s, most of his stu-dents had proved far more conservative than corporate lawyers.)

Finally Kim said "He's showing off"—the class beauty queen, lacquered and painted and grade-obsessed.

Whitney said "Milton's almost thirty years old, right? Then I figure he's stretching—he's using King's death as a chinning bar to test his own strengths. *Can I write this thing?* he seems to be saying, right through to the end." Since Whit was one of the midday nappers, his contributions were always surpris-ing in their sane precision.

Still fire-truck red, Karen finally said "I think Milton's discovering, as the ink leaves his pen, how terribly his friend drowned and vanished—they never even found the friend's corpse apparently. I think it sounds like Mil-ton truly longs for him back."

Hutch said "Does it *sound* like longing, or does he really long?"

Karen winced and withdrew.

Whitney said "What's the difference? Nobody can gauge that, now any-way."

Hutch said "Why not?"

"It's too far behind us, nearly four hundred years. The words have all changed; we can't hear their meaning." Whit lowered his near-white lashes like scrims down over green eyes.

Alisoun said "Then let's all go home." She was six foot one, and any threat to unfold her long bones to their full height was always welcome.

Hutch asked her to explain.

"If four hundred years in the life of a language as widespread as English add up to nothing but failed communication, then I don't see any point in encouraging the human race to live another year. Let's just quit and vacate." She was genuinely at the point of anger.

The other women looked officially startled; their mothering genes had felt the assault.

Erik turned his face, that was always stern, a notch or two sterner and set it on Alisoun. "Get serious. *I* anyhow understand every syllable—not one of them's moved an inch in three centuries—and I'm no genius of a reader, as you well know. Milton is literally desolate here, right here on this page, all this time later. The fact that he's also phenomenal at words and rhyme and music doesn't disqualify him for sincere grief. If that's been the problem about the poem since old Dr. Johnson, then it looks like critics are short on reasons to fan their gums."

Hutch said "*Touché.* They mostly are."

But to general surprise, Karen recovered gall enough to say "I have to disagree. Milton's mainly bragging, the way Kim said. The poem's primarily about himself—'Watch my lovely dust. Recommend me to God. Buy all my books.'"

Hutch smiled but raised a monitory finger. "Milton didn't publish a book of poems for eight whole years after 'Lycidas.'"

So tremulous Karen took another long breath, faced Hutch unblinking and thrust toward the subject that no other student had found imaginable. "Mr. Mayfield, have you written poems about your son?"

Startling as it was to have the question come from Karen, Hutch realized he'd waited months for someone to ask it. *Now the demon's out and smashing round the room.* In Karen's halting, plainly sympathetic voice, the question sounded answerable at least. Her boldness surely had to mean that the news of his son was widespread now and accepted as mentionable. Yet when Hutch looked round to all the faces—some class was breaking up early outside; the hall was a din through the shut glass door—all but Karen were blank as slate again. So Hutch offered the minimum he thought they could use. "My grown son is sick with AIDS in New York. Till today no known AIDS patient has won. And no, Karen, I haven't written a word, on that subject anyhow. I doubt I ever can."

Karen had the grace not to push on and make a connection with Milton, though she thought *Anybody in genuine grief couldn't sit and write an intricate poem, not one we'd keep on reading for centuries.*

But Hutch could read the drift in her eyes. "Don't for an instant make the tempting mistake of thinking that I share Milton's powers—nobody else in European poetry, not since Homer anyhow, can make that claim."

Kim said "Not Virgil, Dante or Shakespeare?"

Hutch shook his head No and suddenly felt a surge of pleasure—a strange boiling from deep in his chest of pleased excitement to plant his feet down and crown John Milton supreme in all the great questions of life. He said "Milton knows more than anyone else, in the western hemisphere in any case, in verse anyhow; and he's nine-tenths right on almost every question. Shakespeare is all a zillion bright guesses, bright or pitch-dark—not one single answer. Dante knows just one big urgent thing."

Whitney said "Which is?"

Hutch said "'No rest but in your will'—the *your* means God of course."

Kim scowled, the regulation atheist.

And Karen's eyes plainly showed that she felt Hutch had short-changed the subject she raised—his son's present illness.

So he faced her directly and tried to give more. "Even Milton will have found that not every loss, however picturesque, and not every joy, however rhythmic, will submit itself as poetry fodder—as food for new poems."

Karen accepted that but wanted still more. "Can you think of a sadness or a genuine pleasure that wouldn't submit when you yourself tried to write it out?"

Hutch knew at once. "In fact, I can—oh many times over. But one in particular strikes me today. I'll be dealing with it again—in my life, not my work—in another few hours. Soon as I leave you today, I'll be driving up to my family's homeplace in the rolling country north of here, up near Virginia, for what should be a mildly pleasant occasion. We'll be celebrating the 101st birthday of a cousin of mine, named Grainger Walters. I've known the event was coming for a long time and have tried more than once to write a poem that would say what that man's meant to me since the day I was born—a kind of older brother when my mother died, a surrogate father when my father died young, even a species of bighearted alien from some kind of Paradise, guarding and guiding me fairly successfully for six long decades. But a poem won't come, or hasn't come yet."

Whitney said "Do you understand why?"

"Not fully, no I don't. But I'm fairly sure the problem's buried somewhere in the fact that I'm all white—pure Anglo-Saxon and Celtic genes, to the best of my knowledge—and Grainger Walters is part black, the grandson of one of my Aryan great-grandfathers on up in Virginia, in Reconstruction days."

Whitney suddenly strummed an imaginary banjo and sang to the tune of "Way Down Upon the Swanee River,

> "Hankey-pankey on the old plantation,
> Far, far away."

Alisoun said "It's already been written."

Hutch was puzzled.

"By Mary Chestnut in her famous diary; by Faulkner, in every paragraph—by Robert Penn Warren too, a whole slew more. Won't that be the main reason you're stymied? The job's been *done*."

Since Hutch was a poet, not a novelist, the fact had never quite dawned that harshly. He instantly suspected *She's at least a third right*. But he said "Wouldn't the fact that every one of you is white, that a black student at this university—or any other—very seldom takes courses in literature, mean that you're wrong? Far from being done to death, the subject of race in America— race in its deepest historical and moment-by-moment contemporary ramifications—has barely reached the level of audibility in our literature, much less the level of sane portrayal. A world of explaining remains to be done."

Alisoun's answer was long-since ready. "I've noticed how scarce blacks are in this department, yes; but the reason for that has got to be, they *know* you'll tell them nothing but lies—our solemn white poems and stories about human one-ness, all our feeble alibis for common greed and meanness and worse: torture, murder. Every black student here, and I know quite a few— I've made it my little white-girl project for the past three years—has got those lies bred into their *bones.* They don't need to read Old Master's effusions. What have we got to tell them, we Western white folks, in poems and plays?"

Her immaculate pale green cotton sweater and short string of pearls had misinformed Hutch; he was shocked by her force. *I'll think about that on the road today.* For the present he could only say what he trusted. With all the self-trust of a lifelong teacher, his mind chose to seize the wheel of the talk and turn it his way. "What conceivable subject—any subject comprehensible to humans at least, of whatever color—hasn't been done to death? The fact that Milton wrote 'Lycidas' has hardly prevented the writing of later great poems about dead youth."

Alisoun said "Name two."

Hutch said "Take three, off the top of my head—Tennyson's 'In Memoriam,' Arnold's 'Thyrsis,' Robert Lowell's 'Quaker Graveyard in Nantucket.'"

Erik said "But isn't the theme of early death a whole lot more universal and available than the historical accident of Anglo and Afro-American miscegenation for three hundred years in a highly particular steamy place called the old Confederacy?"

Hutch waited, then had to say "Thanks for the question; I need to think it over. I will admit I don't think William Faulkner is a genius compared to, say, Tolstoy or Dostoevsky. Faulkner knew a small hot patch of ground he invented; it lacked huge chunks of the actual world—real women, for example: just half the human race unaccounted for. And responsible fathers, which many men are. Mothers who can love and not smother their young. Faulkner *was* the best student of wild and tame animals I've yet found in fiction; but as for his using up any large subject you'd meet in the real world, except maybe whiskey—you recall Hemingway always called him 'Old Bourbon Mellifluous,' a well-aimed spear from one who'd consumed his own share of gin—well, all Faulkner exhausted was runaway English; country show-off prose.

"And no other writer, since Faulkner drank himself out of sane action by the age of fifty, has really dived deep into that huge maelstrom called miscegenation on Southern ground—the feeding of white on black, black on white—though the problem has gone much further toward both solution and utter insolubility than Marse Will Faulkner ever dreamed possible."

Hutch looked up to Alisoun, who'd waited him out, and smiled broadly at her. "I'll prophesy for you what I'm likely to feel, if I think your question through for years—I very much doubt that any reality that's widely experienced by human beings is ever worn out, not so long as the right he or she takes it up in flaming-new language."

More than half the class now realized that the teacher had left himself open for a body blow. *Are you the right man, and where're your deathless flaming-new words?* But every watch showed the hour was ending.

So Hutch said "I promise you more of an answer; but for now, one final word from the foreman here—words as freshly minted and potently thrusting as the words of 'Lycidas' all but never come out of a human mind for any reason less than enormous feeling, a nearly stifling pressure to *speak*. My money anyhow is on John Milton's being mightily moved by his young friend's drowning—by the chance that such a random disaster could fall on himself—and by the near-sure existence of a just afterlife. But believe what you will, if the poem will support you. I'll see you on Wednesday. Read Andrew Marvell."

Only Kim slid her chair back to rise.

Late as it was, the others seemed held in place, unsatisfied.

Hutch actually asked himself *Are they facing their own eventual deaths?*

And they held still another long moment—even Kim balked, unsatisfied but gripped.

To free them, Hutch said the only thing that came. It was anyhow truthful. "This poem—'Lycidas'—means more to me than all but a few of the humans I've known, more than most anything I've ever owned or tried to keep. Except of course for my lost son—he's lost to me; *how* I can't bear to tell you. If the world hadn't turned up creatures like Milton—or Keats or Handel— every century or so, I doubt I could live through the thought of my young son dying in pain, too far from me, refusing any help and even his mother's." He knew it sounded a little mad, maybe more than a little.

But none of their eyes betrayed fear or laughter; and even when they'd filed silently past him toward their crowded unthinkable lives—Whit's hand touched his shoulder as he went—the rising in Hutch's chest boiled on. *What in God's name has got me happy?*

2

The rising continued as Hutch stopped by his office to check the mail. He'd no sooner sat, though, before someone knocked—a tall man behind the opaque glass. A little annoyed, Hutch called "Come in." The dark-haired, dark-bearded man was familiar on sight anyhow—Hutch had noticed him on the stairs and in the hallways for maybe two years. He was almost certainly a graduate student; but he held in place on the threshold, not speaking.

Hutch stood. "I'm Hutchins Mayfield. May I help you?"

Entirely serious, the man said "I very much doubt you can."

Then check out immediately. But all Hutch said was "We may never know if you don't fill me in." He motioned to the single red-leather chair that stood by his desk, for student callers.

Then the man launched a sudden spectacular smile, stepped in, shut the door and took the red chair. When Hutch was seated, the man held out a hand. "I'm Hart Salter, sir, a doctoral candidate. I've watched you for years."

"I've noticed you around, yes, but didn't see you watching me. You're bound to be bored."

Again Hart took it seriously. "Not bored exactly. Not fascinated either. I guess I've always tried to guess how poems get into your head from space."

Hutch had taught one genuine lunatic student a few years back. *Is this a fresh psycho?* He thought he'd try first to lighten the tone. With both hands far above his head, he indicated the shape of a drainpipe running from thin air through the top of his skull. "There's a long invisible pipeline, see, from the spring of the muses directly into my cerebral cortex."

Hart said "I've got no doubt about *that.*"

"Good. I only wish it were true."

Hart said "You fooled me. I've read all your poems; you're a real self-starter."

"Warm thanks, Mr. Salter. I'm a cold engine now, a minor dud." Then dreading what was almost surely the answer, Hutch asked the question that seemed required. "You write poems yourself?" The thought of a manuscript thrust at him here felt as real as a knife.

"Not a line of poetry, not since high school. No, I guess you're wondering why I'm here."

"I had begun to wonder. I'm due out of here in the next ten minutes—"

Hart sprang up at once. "I don't want to hold you."

"No, sit by all means and tell me your errand."

So Hart folded his endless legs again and sat. "I'm in deep water, sir. It's in my marriage. I figured a poet might help me swim out."

For the past three decades, student strangers had occasionally dropped in

with personal problems for the resident poet. One excruciating twenty minutes had followed when a young man with hideous face burns had walked
in to show Hutch the poems he'd written about his fate—a gasoline bomb
that had left him a monster. *But has any lovelorn certified adult ever asked for
love-help? Almost surely not.* Hutch said "My record on love is dismal, Mr.
Salter. I'm alone as a dead tree."

"Call me Hart, please—Hart." He smiled his winning smile again. "This
is idiotic of me, I know; but since I've committed this ludicrous folly, let
me ask one question."

Hutch held up a finger and laughed. "One question then, entirely free
of charge."

"How do you ever convince a woman that you actually love her?"

Hutch had noticed Hart's wedding band. "You're presently married?"

"Yes sir, for three years, fully sworn at the altar with God and man watching—"

"God and *humankind*, Hart. Maybe you need a crash course in—what?—
'gender-sensitive language'?"

"Sir, if I get any more sensitive, my blood will ooze out of these fingernails."
Hart showed ten long thick fingernails, well tended. "The problem is, my wife
can't believe me. I'm loyal as any Seeing Eye dog, I do well over half the
chores (she works full-time in the Botany greenhouse), my body has never
once cheated on her, I say the word *love* to her on the quarter-hour whenever
we're together, but she says she literally cannot believe me. This morning she
said she felt as abandoned as the world's last swallow."

Hutch smiled. "Assuming she meant the last *bird*, I like her image."

"Oh she can crucify you, by the minute, with images."

Hutch said "Try writing her short letters maybe, that she can keep and
reread at will. Try your first adult poem."

"I guessed you'd say that."

"What else could I say?—you called on a poet."

Hart flushed as fiercely as Karen, last hour. But he leaned back, thrust a
broad hand into his jeans and brought out a single folded index card. "I
wrote the poem, just now in the local men's room. May I read it to you?—
I think it's a haiku."

"By all means then—no epic recitations though."

Hart opened the card, spread it on his right knee but never looked down
as he said

> "In all this thicket of straight white trees,
> A single burning bush, concealing you."

Hutch said "Well, it may be a little too bold to be a haiku; but it's strik-ing all right. Will she mind the touch of eros?"

"No, that's one thing that's never been a problem."

Hutch said "Oh bountifully lucky pair!" Then he pointed to his phone. "Call your wife right now; read the poem to her, more than once. *I'd* be glad to hear it from any mate of mine." He was suddenly eager for Hart to succeed, so eager he threw off his usual caution about recognizing real poetry, how-ever modest. "I've got to leave, Hart. I'm overdue for my own family business. But use my phone for as long as you like; just shut the door as you leave—it locks itself."

Hart half rose. "I couldn't."

"You can. You already have, with your poem. Now read it to—who? You never said her name."

"Stacy. Stacy Burnham—she's kept her old name."

Hutch was on his feet now. "If you think it's appropriate, you can say *I* believe you."

Hart said "I may need to deep-six that." But then he could smile. He rose too, shook Hutch's hand again, then sat and carefully placed the phone call.

Only when he'd heard Hart's voice say "Stacy?" did Hutch shut the door behind him and go.

3

Two hours later, for whatever reason, Hutch was still nearly happy. The feel-ing that had sprung up at noon, in class, had only strengthened with the start of his trip. And against strong odds, it had lasted till now when he was in sight of his destination. At first he'd thought the change was caused by the day itself—an early April afternoon, new leaves overhead, the deeps of the woods splodged with redbud and dogwood, the air desert-clear. The landscape twenty miles northeast of Durham had begun a slow change through another forty miles into what was still the land of Hutch's childhood, the only nature he'd loved on Earth, though he'd stood in various stages of awe in the pres-ence of sights from the Jericho wilderness north to Lapland, west to Beijing and south to Rio.

In calm defiance of rusting billboards, trailer parks and all other man-made waste and ruin, the country Hutch drove through briskly was caught in its nearly invisible rolling—a broad-backed brown and green undulation beneath dense evergreens and a wide pitched sky as royal-blue as the eyes of a watchful year-old boy or the banner at a high chivalric tilt in dark-age

France. To Hutch it seemed, as it always had since his own father told him, the actual skin of a slumberous creature the size of a quarter of east Carolina and southside Virginia—a creature that might yet prove benign if it ever roused and faced the living.

And as always, again Hutch pushed on silently across the broad hide, hoping at least to pass unseen in his odd elation. Or was his pleasure a simple prediction of the evening ahead, a birthday supper for his ancient cousin? Hutch slowed a little for the final curve, glanced to the rearview mirror above him and grinned at his face.

After all these years it still surprised him to see how, this far along in life, he'd come to look like Rob his father who'd died a younger man than Hutch was today. Not that Rob was an unlikable model—the same braced brow and jaw, the brown unflinching eyes, the still dark hair with its broad swag of white. So Hutch actually spoke to himself, "You're bearing up better than you ought to be." It was true but the words hardly touched his pleasure as he entered the drive and stopped past the main house, by the vast oak—his father's old homeplace, which Hutch had rented to friends years ago.

He sat still a moment and tested again this strange new feeling. Despite the bitter sadness and loss he knew was bound toward him—him and his family—Hutch felt like a lucky man on a hill. And he guessed it was not some temporary boost, ignited by the weather or a quick jet of natural endorphins in his blood. He'd had long stretches of joy all his life and he trusted pleasure. It had lasted for two hours alone on the road, and it somehow promised to last a good while. For an instant, it even crossed his mind that his sexual force might come back again. Except for occasional bouts with his own hand, sexual will had all but left him months ago when he learned for sure that his son was desperately ill at a distance. Yet he knew all feeling, all longing for love, must hide now—for weeks or months—till he buried his only child, his son who was dying in upper Manhattan, refusing phone calls or visits from home.

Hutch reached for his cousin's birthday gift and climbed out into pure good-smelling sun. He shut his eyes and let the light warm his face and neck. Then he looked around him. No other car or truck, no other human in sight or hearing—Strawson and Emily must be in town. But Hutch had known this house and its setting all his life. He'd spent the best part of his boyhood here; it knew him well enough to let him arrive with no boisterous welcome. Only the fat old Labrador bitch on the porch turned to check; and once she knew him, she spared herself barking. Hutch called to her "Maud, it's the Friendly Slasher—go back to sleep."

Maud ignored the news and resumed her watch on the empty road.

So Hutch walked on toward the squat white guest-house beyond the stable. The clapboard was freshly painted, the roof was sporting new bright green shingles, and every window was shut and shaded against the light. Once Hutch was there though, the door stood open. Even the rusty screen was propped wide.

A single day-moth made a lunge to enter, then fell back as if a broad hand had struck it.

Hutch paused at the foot of the three rock steps and spoke at a low pitch. "Anybody breathing?" A keen-eared child, or a bat, might have heard him. He was testing his cousin's ears and brain.

The voice that answered was lean and light, a note or two higher than in the old days but firm and unbroken with no growl or husk. "One mean old soul in here; that's it—enter at your own risk."

Hutch said "I'm hunting a birthday boy named Grainger Walters. You seen him today?"

The voice stayed put but spoke even stronger. "He's not your boy but I've seen him every time I looked in the mirror for one-damn-hundred-and-one years today."

"You're not in there with some young girl?"

"Haven't seen a girl in thirty, forty years. You coming in or not?—I can't stand up." But there were sounds of a creaking chair, a tall body unfolding itself and then steps toward the door. A man was slowly there in the doorway behind the screen—long powerful hands, skin the color of the starched khaki pants and shirt, brown eyes that had turned almost a pale sky-blue.

At first that seemed to Hutch the one sign of unusual age—the eyes and the skin that lightened with every year as if time were canceling the first fact about this palpable body: its mingled blood. Hutch hadn't seen the old man in nearly four months. If there'd been a real change, it was maybe the eyebrows. The last of the snow-white eyebrows were gone, and the head was as hairless as any bronze bust. Then Hutch realized that the skull itself seemed larger and grander, grown to accommodate the huge filmy eyes. Otherwise the old man stood straight as ever since Hutch had known him—a little shrunk in the chest and thighs but bolt upright and balanced steadily. "Happy birthday, Cousin Grainger—and a hundred more."

Grainger Walters had given up smiling long since, except at unpredictable moments for unannounced reasons; but he showed the remains of his strong teeth now, and he tipped his bare head. "Fall down here in the dirt on your knees, and pray I die after supper tonight."

Hutch said "Whoa here."

"Whoa nothing—I'm tired. Haven't slept since Christmas."

"Why?" Hutch had asked without thinking.

"If you don't know my reason, fool—if you been sleeping good yourself—then leave that package here on my stoop and head on out." Grainger turned and vanished back to his chair.

At first Hutch edged his way to the door and laid the gift where he'd been told to leave it. A powerful urge to *run* shot through him. If anyone living knew Hutch Mayfield from sole to crown, it was this old soul who'd say what he meant if he felt the need or the merest whim. Hutch waited the urge out; then climbed the steps and entered, shutting the screen door behind him. It took a whole minute before his eyes had opened to the indoor darkness, and while he waited he said "You'll ruin your eyes in this dark."

Grainger said "*Trying* to. What do I need to see?"

"You might like to see how well I'm doing. I've trimmed off eight pounds since last Christmas; everybody thinks I'm ten years younger."

"Not me," Grainger said. "You're sixty-three years old and look it—sit down."

Hutch said "My birthday's not for six weeks. Don't rush me please." But he sat in the rocker across from the automatic chair he'd bought as a gift the previous spring when Grainger turned a hundred. You pressed a button; it gradually rose and stood you up with no exertion. When Hutch's eyes could finally see, he looked around the space for changes.

Nothing obvious, just the same strict order Grainger had laid down all his life, wherever he lived. This main room had its two good chairs and a long pine table against the wall with dozens of pictures framed above it—various kin whom he and Hutch shared, caught in photographs ranging from the 1850s to now.

The center of the cluster was a single oval tinted picture of Grainger's wife Gracie, long gone and dead. The other face that caught at Hutch was his own child Wade at about age ten, in a fork of the oak tree not fifty yards from this dim room. Beside it was a tall dark picture of Rob, his own dead father and Grainger's great friend. No one had ever looked finer than Rob, not the way he was here, in summer whites for high-school commencement more than seventy years past—a smiler as charged with electric attraction as the magnetic poles. All the others were distant kin and friends, a few stiff generals from the First World War (and oddly the Kaiser with his comical mustache) plus three or four modern Democratic politicians and Jacqueline Kennedy, a stalled gazelle of inestimable worth.

Otherwise there was only a big oil stove, a television and the neat narrow bed. It all looked as new and nearly unused as when Hutch had paid for

Grainger and two boys to build the place thirty some years back. The kitchen and bathroom doors were shut.

When Hutch didn't speak but went on looking, Grainger said "You planning to sell me out? It's worth every penny you paid me to build it—two thousand, three hundred, twenty-two dollars and eighty-six cents. I got the receipts." He actually pressed his chair button to rise.

"Sit still please—sit as long as you want. Every piece of this is yours and has always been."

"Emily don't think so."

It riled Hutch instantly. "Emily's dead wrong."

Grainger pointed through the wall toward the main house. "She's all the time saying how much it cost them to keep me warm."

It was then Hutch realized the oil stove was burning, though the front door was open. He put his palm out toward the heat. "You know this blast furnace here is roaring?"

Grainger said "I do."

"Shall I shut the door?"

"Shall not. Mind your business." But he may have smiled again. "I'm drying my clothes."

Hutch looked—had Grainger started fouling his pants? Then he noticed another khaki dress shirt, neatly hung on a wire hanger from the window ledge near the stove, and a pair of white socks. "You put out a wash? I pay Emily money to wash your clothes."

Grainger said "She don't get them dry enough—make my bones ache."

"I warned her about that here last Christmas."

"Remind her again; her memory's failing."

Hutch said "She's a whole lot younger than me."

"You failing too." Grainger suddenly focused on Hutch's face and gave it a thorough search. He'd watched it make every change it had made, through six decades.

"Me failing?" Hutch grinned. "I'm in fairly good shape; taught school today." He flexed both arms in their blue sleeves.

Grainger shook his head firmly No. "You're worse than you ever been in your life; you'll be worse soon."

At first Hutch thought it was old-man meanness or hard-edged teasing. But then he wondered what Grainger knew. Hutch had never mentioned his grown son's illness; Emily and Straw knew little about it, if anything; surely Ann hadn't blabbed. Hutch said "You know something I don't know?"

Grainger froze up slowly through the next long minute. He sat in place perfectly still; then again his eyes found Hutch's face as if they'd dug up the bones of a hand with scraps of skin. His old eyes were brimming.

So Hutch said "Wade? You heard from Wade?"

Grainger nodded but offered no more.

"When?"

"Just now. First thing this morning, still dark outdoors." Grainger pointed to the telephone screwed to the wall by the head of his bed.

"Wade called you today?"

"Wade calls me every birthday I've had since he could talk."

"He told you he's sick?"

Grainger said "I could hear it."

"You ask how he was?"

"He told me himself."

Hutch suddenly felt cut loose from a chain and flinging through space. "He tell you it's this terrible AIDS?"

"What?"

"This plague that's speeding all over the world, that kills you by wiping out your whole immune system so you're helpless to every germ and virus—"

Grainger said "I watch the TV. I'm not on the moon yet."

Hutch could grin briefly. "But Wade told you himself, today?"

"You don't know how your one child's doing?"

That hurt more than Hutch's own deep self blame. He said "Wade hasn't talked to me in three months."

"Try calling him up. They invented the phone when I was a boy."

Hutch said "He won't answer me, hangs up soon as he hears my voice."

Again Grainger waited to estimate if Hutch could take the fresh news. He finally said "Then you don't know he's blind."

"Oh my Jesus—" For an instant Hutch felt he'd pitch flat forward on the bare oak floor.

Grainger just nodded.

Then another man's voice called from well out of sight somewhere in the yard. "Mr. Walters, you seen that out-of-work poet we used to know?"

Hutch knew it had to be Straw, Strawson Stuart—the friend to whom he'd rented the place for nearly thirty years. Nobody but Strawson called Grainger *Mr. Walters.*

Grainger looked to Hutch and waved his hand slightly at the door. "Go show him it's you. Tell him I ain't dead."

Hutch was still too dazed to obey. So he and Grainger waited, silent, as footsteps came toward them.

Though Hutch had seen Straw on campus at Duke for a basketball game a month ago, there was always a welcome jolt in running across him in person and seeing how little his excellent face and body had changed in the forty years since he was Hutch's student in prep school in Virginia—Hutch's first real job and his first strong taste of what seemed love at its full hot tilt. And here, for all of Grainger's news about Wade, Hutch stood up smiling to shake Straw's hand—an enormous hand that always engulfed you a second longer than you intended and, above it, the nearly black eyes that would have looked natural in the face of a hurtling Mongol rider.

They were set, a little slant, in a head as strong and encouraging to see as any antique head of a grown man—the Dying Gaul or Augustus Caesar in the prime of power, a face you'd follow through narrow straits. Hutch had lasted well enough too, but he always had to remind himself that Straw was only seven years younger—fifty-six years old and tanned by bourbon like a well-cured hide yet untouched at the core by the years he'd breasted.

Straw let go of Hutch's hand and turned to Grainger. "How long's he been here?"

Grainger said "Time don't mean nothing to me. You ask him." He hooked an enormous thumb toward Hutch.

Hutch went to his chair; but since there was no seat for Straw but the floor or Grainger's bed, he stood and faced Straw. "I've still got some of my faculties intact—I can estimate I got here twenty minutes ago. You charging parking time in the drive?" Hutch was only half joking; something was wrong here. Was Straw on the verge of one of his drunks (they'd grown increasingly rare in recent years but could still throw him badly for weeks at a time), or had Grainger let Straw know about Wade?

Straw said "Oh no, I'm just guarding Mr. Walters. He promised he'd rest all afternoon so we wouldn't wear him out tonight."

Hutch looked to Grainger and could see no sign of impatience or fatigue. But he also reminded himself he could see no adequate sign that this live body had lasted one year more than a century.

Grainger lifted a hand for quiet. "Old Mrs. Joe Kennedy—Miss Rose Fitzgerald, you know, the President's mother? She just turned a hundred and three, going strong up yonder on the Cape Cod beach. Nobody tells *her* when to sleep or wake."

Straw was suddenly as peaceful as the boy he'd been when Hutch first knew him, before the first drunk. He said to Grainger "Well, Hutchins and I aren't President yet and you're no rose. Emily's up at the house now cooking the party. It's the size of a circus and headed your way. So Hutch and I plan to find beds and lie down to rest up for it. Let's stretch you out for a little nap too." Straw went to the old man and took his elbow to help him rise.

Grainger shook Straw off and pressed his stand button.

Hutch went to the other side to help Straw guide the frail bones to bed.

But once the chair had stood him upright, Grainger held in place to loosen his collar—the pearly button; he never wore a tie. Then on his own he moved to the bed with no sign of age but a kind of dream slowness like fleeing in a nightmare with no hope of rescue.

First Grainger sat on the edge of the bed, then laid his head back and drew up his legs. Only then did he ask for help. "Strawson, take my shoes off."

Straw untied the clean black brogans and slipped them off. Beneath them the feet were in high thick cotton socks, spotlessly white.

Grainger said "Hutchins, help smooth out my pants."

Hutch arranged the khaki pants along and around the legs they covered—smoothing wrinkles, straightening creases.

The old man's eyes were shut by then, the eyeballs big as pullet eggs through the thin tan lids. He hooked his thumbs in the waist of his pants. "Now both of you cover my feet. I'm cold."

Straw looked to Hutch; both silently grinned and together unfolded the green summer blanket and laid it over the legs, to the knees.

They were shutting the door when Grainger said "Too mean to die."

As Hutch glanced back, he met the opalescent eyes, open on him again.

Grainger told Hutch "I'm talking about nothing but me. Nobody you know."

Hutch said "I've known you every day of my life." It was literally true and he had clear memories from as early as two and three years old of this same soul here.

But the old eyes shut again. "That's what you think. Live on in the dark." Grainger gave a rough grumble and waved the boys off—two tall men in late midlife, whose ages combined exceeded his by a mere eighteen years. Before they'd both got down his front steps, he was gone in sleep, entirely serene.

4

Outside Hutch turned toward the main house. A nap might not be a bad idea, or an hour alone in deep country quiet.

Straw, though, had turned left toward the pine woods. From a hundred yards' distance, the trees were so dense they looked more like a bulwark than trees, some old fortification abandoned but guarding still its forgotten cause. When Hutch didn't follow, Straw looked back. "We need a short walk."

Hutch fell in five yards behind him. They didn't make a sound between them till they were deep enough in the pines for all other signs of human life to be screened out so thickly that civilization seemed denied. Hutch thought he and Straw might have been air-dropped on an island owned by nothing but evergreens, a brown bird or two and the dark gray owl they startled awake (it flew ahead like a spirit guide in an Indian tale).

He and Straw were in sight of a small clearing with a single white-barked sycamore before Hutch knew he was being led down the same dry path they'd taken thirty-seven years ago after they'd buried Rob, Hutch's father, and Straw had flunked out of Washington and Lee in his first semester and moved here with Grainger while Hutch went back to England to finish his graduate study. Hutch even spoke out now. "You picking this same old trail on purpose?"

Straw never turned. "What trail?"

"The one we took in '56 when I flew back from Rome for Rob's funeral."

Straw said "Sure, since you noticed, I *did*. Walk on a short way."

The leafy ground began a slow decline toward the valley, and step by step Hutch could barely believe the near-silent show of early spring fullness. There were spry red cardinals every few yards. At his feet there were frequent blooms of a shape and color he'd never seen, and overhead there were glimpses of a sky so blue it seemed to be working to match the pleasure he'd felt today on the road. But what kept slamming against Hutch's eyes was not this masterful calm unfolding—a natural life indifferent to him and all his kind, proceeding along its immortal rails—but the new raw idea of his son's face, blind with all its other punishments, if Grainger was right. And what Hutch asked himself every step was *What am I doing on a sightseeing hike five hundred miles from my only child, who needs me whether he'll say so or not?*

After the better part of a mile, Straw pushed on faster ahead, then stopped with his back toward Hutch and waited stock-still.

Hutch came on and stopped in reach of Straw. Only then did he realize they'd come to a place he'd never seen, not in the childhood years he'd roamed these woods alone or with Rob or Grainger. Fifty yards downhill from where he and Straw stood, a wide creek ran in banks so even and clean that the whole scene looked man-made and tended.

The bed of the creek was deep and apparently clear of rocks; but hundreds of rocks in every shade of brown and white paved the banks and made a thick border, far as Hutch could see, to left and right. In broad clumps, scattered among the boulders, were flowers a foot high—a bright egg-yellow. *Late wild jonquils maybe?*

The scene was admirable but a little funny. It had the look of an accidental stretch of city park, spliced in here and lost. Hutch looked to Straw to check

for signals. Was he meant to laugh at the incongruities or praise whoever had
curbed raw nature into this tame stretch?

Straw's eyes brimmed tears, though none had yet fallen.

Hutch said "It's handsome. Who do we thank?"

"Grainger."

"Grainger gets down here to tend all this?"

Straw hadn't faced Hutch, but he knuckled at his eyes and sat on the dry
ground. "Grainger spent most of his spare time, twenty-odd years ago, making this place right. He'd sometimes be down here in the near-dark, hauling
rocks till I'd come down and make him quit."

"What was he planning?"

Straw said "He never told me and I never asked. You know me—I leave
people to their own designs."

"But somebody's keeping it up, I can see—not Emily surely?"

Straw said "Emily doesn't know it's here. Hell, Em doesn't know we live
in the country, not for all the looking around she's done. Never walks an inch
beyond the garden. No, I keep this place up, after every big storm—pull on
my hipboots and gouge it out again. I put in a hundred new bulbs last
winter; every one of them lived. I take pictures of it for Grainger to see—he
hasn't been down here for, oh, eighteen years."

Hutch had also sat and by now the sight looked more appropriate. The
water even sounded pure and free-flowing from some intentionally guarded
source way uphill from here. "Why do you think he did it, back here where
nobody much would see?"

Straw finally faced Hutch; his eyes had a trace of their old ferocity—eyes
you might see as your last sight before violent death. But his voice was low
and steady on. "Mr. Walters told me, flat-out plain, the day he finished. He'd
asked me, weeks before, to leave him be—just let him work down here alone.
But finally late one fall afternoon, he quietly found me when Em was in
town. He led me to this spot, sat me down and said 'It's all I can leave you,
Strawson.' I begged his pardon; I didn't understand. So he tried again. He
laughed a long time—he'd almost quit laughing, even back then—and he
said 'Your *inheritance*. My deathbed gift. Keep it clean in my memory.' I
thanked him and then said 'You killing yourself some evening soon?'

"He picked that over in his mind and laughed again. 'It hasn't come to me
that directly, no. Very few black people kill themselves—you noticed that?—
not with razors or guns, not fast anyhow. No, I'm just thinking I'm past eighty
years old. The Bible doesn't promise but three score and ten; and very few
of my family, black or pink, lived nearly that long.' So I told him I was sure
we'd celebrate his hundredth together. He said he partly hoped I was right.

Then he never mentioned the place again—never came back down here, not to my knowledge; never asks me one word about it, even when I show him the pictures I take."

Hutch owned all the land they'd crossed to get here; he owned this valley. Years back he'd tried to give it to Straw when Straw's daughter was born, an only child. But Straw had said he didn't want to "lay up treasure"; instead, let him keep on supervising the Negro tenant who worked the tobacco and running the place on straight half-shares (Straw had money from his own dead mother). So Hutch thanked Straw for tending Grainger's peculiar improvement.

And Straw agreed as solemnly as if they'd concluded a treaty exchanging some isthmus or bridge.

Hutch couldn't help smiling. "Hell, we may have the core of a gold mine on our hands—buy the rest of the county, clear-cut all the trees, build a cinderblock music hall for tacky stars from Las Vegas and Nashville, run a paved road back here, build parking lots, lure in busloads of senior citizens; and I'll sell tickets when I retire. That'll be any day."

For a moment, as he generally did, Straw took the idea seriously. Then his mouth seemed to fill with bile; he turned aside to spit. When he spoke to Hutch's eyes, it came straight as a tracer. "I can *see* what you've turned into, friend. You can thank your Jesus that Wade is blind; he won't have to watch."

Hutch actually thought *Nothing anyone's said till now in my life was harder than that.* In another ten seconds it still felt true. Hutch still hadn't smelt any liquor on Straw; he couldn't recall an offensive word he'd said to Straw in two decades (it had been twenty years since he'd criticized Emily for her Puritan-mother primness and jealousy). Had some postponed toll for years of self-loathing come down on Straw and poisoned him bad enough to flush hate from him—not only hate but unearned nonsense, however well phrased? *What does he see I've turned into?*

Hutch thought through that before he registered Straw's main news. *Straw knows about Wade. So Grainger's told him.* Hutch had known since Christmas that Wade still phoned Grainger every few weeks, but he'd had no inkling that Grainger knew about the plague and its symptoms. And he'd never asked Grainger to keep anything he knew about Wade from Straw and Emily. Hutch himself, though, had kept it from Straw and everyone else except his own ex-wife—Wade's mother Ann. Ann had been on her own for more than a year since leaving Hutch when she passed sixty-one.

Straw said "You don't deserve that from me." He knocked a fist on Hutch's shin.

Hutch waited, thanked him but then said "What have I turned into?"

Straw looked him over thoroughly again, shook his head in honest bafflement and said "Can we talk about Wade instead? We might help him."

"What don't you know?"

Straw said "How long have you known Wade's sick?"

"Since late last summer, eight or nine months."

"Did Wade tell you outright or call his mother first?"

Hutch thought *Might have known Straw would go for the quick*. He
almost laughed. "Wade came for a visit two winters ago. I hadn't quite
guessed what Ann had in mind, and I doubt Wade knew before he arrived,
but Ann had her own plans cooking by then. She was already hunting modest quarters to start her 'lunge at self-reliance'—honest to God, she was calling it that. So sometime during that three-day visit, she brought young
Wade in on her thrilling secret, and he helped her find the place she's
rented out toward Hillsborough on Pleasant Green Road.

"Sometime on that same visit, Wade told her his trouble—by then he'd
only had minor infections—and asked if he could count on coming home
when he got bad. According to Ann, Wade asked if she could stand to move
back in with me long enough to see him through to his own end, if the end-
time came and he needed help? You know how Wade had shied off visits this
far south in recent years, how he'd barely see us when we went to New York
and then nowhere but in public restaurants or dark theaters—he and his
super-Afro friend."

Straw said "Wyatt Bondurant?"

"None other, the scourge of pink Caucasians. Anyhow, back to my sad
story—Ann's squatty little self-reliant house can barely hold her and her big
designs on self-improvement, much less a man at least as sick as anybody left
on Earth. But Ann told Wade she'd give all she had; she couldn't speak for
me—he must ask me himself. For whatever reasons, though, Wade left
without asking me; and Ann didn't mention one word of his trouble till after
she'd been on her own for long months.

"Then she called me one evening and asked to come by on the pretext
of bringing me some jackass gadget she'd bought for my kitchen. In fifteen
minutes she backed up that great truckload of sadness and poured it on me.
Till then I'd got fairly used to the idea that Wade's friend Wyatt had turned
him against us. But hearing that my son couldn't trust me with the news of
his death—and hearing it from Ann in the midst of this skit she's waltzing
through—well, it put an even harder freeze on our dealings, Wade's and
mine." If Hutch had more to tell, it failed him.

Straw said "So Wade is at the point of death in New York City, alone as
any street-corner psycho, because you and Ann are peeved with each other?"

"That's likely to be a small piece of it, yes. It may be part of why he won't take my phone calls."

"Forget the damned phone, Hutch. *Walk* to New York, if that's what it takes."

"I've thought this through a billion times—Wade's still a grown man, Straw. I don't have the right."

Straw said "Pardon me but I fail to comprehend how any quibble about your rights can be strong enough to keep a man, kind as you've been in your best days, from a son in a pit as low as this?"

Hutch was too full to speak.

Straw said "Set me straight on a few things here—Wade is not a junkie, right?"

"Don't cheapen this."

"Don't worry; I'm not. I'm exercising my rights as I see fit. You may have forgot but I remember, clear as this minute, standing by Wade when he was an infant at the christening font and swearing to be his faithful godfather."

Hutch shut his eyes and agreed. He could see it plain as Straw.

"Last time I looked, Wade wasn't a needle-drug addict. He's sure-God not hemophiliac."

Hutch said "No, Wade would barely take aspirin till this came on him."

Straw's voice was like a voice that has reached the last conclusion available to humans, that exhausted and mild—"What other brands of adult catch this plague?" When Hutch stood silent, Straw stated his finding. "So Wade is queer." It was far from a question.

Hutch faced him; their eyes were no more than three feet apart.

Straw could watch you for hours on end and not blink once; he was steady-eyed here.

Hutch said "That's an admirably educated guess."

"It's the truth, mean as barbed wire; it's been the truth since before Wade finished grade school surely."

Hutch said "I doubt it was early as that; recall he loved more than one fine girl." He paused, then mutely agreed to Straw's finding. *All right, we've both known it always.* But he and Straw had never so much as broached it between them, not till today.

"Is there some kind of freeze-dried Baptist hypocrite hid down in your soul and holding you back from Wade Mayfield at the edge of his grave?"

Hutch said "Not to my knowledge, no. I was never a Baptist, as you'd remember if you honored our past. If any one of your friends has loved pleasure, it's surely been me—taking *and* giving." Hutch paused and met Straw's unbroken stare. "I'd have thought you remembered. God knows, I seldom forgot our times."

Straw watched Hutch again for a long quiet minute. Except for handshakes, no parts of their bodies had touched in nearly four decades. And for Straw that had never seemed a real deprivation, despite their pleasure. Now though, this close to Hutch's body, Straw saw again how well made his friend was, how nearly his face had refused to age and how his eyes had only strengthened in both directions—Hutch drank in the world and sent it back out; something in his eyes always said *Come. There's a better place here, an actual dream.*

Straw asked himself now why he'd stopped answering. He broke his gaze and looked down to Grainger's all-but-maniacal water park below them. Then a memory he'd lost came back. "You remember Wade nearly drowned, right there." Straw pointed to the central pool of the cleaned stretch.

Hutch said "Lord, no." They'd kept it from him. "When was it? Who saved him?"

Straw thought Grainger's name and recalled the event. But all that past suddenly seemed meaningless against the pressing weight of now. He faced Hutch and said the unavoidable thing. "Let me drive you to New York tonight. We can bring Wade back. He'll listen to me." Straw suddenly drew back and flung a small white flint, an arrowhead he'd found underfoot. It missed every tree between them and the valley and thunked down in the midst of the creek.

Shocked as he was, Hutch at least turned the idea over. *Wade tonight? Would he so much as answer the door, much less join them?* At first Hutch could only think to ask "Where would he stay? I'm teaching straight through till the end of the month."

"There's Duke Hospital, for an obvious start. There's his mother in her house, ready to serve. Emily wouldn't object to Wade being here; I'll take him on gladly."

Hutch said "He won't move."

Straw waited through half a long minute. Then he said "Christ, do you love your son or not?"

"Friend, I honest to God don't know," but by then Hutch's own eyes had watered, and the sound of the words was criminal nonsense. The total weight of the postponed fact that Wade Mayfield was dying blind five hundred miles north, the only thing Hutch had expected to last of all he'd had a part in making except a few poems, the only human he'd loved with no real reservation since his own father died—that whole weight caved in on him here. All over his body under the clothes, his actual skin begged to be held and touched. Hutch had waited too long, much more than a year, since any welcome hand had touched him. Now though, he couldn't ask or reach out for touch. So he stood, looked down to the creek a last time, then turned and headed back toward his car—the main house, the car, the road, wherever.

Straw called out "Answer yourself soon, boy. You've got to know"—know whether Hutch truly loved Wade or not. It didn't feel like a cruel question to Straw.

Hutch failed to answer though, failed to look back. And soon he was almost out of sight before Straw fell in behind him and followed. Straw made no effort to overtake Hutch; and when they were out of the woods into day-light, Straw paused at Grainger's to check on his nap while Hutch walked straight to the main house, the upstairs room that was always his on overnight visits.

5

An hour later Straw had already gone on to Grainger's with most of the meal, so Hutch and Emily came down the high back steps with only a tray of the last hot dishes and a box with the gifts. In the short walk Emily said, out of the blue, "Hutch, we're heartbroken for all your family."

If she'd flung off her darkish old-maid clothes and thrown herself on him, Hutch could hardly have felt a stranger surprise. In thirty years Emily had said very little to him that an unbiased witness might have called warm or generous. And it took Hutch a few yards of silent walking before he could say "Em, it's awful. Thank you."

"Whatever we can do, whatever on Earth—"

Have she and Straw huddled on some plan to bring Wade here and see him through to whatever end? Have they told it to Wade and has he agreed? It was hardly the worst thing that might happen next, but the thought of shouldering what was his duty onto others here—even onto Strawson who truly was Wade's godfather and had loved him—was painful for Hutch and scraped on his sense of failing to tend the single person alive who had full claim on his care. He shocked himself by saying "Strawson just mentioned us going to see Wade—him and me, soon."

Emily's small white face burned a kind of fervor that Hutch hadn't seen since the early days when she'd tear into him and fight for her share of Straw's time and notice. "Strawson very much wants to go with you, I know."

"Since when, Emily?"

She paused to answer carefully. "I think it was two nights ago, maybe three—Strawson came back up to the house from Grainger's and said the old fellow had made him call Wade."

"Straw talked to Wade a few days ago?"

"I thought Strawson told you—"

They were in earshot of Grainger's door; it was open again. Hutch quietly said "Straw's barely told me he's alive, not for some years." He thought it would please her.

But again she surprised him. "You're the only person, alive or dead, that I've never heard Strawson low-rate or laugh at or slash to ribbons."

"He's known a lot of people."

"In the Biblical sense." Still Em's face was showing a life it had seldom showed, a fined-down purpose that could drill through rock. "I well know people have lined Strawson's road; but I've told you the truth, Hutch, the bare-knuckle truth. I thought you were in the business of truth—teaching school, writing poems."

By then they'd arrived at Grainger's front steps, and Emily had climbed the first one before Hutch touched her elbow to stop her. When she turned, he said "I needed reminding." His eyes were not cutting.

And she understood that. She also knew it was as near to thanks as she'd get from Hutch Mayfield. She shut her eyes, ducked her chin, then raised her voice and called "Mr. Grainger, we're all here with you."

Hutch wondered since when she'd called Grainger *Mister.*

Inside Grainger said "Stop where you are."

Straw's voice laughed. "Easy, Mr. Walters. We know them both. They're bringing provisions. Just let them unload."

Inside, when the screen door shut behind them, Hutch saw that Grainger had changed his clothes—a starched white shirt and gray wash pants with sharp creases, the small gold eagle-pin he'd found and polished not long ago (some relic of his infantry service in France in 1918). *Can he dress himself; does Strawson help him?* Again Hutch felt accused of failure—this old man was literally his nearest live cousin, of whatever color. Grainger had been as strong a prop to Hutch's childhood as anyone, alive or dead—as watchful, honest and guard-dog loyal. *I should come on up here, soon as class ends, and stay till he dies.*

But the clear fact was, Straw and Emily had been far closer to the old man than Hutch for decades. They'd lived with him daily throughout their marriage; they'd worked beside him as long as he could work; and they'd brought him up to the main house and nursed him through double pneumonia just last winter, not to speak of a hundred daily attentions. Hutch moved toward

Grainger, gathered the long bird-bones of his shoulders into an embrace and said "I owe most of my life to you."

Grainger whispered slowly at Hutch's ear. "Colored men bearing down on you tonight, big knives in their fist. Haul out of here now." It was said in urgent indelible conviction.

Hutch stepped back but said "I think we've got a little time. Let's eat Em's supper."

If that assurance meant anything to Grainger, he gave no sign. His eyes were still urging Hutch toward the door.

By then Straw and Emily had slid the table out from the wall, set the extra chairs that Straw had brought and spread the food. There was a good-sized roasted turkey breast with dressing, baked yams in their skins, macaroni and cheese, home-canned green beans, fresh biscuits, corn chowchow, a pitcher of milk and a bottle of good California red wine. Straw guided Grainger to his place at the head, assigned the right-hand chair to Hutch, the left chair to Emily and the foot to himself.

Then Hutch said "Old cousin, you bless it."

Grainger looked as distant as the outskirts of Cairo, not confused but gone.

Straw said "Mr. Walters has pretty much quit on the Lord Above. You bless it, Hutch."

Hutch had likewise been far less than observant since he gave up on all known Christian institutions during the boiling acid and blood of racial integration in the South, when the churches behaved at least as abominably as the Klan (a good deal more so; the churches knew better). But after a short pause now, he said "Thanks for the three of you and this much food. Thanks above everything for Grainger Walters' life that has given us such long care and that goes on among us. Watch everyone we love who's not here with us." Only at the end did Hutch realize he'd addressed his blessing more to Strawson than God.

But eventually Emily said an "Amen," then began to serve Grainger's plate a heaping plenty. If she knew what she was doing, then his appetite was healthy.

And once he had the food before him, Grainger set in at once to salt it heavily and slice the turkey into minute cubes. Then he ate it, not stopping, the way they'd all seen him eat for years. He'd neatly consume a particular item till it was exhausted—the beans, the bread—then move to another, around his plate clockwise. With each new item he'd fix his eyes on one of the three white table partners. He showed no detectable smile or frown to any of them. Maybe he couldn't see them at all but watched some memory from his long supply; but he never spoke, even when he turned to his tall glass of wine and downed it slowly in an unbroken swallow.

The others ate Emily's likable cooking in normal ways and traded the all but meaningless remarks of longstanding friends; but though the three of them kept mild faces, their separate minds were circling tightly.

Straw thought of nothing but Wade—alone, he guessed, in a city where no strong man should live, much less a godson with the worst disease since white men sold smallpox-ridden blankets to American Indians and wiped out whole tribes, no trace left, not even their language. Straw's own child—a textbook editor now in Georgia, pleasant to see and as cold as a bottle—was as far from his mind as the strangers of Asia.

Emily thought *Someway I'll wind up with Wade on my hands. My hands are full. How in God's name can I hold on to more?* None of that was just mean-minded; with all her fears, she'd kept a decent heart alive in her.

Hutch thought almost entirely of Grainger. Whatever secret personal things this old man had been throughout his own life, he sat here tonight for Hutch as a relic of more than a century of his own family's unfillable hunger—its adamant aim to survive and print its demands on a line of faces called Mayfield, Drewry, Kendal, Gatlin and whatever part-black Walters kin lived on from Hutch's white great-grandfather who'd wasted no chance to pass his traits down whatever human route would give him hot entrance.

Only for a moment did Hutch let himself think that—with Grainger barren of any offspring and Hutch's own son racing toward death now with no more leavings than the memory of pleasure in a few young men as barren as Wade—then one long line of bold contenders from one patch of ground was fading and sinking to Earth at last.

And though all the others assumed that Grainger was either asleep, upright in his chair, or had wandered into some thicket of memory, it was simply a fact that none of them except Grainger Walters—in their thoughts here now—had moved on into fresh knowledge and hope. Since a year ago when television brought him the ghetto riots from Los Angeles—whole days and nights of fire and pillage by young black men—Grainger's mind had frequently called up memories he'd heard in childhood from his slave-born great-great-great-grandmother Veenie.

Veenie had been born around 1820 in southeast Virginia and was halfway grown when a preacher named Turner led his short revolt of a few black men that managed to kill some fifty white people in the summer of 1831. Veenie had even told Grainger she'd stood not twenty yards from the scaffold and watched Turner hanged in the county seat when she'd been sent to town for one spool of thread. And somewhere in his trunk in this room, Grainger still had the buckeye—the dry horse chestnut—that Veenie had found near Nat's swinging corpse as she left the sight that morning and walked to the master's kitchen where she worked every day from sunrise to bedtime. That much pain and iron endurance had come and gone in the live presence of a woman Grainger had loved and leaned on, not fifty miles from where he sat tonight with three white people he'd worked to serve, one of whom was his cousin. Yet Veenie's cold blood, thick as a dragon's, crept through him tonight.

So the mixture of those two ominous thoughts—the California riots and old Veenie's memories—had preyed on Grainger ever since; and lately he'd spent long hours each day, and many whole nights, in the vivid certainty that wholesale righteous dreadful slaughter waited for every soul he'd cared about, live and dead (he specifically thought that the dead, white and black, would also rise at the Judgment with their strength renewed and turn on one another with pitchforks, butchering axes and hand-forged knives). And none of it worried him all that much since, in his mind, Grainger likewise knew he had enough Negro blood in his veins (he was more than half black) to be permitted to save two souls when the gore streamed at last. He'd long since chosen the two he'd rescue—his dead wife Gracie, who'd abandoned him many years ago, and one young white man that sometimes (now in Grainger's shifting mind) wore the face of Rob Mayfield, then Hutch's own face and sometimes Straw's, then Wade's face the way it had looked in childhood: clear as a clean plate with two keen eyes, not bone-thin and blind, which it must be now.

The other thing that wove through Grainger's mind as he sat at the head of this bountiful table was a line of numbers he tried to recall—1-1-2-2 something-5-8-9-9. He barely knew it was Wade's phone number his mind was hunting; but he finally thought it was urgent to ask for somebody's help, whoever these people here might be—he was no longer sure. So he reached for the fork on his empty plate and rapped the plate hard.

Straw said "You don't plan to eat more tonight, Mr. Walters? We'll be up till day."

Grainger ignored him but looked to Emily and said "Tell me what this number means." This time he could only say "1-1-something," then "9-9-9."

Emily went blank.

Even Straw was stumped.

Hutch quietly said "He's working on Wade's telephone number." Then he said the whole number clearly toward Grainger. "Wade's telephone number in New York City is 212-732-5899. You want to call Wade?"

Emily gently said "No—"

Strawson said "Let Mr. Walters say. It's his damned party; he's got his own plans."

But Grainger's eyes had shut down firmly. He might very well have been dead upright.

And Hutch took the possibility seriously. He reached out, turned Grainger's wrist and held two fingers against the skin that was dry as any adder's. It was chill to the touch, and at first Hutch could find no pulse or motion. But he lightened his pressure till, finally, there seemed to be the wide-spaced thud of ongoing life. He moved his fingers to Grainger's neck, the hollow below the back of his jaw. There Hutch could sense an actual beat, still faint and slow.

Emily whispered "The wine was too much for him, this late."

Straw said "He fades off like this a lot." When Hutch had taken his own hand back, Straw said "Mr. Walters, we've got this cake to eat."

Emily said "He can have cake anytime. Let's put him to bed."

Straw said "He's fine, just playing possum."

Hutch said "First possum to live past a hundred. Let's lay him down."

But though he spoke gently, Straw insisted on his own rights. "I want to remember this night; get the cake." He'd drunk more than half the bottle of wine, though he showed no sign of more than his daily heat and focus.

Through the screen Hutch saw that the night was almost on them, and the air had turned cooler than he'd expected. He'd already seen Straw's camera by the door; so he said "Take a picture if you want to now, but I doubt we'll need reminders of this."

Grainger said "I don't show up on film no more." Then he actually laughed, the first time in three years. His eyes stayed shut another long moment; then Grainger looked to Emily. "Em, let's light us a bonfire and eat it."

At first nobody quite understood; then Emily realized he meant the cake. "I just put one candle on your cake, Mr. Grainger. Last year you started over on your age."

Straw laughed. "Last year we nearly had our own firestorm."

Emily stood and went to the kitchen counter, lit the one green candle and brought the cake forward—the caramel cake that Grainger had asked for, rich as any oil billionaire and made by a half-cracked widow down the road. Emily waited for Hutch or Strawson to sing; but though they faced her, they both stayed quiet.

So Grainger said "Everybody's too old to sing but me" and croaked his way through a curious version of the first line of "Happy Birthday." Then he went mute again to eat the sizable slice Emily gave him. And when Straw stood to bring on the presents, Grainger only said "I don't need a thing cash money can buy" and held out his long raised palm to Straw.

Straw set the three boxes back by the door. "You'll enjoy them tomorrow." The contents were socks and a pair of red suspenders and, from Hutch, a framed photograph of his mother—Hutch's own mother Rachel, whom Grainger had known and helped years back. Till now she'd been absent from Grainger's wall of pictures; her death, in childbed, had pained him too hard.

To that point Straw had seemed cold sober, his alert best self. But when Grainger balked him from giving the gifts, Straw's face had gone slack. Then every cell around his eyes and mouth had crouched.

Hutch thought *He's about to say something else mean.*

But what Straw did was stand up soberly and go to Grainger's bed. He sat on the near edge, took up the phone and punched in eleven digits slowly.

If Grainger understood, he sat very still and thought *I was right. Here comes what I dread.*

Emily guessed at once what Straw was attempting.

Strangely it didn't dawn on Hutch. He was watching Grainger again, that lordly face, taking the sight of it back to his own first memories.

When they'd put the phone out here a few years ago, they'd hooked it up with a twenty-foot cord so Grainger could call for help from anywhere. Now Straw walked with the white receiver toward the table; and a moment after he stood by the old man, the number answered. Straw quietly said "Wade, did I wake you up?" Then, with waits, Straw said "We're all down here for this big event" and "I'm glad to hear it" and "Tell it to Grainger." Straw put the receiver against Grainger's left ear.

Grainger's hand didn't come up to hold it, but he seemed to listen for half a minute. What he finally said was "You can't see me." Wade must have answered something like "No, not on the phone" since Grainger said "Here now in this room. You're looking right at me but I'm all gone." If Wade was still there, he either said nothing or launched a monologue—Grainger said nothing else.

So Straw took the receiver back.

But Grainger's hand came up and seized it. He said to Wade "Just do this for me." Then he leaned to hold out the phone to Hutch, to give him this chance.

It didn't startle Hutch or rile him. It was plainly as much a piece of this day as the ancient life that was still beside him in Grainger's body, a part of the course that Hutch had always understood to be laid down before him, a step or two ahead of his feet. He said "Evening, Son."

"Evening sir." Wade sounded younger, by maybe ten years, than the last time they'd talked.

"I've missed your voice."

Skittish as Wade's mind had got in recent days, he'd thought of such a moment for months. A great run of stored scalding words waited in him. But he held himself back enough to say only "I've missed a lot more than your voice, believe me."

Grainger was still in his chair, watching Hutch. His eyes hadn't blinked in maybe two minutes.

Emily and Straw were in the kitchen, scraping plates.

That near to Grainger—and all Grainger signified of their shared family's reckless waste—Hutch was suddenly free to say to his child "When can I see you?" It felt like the first words ever between them.

And Wade's voice was still young and hard as a child's. "I can't see you."

Hutch thought he referred to the blindness Grainger and Straw had mentioned. "I've heard about that. I'll help all I can."

But Wade had intended a bigger refusal—he couldn't imagine the sight of his father, after what had passed between them in recent years. He said "I've got all the help I can use."

"That much relieves me. But I'd still value the chance to see you. I finish classes in three more weeks."

Wade seemed to be gone—the wait was that long. Then a voice that was almost certainly his, though younger still, said "What if I told you to come here right now—by dawn at the latest?"

Hutch said "I'd start driving."

"Tomorrow?"

"Tonight."

Wade took a real wait. "How long could you stay?"

"Long as you need me, Son."

"You just said you had three more weeks of class."

"I'll get a stand-in; that's my least concern. You say what you want."

Wade drew a long breath but couldn't speak.

"Some friend's there with you tonight, I trust?"

Another pained wait, then finally Wade said "I'm by myself."

"For how long?"

"Another few minutes, maybe an hour."

"Wyatt's still with you, right?" Wyatt had been Wade's companion for nine years; he'd quickly become the main obstruction, and then an all but impassable wall between Hutch and Wade.

Wade said "Not Wyatt."

"He's left?"

"He's dead." On its own, Wade's voice made a high rough cry like a wail on the TV news from Palestine.

Hutch thought *Thank God* but he said "Oh no. I thought he wasn't sick at all."

"Wyatt shot himself, downstairs, out on the street—February 18th."

At first Hutch could only think *Has Ann known this and not told me?* But he knew not to ask it. *Keep pushing on.* So he said it again another way. "Wade, you're not all alone there, are you—not in the night?"

"My neighbor checks in twice a day and runs errands for me. A man from the AIDS center comes every morning. I haven't seen a doctor in weeks, haven't needed to—thank Christ for that."

"But you're blind, they say."

"Did Grainger tell you? I asked him not to."

Hutch said "He's here beside me right this minute. We've eaten his birthday cake, and it's past his bedtime by hours." Hutch could see that Grainger's eyes had shut and his head had drifted down onto his chest.

In the kitchen Straw and Emily were quiet, clearly waiting on Hutch to end the call.

Hutch was so overloaded with feelings, he could hardly think. "Son, we need to let Grainger lie down. Can I call you back in half an hour?"

"No, professor. I need to get quiet."

"Then I'll be there tomorrow."

"No. Leave me *alone*, Hutch." Wade had called Hutch *Father* all his life till today.

Hutch heard the change and thought it was hopeful. He said "I'll call you back in a little. If you don't want to talk, don't answer the phone."

But Wade was gone—had he heard the last words?

Hutch called his name again once, then rose and replaced the phone.

By the time Hutch turned back toward Grainger's chair, Straw was leaning to the old man's ear. "Sleepy time down South."

Grainger didn't respond; his head stayed limp on his chest, no sound.

For whatever cause, Hutch felt again the rush of strong pleasure—was it pleasure or a strain of panic, he wondered?—and he thought *Let him go.* It was Grainger he meant—let him go on now to death and eventual rest, at the end of this night when the old man had flung what might be a bridge between father and son, both frozen in silence till this full night.

Straw already had Grainger out on the bed. Hutch watched him unbutton the collar button, the cuffs of the starched shirt; then as Straw moved lightly to loosen the belt, Hutch untied the high-topped shoes and shucked them, then laid the blanket back on the old man, foot to chin (Grainger often spent whole nights in his day clothes).

Grainger said to the air in general "I told you they're coming with sickles, cutting a road, but nobody heard me." He was gone then, asleep, not ready to die; or death was not yet ready to take him—no one else ever had or would.

When Hutch followed Straw down the steps, he walked a little behind in hopes of a quiet few minutes to print on his mind that last sight of Grainger. He might well see him tomorrow morning before he left—he might be leaving tonight if Wade said "Come on" again—but Hutch understood that, once he'd spread that blanket up three minutes ago, he'd made his final try at thanking a man: an openhanded unsparing kinsman, whom he'd never see matched in this world again.

The mold was as long gone as whatever mold made the architect of the Great Wall of China, the goldsmith who beat out the pure death mask for Tutankhamen's withered face; as gone as the captain of the last clandestine slave ship that worked the south Atlantic in the girlhood of Grainger's great-great-great-grandmother and who still plowed on through the old man's mind, though powerless to appall him now.

At the foot of the steps to the main house kitchen, Straw turned and saw Hutch lingering in the dark yard. Straw spoke out clearly. "Take the air you need. I'll be inside. Call for me if you need me. I'll ride to Mars if you need me that far."

Hutch bowed his head and waved and stayed by the big oak, seated against it, looking back through his blind son's life to the days when they'd run around this same tree—Wade in the years before he was twelve, Hutch in his thirties, both flung by love like hawks by a storm.

6

It was past nine o'clock and fully dark before Hutch entered the main house and climbed to his bedroom on the second floor. It was the space he'd occupied when he lived with his father Rob in the country—usefully lonely adolescent years with a man more likable than most, though one who was apt to cause frequent pain, and with Grainger beside them much of the time. Straw and Emily, for thirty-odd years, had used Rob's old bedroom downstairs. It was directly under Hutch's; but though Hutch had left his door open now, he heard no sound except the normal creaks of a dry house older than Grainger.

Hutch had cleared his thoughts fairly well in the yard. He thought he understood that his forced encounter on the phone with Wade was the cause of the clairvoyant pleasure he'd felt through the day—not pleasure in a son's far-off agony but in contact restored—and Hutch had planned his next sure move. He wanted to sit here a few more minutes in a room that had sheltered much of his life, then to go back down and phone Wade again as he'd promised.

He'd repeat his offer to drive north tonight; he could be at Wade's West Side apartment by early morning and do what was called for. If Wade would agree to accept his help and come home, Hutch could simply lock the New York apartment, get Wade to the car by hook or crook and leave the chores of packing and shutting down a life till some decisive choice had been made, by death most likely. Life with a dying son in Durham would need its own plans. Hutch had a shaky confidence that somehow a path would open before him once he had the boy home.

A boy—right—thirty-two years old who had strong warnings of the danger he risked but who walked, open-eyed, into this destruction. The first need would be some reliable help, a companion or nurse. Surely Durham, a town with three huge hospitals, could offer qualified practical nurses to tide them through the last weeks of school. Then Hutch could take over full-time till the end. He'd already set his mind on the hope that Wade could die at home, the comfortable house where he'd grown up.

What will Ann try to do? Once Hutch had helped Ann move into her new life, he and she had hardly communicated except for business matters (and then mostly by letter); and—strangely, though they used the same grocery store and shared many friends—they hadn't met face-to-face in nearly ten months. Their mutual friends were not talebearers. Ann's new job kept her off the Duke campus. And Hutch had gradually managed to fill, with friends and work, what had seemed like a sucking wound when Ann spent her first night in three decades outside their marriage—outside the idea of their marriage at least; they'd of course been briefly parted by business trips. The thought of Ann tonight, with Wade's phone voice still strong in Hutch's ear, felt as distant and cool as a handsome old house seen from a fast car, trailing off in the dusk of a rearview mirror. *It's me Wade has asked for, if anybody.*

Hutch looked up, intending to head downstairs toward the nearest phone; and there stood Strawson, silent on the doorsill, both hands raised like a cornered thief. He'd changed into a dark blue polo shirt and black cotton trousers. Oddly Hutch thought *Pallbearer's clothes.*

Straw said "Don't shoot."

Hutch said "Why would I?"

"I've stood here watching you a whole long minute. I know all your thoughts."

Hutch shook his head No. "We've lived apart much too long, old friend. I'm in deep hiding." It was only halfway meant as a joke. Like everyone, Hutch overestimated his own complexity.

Straw said "You want to go get Wade tonight. You want to have all his death for yourself—you and him in a room till it's over."

"Tell me what's wrong with that."

"You well know, Hutchins."

"I wouldn't have asked you if I really knew."

Straw said "There's somebody still alive called Ann Mayfield, born Ann Gatlin—used to be your wife; gave birth to your child. Wade loves her too."

"You don't understand that Wade ordered both of us out of his life, long years ago; or so his friend Wyatt said by phone and fax and every other known means but letter bombs. Once you got Wade on the phone just now though, it was me he asked for—not his mother."

Straw said "You truly sure Wade was in his right mind?" It was not meant cruelly. Straw had read that dementia was often a late result of this plague.

"I'm going downstairs right now to call him back."

Straw said "Can I go with you?"

"Downstairs?—it's your house, friend."

"No, it's yours; I'm just the loyal tenant. I mean can I ride with you to New York?—you'll need some help."

Hutch said "No I won't."

"Hutchins, the last thing Wade Mayfield needs is a doting father dragging his pitiful body downstairs through a big apartment building and trying to navigate the eastern seaboard single-handed."

Hutch said "Look, I don't even know that I'm going. When you called Wade at Grainger's, the first thing he told me was 'Come tonight.' The longer we talked, the more he circled; then Grainger conked out. So I told Wade I'd try him one more time before bed. If he doesn't want to answer, he won't. He hasn't in months."

"Christ, Hutch, of course he'll want to answer you."

It came out of Straw with the old singeing force that had brought them together, almost as a matter of logical course, weeks after they'd met in a prep school classroom.

And it moved Hutch nearly as much as in those days—few men past sixty get bearable tributes from a trustworthy source. "Thank you, Strawson, but Wade may be exhausted."

"Wade's still got ears." Straw glanced at his watch. "It's past ten now; go call him. I'll wait here."

As Hutch pushed past him, Straw entered the room and—once he heard footsteps going down—he silently stood in the midst of the rag rug, nothing to lean on, nothing to brace him. His arms extended a little from his sides, and he tried to ask for whatever mercy was possible this late in his life, a life that he knew was littered with failure and was not done yet with small but calculated meanness. Whatever hopes or demands for payment went through Straw's mind, his body stayed perfectly still in place, though the last time he'd worshiped anything but a naked body was in his lost childhood.

Straw stood in place the best part of two minutes till at last an enormous blunt shaft of pain forced downward through him, shaking him brutally. A mute bystander might have thought this excellent man with perfect eyes was dying where he stood, bludgeoned somehow by an unseen hand. Straw, though, took it to be the only answer he'd get, the only answer he'd had in years of terse claims on God or fate; and he knew he must take the answer straight to Hutch.

7

When Straw got to the dim long kitchen, Hutch was still at the counter by the hung-up phone. It looked like a baited iron bear trap in reach of his hand. Hutch seemed alarmingly older than he had a quarter hour ago—gray and slumped. He didn't look up but at least he didn't ask Straw to leave.

Straw said "I know the number if you lost it."

"I got the number."

"Somebody else answer?"

"No, it was Wade—pretty certainly Wade. He sounded really stunned but he asked me if I'd ever lived through a dream where I couldn't find the walls or the floor, however high I flew or dived. I told him No; he waited and said 'A man I know is there this minute. Right this red minute.' Then he dropped his phone or left it off the hook—I've tried twice more and just get a busy."

Straw came a step closer and said "I'm driving you up there then."

Stunned as he was, Hutch could think of no reason to wait. "When?"

"I can leave this minute."

Hutch slowly looked around this room where he'd spent so much good time as a boy. *Any rescue here?* In fact, though the room still had its old long proportions, its old self was smothered under long years of Emily's apple-green paint, framed spurious coats of arms, stitched mottoes and furiously cheerful refrigerator decals. Apparently no rescue at all. So Hutch said "Lead the way." Then he risked facing Straw—he dreaded a collapse if he met those wholly demanding eyes. But here they were milder; and Hutch felt a little steadier, on a new pair of legs. "Many thanks, old friend."

Straw would have liked to leave it at that and hit the road, but he had to deliver the hurtful message he'd got upstairs. "First, you need to call Ann Mayfield."

At once Hutch agreed and touched the phone, but then he said "Why?"

Straw prodded him onward. "Just say I told you to do it, tonight."

"What else do I tell her?"

"You're a grown man, Hutchins. You take it from there." When Hutch made no move to pick up the phone, Straw said "What do you really want to say?"

Hutch knew right off. "I want to tell her I'm bringing our son back home to die, the home she left long months ago. Wade spent the first two-thirds of his life in a house she's abandoned; she can stay gone now."

Straw grinned. "You used to be a Christian gent."

"About ninety years back."

"Wait—ask Ann to help you. Just two or three words."

"I don't want to see Ann. Not in this life."

"She's got rights in this," Straw said. "Look at me."

Hutch actually looked at Strawson's eyes and recalled a fact that was easily forgot—Straw was the fairest referee he'd known, however crazy.

Straw told him "This is no child-custody case. A grown man's dying like shit in the road."

Hutch took up the phone and surprised himself by knowing Ann's number (he'd called no more than twice in the past year).

In twenty seconds Ann's firm voice said "Yes." Even here, its smoky resonance was sufficient warning of her steel-trap mind and her heart that had never yet trusted anyone's love for two steady hours.

Hutch said "Don't tell rank strangers 'Yes' in the night, alone as you are."

Ann was silent but she stayed on the line.

Hutch could taste her confusion and anger, so he tried to talk straight. "Ann, I don't know when you saw Wade or talked to him last, but I've had no recent news till tonight. The quick truth is, he sounds really awful; so I'm driving up there tonight to get him. I thought you should know."

"Are you at home?" Ann's voice wasn't choked but odd and uncertain.

Hutch heard her word *home* and wondered if he'd waked her. Was she drinking? Surely not. No company with her surely. Anyhow he said "I'll bring Wade back to one of my homes—I'm at Straw and Emily's; Straw's riding up with me."

Ann said "Let me speak to Strawson please."

Hutch knew she lost no love on Straw, but he held the phone toward him.

Straw refused. "Tell her No. This is your and her business entirely."

Hutch agreed, then told her "You and I'll settle this."

Ann thought she'd glimpsed the trace of a chink in the wall Hutch was already building against her. "Settle what? What's this we'll settle?"

"Wade Mayfield's death."

Ann was adamant. "You don't know he's dying."

Hutch said "This thing kills everything it touches."

"It may have looked like that till now; but Hutch, there are people who've been infected for years, some for more than a decade—I just read about them in *Time* magazine. They're somehow hanging on, doing their jobs. Don't kill Wade yet. Don't scare him to death—you know how contagious anxiety is." When Hutch kept silent, she thought *This won't sound maternal, whatever I feel*; but she went on and lightened her voice to say "I finally talked to Wade night before last; he seemed clear-headed and said not to worry." Then for the first time in many weeks, Ann lost grip on her own smothered feelings. Still she thought she managed to muffle the groan that broke from her, helpless.

Hutch heard it though. "We'll know a lot more when Wade's back home. I'll very likely need you." He hadn't foreseen he'd say that much; and for a bad instant, he thought of denying it.

But Ann said "You know I'll help, day and night."

There was only one thing left for now. Hutch lowered his voice. "You know Wyatt's dead."

"Yes, his sister wrote me."

"Wyatt had a grown sister?"

Ann said "Very grown; she writes a fine letter."

"And you didn't feel compelled to tell me our son was alone?"

Ann paused a long while. "No, Hutch, I didn't. Wade asked me not to."

"Asked you tonight?"

"In the letter—Wyatt's sister's letter."

Hutch felt a surge of revulsion that, though he'd never touched Ann in anger, might have ended in violence if they'd shared the same room. He waited it out, then could only say "I guess this means Wade is ours again." Before the words were out of his mouth, Hutch heard their strangeness. He'd always half concealed from himself his conviction that Wyatt Bondurant had shanghaied Wade Mayfield from his home and borne him off to the glaring impasse where they'd all stood wordless till tonight. Hutch had never quite said as much, even to Ann.

But Ann echoed his sudden discovery of an old sense of ownership in Wade. "Ours?—I guess."

"You say you talked with him two nights ago?"

Ann realized she'd stretched the truth. "It was probably more like a week ago. We talked fairly normally for maybe five minutes; then he hung up on me; and when I've phoned him since, nobody answers." Whatever desertion Ann had doled out to Hutch, her voice here sounded bruised with regret.

Hutch said "All right. I'm leaving for New York."

"Will you let me know exactly what happens?"

"I'll call you from there—you working tomorrow?"

Ann said "All day. I'll tell them to put your call straight through."

Hutch said "Till then."

But Ann held on and gentled her strength. "I'll go anywhere or do anything that you or Wade need."

That was one more piece of news to Hutch, so new that it almost angered him again and he almost laughed. *She won't take simple requests from God, much less her legal mate.* But the sight of Emily standing in the kitchen door made Hutch say at least "Thank you" to Ann.

When he'd hung up, Emily said "Sandwiches and coffee won't take me a minute. Strawson, find the quart thermos; then you won't need to stop." No mention of how she'd heard or guessed that Straw was in on this belated lunge.

Hutch didn't know how long Emily had stood here or what she'd heard, but she had it all right—no word to slow him or to stop Straw's going—so he thanked her too.

She went to the counter and began to slice turkey.

Then there in the midst of Rob's old kitchen—a kitchen that had served nearly two hundred years of kin and slaves, returning freedmen and the rickety children of wormy white tenants—the wall that had held grief back inside Hutch broke and fell. He gave a single cry like an animal watching its own leg torn from the socket.

Straw acknowledged the sound. "That may be all any of us can do. Let's go anyhow."

Hutch agreed and sat with Straw at the table while Emily packed food; and though Hutch tried to think of old Grainger to steady his mind, he thought *What if Grainger dies in the night?* and was briefly troubled till again, in the silence as his mind turned to Wade, a slim flow of pleasure began in his chest.

8

It had been twenty years since Hutch had actually driven to New York, longer still since he and Straw had been alone together in a car for more than ten minutes; but exhaustion swamped him in the deep night in Delaware, and Hutch had to ask Straw to take the wheel. For half an hour Hutch stayed awake, feeling a duty to keep Straw company (though they barely spoke); but as they crossed the New Jersey line, Hutch settled his head against the side window. In five seconds he was deep asleep; and after three miles—once Straw had looked toward him and silently granted his greater need for rest—this dream came to Hutch, an astonishing gift.

The moment it started, his watchful mind recognized it as fact—mere history, an accurate memory of an evening forty-four years back, the day he'd first made love to Ann. They'd met in their freshman year of college, both new students in a bonehead composition class; and though they were each as virgin as snow, they'd seriously liked each other on sight—their looks, the keen young air around them—and after a month of smaller meetings, Hutch had quietly worked toward a way they could meet entirely while the fall warmth lasted. Meet and go past the little they'd learned apart, in separate high schools with high school loves about as adventurous as day-old calves.

He'd borrowed his friend Jack Hagen's car—illegal for a freshman—and driven Ann out one Wednesday near sundown to a place he'd already scouted in the woods. They'd parked on the road, walked inward (not even holding hands) to a site as thunderous as any Hutch knew of between Carolina and the caves of Virginia—a range of granite bluffs that climbed some hundred feet above a small river with its own serene rapids. They'd drunk the bottle of cider Hutch brought, tart but unfermented, with a box of cheese crackers; and then he'd actually fallen asleep to the sound of the water, darkening below them—no sleep at all the previous night, a zoology exam. The nap was wildly unexpected and no part of his plan; he was still too green not to be overcome.

And he'd have slept hours if Ann hadn't waked him a half hour later by stroking his eyes. When Hutch looked up, she was curved above him—her face some twenty inches away. In a few more seconds of bearing that awful distance between them, it seemed a literal prohibition against life itself. Ann was that good to see, that good to smell close. He didn't reach out though; she didn't reach down (her stroking hand was back in her lap).

So Hutch did the next thing he knew to do—it boiled straight up from some old but never-used chamber of his brain, some legacy maybe from his bold grasping father. Very slowly, moving like a man in dense water, he stripped his clothes from neck to toe and stood bare beside Ann Gatlin, still seated. Hutch couldn't see it but his face, chest, arms, his groin and sex were shedding around him, like clean strong light, the only half conscious splendor of his frame, his flawless skin and the promise of his power.

Ann studied it all, grave-eyed as a girl on a Greek tombstone; then she also rose and — a whole yard from him — she followed suit with no trace of shame: a slow but determined unveiling of gifts even grander than any Hutch owned or had dared to want. The hair of her sex alone seemed both the safest thicket for hiding and rest and likewise a masterly crown of thorns, some medieval jeweler's handiwork to set on an ivory Christ in glory, back in victory from death and famished.

When Hutch reached toward her, to close the gap, they found they knew — from longing and dreams — each move to make next, each move in order, each more stunning than its previous neighbor: Paradise. In the dream, as it had in actual life, no sight had ever given Hutch more; no human being had known like Ann (that first best evening) his every hope and how to win them in smiling silence, passing them on with open hands.

And in the car, four decades onward, as Straw sped through the last of dark New Jersey, each moment of that hour — instant by instant, purified of the spite and grudging of Hutch and Ann's long months apart — rose in Hutch's starved mind again and not only gave him the useful reminder of all he'd won in better days but also smothered for actual minutes his dread of morning. Morning, Manhattan and Wade all but gone.

As a dim shine began to leak through the murk in the east toward the coast, Hutch gradually woke and tasted again the nearing core of his aim and purpose — the bitter intent to save his child.

In the lingering night, Straw had got them onto the Jersey Turnpike and borne them on, by the dangerous moment, through an outrage of traffic like the silent forced evacuation of Hell. Its hard demands had him focused ahead as he'd barely been focused since his all-night lunges up and down the roads of his youth, mostly hunting for women to fold him in briefly and then fade off.

In Hutch's memory of the crowded road, it had never run through a likable landscape; but the past two decades had thrust the land, the houses and buildings deeper than he'd known into a frozen degradation or, worse, a total failure of human shame to burden the Earth and its live creatures with the active evil of outright greed and willful blindness to what the planet will bear till it recoils and wipes itself clean. *No wonder at all the country's gone mad. Let it all come down soon, one silent crash. Let the plague roar on.*

Hutch reined himself in. *You're more than half asleep. This is normal America, love it or leave it.* But then they passed the all but extraplanetary miles of oil refineries, fuming and hung with a million red lights, and then the final poisoned gray-green marshes; and Hutch was literally speechless with anger at an idea—America—botched very likely past redemption by the knowing hands of men no stronger than himself.

Only Straw could manage the adequate words as they plunged on through the lifting dark, toward the still-hid west bank of the Hudson. "Don't you hope old God turns out to be *just?*"

Hutch said "Oh no. I'm banking on his mercy."

Straw waited a whole mile, then managed the tired start of a grin. "Old-maid alarmist that you are, you *would* be in the mercy market. What have you ever done that could upset even the crankiest God?"

Grogged as he still was, Hutch turned and took in the full sight beside him—not the blasted world but the one man driving. "You say I failed you."

Straw faced the road. "That's my complaint, not God's."

Through their years of friendship, Hutch had often misplaced the rock-ribbed fact of Straw's undamaged conviction of God, a thoroughly handmade spacious God with rules that resembled no other creed's but that kept a present and active hold on Strawson Stuart. Hutch said "You think old God ever minded the times we had?"

Straw calmly turned his eyes from the road. "Of course he did. I loved you, Hutchins. Nobody but you, not truly, not then—not God nor woman nor trees nor deer, just Hutch Mayfield. Have you lost that?" Straw faced the road again and righted the car.

Hutch shook his head at the clean-lined profile of a head that was still as fine as any, on any old coin. "Never lost it, no. I recall every time our two hides touched—right down to the look of the rooms we were in and how the light fell, how the instants tasted. They're memories strong as any I've got and I'm still grateful."

Straw said "I'm not just speaking of bodies. I'd have spent my whole life bearing your weight, if you'd said the word."

Hutch could smile. "I think you truly believe that. I think you may well believe you wanted that, forty years ago. But don't forget you were cheerfully mounting married women, virgins and spinsters by the literal dozen, in between our rare good innings together; and I was deep over my head with Ann before you ever stepped into my life."

Straw said "I can love anything on Earth with a body heat of eighty degrees, or anything higher, and a calm disposition—I *mean* it; you know it or knew it years ago." Then, unexpected, he laughed the laugh of his own boyhood—the laugh that had brought such steady rafts of excellent human bodies toward his own keen beauty and the power of his heart, well before he was grown.

Hutch saw him even more clearly again, remembered each atom of his face at its best; and not for the first time, he grieved at the choice he'd made against the boy Straw was. Even if the softer man here in the night burned slower and asked for far less worship, Straw was nonetheless a welcome presence—a tangible gift to any close watcher. Finally Hutch thought of the question he'd asked himself years ago; it was still the main question for him and Straw. "But what in God's name could you and I have done—two thoroughly opposite brands of gent, trapped there in the country in too-big a house with an old Negro man and the rest of our lives to kill while the world snickered at us at the grocery store: two old sissies, harmless as house dust?"

Straw knew at once. "Aside from the fact that you and I are about as sissy as Coach Knut Rockne, we'd have had everything any man and woman have."

"Not live babies, Straw."

"To hell with babies—since when did America need more babies? We're strangling on babies."

Hutch said "Steady, friend. We'd have never had children, which is one huge lack in any arrangement that means to last; and worse, we'd have both had male-thinking minds. We'd have run out of things to talk about or to care for in common, and then we'd have just butted skulls round the clock like exceptionally dumb bull elephants. We'd have understood each other far too well before six months passed—all our big and small testosterone traits.

"Every mystery we'd had for each other would have worn out fast—we'd be as obvious as cheap fireworks. And that would have led to despising each other, then hate, then worse. We'd have loathed what time did to each other's bodies. And sooner or later, hot as we were, we'd have been sneaking out to cheat each other with every willing youngster in sight till we got so old we were paying for sex in motels and car seats." Hutch honestly thought they'd avoided just that.

Straw couldn't relent. "What would have been worse than you killing me or vice versa? No great loss to anyone but Grainger, and he might not have noticed the absence. Or we could have made a suicide pact—more people ought to take themselves out early and not ruin other people's outlook on life." Straw was plainly earnest.

Hutch had to grin.

And once Straw glared and failed to stop Hutch, he decided to join him. Their laughter rocked around in the fast car like stones in a bowl. But once they were quiet, Straw said "We failed at our one big chance. Don't ever again, not in my presence anyhow, try to wiggle your hips and slide past the fact. The two of us together had something a whole lot better than we've ever had since; you chose to ignore it and here we stand, two pitiful starved-out men out of luck."

Again Hutch felt the need to smile. There might be more than a gram of truth in Straw's tirade, but any chance they'd have had at a life was so far gone as to look like the smudge on a summer-night sky of the farthest star. So Hutch smiled and said "I've been grateful to you every minute I've known you."

Straw said "That won't buy me a dry dip of snuff." He'd never dipped snuff and soon realized it, which caused him to laugh again. There were few better laughs on the whole East Coast.

9

In another half hour they'd crossed the jammed George Washington Bridge and in twenty more minutes were standing in a dark narrow hallway at the black steel door to Wade's apartment. The rooms Wade had shared for a decade with Wyatt were high in a well-kept building in the upper nineties over Riverside Drive, a neighborhood that had seen better times quite recently. The scattered filth, the broken heaved pavement, the rattled abandoned men and women posted every few yards with lost or frantic or merely dead eyes were plainly the normal state of things now.

Hutch hadn't stood here in at least four years, a little longer maybe; but surely it hadn't been this rejected by all human care. *Forget it, nothing but nuclear holocaust could mend this now, do your own hard duty.* He'd even dreamed, more than once in recent months, of standing at Wade's door, paralyzed to move; and now that he'd actually come, something balked him. His hand refused to reach toward the bell.

So at last Straw touched it—no audible ring. He pressed it longer—still no answer.

They waited more than a minute. Nothing.

Then the elevator door behind them opened on a single rider, a tall young woman.

When she saw Hutch and Straw, she stayed in the elevator but held the door open. The landing was maybe twelve feet by nine. The woman was no more than five feet from Hutch, and their eyes met at once.

Hutch first noticed her height and color. She was maybe six feet tall. Her skin was the shade of dry beach sand; and her hair was abundant and strong as horsetail, a lustrous natural black and long with the deep-set waves of a forties movie star. Warm as it was, she wore a black raincoat halfway to her shoes.

A quick automatic smile crossed her lips; then she went nearly grim with her dark eyes wide. She held a paper bag of what seemed milk and bread, and she still didn't move.

Hutch said "My name is Hutchins Mayfield. Do you know my son Wade?"

That brought her out of the elevator, though she pocketed her keys again.

Silence seemed so much a part of her nature that Hutch told himself she must be mute. He asked an easy Yes or No question. "Have you seen him this morning?"

She shook her head No, then finally said "I'm Ivory Bondurant."

An appealing voice, unmistakably black in its complex harmony. And *Bondurant* had been Wyatt's family name, though at closer range this woman looked ten years older than Wyatt, the last time Hutch had seen him at least. She'd be in her early forties then, remarkably preserved. Hutch extended his hand.

She took it lightly, meeting his eyes.

Hutch introduced Strawson and said "We rang two minutes ago—no answer yet."

Ivory agreed, as grave as before. "Did Wade expect this?"

What's this? Hutch wondered but he said "Yes, I spoke with him late last night—twice in fact."

She persisted. "I put him to bed at ten last night; he didn't mention visitors this morning."

Hutch drew out his wallet, found his driver's license with the small photograph and held it toward her. "I'm who I said. We've come to get Wade."

Self-possessed as she was, for a moment Ivory was shocked and she showed it. Her eyes and mouth crouched. But she refused the license, brought out her keys and stepped toward the door.

Hutch touched her arm to slow her. "What should we know?"

"I beg your pardon?"

"We've heard Wade's blind. He mentioned Wyatt's death. He sounded confused."

Ivory's shock was relenting; she studied Hutch's face, then gave a smile that was startling in its force. "Mr. Mayfield, all the above is correct. Your son has a ghastly disease that we're all but sure he got from my brother Wyatt. My brother took his own life when that was established—shot himself downstairs in the street ten weeks ago. Wade Mayfield is on his way to being nearly as bad off as any starving child on television. But come on in; it's clean anyhow." Her sentences made a real shape in the air; she let the shape hang in place for a moment like a carefully drawn, remorselessly perfect Euclidean figure. Then she opened the door and stood aside to beckon the men in.

As he came, Hutch watched her unbutton her black coat. Beneath it, she wore a blood-red linen dress. He recalled that Mary Queen of Scots had dressed identically for her own beheading, astonishing all the bystanding henchmen of her murderous cousin Elizabeth of England.

The room was empty or it looked so at first. The spare but handsome chairs and tables that Hutch remembered—the buffalo rug, the banks of records and tapes and playing machines: all were simply gone. A few dog-eared books stood by the baseboard, a sickly fern, a worn-out butterfly chair from the sixties, a radio playing what seemed to be Handel, a huge crumbled cork dartboard still bristling with darts. Hutch had bought that for Wade's ninth birthday, a gift that had seemed to displease the boy; yet here it was, a plucky survivor. Even the wood-slat blinds at the windows were gone; and the river was plain to see—the filthy Hudson, still iron-blue and stately in the visible pace of its final surrender to the sea.

Ivory entered and locked the door behind them. When she saw the two men's baffled stares, she said "They sold the things, piece by piece, for pittances."

Hutch was speechless.

But Straw said "Surely they had some insurance to help them along—"

Hutch realized he'd counted on the same thing. He only said "Surely—"

But Ivory said "Wade has a policy that covers more than half. But Wyatt's insurance canceled him out when they knew he was ill incurably. Then they were both hard up in no time. It broke my heart."

Hutch took the four words as a hopeful break in Ivory's daunting mastery here. "I understand you've been through hell."

"I didn't know I was out of it yet"—her great smile again.

Hutch said "I'll lighten your load today." He thought that was the literal truth; but once it was out, it sounded too grand.

Ivory heard the same sound. "Are you sure, Mr. Mayfield? You don't know me—"

"Miss Bondurant, I didn't know you existed. Why did I come here so many times in the past decade and never see you?"

Ivory's voice lowered and hurried to say "They didn't want you to know about me." But then she calmed herself. "I didn't live here when you used to visit. I was married then."

Hutch said "Thank God you've been here lately. We clearly owe you a great debt of thanks. Tell me anything else I should know."

She looked to Straw. "Can you believe this?" Her eyes narrowed down to contain their fury, but somehow she'd managed to gentle her voice.

Straw said "I never believe anything my eyes or ears tell me."

She said "Lucky man. Stay put where you are. The world up here's a torture factory." Then she abruptly smiled. "Tell your boss he'd need a very long year of time if I told him half of what he ought to know."

Hutch accepted the strike; his only reply was to turn away to the window again.

But Straw touched Hutch's shoulder and said "This man is nobody's boss, believe me; he's a sick man's father. Where have you put Wade?" Straw's eyes were among the rare eyes in Manhattan that could meet Ivory's blistering stare, instant for instant.

She finally whispered "Brace both of yourselves, hard, and step through that door." She pointed to a shut door off the main room.

When Hutch balked again, Straw took the lead. At the door he looked back at Hutch, who was pale as tallow on a white plate. Straw bent, being taller than Hutch, and pressed his lips against his friend's taut forehead. Then Straw opened the door, a wall of stifling air fell on him, he stepped inside. The space was dark; a torn sheet was stapled across the one window. Straw said "Old Wade, your godfather's here."

From somewhere in the hot brown air, a young voice said "Oh Godfather, I owe you a favor. Take a chair, sit down, exterminate me." What seemed an attempt at a laugh grated out.

Hutch's hand had found the switch for an overhead light.

The white glare rocketed round the space, then gradually showed another sparse room—no chests or tables, one rocking chair that had been on Wade's great-grandmother's porch the night she eloped and started her branch of the Mayfield family, nothing else but a mattress on a rolling frame and bleached blank sheets.

It took a long moment before Hutch could see that—pale as the sheets— a body was lying on them, naked. Maybe forty or fifty pounds too thin. A chaos of bones, white skin thin as paint, tangled islands of dark chestnut hair, a skull that was helpless not to grin. Hutch thought *Christ Jesus* but he also smiled and held in place.

Straw went forward though, knelt by the mattress, took the thin shoulders lightly and bent to kiss the skull.

Wade whispered "Hearty thanks" and tried to say more, but his voice broke up. His eyes looked normal, they both stayed dry and fixed on Straw-son, he'd still to meet his father's gaze.

Hutch reminded himself *He can't see this*; he stepped onward then and knelt next to Wade. His hand went out to the head and smoothed the sweaty hair.

Wade's eyes found him then and, so far as they could show feeling at all, they looked surprised and gratified. He said "I'm pleased to see you, sir." When his lips closed again, the print of the teeth was stark through the skin.

Helpless, Hutch smiled. "Do you see me?"

"Not to know who you are, but I recognize your outline." Wade stopped as if he'd never speak again and both eyes shut. Blinded, he put up a finger and traced the line of Hutch's head on the air. Then he looked out again and said "You're giving off too much light." What seemed like another try at laughter rose and quit.

And a dry unwilling laugh escaped Hutch. "Son, I'm in deeper dark than you."

By then Straw had found a tan bedspread and laid it on Wade, up to the chin.

Wade's eyes had stayed shut; he was barely breathing—asleep or in some private trance.

Straw felt for a pulse in the throat and faced Hutch. "Let's get this child packed."

Hutch confirmed the pulse for himself, then stood and followed Straw back to the front room. There they could hear low sounds from the kitchen. Again Straw led the way, Hutch behind him.

To Hutch at that moment, Straw's upright back was a sight as necessary as air, the slim last promise of a chance at survival.

Ivory, vivid still in her red dress, was warming milk on a low gas flame. She'd already made toast, buttered it and laid it in a deep blue bowl.

Hutch saw she was making old-fashioned milk-toast, a thing his father had craved when sick. It seemed another small promise of strength, the hope of home.

Ivory said "If you gentlemen haven't had breakfast, I'm sorry to say this is all I've got—I make milk-toast for Wade twice a day. There's a coffee shop two blocks due east."

Straw said "We've eaten"; and as if on signal, he and Hutch both stroked the grizzled stubble of their chins.

Ivory opened a drawer and Hutch could see a small scattering of white plastic cutlery—knives, forks, spoons. He recalled his grandmother Mayfield's silver, ornate and heavy in the hand as a club. She'd left it, dozens of pieces, to Wade when he was a child. He'd stored it at home; and it hadn't been more than eight or nine years since Hutch himself had packed it carefully and brought it north, on his normal spring visit, hoping it might help propitiate Wyatt, who was already fending off Wade's kin. Surely silver hadn't survived the great sell-off?

Ivory had seen Hutch glance at the drawer. "Sorry, Mr. Mayfield, that went also—every silver piece the two of them owned. Wyatt had some too."

In these blasted rooms, like swamped lean-to's to Wade's own fragile bones, that was no loss at all. Hutch thanked her again. Then he wondered *Why thanks? Thanks for what? Why's she still here?*

As if mind reading, Ivory said "I've been the treasurer, the past six months, for my brother and Wade. It's all accounted for in that book there, by the day and to the penny." She pointed to a composition book on the counter—blue back, green spine.

Hutch took a momentary writer's pleasure in the sight of a well-made waiting blank book; then he said "I had no idea he'd run out of funds. He told me his firm paid him disability."

"They did, Mr. Mayfield—they still do—but this plague eats money faster than people. And I told you Wyatt was completely bereft weeks before he died. Wade carried him gladly; he can still swear to that."

Hutch said "I don't doubt that for an instant." Still he rightly felt small. He'd had no thought of theft or deceit; he had none now. It was almost the only cardinal virtue he claimed to possess—a genuine despisal of money, though he'd mostly had enough. This woman had apparently kept Wade alive for the past ten weeks since her own brother buckled and quit—Wade was a likable gifted man, no mystery there, none greater than the sight of human kindness, always a shock. Hutch said "What finally got Wyatt down?"

Ivory looked puzzled.

"Did his eyes fail too?"

The milk had begun to bubble and steam. Ivory drew it off the burner, poured it slowly on the toast and looked to Hutch. "My brother never really got too desperately sick—just a long succession of small but wearisome intestinal infections, nerve parasites, then a rush of lost weight, then finally a patch of Kaposi's sarcoma in the midst of his forehead like an Indian caste mark. At first he laughed that it made him a Brahmin. His doctor said he could have survived for months or years longer. He seemed to be one of these rare lucky people who somehow manage to keep the virus at a near stand-still. No, I honestly think Wyatt Bondurant died from watching what he'd done to Wade Mayfield. He was sure it was him that gave AIDS to Wade; he never said why. Wade was grown when they met. Anyhow when the parasites got to Wade's eyes, Wyatt asked me here—here by this stove—if the two of them could count on me."

Ivory took ten seconds to think her way onward. "I took him to mean would I see them through to peaceful deaths. I'd have rather been asked to kill a new baby, but I told him Yes. Wyatt was the last of my generation. We'd seen each other through a South Bronx childhood, losing two sisters along the way; I couldn't leave him now. At the time I didn't know he meant to check out and leave Wade with me. But that was his plan. He got his own business matters in order, left a short message for me to read to Wade—the last sentence was 'Now you're in safe hands.' That had to mean me; there was nobody else, that was safe anyhow. Then he found a short alley between here and the river and took himself out with a gun I forgot our father had brought up north from Virginia, sixty years ago. A schoolgirl found his body, coming home at dusk from band practice."

It was simple as that then, in her eyes at least. Ivory Bondurant had made a deal with her brother; she was sticking by it now he was gone. She set a plastic spoon in the soaked toast, took up the tray and went toward the bedroom.

Hutch said "You're bound to be a saint."

Ivory thought about that and searched Hutch's eyes but found no clue to what he might mean, so she said "I've had my own good reasons. It's been painful as anything I've ever known, but I don't claim any public-health medals. It was what I wanted to do, while I could. Wade mattered to me too."

Hutch heard her past tense; but he mouthed the words *Thank you*, knowing his debt was too great to pay or to speak of here in these parched walls. When Ivory watched him but gave no answer, Hutch realized Straw was not there with him. He turned and called his name.

"In here." Straw had found the spare bedroom.

Hutch had assumed that Ivory was living in this space now; but when he entered the one spare room, he saw it was crammed with cardboard boxes, crates and two steamer trunks (one of them was the trunk Hutch had carried to Oxford near forty years ago).

Straw was seated by the river window on a solid box, and his face was bleak. In recent years he'd wept too often, always when sober; but he'd shed all the tears he had for this place and the sights it had seen—his eyes were dry. In silence he reached into a shoe box beside him, gathered a thick handful of letters and held them toward Hutch.

Hutch said "No, they're Wade's."

Straw said "There you're wrong. They're yours and Ann's—every one of them are recent letters from you two, addressed to Wade and all of them sealed, the way you sent them."

"Strawson, Wade's blind. We didn't know that."

Straw whispered hard. "That woman can read." He pointed through the wall to Ivory.

Hutch worked a slow path in through the crates and stood by Straw, looking down toward the river. A barge so rusty it seemed in the act of quick dissolution, an orange sugar cube; a big white dog like the hero of some Jack London story overseeing the battered stream, a woman with honey-colored hair who took what were almost surely two lobsters—giant live lobsters—from a pail and pitched them far out over the river. They sank like plummets, and Hutch asked Straw "Would you rather be boiled to death in a pot and eaten by humans or thrown back live to the mercy of a river of human shit?"

Straw had seen the woman. "I vote for the river. I've eaten my share of mammal manure; it hasn't stopped me yet."

Hutch said "You vote for leaving today?"

"What about Wade's doctor? We should notify whoever's been seeing him anyhow and ask for his charts to be mailed home. You settled the business with that smart woman?"

"She does seem fine—no, we didn't get into details yet. She's feeding Wade."

"Has she got a job, other than here? A few sticks of furniture can't have brought them much capital. Maybe she's well-fixed on her own."

Hutch said "She and Wyatt were from the South Bronx. Or so he told me one hateful night, and she just confirmed it."

"Then you want my suggestion? I think I should go out and get us some breakfast—a big hot feed for you, me and her. You make your final arrangements with Ivory, she tells us what we need to take, we make Wade a decent pallet in the car and head for home."

Hutch was still facing the river and the white dog. More than ever, its size and patent vigor seemed the answer to a lonely boy's prayer—a perfectly faithful creature who'd understand every thought you had. At last Hutch laid a hand at the back of Straw's broad neck. "Whose home, old friend?"

Straw reached back and briefly covered the hand. "Well, he grew up where you live; you're rattling around there in too much room. Ann's place is likely temporary. Emily and I will take him in a heartbeat—we've got plenty of room, never sleep. But you make the choice, or ask Wade to choose."

Hutch stayed quiet till he heard Ivory walk toward the kitchen again. Then he quietly said "My place, no question."

"You know I'll come there and stay to the end—just say the word."

"The end could be a long way off."

Straw said "You saw him. He's looking at the grave at fairly close range."

Hutch felt a strong need to say Straw was wrong, but quietly again he said "People do that sometimes for years."

Straw laughed. "Yes, Doctor, the human race for a start—"

The laugh had been short; but Wade heard it somehow and called out "Godfather, come laugh in here." Weak as his voice was, its youth carried well.

Straw went at once.

Hutch followed him as far as the kitchen.

Ivory was rinsing the milk pan and bowl. "I've got to get on to work, I'm afraid."

"Excuse me but are you living here?"

At first she looked offended; then she understood. "Oh no, I was in this building long before Wade and Wyatt. With my ex-husband, two floors down."

Hutch heard the contradiction of what she'd said a short while back—that she hadn't lived here through most of Wade's tenure. But at the same moment, he first saw the wedding band on her left hand—a ring at least, plain platinum—and decided not to question her story. "Where do you work?"

"Far downtown, an art gallery in Soho."

"I'd be glad to drive you."

She smiled, a glimpse of a whole other person—one not seen in these walls for months or years. "No you wouldn't" she said. "You get in morning traffic with me, and you'll never want to see Ivory again. I take the subway five days a week."

Hutch said "You know I want to take him home."

Ivory said "I've prayed you would. You know he couldn't ask."

Hutch believed her but he had to ask this last soul alive a question that only she might answer. "Why has he been so set against me?"

"My guess is, mainly pure loyalty to Wyatt."

Hutch shut his eyes and agreed.

With no sign of vengeance, still she pressed ahead. "You know Wyatt hated you and all you stand for—all he could see; Wyatt *trusted* his eyes." She was suddenly splendid as any oak tree lit by lightning.

Hutch managed half a smile. "I'm glad Wyatt knew so well what I stand for. I've yet to solve that mystery in more than six decades; and I've really tried—Wyatt may have spent, oh, twenty conscious hours in my presence."

Ivory was free to laugh in relief. She'd launched her attack on behalf of her brother; now she was free of that final duty (not that she'd ever thought Wyatt was all wrong).

But Hutch was not finished. "Was it just the fact that I'm white and Southern?"

"That was part; Wyatt was *radical* back in college. So was I but I got my edge dulled as time passed, and Wyatt never did."

Hutch said "Oh he was keen with me."

"Maybe you earned that?" Though Ivory's voice had made it a question, her eyes confirmed that she fully believed the answer was Yes.

Hutch waited. "Did he think I condemned the way they lived?"

"He knew you did; you told him so."

Hutch said "Wyatt may have thought I did. We had a bad meeting, the last time I saw him—all three of us badly lost our heads on the subject of race and sex and all else. But no—God, no—with the life I've led, I've got very slim rights of condemnation over the worst soul alive on Earth."

"But you never contacted them again?"

"I didn't, no—not the two together. I was standing on form, I was Wade's only father, he was past twenty-one and he knew my address. Even so, I wrote him a good many letters that he never opened."

Ivory took awhile to grant Hutch's premise. "They were much too close—I could see that myself. They were all but Siamese twins, most days. They doomed each other, is what it came to."

To Hutch there seemed only one question left. "How did Wyatt's hatred for so many white people part and make way for Wade?"

Ivory said "My brother would pick at that subject, fairly often—right here in Wade's presence. Wade always laughed and said he was the master Wyatt wanted, deep down. Wyatt would blare his hot satanic eyes and say 'Dream on, sweet honky—little white sugar-tit. I'll get you yet.'" She held in place and watched the words pierce Hutch: and for the only time today, her eyes nearly filled.

So Hutch only waited till she'd got her grip again. "We're hoping to take Wade home today. Any reason why not? Anything or anybody we need to consult, any bills to pay?"

Ivory said "His volunteer comes at ten to bathe him. All his medicine's in the bathroom cabinet; he usually understands what he takes and why. If not, the bottles are clearly labeled." She pointed again to the composition book. "I've kept a record of all he's been through—the names of the illnesses, the doctors and dates. You'll need that with you. There's a big box of Wade's papers in the spare bedroom; better take that too."

Hutch said "You think he can stand the drive—eight or nine hours?"

"Mr. Mayfield, Wade's so up and down, I really can't tell you. Some days he has the strength to dress himself and walk with me around the block, very slowly. We got as far as the river last week, then sat down awhile and came back with even a little strength to spare. Other times he's too weak to raise his head, and I have to diaper him three times a night. His eyes are either three-fourths blind or fairly sharp, depending on circumstances I've never fathomed; and as you know from your call last night, his mind's not reliable. Some days he talks like a lucid gentleman. Other days, and a lot of nights, he's flinging way out on spider thread. No harm in him, though. Never says a mean word, not to me at least. Begs my pardon all day—"

"That's a Mayfield trait."

"He's told me as much; he's a kind-natured man. I can tell you I'll miss him—" No tears fell but Ivory's dark eyes widened further, and she bit at her lip.

Hutch said "Please don't take this the least bit wrong, but we must owe you substantial money."

"Thank you, I never doubted you'd be fair. May I write you about that later on?"

"Any day you're ready."

Ivory said "It won't be anything steep—less than three hundred dollars, little odds and ends."

"Is there anything left here that you want or can use?"

Her attention was already moving toward her job; in another few minutes she'd be seriously late. "May I also think that over awhile?"

"By all means, please. I'll just pay the rent till I can come back up and clean things out—if that's ever appropriate." Hutch could hear his refusal to face death's nearness.

Ivory looked round the bare room again. "I've kept it as neat as I knew how." No ship's galley was ever cleaner.

Hutch said "You've done a magnificent job—I wasn't complaining. If I start in to thank you finally today, I'll just go to pieces."

She was in the same fix. "Let's both of us wait till we're ready. There's the phone and the mail; we'll communicate." She'd taken her black coat off a wall hook.

Hutch helped her put it on, concealing the bright dress. "Then Strawson and I will likely clear out here before you're back. I guess we'll wait till the volunteer comes—will she know details like the doctor's number?"

"It's a he, Mr. Mayfield. Yes, he knows more than me—details anyhow. *He's* the saint you mentioned."

"What's his name?"

"Jimmy Boat—we call him Boatie. He'll be all the help you need." She was leaving; she put out a long hand in parting.

Hutch took it for maybe a moment too long. "Wade may have told you that I've spent my life writing, when I wasn't teaching college. I've seldom felt at a real loss for words—" He bowed and pressed his forehead to her hand.

Ivory held in place, uncertain of how to use the old gesture or whether to refuse it. When she knew, she said "I've read every word you've published, I think. I've had hard times of my own to weave through; you've been some help. I promise a letter in the next few weeks." She moved toward the hall door.

"Did you tell him goodbye?" The moment it left Hutch, he was sorry he'd said it.

Ivory held in place at the door a long moment, her strong shoulders squared. But her face, when she turned, was the ground plan of pain. Her mouth moved to speak but nothing came, so she shook her head No and went her way.

In his mind, Hutch barely heard his own last thought as she vanished through the door. *Wade was loved, all ways.*

10

They'd eaten the breakfast Straw brought in from two blocks east; and they had Wade propped up, in his robe, in the rocker when the volunteer let himself in with a key at ten o'clock. He came in, back first, carrying a satchel; so at first he didn't see the company; and when he faced the room, he yelled out "God on high!" He was tar black, maybe five foot six, built like a reinforced concrete emplacement in a World War II antitank defense; and his reddish hair was high in an old-fashioned Afro arrangement above a round face, no neck at all and a silver-gray and spotless jumpsuit.

Hutch and Straw got to their feet; but before they could speak, Wade said "Boatie Boat, this is my father Hutch and my godfather Straw."

Boat said "I thought both of you were *dead.*" But he set down the satchel and strode on toward them for crushing handshakes. Then he stood back and studied Wade in his chair. "*You're* resurrected, child! I told you you'd live." To Hutch, Boat said "Wade called me last night, told me you were on the road; and he made me promise not to let you see his frozen corpse." He touched Wade's wrist. "You're still beating anyhow. No icicles yet."

Wade said "Boatie, these men are kidnaping me south. Next time you see me, I'll be warm as toast."

Boat said "South got too hot for me." He put out a flat hand and felt Wade's forehead. Then with both hands he lightly probed Wade's throat; the lymph nodes there were hard as kernels. "No fever in you today at all. Sugar, you're cooling down."

Straw asked Boatie "Where you from in the South?"

"Take a flying guess."

"Society Hill, South Carolina."

Boat laughed. "Way off."

Hutch said "Social Circle, Georgia?"

"Getting closer but *wrong*."

Straw said "Where exactly?" He was only indulging the common need of country dwellers to place everybody they meet on a map of the actual ground.

But Boat slid into minstrel-darky tones. "You honkies still hunting us runaways *down*—lay back, white man; we *free* at last!"

Straw grinned and raised both hands in surrender. He'd been involved in no such complex racial theatrics since Martin Luther King opened so many eyes.

Despite his kidding-on-the-level, though, Boat showed no malice. For blind Wade's sake, he was eager to jive. "I'm from Little Richard's hometown—who know where that is?"

Hutch said "Macon, Georgia—the cradle of rock and roll, birthplace of Little Richard, all-time king!"

Boat folded both hands. "Amen, pink Jesus."

Wade crossed himself. "Mother Mary, Amen."

By then Boat was combing Wade's hair with his fingers and neatening his robe.

Wade accepted the service as a small welcome pleasure. He shut his eyes and, for a long instant, assumed unconsciously the look of a boy-pharaoh on his gilded barge, borne toward death and endless judgment, very nearly smiling.

Boat looked to Hutch. "You taking this lovely friend out of here?" In the course of eight words, his voice had changed again—realistic now and sober.

Wade's eyes were still shut; he still looked serene but a wiry snake's voice came from his lips. "Don't let this bastard here lay a hand on me."

Boat laughed. "Which one?—there's three bastards here."

Wade's eyes found Hutch. "This main man, grinning like nobody's gone."

Hutch thought *That's me   he's struck the truth finally: Wyatt Bondurant's truth*.

Boat only continued stroking Wade's hair.

In ten more seconds Wade spoke again, the same cold voice. "We'll *cut* if we have to."

Boat brought two knuckles around and rapped lightly on the crest of Wade's forehead. Then Boat looked to Hutch and Straw; he shook his head sadly and mouthed four clear words—*Out of his mind.* But what he said was "Wish I was traveling toward green trees and water."

And Wade's head moved to sign *Come on,* though he said no more.

So Hutch turned to Boat. "Please come on with us." It was not an idle offer. He'd sensed at once that Boatie would be the perfect help.

And Wade moaned confirmation of the offer.

Boat couldn't bear to turn Wade down, and he said it to Hutch. "Don't *both* of you break my heart. This friend Wade here means as much to me as the rest of the friends and miserable boys I've helped up and down this town for a long mean time. Wade's got his own people though—you fine gents and his mother's live, right? A lot of my boys don't have blood relations, and a lot that have got whole *housefuls* of kin get turned down by them as hateful as rats—but I see you're strong enough to take what's happening."

Hutch said "I guess we'll know soon enough."

Wade turned to his father. "I doubt I'll be all that much trouble."

It nearly downed Hutch; he literally swayed as in a wind.

But Boat leaned to Wade's ear with a secret, though he said it plainly. "You going to live till the man says 'Quit.' That may not be for long years to come if you got loving care around you, steady like you need. You been here alone; that'll kill a big horse."

Wade's eyes were still shut; and his voice was thin again but cheerful. "I may not make it to Maryland."

The three strong men considered that.

Then Straw said "No, Wade, your godfather's driving every mile. You'll make it. I promise. I never failed yet."

Wade said "You never saw me this far gone either."

Straw had to say "Right."

"Then promise me we'll make it again." Wade was in earnest.

Straw said "Wade Mayfield, you're golden with me."

Wade said "Is that safe? What does *golden* mean?"

Straw said again "*Golden.* You wait and see." He had no clear idea what he meant, but in his mouth it felt like the nearest thing to usable truth.

11

By noon Boat had bathed Wade, diapered him and dressed him in what seemed like too many clothes for a mild spring day. Then he laid Wade back on the bed to rest while he packed everything they'd need or could use in the way of clothes and medical equipment. He'd helped Hutch reach Wade's doctor by phone to learn any vital details and procedures—the main advice was simply to continue all medicines till Wade was back in the hands of another AIDS specialist; and when Hutch thanked the brusque man and said goodbye, the doctor suddenly lowered his voice and said "You must have had a fine son." Then he was gone.

So while Hutch and Straw made several trips down to load the car, Boat sat on the floor by Wade's bed, near his wavering eyes, and worked in silence—as he'd worked so often, near so many young men—to call death closer.

Though he'd been raised in Georgia by his mother's mother in an African Methodist Episcopal church and had sung in the choir till the day he boarded the train north to Harlem, these hard recent years Boat had been forced to go his lone spiritual way. Now in the room where Wade Mayfield and Wyatt Bondurant had known good hours for actual years, a room that Wade was leaving soon and surely forever, Boat called up the face he always pictured for death itself—a thin dark woman, very much like his mother who'd vanished long since on a bus toward Chicago—and he said a silent respectful prayer as that tall woman answered his call and stood in his mind at the foot of Wade's bed here, eight feet from Boat. *Keep this child from messing his pants on the road. Let him get back far as his home and his mother, and let him see her face someway. Put him on whatever bed he slept in when he was a child and let him breathe easy till you're ready for him. Then come on into his clean safe room and lead him while he's picturing Wyatt in the days when they didn't know they'd killed each other like this and deserted a child.*

When the packed car was ready and they'd got Wade up onto his feet, Boat stood on Wade's left with the boy's arm around him. Then he told Straw to stand on the right. Once they got their balance and Hutch was standing with two hands free, Boat said to Wade "You got everything?"

Wade signified Yes.

"You sure you got all your papers and things—your picture albums?"

Wade said "Oh yes, I'm well stocked with pictures. I plan to meet Jesus in northern Virginia and get my eyes healed."

Boat said "You hold your tongue about Jesus. Be sweet to him, baby. He got us in this fix we're in."

Wade said "I don't believe that a minute and neither do you."

Boat said "All right. I was racing my lip." Then he was satisfied they could head down. He asked Hutch please to bring the satchel of soap and lotion and natural sponges he'd use on the five men he still had to see today; then he said "Let's boogie on down the road."

They'd gone three steps when Wade said "No—"

Each of the able-bodied men had privately thought that Wade might balk at the fence. Now they faced one another in blank disappointment.

Wade tried to think—not a good day for thinking. So he said again "No."

Hutch thought *Wyatt's got him and is hauling him back.* It seemed more credible than what his eyes saw—a splendid man, crushed and all but gone.

But finally Wade could recall what he wanted. "Hutch, please step in the bedroom and bring that frame that's over the bed."

Hutch couldn't recall a picture there, but he quickly obeyed and took the silver frame off the dark wall. Only in the window light of the main room could he catch a glimpse of what he held—a landscape he himself had drawn near his mother's home in Goshen, Virginia when he was a boy and visiting there with Alice Matthews, his dead mother's friend: in the summer of 1944. Now was no time to think of meanings or omens in the clean-lined picture of a spine of mountains cloaked in dense evergreens. *Why this of all things?* Not thinking of blindness, Hutch showed it to Wade. "This what you want?"

Wade's right hand came out and sized up the frame. Then he nodded Yes hard and took the next step to pass through the door into the dim-lit hall. In those last inches Wade told himself *This vanishes now. Never again.* It felt worse than all his life till here, worse than the prospect of oncoming death.

Nobody spoke as Hutch double-locked the door, called the elevator, and they all rode down in its weird light to cross the lobby into strong April sun—the morning of Passover, though they didn't know it, the night when God killed the firstborn son in every Egyptian overlord's house not marked with the blood of a slaughtered lamb.

In the light Wade looked even more devastated, gaunt as a flail. Not having seen himself for weeks, still he understood that and rigged a taut smile on his face, a try at pleasantness that looked like famine. So if you'd watched him every inch of the way toward the loaded car, you'd have seen no outward sign of the pain that went on tearing him like a tattered doll—leaving the site of most of the good he'd tasted in his past grown life or would ever taste: the walls that held the memory of Wyatt Bondurant's beauty, his sudden ambushes of a stunning kindness, through long nights of juncture and mutual joy.

Hutch silently tried to tell himself that the source of all the strange elation he'd felt these past two days was finally shown to him as he led his son, his only child, toward the only home they'd had or would ever have.

As Hutch and Straw worked to lay Wade out on the pallet they'd made on the long backseat, the passersby barely slowed their headlong pace through the day, though some of them veered a little aside from a face and body as near gone as whoever this ghost was.

At the final moment of stillness at the curb—Straw had cranked the car and was turning the wheel to enter traffic—Wade somehow managed to raise himself and look to the street. No one heard him, even his father, but he said "Adiós." Then he sank again and, before they were back across the great bridge, he'd drowned in the misty fatigue that lapped him constantly—the main mercy now.

T W O

HOME

APRIL–JULY 1993

April 23, 1993

Dear Strawson,

 This will be just a quick line from campus to keep you posted. I'd have phoned before now, but with Wade in the house—even when he's asleep—I somehow can't discuss him with anyone. He's so wholly dependent that I won't risk beginning to think that he's, above all, somebody to manage—even if I say it to my oldest closest friend, which (despite your doubts) God knows you are.

 I've told you that your presence on the trip north and through those first days with Wade at home was much more than a practical help, but the truth bears repeating. More even than I could, or Ann in her visits, you let Wade know that he's still very much alive and a pleasure to know. Your ease and good humor and steady attention set the pitch for us all; and I won't forget, if and when the time comes, that you've promised to come back and stay when we need you and until we're done. Meanwhile, by the way, the hospital bed you ordered is here and makes a real difference. Wade raises and lowers himself with ease and sleeps through the night almost upright—it helps keep his lungs clear and maybe his mind, which is much less likely to streak off into meanness or nonsense or self-punishment than it was at first.

 Also in the past three weeks, he's recovered more strength than I expected. I'm trying to tell myself it's the outcome of being at home with reliable care, regular company and sensible food, though he still barely eats any more than the liquid protein you found and sometimes a small dish of frozen yogurt. That seems to stay with him when nothing else will. Even so, he can't stand any flavor stronger than vanilla—it's odors apparently that trigger his nausea.

 In any case I'm also trying to remind myself that whatever strength Wade regains is bound to be brief. The graduate student that I found to sit with him, when I teach or run chores, is also a big help. His name is Hart Salter. He's a good-looking, huge—not fat but muscular—twenty-six-year-old medievalist; and he knows more dirty jokes than Chaucer. He already seems to have known Wade forever, and they actually manage to laugh a good deal. Hart's marriage has apparently been rocky lately, so I think he actually gets a real benefit from cheering a fellow creature up—Wade that is; the wife seems to be one of those black holes for love, incapable of the simplest trust. If only Hart weren't due to leave us soon—he's finished all his course work and prelims and will need to travel to London this summer to start his research, but for two more weeks he'll still be available. Once he's gone, I'll be in the lurch if I can't find an honest substitute soon. That's when I may need to call you back.

Which reminds me that I've told a few of my colleagues the truth and have got only genuine concern from them and offers of help. Not that I expected otherwise. Life in an English Department can often feel like a bad day at the beehive; but the few times I've ever let it be known that I needed help of the human variety from my colleagues, they've laid it out with generous tolerance, unstintingly.

The woman doctor you said you trusted when we took Wade to Duke—Dr. Margaret Ives—she's become his main doctor and has even been out to the house for a visit. Entirely out of the blue last evening, she phoned from the hospital and asked if we'd give her that drink we'd offered. I put it to Wade, who was napping on the sofa while I watched TV (the Court channel, to which I'm addicted). Wade said "Bring her on"; so out she came and stayed past nine— Wade awake the whole time, participating more than he has till now in the talk and laughter.

Just being with people and practicing words has likewise helped to clear his mind, though his vision has definitely not improved except for brief spells when he'll suddenly be facing the window and say "There's an eagle surely" (he was right, a male golden eagle; the first I've seen in all my years out here and, according to my bird book, way off course). Or he'll suddenly ask "Where's Mother's portrait?" (I'd stashed the picture he drew of his mother in grade school; it had hung in the kitchen till Ann went her way). Ten seconds later he won't be able to find me in the room.

Anyhow Dr. Ives's visit was the first house call I've heard of from a doctor since steam was invented; and though we all pretended it was social, I knew that she was watching Wade closely and with more sympathy than may turn out to be good for her peace of mind and soul. It turned out she's an avid reader of poetry and has known my work since high school in Utah. We didn't talk too much about that; I didn't want Wade to feel he was her alibi for knowing me—

I don't think he was that, by the way. I long since gave up feeling like anyone a sane modern reader could want to meet.

As for Wade's health, she's sticking to what she told us that day you were with us in the Infectious Diseases clinic—the same medications he was taking in New York, as much exercise outdoors as he can take, and as many meetings with people he likes as we can arrange and he has strength for. She puts special emphasis on the inhalations to prevent further bouts of parasitic pneumonia, so we're loyal with those.

Last night, when she was close to leaving, Dr. Ives turned to Wade in my presence and said "If you want us to, we can try to treat this blindness. We might even stop it before it goes further." She understands that he still has a certain amount of sight which goes and comes unpredictably, and she went on to say she could give him a fairly high-powered drug that would likely clear out the parasites and keep his eyes from failing any worse. The drug however is given through a permanent tube implanted in a hole in the chest.

I was ready to take her offer on the spot, but I left it to Wade; and once he'd thought for twenty seconds, he said "Thanks, I've known about that for some time. I decided against it."

She seemed a little rebuffed but hardly showed it. When she left she did say again that she'd be at Wade's disposal for whatever she could do; and he said again "Thanks, I'll try not to crowd you." When she still looked puzzled, he said "I'm letting it come on now." Neither she nor I had to ask what he meant. And then Wade confirmed it. He said "All I want is enough morphine when the howling starts." She said "We keep it on hand, all hours. You let me know when you feel the need." He gave a short wail on the spot, then laughed and said "Not yet." And she left us smiling. Remind me to ask for all-female doctors when my time comes, if I don't pitch over cold-dead in class or at my home desk like a lucky man.

Ann has stopped by at least once a day; she phones Wade frequently, which he seems not to mind. I pretty much leave them alone when she's here; but when Ann and I wind up in a room, we give our best imitations of civility. I'll have to say I've genuinely enjoyed the food she cooks and brings every few days and the laundry she does almost every day for Wade. The other night, when Wade had us both in his room, he cranked up the head of his bed and said "Am I right in thinking that you two will stay here under this roof when I'm bad off and see me out?" Ann and I said Yes and faced each other. I could see she meant it. I'm not sure I did; but time will tell, I guess.

I've got to run. Today's the final day of classes before exams, and I'm risking a good deal by going through with my long tradition of having the writ-

ing class out to the house for a final discussion and a rough-and-ready supper. Last week I told the students that my son was now with me and was seriously ill—no more details. Wade knows they're coming and that he can either ignore them completely and rest in his room or be entirely welcome if he feels up to joining the students at any point. Two of them really mean to be writers and may not be deluded in their hopes. If they see Wade at all, I can hope they'll see him and his situation as life *anyhow, the Great Subject.*

I don't doubt Wade can handle what comes. Christ knows he's handling himself and me with a grace and strength I've never had to summon. He feels like the purpose of my life till now, even though he's ending in this blocked alley. I mean that very seriously. Slim or nil though his chances are, I feel fairly sure that whatever Wade and I have throughout these weeks will outlast us both. It'll be our good-will effort to get something right in a family that's never engineered a right *thing yet—an open-eyed, willingly paired walk on to the grave in dignity if nothing better. So I'm working to give Wade all I've got while he can still use it—and the* all *includes whatever I've held back from him in the past. If he wants it, that is. I'm sure you won't grudge him your role in the story, if he probes that far. We almost certainly owe it to him.*

None of which means that every hour of this doesn't blast on through my head like a cold jackhammer that's somehow silenced but pounds on still. The sight of this boy alone in deep water, far past my reach or anyone's apparently— well, you've seen him and know the worst.

I'll phone you this weekend. Wade will likely call you too—he says that's his plan. But I wanted you to have this much in writing first. Drive down to see us as soon as you've got the planting in hand—let me know if the business account is too low. I trust Grainger's upright and running the world still. Wade mentioned yesterday that he meant to see Grainger soon somehow. I can't be sure such a plan is realistic, and I certainly can't ask you to bring Grainger down here—even if his body could stand the trip, he very well might not recognize Wade when he got here, changed as Wade is. But we'll talk it over soon, you and I. Love to Emily and thanks for her care, love to yourself and unpayable thanks.

Ever,
Hutch

That same night, after Hutch was asleep, Wade managed to reach the operator and ask her to place a call to Grainger. On the third ring, the old man answered. *"All right."*

"Mr. Grainger?"

"Him."

"*This is Wade, your old friend.*"

"*Younger than me. Everything else alive is younger than me.*"

"*Well, except for a few trees, I guess you're nearly right.*"

"*You said you were Wade? Don't sound much like him.*"

"*It's me—guaranteed. I'm just getting younger.*"

"*Your eyes improving?*"

"*I think maybe Yes. Some days anyhow, minutes at a time, I can see moving things.*"

"*It's the still ones that kill you.*"

"*Don't make me laugh please. I'm sore all over.*"

"*Somebody beating on you?—I still got my gun; just say the word.*"

"*The word? The word. Grainger, I can't think of but one word most days.*"

"*Your mind failing on you?*"

"*No, never been clearer. But all I think about is one word, Wyatt. Wyatt Bondurant—remember him?*"

"*Can't say I do, thank Jesus Above.*"

"*He was hard on you, I well recall—hard on most everybody but me.*"

"*Ain't he killing you now? Ain't that fairly hard?*"

"*He thought so at least—Wyatt thought so. It killed him to know it. But no, I blame nobody, live or dead. I walked, eyes open, into one big set of blades, grinding live meat. Still I liked my time on Earth, short as it's been.*"

"*You lucky as a racehorse.*"

"*Want to tell me how?*"

"*You leaving on out while you're still yourself.*"

"*You're who you've been since the day I was born—that long anyhow.*"

"*No, child, Grainger Walters turned into this warm corpse, oh, fifty years ago—when did Gracie Walters die?*"

"*I never knew Gracie, I'm sad to say. Recall she was gone well before I came.*"

"*You missed a good sight.*"

"*I'll miss a lot more.*"

"*Child, you've seen every bit of the story. Nothing much to it that you hadn't seen once you tried your body on one other soul.*"

Wade took a long wait. "*I thank you for that.*"

"*And it's true as a knife—*" Grainger hung up then, high in midair.

April 24, 1993

Dear Emily,

I was so grateful for your kindness and sympathy in phoning last evening; be assured I won't speak of it to anyone. The whole situation here is harder than anything I've been in, except for the long months of silence from Wade when he was in New York, refusing most calls and accepting nothing by way of help. Those months were the nearest I've ever come to losing all grip. Now that Hutch and Strawson have brought him back south, what the new problem comes down to is terribly simple. Hutch wants as little of me as ever. He lets me stop by with food and clean clothes for Wade and, those times, he mostly manages to be polite. But I know he'd rather I vanished today and left no traces, surely no claim on Wade.

Even more painful, as I tried to tell you before I broke down, I can't be certain Wade wants my visits either. Oh he thanks me for favors and answers small questions; but more than not, he's silent and pulled back—dozing or pretending to, though I well know he's tired from the moment of sunrise onward.

All I'm trying to do is keep my loving presence in his mind. I tell myself that's my minimum duty, however much less it amounts to than I hope for. I try to believe that, somewhere in his mind, there's a memory of having a mother that cherished him above all others and that, if I keep up a gentle persistence beside him, he'll connect who I am with the memory of me in his earlier days. I'm the same girl anyhow. Do you feel that as strongly as I do—that you don't get any older inside but are always who you've been since birth? I generally feel like me at the age of about eleven, smarter some ways but the same general girl; and it's only when I wander past mirrors and see the changes that I shiver and think "Who's that old stranger in here with me?"

I've got to get back to work right now, but let me just ask one thing in closing. I think you know that, all these years, I've never asked you to press Straw for help with me and Hutchins. And I wouldn't today, if time weren't almost certainly short. But if you can find a natural way to say to Strawson that Ann is Wade's mother—and never was less, in spite of his refusals—then maybe Straw could find it in his heart to see Hutch and ask him to find a way to give me natural rights in this sadness. If you think it's too awkward, then thanks all the same. I wouldn't want to tread into tender ground.

Any chance you could ride down here one day soon and eat lunch with me? I hate myself for still needing food; but I do eat lunch, though very seldom dinner.

Keep us three in your prayers.

> *And love from,*
> *Ann*

> *April 25, 1993*

Dear Ann,

Your letter is just here. Since I'm heading into town for groceries in a minute, I'll jot a quick word and mail it myself, to prevent suspicion.

Rest your mind on one subject at least. Strawson has said to me at least once daily that Hutchins is walling you out of this and that that's less than fair. I've told Strawson that fair is not the word, and he agrees to that too. But you know how much he reveres Hutchins Mayfield and all H's plans, so I cannot hold out a great deal of hope that Strawson knows any way to help right now.

If he forgets that he saw your writing on the envelope an hour ago when he brought in the mail, then tonight I'll slip in a word along the lines you suggested. The sooner the better but I can't let S think you have coached me in this—you understand.

What I don't understand is, where are you finding the strength to watch the sights you are watching? You asked for my prayers and, Ann, they are yours. The last thing Strawson would admit to me is that he prays too, but I know he does, and you are high on his list. He has always said you were "Very top-grade," which is far as he goes in human praise!

I will phone again soon. Till when,

The best love,
Emily

April 29, 1993

My dear Ivory,

I am dictating this to a man who is helping me come to life the best I can hope to. His name is Hart and he has plenty of it—heart, I mean. He is working on his doctor's degree in English literature and has studied with Hutch, so this will all be spelled correctly and in proper grammar. Not that it needs to be all that proper to say what I mean. Not that you don't know all I mean already. Or so I trust, God knows, God knows. I asked Hart to write those words down twice.

What I mean is, you have been better to me for nine years now than anyone else ever was in all my time. Everything I ever did to hurt you is clear in my addled brain this instant as any needle stuck in an eye. You said more than once that you pardoned me, and I more than half believe you have. But since I've been down here, I wake up in the night—most every night—and see your face that awful day I turned on you, when you were needing help I didn't know how to give. Or so I thought. I was full grown though, as you pointed out, and had nobody but me to blame for the preservation of terminal adolescence.

Don't feel like you need to call me up and say any words. Don't think I'm asking for written forgiveness. But sometime soon, when you find yourself in a quiet place and the light feels right, see if you can manage to say inside your head "I wish a peaceful rest for Wade Mayfield, I and my kin, through all time

*to come." Just those few words, between you and the air, will very likely reach
me and help me on, wherever I'm headed, however soon or late.*

*Again, dear friend, you are matchless in the world. Long love to yourself
and all you care for*

From your hopeful
Wade

2

When Hart had finished transcribing the letter and addressing the envelope, he brought it to Wade who signed it the best he could, folded it carefully, then gave it back to Hart and said "You lick the envelope please."

Hart laughed. "Lazy dude, your tongue still works."

Wade said "Too true. No, my spit's infected—I already warned you. I try not to export the virus to friends."

Hart said "Eureka!"

Wade pointed a finger in Hart's direction. "Everything you write for me's a deep secret—swear to that please?"

"Absolutely," Hart said. "I'm the dark grave of secrets."

Wade said "I'm glad I've met him at last."

Only then did Hart hear the tactlessness of his metaphor. He laughed. "I'm sorry to bring up the grave!"

"That goes without saying" and Wade laughed too.

They were in Wade's room in strong morning light, Wade was dressed in a sweat suit and lying on his bed, Hart was at the small desk Wade had used in childhood. When the letter was sealed and stamped, Hart said "I'll walk this down to the road and leave it for the postman." He stood to go.

Wade agreed, then quickly said "No, wait." His hand came up on the air like a painter's, and he drew a complicated line that copied the outer boundaries of Hart—his head and trunk at least. When it was finished, Wade lapsed into silence.

Finally Hart said "Wait for what?"

Wade said "Just stand still another ten seconds—I can suddenly see you." In fact he could. Wade's eyes had slowly clarified as they wrote the letter; and now Hart Salter was here before him, the first entirely visible creature that Wade had seen in three or four months. Only at the outer limits of Hart, a kind of flickering silver aura that clung to his outline with small explosions, was there anything less than honest facts. Maybe six foot five, with a full head of thick chestnut hair and a long ingratiating face with a Jesus beard—all so real and pleasing to the eyes and mind that it sent a terrible bolt through Wade, like a single blow from a battering ram. *I'm leaving this. I'm worse than dead.* He even shut his eyes and spoke the knowledge aloud, in a whisper. "Let me be really blind."

Except for occasional shaves and trims, Hart had never spent more than an hour, all told, in front of a mirror, regarding himself. Like most well-put-together creatures, he'd been told often he was no eyesore. In fact everybody important in his path, except for his wife, had sooner or later praised his looks. But the news had weighed very lightly on him; he'd all but never relied on his looks in any exchange. So now he was mildly puzzled by Wade's wish. "I'll stay, sure, if you're hurting any."

Wade said "I am. But you can't help."

"No, try me. Say the word." Since Hart got here at nine o'clock, he'd already helped Wade bathe and dress.

Wade's eyes opened and saw Hart again almost as clearly, blurring slightly at the edges like a spirit materializing before you or slowly leaving. After a long time Wade grinned and took his biggest gamble in maybe three years. "Would you just strip and stand right there—oh, for one whole minute?"

It took Hart less than five seconds to find sufficient permission. *I'll be four thousand miles from here in another few days. Before I'm back, this boy will be dead* (he'd always thought of Wade as a boy since the first day he saw him). So Hart smiled slightly and said "You bet." Then he laid the sealed letter on the desk, briskly slid off his frayed jeans, T-shirt and underpants and stood in place where the sun was brightest. In general, he was always at home in his body—no excess modesty, just a real ease in the amplitude of the irreducible skin and bones in which he'd met the world from the start.

There were no more than ten feet between him and Wade; and after a moment when Hart felt a little more like a target than he'd planned to feel, he shifted his weight to his broad right foot and hung his right hand like a hinge at the crest of his massive left shoulder. Unthinking, he'd assumed the stance of a thousand athletes—dead for two thousand years—in shattered Greek and Roman marble, unthinkably generous in offering the world their private portion of eternal perfection.

Wade took in the sight in full awareness of both its blessing and what he guessed was its bitter finality. The splendor of the pale taut skin of the chest and belly, the smiling wings of muscle suspended from the corners of the groin, the full heavy sex—strong as they all were, they looked alarmingly fragile to Wade: one more thing he'd failed to protect and now must abandon.

One more last thing. Even as he thought it, Wade's eyes were clouding. Hart's arms were already swimming in a vague light. *Ask to touch him once quick, only one touch.*

At the same instant Hart thought *Take the four steps forward; put his hand on your chest.* For the first time, Hart saw the face of Stacy his wife, who was four miles from here at her greenhouse job, still hungry for far more than Hart had to give—he or any man he'd yet known. *Well, she'll never know anything that passes here. This is between just Wade, me and death.* Hart took two steps.

Wade's hand came up, palm out toward the shield of his new friend's chest. *New friend and last.* Then the hand drew back of its own accord; and Wade told Hart "There. Many thanks but no, just there forever." Nothing had ever looked finer than this—worth a whole life's service—and Wade well knew that he'd watched the world more closely in his three decades than anyone he'd known, maybe barring Hutch. Nothing had ever looked farther away than this present goodness. Nothing—that Wade could recall at least—had ever brought his mind more joy or the weight of more desperate loss than this sight here, this kind young man. Wade's hands went flat on the sheet beside him; and he lay on watching, still saying "Just there."

So Hart stayed there, entirely at ease in the unblocked light of a day in progress far beyond them on the actual Earth, till Wade's eyes shut and he fell back to sleep—gone quicker than any feverish child.

3

There were fourteen members of Hutch's class in Writing Narrative Poetry—eight men, six women. The oldest were two postgraduate renegades, moonlighting from the Law and Divinity Schools. The youngest was twenty-one, named Maitland Moses, a senior burdened with talent and a mind as attentive as a small threatened creature, though he seemed fearless and undownably cheerful. By four that afternoon they'd all assembled at Hutch's place in Orange County, four miles from campus in the evergreen fringes of Duke Forest. The forest itself was eight thousand acres of pines and cedars, streams, lost ponds and the odd deserted farmhouse biding its time with plentiful deer, foxes, crows, hawks, wild turkeys and herons, the raccoon and snake and indomitable beaver, even the occasional Madagascan lemur escaped from the high-fenced Primate Center just up the road. And Hutch's twelve acres abutted the woods on three sides.

The late afternoon air buoyed itself on a unique slanting amber light native to Hutch's corner of the county, a ridge that his oldest neighbor called Couch Mountain, the highest point for many miles around. Hutch and Ann had built the house in the 1960s on an outcrop of rock at the ridge of Couch Mountain. It was ten spacious high-ceilinged rooms, a small greenhouse, an old-fashioned basement stocked with nothing more valuable than prehistoric paint cans and exhausted appliances, and a wide brick terrace facing due south from which on clear days you could see farther than Chapel Hill, which was ten miles away beyond the broad pasture where a neighbor's cattle still grazed in monumental stupor broken only by unpredictable mountings, couplings and outraged bellows.

By five o'clock, four of the pleasant but talentless members of the class had read their final installments of verse. Hutch had listened quietly through the criminally flattering student comments on one another; then he'd offered his own slightly keener observations and was near to calling on Maitland Moses to end the session with what promised to be the concluding part of either a long verse memoir he'd been writing all term or a newer attempt at a truly bizarre tale. Hutch had even asked Mait to start reading when it came to him suddenly that he'd failed to tell the group about Wade — the details anyhow; he knew they'd heard the rumors.

Earlier in the day, Hutch had told Wade to join them outdoors at any point if he felt up to it; and now through the open door behind him, Hutch could hear Wade shuffling somewhere inside. So he faced the students, kept his voice down and briefed them honestly. "My son Wade Mayfield moved back in with me three weeks ago. He's been an architect in New York for some years but has been ill lately and is resting up here in the house where — strangely for a modern child — he was actually born. His mother went into fast unexpected labor; and yours truly birthed him on the living room sofa, not ten yards back of where we're seated. By the time the rescue squad arrived, he was wailing strongly. I've told Wade to join us if he feels the urge, so at least you'll know him if he chooses to join us." Hutch ended even softer. "His eyesight is bad."

And while young Mait was clearing his throat and giving his usual abject rundown of what he'd reached for and failed to grasp in this final installment, Wade chose to appear. He'd dressed in a pair of his boyhood jeans that fit his narrow waist again and a long-tailed black shirt that swallowed his shrunken shoulders and chest; and as he came toward them, Wade paused in the doorway to brace himself against the full light.

Mait saw him first and, with premature courtesy, said "Join the firing squad." When Wade was plainly confused by that, Maitland tried again. "I'm about to spill my last mile of guts here. Listen at your own risk."

By then Hutch had risen and gone toward Wade. "You and I'll sit over here in the shade where it's cooler." Hutch made his elbow available for guidance.

But Wade had been seeing better all day, never so well as he'd seen Hart Salter but snatches of what seemed visual fact. He said to Hutch "Let me try the sun first" and took slow steps on toward a broad flat rock that rose in the midst of the paving bricks and took the steady light. Wade sat there carefully and looked round the smeared and jittering faces. By some kind of instinct he settled on Maitland Moses' face and said "I'm the dying homo son." Then Wade gave a grin to the whole wide circle. In the light he looked a good deal less thin—he barely weighed a hundred pounds—and in three weeks of short sunbaths, he'd replaced his pallor with a yellowish tan.

Hutch heard the self-introduction calmly with no sense that Wade meant to cause a stir. As for the students, Hutch thought only *All right, they claim they're adults; let's see them take this.*

But in fact only Mait and two of the women had heard Wade's words, and only Mait had taken the next step—*This man's got the plague.* He looked to Hutch.

Hutch told him "Read, Mait."

Whenever Mait read his rough drafts aloud, his voice was still subject to the woozy pitch of adolescence—steep climbs and plunges, hilarious yodels but he'd long since mastered a way to read blank verse and make it sound like the pulse of a curious heart, a life that was not quite human but benign and entirely reliable. Though he'd only finished the lines last night, Mait already all but knew them by heart; and in a situation where most young poets read like whipped dogs—head down, avoiding eye contact—Mait read fairly straight at Wade's face.

What he'd brought today was the weirder of his two unfinished poems, one that he had started four months ago as a kind of Browningesque dramatic monologue—the first-person and unintentionally comic account of a young husband's first adultery. In Seattle on a business trip, and exhausted at midnight, the husband goes to his hotel bar. There he meets a friendly and mildly exotic woman, whom he winds up taking back to his room. Only at the end of lengthy foreplay does the errant husband detect two faint crescent-scars beneath the woman's breasts. He politely asks if she's had breast cancer. She says "Guess again." He says "Implants?" The woman then gives an account of her sex change five years ago. As a man she'd been a successful yacht builder with a wife and two daughters; as a woman, she goes on building yachts but is very much alone. Tonight is the first time she's dared herself to find a man, and her success quickly reduces her to sobs which the husband is powerless to console, though he goes on trying throughout the long night. It was an allegedly true story that a young computer salesman had unloaded on Maitland, in urgent confession, on an airplane high over south Georgia last winter.

But before Mait had forged far ahead with his latest draft, the class lost its professional composure and collapsed in mirth. More than half of them were exquisitely trained in the taboos of political and social correctness, but till now they'd never been challenged by a story so fraught with the heartbreak of various minorities—men-made-women by courtesy of knives and chemicals, adulterous but sensitive husbands, the vagabonds of business life in contemporary America, the unseen but surely downcast wife and whomever the man/woman had abandoned in his quest for fulfillment.

After two minutes of restraint, however, the whole class took a genuine dive into helpless laughter. The dive included Hutch as well, a teacher who always tried to obey Ben Jonson's advice never to tell a young poet all his faults. Finally he managed to sober himself. Then he calmed the group and asked Mait how conscious he was of the laughter implicit in any such tale when told in such a flat-footed fashion.

At the first hilarity, Mait had been stunned—irony was not his strongest suit—but in twenty seconds he'd seen the point and joined the laughter. Then he literally ripped the pages apart in the class's presence and promised them better. The promise amounted—on the spot—to the final installment of another slow but quite different confession, one doled out in pieces through the term, of a fact he'd kept to himself till now—that he was both a virgin at twenty-one and "queer as a pink hairnet" (it was Mait's own simile; he dodged the demeaning label *gay* by saying he felt far more nearly *glum* and that *queer* was something he was glad to be if the world was *normal*). And the final pages he took from his notebook and read to the class now were cast as a letter from Mait to his father, a career marine who'd died in Vietnam the year the boy was born.

Right off, Hutch heard the resemblance to a poem that he himself had written for his own father Rob, thirty-seven years ago, as Hutch left America after Rob's funeral and flew back to England and his graduate studies.

At the end of Mait's second poem, three of the students tried valiantly to feel their own way into its naked heart. The lines more or less conveyed a child's awareness, at the age of seven, that men were the magnetic pole of his mind and would always be—mind and body eventually. All three of the well-intentioned students failed in their try at understanding (they'd have bedded with wolves quicker than their own gender, though they didn't quite say so). One of the law students was repulsed, though he managed to hide it in a rambling attack on iambic verse as being un-American—one of the oldest critical chestnuts and one that Hutch demolished in a sentence: "The only American line, if there were one, would be in the rhythm of an Indian heart-beat, whatever that was four centuries ago."

One student, Nan Benedict, had made her own version of Mait's discovery in her freshman year and had yet to tell anyone but the roommate who'd accepted her love as a mildly pleasant matter of course, due to end now that both would graduate next month—the roommate called herself "a four-year dyke." As Nan responded warmly to Mait's lines, she unloaded her own brisk confession onto this last class as a kind of tribute to their four-months' closeness in the crowded dinghy of a writing class.

The others heard mainly, in Mait's lines, a single message—nothing to do with eros or oddness and nothing that meant to be proud or cruel. Both Nan's lean confession and the sound of Mait's lines, in his frail voice, joined to tell the talentless watchers that *We can do all we want with these words while the rest of you'll fall further and further behind as you choke, in untold feeling, through the rest of your lives.*

It was only toward the end of Mait's poem, however, that a genuine strength broke through to Wade. In mildly archaic but dead-earnest lines, Maitland's hand reached toward his own father who'd fallen, shot through the temple, at the edge of a boatbuilder's hut he'd burned in the mouth of the Mekong River near Vung Tau.

> "Sir, this untried unused hand has traveled
> Worlds, or half this Earth, and guards you now.
> Replay the fatal moment for me. My innocence
> Can helmet, shield and glove your life—that
> Life which gave me mine and which, even here,
> I taste by night in dreams, your fleecy pelt."

When the word *pelt* brought a hush behind it, and no one spoke, Wade jerked upright to his feet and said "Christ-in-a-rowboat! *Thank* this man." His eyes were dry but the skin of his face contorted in pain when, still, no one spoke.

Hutch waited, then chose not to break the standoff.

Mait finally said "Thank you, Wade."

Wade stood on in place by his rock, a little rickety. He was suddenly baffled—where was he, why this crowd of voices, who were these blank faces? Then he found what seemed to be the head of his father, a head that seemed to be facing him knowingly; so he said to Hutch "I dreamed about you, old handsome sir, most nights of my life" as though his life was far behind him. Then he sat again on the sunny rock.

Hutch said "Thanks, Maitland. I share Wade's feeling—you've come so far in four months, I'm pleased. All of you know I almost never push anybody to try publishing anything, verse or prose, till it's smoking on the desk with sullen impatience or felonious narcissism at least; but I think Mait Moses has an actual poem that—once he's let it lie awhile to purify its diction, which is still a little crusty—others should read. Mait, plan by late summer to send it to *Poetry* magazine in Chicago—they might well take it. If not, whatever you do, keep it moving."

Mait flushed scarlet and his eyes had a life he'd hid till today.

A few others murmured "Excellent," "Write-on"; "Good luck, man."

Wade said "I'm just glad I lasted to hear it." By then the late light had deepened in tone, and Wade's eyes just barely registered the change. All the air around him this minute was a rich brown as deep and virtually narcotic as the shadows prevailing at the edges of late Rembrandt self-portraits. Slowly the shade was mounting round Wade like a strange welcome fluid in which he could breathe with a freedom he'd seldom known till this moment. He even turned his head through a long arc, hunting for west and the sinking sun. He discovered it finally and fixed on its brightness, then lifted his chin toward the vanishing disc. It hadn't crossed his mind that others were watching him; the light and warmth felt like a brief health, for eight or ten seconds as his eyes dimmed again even further toward blindness.

Hutch was watching though and, to him, Wade looked like one appalled face in a Rodin bronze of teeming Hell or like a rescued drowner. From eighteen or nineteen till two years ago, Wade had struck Hutch as one of the three great stunners he'd known, among men at least—that handsomely formed and carefully tended and moved by an open generous heart. Much of the beauty survived here today but only as the fragile planes and struts of a crumbling building, struggling to hold off a barely arrested downward fall. To change the present feeling, Hutch was compelled to stand and speak. "I need volunteers please to help with the food. It's all in the kitchen, thanks to the caterer, waiting to be spread."

Wade said "Wait." When everybody faced him for final orders, Wade said "Nobody's asked to hear *my* poem."

Most of the students exchanged doubtful glances.

But Hutch sat again and said "Tell us, Son." In adolescence Wade had written some genuinely likable short poems; so Hutch was curious and, for the first time since they'd left New York, he smelled again the elation he'd known when he found Wade willing to come back south. *This boy is going to surprise us yet.*

At first it seemed Wade had only been joking; his face was tranquil again but empty.

Hutch finally moved to stand.

Wade motioned him down and laughed. "Lost my mind for a minute—" No poem came though and finally Wade noticed the circle's discomfort. He rigged a broad grin. "Anybody want to ask me a question?" When no one spoke, he said "I hope you're not scared; I'm not contagious, not in formal relations." He laughed a dry note.

It dawned on Hutch that Wade might want to tell his own story, some part of it anyhow. He said "Wade, these are very thoughtful people. I've trusted my own new poems with them; they were smart and too kind. Want to tell them about what you're living through?"

Wade took the suggestion like a starved man, snagging at the word *Yes* fiercely with his chin. Then he found a voice much like his old voice, deep and affable. "I'm thirty-two years old and almost surely can't hope to make it to thirty-three. Once I completed my apprenticeship, I worked six years as a licensed architect; so I have some feeling for what you people try to make in poems—there's a sturdy serviceable building in Brooklyn, a three-story brick night-college for immigrants; it's got my name on the cornerstone. Barring nuclear war, that'll probably last somewhere between fifty and a hundred years till some real-estate mogul in the twenty-first century tears it down or blows it up. Who gets much more, when it comes to lasting? What killed me though was not hard work—" Wade stopped, looked straight in Maitland's direction and laughed. "This sounds more like a bad song from the forties than anything else, but *I died for love.*" He stopped there; it seemed to be all he meant to give.

Hutch said "You're *alive*; don't use the past tense. It's hard on your pa, not to speak of the poor old English language."

Wade smiled. "I stand corrected, Doctor. No, all I'm meaning to say to you people—all I know now with my brain ruined—is that I represent a few hundred thousand Americans of a certain breed who're dead or dying or doomed but don't know it yet for no better reason than the fact they trusted their bodies with each other when nobody guessed that love or rut could kill you. For a short thirty years there, starting in the forties, penicillin cured the clap and syphilis. A vaccine fixed you for hepatitis B, they had killer lotions for crabs and fleas, and other drugs killed off intestinal amoebas. That didn't leave much but herpes and murder to worry about in the love bazaars, whatever your pick of species or gender.

"Since I never went with more than two men—honest to God, I never had sex with but three women and two other men; and the men were plainly not psychopaths—I knew I was safe. Turned out I was wrong. What you're seeing, this minute, is a young man that ought to weigh 175 and be looking at least as presentable as anybody here and who ought to be ready to build good buildings for forty more years. And what this fucked-up poem of mine says is not that you should prowl around sex, scared cold to death, or not to have sex unless you're wrapped in some stainless steel condom. No, what I mean is, if any of you wind up being writers or even just competent witnesses, then tell the world what it means now to live—till some cure's found, if a cure exists—in a whole new world where, for the first time since penicillin dawned, the acts of love and the best kind of pleasure, the only good acts most humans get to do, can kill you dead in this slow dreadful way." By then, though Wade hadn't seen himself clearly for some four months, he knew he stood as his own best example, in the students' eyes at least—his broad flayed skull in setting sunlight. In that many words he'd burned all his strength but the last few traces which let him say "I better lie down."

Hutch looked to Maitland.

Mait stood, and together they walked Wade in to his bed.

4

From his decades of teaching, Hutch well knew that American students never leave a party of their own free will. Even self-possessed graduate students must be given strong hints that it's time to leave; most undergraduates won't think of budging before sunrise unless the host specifically orders them out. Tonight though—once they'd ravaged the spread of sandwich makings, baked beans, wine and deep-dish pies—they trailed off quietly into the evening. Some parted with the classic student vow to stay in contact through the years when Hutch understood he'd likely never hear their names again and would never miss them individually, despite his pleasure in their brief company and the things he learned in their presence still, after so much time.

When the last car had gone down the drive, Hutch thought he'd check on Wade first—the students had pretty well cleared the mess and washed the few dishes. Wade's light was out, his door was open, Hutch stood at the threshold long enough to hear his son breathing slow and raucous as if each breath was a separate achievement. For an instant Hutch felt his own heart shut, a desperate fist; and a wild thought racketed through him in words. *I'll get Rob's pistol and finish this*—he meant Wade and him both. *But Ann would find us.* Hutch almost grinned to think that would stop him if nothing else could. Did he mainly want to spare Ann the shock or deprive her of a grisly moment she'd dine out on the rest of her life? *You're not this vicious, Hutch. Go do some harmless work.*

As Hutch turned toward his study, Wade spoke from where he lay flat on his bed. "You ashamed?"

"No more than usual. Did I do so badly?" Hutch walked to the bed and switched on the lamp.

Wade turned, with open eyes, to face him. "You were smart as ever, smart and the soul of Dixie hospitality. No, I meant me—are you shamed by me?"

Hutch sat on the edge of the mattress and laid a hand on Wade. "I'm as proud of you as I ever was."

Wade waited so long he seemed unconscious; then he laughed two notes. "That's begging the question, Doc—how proud of me have you ever been?"

"Son, that's one rap I really won't take. You well know what you've meant to me."

"Tell me again—I must have forgot."

Hutch said "You're my beloved son, you're a good human being, a superb architect, you've carried our family's line on in style."

Wade shook his head. "I'm crashing with it now." His right hand imitated an airplane crashing to Earth; and for the first time since he'd been home, his eyes were full.

Hutch couldn't speak either.

Finally Wade said "No, what I really meant was, I'm sorry I gave that lecture to your class—that and my sizzling true confession."

"They're certified grown-ups, legally at least. They took it in stride."

Wade said "That's a lie."

Hutch said "I watched them; maybe two or three flinched. But it did them good—welcome to life."

"Amen to that. Now say you forgive me."

Hutch said "'You forgive me.'"

"I'm serious."

"Forgive what?" Hutch truly knew of no grievance to pardon, not here in this room.

Wade's eyes focused so precisely on Hutch that anyone watching would have sworn they could see as keenly as a condor's. "Pardon me for running my life in the ground—" Again Wade gave his little airplane gesture.

"You haven't done that. And anyhow, if this monster virus had been around four decades ago, I might very well be sicker than you." That was an opening he'd never quite offered to Wade before.

But Wade was fixed on his own rail. He put up a hushing finger; *Let me finish.* "Pardon me for choosing and loving forever—you've got to know I'll love Wyatt Bondurant forever: a man that flat-out hated you."

Hutch said "There are whole broad pieces of me anybody in his right mind would hate."

Wade said "Amen" and waited.

Hutch wouldn't object but he wouldn't ask for clarification. *What does he hate in me?* Hutch still couldn't ask.

So Wade pointed past him. "Just say the word *pardon.* It's a good English word."

"Pardon. Pardon."

Wade's hand fished around, found Hutch's and pressed it.

Hutch said "You say it too. Say it to me."

Wade's lips barely parted and made the motions that might have been *pardon* if he'd found the strength. In a moment he'd slid into sleep like a week-old infant. Sleep closed around him.

Hutch sat for two minutes, then quietly rose, switched off the light and was halfway toward his study again to read a few last papers from his seventeenth-century seminar when he thought he heard the front door close. They'd had several break-ins out here in the seventies, but he didn't feel scared. He quietly walked toward the hall to investigate.

There, with the door half open behind him, was Maitland Moses—big-eyed and edgy.

Hutch said "Did you try to ring? The bell doesn't work. I was checking on Wade."

"No, I'm afraid I just walked in." Oddly Mait's voice was under control; had some new hormone just kicked in and anchored his yodeling?

"Well, you're under arrest." Hutch almost meant it; he was private to a fault and had always been. But the sight of Mait's collapsing face brought him around. "You forget something?"

"I'm pretty sure I did."

"Run find it; I've got a million papers to mark."

Quick as a burned child, Mait turned toward the door. His shorts (a pair of hacked-off jeans), the poisonous green of his baggy T-shirt, the rosy face of a Dickensian chimney sweep completed the picture of an innocent hapless Chaplinesque clown—a genuine orphan bound for the night.

"No, find what you lost, Mait."

"Sir, it's nothing I lost; but my bike and I were halfway down the drive when it just came over me that soon I was leaving this good place forever, and we'd never really sat still and talked—not off campus at least, you and I. Not in a real home."

Tired and dejected and busy as Hutch was, he had all the teaching instincts of his family still in him, ticking infallibly. Every student plea that was not plainly fraudulent demanded his attention. *You can't turn this wet dog out yet.* So he told Mait "Get yourself a drink from the kitchen and bring me that last 7 Up I saved. I'll wait in here."

While Mait found a beer, Hutch sat in his main chair and actually dozed for ninety seconds (the ease with which he could nap anywhere was a life-long boon). When his eyes reopened, Mait was in the opposite chair, looking whole years older than he had in the afternoon—older, calmer and somehow wiser across the eyes and brow. Hutch had a sense that decades had passed or hours at least. But he looked to his watch and saw it was just past nine o'clock, same day. Near him on the table, his 7 Up fizzed in a silver goblet he hadn't seen for years—the first prize he'd ever won for poetry, in high school. Mait must have gouged deep in the cabinets. *What's this boy hunting?* Hutch took a long swallow of the cold tart drink. "You want to just start in and see where it leads?"

Mait was puzzled.

"I believe you said you forgot to tell me something—please don't confess you copied your poem from an Urdu original of the fourteenth century."

Mait gave a good imitation of *You caught me!* "I did copy, sure, but just from you. You're bound to have heard it."

Hutch smiled. "I may have detected an echo of olden days in the vaults of the Hutchins Mayfield canon, but I meant what I said. You're very possibly the thing itself, if you need to be—a live working poet. I'm fairly sure of that much, or I'd never say it." Through the years Hutch had always told his writing students that he wouldn't manhandle them in class for being less than geniuses; but if they cared to hear his honest opinion of their poems at the end of term, he'd give it to them privately so long as they knew it was just one opinion, subject to error.

None but the really good students ever asked—maybe a total of six in all the decades, and four of them had published volumes by now. Mait hadn't asked yet; Hutch had told him anyhow this afternoon and in front of the others. What was left to say? (Hutch tried to wean students once they'd left him—no lifetime correspondence courses. He and every honorable writer he knew had made their own way with bare hands through granite; he thought others should.)

Mait sat forward and gave an oddly formal speech of thanks—he was from rural upper-class Virginia and a little hypercourtly. Once the speech was past, Mait said "Next I need to know if you despise me."

Hutch was surprised. *Is this some penitential feast tonight?* "Despise you?—absolutely not. What gave you that notion?"

Mait was agonized and blushing again, and his voice broke loose. "This endlessly prolonged initiation of mine into the sodomite tribe. You've had to put up with a lot of navel gazing—or is it weenie gazing?—and I've got the sense every now and then that you'd have liked me better if I was a functional lumberjack with a ring of dumb girls hung round my studly shoulders."

Hutch laughed. "That might have been picturesque; but no, you're who you are, my friend. That's been enough for me. I'll miss your avid mind and kindly wit, but I know I'll see your work in print in the next five years."

"That still doesn't say you don't despise me."

Hutch said "For *what?* What I know about you is what I've seen, none of which repels me. Granted, I haven't trailed you around with a night-vision scope, spying on your murky secrets. But in any case, 'Nothing human is foreign to me,' as some Roman said." After nearly four decades of teaching, like most workers at any trade, Hutch was finding it nearly impossible to produce anything like a fresh reaction to a youthful question. However well-meaning he meant to be, he'd hear his words limp out from his face and creep like tattered tramps toward the young; or he'd pick up an imaginary needle, set it down precisely on his mental record and play them a paragraph or two from his greatest hits—home truths, convictions, lines from old poems: things Hutch had mouthed a thousand times.

Mait was not satisfied with secondhand wisdom, and he winced hard. The sudden age and depth of his face were holding up. "Then I need to ask you a violent question."

Hutch laughed. "What's a violent question please?"

"I feel like, deep down, you understand everything I've ever felt. You've done everything I want to do—that's made you mighty awesome to me."

Hutch smiled to think he'd at last understood. "Are you asking me if I'm queer too?"

Mait's eyes looked doused in welcome relief. He was plainly heartened by the opening, so much so that he doubted his luck. "What makes you think that?"

Hutch said "You're claiming I understand you, to the shoe soles and sockets. All right then, my world-famed understanding tells me you're feeling like nothing *but* queer; and you're hunting down volunteers for your little lifeboat."

Mait said "Bingo!" in a scooping yell.

Hutch pointed behind him toward Wade's room and whispered "He's sleeping." Then he drank the rest of his drink and faced Mait, working with more than a little amusement to drain the chalky professor from his look. "Queer—me? No, not now nor any other night—not that pure a label, no one pigeonhole." That seemed truth enough.

Mait leaned in. "Bisexual?"

And Hutch thought it through but finally laughed. "No, every man I've met who claimed bisexuality was a full-time queer in under six months."

Mait agreed. "Me too. But you understand loving your own cut and kind?"

With no trace of compunction, Hutch grinned and agreed. "Still there's never been a slot or group or club I was comfortable in. God—for instance—I voted as a yellowdog Democrat at every election since Jefferson ran; but I've never once worn a campaign button, never confessed in a telephone poll, never felt a hundred percent like a donkey. As for love and rut, I can freely tell you I've loved more than one man—oh Christ yes, loved men in every practical way from stem to stern, plus a few ways that strained the laws of physics; and I enjoyed the hell out of most of those nights.

"I can even say that, looking back, those days and nights were my main pleasure—the height of the pleasure my body's known anyhow, actual joy down the length of my skin. Men do know how to ring men's bells. And I think of those few men, all my time near them, with a lot of thanks and very slim regrets. The only regrets are for my own skittish meanness when people leaned on me. Somehow I couldn't bear another man's weight for long at a time—maybe because I bore a lovable breakable father right through my childhood. But I can't recall an act I've done with my bare body that I'm sorry for—I say that with full awareness, I think, of the moral codes of most religions.

"Still when I was only a few years older than you tonight, toward the end of my years of study in England, I honest to God felt my mind undertake a wide slow turn westward. It felt like some strong gyrostabilizer moving a ship onto some new course and locking it there. Whatever, I gradually found my mental, spiritual, sexual needs homing in on one certain young woman—my girlfriend for years, whom I'd mistreated on more than one continent. Her name was Ann Gatlin. We married once I was home from England, we had our son Wade, and I thought we were doing as well as old yoke-horses after decades together; but Ann thought otherwise a short while back and went her own way. You met her two years ago, when I first knew you—"

Mait said "I did. She's a striking lady."

"I'll tell her you said so. She's fine all right."

"So you see her still?"

"She comes by regularly since Wade is home."

Mait said "Don't answer this if I'm out of line, but surely you were tempted hard after you chose her."

"To go with other men? I can tell you this much and it's simply the truth—you may not believe me; I barely believe myself in the matter—but though I've looked at a good many men and imagined my way into their hid places, I've literally never cheated with anyone, male or female, since the day I married Ann."

"How much did that cost you?"

Hutch had never calculated. He paused to try. "Not more than a few thousand dollars a year—to translate it crassly. Nothing I couldn't fairly easily afford."

"But now you've been alone out here for—what?—at least a year."

"Longer. And I've kept to myself. I've never been a barfly or bus-station hound. Still, just when I might have looked elsewhere to feed my mind, Wade Mayfield got dreadfully sick and that grounded me."

Mait said "I hate to ask this too, but isn't it the plague—Wade's thinness, his eyes?"

"Didn't he tell you outright this evening, you and the others? I thought that was clear."

"He never said the word."

Hutch said "No but he drew a stark picture. All his life, Wade's been a poor liar."

"Did you know he'd talk the way he did out there today?" Mait pointed outside as though Wade were still there, confessing in the dark.

Hutch could see Mait was back on his best calm stride; his eyes were drinking up information like a ditch of dry sand. "No, but once he'd started, I knew I was glad."

"Glad of what?"

Hutch studied this boy before him intently. *Why should I tell this raw near-stranger?* But he knew this stranger was at least as magnanimous as any captive dolphin so Hutch went ahead. "I guess I'm glad because what Wade confided to you and the class tonight means I'll get to talk to him now myself and tell him all—he knows next to nothing about his father."

"—Which is you, his blood father?"

"Absolutely. Can't you see my eyes in him and the shape of his head?"

Mait said "Oh yes sir" as if caught in some implication of bastardy. When Hutch said nothing, Mait said "I told you I'll be around this summer, right?"

"You got the grant then?"

"Three thousand dollars to live, eat and scribble on."

"Will you keep your apartment?"

"I doubt I can. My well-heeled roommate's leaving for a year in Japan next week, and four hundred dollars a month's mighty steep for an unpublished poet. I'll get something smaller or move in with the Poufs—they've got a cheap old barny house just off east campus." The Poufs were an ongoing, only mildly embarrassing, pair of near-transvestites in sequins and pumps and Joan Crawford shoulder pads.

Hutch said "Do yourself a favor—find an ex-convict or a nice axe-murderer, but don't stay long with those painted queens."

Mait grinned and mugged. "They speak well of you." But Hutch was in earnest. "Don't narrow your choices sooner than you have to. Just because your miserable Poufs have cut themselves a path one micron wide and a millimeter deep through the whole of human feeling, please Mait, don't you. Drive off in every direction you can manage, and crash if you must—you likely won't die—but don't slim your choices down too soon. Not to feathers and lizard bags. You've got a real chance to understand the world, not just one tribe and its rhinestone blinders."

Mait's face assumed a generic expression Hutch knew too well—the universal muscular response when a student hears the teacher babbling outdated nonsense and seals himself off without saying so, least of all contradicting: the eyes go glassy and the lips beam thinly. In Hutch's silence the boy said finally "I came back mainly to say I can help you any way you need me all summer long, maybe longer than that."

At first Hutch was puzzled. *Help, what help?* "With Wade, you mean?"

"It's the least I can do, much as you've given me."

"But I've hardly seen you outside class."

Mait said "In my work, in the way I'll try to live."

To hear that was harder than any sympathy Hutch had got lately. All the others—Grainger, Straw, Emily, Ann, Ivory, Boatie—had blood or near-blood stakes in Wade's life. This tenderfoot poet at hand here tonight, with his naive offer to enter a tunnel as bat-lined as any since the black death killed a third of all Europe, seemed a sudden return on Hutch's years of teaching, a trade that amounts to work in the dark with almost no immediate rewards (it was after all a teacher's long dream, to know he's connected and moved a young mind a few yards forward toward a sane useful life). At least Hutch managed to say what he felt. "That's as welcome an offer as I've ever got."

Mait said "I mean every syllable of it."

"But, friend, we'll be in black water soon—right here in this house. This will get truly awful. I already diaper that dignified, powerfully accomplished young man, who only happens to be my son, six or eight times a day."

"It'll teach me a lot I need to know." Mait's face had taken on an old-fashioned fever of righteous ambition.

"Is that your main reason?"

Mait said "God, no. I liked Wade immediately. I've loved you for four years—a fifth of my life."

Hutch was genuinely ambushed by the claim. "Me? I'm more than forty years your senior, a scarred old walrus."

"You know you're magnetic."

Hutch said "I feel as magnetic as lint. But thanks anyhow." He thought of a necessary stipulation. "We'll work out a way to recompense you fairly."

Mait looked struck across the eyes; he shook his head. "Not a penny, no sir. I've thought about this for more than a week, thinking I might meet Wade here tonight; and I'm sure as a bullet on one main point—this'll be my first contribution someway to a world I've barely visited yet. I guess it's also a partial payment to God or whatever for who I'm turning out to be."

At that moment, out the window on the lighted terrace, a female raccoon made a fearless appearance. Surprisingly tall in the arch of her back and magisterial in cool neglect of the house behind her, she smelled her unquestioned way round the bricks and the rock where Wade had sat. *Nothing of any serious interest in the fading scents of an irrelevant species*, she seemed to say. But then at last she faced the wide window; and whether or not she saw Hutch and Mait, she raised her nose in a comical snub—a dowager's proud dismissal of a sighting unworthy of notice. She ambled off.

But a dry voice behind them said "What day is this?"

When they turned, there was Wade again in the hall door. He'd somehow slipped out of his diaper and waited, naked and stunned, just beyond them.

For eyes trained like Hutch's and Maitland's, Wade seemed to be two things—a young man suffering intolerably, far past their reach, and also a likeness of hundreds of images in Western art. All of them were young men tortured toward death—the lynched dying Jesus, starved desert saints, impaled rebels in Goya's *Disasters*: all long past help and as pure as new light in their unearned agony.

Hutch stood in place and smiled toward Wade, though the eyes were plainly blind again. "It's the same night you fell asleep in, darling." He realized he hadn't called Wade *darling* in ten years, maybe fifteen. When Wade said nothing, Hutch said "You been dreaming?"

Wade was sure of that much. "I haven't dreamed for two years." It seemed to be all he had to tell them. With his arms out stiff from his sides for balance, Wade slowly steered himself around and back out of sight.

Mait said "He'll freeze before morning; it's chilly out."

Hutch said "I'll cover him up in a minute."

"I could sleep in his room tonight, if you need me to."

"I'll need you more later on," Hutch said. "Get some rest while we can. And deep thanks, Mait."

They parted in a silence that felt to Mait like actual music, sober but useful.

5

By half past midnight Hutch had slogged his way through four more papers from the daunting stack. As ever he came away from the task numbed by a question—*What can have happened in America, in the past hundred years, that a people who readily speak to a friend in a room with human force and directness will seize up like an oil-drained engine when they try to commit those words to writing?* Why do so many—most of them veterans of long years of schooling—melt down, when they attempt to write, into a gummy mass that not only lacks grace and economy but, worse, conveys no legible message? Any half hour's look at a volume of eighteenth or nineteenth century letters or diaries by ordinary frontier Americans—from semiliterate riverboatmen to newly arrived East European immigrants and escaped African slaves—will show a sweet or searing intensity of feeling and a taken-for-granted trim eloquence that passes from writer to reader with no smoke or flame. Why are those qualities as rare today throughout the nation as wit and elegance? And what huge, or silent, disaster does the loss predict? For surely no republic unable to write its chosen tongue with lean precision can do its civic and personal business for long, not in clear-eyed justice and compassion.

It can't all be charged up to TV or miserable schools that can't even babysit murderous kids, much less teach language. What broke loose and why? In recent years Hutch had sensed the breakage in his own life and poetry. His emotions came and went with the same force as ever, but his writing hand could seldom move now in the close shadow-dancing it had managed before, the near-perfect fit of feeling and word. And despite a run of good new poems—some angry as hornets—just after Ann left him, Hutch had pretty much surrendered serious hope that the tide could be turned in the visible future, not for himself or for other balked Americans, not by human intervention. Now with the savage plague on hand, and the human body threatened with death at the mere touch of pleasure, wouldn't language itself only go on withering and vanishing within us?

Yet somehow the prospect hadn't soured his teaching, partly because his students selected themselves for competence and partly because—despite his age—Hutch had never quite lost his family's daily reborn taste for a given stretch of predictable hours, the time from here till tonight's oblivion. No one he could think of in all his past, except his great-grandmother Kendal, had chosen to die (she'd swallowed lye and foamed to an agonized death on the floor). But no, that same great-grandmother's father—Thad Watson—had shot himself and fallen on his young wife's just-dead body (she'd died in childbed).

That of course led Hutch irresistibly to Wyatt, Wade's companion. *A family member? All right, call him that, posthumously anyhow—a third family suicide, less grisly than the first but still an unpardonable wound to the living, the kin and friends.* The next thought had to be *And why not Wade? Has he thought of quitting on his own schedule, not waiting for agony?* At that Hutch shook his head to clear it, then stood and walked quietly to Wade's open door.

At some point in the past two hours, Wade had waked, raised the head of his bed still higher and switched on the lamp; but now that he was far gone into sleep again, there was no sound of life. He was still uncovered, his body still carving itself to the bone from instant to instant.

Let this be it, in his sleep, this easy. Hutch stopped at the foot of the bed to listen closely. Still nothing.

Thank God. Hutch went to the edge of the narrow mattress. He freed the bruised feet from a tangle of cover (they had no more flesh than a hawk's dry claw), and he drew the blue sheet up to Wade's waist. Then he sat, his hand settling on Wade's left arm. *Warm, still soft.* Hutch lightly touched the pulse in the neck. It was there, weak but game. *Then it's all come down to this, here now on a single dry bed.* By *all* Hutch meant what he knew of his family, from old Rob Mayfield his great-grandfather and his grandmother Eva, till tonight—this young man tortured to death in sight of his father, the end of a line.

Wade's eyes stayed shut but he said "I'm just playing possum; ignore me."

Hutch's thumb stroked the ridge at the crest of Wade's eyes. It was handsome as the arc of a Chinese bridge in the mountains or the brow of a silver-backed gorilla, wiser than man. When Hutch stopped finally he saw that, gentle as he'd tried to be, his thumb had uprooted lashes from the dark brows. He carefully brushed them into his handkerchief and folded them neatly. They seemed worth saving; he didn't think why. Then he slid a hand beneath the cover and felt Wade's waist—still no diaper. *Can I put one on him and not break his rest?*

Wade said "I'm giving you an incomplete grade."

"Sir?" Hutch chuckled.

"You're the only class member who didn't recite."

"They've heard too much of me all term."

Wade said *"Incomplete."*

Hutch said "Pick a poem then—quick, as long as it's not by me—I bet I can say it."

This tack was peculiarly urgent for Wade. "I told your class a very true story; so did young Maitland Moses—I could tell."

Hutch said "Did you like Mait?"

"I thought he was bold for his age, yes sir. And he's got good eyes, the best I could see."

"Mait'll be calling on us this summer."

Wade said "You're changing the subject, O Bard of the Pines. Recite me a story." His voice was thin, high and drifting, as if he was teasing a child or had gone insane since sundown.

Hutch had read stories to Wade, and reams of good poems, all through his boyhood. And through long repetition together, they'd painlessly memorized hundreds of lines. By the time Wade was nine or ten, he and Hutch would sit or lie most nights in this room and recite in unison a poem that one or the other had chosen as fit to close a particular day. Tonight as Hutch faced what had become of his son, the only lines he could hear in his mind were John Keats's last poem, written in unflinching knowledge of the fact that Keats was dying of TB at twenty-six. Oddly the poem had been a favorite of Wade's in adolescence. *Maybe not so odd; adolescents are morbid. But we can't say those lines, not tonight.*

Merciless, Wade raised his own left hand from the cool sheet and held it up in the air between them. Even in dim light it was nearly transparent; the fingers looked endlessly long and fitted with abnormal extra joints, knobby and bluish.

Hutch reached to clasp the hand.

But Wade took it back and hid it in cover. His eyes were smiling with a high glitter though; and in the new thin voice, he said *" 'This living hand' —"*

It had never seemed strange on the frequent nights they'd stumble on the same poem at the same moment, but to have Wade read his mind this closely here was ominous for Hutch. He said "We couldn't get through that tonight" and reached again to stroke Wade's forehead.

Wade rolled his head aside, then looked back at Hutch with the punishing smile. "Sure we could; we're both realistic as apoplexy." Wade started Keats's poem again; and after three lines, against his better will, Hutch joined him to the finish.

> "This living hand, now warm and capable
> Of earnest grasping, would, if it were cold
> And in the icy silence of the tomb,
> So haunt thy days and chill thy dreaming nights
> That thou wouldst wish thine own heart dry of blood
> So in my veins red life might stream again,
> And thou be conscience-calm'd—see here it is—
> I hold it towards you."

It took them a moment to weather that powerful shudder of words from a century when words served gladly, in utter perfection. Then knowing the gesture might seem soft or lurid, Hutch searched in the cover and found Wade's hand.

It was hot as a small fire; and this time Wade let him hold it, unflinching. Finally Wade said "More, please sir."

"More?"

"Father, *Father*—I can ask for more now, and you can tell me safely." His voice took on the conscious creepy tones of a ghoul in a forties horror film. "I'm beyond the grave, I keep all secrets, you're safe with me." Wade laughed but still he waited for Hutch to agree. When he got that permission through pressure to his hand, Wade went for the throat. "Hutch, I'm as grown as I'll ever get. Tell me as much as I told the class."

So Hutch thought awhile and convinced himself that now might well be their last chance before Wade went past comprehension; then he gave Wade the story. And though he gave it for the second time tonight, to someone in a world as far from Maitland's as the star Arcturus, it came more easily and felt still truer as it moved into words. "What you're looking at, Son—whatever you see—is a sixty-three-year-old man who's hauling a hundred and seventy-eight pounds round the world on a six-foot frame. He's finishing up his thirty-fifth year as a college teacher and trying to write a few last poems for his fifth lean volume, a *New and Selected*. He's well thought of in the minuscule world of American verse, a few of his poems have been translated into French and Spanish and Japanese; and he's been tapped into most of the right self-congratulating clubs and academies, though they tend to give him attacks of the creeps if he goes to many meetings. But if he'd give you his honest guess, he'd reckon that not more than six of his poems have a chance of being read, much less memorized, fifty years from now."

The strain of distancing himself from the story broke Hutch's pose. When he started over he spoke as himself, in his naked intent. "Wade Mayfield, you're still set to be the main thing I bequeath this starving planet;

and whatever happens in the time we get, I know you'll go on being that, among a lot else—a man that started life as a pleasure for everyone near him and who only gets better and better with time."

Wade said "Tell the truth."

"Wait—I am." Hutch lost his grip briefly. "Hutch is hard up for knowing the whole truth tonight, not with his wife far off on her own and his son in trouble—"

Wade said "Say I, if it's *you* you mean."

"Am I telling this story or you?"

"I'm starting to wonder." Both their voices had veered into harshness, so Wade kept silent from then on and focused his mind to guide his father's account toward what he'd wanted to know in all their adult years together and then apart.

Hutch sensed the guidance and was all but relieved to bow to it finally. "You asked the class to witness this world we're caught in here, where love can kill you as sure as gunfire. I think close watch is the main thing my work has tried to offer since nearly the start, once I'd given up trying to draw and paint things anyhow. And if I've really seen anything at all in these years, and passed it on, it's been just this—the only thing that matters a whit in human life is using your mind and body, *throttle-out* as long as you last, to spark the gaps and to hook you to people you need and can give to.

"I well understand I'm the ten-billionth watcher that's seen as much and said it legibly, but I'm fairly easy these days with the fact that I'm not Wordsworth or even Frost and likely won't be. I know this though—the single really good thing I've done, apart from helping get you underway, is to tie myself to a few human shapes too beautiful to resist for long and then to give them at least as much nourishment as they give me. All but one of them are still dear friends—as near as Strawson, you're bound to know—and the only one I've lost is dead, not abandoned by me: a likable baffled young man named James, an Oxford stonemason with a prison record who treated me kinder than a convent of nuns in swansdown gloves. You surely must have known for years that, before you were born, a reasonable number of my intimates were men."

Wade's eyes were still shut. "I've estimated as much, yes sir."

"Since when?"

"More or less from the first, I guess, when I was maybe eight or nine—soon as I looked out and really knew I was watching other bodies too."

Hutch laughed. "Whoa here, I resisted you at every age. I've been many things but no child molester—"

"Easy, I'm not on the vice squad yet. I *wanted* you to touch me more ways than one, but you were a gentleman round the clock always and a knockout to boot."

"I'm a blighted cabbage leaf to what I was. You're pretty grand yourself."

Wade said "—If you're drawn to the human skeleton." But he smiled at last before he went silent and lay still so long he seemed asleep. Then in a thin voice, he said "You're saying you're the worst thing of all—the unhappiest anyhow?"

Hutch said "What's that?"

"One of the all but nonexistent genuine bisexuals."

Hutch laughed. "I was talking about that mythical species earlier tonight."

"Who with?—the walls?"

"No, Maitland came back once the others left and stayed awhile—you remember you walked in on us, in the living room?"

"I don't," Wade said. He let that pass. "You weren't telling Mait you'd been bisexual, I pray to Jesus."

Hutch laughed again but gave the question a minute's thought. "Not at all, no. I honestly think I've always been *sexual*, nothing any more focused than that—though for more than thirty years, I was aimed at no one but your mother."

Wade's eyes were still shut. "What was the one thing you liked to do most— whoever you loved, wherever you were, whatever hour of day or night or sun or snow?"

Hutch thought *Wade's far past dead; tell the truth.* But then he half hedged. "Without getting down to the sweaty home movies, I always aimed to *give* real pleasure to who I was with. That was always the best reward for me. Remember what Blake said?

"What is it men in women do require?
The lineaments of Gratified Desire.
What is it women do in men require?
The lineaments of Gratified Desire."

With his eyes still shut, Wade hacked out a chuckling that lasted longer than his breath. When he'd eased again, he said "Billy Blake was the craziest coot; but he hit that one, didn't he? For me anyhow. I could look, a whole year, at a body I loved and the mind that drove it. Then all I asked was to let my hand do the necessary pleasing on that loved body—my hand or some other piece of my skin that wouldn't repel or sicken my love." Wade waited, then abruptly turned to his father and tried to see him. When he failed, he asked Hutch a genuine question. "Still, where does that leave the Poor Local Blind Boy?"

It went more than halfway through Hutch's whole body, but he smiled on the chance Wade could see him at all. Then he told him "Like me, I guess, you've got your memories." He'd sung those last four words like a sob song from a twenties operetta.

Wade eventually shook his head, a firm *No*; but he offered no more explanation.

Hutch thought *He's blind in his mind as well*. It was so hard to think, he smoothed the cover and moved to rise.

Wade looked out and found his father's face, a momentary milky patch on the air above him. "Wyatt told me, the first night he met you, that you'd cut your heart off from the world the day you got married—he knew it on sight." Before Hutch could answer, Wade grinned out wildly to the room in general. "You're worried about my diaper, I know. I promise if I mess up these sheets, I'll wash them myself." Both of them knew Wade could never manage that; he was weakening daily.

But in spite of the posthumous thrust from Wyatt, Hutch agreed, smiling; then gave a slight wave as he faced the door.

Wade wasn't done. "Hutch, you know it was Wyatt between us, don't you? You and me—nothing bigger than Wyatt?"

"Wyatt loathed me, Son; I mainly knew why—partly at least, though I knew he was wrong: half wrong at least. Some of his reasons were understandable, though he distorted my meanness unfairly. I had very little to do, you must know, with importing black Africans to these cruel shores or fueling the torture machine built for them. I was, honest to God, never Simon Legree; not even a genial white-country-club member." Hutch knew it was too late to add the other fact—that Wade had let Wyatt *stand* between them and had never once tried to wave him aside or bring him to heel, not so far as Hutch or Ann ever knew. Before he could go on, Hutch heard his own thought—*Bring Wyatt to heel*. But Wyatt was dead, cold dead underground. *He scares me still; I'm not cured yet.*

As if eavesdropping, Wade said "Wyatt's reasons were fairly sound, yes sir" as calmly as if he'd said *Evening* or *Rain*. He took a long silence, though his eyes stayed open. Finally he said "You understand I'm totally blind now."

Hutch said "You were seeing this afternoon, out on the terrace. I could tell you were."

Wade said "I get little spells of sight—somebody's outline, the taste of the light as it's dimming for evening."

Hutch said "Surely you saw Mait Moses."

"I could tell he was lively; he was giving off streaks like the northern lights—mostly blue and blood-red."

Hutch said "But you're not seeing me here with you?"

Wade's face slowly sought out his father, and the eyes moved slightly as if they were stroking a welcome object. Finally he said "You're there, I can tell."

Hutch had returned and was standing at the foot of the bed. He took two steps back, farther away, and said "How can you tell?"

Wade said "I'm not sure—just some sort of radar that I've slowly got as my eyes went out. It's an interesting skill, one I wish I'd had in my architect days. Things almost seem to be playing a music nobody can hear till they're blind as me; even now it's faint, but I mostly can hear it. I bet you could lead me to the strangest room right now, stand me on the threshold; and I could tell you where they've placed the bed, where the windows are, which chair is the oldest inhabitant's favorite."

Hutch had stayed in place, between the foot of Wade's bed and the door. "Do you get any feeling of me?"

"Oh sure."

"What's it like?"

Wade knew at once. "You're somehow separate from the rest of the dark. You're—what?—embossed, slightly raised from the background, a kind of bas relief but *there*."

Hutch said "No, *here*. And I'll be here as long as you need me—God couldn't make me quit."

Wade grinned. "I'll pretend you didn't say that. Friend God can shut you off like a flashlight, any instant he chooses, O Seer Blest!" The grin survived a few seconds more; then Wade was gone like a shot-down quail.

These instant vanishings were badly unnerving, maybe even too convenient for Wade. But Hutch sat there another few minutes, hoping the boy would come back again and work his way past the last low hurdles left between them to some kind of justice on both their actions in the past ten years. *There's almost no time, Son—come back.*

Wade needed rest more or was overwhelmed by the gulf still between them.

So Hutch tried to find a way into prayer, a kind of thinking he'd more or less ignored through the past four decades. How does a sane human being address the mind that conceives—and goes on conceiving—the walls or infinite reaches of space, the real or unreal nature of time and the purpose, if any, of a species as infinitesimal as *Homo sapiens*, not to speak of a single man, woman or child? Quite aside from the mystery of whether any such speech could rouse that unimaginable mind and hold its attention for a private request smaller (say) than the hydrogen atom, for Hutch the quandary came down to words as most quandaries did—what words in what order? The Buddha says only *Consume me utterly*. Jesus says *Your will be done*. Dante says *In your will is our peace*.

All Hutch could think of saying here was *Spare Wade Mayfield*. Or again *Take him now*. But he wouldn't say either. And he'd never given a moment's thought to anything as ludicrous as cursing the sky. As if the sky gave a good goddamn—the sky or its veiled shut-mouth endless boss, eyeless as any fish in the back of a mile-deep cave, afloat in pure black oakgall ink.

For the first time clearly, Hutch knew he needed each conscious hour this boy might get. And he needed them for both his own and Wade's sakes—to finish their lives and ease them out with a clear-eyed dignity, blind or not. So Hutch said to himself *Heal him someway. Bring him back*. Then he held his palm over Wade's shut face as if a father might raise the dead with nothing but skin and a weight of care that was all the greater for being reclaimed from years of silence.

The phone rang two rooms away in the study (Hutch had muted all the other phone bells). He checked his watch—past one in the morning—then walked toward the rings and waited till the message machine clicked on and the caller spoke.

"It's late, I know, but I need to talk if you're hearing this." When Hutch didn't answer, the voice said "Hutch, it's Ann. Do you hear me?"

Hutch thought Forget it. But Ann didn't quit; she was waiting him out, as she'd almost always known she could.

He took up the phone. "I'm here. What's the problem?" Ann was silent.

Hutch thought she'd hung up. Only when he said "Good night" did she speak.

"The problem, ex-friend, is our son's on his way."

Hutch said "No, he's sleeping quite peacefully. I just this minute left him. He's had a strong day."

"You had your class supper?"

"I did. They're long gone. Wade enjoyed them."

"When will you be done with your chores?" Ann had always referred to his teaching as chores.

"I should finish reading my last exam by the 28th."

"Then you make your annual May trip north?"

"The Academy shindig? No, I'll bypass that, this year anyhow."

Ann said "I was going to offer to spell you that week."

"We're covered, thanks. Hart Salter is excellent help when he's here, and just tonight one of my seniors offered to help us this summer."

Ann said "I talked with the doctor again, just today. I like her, on the phone at least. She says Wade's stronger since the first time she saw him. I wish I agreed."

Hutch couldn't resist a knowing lie. "You're wrong. Wade's come a good way since getting home." He hadn't purposely chosen the word *home*; but as it passed, he felt its weight in Ann's lone mind. *We know too well how to maim each other.* Even after so many months apart, Hutch and Ann had fingers poised on one another's prime destruct-buttons and could trigger a mauling with the merest flick.

Ann let *home* pass. "I've just pulled a pork roast out of the oven; can I run it by before work in the morning?"

"You've got your key; come in and leave it."

"You know I don't like to use that key."

Hutch said "Remember what the sheriff said after that last break-in—'Locks are just to keep your friends out.'" Hutch laughed a little. "No, come on in."

"Will you be there tomorrow?"

"Most of the day—or have you forgot your old contention that college teachers are underworked and overpaid?"

Ann sidestepped the taunt. "I'll run by then about seven o'clock."

"You're rising early in this new life." With Hutch, Ann had always slept like the floorboards.

"We're starting a big case—the man that carved up his trailer-park neighbors near Hurdle Mills."

"So all paralegals are scrambling day and night to save his precious hide?"

Ann said "Why does that disturb you so? I thought you valued all forms of life."

"That was years ago. I'm a seasoned killer now." His voice went cold and metallic as a psychopath's. "I'm *fascinated* by your taste for crime, madam."

"It's not my taste—you're the neighborhood vampire; you hate me saving a single warped soul." By the end of that, she was half joking too.

"On the contrary, madam—I'm delighted your hands are occupied. Just don't get left alone with the defendant—you're still too well-knit to undergo whittling."

Ann chose to hear a small compliment. "Thanks, Doctor. I need that."

"It's the visible truth. That student of mine said so tonight."

"Do I know him?"

"Maitland Moses, the one that's not just gifted but rolling full tilt already."

"The one with the choirboy frog in his throat? I liked his red cheeks. I'll send him a jar of honey for his vocal cords with my sincere thanks, if he really said that."

The thought that Ann could even doubt that much—a student compliment—reminded Hutch of how much lighter his days were now without that infinite pressure of waiting from Ann: *Award my life your consent to proceed.* But all he said was "Hold off on the honey. We may owe Mait more than any honey made, if he does what he's volunteered to do."

"What was that?"

Hutch said "I told you—he offered to help out all summer long, as much as I need."

Ann took a wait. "You moving him in?"

"Not any time soon, far as I can see—though since you mention it, I do have space. Maybe I'll take in boarders soon. No, we don't know what we may need down the road; but Maitland's offer is a bankable asset."

Ann said "Who is *we*?"

It had been the main question of their years together. Hutch smiled, but not ironically, to hear it. "It's our son and us—the Mayfield-Gatlin ex-family alone again, against all odds: remember them?"

"Why is it *ex*?"

"You made it so." When Ann took a pause to work through that, Hutch said "Ms. Mayfield, I'm whipped—turn me loose please."

She said "Don't you conk out, for God's sake."

"I love this, Ann."

"You *love* it?"

Hutch said "You know I do."

"Our son's pain and death?"

In some huge way the answer was Yes, but Hutch didn't say it. He said what was also true—"I love this chance to help him when he needs me. He hasn't needed you or me for nearly twenty years."

"Wade was not a grown man at twelve years old."

Hutch said "He was. If you and I had vaporized, Wade would have lived."

"*Lived* maybe but not much else."

Hutch said "He had you and me here squarely behind him till he finished college. Then he lit out, put a long distance between us, found a crazed mate and signed us *off*. So much for *us*."

"I always thought they were right about us—Wyatt anyhow. Wyatt Bondurant wasn't crazy, Hutch; he saw too clearly."

"Ann, if that's the case, Wade and Wyatt were also right about ninety percent of the American populace who'd find it exotic—to say the least—if they were cast as the main in-laws to a mixed-color monosexual union with the new in-law as vicious as a mongoose."

Ann laughed. "If Wyatt Bondurant was a mongoose, that makes us cobras."

Hutch said "Oh right, great hooded viperess."

"No, I grant that Wyatt was from a very different world. But he had good sense when we weren't around; he looked like a Congolese river god and could smell racism through ten feet of concrete and five hundred miles."

Hutch said "You and I are were indictable racists then?"

"At times, sure—were and are. So is every black, white, red or yellow American—"

Hutch stopped her. "I lack your trained legal mind; but if one sin's committed by all live citizens, who the hell's got any right of condemnation?"

In the face of his logic, Ann rushed ahead. "I don't think you and I are abnormal, Hutchins—not in that one department."

"But our son bought Wyatt's whole blanket indictment on Caucasoid man for nearly ten years." Hutch had calmed a little. "I think Wade's quietly letting it go, as he settles in here. I haven't heard a mean word from him yet, and we've had several crises already that might have provoked him—I told you he passed out on me in the bathtub?"

"You did, yes." Ann took a seamless breath and held it. It gave her the force to say "You know you're walling me out of all this."

"What's *this?*"

"Our son's tragedy—yours and mine."

"I'm still not sure it's a tragedy," Hutch said.

"A young man dying in agony, for no just cause, is not tragic to you?"

"It's horrific, Ann—no question whatever. No question it's the worst thing I've ever witnessed or tried to bear, and I've borne at least a normal load of hard sights. But I guess I'm starting to see it Wade's way. He's so completely uncomplaining, so ready for whatever slams in on him next. So maybe he feels like a tall lean hero at the end of something like Shakespeare's *Tempest* or Sophocles' Oedipus near his own death."

Ann said "Wasn't Oedipus a very old man when he died?"

"Fairly old, yes. But he just disappeared, no corpse at all—remember?"

She took a long wait. "Hutch, listen to yourself. This is no seminar for dazzled sophomores. A very young man is dying blind in agony, against his best will."

"Wade doesn't act that way."

Ann said "Wade's sparing you. He's spared you forever."

"Then I thank him profoundly."

"Can I come back?" If Ann had phoned with the news that an asteroid would crash between them in the next thirty seconds and atomize the world, she couldn't have made a firmer impression.

Hutch felt almost assaulted and robbed. *This thing is mine now.*

"Did you hear me, Hutch?"

"Yes ma'm, I did."

"Could I have an answer soon?"

"It was you that left, Ann."

"I quit our marriage or what was left of it. I never meant to quit all care for my child."

"Our child," Hutch said. "Wouldn't that be fair? No, I never said you quit on Wade; but if you've discovered this intense need to nurse him, then why didn't *you* go to New York and get him? You can drive; some junior lawyer would have ridden up with you. I went; I rescued my son—" The words were still in the air between them when Hutch heard their self-love and cruelty. He could neither call them back nor ask Ann's pardon.

She let them pass her by. "Hutch, I wrote to Wade with numerous offers for the whole past year. I never heard a word."

"That's because he never opened a single one, yours or mine. They're all here beside me, in a box he brought home, each one still sealed. Come get them when you're ready."

Ann said "I couldn't stand to see them again. And please don't you."

Hutch was suddenly exhausted—the long day, the class, this familiar arm wrestle over a son's life, a life that was leaking through their actual fingers before their eyes. Hutch said "Let's talk tomorrow then. I'm past thinking clearly."

"*Thought's* not required—just average human feeling."

Hutch said "Tomorrow please."

At that Ann was gone, not a slam-down but a silent disappearance.

People are vanishing on me by the hour. But Hutch was safe again in his house with his son; for a sweet moment he tasted the fact. Then as he moved toward bed and sleep, he thought *Cheap and stingy* and he meant himself.

6

May 9, 1993

Dear Wade and Pops,

I know it's Mother's Day not Father's Day but I've been meaning to take pen in hand ever since you two left me up here and I've been so busy that this is the first slow minute I've had to tell you both "Hey!" like they say down yonder in the cotton fields and to gripe about how much I miss my friend Wade but how glad I am that he's with you Mr. Mayfield. Happy Mother's Day to both of you—Dad and son—from your pal The Boat.

I was so glad, Wade, to get your call the other night and to know that you been gaining strength with the good homecooking and personal doctor care. Like I said I watched more than one miracle happen in my days. Just don't overdo it with the fatback and chitlins, your belly is tender, but if you get a chance just ship me a thermos full of warm pot liquor from your next turnip greens. That'll heal some bodies and souls let me tell you!

Speaking of which you don't want to hear my news, it's so pitiful. Two of my boys passed on last week, Sellers and Larry. I don't believe you know either one but I'd been tending to them since back at the start, back about '82, and they had worn themselves deep in my heart. Larry especially had been doing so well gaining a little weight and hadn't been badoff sick since winter. But he hit the ice, let me tell you, and went.

Don't let that get you down a bit. Every boy in this mess, and every man, woman and baby is a whole different thing and you can't foretell. You remember, Wade, I've still got Monte that's had a full case of it since '83 and has still not missed a day of work, never has any trouble that's harder to fight than a summer cold or a little athlete's foot from swimming at the gym. I wasn't ever too good at the books but Monte amounts to a miracle in my book.

Haven't run into Ivory to speak to since you all left but I saw her crossing the street this morning with a white flower on toward the subway station looking fine as ever. I wonder if it means her mother is dead or if Ivory's still in mourning for Wyatt? Let me stop right here or I'll get you both down and let me end with a cheerful hope. You both invited me to visit you. I may be planning to ride the bus to South Carolina for July 4th.

My grandmother is leaning on me for one more look at my homely face before Jesus calls her. I told her in that case she was safe. Since she's deaf as a post, she couldn't hear Jesus with a bullhorn no how! If you two gentlemen are not too busy it would do me good to stop by and see you. Don't let me get in the way of your plans though and don't let me weigh on your mind at all. I couldn't stay more than an hour or so or maybe one night if you got an army cot. You know my number so if the word is Yes just call me collect. If not I won't think you mean any harm.

Lord bless and keep. Pray for Boatie and the world. He is watching over you

Like a friend
Jimmy Boat

May 9, 1993

Dear Mr. Mayfield,

    You asked me to send you a list of what I might have spent on Wade's behalf. I've finally had a chance to sit down with my receipts and add things up. It comes to even less than I thought — $217. If you'll check me against the composition book you took home from Wade and Wyatt's kitchen, I believe you'll find me accurate. If there's any question, don't hesitate to write me. One reason I spent so little on my own was that, after Wyatt's death, Wade gave me check-writing privileges on their joint account. I terminated those, in writing, at the bank last week.

    I got your kind letter after you reached home. Everything you say about my time with Wade is thoughtful of you, but don't fail to know that I did it because I wanted to. Tragic as things have been in my family lately, it meant something to me to help Wade when needed. He has done me more than one kindness, and I will never forget him, I or the remains of my kin. Tell him please that I went out to see my mother this morning in Sea Cliff, that things are going well out there with everybody and that Mother sends him her love and prayers. She thinks Wade will "live a long life" and she's only been wrong half a dozen times in the years I've known her. She will be seventy-six next month and is strong as she's ever been but still grieving for my brother.

    Please keep me informed on how things go and don't hesitate to call on me if you need anything sent from the apartment or if Wade has any unfinished business up here I can handle. As you requested, I check the apartment two or three times a week and water the fern. Everything except what you packed up and took is still right there where you left it and will wait for your plans long as you pay the rent, which I hate for you to keep doing.

    With many good wishes from me and my family to you and yours,

Sincerely,
Ivory Bondurant

May 16, 1993

Hello to you, Mr. Wade Mayfield. This pretty get well card hits the spot with what we are feeling about you today. You just keep your mind set on strength like I told you to and keep your blood purified with lemon and water hot as you can stand it plus your doctor medicine and we will look for you back up here at work and visiting us before much longer. Call us on the phone late some afternoon, we are always home with the TV on so let the phone ring awhile till I get to hear it. It would be a real tonic for me and mine to hear your voice. You recall I grew up in Virginia and I still get homesick when I think of the beautiful land down there near my dear grandfather's place and all of us children

*running round outdoors in the old times not scared of a single thing. My old-
est brother Bankey is still alive, by himself in the family home, last I heard. I
would dearly love to see him once more, a serious boy that could read all night
if you left the light on. I take fresh flowers to Wyatt's grave every Sunday after
church and I always tell him your name to remember, Wade. Please give my
good thoughts to your mother and father. They raised a good boy.*

Respectfully yours,
Mrs. Lucy Patterson Bondurant and Raven

May 19, 1993

Dear Emily,

   *You're good to keep bracing me up with calls and letters. I wish there were
other causes for cheer from down here today, but no there are none. Wade goes
on more or less the way he's been since the day he arrived in early April. Hutch
and even the doctor try to claim he's stronger, but a mother's eyes and intuition
say no. As I told you, I take everything Hutch will give me—daily visits with
food and clean laundry—but when I'm there with just Wade alone and Hutch
not trying to hide the truth, I generally see a steady decline.*

   *Wade's vision is pretty much completely gone; and again when I'm alone
beside him, he'll say occasional things that show he's not entirely sure who I
am or where he is at the moment and why. Just this afternoon I sat there by
him through a ten-minute nap; and when he woke up and turned toward
me, he said "Take a pen and write down this instruction." I thought he might
have some important request, so I got stuff to write with and told him to tell
me. He put all ten fingers up to his temples, rubbed at them hard, then
finally said "Wade Mayfield plans a fair distribution of all he owns to any
child under fifteen years old who grew up an orphan like him and can prove
same in writing." When he finished he asked me to sign it for him. I continued obeying but he suddenly scowled at me quite wildly and said "You've
forged my name all your life." I begged his pardon but before he could give it,
he was out again, another feverish nap.*

   *Without going deeper than you could stand into this domestic tragedy—I'd
just be repeating—I have to report that Hutch goes right on doing it all and
refusing help, except for a student that sits with Wade for brief spells some days.
Otherwise Hutch is cook, bottlewasher, trained nurse and constant companion. I'll give him this much—so far he's got the endurance of a mountain. He's
never looked stronger; he's literally thriving. In meanness the other day, I told
him if he'd been an undertaker and frequented the dead a lot earlier in life, he
wouldn't have a gray hair to show, even now. He laughed and said "Maybe."*

   Every offer I make—beyond the two chores—is coolly rejected; and I can't

ask Wade, bad off as he is, to enter the fray on my behalf. I understand Hutch
loves Wade in his own way as much as I do, so I'm straining every nerve to be
fair. But still I know Hutch is paying me back by the bitter minute for saying
I wanted a separate life, when I moved out. When I left, though, my son was
still strong—so far as I knew. Now I'm forced into what amounts to practical
abandonment of the main thing I've cared for in my life. I honestly think if I
turned up on the doorstep with my bag, saying I meant to stay to the end,
Hutch would call the sheriff to escort me out.

I know that sounds like trailer-park news, real white-trash behavior. But that's
where I stand and, even with a good deal of legal advice, I don't see any way to
reach my son for more than quick drop-in visits, with Hutch standing by and
checking his watch. You and Straw mean the world to him—Straw means more
than ever to him these days—so again if either of you can think of a word that
will gain me greater natural access to my sick child, I'll be your debtor till Judg-
ment Day—which feels a lot closer than it has till now.

Meanwhile, love from

Ann

7

Though it was only a two-hour trip on such a clear day, they were almost
surely the bleakest hours Hutch had known on the road. He'd tried for days
to resist Wade's wish to see the old Kendal place again, his great-grandmother's ancestral home, and Grainger there still. Hutch had told Wade
lies about Grainger's poor health, he'd told Wade how busy Straw and
Emily would be in the growing season, Hutch had finally even said to
Wade "Don't make me do this."

But at that, Wade had shut his eyes in silence and made the wish an
unmistakable demand. Though Wade could no longer see Hutch's face, he
said "I want you to scatter my ashes up there by the creek where I used to go
with Grainger. I want to pick the spot."

So Hutch called Strawson with the ultimatum; and Straw suggested Sunday, May 30th. Emily would make up a daybed in the dining room where
Wade could rest in the course of the day without climbing steps. Straw
wouldn't tell Grainger till the day itself; the old man would only dwell on it
too hard and be confused when, and if, they got there—he'd already spoken
more than once of Wade Mayfield as a friend of his childhood, ninety-five
years back.

On the morning itself Hutch lost whatever nerve he'd had and lay on his bed just after dawn, thinking *This is the first thing I can't handle—can't and won't.* But then he heard Wade awake down the hall, coughing and feeling his way round the room to dress himself. Hutch sat up, put his glasses on, found Maitland's number and called him—ten or twelve rings and still no answer. Hutch recalled telling Mait last week that he wouldn't need him over the weekend. *Go calm Wade down; tell him you're feeling sick—whatever it takes.*

But by the time Hutch had put on his robe and walked to Wade's door, the boy had finished dressing and sat on the edge of his bed, waiting silently.

Hutch stood there, looking.

The boy did seem a little stronger this morning; and though his face was mostly blank, it wore a new kind of unanswerable demand. He said "You're trying to fail me, aren't you?"

Hutch said "Pardon?"

"You've thought of a way to cancel my trip."

"I have been feeling pretty awful all night—some stomach bug."

Wade said "I'm the host to every bug species on Planet Earth and *you're* feeling poorly." He grinned; by now the sight was appalling, all teeth and white gums. "Go lie down then. I'll call Ann Gatlin." It was the only time Wade had used his mother as a threat between them.

Hutch said "Now you've turned mean."

"Not mean at all, Hutch—just realistic. I'm making this trip, by car or taxi, alone or with one of you. I know Ann's ready."

"You call her in the night?" Wade's late phone calls usually waked Hutch; more than once he'd had to get up and go in at three in the morning and hang up the phone after Wade had dozed off in the midst of a call.

Wade said "No sir, but she asked to come with me."

"When?"

"Every second since I told her we were going."

All right, use this. You'd rather drink lye, but call and ask her. Hutch gave Wade a last chance. "You're serious now? You want Ann to join us?"

Wade said "I seem to remember a girl named Ann Gatlin brought me to life. Am I wrong on that?"

"Ann Gatlin Mayfield—you were no way a bastard."

Wade said "She's *Gatlin* to me these days. She did all the work, to the best of my memory—I know my mind's failing."

That was as near to a direct strike as any Hutch had taken since Wyatt's first days on the edge of the family, sighting and firing on social occasions with the lethal arms and precision of a renegade African guerrilla. Hutch thought *Take it gracefully; his mind is weak. Just call Ann and tell her you need her help.* But he said to Wade "You're making me do this."

"I know I am." Wade tried to laugh, then broke up coughing. At last he could finish. "You made me *be.* You started all this."

Hutch said "You just now said Ann did it all."

In the black bass voice of Hattie McDaniel in *Gone With the Wind,* Wade said "Mistuh Rhett, Lord, you is bad. I nevuh told you no such of a thing." It was a voice Wyatt had used more than once on his visit here, kidding on the level with his fine hot eyes.

It felt unnecessarily cruel but Hutch turned and went, with no further persuasion, back to the phone in his own room.

Ann answered on the second ring; he could tell he'd waked her, though she denied it—her role in the trial of the Hurdle Mills Strangler was pressing her still.

Hutch said "You know about this planned trip to Strawson's?"

"Wade told me, yes."

"Can you help me with it?"

Ann said "Are you sure?"

For the first time in weeks, Hutch's throat shut down; and what he said was audibly painful. "This is something I just can't tackle alone."

When Ann finally spoke, there was no sound of gloating. "Are you and Wade ready?"

"I'm not, God knows. Wade's dressed himself in a strange mixed getup; I've still got to shower. They're not expecting us till late morning anyhow."

Ann said "Shall I be there by nine-thirty then?"

"I'd be grateful, yes."

Ann hadn't spent long months with lawyers for nothing. She'd always listened closely to words; now she heard them like a radio telescope. "*Grateful* but not *glad.* I feel the same way. Anything I should bring?"

Her voice was milder than Hutch had heard lately. He lowered his own, "Bring an extra handkerchief. This'll be hard."

When Hutch hung up, Wade was standing in his doorway, smiling still in a shrunk knit shirt that said *I'm The One Happy Homo* and khaki trousers from his Boy Scout days, five inches too short. He grinned toward his father. "Nothing on Earth that can happen today will be any harder than being *me.*" It was only a fact, no trace of self-pity.

It was, and would be, the only time Hutch ever heard Wade confess to the horror that was clawing him down. Hutch carefully led the boy back to his room to help him change the clothes he'd chosen blind at dawn.

8

Straw and Emily were as ready as they could be for the visit. In the old front parlor, the daybed was made up and ready for Wade when he needed rest. Beside the cot they'd set a china slop jar and a pitcher of water with glasses on the table by a small ice bucket. Emily had gathered a cold spread of food for whenever they were hungry; and when Hutch phoned to say they were starting the trip and to look for them somewhere around midday, Straw had walked down to Grainger's to break the news as clearly as he could. He'd already made his early morning check to see if the old man had lasted the night and to cook his breakfast, so he had some confidence that Grainger was up and watching TV—Grainger liked Sunday morning political shows such as "Face the Nation."

Without knocking, Straw opened the screen and stepped into the heat which Grainger had needed year-round for decades.

The old man was immaculately dressed in his stand-up chair at an awkward height, nearly half stood up and plainly awake. The TV was off and the air around him was all but crackling with the force of his ancient patience and readiness.

Straw said "Where you headed?"

Grainger said "You tell me. Been thinking all night I'm going somewhere. Sitting here ready."

Straw leaned to the switch and lowered Grainger's chair. With his hand he stroked the polished top of the enormous skull. Any touch of Grainger was likely to make Straw feel the scary power of his own long loneliness—this life that had burned on, unpaired for so long, gave off its strength like a tangible radiance. Then Straw took the straight chair opposite. "No good news on the TV this morning?"

"Nothing but white folks trying to preach. Blond-headed strumpets and pitiful-looking sissified men in light blue suits with red hair dye."

"I thought you sent those preachers contributions."

"Do," Grainger said. "Some of them, I do; but that don't mean I got to watch them talking. I just pay them to pray for me every few months."

Straw said "I thought you could do your own praying." Grainger and churches had seldom seen eye to eye.

The head shook slowly. "I gave up praying after Gracie died. Can't see prayer ever helped me anyhow."

Straw said "*Somebody's* been looking out for you."

"You."

True as it was, that came to Straw as a considerable surprise. He'd lived in close touch with Grainger Walters for near forty years. He'd hardly felt scorned or disvalued by the old man; but no, Straw had never heard him come so near to thanks before. He said "I've enjoyed every day we've had."

Grainger said "You been short on stuff to enjoy."

Straw waited for some expansion of that—he'd had his disappointments and persistent aches but no long bitterness, despite his drinking. Still Grainger had shot his bolt for now. Straw had to move on. "You're feeling all right this morning then?"

"You can see. How I look?"

Straw said "Three or four years younger than me—you look first-rate. But we've got a problem here. You know how sick Wade Mayfield's been; you know Hutch and I brought him home last month. He's feeling a little stronger, and Hutch is driving him."

Grainger said "Wade called me up last night on *that thing*." He still called the telephone *that thing* and often wouldn't answer it, claiming he could tell from the ring whether a call was long distance or local—he honored long distance.

Straw said "Hutch called you up last night?"

"Wade called—I told you."

"What time; what did he say?"

"In the dark sometime. Said he's coming today. That's why I'm waiting, fool."

Straw felt the need to test for Grainger's clarity; he feared the old man might upset Wade through misunderstanding. "How old was Wade last time you saw him?"

"Saw him this past spring; he come here with Ann."

"Did he look full grown?"

Grainger bowed his head deeply. "Son, I know who Wade Mayfield is. And he told me plenty about what's killing him. When he comes, lead him down here and leave him with me. Don't want you or Hutch or nobody else—black or white—hanging round, tuned in to what we say."

Straw said "Yes sir, Mr. Walters. But understand—last time I saw Wade, he was very confused. His mind's badly affected by the illness, and he's totally blind most all the time. He may not really know what he's telling you."

Grainger shook his head again. "Wade's called me plenty of times in the past year, crazy as a cat. I've known crazy men all my life, some women too—they've been good to me; I can talk every one of them down to being peaceful. Wade gets peaceful with me every time, once I talk him down some. Known heap worse fools than Wade in my time."

Even a short conversation with Grainger almost always set Straw, who still read mountains of history and lives of the great, to thinking of the scale of human time—how short it is and how long it feels. Now Straw thought of a question, entirely off the subject of Wade, that his mind had raised in a dream last night. If he didn't ask questions when he thought of them now, he'd likely forget; so he said "Mr. Walters, who was the oldest person you met when you were a boy?"

Grainger knew at once and, leaning back, told it to the ceiling. "I met an old woman in Washington, D.C. when I was changing trains on my way down to Virginia from my father's in Maine—coming to stay with my great-great-great-grandmother, old Miss Veenie that you never knew: something else you missed. I was sitting in the station, scared to death—eight years old and heading to where the slavery times were scarcely over, in spite of what every calendar said—when this old colored woman, size of a sparrow, come up to me and asked me would I take her somewhere to 'do her business.'

"*Old*—she looked a lot older to me than any burnt-out chimney by the road. She had to be somewhere near the age I am today. That would have been around 1900. She was near blind like Wade's going to be; so I took her hand and led her to the only place I knew about, the big men's room—a gray marble place about the size of this county. She looked like a man, bald as me now; but she wore a long dress. Still nobody stopped us and she got her skirts up and set herself down like she'd been using indoor toilets all her years. Then she held my hand while she did her business—her skin was drier than mine is now, worse than gator hide.

"It took her a long time; but when she finished and stood back up, she said 'You a mighty respectful little man.' I thanked her for that, and she said 'You bound to know who I am.' To hush her up I said I knew her; but she said 'You lying' and hit me a lick on the head, not hard. By then I'd led her back to the bench for colored people, hard as a rail; and when she sat down, she said 'Tell your children you know old Lacey.' I said 'Who's Lacey?' and she said 'One of Miss Martha Custis's niggers—Miss Martha Washington at old Mount Vernon.' Said she was a slave on the Washington place out by the Potomac when she was a girl, born a little bit after 'old General died.' That made her younger than I am today—like I said maybe just by a year or so.

"Course she may have been lying, bragging on herself; but if you sit down with your history book and do some arithmetic, you'll see she could have been telling me the truth. I thought she was then, I still think she was; she looked like the truth. I see her right now. Ugliest old woman I ever watched; but she knew her story, old as she was—less she was lying."

"And you think she was?"

Grainger said "I told you No. She was too old to make up something that hurt that bad to hear and still be smiling."

Straw had heard most of Grainger's stories many times through the years but never this one. It made him want to stand and wail to the open sky—the fact that one man, a man you'd known and watched all your life, could ram you back that far in time through direct knowledge, hand-to-hand. And here this morning they were all torn up and grieving for one particular boy who'd killed himself by strowing his seed where the ground was poison. It made Straw long, as he longed so often, to walk out of this room and keep walking straight through woods and creeks till he found the one safe place on Earth where he could pause—it had to be there, though he'd yet to find it— and then to take a dry seat on the ground, shut his eyes and never leave, never retrace his steps, never see his home and kin again.

Grainger said "Don't let this get you down."

Straw came to himself and touched the old man's knee. "I'm trying hard."

"Try harder then—this many people leaning on you, you can't cave in."

Straw said "Don't worry. I'll tend to you."

"Not me I'm thinking about, not now. You could go on and stretch me out today and I'd be glad. Hutch and his boy though—they driving up here right this minute for me to save; and I can't walk ten steps to meet them, much less ease their misery."

"They know that, Mr. Walters."

"Why else they coming then?" Grainger's eyes were crouched and gleaming with the helpless need to do a duty he'd felt all his life to a few white men that were his blood kin, though they'd let him live like a whole different creature in a parallel world that ran—when it moved at all—beneath their feet, never higher than their knees: a world that was generally either ice-cold or blistering hot, furnished with big-eyed hungry children and men and women old as Grainger, harder than ironwood and wild in their minds. All the same, a great part of Grainger's pain rose from the fact that all he wanted to do and give now was far past giving. He understood he was nothing on Earth but eyes today—useless eyes and a wakeful mind that, he well knew, came and went like daylight.

9

With all his failings Straw's body was still as strong as an engine—arms, legs and back. So in late afternoon when Wade had rested from the hard trip and managed to eat two slices of bread, and Hutch had put a clean diaper on him, Straw solved the problem of how to bring the two frail men on the place together. Grainger could never have walked to the main house and climbed the porch steps; today Wade couldn't have made it to Grainger's. So Straw led Grainger out of doors and sat him on a chair by the nearest hickory in cool dry shade. Then Straw went back to the main house and, with Hutch beside him, took Wade in his arms and brought him down the steps and over the seventy yards of shadow and sun to another chair three feet from Grainger. Then Straw and Hutch left the two men alone and waited on the back steps, in sight but not hearing.

Grainger had seen Straw set the boy down and help him get his balance in the chair. By the time Wade had faced him and said "Old friend," Grainger's morning memory had faded to where he had no recollection of this starved face or who lived behind it; but he answered politely "Fine, thank you, sir. How you making out?"

Though Wade knew that his smiles were frightening, he had to grin for the first time today. "I'm bound to tell you I've seen better days. I got carsick on the way up here and had to keep stopping along the road. I can't vomit though; there's nothing left in me."

"You're slimming down all right—scarcely see you."

"I told you I don't see much now, remember?" All Wade could see, even this nearby, was a darker patch on the screen of his mind where he felt Grainger's force. Wade's hand came up in the air between them and traced what he could see of Grainger, the faint tan shimmer.

"Not missing a thing, Son. Nothing left of me. Right pretty leaves on these old trees though." Grainger was still not sure who was here, but the boy seemed to know him.

Wade understood that much—the blind were leading the blind again. And he managed to wonder why he'd gone through this strenuous trip, and put his parents through it, to sit here briefly by an ancient man who hardly knew him and might well die before Wade himself. In their feeble strength though, both men were patient with the quiet calm of prisoners; both pairs of hands lay harmless on their knees. And after a while, Wade thought of his point in coming at all. He took slow care to lean toward Grainger and not lose balance (his blind sense of objects had grown even keener; the way they reflected his voice would tell him what was near; sometimes he only had to think like radar, and he'd locate things and people precisely). Now when Wade thought the old eyes had found him and recognized his face, he said "You know that place back here in the woods, down by the bend in the creek? You used to watch me swim down there, saved my life that time?"

Grainger's scaly hand came across the cold space and found the boy's bone wrist. He pressed it once.

Wade thought that was Yes. "I'm going to die fairly soon after this. I've asked Hutch to bring my ashes up here and scatter them on that pool in the creek where you rescued me. Can you show him where?"

"That drowning hole where you fell in and I drug you out—nineteen and seventy?"

Wade sat back. "Yes sir. I was nine years old."

"I know my way down yonder like my hand." Grainger stopped as if to think his way again into the woods and on downhill. Then he may have tried smiling; the muscles had forgot. "No, I fixed it for you. Safe as can be. Widened the banks and filled up the deepest hole with rocks. Bring your boys anytime."

Wade laughed. "I will; thank you. You remember my friend I brought up here a few years back—a Bondurant fellow, older than me?"

Grainger said "Colored boy with the sharp gray suit?"

Wade had forgot Wyatt's handsome suit, bought specially for the one trip he'd made south with Wade. "Those were fine clothes."

"Set him back a fair piece of money, I could tell."

"Money meant less to Wyatt than ruts in the road."

Grainger said "Me too. And look at me now—" He patted around his chest and flanks as if frisking himself for hidden cash. "I'm trusting to be a big banker in Heaven though."

"You going there?"

"No doubt about it. Any minute—"

Wade said "You'll outlast me, for sure."

Grainger looked him over as if for a written date of death. "Never happen," he said.

Wade smiled but said "I'm too weak to argue."

"Not arguing one bit at all here, Son. I'm bound for Paradise is all I know."

"And you're looking forward to that prospect?"

Grainger said "I'll tell you the honest fact—in the Bible it sounds mighty tacky to me: a whole city made out of jewelry and gold. And I doubt I can stand to sing all day or listen either, not all day, not if they let many white women sing. But no, I'm planning to take plenty rest and get some questions answered finally."

"Want to say what they are?"

Grainger said "I don't; you not old enough." But the faint start of a smile tugged at him, and he said "You drop by and see soon's you get there—I'll tell you then, everything I know."

Wade agreed to that. "And vice versa. Between now and Paradise though, do me a favor? Show Hutch the place I mentioned, in the creek?"

Grainger's slow head agreed. "Ease your mind." Then his mind hooked back to the memory of Wyatt, the sharp gray suit; and he said "That colored boy called me a house pet—you hear him?"

Wade could no longer call the phrase to mind; but he guessed it sounded like something Wyatt might have said, half whispering near Grainger. Rather than deny it, Wade said "People have all grades of pets, you know. There's people with royal tigers asleep on their beds every night, tamer than rabbits."

Grainger said "He didn't mean that but thank you." The moment in which their vague minds had met at last hung on around them, a mild reprieve.

From the faint direction of the main house steps, Wade could hear the mixed voices of his father and Straw. It was one of the better sounds of his childhood on summer visits here, the undercurrent of safety mixed with the coiling invisible scent of his early body's unspoken desire—the lives and shapes of men worth reaching for and tasting. It turned Wade's mind completely away from the old man near him; and he rose in place, facing the main house. Then he gave a wide wave toward his father and waited for guidance.

Grainger said "You're the luckiest child I know."

Wade tried to laugh; it sounded like leaves. But he said "You've known a million children; how did I win the lucky crown?"

"Win what?—you losing, Son. You fading on *off*."

Wade finally laughed. "You said I was luckier than all the kids you've known. I need to ask how."

Grainger took the time to recall his meaning. Then he lined it out on the air with a finger as if Wade could read the actual words. "You dying in trusty arms like you are. Like me and you. That's some kind of luck. I seen men die in the mud like hogs—" Grainger didn't sound finished but he stopped there firmly.

Wade barely recalled Grainger's service in France, but he said "It does beat jumping out the window."

"—And leaving young. I ought to left this world, young like you, with my teeth and good health. Would have left a better memory behind me, not this old gunny sack of gristle and bone."

Gristle and bone—Wade knew that Grainger could see him at least, whether he truly recognized him or not. There was nothing else to say except "Show Hutch the place but wait till I'm gone." Then Wade balanced himself upright for Hutch and Straw—he'd gained a little strength in the shade. When they reached him, Wade said "I better lie down awhile before the trip home."

Straw said "Mr. Walters, I'll get Wade in; then come get you."

Grainger said "Take your time."

In his old half-comic grumbling way, Hutch said "Nobody but you's *got* time."

Wade laughed. "Nobody." He put out a hand again, straight to its target, and found Grainger's ear. He slowly leaned and whispered "Adiós."

Grainger said, full voice, "I don't speak French no more."

Wade paused, reeling a little to be upright in warmer air. Then he decided against the clear word *Goodbye*. He reached for where he knew Straw stood.

Straw gathered him in again and lifted him gently in one long move.

Hutch recalled for the first time in maybe three decades how Straw had lifted him similarly one night in Oxford, as easily as if skin and bone were weightless. *He's not a bit less powerful now.* That constituted a small reward.

As Hutch and Straw took Wade away, Grainger could see them through the first few yards of gradual distance; and he thought *I finished my whole job now*. It meant he could leave any day he chose — he meant to die in broad daylight, to spare anybody finding him cold with his mouth gapped open some early dawn.

10

Wade had slept so deeply through the afternoon, even with his family moving around him, that Hutch and Ann felt able to stay on at Straw and Emily's till nearly dusk. The women had served the food, washed the dishes and gone for a long walk up the road (by then the heat of the day had broken). The men had sat on the front porch, waving toward the scarce cars of a holiday weekend, calling out to a few familiar walkers — all of them black and lifelong acquaintances. They were trying to cool their minds with small talk.

Straw as usual had just read a new and inflammatory book on the Civil War, an occurrence he still chose to call the War of Northern Aggression; and he had to give Hutch a feverish summary — some overeducated son of a bitch had published a book claiming Robert E. Lee was a mediocre general and a dishonest man.

Hutch responded with the latest foolishness at Duke — a campus fracas on the question of whether or not the all-male, ninety-nine-percent-white-and-alcoholic fraternities had the faintest right to continue existing (Hutch was sure they didn't; Straw oddly agreed). Then Hutch said his newest poem for Straw, written this year at the first sight of spring, a week before they brought Wade south. The poem was a ten-line memory of a day Hutch and Straw had spent at Warm Springs, Virginia many years back—both of them stripped in their best young bodies, suspended in thoughtless fetal ease in the huge natural spring at precisely blood heat.

Straw responded with thanks and a reiteration of the blanket request he made each time Hutch wrote any poem about him. "Don't let Emily see it."

Since Emily had never read a serious poem in her life, Hutch had always known their past was safe. Even Ann had barely responded to anything Hutch had published in the past dozen years.

On the porch after that, Straw and Hutch turned to making whatever plans seemed sensible for the time left to Wade—what Straw might be called on to do by way of help. At about five-thirty, as the light dimmed a notch and Hutch was thinking it was time to find Ann and start home with Wade, Straw leaned in closer. "Was this Ann's idea today—coming up here with you?"

"Not really. My student helper's gone for the weekend, my nerve failed me for coming single-handed; and at the last minute, Wade asked for his mother."

"I'd have run down and got you."

Hutch said "I always know that. You saying I'm wrong to give her this much?"

Straw took his time. "No, it may well be the best thing you've agreed to in years." He grinned at the road first, then brought it back to Hutch.

"What's the joke here, friend? You and Emily stage this someway?"

Straw looked back to the road. "Oh no, this has the unmistakable handprints of Fate all over it." Now the grin was a laugh. Straw had drunk three glasses of wine with lunch, but there'd been time to sober.

Hutch couldn't quite laugh but he lightened his tone. "Read the handprints for me."

"You think you can do this alone; you absolutely can't."

"I've got good help and, hard as it sounds, this can't last long."

Straw said "It'll last the whole rest of your life. How in God's name could you ever blot out the memory of your one child in a hell like this?"

"I don't plan to blot it. I wouldn't if I could. If I outlive this, it's bound to be at the awful center of anything else I ever write. You well know I've dwelt on the past too much and am too old to change."

"Then ask for Ann back."

Hutch said "I don't follow you. It was Ann that left; I never asked her to."

"Hutchins, there are millions of ways to ask. You hadn't *seen* Ann for the last twenty years till the day she left."

"That's your flaming imagination again. I loved Ann Gatlin every day we spent together. That wasn't enough, not for her anyhow; she said I couldn't make her believe it. So frankly I've learned to like the relief she left in her wake. There's a lot of things worse to live among than quiet empty air."

Straw said "You're how old—sixty-two?"

"Sixty-three on the twelfth of this month; you missed it."

"Twelfth of May?"

Hutch smiled. "Falls on the twelfth almost every year."

"Well, damn. I'm sorry. I miss a lot don't I?"

Hutch laughed. "That's all right; some of my young friends remembered." By now they were back in their old slow teasing; these days they seemed to manage it only when one of them hurt.

Straw said "I know you see yourself stumbling on to the grave like some old sourdough trapped on the salt flats; but don't plan to do that, Hutch— I couldn't stand to watch."

"Who says you're going to outlast me?"

"The handprints of Fate again—don't forget my forebears: Mother's still living at a thousand years old."

Hutch said "She's eighty-three."

"And looks a lot older than a redwood thicket."

"That's because she's chain-smoked unfiltered Camels since before Walter Raleigh brought the blond weed to white folks."

Straw said "Exactly. If she's eighty-three under all that tobacco tar, then I'm bound to last till a hundred at least."

Hutch's voice was little more than a whisper. "Take me in then. Otherwise I'll croak in a nursing home."

"Oh no, not me; hire yourself a trained nurse. Cranky as you are, set in your ways—I won't come near you. You had your chance."

"At what?"

Straw faced Hutch and, simply by thinking back, produced a strong live trace of the power of his young face and eyes—the boy he'd been. "Your final chance at young Strawson Stuart. He's beyond reach today." The power held on, at a high hot burn.

For an instant Hutch looked and saw Straw was right. It felt like an immense hot loss and worthy of grief. But he said "Look, if you're in touch with that fine boy still, give him bountiful thanks from an antique friend."

Slowly Straw let his present face return. "He accepts all gifts with shameless gratitude." In his chair Straw bowed from the waist toward Hutch.

Hutch had just seen Emily and Ann top the rise in the road to his right. They were each walking with five-foot sticks like shepherds in an old Bible engraving. Hutch pointed to them. "Lo, Ruth and Naomi come leading the herd."

Straw said "Thank Christ. You be good to yours. Emily Stuart may be a Methodist missionary, but she's saved me from drowning more times than I know." Straw waved broadly to the distant women.

They seemed not to see him, but still they came on.

11

In fact Ann had seen both men as soon as she and Emily topped the rise; and for a bad moment, she felt the chill of abandonment she'd always felt at the sight of Hutch and Straw together. Till now she'd put off asking again the question she'd asked in her letters to Emily—the second letter had never been acknowledged—so these few yards of distance would be Ann's last chance to ask for help again. She said "Do you think Straw's spoken to Hutch?"

At first Emily was honestly puzzled and creased her brow.

"About me, Em—asking Hutch to let me share in this, just a rightful share."

Emily said "Ann, I feel awful about this; but I need to tell you the local facts. When you first wrote me, I spoke to Strawson; all he did was turn his back and head down to Mr. Walters' house. So I can't say more. See, I promised myself to give up mingling in Hutch and Strawson's business, oh, twenty-five years ago. It had truly eaten me up by the day, just knowing how fully they'd shared each other before I came into Strawson's life. I finally had to step back and ease off or die."

"Can you give me the directions for *how* to ease up?"

"You've made your break."

Ann said "Making a break and changing your mind—the whole way you think—are two different things."

Emily said "But I did it." Her face was as firm and self-confident as a young reliable terrier's.

Again Ann wanted to press for more than she knew. She'd never learned the entire story of Hutch and Straw and had never asked. But she'd somehow known from the start not to seek possession of facts and mental images she couldn't use or live beside. And here with Emily walking so near, with what Em implied was available knowledge, Ann told herself *Stop her right here, girl. Spare your mind.* So she said "Don't worry yourself a moment. I'll find a way to speak to Straw, or I'll phone him from Durham."

"Strawson won't support you—you're bound to know that."

With those words, Emily's face changed again in a way Ann had never seen till now—an almost scary intensity that looked like something you'd glimpse at the scene of a bloody collision and turn from at once. Ann said "I honor

Straw's loyalty to Hutch. If Hutch doesn't see his own way to decency, the next few days, I'll have to ask Wade himself to speak up."

The glare in Emily's face hadn't dimmed, but her hand moved over the gap between their moving bodies and took Ann's fingers. "Don't tear that pitiful boy any worse than he's torn already. He's plowed up my heart—I've loved him too—so I know he's ruined yours."

In all the years Ann had known Emily Stuart, she'd never had one firm word of warning from her; and the sudden freshness of this demand cut all the deeper. Ann couldn't face Emily's eyes, here and now; but as they reached the mouth of the drive and turned toward the house, Ann said "I thank you for taking me seriously."

Emily said "I guess that's my worst failing—seriousness. Strawson says I treat the damned birds in the *trees* like they were angels of God."

Ann said "Which they are." And in the sudden relief they felt—near as they were to Straw and Hutch, still there on the porch—both women laughed.

12

Hutch and Straw had to wake Wade up to get him to the car. He sat up, fairly alert on the backseat, for the next twenty minutes as Hutch detoured them through the small and moribund town of Fontaine on a mission that Wade had failed to mention but might be glad of. Fontaine was where Hutch's own father's maternal family had lived when they moved off the Kendal land in the 1880s. The boxy two-story white frame house where they'd stayed for so long was still upright on its ample lot by the train depot at the north end of town—the actual roof and walls from which his grandmother Eva had eloped on a warm spring night ninety years ago with Forrest Mayfield, where Eva's mother had drunk lye and died in agony on the kitchen floor, where Rob had spent his peaceful but longing childhood and where he'd brought the infant Hutch when Rachel died.

The depot was long since abandoned by trains, to be rescued ten years ago as a play-and-hobby center for the old and idle. But the Kendal house was barely fazed by its new coats of paint—a glossy blue-white with firetruck-red window frames and the plaster statue of a Mexican boy with a wide sombrero and a balky donkey near the stones of a walkway that still bore all the Kendals' initials and every Mayfield's who'd ever lived there.

Hutch paused at the curb and leaned to look past Ann. The house and its old trees could still move him strongly, in the right circumstances; but now it might as well have been foreign—a small dead factory.

Wade's head turned too, for what that was worth. He recognized the air of the place but couldn't really see more than shadows.

Ann said "Who painted the window frames red?"

Hutch said "The lawyer's wife, I guess." A Pennsylvania civil rights lawyer had bought the house back in the seventies once Eva died and, however tasteless, had kept it up.

Ann said "I like it—especially the windows: a nice whorehouse touch, might wake the town up. And the sculptural ornaments are equally welcome." She was honestly trying for pleasantry.

Wade quietly said "What ornaments please?"

Ann suddenly found she could barely speak.

So Hutch said "A Mexican midget and his burro." The yard behind the sculpture was cluttered with some child's toys—a yellow tricycle and numerous pieces of bright equipment: a stroller, a playpen. The lawyer and his wife had never had children; whose could they be? But then Hutch recalled a possibility. "Maybe they've adopted a Chinese girl. The wife told me she'd been thinking that over, a year ago. You can rescue unwanted Chinese girls from death now, easy—there's a place in Seattle makes all the arrangements, door-to-door."

Wade nodded once as if any news about this house, with its outlandish weight of memory, had long since lost the power to shock. In another moment, before Hutch faced the road again and drove them off, Wade drew his legs up tight to his chest, bent himself together and lay on the seat.

Before they were on the main highway, Ann had reached back and spread the two light cotton blankets up to Wade's shoulders—he was already gone.

And his deep-drowned sleep lasted through the first three-fourths of the trip home. So Ann and Hutch had a further reason to ride in silence, speaking only at curious sights by the road—a palmist's sign saying *Mother Mindy's Mysteries*, three black children driving a mule and wagon so decrepit it looked like a natural object, not made by hands; and an early moon that was literally gold.

But when they were twenty miles from Durham in the full spring night, Wade suddenly spoke in his old normal voice. "I told Grainger where to strow my ashes—they won't amount to much, just three handsful."

Too quickly, Hutch tried for levity. "I heard we amount to three *quarts* of ashes. Don't sell yourself short."

Wade said "You heard wrong again; I *know* — I've scattered more than one friend these last few years. Anyhow, old Grainger will show you the resting place, when it's time." Wade waited a long time and then said "Rest," like a long-sought name that had dawned at last.

Ann looked to the side of Hutch's face. It was the first time she'd watched him challenged for a sizable response since she left their house. *You answer him. Now.*

Hutch laughed and glanced back to Wade. "You better draw a good map and file it with me; you're going to outlast Grainger by years."

If Wade heard that, he didn't speak again.

And when Ann looked back a minute later, Wade seemed plunged again into sleep like a river too swift to touch. She got to her knees in the passenger seat and reached to his forehead. It was burning hot and his hair was drenched with an oily sweat. She adjusted his blankets, then faced forward. "He's got a fever, Hutch."

"I know. I could feel it when we laid him down."

"Then we should head straight for the hospital now." Ann hadn't delivered that strong an opinion since Wade's return.

Hutch said "No, we'll go home and check. If Wade's really feverish, I'll call Dr. Ives."

In that short time Wade's breathing had gone from quiet to grating, slow but painful to hear.

Ann lowered her voice. "You know he's had pneumonia once already?"

Hutch said "In early March — he's told me the grim details several times. I doubt this is it. We've taken all the preventive measures." But Hutch did silently recall the times Wade would claim to be too exhausted for his inhalation treatment.

They continued in silence till they got to the bottom of Hutch's drive. It had been a long time, nearly four decades, since they'd been this sad and thwarted in one another's presence; and that had been over the transatlantic phone lines when Hutch learned Ann had aborted the child they conceived at Christmas in Rome during his first year abroad. They understood tonight that the fact of their separate nearness in the car, with their sick child behind them, was increasing the pain — a pain neither one of them could touch, much less banish. And though they literally hadn't touched for nearly a year, Hutch took his right hand off the wheel and laid it on the seat between him and Ann.

Ann waited a moment, not denying the offer but meaning to brace her feelings first and not think ahead. *No further than here.* Then she laid her left hand above Hutch's and kept it there till they stopped at the side door of the house.

Odd as it felt after celibate months; and in this space with a dying man, Hutch was stirred in a way he'd only known in dreams the past year—his cock still blindly faithful after so long, such gain and loss. Sad as he was, he almost grinned to think it might moan aloud any instant; it had been friendless so long.

Ann was still faced forward, unsure of how she could manage to turn and meet Hutch's eyes.

But he turned and saw her clean profile, her finest side always. Only just lately the edge of her jaw had begun to loosen; that and the slightly hooded eyelids were all the genuine change Hutch could see. Finally he could tell her "It's meant a good deal, having you along today."

That brought on her tears, the few quiet tears Ann could ever shed. And they came always for someone else's authentic trouble, never for her own— Hutch's feelings had always shown themselves more freely than Ann could manage. She dried the tears with her one free hand and finally turned to Hutch.

His eyes looked worse than Wade's, already somehow bereft of his whole world and as far past reach as any lost astronaut.

Ann had never for an instant thought Hutch could come to this. She'd never seen him break; he was plainly close to breaking. She pressed his hand lightly once, then left her own in place above it. "I'll be with you both, anytime you say."

"Then why did you leave us?"

"I left *you*, Hutchins. No way I could stay." Ann waited, then whispered "Let's don't start this again, not here tonight."

Hutch whispered too. "No, tell me why you'd want to come back."

"You're what I've got."

"Me? Or Wade and me?"

Ann said "Both of you. Or either one."

"Come back for good, you mean?"

"I'm an old woman, Hutch; but I'm not on trial nor volunteering for a polygraph test. I'm offering the little I've got to give; please take it or leave it."

So Hutch left his hand on the seat under hers and shut his eyes a moment. "Let's see if we can get this boy indoors. If not, I'll call somebody for help."

But the two of them managed it; Wade was that nearly weightless and easy to help, though every atom of his body hurt—one more fact he kept to himself.

13

Wade was running only three degrees of fever when they laid him down; and though he was still in the curious daze he'd moved in through the entire day, Wade told Hutch and Ann, who were by his bed, "Nobody's calling a doctor tonight. I'm just worn out. Go cook your supper and bang some pans—it'll cool me down, just to hear you in the kitchen."

While neither Hutch nor Ann had thought they were hungry, they obeyed Wade's instructions, cooked a mushroom omelet and ate every morsel with Ann's fresh soda bread and a glass of wine. When their plates were empty, it was past ten o'clock; and they each felt nearly as tired as Wade.

Ann glanced to her sensible big-number watch and said "You tell me what to do next." When Hutch looked quizzical, she said "Do you need me here tonight? If so I'll run home and get a few clothes."

Home, she says—meaning St. Mary's Road, eight miles from here. What needed Ann here and now was Hutch's body, beat as it was, and his mind that had starved itself for so long of any assurance that his skin and bones were welcome in someone else's life. But he couldn't ask to feed off Ann tonight, not in these straits, unless she flagged a similar need. *Has she stayed as dumbly faithful as me? No sign she hasn't.* Hutch sat there beside her another half minute, but all he could sense from Ann was exhaustion. He ringed her wrist with his hand. "Go rest in your own bed. Let's talk tomorrow."

She was mildly relieved that he'd made the choice, for now at least. Much as she needed to stay near her son, she knew what a thicket of choices would follow—to spend the rest of her daily life near Hutch Mayfield, or another agonized disengagement and a gypsy move to smaller quarters. "You'll call me if Wade takes a turn for the worst?"

Hutch agreed. "The minute he's worse but I doubt he'll get worse tonight somehow. The trip was just hard, seeing weird old Grainger and the house Wade loved so much as a boy." Hutch stood and gathered their few dishes.

So Ann rose too. "Does it feel like I'm asking to come back for good?"

Hutch couldn't quite face her; he rinsed a plate. "I never went anywhere, Ann—swear to God. I've just never been the world's most *present* man. You may well remember, I don't turn up—not fully armed—till most bystanders have given up and gone. But I somehow thought, anybody who waited, would somehow collect on his or her patience—I'd have some feeling or fact ripe to give." At last he turned with one hand raised to back his oath, his strong right hand, as if it were proof that even as close a witness as he could still drift farther off than most lone voyagers and could only signal *Farewell* or *Save me*, knowing both were useless.

"Oh Hutch, you *went*—you're out there now, on your fragile wings, insisting on bearing all the weight of a death that's at least half mine. I made that child, with this same body you're looking at here." She had the grace not to touch her own body; it stood for itself.

Hutch knew she was right. Distance was his oldest instinct, seizing what looked like the full brunt of something—death, love, failure, abandonment—then winging off with it for lone decades of slow ingestion, concoction, assimilation, then a guaranteed (if long overdue) return. He sometimes thought the tendency came from the enormous fact of his mother's death the day he was born and the ensuing fact that his lovable destitute father quickly became more nearly a son than a father to Hutch. For the first time, in his memory at least, he told Ann now "I've borne the weight till today, yes ma'm. Let's talk tomorrow. Maybe we can shift the load."

Ann agreed. "Good night." She was already moving to check Wade's room and drive home alone.

Wade's light was still out and his breathing was maybe more regular.

So Ann went on.

14

But it was pneumonia, the parasitic swamping of the lungs so common to this plague and so often lethal. Hutch had waked on his own at three in the morning, dreading the duty to check on Wade and maybe find him worse than before. But Hutch rose finally and went to Wade's doorway. At first the slow breaths sounded normal, but Hutch went on in and leaned to feel the boy's hair.

It was soaked and snaky, the pillow beneath Wade was drenched, his chest and sheets were sopping wet with the desperate effort to break a fever that only descends on very young children or dying adults. When Hutch took a step to find the thermometer, Wade sang "*'Old Paint, I'm a-leaving Cheyenne.'*"

"Did I wake you up?"

"Oh no, I've been swimming laps for an hour in this cold bed." Wade gave a hard shudder as a chill wrenched through him.

Still in the dark, Hutch sat on the edge of the mattress and felt the forehead again. Surprisingly cool, if this was fever—maybe the bedtime aspirin had finally broken the heat. *Some minor bug surely.*

But Wade said "Hutch, this is pneumocystis."

"You're breathing easy—"

"I recognize the thing I've got, my lungs are filling, it's only just starting."

Hutch could hear a trace of burr on the voice—the distant warning of a real death rattle from deep in Wade's lungs. "Then I'll call Dr. Ives." Hutch stood to go to the kitchen phone.

"Wait, Father—I don't plan to fight this again." Wade hadn't called Hutch *Father* more than twice in the past decade.

"The hell we won't fight it." Hutch went to the door. Any minute or second he could add to Wade's life was a monumental gain.

But Wade found strength to give what was almost a bellow of rage in the silent house—rage to do his own will this instant, to let death in and bend to its power. When Hutch turned to face him, Wade said "We're riding this through, or out or whatever, under this roof. You, Mother and me. Please help me *go*."

Hutch came back, sat and stroked the damp brow. "You'll let me call Dr. Ives at least?"

Wade shook his head ferociously.

"Then you're asking us to watch you drown with our hands tied."

Wade said "That well may be. Many parents have done it, from the edge of the pool." He took a long wait, then managed to laugh, then coughed convulsively. At last he could whisper "How crazy is that?"

"Not crazy at all. It's *cruel* as hell." Hutch had almost whispered it; but once it was said, he wanted it back. *Any parent's volunteered for this. Stand and take your punishment.*

Before Hutch could speak again, Wade said "Cruel? To you and Ann? It's no big moonlight hayride for *me*."

"Look, Son, the hospital's ten minutes away. We'll put on your robe, I'll call Margaret Ives, she'll tell us where to go, they've got the right drugs and the oxygen."

Wade's hand fumbled up and found Hutch's mouth, trying to mute it. "Promise me?"

"Yes. Wait—promise you what?"

"—That you and Ann won't keep me alive when it stops being me."

"How will I know that?"

"Say *we*—you and Ann. Ann Gatlin's my mother."

Hutch said "Ann *Mayfield*—don't forget we're legal still. But all right, how'll we know when you're ready?"

"I'll either tell you or—didn't you used to pray every year or so? Try that again maybe; ask God or somebody in his line of work."

Wade's skin still felt strangely cool to the hand, but he was plainly skirting delirium. Hutch leaned to speak clearly. "Let me be sure I understand you. You're willing to go to the hospital, aren't you?"

Wade shut his eyes and slowly agreed, barely moving his head.

Hutch accepted the signal and switched on the dim lamp.

The skin of Wade's face and neck was purplish; his eyes were wide but fixed on a far point—the eyes of some sky god hacked out of granite five thousand years back but fulminant still.

At the edge of the commanding gaze, Hutch could say only "I make you that promise, I'm sure Ann will, we won't hang on when you give the sign." Though Hutch knew it was only the simplest humane good sense, he'd have made the vow to nobody else, alive or dead. But what else can you say to your own crushed child who begs to die? Hutch pressed the switch that slowly raised the head of Wade's bed till the boy was half upright. As it rose, Wade's face—even with the eyes shut—looked like some corpse, long sunk in peace but dragged back to life and mindlessly tortured.

Wade said "Make your plans before I start howling." By now, he couldn't have howled in a firestorm; his wind was that scarce.

Hutch went toward the kitchen to make the two calls—the doctor and Ann. He'd rather have called in nuclear ruin on the entire American continent at sunrise.

15

On the fourth day in Duke Hospital, Wade took a sharp fast turn for the worse. He was mostly unconscious or, when he woke for snatches, he was wildly reeling through scraps of lunacy and terror. His lungs were chocked with microscopic creatures, drinking his life; and a rank web of tubes brought him full-time oxygen, drugs and nourishment. Hutch and Ann visited several times a day and stood alone or together by the bed to watch the course of a war they couldn't speed or hinder. They saw Dr. Ives at least once in the course of each day or night. Her reliable warmth and her pale clear eyes seemed a kind of outrage in the rackety life of a huge hospital, a place that was less a refuge than a nonstop foundry steeped in gloom and producing at contradictory rates of urgency and torpor some mysterious artifact, never shown to humans.

But with all her sympathy and ungrudging words, Dr. Ives never gave them an atom of excess hope for time or rescue. The nearest she came to a firm prognosis was to face them both in the hall outside and say "You might want to think about last arrangements. Wade could go any minute or fight his way back for a few weeks or months." This crisis was simply uncallable—Wade was drastically weak before it started. His kidneys and liver had suffered from

the two years of toxic drugs; they were functioning far below par now and
could fail at a moment's notice.

All that Dr. Ives would allude to, by way of a future, was that, when she
asked Wade if he'd made a living will with his plain intentions should he lose
all consciousness, he'd only smiled and said "I somehow doubt this is curtains.
Don't order the coffin unless they're on sale." And she'd added that, over the
past decade, AIDS patients had taught her something she'd never quite trusted
before—within certain limits an adult, even a very young child, can choose
the day, sometimes the instant, to let death in. Her sense was that Wade was
gearing up to make that choice.

Both Ann and Hutch thanked her, silently acknowledging that almost
no male American physician—skittish as they were at the risk of error—
would have made that considerate a prediction.

The night of the fourth day, Hutch had stayed well past the legal nine
o'clock in the chair near Wade, in reach of his shoulder, though the boy
hadn't spoken since midafternoon. And Hutch left only when the splendid
young black nurse named Hannah Bertram convinced him again that he'd
be no good to Wade or anyone if he didn't go home and try to rest—she'd
call him if anything changed either way. As always before he left Wade's side,
Hutch bent and kissed the boy's tall brow. It was so dry and thin-skinned that
it felt like actual bone to normal lips. On the chance that a single cell in
Wade's mind was still keeping watch, Hutch said "I'm going no farther than
the telephone. Keep resting, Son; I'll be here when you need me."

In his trance, Wade heard that. He thought *No, nobody's ever been near,
not when I'm truly needy.* Drugged as he was, it was almost the truth; but even
when he heard Hutch turn to leave, Wade kept his own counsel, a hands-
breadth from death, still refusing to yield. *Why? Why not now?*

16

Back home Hutch had drunk two ounces of scotch and watched the news
on television—the daily butcher's bill of children shot at random and beat
by their kin, women raped by strangers or close relations, dead human
fetuses paraded in priests' arms past abortion clinics, men burned for their
race or their choice of partner, women pounded to pulp by mates or sons.
In its muffled horror, a daily dose of such meaningless leering had come to
be oddly calming for Hutch—like an evening spent at a knockout produc-
tion of some fifth-rate Jacobean tragedy: a feast of cadavers in velvets and lace,

their chalky faces specked with the ulcers of syphilis. But toward the end of this night's news, tucked in before the zany sportscaster, came the story of a young Chapel Hill man—known to be in the early stages of AIDS—who'd burned himself, his bedridden mother, the collie dog and their gnomish bungalow all to the ground just this past morning.

It was so god-awful, if Hutch hadn't felt exhausted, he'd have laughed. As it was, when he rose to switch off the set, a clear thought pierced up through his mind like an iron spike. *Wade dies tonight.* It felt as true as any thought he'd had since childhood. Hutch stood in place, letting the shock drain off through half a minute. Then he thought *Thank God*—thank God for Wade's sake, his own sake and Ann's. Hutch felt the dazed but spacious relief he'd felt at the sight of his own father's death—*Thank Christ he's gone.* Should he drive back and sit out the night beside Wade's bed or wait here for Hannah's call near morning? *Wait here and lie down anyhow.*

Before Hutch took the first step toward his bedroom, his mind brought up a whole second thought. For the first time since they'd hauled Wade's papers down from New York, he recalled the big box and the record book that Ivory had kept in the kitchen. Far as Hutch knew, they still lay shut on the floor of Wade's closet. *Do I open them now?* What would the need be? Any will or notes about last wishes could wait till the end. But it came to Hutch powerfully, tired as he was, that there might be something in the sizable box which would clear a final block between them while Wade was still breathing—some possible light on Wyatt Bondurant, Wyatt's hatred of Hutch; or some slight clue to the unknown life that Wade concealed in the midst of all those years when Hutch and Ann had hardly seen him.

To break the seal on that box now, with Wade alive, could only be right if Hutch really hoped that the boy would last through a stretch of sane days for healing the years of silence between them—if Hutch and his son's old laughing ease could someway return. *I beg for that, yes.*

17

It was two in the morning before Hutch had gone through all the papers. Either Wade was a neater man than the pack rat child he'd been, or he'd weeded these papers in recent months, or someone else had weeded them for him. There were none of the pointless souvenirs that litter most drawers—receipts, matchbooks, hazy snapshots of vague and inexplicably grinning strangers. Every letter that Hutch could recall sending Wade seemed to be here, a thick handful of letters from Ann; early letters from Hutch's grandmother Eva, from family friends like Polly Drewry and Alice Matthews, Strawson and Grainger. There was even a diary Wade had kept in his first stay at summer camp at the age of ten, a detailed record of thirty days that still had the power to summon a taste of the hopeless misery of a homesick child—a misery Wade had never confessed.

There was nothing from his college days and little in writing to represent his early years in New York. There was, though, an unsealed envelope of photographs of young men, all in various stages of undress and many of them naked, all taken in rooms Hutch was almost sure he could recognize as Wade's—Wade's first small apartment on Bleecker Street and Seventh Avenue, above a Greek nightclub. The faces, white and black, were strangers to Hutch; but none of the dozen-odd photographs had the musky thrusting air of real pornography. Most of the men had the startled and slightly bruised air common to undressed Americans, a people not quite at ease in their skin—surely no Mediterranean poise in the body's frank grandeur or the perky indifference of Amazon tribes who wear their genitals matter-of-factly as household implements, handy conveniences. The single other shared quality that Hutch could see in the photographs was a high proportion of striking faces and cared-for bodies, the equal of a swarm of lesser classical heroes or minor gods. *Wade told the class he'd slept with only two men. Maybe these are Wyatt's. But did Wyatt know Wade in the Bleecker Street days?*

What held Hutch longest were the letters from Wyatt. Hutch hadn't realized till tonight that the two men had been separated so often, but each had occasionally traveled in his work (Wyatt was a book designer at Pantheon), and a thick run of letters survived from their weeks and days apart through the years together. Like most modern letters, Wade's and Wyatt's mainly amounted to less than the average long-distance phone call—some quick reminder of a bill to be paid, a line of greeting on a birthday or an anniversary apart, a joke overheard or some cryptic direction like *Act your own way; do what tastes true.*

There was one long letter in Wyatt's imposing and impetuous hand in dark brown ink, pages that looked like credible news from a general pausing in the midst of battle to scrawl a command—say, Stonewall Jackson at Chancellorsville or Shaka Zulu in full lion skin. It amounted to a scorching self-justification, written in late 1984 from the opposite end of the two men's apartment, at what seemed the first big impasse they'd reached. The final sentences were only the starkest from a blistering sequence.

Wade, If you think I've agreed to go on being the sweeper-up of the dry little turds from your meager past while you glide on with an appetite at least the equal of a starved hyena's, you've got less mind than even I thought you had.

I burn my push broom, here and now. Scour up your own shit or pack your boxes, clear out of my place and leave your key in the vase by the door. I want you to stay but not like this—not another day, not to mention a night.

And like the long-unsuspected Rosetta stone of Wade's estrangement from his parents, there was one last incendiary letter, separate from the others, at the bottom of the box. It was dated *New Year's Eve 1985*; and even before Hutch read a word further, he knew that the letter was written at the end of Wyatt's only visit to Durham with Wade.

They'd come down on December 27th to spend a week. Hutch and Ann had met Wyatt several times at dinner in New York; and those hours had seemed to go smoothly enough, though Wyatt said little and smiled to himself too often for comfort. But in Durham suddenly on the morning of New Year's Eve, Wade had walked into the kitchen to say that Wyatt was having to leave unexpectedly. Hutch and Ann wondered at the time if Wyatt had somehow taken offense—they'd spent the previous day at Strawson's with a visit to Grainger's—but Wade said "No, Wyatt has family duties." And Wyatt himself departed with thin smiles and thanks for all. When Wade left a few days later, on January 4th, it marked the end of his last really natural meeting with his parents till eight years later when he came home dying. The interim meetings had sooner or later turned skittish or silent. And neither Hutch nor Ann had ever seen Wyatt again, not face-to-face.

The relevant letter still smoked on the page.

Wade,

You know I didn't want to come along on that scenic voyage through upper Dixie, but you said you'd run interference with the Klan, the Carolina Nazis etc. and I trusted you. What I didn't guess, and it's partly my fault (I'm old enough to know when a road's booby-trapped), was that the real roadblock would be your lovely family.

The times we'd met them here in the city, I thought they seemed a little brittle and a little more seedy by the month. But I didn't plan to feel like I did from the hour I entered that handsome house in the piney woods—like the field hand buck that had ravished their darling, kinked his hair, inflated his cock and rinsed his brain in indigo till all he could want was The Negro Organ of Generation and Wyatt Bondurant's grinning eyes with the white teeth above it.

I know you think I'm criminally wrong or ridiculously off track anyhow. I can see your mother and father have never done a deed that they'd call impolite, not to mention cruel. I can see what's lovable and likable about them— they look good, smell good, talk smart and funny, and roll with the punches life throws their way. I can imagine they sit down Sundays in some well-

furnished church—Episcopal, I bet—and come out thinking they stand a fair chance of eternal life near God in Glory, a dignified Paradise with no voice raised and loyal colored washerwomen for the white satin robes.

My mother, as you know, believes the same nonsense—especially since we moved her to Sea Cliff, that crumbling beachhead of the old Anglo lower middle class. But I bet you all of my life's possessions that, come Judgment Day—if Judgment comes—my mother winds up in an eighteen-karat martyr's crown being fanned by coal-black pickaninny cherubs while your two progenitors are rushed up against a concrete wall by blazing archangels and mowed to a pulp with whatever brand of automatic weapon the angels are issued for simple justice.

That doesn't mean that I qualify as a justice agent on Earth for now, and it does not mean what I know you'll say—that I see racists in every skin that's not beige-to-black. What I realized it meant last night, when we got back from that drive to the country to see poor old Mr. Grainger Walters, was that any people who could use ninety-some years of one man's life like it was a substance they could wear to protect their hands and eyes from the winter wind—and him a frail man that's your father's cousin, and yours as well, and that your family's turned into a tame crippled monkey in a dry little shed you threw up around him, a shed that's really nothing but his last cage in a century of cages—well, what it told me was Wyatt Bondurant, you are out of your element. Swim fast for the shallows.

I know I've got every fault on Earth myself, in triplicate flaming letters on the sky. I know I've asked you to live beside me and put up with it. I know we spent our adult time, before we met, living lives that my dear ignorant mother would think lead to ruin, if she knew the facts. I know we've already done together more than a few things that every Gallup poll says most Christians abominate (many Jews and Muslims thrown in)—not just with our bodies attached to each other.

You know what other act I mean and its coming result that I still dread for my sister's sake—she's paid too much already for her life.

But I want you. From here on out. I want you free of that courteous Murder Incorporated you grew up in and that's round your feet this very minute like a pet anaconda crushing you to ooze as you sit reading in their tasteful rooms. Get out while you can and come back, come home to me. At least I love you and tell you the truth.

> Till I see you here, or whether I see you
> again or not, I'm nothing but
> Take-Him-or-Leave-Him Wyatt

When he'd read through it twice, Hutch knew his first response was right—again a focused sense of elation that boiled up through him. He'd been found out, in one of the vital cores of his life, for the first full time by a watchful witness other than Ann. Hutch had always known that, if the universe was just, his and his loved ones' chances of escaping execution in the first round of burnings were virtually nil. His sense of the appalling poison of slavery—a freezing poison that had no antidote, in his own life, his family's fate, and the whole nation's ruin—had been born in Hutch and had only grown. He saw, as plainly as he saw the oak floor, the unstemmable progress of the spreading stain of human chattel on his home country through nearly four centuries and its outward seepage now through the nation and the world beyond. And here in Wade's enormous pain and Hutch's powerlessness to ease it, here surely at last was the measured stroke of vengeance—a vengeance delivered far too late to teach or mend.

What it came to of course was unthinkably simple. An entire people from a vast continent had been seized by the millions, abducted, molested, raped in every conceivable posture and forced to tend the fruit of those unions or watch them sold into still crueler hands, worked under torture, then freed in a cataclysmic war to live abandoned—in fact, *abandoned*— by master and righteous liberator through all the years since. So while a great earth-movement of freedom had lifted millions in the past thirty years, hundreds of thousands of unmoved, unreached but justified sons of those dead slaves were foraging still in tight bands of vengeance, exacting their due and the unpaid loans of an impatient fate from generations that were undreamt of when the first black Africans strode in chains onto these mild shores, their endless exile.

Recalling the conversation with his seminar back in April, Hutch knew his conviction was hardly fresh—it was, spoken or not, the central theme of American life, its history and literature for nearly four centuries with no sign of flagging. Even the wound from the systematic slaughter of millions of native Indians had begun to heal almost everywhere except on the stunned reservations themselves. But the force that endured as the legacy of slavery, in every city and town tonight, had swelled to a din still unsuspected in the books and visions of older prophets who'd barely seen beyond their own moment, from John Brown and Lincoln to Faulkner and Baldwin. A whole irresistible limb of one strong race— a matchless arm, say—was moving now like a gleaming scythe to level the rows of the guilty, the great-grandchildren of the guilty, and the pure newborn.

Hutch also knew that all he'd managed to do about the horror and its constant survivals in his own existence and his family relations was pitifully small—a trim set of fairly consistent kind acts, more decorous than lasting, and a steady effort at trying to understand all the minds involved: the male and female overlords' minds, the male and female slaves and their present heirs, a single mind like Grainger Walters' or half-crazed Wyatt's or Wade's sacrifice to the wrongs of his kin or Hutch's own mind that had grown its callus early and accepted the service of a part-black kinsman who nonetheless lived in exposed solitude.

Hutch's whole life then amounted to long years of quiet assent to the most colossal act of theft and murder in human history—assent by Hutch and, again, all he'd loved except maybe Wade. But in sixty-three years of Hutch's life no one but Wyatt had pointed toward that lasting assent and called its name, an unstopped crime.

For the first time ever—with Wyatt's dead unanswerable voice aimed level at Hutch in the empty house this late spring night, and the wreckage of his son's life strewn round his feet—the chance that poor Strawson had also been right bore in on Hutch as another giant failure. *"I loved you, Hutchins. Have you lost that? I'd have spent my whole life bearing your weight, if you'd said the word."*

Hutch had leaned instead on a woman strong enough to bear six men for however long their lives might take—no, he'd never leaned; that had been half the trouble. Ann had asked for burdens that he'd never give her. Had he truly borne, in childhood, too much of his father's pain to volunteer for much of a burden from anyone else? Could he somehow have managed full trust in Straw or another man, the kind of trust he'd placed on their bodies forty years back? Wade and Wyatt plainly managed it; it killed them both. But that was the outcome of nothing more fatal than the accidental convergence of time with one especially crafty virus, no condemnation of their human bent or choice. Hutch and Ann had likewise ended each other's lives—at least their chances of usable nearness, a merciful contingency of care and trust— for now and maybe from here on out.

Hutch had worked through that to the point of realizing how entirely, with a son dying four miles away, he'd spent half a night confronting himself in one more looking glass, clearer than most he'd faced till tonight. *But there's nothing else I can do for Wade; Wade's gone past me into some new world I've never known—total silence or punishment or unthinkable reward.* The thought gave Hutch no pain or ease; he was exhausted and ready to sleep.

The phone rang; it was three in the morning.

Wade had grown so strong in Hutch's mind as he read through the box that, at first, he didn't think of Hannah Bertram's promise to call with any trouble. When he answered though, it was her unruffled voice.

"Mr. Mayfield, Wade is asking for you."

By reflex Hutch said "I'll be right there." Then he needed to know. "Is he any worse off?"

"His signs have been pretty steady right along, but frankly he's been very troubled since midnight and calling for you."

Hutch said "You could have called me sooner," then regretted his haste. Before Hannah could defend her choice, Hutch said "I'm sorry. You're the person in charge."

Hannah said "All right." Then she paused. "Mr. Mayfield, Hannah is not in charge of this, nobody else either—not on this Earth. You come on soon or send somebody to ease Wade down." Young as she was, her voice had the weight of a qualified judge's bleak instructions.

Her gravity let Hutch ask a last question. "Will he make it till morning?"

Hannah said "I wish I could promise you Yes; but like I told you, I'm not the Lord." For that last moment, she sounded no older than ten or twelve—very nearly the Lord but a year or too short.

When he'd hung up, Hutch thought next of Ann. Should he call and tell Ann to meet him there? Maybe she'd left some request of her own with a nurse or doctor. *What Hannah said was, 'Wade's asking for you.' Go on by yourself. If he's asked for his mother too, she'll come on her own.*

Hutch left the box of papers on his desk and went to his bedroom to find the keys. Beside them on the bureau was a framed photograph of Wade and Grainger in the woods back of Straw's, a small bright clearing. Wade was maybe five years old, though going on fifty with his bright-eyed somber look at the lens—eyes that were all but blazingly wide and penetrating. Grainger was already seated on a stump but in full daylight and not yet eighty; he faced whatever stood outside the frame—away from Wade and Hutch himself, who'd snap the shutter.

For an instant the picture felt like a thing Hutch should burn on the spot; its chance of giving future pain seemed too great a threat. Hutch opened the back of the frame, slid the picture out, almost ripped it long-ways before he stopped and—still not studying it again—brought its blank side up to his lips and touched it. Then he went toward his car, not pausing to lock the house behind him.

18

Since his own father's death in a small county clinic, Hutch had dreaded every visit to any hospital. In fact he'd often shirked the visits he owed colleagues or family friends—the dingy carbolic air that signals untreatable germs in every breath, the raking white glare of inhuman light from overhead tubes, the glimpses through open doors of bald distress or the unextinguished hope in eyes that are plainly hopeless. But late as it was, Hutch got through the lobby, up the room-sized elevator and down Wade's hallway without the sight of another live soul. Wade's door was shut; Hutch pushed inward.

The air was pitch-dark, and the only sound was a high hiss of oxygen flowing into Wade.

Hutch paused on the doorsill, looking behind him for Hannah Bertram or anyone sane. But no one appeared; he stepped in and shut the door behind him.

No sign of life from Wade.

Hutch stood in the dark till his own eyes opened as far as they could. Gradually through the single window there came enough starlight to show the bed and a humped covered body. Hutch all but whispered "Son?"

And at once Wade's clogged voice said "I'm dreaming."

Hutch said "Don't stop." He could just see his way to the bedside straight chair. When he'd sat there silent for two long minutes, Hutch had to say "You're sounding better."

Again Wade answered promptly. "Better than what?"

"Than when I left you earlier tonight."

Wade said "You never left me once." He seemed to chuckle. "That's been half the problem."

Hutch knew not to probe for clarity; the drugs seemed to cast a dense mental haze and then short flicks of keen understanding. "Hannah Bertram said you were calling for me."

"Oh Hannah—Christ, *no.*"

"Was she wrong?"

Wade waited a long time. "I said I was dreaming."

"Remember what?"

"Too crazy to tell."

Hutch said "Was I in it?"

"*In* it?—Lord, you wrote, produced, directed, starred, sold tickets and taffy and seated the crowd." Even to Wade, it seemed a phenomenal burst of words to come from struggling lungs; at the end he was seized in a barking cough.

Hutch tried to keep the dream intact. "Glad I drew a crowd—hope I didn't fail to entertain."

Again Wade seemed to have glided away.

So Hutch stayed on in the one easy chair, trying with some success not to think or dwell on what he couldn't change. By four in the morning, he was nearly asleep when Hannah walked in and switched on the light. It brought Hutch awake and onto his feet.

Wade seemed to sleep on.

Hannah's small dark body in its starched white uniform brought with it an excess charge of hope—she looked that capable of healing. First she acknowledged Hutch's presence with a duck of her chin, then went about her tasks in silence—a thermometer into Wade's left ear, his pulse, a blood-pressure sleeve on his broomstick arm, a careful look at the oxygen gauge and the intravenous bags.

Wade still never gave a sign of awareness.

And only when she was ready to leave did Hannah face Hutch and speak in a normal voice. "His fever's down again. You managed to ease him."

"You're kind to say so. He saw me come in, but since then we've hardly spoken."

Hannah said "It doesn't take words, not with most of them. They just want you here."

"You've seen a lot of patients with this?"

"Ten years' worth," Hannah said. She barely looked twenty years old, even here. Then she glanced to see if Wade was sleeping. "Every day I feel like I need to quit. I'd rather crawl naked across an acre of rusty nails." Her eyes plainly meant it.

Hutch said "Oh don't"—he meant *Don't quit us here tonight.*

Hannah said "It's all I know how to do—this and one other thing: nursing burned children and that nearly killed me, eight years on the burn ward. I'm here with you both; no fear about that. You go on and sleep." She gave a slight smile and reached for the door.

Hutch made a sign of wanting to speak with her in the hall.

But as Hannah stepped out and Hutch tried to follow, Wade said "Don't ask that lady my secrets." The oxygen tubes in his nostrils hissed, but they also deepened the pitch of his voice.

Hutch stopped, took Wade's hand and gave a quick laugh. "They're safe from me."

Hannah was gone and the door shut behind her.

Wade said "I dreamed you were pardoning me."

Hutch pressed his fingers lightly on Wade's mouth. "Nothing on Earth to pardon you for."

"You can't be serious."

"I am, absolutely."

Wade shut his eyes. "We tried to *harm* you."

"I volunteered—your family volunteers."

"Not everybody's family, not for this." Wade's two hands indicated the length of his body; it hardly raised the covers.

Hutch had heard stories of sons rejected on their parents' doorsill and infants abandoned with this frightening scourge. He said "That's the least of your worries, Son. I'm a lifelong volunteer; count on that."

Wade's eyes stayed shut but he shook his head No. "I'm trying to get out of this thing clean."

"What thing?"

"My life. You notice I'm dying. I'm meaning to do it on my own." Wade faced Hutch then and started to laugh, but his breath gave out, and in ten seconds he was silent and gaping. Only when he'd drawn in a long gasp of oxygen was he able to laugh again. "I'm making a piss-poor job of bravery, aren't I? I'm about as alone as a bitch in heat."

Hutch had never released the boy's hand. "You're a man strong as any *I've* known. Fight through this skirmish and come on home. We need some time yet."

For the first time in weeks, Wade's eyes seemed to see his father and know him. He strained his head up off the pillow as if to reach him; then he fell back blind. "I doubt I could stand it."

"Son, you don't have to stand a thing. Get through this crisis, I'll take you home, we'll tell some stories and heal some wounds."

Wade's head came up again, well off the pillow; and he clamped down hard on his father's hand. "Pardon me, sir. I need to go on." His face said plainly that by *go* he meant *leave*.

Hutch could only say "Make your own choice."

Wade lay back, shut his eyes, slipped his hand from Hutch's and turned away. It was a long time before he said "Anything left of my lemonade?"

Hutch shook a paper cup on the bed stand—some liquid, no ice. "I'll get you some ice."

"Don't go; help me drink it."

Hutch moved the curved straw to the burned blue lips.

Wade took a long draw of the lemonade and strained to down it. When he turned away again, he said "Nothing wrong with that, nothing a shot of good gin wouldn't cure—gin and bitters."

"You want some gin?" Hutch had seldom known Wade to drink spirits stronger than wine; but if gin would ease him, he'd smuggle some in.

Wade thought through the offer like the final puzzle he'd ever confront. He whispered clearly through a withering smile. "I've wanted six or eight things through the years that history has somehow denied me till now."

Then his grin relaxed over half a minute into the strongest afterglow that Hutch had seen since his own father died. Wade fell asleep there.

Or fainted or died. It took a hard minute, but only when Hutch saw Wade's throat draw the first shallow breath could he make himself leave.

19

It was well past four o'clock in the morning when Hutch reached his car in the hospital parking deck, the scene of sporadic assaults on staff and visitors in recent years. As he opened his car door, Hutch paused to look round him in the expectation—even the chill hope—that some marauder lurked in wait, a creature starved through its whole short life and eager to spring. *Quick death by knife or a merciless beating.* Since Hutch had less than the average masochist's need for damage, the thought was as new as the duties pressed from him by a son who was literally dying of love for a man who'd loathed Hutch and Ann Gatlin with a permanent fury.

There was no one in sight, no sound but occasional cars on the street; and though Hutch knew dawn would break in an hour, he was suddenly swamped by a scary loneliness, an unaccustomed fear of being on his own in the dark. *Who's awake that'll take me in and talk?* The two or three colleagues to whom he'd confided would be deep asleep. He didn't think of trying Ann, and Strawson was more than an hour away; so he cranked the engine, paid his parking fee to a near-albino man who must have weighed four hundred pounds and drove three blocks to Maitland Moses' small apartment in a concrete wilderness of student lodgings. Mait had told Hutch only last week that he woke most mornings at five o'clock to read and write before heading off to the printing shop where he worked a full shift three days a week as a trainee typesetter and general factotum.

Stopped at the curb, Hutch could see Mait's two windows, curtained and black. *He's already left. Or is still asleep. Or somebody's with him.* Though Hutch had never felt drawn to Mait's body, in the next long minute, that third possibility felt intolerable—that Mait was bedded in with a guest, either spent from sex or ready for more. In any case, in the past thirty-odd years, Hutch had never yet tracked a student to his lair for any purpose, much less a home visit in the predawn dark with no business pending. Again he tried to think of a friend who might take him in—no, none of his colleagues, all regular souls, and still not Ann. So he left the car, climbed the outside iron steps to Mait's door and gave two firm knocks—three or four would have felt like begging. *Let him come.*

After an endless twenty seconds, the door cracked open three inches on an eye that might be anyone. It stayed in place, silent.

"Maitland?"

No answer.

"I've got the wrong door. I beg your pardon—"

"Mr. Mayfield?" Slowly the door opened farther. "Are you all right?" Mait was there in boxer shorts, his face still dazed, the skin of his chest and arms white as sheeting.

Against his better judgment, the rags of his pride, it came out of Hutch in a powerful stream. "Excuse me, friend. I need to see someone—" He broke up there; two dry sobs wrenched through his teeth, then a moan.

Mait reached for Hutch's arm, stepped aside and pulled him in.

The small front room was all but totally dark; the air had a mordant smell of rut laid over the usual fug of young-male lodgings—a slightly sour icebox, a mildewed shower, discarded sweatpants and the clean strong chlorine smell of cum. Again Hutch knew he'd bumbled into some first overnight encounter of Mait's (he knew the boy had been on the hunt since gradua- tion); so when Mait bent to switch on a lamp, Hutch whispered "I'm sorry. Go back to your guest. I'm not really sick; I'll be all right." Even then the thought of leaving two postadolescents to root each other on a stale narrow cot felt like a grim expulsion from life, but Hutch moved toward the door.

With unaccustomed force, Mait said "Hey, you woke me up, sir. You owe me two words." The light came on and showed the boy's face again, still fogged with sleep but intent on facing this novelty—an uninvited senior pro- fessor, a poet of note, on his doorstep at dawn.

Mait hadn't whispered so Hutch raised his own voice. "Two words? Help - me. Please - sir. *Four* words, sorry."

Mait said "Wade's passed away." Despite the euphemism, his eyes were as certain as if he'd dreamt the whole rest of the day and could foretell its heavy news, this early. Except for his baggy shorts Mait was naked; he suddenly shud- dered in the damp air and held himself. "I'll go make some coffee. You sit here and rest." He swept a clutter of books and magazines onto the bilious green shag carpet.

Hutch said "Wade's alive. He may even have passed the crisis one more time. I just came from him; his fever's broken. The nurse called me at three o'clock, said Wade was calling steadily for me, I rushed in and found him fairly clearheaded and breathing better. He and I managed a few sane words before he slept. Then he dropped off, I waited awhile, the nurse told me to go home and rest. But by the time I cranked my car, I felt like a drowned dog and stopped off here to see a human face. I'm all right now; you go back to bed."

But Mait held his ground and shook his head No.

The boy's short body—maybe five foot eight, bare chest, arms, legs—showed a lean compacted promise of competence that ambushed Hutch. In his clothes, Mait had always seemed underpowered; the teenaged doofus. *But none of it's one bit of use to me.* Hutch tasted the acrid stench of that but couldn't unthink it.

Mait pointed again to the empty chair, stepped to the dwarf kitchen behind them and started drawing water for coffee. When Hutch had followed him and sat on a stool, the boy smiled crookedly. "I *do* have company—can you believe it? First time in my life; let's celebrate."

Hutch's first thought was *Some brand of killer,* some guy off the street who'd already pumped the virus into Mait. But he told himself *Steady* and only smiled back.

"I met him last weekend at the new AIDS hospice. I was trying to volunteer a few hours; he's a full-time staffer."

"But he's here this minute?"

"He gets a few nights off, three nights a week and one afternoon." Mait pointed down the hall, the one bedroom. "He's out, like a coma."

Again Hutch felt not exactly robbed but thoroughly sidelined by young men living his old life near him. "I was hoping you could help me with Wade from here on, Mait. He needs young company to break the monotony of me and his mother." It hadn't been a hope till the instant Hutch said it. Though Mait had visited once or twice in the past month, Hutch hadn't called on him for serious help.

Mait said "Absolutely" with the ready surrender and eager loyalty that nobody much past twenty-one can muster.

"Just a couple of hours every two or three days. I've run out of subjects that Wade hasn't heard me preach sermons on since before he was born."

Mait was facing the coffee machine when he said "Mr. Mayfield, how much longer has Wade got?" When he turned, his eyes belied the hardness of the question. Mait had promised to help any way Hutch needed from here to Wade's death; how long would that be?

So Hutch tried to answer soberly. "My guess, from what I've read and heard, is somewhere between the next five minutes and another few months. Wade's only got so many cells of flesh to lose; they melt off him daily. His eyes are finished, as you well know; his mind's affected off and on; his lungs and kidneys are worn out from fighting."

Mait came to the opposite side of the counter, two feet from Hutch. "Do you know Wade's thought about suicide?"

It shocked Hutch cold. "I don't know that—no sir, I don't."

Mait stood in place, two cups in hand, and signified Yes.

Hutch could only say "When?"

Mait knew he'd betrayed Wade—too late though. He forced himself to meet Hutch's eyes and said "Last time I came out to your place—what, last Tuesday?—when you left us alone, Wade asked me if I could find him some cyanide."

"What did you say?"

"I said I could try. At the bars I've met a couple of chemists from Burroughs Wellcome; they seem very friendly—" Mait carefully filled the cups with coffee and held one to Hutch.

"Do you plan to try?"

"As I said, I've got more than one chemist friend. Please say if I should." When he'd thought for a moment, Mait said "I know that sounds awfully flip, but it could be easy if we did it right—the dying at least: we could bring that off, with the simple right substance, in a matter of seconds."

Hutch waited a long time. "No soul in my family has managed his own death in ninety years—my great-grandmother Kendal drank lye and died on her own kitchen floor." He waited again. "But you and Wade are both grown men."

"Is that real advice or are you just polite?" In all Mait had said since waking today, his voice had served reliably—no highs or lows.

The scent of the brewing coffee had jostled Hutch's exhaustion. He almost smiled to Mait. "I'm cursed with politeness, as you recall; but no, I've got no wisdom to give you. It's Wade's life and death; he's been through more than I'll ever imagine—far more pain than you'll ever need to know, I hope." That last was a warning which escaped unintended. *Guard your body, whoever you're with.*

Mait said "Let's talk about this later. It's still not day."

Hutch knew why he'd stopped here, not for simple company but on the off chance that Mait might finally be old enough to give what Hutch needed and had needed for weeks—a precocious offer of fatherly guidance, a strong voice to say *Do this, now that, now stretch out and rest.*

And there in his shorts, Mait seemed to bend to the role with no fear. His eyes looked wiser in an instant. But then, though his voice had kept its firmness, his face flushed brightly; and he said "Good morning" past Hutch's shoulder.

Hutch looked behind him at a man as arresting in face and body as anything torn off a Roman basilica and painted again in the colors of life—black hair, dark eyes and biscuit-colored skin. Older than Mait, he also was naked except for a towel round his hips, and he'd stopped in the hall on the kitchen threshold. Hutch gave him a brief instinctive bow.

The man came on and held out his right hand. "Cam Mapleson, sir."

Hutch said his own name and took the strong hand. "I'm more than sorry I woke you up. My son is ill in Duke Hospital. I was feeling lonesome and stopped to see Maitland."

Cam said "He's told me. I'm proud to know you, sir."

Hutch thought *You don't know a thing about me. Don't grab for more than I can give.* But he only smiled.

Hoping to revert to cheer, Mait said "Is everybody hungry?"

Cam said "Are we up?"

Hutch said "No, I'm leaving—"

Mait said "*I'm* up and a carnivore to boot. Bacon and toast?"

Cam laid a light hand on Hutch's shoulder. "Please stay. I'd welcome a chance to know you, sir."

Hutch said "But if you keep calling me *sir*, I may well drop down dead on the floor of sheer old age."

Cam said "I'm sorry—it's my marine training. My dad objects as much as you, but it's in my blood—maybe too late to change." His hand had stayed on Hutch's shoulder.

Mait was searching the refrigerator. "Mr. Mayfield, what's the difference between a marine and a queer?"

Cam's hand clamped tighter on Hutch's shoulder.

"I surrender—what?"

Mait said "A six-pack."

Hutch laughed but, by now, was resenting the weight of Cam's hand. He'd begun to sense he was being lured into some narrow trap. *What does this new boy want, from Mait and me?* And in the next minutes, as he moved at Mait's suggestion and sat at the bare dollhouse table, Hutch felt more and more like an excess wheel beside this pair who were young enough to be his sons, nearly his grandsons. They'd already shared more than Hutch could guess; and their readable faces had plainly known more pleasure in the last few hours than he'd known in months, if not years. But still the thought of heading home alone, or of waiting in his campus office till ten o'clock when he could visit Wade again, was harder to manage. Hutch said "Thanks, Mait—just toast for me; I'm giving up fat."

Cam had lifted his hand and was standing in their midst, in his towel. His eyes frisked Hutch. "You're too thin, man; keep your energy up."

Hutch thought *Your eyes are flat as a puppet's; is there anyone in you?*

But he told Cam "Relax, endurance is my strong suit." The pompous sound of that on the air made Hutch laugh first.

Mait and Cam joined gladly in the noise.

And Cam's towel fell to the floor round his feet. His whole body, pure white in the loins and bushed with black, flared like a phosphorous fire in the kitchen.

Mait roared "Help! A *man!*"

Not rushed, Cam bent, retrieved the towel and fastened it safely.

At once Hutch took the glimpse as an omen on Wade's behalf. All his life Hutch had trusted in such quick meetings with another human's grace and worth. This strange bare man—some kind of nurse and as easy to watch as any man in Wade's sheaf of pictures—was signaling better times for Wade or, at the least, an easier death. When Maitland reached above the sink and opened the blinds on first daylight, Hutch suddenly knew and actually said seven words in his mind. *This whole story can end soon now.*

He meant the story of his joined families, all the story he'd witnessed or heard from kin whose memories ranged two centuries back—most of them burning what they called *love* as their treacherous, always vanishing fuel when what they craved was merely *time:* more time above ground anyhow to feed their dry unquenchable sovereign hearts. That story was ending in Wade Mayfield, who was hardly breathing less than a quarter mile from this room and from these two ready likable boys whose excellent bodies, a few years back, Wade might have plumbed in thoughtless safety or held and honored for long paired lives.

By the time Hutch worked his way through that, drinking coffee, Cam and Mait had dressed for the cloudless sweltering day at hand and were laying out food like a four-handed creature, with that little waste of minutes or motion.

Those smooth moves gave Hutch even more hope that someway Wade's hurried dissolution had slowed and leveled and could now be guided or aimed at least toward a dignified close. Hutch said to Mait "Thank God I woke you."

"Don't mention it please."

Cam kicked out at Mait's butt. "Take the compliment, child; the man clearly means it." And only then did Cam look to Hutch; he thought he could see in Hutch's eyes that his own hawk-face was as fine to see as the rest of his hide when the towel had dropped.

Hutch was thinking *He's maybe eight years older than Mait, those eyes want something Mait doesn't have to give, when did they meet?* But all Hutch said was another fact. "I'd got fairly near the end of my rope."

Cam brought bacon, toast and jam to the table and said "Jump or fall. We're a good strong net; Mait and I'll catch you."

Hutch knew they were promising more than they'd give—more than they had, whoever they were to one another (and hadn't Mait said this was their first night?)—but he thanked them again and buttered the bread.

20

When Hutch turned the curve and saw his own house, it was seven o'clock and growing clearer and brighter by the minute. When he reached the backyard, Ann's car was parked in its old place—no sign of her in it. *Wade's worse; she's here to get me.* Hutch paused long enough to face due south and see the highest roofs of Chapel Hill over green intervening miles of trees. For a moment he felt he was calmed. *Life at a distance anyhow. We'll last some way. He didn't think who he meant by we.* He turned, walked around to the front door and tried the knob. Generally double-locked, it was open. Hutch entered the hall and listened—silence. He froze in place, invaded and offended. Ann had long since carried off every thread and book that was rightly hers. *She's rummaging through my desk, on a hunt.*

She almost was. Though Hutch hadn't tried to muffle his steps, Ann was startled when he got to the door of his study and found her seated near the desk. Like a child, she held her hands up empty. "I was reading this sadness—" Wyatt's long hateful letter to Wade was open on her lap.

"It isn't yours."

"You haven't read it?"

Hutch said "Wade left it here with me."

"And told you to read it?"

Hutch wouldn't lie. He shook his head No. "I read it in the night, when I couldn't sleep. I thought it was something I might need to know if Wade lasts long."

"He's better this morning; I called the ward. They said his fever's down and he's breathing better. I stopped by here to wash some nightshirts and sheets." As proof, the washing machine in the kitchen pumped and chugged beyond them. Ann gathered the furious pages and laid them neatly facedown in the box.

Hutch could see her own letters to Wade, still sealed at the side of the box. But he only said "You think Wyatt's dead right, I very much bet."

"I beg your pardon?"

"Wyatt. In his letter. About you and me."

Ann intended no harm when she said "Are you sure he included me?"

Hutch was also calm when he nodded Yes. "Everybody with eyes in the past three centuries knows that white women were the engines of slavery."

"You want to defend that wild proposition? It's new to *me*."

Hutch rushed it out toward her. "White men shanghaied slaves to America, bought and sold them, worked them to death in sugarcane fields or treated them like pet minstrel dolls you can slam up against the wall anytime you're tense or a little discouraged with your day; but unless the perpetual-virgin white wives and daughters had stood on the porch or at the field edge, broadcasting hate and fear and attraction, the worn-out men would have given up such a costly burden long years sooner—the whole monster business— and done their own work, just killing each other and occasional Indians."

Ann eventually smiled, suppressing a laugh. "That's appropriately weird."

"It's true."

She still smiled. "Some part of it may be—Lord knows, my mother and all her sisters suffered most from the simple fact that they had to have black women cooking and cleaning all day behind them while they sat idle, depressed and picking at the slightest flaw in every life near them."

Hutch said "So Wyatt was more than half right."

"Wyatt got his revenge."

"How?"

"Look, Hutchins—Christ Jesus, he's killing our child."

Hutch said "We can't lay that on the dead."

"You just laid slavery on a million dead women."

He waited to think of one more answer, then raised both open hands. "Truce. I'm too tired."

"You didn't sleep either?"

"I got scared in the night and drove in to see Wade. You're right; he's better. Very slightly better. For a day or so, till this afternoon maybe when some barely harmful germ blows in and carries him—"

Ann stood. "You want me to fix you some breakfast?"

"I've eaten, thanks. You're not working today?"

"I took the day off. I needed some quiet."

"Lucky job," Hutch said. "The Hurdle Mills Meat Man get the day off too?"

Ann said "Read the newspaper, Hutch. We're saving his skin. Last week he got his charges reduced—stands a good chance of nothing worse than life with no parole."

"Who doesn't get more or less that exactly?"

"Well, you." Ann took a step toward him and studied his eyes.

Hutch realized she hadn't been this good to see for a very long while—a new kind of force flushed all through her skin; her hair and eyes, her elegant bones. He studied her, silent.

Then she finally said "You've had a full life. You *used* yourself. You liked most of it."

"Didn't you? Sure you did—"

"The jury's still out on me." But she smiled. "Permission for coffee?"

Hutch gave it. "Permission."

Ann turned toward the kitchen and Hutch came behind.

Twenty minutes later, with nothing transacted beyond small talk, Ann headed out "to mow the lawn"—she had a little hearthrug of grass by her back door—and Hutch moved toward his study in the slim hope of starting at least to choose the poems for his new selected volume. The box of Wade's papers was where Ann had left it—Wyatt's letter on top, Ann's own sealed letters untouched where they'd been. It came to Hutch suddenly. *Read just one letter; you need to know it somehow.* If the thought hadn't come with a taste of hope in it, he'd have pushed it back. All his novelist friends were abject snoopers; Hutch had seldom shared the urge.

Now with no qualm, he sat at his desk and asked himself which letter to choose. *The last one she sent.* But that was still sealed, dated *March 29.* Breaking Ann's seal was not yet allowed, not under the rules that were running Hutch here. So he rummaged carefully through the box, hunting the most recent letter from Ann that Wade had opened—Wade or Wyatt or Ivory or Boat. At last he found one, slit neatly open, and postmarked just after this past Christmas.

December 30, 1992

Dear Wade,

I hope you're weathering the post-Yule blues a lot better than me. Don't mean to burden you with my small troubles—and not to imply that I'm standing here, armed to kill myself—but my first Christmas entirely alone was an awful idea. Oh I had three invitations to parties and one to dinner with my boss and his clan; but believe it or not, I was fool enough to sit out here with the bare trees around me and wait on the phone. I even picked it up more than once as the day went on, to see if it worked; and there Oh Lord was the healthy dial tone, saying "Yah, yah, yah, nobody needs you." The rest of the day and the whole night proved it, not even one wrong number or a pitiful handicapped lightbulb salesman.

You're right if you're thinking "She volunteered for it with both eyes open."

I did, you warned me, Hutch warned me, God warned me. But Wade, let me tell you what you already know. My last four years under Hutch's roof—and it was never my roof, not the smallest shingle from the day they were laid—I'd wake up beside your father in the night and feel the weight of every object in the rooms stacked on me. Every bed and table, the stove and freezer and washer and both cars, my own small lot of precious possessions (most of which pertain to you) and—topping the pile—your father's billion souvenirs from a rich strong life, everything from the carved-bark man with the workable penis to your father's books and pictures and the manuscript mountains. I thought I'd loved them, or been glad to live near them; but in those last four years, I couldn't stop thinking They were all meant to kill me. That's why they're here. You stand up and run, girl.

Eventually I ran; as you well know, I ran. Nobody but me; nobody forced me, least of all Hutch—not consciously, never.

So why am I sitting here moaning to you, when your outlook is what it is? I'm not too sure what the answer is, but I have learned one thing I didn't quite know. There's not much out here for any woman my age, unless she wants to take the veil (and even that convent of cloistered nuns on the Roxboro road shut down years ago; they ran out of sisters). If I'd started life as a virgin martyr and taught long division for the past forty years, I might at least get occasional cards from giants of industry that I'd helped launch on their grisly course. If I'd had real friendships outside my marriage (which all but no American mates do), there'd be somebody I could eat supper with at least or join at the movies on my day off. If I'd had a real mind (a strong imagination as opposed to a dedicated homemaking robot inside my skull), I'd have sure-God never let my private soul just die down to nothing but a warm coal or two the way I did.

You're surely asking yourself—if you've read this far—"What's she want from me?" I trust I don't need to restate my offer to care for you—here or there, any place you say. Beyond that, I sometimes pray for the phone to ring and you to be there saying "Call him up, Ann. Start talking anyhow about what's left, if anything, between you and what you could stand—you and Hutch, both alone now." Second to praying you call with the news that a cure's been found, I pray for that—a way we could all live together a few years longer.

Is that what you mean, when you think about us—assuming you do? Again, forgive this burden from me. But the Season of Hope has very nearly killed me. What I may have learned in this new life is clearer, though, after these lonely days—I'm as good a woman as I know how to be (and I'm at least normally smart for my age), and the same is surely true for Hutch. He's got a whole lot less greed and malice than the average songbird—I know; I watch my bird feeder closely.

And the absolute unquestioned truth of my life is, I love you and am yours—with whatever good I could bring—for the simple asking. A premature Happy New Year, Wade. Ignore this if you need to.

All the love left in
Ann Gatlin Mayfield

Hutch placed the pages back in their envelope, then buried the letter deep in the box. He'd barely thought that it might have snagged a hold in his mind.

21

Ten days later at Hutch's house, on a bright dry June afternoon, Cam Mapleson stood up to leave Wade and Maitland. Cam was due at work in the hospice; Mait was going to stay on with Wade since Hutch was in Richmond to read his poems at a summer writers' conference. When Cam had stroked Wade's forehead by way of saying goodbye, he noticed for the first time the drawing that hung above Wade's bed—Hutch's childhood drawing of mountains and trees, the one Wade had wanted at the last moment as they left New York. Cam had spent a good part of his own childhood painting and drawing landscapes near Nags Head where he'd grown up, and Hutch's drawing of Virginia mountains struck him as fresh and oddly impressive. It had the homemade but masterful quality of certain unique accomplishments— things done just once, got perfectly right, then never repeated. Cam said to Wade "Did you draw this?"

The head of Wade's bed was cranked up high. He slowly groped back with one hand and found the picture frame; the feel of the gilded wood told him what was there. His crooked smile was a gauge of the pleasure he took in its memory. "Don't you like this a lot? But no, don't thank me—I couldn't draw, even when my hands worked. This was done by Hutch, before he wrote poems. I think he was fourteen. I can look at it more or less endlessly."

Both Cam and Mait silently noted that Wade had never mentioned his blindness to either of them.

Cam said "He had some serious gifts; has he kept up his art through the poetry years?"

Confused as Wade had begun to be lately, he treated the question with greater care than Cam intended. Finally Wade pulled his hand back off the picture and extended the fingers toward where he thought Cam stood.

Cam was nearby and took the hand, holding it as lightly as any moth wing—by now it was plainly that easy to ruin.

Wade said "My father is Hutchins Mayfield, born in 1930, month of May, twelfth day." For a long moment that seemed his only finding. But he suddenly withdrew his fingers from Cam's hand; his dead hot eyes found Cam's face—its locus at least. "My father saw through the world long before he had me. When he drew that picture, he still believed something he'd thought of in childhood—that there was something buried, buried and worth finding—beneath the world: the part we can see, beneath the skin. Or so he told me when he gave me the picture; that was the Christmas I left home for good. The only other thing he said was he wanted me to have it as a memory of him and his mother Rachel Hutchins. She died just a few minutes after he was born, so he never really saw her, and God knows I didn't." Though still Wade hadn't acknowledged his blindness, he gave a high laugh.

It took him awhile to refocus his mind. "The picture was drawn near where Rachel lived—near Goshen, Virginia: a really gorgeous piece of the Earth. Hutch and I drove up there several times when I was a boy. That was when I got the idea of having at least one daughter that I could name *Rachel*—my favorite name, for girls anyhow. God had other plans for my plumbing fixtures. But those trips to Goshen were my best days till I knew Wyatt. Wyatt Bondurant—you've heard about him, right?—was best of all: we killed each other." Nothing in Wade's face betrayed the pain of that, though he'd stopped again. Then his hand went back a second time and pointed to the picture. "Look at how spooky the *drawing* is, all there in the middle—all those thick leaves down the side of the mountain, like some dense screen they wove with leaves over something they're hiding. I asked Hutch what was hid there in the middle—" Wade waved a final time at the picture; then he went cold silent.

Cam studied the drawing and didn't speak.

But Mait asked Wade "Did he say what was there?"

And Wade remembered; it hooked in his mind, and his skull ducked eagerly. "He said 'It's a giant that's dreaming the world.'"

Mait said "That's an idea almost all children have, through the whole world apparently. I know I had it when I was five. I thought the dreamer was a great gold dragon, and somedays I would literally walk around, light on the sidewalk, not to wake it up. I knew I'd vanish when the dragon stopped dreaming. I'd forgot till last year when I took a course in world religions; the teacher said most cultures have the same idea—we're all somebody's, or something's dream: a giant's or a butterfly's, paused on a rose in the warm sun of some perfect place."

Wade nodded, a little calmer again but earnest still. "I'm there," he said. "Believe it; I'm *there*. I'm dreaming all this."

Cam said "'A dream is dreaming us'—who said that?"

Mait said "Me, I told you—no, an African Bushman said it to some big anthropologist, in the 1920s."

Wade's head ducked Yes again and again.

Cam thought *Oh Wade, if this is a dream, for God's sake wake up and save mankind*; but he understood Wade was past clear reason, so he told him "Dream on."

Wade said "Christ, no—oh, *wake* me please." But as Cam looked toward Mait, really disturbed, Wade laughed in a voice very much like his old voice—kind and all but endlessly pleased. As he heard the sound, Wade thought *That's my last laugh.*

Cam was late for work, so he took the laugh as permission to leave. He bent to kiss Wade's forehead and asked him the riddle he'd heard only yesterday from another blind man at the hospice, scarecrowed worse than Wade. "What's the difference between Cleveland, Ohio and the S.S. *Titanic?*"

Wade's eyes were still trying to find human faces, though they couldn't now, but his grin survived. "I give up—what?"

Cam said "Cleveland had a better orchestra"; then he scissored to the door in three comic strides as if he were seen. From there he looked back. Just those few seconds away from Wade had eased Cam's mind; and when he saw him, the sight was shocking one more time—worse than any he'd seen in five years of military service or his months at the hospice: a grown man weighing maybe eighty-five pounds, not ready to die. The eyes were still wide open and hunting. Cam kissed the palm of his own hand and held it to Mait and Wade. "You two get a very tight grip on yourselves and hold it till I'm back."

Wade laughed. "Oh Christ, a *grip!* I wish I could. It's been ten months since I touched the old rascal."

Before he thought, Mait said "I make up for everybody." Laughter covered them all as Cam left.

But Wade's mind managed to hold the thought till they heard Cam shut the front door. Then he turned to Mait. "I said ten months but I can't remember when my cock worked." It was only a fact; Wade hadn't had sex with Wyatt since nearly two years ago, and even self-service had proved impossible for—what?—long months, maybe more than a year. If the urge dug at him, he'd try to reward it; but almost always, before he could run the mental pictures to fire him onward, he'd recall that his cum was now a poison, a lethal substance; and that would down him. Oddly today, that long-lost pleasure seemed the least of Wade's problems. The better memories of his times with Wyatt seemed more or less sufficient now, the times when Wade could remember to let himself dwell on those thousands of indescribably excellent junctures with Wyatt.

Mait said "I sometimes wish my rascal didn't work at all."

That soon, Wade was puzzled. "What rascal you mean?"

"My red fire hydrant, the flaming weenie that runs my life."

"Oh child, don't let it. It's the whole wrong century for that lovely failing." Those were far more words of real warning than Wade had attempted in all the years since the plague arrived; they left him empty.

At such stalled moments Mait had learned to sit still and wait till Wade either dozed or regained his footing on breath and clarity and could speak again.

The eyes stayed open and the lips were gapped, no sign of pain or suffocation though. Finally the bony head turned to Mait and worked at a smile. "You talk. Let me listen."

So Mait took that as maybe a last chance to hear the answers he'd never got from anyone more likely to know the truth than this aggrieved man, vanishing by the instant where he lay. Mait said "You can just nod or shake your head a little, but help me please. I trust you, Wade." Mait took a long breath, then was shamed to think of his own body's ease in a room like this—his healthy ease and opulence in young skin and joint. Still he said to Wade "You regret your life?"

Wade replied at once, a silent No.

"You sorry you were queer?"

Wade said "Still queer—queer, dead or alive. The answer's No. I loved most of it; I was one strong lover. I don't just mean sex either but love—I could evermore watch the person I loved and figure his needs and set out to fill them. Damned nearly did too, till the time it really sunk in we were sick. I'd have loved Wyatt right on, cell for cell—we were past hurting each other any worse—but he called it off, stopped sex on a *dime* like it was a skate." Wade imitated a braking skate with his long right fingers. Then he shut his eyes. "You understand Wyatt killed himself?"

Hutch had told Mait that much, days ago. Now was no time to ask for more; Wade was plainly exhausted. So Mait raised a hushing finger, then recalled that Wade couldn't see it. "Are we some kind of monsters—you, me, Cam, Wyatt, whatever percent of the human race we constitute?"

Wade very slowly signified Yes.

"Truly? Actual felons?"

"Not felons, except in the idiot terrified law, just not quite *Homo sapiens* either but mostly well-meaning monsters, I think—a different and partly benign neighbor-species. *Monster* in that sense. Better at some things, worse at others."

Mait said "Aside from this new plague, what's the worst thing about us?" When Wade stalled a moment, the boy pushed on with the Yes or No rite. "Adultery, alley-cat promiscuity?"

Wade shook his head No.

"You don't regret knowing so many men?"

Wade said "I told you—I knew two other men besides myself. Exactly two. Few lily-white martyrs were chaster than me."

Mait smiled, though he couldn't stop himself. "But all we think and talk about is sex—the queers my age at least."

"You ever sit down with two other straight guys, anywhere else but the State Department? Every coffee break is a pussy op—pussy and money: all they talk about. No classic queer that ever lived was as hipped on cock as straights on cunt. I doubt Plato told many cock-jokes."

"I bet Socrates did." Mait laughed, real cheer.

Wade joined him, the best he could—his lungs were still weak. When he'd rested awhile, he suddenly knew the answer to Mait's flat-footed question. "If straight men weren't hardwired for women, with all women's training and doubts and plumbing problems, they'd fuck as many times a day as the most crazed queer on the south side of Eighth Street. No, what's wrong with queers—the only wrong thing they don't share with straights—is nothing but children. Queers don't make children, not as a rule. I figured you'd noticed."

Mait said "Oh yes. But that didn't seem to throw too big a monkey wrench into some of the Homo Great's working plans—"

Wade shut his eyes and, in his most bored voice, reeled off a stretch from the sacred litany of queers. "Donatello, Botticelli, Leonardo, Michelangelo, Caravaggio, Handel—"

Mait took up the chant. "Sophocles, Virgil, Shakespeare, Melville, Whitman, Tchaikovsky, Mann, Auden, Britten, Barber, Copland—"

Wade raised a finger. "Mann and Melville and Shakespeare had children." Wade's blank face slowly produced a grin; he beamed it toward Mait. "Reminds me of a joke—why did God make queers?"

Mait said "I give up."

"Because he looked down at the Earth one day, well after that dustup in the Garden of Eden; and he said to himself 'They're just getting nowhere at *all* with the arts.'"

Mait laughed but was still too riled by Wade's diagnosis of the great lack in queerdom. He said "Now back to us not having children. A good many straights are born barren as coal mines; they sometimes manage whole faithful lives together."

Wade smiled for an instant longer but then went stiller than any sunk ship. In a long wait, his eyes seemed to fill with the only water left in his body—too few tears to run.

Mait started to change his tack. "For me, the main problem seems to be—"

Wade raised his whole right hand from the sheet and moved it toward Mait, three or four inches nearer.

Mait took it, as Cam had, with serious caution not to crush the stark bones.

And then Wade agreed. "It's children, truly, most of the time—just not having children underfoot for years at a time, leaning hard on you for life itself. In general a queer's got nothing at home but one other man and him the same model as you in the head—the same age and, deep-down, the same brand of wiring: same instincts, same thoughts, same unstoppable testosterone boil-ups that sabotage a whole day or night in a flash. I'd have been a fair father to a likable child; I had things to tell."

"You could still tell me. I'm going nowhere."

Wade shook his head and withdrew the hand. "My mind's burnt up, Son."

"So I should have children?" Mait was as poised to act as any hot axe.

Again Wade was silent, refusing to face him.

"What's so urgent about more children? Children, all sizes and shades, are starving by the million from right here near us to the high snows of Asia."

Wade shook his head in furious denial. "Someway. Have children. One child anyhow."

Mait could think *Wade's crazy—keep that in mind.* But the answer caught in his mind like a gaff.

22

Next morning when Hutch had phoned home from Richmond, spoken with a confident-sounding Mait and even with Wade, who was weak but sprightly, he felt safe enough to pause on his drive home and run a brief errand. After an early hotel breakfast, Hutch drove toward the street in the dead heart of town where—ninety years ago—old Robinson Mayfield, his great-grandfather, had lived with the girl Polly Drewry who'd nursed him through the last days of TB and warmed his body, though he'd never married her. Polly herself had stayed on in the house, vital as a lit lamp and brave as a sled dog, when old Rob died. Then she'd stayed on as housekeeper, and eventual common-law wife, to old Rob's son, Hutch's grandfather Forrest—a Latin teacher and an amateur poet with a certain gift, however restrained by his time and reading.

Over long years Polly had proved to be the soul who could give Forrest all the love he'd failed to find in his young wife Eva Kendal, who'd abandoned Forrest when their son was born—young Rob, Hutch's father. When Polly had finally outlived Forrest, she'd lingered on in the same house still—alone but industrious, a talented seamstress and all but indomitable veteran of time. Once his father had died and Hutch was home from England for good, he'd finally done what the family should have done ages ago—deeded the Richmond house to Polly, paid her annual taxes and otherwise helped her with small sums of money and irregular visits through the rest of her days till, in her late eighties, she lost clear sense of who she was and what was expected of an elderly spinster. Even then, she generally recognized Hutch on his unpredictable look-ins till she died upright in her sewing chair in 1980, having all but finished a needlepoint cushion she was stitching for Wade, who was then a boy. It bore a plain message, threaded in green, in her own forthright script—*May You Never Know Sorrow.*

Though Hutch hadn't tried to find the house since Polly's funeral, this morning he found it easily—disheveled as it was and derelict in its tiny yard of shattered glass and knee-high weeds. He stopped by the curb and paused to think of what the actual house had been when his kin owned it (Polly had left the house to Wade; Wade had turned it over to Hutch, and an agent then sold it for less than a song). Since there was no other human in sight in the early sun, Hutch sat in his car, with some amazement, for at least two minutes in quiet respect to the several powers that had lit those rooms through nearly a century of his family's life. No single one of them had ever matched Polly for sheer satisfaction in the passage of time and for an apparently native gift of love without hunger or even demand, the love commended by virtually all the world's religions but scarce as pure water—now as forever.

While Hutch waited a few yards distant from where Polly Drewry had led a life as openhearted as any since the saints, he missed her intensely and thought *Nobody left alive on Earth can help Wade die the way Polly could have; bring her back just long enough to see Wade through.* Hutch's longing and practical need were so strong that, in the next instant, he saw Polly's likable tidy body and her intact face, here on the cobblestone street before him and clear as she was till her mind had clouded. She was dressed in black from neck to ankle; and she carried a small leather overnight satchel in her powerful left hand, ready to serve.

Hutch well understood she was not really there, not palpably, though some real part of her presence was there—her healing eyes and her readiness. He also knew this was maybe the only vision of his life, the single all but credible return of someone irrecoverably gone and lost. So he held both palms toward the warm windshield to offer the sight whatever piece of his own life it might accept in a bargain for help. *Take anything left alive in me but come here. Nobody known to me but you can send the dying out in an honor that precludes no trace of love.* Hutch knew he was nudging the thin edge of sanity; he was calm in the knowledge.

As the sight faded slowly, he thought of the only conceivable substitute—his long-dead mother's great friend Alice Matthews in Petersburg, south of here on his route (with the years, Hutch had come to assume that his mother and Alice had been some brand of lovers, before his mother met Rob anyhow). As different from Polly as Eve from Ruth in the Hebrew Bible, still Alice had meant almost as much as Polly to Hutch in his childhood and youth. Lately their correspondence had come down to Christmas cards and occasional phone calls.

Hutch hadn't seen Alice for three or four years, though she'd phoned on his birthday this past May and said she was nearly eighty-nine years old, still living in her own apartment and battling to stand on her own till she "quit." Hutch recalled that Alice often referred to death as simply *quitting*; it seemed an accurate personal banner for someone as forceful through a long life as she; Hutch hadn't told her about Wade's illness.

He looked one last time to where the sight of Polly had waited—mere early light, the start of a day that would never know Polly. He turned the car in a wide circle on the broad cobbled street and headed south.

23

As a rule Hutch never visited any friend unannounced, but a half hour later he parked at Alice's with no prior warning. He'd thought a surprise appearance might please her more, sparing her hours of sprucing the place. But once he'd knocked, he thought *Oh God, she may be cracked or bedridden too.* When they'd talked in May, Alice had mentioned her balky heart—"this tremulous pump that's seen better days." And when light footsteps came to the door and paused on the locked side, silent, Hutch thought *I've scared her.* So he said "It's maybe your oldest friend."

Another long silence; then with no hint of joking, Alice's voice said

"Insert passport beneath the door." Odd as it was, she sounded as clear as she'd sounded in May.

But again Hutch wondered if she'd lost mental ground. Still he said "I'm traveling on confidential documents; give me the password."

At last Alice said the word *pearl*, then laughed a high note; then "Pearl, Pearl, Pearl—Great Pearl of the South, swim into my cave." She proceeded to throw back a series of locks and opened on Hutch.

At first Hutch thought *She's younger by years. Everybody but me gets younger.*

And Alice was startlingly like herself, for all the years—a little shrunk maybe but straight-backed still and with hair so white it seemed the source of a curious intermittent shine, harmless but unprecedented in Hutch's memory.

He bent to kiss her.

She smelled as ever of lemon cologne, and she wore an immaculate dark-blue dress as quietly costly and dignified as if she'd expected a presidential call. She bore his kiss calmly; and once she was free of his arms again, she said "I haven't been kissed in so long it feels like a primitive rite in Samoa."

"Sorry," Hutch said.

"Not a bit. I miss a little savagery now and then. Of course I could leave my door unlocked any hour of the day and stand a good chance of winding up flayed and nailed to this door in an unbecoming pose." When Hutch looked puzzled, Alice said "The neighborhood is sinking by the minute—you're bound to have noticed. Six more months, it'll be a bona fide slaughterhouse out there." She turned and led the slow way inward down the hall with its striking framed photographs of little-known statues from hidden piazzas and backstreets in Italy, Greece, Crete and the islands—all taken by Alice in midlife solitary tours and enlarged in the kitchen, just yards away.

"You planning to move?"

"Oh no. I'm considering volunteering to be the next victim. I hear if you call the police and they fail you, the county pays to repair and embalm your scattered remains."

Hutch said "I'd double-check on that. Sounds far too logical."

"Darling, I made it up—give me a laugh." Alice paused to study his eyes for the first time. "What's gone wrong?" Before he could answer, she sat in her favorite chair, blue velvet now.

Hutch sat on the forward edge of the sofa, then couldn't speak.

"Is it Wade?"

Hutch signed Yes with his eyes.

Alice shut her own keen gray eyes and turned her small sharp face toward the ceiling as if she kept hints for wisdom posted there. At last her eyes looked back to Hutch. "I've known, deep in my bones, it was coming."

"What?"

"He's got this dreadful plague, I'm afraid."

Hutch said "Has he called you?"

"Not a word from Wade, no—not for three years. But I've felt it bearing down for months."

"How?"

"I've known Wade, darling. I guessed at the danger. I've known for a decade he's been in the eye of this fearful storm."

Hutch was genuinely thrown by her foresight. "When was the last time you saw him then?"

"In New York—my last trip up there, four or five years ago. I went with a cousin older than me, and we got out with unbroken bones but not much else. Wade took us to dinner with his young man."

"Wyatt Bondurant?"

"I think so, yes—a light-colored gentleman of African extraction."

"And Wyatt didn't ruin your trip?"

"Ruin it?" Her eyes were bemused by the thought.

"With meanness; he didn't tongue-lash you?"

Alice laughed. "Lord, no—the soul of well-bred politeness. I thought Wade had freed him from some ancient spell; he seemed so much like a resurrected gallant rake from Restoration days, in pale plum satin."

"Wyatt? You understand Wyatt was black?"

"I just said as much—are Negro men exempt from elegance?" Her eyes went cold and narrowed slightly. "And what's this *was*; where's Wyatt now?"

Hutch knew he was caught in a just rebuke, but his news impelled him. "Wyatt died last winter—the same plague as Wade, though he killed himself first. He'd infected Wade; he couldn't live with that, couldn't stay to help Wade."

Alice studied her hands. As much as her face, they'd refused to age—almost no spots and few ropey veins. She finally said "My eyes are as good as they ever were, Hutchins. I see you here now—welcome as rain, which you've always been. And I saw Mr. Bondurant that one night as a beautiful Negro man straight out of my great-grandmother's parlor—the finest of manservants, perfectly trained. Of course I hated myself for the thought. I also saw he would spring like a wolf and tear my throat out if I gave him *that* much cause." With her thumb and finger she'd measured off a slim half inch.

"He sprang at us, God knows—Ann and me, throat and eyes. He kept

Wade away from us the past few years, right up till he shot himself in an alley last February with Wade already bad off. That left Wade all but alone in the city and desperately weak. When I found out early this past April, I went up and got him."

"Wade's with you at present?"

"For however long. He's trailing off by the day, skin and bone." Hard as the past two months had been, in close sight of Wade, the boy's fate had seemed just bearable till now. In reach of a woman as self-contained and fearless as Zenobia Queen of desert Palmyra or Portia the wife of Marcus Brutus, eating live coals, Hutch suddenly felt done in by a judgment precisely hurled at his own private failings, a plunge dead center to the heart of his error—the secret central wrong of his life. *Which is what—what's the secret?*

Before Hutch could even start an answer, Alice said "We both need a glass of good sherry." And she rose to get it.

By the time she was back with the usual tray—a bottle of excellent amontillado, a plate of homemade cheese sticks and two glasses, Hutch had calmed himself and could watch her pour with pleasure in the sight of how little she'd lost. When she gave him his wine, he offered it up at once to toast her.

But she said "Not so fast. It's still my house so it's my first toast—to you, dear blessed one."

Hutch thanked her and drank. "I'm feeling deeply unblessed here lately."

"Of course you are. You're past sixty, aren't you?"

"By three full years."

Alice smiled. "Sure, the blues are a sixtyish burden. Once you strike eighty though, you're suddenly young. I wake up every day before daylight, full of curiosity and a whetted appetite to say what I know, to give what I've got and then get something new. Then I rise on my old feet and face my mirror, which is ancient as me but exceedingly literal and realistic. At the gruesome display, I think *Old girl, you've had your run. Lie back down and sleep.* Sometimes I do—nobody to stop me. I slept past ten o'clock this morning, a well-fed baby."

"You look very rested."

"I am—that's the horror. Nobody's used me in thirty-odd years."

Hutch said "I feel like a worn-out broom, used up to the stick."

"It must be awful—I see these deaths, by the day, on television: far more merciless than anything known when I was a girl. I trust you and Ann have got good help."

So Alice didn't know about Ann's experiment. Had he failed to tell her or had she forgot? Should he pile that onto the news about Wade? *No, spare her something.* Hutch said "Two Duke students have helped us a lot; Wade has liked them both. We've so far managed the rest on our own. I can't guess for how much longer; it's worse by the day."

"Wade's failing that fast?"

"As a matter of fact," Hutch said, "he's rallied a little this week—that's how I could dash off to Richmond and earn us a small piece of money. But the fact is, it's all an ice chute from here on. Wade's had parasitic pneumonia twice, half the microbes known to man are nesting in him, his eyes have failed to where he can only sense light from a window, and one of my students who sits with him often tells me that the boy's asked him for cyanide."

Alice had always been as unflinching as the brow of a sphinx, but she waited to be entirely sure of her ground. Then she said "Get the poison. Let Wade make his own way while he still can." There was not a gram of uncertainty in her level gaze.

And it shook Hutch hard. For the first full time, he thoroughly knew Wade would die very soon. All his frank words up to this point had merely concealed a shocked man's delusion that the lethal axe would freeze in midair, remorseful somehow, just short of his son. But of all his friends alive on Earth, Alice was the last sane one who'd never lied. Hutch said "You're serious."

"Darling child, I was never anything else, not ever; it's been the bane of my long life." And when Hutch sat speechless, facing her eyes, Alice said "You've walled Ann out of this."

"Has Ann called you?"

"Not once in her life."

"Then Wade."

"Not Wade. Give me credit for some degree of sense, Hutch. Even if it was a millennium ago, I loved your mother like night-blooming lilies; I somehow managed moderate fondness for your helpless wonderful-looking father, I met his cold mother and that little terrier of an aunt you loved—both of them powerful as iron locomotives on pig iron rails—so you couldn't hold a secret from me if you strained every nerve. I wish you could. You want all this ghastly death, I know; and you want it alone." She could even half smile.

Hutch accepted it again as her verdict, relieved that someone beyond him and Ann comprehended the need to possess—actually to *own* a son's death. He'd heard no reproof in all Alice said, and rightly so—she intended none, only simple description and the venting of a backed-up private knowledge she could seldom spend in her lonely days. He said "I'm the child of both my parents—no less, little more."

Alice said "I'm asking, not telling, but have you got their big luckless hearts?"

"I think so, yes. I'm seldom stingy or really indecent." He offered a laugh, which she barely received.

"You froze Ann out, I'd estimate."

At last Hutch knew he had and he agreed. "I never wanted all Ann had to give; she was way too gifted and starved as a snake."

Alice said "Good people tend to be. Send her up here to me. I'm vanishing alone."

"You'll outlast me."

Alice took the proposition seriously, then said "I may. Is there anything I should say in my prayers for your poor soul, any errands you might want me to run?"

Hutch said "See that I'm near Wade please—wherever he goes, however hard. See he knows me there and grants my rights."

Again she gave it careful thought. "You're not imagining Wade Mayfield in some private Hell for men who've used each other in love or even quick pleasure? You're not that evil or ignorant?"

"I'm not, no, truly. I'm just dreaming, in my weakest fantasy, of some cool place with more serenity—a place where Wade can finally comprehend his mysterious father."

Alice's eyes began to relent. "My darling, the purpose of human life has little to do with understanding your parents. In any case, I never thought you were that hard to plumb. But you're speaking of filial respect, aren't you? You still want that?"

Hutch said "Partly—maybe. I'm thinking of the after-life just now. No, what I'd really give a great deal for would be some brand of laughing welcome from Wade—not frequently but often enough to keep whatever blood's still in me alive and running."

"You're convinced we last on, somewhere past death?" The set of her eyes showed she asked in all seriousness.

"I wouldn't lay all my funds on it, no; but the last time I was in church—Good Friday a year ago—I listened to the creed as I said it with the others. I got through 'I believe in the resurrection of the body and the life everlasting' nearly as smoothly as if I'd said I trusted water ran downhill."

Alice said "Water does that mostly—" She suddenly chuckled. "I've seen exceptions. But yes, I find myself talking to the night air more often as I wade onward here; a sane bystander might call it prayer. I'll talk my damnedest for you and Wade, from today to the end—rest easy on that. I've built up a sizable head of credit, if the Maker keeps books (I assume that there's a Maker with account books). Nobody's got less love from the world than tough old me, not since your mother married at least.

"I used to bear the world an almighty grudge; but oh about thirty years ago, I saw I'd made a whole life in the famine. An enviable life compared to most of the ones I've watched, in close quarters anyhow—a Virginia Vestal Virgin of solitude who taught that virtue to decades of students, almost none of whom listened but you; and you disobeyed me. Ever since that realization, I've admired myself—within reason of course, no greatly swelled head. I took what time gave, mostly hardtack; and I came back for more. I'm ready still." With eyes as gleaming as they'd ever been, even in the long-gone presence of Hutch's mother whom she'd loved above all, Alice took up her glass and drained the final thick drop of her sherry as if the prospect of eventual welcome was a foregone conclusion, not subject to doubt.

Whether or not her certainty bore a chance of being the bankable truth, Hutch finally saw why he'd made this detour and borne this old woman's reckless honesty, straight as a javelin flung at the eye. For a last time he toasted her silently and drank.

24

On the fast trip home in midafternoon, Hutch's car broke down near the first turnoff in North Carolina. The engine simply quit in the road—no warning, no smoke. When he'd spent ten minutes trying to crank it and gazing under the hood in bafflement, he trudged up the ramp, found a crossroads mechanic who said he could either tow it to Durham for $100 or fix it here for a good deal less by late afternoon.

Before deciding, Hutch phoned home to check on Wade.

Mait answered, said things were even-keeled and not to worry—he'd stay till Hutch was back, whenever.

Hutch asked to speak with Wade for a moment. But Mait said "Wade's been a little mixed up—not unhappy though. Should we let him rest?"

It troubled Hutch but he held to his plan, only exacting a promise from Mait to phone Hutch at the garage in an emergency and then to call Ann.

No call ever came and the sun lunged on at the helpless Earth—a dry heat, almost deadly in its force. Soon Hutch felt that the hair of his head might ignite any instant. And to find some shade beyond the reach of the voices of the mechanic and his wife, Hutch walked out through a thicket of junked cars into a stand of tulip poplars behind the station and sat on old leaves against one thick trunk. In a silent three minutes, he began to cool; and soon he'd shut his eyes and was hoping for the first time in months that a new poem would come—one line at least, what Paul Valéry called the "one given line" that comes unbidden to a natural poet (Hutch would never have called himself a large poet; but he knew he was born with the gift in his brain, a native tendency to think in rhythmic words that reached a few thoughtful souls and lodged in their memory).

To aid the hope for a start at least, he sat on—oblivious to the day around him—and tried to accomplish the gray erasure he could usually manage on his working mind, the calling up of an empty screen with no thought or message, just a patient pregnant waiting.

He could work it for five or ten seconds at a time; then Wade's face would come, not now as it hurled downhill toward disaster but as it had been on the crest of his life. A tall strong-limbed boy, twelve or thirteen, slowed for a moment by the last step to manhood and toward all the pain that closed around him once he took that final rise in the even ground that must have looked welcoming but led him on to life in a city as cursed as any since Nineveh and into however many poisoned bodies he'd plumbed in nine years. Hutch finally gave up trying for blankness and dwelt on the valuable sight of young Wade, smiling gravely at the pitch of his noon.

Only then, when a live boy yelled out beside the filling station's air pump—"Foster, goddammit, you'll bust your tube!"—did eight words come into Hutch's mind, ready-made and dressed in authority, his given line maybe: *This child knows the last riddle and answer.* Hutch said it aloud, convinced at once that the *child* was Wade and not the yelling boy there beyond him. He repeated it twice; then fished out a pen and a scrap of paper napkin and wrote down the line. Somehow it would turn into Wade's elegy, in time for his grave. It felt like the one trustworthy thing that had come free to Hutch since spring at least, and it heartened him to stand again and walk toward the boys. "You fellows traveling north today, are you?"

The older boy said "No sir, we're at home."

But the younger—Foster—said "You want a ride? I'm heading for Spain."

"Spain? Why Spain?"

"I'm an ace bullfighter."

The older boy cuffed out at his brother. "You won't even step in the field with a bull; tell the man the damned truth."

Foster faced Hutch as seriously as if this was court and his life was at stake. "I'm just who you see."

Hutch said "You look fine. What are you—eight or nine?"

The older boy said "Man, you bound to be blind. That little flea ain't but six years old."

Hutch fished in his pocket, found a dollar in change and held it toward Foster.

Foster said "What you buying?"

Hutch said "Not buying. I'm thanking you, Son."

"For what?"

"Don't question your luck; just take it."

The older boy said "Take it, fool."

But Foster was already on his bike and bound away.

The older boy said "I'll give it to him for you."

Hutch gave him the change; and as he left too, Hutch called to his back "Go straight home and *stay.*" In the backwash of both boys' vanishing scorn, he felt like the primal sire of the race. It helped him smile.

25

At that same moment Wade's eyes came open in his darkened room in Hutch's house—not that he knew any name for the place. By now he could see no more than a kind of pearly light in which occasional tall or round shapes stirred faintly at a distance like hands in milk. He said "Well, I'm here"; and his left hand scratched toward the edge of the mattress, feeling for his exact whereabouts. He found another hand, warmer than his and softer, though large. The arm above it was bare to the shoulder, where he felt a soft shirt. Wade started to say "Fe-fi-fo-fum, I smell the blood—" Then he lost the rest of the saying. So he laughed. "Who's in my bed?"

Mait said "Your Mait." He was lying full-clothed on the top of Wade's cover, a handspan apart.

Wade said "Hey, Mait." Then "Who the hell are you?"

"A young short guy—twenty-one years old though: no minor, don't worry, no charges are pending."

Wade's whole head seemed to retreat a long way. He finally said "I beg to differ."

"How?"

"I'm convicted. And sentenced."

At once Wade had pushed Mait past his calm moorings. Mait laughed anyhow. "Convicted of what? Nothing worse than roadhogging."

Again Wade paused. Mait's hand was still in reach, so Wade took it again and thought he pressed it—the pressure was barely detectable. "I think I'm guilty of just one thing."

"Want to tell Father Mait?"

"If I do, will he trust me and not make the same mistake again in his entire life?"

"A promise—Mait'll give it a serious shot."

Wade's lips were so dry they stuck together and only opened when he shook his head. "I was stingy as some old village miser."

Mait said "I heard otherwise—rumor says you were truly a gent and a spender."

"Too much of a gent—way too much. But barely a spender. Oh Jesus, no."

"You failed to buy what?"

Wade knew right off. "Oh love. Fine bodies. Warm cries in the night."

Mait laughed again.

"I mean every word. Don't hoard your body."

"But Wade, your body's what's punishing you—*using* your body any-how." Mait bit his lip to have said the word *punishing*; too late now.

The huge skull agreed. "For a few good years with one splendid man. One woman, for a few months before I actually figured who I needed, before I knew Wyatt. One tacky boy before I left home, a senior at State. God, I could have known every man in the nation, from stem to stern, and not be dying faster than this."

Mait said "You've got a point. It's scary as hell."

"It's *waste* and you know it. No, child, listen and recall this forever— remember Wade Mayfield tried to save you from stinginess, as mean a fail-ing as anything else but strangling children." Any person with eyes, seated by Wade, could have seen he was sane and urgent in his warning. What a watcher might have failed to see was how unstoppably the whole past life of his family surged in Wade and pressed out the news he'd passed to one boy, one who might or might not have the wits and courage to use it well.

Young as he was, Mait knew to thank him, though he thought at the time *Wade's waving me on toward a death like his own.*

26

It was well past six in the evening before Hutch took the last turn in the drive and saw home, broad on its green hill, no sign of trouble, a rest for the mind. In the final twenty minutes of the trip, he'd all but panicked in the simple need to see Wade again and know that the boy had waited to see him and would recognize his face and accept his gift. Hutch had brought Wade a gift from Richmond, a small piece of staurolite, a dark brown stone that occurs in the natural shape of a cross and is mined in the mountains of Virginia.

Hutch checked his pocket for the stone cross, found it, then searched the house windows for life. The sun stalled, ruthless, above the tree line; but in every window some lamp burned. Hutch thought *They're gone and they left in a hurry.* Mait's bike still waited in the back turn circle and a strange old Buick. *They called the ambulance or Ann came and got them.*

By the time Hutch reached the door, he nearly believed it. But he turned the knob—open on cool air and the sound of laughter, a man's voice deeper than Wade's or Mait's. Hutch waited in place. *Who on Earth?*

Then Mait's voice called out "Welcome back." His undiscourageable face appeared at the end of the hall, in Wade's doorway. He was wearing khaki shorts and a green tank top.

Behind Mait, a taller darker man stood and faced Hutch squarely. He was in the act of donning a T-shirt.

Hutch failed to recognize the man; and when a surge of resentment struck him, Hutch heard himself say to Mait "You called in strangers?"

Mait's face collapsed.

The other man said "Mr. Mayfield, I'm Cam—Cameron Mapleson. We met at Maitland's." When Hutch stared on in obvious anger, Cam said "I was badly dressed at the time—it was dawn—and I'm still sorry."

Then Hutch remembered their awkward meeting and nodded curtly; but he went on feeling invaded, assaulted. *Why did Mait feel the right to bring in company?*

Cam understood. He came halfway down the hall toward Hutch. "Sir, this visit was my idea. I had the evening off, I knew Mait was staying out here with Wade, I wanted to see them both and I stopped by. I thought I might help someway, with my background." He extended his massive right hand to Hutch.

Finally Hutch came to meet him and took the plainly guileless greeting with the trace of a smile. "I'm just an old bear, sorry—guarding my cave."

Mait's guilty face was still at Wade's door, well beyond them.

So Hutch said "Who's feeding this great multitude?"

From his bed Wade tried to call out "Me," a broken syllable.

Hutch could hear it but, to Mait and Cam, it sounded like trouble. They both looked to Hutch for directions. *You deal with the crazy.*

Hutch lowered his voice. "Let me see Wade alone. Then I'll cook us supper."

Relieved, the two young men agreed and moved past Hutch toward the bright-lit front room.

When Hutch got to Wade, the boy was lying flat with both eyes open toward the ceiling. For the first time in weeks, the eyes had the look of real connection; they were almost surely seeing something beyond them in the world.

Hutch leaned to the forehead and kissed it—cool. "What're you watching, dear friend?"

Wade tried to find him but settled on the wrong place, the foot of the bed. "I'm running our old home movies by the mile."

"Which reel?" There were years of old eight-millimeter film in cans in the attic—Hutch and Ann's honeymoon in Charleston, Wade's whole childhood; Hutch's grandmother Eva in the year of her death, daunting as any Cretan priestess brandishing gold snakes; Wade's graduation from architecture school at N.C. State and departing from the airport for his job in New York.

Wade said "I'm watching, over and over the ones of you as a boy up at Strawson's." There were no such films. Any movies Wade watched were confined to the screen of his uncertain mind.

Hutch understood that, but still it set off a recollection. He'd bought the movie camera just before he and Ann were married in the fifties. To a mind as visually grounded as Hutch's, in those years even his private events had hardly seemed real until they'd been witnessed by some kind of camera and stored as proof for future reference—*We had this life, it's not all gone, I can bring it back partway.* So he said to Wade "I wish we did have some record of me. I've got no idea how I really looked or moved in the early years, just that I never smiled in snapshots. I was always posing ferociously as the Hope of Mankind or the Blazing Avenger of Sensitive Souls. There's an all but daily record of you in your first year, your first six Christmases until you told me I was Santa Claus, and I beat a retreat."

Wade said "I'll burn those."

You couldn't strike a match if your life depended on it. But Hutch said "They'll just mean more and more to me."

"You can't ever watch them again though, can you?"

"Why?"

Wade's voice slid into the high singsong he used more and more. "Go incinerate every one of them *now*. You're in my command."

Hutch said "I don't watch them more than once in ten years; but no, they'll be precious further down the road."

Wade said "They'll kill you—on sight—you well know that: watching me young and well, in my right mind."

Hutch agreed in silence, then quickly moved the subject aside. "Enjoy your break, your two days with Maitland?"

Wade waited a long time, then ducked his head hard. "They stripped buck naked for me, let me feel skin. Mait and Cam—they mainly let me listen while they did it." Wade was plainly not joking, he seemed clearheaded, then he faced Hutch and smiled the first abandoned smile he'd managed in months. "I'd forgotten *hair*, Hutch—sweet private hair. Don't it heal your heart?" It sounded like unimpeachable thanks.

And it took Hutch awhile to process the news with no resentment. Finally he granted the truth of Wade's question. "Hair's one of the absolute good things, true—the right kind of hair." He reached for the bones of Wade's hand on the sheet, lifted them gently toward his own dry lips and barely brushed them—the withered whorls that had been fingerprints.

Wade said "Don't stop. I'm living for pleasure entirely these days." Then he gave the strongest laugh he'd given since before Wyatt died; he heard it himself and wondered at his strength.

Hutch laid the cross-shaped staurolite in the palm of Wade's hand. "A little gift from Old Virginny."

Wade's fingers felt it hungrily, then took it to his lips, forced the long teeth open and the lips sucked it in.

Hutch thought *Oh Son, don't swallow a brown rock.* But he only said "It's not candy, boy. Don't break a good molar."

Wade said "I know it's the Holy Cross. I'm draining it dry. It knows my name." In another five seconds he'd sunk into sleep.

Taking a clean rubber glove from the drawer, Hutch carefully opened the clenched jaw and teeth, felt for the staurolite with his finger and fished it out. He set it on Wade's bedside table, went to his own room and washed the trip from his face and hands, then went to see if Mait and Cam were gone.

No, they were silent, back in the kitchen, well into cooking clam sauce for pasta—their own idea.

Hutch was too tired to feel resentment.

27

But an hour later, with the food and wine and low-keyed laughter, Hutch was partly restored. The ache for Wade was a steady presence, sure to last as long as Hutch lasted and to blare out unpredictably in solitude. Yet the nearness here of Cam and Mait had worked to remind Hutch of time's persistence and the hell-bent course of every life except the self-haters who circle, slow-motion. Finally, when the dishes were washed and the two guests stood to leave, Hutch confronted them, smiling. "You gave Wade a brief *exhibición* I hear?"

Mait didn't know the word.

But Cam had heard it years back from his father, a U.S. Navy vet from the days when Havana offered sailors a wealth of booths and small theaters where women, men and assorted animals supplied their starved eyes with live exhibitions of mammal flesh at the outer limits of its will to join, delight or torment other flesh. So it was Cam's turn to look trapped and sheepish. Still he tried to put his best foot forward. "Wade remembered and told you?"

Hutch said "Long enough to tell me he'd felt skin again."

Mait understood at last and went through his full regulation response—flushing, stammering at various pitches. "Sir, Wade asked *us.*"

But Cam faced Hutch. "Not truly, no, he didn't. It was my idea and it went a little further than I intended. You feel insulted?"

When Hutch kept silent, Mait said "We just sat lightly on the bed by Wade and talked—in our birthday suits for half an hour."

Not glancing to Mait, Cam said straight to Hutch "That's a lie, sir. We made flat-out love in easy reach of Wade."

"On that narrow bed?" Hutch was asking Cam.

But Cam looked to Mait and gave a slow gesture. *Over to you.*

So Maitland said "Wade asked us to—"

In a calm whisper Cam said "No Wade didn't. We offered it to him—I made the offer. I'm his age, I can feel his loneliness, I had the right."

Hutch bridled. "The *right?* Where's your half of the deed? This is my house, Cameron, while I draw breath."

Cam held in place at the table and took it, eye to eye with Hutch.

Mait's face had reddened to the point of real danger. He nodded to Hutch though. "Wade liked it, right off."

Cam leaned forward finally. "Sir, I don't think we harmed your son in the slightest. He's been so far gone from life and caring, I'd all but guarantee we did him a kindness—a service at least."

Hutch said "I'm sorry you can think that simply." He didn't feel puritan outrage or envy, just one more taste of bone-aching regret that once again Wade had been forced up against a human pleasure he'd never share again.

Cam said "Don't be sorry. And think how wrong you may well be. Whatever Mait says, I can tell you this—I never did anything any more intimate with anyone else, male or female, than what the two of us did for Wade. I'll never forget it."

Hutch said "You both took precautions?—Wade's a very sick boy."

Cam said "Rest your mind. I work with the sick."

Then oddly, for the first time in years, Hutch was ambushed by concern for Ann's rights in this. *Ann would hate this; she'd blister us all, the moment she knew.* He even said to Mait "Did his mother drop by?"

"This morning early. Then she called up again in midafternoon."

"How much did you tell her?"

Mait said "Cam wasn't even here that early. I told her the truth—Wade and I were fine; you'd been delayed but would be here by dark."

Hutch had to say "But what if she'd walked in on you?"

Mait looked to Cam.

Cam said "We'd have stood up and acted polite."

Hutch imagined the scene and couldn't think whether to laugh or howl. "She'd have shot you both dead—she packs a pistol" (Ann did, quite legally in her purse, ever since she moved to the deep sticks alone). By then Hutch could risk a smile.

Mait said "Mr. Mayfield, I'm apologizing."

"To me?" Hutch said.

Cam said "I'm not."

Hutch said "I wouldn't accept it if you did." He turned to Mait, who was still humiliated. "Friend, thanks for the time, if not the sideshow. We may need more of your presence yet; I'll make it worth your while, as I told you."

Mait said "Your money won't work with me."

Hutch was stumped.

Mait said "I owe you anything you can ask—you gave me my life. Don't even say *money*, sir."

Cam was standing by, behind Mait's chair. Now he leaned and folded Mait into his arms, rubbing his chin on the crown of Mait's head.

And to Hutch, Mait's outburst felt like as good a reward as he'd ever get for his years of teaching; the sight of Cam's eyes and face were a gift too. So Hutch said "My friends mostly call me Hutch—please no more *sirs*, not from either one of you." When he'd shaken their hands, he felt so empty that he nearly begged "Better let me go rest."

But Wade's voice sang out through his open door yards away, a high soft line from "The Last Rose of Summer"—"*Left blooming alone.*"

Frail as the sound was, Hutch knew the voice well enough to know that Wade's lips were grinning.

Everyone chuckled and Mait and Cam left, not turning back on their full day.

28

By half past nine Wade was washed and diapered and back asleep. Hutch had locked the house and was in his own room, ready for bed, when the telephone rang. Two rooms away, the message machine broadcast Ann's voice. "Hutch, can you hear me?"

He badly wanted to ignore her, but he knew she'd panic and drive straight over to check on Wade. So slowly he took up the nearest phone. "—Just barely. I'm exhausted."

"The trip was hard?"

"I had some car trouble; but no, I'm just not the wandering bard I was."

"You're no worse than tired though?" Her time among lawyers was telling on Ann; she sounded relentless as any prosecutor.

"Christ, no, lady—I'm no worse than beat. Not to the best of my knowledge at least."

"You can't fail, Hutch."

"I don't plan to fail. But I need to rest." He was rushing her. "What's on your mind?"

She balked. "You're conceding then that I've got a mind?"

"Games, Ann, games. I resign; play solitaire. Sincere good night."

"Wait—it's been a rough two days."

"It's been a rough life." When she didn't agree, Hutch briefly heard Alice back this morning—*You've frozen her out*—so he said "What's the latest?"

Her voice moved through it like a memorized speech, with pauses and feeling but clearly practiced (which made Hutch despise it, from the first word on). "I need one promise from you, just one. I'll even pay for it—don't hire young Maitland Moses again to sit with Wade. I'll pay for a nurse if you have to leave. When's Hart Salter coming back from England?"

Hutch said "Hart's gone till the fall at least. No, save your cash; young Mait worked fine—he's honest and careful. Wade told me so."

Ann said "Give me this much."

"You've scarcely seen Maitland; what's so bad about him?"

"You'll say I'm a bigot, but I'm also Wade Mayfield's only mother. He's dying of the kind of life he chose; it seems very wrong to me that, in these straits, we should leave him alone with one more man who's made the same blind and killing mistake." It was literally the first time Ann had broached the subject with Hutch in all their years. For all the recognition she'd conceded, Wade and Wyatt might have been blood twins or orbiting astronauts, chosen by lot.

Instantly Hutch felt bathed in the lights of a television panel show of idiot simplicity—*Our Sexual Roles: Genetic Fate or Adult Choice? Choose one and justify*. All he might have learned from Alice that morning flushed through him and vanished. He wanted to tear the phone from the wall; but he finally said "Yes, Counselor Mayfield, you're right as always—your son and mine chose his own life and death exactly the way presexual children choose brain tumors or pediatric AIDS, just that freely—so has Maitland Moses. Christ, wake up, Ann. Or *wise* up, at least. You're too smart to mimic some nineteenth-century Baptist deacon who thinks Jonah spent three days in a whale and that women who lie with donkeys must be stoned. I fear you've spent a few hours too many with the criminal element—or is it just Christian TV you're watching? Whatever, it's plainly dulling your mind and damning you to Hell."

Ann said "I haven't mentioned a donkey yet, though the word *jackass* does come to mind often. But no, just because you ruined your and my life through cowardice doesn't make me wrong."

"Cowardice?"

"Hutch, I trust you've known for decades—God knows, I have—that you made a choice and made it wrong. You loved Straw Stuart but married me."

To his surprise, and shocked as he was by this delayed charge, Hutch had a ready answer. It came so smoothly that he thought, as he said it, *This has waited for years.* "Ann, I've loved Strawson nearly all his life. He's a lot more loyal than the average collie—not to speak of humans including my mate, who abandoned me for nothing worse than the normal atmospheres of a marriage that's lasted awhile. But I couldn't have lived with him forty-five minutes—Straw or any other man I've known. So your brilliant diagnosis of my wrong turn is so inaccurate that I won't dignify it with a full answer. From somewhere around age fourteen and onward, I've steadily done what I meant to, in my main choices, with you at least and in starting our son on his way to life.

"I reached out and tried for a sizable life with a woman as different from me as a panther. And up till last year, I thought we had a life—a good-sized existence, give or take normal failures—till you skipped out for your experiment in radical secular hermitage. Anyhow, whoever ended our marriage, the main result of what we did is dying now, way past our help. That much is tragic; what's left of you and me is ludicrous—you just made it so."

Ann held a long moment. "I told you the truth, and you well know it. What you wanted was wrong—and it's caused our pain, all ours and Wade's—but I wish to God you'd gone with Straw and left me free. There ought not to *be* anything left of us."

If Hutch could have found the energy for one more speech, his actual fury might have caused Ann harm, even at a distance. That at least would have been a true sign of what he felt. But finally he only said "Good night. I'm gone." And he was; he hung up. He sat still a minute, in case she called back. No call came and, in ten minutes more, Hutch was on his own bed— stripped and out like a smothered child, desperately unconscious.

Over again, till Wade called for him a little after dawn, Hutch dived and surfaced in a tangled continuous dream of paralysis. In all its parts, Hutch could see his real body, laid here on his bed and frozen to stone in every cell. On a straight chair against the wall beyond him, he could sense Wade's presence—huge now and strong again but still blind and stunned. The one great need was for Hutch to make a simple request, a single demand of Wade, requiring an answer; but his lips couldn't move. And a spot on the surface of his locked brain, the size of a stamp, was all that could think. In that small spot, on through the night, Hutch repeated the single request in silence, trapped in his skull but meant for Wade—*Will you give me an answer?* Whether or not it ever reached Wade through the air between them in the dream, no answer came, not all night long, though Wade sat on in reach of his father and had sufficient strength to free him.

29

At five forty-five in the morning however, the actual Wade called Hutch's name between their rooms; and Hutch came at once, not pausing to put on more than his briefs. In the doorway he paused and tried to see Wade's shape, trusting he'd still be down in bed, weak as he'd been since the last pneumonia. But when Hutch's eyes came open in the dimness, the bed was only a tangle of sheets.

Wade had somehow got himself up and dressed in a flannel robe from his childhood, a remnant that fit him once again. He was crouched on himself in the one easy chair. When he sensed his father, he said "I've been up a very long time, sir, waiting for you."

Hutch said "I'm sorry; I must have been even tireder than I knew. You should have called me."

Wade said "I did, about five hundred times. You never heard me and I couldn't walk closer."

By then Hutch had moved to the bedside table and switched on a lamp. The boy looked no worse than yesterday, but Hutch said "What's wrong?" and sat on the bed.

Again Wade took slow time to decide. The message would sink, then rise and hook at the base of his brain, then vanish again. Finally it rose for long enough to let Wade say "I'm a whole lot stronger suddenly." To prove it, he did a physical trick the neurologists had taught him—shutting his blind eyes, extending both arms, then finding his nose with his straight forefinger—first one arm, then the other. Each time the finger found its way with no detour.

Hutch said "No doubt about it; you're better."

Wade put a silencing finger to his lips. "I know this means I'm close to dying. *No*, don't shut me up, Hutch. I've watched it in others—we get a few of our faculties back, like a small tip from fate." Wade chuckled deeply. "There's something I need to tell you soon, before I'm gone." He stopped and wiped his dry blue lips as if they were wet. He'd lost his subject.

Hutch said "I'm listening."

Wade ran a hand down the length of his face as if clearing cobwebs but nothing more came. So he finally smiled. "Remind me every day from here on out. There's something in me that you need to know."

The announcement of death was all Hutch heard, and he knew at once that Wade was right. He went to the bathroom, filled a pail with water, brought soap, a rag, and a small soft towel; then he went back, stripped and bathed his child where he sat in the chair as dawn progressed at every window.

30

That morning Ann drove the ten green miles to Hillsborough, the small county seat with its pillared old court house, the town green where the leaders of a protorevolutionary force called the Regulators had been ceremoniously hanged by the Royal Governor in 1771, the airy home of a signer of the Declaration of Independence, and a small jail that still looked like a holding pen for cutthroats dragged from a pirate hulk off the Outer Banks, which had been a bolt-hole for the dreaded Blackbeard, Edward Teach.

Those facts—and the strata of pain they implied—were hardly foremost in Ann's mind as she paused at the first stoplight in town; but the peace of the place, its slow air of entire self-confidence and serene faith in its chance of enduring centuries longer were parts of the ease Ann felt as she parked just off the main street. Today she and a younger woman attorney had had an appointment to talk with the law firm's most urgent client; at the last moment, the attorney got sick; so Ann had come on her own, unruffled, to ask more questions of that dire client—the young man whom Hutch called the Hurdle Mills Strangler (Hurdle Mills was fifteen miles north, a quiet village).

The man's name was Walter Wilk, called Whirly or simply Whirl by all; and what he'd done—unquestionably, this past Easter morning—was strangle his mother with a Donald Duck necktie, a gift she'd brought him from her Thanksgiving trip to Disney World with the women of her church. Then two days later when no one had yet discovered his mother, who lived alone, Whirly suffocated his passed-out alcoholic brother-in-law with a pillow in the early hours of a Sunday morning as the drunk snored on beside his drunk wife, who never heard a peep, in their double-wide mobile home in the woods.

In the weeks that Ann had worked with the killer—taking his increasingly hair-raising confessions and his simultaneous fevered mission to win her and all her colleagues to Jesus—she'd developed an undownable sympathy for what Whirly had endured in his thirty-six years (a father like something from the Brothers Grimm, a runaway wife as ravenous for love and money as any debutante, a string of early felonies involving drugs and break-ins, and the sight of his sister delivering a stillborn baby in her kitchen with nobody present but Whirly and her husband's deranged pit bull).

The day Ann had first seen Whirly in jail, three months ago, she'd noticed—as he turned to leave their cubicle, chained hand and foot—that the back of his head with its thick black hair beginning to curl, the wide level shoulders and rail-straight posture all but made him a twin to Wade Mayfield: a lost twin mangled by the hands of his kin but waiting still for some hope of rescue, a hope as surely futile as Wade's.

Now as the jailer led Whirly in to the same green conference cubicle, he still wore handcuffs but no leg irons. His hair was even longer, he'd thinned down further in the week since Ann had seen him, so even his eyes were now moving in Wade's direction—the blank and unbearably helpless stare of the volunteer martyr, oblivious to his crime.

Since Ann was part of Whirly's defense team, the jailer was forced to leave them alone—checking at intervals through a glass slot to see if she was staying alive in such proximity to a known madman.

As the madman faced her across a three-foot-wide oak table, Ann saw that his face had gone on clearing in the past eight days—a well-shaped landscape, purging itself of mountainous waste and a lowering sky. Ann opened her notebook, reminded herself *He's not Wade, Ann; he's killed his own mother; you're not his Aunt Jesus;* and then she amazed herself by saying a thing she'd never mentioned before, not in this death house. As each word came, it sounded more unprofessional than the last; but she gave in and told him. "Whirly, my son's at the point of death; so talk plainly please, fast. I need *out* of here." At once she felt like fleeing in shame. She'd never so much as acknowledged being human, much less a sad mother—not in this awful room—but she begged no pardon and waited for his answer.

Whirly said "It's AIDS, right?" His eyes were as flat as aluminum washers.

That he'd gone for the throat like that, in an instant, barely seemed strange to Ann. *Somebody from the firm is bound to have told him. But surely not.* "Who told you that?"

Then slowly Whirly's eyes went hot as an ermine's at the throat of a mouse. "Mother Mary, in the night. She tells me a *lot.*"

Whirly's strain of Christianity, from what Ann had gathered, was a holy-rolling Protestant sect with a self-anointed woman bishop weighing three hundred pounds and called Sister Triumph. Sister's theology, oddly, included a few Roman saints and the Virgin Mary in exotic doses—Whirly wore a black rosary around his neck every time Ann had seen him; he claimed to use it hourly at least. Now Ann said only "Ask her to pray for him then."

"Who?"

"Mother Mary."

Whirly's eyes were puzzled. "What's your boy's name then?" When Ann balked, Whirly said "I got to have his name—she don't take nameless requests nohow." Then he smiled broadly; his teeth were calamitous.

"Wade—Wade Mayfield, Raven Wade Mayfield. As good a man as breathes." Even more certain she was on crazy ground, Ann glanced to the window in the door—no sign of the jailer. *I've crossed completely over, someway. I'll never leave this room, not today.*

Whirly's voice stayed level. "Young Wade's a queer?"

Of course it all but stupefied Ann. N*ow, like the rest of the hateful Christians, he'll damn him to Hell* (Ann's own youthful Christianity had been scorched out, long since, by her notice that groups of Christians bigger than three, tend to grow scornful fangs and dream at least of executing God's vengeance on their neighbors). But since she'd constantly stressed to Whirly that he needed to tell the full truth at all times to all his defenders, she couldn't lie here. "Wade lived for some years with a man in New York, a black man that hated his father and me. No girlfriend ever, not that I ever saw—not since his college years at State. But nobody I ever met or watched in any brand of news was a kinder soul. Wade could watch you every day of the week and still act kind."

Whirly said "*Was?* Nobody else *was.* Ain't Wade alive? You just said he was." Whirly's hands had joined on the table between them, making a flat empty pyramid against the dark oak. Big as they were, they could easily suffocate a Doberman, an ox.

"Wade's hanging on, yes, by the thinnest strand. Nobody yet has rounded a curve with AIDS and come back." Ann could hear that, already, she'd said the word AIDS in this dim room more times than elsewhere. But then these walls had heard the worst the human race could dream or do, for well over two hundred years and counting.

"There you *go,*" Whirly said. "Ain't that everybody's boat? Who gets back alive?"

Helplessly honest again, Ann said "Well, you're hanging on, my friend, in fairly good shape."

"Hold your phone here, lady. Everybody's warming up the gas chamber—ain't they?—making little signs that say 'Whirly Wilk, *die* in your own shit and stink'; but I'm swimming for *land*." Whirly raised both giant hands and stroked at the hot air, an Australian crawl.

Ann pushed back a little from the table, tried to smile, and stroke a few yards of her own beside him.

Whirly said "Where to?"

"Pardon?"

"Where are *you* headed?"

Ann said "You tell me *your* destination."

Whirly likewise pushed back, some six feet from her. In a full minute's wait, with his eyes shut calmly, what he came up with was "A piece of high ground. Plenty light, a cold spring, shady groves and music—deep banjo music all night and noon, not too near to drown you or upset your rest. No in-laws present, no blood kin but maybe a deaf old aunt, a few distant cousins—beg your pardon on that." He smiled thinly but looked as sane as any magistrate, exercising pardon on a room of young children. "I'll wait for him there."

"*Him* is my son, Whirl? *Him* means Wade?"

Whirly smiled an entirely new credible smile, then ducked his chin in a fix-eyed surety. "Wade Mayfield, sure. He'll be safe as trees."

Mad as she understood Whirl was, Ann half chose to trust him. *Even so,* she thought, *that leaves me lost.*

31

Two days later at the end of work, Ann came to the house, knocked at the front door and waited while Hutch put down his book and answered.

His first sight of her, in the late oblique light, was the same fresh shock she'd given him often in the past forty years, the most reliable gift she gave—the jolt of her beauty even here, this far along; the depth of her eyes, her lustrous hair that was more than half white now, the delicate and tacit promise she'd always offered to join him in private acts of pleasure with a steady daring grace that could bring down immense rewards. It took Hutch a moment to raise his resistance to such a body and its intricate, forbearing, feral mind. Then he said the first two words that came. "Lose something?"

Ann had lectured herself all the way out here to turn his first thrust, not to flare and explode. So in a low voice she answered him literally, then said what she planned. "I'm losing the same son you are; and, Hutch, I need to move back."

"Back where?"

"My home, the legal address of my child and the man I'm still married to."

In its single blast, it nearly thawed Hutch; he was startled again to feel how hard he wanted her—not *for* anything but her frank handsome presence and the matrix of shared time and acts they'd laid down beneath them as food and shelter precisely for this late time in both their lives: the chance at a peaceful evening glide before full desolation and age. But he said "I can't fall down here, Ann, and let you walk right over and past me suddenly. You dug this whole bizarre canyon between us; I can't just ignore it and—"

"I dug the canyon?"

"We both did—sure, I dug along with you—but you chose to move to the far rim, right?"

Ann yielded his point with her eyes, her best argument.

So Hutch drew back from blocking the entrance and stood as she walked in.

She went up the hall to the living room door and paused there, looking back for further permission.

"You can go on to Wade's room."

In her normal voice, not whispering to spare Wade, Ann said "I'm asking for the back bedroom—not for life, understand, but just the duration." She pointed toward Wade's room—the term of Wade's life, she plainly meant. When Hutch failed to answer, she said "I'll pay rent, my share of the groceries, the phone and lights, anything else you say." By the end, when she understood she was begging, she'd begun to whisper. She was whispering now, though few other humans could have yielded so much and still looked upright and straight as an elm.

Hutch pointed to the kitchen and also whispered. "Let's talk back there."

For all their problems, neither one of them ever had leaned on alcohol. Generations of drunks in both their families had warned them off it. So Hutch knew not to bring out the wine or Ann's preferred brand of unblended scotch; they'd need full clarity. There was ready-made coffee on hand by the sink. Hutch poured that out into two tall mugs, sugared Ann's her way, heated the mugs in a microwave big enough to roast a grown pig, then sat opposite Ann at the breakfast table. When they'd each downed swallows, he said "You know it nearly killed me when you left?"

She shook her head No. "You never said."

"It did—the pure truth."

"Hutch, if that's meant as flattery, I can't take it here." Yet his deep-set eyes met hers—unaged, undimmed—the one part of him that could always reach and, most times, hold her.

He shook his head No and again said "The truth. I thought I'd die for the first few days, flat-suffocate. It's still like another great rock on my chest."

"Then I'm more than amazed." There was no keen edge or burr on her voice; she was aiming at honesty buffered by the years of sympathy she hoped they'd laid down, a hanging bridge between them.

Hutch met that offer with his own precision. "You know I've had trouble all my life telling people I love them. I'm afraid it'll spook them, maybe even kill them. It killed my mother."

Ann said "Hutch, your mother died of a hemorrhage."

"—Caused by me."

"Not *you*, never you. She'd loved Rob Mayfield and wanted to bear his child—plain as that. She was grown when she chose to bring you to life; her eyes were wide open. The doctor couldn't stop her bleeding the day you came; it was plain as that."

Maybe it was. Hutch had never seen it that way, not that simply. It might even serve as a skeleton key to some old locked gates. But he still owed Ann more explanation. "You and me though—I couldn't convince you we were barely two people. In forty years we'd grown into being all but one thing, one thing with two minds. I was fairly content. You seemed to need proofs of love, on the hour—proofs of how separate we were but how needy—and I couldn't give that. All I had to offer was a visible fact, the homely fact that *there I was.* I couldn't and wouldn't, not two years ago and maybe not now."

Ann said "Let's don't even mention love yet, not between you and me. What I'm asking for is a room in this house, whosoever it is, and the right to do my duty to our son. I can't love Wade one bit less than you; grant me that much, Hutchins."

"It's not up to me to grant you that. I've never doubted your care for Wade."

"Then let me near him, any hour of the day or night."

Hutch said "I remind you you've got a key. I've never once bolted these doors against you."

"You bring people in here that I can't face—"

"They're not yours to face, Ann. They're my trusted help."

Before her lips had closed just now, she'd heard her mistake. *I left this house; it's his to fill—or torch if he chooses.*

Hutch gave no sign of hearing; but he took a second draft of his coffee, then got to his feet. "Wade's waiting. He's called your name all afternoon."

Ann heard the small compensation in that, the tidy offering—*Wade still knows you*—but as Hutch turned from her and moved toward his study, she knew she wouldn't be sleeping here soon.

32

At nine that night Hutch phoned Ivory Bondurant. There were nine or ten rings, then a silent pick-up; then nothing but the distant weaving of music, Debussy or Ravel on a harp. He finally said "This is Hutchins Mayfield. Is Miss Bondurant there?"

After five more seconds of music, Ivory said "Good evening"—no trace of surprise or welcome.

Hutch had to say "Are you all right?"

"I think so, yes"—very cautious and slow.

She's drugged or sick. But he said "I'm afraid I've waked you. Sorry, I'll call another time."

"No, no, Mr. Mayfield. How are you?"

Only then did he realize *She must think I'm calling to say Wade's dead.* "Thanks. I'm well, Miss Bondurant. Wade's had pneumonia but is back home again and a little stronger maybe."

Ivory said "And his vision?"

Hutch had noticed, from the start, how everyone's dread at the thought of Wade went straight toward his blindness (as recently as two weeks ago, Dr. Ives had repeated her offer to treat Wade's eyes with the single drastic remedy at hand, however late). So Hutch lied now, to ease the news. "He sees a little, odd times of the day; but no, his eyes are a good deal worse than when you saw him last—I think so at least. He's confused more often, and of course he's thinner still."

Ivory said "That's expected," then waited for more. Behind her the music solved its way toward a tentative ending, followed by silence.

Had a radio died? Had some live harpist been in another room of Ivory's apartment and shut down this moment? In the calm Hutch couldn't remember why he'd called, and his uncertain wait stretched out like tension.

At last Ivory said "Mr. Mayfield, what has Wade told you?"

Late as it was, Hutch heard nothing strange in the question. It even triggered the memory of his purpose. "Wade mostly lives in the here and now—I think his memory's almost gone. But today he did bring up the apartment; he asked me if we still had Wyatt's portrait. I can't recall seeing any such picture. I thought you might."

"I have it, yes. It's safe with me."

"Is it a photograph or a painting?"

"A painting—the absolute soul of Wyatt Bondurant."

"Who painted it?"

"I did, years ago, when I still painted—when my hand could still do it. I gave it to Wade once Wyatt died; but even with his failing vision then, Wade told me he couldn't stand to have it in sight—he regretted Wyatt so grievously. It's been here with me, turned to the wall. I can't watch it either. Wade can have it anytime."

"I'll tell him that you said as much. If he wants it down here, I'd pay of course for your gallery to crate it."

"Just let me know."

"Did you ever paint Wade?"

Ivory paused. "I did, eight years ago, but now that's gone."

Hutch was interested. "Sold?"

"No, it's with my mother out on Long Island. She cherished Wade and asked me for it."

Hutch said "Thank her for me, over again. She's written us kindly."

"She's far more than overqualified for a saint—my sainted mother. I wish I had a tenth of her grit." Ivory waited again.

So Hutch came to the point. "You're getting the rent checks I send on time?"

"No problem with that, except I wonder if you don't want me to clear out those rooms and let them pass to a new set of people. I could ship everything that matters on down; it wouldn't fill up more than three more boxes. It may be a crime, paying this much rent on useless space."

Hutch said "It's useful to Wade, I believe. Shutting it down might actually kill him."

"Would Wade have to know?"

"I couldn't lie to him; he grills me occasionally, to be sure it's there; that we haven't ended his old life without a sign at least from him."

Ivory said "I didn't know his mind was that clear."

"*Clear*'s not the real word. But even now he sometimes speaks of going back up there to work again. He knows the last drawing he left on his desk." Hutch hadn't quite understood he felt that till then, though he knew he'd never grudged the steep rent, both Wade's and Wyatt's shares (Ann's absence from the house had freed up some cash).

Ivory said "Then I see what you mean; that might well throw him. I know my brother's empty space in this building keeps *my* hurt strong."

"I hadn't considered that."

"Then don't—Lord, don't. I can last it out. It's a small task compared to yours and Wade's mother's."

Hutch couldn't recall that Ivory had mentioned Ann before, and he wondered what contact they might have had. Had Ann ever phoned her or vice versa? *Stay out of that.* So he only thanked Ivory.

She politely denied that Hutch bore her a debt; but when she could hear he was near hanging up, she said "Mr. Mayfield, is there something else?"

"No, not really. Nothing but the sadness, and you share that. It doesn't slack, does it? I thought it would."

"You're terribly right. No, I just thought you might have something on your heart or mind."

Her tone was so gentle Hutch couldn't imagine she meant Wyatt's hatred of him and Ann, but he said "You mean about Wyatt's refusing us?"

"No, sir, I didn't." With that she went silent, plainly finished.

Hutch heard it. "Would you say the name *Hutchins* once please?"

Ivory said "Hutchins" in her richest voice.

For a moment it gave Hutch his old childhood thrill at hearing his name, two syllables of noise that were somehow him. "Thank you, Ivory—if I may call you that." For an instant he thought *God, she'll think I'm playing massah*; but he said "I'm almost old enough to be your grandfather. Please call me Hutchins or Hutch from here on." Awkward as it felt, Hutch wasn't embarrassed. He'd suddenly needed a woman's kind notice; it might help him through one more restless night.

Ivory said "I'll try, if we meet again."

Just as the phone moved down from his ear, Hutch thought he could hear her music renewed—one wide and darkly chromatic chord.

33

But well after midnight Hutch still hadn't slept, so he reached out into the dark and dialed the operator. For some odd reason he lied to the woman and told her his lights had suddenly failed, he couldn't see to dial, would she please connect him to a long-distance number?

That late, the woman took time to be pleasant. "In the dark all alone, eh? *I know* how you feel—believe you me." She assured him he'd get the cheap rate all the same, and the number rang twice.

Strawson answered *"Late,"* sepulchrally. No one alive could be far off and still establish, with voice alone, the vivid sight of his physical body and the air around him quicker than Straw.

"It's nowhere near late for you, old watchman."

"I was just lying here awake thinking of you."

Hutch said "Much obliged; your thoughts must have reached me."

"They do that, yes. It's the last of my powers; all else has failed me." But he laughed around in the lower reaches of his deep bass register for a good while longer.

Hutch had not spoken with Straw in ten days, not since Ann's nighttime phone attack; and he suddenly needed to mention that surprise and hear the effect on whatever Straw had meant last April when he said Hutch had failed to request his life — Straw's own young life as it sped through its brief prime. Now was almost surely not the right time to ask; still Hutch said "Where are you at present?"

"Lying beside my legal spouse, who's snoring nicely."

Hutch said "Good" and felt he meant it.

Straw said "Wade" — more a hope than a question.

"Wade's about where he was when we talked last."

"Would he know me if he saw me?"

"Pretty surely," Hutch said. "For part of the time; he still goes and comes."

"Then I'll be there soon." Straw had never been prone to guilt; for once, he sounded caught out and sorry.

"How about tomorrow? Come spend the night anyhow." Hutch knew that Straw had the countryman's aversion to spending a full night away from his groundings; he'd never spent a night in Hutch's Durham house.

"I'll do it soon but, no, it can't be tomorrow."

"You busy watching weeds grow?"

Straw's wait was so long Hutch thought he'd hung up or drifted to sleep. Finally he said "I'm drunk at the moment. Been drunk five days. I'll be there when I can face you and Wade."

"You sound clear to me."

Straw laughed. "Cast your mind back through the slow centuries, friend; the pageant of S. Stuart's profligate course — when did you ever hear me sound less than clear as the evening lark at dusk?" By the time he'd reached the end of the sentence, he was more than half serious.

Straw Stuart, soused, was several notches clearer than the average air traffic controller; and Hutch well knew it. "Then come on here. I've weaned you before."

"You weaned me from you — that's absolutely all. No, I'm tapering off my usual way, a half pint less a day. I don't want Wade to smell a drop on me; he never has yet."

That instant, Hutch felt painfully single. *I can't see this thing through alone.* He could think of nobody else alive, since Grainger was ancient and Ann disqualified, whom he'd trust to watch Wade's last days with him. But he also knew Straw meant what he'd said—Straw had always kept his drinking from Wade. Even in the worst times, twenty years ago, the surest way to sober Straw was to tell him young Wade was on the way up for a few country days (Wade had literally never seen Straw high, much less drunk). So now Hutch only said "Hurry please. Wade's all but gone. I'm running out of guts."

"You're not and you know it. You watched your father die, hard as this; and you helped him right through."

Hutch said "Not so, old friend. I watched Rob, sure, for a few long days just before he went; but even lung cancer's a moonlight walk compared to Wade's plague."

"You mentioned—who was it?—young Jimmy Boat awhile back. He seemed like a truly old-fashioned gem. Is he still coming down from New York for the Fourth?"

Hutch had forgot the letter from Boat; the thought encouraged him. "Boatie wasn't really young and anyhow the Fourth is still a good while off."

"Call him up. Speed his plans. You could put him on salary as long as you need him."

"Straw, Boatie's got his hands full up there."

"Boat's taking the Fourth off somehow—remember?—to bus himself to—where?—Macon, Georgia and his old grandmammy in her cabin in the cotton. Call him tonight and tell him you'll pay his substitute to work a while longer if he'll help you out."

"Did Boatie say he'd arranged a substitute?"

Straw said "Bound to. He's an angel of God; wouldn't leave his boys to starve alone."

"You got his number then?"

Again Straw lingered as if paging slowly through a universal phone book. At last he said "You do, in that book you brought from Wade's kitchen—Ivory wrote all the numbers down there in the back."

So she had. And Hutch had not called one, not since New York. He'd barely ever cracked the book open; it threatened to unleash its piece of the past. But even before he finished with Straw now, he reached for the lamp on his bedside table. The clock said twenty minutes to one. *No, Boatie works hard; let him sleep till day.*

34

Still Hutch couldn't wait. When he'd hung up on Straw and gone to Wade's door to check on his breathing, Hutch went to the study, found the composition book and Jimmy Boat's name with a number beside it. After eight rings Hutch was ready to quit.

Then a woman said "*All* right," an old black voice more native to here than the heights of Harlem.

She repeated herself before Hutch could ask for Boatie or Boat.

"Nobody named that."

"Is Jimmy Boat there, please ma'm?—I'm sorry."

The woman said "Man, I'm sicker than you'll ever know, to get woke up here, dark as this place is; but hold your water, I'll try to get James."

It took three minutes and Hutch would have quit except for the fact that, right through the wait, he could hear the old woman shuffling through rooms and muttering sentences to what seemed cats or maybe dogs named Arthur and Pepper before she finally knocked at a door and said "James, some sick man in trouble out here."

Eventually James picked up the phone. "Boatie's awake. Can he help you please?"

The way Hutch felt, few questions could have been more welcome. "Boatie, this is Wade Mayfield's father—Hutch Mayfield—in North Carolina. Wade was Wyatt Bondurant's friend, remember?"

"Mr. Mayfield, sure. And Wade—Wade's on my mind every other second." Boat felt a reflex moment of cheer before it dawned on him that Hutch's news could hardly be good. So he rushed to say "Jesus, say it's not so."

"No, it's not, not yet. Not tonight anyhow. But we need you, Jimmy."

"Well, I'm hoping to see you—like I said—round the Fourth of July. That still sound good?"

"What would sound like manna from heaven tonight would be you saying you could fly down here tomorrow morning. I'd make all the plans, make it well worth your while."

Boat seemed to be considering the plea.

Behind him the old woman cranked up again with cries at her cats and loud swats with what seemed like an old slapstick.

Then Boat said "Mr. Mayfield, excuse my aunt; she's crazy as me. Fact is, we're no kin on Earth; but she took me in when I was a raw kid up from Georgia with no more sense than to know I should *run* from where I'd been. She'd fold now without me—eighty-six years old. And don't you know I got men up here counting on me, by the hour and minute, for air to breathe? I can't cut loose. These boys up here would strangle alone, and then I could never forgive myself."

The voice was mild and stripped of the blackface-comic growl it had by day, but Hutch felt a sting of shame. *Marse Hutchins givin his orders to de hands.* "I understand that," he said. "Forgive me, Jimmy."

Boat said "No sooner said than done. But listen, you haven't got no help at all?"

It felt like a dead-right diagnosis. *No help, no. Not a soul I truly want, anywhere near me.* Hutch's throat dried on him; but finally he said "I'll get by, sure. I was just feeling sorry for myself in the night."

"Every reason on this wide Earth to feel sorry. Go on and bawl, sir; I'll sit till you're through."

The thought of Jimmy—the size of a jockey—waiting through long-distance tears in a room with a cracked old aunt and her stray cats was a palpable relief. Hutch said "I'll try to spare you tears. Truly though, if whoever's spelling you in early July can help awhile longer, I'll gladly pay him for all his time so you can stay longer with Wade and me. Of course I'll pay you too." Even laid out meekly, it sounded too grand. "Jimmy, help me—I sound so goddamned rich. I'm not, not in *nothing.*" Hutch had never confessed that much bankruptcy to anyone before.

Boat said "Course you're not. Everybody's broke now, everybody I know or want to know till this nightmare's over."

"Say it's a dream, yes."

"Child, I wish I could." Boat heard himself and said "Mr. Mayfield."

"*Hutch,* please—just Hutch."

"All right, sir, next time I see your face. But is Wade failing fast?"

"I wrote you he had pneumonia again. He's back home from that and barely holding his own. His throat has got patches of yeast infection the size of half dollars. Just this morning an apparently healthy tooth simply dropped from his jaw and he swallowed it. His hair's lost color till it's nearly transparent and breaks at the touch."

Boat took that in, old news but still stunning. "His eyes all gone?"

"Afraid so, yes—his eyes and his mind. He drifts in and out. He'll know you though. He asks about you several times a day."

Boat said "Then tell him to hold on for me. I'm coming if God gives me strength to travel, and I love him good as ever—don't fail to say that. Tell him Boat says Wade Mayfield *deserves* it—all the love in the world. I truly mean my words."

"Will you call me collect the minute you've got your travel plans?"

"Guaranteed, sir. You'll be the first to know."

Hutch said "I don't think we've got much time."

"Course not," Boat said. "Not one of us has." But then he managed to laugh and whisper "I wish you could see my poor aunt now, here reading scripture to these wild cats—she thinks they'll talk any minute, quote the Bible. They're learning too; they're calling my name! Don't never wake her up again this late!"

"Please tell her I'm sorry."

"Mr. Mayfield, everybody alive is as sorry as you and me and Wade, or they ought to be."

Hutch said "I believe you."

35

All that was toward the end of June. Then the days geared down for the coming swelter of July; and when its humid hand clamped down, Wade had very nearly vanished. Confined full-time in the chill clammy house, he now had no flesh left to lose. What coated the awful rack of his bones, that had once been the armature of such welcome beauty, was more like a thin glove leather than skin. He never left bed except in the arms of his father or Maitland; he slept through most days and all of each night in a frail fast dreaming that juddered in his eyelids; and when he woke, he swung from minutes of perfect clarity—recalling his whole life in close detail—to hours of serene but unreadable confusion and long paragraphs of speech in a language unknown since Babel.

For Hutch the single blessing of the time was that he, with help from Mait and Ann and occasional generous visits from the doctor, was able to fill Wade's apparent needs. Hutch gave the medicines, replenished the intravenous nourishments, held urinals and bedpans, emptied and washed them, and fitted the oxygen tubes to Wade's face when his breathing slackened to inaudible wisps. Hutch bathed Wade's skin with the lightest touch each morning and every time Wade fouled himself—less often since there was so little of him and such slim waste to flush through his bore. Hutch sat at the bedside, long parts of each day and much of the night, to answer Wade's deranged requests, his fears and outcries of weak delight, and to tend his remains with the deference due any agonized loved one.

Often Hutch would read aloud from old anthologies of verse—the Greek anthology (its epitaphs for a world of lost boys), the silver Roman poets of friendship and loosely worn love and the splendors Hutch could tap at will from Britain's inexplicably long run of genius (Elizabethan, Jacobean, Metaphysical, Augustan, Romantic, Victorian, Modernist) on down through America's Whitman, Dickinson, Robinson, Frost and Elizabeth Bishop. One afternoon, when he thought Wade was sleeping, Hutch read out—for his own lost sake—Bishop's villanelle on the death of her longtime companion Lota Soares, a suicide.

> "The art of losing isn't hard to master;
> so many things seem filled with the intent
> to be lost that their loss is no disaster.
>
> Lose something every day. Accept the fluster
> of lost door keys, the hour badly spent.
> The art of losing isn't hard to master.
>
> Then practice losing farther, losing faster:
> places, and names, and where it was you meant
> to travel. None of these will bring disaster.
>
> I lost my mother's watch. And look! my last, or
> next-to-last, of three loved houses went.
> The art of losing isn't hard to master.
>
> I lost two cities, lovely ones. And, vaster,
> some realms I owned, two rivers, a continent.
> I miss them, but it wasn't a disaster.
>
> —Even losing you (the joking voice, a gesture
> I love) I shan't have lied—"

Hutch had got that far, barely whispering not to wake Wade; but at the word *lied*, Wade's voice came alive and said the final lines from memory with all the remains of strength he had.

> "—Even losing you (the joking voice, a gesture
> I love) I shan't have lied. It's evident
> the art of losing's not too hard to master
> though it may look like (*Write* it!) like disaster."

It was a poem they'd never recited together, published after they'd stopped their bedtime poems; and Hutch was amazed that Wade had learned, on his own, a poem that meant as much to Hutch as any published in the past fifty years, since Eliot's *Quartets*. But once Wade said the final line, he sank back into what seemed a deep trance, maybe something deeper; so Hutch couldn't ask him how and where he'd found the poem and why he'd learned it. *What's the worst loss he's known? Losing Wyatt, or his home and us, or his body and life here now by the inch?* Lately Hutch had managed to invent quick snatches of prayer he could say with no embarrassment, though with next to no hope. So here by his son, he silently said again *Take Wade this instant.*

But Wade breathed on.

36

Then on the Friday before the Fourth, in the midst of a suddenly cool afternoon, Hutch was in his own room for a rest when he heard a car stop near the house and slow footsteps toward the kitchen door. The steps were much too heavy for Ann, and no one else was expected to call. *Some homicidal kid out to steal TVs. Let him on in, sure.* For a minute the thought seemed serious—a young crazed killer would simplify things. Hutch got up, quickly brushed his hair and went toward the kitchen to meet whomever.

Straw was standing on the back porch, facing the hill and the natural terraces of pine and juniper and honeysuckle thicket that rose toward the crest and its unblocked view of more green miles. There'd been no word from Straw since the phone call, no sign he'd tapered off from his binge, no apparent interest in Wade.

So the sight of Straw was not really welcome. Hutch thought of hiding—all doors were locked; he could crawl to his own room and ride out the visit. He even got as far out of sight as the windowless hall and waited for the knock. But no knock came. Maybe five minutes passed and still no knock.

By then Hutch was thinking of Straw as more threatening than any housebreaker. *What's he after? He'll somehow burn the place down*—not remotely sane thoughts but they came nonetheless. *Where is he this moment?* Hutch went back then and opened the kitchen door.

No one in sight, though Straw's car was still there. Hutch called out "Strawson—"

Nothing, no reply.

Hutch stepped out and walked around the whole house.

Nothing still.

Is he up in the woods? Hutch estimated that had to be it, but he couldn't leave Wade long enough to check. He went back indoors and tried to proof-read the typescript of his recent poems, with very slim luck. None was more recent than the one for Straw, written months ago; and they all felt feeble with repetition of his own trademarks and his disconnection, for criminally long, from the brutal present.

It was past four o'clock when Hutch finally heard a tap at the front door. By then he was more than ready to answer; and there was Straw, unshaven, gray-faced and looking years older than when Wade had visited Grainger in May. Hutch said "What's wrong?"

Straw said nothing but stood facing Hutch, looking for a while as if he couldn't speak.

Some kind of stroke? Hutch reached for Straw's arm and drew him inward.

In the dim hallway Straw drew two long breaths, as if he'd run a hard race to get here. Then he bent at the waist and laid the palms of both hands on the floor—he was still that supple.

Hutch said "Your *joints* work at least—"

"Every goddamned thing on me works, and in spades." Straw faced Hutch and grinned. "That's the awful thing."

Hutch could smell Straw's breath—no trace of liquor. "You been on a nature hike?" When Straw looked baffled, Hutch said "My woods—you took a long walk." His tone was edgy with the threat of impatience.

Straw ignored the swipe. "It's *all* nature, Hutch, everything I do—all natural as humping. But yes, you could call this a nature trip."

Hutch motioned to Wade's open door and signed that they should lower their voices.

"Is Wade asleep?"

"Most of the time. He'll want to see you though." *But aren't you half drunk?* Hutch stepped forward to where he'd smell the bourbon if Straw had had a drink today. *No smell at all.*

Straw said "I doubt Wade ought to see me."

Neither one of them had heard himself use the word *see*. But Hutch said "You're sober. What's on your mind?" Whyever, it was plain that Straw was far off his stride.

Straw turned and led the way to the kitchen.

Then only when they'd each drunk swallows of coffee, ten minutes later, did Straw speak again—nearly whispering now. "You remember Charlotte Arm-field?"

"Afraid not, no."

"The girl that owned the wolf—from Virginia, right after you got back from England. Recall her?—tall, stunning girl, eyes that could fell you at two hundred yards."

Hutch said "Fell *you*." But then he recalled the wolf at least, only a small cub yet already fitted with the gimlet eyes that were meant to see him through a lifetime of killing every morsel he ate. "I remember the wolf but not the owner. Weren't you and I at that steakhouse in Roanoke, and didn't the manager make one try to evict the wolf and then beat retreat when it stared him down?"

"You got it—Roanoke. And Charlotte was there. I spent a lot of nights beside her that summer. She asked me to save her from a fate worse than death—something to do with her awful father: all hands and assorted appendages. I let her give me the wolf and walked out like the virtuous gent I was in those days. You recall those days—"

Hutch remembered Straw bringing the wolf to the old Kendal place as a Christmas gift to Grainger. Hadn't Grainger set him free in the woods in a matter of days? "Where's Charlotte these days?"

Straw turned to the window.

"You seen her lately?"

"All of last night, just up the road." Straw pointed west, the germ of a smile at the edge of his mouth.

"She live in Durham?"

Straw said "Pittsburgh. She's visiting her daughter, a Latin professor at Chapel Hill."

"Charlotte called you up after—what, thirty years since you walked out on her?"

By then Straw had decided to tell it; he faced Hutch again and laid it out. "Charlotte called me at home yesterday morning. Emily was outside, digging up weeds; I was reading *Nostromo*—the final book on that reading list you gave me last fall—and I just tried to ignore the phone. It finally stopped but rang again at once; so I thought it might be you, needing help with Wade. I hadn't heard Charlotte's voice in—right, thirty years: more like thirty-five. Soon as she said my full name though, I knew her and saw her. Even on the phone, keen as ever, I could see her face and her whole long body; and I wanted to hold her. She said she'd found me through Information and was calling on a hunch—she'd be at her daughter's in Chapel Hill for another two days, any chance we could talk? I told her I'd get to her somehow by dark."

From Wade's room there came a high yip like a dog's.

Straw watched Hutch wait for a second call; but when none came, Hutch said "You're referring to dark yesterday?"

Straw nodded. "And I kept the promise. I told Em and Grainger I was coming to you and Wade; I'd see them by bedtime. The minute I laid eyes on Charlotte though, and realized she was just baby-sitting her daughter's parrot while the daughter left town, I suspected I wouldn't head home for a while."

A taste of rot was spreading in Hutch's mouth, yet he felt compelled to know the whole story. "She looks that good still; she's what—fifty-six?"

"Fifty-seven going on thirty-five. She looks like she's slept inside clear amber every night since I saw her. She never was exactly beautiful—was she?—more like haunting, with those slate eyes that never shut and that amazing mouth. They're strong as ever, and everything else that mattered about her is with her still."

"So you spent the night?" It was not said harshly. With Wade down the hall as light as a locust—a locust in flames—Hutch hardly cared where Straw laid his head.

"As a matter of fact, I didn't, no. We went to bed, all right, naked as minnows. But those few hours were shocking as hell—I haven't been used like that for years."

"You look a little used—like a car wreck really." The taste of rot was fading in Hutch.

"No complaint, God knows."

Hutch managed to smile. "I trust you took precautions against the lover's plague, for your sake and Emily's if not for Charlotte's."

"I did, thanks for asking."

Hutch said "So you went prepared?"

"As a matter of fact, Charlotte saw to that before she called me." Grim as the details felt, spelled out, Straw's excitement was undiminished. He actually seemed thrust back through time, some thirty-five years—that ready and rising, that eager to fling himself on his sword for an abstract cause: his right to feed his mind and body whatever it craved, and damn the torpedoes.

Hutch had always, and rightly, seen Straw as a sexual mystic. Since boyhood, Straw had always tried to use his body, at every chance, as an instrument of knowledge—the nearest implement any human possesses for truly exploring the limits of knowing his human companions and maybe the angels. Hutch himself had got many powerful signals from the same dark notion—moments and hours with beautiful others in whom he found real ease and reward, whole unexpected islands of knowledge surpassing speech and as unmatched as music—but long ago, for whatever reason, Hutch had agreed to a simpler life than Straw would settle for. So now, facing Straw on fire from his meeting, Hutch could only say "Where've you been between your thrilling night and this dull minute?"

Straw looked as if he'd been struck broadside.

"You said you didn't spend the whole night with Charlotte."

"Did I? I guess not—I left before dawn. But when I tried to aim the car home, it wouldn't go."

Hutch said "Where does Emily think you are?"

"She's guessing as usual." Vicious as it sounded, it wasn't meant to be. Again Straw was speaking from the core of his hunger, a lifelong need that no one person had ever filled—never volunteered to fill. By his own lights, he'd mostly tried to treat others fairly. They were all adults, they'd watched him well before they'd joined him, then they'd chosen to know him and stay beside him, they could only accuse him of so much treason when he turned elsewhere. In fairness he'd always accepted that brand of betrayal from others with slim resentment.

Still Hutch knew what Straw was asking. "I'm guessing you want me to phone Emily for you."

"That had crossed my mind, yes."

"And tell her what?"

Straw said "You're the poet—call up your muse."

That rubbed Hutch wrong. He knew he had no earthly right to judge Straw for cheating. He'd lied for Straw many times in the past; and he'd perpetrated cheats of his own, though never adultery—but the thought of inventing excuses here for one more dingy pelvic cheat collided with the sterile but vehement concentration of his care for Wade. Hutch said "I'll gladly pay for the call, but you do the talking." He pointed to the wall phone three steps away.

For most of a minute, Straw was angry; but in real exhaustion he finally thought his way into Hutch's mind, its scalding white light. Then Straw rose quietly and placed his call.

Hutch was nearly out of the room when he heard Straw say "Grainger?" He paused and looked back.

Straw said to Grainger "Old gentleman, you feeling all right this afternoon?" Apparently the answer was Yes. So the rest of the conversation consisted of asking who Grainger had seen today and whether Emily had fed him on time. Was Emily there with him by any chance? No? In that case Straw would see him by dark. His voice had the sound of saying goodbye; Straw said to Grainger "Say hey to Hutchins" and held the receiver out to Hutch.

Hutch shook his head No and thought *I've never refused Grainger yet, and he'll die any day. Make it up to him soon.*

Straw gave the old man a few more words, hung up and quickly called another number.

Hutch stayed in place in the kitchen door, disgusted to think Straw had left his tawdry errand to Grainger. Emily would come down with Grainger's early supper; the old man would tell her Straw was on his way home.

But the number answered and Straw said "Emily?" Then with few words from Em, Straw begged her pardon for his absence—no explanation, false or true—and said he'd see her well before bedtime.

By then Hutch was half hoping Emily would strike back. It showed in his face.

When Straw hung up, he said "You hate me."

Hutch all but agreed. "Almost."

"Where's your license to hate—hate me anyhow?"

Hutch shook his head at the flagrant nonsense, the foul idiocy of Straw's self-defenses.

But Straw said "You've told me some of your cheats. I don't recall they smelt sweeter than mine. Hell, you dealt your biggest cheat to me, when I'd offered you nothing less than my life. What have I done worse?"

Hutch knew the accurate answer was *Nothing*, but he couldn't say it. He knew Straw deeply believed he'd offered his entire life on the threshold of manhood, and Hutch had refused him. Maybe Straw was right. So Hutch went on watching Straw's disarranged face, baited as it was with remnants of his shine from years ago.

Straw sensed that Hutch was aimed at the past, and a splendid piece of it rose up in him. "Forest Hill," he said. "Remember us at Forest Hill?"

At first Hutch didn't and shook his head No.

"The church where you said John Milton got married to his first wife; the girl that left him straight from the honeymoon, dick in hand—what was her name?"

Hutch said "Mary Powell, age sixteen; John was twice her age. I seem to recall us driving out there, yes." Forest Hill itself was barely a village, a few miles from Oxford on the London road—several low cottages, stands of old trees, a pleasant but undistinguished early church where Milton and Mary had recited their vows, a disastrous union that maimed them both—and, yes, Hutch had driven Straw there in the three days they spent together in England, July '55.

"You don't remember the offer I made?" Straw's eyes were clearing by the moment, firm in the memory they were still seeing.

"I know I've got a snapshot of you, in the churchyard, pouting."

Straw said "Surely a famous American poet can tell the difference between a pout and a bruised damned heart." No one else could have made that sentence sound almost sane.

"We were happy those days, in my mind at least."

Straw said "You refused to take my hand."

"Beg pardon? When?"

"In Forest-damned-Hill that hot afternoon. We had that dim church all to ourselves, you were up by the altar, I came up behind you and reached for your hand, you let me take it for one cool second, then pulled it away."

Hutch thought *This is more than mildly crazy.* "We'd held a lot more than hands, the night before."

Straw said "Amen—I feel every minute still. But in Forest Hill I offered you my time, my whole life to come."

"In the form of a handshake? You were eighteen, friend; your mind and your cheerful cock were headed off in six or eight directions—no hint whatever of a real destination. And I was in no state, psychic or otherwise, to give or take anything or anybody, not anybody that threatened to last." When Straw's eyes heated and fixed Hutch in place, Hutch said "I'm sorry I ignored your gesture."

Straw held stock-still. "Get it *straight*, here now where it's past too late—it was no gesture, Hutchins; no offer to shake hands and pledge blood brotherhood. I *wanted* all of you."

Hutch quickly said "*All* of it would have killed you—it killed Ann Gatlin; it may be killing Wade." At once Hutch thought *What the hell do I mean? I'm crazy as Straw.* But as he watched Straw's face respond to the wild outburst, Hutch understood fully—and for the first time—that, in the raddled mind Straw brought here today, he believed himself. Straw fiercely believed in his right to have borne this mammoth grudge through four decades, minus two years and counting.

Whatever the buried facts of that summer afternoon in '55—lazing through a musty church that had seen John Milton at the pitch of his pride, on the ledge of a fall—Hutch felt he should honor Straw's maddog force: it was scarce as valor, words like *honor* and *valor* and the force they'd once had to shape whole lives. So he said "Old friend, I've loved you as long as anybody breathing. Through the years, I haven't had as much to give as you."

Straw's head ducked gravely. "You're goddamned right."

For a moment Hutch thought *Straw's the lightning rod; I'm just the rain barrel.* It snagged up a laugh from deep in his chest; but in respect to Straw's ravenous heat, Hutch swallowed it down. He thought *I can't use this; get Straw out of here, quick as you can.* Then he turned his back and went toward Wade.

37

Two minutes later Hutch was sitting by Wade, who seemed asleep, when Straw came to the door and stood. Hutch didn't speak or even look back. He was aiming a powerful thought at Straw, a thought that was very nearly an order. *Leave now. I'll call when I'm calm.*

Straw understood but wouldn't leave. He had a strong sudden knowledge that this would be his last sight of Wade. He'd always liked the boy, had always felt at least partly his father; but not till today had he felt that Wade's leaving would tear his own heart, which Straw dreaded tearing. The least he could do here was have some sober last word with the boy. He came forward quietly and whispered to Hutch "Can I wake him a minute?"

Hutch leaned toward Wade; the sleep seemed genuine, though dreamless. In his normal voice Hutch said "All right," then stood and moved toward the door. "I'll leave you. Don't wear him out, don't beg him for pardon, and call me when you leave." Then he went to the study.

Straw stood awhile longer, moving the last few inches to the chair and sitting beside his young friend's bed, among the futile defense equipment of tubes and wires against a death manned by ten billion enemies, visible to nothing but electron microscopes. Straw slowly shifted his mind off the shock of new life he'd got in the hours inside Charlotte's body and her avid mind; and eventually he was reeling back through pictures of Wade from infancy on through late boyhood to the time when Straw had ceased to see him often, the day Wade took his degree at State and headed north.

Straw's own child had given no tangible cause for offense—a pale tall smart girl, now a married woman in suburban Atlanta, certifiably successful, though barren as sand and with less family feeling than most third cousins. Wade had won all hearts from the day he was born, a child with each of his parents' strengths and no great weakness except his constant aim to please every soul around him. After maybe five minutes, Straw actually said, in the lowest whisper, "Take what's left of me and let Wade be." By *be* he meant *live—Let Wade live on past me, years longer. I've had too much; I've used up me and too many others.* Warmed as he'd been by his hours with Charlotte, Straw was intent as any threatened creature longing to last in the wild—the black rhino or the snowy egret. He literally hoped to die in this chair here and set Wade free into new healed life, a calm eternity or pure oblivion.

And Wade's head finally turned toward Strawson. In the past two weeks, since shaves had proved painful and dangerous, the boy had accumulated a beard—short and patchy, as if the hair itself were exhausted, but still a surprise. Now his eyes opened as if they still worked; and when he'd sensed what lay beyond him in reach of his hand, Wade put out his arm and said "Thank God."

Straw took the hand and said "What for?"

Wade had to decide. At last he said "For somebody happy to be here now."

Straw thought at first *You couldn't be wronger;* but as he felt the chill fingers heat in his grasp, he knew Wade was right as he'd mostly been. After they'd got through minutes of silence, joined that closely, Straw finally leaned to kiss Wade's wrist and replace it carefully under the sheet. He told the boy "I recall every *hour,*" and he felt that was true—all their hours at the Kendal place, in the woods and fields, whole years of laughter and ten thousand stories.

When the words were out in the air between them, Straw suddenly hoped for the least hint that Wade had heard him and halfway agreed. But the glazed eyes held on Straw's face, unblinking; and the dry lips were set. Then after a long time the lips said "Minutes. I know all the *minutes*—" Nothing else came.

So at last Straw stood and forced himself to turn his back on the vacant face and its awful eyes. Then he left the house in total silence, without so much as a sign to Hutch, and was gone toward home.

38

On the fifth of July, a blistering Monday, Hutch met Jimmy Boat at the Durham bus station. By then it was past eight o'clock in the evening, and the heat had relented, so Boatie could say as he came down the steps "Ocean *breezes!* This is cooler than Mama's."

Hutch told him not to get his hopes up; they were locked in a drought. But the sturdy refusal of Boat's short body to show discouragement cheered Hutch enough to let him laugh for the first time in days. He made Boat let him carry the suitcase; and all the way to the car, they talked about nothing but Boat's family and the feast they'd offered him yesterday in rooms as hot as any brick kiln.

Since Wade was sleeping at the house with Maitland reading beside him, Hutch took the chance to drive Boat through both halves of Duke campus, locked in their annual chaste summer daze.

Not till they'd passed the chapel tower did Boatie speak of why he was here. He'd talked on the phone with Hutch yesterday, so he felt fairly safe in saying "Our boy bearing up all right?"

"He's been a little stronger all afternoon, I'm glad to say. I honestly think he's waiting for you."

Boat looked to Hutch's face; any trace of the jockey or clown had leached from him. "For me to do what?"

Hutch could only laugh again. "For your kind face."

"He won't see that." Then after they'd left the campus gates, Boat said "You mean he's waiting on me to die, Hutch?" It was the first time Boat had said only *Hutch*, and it didn't feel right.

Hutch said "May be." The chance implied in Boat's last question had not quite dawned on Hutch till he heard it. *Boatie's his last bridge to Wyatt and that world.*

Boat's head moved slowly. "Lord Jesus, again. You know I've been to forty-eight funerals in the years since this thing took real hold—eleven years?" Though he managed to hide it, Boat felt a sudden longing to open the car door and fling himself out, anything now but the fresh sight of Wade after three more months of a pain and wasting more savage than any locust plague in the Bible—a book which Boat read nightly in his narrow room, a room Boat scrubbed on his hands and knees nightly and loveless as any field of chalk.

39

But when they reached Wade, he was propped in bed on a thick nest of pillows; and Mait had shaved him and tamed his long hair.

Boat had learned, in the years of the plague, to freeze his face against the ambush of a person's changed body or the air that clung round him. He'd learned to scent, sharp as any deer, the distant signs of a new assault—bacterial, viral, parasitic—or the inevitable rush to surrender, after years of drawn-out hope and fight, to a matchless foe. Now Boat kept his smile at full white blast as he faced Wade and thought *You can't weigh eighty pounds.* He saw right off that Wade had passed through the narrows at least toward the broader water that would be his death soon, and the first thing he said was "If you get any handsomer, baby, I'll call the cops." In a strange way, he meant it.

Boat's voice and the crisp charge of his attention reached Wade quicker than most things lately. In under five seconds he also grinned. "I'm out of the running, I lost the bikini competition, save the public funds."

Boat said "Naw, boy. You're too hot to handle—Mr. America in Technicolor!"

Wade said "I've settled for the Mr. Congeniality prize." His hand pointed to the bedside chair where Mait was sitting.

Mait stood at once and Hutch introduced him to Boat. Mait said "Boatie, sit here. It's the best seat we've got."

Boat said "Keep your place. I been sitting all day. Anyhow I need to hug this child." He went to Wade, touched the dry hair lightly, then bent to his forehead and kissed him there. Boat glanced back and—quick, while no one saw him—he made a short sign of the cross on Wade, where his lips had touched the disappearing child.

As Boat leaned back, Wade said "You scared to kiss my mouth?"

Boat understood at once. "Come on—you know me better than that. I just didn't want to be overfamiliar after so long apart and give you all my big-city germs."

Wade looked like Death on his cold white horse, but he said "Nobody's kissed me head-on since I left New York."

Hutch knew it was true and felt rebuked.

Boat bent again, with no hesitation, and met Wade's thin lips—dry as clean cloth.

Wade said "Many thanks."

"My pleasure, all mine." Boat took the chair then and laid a hand on the bone of Wade's arm. "Tell me all the trash you seen since you left me. I'm starving for news."

Mait and Hutchins left him there.

40

It didn't seem strange to Hutch that—once Wade fell asleep and he and Mait fed soup and sandwiches to Boat, who was finally showing hunger from his trip—Boat said "You mind if I sleep in yonder with Wade?"

Hutch thought Boat meant to sleep in Wade's bed with him; even then he could think of no objection except the chance that a healthy body might bruise or break Wade, but he said "If you think that can help him any—it's not a wide bed."

Boat could hear, in just those words, that Hutch had watched this death too closely; he was losing grip. What Boat had meant was a cot or a pallet beside Wade's bed.

And there was an antique folding cot. Hutch and Mait brought it up from the cellar, opened it in the kitchen to check for mice or flying squirrels' nests, found it clean and dry, and rolled it into Wade's room where Boat insisted on fitting it out with the sheets Hutch gave him—Wade had long since drifted off.

That got them to nearly eleven at night; and though Boat was plainly tired from his trip, Hutch offered him and Mait a drink. So the three men sat in Hutch's study and drank small quantities of good apple brandy, atom by atom, making it last. They were that slowed down by the weight and heft of oncoming death which was pressing now at all the boundaries of the house and at every window. There was no sense of fear or dread in anyone, only the mild hope to huddle down with reliable friends and see death work its final will.

Exhausted as he was, between sips of brandy, Boat went on responding with pleased surprise to this or that picture on the walls or the odd arresting object nearby—an ostrich egg brought from Africa by a cracked old missionary woman Hutch had known in boyhood, a framed lock of what claimed to be Thomas Jefferson's hair (given to Hutch by a student years back, a red-haired boy who was Jefferson's great-great-great blood nephew); a brass bugle that had sounded taps in France on November 11th, 1918 (a gift from Grainger, who'd blown the call for his own black contingent and could guarantee it). Boat touched, then stood before each object as if each one were giving off rays—invisible power he could feel but not see. Wherever it came from, Boat sensed it was good; so he let it flow through him, hoping it had some strength to give, some guidance in moving this house toward its end.

Watching Boat stand in such mute patience deepened Hutch's trust in the small burdened man. All Hutch's life he'd noticed with puzzlement the fact that ninety-eight percent of his visitors never gave a moment's attention to any man-made or natural thing in the house. They were not only legally blind, like most Americans in a swarming television-blinded century; they were likewise trapped in the tunnel vision of self-absorption or were swaddled to the ears in the devastatingly barren legacy of a puritanism that refuses all worldly pleasures to the eye, not to speak of the mind or the lonely body.

When the three men had gone for ten minutes more with very few words, Boat walked a straight line toward the mantel. Most of the rocks Hutch had gathered through life were laid out there in long months of dust—flint arrowheads he'd found in childhood at the old Kendal place, an almost perfect Indian axe-head Grainger had found when he dredged out the creek, a stained shard of marble from the days Hutch spent with Ann in Rome when she met him there on his first Oxford Christmas; and a flat white pebble from the town of Capernaum on the northern shore of the Sea of Galilee, Simon Peter's home.

What Boat picked up though and held toward the light was something

Hutch had almost forgot. A primitive carving in thick pinebark five inches long. It was all Hutch had of his great-grandfather, old Robinson Mayfield, the family starveling who'd consumed so many lives, white and black. Well over a century ago, Rob had whittled it brutally into the rudimentary shape of a man and had hung in its crotch, on stiff copper wire, a half-inch cock you could flip up or down. (Polly had persuaded old Rob to remove the prong; Hutch had restored its full flagrance, in his childhood, when Polly gave it to him.)

Boat worked the toy cock up and down twice, then shook his head. "One piece of skin has killed all my boys."

Hutch smiled bleakly and agreed.

But it struck Mait wrong—a small attack on his own person; the choice his body had made, whenever. He said "Skin is mainly what's killed men always. And women have certainly used theirs for harm."

When Boat looked embarrassed, Hutch defended him calmly. "I don't think Boatie's indulging in blame, Mait. That's just an old carving an ancestor made—my great-grandfather. He all but killed four or five of my kinsmen with the works of his cock—the acts it led him to anyhow. Nothing new about that—right—but don't take it personally."

Boat set down the carved man and came to his chair. "Some nights I get back to my room late, after spending fifteen hours or more with boys that are dying in shit and shame just because they ran their cock into one wrong socket or got run into; and all I can think to pray is 'Lord, let people just cool off from here out; let em stop hunting skin like skin is *coal* or oil for their fire.'"

Hutch accepted that, then turned to placate Maitland. "Mait, this hard time is not really new. Sex has been part-time lethal almost always, especially to artists. Syphilis alone killed half the best male writers, composers and painters of the nineteenth century." It was not quite true, but it rang true enough for Hutch to brace it with a partial roll of the actual names. "Maybe Beethoven—that's not quite certain. But definitely Schubert, Donizetti, Flaubert, Schumann, Verlaine, De Maupassant, Wilde, Nietzsche, Van Gogh (whom it drove to crazed suicide), Gauguin, Hugo Wolf and a whole slew more, including Rimbaud almost surely, Scott Joplin, the female Isak Dinesen, and that great painter in gore—Al Capone.

"Just lately here I read in the *Times* where they've found the remains of syphilitic skeletons thousands of years old in the Middle East, so Columbus didn't invent it at all. No, the simple act of rubbing your joy knob—to make more babies or soothe your mind—has always been subject to slow awful death. Sometime in the next decade or so, we may well find a treatment at least for this latest plague, then we'll pull out the old skin throttle again and go at it hard; then eventually—when our poor successors expect it least—death'll stalk back in through somebody's cock."

"Or cunt," Mait said.

"Not mine," Boat said. "I'm the first male Afro-American *nun*."

Mait said "I know I'll die of it too."

Hutch and Boat looked toward him, in real surprise.

Boat leaned to lay his hand on Mait's mouth. "Take it back while you can."

But Mait shook his head free. "I know it, that's all. It's in my bones. I can't use myself and love anybody else without this plague slamming in on me soon."

Hutch said "Mait, it's not that easy to catch. You're taking precautions, right?"

Mait said "Not really. Oh condoms, sure, and spermicidal jelly; but Jesus, who can even think about love—not to mention pleasure—when you've got to suit up like an astronaut on a poisoned planet?"

Boat said "Then you're right, if that's how you're thinking. You'll go soon, child." He put both hands up over his eyes. "Don't ask me to watch. Don't let me even get to *know* you, not if you're bound to die like a fool on a window ledge."

Even Hutch agreed.

They all sat a moment, then abruptly Mait stood. "I better go then."

Neither Boat nor Hutch could find the will to stop anybody who was that bound to die.

Mait stopped at Wade's door to say good night—Wade was deep asleep—so he was actually out on the front stoop before Hutch caught up and hugged him close. "You're the best young writer I've known for a long time. Even better, you're a good human being, Mait. You need to last; I need you to last."

Mait stepped back and thanked him, but the smile was false; and for the first time in Hutch's presence, the boy's face bore a trace of hot despisal.

41

It was one in the morning before Hutch was in his room, ready for bed. He'd seen that Boat had all he needed and thanked him again for being here; they'd quietly checked the sleeping Wade and smoothed his covers. Then they'd signed good night to one another, though no doors would be shut between them. So Hutch was mildly startled when he threw his own covers back and suddenly noticed Boat there on his doorsill. "Whoa, man, you scared me."

"I scare nice people everywhere I go." Boat was barely joking; he knew that his dark knotty face, his short bow-legs had either scared or tickled strangers from the day he was old enough to walk outdoors and meet the public.

Hutch could see that his guest's eyes were wide awake and troubled. "Something on your mind?"

Boat's head shook. "I know Wade's not a praying man; but you are, aren't you—being such a big poet?"

Hutch smiled and sat on the edge of his bed. "Oh sure, I pray several times a day—more often than that, with Wade on board—but I don't claim to know God's full name. I don't offer guarantees he hears anybody."

"You a Catholic, I bet."

There were several Byzantine icons in the house, an ivory Spanish Corpus Christi on the wall by Hutch's bed; but he said "No, I neglect my soul. I never found a church that didn't turn my stomach."

Boat agreed. "Me too. Oh I got drug to the Methodist church with my grandmama two times every Sunday; but once my body struck out on its own, all I could hear in church was meanness—old women dry as navy beans, old men limp as dishrags and all of them shipping us young ones to Hell for doing what our minds *made* us do."

Tired as he was, Hutch had heard all he needed about sex tonight, sex of whatever brand; and he guessed Boat's was queer. He smiled to try to seal off the subject. "You sure it was your *mind* making you act up? It's time you put that mind to rest."

"It is, I know it—mine and yours. But you got to be the smartest man I ever been near."

Hutch said "Much obliged; you've got the wrong man. I'm your average jackass."

Boat shut his eyes tight. "Most educated man I'll ever meet, I can swear that to you." When he looked out again, Boat raised his hand to stall Hutch's clear will to send him to bed. "Tired as you are, please answer me one thing. I come all this way for just two things—to see Wade a last time and ask you one question."

So Hutch said "Thank you. Fire away—one shot." He pointed to an easy chair beyond him.

Boat came two steps into the room but stopped in the pool of pale light from a single hanging lamp, centered above them. More than ever, Boat knew he looked like a creature you beat when you're mad, a troll in the one book he'd owned as a child—*Three Billy Goats Gruff.* He nearly laughed, then recovered his bent. "I need you to tell me where Wade and I are bound—in your best opinion."

"Where you and Wade are *bound*?"

Boat nodded deeply. "Which way are we headed, do you think—up or down?"

Hutch guessed, on instinct. "Heaven or Hell?"

"That's the two choices, right?—so far as we know."

"If choices exist at all, maybe so."

"You're bound to believe in God and the Devil." When Hutch kept silent, Boat rushed ahead. "You been watching Wade in all his shit and poisoned blood and pain; you *bound* to believe."

Hutch said "Boat, I'm trying to trust one thing—" His voice failed him there.

"Tell Boat; get it out."

"I'm trying to trust that pain as hard and long as Wade's—pain that I know could crush rocks in the road—leads to something at least a little better than a blackout: numb darkness forever."

Boat's face went hot as any iron stove. "Boat *knows* it does."

Hutch was nearly as serious. "Then tell me how, how you know anyway."

Keeping his distance, Boat searched Hutch's eyes—could he trust this man with his chief secret? He soon saw he could. "Hutch, don't tell a living soul I shared this with you; but see, I talk to Jesus every night—that's how I *know* Wade's bound somewhere better."

"In prayer you mean, you and Jesus in prayer?"

Boat said "Not prayer exactly. See, when this mess started ten years ago, I was scared as most queer boys—scareder than most, praise God on High; so now I'm well while my friends are dead or dying by degrees, black and white together, no prejudice at all. Scared as I was before they found the name of the virus and I tested clean, I got into coming back to my room every night in my old crazy aunt's apartment and scrubbing my skin, my nails and mouth, the soles of my feet and every square inch of the floor in my room. I'd push back my pitiful furniture and mop with Lysol every night. I could *hear* germs dying to left and right; but it wore me out, hard as I worked daytimes.

"So I kept asking God Above to give me a break, let me calm down and take his lead through the trouble, let me trust he'd keep me healthy to lead his miserable boys on into their peace—some few of them anyhow, if he'd accept them. I didn't hear an answer for the longest time, so I kept my job delivering prescriptions for a big drugstore.

"Then maybe two months before they found out the test for AIDS, I was washing my poor floor again one evening—now I scrub it every night of my life—when up in the corner, up in the dim ceiling, this man's voice said to me 'You be my help.' I recognized it was Jesus' voice from the movies I watch on late TV; I never doubted that—he's got a good voice, even deeper than yours. So then when, two nights later, he said 'You help me but first get your own soul free,' I asked him 'Lord, get free of what please?'" Boat stopped in midair, with his voice pitched firm on a clear tenor note. He held there silent for maybe half a minute; then he took another step nearer Hutch, who was half laid back across his wide bed.

When Boat didn't speak again, Hutch said "You think he meant free of being queer? You asking me that—did Jesus mean that?"

"A lot of people say so, left and right—church, TV, radio, nuts and crooks in the gutters and some powerful people I used to respect: bishops, you know; big senators."

Hutch said "A lot of such people claim white is green too, and day is night. Walk down the street, doing your level best to honor the Earth and all its creatures—a fourth of the people will think you're an asset, another fourth will think you're an ass or a rabid felon, the other half won't even know you're there. You can't pay that much attention to people. I seriously doubt that whatever God or force of nature made an infinite universe, with endless zillion stars, cares a lot about the whereabouts of my pee-pee at any given moment, long as I don't rub it on the skin of a child or ram it into someone that's told me plain No."

"You don't see nothing at all wrong with queers?" Boat's whole face expected an answer at last.

So, while he laughed one tense dry note, Hutch had his answer fast. "Nothing deeply special, no; and I tell you that quick since—to be honest, Boat—I've played long innings with fine men's bodies and never felt a trace of guilt, except for occasional stingy meanness that I laid down in other departments besides my cock." Hutch paused to hear how far he'd gone. *Be true; you can't lie to this kind man.* When he faced Boat again, Boat was patiently waiting. "No, Boat, I don't claim to be pope; but I've really never seen anything especially wrong with queers, nothing that's not wrong with everybody else I ever met—self-love, planned cruelty, ignorance and greed."

Boat's head half consented, though his eyes were dubious. "You don't object to us not having kids? Preachers always talking about 'God made Adam and Eve, not Adam and Steve.'"

Hutch quickly thought of his talk with Strawson back in the spring—how with no child between them, they'd have never made a life. He felt the strength of that barrier still. "I strongly suspect that most queer couples run out of ways to feel and act to one another; they're likely to perish for lack of anything else than them*selves* to think of or do for. But think of this too — and tell it out loud to the next flip preacher that lowers his boom on Adam and Steve: I heard the clear fact on the news this morning — 250,000 children were born on the planet Earth just today, these twenty-four hours.

"A great slew of them will die starved or agonized, a scary part of all the survivors will grow into monsters, even the balance of law-abiding citizens will almost surely pollute the planet with their trails of waste and excess kids. No, thank Christ for queers." Hutch could suddenly hear Straw's voice speaking through him, edging him off his old objections. In sight of Boat's near smile though, Hutch recalled one objection that needed making. "I will say this — for the past twenty years or so, queers have been turning way too fundamentalist. Few country Baptists are as shut to the full truth as many young queers — such flaming evangelists."

Again Boat half agreed. "You're saying you got the full truth on your side?" If he meant sarcasm, he'd flushed it from his eyes.

Hutch smiled. "I didn't mean to claim full truth, no — just that I loathe any self-anointed team of two or more humans who claim they're righter than any bystanders in the range of their voice."

Hutch had gone past Boat; and to show he was lost, Boat raised both hands, shut his eyes, sealed his lips and shook his head wide. When he looked again, Hutch was waiting, still and silent. So Boat changed his tack. "See, I search the scriptures fairly steady, most nights. Old Testament gets right rough on the boys; St. Paul throws *fits* every time they come up."

"You notice how Jesus never turns on them once?"

Boat said "You notice too? Why don't people preach that on the TV? — not one word from Jesus anywhere in the Bible where he damns queers."

Hutch had noticed long since. "And he surely knew some — roaming round Palestine with those twelve lonely men, those rich young rulers with big crushes on him and all those clerical lawyers and priests."

Boat wanted to grin but wrestled it back. He also felt an official reluctance to take any views, just because they were white. Yet Boat was held by this talking man who made more sense than he'd dared to hope for.

Hutch said "On the contrary, come to think of it, Jesus may well bless queers by name, in person. Remember where he says 'Some men are born eunuchs, some make themselves eunuchs, and some are made eunuchs for the Kingdom of God'?"

"A eunuch's cut off his own balls, right?"

Hutch laughed. "Cut off? No balls at all." Then bleared as he was, he remembered a song from the Oxford pubs and sang a quick chorus.

> "No balls at all, no balls at all;
> She married a man who had no balls at all."

Boat was frowning by then. He was still in earnest. "I wish more of my boys had cut off *something*."

"No you don't."

"You see Wade dying like a dog in the road. You don't wish he'd of stopped using himself that way with Wyatt?"

Hutch said "No I don't."

"So you think Wade and me got a chance at Heaven yet?"

Hutch saw that he owed this anxious man—an undoubted angel of tireless heart—one serious answer, late as it was and dazed as he felt. He finally said "Boat, if there's any Paradise, with any crystal river, you'll be there in *hip boots*."

"And Wade?"

"You and Wade."

Boat waited. "And Wyatt?"

It took a long moment, but at last Hutch agreed. "I'll let Wyatt argue his own case in Glory."

Boat's face had eased slightly; he'd waved good night again and turned to go, then wheeled around. "What you mean by *hip boots?*"

Hutch laughed. "Nothing special—the word must have poured out of what I feel. Unlikely as it seems, if there's any place where good is repaid, Jimmy Boat, you'll need hip boots just to breast your floods of reward."

"You're not fooling me? I've read less than ten books in my whole life, except for some filth—you wouldn't confuse me?"

Hutch said "I've told you the absolute truth, so far as I can guess it. *Guess* is all I can give you, this late and this beat."

Boat said "I may ask you again in the morning then."

"Help yourself, friend; but morning or night, your host is a fool next to you; and he means it."

Boat couldn't bring himself to thank Hutch for that, but he looked to Hutch with a trace of fear. "You really want to know what I think about all this?"

"I'd be glad to know."

Boat said "I been thinking here lately—God's bound to love queers; he's killing them so fast."

Hutch guessed there was more than a trace of discovery buried in that; he was too beat to pursue it. "You may well be right."

Boat left with that one sentence clear before him. He said it over more

than once to himself till he slept at last on his cot next to Wade. Several times
he replayed Hutch's voice just now, laying out broad calm answers like a banquet, not spilling a morsel; and he thought *Boat, you know as much common
sense as him. Make up your own mind.* Then he'd tell himself *The man
respects me.* Boat was right about that too, as his whole life was right in its
unstinting gift of all he owned and could do with the hands his tireless mind
freely offered to boys in howling need, boys from his native country on
Earth.

42

Well before daylight Wade woke and lay on his back a half hour, silent and
still. He could hear the sound of another creature breathing slowly, off to his
right. Wade had barely registered Boat's arrival, hours ago, or the setting up
of a cot by his bed; and he had no memory at all of who was with him, asleep
at his side. By now his mind was mostly a sheet of clouded glass, an undamaged but thickly frosted window. He understood that much—how the plague
had brought him one kindness at least, a calm blank mind most waking minutes. And though he knew he was safe from external harm, that he had guards
around him, whatever their names, still he wondered who was here with him
this instant.

   And he strained to guess the name and the reason. The main thing he
guessed was, it couldn't be Wyatt; Wyatt was almost certainly gone from
the Earth. *Don't count on it though.* And the sound of the breathing was
too high and easy to come from Hutch—Hutch struggled through sleep
like a distance swimmer. *Maitland maybe?* But Wade couldn't think why
Mait would be here unless Hutch had gone again and not left word. *Ann,
surely Ann.* Wade thought he recalled that his mother was still alive and
strong, though mostly out of sight for some reason he'd long since forgot.
Not Ann then, no. Not Strawson nor Grainger. Not Ivory surely.

   That really left Wade with only one choice, the most unlikely guest of
all—the only one he'd actually wanted. *Wyatt after all. Bound to be. How'd
Wyatt get here?* Despite his blind eyes Wade turned to his right side, careful
not to detach his intravenous needle—he was down to a single needle
tonight. On his side, he was facing the regular sighs that came from maybe
a yard away and—*Christ*—came surely from Wyatt, here.

   Wade forced back a smile and tried to whisper "When did you get in?" The
words came stronger than he intended. *Careful here.* He'd wake Hutch and
start some painful scene—he still recalled Wyatt's scorn of Hutch. So next

Wade only wrote the words out on a scrim in his mind, a nonexistent surface. He and Wyatt had long since reached the point where words could pass between them in silence, intact on the air of a quiet room. *Move closer to me. You won't catch anything you haven't had. I'm safe to hold—easy though; these bones are sharp and every joint aches.*

When no one moved—to come or go—and the sighing breath went on at the same rate, still Wade's hope survived. Wyatt Bondurant was here again, wherever he'd been these last hard months; no one else knew. *He'll see me out of here before day anyhow. Now we can go.* At last Wade allowed himself what felt like a final smile, and in another minute he slept again.

Boat's exhausted trance, not six feet from Wade's skull, never wavered but kept him locked in a dream of swimming and walking deep beneath the surface of a broad stretch of water—a warm lake, clear as any glass, that was secret to all but Boat and his brother who'd died years back: a funny boy named Bloodstone Boat, named after the stone in their mother's ring, a ring that had come her way through the family from a great-grandfather who'd been born a slave in the flooded rice fields of coastal Georgia— fields that were as lost as he today, choked with marsh grass, cottonmouth snakes and the houses of idling doctors and lawyers.

In the dream Bloodstone would swim beside Boatie, then dart ahead out of sight for a while till he'd suddenly come back smiling through the murk and always holding out, as a gift, some precious thing he'd found alone. In the course of the night, Blood offered Boatie numerous seashells made out of silver, broad purple flowers that grew underwater and a palm-sized carving in pure white rock of a child that had to be Wade Mayfield in the days before he'd bowed to his death and all but pared his body to bone.

43

At ten that morning, after Hutch drove into town for supplies, Boat sat down alone by Wade and began to read him one more chapter in a book he'd asked to hear for some reason, Sir Walter Scott's *The Heart of Midlothian*. As always the act of reading soon lulled Boat toward the edge of dozing.

Wade could hear Boat's oncoming torpor, so every few minutes Wade would lift his right arm and say "Please wait."

Boat would wait and, after three waits when Wade asked for nothing, Boat finally said "You need the bedpan, baby?"

Wade's head shook hard and his face went dark as if a great vein had burst in the midst of his stark-white forehead. Then both his eyes focused square on Boat and seemed as clear as they'd ever seemed (Boat would have sworn Wade could see him plainly). At last Wade said "You want to try to persuade me I'll meet Wyatt Bondurant again?"

"No, baby, no. I'm no big preacher."

That helped clear Wade's mind for a moment; he gave a wide smile. "You told me you were a shouting Methodist—passport to Heaven."

"Recall I told you that years ago. What I've seen these past years, baby, I'm flying blind as you, every day."

"Then you're not much of a navigator—" The sentence dissolved in a deeper grin that cut across Wade's face like a slash.

"Never said I was nobody's navigator; won't claim to be neither. I'm just an old boy that empties the slop jars and cheers up his friends."

Wade darkened then. "Christ, man, I'm aiming to get *out* of here. Lend a hand or *leave.*"

Boat sat till he had the start of what might constitute real help. "Baby, I haven't had your education—I quit the eighth grade—so I've missed a lot of the world from not knowing what to look at or what I was seeing if I did look at it. And I didn't know you all that long before you and Wyatt hit onto each other and left me swinging at the north end of Harlem like a cat on a string; but what I've seen you turn into through the past mean years is a lot better man than most I've known, maybe any other man since my brother died when him and me were kids. Bloodstone Boat, his true exact name, was some kind of magic. I miss him every day, sweetest man God made—beside you, like I said. I mean, just the way you set up Ivory and her little child was a lot damned further than my dad went for any of us. Ivory knows it too—I made sure of that, told her nobody I've known has had better luck."

Wade held up his arm again; and when Boat stopped, Wade said "You seen him lately?"

"My dad? No, baby, my dad's long gone to Hell. Thank you, Jesus, for that."

Wade said "—Ivory's child." Then he found the name. "Raven."

"Haven't laid an eye on Miss Ivory's child since she moved him on out to her mother's on the Island. When was it?—five or six years ago."

Any power to gauge the passage of time had left Wade by now. The things he recalled stood separate in his mind, untouching inside the bounds of a narrow hoop in his shot memory, all paler than they'd ever looked in life but stiller as well. Wade tried for a moment to answer Boat—had the boy Raven lived in Manhattan ever? Didn't he go straight to his grandmother once Ivory left the clinic? Or was it months later? But the idea slid like water through Wade's hands and soon was gone. He faced the general direction of

Boat and gave a short lift of his naked chin to whatever Boat had just asked or said.

Boat gathered courage from the sign and eventually felt he had the right to say "Is there anything on this Earth you want me to know while I'm here with you?"

Wade stayed blank.

"Any business you want me to do for you, down here or up yonder, whatever comes next? Any message you got for God or man—I'm a first-rate messenger boy, remember?"

Wade nodded again, then thought through his needs. At last he said "I want you just to remember how Wyatt looked in his prime."

It was not the errand Boat had hoped for. Still he said "That won't be no big problem. I see Wyatt this minute, fine as wine." And he did—young Wyatt, the finest-looking black man he'd ever known, though *black* was not the name for the color of Wyatt's skin: more like some kind of expensive beige cloth with good blood streaming behind it in sunlight, giving the surface a high fast life, like nobody else ever seen on land.

After that Boat gave up asking for more about Ivory's child. And in a while he was more than glad that Wade had stopped him there, for whatever cause. Those questions anyhow were things that Boat would never have asked a stronger Wade—young Wade before this terrible hand struck him broadside in every cell and left him nothing but coated bones with a smoky candle lit in his skull in a wind as hard as any tornado. So in the next minutes, as Wade went quiet, Boat also drifted peacefully off in his straight-backed chair.

At one o'clock when Hutch returned and looked in before sorting groceries in the kitchen, he saw Boat asleep upright in his chair, though Wade was watching him steadily with eyes that still were clear but useless.

44

That evening at half past eight, Hutch and Boat were back in the kitchen, cleaning up after their light supper when the sound of a nearing car broke through their mild but pointless talk. Entirely separate, the two men thought it was Ann Mayfield. Hutch felt annoyed—he was nearly exhausted from the long day and couldn't imagine another round of tilt and shove. Boat felt the slight dread he'd come to expect at the prospect of meeting any white mother of one of his boys—he'd seen so many monsters, nearly ten in ten years.

But when the car showed, out back in the dusk, at first it was strange to Hutch, a deep green color he hadn't seen on a new car in years. This was surely not Ann, but a single woman turned the wheel and stopped. She'd opened the door and taken a step before Hutch remembered the car and the standing woman's outline.

It was Margaret Ives, Wade's chief physician. A tall thin woman—maybe forty-two, black hair to her shoulders—came briskly forward in a lapis blue dress and managed to touch the back door knocker before Hutch opened on her. A wide and all but heart-easing smile broke out as she saw him; it nearly concealed her own bone-tiredness. She hadn't slept in nineteen hours.

Hutch said "Oh welcome. You need a good chair." He hadn't seen her since Wade's pneumonia, though they'd talked on the phone every three or four days. As ever, he scented a whiff of hope in the fact of her nearness— young enough to be his own daughter, still she seemed so patently dauntless. So worthy you'd seek her out in any disaster scene, knowing she'd last and lead you onward.

Her smile endured. "Welcome? Truly? Sure I'm not interrupting?"

Hutch said "Never. We were just drying dishes."

"This is flat rude, I know. I should at least have called you; but I had to drop off a friend's cat farther down the road—I've been cat-sitting the past two weeks, an antique Persian demanding as an empress—so I thought I'd see how you and Wade are faring."

Hutch stood aside and waved her in; then looked for Boat, to introduce him. He'd vanished or fled. So Hutch lowered his voice. "A good friend of Wade's from New York is here; he was Wade's best help in the hard last days— not quite a practical nurse, I guess, but still a godsend. He's in with him now."

Though the smile she'd launched at the door had faded, Margaret's face still literally beamed; some innate unquenchable power worked in her steadily.

Hutch had never quite registered her beauty and its elegance, its veiled but potent strength—even this far from Duke Hospital, she seemed to have damped her fineness quite consciously. *Does she think it's irrelevant or an actual hindrance?* He gestured to a chair at the kitchen table. "We've got some fairly sinful homemade ice cream a neighbor hand cranked—fresh Sand Hill peaches, make your last artery clamp down and die for joy. Let me fix you a dish."

"I just ate, thanks."

"At the hospital?—ugh."

"You're looking at a hardened soul, Mr. Mayfield."

"It's not your soul I'm hoping to feed. And call me Hutch. A drink, some wine?"

Margaret shook her head No. "I need to get back to a patient by dark; but if you think this is not too sudden—too sudden and bald—and if Wade is strong enough, maybe we could ask him a question or two about his own wishes."

With a silent thud like a great fist descending, Hutch understood; but still he said "Wishes?"

Her wide eyes shut for a long two seconds. "For treatment. Last wishes. We both may need to know Wade's intent, when he can't really tell us."

Hutch said "This soon?"

"It's not really soon, if you think about it. I don't know how he's living this minute; he's long past exhausted in every cell. But not if you think it's premature tonight, no. I've just admired Wade's spirit right along; he asked me to see him through to the end with the absolute barest minimum of brakes."

"Did he say 'the *end*'? Did he truly say '*brakes*'?"

Margaret gave it a careful moment's thought. "Those two words, yes."

Hutch said "Then that's all I need to know." He signed for her to precede him toward Wade.

As they moved up the dark hall, well apart, a whippoorwill in the thicket to the east was turning out its manic cry like a stuck organ grinder.

It had taken Hutch a slow ten minutes to introduce Boat, who was deeply abashed near an actual doctor; then to wake Wade carefully and help him know who was here beside him—his father, his New York guest, his doctor.

Wade held his left hand out in the air toward Margaret Ives. "You do me great honor, ma'm."

Margaret took the hand and stroked his forearm. "Your trust honors me, Wade, kind sir." When he stared on at her, with no further words, she said "Please say my name, if you would."

Only silence.

"Wade, I need you to say who I am—"

Hutch longed to coach him but knew that Margaret was working to establish his sanity for the last decisions.

Wade's eyes searched her face as if they were floodlights hunting a killer. Then his lips jerked up in a wild grin. "You're the Queen of Doctors, from the flatlands of Utah."

Margaret stroked his arm again. "Right, the Utah part anyway. Recall my name?"

It turned out he did. "Mag, Meg, Maggie, Margaret. Margaret Ives."

She said "At your service, sir. You've had a fair day?"

In a stage whisper Wade said "Wait right there." Then he waved his right hand out toward Boat; it could barely stir air.

Boat came up and took it.

Wade shut his eyes and held a long moment. "Hutch, aren't you down there near my feet?"

"I am, exactly."

"Then lay your hand on my feet. Please, Father."

Hutch lifted the sheet and obeyed.

Wade held again, with his eyes still shut, till all the others thought he was sleeping. Only when Boat squeezed the right hand a little did Wade look up—at the ceiling, no face—and in one sentence, dispel the weight of dread above them. "The instant I can't draw my own breath, the instant you can't recognize Wade in who I am, then cut me loose—wave me on off."

No hand released him, none of them pressed, and no one answered.

So Wade said "*Swear*—"

In Hutch's head, he could hear the ghost of Hamlet's father compelling Hamlet's balky vengeance. "*Swear, oh swear.*" But Hutch couldn't speak, though Boat's eyes waited.

At last Margaret Ives bent and kissed Wade's arm at the elbow hinge. Her voice said "*Swear.* Every one of us swears. You sleep on that."

Boat said "Amen."

Still amazed that a live American doctor had earned the grace to greet a dying man so closely, Hutch could only go on looking, silent. He knew his own eyes had little time to see even this last shadow of his son.

45

That was the Tuesday after the Fourth. Boat had said he could stay till the Thursday night bus, then would need to head north and resume his duties before another weekend. So with that slight reprieve, Hutch took the chance to leave the house for the long afternoon and do neglected chores in town. He told Boat he'd phone every hour or so; Boat said not to worry—things would likely be fine. To his own surprise by then, Hutch agreed (he hadn't expected ease again till Wade was gone). So he left Ann's office number on the table beside Wade's bed.

And Boat spent the second half of Tuesday cleaning Wade's room and the nearest bath. He'd hoped he could wash all the clothes and maybe cook a few things that Wade could eat. Boat had long since learned how to cook soft foods that some of his sick men, men who'd barely chewed in years, could swallow at least—mostly childhood food: warm, bland, mouth-crowding. But when Boat found that Wade's mother washed the clothes, and Hutch was firmly in place in the kitchen, he chose to fill the only other need he saw.

Wade's room was reasonably clean and neat; but with Hutch's permission, Boat moved the small furniture into the hall, swept the floor quietly, then mixed oil soap with scalding water, got down on his hands and knees and scrubbed the oak boards to an unaccustomed shine. Asking Wade no questions at all, Boat sorted clothes in the jam-packed closet, culling out stacks of mouth-eaten sweaters saved over from grade school and trousers and coats from Wade's college days. With every piece he touched, Boat thought something like *This jacket would look good on poor Sam Butler* or *A sin in this world to leave stuff here while so many creatures are wrapping their sores in stinking rags and walking barefoot.*

As each of his New York boys died off, Boat took every chance to ask the heirs for any old clothes to pass along—the homeless gave him genuine nightmares, the thought that a country rich as America still was throwing people away like old rags and paper. But he knew not to mention such thoughts here. *Never strip the dead; you'll die cold yourself*—he'd heard his grandmother say that when they found an old man cut down by the train one Sunday dawn.

Though Boat had got short glimpses of hope, throughout this plague, that some kind of miracle might intervene—some one boy anyhow might rise up from his bed, healed and whole, to prove some human at least could outlive it; some few might silently die in their sleep, not looking like husks of ancient monkeys—he'd learned to spot the angled glance, the flaky dryness in the hands, the lank brittle hair that meant a boy was ready to die. *Wade's ready. Good Jesus, let him go while I'm here.* With some of his boys, Boat had actually bent to their ear when he saw those signs and whispered permission to let go and leave. He thought he'd wait till late tonight and then give Wade that last encouragement.

But when Boat had finished the floor and closet, when he'd sorted every drawer and shelf and dusted each souvenir of Wade's past, he saw he'd come to the end of his chore and that Wade, who'd slept through most of the day, was awake again.

Wade's eyelids were shut but his breathing was smooth; and once Boat noticed him, Wade put up a hushing finger and beckoned him closer. When Boat had bent almost to his lips, Wade whispered "Much obliged."

Boat whispered "What for? I'm just your old pal."

"For getting me ready."

Boat couldn't deny that. "Baby, I'm not doing nothing for you. I wish I could. But you know that."

Wade's hand found Boat's mouth and muffled it. "One more thing—"

"Name it, anything the Boat can do."

"Bring Mother in here."

Boat had never seen or met Ann Mayfield. All he knew was that Hutch had told him Wade's mother dropped by every day or so with laundry and food, so Boat surmised a local minefield that Ann took only one pathway through. Through all his nursing, he'd run up against a hundred kinds of family trouble—parents who flatly refused to bring a sick son home, some who even refused phone contact; others who'd send no more than checks and only appear after their son died, just in time to confiscate his property, denying his loyal mate so much as recognition. Boat was hardly likely to plow in here and raise the dust. He said to Wade "Your dad'll be here shortly, baby. You tell him you need her."

"I never said that."

"You just *want* her, don't you?"

Wade took awhile to agree to that. Then he persisted. "Tell Hutch you think he ought to call her. Not later than now. Hutch worships you."

Boat laughed and tapped his own brow. "Nobody ever worshiped *this* fool midget."

Wade shook his head hard, and splotches of color came to his cheeks for the first time in days. "My father literally worships black people."

"He's been kind to me—"

Wade's color stayed bright; he was oddly thrilled to find again and say aloud here what he'd always known but never quite faced. "Hutch thinks black people, all bound together, are the angel burning to fuel human time. His words exactly. And wild as it sounds, I think he's part right. I've thought at least that much, since my own childhood. Black people have burned—truly *burned*, I mean, for more than their share of all known history, them and the Jews (though Hutch never knew many Jews as a boy, not here in the South)—but also odd bands of most other people in various ages: brown, yellow, red, white, queer as coots, straight as rails. It's nothing else—is it? all this old history— but a permanent bonfire, maybe a holocaust if that means anything, old at least as human time and somehow the literal oil it takes to turn the big wheel."

"What wheel?"

"Oh the world, like I said. The poor old world. What African country is it today?—every month it's a new little desert or valley where millions of children, gorgeous as ebony carved by saints, are starved to bones or hacked to ribbons in their dead mothers' arms: all burning, burning. For me and you."

The smile that spread on Wade's dry lips was as awful a wound as Boat had seen in all these years. He laid cool fingers on the lips to smooth them, then told Wade "Baby, you rest your mind. No need for you to be this far gone, in this fine house with your own people, not if you'll rest more."

Wade frowned to warn off any break in his frail line of thought. "Hutch tries to convince himself he's a Klansman—see, he let Wyatt ruin his self-respect, when all of us knew Hutch bowed down deep in his mind to every black face he passed."

By now Boat was used to most kinds of dementia. You listened and patted their hand and said Yes. He tried that here.

But Wade's voice hardened. "Listen to *me*."

So Boat tried his next trick, changing the subject or reverting to an old one. "I'm listening, baby, but I'm not God Above. If your folks don't want to be here together, Jimmy Boat can't force them—can't and won't."

In all the years that Boat had known Wade Mayfield, in all the months he'd seen Wade through this hard slow fall and Wyatt's brutal death, he'd never seen the trace of a tear on Wade's face. Boat himself was a regular fountain of tears—he'd weep at television commercials where grown men phoned their fathers on Father's Day—and more than once he'd felt real pity for Wade's refusal or inability to vent his stifling grief.

Now, though, the sockets of Wade's blind eyes were brimming water.

Knowing that even tears could carry the plague virus, still Boat leaned again and wiped at the tears with his bare thumb. He stood back and listened for Hutch's presence—no sound from the kitchen or elsewhere near—so in almost a normal voice, Boat said "Oh baby, I'll ask him someway or other between here and dark. Maybe your mother will even drop in."

Wade waved away the thought of any drop-in. He said "*Tell* Hutch. Get Mother back here tonight. I'm ready to go."

Standing that near a face as wild as Wade's, Boat thought *This boy can still do a good many things but no way left for him to stand up and call his mother in here for the final end.* And all he could think to tell Wade here was that, yes, Jimmy Boat would find a chance to relay the message between this minute and tonight someway.

46

At seven o'clock though, Hutch was still in town; and Ann stopped in on her way home. By then Wade had been asleep for hours. Boat had long since finished his cleaning and was in the kitchen, making rice pudding and vanilla milk junket when Ann let herself in through the back door. She'd known that a helpful friend of Wade's would be there from New York, but she'd never met Boat and was startled to find a tiny black man busy at the stove. She thought she managed to cover her fear and at once went toward him, extending her hand. "I'm Wade's mother, Ann."

Boat had seen her clearly from the moment she left her car, walking toward him; so while he seldom thought of himself as the kind of black man always harping on how white folks have ruined the world and him in particular, he went a little cold and reached for a dish towel to hold in his hand. That would ease this rich-looking woman right off—him being an old-time kitchen boy. Still her sudden smile and hand were unexpected. Boat put down the towel, accepted her hand and said "I'd have known your face on Mars or in Panama." The moment he spoke, Boat thought *Crazy fool*—he'd seen Panama in his navy years.

Ann went on smiling; she well knew how much Wade was like her. "Mr. Boat, I don't think we can ever thank you."

Boat wondered who she meant by *we*. He'd gathered that she and Hutch were as far apart as parents get. *She means her and Wade.* So he told her "Wade's been good to me ever since we met long years ago. If I didn't have my duties up north, I'd be his main help."

"I know you would." A quick look showed Ann what Boat was cooking. "That rice pudding smell takes me back a long way. I hope Wade can eat it."

"No doubt about that. I fixed it for him up in New York every chance I got. He loves the raisins mainly." Boat pointed north as if the city were closing on them and would be here soon.

Ann had long since forgot Wade's childhood love of raisins. She'd tried every other food she could think of and failed to rouse Wade's appetite, and now Boat's memory rebuked her own, but she didn't say she doubted Boat's chances. She said "Is Wade sleeping?"

"Last time I looked. He's barely been awake all today."

"I'll just tip in then and get his laundry."

Boat pointed again, toward the washing machine and dryer in the pantry. "Every stitch is clean." Ann's face looked so forlorn to hear it—he wished he'd thought to save her a chore. "The dryer just finished; clothes'll still be warm—you can fold them easy."

She washed her hands at the sink and went to sort Wade's clothes. Only at the door of the pantry did she look back. "Is Hutch all right?"

Boat said "As all right as any of us can be in these mean days. He's in town catching up on things. Called and said he'd be back soon as they changed his oil at the shop."

For Ann that sounded like a short reprieve. To her own surprise she folded a few of Wade's white briefs and a green T-shirt, then came to the door and said to Boat "You understand I want to be here?"

By then Boat was seated at the worktable, reading a story in *TV Guide.* "Yes ma'm, I do."

Ann managed a slight smile. "No *ma'm*—please, sir. I answer to *Ann.*"

Boat smiled and agreed.

"The reason I moved out of here had nothing to do with Wade."

"I doubt he knows that. He wants you back. Told me so just now."

Ann took a long wait. "That means he's near to—"

Boat said "It mostly means that. I've seen it a lot, even when their mothers have shut them off. I've seen boys' natural parents shut them off like rats in the walls; slam the door in their face and them as harmless as day-old pups, just needing attention—"

Ann said "Do you understand Wade's father has made me keep this distance, ever since he was home?"

"Mrs. Mayfield, I can't touch your business—Mr. Hutch's and yours. All I know is, Wade wants you. When he told me this afternoon, it burned me bad. I couldn't see a way."

Ann's face was wan in the late sun that broke through the windows beyond her, but it also looked remarkably young and as strong as she'd ever been. With Wade's green shirt still warm in her hands, she came halfway back toward Boat's chair and told him plainly "Hutch'll have to call the Law to make me leave here tonight."

Boat thought *The mothers, even the monsters, always smell death coming first.* But he said "No way Hutch'll do that much."

Ann said "We'll never know till we test him." When Boat was quiet, she said "Will we now?"

"Let me say it one more time, polite as I can—this is your business, lady. Don't make trouble for me. I'm just here to be an invited guest."

Ann said "You claimed you were here to help Wade—"

"I wish to God I was. If you'd seen that sad boy today, you'd know nobody in this weak world got help for him—not where he's at."

Ann's eyes flared up. "What a thing to say—"

Boat stood in place and shut his magazine. *Leave out of here, Boatie. Call a taxi and run.*

But as distant-sounding as if it came by satellite, Wade's voice called out a long high "Ann?"

She held in place, still facing Boat.

Wade called again. "I heard my mother's voice."

When Ann held still another slow moment, Boat called "You did. She's on her way, baby." When he finally faced Ann, he said "All yours. Go fix him please."

That broke the lock on Ann's last restraint. She laid the green T-shirt near Boat's elbow, smoothed it carefully, then said "I'm sorry. I'm not my best self."

"Few of us ever is." Boat reached for the green shirt, opened it out and folded it again—a neater job.

So Ann went toward Wade, whoever he'd be when she got there.

47

When Hutch phoned again a few minutes later to say his car was finally ready and he'd be home soon, Boat answered in the kitchen, said things were steady but didn't mention Ann's presence. She'd stayed on in Wade's room. Boat had heard no words or moves; so when Hutch came in through the kitchen door, the house was still. Boat was reading *The Farmer's Almanac* in a chair by the table and copying down the full-moon schedule for the rest of the year.

Hutch set two bags of groceries on the counter, quickly put a few things in the freezer and washed his hands.

Boat said "I'll shelve the rest of those."

But Hutch said "I see my wife's car. How long has she been here?"

"Maybe half an hour. She's in there with Wade." Nothing on Earth made Boat feel weaker than family strife.

Hutch could see the misery, so he tried to smile. Then he gave his arms and legs a mock hand-frisk. "We don't pack guns, Boatie. We can be civil."

For all his unease, Boat knew he had to speak. "Mr. Mayfield, she's back here for good."

Hutch said "How's that please?"

"Your wife told me she's staying here till Wade passes on. She knows he's close—"

"Close to what?"

Boat said "You know—to passing."

"Who told her that?"

"Mr. Hutch, that woman's his natural mother."

"And that makes her magic?"

Boat well understood that the answer was *Yes*, but he held out his two flat palms—empty-handed.

Hutch kept his voice calm, but he said "No she's not." He stepped off in the direction of Wade.

So Boat stopped him with a powerful whisper. "Mr. Mayfield, Wade needs her with him here."

"Did he tell you that?"

Boat's head shook hard. "Right after you left."

"How did he say it?"

"He told me he was ready to go; so he wanted her by him, along with you."

Hutch was in the doorway that led to the hall. He stayed there, both arms raised and pressed to the doorframe. Again he meticulously gentled his face. "Were those his words?" When Boat hesitated, Hutch said "About me—wanting me with him too?"

Boat knew what he said was a technical lie; but since he'd heard Wade in New York talking so often about his dad and their good times together so long ago, he compounded his lie. "Yes sir, he asked for both of you with him."

"You think Wade's right?"

"About what?"

"Dying soon."

Boat whispered again. "Maybe tonight, around four in the morning. No later than sundown tomorrow for sure."

The odd precision somehow convinced Hutch. "How many of these boys have you watched die?"

Boat said "Mr. Mayfield, they were all grown men. To answer your question, I believe it's twenty-three I actually watched. I may have lost count, it's hurt so bad."

An old high wall of Hutch's pride crashed silently down. The nearness and service of this stunted young man, here at hand in the kitchen—apparently some kind of valid angel—was the strongest rebuke Hutch had met with in years. Boat's face and level voice alone were a justified and fair reproach to feelings that Hutch still thought were his due, his right to rancor in Ann's abandonment. But any will to usher Ann back to her car tonight, to refuse her presence, seemed not only petty but an actual evil. And Hutch believed that very few things were evil in the average life—the normal run of men and women being seldom awarded the chance or the force to make mistakes with enormous outcomes. He felt a new and deep-running relief, so he brought his arms back down to his sides and said to Boat "This kitchen smells better than it has in years. Anything ready to eat for supper—just the three of us: you, Ann Mayfield and me?"

Boat said "You brought in a big load of food, looks like. Go in and check on Wade and his mother; I'll have something ready in, oh, twenty minutes. Any special requests?"

Hutch had heard Wade praise Boat's kitchen skills, and he tried to think of something quick and good. Nothing came. "You choose, please sir. Maybe a little surprise would help us."

"That's exactly my intention, Doctor."

But before he left, Hutch had to explain. "I understand you're here as our guest and ought not to work as hard as you're doing. But if you wouldn't mind cooking a little, I'd be much obliged. So would Wade if he could thank you clearly."

"Don't give it a thought, Mr. Hutch. Not a thought. I'm here to help any way I can."

"*Hutch* — call me Hutch."

Boat smiled. "Sure — Hutch. You leave this to me."

Hutch said "I wish I could leave the rest of my life to you." Then he knew he meant it.

48

Ann was sitting by the side of Wade's bed, her hand on the bones of his left hand, lightly riding the pulse that was only a feeble transmission. The main light came from the desk across the room, Wade's old student lamp at its lowest power.

Hutch waited in the door, trying to gauge Wade's rate of breath. It was all but inaudible, so wide spaced and shallow it barely moved the sheet that covered the leg bones and ribs and on to the chin. The eyelids were shut on eyes that had shrunk inward so far they seemed no bigger than the waxy fruit from chinaberry trees or healthy blueberries.

Ann didn't turn; she hadn't sensed that Hutch was there. By now she felt almost a part of the house again; and though she'd heard Hutch's voice at a distance, talking to Boat, she'd heard none of their words nor Hutch's steps toward her. As she sat on motionless, she was only fixing the line of Wade's profile deep in her mind by gouging it again and again on her thigh — just her long dry finger on the cloth of her skirt.

At last Hutch cracked the joints of his right hand.

Ann looked round, then got to her feet and stood by her chair.

Hutch came on to the foot of the bed, touched both of Wade's feet beneath the cover. "Son, I'm back." Though he'd said it as a final claim on the boy, Hutch understood that Wade might not hear him—*You're mine; I'm with you.*

But slowly Wade heard it. His head raised an inch from the pillow toward Hutch. The eyes stayed shut and he said "Aye, aye, sir."

Ann was still in place; but she said "Sit down, Hutch, and rest a minute. I'll go help Boat" (the sounds of work were coming from the kitchen). The set of Ann's eyes and mouth left no question that she meant to eat, and stay, here tonight.

And Hutch raised none. As Ann came past him, his hand went out of its own accord and brushed her wrist.

She gave a slight sound, nearly a moan, but never broke stride.

So Hutch went on to the chair and sat in Ann's narrow warmth.

When her footsteps faded off, Wade's eyes opened, though his head still didn't move toward Hutch. His mind had given up trying to see. When Hutch's hand touched the crown of his skull, Wade drew his right arm out of the sheet and held it straight in the air above him like a lightning rod or a white antenna. Finally he got whatever message he waited for, and he said to the ceiling "Call Ivory and tell her."

"Tell her what, Son?"

"That this whole tour is still underway, and I'll be seeing her and her family any week to come. Soon."

That seemed the first guarantee of dementia Hutch had heard—all the other strangeness, he'd half suspected of being intended for various reasons—but he said only "Fine, Son, I'll call Ivory later this evening."

"Remind her I want to be buried with Wyatt."

"You told me you meant to be scattered on the creek behind the old Kendal place, on Grainger's pool where he rescued you." When Wade stayed silent, Hutch said "Remember?"

Wade appeared to try, then said "That's not the first thing you've got wrong." When the words had faded on the air, Wade laughed—a parched chuckle, the first in days. He turned his blind face in Hutch's direction.

Hutch was compelled to turn aside.

"Don't take this personally—you're my good friend—but you know less about me than these birds here."

Hutch tried a short laugh. "Aren't the bluebirds especially smart this summer?"

Wade said "I'm talking about these birds that are helping me travel."

"Then thank them for me, Son. Many thanks."

Wade lay on, facing his father; and his eyes stayed open. But long minutes passed before he said "Big tall brown birds. Maybe storks but taller." Then he said nothing else.

Hutch sat on, determined to bear the sight. The sounds of peaceful work came from the kitchen, the mingled voices of Boat and Ann. Hutch could feel no objection; he knew he was far too tired and sad to fight old battles and lick cold wounds—those scores could wait. What chose to rise from the depths of his mind was that single line he'd got, days past, as he waited for his car to be fixed in the country—the possible start of a poem for Wade.

It repeated itself two clear times in Hutch's head. *This child knows the last riddle and answer.* The line had come to him an instant after he heard the distant voices of two boys on their bicycles at a country crossroads. Was the waiting poem meant to be about them?—they were brothers, the younger one named Foster who claimed he was bound for Spain, a bullfighter. Surely the poem had to be about Wade, the only child Hutch had really known or wanted to know.

But the dreadful pitiful husk of a body that breathed beside Hutch seemed drained of any question or answer that a living creature could hear or use.

Almost unaware that his voice was audible, Hutch said the only thought he had, as natural as air. "Pardon for any harm I caused."

The word *harm* snagged Wade back from his daze. His skull signed Yes and he said "Sure. *Harm.*"

The single word in Wade's voice, weak as it was, tore a hole in the air; and in a stiff rush, Wyatt Bondurant pierced the wall of the room—his presence and force undoubtedly plunged in from whatever place they'd lingered for so long. The force went straight to Hutch and poured all through him instantly, freezing him deep. Though Hutch was a man more susceptible than most to the unseen world of the lingering dead, only one other time had he been in touch with the actual power of a vanished life; and he'd kept no memory of that benign visit. (The night after his father Rob died, Hutch had slept alone in the old Kendal place; and the thinning shape and fading force of Rob's vanishing spirit had searched the house one final time, touching Hutch's unconscious body lightly as it left for good.)

Here beside Wade, Hutch knew at once whose ghost was in him. For a long minute he sat in calm terror, thinking his own death was maybe at hand. All he could ask was *Let me outlast Wade just long enough to see him buried the way he wants.* That freed him to think *I'll take his last wish and put him by Wyatt.*

If the promise somehow reached Wyatt, his cold strength gave no sign of mercy.

So Hutch sat on for another minute, breathing carefully and trying to quiet his thudding pulse. With all he'd felt and thought in these moments, he'd never questioned the hard-eyed sanity of his gut knowledge. *Wyatt Bondurant is here in some form, real as the one I knew.* As a kind of amulet against that certainty, Hutch repeated his single line many times—*This child knows the last riddle and answer*. No other lines came, Wade never roused to speak, but slowly Hutch felt his own chill body reclaim itself from Wyatt's assault. Only then could he start to wonder *Does Wyatt mean us harm?* Before Hutch could think, he heard steps behind him and turned to the door.

Jimmy Boat stood there, small as he was, a welcome sight. "Hutch, you go eat a little something please. I'll sit here with Wade."

Hutch tried to say No.

Boat shook his head and pointed to the kitchen. "You need all your strength. We got a whole night, maybe some bit longer."

Hutch agreed, then wondered if he should mention Wyatt. *No, Boatie knew Wyatt. Let Boat deal with him if he's truly here someway.* But before Hutch stood, he leaned to Wade's ear and said he'd only be back in the kitchen—call him if needed. Then he thought he should say "Son, your mother's here too. For as long as you need her."

That seemed to reach Wade. The boy didn't rouse but he took what looked like the first painless breath he'd had in more than a week of long nights; and he made a sound like the liquid hum that escapes some sleeping birds, mysterious as to meaning or purpose. Then as Boat stepped forward and Hutch reached the door, Wade said "My mother died the day I was born."

Boat's eyes went to Hutch.

Hutch frowned, unable to think or speak an answer. Wade was imagining some new path through Hutch's own story, Hutch's own mother's death. *Is he somewhere already, forced to relive it?* Hutch wanted the words to clarify that much anyhow. "No, your mother's here, Son."

But Wade was still again.

So Boat came on past Hutch on to the bedside, touched the cover above Wade's chest and said "Baby, everybody you love is here."

Hutch thought *Then Boatie's felt Wyatt here too.*

But in a stronger voice than before, Wade told Boat "That's a lie. Thanks anyhow." They would be his last words.

Hutch thought *Then somehow Wyatt hasn't reached Wade yet.* But he knew he couldn't describe his own meeting, not to this fading mind that was maybe half elsewhere, in some further life. Hutch thought it wasn't his duty even, weak as Wade was. *Wyatt Bondurant can tell his own news.* Hutch was also ignorant of what Wade was dwelling on when he called Boat a liar.

Boat said to Hutch again "Please keep your strength up" and pointed toward the kitchen.

So Hutch went to eat.

*   *   *

Wade heard his father's footsteps leave; and when they were gone, the grip of Wade's mind slowly released its hold on the world. The few remains of his body went weightless, no anchor or ballast to hold him back. The eye that had stayed alive in his mind through all his trouble went entirely clear again—Wade could see all he needed to see. And what he saw was a tall narrow room maybe twenty yards long, with beechwood floors and smooth bare walls that showed all the colors of pigeon wings—gray with shifting blues and purples. Wade was standing at one end of the room—the west end, he thought. He also thought *I'm on my feet for the first time in—when?—oh, years or days.* And then he knew, for the first clear time, that in his dreams he'd never been sick. *But is this a dream?* The answer came in his own strong voice, *No, no dream.*

And in that moment a live companion suddenly stood at the room's far end. By now, all human names were leaching from Wade's new mind. What he understood plainly was that this guest here was a young man, maybe twenty-five years old, in the nearly perfect body and face that made him a bare strong manifestation of all Wade had hoped for, ever on Earth— an entirely admirable welcoming man, at ease in both his mind and body and eager to give both freely without stint.

As Wade made a slight courteous bow toward the guest, the dazzling body took the first step toward him.

Wade thought *He'll reach me in maybe ten seconds.* He still tried to think it was Wyatt, renewed. But it took the guest well under ten seconds; and when he'd arrived at the edge of the bed and held out open arms and hands, Wade felt the pouring out in his chest of unthinkable joy. By then all human names were wiped from his mind—Wyatt's, whosever—so he never quite learned that the guest wore the ageless face of his dead grandfather Rob Mayfield, young again, a man Wade had never seen alive above ground. Wade stepped on forward into the harbor of powerful arms, and the light was blinding.

49

Ann was already seated at the kitchen table, under the hanging light. Boat had thawed two quarts of Brunswick stew that Hutch had bought at a roadside church sale back in the fall, and he'd somehow managed to make real corn sticks in an old iron mold that Hutch and Ann had forgot they owned. When Hutch walked in, Ann was staring at the clean empty bowl before her as if it held answers she'd need before day.

Hutch sat across from her, unfolded his napkin, then suddenly surprised himself. His right hand, of its own volition, went out and covered Ann's hand on the table.

At first she flinched and nearly retreated; then she held in place, though she didn't look to meet him.

Against his better judgment, Hutch said "What's wrong?"

"It would only ruin your night to hear it."

"Ann, this is not one of my good nights."

She went on drawing a tall abstract figure on the table, but she finally said "—How awful it is that you and I sit here, in fairly clear sight of three-score-and-ten, and our son's leaving with no remains. Nothing we can hold hereafter."

"What exactly do your hands want?" His voice was not hard.

"Oh Christ, Hutch, look."

When he looked he saw, not the worn woman here but the girl he'd loved in Rome and Richmond, more than half their lives ago, forty years—the girl who'd gone to a back-alley kitchen (on her own, uncomplaining) and ditched the first child they conceived when she thought Hutch had left her. He said "We ought to have covered our bets, yes. Is it too late for you to adopt a grand-child?" The moment he heard it, it sounded cruel and crazy.

Ann let it pass but her eyes still searched his face and eyes. "I want you to know that never—never, I'm thoroughly sure—can I agree that Wade chose rightly: Wade nor none of these miserable men that choose each other."

Hutch only said "You know I think you're tragically wrong. You know I'll never understand why you punish yourself with simple lies about the human race through all of history—you're smarter than most Supreme Court justices; *use* your mind, Ann."

She let that settle around them in the stillness. Then, smiling a little, she took up her spoon and clinked on the bowl. *Food, nothing but food now.*

After fifteen seconds Hutch drew back and stood to serve the stew.

"Just a mouthful for me." Then conscious that the food had been bought by Hutch, Ann said "It looks fine; I'm just barely hungry."

Hutch repeated Boat's warning. "We may need extra strength through the night."

Ann waited, then managed the start of a smile. "I think I've got the strength—"

Hutch said "I can't remember when you didn't." With a full bowl of stew, he came back and started to eat.

He'd finished a corn stick before Ann said "You think it's safe for me to run home and get a few clothes?"

"Boat could go; he told me he drives."

"Boat wouldn't know where to start with my mess."

So Hutch said "I think if you tell Wade now that you're going out for less than an hour, he'll wait for you."

"You think it's that easy?"

Hutch said "About as easy as chewing barbed wire. But no, I think Wade is running this thing. He's in some kind of temporary control. He'll tell you if you shouldn't leave."

Ann reached for a corn stick, buttered it slowly and ate a small bite. "He's told me, Hutch. You know he's asked for me."

"I do, yes. We'll make up the guest bed."

"I can't move Boat."

"Boat sleeps on a pallet by Wade—he asked to."

Ann said "I doubt any of us will sleep for days to come. Wade's got a timetable. I feel it in my bones."

Hutch could only agree. "It won't be days." Before his throat cleared, the wall phone rang with startling force. He scrambled up to prevent a second ring. "Hutchins Mayfield."

"Hutch, it's Maitland. How's Wade this evening?"

It was the first time Mait had phoned since his coolly threatening departure on Monday night; and Hutch was constrained, not just by Ann's objection to Mait but by his own recent knowledge of what seemed Mait's fool recklessness. "Thanks, Wade's about the same as he was."

"Is Boat still there? I'd like to see him again before he leaves."

Hutch was trying not to say Mait's name. "Boatie's got his hands pretty full tonight. We both have, in fact."

Mait smelled trouble if not the precise kind. "You can't talk now or you're mad at me—which?"

"Neither one, truly. Wade's on his last legs. I'll keep you posted. Thanks for calling."

Mait said "I've hurt you—"

"No, you couldn't do that." Hutch heard his own words; what they really meant was *You don't matter enough in my life to* hurt *me now.* So he tried to blur the message a little. "I'll call when I can. Take care of yourself." When he got that far, he realized Mait was no longer there.

He'd hung up somewhere in Hutch's last words.

With all the other causes for pain, still this slight impasse was the one that chose to fall on Hutch and bring him down. As he hung up the phone, tears flooded his eyes. To hide them from Ann, he went to the sink and ran cold water.

Still, when he turned, she said "Oh please don't give in yet."

That rubbed Hutch wrong—he'd borne up at least as well as she. But strangely no hot words came to him. And stranger still, his next move was slowly to walk up behind her, lay both hands on her shoulders and press. They'd barely touched in more than a year, and in those months she'd lost no serious trace of the fineness she'd borne all her life—all the years Hutch had known her. Even here his hands only touched Ann's blouse; but when she didn't shrug him off, Hutch extended his thumbs and found the bone at the base of her neck. He'd only begun to rub there gently when he realized Boat was standing in the door, in the stillest air Hutch had seen in long years. Again Hutch couldn't speak.

Finally Ann said "Mr. Boat, here, let me fix you some stew."

Boat shook his head and gave a slow smile that darkened the whole room—nothing in sight was as bright as his eyes. "Thank you, Ann. I'll wait a little while on that. I just came to tell you Wade's gone on off."

Hutch didn't understand at once. "Off?"

Ann knew. She only said "No—"

But Boat's head signed Yes over and over, and his smile burned on. "Yes ma'm, he's passed. Peaceful as any child asleep. I was two feet from him and couldn't hear him go. There was no time to call you."

Hutch's mind lunged hot into anger. *Of course there was time to call us, you fool.* But he kept his silence for the moment it took to search Boat's face and confirm his good intent. Hutch stood in place, his eyes bone dry.

Ann didn't face Hutch but, as she stood too, her right hand came up and found his hand behind her. Separate as that, they held each other a long minute till Boat turned and led them on in to Wade.

In death what was left of Wade Mayfield seemed the absolute proof that life is a power that fills real space with its mass and force. The cooling bones and hair and skin were hardly enough for a ten-year-old boy harrowed to death, much less a grown man whose shape had contained ten billion memories of life lived and stored, for reward or fear. Though Boat had shut the eyes before calling Hutch and Ann, they'd opened slightly. Through the long dark lashes, the enormous pupils had set at an angle like the angle in portraits whose eyes can follow you round a room. But they showed no threat now and made no plea.

Ann reached out and carefully shut them again.

This time they stayed down—they and all the rest of the body.

Though Ann and Hutch and Boat were silently sending out the last of their care and the start of their grief like a final healing or at least a balm, the abandoned body was already past such negligible wants. In Boat's word, the substance of what had been a life—a life with serious weight and reach, and with numerous thousand unmet hopes—had plainly *passed.*

50

By ten o'clock they'd done what they could. Hutch, Ann and Boat together had washed Wade's body and dressed it in a clean nightshirt. With very few words they all decided the body should lie in its own bed tonight; early tomorrow Hutch would call the undertaker and gave him instructions for a simple cremation (they'd plan a memorial service for later). Then once they'd each touched Wade a last time—each kissed his forehead—and left the one lamp burning by his bed, they still had to find small tasks for their hands, tasks to numb their minds. They were wide awake, and no one had mentioned Ann's leaving again.

Hutch felt compelled to pack every bottle of pills, every dressing and diaper and intravenous tube in a single big box and take it to the laundry room, out of sight.

Boat helped Hutch root out the last signs of illness; then he turned to the kitchen and swept and scoured the floor and counters as if nothing but the sight of unvarnished wood could satisfy him or ease Wade onward—Wade and Wyatt, whom Boat knew was with him.

In the dim bedroom, ten feet from Wade, Ann sorted the clothes in the old chest of drawers. She'd meant to set aside for burning anything that was frayed, and give the rest to the Salvation Army for needy children. But then she got to the bottom drawer and found the one old sunsuit that had lasted, a sole survivor from the year Wade was five—a white sailor shirt with navy piping, a whistle on a lanyard and short white pants with a button-front flap. Though it was cotton, some bug had got to it and made lace of the middy shirttail. There was no way Ann's hands could discard it though, not here tonight. She folded each piece meticulously and laid them all back into the chest. There'd be time for them later. Then she went to the kitchen to make strong coffee. Never in their lives had coffee ever fazed her or Hutch's chance of sleep.

Boat followed and stayed with her there, finally eating the supper he'd missed. They said no single word that didn't pertain to food or washing dishes.

Hutch spent twenty minutes alone in his study, turning through handfuls of pictures (his long-gone mother, his father, Grainger, he and Ann near Rome in the fifties with a lanky American airman they'd met in their semi-whorehouse pensione, a homesick stunner; then dozens of views of Wade in every year of his life till he left for New York). It came to Hutch that, here tonight, he should find that cache of naked men he'd discovered in New York, the small stack of snapshots — whosever they'd been — and burn them in the fireplace before Ann could find them and turn them against herself. *No, not tonight. They're genuine relics, not mine to destroy.* So Hutch stood and went to join Boat and Ann in the kitchen.

They were still seated at the center table, quiet as animals stalled for the night.

Boat was darning a knee-length argyle sock of his own (his crazy aunt could still knit).

Ann was reading through papers from a full briefcase — the pitiful strangler, committed to paper, still mad as a breakaway threshing machine.

When Hutch had poured a cup of coffee and found the box of dry saltines, he sat between them.

No one met anyone else's eyes, and the better part of two minutes passed before Boat spoke. "Mr. Mayfield, is it too late to call Ivory?"

Hutch glanced to the wall clock — just past eleven. He'd forgot his promise to Wade to call her, but it seemed late to disturb a working person with desolate news. "I guess we'd better wait till morning."

Boat said "Wade asked for Ivory several times today, while you were out."

"And Strawson," Ann said. "Straw never sleeps."

Hutch had forgot Straw too. Well, it had to be unmerciful to rouse anybody for news they couldn't act on, not tonight. "I'll call them both first thing in the morning."

Ann agreed.

But Boat met Hutch's eyes a long time.

Hutch said "Am I wrong?"

"Mr. Hutch, this is your business to run. But if I was up in Harlem this minute, hearing nothing but garbage trucks in the street and men killing kids, I'd want you to call me soon as you could, any hour of the dark — I loved Wade that much. I could anyhow get down on my knees and beg God to ease him passing over and guard him from worse than he's known already."

Hutch looked to Ann.

She said "The same for me." No tall sycamore in late December was ever stripped cleaner.

So once they'd each lapsed back into silence and Hutch had drunk the last of his coffee, he said "I think I'll say good night. I'll try to phone Ivory and Straw from my room. If anybody needs me, don't hesitate to knock." He pushed back his chair to stand.

But Boat leaned toward him across the table, both hands extended.

Hutch reached to take them and press them hard. They were tough as new leather and nearly dry as Grainger's.

Boat freed one hand and held it to Ann.

Hutch met her eyes and mouthed a silent Yes.

So she gave her own two hands to make a full circuit. The three of them held there, quiet together, for maybe ten seconds. Still no force moved among their hands—none but their own alert exhaustion, their bone-deep sadness.

Hutch stood and left them.

51

This time a machine answered Ivory's number, a deep strange man's voice. "Please leave a message."

Hutch almost hung up but then chose to gamble. "If this is Miss Bondurant's residence, I'm Hutchins Mayfield in North Carolina." He waited a moment.

Then Ivory's voice said "Good evening, Mr. Mayfield."

"I'm sorry to wake you."

"You didn't. I was lying here, knowing you'd call tonight."

"And so I have."

"Wade's gone then," she said.

"Very peacefully, yes. Jimmy Boat was with him in his old bedroom; his mother and I were just a few yards off in the kitchen—no sound or struggle."

Ivory took a long wait. "Well, God, now we can all stop hoping."

Though plainly not harsh, it struck Hutch as a very odd thing to say. "I guess I'd given up hope way back."

Ivory said "You had to. I'm just a fool. But then I guess I need to be."

Again the words seemed so unlike her, Hutch wondered if she was drinking maybe or confused from sleep; and who was the strange man's voice on her answering machine? "Whatever, Ivory—you helped Wade live as long as he did. He mentioned you today."

"How was that, Mr. Mayfield?"

Again he asked her to call him *Hutch*.

"That doesn't seem right—not yet at least."

So he answered her question. "Wade said to tell you his tour was finished—he may have said *trip*, but I think it was *tour*. Then he said he'd see you and your family soon."

Ivory said "Wade Mayfield was one gentle man."

"That he was, to the end."

"Do you believe he's ended then?" Her voice made it sound like a genuine question.

Hutch said "How do you mean that exactly?"

"Do people outlast death, as themselves somehow?"

He said "I've got a lifelong hunch they do, no personal proof though. One of my old college philosophy teachers used to say 'The human race in general has believed in immortality; the opinion of a whole race is worth consideration at the least.'" When Ivory was silent Hutch said "And you?"

"I pretty much gave up faith, back in college; but lately I've had strong feelings again, like messages almost."

"From Wyatt or who?"

Ivory said "As a matter of fact, my brother, yes."

"You've felt him near?"

"Just twice," she said. "Both times *strong* and close at hand. The second time he brushed my hand, along the back, barely raking my knuckles."

So Hutch had to tell her. "I felt him today—Wyatt, *strong*, yes. I was in Wade's room just before he died—just Wade and I in the space alone—and I'll swear Wyatt's presence swept in on us."

Ivory took the report as a credible fact. "He's furious, isn't he?—still, poor child."

"Frightening, yes."

"He'll start to calm." Her voice was free of tears.

"How's that?" Hutch said.

"Wyatt has all of Wade on his side from here on."

Hutch couldn't think how to go further than that. *Can't and maybe won't ever need to.* He said "I'll let you sleep on then—deep thanks again. Wade's asked to be buried up there by Wyatt. When we've had our memorial service among his friends down here, in a week or two, I'll bring the ashes north and shut the apartment. Then if you and your mother don't object, we'll bury Wade with Wyatt—I think you said Wyatt's buried on Long Island?"

Ivory took a long wait. "He is, in Sea Cliff next to our father. Mother and I won't object, no sir. Not if that's your wish."

"I'll call again when I've got clear plans. But get some sleep."

Ivory balked at saying goodbye. She said a long "Ah"; then "Would I be welcome at Wade's service, if I could get off?"

"You'd be welcome as the day, absolutely. We'll have it on a weekend if that will help. Please come."

"If I can," she said, "I owe him that much."

"Ivory, you've paid any debt many times with the care you gave him. But I'll call the moment we have a firm plan."

For all her self-possession, Ivory said "Promise—"

"A strong promise, surely."

Then she was gone, no word of goodbye.

That chilled Hutch a little; but before he could dwell on Ivory's strangeness, he punched Straw's number. Two rings, then Strawson's deep "All right."

At the sound of that voice, Hutch's own throat shut again.

In his deepest bass, Straw carefully and politely said "If you're the psycho son of a bitch that's been calling here and scaring my wife, you've met your match tonight, hot stuff. Here comes ten thousand rads of pure X ray down the wire to your ear." He made an ominous crackling sound; then "There, your brain is hopelessly fried."

At least Hutch could chuckle. "It's nobody but me."

"Hey you. You holding your own tonight?"

"That's the point," Hutch said. "My hands are fresh empty."

"Since how long ago?"

"Three hours maybe. We've all been busy, doing small chores."

Straw said "You're saying he's already gone?"

"Wade died tonight. In a good deal of peace."

Slowly Straw said "Please understand me. Is Wade still there at the house with you?"

"His body, in his bed, clean and ready, yes."

"I'll be straight down there then, all right?"

"We've got a full house—Ann's here and Jimmy Boat."

Straw said "I won't lie down; I won't press on you. I just want to see that boy on human grounds, not in some creep's embalming parlor."

"No chance of that. Wade asked for cremation."

"But you said he's still there."

Hutch said "Till morning. Then the undertaker comes."

"I'm leaving this minute."

Hutch couldn't pretend he wanted Straw's presence this late in the night, but he knew Straw had true rights in this—all his care for Wade through the years. He said "Don't knock. Just tap on my window."

Straw said "I'll sleep in the car till dawn."

Hutch knew he meant it, no point in a quarrel. "I'll see you at daybreak; watch your step on the road." Then "Thanks, old mate."

"None older," Straw said. "Lean on that at least."

In under ten minutes, and fully dressed on top of his sheets, Hutch was deeper asleep than he'd been in weeks.

52

At four forty-five in the sounding dark, Hutch's eyes clicked open. The moment he knew he was truly awake, a thick shaft drove right through his body from head to feet—*You are utterly alone.* In fact, he was. With Wade gone, there were no blood kin to whom Hutch felt remotely close except old Grainger at the end of his century. No friend any nearer to hand than Strawson. And Ann had made her choice to leave, a choice Hutch still couldn't make himself fight. So a fairly enormous story had ended, as human stories go at least—a story whose long path was visible for ninety years anyhow, from a night in the spring of 1903 when his young grandmother had abandoned her family to flee with her high school Latin teacher and start the line that ended here in Hutch.

All his adult life he'd been a namer, a man whose trade was an effort to transcribe the living and dead in durable words—the minimal words that can summon an essence before the eyes of distant strangers and leave them better endowed for time than they presently are, alone in the solitary cells of their own lives—so now Hutch lay on flat in the thick dark and tried to name his family's journey. All he could find, here anyhow, was a single word—a word he'd dreaded most of his life: unmitigated *waste.* What was left of ninety years of Kendals and Mayfields, them and all their close dependents, but the barely phosphorescent trail left by the burning of what they'd all called *love* as their fuel?—their treacherous, always vanishing fuel, their craving for time. With Wade's abandoned shell of a body just yards away, that finding seemed unbearably right to Hutch and too hard to live with, this close to daybreak.

Hutch got to his feet, found his robe in the dark and quietly made his way to Wade's room. In the doorway he paused and listened for Boat— Boat had chosen to sleep again on the floor by Wade.

And there was faint breathing, steady enough to indicate sleep.

So Hutch stepped in. The chair that had sat by the bed was gone. With slow care to make no noise, Hutch sat on the edge of the mattress at the level of Wade's sharp hipbone encased in the dry nightshirt and the sheet.

At first he felt he shouldn't touch Wade; the skin would be cold and the rigor of death would have surely set in. But as Hutch sat on, working back toward pictures of a live smiling Wade—ten, twenty years ago—he soon was silently telling himself *This is truly the end of the best thing you made; touch him one more time for memory at least.* Slowly again Hutch ran his left hand under the sheet toward Wade's upper arm.

It was cool, not cold, and still yielding to the touch.

Hutch's thumb tried to brush the skin lightly.

Only then did a force as repellent as high wind pour out of Wade into Hutch's own body.

Tired and grieving as he was, Hutch still could think of no name but Wyatt's. Ivory, nearly five hundred miles north, had known that Wyatt owned all of Wade now. Hutch kept his thumb in place and tried to tell the source of that power how thoroughly he ceded his rights in the last remains of his only child. In his mind he said three times *Take him, yes.*

But the force became an actual blast of silent demand, as strong as loathing.

Hutch bore it ten seconds more—it was surely reaching Boat's sleep too. What would Boat do or say?

When Hutch couldn't stand it any longer and drew his hand back free from the covers, Boat spoke plainly from his mat on the floor. "You know who it is here this minute, don't you, Hutch?"

"I do. And I've given Wade up to him—"

Boat waited so long Hutch thought he was gone into sleep again; but then Boat said "Excuse me, Mr. Mayfield, but maybe you still need to know—Wade hasn't been yours to give for long years."

Hutch thought *I've known that longer than you;* but he had the grace in the dark to thank Boat, then stand and leave.

53

Where he went was toward Ann. She'd shut the guest room door and no light showed; but the last few minutes had left Hutch gravely in need of a presence that stood a chance of welcoming him, tolerating him at least. Without a knock he turned the knob and entered dark air. A good deal of starlight fell through the one big window that Ann had opened beyond her.

Her body was clearly outlined on the bed, a wide double bed. She was on her side, facing the window, apparently wearing only her slip. Her legs were covered to the knee by an afghan.

Hutch went to the near edge of the mattress and waited long enough for Ann to send him out if she wanted, if she sensed his presence. What felt to Hutch like a long time passed, a stretch of minutes in which his right hand burned on still with the memory of Wyatt. Finally he couldn't make himself wait longer. With gradual care to lighten his moves, Hutch laid his body in the tangled space on the near side of Ann. She was still turned away, though she'd silently waked; Hutch was on his back.

Separate but near, they each soon thought of their bodies' long denial. Neither had touched another body, not in intimate need, since Ann left here. Alone on their own beds, they'd fed their bodies the best they could manage in their first weeks apart. Then as Wade came home, and his desperation gripped them, they'd silently lost all secret need and lived in their own skins, chaste as clean linen. Now with Wade bound outward, Hutch and Ann lay on, wondering if some kind of trusting union might come down on them in a new natural craving, for partial ease. But neither one's mind could raise itself to that pitch of want; neither one's voice had the modest daring to speak in this quiet room and own up to what had become for each a slow starvation.

Eventually, as the starlight dimmed for the endless minutes before sunrise, Ann turned to her back and lay, facing upward, a handspan from Hutch. When she could hear he was still awake, she said "You're thinking of Wyatt, right?"

"Right, as ever."

"He's been all in here, all night, hasn't he?"

"In my mind at least. And Boatie's felt him."

"God damn his soul then." Ann plainly meant it.

Hutch waited till he felt he had the full right. "Oh no. Wade's his."

"I understand that, yes. It hurts worse than Hell."

"It'll pass," Hutch said. "Hell doesn't exist—not for Wade Mayfield, not after tonight."

"You can't promise that." Ann's voice was level but still firmly convinced.

"No, I can't—no promises ever again. But both of us need to believe we'll outlast even this."

Ann said "I'm sorry to repeat myself; and Hutch, I'm half glad you think I'm so wrong. But still I very much doubt I'll outlast my soul's deep suspicion that, if there's a place of long damnation, then Wade is in it."

That stopped Hutch for minutes. He finally said "You're *willing* Hell, listen. That's all Hell is—pure human sadism: you want Wade to burn, for your wild reasons."

"I've got no choice; my whole life believes it."

Hutch had always known that the unseen world—of gods and fate, yes or no—had come to him much more strongly than to Ann. The simplest child's prayer was a trial for her; was she telling the truth or sucking sweet lies?

1128   *The Promise of Rest: Home*

So he knew he couldn't press harder tonight. But he found what felt like a sizable fact and offered that to her. "I've known a big lot of smart women in my life. Not one of them ever outran you for smartness. You can't scald yourself in ignorance forever; trust your mind. Wade died a good man. Teach yourself that at least. Two people as bent on life as we've been are bound to survive, so we owe Wade simple justice at least—intelligent memory."

Ann had no answer, or offered none. Like Hutch, she'd lost too much through the years to doubt her own adamant strength—the child she'd aborted (that still came at her in dreams, begging life), her long-gone parents, a dozen or so dear missing friends: none of them had downed her, deep as they hurt. So she lay in reach of the warmth from Hutch, not speaking or touching, till daylight first pierced the wide east window. Then she quietly rose and went to look out. It took her awhile to understand, but then she turned and said to Hutch "Strawson is waiting out there in his car."

In the threatened night, Hutch had forgot that Straw was coming; but he only said "He's expected, yes." What he hadn't expected was the hope that suddenly shot all through him from the sight of Ann's face.

Even this early, and her hair disarranged, the strength she'd promised last night to bring was visible on her, in her face and eyes. It even seemed greater than ever in her life. And to Hutch that strength felt almost ready to open again and offer him anything he could use. He thanked her simply for being here; but when she only nodded and moved toward the door, he thought the prospect of Straw had troubled her. He said "No way we can wall out Strawson. Straw was in at the start of Wade's life, and you well know it." Then Hutch got up too and went toward his friend, the first hope of ease.

Ann reminded herself that she'd urged Hutch to call Straw last evening. She had no grounds for real complaint then; and for the first time in more than a year, she felt none at all. Age and loss—she'd started to see—were the normal acids in every life, eating away the iron spine of anger and greed and unjust demand. She'd wash and dress in yesterday's clothes and offer to cook a big breakfast for all. Even she was hungry. So what she said was "Bring Straw in, any time you're ready."

54

July 7, 1993

Dear Professor Mayfield,
    I'm extremely sorry I crashed in on your privacy today. I was feeling two strong emotions at once—homesickness and pleasure in my findings over here

in the British Library—and since my father had sent me a check for my birthday last week, on a whim I decided to place that call to you and send my greetings and thanks in person. Thanks for all your encouragement in everything, life and work. Then you told your news, and I've been regretting my impulse ever since.

Of course I'd known that Wade was bad off before I left. And my wife has kept me posted at intervals on his progress—you recall that she knows Wade's mother who shops at the greenhouse where Stacy works. But hearing he's gone, in your controlled voice this afternoon, has struck me harder than I'd have guessed, even with all the liking I felt and all my admiration for his courage and remarkable cheer in the times I was with him this spring—that long ago.

Because I've been the receiver so often of your own kindness and openness to—what?—human failings maybe, I want to risk a few words to you now that may prove a surprise and a gift, I hope. I mean *them* anyhow as my main gift in Wade's honor here, all I can send you from as far off as London.

The gift is one fact. Almost the last day I sat with Wade while you were on campus, he told me his eyes were having a good day and would I please strip off my clothes so he could see me—altogether me. We were out there, alone as any two hawks on a thermal updraft; so I thought "What the hell?" and gave him his wish. He watched me closely; I felt like it helped him. I can honestly say I know it helped me and bucks me up still when I get low. You recall I was having problems just then with my scrappy marriage, so any word of a hint that I or any part of me was of serious use to another live creature—well, it came as a help.

You understand that I'm aimed at women like a heat-seeking missile of the most abject kind; but that day with Wade, I even stepped near enough to take his touch if he'd felt up to that, but he turned it down—all very polite on both our sides, and a memory that gives me the little comfort I feel, here at this distance with the weight of his death on my mind and your grief. He'd said I was something worth watching with the eyesight left him by then. I've never felt nearly watchable enough, despite my mother's praise.

That's meant of course for nobody but you. Even though I've invested in express postage here, please burn these pages, to spare any hurt it might cause another, if other eyes see it. And if learning that fact has anyway deepened your present pain, I send you my deepest apology ahead of time to say I'm thinking of you by the minute, with the best hopes for strength and that somehow your own work will see you through again, as I know it has before. I'll phone again soon. Meanwhile,

Yours,
Hart (Salter)

Dear Hart,

   That news means a very great deal to me. I thought Wade had died in an unbroken drought. Now I know I was wrong. I've burned your letter but the picture it gave me will last, I'm all but sure, the rest of my life.

   I'll look forward to your call.

                                                    Grateful affection,
                                                    Hutchins Mayfield

July 10, 1993

Dear Strawson,

   A bright cool Sunday morning here—the first chance I've had to draw a long breath for what feels like weeks. And first on the list of people I need and want to thank is you of course. I only wish I'd had the foresight to ask you to stay another day or so and answer the phone, distribute the excess food and flowers, and in general stand between me and life till I got a little better balanced on my pins.

   It turns out that even the simplest plan to cremate a body and scatter the ashes, as directed by the dead man, is mined with traps of various sizes—none of which is your concern, so I'll spare you the moan of a father aged sixty-three who had to stand helpless and watch his one child vanish this awful way (I have to remind myself I can say that *awful way* now, that it's finished at least—it died with the boy).

   There is one sizable dilemma I failed to mention while you were here. You know how Wade insisted on visiting Grainger in May and that he asked Grainger to oversee the scattering of his ashes on the creek behind the house. He went on to stress that intention to me on several occasions afterwards. Just before he died, though, he told me twice to bury his remains with Wyatt Bondurant in Sea Cliff, Long Island.

   Confused as he was those last few days, I couldn't take an oath that he was demented when he changed his plan—my guess is, he understood what he was asking and had weighed it sanely. In fact the only credit I can take from these last weeks comes from promising Wade I'd follow his wishes. I even phoned Ivory the night he died and let her know that Wade would be on his way north as soon as I could bring him. She calmly agreed.

   The hitch of course lies mainly with his mother. Ann didn't hear Wade express a last wish, and now she's all but dug her heels in and defied any thought of taking him farther than those backwoods and the creek Grainger dredged. You'll understand what a concession she's making, just in agreeing to that first plan—spreading him on my own family's ground, not a neutral cemetery plot in Durham or in southside Virginia with her own gruesome clan.

I suspect you're straining to suppress a grin. Sad as it all is, as quandaries go it does sound a lot like the unholy wrangle over D. H. Lawrence's ashes in the thirties. In his case—Frieda Lawrence (the spouse) and Mabel Dodge Luhan (the patroness) had decidedly separate plans for the remains, and Frieda finally resorted to mixing every particle of the ashes into wet cement and letting it harden. In no time thereafter she had Lawrence safe in a ton of concrete that Mabel with all her millions couldn't haul.

I'm nowhere near that desperate yet, and I won't claim to like Wade's last idea, but I feel a deep loyalty to a deathbed promise. So I may yet ask you and Emily to speak about the matter with Ann and help her see what's understandably all but as painful as the loss itself—that her son, in his right mind, chose to leave her again in a choice she loathes, and this time for good.

Whatever, we're planning a small service here for Saturday afternoon, July 31st. If the weather's good we may try to have it right here at the house where Wade after all lived two-thirds of his life. I guess I could get Duke Chapel for a half hour—Ann seems to want that—but I'm not sure I can be responsible for bearing up the way I'd want to in those huge surroundings. When that great organ gets underway, in those levitating vaults, I forget that the whole place was built with the proceeds from a billion lung cancers; and I more or less instantly revert to the worldview of, say, an Anglo-Saxon mason—the ceiling peels back, clouds evaporate, I contemplate God's face at point-blank range and find slim reflection of me or my life anywhere in his eyes: slim or none at all. (I'm prepared to learn in any case that Wells Cathedral was built with, say, the proceeds from the archbishop's chain of licensed brothels and that God Itself cares nary a whit for anything but the sight of our awe, facedown on the pavings.)

In any case I'll keep you posted as arrangements are made. Ann and I both want you to participate as you think best—remarks or the reading of something you think will suggest Wade best to his few survivors. When I spoke with Ivory the night Wade died, she said she might also come down to join us. Again you can guess Ann's feelings on the prospect, but so far she's issued no ultimatum, so I'm writing to Ivory later today with full details. Should I ask her to speak?

I may drive up toward you late next week, if you mean to be home—see Grainger and you, beg Emily to feed me old childhood favorites (are the butter beans in?), maybe spend a quiet night. I'll give you fair warning. Till when, more thanks than even an aging Mayfield can send. You know we've always been big thankers, whatever our faults.

Love always,
Hutchins

July 10, 1993

Dear Ivory,

    I'd never in my life seen an entire orchid plant, so the one you sent was not only beautiful the hour it arrived but is by me still as I write to thank you — even more blooms, each one more mysteriously made than the others.

    I don't need to tell you that it's been a hard week, a hard three months; but just today I begin to feel that the tunnel of numbness may well end. Not that I'm eager to start responding with sober nerves to all that's happened since I last saw you — and to all that happened to Wade and Wyatt and you for months before I blundered on the scene. I hope you'll also understand how deeply I feel relieved — many hours of the day and night, to the roots of my bones — and how guilty I feel at even the chance to shut my eyes for more than ten seconds and not expect a voice to call me. I've never been much of a believer in "blessing in disguise," not even when the blessing comes as death. I've never thought any one I love should need to die. I still don't.

    We have made a practical plan or two, though. On Saturday afternoon, July 31st, we'll ask Wade's closest friends to gather for a brief chance to honor his life and recall his best. I was grateful when you said you might come down for that occasion. I very much hope you can still be here. The guest room in this house is quiet and cool with a bath of its own; no one on Earth could be more welcome. I'll hold it, waiting for word from you, and will also reserve you a room in town in case you prefer. If you can be here, may I ask you to speak your heart at the time? If for any reason you feel you can't, no need to explain. Wade's family — his mother, his godfather Strawson and I — know how much you've done.

    After the service, you and I can talk a little about the only two remaining problems. I need to face up to shutting that haunted New York apartment, and I need your advice on the final disposition of Wade's ashes. I told you that the last wish he expressed to me was to lie by Wyatt. Earlier he'd told an ancient cousin and his mother about a different plan, and I trust you'll realize that she's distressed at the contradiction.

    Long Island's a long way to go from Durham to visit a grave. By the time you're here, we should have a solution — one way or another. Conceivably I could drive you back north, finish emptying out Wade's apartment and then inter him by Wyatt in Sea Cliff, or you might stay a day and drive up with us to my old homeplace an hour from here and spread him there on a creek he loved back deep in the woods. That was Wade's original plan, expressed in strong terms to several of us.

    Please let me hear soon. I don't want to burden you with one ounce more of my family's business than you've already borne, but let me say one last word in closing—your presence here on the 31st of July would mean an enormous amount to me.

Ever in gratitude,
Hutchins Mayfield

14 July 1993

My dear Hutch,

I never dreamt I'd have to mark French Independence Day in my old age by learning of Wade's death and your plans to remember him. I've been permitted, for whatever cruel purpose of fate, to outlast the ranks of all I've loved except your good self. What else can I tell you but King Lear's monosyllabic response to his one good daughter's murder—"Howl, howl, howl"?

As for your invitation to come and speak for Wade at the chapel service, can you understand how hard I want to refuse you flat, then to sit right here—bolt every door and window, chink every keyhole—and refuse to acknowledge one more departure?

I'm coming, though, if I live and can walk downstairs on the morning in question and get past the Petersburg city limits sign. Don't think about sending somebody to get me, but thanks for the offer. I've got an elderly Negro gentleman who drives me places I can't help going, and I've already phoned to book his assistance. I won't spend the night, so forget about hotels. If I'm not there by the hour appointed, you'll know I'm prostrate or have quit myself.

It's all I can offer you, dear boy, now or ever after. You'll never get over this; don't even try. It will make you strong as a heartpine knot though. You'll be minting out poems and sterling pupils when Western Civilization is back in the hands of the wolves—speed the day! Wolves constitute a far more admirably organized species in every way than we and our brethren. I even read recently that wolves seem to have a developed religious sense—their love of the moon and worship of it—but as yet they have no known TV evangelists raking in the shekels. No doubt their basic decency has spared them any such vulgarity. May your own wolf nature serve you at present.

I send you a lifetime's love at the least,
not that my love ever cured any pain yet,
least of all my own, though I'm breathing
still and glad to be

Alice

July 15, 1993

Deep Sympathy in your Time of Grief, Mr. and Mrs. Mayfield,
I am Wyatt Bondurant's only mother as you well know and I think I can guess

in the pit of my chest how you are looking at life these days. I have seen both of you in pictures Wade showed me in happier times and I know you are younger than me by some years. So please don't think I am forward in saying the Lord will answer your need if you ask him in coming weeks. I have seen a lot, from old Virginia where I grew up to Long Island presently, and one thing I know about the Lord is, he may take you by the scruff of the neck and shake every last tooth out of your head but he very seldom cuts you off at the knees, or much below. Once in a great while but very seldom. To be sure, you may have to hunch down deep to bear his will. I am bent nearly double with all I watched since I was a girl in a family of nine. I have buried twenty-three loved ones in my life, including two children from my own body. But God won't press you lower than you let him, not till your time is up and he's ready. I wish we could be with Ivory at the service but will think of each of you through that day. And every other day till I am called home.

Respectfully yours,
Mrs. Lucy Patterson Bondurant and Raven

July 15, 1993
Dear Hutch,

I'll be there to help you with the service. Won't even attempt, however, to advise you or Ann on scattering the ashes—here or Long Island. To my mind, they're ashes, no more precious than woodsmoke. Everything that mattered and will last of Wade Mayfield will hang all around us every day of our lives till we follow on. Flip a coin, I'd say—but I said I wouldn't say, so just ignore that.

Meanwhile Mr. Grainger finally responded to the news I gave him eight days ago, soon as I got home from seeing Wade last. When I sat down and told him then, he didn't move a muscle. After ten minutes when I stood up to leave and asked if he recalled what I'd told him, he looked at the TV and said "Strawson, you couldn't tell me news if you tried. I foretell every breath you ever draw." Still, this morning when I helped him dress and had made him his breakfast, I opened the door to start my day; and he said "Go post this message to Hutchins." He held out this little wad of folded paper. I have not opened it but send it on for what it's worth.

Love anyhow from
Strawson

The enclosed tight-folded plain sheet of paper with pale blue lines seemed to say in the faintest readable hand, which was all but surely the remnant of Grainger's old strong script,

> *Raven Hutchins Mayfield*
> *Raven Wade Mayfield*
> *Grainger Walters: kin people.*

In all the years any white Mayfield had known him, since he came south in 1904 from Maine where his father (who was old Rob's mulatto son) had taken the family in flight from Virginia, none of his white kin had ever heard Grainger claim blood relation.

For most of his own life, Hutch had understood how immense the distance was between the lives the white Mayfields had led in their well-built homes and Grainger's adjacent tacit pain and solitude. But still this glimpse of the old man's spider-silk words on paper shook Hutch to the sockets like nothing he'd seen since the last glimpse of Wade. It partly braced Hutch for what came to him the following day by express mail.

July 16, 1993

Dear Mr. Mayfield,

With any luck I'll be there on the evening of July 30th, but please don't count on me to say anything at the service. I couldn't. I saw too much in this past year and felt too many feelings, being powerless to help; so anytime I let myself recall it, I seize up cold and simply can't speak. Wade knew he mattered in my life, more or less from the day we met; that's what counts with me.

Since you've been so decent to me and my mother through this, I hate to complicate matters this late. But better now than when I'm down there, in the midst of your guests. The fact is that, once Wyatt died, Wade sat down on the night of the funeral and wrote a letter to you and Mrs. Mayfield. He sealed it just as it is today and made me promise to mail it to you when he was gone.

I don't know all of what it says; but I've held off this long, trying to find a way to burn it and maybe spare you a further hurt. I'm too much of my Baptist mother's child, however, to fail a dead man if I can avoid it. If anything Wade has written makes you want to stop my visit, just leave a message on my phone machine. I will understand far more completely than you know.

Till whenever then, I send you and all Wade's people my thoughts, my strongest good hope.

> *Truly,*
> *Ivory Bondurant*

The letter she enclosed was sealed in a business envelope, no sign of tampering with the flap. In Wade's unquestionable script, already shaky, it said *For Hutchins Mayfield and Ann Gatlin once I am gone.*

Dear Hutch and Ann,

We buried Wyatt today on the Island, so I don't have the will to copy this twice. I trust whichever one sees this first will share it with the other, however far apart you are at the time. It's the only thing you need to know about me that you don't already know or haven't surmised.

Wyatt has a living sister named Ivory Bondurant, a good-looking, smart and admirable woman. Through my work I met her my first week up here, summer of '84. At that time she worked in the same firm as I, a first-class draftsman. She was only just recently separated from her husband, I was lonesome as a cactus and still hadn't set my big sex drive on a single last rail, so she and I got very close in a hurry and stayed that way all the slow steaming summer. So close that, when Ivory realized she was pregnant that fall, we frankly didn't know if the child was mine or hers and her husband's. They'd gone on meeting occasionally.

At the time I knew I loved her in a real way. I also knew I was built to need men, pretty much exclusively, and was headed that way at the first sign of promise. Ivory had more or less understood that from the start; and once she found she was carrying a child, we discussed her having the blood tests done to answer the question of whose child it was, but she wouldn't hear of asking her ex to participate—the last thing she wanted was for him to think he had a claim on the baby; by then they were parting bitterly. He was incidentally also white. The other last thing she wouldn't hear of was shedding the baby. Till then she hadn't felt safe to get pregnant because her marriage had been so rocky. So I stayed near her till the child came safely and have ever since helped her each month with the bills. As I say, she'd pretty much understood from near the start of our friendship that I couldn't spend my whole life with a woman, however fine, though I surely meant to honor the child if time proved him mine.

In the fall of '84, Ivory moved uptown to be near her brother in a better apartment. And that was when I got to know Wyatt. In fairly short order he and I seemed to understand that we were set for the long haul, despite our loud disagreements and crises, which mainly arose from the unavoidable fact that we were built as differently as Memphis and Mombasa. It didn't hurt Ivory, not that she ever showed, not for long anyhow (though I've also suspected her of being the greatest actress since Eve). By then her and Wyatt's good mother had taken the child to Long Island, except for occasional visits in town. So Ivory, Wyatt and Wade became a working family of three, with a likable weekend guest on occasion.

What am I telling, or asking, you? First, the child may be half mine. Sec-

ond, you owe me or Ivory nothing by way of moral or financial support. She will be the sole beneficiary of my insurance and the money I've got in my firm's pension fund. I know you won't dream of contesting that. She's also got quite a decent job, Wyatt left her good money, and—knowing the Bondurant pride as I do—I'm certain she wouldn't accept a dime further. No, I guess all I want is for you to know that Raven Wade Mayfield may have a son to live on beyond him, whatever he's called and wherever he lives. You two may have a survivor on Earth. I wish I could leave you more than that. You'll have to lean on memories, I guess. I've done that for months.

I trust each of you will do whatever is right by your standards. I also wish I had the time and sufficient strength to admit here fully how very much pain I've caused you—and suffered for causing—how wrong I feel about all I'll never get to do for Ivory and her likable boy. The strength to tell you just is not *available in my body and won't ever be.*

So love for now—and, sure, always—from
Wade

55

That news reached Hutch the next afternoon. He had spent the morning alone in the house, whittling through the thicket of letters he'd got since Wade died. However kind, most of them had come from fellow writers— poets, novelists, playwrights—and their guaranteed eloquence had made each one a hardship to read: the words went so unerringly straight to the core of his pain. When he'd thanked as many as he could bear in a two-hour stretch, he turned to the all but mindless job of choosing from his own lifetime stock of poems for a *New* and *Selected* volume he meant to publish in '95. That would be the thirtieth anniversary of his first small volume.

He worked by writing the title of each of the poems from the past forty years on a separate index card. They came to a dauntingly thick stack of cards, nearly two hundred poems. But undeterred, Hutch dealt the cards out on the desk before him—grouping, rearranging and finally winnowing. At first he winnowed mercilessly, saving only the poems he suspected would last another fifty years, maybe even a century, as useful objects for a brand of reader scarcer nowadays than clean air to breathe. That left him with less than a twenty-page book. He shuffled his deck again and started a slightly more tolerant game, one in which he worked again to forgive himself for all he'd omitted.

For years Hutch had known that, because he'd confined his work to verse and, specifically, brief lyric meditations—like the vast majority of American poets since Robert Frost's narrative prime—he'd arrived at the edge of what might well be his last decade without having dug, with words at least, into ninety percent of what he'd seen in his family and the world and what he'd learned and deduced of the past that stretched behind him and the places he'd known. If, forty years ago, he'd tilted toward the novel and learned to convert his gift and his findings into sizable stories—and one of his teachers had urged that on him, fruitlessly—he might have something more to show now than what felt like a few dozen bright chips off enormous, deeply socketed stones that were long past his reach.

In the midst of that, Maitland Moses arrived a little early for lunch. So Hutch gladly broke off and made colossal sandwiches which he and Mait ate with cold beer in the kitchen—it was far too hot to sit on the terrace. Neither of them mentioned Mait's behavior the last time they met, his volunteering for an early doom; they kept to milder subjects. Mait claimed that his friendship with Cam was strengthening steadily, and Cam was looking for a less demanding job than the hospice. As it was, they had so few nights together. They were homing in on the thought of sharing a larger apartment than Mait had presently, if they could afford it—after Wade's death Mait had taken a job in the Duke Library, the manuscripts collection.

Hutch began to tell Mait about his plan for a *Selected Poems*, asking his advice on what to exclude. And soon that had them moving to the study and fiddling again with the index cards. Finally Hutch asked Mait to lay out his own idea of a volume. "Keep all you think you'll want to recall from an old friend's work when you're sixty years old and discard the rest."

Mait faced him squarely. "You know I don't think I'll get to be sixty?"

"Don't depress me again. Just do what I ask."

So while Hutch shelved a few dozen books that had come in the mail when Wade was dying—most of them new poems by friends and ex-students—Mait stood at the desk and played out the white cards carefully. In twenty minutes he turned to Hutch, grinning, and gestured to a wide star of rescued titles. "I gave you sixty-five, one per year for the age you'll be in 1995."

From across the room Hutch said "Way too many."

"You haven't even looked yet."

Hutch said what he suddenly felt in his gut. "I couldn't bear to. So many dead little dinghies in the shallows."

Mait laughed his old high-low croak. "*Now* who's being reckless? These are all trim craft, all still at sea; a few of them qualify as dreadnoughts at least."

Hutch shook his head in honest rejection, but he walked to the desk and studied the titles. In another two minutes he felt a quiet surge of surprise. There seemed at least an even chance that Mait had built, not simply a star of cards but an honorable—maybe better—showing for a lifetime's witness and silent labor. Hutch knew it might all crumble in his mind in the next ten minutes, but for now he looked up. "Don't let me destroy it."

"Sir?"

"Remember it, Mait, just the way it lies. Don't let me hack it up in self-loathing."

Mait was smiling still but he spoke, quite firmly, "Not on your life."

Before Hutch could ask him to gather the cards in order and keep them, the sound of a truck moved up the hill; and a Federal Express man brought Ivory's letter with the separate news from Wade.

Hutch asked Mait's permission, then sat across from him and read both pages in a deepening calm. The peace surprised him more than the news in Wade's few lines. *Is it news at all? Have I always known it?* As the words passed through him, Hutch knew he'd partly dreamed or guessed them—when? *Ages since.* It likewise strangely raised his spirits to meet, head-on, a fresh and surely insoluble mystery (Wade's death had seemed such a terminus to questions of hope). When Hutch scanned both pages a second time, he held them toward Maitland.

Mait grinned but stalled. "Secret dispatches?"

Hutch shook his head No but insisted "Please read them."

Mait took what seemed like abnormal time; then looked up, solemn. "Is this as big a shock as I suspect?"

"Strangely not."

"But it's really weird, right?"

"*Weird*—as in what? In a country as hopelessly sick on the subject of family as ours, with the whole millennium speeding down on us, this sounds like fairly old-time human news—surely nothing weirder than what goes on behind barely closed curtains in middle-class houses down every street I travel anyhow."

Mait said "You've got a point."

"I've got a lot more than a point, young pal."

"I guess you could do some DNA tests, if the mother would let you."

As calmly as he'd tracked the sight of the news, Hutch said "No, never."

"Won't Wade's mother really want to know?"

Hutch waited. "Ann put up with me for four decades; I think she's earned her spurs in the dire uncertainty department."

"But will you tell her?"

Hutch hadn't yet thought there might be a choice. Ann's name after all was plain on the envelope, no smaller than his. But he wondered if he might not wait till after Wade's memorial service, when Ivory and the others had come and gone, and then tell Ann. That way she could respond in the slow aftermath, with no threat of panic. So he said to Mait "I may hold off a day or two; but no, clearly Wade meant his mother to know."

"Then hadn't you better tell her before the child's mother comes down? She may have her own plans to tell both of you her side of the mystery."

Hutch saw Mait was right. He'd need to reach Ivory tonight, no later.

56

It was nearly midnight, and again the mechanical man's voice answered; but when Hutch spoke his name, Ivory picked up the phone. Her voice was tired but not unwelcoming. "I'm sorry I've missed your calls more than once. I've been at a friend's."

Hutch said "Your message got here this afternoon."

"There were two separate messages, Mr. Mayfield."

"Both arrived, clear as day."

Ivory took a long moment. "No sir. Wade's message to you is uncertain."

"How's that?"

Again she waited, this time for so long that Hutch thought she was gone. Then at last her voice came, with more life in it. "I'm assuming he told you about my son. Whatever else Wade said, the name of the father has *never* been clear—not to me at least. And if I don't know, nobody else can. Nobody ever chloroformed and raped Ivory Bondurant."

"What's the child's last name?"

"My name—Bondurant, as I just told you. I never gave it up."

"But you know Wade and I both have *Raven* as part of our names."

Her voice came like a speaking statue's or a sleepwalking child's. "I well understand where *Raven* comes from. Wade and Wyatt and I chose it together. All that meant to us that long summer was, we liked the name. It may seem odd from this far along; but we also thought it was mildly funny since, either way, the boy was half white—more than half; Wyatt and I are both quadroons."

Hutch said "Will it feel right to you and your mother if you bring him for the service?"

"Young Raven? No, that hasn't crossed my mind. He's in day camp out on the Island, at Mother's. He's well settled in and has been for years."

Hutch saw himself barging through pitch-dark water with his eyes half blind. *Why am I more lost, here with this creature who seems at least kind, than anyone near?* But he told her still. "Wade's mother and I would surely value the chance to meet Raven."

"That's kind of you both. I've thought more about this than you've had a chance to, and I'll have to say you'd be complicating your lives a good deal."

"How?"

"Raven's that fine a child."

Hutch said "How old is he, Ivory?"

"Eight, going on eighty." She managed a smile that colored her voice.

Hutch could hear it. "Eight is one of my favorite ages. I honestly think I knew more good sense at eight than ever since."

Ivory said "Oh, me too—maybe nine with me. If you told me at nine I'd be sitting here tonight, having this talk with you ten thousand years off, I'd have no doubt said 'Girl you're stark-raving nuts.' No, at nine I knew that the world was divided into *Fair* and *Unfair,* forget *Good* and *Evil*—"

"And of course you were right. The average child is."

"I was way past average, if I do say so. I'd have never sat still while this whole mystery around a fine child turned half rank and fishy."

Hutch said "Well, no. Far stranger things turn up every day on the evening news or the afternoon talk shows—children waiting in pain for long decades, then crawling through fire to find a lost parent, cascades of tears."

"Mr. Mayfield, listen—I've never been lost. Neither has my son." She was peaceful and still self-possessed as a heron.

"Ms. Bondurant, I have never doubted that once, not one hot instant." With that, Hutch suddenly felt he'd lost some final chance at continuance: another tack for a dying story, the telling out of his and his family's path on the ground, which was otherwise what now?—Wyatt's dry ashes in a bowl.

"Then thank you, sir. I'm glad you know."

"Shall I call you *madam?*"

"Pardon?"

"You're calling me *sir*. I'm a U.S. citizen, nothing grander." But for a harsh instant, he thought *I've paid mine and many others' way. That's fairly grand.*

Ivory said "Sir, suh, oh suh. Maybe I'm just an old-timey girl—my mother's child from old Virginny, one of the Pattersons from Patterson Hall." No trace, though, of a smile or a sneer.

"Remember I asked you to call me *Hutch?*"

Again Ivory paused for a long breath, then "Hutch, Hutch, Hutchins."

Torn as he felt, in her rich voice finally, it sounded to Hutch like a chain of long-sought hopes amply rewarded, partly earned but never entirely— decades of pardon and boundless bigheartedness, the promise of rest. He understood he was hearing too simply. No human voice could give that much in that little time to any live soul. But for some reason, gently, he told Ivory "Thanks, sleep now, good night." Then he suddenly found he'd said all he knew. Not waiting for an answer, he hung up quietly.

T H R E E

BOUND AWAY

JULY–AUGUST 1993

From fifty yards' distance, the child was as striking as a palomino colt, a privilege to see; and he watched the car from the moment Hutch turned at the stoplight and drove through the greenery toward him.

The day Ivory's letter came, in mid-July, Hutch had reserved a room for her at the Washington Duke Inn, ten minutes from his house. She'd arrived by plane on Friday night and gone, at her insistence, straight to the inn. Now it was Saturday afternoon, a quarter past two, as Hutch came down the drive to the inn and saw them both, already waiting at the curb. Good as Ivory looked in a dark purple dress and a wide-brimmed straw hat, Hutch naturally focused at once on the child who stood beside her peacefully—a little small maybe for eight years old, in a tan summer suit with an open-necked white shirt, a face the excellent color of his mother, and with eyes as dark as any polished onyx.

Hutch felt a swift flood of expectation—Ivory had never promised she'd bring the child—but he knew he must rein himself in hard. He thought firmly *This child's real, Hutchins. Get one thing right in your life, starting here.* He stopped at the curb, got out at once and stepped toward the two.

For a long moment they looked like the sudden embodiment of all Hutch had lost in his life till this moment—his own young mother whom he'd never seen, young Wade, young Strawson and even Ann herself in her own best days. As Hutch neared them though, they were only themselves, not echoes of others; and that felt like enough of a bounty. He knew not to rush the boy at once, so he put out his hand to Ivory. "You're a friend to be here. Wade's mother will meet us at the chapel."

Ivory shook his hand, then touched the boy. "Hutch, this is Raven Bondurant, my son. Raven, this is Mr. Mayfield—Wade Mayfield's father."

At close range the child was almost too good to see. Hutch refused the urge to hunt for Wade in the flawless skin of the face, the eyes, the black hair and lashes, the silent poise of his whole body in its raw linen suit and starched white shirt. Hutch bent a little and offered his hand. "That's a handsome suit, my friend. Welcome down."

In general, children shake hands like the dead; but Raven Bondurant took hold of Hutch with surprising strength, though his eyes were fixed beyond him. "Brand new," he said. He stroked both palms down his wide lapels.

So Hutch opened both doors on their side of the car and stood while they chose the front or backseat.

Ivory took the back.

Raven slid up front; and when Hutch had joined them, asked the two to buckle their seat belts and then moved out, Raven said "Mother, this place is all green woods."

Ivory said "More trees than you've ever seen. Or may see again. This is how the Earth was meant to look, Son, on weekends at least. You remember it, hear? It's vanishing fast."

Hutch thought *It's vanished already, long gone. These are stage-set trees. But remember me.*

Raven said a single word.

Hutch said "Pardon?"

The child's face was pressed to the window on his side. He took his time before repeating the word. *"Hideout."*

Hutch said "You're in hiding?"

Again the child waited; then still not looking round to Hutch or Ivory, he said "This whole place is some kind of hideout."

From memories of his own childhood and Wade's, Hutch had to assume that the child liked the sight of so many trees—what child doesn't dream of the perfect concealment, the invisible ambush, the cave with two exits? But when he asked whether Raven liked the idea of hiding out here, he got no answer but a shake of the small head. By then they'd reached the first stop-light and could see the chapel tower beyond them. Hutch pointed. "We're headed there."

The boy turned back to his mother and laughed. "Looks like a big old funny church, see?"

Ivory smiled; Hutch saw it in the rearview mirror. "It's a big church, baby. You know what I told you?"

"To hush up and sit."

"And you promised me?"

Raven said "I know it."

"You know it *what?*" Ivory said.

"I know it, yes, Mother."

In the rest of the three-minute drive through campus, none of them said another word, though the boy pointed silently to tree after tree — enormous cedars, pines and huge water oaks. On the air, his finger would trace a whole outline — trunk, branches and leaves — then start another.

Hutch couldn't help thinking the boy was hunting some trace of the sleeping giant who dreams this world and its contents, and he nearly asked. But then he knew *If I'm wrong, it'll be too big a disappointment;* so he drove on in silence.

Only then when he'd stopped in front of the great wide limestone steps to the chapel did he look back and meet Ivory's face. "My wife hasn't seen Wade's letter, the one you sent me. I haven't found the right time to tell her yet."

Ivory registered the fact serenely. "That's entirely your business." Then she and Raven waited in place, still as soldiers, till Hutch came around and opened their doors.

2

Hutch and Ann had planned the memorial service days ago; and early this morning, Hutch had come in and checked on the flowers and programs. But as he walked in now, twenty minutes early with Ivory and Raven, and felt the chill of the steep gray walls, it seemed as foreign a place as the pole. *What are we doing here, in so much peace? And who are we kidding? — Wade Mayfield died in agony.*

Ann was standing in a corner of the narthex. As Hutch and the Bondurants moved toward the final steps and the long nave, she joined them quietly and met both visitors. Then she looked to Hutch. "Strawson and Emily are here, down front. I told them we'd join them."

Ivory had stepped slightly back from the Mayfields. She meant to signal she'd follow them in and sit some distance behind the family.

But Ann touched Ivory's arm. "Please sit with me."

Hutch said "Yes, with us by all means."

So — Raven with Hutchins, and Ivory with Ann — they climbed the tall steps, entered the towering aisle lit only by the flaring reds and blues of the stained glass, which swarmed with blared-eye faces of prophets, saints and (at the peak of the huge altar window) the terrible bearded head of God aimed at all watchers.

Raven's eyes followed the rising vaults to the pale height of what was, after

all, an upturned stone boat the length of a warship. Even a child could see
the likeness, a long keel overturned.

Beached or abandoned?—Hutch often wondered; but now he silently
led them past rows of maybe eighty friends and strangers to the very front
where Straw and Emily sat in a shaft of brown light.

Straw stood in place, hugged Ann and Hutch and sat again after bowing
to Ivory.

Beyond him, Emily smiled faintly and bowed. Despite her severe dark
dress and small hat, her thin plain look seemed to Hutch like a hint that the
actual country might never quite vanish—the fields and thickets and patient
faces prepared to last till time relents in the speed of its pace or lifts its hand
for a run of days unmarked by pain.

All of them sat but Raven. With the slow deliberation of an old man, he
got to his knees on the cold stone floor, folded his hands beneath his chin,
shut his eyes and seemed to pray.

If it was a new idea for the boy, Ivory gave no sign, though when he finally
sat beside her, she circled his shoulders and gathered him inward. For a
moment he entirely surrendered to her, and that left him seeming younger
than he was—a precociously well-dressed six-year-old. But then Ivory kissed
the wiry close-clipped crown of his skull and set him free.

From that moment on, Raven sat with the grave self-esteem of a bronze
head from Benin or Delphi, unconsciously giving the color and line of his
unmarred face to all who were lucky enough to see him.

Behind the family, a quiet hubbub of others filed in; and then at precisely
three o'clock, a friend of Hutch's from the music department started on the
massive organ behind them to play a *Siciliana* of Handel's, so effortless and
gravely joyful in its winning try at perpetual motion that it seemed yet
another guarantee of survival. *Who could make such a sound and then die out?*
When the last notes had died in the echoing space, a short line of witnesses
rose one by one and spoke from a lectern at the top of the choir steps.

The first was a high school teacher of Wade's from Durham Academy,
a plump-faced woman in a lace jabot above a yellow suit. She'd single-
handedly noted Wade's skill at design when (as a sophomore) he wrote a
term paper on the pattern he saw in the plan of George Eliot's *Silas
Marner*. In under five minutes now, she managed to summon Wade's high
adolescence with credible force—"a good-hearted looker, dangerously
generous with all he owned" and "the most charged boy I've known till
today; oh I've known some *magnetos*." She ended with a memory of seeing
him walk beyond her one day after graduation, in a shopping mall. He'd
worn a new "absolutely blood-red shirt," and all she'd seen was the back of

his head in a crowd of others; but that live sight had come back to her the night of his death, well before she heard the news. When she'd addressed him directly at the end of her memories—"Wade, thank you for a splendid sight"—she was followed by Hutch's faculty friend who'd helped him most in recent weeks, an eminent Shakespearean.

George Williams stood in his eternal pinstripe seersucker suit and green bow tie. He'd spent more than forty years, in Charlottesville and here, teaching Shakespeare with the tireless vigor of a November cricket or a smart and willing young guide dog. Now he looked straight to Hutch and said "I knew Wade Mayfield all his life and thought it a privilege as each year passed. I know I was not wrong and not misled. Most of you, I trust, share my strong sense of being his debtor for a long time to come. Let me bid him what I see as temporary farewell with this sonnet of Shakespeare's—number 146." Then in his crisp unsentimental voice, not looking once to the book in his hand, he recited the brief indelible poem.

> "Poor soul, the center of my sinful earth,
> Thrall to these rebel powers that thee array,
> Why dost thou pine within and suffer dearth,
> Painting thy outward walls so costly gay?
> Why so large cost, having so short a lease,
> Dost thou upon thy fading mansion spend?
> Shall worms, inheritors of this excess,
> Eat up thy charge? Is this thy body's end?
> Then, soul, live thou upon thy servant's loss,
> And let that pine to aggravate thy store;
> Buy terms divine in selling hours of dross;
> Within be fed, without be rich no more:
> > So shalt thou feed on Death, that feeds on men,
> > And Death once dead there's no more dying then."

In the pause that followed the resonant end, the next speaker—a friend of Ann's who'd likewise known Wade from his first year—had barely stood when a man strode fast up the center aisle and faced the pews. Hutch had never seen the man; and when Hutch looked to Ann and Ivory, they shook their heads too—plainly a stranger.

A well-dressed stranger, maybe thirty-five, in a well-cut blazer and stiff white trousers that looked like U.S. Navy surplus. But his face was flushed an unnerving purple; and though he faced no one in the pews, his eyes were wild as they scanned the air above all heads. Finally he said "I'm a friend of

Wade's from way way back. But I hadn't seen him for more than five years, and then I saw his obituary in the Durham paper and called the English Department at Duke to find out when this service might be—I knew he wouldn't go under unwept. I felt like I had one thing to tell that nobody else would—I've heard his longtime partner is dead too—so here I am, the first human adult Wade ever slept with after high school. He told me that fact anyhow right off; and even when we parted company later, he never denied it; and I still believe him. He was my first too and the start of my luck—I'm one lucky fool.

"What I know then is the personal truth of a living witness to a life that's gone. Wade Mayfield was one enjoyable sight in any room or under the sky, by day or night. His skin was as sheer as any good silk. He never stopped laughing when the going got fast; and while I've somehow escaped AIDS myself, I know for certain I'll never love anyone as thoughtful as Wade, or anyone else that can watch you as steady or be gladder to see you just when you feel less respect for yourself than any blind mole; and above all things—" The voice failed a moment and the silence lengthened.

Though Ann had looked to Hutch's profile from the start of this unexpected splurge, trying to make him hurry it on, Hutch had stayed seated. In the man's silent falter, Hutch leaned toward Straw and signed *Get up, go stop him somehow.*

But Straw kept his seat another ten seconds.

And by then the speaker had mastered his throat. "Above all things, Wade had the best eyes south of Fairfax, Virginia—that's my bailiwick; I'm a student of eyes. Thank you, Wade. You've left a hole in the local air, but sleep on for now." He left the microphone, still nameless and flustered, and fled down the aisle on hard leather heels.

Hutch thought *Well, we're here still. The vaults haven't cracked and his speech may have been true. God's heard worse.* He looked to Ann.

She was clear-eyed but riled. Still she sketched a smile at the edge of her mouth. This space after all was a vast well of secrets—mostly from young lives, decades of students.

Ivory and both the Stuarts were calm. In the space next to Hutch, Raven's face still poised on the air, a motionless setting for eyes that surely must match any eyes between here and—where?—surely Fairfax, Virginia if not Long Island or Ultima Thule.

From that point, the service went according to plan. Ann's friend, whom the stranger had balked, spoke barely audibly about Ann's early care for Wade—how lovely they'd both been, "madonna and child."

Then another friend of Ann's rose, a colleague at the Rape Crisis Center where Ann volunteered two nights a week. She'd met Wade twice at dinner on his last healthy visit home; so she spoke only of his manners and wit, both of which she defined as "rare and delicious."

The chairman of Hutch's department spoke briefly, then a junior partner from Wade's architecture firm (a rabbity man who'd barely known Wade in his healthy days), and then the girl Wade had dated through high school. A painter with a husband and numerous children in Tennessee, she'd never lost touch with Wade through the years; and she ended by saying "Wade saw more things, with his good eyes, than any three artists I've ever met."

Then Strawson rose.

Hutch dreaded the prospect, knowing that these words were bound to cut deepest; but Straw looked sober and in full control as he reached the lectern, so Hutch shut his eyes and braced his mind.

Straw said "I've known Wade Mayfield's father since I was a child myself— he taught me the best part of what I know, if I know anything. Hutch and I spent a lot of time together forty years ago; so when he and Ann finally made their choice and started a child, I asked them if I could stand as one of the godparents once the child arrived. I forced their hand; they couldn't say No. But being themselves, they said 'Go to it.' When it came and was Wade, and they christened him soon, I bit right down on the duty I'd sworn to God to perform. All I knew how to do, though, was show him the Earth the way I'd learned it and try to tell him what seemed like to me the very few laws God means us to heed—laws about decency to everything breathing, which includes the whole planet and the distance beyond.

"I don't mean to say I set an example that Wade could learn from—I'm a reprobate. Or a renegade, more like a renegade. Anyhow he outstripped me fast. By the age of seven, he knew more about the Earth and animals than any six Cherokee medicine men; and he'd still never done an indecent, thoughtless, mean-spirited thing—excepting the normal lies and jokes involving body functions and his growing parts. That pretty much lasted, the times I saw him, till he left here and moved north to earn his keep. Up there he found out something I'd known forever—that he was not your average boy.

"It suited me fine, I never tried to stop him, I couldn't have managed if I'd wanted to stop him. He was born ready-set, I'm fairly certain. Which is all the more reason for sadness today, that the power deep in him finally thrust him out in the path of the cruelest plague in six hundred years. I don't need to tell this smart a crowd the low-down truth—that when people say this curse was sent by Fate to punish a special brand of human, we ought to ask—right back in their teeth—whether they think leukemia is sent to punish the millions of children that die of it everywhere, not to mention God's exquisite care for the children tortured by the thousand today in the Balkans or the bruised and starving everywhere from Durham to Durban."

Straw's voice stopped there; his mind was blank—he hadn't intended to say that much; anger and fierce devotion to Wade had burned him severely. But he looked to Hutch and recovered his plan. "I'd like to close by recalling a verse from Paul's letter to the Romans, chapter eight.

'I reckon the agony of this present day is not fit to be compared to the glory which shall be unveiled. For the anxious expectance of all creation eagerly waits for the last unveiling of the sons of God.'

Wade may not have known those words in his life—I doubt he admired the Apostle Paul—and I stand before you as the last man alive who can swear to the future with no trace of doubt, but I'll make you a fairly confident bet Wade knows those words and their full meaning now."

As Straw came down and moved to his seat, the organ broke into Bach's giant fugue "We All Believe in One God." Like the Handel, Hutchins had picked it himself—not favorites of Wade's but then Wade was not the one needing strength here. As the massed unanswerable statement rolled through the crowd and onward through the altar window and the baleful eyes of God on high, Hutch told himself in the wake of Straw's speech *We don't all believe God gives a damn, though.* It even seemed urgent that, here this moment, Hutch stand when the fugue had solved its conundrum and state his own sense of where Wade was, if Wade stood the chance of being anywhere more desirable than a funeral urn that was back at the house, barely full of ashes (Ann had resisted his instinct to set them here in their midst). But the fugue compounded Bach's rock-ribbed conviction through its three-minute claim with such immense power that, when it ended, Hutch could only look down to Raven beside him.

The boy had already looked up to Hutch; and when their eyes met, Raven shook his head as if throwing off water. Then he said "Lord, Lord!" in his grandmother's voice, having never heard an organ in full cry before.

Hutch smiled at the eyes and touched Raven's warm hair. "Wait for me," he said. Then he rose, went forward, faced the crowd—more nearly a crowd than anyone expected—and said "Wade's mother and I won't easily forget that you came here on this hot afternoon to back us with your presence and your memories. Surely your generous share in Wade's death will help tide us through the daunting pictures of his last days that are still fresh with us. Wade, to be sure, is beyond us all. Or so I very fervently hope, though I'm also more than half persuaded that he's conscious, not of us and our errands but of whatever peace lies still at the hub of actual things. The final piece of music we'll hear will be the only piece that Wade requested, three weeks before he died, of his mother. It's the last great song of a band whose records he loved as a baby, early as two or three years old in the early 1960s when Vietnam had us all in despair. By the time the band scattered, Wade was nine years old; and their last song was always his favorite. More than once I've watched it move him deeply. May we leave here then to the sound of the Beatles in 'Let It Be.'"

Hutch had got permission from the dean of the chapel for such an unorthodox conclusion. So the man Hutch had hired from the sound department cued the tape perfectly; and before Hutch even returned to his row, to stand while Ann and the others filed out, the truculent-choirboy voice of Paul McCartney started the song.

Anne's face, that had hardly met Hutch's today, turned quickly toward him. Her eyes looked helpless to bear another note.

Hutch knew that she could; he silently mouthed the one word *Surely*.

She chose to trust him.

As young Raven stood and entered the aisle, his head was strongly affirming the beat of a song as foreign and old to him as the farthest keening monk in Nepal, frozen in snow and adoration.

Hutch reached for the boy's hand; and they went out together back down the nave through the song's big jubilant but still sad ending, itself a claim of eventual solace as firm as Bach's. By the time they reached the steps out to sunlight, what had surprised and moved Hutch most was the sight of Alice Matthews standing beside her old black driver and turning her unblinking eyes toward Hutch. Mait's splotched white face was also a welcome sight. Then the sunlight took Hutch, and Raven broke loose to run ten yards onward into its power—the force of a guarding or killing hand.

3

It was just past eight, and dusk was rising, when Hutch and Ann saw the last guest off down the winding drive. Some thirty of them had come straight out from the chapel to the house. They'd stayed indoors for the air conditioning—with drinks, mounds of ham biscuits and artichoke pickle—and all of them had gone on speaking of Wade. But as the glare and heat of the afternoon eventually slid through gold and tan to the indigo of summer night, Wade's lingering presence likewise dimmed. And when the more watchful guests realized that now they were laughing and weeping toward his back as Wade turned his face away forever and was finally gone, the heart went out of the day at last, and they all started leaving.

The first to go had been Alice Matthews and her immensely dignified driver, bound north to Petersburg—a two-hour drive. Because Hutch had known it might unnerve Alice to see the picture unexpectedly, he'd taken down his childhood drawing that Wade insisted on bringing from New York—the landscape Hutch had drawn on a day's sketching trip with Alice near Goshen, Virginia nearly fifty years back. When he'd known for sure that Alice would come for Wade's service, he'd wrapped the picture; and now he carried it under his arm as he guided Alice's careful steps downhill to her car.

Neither one of them spoke till Alice was seated by Herc, the driver who'd napped through most of the blistering day. Her eyes went to Hutch, and she actually smiled to guarantee the truth of her words. "It won't get worse than this, old friend. They haven't got anything worse in their quiver." For years, she'd referred to *fate* as *they*.

Hutch bent to kiss her upturned forehead. "I sure to God hope not."

And for an instant Alice's certainty broke. It made her eyes crouch—Hutch saw the fear—but then she literally waved it off. "I was right the first time. Start living again."

Hutch agreed. "Yes ma'm." He opened a back door and laid the drawing in the midst of the seat. "A bolt from the past," he said.

Alice said "Oh no—"

But Hutch had shut the door and faced her again. "It's a pleasant surprise, from our best old days." When Alice looked back, he said "Don't open it—not till you're home. Let it be a surprise."

She looked confused for the first time yet. "It can't be anything valuable, darling. I'm too old for that."

"You're younger than me—in heart anyhow. If it makes you enjoy it any better though, put my name on the back. I'll collect it someday if you quit first."

"What is it? Don't surprise me."

Hutch could somehow not tell her. "Oh"—he suddenly remembered the instant he'd finished the last branch and leaf of the scene, the last pencil stroke and the title he'd thought of in his green grandiosity—"it's nothing but the meaning of things!" He laughed a little and said it quietly.

Alice showed no sign of recognition but she managed to smile. "Then I thank you. I was short on *the meaning*. I'll write you tomorrow." Her gloved right hand made one short wave; she rolled up her window and the car moved off. She made no effort to mime through the glass, but she turned as she left and watched Hutch standing alone in the yard. *Never more than alone* was all she could think as long as she saw him. But another thought came to her clearly as the car took the first curve and Hutch disappeared. *Another soul I won't see again.* Again she was right; she'd quit by Christmas, asleep in her own bed, no pain or awareness.

The last to leave was Maitland Moses, a little drunk but quiet and polite (he and Cam had argued last week and were split at present, though Cam had sat alone today at the back of the chapel and bowed to Hutch). Hutch also walked with Mait out to the terrace; and in the full dark, Mait suddenly took him in a long embrace.

Mait's earlier threat to court the plague still troubled Hutch. So when they were separate again, he said "You owe me a solemn vow."

Mait was already looking away, but he said "I know what it is."

"Swear to live—or at least try—or don't come back here. I can't take this again."

Mait said "But isn't that radically stingy?"

"May very well be; but Son, I'm as earnest as a fractured skull." Hutch was almost sure that would reach Mait now, in the live quick flesh, whether Hutch ever saw him again or not.

But Mait took a long look toward the dark south above the trees. Then he turned and managed to see Hutch's eyes. "I'll have to let you know about that—"

"Again, I'm earnest."

"—And again Hutch, I really can't be your son. One father has all but killed me already."

Oddly Hutch was too tired to take it amiss. He even grinned.

So Maitland finally had the nerve to say "You're scared and sad. I understand why. You sidelined yourself so long ago you've forgot how it feels to have a live body and need to use it." Surprised by his force, Mait gave a slight stage-idiot chuckle.

"I can't tell you how wrong you are." Then Hutch turned silently toward the house, no word of goodbye.

Mait took the refusal and went his way.

From outside, through the living room window, Hutch could see only one thing—Raven Bondurant stretched on his stomach, in his new linen suit, asleep on the couch in a deep exhaustion as pure as the night. Hutch tried to think *This child knows the last riddle and answer.* But it felt staged and false, like a poet in a movie receiving his lines from birdsong and clouds. So he moved on toward the actual child. With Ivory's permission, he'd wake the boy and maybe show him pictures of Wade's own youth, which felt like a thousand years ago.

When he opened the door though, Ann stood in the entrance, taking down the black hat she'd worn in the chapel. She was plainly readying to leave. When Hutch looked puzzled, she said "I've got every glass and dish clean. Ivory has offered to clear up the rest. I need to leave."

"You need to leave, or you think I want you gone—which one?" Hutch had no immediate preference of an answer.

Ann managed to smile. "A good deal of both."

"Then you're at least one-half mistaken. We need to sit down with Ivory here and settle this question about Wade's ashes."

Ann's whole face tightened. "That's immaterial to me—believe it."

Hutch agreed. "I believe it. I also know you'll live years longer. Time may come when you change your mind and want Wade nearer at hand than coastal Long Island."

"I've got him all in here, for good." With one hand, she ringed her throat lightly. "I *made* him, Hutch."

"You did. With some help." But then he could smile too. He reached to take her hat. "Please stay. We need you."

So while Ann heard him avoid the claim that he alone needed her for anything tonight, she let him hang the hat back up.

Together they paused to look in at Raven, still skewed and drowned. Till now they hadn't been near him without some other adult.

In her lowest voice Ann said "Who's he look like to you?"

Hutch waited. "His mother."

"Even better," Ann whispered. "His mother and Wyatt."

It chilled Hutch to feel the words in his mouth, but he let them out at normal volume. "And maybe Wade."

Ann faced Hutch. "You don't think there's any chance of that?"

Hutch thought he detected the trace of a hint that Ann had made her own discovery, or had she been told some new fact by Ivory? He wouldn't press to know. "I've given up hunting for answers long since."

Ann took that as though it were all she needed. Then they went on to Ivory.

4

Ivory had made surprising progress in the minutes since Ann first tried to leave. The kitchen was almost alarmingly clean—blank stretches of space, the cactuses watered and draining in the sink. Who could ever bear to eat here again? As the Mayfields entered, Ivory smiled to acknowledge that Ann was back. "Oh good. How about I make some fresh coffee?"

Ann said "Not for me, thanks."

But Hutch said "A gallon—and strong as tar."

Ivory stopped an instant to let the order pass. Then she chose to curtsey to Hutch and say "Yassuh, Mr. Rhett."

In a quick recovery he said "Much obliged, Miss Scarlett—oh yes" and bowed from the waist.

Ivory turned to grinding coffee beans.

Hutch joined Ann at the bare table, both vacant-eyed.

And soon Ivory sat in the one free chair, at the head, slightly dim (she was farthest from the hanging lamp).

At last Hutch said "Let's agree on the ashes."

When Ivory tucked her chin and kept silent, Ann told her "I've tried to back out of this. Wade knew I loved him like shade in August. Anywhere those ashes go is fine by me; they're not mine at all." She took a long breath. "They're not Wade either."

Ivory said "I feel very much the same way—not that I claim I shared him with you or mattered anywhere near as much through the years as you. But no, Wade's gone for me and mine."

Hutch waited through a lengthy silence. Then, not quite thinking that Ann might hear his words as insane, he risked a new tack. "Wade's either gone or he's napping in there on the couch this minute, not ten years old." When Ivory and Ann both looked mystified, Hutch pointed behind him toward the living room. "Maybe Raven Bondurant is half Wade anyhow, the only part left. At some odd angles, he helps *me* feel that Wade's not all gone."

Whatever she thought, Ann's face held its own. Nothing on Earth could amaze her tonight.

But for the first time in either Hutch or Ann's presence, Ivory flushed; and her eyes sought her own long hands laid before her. So far as she knew, Ann still hadn't read the note Wade left; but she faced both Hutch and Ann and finally said "Both of you—understand this, if nothing more. There was a time, way back, when I loved Wade and thought he loved me—in every sense of the word, I mean. That didn't turn out to last in our lives, but we stayed close friends, and he always mattered seriously. From here on, though, I make no claim whatever, now or doomsday, on Wade or his leavings or either of you. Neither will my son, who liked him too. You've been kinder than I had any right to hope for; but don't give me and my son a *thought* when you make your plans, not a single thought from here on out. We're taken care of and

I'm a strong soul, my mother's real child—I'll get us through, young Raven and I."

Though Ann still knew nothing of Wade's message to her and Hutchins, she'd sensed from the moment she saw Raven's eyes and heard his name that the boy leaned her way somehow in space, not a visible tilt or the trace of a plea to her or to anyone in sight but something unbroken and strong nonetheless. What Raven cast her way—and she knew it was cast unconsciously—was more like a net or an unseen globe with a powerful draw all round his body, a draw that pulled at her mind and the stump of her love for Wade. Ann was too sad and tired to feel more than faintly warmed, warmed from a distance as if by a lantern set on a raft in the midst of a broad river she stood beside. She faced Hutch wondering what to ask—had his mind broken slightly, and what could he mean, and why more wrangling now about ashes?

Before Ann could speak, Hutch said "All right, can we do this then—the three of us and Raven? I'll call Straw and Emily so they know we're coming— I warned them we might; they said whatever we wanted would work. We'll leave after breakfast tomorrow morning, drive up there, pay our respects to Grainger and spread Wade out where he said he should be when he still knew clearly." He looked to Ann and then Ivory. "Agreed?"

Ann said "I'll be ready."

Ivory said "Whatever you believe is right—and you know I think that's the better plan—but let me just say one more thing now: Wade was in his right mind to the last, I very much believe. He phoned me, the night Jimmy Boat got here."

Nobody, not even Jimmy, had known that. Still Hutch heard it calmly. "Anything we should know, from what he said?"

"He asked me to talk like Wyatt, a last time. Since I was a child, I could imitate Wyatt and fool everybody. I played jokes on him and Wade to the last."

Ann said "Did you do it again when he asked you?"

Ivory said "Oh yes, I called his full name the way Wyatt would when he got home at night. 'Raven Wade Mayfield, show your fine face.'"

Her voice had easily become Wyatt's voice.

It shook Hutch. He said "Can Wyatt bear this?" as though Wyatt stood in the doorway, assaulted and bracing to answer.

Ann said "Bear what?"

Hutch said entirely seriously "Us talking like this."

Ivory said "No question. He's got all of Wade now—but I told you that. That was Wyatt's only plan, from the week they met." Her face was pained for the instant it took to make the last concession.

Hutch covered her hands with his own.

Ivory met his eyes to thank him, then withdrew her right hand and held it to Ann.

When Ann had again closed a circuit among them, Hutch could withdraw. He stood and moved toward the inside door, meaning to check on young Raven's nap; then find Wade's letter and pass it to Ann, out of Ivory's sight, before Ann left for her own house. She'd said again just now that she was going and he hadn't objected. With Ivory and Raven here (Hutch had persuaded them to move from the inn), there was no spare bed, unless Ann wanted to sleep in Wade's room—the bed he died in or a pallet on the floor.

Hutch couldn't offer her that, not yet; and for all the help they'd given each other in the past few weeks, he couldn't yet want to fold Ann back into his own life for good—not before they'd managed a drastic coming to terms with all her own years of grievance and want, and his own cooled bitterness: his ingrained distance. She'd need to make her own choice on that, then to tell him somehow and let him decide what he could take and whether he could learn to stand in closer. For all the margin of space around him, by his own lights, Hutch had never abandoned anyone yet, not anyone who mattered in his life; he didn't plan to start this late.

But he quickly thought of a fresh exception. *Young Mait Moses. I've turned him out.* And as Hutch reached the door of the living room, with Raven snoring lightly beyond him, he saw Mait's face in his mind this evening, trailing his hellbent body downhill. *I'll phone him later; Mait's too good to lose.* Then Hutch walked silently over to Raven, got down on one knee beside the boy's head and held the palm of his hand a half inch above the damp hair. Though Hutch couldn't know it, some form of the same cloud of force that had drawn at Ann was reaching for him. Hutch brushed his chin to the warm whorled ear and told himself *This child knows me somehow. He's trusting me here.*

The child's rest, though, was fabulously deep—way past fear or hope or any plain dream. At its lowest ebb, still Raven's mind could know that it and all his body was safe as any child alive, banked with care like a fast horse with roses.

Hutch knew he mustn't turn strange here. *No plans for this child. His mother's leaving and he's going with her.* So he rose and went to find the letter that Wade had written for his parents to read. In the two weeks since Hutch had first read it, he'd felt a conscious low-grade shame, withholding it from Ann—her name after all was in the address as plainly as his. Why had he waited? *Part meanness no doubt but also maybe the fear that Ann might have plunged off on some errand of her own and pressed on Ivory for hard details, or even flown to New York and tracked down the child and blundered into some innocent harm. No way to hide it another hour though.*

Before Hutch had taken two more steps, he knew—he all but knew for a certainty—that the letter was not just the last news from Wade but was also maybe the main truth he'd left them: a last open door. *This story may not be ending yet.* No way he could keep the news from Ann beyond tonight, and no wish to keep it.

5

Ivory and Raven had been in their room, asleep, since ten o'clock that evening. Hutch had managed to stay awake till midnight, listing the names of guests while he recalled them and reading all the sonnets of Shakespeare. He hadn't read straight through the whole cycle—a hundred and fifty-four poems as mysterious as any ever written—since his years in Oxford when he'd sometimes drive the forty-odd miles between his college and Shakespeare's home in Stratford-upon-Avon just to stand on the bridge there or poke through the streets and silently think through a speech from the plays or a few of the sonnets. He'd known a handful by heart since the ninth grade; they'd clung to his mind with the hooks of young memory.

Even here when he'd read to the end of them all, and the clock said quarter past midnight, Hutch shut both the book and his eyes and lay still to run through the bristling power of

> They that have power to hurt and will do none,
> That do not do the thing they most do show. . . .

And

> What is your substance, whereof are you made,
> That millions of strange shadows on you tend?

His light was out though before he recalled, and found he still knew, the whole of the poem that—forty years ago—had seemed the flag of his care for Strawson.

> Lord of my love, to whom in vassalage
> Thy merit hath my duty strongly knit,

To thee I send this written ambassage
To witness duty, not to show my wit:
Duty so great, which wit so poor as mine
May make seem bare, in wanting words to show it,
But that I hope some good conceit of thine
In thy soul's thought all naked will bestow it,
Till whatsoever star that guides my moving
Points on me graciously with fair aspect,
And puts apparel on my tatter'd loving
To show me worthy of thy sweet respect:
    Then may I dare to boast how I do love thee,
    Till then not show my head where thou mayst prove me.

Now in the dark of his house, Hutch lay and let tall waves of amazed thanks and charred loss pour freely through him—thanks for the plentiful love he'd got, through the length of his life, from sane other souls and harsh regret for his monstrous failures to take and honor every gift of flesh and pleasure, trust and pardon, that was offered his way. The failures came to him as they always did, stark separate faces—Straw's, Rob's, Ann's, Grainger's, Wyatt's, Wade's. Before he could check the hurtling speed of his runaway guilt, Hutch had run through dozens of students, friends, loves, all the lost names of lives he'd skimped or cheated on. *Waste, grim waste in the teeth of plenty.* He was almost asleep when the bedside phone rang; he caught it at once. "Yes?"

"Hutch, it's Ann. I'm sorry to wake you—"

"You didn't at all; I'm up reading Shakespeare. Thanks for the company today; it truly counted."

Ann pushed that aside. "I've read Wade's letter and I guess I can maybe half understand why you felt you should hold it back till tonight—you were wrong; still I can't fight you now—but before we meet in the morning, I just need to know a few things."

"Me too. It's still a deep mystery to me."

"But you've discussed the details with Ivory?"

Hutch said "In about four cloudy sentences only, not a real discussion. I honestly haven't felt I had the right. And Ivory's said nothing really, not to me, that throws any further light on the boy. She's said we have no debts to her at all, but you heard her say that much again tonight."

"You think Raven's ours?" Raw as the words were, Ann's voice had its old patient candor. *I can take what comes; so can you, beside me.*

Hutch almost laughed. "He's not ours, no ma'm."

"You know what I mean—is Raven actually kin to Wade?" Even Ann heard the quaintness of her question.

"I very much hope he is—kin to us too. We may never learn."

Ann said "Don't be so sure we won't. As he goes, Wade's traits may well show in him. Meanwhile, we can't just let him and Ivory drift off and pay them no mind at all, not for the entire rest of our lives. She'll need boxloads of money through the years and practical help to raise a child alone in New York."

"She can do it, Ann. She plainly means to. She may never want us to see him again."

"And you don't plan to ask for anything—some reasonable visits, a hand in the child's life? You don't think we should contribute to his care?"

Hutch said "I want every bit of that, yes; but Ivory Bondurant owns her own mind—I've learned that well. I very much doubt she'd smile on our hopes. Never forget she's Wyatt's sister."

"Oh I haven't, not once." Ann waited so long Hutch thought she was gone; then she suddenly said "You think that Wyatt will give us some peace now?" Ann was as likely to mention ghosts as any particle physicist.

Hutch was stunned for a moment. "Wyatt? Peace?"

"You know what I mean."

I do; too well. They hadn't mentioned Wyatt since the night Wade died, when they'd both acknowledged his nearness and power all through the house. Hutch said "Wyatt's gone, I'm fairly sure; but Ivory's got to be as scorched as we by memories of him—what he thought about us as Wade's close kin, the ghastly way he chose to die."

"Don't blame poor Wyatt for that; God knows, he was not himself then."

Hutch said "How do you know that? And don't call him *poor.*"

"Ivory told me that much, tonight in the kitchen when you walked out."

"How did she put it?"

Ann said "Just that plainly—you were barely out of sight; she turned those strong eyes on me and said 'You know my brother lost his mind before he died.' Since she'd been that honest, I pushed a little. I asked her how far back that confusion went, in his life and ours—"

"Oh, careful, Ann."

"No, Ivory took it calmly. I could see she knew I was fishing for hope that all he'd thought and said about us was truly insane, but she didn't stretch an inch past the truth. She said 'I date it from three weeks before he picked up the pistol. Till then he was clear-headed—wild and sure he was right but clear-headed.'"

Hutch waited for Ann to go on.

She didn't; she'd apparently finished for the night.

So he opened his mouth to say "Till morning then" but other words came. He heard himself say "Could you come back here?"

"Now, tonight?"

"Whenever, for good."

Ann said "You can't mean that."

Hutch wondered if he did. It had shocked him to say it; it could be anything from a moan to a lie. Still he said "I very well may mean it, yes."

"You're thoroughly worn out and sad like me. Sleep awhile anyhow; we can talk tomorrow." Her tone was a little too sensible.

Hutch said "Are you at the office or home?"

"Home—great God, I don't work till Wednesday."

"Till breakfast then."

Ann said "Till when. Or whenever, friend."

Hutch said "Old friend—"

But by then she was gone.

Once Hutch had lain on another ten minutes, asking himself to explain the plea he made to Ann—was it a plea or a hurtful probe?—and finding no answer, faces began to rise again and challenge his failure. This time the clearest face was Maitland's. Hutch remembered he'd promised himself to call Mait later tonight, after their bleak parting. The lighted clock said nearly one, but he seldom hesitated to call students anytime—they hardly slept except on Sundays. Yet it took a long ten rings before Mait answered. "Moses," he said.

Hutch said "Mayfield."

A wait, then Mait said "Morning there, Mayfield."

In a shy reflex Hutch said "You alone?"

"No, I've got Barnum and Bailey here with matched white tigers and a small troupe of midgets."

Mait seldom joked and Hutch felt shut out, so he only said "I'll leave you to your midgets then. I just meant to tell you I spoke too harshly, way too harshly, tonight as you left."

"No you didn't. You were telling the reasonable truth; I still wouldn't hear it."

"I was too harsh though."

"You were honest," Mait said. "It's all harsh news, here where I'm living. I just can't live by your fears, Hutch."

"Then by all means don't. Nobody yet ever got happy from me."

"Now you're lying. You've cheered me a lot. I told you you've given me a whole sense of life, of somewhere to go and a way to get there."

"Can I lean on that? Will you try to keep living?"

Mait said "Absolutely, for what it's worth. I just can't promise to obey you though. My body can't. Or won't anyhow."

Hutch realized Mait's voice hadn't cracked once in maybe two weeks; the boy had pushed through some final membrane and stood tall and ready for stripped-down life. In the dark Hutch's own eyes were suddenly exhausted; a kind of mist had settled on his face, a dense cold webbing. He said "Please come to supper on Tuesday."

"Cam and I both?"

"Well, if you like. I thought the two of you were on outs."

Mait waited. "We were but he came by an hour ago. Wade's service really moved him."

"He's not still with you?"

"No, but we talked calmly. I'll go by to see him at the hospice tomorrow."

Hutch said "And you want to bring him here Tuesday?"

"Do I hear a suggestion you don't want Cam?" Mait was calm at the thought.

Hutch managed a laugh. "Oh no, I've mostly been a third wheel, some sixty years and rolling."

Mait thought he heard a trace of self-pity. *I'd better ignore it.* So he just said "We'll bring the groceries and cook them. Cam's a dynamite chef."

"I doubt I can easily eat dynamite."

Mait said "No, *dynamite* means he's really good." Then he guessed that Hutch was joking after all. "You know that, right?"

"My ears can still just barely hear what young people say, yes. And sure, I'll be glad to let Cam cook—some night next week." Then Hutch thought *What if Ann's back here by then?* But he said "I'll be hungry and waiting at six."

Mait said "Adiós," not knowing he'd echoed Wade's farewell on leaving New York.

Neither did Hutch but the word snagged in him, a strong clean hook. He could only think to sign off with the simplest translation, inaudibly whispered. "Yes, Mait, *to God.*" Then before he hung up, Hutch thought he should also have phoned Straw with word of the plans for morning. *Not tonight. I'm finished. I'll call him at dawn; he'll be there the rest of his life anyhow.* The phone was barely back in its cradle before Hutch slept.

6

So in all the house no one was awake but Raven Bondurant, flat on his twin bed six feet from Ivory's in the back guest room. In the perfect dark the boy was not scared, despite the depth of stillness around him—a stillness he'd never heard, even on Long Island. He was holding in both hands, atop the sheet, a doll that had been Wade's. Hutch's father had bought it for Hutch, the summer they visited Jamestown together, the site of the first white permanent English-speaking colony on the continent and the harbor into which the first black African captives were brought and sold as things.

The doll was a well-made realistic copy, ten inches tall, of a Stuart cavalier in his doublet and soft boots, his ruddy skin, blond beard and one earring—hardly the kit for life on the rim of a country settled by six million red men with plans of their own. The doll's painted china face wore the gold-struck inner gaze of a murderous innocent, bent on triumph if it could just master the starving icebound winter ahead.

When Raven had gone in tonight, at Ivory's urging, to thank Hutch for all his attention today, Hutch had reached to a shelf by the living room fireplace, found the doll and held it out to him. "This is yours from here out, Raven. Wade used to love it when he was a boy."

Though Raven himself would never quite know it—nor his mother or grandmother, Hutch nor Ann—the lasting traits of Wade Mayfield, who was Raven's father (Wade's merciful wit and early decency), would seep into the child's growing body through this small likeness of a body both paler and older than Raven's, the artful token of three whole peoples (two of whose blood ran in the child's veins) locked in the toils of a mortal combat still undecided but apparently endless. And while it was still three hours till dawn on Hutch's green hill in the midst of quiet woods, that nonetheless harbored their own nocturnal raptors and prey, the expectant boy took only short naps till daylight showed him this latest treasure—an unthinkably intricate potent doll, in his small hands, that would be his for good.

7

When Hutch phoned Strawson at six that dawn, Straw showed no surprise and said that Emily was anticipating the Mayfields and Bondurants for lunch. So Hutch and Ann—with Raven and Ivory—headed out in a bright and remarkably dry midmorning for the short trip north. Raven sat by Hutch up front with Wade's ashes boxed on the floor at the child's feet. Very little was said by anyone, though Ann would occasionally point to a distant house or tree or a lone white horse and describe it to Raven.

They even passed a solitary mule in a huge mown field; and Ann said "Raven, remember that sight. Mules are all but a thing of the past; they used to *own* the country."

Ivory was the one who laughed and showed interest. "My mother's favorite brother was Mule—she's always saying he was just that stubborn. But I never knew Muley; he died too young." She leaned forward near enough to tap Raven's head. "Maybe I ought to start calling you Mule, Mr. Set-in-His-Ways."

Raven didn't look back but, once he'd watched the mule out of sight, he said "You talking about that boy who died when I wasn't born?"

Ivory said "Yes, he was your great-uncle."

Still watching the road, Raven said "Don't mention him dying again."

Hutch said "Why not?"

"I can't stand to hear how children die." From then on Raven faced only the woods.

So Hutch tried to think how this world looked through this boy's eyes. If Raven had watched as much television as most young children, and since he'd barely left Long Island till two days ago, these hardwood thickets and evergreen jungles must look more like the surface of Venus than anything common to New York state—some planet anyhow where men, women, children were far from the center of anyone's gaze. And surely, Hutch knew, the child who grows up watching nothing more self-possessed and reliable than people and cars, buildings and madmen is cruelly blighted from the start. *Is it too late here to let this child watch fields and trees and feed his mind every element it craves?* They were no more than five or ten minutes from the Kendal place when Hutch said at last "You enjoying the scenery?"

Raven still didn't turn and he offered no answer.

Ivory said "Son, answer Mr. Mayfield."

Finally the child said "If I tell the truth, it'll hurt his feelings."

Hutch laughed. "No you won't; I'm a tough old turtle."

Raven said "I don't see *nothing* I recognize. Lord, I feel like I'm lost for good."

Ivory heard the sound of her own mother's voice; still she said "You don't see *anything*—"

Hutch said "Trust me—this is my native ground." He chuckled again.

Raven said "That's the problem. I stopped trusting people."

Now Ivory laughed. "Don't talk crazy, Son."

Raven pressed his face to the window glass. "It's not me that's crazy. People killing children everywhere. You watch the TV, you'll learn some news."

Everybody let the child's words settle slowly; then Hutch said "Son, you're safe with me."

Raven looked round and studied Hutch like a hard lesson. Finally he said "I'm not your son."

Ivory said "What a thing to say. You mind your manners."

Hutch grinned at Raven. "You're right as rain. I'm a well-wisher though; I could still be your friend."

Raven said "Well, I'm thinking that over."

All the adults laughed.

But the child faced Hutch. "Man, I'm telling you the truth."

Hutch said "I never doubted you were."

8

It was past noon then when the car drew up in the shade of the oak at the Kendal place and Straw came down the back steps to meet them. The previous day, after the service, Raven had taken a shine to Straw and followed him up the slope back of Hutch's—the bare crest from which they could see for twelve miles south. Beyond the spires of Chapel Hill, Straw knew very little about what lay there peaceful before them; but he got the boy to join him in populating the wide sea of woods with buildings and creatures designed to fulfill their joint pleasures—horse-riding schools full of pretty girls in various shades, an ice-skating rink with giant benevolent dinosaur-instructors, tremendous rooms with women and tall men boldly dancing in long white clothes, and numerous other houses and contests: all likewise benign, though some hilarious and some fairly risky.

So as Raven was the first to climb from the car this Monday noon, he ran toward Strawson till Straw stopped midway and crouched to greet him. Somehow the unaccustomed sight of an open-armed grown man stopped the boy in his tracks till Ivory came up behind him. "That's Mr. Stuart, Son. From yesterday. He took you walking. Show him your new friend."

Raven stayed in place but slowly extended the cavalier doll.

Straw knew it on sight; Wade had brought it up here on numerous visits. But he accepted it from Raven, studied its face a moment, then handed it back. "You know who that belonged to, don't you?"

Raven nodded, silent.

Ivory said "Tell him 'Yes, thank you.' "

But Raven waited, then said "That dead man" and suddenly laughed.

Hutch and Ann had caught up by then; so everybody could laugh with the boy as Straw stood and led them on into the darkened cool house, the roof that had sheltered a sizable portion of Hutch's long-dead kin a century back and further still. Their faces hung on in the least used rooms—Straw had bothered to round up portraits and photographs, from Hutch's grand-mother Eva, when he first moved here. They were all plainly marked by their own ancestors with the long broad foreheads and splendid eyes that, even in painful antique poses, burned with a heat that could still be felt—a heat trans-formable to love, hate, victory at a moment's warning and tirelessly ready. One by one, as Straw showed Raven through the rooms, he pointed the pic-tures out with histories and family names.

The boy absorbed as much as he could of an almost foreign world and time. Then at the picture of one hefty woman, swathed in black and coiled with braids, he finally told Straw "I think I need to stop doing this."

Straw said "I may agree with you there." Then he led Raven down to join the others for the bountiful meal that Emily had worked on since nearly dawn—eight vegetables (picked in the garden today), endless fresh crisp fried corn cakes, iced lemon tea and a strawberry pie with cream from half a mile down the road—a cow named Battleaxe.

Through that, Wade's ashes waited on a table on the shady back porch among the day's harvest of ripe tomatoes—maybe fifty big fruit. Thin as Wade had been on the night he died, his ashes filled the salt-glazed urn that Hutch had driven to Jugtown to get three days ago, made for him by his friend Vernon Owens there—a master potter from a line of potters that went straight back to Staffordshire, England more than two centuries past. The urn was eighteen inches tall and a high tan-gray with the figure of a dark horse running on the curved face.

The horse was the potter's own idea—he'd met Wade more than once in Wade's childhood and said he recalled the boy asking him once to make a horse's head, life-size, in clay and then bake it hard. Vernon claimed Wade said that horses knew more than people at least. That would have been maybe twenty-five years back; Wade would have been maybe seven years old. Hutch had no memory of such a request, but he'd taken Vernon's memory as true. So he brought home the urn, poured in the two quarts of Wade's grainy ashes with small knots of bone and left them to wait for whatever plan developed for their scattering.

They were minerals now and dumb to the voices that washed out past them through open doors from the dining room. The voices, though, were gladder than not to be alive—well fed and gathered for this brief pause at the edge of Wade's last traces on Earth.

9

By the time they'd got to the end of lunch, Ivory could see that Raven's sleeplessness from last night was calling for rest. They were still at the table, she was sitting by Hutch, so she asked if they had time for Raven to lie down for maybe half an hour.

Everyone present had reared a child, and Hutch said "By all means."

Raven objected seriously, though his eyes were closing.

But Ivory said "Everybody else go right on with your plans. I'll stay here and let this rascal nap awhile. Otherwise he'll be mean as a hornet all evening."

Hutch turned to Ann. "We're in no hurry, are we?"

Ann said "Not I."

Hutch said "In that case, we could all stand a breather. Let's wait in the cool here while Raven snoozes."

Straw had known, since he first laid eyes on Raven, that Wade was somehow involved in his life. And here he could sense that Hutch shared the feeling. *Hutch wants this child to scatter Wade with him.* Straw said "Raven, you and your mother can rest in the upstairs room with that fat lady's picture you loved so much."

Much as he hated yielding to it, Raven was at the mercy of his age. Like most children, his strength had quit him in an instant with no warning; and he was almost asleep in his chair. But before Ivory led him off toward the stairs, he said "Don't anybody *do* anything here till I get back."

Emily said "We won't, Son. Go have a nice dream."

It was natural enough, even for a woman who'd borne one daughter and no male child, to call Raven *son*; but Straw heard the word in Emily's mouth as a punishment on his own past and future, his silent refusal to give her children beyond their own daughter, so far off now. In the instant, his whole life stretched like a salt plain, behind and before him. All he said however was "A first-rate meal, Em. You're better by the day."

Not meeting Straw's eyes, Emily thanked him. Then she and Ann stood to begin clearing up and washing dishes.

10

Hutch and Straw went to the front room and took easy chairs for a snooze of their own. First, Hutch leafed through the day's *News and Observer*. It had been twenty years since he'd read the news daily; so whenever he came across a copy of a small-city paper, he was always surprised how full it was of possible lumber for stories and poems—vanished children, an adult male dwarf beat to a pulp in domestic combat somewhere in east Durham (the article noted that "Officer Pulliam said 'He was nothing but gristle when we got there'") and the perennial fuming letter-writers, flashing their crank convictions like road flares with nuclear fuel.

Hutch looked up and read Straw an item on the claim of a twelve-year-old black girl that she'd walked to Raleigh from Cordele, Georgia with a month-old baby and an old bulldog to celebrate her great-grandmother's birthday. The piece made the girl seem smart and credible, despite her grandmother's stated doubt—"She may be telling the truth. I can't say. I got so many descendants, you know, I wouldn't recognize most of them stretched out on the bubbling road under my flat feet."

Straw laughed, took a long breath and said straight out "You recognize Wade in Raven, don't you?"

"Amen."

"Was it news to you?"

Hutch said "It was news all right, big news; but we'll never be sure the news is true—not short of far more tests and studies than Ivory Bondurant would ever agree to or I'd ask for." Then he wondered *Did Wade discuss this with Straw?* So he said "How long have you known about Raven?"

Straw said "The minute I laid eyes on him. First time I saw him tilt his head—Wade Mayfield's hid in his spine like a great spring."

Hutch almost agreed. "I hope that's the case. We'll never know."

Straw said "If there's any question of leaving the child any land or money in your will, you could probably get a court order for tests."

Hutch stopped him with a flat palm, firm in the air. "You, of all people, know I thrive on mystery. Anyhow what's to say I can't leave every scrap I own to the nearest bird dog, if that's my whim—not to speak of a likable healthy child that may be my dead son's only leavings?"

Though Hutch smiled to say it, Straw knew he was earnest and wouldn't budge further. Through a drowsy half hour then, they sat at the ancient roll-top oak desk and looked through Emily's meticulous records of every seed planted since January 1st, every nickel paid out for help or supplies, even the pints of bourbon Straw bought to tide his tenant through quarterly three-day drunks and recoveries (she kept no record of Straw's own quarts).

Numbingly familiar as the process was, Hutch took some comfort in Straw's hot nearness beside him at the desk and in the certainty that, at the least, they were once more performing a major rite of the human race, as old as man's descent from the trees—far older than any glimpse of art more durable than the blankets of wildflowers laid on their dead kin by roving Neanderthal bands in Asia sixty thousand years back.

When Straw gave signs of dozing again, upright at the desk, Hutch said "Put your head down and dive for five minutes."

Straw obeyed, laid his arms and head on the desk and was gone in three seconds.

Hutch took the time to rise and walk silently toward the far bookcase, lift its glass door, then choose the last volume of *Lee's Lieutenants* from Straw's miles of Civil War lore. With a glance to check on Straw's snoozing breath, Hutch reached in his pocket and brought out the wrapped small stack of pictures he'd found in Wade's papers—the nude young men: some nude, some naked as peeled raw eels. He'd thought of them at sunrise today. *Get rid of them quick, or they'll break Ann down.* Again, though, Hutch hadn't managed to burn them. Whether they were Wyatt's or Wade's brief companions or store-bought outright provocations, they still were live traces of a vanishing warmth.

With no clear plan, merely acting on the instant—half joking in fact— Hutch slid the pictures to the back of the shelf behind *Lee's Lieutenants.* Given the depth of cobwebs and dust, it was guaranteed Emily never touched these books. Straw might find them, though, years down the road and think of—what? A *life I denied him, for good or bad? Or simple human pleasure in itself, these vulnerable young men—many surely dead now.*

As Hutch slid the one concealing volume back into place, Straw roused and said "Now—" He plainly meant Wade, *Now we lose Wade at last.*

11

At the final moment Ann touched Hutch's arm and said "Friend, I'm going to wait here with Emily."

The pain in her eyes kept Hutch from urging a change of heart. So it was past two when he took up the urn and walked with Strawson, Ivory and Raven down the back stairs and out to Grainger's. By then the heat had climbed past ninety, but the window air conditioner at Grainger's was plainly not running, and every door and window was shut.

Straw said "Everybody brace yourself; here comes a brick kiln. This old gent's been a little cold-natured for the past few decades. We won't stay long." Straw climbed to the door, knocked twice, then opened it and leaned inside. When he'd said "You ready?" and got Grainger's nod, he waved in the others.

Few brick kilns could have been appreciably hotter; but Grainger was in his automatic chair, fully dressed in his usual khakis with his neck buttoned tight and a cardigan sweater. Straw had stood aside to let Ivory enter first; and when Grainger saw her, he stood on his own—not waiting for the chair lift and lurching only slightly. Straw had prepared him for a lady from New York, with her young son, and Hutch of course; but he'd mentioned nothing about the lady being colored or who the child might favor. If Grainger was surprised, he gave no sign. He did bow deeply, though, when Straw introduced her as Miss Bondurant; and he offered her his chair.

Ivory declined but introduced Raven. "Mr. Walters, this is my son, Raven Bondurant." When Raven stepped forward to take Grainger's hand, Ivory said "Son, Mr. Walters helped raise Wade."

Oddly, Raven said "Thank you," not quite sure for what; then he felt mildly shamed and fell back silent.

Grainger faced the boy long enough to say "Pretty name"; then he had to sit—his knees were unreliable in such dry weather (his joints worked opposite to everyone else's). As he sat, his eyes found Ivory a last time. "You'll have to excuse my feebleness—no disrespect to you, ma'm."

Ivory reassured him.

But by then he'd fixed on Hutch and the urn. "You finally going to keep my promise to Wade?"

Hutch said "Yes sir, it's only right."

Grainger said "You've done a fair number of wrong things, you understand—I been mighty worried." His old dragon eyes could well have been smiling—even Straw wasn't sure—or they might have been merely pleased at their victory.

Either way, Hutch was easy. He'd mainly been watching to see whether Grainger paid close attention to Raven here by him. *Who can he see in this child's eyes?*

Grainger was done with Raven though. He'd quit liking children once Wade was grown, and was making no exception today.

So when the old man seemed suddenly gone on one of his driftings, Hutch said "I wish you could walk down with us to scatter these ashes. We better head on."

Straw said "Mr. Walters, you had your nap?"

Grainger said "Haven't had a good nap since the war." As always he meant his war—France in 1918, the trenches, cooties, mustard gas.

Raven laughed and looked to his mother.

Ivory put both hands on her boy's strong shoulders and said "Mr. Walters, we're honored to meet you. I've heard Wade speak of you many many times—Wade and my brother both appreciated you, and I only wish my mother could have been here. She hails from Virginia, a good while back, and misses the South."

Grainger didn't face her but said "She had her head tested lately?" Before anyone could decide to laugh, he said "I'm from Maine" (it was literally true; his father Rover had left Virginia in early despair and gone north to build boats in the late 1880s). If he'd meant anything by that sideswipe, Grainger gave no further sign.

So with no more to say, and no lead from Grainger, Ivory steered Raven toward the door. They'd wait outside; the sun was cooler than this stifling room.

Straw said "Mr. Walters, you better rest a little. I'll be back down with your supper at four. Call if you need us—Emily's up at the house."

Grainger raised his right arm, as if in school, to speak; but when Hutch and Straw moved closer on him, he found no words.

Hutch thought he'd simply forgot his point; he said "Just wait. It'll come back to you."

But Straw understood. He grinned broadly and slapped his own thigh. "So you're saying you want me to leave you and Hutchins?"

Grainger still didn't speak. He was facing the blank television screen as if it would, at any moment, flash instructions for his imminent departure or as if he might learn from his gaze alone a whole intelligent new brand of speech and the hard-earned power of generous judgment.

Straw said to Hutch "He wants you by yourself. I'll be outside with Ivory and the boy." As he left, Straw said "Mr. Walters, when they made you, they threw away the door—much less the key."

Straw's hand had hardly touched the doorknob when Grainger said "You let Hutch walk down yonder by himself, hear?" When Straw was silent, Grainger raised his voice. The ghost of its old self, its old bull bellow, it was still astonishing. "You hear what I said?"

Straw didn't look back but he said "Aye, aye, sir"—not harshly but whispered.

So when Strawson had shut the door behind him, Hutch went to the edge of the bed and sat. The urn was in his hands, resting on his knees. He thought *I ought to be pouring tears; this is straight out of* Homer *or late Shakespeare.* But he'd wept all his tears, very likely the tears of the rest of his life. What he felt was ease in the silent presence of a permanent feature of his usable landscape, the shadow of a broad hill he'd grown up beside. *Don't even think of the day he'll die.* After a minute with nothing from Grainger, Hutch said "They're waiting for me out there in the blistering sun. I better join them. I'll be up here again next week to see you with less on my mind. Tell Straw to call me if you need the least thing."

Grainger faced him then, the only judge Hutch had ever acknowledged.

It almost bowled Hutch over on his back—the total recognition in that broad skull, the record of all his life that survived in this lean face, the man that moved it, the ancient eyes that even here were still feeding constantly on what the day offered. *The only live thing, myself included, that's seen my whole life.* Hutch couldn't speak.

Grainger said "Son, let me see Wade please." The *please* was the shock; *please* had disappeared from Grainger's speech forty years ago.

The lid of the urn was taped neatly shut with silver duct tape. For an instant Hutch hesitated to obey; he sat upright on the edge of the bed still. But once the old man leaned far forward and waited for the sight, there was no more question of refusing consent. Hutch peeled back the tape, set the lid beside him on the taut bedspread and tilted the open urn toward Grainger.

Grainger leaned still farther till his eyes were less than a foot from the ashes. "You sure that's him?"

"As sure as anybody could be that didn't watch him burn. No sir, I trust the people that did it."

Grainger said "People didn't use to do this, you know—just cook people down like sand in the wind. You think Wade Mayfield can rise up at Judgment, all parched like this?" His right hand went to the lip of the urn.

Hutch knew that God or the likelihood of punishment had meant less to Grainger, in the past fifty years, than money or vengeance. *Is he changing here on the verge of the grave? No clean way to ask—he'd never tell me.* So Hutch said "I feel fairly sure Wade can rise, yes sir, if there's any such day. A lot of saints burned—you recall Joan of Arc, old Nero's martyrs, soldiers in firefights, your own friends in France, young children in buildings every night of the year."

Grainger was not fully satisfied, but he said "All right." He saw no reason to alarm Hutch further. Then again he moved to stand on his own.

Hutch reached for the lid.

"Leave it open, I told you." Again Grainger got to his feet, unaided. He went to the nearest kitchen drawer, reached toward the back and brought out a box maybe three inches long—an old cream-colored box tied with a ribbon that had once been red.

Hutch had never seen it.

Grainger came back with enormous care, stood before Hutch, untied the ribbon, reached under a yellowed scrap of cotton and drew out a gold ring—a wide plain band.

At first Hutch failed to recognize it.

But Grainger held the ring between thumb and finger and met Hutch's eyes again. "Make up your mind who this is for next." He didn't hand it over.

Hutch suddenly knew. It had to be his family's wedding ring—the one old Rob Mayfield gave his bride well over a century ago in Virginia. Nearly four decades had passed since Hutch had seen it. After his and Ann's sad inter-rupted Christmas in Italy, she'd abandoned the hope to use it as their wed-ding ring. Hutch had left it with Polly Drewry in Richmond; she'd warmed old Rob in his last sick years, then Rob's son Forrest (Hutch's own grandfa-ther). Polly had conditionally accepted the ring but for safekeeping only. She'd written to say she'd hold it for Hutch, taped to the underside of her bed. Then while the years passed, Hutch forgot the ring. Polly had never mentioned it again; and when she died, in her peaceful confusion, Hutch sold her few sticks of furniture for minus nothing—no thought of a ring worth maybe no more than eighty dollars, with a burden of suffering locked in its round. Yet here, in its shining life, it was. Had Polly sent it to Grainger somehow before she died? She and Grainger had never been great friends; they loved the same men. Still seated on the bed, Hutch could only say "Is it what I think?"

Grainger said "Don't matter what you think."

"Polly sent it to you?"

Grainger only said "You do what you know is right with it next."

In real uncertainty, Hutch said "I'd appreciate some advice." With all its other history, he also knew that the ring had spent some years of its life on Grainger's wife's hand—hard beautiful burnt-out Gracie Walters, who'd abandoned Grainger and drunk herself deep into the ground, a young woman still.

So Grainger reached inside the urn and pressed the gold band into the absolute center of the ashes till it barely showed.

Hutch said "You want me to scatter it with him?"

Grainger said "I told you I got no plans. You the man here now."

It was hardly the first time Hutch had felt grown, though like most humans he secretly felt the same age always—some tentative year in midado-lescence. Yet with this sudden license from Grainger, he did feel stronger. He stood in the short space between himself and the harsh old man and looked all round him.

The crowded wall of pictures beyond—poor scorched-out Gracie, Rob in his prime, Wade in his childhood (vivid as paint) and the whole constella-tion of kinfolk, statesmen, and murderous generals from Grainger's war—

they all seemed spokes of a slow-turned wheel in which the old man was somehow, for lack of another, the hub and axle. As Hutch cradled the ashes and moved to leave, his left hand grazed the cloth of Grainger's shoulder.

Grainger said "Go on."

12

Outside, Straw stood with Ivory and Raven in the deep oak shade. The heat had stilled them, and they stood as separate as horses in a field; but when Hutch came down Grainger's few steps, he saw how the three of them looked like the harbor he'd longed for all his life and never found. *Ask for them, here and now — then they'll* know *I'm crazy.*

When Hutch reached them though, thinking of some right way to ask for such a gift, Straw spoke first. "Ivory and I want to give you privacy, if you want that, down there at the creek." He pointed to the woods.

It seemed unthinkable — coming from Straw who'd cared for Wade as much as anyone left alive (except maybe Ann; who could speak for Ann Gatlin?) — that Straw would surrender his place in Wade's last moments among them. Hutch was all but ready to say "God, no, I need you all."

But at that moment young Raven ran off toward the single-strand barbed wire fence that lay between here, the woods and the creek in its steep valley. The fence was thirty yards off in full sun; and when the boy reached the ugly strand of wire, he looked back toward the solemn adults and burst out in a low hilarious unbroken laugh.

It felt to Hutch like the first authentic joy the human race had earned.

Raven spun in place a few quick times, then stopped with arms out to calm his dizzy head. Finally he looked back and called out plainly. "Mother, I'm *gone* from here." Then he bent to pass through the wire to the strip of field that lay between him and the trees.

Ivory kept smiling but she said "You hold on right where you are, Mr. Smarty." She looked to Hutchins and, though her face was empty of anything like a threat or plea, she said "You think you could stand for him to walk down with you?"

Hutch thought *Wait — what are you telling me?* But in the presence of Ivory's commandingly peaceful eyes, he knew *She wants the child to go;* so he said at last "I'd be more than pleased."

She said "Then I'll wait back in the house." Her eyes had always seemed past weeping; they were still in her mind's full control, but what showed through them was a sorrow beyond what Hutch could have guessed.

Straw, in a sudden pool of green light, was his best old self—more vulnerable than any young runner at the end of his sprint, far more likely to last. He said to Hutch "You're really sure?"

"Of what?"

"Of me not walking down with you this time."

Hutch accepted that. "You'll be here the rest of your life though, right?"

Straw said "To the best of my knowledge, yes—it's my intention."

By then Ivory had walked halfway toward Raven. When he'd slowly obeyed her beckoning hand and stood before her, she told him to help Mr. Mayfield politely, not to act silly and to show his respect for Wade and Wyatt.

Straw followed closely and gave his own warning. "Don't fall in a hole—there's an old well back there that eats careless boys."

Ivory looked concerned.

Straw shook his head and grinned.

Raven said nothing but ducked his chin. He'd been to funerals with his old grandmother, but this was the first time he'd known the dead man. He'd do what he could, as events unrolled.

By then Hutch had joined them, still waiting for fate to choose his companions.

Ivory turned and faced him a moment. The loss in her eyes was glaring and endless. She said "I'd go if I thought I could, but Raven will help you." Then though her composure had held, she passed Hutch and headed back toward the house. After a few steps, she looked round and said "Don't forget young Raven's a city boy; he wouldn't know a snake from a rolled-up sock."

Hutch silently mouthed two words—*He's safe*—and waved as if they were leaving for good.

But Straw told her "Put your mind at ease. No bad snakes around here." It was not strictly true—the odd copperhead turned up every few weeks.

Ivory took it though and went her way.

When she'd gone past earshot, Raven whispered "I'm hoping to see me a cobra."

Straw said "You're on the wrong continent, Son."

Hutch smiled. "That's a fact, more ways than one."

If anyone heard him, no one gave a sign.

Then the two men and the eager boy were silent for a moment, their eyes on the ground.

Straw stood long enough to reach out and touch the urn once more. Half facing Hutch, he said "So long"; then he touched his friend's shoulder and followed Ivory.

*   *   *

When a safe distance had grown between them, Raven called to their backs—a notch louder than a whisper—"I'm big enough to take care of me *and* this man."

No one heard him but Hutch. He touched Raven's forehead and said "I hope you are."

But Raven tore off eight or ten giant steps toward the trees.

And Hutch saw that Maud, Straw's old black retriever—broad-backed as a pony—had come up beside him and was fixed on Raven, running beyond her. She'd never harmed a live thing in her life, nearly thirteen years; and in her youth, Wade had been her favorite from humankind, an instinctive bonding that had pleased them both through hundreds of walks and hours on the porch. Hutch suspected she'd come to follow him down through shade to the creek, and he knew a single word would stop her. The day was hot for her age and her thick coat; Hutch also didn't trust his strength to be with her. So he scratched the loosening skin of her muzzle and said "Old lady, you guard the others."

Maud didn't look up—she was still calculating the distance before her, down through the woods. But finally she took Hutch's order and turned. No look, no trick, just a slow stiff-hipped surrender and exit.

Raven had stopped at the line of trees and was looking toward Hutch.

So Hutch went on.

13

Hutch set the urn down and crouched to thread himself through the rusty barbed wire.

Before he could stand upright again, Raven ran back to watch his progress; and as Hutch reclaimed the urn, the boy said "Who burned up the man?"

"Call him Wade. His name was Wade Mayfield. You remember Wade, your uncle's friend."

Raven's eyes were blank; he was making no commitment. In fact he hadn't seen Wade since Christmas, seven months ago.

Hutch reached his right hand out to Raven.

The boy looked it over, then surrendered his own. It was deeply lined already, a shrunk man's hand but fully fleshed.

When they were nearly into the pines, Hutch asked again "You remember my Wade?"

The boy watched the ground, unlike any ground he'd crossed till today. "Nobody told me he was yours."

"Well, you're right he wasn't, not mine to keep. But I was his father."

"When he was a child?"

Hutch said "That's pretty much how it was, yes—when Wade was a child very much like you." And for the first time, Hutch wondered if Ivory or Wade or Wyatt—or old Mrs. Bondurant on northshore Long Island—had given the boy any clue about Wade. *No way to ask, not for years anyhow.* Possible questions ran through Hutch's mind, but all seemed mildly obscene or cruel.

Then Raven forestalled him. "My mother and father have got a divorce."

"I heard that, yes. Do you see your father?"

"Too much. I hate him. One weekend a month way off in New Jersey. I hate that place."

Hutch said "Hate's probably not a good idea."

Raven looked up till he'd drawn Hutch's eyes to meet him. "You must not know my father then."

Hutch noted the courtliness with which the boy called his parents *mother* and *father* when the rest of America had accepted *mom* and *dad* from TV, but he dodged the boy's question. "I just meant hate hurts the person that hates more than anybody else."

Raven said "Man, you're wrong again."

"How's that?"

"Meanness is getting to be the big style. You never been to New York City, have you?"

Hutch laughed. "Not lately. I hear it's bad."

"*Bad!* They'll shoot you in kindergarten; don't wait till you're grown."

"But you're being extra careful, aren't you?"

"I can't stop bullets if that's what you mean." Raven held up both palms as if to show holes.

Till here it hadn't really struck Hutch that, if Wade was truly this boy's father, then his and Ann's one grandchild and their only heir was living up north in even more danger than he'd meet down here in the worst imaginable hands—the all but vanished white-trash Klansman or defeated punk. The apparently endless slaughter of innocence underway in American cities, a mindless raking down of bystanders, had overtaken hatred in its tracks and bludgeoned its way on at unchecked speeds. *Anything I can do about that? Not short of moving him down here with Ivory, no; and that can't happen— can't or won't.* Hutch said "You wish you lived somewhere else?"

"Not down here anyway if that's what you mean."

Hutch said "What's the problem with where we are?"

"*Hot*, red hot." The boy fanned his face.

"It's hot up north."

Raven said "Sometimes. But we got the ocean. Remember I live in *Sea Cliff, New York*."

Hutch laughed. "I'll do my best to remember." Yet even alone now he felt the need to cover his tracks. "I wasn't exactly inviting you down here. I just thought you said you liked all the trees."

They were well into the serious woods, the soft floor deep in dry leaves and pinestraw, the gradual downgrade toward the valley. In ten more yards the shade was dense as dusk.

Raven pressed Hutch's hand. "I didn't say that to hurt your feelings."

Hutch said "I understand—you're a city boy. You think you could come down and visit sometime though? We could go to the beach or the mountains maybe."

"Just you and me?"

"Ivory could come if she wanted to."

Raven's head all but agreed to the plan. "She does like it better than me down here." He went on thinking the option through. "Would that lady back at the house be with us?"

"Wade's mother? Ann?"

Raven signed a strong Yes again. "The dead man's mother—"

"Wade's mother—she might be; yes, she might. Her plans are still vague. But that wouldn't affect you."

"I like her." Then the boy looked around in half-comic carefulness and whispered "She gave me a five-dollar bill." He patted his hip pocket where a small wallet guarded the crisp new bill, plus the five and two ones he'd brought from New York (his grandmother gave him money to phone her in case he got lost).

Hutch said "Good. She's smart and well paid."

Raven seemed to consider that matter closed. He struck off on his own. "My mother is scared of airplanes, but I'm old enough to fly by myself. Children fly everywhere, tickets tied round their neck to show who they are."

"They do," Hutch said. "You name the day."

"You'd need to make those arrangements with my family." The boy's high-spoken gravity amused even him; when he'd heard his sentence, he beamed up at Hutch.

"I'll remember that, when the time comes, surely."

They'd gone a good way downhill before Raven said "When will that be?"

"Sir?"

"You said 'When the time comes.' What time is that—when you ask my mother?"

Hutch said "It could start anywhere from the minute we're back in Strawson's house till sunup tomorrow."

"And last for how long? How long would you need me?"

"Oh till you're a grown man and I'm out of sight."

Raven consulted himself in silence. "I don't think that's going to work, Mr. Mayfield. I'm missing day camp just walking with you in all this heat." He elaborately dried his neck with a hand, then fanned himself again.

"Call me *Hutch*, please sir—I heard about your camp. Sure, you need to finish that."

"And high school and college and the rest of my grandmother's life, I guess."

"How's that?"

"She'd die without me."

Hutch thought *That's very likely the truth.* "That doesn't leave us much hope then, do you think?"

Raven said "I wouldn't go far as that." His voice was plainly an echo of his elders but likewise in earnest.

"You got some spare time, somewhere in your life?"

"I'll see can I manage to work - you - in." Again the boy smiled his enormous delight at Hutch.

It found its mark. Hutch felt the slow rise in his chest and throat of that strange elation he'd felt in the early hours of rescuing Wade and bringing him home. When he could speak, he said "You phone me collect when you know."

"No way, Hutch," the boy said. "I'll pay for the call." He held up his pale small hand to offer a genuine high five, nobody's beggar.

As well as Hutch could, with the cradled ashes, he met the hand and confirmed the greeting.

By now they were near enough to the creek to hear its slender late-summer flow and the heartened birdcalls that signaled a cooler air and light than any available elsewhere for miles. Hutch recognized each sound as it came—the furious challenging cluck of a squirrel, a far-off dove in its lunar moan, the piercing *scree* of a red-tailed hawk nearby overhead. It all drew him down more surely toward his goal.

Raven had never been this near a wilderness, but the deepening peace above the strange sounds and the separate odors of natural water and ripened leaves were welcome findings.

Hutch said "This place where you and I are going was Wade's favorite place when he was your age. He used to come up here every summer and stay with the Stuarts and old Mr. Walters, and this was the place he made his own."

"For what?" Raven said.

"Oh being alone, thinking his own thoughts with nobody leaning or holding him back."

Raven said "I spend most of my time alone, when I'm home from school. My grandmother works till time to cook supper; then she watches TV past my bedtime."

"You mind that at all?"

"Shoot, no, I love it. I'm good company, Hutch."

"I'm beginning to notice. You'll almost certainly like Wade's creek then. With a little luck on the food and weather, a smart sane man could live a whole life here and never need more."

"How about a young boy? Could he make out?"

Hutch said "Maybe if he was, say, thirteen."

"That's five years from now."

Hutch said "You could probably manage it, with occasional visits from Strawson or me."

Raven let go of Hutch's hand and stepped ahead faster, but he still asked clearly "Why did Wade leave then?"

"Wait please," Hutch said. "Don't get there before me." He wanted to see the boy's eyes take in the heart of the place—first sight, first pleasure.

So Raven halted in his tracks, with his back turned, and waited till Hutch was precisely beside him. He asked again "Why you think Wade left?"

Hutch said "He had his grown life to find." For a moment he wanted to sit down here, beg the boy to sit and try not to leave. *Crazier still. Lead him on; do your job.* He said to Raven "You walk in my tracks," not explaining that his tracks would be safer on the slope, when they reached the downgrade.

So the boy looked to Hutch's feet and fell in behind him, stride for wide stride, till they came to the crest of the valley and stopped.

Full as the summer growth still was, this deep into shade, the stretch of creek that Grainger had channeled was plain below them. Its edges were softened by moss and vines since Hutch's visit in early spring, and summer rains had gnawed at the banks, but the big smooth boulders still broke the flow into tamer strands of water that now looked clear but dark brown like strong cold tea.

Raven's face was calm but his eyes had widened; and he said "Man, this is a Tarzan movie."

"Exactly. Hear him swinging our way—him and his monkeys?"

Raven gave Hutch the benefit of the doubt; he actually listened, then shook his head Yes and pulled ahead on Hutch's wrist. "Come *on*, man." The boy ran three steps down the steep embankment, then tumbled over, rolled a fast two yards, stopped himself and sprang to his feet.

Hutch had thought *God, don't let him be hurt with me. We've only started* and moved to help him.

But by then the boy was brushing leaves off his suit, picking at a narrow scratch in his right palm, then laughing to Hutch and giving a formal bow from the waist. "Son of Tarzan, at your service, sir."

Hutch said "Well, greetings" and returned the bow. For that long instant he felt all but fully rewarded for the spring and summer's pain.

Raven said "For a white dude, you doing all right."

"Thank you, friend—I try. I try when I can."

Raven was already thinking ahead. "Can I see the dead man now?"

Hutch was holding the urn in both arms, against his chest. "These are ashes, Son. They're all that's left of Wade Mayfield's body. Wade was my only son. You said you remembered Wade."

"A little bit. I think we had a picnic."

Hutch could see he was hedging. "When was that?"

"When I was a child, *way* back when." Raven's eyes were still fixed on the urn.

Hutch said "Let's do our duty then" and took the first careful step down the steep slope.

Reminded again of their serious errand, Raven came on several yards behind Hutch in long slow strides.

At the edge of the creek, Hutch waited till the boy had caught up beside him. Then he crouched to the ground and again peeled the tape from the lid of the urn. He paused a moment to brace himself for what he might feel at this last sight. Then he looked to Raven who was in reach behind him, waiting too with eyes on the lid. So what Hutch felt was, again, the oldest feeling of his life—the literal medium in which he was born and had swum ever since: a bitter mix of pleasure and grief, thanks and irrecoverable loss. He took off the lid; the ashes were just as Grainger had left them. The gold ring barely showed, still pressed in the center. Hutch tilted the urn so Raven could see.

The boy crouched too and took a long look. Without facing Hutch he said "Is this all you got?"

"All of what?"

"The dead man—your Mr. Wade."

Hutch said "Not all, no."

"Who's got the rest?"

Hutch said "All of us, deep down in our minds. You'll know more about Wade once you get grown."

Raven said "I see him right this minute." When he looked across to Hutch, it was clear that the boy meant he was watching memories, however unsure and far in his past. Then his head bent closer to the urn. "Are they safe?"

"From what?"

"For me to touch—my uncle Wyatt wasn't safe when he died. They locked up the casket; said he was *catching.* I wouldn't even go in the room where they had him."

Hutch said "Wade's ashes are safe as sand. You do what you want."

Raven put out his right hand and set two fingers on the gritty surface. "That's his finger ring?"

"It should have been."

"You throwing it away too?"

Hutch said "Maybe. What do you think?"

Raven touched a single finger to the ring and pressed it deeper into the ash. "I think some child'll get a nice finger ring when he finds it down here."

"Or maybe it'll wash on down through the river and land on the ocean floor."

"A shark might eat it." The idea lit the boy's whole face.

Hutch said "He might."

Then they both were silent a long time, seeing only their private needs— Hutch searched for a small still cove by the bank; Raven scanned the tree limbs for pythons.

At last Hutch reached in, uncovered the ring and hooked it onto his right little finger. It hadn't touched him in so many years, but it felt normal here. He said to Raven "You still want to help me?"

"Yes, just say the word." The boy's face lit again with the solemn force it had in the chapel yesterday, not a ritual funeral look but the image of innocent awe at the final mystery left.

Hutch said "Reach in then, take a good handful and spread it on the water."

Careful as a good young priest, Raven performed the gesture like something he'd learned years back and brought to effortless ease today.

The tan ashes lay on top of the water for an instant, then sifted downward and on with the stream.

Raven kept his eyes on their course. "Let me do one more."

Hutch waited with the urn while the boy spread a second handful.

In a quick shaft of light, the ashes spread on the surface — rainbowed for a moment in their startling colors of tan, white, ochre, blues and purples. The bits of bone cast circles around them that rode out of sight.

But Raven stood where he'd stopped and watched them, his dusty right hand held out from his side.

Hutch had crouched through that. Now he stood, walking slowly upstream to scatter the rest. If he'd been thrown forward, dead of grief and regret in the dirt any instant here, he'd have felt no surprise. But his blood beat on, he stayed upright, and the ashes were gone even sooner than he'd guessed. He was left with the urn and a weight of loss — iron desolation — like none he'd ever borne till today. For half a minute again he thought he'd pitch to the ground. His heart contracted like a terrified fist and slammed at his ribs.

It was then Hutch knew that, against all reason, he still dreaded Wyatt — Wyatt Bondurant here in this real day. Whoever had fathered Ivory's Raven, there could be no doubt the child was Wyatt's nephew. *Wyatt may slam in here, any moment, to take this child. He'll never let me know him.* Wild as that tasted and felt in Hutch's mind, he half believed it; half expected it in this real daylight on land his family had owned for so long and worked with the usable entirely expendable lives of others, all of them buried in long-lost graves within reach of his voice, if he'd raise his voice here.

In Hutch's crowded head, he even saw an image — the child crushed down, with blood on his lip, by the unseen weight of a famished dead man. *We all end here — Wade, Ann and me; maybe even this child, whoever he is. And all my kin, back far as they go toward Eden and Gomorrah.* The entire story (the little Hutch knew of it and all the hidden mass with its thousand feeders) — all the likable, darkening, execrable routes each private life had dug toward its goal, its hunt for care and heat in the world, the self's desert triumph over others, over land and God; and the promise of some eventual rest: all the history of the world ended here, in no more than six or eight fistsful of ashes.

Oh to roll it back and scotch it at the start. Absurd as that sounded in his head, Hutch flushed it away but then felt his mind lunge forward at the boy here, with more real threat than he'd felt toward anyone since the awful moments of balked lust and abandonment in his early manhood. He was literally helpless not to think *End this child now, here, end him yourself. Spare him the slow and poisonous trek.* He turned to the boy.

Raven had followed three steps behind Hutch; he'd also watched the last of the ashes rest on the water and then sift inward. When they'd sunk and Hutch had swung round to face the boy — thinking any instant he must beg for help — Raven went on watching the creek as if the world harbored no threats stronger than pine trees and gangster jays. Then the boy said "Your Wade can enjoy himself from now on."

Hutch stood and took that, knowing not to ask for more by way of explanation. *All right; he ought to.* Hutch's heart opened slightly; he drew a short breath, ready at least to believe they were safe again. "Let's hope Wade enjoys the whole rest of things, as long as things last. God knows he paid for it." Then a second breath offered itself and went deeper into his lungs and mind. So Hutch walked forward, found the lid on a flat rock and closed the urn. He hadn't anticipated having a handsome empty pot to keep or destroy. *Smash it on the rocks. Leave it here with the dust.* That would break the enormous quiet around them. *Give it to Raven.* Hutch actually held it out before him to see if the boy would ask to have it.

By then though Raven had seen a red salamander on the moss and was watching it closely.

It eyed him back more urgently than any two eyes had watched him till now.

Hutch gave the boy another few seconds, then said "We need to climb back and head for home."

Raven said "There's four states between here and *my* home."

Hutch could smile. "Then we need to ball the jack." Again he offered the boy his hand, and they climbed carefully up the steep valley and on through gradually thinning trees—through Hutch's racing thoughts of a lifetime, long lifetimes behind him, the unseen future—till open ground was no more than fifty feet ahead, still flat under unblocked pounding sun. Hutch paused there, mainly to catch his breath.

Raven waited beside him, staring ahead.

Hutch finally said "You ready?"

"For what?" The great dark eyes went to Hutch again.

"Oh for life to start."

"Man, it's *started*," Raven said. "I'm near about grown."

There was more than a grain of truth in that, Hutch well understood. This boy might never come back here again; they actually might not meet again. However hard Hutch might want to see Raven through the years, that was Ivory's choice and must never be seized without her full assent and blessing. *Now, this instant, is all you know you'll get on Earth.* So Hutch bent and set the urn at the foot of a monumental beech, a giant elephant's leg. He slid old Rob's gold ring from his right hand, reached silently out, won Raven's consent and slid it onto the boy's left thumb.

Raven studied the wide band, still several sizes too large for his hand. He turned it slowly as if he already knew its power, the rune that perfectly worked its strength to bind whole lives and outride time. Not looking to Hutch, Raven almost whispered "You trying to say this is mine to keep?"

"Yours to keep or give away or fling in the sea."

"I live in Sea Cliff, you know that, right?"

"I do," Hutch said. "I'll know it forever."

Still not looking up, the boy said "Thank you."

"You may want to let your mother keep it safe till your hand grows to fit it." Raven agreed to that. "It won't be long."

Hutch said "I bet it'll feel like forever, but really you're right. It'll come very quick."

The boy's smile broke out against his resistance, one of the last bursts of uncrossed joy he'd feel till his own middle age. He turned that actual beam on Hutch, said "Roll right on!" and pointed ahead.

For the first time since the line came to him last month at the crossroad mechanic's, Hutch suddenly knew he'd build a poem from the first given words. A second, a third, and part of a fourth line clicked into place here.

> This child knows the last riddle and answer.
> They wait far back in these mineshaft eyes
> Till he concedes your right to know them,
> Which may be never.

No other actual words arrived, neither riddle nor answer and no firm sense of a shapely life on a page of print or a possible length, just the strong assurance Hutch had barely known since his first mature poems—that a thoroughly sizable living creature was forming down in him, below his sight or natural vision. The creature would surface in its own time and cut its own path.

Not that a single poem, however deep, would count for much in whatever scale his life hung from or would hang from at the end. *An honorable piece of handiwork anyhow, a clean piece of carving to set in the long American gallery of cigar-store Indians and Abe Lincoln busts. That much, if no more.* The only other thing Hutch knew, here on the final edge of shade, was that somehow the poem would resurrect Wade in words more durable than any of his kin and join him finally with this likable child. The prospect felt like strength enough for days to come; and Raven's eyes were still fixed on him, still ready to guide.

So whoever they'd be for one another in the years between here and Raven's full manhood or Hutch's death, the two of them went on, hand in hand, through the last of the shade and broke into blinding clean sunlight. Though their stunned eyes saw only wavering heat and the withering grass, all that lay beyond Hutch and his new kin seemed to them both their only goal—Grainger's, the main house, the durable oaks, whatever people had waited them out, the car that would drive them south to the airport and part them again for months or for good. They could hardly see to walk toward shade and find the others to say they'd done one duty at least—one man's return to the bottomless ground; maybe even a family's end, its story told— but they looked on forward and took the first steps.

PRIMARY CHARACTERS

A GREAT CIRCLE

The Kendals

Bedford Kendal, 1850–July 1929
Married Charlotte Watson. Father of Kennerly Kendal, Eva Kendal Mayfield, and Rena Kendal. Lived in Fontaine, NC.

Blunt Powell Kendal
Wife of Kennerly Kendal. Sister-in-law of Eva Kendal Mayfield and Rena Kendal. Lived in Fontaine, NC.

Charlotte Watson Kendal, 1860–16 March 1904
Daughter of Thad Watson and Katherine Epps Watson. Wife of Bedford Kendal. Mother of Kennerly Kendal, Eva Kendal Mayfield, and Rena Kendal. Lived in Fontaine, NC.

Eva Kendal Mayfield, February 1887–1970s
Daughter and middle child of Bedford Kendal and Charlotte Watson Kendal. Sister of Kennerly Kendal and Rena Kendal. Married May 1903 to Forrest Mayfield. Mother of Robinson Mayfield. Grandmother of Raven Hutchins Mayfield. Lived in Fontaine, NC and Bracey, VA.

Kennerly Kendal, born 1886
Son and oldest child of Bedford Kendal and Charlotte Watson Kendal. Brother of Eva Kendal Mayfield and Rena Kendal. Married to Blunt Powell. Uncle of Robinson Mayfield. Lived in Fontaine, NC.

Rena Kendal, born August 1888

Daughter and youngest child of Bedford Kendal and Charlotte Watson Kendal. Sister of Kennerly Kendal and Eva Kendal Mayfield. Aunt of Robinson Mayfield. Never married. Lived in Fontaine, NC.

THE MAYFIELDS

Ann Gatlin Mayfield, born 1931

Married in 1960 to Raven Hutchins Mayfield, whom she met in college. Mother of Raven Wade Mayfield. A legal secretary and paralegal. After college she worked in Richmond, VA. After her marriage she lived in Durham, NC.

Anna Goodwin Mayfield, 1848–1883

Married in October 1866 to Old Robinson Mayfield. Mother of Hattie Mayfield Shorter and Forrest Mayfield. Lived in Bracey, VA.

Forrest Mayfield, 28 November 1870–May 1944

Son of Old Robinson Mayfield and Anna Goodwin Mayfield. Brother of Hattie Mayfield Shorter. Teacher and poet. Married in May 1903 to Eva Kendal. Father of Robinson Mayfield. Grew up in Bracey, VA. Lived in Fontaine, NC; Bracey, VA; and Richmond, VA. Died in Richmond, where he was living with Margaret Jane Drewry.

Hattie (Hatt) Mayfield Shorter, June 1867–1945

Daughter of Old Robinson Mayfield and Anna Goodwin Mayfield. Sister of Forrest Mayfield. Married in 1883 to James Shorter. Mother of Gid Shorter and Whitby Shorter. Aunt of Robinson Mayfield. Lived in Bracey, VA.

Rachel Hutchins Mayfield, 27 May 1905–12 May 1930

Daughter of Raven Hutchins and Carrie Hutchins. Grew up in her family's hotel in Goshen, VA. Married to Robinson Mayfield 28 November 1925. Mother of Raven Hutchins Mayfield. Died in childbirth in Richmond, VA.

Raven Hutchins (Hutch) Mayfield, born 12 May 1930

Born in Richmond, VA. Son of Robinson Mayfield and Rachel Hutchins Mayfield. Married in 1960 to Ann Gatlin, whom he met in college. Father of Raven Wade Mayfield. Taught at a boys' school in Edom, VA, 1952–1955. Studied at Merton College, Oxford University, 1955–1958. Poet. Professor of English, Duke University, Durham, NC.

Raven Wade Mayfield, 1961–6 July 1993
Son of Raven Hutchins Mayfield and Ann Gatlin Mayfield. Graduated from the School of Design, North Carolina State University, Raleigh, NC, May 1984. An architect who lived with Wyatt Bondurant in New York. Died of AIDS at his father's home, Durham, NC.

Robinson (Old Rob) Mayfield, March 1839–21 February 1905
Born in Richmond, VA. Son of Forrest Mayfield and Amelia Collins Mayfield. Married to Anna Goodwin October 1866. Father of Hattie Mayfield Shorter and Forrest Mayfield. Also father of Rover Walters, whose mother was Elvira Jane Walters, who was born a slave. Grandfather of Robinson Mayfield and Grainger Walters. Died of tuberculosis in Richmond, VA, where he was living with Margaret Jane Drewry.

Robinson (Rob) Mayfield, 11 March 1904–29 December 1955
Born in Bracey, VA. Son of Forrest Mayfield and Eva Kendal Mayfield. Grew up in the Kendal home in Fontaine, NC. Teacher. Married in Goshen, VA to Rachel Hutchins 28 November 1925. Father of Raven Hutchins Mayfield. Lived in Bracey, VA; Richmond, VA; Goshen, VA; Raleigh, NC; and in the Kendal homeplace near Fontaine, NC.

Black Kin and Help

Jimmy (Boatie) Boat
Raised in Macon, GA, by his grandmother. A volunteer nurse who cares for Raven Wade Mayfield and other AIDS patients in New York. Comes to Durham, NC in July 1993 to visit Raven Wade Mayfield and help Wade's father, Raven Hutchins Mayfield, care for him.

Ivory Bondurant
Born in the early 1950s. Daughter of Lucy Patterson Bondurant. Sister of Wyatt Bondurant. Mother of Raven Bondurant. Grew up in the South Bronx. In 1993 living in New York and working at an art gallery in Soho.

Lucy Patterson Bondurant, born 1917
Mother of Ivory Bondurant and Wyatt Bondurant, living on Long Island in 1993. Grandmother of Raven Bondurant. Grew up in Virginia. Oldest brother, named Bankey Patterson, alive in 1993.

Raven Bondurant, born 1985

Son of Ivory Bondurant. In 1993 living on Long Island with his grandmother, Lucy Patterson Bondurant.

Wyatt Bondurant, died 1993

Son of Lucy Bondurant. Brother of Ivory Bondurant. Uncle of Raven Bondurant. Grew up in the South Bronx. Companion of Wade Mayfield from 1984 until Wyatt's death in 1993.

Veenie Goodwin, born 1815

Born a slave of Anna Goodwin Mayfield's family. Still alive in 1919, died before 1925. Mother of eleven children. First live child was Mary Lucretia. Great-great-grandmother of Rover Walters. Great-great-great-grandmother of Grainger Walters. Living in Bracey, VA in 1904.

Mag, 1857–1919

Mother of Sylvie. Worked for Bedford Kendal, Charlotte Kendal, and their family. Lived in Fontaine, NC.

Bowles (Bo) Parker, 1907–1944

Son of Flora Parker. Wife named Lena. Father of three children. Drafted into army in 1942. In June 1944 he was an army cook at Fort Bragg, NC. Died in car wreck June 1944. Lived near Fontaine, NC.

Flora Parker

Mother of Bowles Parker. Cousin of Sylvie. Grew up in Fontaine, NC. In 1921 living in Baltimore, MD.

Bankey Patterson, born about 1824

Born a slave of the Fitts family. A blacksmith. Mother named Julia. Had several wives and several sets of children. In August 1904 living at Panacea Springs near Fontaine, NC, where Forrest Mayfield met him.

Julia Patterson

Abortionist in Richmond, VA in 1956.

Della Simmons, born 1906

Mother named Lucy. Grandmother named Julia. Worked in the hotel in Goshen, VA, which belonged to the family of Rachel Hutchins Mayfield. In November 1925 went to Philadelphia, PA where she worked as a maid. In

June 1944 she was back in Goshen at the Hutchins hotel. Never married. No children.

Sylvie, born 1887
Daughter of Mag. Worked for Bedford Kendal, Charlotte Watson Kendal, and their family in Fontaine, NC. Never married. Bore a son, who died at birth, in 1904.

Gracie Walters, 1902–1953
Wife of Grainger Walters. Died at the home of her cousin Gladys Fishel in Richmond, VA.

Grainger Walters, born 5 April 1892
Son of Rover Walters. Grandson of Elvira Jane Walters and Old Robinson Mayfield. Great-great-great-grandson of Veenie Goodwin. Husband of Gracie Walters. Served in U.S. Army in France in World War I. Worked for the Mayfields and the Kendals. Grew up in Maine. Lived in Bracey, VA; Richmond, VA; Fontaine, NC; and the Kendal place near Fontaine. Still alive in August 1993.

Rover Walters, born 1876
Son of Elvira Jane Walters and Old Robinson Mayfield. Father of Grainger Walters. Great-great-grandson of Veenie Goodwin. In May 1904 living in Augusta, ME, where he built boats.

OTHERS

Lew Davis, born 1930
Cabin-mate of Raven Hutchins Mayfield in June 1955 on voyage to England. Traveled with Hutchins in Wales and the Scilly Islands in June 1955. Grew up in Wales. In March 1956 living in Toronto.

Margaret Jane (Polly) Drewry, 1886–1980
Father was a Confederate veteran from Virginia who owned a Confederate museum in Washington, D.C. Her mother, who died five days after Polly's birth, was named Lillian Drewry. Polly met Old Robinson Mayfield at her father's museum in 1903 and went to live with him in Richmond, VA. After Old Robinson's death, she kept house for his son, Forrest Mayfield, in the Mayfield family home in Richmond and continued living there until her death.

Raven Hutchins, November 1872–May 1944
Born at the Hutchins hotel in Goshen, VA. Grew up at the hotel and lived there most of his life. Married in 1894; wife named Carrie. Father of Rachel Hutchins Mayfield. Grandfather of Raven Hutchins Mayfield.

Cameron (Cam) Mapleson, born about 1964
Grew up in Nags Head, NC. Served in the U.S. Marines. Friend of Maitland Moses. In 1993 worked at an AIDS hospice in Durham, NC, and helped tend Raven Wade Mayfield.

Alice Matthews, 1904–1993
Grew up in Lynchburg, VA, where her father, a doctor, owned a sanitorium. Friend of Rachel Hutchins, whom she met when Rachel was a patient at the sanitorium. Was Rachel's maid of honor when she married Robinson Mayfield. Never married. In 1944 living in Roanoke, VA, teaching art. In January 1955 moved to Petersburg, VA.

Maitland (Mait) Moses, born 1972
In 1993 a senior at Duke University, Durham, NC. A student in Raven Hutchins Mayfield's class in narrative poetry. A writer. Helped Hutchins care for his son, Raven Wade Mayfield, in the summer of 1993. After Wade's death in July 1993, worked in the manuscripts collection of the Duke University Library.

James Nichols, born 1933
Born in Jericho—a district of Oxford, England—where he grew up. Mother named Nan. Nan was also his daughter's name. A stonemason. Served time in Lewes Prison for assault. In July 1955 Raven Hutchins Mayfield met him and his daughter at a pub in Oxford. Dead by 1993 but date of death unknown.

Hart Salter, born 1967
Married in 1990 to Stacy Burnham. In 1993 a doctoral candidate in English at Duke University. Occasionally tended Raven Wade Mayfield.

Emily Stuart
Wife of Strawson Stuart. Mother of one married daughter, an only child, a textbook editor in Georgia. After her marriage to Strawson, Emily lived with him at the Kendal homeplace near Fontaine, NC.

Strawson (Straw) Stuart, born 1936
A student of Raven Hutchins Mayfield at an Episcopal boys' school in Edom, VA, from 1953 to 1955. Husband of Emily Stuart. Father of one married daughter, an only child. After 1956 lived at the Kendal homeplace near Fontaine, NC, and managed land for Raven Hutchins Mayfield, who inherited it from his father Rob. Godfather of Raven Wade Mayfield.

Rowlet Swanson, born 1935 or 1936
From Monongah, WV. Serving in the U.S. Air Force and stationed in Germany in 1955. On leave in December 1955 and staying in the same pensione in Rome as Raven Hutchins Mayfield and Ann Gatlin.

Minnie (Min) Tharrington, born 1905
Born in Fontaine, NC, where she grew up. High-school sweetheart of Robinson Mayfield. Never married. Teacher and genealogical researcher. Lived in Fontaine, NC, and Raleigh, NC. Living at the Kendal homeplace near Fontaine with Robinson Mayfield when he died December 1955.

REYNOLDS PRICE

REYNOLDS PRICE was born in Macon, North Carolina in 1933. Educated at Duke University and, as a Rhodes Scholar, at Merton College, Oxford University, he has taught at Duke since 1958 and is James B. Duke Professor of English. His first novel, *A Long and Happy Life*, was published in 1962 and won the William Faulkner Award. His sixth novel, *Kate Vaiden*, was published in 1986 and won the National Book Critics Circle Award. He has published thirty-one other volumes of fiction, poetry, drama, essays, and translations. He is a member of the American Academy of Arts and Letters, and his work has been translated into sixteen languages.